BLUE HORIZON
and
THE DARK OF THE SUN

WILBUR SMITH was born in Central Africa in 1933. He was educated at Michaelhouse and Rhodes University. He became a full-time writer in 1964 after the successful publication of *When the Lion Feeds*, and has since written over thirty novels, meticulously researched on his numerous expeditions world-wide. His books are now translated into twenty-six languages.

THE NOVELS OF WILBUR SMITH

THE COURTNEYS

When the Lion Feeds   The Sound of Thunder
A Sparrow Falls   Birds of Prey   Monsoon
Blue Horizon   The Triumph of the Sun

THE COURTNEYS OF AFRICA

The Burning Shore   Power of the Sword   Rage
A Time to Die   Golden Fox

THE BALLANTYNE NOVELS

A Falcon Flies   Men of Men   The Angels Weep
The Leopard Hunts in Darkness

THE EGYPTIAN NOVELS

River God   The Seventh Scroll
Warlock   The Quest

Also

The Dark of the Sun   Shout at the Devil
Gold Mine   The Diamond Hunters
The Sunbird   Eagle in the Sky
The Eye of the Tiger   Cry Wolf
Hungry as the Sea   Wild Justice
Elephant Song

WILBUR SMITH

BLUE HORIZON
and
THE DARK
OF THE SUN

PAN BOOKS

Blue Horizon first published 2003 by Macmillan
First published in paperback 2004 by Pan Books
The Dark of the Sun first published 1965 by William Heinemann
This edition published 1998 by Pan Books

This omnibus first published 2008 by Pan Books
an imprint of Pan Macmillan Ltd
Pan Macmillan, 20 New Wharf Road, London N1 9RR
Basingstoke and Oxford
Associated companies throughout the world
www.panmacmillan.com

ISBN 978-0-330-50802-5

1 3 5 7 9 8 6 4 2

A CIP catalogue record for this book is available from
the British Library.

Typeset by SetSystems Ltd, Saffron Walden, Essex
Printed in the UK by CPI Mackays, Chatham ME5 8TD

BLUE HORIZON

This book is for my wife

MOKHINISO

Our first three years have been enchantment
I look forward eagerly to the next thirty

The three stood at the very edge of the sea and watched the moon laying a pathway of shimmering iridescence across the dark waters.

'Full of the moon in two days,' Jim Courtney said confidently. 'The big reds will be hungry as lions.' A wave came sliding up the beach and foamed around his ankles.

'Let's get her launched, instead of standing here jabbering,' his cousin, Mansur Courtney, suggested. His hair shone like newly minted copper in the moonlight, his smile sparkling as brightly. Lightly he elbowed the black youth who stood beside him, wearing only a white loincloth. 'Come on, Zama.' They bent to it together. The small craft slid forward reluctantly, and they heaved again, but this time it stuck fast in the wet sand.

'Wait for the next big one,' Jim ordered, and they gathered themselves. 'Here it comes!' The swell humped up far out, then raced towards them, gathering height. It burst white on the break-line, then creamed in, throwing the bows of the skiff high and making them stagger with its power – they had to cling to the gunwale with the water swirling waist high around them.

'Together now!' Jim yelled, and they threw their combined weight on the boat. 'Run with her!' She came unstuck and rode free, and they used the backwash of the wave to take her out until they were shoulder deep. 'Get on the oars!' Jim spluttered as the next wave broke over his head. They reached up, grabbed the side of the skiff and hauled themselves on board, the seawater running off them. Laughing with excitement, they seized the long oars that were lying ready and thrust them between the thole pins.

'Heave away!' The oars bit, swung and came clear, dripping with silver in the moonlight, leaving tiny luminous whirlpools on the surface. The skiff danced clear of the turbulent break-line, and they fell into the easy rhythm of long practice.

'Which way?' Mansur asked. Both he and Zama looked naturally to Jim for the decision: Jim was always the leader.

'The Cauldron!' Jim said, with finality.

'I thought so.' Mansur laughed. 'You still got a grudge against Big Julie.' Zama spat over the side without missing the stroke.

'Have a care, Somoya. Big Julie still has a grudge against you.' Zama spoke in Lozi, his native tongue. 'Somoya' meant 'wild wind'. It was the name that Jim had been given in childhood for his temper.

Jim scowled at the memory. None of them had ever laid eyes on the fish they had named Big Julie, but they knew it was a hen not a cock because only the female grew to such size and power. They had felt her power transferred from the depths through the straining cod line. The seawater squirted out of the weave, and smoked as it sped out over the gunwale, cutting a deep furrow in the hardwood as blood dripped from their torn hands.

'In 1715 my father was on the old *Maid of Oman* when she went aground at Danger Point,' Mansur said, in Arabic, his mother's language. 'The mate tried to swim ashore to carry a line through the surf and a big red steenbras came up under him when he was half-way across. The water was so clear they could see it coming up from three fathoms down. It bit off the mate's left leg above the knee and swallowed it in a gulp, like a dog with a chicken wing. The mate was screaming and beating the water, all frothed up with his own blood, trying to scare the fish off, but it circled under him and took the other leg. Then it pulled him under and took him deep. They never saw him again.'

'You tell that story every time I want to go to the Cauldron,' Jim grunted darkly.

'And every time it scares seven different colours of dung out of you,' said Zama, in English. The three had spent so much time together that they were fluent in each other's language – English, Arabic and Lozi. They switched between them effortlessly.

Jim laughed, more to relieve his feelings than from amusement, 'Where, pray, did you learn that disgusting expression, you heathen?'

Zama grinned. 'From your exalted father,' he retorted, and for once Jim had no answer.

Instead he looked to the lightening horizon. 'Sunrise in two hours. I want to be over the Cauldron before then. That's the best time for another tilt at Julie.'

They pulled out into the heart of the bay, riding the long Cape swells that came marching in unfettered ranks from their long journey across the southern Atlantic. With the wind full into the bows they could not hoist the single sail. Behind them rose the moonlit massif of Table Mountain, flat-topped and majestic. There was a dark agglomeration of shipping lying close in below the mountain, riding at anchor, most of the great ships with their yards down. This anchorage was the caravanserai of the southern seas. The trading vessels and warships of the Dutch East India Company, the VOC, and those of half a dozen other nations used the Cape of Good Hope to victual and refit after their long ocean passages.

At this early hour few lights showed on the shore, only dim lanterns on the walls of the castle and in the windows of the beachfront taverns where the crews from the ships in the bay were still revelling. Jim's eyes went naturally to a single prick of light separated by over a sea mile of darkness from the others. That was the godown and office of the Courtney Brothers Trading Company and he knew the light shone from the window of his father's office on the second floor of the sprawling warehouse.

'Papa is counting the shekels again.' He laughed to himself. Tom Courtney, Jim's father, was one of the most successful traders at Good Hope.

'There's the island coming up,' Mansur said, and Jim's attention came back to the work ahead. He adjusted the tiller rope, which was wrapped around the big toe of his bare right foot. They altered course slightly to port, heading for the north point of Robben Island. 'Robben' was the Dutch word for the seals that swarmed over the rocky outcrop. Already they could smell the animals on the night air: the stench of their fish-

3

laden dung was chokingly powerful. Closer in, Jim stood up on the thwart to get his bearing from the shore, checking the landmarks that would enable him to place the skiff accurately over the deep hole they had named the Cauldron.

Suddenly he shouted with alarm and dropped back on to the thwart. 'Look at this great oaf! He's going to run us down. Pull, damn you, pull!' A tall ship flying a great mass of canvas, had come silently and swiftly around the north point of the island. Driven on the north-wester it was bearing down on them with terrifying speed.

'Bloody cheese-headed Dutchman!' Jim swore, as he heaved on the long oar. 'Murderous landlubbing son of a tavern whore! He's not even showing a light.'

'And where, pray, did *you* learn such language?' Mansur panted, between desperate strokes.

'You're as big a clown as this stupid Dutchman,' Jim told him grimly. The ship loomed over them, her bow wave shining silver in the moonlight.

'Hail her!' There was a sudden edge to Mansur's voice as the danger became even more apparent.

'Don't waste your breath,' Zama retorted. 'They're fast asleep. They won't hear you. Pull!' The three strained on the oars and the little vessel seemed to fly through the water, but the big ship came on even faster.

'We will have to jump?' There was a question in Mansur's strained tone.

'Good!' Jim grunted. 'We're right over the Cauldron. Test your father's story. Which of your legs will Big Julie bite off first?'

They rowed in a silent frenzy, sweat bursting out and shining on their contorted faces in the cool night. They were heading for the safety of the rocks where the big ship could not touch them, but they were still a full cable's length out and now the high sails towered over them, blotting out the stars. They could hear the wind drumming in the canvas, the creaking of her timbers, and the musical burble of her bow wave. Not one of the boys spoke, but as they strained on the oars they stared up at her in dread.

'Sweet Jesus, spare us!' Jim whispered.

'In Allah's Name!' Mansur said softly.

'All the fathers of my tribe!'

Each called out to his own god or gods. Zama never missed the stroke but his eyes glared white in his dark face as he watched death bear down on them. The pressure wave ahead of the bows lifted them, and suddenly they were surfing on it, flung backwards, racing stern-first down the side of the wave. The transom went under and icy water poured in, flooding her. All three boys were hurled over the side, just as the massive hull hit them. As he went under Jim realized that it had been a glancing blow. The skiff was hurled aside, but there was no crack of rending timbers.

Jim was driven deep, but he tried to swim deeper still. He knew that contact with the bottom of the ship would be fatal. She would be heavily encrusted with barnacles after her ocean passage, and the razor-sharp shells would strip the flesh from his bones. He tensed every muscle in his body in anticipation of the agony, but it did not come. His lungs were burning and his chest was pumping with the compelling urge to breathe. He fought it until he was sure that the ship was clear, then turned for the surface and drove upwards with arms and legs. He saw the golden outline of the moon through limpid water, wavering and insubstantial, and swam towards it with all his strength and will. Suddenly he burst out into the air and filled his lungs with it. He rolled on to his back, gasped, choked and sucked in the life-giving sweetness. 'Mansur! Zama!' he croaked, through the pain of his aching lungs. 'Where are you? Pipe up, damn you. Let me hear you!'

'Here!' It was Mansur's voice, and Jim looked for him. His cousin was clinging to the swamped skiff, his long red curls slicked down over his face like a seal's pelt. Just then another head popped through the surface between them.

'Zama.' With two overarm strokes he reached him, and lifted his face out of the water. Zama coughed and brought up an explosive jet of seawater and vomit. He tried to throw both arms around Jim's neck, but Jim ducked him until he released his grip, then dragged him to the side of the wallowing skiff.

'Here! Take hold of this.' He guided his hand to the gunwale. The three hung there, struggling for breath.

Jim was the first to recover sufficiently to find his anger again. 'Bitch-born bastard!' he gasped, as he stared after the departing ship. She was sailing on sedately. 'Doesn't even know he almost killed us.'

'She stinks worse than the seal colony.' Mansur's voice was still rough, and the effort of speech brought on a coughing fit.

Jim sniffed the air and caught the odour that fouled it. 'Slaver. Bloody slaver,' he spat. 'No mistaking that smell.'

'Or a convict ship,' Mansur said hoarsely. 'Probably transporting prisoners from Amsterdam to Batavia.' They watched the ship alter course, her sails changing shape in the moonlight as she rounded up to enter the bay and join the other shipping anchored there.

'I'd like to find her captain in one of the gin hells at the docks,' Jim said darkly.

'Forget it!' Mansur advised him. 'He'd stick a knife between your ribs, or in some other painful place. Let's get the skiff bailed out.' There was only a few fingers of free board so Jim had to slide in over the transom. He groped under the thwart and found the wooden bucket still lashed under the seat. They had tied down all the gear and equipment securely for the hazardous launch through the surf. He began bailing out the hull, sending a steady stream of water over the side. By the time it was half cleared, Zama had recovered sufficiently to climb aboard and take a spell with the bucket. Jim hauled in the oars, which were still floating alongside, then checked the other equipment. 'All the fishing tackle's still here.' He opened the mouth of a sack and peered inside. 'Even the bait.'

'Are we going on?' Mansur asked.

'Of course we are! Why not, in the name of the Devil?'

'Well . . .' Mansur looked dubious. 'We were nearly drowned.'

'But we weren't,' Jim pointed out briskly. 'Zama has got her dry, and the Cauldron is less than a cable's length away. Big Julie is waiting for her breakfast. Let's go and feed it to her.' Once again they took their positions on the thwarts, and plied the long oars. 'Bastard cheesehead cost us an hour's fishing time,' Jim complained bitterly.

'Could have cost you a lot more, Somoya,' Zama laughed, 'if I hadn't been there to pull you out—' Jim picked up a dead fish from the bait bag and threw it at his head. They were swiftly recovering their high spirits and camaraderie.

'Hold the stroke, we're coming up on the marks now,' Jim warned, and they began the delicate business of manoeuvring the skiff into position over the rocky hole in the green depths below them. They had to drop the anchor on to the ledge to the south of the Cauldron, then let the current drift them back over the deep subterranean canyon. The swirling current that gave the place its name complicated their work, and twice they missed the marks. With much sweat and swearing they had to retrieve the fifty-pound boulder that was their anchor and try again. The dawn was sneaking in from the east, stealthily as a thief, before Jim plumbed the depth with an unbaited cod line to make certain they were in the perfect position. He measured the line between the span of his open arms as it streamed over the side.

'Thirty-three fathoms!' he exclaimed, as he felt the lead sinker bump the bottom. 'Nearly two hundred feet. We're right over Big Julie's dining room.' He brought up the sinker swiftly with a swinging double-handed action. 'Bait up, boys!' There was a scramble for the bait bag. Jim reached in and, from under Mansur's fingers, he snatched the choicest bait of all, a grey mullet as long as his forearm. He had netted it the previous day in the lagoon below the company godown. 'That's too good for you,' he explained reasonably. 'Needs a real fisherman to handle Julie.' He threaded the point of the steel shark hook through the mullet's eye sockets. The bight of the hook was two handspans across. Jim shook out the leader. It was ten feet of steel chain, light but strong. Alf, his father's blacksmith, had hand-forged it especially for him. Jim was certain it would resist the efforts of even a great king steenbras to sheer it against the reef. He swung the bait round his head, letting the heavy cod line pay out with each swing, until at last he released it and sent it with the chain leader to streak far out across the green surface. As the bait sank into the depths he let the line stream after it. 'Right down Big Julie's throat,' he gloated. 'This time she isn't going to get away. This time she's mine.' When he felt the lead sinker hit the bottom, he laid out a coil of the line on the deck and stood firmly on it with his bare right foot. He needed both hands on the oar to counter the current and keep the skiff on station above the Cauldron with the heavy line running straight up and down.

Zama and Mansur were fishing with lighter hooks and lines, using small chunks of mackerel as bait. Almost immediately they were hauling in fish – rosy red stumpnose, wriggling silvery bream, spotted tigers that grunted like piglets as the boys twisted out the hook and threw them into the bilges.

'Baby fish for little boys!' Jim mocked them. Diligently he tended his own heavy line, rowing quietly to hold the skiff steady across the current. The sun rose clear of the horizon and took the chill out of the air. The three stripped off their outer clothing until they were clad only in breech clouts.

Close at hand the seals swarmed over the rocks of the island, dived and roiled close around the anchored skiff. Suddenly a big dog seal dived under the boat and seized the fish Mansur was bringing up, tore it from the hook and surfaced yards away with it in its jaws.

'Abomination, cursed of God!' Mansur shouted in outrage as the seal held the plundered fish on its chest and tore off hunks of flesh with gleaming fangs. Jim dropped the oar and reached into his tackle bag. He brought out his slingshot, and fitted a water-worn pebble into the pouch. He had selected his ammunition from the bed of the stream at the north end of the estate, and each stone was round, smooth and perfectly weighted. Jim had practised with the slingshot until he could bring down a high-flying goose with four throws out of five. He wound up for the throw, swinging the slingshot overhead until it hummed with power. Then he released it and the pebble blurred from the pouch. It caught the dog seal in the centre of its rounded black skull and they heard the fragile bone shatter. The animal died instantly, and its carcass drifted away on the current, twitching convulsively.

'He won't be stealing any more fish.' Jim stuffed the slingshot back in the bag. 'And the others will have learned a lesson in manners.' The rest of the seal pack sheered away from the skiff. Jim took up the oar again, and they resumed their interrupted conversation.

Only the previous week Mansur had returned on one of the Courtney ships from a trading voyage up the east coast of Africa as far as the Horn of Hormuz. He was describing to them the wonders he had seen and the marvellous adventures he had shared with his father, who had captained the *Gift of Allah*.

Mansur's father, Dorian Courtney, was the other partner in the company. In his extreme youth he had been captured by Arabian pirates and sold to a prince of Oman, who had adopted him and converted him to Islam. His half-brother Tom Courtney was Christian, while Dorian was Muslim. When Tom had found and rescued his younger brother they had made a happy partnership. Between them they had entry to both religious worlds, and their enterprise had flourished. Over the last twenty years they had traded in India, Arabia and Africa, and sold their exotic goods in Europe.

As Mansur spoke Jim watched his cousin's face, and once again he envied his beauty and his charm. Mansur had inherited it from his father, along with the red-gold hair that hung thickly down his back. Like Dorian he was lithe and quick, while Jim took after his own father, broad and strong. Zama's father, Aboli, had compared them to the bull and the gazelle.

'Come on, coz!' Mansur broke off his tale to tease Jim. 'Zama and I will have the boat filled to the gunwales before you have even woken up. Catch us a fish!'

'I have always prized quality above mere quantity,' Jim retorted, in a pitying tone.

'Well, you have nothing better to do, so you can tell us about your journey to the land of the Hottentots.' Mansur swung another gleaming flapping fish over the side of the skiff.

Jim's plain, honest face lit up with pleasure at the memory of his own adventure. Instinctively he looked northwards across the bay at the rugged mountains, which the morning sun was painting with brightest gold. 'We travelled for thirty-eight days,' he boasted, 'north across the mountains and the great desert, far beyond the frontiers of this colony, which the Governor and the Council of the VOC in Amsterdam have forbidden any man to cross. We trekked into lands where no white man has been before us.' He did not have the fluency or the poetic descriptive powers of his cousin, but his enthusiasm was contagious. Mansur and Zama laughed with him, as he described the barbaric tribes they had encountered and the endless herds of wild game spread across the plains. At intervals he appealed to Zama, 'It's true what I say, isn't it, Zama? You were with me. Tell Mansur it's true.'

Zama nodded solemnly. 'It is true. I swear it on the grave of my own father. Every word is true.'

'One day I will go back.' Jim made the promise to himself, rather than to the others. 'I will go back and cross the blue horizon, to the very limit of this land.'

'And I will go with you, Somoya!' Zama looked at him with complete trust and affection.

Zama remembered what his own father had said of Jim when at last he lay dying on his sleeping kaross, burnt out with age, a ruined giant whose strength had seemed once to hold the very sky suspended. 'Jim Courtney is the true son of his father,' Aboli had whispered. 'Cleave to him as I have to Tom. You will never regret it, my son.'

'I will go with you,' Zama repeated, and Jim winked at him.

'Of course you will, you rogue. Nobody else would have you.' He clapped Zama on the back so hard he almost knocked him off the thwart.

He would have said more but at that moment the coil of cod line jerked under his foot and he let out a triumphant shout. 'Julie knocks at the door. Come in, Big Julie!' He dropped the oar and snatched up the line. He held it strung between both his hands with a slack bight ready to feed out over the side. Without being ordered to do so the other two retrieved their own rigs, stripping the line in over the gunwale, hand over hand, working with feverish speed. They knew how

10

vital it was to give Jim open water in which to work with a truly big fish.

'Come, my prettyling!' Jim whispered to the fish, as he held the line delicately between thumb and finger. He could feel nothing, just the soft press of the current. 'Come, my darling! Papa loves you,' he pleaded.

Then he felt a new pressure on the line, a gentle almost furtive movement. Every nerve in his body jerked bowstring taut. 'She's there. She's still there.'

The line went slack again, 'Don't leave me, sweetest heart. Please don't leave me.' Jim leaned out over the side of the skiff, holding the line high so that it ran straight from his fingers into the green swirl of the waters. The others watched without daring to draw breath. Then, suddenly, they saw his raised right hand drawn down irresistibly by some massive weight. They watched the muscles in his arms and back coil and bunch, like an adder preparing to strike, and neither spoke or moved as the hand holding the line almost touched the surface of the sea.

'Yes!' said Jim quietly. 'Now!' He reared back with the weight of his body behind the strike. 'Yes! And yes and yes!' Each time he said it he heaved back on the line, swinging with alternate arms, right, left and right again. There was no give even to Jim's strength.

'That can't be a fish,' said Mansur. 'No fish is that strong. You must have hooked the bottom.' Jim did not answer him. Now he was leaning back with all his weight, his knees jammed against the wooden gunwale to give himself full purchase. His teeth were gritted, his face turned puce and his eyes seemed to bulge from their sockets.

'Tail on to the line!' he gasped, and the other two scrambled down the deck to help him, but before they reached the stern Jim was jerked off his feet, and sprawled against the side of the boat. The line raced through his fingers, and they could smell the skin, burning like mutton ribs grilling on the coals, as it tore from his palm.

Jim yelled with pain but held on grimly. With a mighty effort he managed to get the line across the edge of the

11

gunwale and tried to jam it there. But he lost more skin as his knuckles slammed into the wood. With one hand he snatched off his cap to use as a glove while he held the line against the wood. All three were yelling like demons in hellfire.

'Give me a hand! Grab the end!'

'Let him run. You'll straighten the hook.'

'Get the bucket. Throw water on it! The line will burst into flames!'

Zama managed to get both hands on the line, but even with their combined strength they could not stop the run of the great fish. The line hissed with the strain as it raced over the side, and they could feel the sweep of the great tail pulsing through it.

'Water, for the love of Christ, wet it down!' Jim howled, and Mansur scooped a bucketful from alongside and dashed it over their hands and the sizzling line. There was a puff of steam as the water boiled off.

'By God! We've almost lost all of this coil,' Jim shouted, as he saw the end of the line in the bottom of the wooden tub that held it. 'Quick as you can, Mansur! Tie on another coil.' Mansur worked quickly, with the dexterity for which he was renowned, but he was only just in time; as he tightened the knot the rope was jerked from his grasp and pulled through the fingers of the other two, ripping off more skin, before it went over the side and down into the green depths.

'Stop!' Jim pleaded with the fish. 'Are you trying to kill us, Julie? Will you not stop, my beauty?'

'That's half the second coil gone already,' Mansur warned them. 'Let me take over from you, Jim. There's blood all over the deck.'

'No, no.' Jim shook his head vehemently. 'She's slowing down. Heart's almost broken.'

'Yours or hers?' Mansur asked.

'Go on the stage, coz,' Jim advised him grimly. 'Your wit is wasted here.'

The running line began to slow as it passed through their torn fingers. Then it stopped. 'Leave the water bucket,' Jim ordered. 'Get a grip on the line.' Mansur hung on behind

Zama and, with the extra weight, Jim could let go with one hand and suck his fingers. 'Do we do this for fun?' he asked, wonderingly. Then his voice became businesslike. 'Now it's our turn, Julie.'

Keeping pressure on the line while they moved, they rearranged themselves down the length of the deck, standing nose to tail, bent double with the line passed back between their legs.

'One, two and a tiger!' Jim gave them the timing, and they heaved the line in, swinging their weight on it together. The knotted joint came back in over the side, and Mansur, as third man, coiled the line back into the tub. Four times more the great fish gathered its strength and streaked away and they were forced to let it take out line, but each time the run was shorter. Then they turned its head and brought it back, struggling and jolting, its strength slowly waning.

Suddenly Jim at the head of the line gave a shout of joy. 'There she is! I can see her down there.' The fish turned in a wide circle deep below the hull. As she came round her bronze-red side caught the sunlight and flashed like a mirror.

'Sweet Jesus, she's beautiful!' Jim could see the fish's huge golden eye staring up at him through the emerald-coloured water. The steenbras's mouth opened and closed spasmodically, the gill plates flaring as they pumped water through, starving for oxygen. Those jaws were cavernous enough to take in a grown man's head and shoulders, and they were lined with serried ranks of fangs as long and thick as his forefinger.

'Now I believe Uncle Dorry's tale.' Jim gasped with the exertion. 'Those teeth could easily bite off a man's leg.'

At last, almost two hours after Jim had first set the hook in the hinge of the fish's jaw, they had it alongside the skiff. Between them they lifted the gigantic head clear of the water. As soon as they did so the fish went into its last frenzy. Its body was half as long again as a tall man, and as thick around the middle as a Shetland pony. It pulsed and flexed until its nose touched the wide flukes of its tail, first on the one side, then on the other. It threw up sheets of seawater that came aboard in solid gouts, drenching the three lads as though they

13

stood under a waterfall. They held on grimly, until the violent paroxysms weakened. Then Jim called out, 'Hang on to her! She's ready for the priest.'

He snatched up the billy from its sling under the transom. The end of the club was weighted with lead, balanced and heavy in his big right hand. He lifted the fish's head high and swung his weight behind the blow. It caught the fish across the bony ridge above those glaring yellow eyes. The massive body stiffened in death and violent tremors ran down its shimmering sun-red flanks. Then the life went out of it and, white belly uppermost, it floated alongside the skiff with its gill plates open wide as a lady's parasol.

Drenched with sweat and seawater, panting wildly, nursing their torn hands, they leaned on the transom and gazed in awe upon the marvellous creature they had killed. There were no words to express adequately the overpowering emotions of triumph and remorse, of jubilation and melancholy that gripped them now that the ultimate passion of the hunter had come to its climax.

'In the Name of the Prophet, this is Leviathan indeed,' Mansur said softly. 'He makes me feel so small.'

'The sharks will be here any minute.' Jim broke the spell. 'Help me get her on board.' They threaded the rope through the fish's gills, then all three hauled on it, the skiff listing dangerously close to the point of capsizing as they brought it over the side. The boat was barely large enough to contain its bulk and there was no room for them to sit on the thwarts so they perched on the gunwale. A scale had been torn off as the fish slid over the side: it was the size of a gold doubloon and as bright.

Mansur picked it up, and turned it to catch the sunlight, staring at it with fascination. 'We must take this fish home to High Weald,' he said.

'Why?' Jim asked brusquely.

'To show the family, my father and yours.'

'By nightfall she'll have lost her colour, her scales will be dry and dull, and her flesh will start to rot and stink.' Jim shook his head. 'I want to remember her like this, in all her glory.'

'What are we going to do with her then?'

'Sell her to the purser of the VOC ship.'

'Such a wonderful creature. Sell her like a sack of potatoes? That seems like sacrilege,' Mansur protested.

'"I give you of the beasts of the earth and the fish of the sea." Kill! Eat!' Jim quoted. 'Genesis. God's very words. How could it be sacrilege?'

'Your God, not mine,' Mansur contradicted him.

'He's the same God, yours and mine. We just call him different names.'

'He is my God also.' Zama was not to be left out. 'Kulu Kulu, the Greatest of the Great Ones.'

Jim wrapped a strip of cloth round his injured hand. 'In the name of Kulu Kulu then. This steenbras is the means to get aboard the Dutch ship. I am going to use it as a letter of introduction to the purser. It's not just one fish I'm going to sell him, it's all the produce from High Weald.'

With the north-westerly breeze blowing ten knots behind them they could hoist the single sail, which carried them swiftly into the bay. There were eight ships lying at anchor under the guns of the castle. Most had been there for weeks and were already well provisioned.

Jim pointed out the latest arrival. 'They will not have set foot on land for months. They will be famished for fresh food. They are probably riddled with scurvy already.' Jim put the tiller over and wove through the anchored shipping. 'After what they almost did to us, they owe us a nice bit of profit.' All the Courtneys were traders to the core of their being and for even the youngest of them the word 'profit' held almost religious significance. Jim headed for the Dutch ship. It was a tall three-decker, twenty guns a side, square-rigged, three masts, big and beamy, obviously an armed trader. She flew the VOC pennant and the flag of the Dutch Republic. As they closed with her Jim could see the storm damage to hull and rigging. Clearly she had endured a rough passage. Closer still, Jim could make out the ship's name on her stern in faded gilt lettering: *Het Gelukkige Meeuw*, the *Lucky Seagull*. He grinned at how inappropriately the shabby old lady had been named. Then his green eyes narrowed with surprise and interest.

'Women, by God!' He pointed ahead. 'Hundreds of them.' Both Mansur and Zama scrambled to their feet, clung to the mast and peered ahead, shading their eyes against the sun.

'You're right!' Mansur exclaimed. Apart from the wives of the burghers, their stolid, heavily chaperoned daughters and the trollops of the waterfront taverns, women were rare at the Cape of Good Hope.

'Look at them,' Jim breathed with awe. 'Just look at those beauties.' Forward of the mainmast the deck was crowded with female shapes.

'How do you know they're beautiful?' Mansur demanded. 'We're too far away to tell. They're probably ugly old crones.'

'No, God could not be so cruel to us.' Jim laughed excitedly. 'Every one of them is an angel from heaven. I just know it!'

There was a small group of officers on the quarter-deck, and knots of seamen were already at work repairing the damaged rigging and painting the hull. But the three youths in the skiff had eyes only for the female shapes on the foredeck. Once again they caught a whiff of the stench that hung over the ship, and Jim exclaimed with horror: 'They're in leg irons.' He had the sharpest eyesight of the three and had seen that the ranks of women were shuffling along the deck in single file, with the hampered gait of the chained captive.

'Convicts!' Mansur agreed. 'Your angels from heaven are female convicts. Uglier than sin.'

They were close enough now to make out the features of some of the bedraggled creatures, the grey, greasy hair, the toothless mouths, the wrinkled pallor of ancient skin, the sunken eyes and, on most of the miserable faces, the ugly blotches and bruises of scurvy. They stared down on the approaching boat with dull, hopeless eyes, showing no interest, no emotion of any kind.

Even Jim's lascivious instincts were cooled. These were no longer human beings, but beaten, abused animals. Their coarse

16

canvas shifts were ragged and soiled. Obviously they had worn them ever since leaving Amsterdam, without water to wash their bodies, let alone their clothing. There were guards armed with muskets stationed in the mainmast bitts and the forecastle overlooking the deck. As the skiff came within hail a petty officer in a blue pea-jacket hurried to the ship's side and raised a speaking trumpet to his lips. 'Stand clear,' he shouted in Dutch. 'This is a prison ship. Stand off or we will fire into you.'

'He means it, Jim,' Mansur said. 'Let's get away from her.'

Jim ignored the suggestion and held up one of the fish. '*Vars vis!* Fresh fish,' he yelled back. 'Straight out of the sea. Caught an hour ago.' The man at the rail hesitated, and Jim sensed his opportunity. 'Look at this one.' He pointed at the huge carcass that filled most of the skiff. 'Steenbras! Finest eating fish in the sea! There's enough here to feed every man on board for a week.'

'Wait!' the man yelled back, and hurried across the deck to the group of officers. There was a brief discussion, then he came back to the rail. 'Good, then. Come! But keep clear of our bows. Hook on to the stern chains.'

Mansur dropped the tiny sail and they rowed under the side of the ship. Three seamen stood at the rail, aiming their muskets down into the skiff.

'Don't try anything clever,' the petty officer warned them, 'unless you want a ball in your belly.'

Jim grinned up at him ingratiatingly and showed his empty hands. 'We mean no harm, Mijnheer. We are honest fishermen.' He was still fascinated by the lines of chained women, and stared up at them with revulsion and pity as they shuffled in a sorry line along the near rail. Then he switched his attention to bringing the skiff alongside. He did this with a seamanlike flourish, and Zama tossed the painter up to a seaman who was waiting in the chains above them.

The ship's purser, a plump bald man, stuck his head over the side and peered down into the skiff to inspect the wares on offer. He looked impressed by the size of the giant steenbras carcass. 'I'm not going to shout. Come up here where we can talk,' the purser invited Jim, and ordered a seaman to drop a rope-ladder over the side. This was the invitation Jim had been angling for. He shinned up and over the high tumble-home of the ship's side like an acrobat, and landed on the deck beside the purser with a slap of his bare feet.

'How much for the big one?' The purser's question was ambiguous, and he ran a pederast's calculating glance over Jim's body. A fine bit of beef, he thought, as he studied the muscled chest and arms, and the long, shapely legs, smooth and tanned by the sun.

'Fifteen silver guilders for the entire load of our fish.' Jim placed emphasis on the last word. The purser's interest in him was obvious.

'Are you an escaped lunatic?' the purser retorted. 'You, your fish and your dirty little boat together are not worth half that much.'

'The boat and I are not for sale,' Jim assured him, with relish. When he was bargaining he was in his element. His father had trained him well. He had no compunction in taking advantage of the purser's sexual predilections to push him for the best price. They settled on eight guilders for the full load.

'I want to keep the smallest fish for my family's dinner.' Jim said, and the purser chuckled. 'You drive a hard bargain, *kerel*.' He spat on his right hand and proffered it. Jim spat on his own and they shook hands to seal the bargain.

The purser held on to Jim's hand for a little longer than was necessary. 'What else have you got for sale, young stallion?' He winked at Jim and ran his tongue round his fat, sun-cracked lips.

Jim did not answer him at once, but went to the rail to watch the crew of *Het Gelukkige Meeuw* lower a cargo net into the skiff. With difficulty Mansur and Zama slid the huge fish into it. Then it was hoisted up and swung on to the deck. Jim turned back to the purser. 'I can sell you a load of fresh vegetables – potatoes, onions, pumpkins, fruit, anything you want at half the price they will charge you if you buy from the Company gardens,' Jim told him.

'You know full well that the VOC has the monopoly,' the purser demurred. 'I am forbidden to buy from private traders.'

'I can fix that with a few guilders in the right pocket.' Jim touched the side of his nose. Everyone knew how simple it was to placate the Company officials at Good Hope. Corruption was a way of life in the colonies.

'Very well, then. Bring me out a load of the best you have,' the purser agreed, and laid an avuncular hand on Jim's arm. 'But don't get caught at it. We don't want a pretty boy like you all cut up with the lash.' Jim evaded his touch without making it obvious. Never upset a customer. There was a sudden commotion on the foredeck and, grateful for the respite from these plump and sweaty attentions, Jim glanced over his shoulder.

The first group of women prisoners was being herded down below decks, and another line was coming up into the open air for their exercise. Jim stared at the girl at the head of this new file of prisoners. His breath came short and his pulse pounded in his ears. She was tall, but starved thin and pale. She wore a shift of threadbare canvas, with a hem so tattered that her knees showed through the holes. Her legs were thin and bony, the flesh melted off by starvation, and her arms were the same. Under the shapeless canvas her body seemed boyish, lacking the swells and round contours of a woman. But Jim was not looking at her body: he was gazing at her face.

Her head was small but gracefully poised on her long neck, like an unopened tulip on its stem. Her skin was pale and flawless, so fine in texture that he imagined he could see her cheekbones through it. Even in her terrible circumstances she had clearly made an effort to prevent herself sinking into the slough of despair. Her hair was pulled back from her face, plaited into a thick rope that hung forward over one shoulder, and she had contrived somehow to keep it clean and combed. It reached down almost to her waist, fine as spun Chinese silk and blonde, dazzling as a golden guinea in the sunlight. But it was her eyes that stopped Jim's breath altogether for a long minute. They were blue, the colour of the high African sky in midsummer. When she looked upon him for the first time they opened wide. Then her lips parted and her teeth were white and even, with no gaps between them. She stopped abruptly, and the woman behind stumbled into her. Both lost their balance and almost fell. Their leg irons clanked, and the other woman thrust her forward roughly, cursing her in the accents of the Antwerp docklands. 'Come on, princess, move your pretty pussy.'

The girl did not seem to notice.

One of the gaolers stepped up behind her. 'Keep moving, you stupid cow.' With the length of knotted rope he hit her across the top of her thin bare arm, raising a vivid red welt. Jim fought to stop himself rushing to protect her, and the nearest guard sensed the movement. He swung the muzzle of his musket towards Jim, who stepped back. He knew that at that range the buckshot would have disembowelled him. But the girl had seen his gesture too, recognized something in him. She stumbled forward, her eyes filled with tears of pain from the lash, massaging the crimson welt with her other hand. She kept those haunting eyes on his face as she passed where Jim stood rooted to the deck. He knew it was dangerous and futile to speak to her, but the words were out before he could bite down on them and there was pity in his tone. 'They've starved you.'

A pale travesty of a smile flickered across her lips, but she gave no other sign of having heard him. Then the harridan in the line behind her shoved her forward: 'No young cock for you today, your highness. You'll have to use your finger. Keep moving.' The girl went on down the deck away from him.

'Let me give you some advice, *kerel*,' said the purser at his shoulder. 'Don't try anything with any of those bitches. That's the shortest way to hell.'

Jim mustered a grin. 'I'm a brave man, but not a stupid one.' He held out his hand and the purser counted eight silver coins into his palm. He swung a leg over the rail. 'I'll bring out a load of vegetables for you tomorrow. Then perhaps we can go ashore together and have a grog in one of the taverns.' As he dropped down into the skiff, he muttered, 'Or I could break your neck and both your fat legs.' He took his place at the tiller.

'Cast off, hoist the sail,' he called to Zama, and brought the skiff on to the wind. They skimmed down the side of the *Meeuw*. The port-lids on the gunports were open to let light and air into the gundecks. Jim looked into the nearest as he came level. The crowded, fetid gundeck was a vision from hell, and the stench was like a pig-sty or cesspit. Hundreds of human beings had been crowded into that low, narrow space for months without relief.

Jim tore away his gaze, and glanced up at the ship's rail, high above his head. He was still looking for the girl, but he expected to be disappointed. Then his pulse leaped as those unbelievably blue eyes stared down at him. In the line of women prisoners the girl was shuffling along the rail near the bows.

'Your name? What's your name?' he called urgently. At that moment to know it was the most important thing in the world.

Her reply was faint on the wind, but he read it on her lips: 'Louisa.'

'I'll come back, Louisa. Be of good cheer,' he shouted recklessly, and she stared at him expressionlessly. Then he did something even more reckless. He knew it was madness, but she was starved. He snatched up the red stumpnose he had kept back from the sale. It weighed almost ten pounds but he tossed it up lightly. Louisa reached out and caught it in both hands, with a hungry, desperate expression on her face. The grotesque troll in the line behind her jumped forward and tried to wrest it out of her grasp. Immediately three or four other women joined the struggle, fighting over the fish like a pack of she-wolves. Then the gaolers rushed in to break up the mêlée, flogging and lashing the shrieking women with the knotted ropes. Jim turned away, sick to the guts, his heart torn with pity and with some other emotion he did not recognize for he had never experienced it before.

The three sailed on in grim silence, but every few minutes Jim turned to look back at the prison ship.

'There is nothing you can do for her,' Mansur said at last. 'Forget her, coz. She's out of your reach.'

Jim's face darkened with anger and frustration. 'Is she? You think you know everything, Mansur Courtney. We shall see. We shall see!'

On the beach ahead one of the grooms was holding a string of harnessed mules, ready to help them beach the skiff. 'Don't just sit there like a pair of cormorants drying your wings on a rock. Get the sail down,' Jim snarled at the other two with the formless, undirected anger still dark upon him.

They waited on the first line of the surf, hanging on the oars, waiting for the right wave. When Jim saw it coming he shouted, 'Here we go. Give way together. Pull!'

It swept under the stern and then suddenly, exhilaratingly, they were surfing on the brow of the curling green wave, racing on to the beach. The wave carried them high, then pulled back to leave them stranded. They jumped out and when the groom galloped in with the team of mules, they hitched on to the trek chain. They ran beside the team, whooping to drive them on, dragging the skiff well above the high-water mark, then unhitched it.

'I'll need the team again first thing tomorrow morning,' Jim told the groom. 'Have them ready.'

'So, we're going out to that hell ship again, are we?' Mansur asked flatly.

'To take them a load of vegetables.' Jim feigned innocence.

'What do you want to trade in return?' Mansur asked, with equal insouciance. Jim punched his arm lightly and they jumped on to the bare backs of the mules. Jim took one last, brooding look across the bay to where the prison ship was anchored, then they rode round the shore of the lagoon, up the hill towards the whitewashed buildings of the estate, the homestead and the godown that Tom Courtney had named High Weald after the great mansion in Devon where he and Dorian had been born, and which neither of them had laid eyes on for so many years.

The name was the only thing that the two houses had in common. This one was built in the Cape style. The roof was thatched thickly with reeds. The graceful gabled ends and the archway leading into the central courtyard had been designed by the celebrated Dutch architect, Anreith. The name of the estate and the family emblem were incorporated into the ornate fresco of cherubs and saints above the archway. The emblem depicted a long-barrelled cannon on its wheeled carriage with a ribbon below it, and the letters 'CBTC' for Courtney Brothers Trading Company. In a separate panel was the legend: 'High Weald, 1711'. The house had been built in the same year that Jim and Mansur were born.

As they clattered through the archway and into the cobbled courtyard, Tom Courtney came stamping out of the main doors of the warehouse. He was a big man, over six foot tall, heavy in the shoulders. His dense black beard was shot through with silver and his pate was innocent of a single strand of hair, but thick curls surrounded the shiny bald scalp and bushed down the back of his neck. His belly, once flat and hard, had taken on a magisterial girth. His craggy features were laced with webs of laughter lines, while his eyes gleamed with humour and the contentment of a supremely confident, prosperous man.

'James Courtney! You've been gone so long I'd forgotten what you looked like. It's good of you to drop in. I hate to trouble you, but do any of you intend doing any work this day?'

Jim hunched his shoulders guiltily. 'We were almost run down by a Dutch ship, damned nigh sunk us. Then we caught a red steenbras the size of a carthorse. It took two hours to bring it in. We had to take it out to sell to one of the ships in the bay.'

'By Jesus, boy, you've had a busy morning. Don't tell me the rest of your tribulations, let me guess. You were attacked by a French ship-of-the-line, and charged by a wounded hippo.' Tom roared with delight at his own wit. 'Anyway, how much did you get for a carthorse-sized steenbras?' he demanded.

'Eight silver guilders.'

Tom whistled. 'It must have been a monster.' Then his

expression became serious. 'Ain't no excuse, lad. I didn't give you the week off. You should have been back hours ago.'

'I haggled with the purser of the Dutch ship,' Jim told him. 'He will take all the provender we can send him – and at good prices, Papa.'

A shrewd expression replaced the laughter in Tom's eyes. 'Seems you ain't wasted your time. Well done, lad.'

At that moment a fine-looking woman, almost as tall as Tom, stepped out of the kitchens at the opposite end of the courtyard. Her hair was scraped up into a heavy bun on top of her head, and the sleeves of her blouse were rolled up around her plump sun-browned arms. 'Tom Courtney, don't you realize the poor child left this morning without breakfast. Let him eat a meal before you bully him any more.'

'Sarah Courtney,' Tom shouted back, 'this poor child of yours isn't five years old any longer.'

'It's your lunchtime too.' Sarah changed tack. 'Yasmini, the girls and I have been slaving over the stove all morning. Come along now, all of you.'

Tom threw up his hands in capitulation. 'Sarah, you're a tyrant, but I could eat a buffalo bull with the horns on,' he said. He came down off the veranda and put one arm around Jim's shoulders, the other round Mansur's and led them towards the kitchen door, where Sarah waited for them with her arms powdered to the elbows with flour.

Zama took the team of mules and led them out of the courtyard towards the stables. 'Zama, tell my brother that the ladies are waiting lunch for him,' Tom called after him,

'I will tell him, *oubaas!*' Zama used the most respectful term of address for the master of High Weald.

'As soon as you have finished eating, you get back here with all the men,' Jim warned him. 'We have to pick and load a cargo of vegetables to take out to the *Lucky Seagull* tomorrow.'

The kitchen was bustling with women, most of them freed house slaves, graceful, golden-skinned Javanese women from Batavia. Jim went to embrace his mother.

Sarah pretended to be put out, 'Don't be a great booby,

24

James,' but she flushed with pleasure as he lifted her and bussed her on both cheeks. 'Put me down at once and let me get on.'

'If you don't love me then at least Aunt Yassie does.' He went to the delicate, lovely woman who was wrapped in the arms of her own son. 'Come now, Mansur! It's my turn now.' He lifted Yasmini out of Mansur's embrace. She wore a long *ghāgrā* skirt and a *colī* blouse of vivid silk. She was as slim and light as a girl, her skin a glowing amber, her slanting eyes dark as onyx. The snowy blaze through the front of her dense dark hair was not a sign of age: she had been born with it, as had her mother and grandmother before her.

With the women fussing over them, the men seated themselves at the top of the long yellow-wood table, which was piled with bowls and platters. There were dishes of bobootie curry in the Malayan style, redolent with mutton and spices, rich with eggs and yoghurt, an enormous venison pie, made with potatoes and the meat of the springbuck Jim and Mansur had shot out in the open veld, loaves of bread still hot from the oven, pottery crocks of yellow butter, jugs of thick sour milk and small beer.

'Where is Dorian?' Tom demanded, from the head of the table. 'Late again!'

'Did someone call my name?' Dorian sauntered into the kitchen, still lean and athletic, handsome and debonair, his head a mass of copper curls to match his son's. He wore high riding boots that were dusty to the knees, and a wide-brimmed straw hat. He spun the hat across the room, and the women greeted him with a chorus of delight.

'Quiet! All of you! You sound like a flock of hens when a jackal gets into the coop,' Tom bellowed. The noise subsided almost imperceptibly. 'Come on, sit down, Dorry, before you drive these women wild. We are to hear the tale of the giant steenbras the boys caught, and the deal they have done with the VOC ship lying out in the bay.'

Dorian took the chair beside his brother, and sank the blade of his knife through the crust of the venison pie. There was a sigh of approval from all of the company as a fragrant cloud of steam rose to the high stinkwood beams of the ceiling. As Sarah spooned the food on to the blue willow-pattern plates the room was filled with banter from the men, giggles and spontaneous demonstrations of affection from the women.

'What's wrong with Jim Boy?' Sarah looked across the table, and raised her voice above the pandemonium.

'Nothing,' said Tom, with the next spoonful half-way to his mouth. He looked sharply at his only son. 'Is there?'

Slowly silence settled over the table and everyone stared at Jim. 'Why aren't you eating?' Sarah demanded with alarm. Jim's vast appetite was a family legend. 'What you need is a dose of sulphur and molasses.'

'I'm fine, just not hungry.' Jim glanced down at the pie he had barely touched, then at the circle of faces. 'Don't look at me like that. I'm not going to die.'

Sarah was still watching him. 'What happened today?'

Jim knew she could see through him as though he was made of glass. He jumped to his feet. 'Please excuse me,' he said, pushed back his stool and stalked out of the kitchen into the yard.

Tom lumbered to his feet to follow him, but Sarah shook her head. 'Leave him be, husband,' she said. Only one person could give Tom Courtney orders, and he subsided obediently on to his stool. In contrast to the mood of only moments before, the room was plunged into a heavy, fraught silence.

Sarah looked across the table. 'What happened out there today, Mansur?'

'Jim went aboard the convict ship in the bay. He saw things that upset him.'

'What things?' she asked.

'The ship is filled with women prisoners. They had been chained, starved and beaten. The ship sinks like a pig-sty,' Mansur said, repugnance and pity in his voice. Silence descended again as they visualized the scene Mansur had described.

Then Sarah said softly, 'And one of the women on board was young and pretty.'

26

'How did you know that?' Mansur stared at her with astonishment.

J im strode out through the archway and down the hill towards the paddock at the edge of the lagoon. As the track emerged from the trees he put two fingers into his mouth and whistled. The stallion was a little separated from the rest of the herd, grazing on the green grass at the edge of the water. He threw up his head at the sound, and the blaze on his forehead shone like a diadem in the sunlight. He arched his neck, flared his wide Arabian nostrils and stared across at Jim with luminous eyes. Jim whistled again. 'Come, Drumfire,' he called. 'Come to me.'

Drumfire glided from a standstill into a full gallop in a few strides. For such a large animal he moved with the grace of an antelope. Just watching him Jim felt his black mood begin to evaporate. The animal's coat gleamed like oiled mahogany and his mane streamed out over his back like a war banner. His steel-shod hoofs tore chunks out of the green turf with the thunder of rapid fire from a massed battery of cannon, the sound for which Jim had named him.

Riding against the burghers of the colony and the officers of the cavalry regiment, Jim and Drumfire had won the Governor's Gold Plate last Christmas Day. In doing so Drumfire had proved he was the fastest horse in Africa, and Jim had spurned an offer of two thousand guilders for him from Colonel Stephanus Keyser, the commander of the garrison. Horse and rider had won honour but no friends that day.

Drumfire swept down the track, running straight at Jim. He loved to try to make his master flinch. Jim stood his ground and, at the very last instant, Drumfire swerved so close that the wind of his passing ruffled Jim's hair. Then he came to a dead stop on braced front legs, nodding and neighing wildly.

'You great showman,' Jim told him. 'Behave yourself.' Suddenly docile as a kitten Drumfire came back and nuzzled

27

his chest, snuffling at the pockets of his coat until he smelt the slice of plum cake. 'Cupboard love,' Jim told him firmly.

Drumfire pushed him with his forehead, gently at first but then so demandingly that Jim was lifted off his feet. 'You don't deserve it, but . . .' Jim relented and held out the cake. Drumfire drooled into his open palm as he picked up every last crumb with velvet lips. Jim wiped his hand on the shining neck, then laid one hand on the horse's withers and leaped lightly on to his back. At the touch of his heels, Drumfire glided again into that miraculous stride, and the wind whipped tears from the corners of Jim's eyes. They raced along the edge of the lagoon, but when Jim touched him behind the shoulder with his toe the stallion did not hesitate. He turned and plunged into the shallows, startling a shoal of mullet into brief flight like a handful of spinning silver guilders across the green surface. Abruptly Drumfire was into the deep and Jim slipped into the water beside him as he swam. He grasped a handful of the long mane, and let the stallion tow him along. Swimming was another of Drumfire's great joys and the horse gave loud grunts of pleasure. As soon as he felt the bottom of the far shore under the horse's hoofs Jim slid on to his back again, and they burst out on to the beach at full stride.

Jim turned him down towards the seashore, and they crossed the high dunes, leaving deep hoofprints in the white sand, and went down the other side to where the surf crashed on to the beach. Without check Drumfire galloped along the edge of the water, running first on the hard wet sand, then belly deep through salt water as the waves came ashore. At last Jim slowed him to a walk. The stallion had galloped away his black mood, his anger and guilt left on the wind. He jumped up and stretched to his full height on Drumfire's back, and the horse adjusted his gait smoothly to help him balance. This was just one of the tricks they had taught each other.

Standing high Jim gazed out over the bay. The *Meeuw* had swung on her anchor so that she lay broadside to the beach. From this distance she looked as honest and respectable as a burgher's goodwife, giving no outward sign of the horrors hidden within her drab hull.

'Wind's changed,' Jim told his horse, who cocked an ear back to listen to his voice. 'It'll blow up a hell-storm in the next few days.' He imagined the conditions below the decks of the convict ship if she were still anchored in the bay, which was open to the west, when it came. His black mood was returning. He dropped back astride Drumfire and rode on at a more sedate pace towards the castle. By the time they arrived below the massive stone walls his clothing had dried, although his *velskoen* boots made of kudu skin were still damp.

Captain Hugo van Hoogen, the quartermaster of the garrison, was in his office beside the main powder magazine. He gave Jim a friendly welcome, then offered him a pipe of Turkish tobacco and a cup of Arabian coffee. Jim refused the pipe but drank the dark, bitter brew with relish – his aunt Yasmini had introduced them all to it. Jim and the quartermaster were old accomplices. It was accepted between them that Jim was the unofficial go-between of the Courtney family. If Hugo signed a licence stating that the Company was unable to supply provisions or stores to any ship in the bay, then the private chandler designated in the document was allowed to make good the shortfall. Hugo was also an avid fisherman, and Jim related the saga of the steenbras, to a chorus from Hugo of 'Ag nee, man!' and 'Dis nee war nee! It's not true!'

When Jim shook hands with him and took his leave, he had in his pocket a blank licence to trade in the name of Courtney Brothers Trading Company. 'I will come and drink coffee with you again on Saturday.' Jim winked.

Hugo nodded genially. 'You will be more than welcome, my young friend.' From long experience he knew that he could trust Jim to bring his commission in a little purse of gold and silver coin.

Back in the stables on High Weald Jim rubbed Drumfire down, rather than letting one of the grooms do the job, then left him with a manger of crushed corn, over which he had dribbled molasses. Drumfire had a sweet tooth.

The fields and orchards behind the stables were filled with freed slaves gathering in the fresh produce destined for the *Meeuw*. Most of the bushel baskets were already filled with potatoes and apples, pumpkins and turnips. His father and Mansur were supervising the harvest. Jim left them to it, and went down to the slaughterhouse. In the cavernous cool room, with its thick, windowless walls, dozens of freshly slaughtered sheep carcasses hung from hooks in the ceiling. Jim drew the knife from the sheath on his belt and whipped the blade, with practised strokes, across the whetstone as he went to join his uncle Dorian. To prepare all the produce they needed to supply to the ship, everyone on the estate had to help with the work. Freed slaves dragged in fat-tailed Persian sheep from the holding pen, held them down and pulled back their heads to expose the throats to the stroke of the knife. Other willing hands lifted the dead animals on to the hooks and stripped off the bloody fleeces.

Weeks ago, Carl Otto, the estate butcher, had filled his smokeroom with hams and sausages for just such an opportunity. In the kitchens all the women from eldest to youngest were helping Sarah and Yasmini to bottle fruit and pickle vegetables.

Despite their best efforts it was late in the afternoon before the convoy of mule carts was fully loaded and had set off down to the beach. The transfer of the provisions from the carts to the beached bumboats took most of the rest of the night, and it was almost dawn before they were loaded.

Despite Jim's misgivings the wind had not increased in strength and the sea and surf were manageable as the mule teams dragged the heavily laden boats down the sand. The first glimmer of dawn was in the eastern sky by the time the little convoy was on its way. Jim was at the tiller in the leading boat and Mansur was on the stroke oar.

'What have you got in the bag, Jim?' he asked, between strokes.

'Ask no questions and you'll hear no lies.' Jim glanced down at the waterproof canvas bag that lay between his feet. He kept his voice low so that his father did not overhear. Luckily Tom Courtney, who stood in the bows, had fired so many heavy muskets in his long career as a hunter that his hearing was dull.

'Is it a gift for a sweetheart?' Mansur grinned slyly in the darkness, but Jim ignored him. That arrow was too near the bullseye for comfort. Jim had carefully packed into the bag a bundle of salted, sun-dried venison, the ubiquitous *biltong* of the Cape Boers, ten pounds of hard ship's biscuit wrapped in a cloth, a folding knife and a triangular-bladed file that he had pilfered from the estate workshop, a tortoiseshell comb, which belonged to his mother, and a letter written on a single sheet of paper in Dutch.

They came up to the *Meeuw*, and Tom Courtney hailed her in a bull bellow: 'Longboat with supplies. Permission to hook on?'

There was an answering shout from the ship and they rowed in, bumping lightly against the tall hull.

With her long legs folded under her, Louisa Leuven sat on the hard deck in the noisome semi-darkness that was lit only by the feeble light of the fighting-lanterns. Her shoulders were covered with a single thin cotton blanket of the poorest quality. The gunports were closed and bolted. The guards were taking no chances: with the shore so close, some of the women might take the risk in the cold green currents, undeterred by the possibility of drowning or being devoured by the monstrous sharks that were attracted to these waters by the swarming seal colony on Robben Island. While the women had been on deck that afternoon the cook had thrown overboard a bucket of guts from the red steenbras. The head gaoler had pointed out to his prisoners the triangular fins of the sharks as they sped in to snatch these bloody morsels.

'Don't any of you filthy slatterns get ideas of escape,' he cautioned them.

At the beginning of the voyage Louisa had claimed for herself this berth under one of the huge bronze cannons. She was stronger than most of the other wizened undernourished convicts and, of necessity, she had learned how to protect herself. Life on board was like being in a pack of wild animals:

the women around her were every bit as dangerous and merciless as wolves, but shrewder and more cunning. At the beginning Louisa knew she had to procure a weapon so she had managed to prise loose a strip of the bronze beading from under the carriage of the cannon. She had spent long hours of the night stropping this against the cannon barrel until it had a sharp double stiletto edge. She tore a strip of canvas from the hem of her shift and wrapped it round the hilt to make a handle. She carried the dagger, day and night, in the pouch she wore strapped around her waist under the canvas shift. So far she had been forced to cut only one of the other women.

Nedda was a Frieslander, with heavy thighs and bottom, fat arms and a pudding face covered with freckles. She had once been a notorious whore-mistress for the nobility. She had specialized in procuring young children for her rich clients, until she became too greedy and tried to blackmail one. On a hot, tropical night as the ship lay becalmed a few degrees south of the equator, Big Nedda had crept up on Louisa in the night, and pinned her down under her suffocating weight. None of the gaolers or any of the women had come to Louisa's rescue as she screamed and struggled. Instead they had giggled and egged Nedda on.

'Give it to the high and mighty bitch.'

'Listen to her squealing for it. She loves it.'

'Go on, Big Nedda. Shove your fist up that prim royal *poesje*.'

When Louisa felt the woman prise her legs apart with a fat knee, she reached down, slipped the blade out of its pouch and slashed Nedda's chubby red cheek. Nedda howled and rolled off her, clutching the deep, spurting wound. Then she crept away, sobbing and moaning, into the darkness. During the next few weeks the wound had festered, and Nedda had crouched like a bear in the darkest recess of the gundeck, her face swollen to double its size, pus leaking out through the dirty bandage, dripping yellow and thick as cream from her chin. Since then Nedda had kept well clear of Louisa, and the other women had learned from her example. They left her well alone.

32

For Louisa this dreadful voyage seemed to have lasted all her life. Even during this respite from the open sea, while the *Meeuw* lay at anchor in Table Bay, the magnitude of the ordeal she had undergone still haunted her. She cowered further into her refuge under the cannon and shuddered as each of the separate memories pricked her like thorns. The throng of humanity was pressed close about her. They were packed so tightly into every inch of the deck that it was almost impossible to escape the touch of other filthy bodies crawling with lice. In rough weather the latrine buckets slopped over, and the sewage ran down the crowded deck. It soaked the women's clothing and their thin cotton blankets where they lay. During the occasional spells of calm weather the crew pumped seawater down the hatches and the women went down on their knees to scrub the planks with the coarse holystones. It was in vain, for during the next storm the filth splashed over them again. In the dawn when the hatches were taken off the companionways, they took turns to carry the reeking wooden buckets up the ladders to the deck and empty them over the side while the crew and the guards jeered at them.

Every Sunday, in any kind of weather, the prisoners were mustered on deck while the guards stood over them with loaded muskets. The women, in their leg irons and ragged canvas shifts, shivered and hugged themselves with their thin arms, their skin blue and pimpled with the cold, while the Dutch Reform dominie harangued them for their sins. When this ordeal was over the crew set up canvas screens on the foredeck, and in groups the prisoners were forced behind them while streams of seawater were sprayed over them from the ship's pumps. Louisa and some of the more fastidious women stripped off their shifts and tried as best they could to wash off the filth. The screens fluttered in the wind and afforded them almost no privacy, and the seamen on the pumps or in the rigging overhead whistled and called ribald comments.

'Look at the dugs on that cow!'

'You could sail a ship-of-the-line up that great hairy harbour.'

Louisa learned to use her wet shift to cover herself, as she crouched low, screening herself behind the other women. The few hours of cleanliness were worth the humiliation, but as soon as her shift dried and the warmth of her body hatched the next batch of nits she began to scratch again. With her bronze blade she whittled a splinter of wood into a fine-tooth comb and spent hours each day under the gun carriage combing the nits out of her long, golden hair, and from the tufts of her body hair. Her pathetic attempts at bodily hygiene seemed to highlight the slovenliness of the other women, which infuriated them.

'Look at her royal bloody highness, at it again. Combing her *poesje* hairs.'

'She's better than the rest of us. Going to marry the Governor of Batavia when we get there, didn't you know?'

'You going to invite us to the wedding, Princess?'

'Nedda here will be your bridesmaid, won't you, Nedda *lieveling*?' The livid scar down Nedda's fat cheek twisted into a grotesque grin, but her eyes were filled with hatred in the dim lantern-light.

Louisa had learned to ignore them. She heated the point of her blade in the smoky flame of the lantern in the gimbal above her head, ran the blade down the seams of the shift in her lap, and the nits popped and frizzled. She held the blade back in the flame and, while she waited for it to heat again, she ducked her head to peer through the narrow slit in the joint of the port-lid.

She had used the point of her blade to enlarge this aperture until she had an unobstructed view. There was a padlock on the port-lid, but she had worked for weeks to loosen the shackles. Then she had used soot from the lantern to darken the raw wood, rubbing it in with her finger to conceal it from the weekly inspection of the ship's officers, carried out on Sunday while the convicts were on the open deck for the prayer meeting and ablutions. Louisa always returned to her berth terrified that her work had been discovered. When she found that it had not, her relief was so intense that often she broke down and wept.

Despair was always so near at hand, lurking like a wild beast, ready to pounce at any moment and devour her. More than once over the past months she had sharpened her little blade until the edge could shave the fine blonde hairs of her forearm. Then she had hidden away under the gun carriage and felt for the pulse in her wrist where the blue artery beat so close to the surface. Once she had laid the sharp edge against the skin and steeled herself to make the deep incision, then she had looked up at the thin chink of light coming through the joint of the port-lid. It seemed to be a promise.

'No,' she whispered to herself. 'I am going to escape. I am going to endure.'

To bolster her determination she spent hours during those terrible endless days when the ship crashed through the high, turbulent storms of the southern Atlantic daydreaming of the bright, happy days of her childhood, which now seemed to have been in another hazy existence. She trained herself to retreat into her imagination, and to shut out the reality in which she was trapped.

She dwelt on the memory of her father, Hendrick Leuven, a tall, thin man with his black suit buttoned high. She saw again his crisp white lace stock, the stockings that covered his scrawny shanks lovingly darned by her mother, and the pinch-beck buckles on his square-toed shoes, polished until they shone like pure silver. Under the wide brim of his tall black hat the lugubriousness of his features was given the lie by mischievous blue eyes. She had inherited hers from him. She remembered all of his funny, fascinating and poignant stories. Every night when she was young he had carried her up the stairs to her cot. He had tucked her in, and sat beside her reciting them to her while she tried desperately to fight off sleep. When she was older she had walked with him in the garden, her hand in his, through the tulip fields of the estate, going over the day's lessons with him. She smiled secretly now as she recalled his endless patience with her questions, and his sad, proud smile when she arrived at the right answer to a mathematical problem with only a little prompting.

Hendrick Leuven had been tutor to the van Ritters family,

35

one of the pre-eminent merchant families of Amsterdam. Mijnheer Koen van Ritters was one of Het Zeventien, the board of directors of the VOC. His warehouses ran for a quarter of a mile along both banks of the inner canal and he traded around the world with his fleet of fifty-three fine ships. His country mansion was one of the most magnificent in Holland.

During the winter his numerous household lived in Huis Brabant, the huge mansion overlooking the canal. Louisa's family had three rooms at the top of the house to themselves and from the window of her tiny bedroom she could look down on the heavily laden barges, and the fishing-boats coming in from the sea.

However, the spring was the time she loved the most. That was when the family moved out into the country, to Mooi Uitsig, their country estate. In those magical days Hendrick and his family lived in a cottage across the lake from the big house. Louisa remembered the long skeins of geese coming up from the south as the weather warmed. They landed with a great splash on the lake and their honking woke her in the dawn. She cuddled under her eiderdown and listened to her father's snores from the next room. She had never again felt so warm and safe as she did then.

Louisa's mother, Anne, was English. Her father had brought her to Holland when she was a child. He had been a corporal in the bodyguard of William of Orange, after he had become King of England. When Anne was sixteen she had been engaged as a junior cook in the van Ritters household, and had married Hendrick within a year of taking up her post.

Louisa's mother had been plump and jolly, always surrounded by an aura of the delicious aromas of the kitchen: spices and vanilla, saffron and baking bread. She had insisted that Louisa learn English, and they always spoke it when they were alone. Louisa had an ear for language. In addition Anne taught her cooking and baking, embroidery, sewing and all the feminine skills.

Louisa had been allowed, as a special concession by Mijnheer van Ritters, to take her lessons with his own children, although she was expected to sit at the back of the classroom and keep quiet. Only when she was alone with her father could she ask the questions that had burned all day on the tip of her tongue. Very early she had learned deferential manners.

Only twice in all the years had Louisa laid eyes on Mevrou van Ritters. On both occasions she had spied on her from the classroom window as she stepped into the huge black-curtained carriage, assisted by half a dozen servants. She was a mysterious figure, clad in layers of black brocaded silks and a dark veil that hid her face. Louisa had overheard her mother discussing the chatelaine with the other servants. She suffered from some skin disease which made her features as monstrous as a vision of hell. Even her own husband and children were never allowed to see her unveiled.

On the other hand Mijnheer van Ritters sometimes visited the classroom to check on his offspring's progress. He often smiled at the pretty, demure little girl who sat at the back of the room. Once he even paused beside Louisa's desk to watch her writing on her slate in a neat and well-formed script. He smiled and touched her head. 'What lovely hair you have, little one,' he murmured. His own daughters tended towards plump and plain.

Louisa blushed. She thought how kind he was, and yet as remote and powerful as God. He even looked rather like the image of God in the huge oil painting in the banquet hall. It had been painted by the famous artist, Rembrandt Harmenszoon van Rijn, a protégé of the van Ritters family. It was said that Mijnheer's grandfather had posed for the artist. The painting depicted the Day of Resurrection, with the merciful Lord lifting the saved souls into Paradise, while in the background the condemned were herded into the burning pit by demons. The painting had fascinated Louisa and she spent hours in front of it.

Now, in the reeking gundeck of the *Meeuw*, combing the nits from her hair, Louisa felt like one of the unfortunates destined for Hades. She felt tears near the surface, and tried to put the sad thoughts from her mind, but they kept crowding back. She had been just ten when the black plague had struck Amsterdam again, beginning as before in the rat-infested docks, then sweeping through the city.

Mijnheer van Ritters had fled with all his household from Huis Brabant, and they had taken refuge at Mooi Uitsig. He ordered that all the gates to the estate were to be locked and armed sentries placed at each to deny access to strangers. However, when the servants unpacked one of the leather trunks they had brought from Amsterdam a huge rat leaped out and scuttled down the staircase. Even so, for weeks they believed themselves safe, until one of the housemaids collapsed in a dead faint while she was waiting on the family at dinner.

Two footmen carried the girl into the kitchen and laid her on the long table. When Louisa's mother opened the top of her blouse, she gasped as she recognized the necklace of red blotches around the girl's throat, the stigmata of the plague, the ring of roses. She was so distressed that she took little notice of the black flea that sprang from the girl's clothing on to her own skirts. Before sunset the following day the girl was dead.

The next morning two of the van Ritters children were missing when Louisa's father called the classroom to order. One of the nurserymaids came into the room and whispered in his ear. He nodded, then said, 'Kobus and Tinus will not be joining us today. Now, little ones, please open your spelling books at page five. No, Petronella, that is page ten.'

Petronella was the same age as Louisa and she was the only one of the van Ritters children who had been friendly to her. They shared a double desk at the back of the room. She often brought small gifts for Louisa, and sometimes invited her to play with her dolls in the nursery. On Louisa's last birthday she had given her one of her favourites. Of course, her nurse had made Louisa give it back. When they walked along the edge of the lake Petronella held Louisa's hand. 'Tinus was so sick last night,' she whispered. 'He vomited! It smelt awful.'

Half-way through the morning Petronella stood up suddenly and, without asking permission, started towards the door.

'Where are you going, Petronella?' Hendrick Leuven demanded sharply. She turned and stared at him with a bloodless face. Then, without a word, she collapsed on to the floor. That evening Louisa's father told her, 'Mijnheer van Ritters has ordered me to close the classroom. None of us is allowed up to the Big House again until the sickness has passed. We are to stay here in the cottage.'

'What will we eat, Papa?' Louisa, like her mother, was always practical.

'Your mother is bringing down food for us from the pantries: cheese, ham, sausage, apples and potatoes. I have my little vegetable garden, and the rabbit hutch and the chickens. You will help me work in the garden. We will continue your lessons. You will make swifter progress without the duller children to hold you back. It will be like a holiday. We will enjoy ourselves. But you are not allowed to leave the garden, do you understand?' he asked her seriously, as he scratched the red flea-bite on his bony wrist.

For three days they had enjoyed themselves. Then, the next morning, as Louisa was helping her mother prepare breakfast, Anne fainted over the kitchen stove and spilled boiling water down her leg. Louisa helped her father carry her up the stairs and lay her on the big bed. They wrapped her scalded leg in bandages soaked in honey. Then Hendrick unbuttoned the front of her dress and stared in terror at the red ring of roses around her throat.

The fever descended upon her with the speed of a summer storm. Within an hour her skin was blotched with red and seemed almost too hot to touch. Louisa and Hendrick sponged her down with cold water from the lake. 'Be strong, my *lieveling*,' Hendrick whispered to her, as she tossed and groaned, and soaked the mattress with her sweat. 'God will protect you.'

They took turns to sit with her during the night, but in the dawn Louisa screamed for her father. When he came scrambling up the stairs Louisa pointed at her mother's naked lower body. On both sides of her groin, at the juncture of her thighs with her belly, monstrous carbuncles had swelled to the size of Louisa's clenched fist. They were hard as stones and a furious purple, like ripe plums.

'The buboes!' Hendrick touched one. Anne screamed wildly in agony at his light touch, and her bowels let loose an explosion of gas and yellow diarrhoea that soaked the sheets.

Hendrick and Louisa lifted her out of the stinking bed and laid her on a clean mattress on the floor. By evening her pain was so intense and unrelenting that Hendrick could bear his wife's shrieks no longer. His blue eyes were bloodshot and haunted. 'Fetch my shaving razor!' he ordered Louisa. She scurried across to the wash-basin in the corner of the bedroom, and brought it to him. It had a beautiful mother-of-pearl handle. Louisa had always enjoyed watching her father in the early mornings lathering his cheeks, then stripping off the white soapsuds with the straight, gleaming blade.

'What are you going to do, Papa?' she asked, as she watched him sharpening the edge on the leather strop.

'We must let out the poison. It is killing your mother. Hold her still!'

Gently Louisa took hold of her mother's wrists. 'It's going to be all right, Mama. Papa is going to make it better.'

Hendrick took off his black coat and, in his white shirt, came back to the bed. He straddled his wife's legs to hold her down. Sweat was pouring down his cheeks, and his hand shook wildly as he laid the razor edge across the huge purple swelling in her groin.

'Forgive me, O merciful God,' he whispered, then pressed down and drew the blade across the carbuncle, cutting deeply and cleanly. For a moment nothing happened, then a tide of black blood and custard yellow pus erupted out of the deep wound. It splattered across the front of Hendrick's white shirt and up to the low ceiling of the bedroom above his head.

Anne's back arched like a longbow and Louisa was hurled against the wall. Hendrick cringed into a corner, stunned by the violence of his wife's contortions. Anne writhed and rolled and screamed, her face in a rictus so horrible that Louisa was terrified. She clasped both hands over her own mouth to prevent herself screaming as she watched the blood spurt in powerful, regular jets from the wound. Gradually the pulsing scarlet fountain shrivelled, and Anne's agony eased. Her screams died away, until at last she lay still and deadly pale in a spreading pool of blood.

Louisa crept back to her side and touched her arm. 'Mama, it's all right now. Papa has let all the poison out. You are going to be well again soon.' Then she looked across at her father. She had never seen him like this: he was weeping, and his lips were slack and blubbery. Saliva dripped from his chin.

'Don't cry, Papa,' she whispered. 'She will wake up soon.'

But Anne never woke again.

Her father took a spade from the tool shed and went down to the bottom of the orchard. He began to dig in the soft soil under a big apple tree. It was mid-afternoon before the grave was deep enough. He came back to the house, his eyes a vacant blue like the sky above. He was racked with shivering fits. Louisa helped him wrap Anne in the blood-soaked sheet, and walked beside him as he carried his wife to the bottom of the orchard. He laid the bundle beside the open grave and climbed down into it. Then he reached up and lifted Anne down. He laid her on the damp, fungus-smelling earth, then climbed out and reached for the spade.

Louisa sobbed as she watched him fill in the grave and tamp down the earth. Then she went out into the field beyond the hedge and picked an armful of flowers. When she came back her father was no longer in the orchard. Louisa arranged the tulips over where her mother's head must be. It seemed that the well of her tears had dried up. Her sobs were painful and dry.

When she went back to the cottage she found her father sitting at the table, his shirt filthy with his wife's blood and the grave soil. His head was cupped in his hands, his shoulders racked by shivering. When he lifted his head and looked at her, his face was pale and blotched, and his teeth chattered.

'Papa, are you sick too?' She started towards him, then shrank back as he opened his mouth and a solid stream of bile-brown vomit burst through his lips and splashed across the scrubbed wooden tabletop. Then he slumped out of his chair on to the stone-flagged floor. He was too heavy for her to lift, or even to drag up the stairs, so she tended him where he lay, cleaning away the vomit and liquid excrement, sponging him with icy lake water to bring down the fever. But she could not bring herself to take the razor to him. Two days later he died on the kitchen floor.

'I have to be brave now. I am not a baby, I'm ten years old,' she told herself. 'There is nobody to help me. I have to take care of Papa myself.'

She went down into the orchard. The spade was lying beside her mother's grave, where her father had dropped it. She began to dig. It was hard, slow work. When the grave was deep, and her thin, childish arms did not have the strength to throw up the wet earth, she fetched an apple basket from the kitchen, filled it with earth and pulled up each basketload from the bottom of the grave with a rope. When darkness fell she worked on in the grave by lantern-light. When it was as deep as she was tall, she went back to where her father lay and tried to drag him to the door. She was exhausted, her hands were raw and blistered from the handle of the spade, and she could not move him. She spread a blanket over him to cover his pale, blotched skin and staring eyes, then lay down beside him and slept until morning.

When she woke, sunlight was streaming through the window into her eyes. She got up and cut a slice from the ham hanging in the pantry and a wedge of cheese. She ate them with a hunk of dry bread. Then she went up to the stables at the rear of the big house. She remembered that she had been forbidden to go there, so she crept down behind the hedge. The stables were deserted and she realized that the grooms must have fled with the other servants. She ducked through the secret hole in the hedge that she and Petronella had discovered. The horses were still in their stalls, unfed and unwatered. She opened the doors and shooed them out into the paddock. Immediately they galloped straight down to the lake shore and lined up along the edge to drink.

She fetched a halter from the tack room, and went to Petronella's pony while it was still drinking. Petronella had allowed her to ride the pony whenever she wanted to, so the animal recognized and trusted her. As soon as it lifted its head, water dripping from its muzzle, Louisa slipped the halter over its ears, and led it back to the cottage. The back door was wide enough for the pony to pass through.

For a long while Louisa hesitated while she tried to think of some more respectful manner in which to take her father to his grave, but in the end she found a rope, hitched it to his heels and the pony dragged him into the orchard, with his head bouncing over the uneven ground. As he slipped over the lip of the shallow grave Louisa wept for him for the last time. She took the halter off the pony and turned the animal loose in the paddock. Then she climbed down beside her father and tried to arrange his limbs neatly, but they were rigid. She left him as he lay, went out into the field, gathered another armful of flowers and strewed them over his body. She knelt beside the open grave and, in a high, sweet voice, sang the first verse of 'The Lord Is My Shepherd' in English, as her mother had taught her. Then she began to shovel the earth on top of him. By the time she had filled in the last spadeful night had fallen and she crept back to the cottage, emotionally and physically numbed with exhaustion.

She had neither the strength nor the desire to eat, nor even to climb the stairs to her bed. She lay down next to the hearth and, almost immediately, fell into a deathlike sleep. She woke before morning, consumed by thirst and with a headache that felt as though her skull was about to burst open. When she tried to rise she staggered and fell against the wall. She was nauseous and giddy, her bladder swollen and painful. She tried to make her way out into the garden to relieve herself, but a wave of nausea swept over her. She doubled over slowly and vomited in the middle of the kitchen floor, then with horror stared down at the steaming puddle between her feet. She staggered to the row of her mother's copper pots, which hung on hooks along the far wall, and looked at her reflection in the polished bottom of one. Slowly and reluctantly she touched her throat and stared at the rosy necklace that adorned her milky skin.

Her legs gave way and she subsided on to the stone flags. Dark clouds of despair gathered in her mind and her vision faded. Then, suddenly, she discovered a spark still burning in the darkness, a tiny spark of strength and determination. She clung to it, shielding it like a lamp flame fluttering in a high wind. It helped her to drive back the darkness.

'I have to think,' she whispered to herself. 'I have to stand up. I know what will happen, just the way it did to Mama and Papa. I have to get ready.' Using the wall she pulled herself to her feet, and stood swaying. 'I must hurry. I can feel it coming quickly.' She remembered the terrible thirst that had consumed her dying parents. 'Water!' she whispered. She staggered with the empty water bucket to the pump in the yard. Each stroke of the long handle was a trial of her strength and courage. 'Not everyone dies,' she whispered to herself, as she worked. 'I heard the grown-ups talking. They say that some of the young, strong ones live. They don't die.' Water flowed into the bucket. 'I won't die. I won't! I won't!'

When the bucket was full she staggered to the rabbit hutch, then to the chicken run, and released all the animals and fowls to fend for themselves. 'I am not going to be able to take care of you,' she explained to them.

Carrying the water bucket, she staggered unsteadily back to the kitchen, water slopping down her legs. She placed the bucket beside the hearth with a copper dipper hooked over the side. 'Food!' she murmured, through the giddy mirages in her head. She fetched the remains of the cheese and ham and a basket of apples from the pantry and placed them where she could reach them.

'Cold. It will be cold at night.' She dragged herself to the linen chest where her mother had kept what remained of her dowry, took out a bundle of woollen blankets and a sheepskin rug and laid them out beside the hearth. Then she fetched an

44

armful of firewood from the stack in the corner and, as the shivering fits began, she built up the fire.

'The door! Lock the door!' She had heard that in the city starving pigs and dogs had broken into the houses where people lay too sick to defend themselves. The animals had eaten them alive. She closed the door and placed the locking bar in the brackets. She found her father's axe and a carving knife, and laid them beside her mattress.

There were rats in the thatch and the walls of the cottage. She had heard them scurrying about in the night, and her mother had complained of their nocturnal depredations in her pantry. Petronella had described to Louisa how a huge rat had got into the nursery of the big house while the new nursemaid was drunk on gin. Her father had found the horrid beast in her little sister's cot and had ordered the grooms to thrash the drunken nurse. The wretched woman's screams had penetrated the classroom, and the children had exchanged glances of delicious horror as they listened. Now Louisa's skin crawled at the thought of lying helpless under a rat's razor fangs.

With the last of her strength she brought down the largest of her mother's copper pots from its hook on the wall, and placed it in the corner with the lid in place. She was a fastidious child, and the thought of fouling herself as her parents had done was abhorrent to her.

'That's all I can do,' she whispered, and collapsed on to the sheepskin. Dark clouds swirled in her head and her blood seemed to boil in her veins with the heat of fever. 'Our Father, which art in heaven . . .' She recited the prayer in English, as her mother had taught her, but the sweltering darkness overwhelmed her.

Perhaps an eternity passed before she rose slowly to the surface of her mind, like a swimmer coming up from great depth. The darkness gave way to a blinding white light. Like sunlight on a snowfield, it dazzled and blinded her. The cold came out of the light, chilling her blood and frosting her bones, so she shivered wildly.

Moving painfully she drew the sheepskin over herself, and

rolled herself into a ball, hugging her knees to her chest. Then, fearfully, she reached behind: the flesh had wasted from her buttocks leaving the bones poking through. She explored herself with a finger, dreading the feel of wet, slimy faeces, but her skin was dry. She sniffed her finger tentatively. It was clean.

She remembered overhearing her father talking to her mother, 'Diarrhoea is the worst sign. Those who survive do not scour their bowels.'

'It's a sign from Jesus,' Louisa whispered to herself, through chattering teeth. 'I did not dirty myself. I am not going to die.' Then the scalding heat came back to burn away the cold and the white light. She tossed on the mattress in delirium, crying to her father and her mother, and to Jesus. Thirst woke her: it was a fire in her throat and her tongue filled her parched mouth like a sun-heated stone. She fought to raise herself on one elbow and reach for the water dipper. On the first attempt she spilled most of it over her chest, then choked and gasped on what remained in the copper dipper. The few mouthfuls that she was able to swallow renewed her strength miraculously. On her next attempt she forced down the entire contents of the dipper. She rested again, then drank another dipperful. She was satiated at last and the fires in her blood for the moment seemed quenched. She curled under the sheepskin, her belly bulging with the water she had drunk. This time the sleep that overcame her was deep but natural.

Pain roused her. She did not know where she was, or what had caused it. Then she heard a harsh ripping sound close at hand. She opened her eyes and looked down. One of her feet protruded from under the sheepskin. Hunched over her bare foot was something as big as a tomcat, grey and hairy. For a moment she did not know what it was, but then the tearing sound came again and the pain. She wanted to kick out at it, or scream, but she was frozen with terror. This was her worst nightmare come true.

The creature lifted its head and peered at her with bright, beadlike eyes. It wiggled the whiskers on its long, pointed nose, and the sharp curved fangs that overlapped its lower lip were rosy pink with her blood. It had been gnawing at her ankle. The little girl and the rat stared at each other, but Louisa was still paralysed with horror. The rat lowered its head and bit into her flesh again. Slowly Louisa reached out for the carving knife beside her head. With the speed of a cat she slashed out at the foul creature. The rat was almost as quick: it leaped high in the air, but the point of the knife split open its belly. It squealed, and flopped over.

Louisa dropped the knife and watched, wide-eyed, as the rat dragged itself across the stone floor, the slimy purple tangle of its entrails slithering after it. She was panting and it took a long time for her heart to slow and her breathing to settle. Then she found that the shock had made her feel stronger. She sat up and examined her injured foot. The bites were deep. She tore a strip off her petticoat and wrapped it round her ankle. Then she realized she was hungry. She crawled to the table and pulled herself up. The rat had been at the ham, but she hacked away the chewed area, and cut a thick slice, and placed it on a slab of bread. Green mould was already growing on the cheese, evidence of how long she had lain unconscious on the hearth. Mould and all, it was delicious. She drank the last dipperful of water. She wished she could replenish the bucket, but she knew she was not strong enough, and she was afraid to open the door.

She dragged herself to the big copper pot in the corner and squatted over it. While she piddled, she lifted her skirt high and examined her lower belly. It was smooth and unblemished, her innocent little cleft naked of hair. But she stared at the swollen buboes in her groin. They were hard as acorns and painful when she touched them, but not the same terrifying colour or size of those that had killed her mother. She thought about the razor, but knew she did not have the courage to do that to herself.

'I am not going to die!' For the first time she truly believed it. She smoothed down her skirt and crawled back to her mattress. With the carving knife clutched in her hand she slept again. After that, the days and nights mingled into a dream-like succession of sleeping and brief intervals of wakefulness.

47

Gradually these periods became longer. Each time she woke she felt stronger, more able to care for herself. When she used the pot in the corner she discovered that the buboes had subsided and had changed from red to pink. They were not nearly so painful when she touched them, but she knew she had to drink.

She summoned every last shred of her courage and strength, tottered out into the yard and refilled the water bucket. Then she locked herself into the kitchen again. When the ham was just a bare bone and the apple basket was empty, she found that she was strong enough to make her way into the garden, where she pulled up a basketful of turnips and potatoes. She rekindled the fire with her father's flint, and cooked a stew of vegetables flavoured with the ham bone. The food was delicious, and the strength flowed back into her. Each morning after that she set herself a task for the day.

On the first she emptied the copper vessel she had been using as a chamber-pot into her father's compost pit, then washed it out with lye and hot water, and hung it back on its hook. She knew her mother would have wanted that. The effort exhausted her and she crept back to the sheepskin.

The next morning she felt strong enough to fill the bucket from the pump, strip off her filthy clothing and wash herself from head to toe with a ladleful of the precious soap her mother made by boiling sheep's fat and wood ash together. She was delighted to find that the buboes in her groin had almost disappeared. With her fingertips she could press them quite hard and the pain was bearable. When her skin was pink and glowing, she scrubbed her teeth with a finger dipped in salt and dressed the rat bite on her leg from her mother's medicine chest. Then she chose fresh clothes from the linen chest.

The next day she was hungry again. She caught one of the rabbits that were hopping trustingly around the garden, held it up by the ears, steeled herself, and broke its neck with the stick her father had kept for that purpose. She gutted and skinned the carcass as her mother had taught her, then quartered it and placed it in the pot with onions and potatoes. When she had eaten it, she sucked the bones white.

The following morning she went down to the bottom of the orchard and spent the morning tidying and tending her parents' graves. Until now she had not left the security of the cottage garden, but she gathered her courage, climbed through the hole in the hedge and crept up to the greenhouse. She made certain that no one was anywhere to be seen. The estate seemed deserted still. She picked out some of the choicest blooms from the vast array on the shelves, placed them in a handcart, trundled them back to the cottage and planted them in the newly smoothed earth of the graves. She chatted away to her parents as she worked, telling them every detail of her ordeal, about the rat, and the rabbit, and how she had cooked the stew in the black three-legged pot.

'I am so sorry I used your best copper pot, Mama,' she hung her head in shame, 'but I have washed it and hung it back on the wall.'

When the graves had been decorated to her satisfaction curiosity rose in her again. Once more she slipped through the hedge and took a circuitous route through the plantation of fir trees until she could approach the big house from the south side. It was silent and bleak: all the windows were shuttered. When she sidled up cautiously to the front door she found that it was locked and barred. She stared at the cross that someone had sketched crudely on the door in red. The paint had run like tears of blood down the panel. It was the plague warning.

Suddenly she felt lonely and bereft. She sat down on the steps that led up to the doorway. 'I think I'm the only person left alive in the world. All the others are dead.'

At last she stood up and, made bold by desperation, ran round to the back door, which led to the kitchen and the servants' quarters. She tried it. To her astonishment it swung open. 'Hello!' she called. 'Is anyone there? Stals! Hans! Where are you?'

The kitchen was deserted. She went through to the scullery

and stuck her head through the door. 'Hello!' There was no answer. She went through the entire house, searching every room, but they were all deserted. Everywhere there was evidence of the family's hasty departure. She left everything untouched and closed the kitchen door carefully when she left.

On the way back to the cottage a thought occurred to her. She turned off the path and went down to the chapel at the end of the rose garden. Some of the headstones in the cemetery were two hundred years old and covered with green moss, but near the door there was a line of new graves. The headstones had not yet been set in place. The posies of flowers on them had faded and withered. Names and final messages were printed on black-edged cards on each pile of fresh earth. The ink had run in the rain, but Louisa could still read the names. She found one that read 'Petronella Katrina Susanna van Ritters'. Her friend lay between two of her younger brothers.

Louisa ran back to the cottage, and that night she sobbed herself to sleep. When she woke she felt sick and weak again, and her sorrow and loneliness had returned in full measure. She dragged herself out into the yard and washed her face and hands under the pump. Then, abruptly, she lifted her face, water running into her eyes and dripping off her chin. She cocked her head and, slowly, an expression of delight lit her face. Her eyes sparkled with blue lights. 'People!' she said aloud. 'Voices.' They were faint, and came from the direction of the big house. 'They have come back. I am not alone any more.'

Her face still wet, she raced to the hole in the hedge, jumped through and set off towards the big house. The sound of voices grew louder as she approached. At the potting shed she paused to catch her breath. She was about to run out on to the lawns, when some instinct warned her to be cautious. She hesitated, then put her head slowly round the corner of the red-brick wall. A chill of horror ran up her spine.

She had expected to see coaches with the van Ritters' coat-

50

of-arms drawn up on the gravel driveway, and the family disembarking, with the coachmen, grooms and footmen hovering around them. Instead a horde of strangers was running in and out of the front doors, carrying armfuls of silver, clothing and paintings. The doors had been smashed open, and the shattered panels hung drunkenly on their hinges.

The looters were piling the treasures on to a row of handcarts, shouting and laughing with excitement. Louisa could see that they were the dregs of the city, of its docks and slums, army deserters, from prisons and barracks that had thrown open their gates when all the trappings of civilized government had been swept away by the plague. They were dressed in the rags of the back-streets and gutters, in odd pieces of military uniform and the ill-fitting finery of the rich they had plundered. One rascal, wearing a high plumed hat, brandished a square-faced bottle of gin as he staggered down the main staircase with a solid gold salver under his other arm. His face, flushed and marked with drink and dissipation, turned towards Louisa. Stunned by the scene, she was too slow to duck back behind the wall and he spotted her. 'A woman. By Satan and all the devils of hell, a veritable woman! Young and juicy as a ripe red apple.' He dropped the bottle and drew his sword. 'Come here, you sweet little filly. Let's take a look at what you're hiding under those pretty skirts.' He bounded down the steps.

A wild cry went up from all his companions: 'A woman! After her, lads! The one who catches her gets the cherry.'

They came in a screaming pack across the lawn towards her. Louisa swirled about and ran. At first she headed instinctively for the safety of the cottage, then realized that they were close behind her and would trap her there like a rabbit in its warren pursued by a troop of ferrets. She veered away across the paddock towards the woods. The ground was soft and muddy and her legs had not yet recovered their full strength after her sickness. They were gaining on her, their shouts loud and jubilant. She reached the treeline only just ahead of the leaders, but she knew these woods intimately for they were her

51

playground. She twisted and turned along paths that were barely discernible, and ducked through thickets of blackberry and gorse.

Every few minutes she stopped to listen, and each time the sounds of pursuit were fainter. At last they dwindled into silence. Her terror receded, but she knew it was still dangerous to leave the shelter of the forest. She found the densest stretch of thorns and crept into it, crawling on her belly until she was hidden. Then she burrowed into the dead leaves until only her mouth and eyes were showing, so she could watch the clearing she had just left. She lay there, panting and trembling. Gradually she calmed down, and lay without moving until the shadows of the trees stretched long upon the earth. Eventually, when there were still no more sounds of her hunters, she began to crawl back towards the clearing.

She was just about to stand up when her nose wrinkled and she sniffed the air. She caught a whiff of tobacco smoke and sank down again, pressing herself to the earth. Her terror returned at full strength. After many silent, tense minutes she lifted her head slowly. At the far side of the clearing, a man sat with his back to the trunk of the tallest beech tree. He was smoking a long-stemmed clay pipe, but his eyes roved from side to side. She recognized him instantly. It was the man in the plumed hat who had first spotted her and who had led the chase. He was so close that she could hear every puff he took on his pipe. She buried her face in the leaf mould and tried to still her trembling. She did not know what he would do to her if he discovered her, but she sensed that it would be beyond her worst nightmares.

She lay and listened to the suck and gurgle of his spittle in the bowl of the pipe, and her terror mounted. Suddenly he hawked and spat a glob of thick mucus. She heard it splatter close to her head, and her nerve almost broke. It was only by exerting all her courage and self-discipline that she stopped herself jumping to her feet and running again.

Time seemed to stand still, but at last she felt the air turn cold on her bare arms. Still she did not lift her head. Then she heard rustling in the leaves, and heavy footsteps coming directly towards her across the clearing. They stopped close by her head, and a great bull voice bellowed, so close to her that her heart seemed to clench and freeze, 'There you are! I can see you! I'm coming! Run! You'd better run!' Her frozen heart came to life, and hammered against her ribs, but she forced herself not to move. There was another long silence, then the footsteps walked away from where she lay. As he went she could hear him muttering to himself, 'Dirty little whore, she's probably riddled with the pox, anyway.'

She lay without moving until the darkness was complete, and she heard an owl hoot in the top of the beech tree. Then she stood up and crept through the woods, starting and trembling at every rustle and scurry of the small night creatures.

She did not leave the cottage again for some days. During the day she immersed herself in her father's books. There was one in particular that fascinated her and she read it from the first page to the last, then started again at the beginning. The title was *In Darkest Africa*. The tales of strange animals and savage tribes enchanted her, and wiled away the long days. She read of great hairy men who lived in the tops of the trees, of a tribe that ate the flesh of other men, and of tiny pygmies with a single eye in the centre of their foreheads. Reading became the opiate for her fears. One evening she fell asleep at the kitchen table, her golden head on the open book, the flame fluttering in the lamp.

The glimmer of the light showed through the uncurtained window, and from there through a chink in the hedge. Two dark figures, who were passing on the road, stopped and exchanged a few hoarse words. Then they crept through the gate in the hedge. One went to the front door of the cottage while the other circled round to the back.

'Who are you?'

The harsh bellow brought Louisa awake and on her feet in the same instant. 'We know you're in there! Come out now!'

She darted to the back door and struggled with the locking bar, then threw open the door and dashed out into the night. At that moment a heavy masculine hand fell on the back of her neck, and she was lifted by the scruff with her feet dangling and kicking as if she were a newborn kitten.

The man who held her opened the shutter of the bullseye lantern he carried and shone the beam into her face. 'Who are you?' he demanded.

In the lamplight she recognized his red face and bushy whiskers. 'Jan!' she squeaked. 'It's me! Louisa! Louisa Leuven.'

Jan was the van Ritters' footman. The belligerence in his expression faded, slowly replaced by amazement. 'Little Louisa! Is it really you? We all thought you must be dead with the rest of them.'

A few days later Jan travelled with Louisa to Amsterdam in a cart containing some of the salvaged possessions of the van Ritters family. When he led her into the kitchens of the Huis Brabant the servants who had survived crowded round to welcome her. Her prettiness, her sweet manner and sunny nature had always made her a favourite in the servants' quarters, so they grieved with her when they heard that Anne and Hendrick were dead. They could hardly believe that little Louisa, at just ten, had survived without her parents or friends, and had done so on her own resources and resolve. Elise the cook, who had been a dear friend of her mother, immediately took her under her protection.

Louisa had to tell her tale again and again as news of her survival spread, and the other servants, the workers and seamen from the van Ritters' ships and warehouses came to hear it.

Every week Stals, the butler and major-domo of the household, wrote a report to Mijnheer van Ritters in London, where he had taken refuge from the plague with the remainder of his family. At the end of one report he mentioned that Louisa, the schoolmaster's daughter, had been rescued. Mijnheer was gracious enough to reply, 'See that the child is taken in and set to work in the household. You may pay her as a scullerymaid. When I return to Amsterdam I shall decide what is to be done with her.'

In early December when the cold weather cleansed the city of the last traces of the plague, Mijnheer van Ritters brought home his family. His wife had been carried away by the plague, but her absence would make no difference to their lives. Out of the twelve children only five had survived the pestilence. One morning, when Mijnheer van Ritters had been over a month in Amsterdam, and had attended to all the more pressing matters that awaited his attention, he ordered Stals to bring Louisa to him.

She hesitated in the doorway to Mijnheer van Ritters' library. He looked up from the thick leatherbound ledger in which he was writing. 'Come in, child,' he ordered. 'Come here where I can see you.'

Stals led her to stand in front of the great man's desk. She curtsied to him, and he nodded approval. 'Your father was a good man, and he taught you manners.' He got up and went to stand in front of the tall bay windows. For a minute he looked out through the diamond panes at one of his ships, unloading bales of cotton from the Indies into the warehouse. Then he turned back to study Louisa. She had grown since last he had seen her, and her face and limbs had filled out. He knew that she had had the plague, but she had recovered well. There were no traces on her face of the ravages of the disease. She was a pretty girl, very pretty indeed, he decided. And it was not an insipid beauty: her expression was alert and intelligent. Her eyes were alive, and sparkled with the blue of precious sapphires. Her skin was creamy and unblemished, but her hair was her most attractive attribute: she wore it in two long plaits that hung forward over her shoulders. He asked her a few questions.

She tried to hide her fear and awe of him, and to answer in a sensible manner.

'Are you attending to your lessons, child?'

'I have all my father's books, Mijnheer. I read every night before I sleep.'

'What work are you doing?'

'I wash and peel the vegetables, and I knead the bread, and help Pieter wash and dry the pots and pans, Mijnheer.'

'Are you happy?'

'Oh, yes, Mijnheer. Elise, the cook, is so kind to me, like my own mother.'

'I think we can find something more useful for you to do.' Van Ritters stroked his beard thoughtfully.

Elise and Stals had lectured Louisa on how to behave when she was with him. 'Remember always that he is one of the greatest men in all the land. Always call him "Your Excellency" or "Mijnheer". Curtsy when you greet him and when you leave.'

'Do exactly what he tells you. If he asks a question, answer him directly, but never answer back.'

'Stand straight and don't slump. Keep your hands clasped in front of you, and do not fidget or pick your nose.'

There had been so many instructions that they had confused her. But now, as she stood in front of him, her courage returned. He was dressed in cloth of the finest quality, and his collar was of snowy lace. The buckles on his shoes were pure silver, and the hilt of the dagger on his belt was gold set with glowing rubies. He was tall and his legs in black silk hose were as shapely and as well turned as a man half his age. Although his hair was touched with silver, it was dense and perfectly curled and set. His beard was almost entirely silver, but neatly barbered and shaped in the Vandyke style. There were light laughter lines around his eyes, but the back of his hand as he stroked his pointed beard was smooth and unmarred by the blotches of age. He wore an enormous ruby on his forefinger. Despite his grandeur and dignity his gaze was kind. Somehow she knew she could trust him, just as she could always trust Gentle Jesus to look after her.

'Gertruda needs someone to look after her.' Van Ritters reached a decision. Gertruda was his youngest surviving daughter. She was seven years old, a plain, simple-witted, petulant girl. 'You will be her companion and help her with her lessons. I know you are a bright girl.'

Louisa's spirits fell. She had grown so close to Elise, the motherly woman who had replaced Anne as head cook in the kitchen. She did not want to forsake the aura of warmth and security that cosseted her in the servants' quarters, and have to go upstairs to care for the whining Gertruda. She wanted to protest, but Elise had warned her not to answer back. She hung her head and curtsied.

'Stals, see she is properly dressed. She will be paid as junior nursemaid, and have a room to herself near the nursery.' Van Ritters dismissed them and went back to his desk.

Louisa knew she would have to make the best of her circumstances. There was no alternative. Mijnheer was the lord of her universe. She knew that if she tried to pit herself against his dictates her suffering would be endless. She set herself to win over Gertruda. It was not easy, for the younger girl was demanding and unreasonable. Not content with having Louisa as a slave during the day, she would scream for her in the night when she woke from a nightmare, or even when she wanted to use the chamber-pot. Always uncomplaining and cheerful, Louisa gradually won her over. She taught her simple games, sheltered her from the bullying of her brothers and sisters, sang to her at bedtime, or read her stories. When she was haunted by nightmares, Louisa crawled into her bed, took her in her arms and rocked her back to sleep. Gradually Gertruda abandoned the role of Louisa's tormentor. Her own mother had been a remote, veiled figure whose face she could not remember. Gertruda had found a substitute and she followed Louisa about with puppylike trust. Soon Louisa was able to control her wild tantrums, when she rolled howling on the floor, hurled her food against the wall or tried to throw herself out of the windows into the canal. Nobody had been able to do this before, but with a quiet word Louisa would calm her, then take her by the hand and lead her back to her room. Within minutes she was laughing and clapping her hands, and reciting the chorus of a children's rhyme with

Louisa. At first Louisa felt only a sense of duty and obligation towards Gertruda, but slowly this turned to affection and then to a type of motherly love.

Mijnheer van Ritters became aware of the change in his daughter. On his occasional visits to nursery and classroom he often singled out Louisa for a kind word. At the Christmas party for the children he watched Louisa dancing with her charge. She was as supple and graceful as Gertruda was dumpy and ungainly. Van Ritters smiled when Gertruda gave Louisa a pair of tiny pearl earrings as her Christmas present, and Louisa kissed and hugged her.

A few months later van Ritters called Louisa to his library. For a while he discussed the progress that she was making with Gertruda, and told her how pleased he was with her. When she was leaving he touched her hair. 'You are growing into such a lovely young woman. I must be careful that some oaf does not try to take you from us. Gertruda and I need you here.' Louisa was almost overcome by his condescension.

On Louisa's thirteenth birthday Gertruda asked her father to give her a special birthday treat. Van Ritters was taking one of his elder sons to England, where he was to enter the great university at Cambridge, and Gertruda asked if she and Louisa might go with the party. Indulgently van Ritters agreed.

They sailed on one of the van Ritters ships, and spent most of that summer visiting the great cities of England. Louisa was enchanted by her mother's homeland, and took every opportunity to practise the language.

The van Ritters party stayed for a week in Cambridge as Mijnheer wanted to see his favourite son settled in. He hired all the rooms at the Red Boar, the finest tavern in the university town. As usual Louisa slept on a bed in the corner of Gertruda's room. She was dressing one morning and Gertruda was sitting on her bed chattering to her. Suddenly she reached out and pinched Louisa's bosom. 'Look, Louisa, you are growing titties.'

Gently Louisa removed her hand. In the last few months she had developed the stony lumps under her nipples that heralded the onset of puberty. Her breast buds were swollen, tender and sensitive. Gertruda's touch had been rough.

'You must not do that, Gertie, my *schat*. It hurts me, and that is an ugly word you used.'

'I am sorry, Louisa.' Tears formed in the child's eyes. 'I didn't mean to hurt you.'

'It's all right.' Louisa kissed her. 'Now what do you want for breakfast?'

'Cakes.' The tears were immediately forgotten. 'Lots of cakes with cream and strawberry jam.'

'Then afterwards we can go to the Punch and Judy show,' Louisa suggested.

'Oh, can we, Louisa? Can we really?'

When Louisa went to ask Mijnheer van Ritters' permission for the outing, he decided on an impulse to accompany them. In the carriage Gertruda, in her unpredictable fashion, returned to the morning's topic. She announced in a penetrating tone, 'Louisa has got pink titties. The tips stick out.'

Louisa lowered her eyes and whispered, 'I told you, Gertie, that's a rude word. You promised not to use it again.'

'I am sorry, Louisa. I forgot.' Gertruda looked stricken.

Louisa squeezed her hand. 'I am not cross, *schat*. I just want you to behave like a lady.'

Van Ritters seemed not to have overheard the exchange. He did not look up from the book that was open on his knee. However, during the puppet show, when the hook-nosed Punch was beating his shrieking wife about the head with a club, Louisa glanced sideways and saw that Mijnheer was studying the tender swellings beneath her blouse. She felt the blood rush to her cheeks, and drew her shawl more closely around her shoulders.

It was autumn when they sailed on the return journey to Amsterdam. On the first night at sea Gertruda was prostrate with seasickness. Louisa nursed her, and held the basin for her as she retched. At last she fell into a deep sleep and Louisa escaped from the fetid cabin. Longing for a breath of fresh sea air she hurried up the companionway to the deck. She stopped in the hatchway as she spotted the tall, elegant figure of van Ritters standing alone on the quarter-deck. The officers and crew had left the windward rail to him: as the ship's owner this was his prerogative. She would have gone below again immediately but he saw her, and called her to him. 'How is my Gertie?'

'She is sleeping, Mijnheer. I am sure she will feel much better in the morning.'

At that moment a larger wave lifted the ship's hull and she rolled sharply. Taken off balance Louisa was thrown against him. He put an arm round her shoulders. 'I am so sorry, Mijnheer.' Her voice was husky. 'I slipped.' She tried to draw back, but his arm held her firmly. She was confused, unsure what she should do next. She dared not pull away again. He made no move to release her, and then – she could hardly credit her senses – she felt his other hand close on her right breast. She gasped and shivered as she felt him roll her tender swollen nipple between his fingers. He was gentle, unlike his daughter had been. He did not hurt her at all. With a terrible burning shame she realized she was enjoying his touch. 'I am cold,' she whispered.

'Yes,' he said. 'You must go below before you catch a chill.' He released her and turned back to lean on the rail. Sparks streamed from the tip of his cheroot, and blew away on the wind.

When they returned to Huis Brabant, she did not see him again for several weeks. She heard Stals telling Elise that Mijnheer had gone to Paris on business. However, the brief incident on shipboard was never far from her mind. Sometimes she woke in the night and lay awake, burning with shame and remorse as she relived it. She felt that what had happened was her fault. A great man like Mijnheer van Ritters surely could not be to blame. When she thought about it her nipples burned and itched strangely. She felt a great evil in her, and climbed out of her bed to kneel and pray, shivering on the bare wooden floor. Gertruda called out in the dark, 'Louisa, I need the chamber-pot.'

With a sense of relief Louisa went to her before she could wet the bed. Over the following weeks the guilt faded, but never quite left her.

Then, one afternoon, Stals came to find her in the nursery. 'Mijnheer van Ritters wants to see you. You must go at once. I hope you have not done anything wrong, girl?' As Louisa brushed her hair hurriedly she told Gertruda where she was going.

'Can I come with you?'

'You must finish painting the picture of the boat for me. Try to stay inside the lines, my *schat*. I will be back soon.'

She knocked on the door of the library, her heart racing wildly. She knew he was going to punish her for what had happened on the ship. He might have her beaten by the grooms, like they had done to the drunken nursemaid. Worse still, he might dismiss her, have her thrown out into the street.

'Come in!' His voice was stern.

She curtsied in the doorway. 'You sent for me, Mijnheer.'

'Yes, come in, Louisa.' She stopped in front of his desk, but he gestured for her to come round and stand beside him. 'I want to talk to you about my daughter.'

Instead of his usual black coat and lace collar he wore a dressing-robe of heavy Chinese silk that buttoned up the front. From this informal attire and his calm, friendly expression she realized he was not angry with her. She felt a rush of relief. He was not going to punish her. His next words confirmed this. 'I was thinking that it might be time for Gertruda to begin riding lessons. You are a good horsewoman. I have seen you helping the grooms to exercise the horses. I want to hear your opinion.'

'Oh, yes, Mijnheer. I am sure Gertie would love it. Old Bumble is a gentle gelding . . .' Happily she started to help him develop the plan. She was standing close to his shoulder. A thick book with a green leather cover was lying on the desk in front of him. Casually he opened it. She could not avoid seeing the exposed page and her voice trailed away. She lifted

61

both hands to her mouth as she looked at the illustration that filled the whole of one folio-sized page. It was obviously the work of a skilled artist. The man in the painting was young and handsome, he lolled back in a leather armchair. A pretty young girl stood in front of him, laughing, and Louisa saw that she might have been her own twin. The girl's large wide-set eyes were cerulean blue, and she was holding her skirts up to her waist so that the man could see the golden nest between her thighs. The artist had emphasized the pair of swollen lips that pouted at him through the curls.

That was enough to stop her breath, but there was worse – far worse. The front flap of the man's breeches was undone, and through the opening thrust a pale shaft with a pink head. The man was holding it lightly between his fingers and seemed to be aiming it at the girl's rosy opening.

Louisa had never seen a man naked. Even though she had listened to the other girls in the servants' quarters discussing it with gusto, she had not expected anything remotely like this. She stared at it in dreadful fascination, unable to tear her eyes away. She felt hot waves of blood rising up her throat and flooding her cheeks. She was consumed with shame and horror.

'I thought the girl looked like you, although not as pretty,' said van Ritters quietly. 'Don't you agree, my dear?'

'I – I don't know,' she whispered. Her legs almost folded under her as she felt Mijnheer van Ritters' hand settle lightly on her bottom. The touch seemed to burn her flesh through the petticoats. He cupped her small round buttock, and she knew she should ask him to stop, or run from the room. But she could not. Stals and Elise had warned her repeatedly that she must obey Mijnheer always. She stood paralysed. She belonged to him, like any of his horses or dogs. She was one of his chattels. She must submit to him without protest, even though she was not sure what he was doing, what he wanted from her.

'Of course, Rembrant has taken some artistic licence when it comes to dimensions.' She could not believe that the artist who had painted the figure of God had also painted this

– 62

picture, yet it was possible: even a famous artist must do what the great man required of him.

'Forgive me, Gentle Jesus,' she prayed and shut her eyes tightly so that she did not have to look at that wicked picture. She heard the rustle of stiff silk brocade, and he said, 'There, Louisa, this is what it really looks like.'

Her eyelids were clenched tightly, and he ran his hand over her buttock, gently but insistently. 'You are a big girl now, Louisa. It is time you knew these things. Open your eyes, my dear.'

Obediently she opened them a crack. She saw that he had undone the front of his robe, and that he wore nothing under it. She stared at the thing that stood proud through the folds of silk. The painting was a bland and romanticized representation of it. It rose massively from a nest of coarse dark hair, and seemed as thick as her wrist. The head was not an insipid pink as in the painting, but the colour of a ripe plum. The slit in the end of it glared at her like a cyclopean eye. She shut her eyes again tightly.

'Gertruda!' she whispered. 'I promised to take her for a walk.'

'You are very good to her, Louisa.' His voice had a strange husky edge to it that she had never heard before. 'But now you must be good to me also.' He reached down and under her skirts, then ran his fingers up her naked legs. He lingered at the soft dimples at the back of her knees, and she trembled more violently. His touch was caressing, and strangely reassuring, but she knew it was wrong. She was confused by these contrary emotions, and she felt as though she were suffocating. His fingers left the soft back of her knees and moved up her thigh. The touch was neither furtive nor hesitant, but authoritative, not something she could deny or oppose.

'You must be good to me,' he had said, and she knew that he had every right to ask that of her. She owed him everything. If this was being good to him, then she had no choice, yet she knew it was wicked and that Jesus would punish her. Perhaps He would cease to love her for what they were doing. She heard the rustle of the page as he turned it with his free hand, and then he said, 'Look!' She tried to resist him in this at least, and shut her eyes again. His touch became more demanding and his hand moved up to the crease where her buttock joined the back of her thigh.

She opened her eyes, just a fraction, and looked through her lashes at the fresh page of the book. Then her eyes flew wide open. The girl who looked so like her was kneeling in front of her swain. Her skirts had hiked up behind her, and her exposed bottom was round and buttery. Both she and the boy were gazing down into his lap. The girl's expression was fond, as though she were looking down at a beloved pet, a kitten perhaps. She held it clasped in both her small hands, but her dainty fingers were not able to encompass its girth.

'Is it not a beautiful picture?' he asked, and despite the wickedness of the subject, she felt a strange empathy towards the young couple. They were smiling, and it seemed as though they loved each other and were enjoying what they were doing. She forgot to close her eyes again.

'You see, Louisa, that God has made men and women differently. On their own they are incomplete, but together they make a whole.' She was not sure exactly what he meant, but sometimes she had not understood what her father had told her, or the sermon preached by the dominie. 'That is why the couple in the painting are so happy and why you can see that they feel full of love for each other.'

With gentle authority his fingers moved between her legs, right up to the juncture of her thighs. Then he did something else to her there. She was not sure what it was, but she moved her feet apart so he could do it more easily. The sensation that overtook her was beyond anything she had experienced before. She could feel the happiness and love he had spoken about spreading out and suffusing her entire body. She stared down again into the opening of his robe, and her feelings of shock and fear faded. She saw that, like the picture in the book, it was really quite pleasing. No wonder the other girl looked at it like that.

He moved her gently, and she was pliant and unresisting. Still sitting in the chair, he turned towards her, and at the same time, drew her closer and placed one hand on her shoulder. She understood instinctively that he wanted her to do what the girl in the picture was doing. Under the pressure of the hand on her shoulder she sank down to her knees and that strangely ugly, beautiful thing was only inches from her face. Like the other girl she reached out and took it in her hands. He made a small grunting sound and she felt how hot and hard it was. It fascinated her. She squeezed gently, and felt a leap of life as though this thing had a separate existence. It belonged to her, and she felt a strange sense of power, as though she held the core of his being in her hands.

He reached down and placed his own hands over hers. He began to move them back and forth. At first she was not sure what he was doing, then understood that he was showing her what he wanted. She felt a strong desire to please him, and she learned quickly. While she moved her fingers as rapidly as a weaver working at the loom he lay back in the chair and groaned. She thought she had hurt him and she tried to stand up, but he stopped her with the hand on her shoulder again and, a desperate tone in his voice, said, 'No, Louisa, just like that. Don't stop what you're doing. You're such a good, clever girl.'

Suddenly he let out a deep, shuddering sigh and whipped a scarlet silk kerchief out of the pocket of his robe, covering his lap and both her hands with it. She did not want to let go of him, even when she felt a hot, viscous fluid pouring over her hands and soaking the silk cloth. When she tried to keep on with what she was doing, he grasped her wrists and held her hands still. 'That's enough, my dear. You have made me very happy.'

After a long time he roused himself. He took her little hands one at a time and wiped them clean with the silk cloth. She felt no sense of revulsion. He was smiling at her kindly, and he told her, 'I am very pleased with you, but you must not tell anyone what we did today. Do you understand, Louisa?' She nodded vehemently. The guilt had evaporated, and she felt instead gratitude and reverence.

'Now you can go back to Gertruda. We will begin her

riding lessons tomorrow. Of course, you will take her to the academy.'

Over the next few weeks Louisa saw him only once and at a distance. She was half-way up the staircase, on her way to Gertruda's room, when a footman opened the doors to the banquet room, and Mijnheer van Ritters led out a procession of his guests. They were all beautifully dressed, prosperous-looking ladies and gentlemen. Louisa knew at least four of the men were members of Het Zeventien, the directors of the VOC. They had obviously dined well and were jovial and noisy. She hid behind the curtains as they passed below her, but she watched Mijnheer van Ritters with a strange feeling of longing. He was wearing a long, curled wig, and the sash and the star of the Order of the Golden Fleece. He was magnificent. Louisa felt a rare flash of hatred for the smiling, elegant woman on his arm. After they had passed her hiding-place she ran to the room she shared with Gertruda, threw herself on the bed and wept.

'Why does he not want to see me again? Did I displease him?'

She thought about the incident in the library every day, especially after the lantern was out and she was in her bed across the room from Gertruda.

Then one day Mijnheer van Ritters arrived unexpectedly at the riding academy. Louisa had taught Gertruda how to curtsy. She was awkward and clumsy and Louisa had to help her back on to her feet when she lost her balance, but van Ritters smiled a little at this accomplishment, and returned the courtesy with a playful bow. 'Your devoted servant,' he said, and Gertruda giggled. He did not speak directly to Louisa, and she knew better than to address him uninvited. He watched Gertruda make a circuit of the ring, on the lead rein. Louisa had to walk beside the pony, and Gertruda's pudding face was screwed up with terror. Then van Ritters left as abruptly as he had appeared.

Another week passed and Louisa was torn with opposing emotions. At times the magnitude of her sin returned to plague her. She had allowed him to touch and play with her, and she had taken pleasure in handling that monstrous thing of his. She had even begun to have the most vivid dreams about it, and she woke in confusion, her newly fledged breasts and her private parts burning and itching. As though in punishment for her sins her breasts had swelled until they strained the buttons of her blouse. She tried to hide them, keeping her arms crossed over her chest, but she had seen the stable boys and the footmen looking at them.

She wanted to talk to Elise about what had happened to her and ask her advice, but Mijnheer van Ritters had warned her against this. So she kept silent.

Then, unexpectedly, Stals told her, 'You are to move to your own room. It is the Mijnheer's order.'

Louisa stared at him in astonishment. 'But what about Gertruda? She can't sleep alone.'

'The master thinks it is time she learned to do so. She, too, will have a new room and you will have the one beside her. She will have a bell to call you if she needs you in the night.'

The girls' new apartments were on the floor below the library and Mijnheer's bedroom suite. Louisa made a game of the move, and stilled Gertruda's misgivings. They took all her dolls up and held a party for them to introduce them to their new quarters. Louisa had learned to speak in a different voice for each toy, a trick that never failed to reduce Gertruda to shrieks of laughter. When each of her dolls in turn had told Gertruda how happy they were with their new home, she was convinced.

Louisa's own room was light and spacious. The furnishings were quite splendid, with velvet curtains and gilt chairs and bedstead. There was a feather mattress on the bed, and thick blankets. There was even a fireplace with a marble surround, although Stals cautioned her that she would be rationed to a single bucket of coal a week. But, wonder of wonders, there was a tiny cubicle that contained a commode with a lid that lifted to reveal a carved seat and the porcelain chamber-pot under it. Louisa was in a haze of delight as she crept into bed that first night. It seemed that she had never been warm in her life until this evening.

She came out of a deep, dreamless sleep and lay awake trying to place what had woken her. It must have been well past midnight for it was dark and the house was silent. Then the sound came again, and her heart raced. It was footsteps, but they came from the panelled wall at the far side of the room. She was gripped by superstitious dread, and could neither move nor scream. Then she heard the creak of a door opening, and a ghostly light glowed out of nowhere. Slowly a panel in the far wall swung wide open and a spectral figure stepped into the room. It was a tall, bearded man dressed in breeches and a white shirt with leg-o'-mutton sleeves and a high stock.

'Louisa!' His voice was hollow and echoed strangely. It was just the voice that she would have expected from a ghost. She pulled the covers over her head and lay without breathing. She heard footsteps crossing to her bedside, and she could see the wavering light through a slit in the bedclothes. The footsteps stopped beside her and suddenly her coverings were flung back. This time she screamed, but she knew it was futile: next door Gertruda would be sleeping in a mindless stupor from which nothing short of an earthquake could waken her, and there were only the two of them on this floor of Huis Brabant. She stared at the face above her, so far gone in terror that she did not recognize him even in the lantern-light.

'Don't be afraid, child. I will not hurt you.'

'Oh, Mijnheer!' She flung herself against his chest and clung to him with all the strength of her relief. 'I thought you were a ghost.'

'There, child.' He stroked her hair. 'It's all over. There is nothing to be afraid of.' It took her a long time to become calm again. Then he said, 'I won't leave you here alone. Come with me.'

He took her hand, and she followed him trustingly in her cotton nightdress on bare feet. He led her through the door in the panel. A spiral staircase was concealed behind it. They went up it, then through another secret doorway. Suddenly they were in a magnificent chamber, so spacious that even with fifty candles burning in their chandeliers the far reaches of the room and the ceilings were in shadow. He led her to the fireplace in which tall yellow flames leaped and twisted.

He embraced her and stroked her hair. 'Did you think I had forgotten you?'

She nodded. 'I thought I had made you angry, and that you did not like me any more.'

He chuckled and lifted her face to the light. 'What a beautiful little thing you are. This is how angry I am and how much I dislike you.' He kissed her mouth and she tasted the cheroot on his lips, a strong aromatic flavour that made her feel safe and secure. At last he broke the embrace and seated her on the sofa in front of the fire. He went to a table on which stood crystal glasses and a decanter of ruby red liquor. He poured a glass and brought it to her. 'Drink this. It will chase away the bad thoughts.'

She choked and coughed at the sting of the liquor, but then a marvellous glow spread through her, to her toes and fingertips. He sat beside her, stroked her hair and spoke to her softly, telling her how pretty she was, what a good girl, and how he had missed her. Lulled by the warmth in her belly and his mesmeric voice she leaned her head on his chest. He lifted the hem of her nightdress over her head and she wriggled out of it. Then she was naked. In the candlelight her child-like body was pale and smooth as cream in a jug. She felt no shame as he fondled her, and kissed her face. She turned this way and that at the gentle urging of his hands.

Suddenly he stood up and she watched him as he pulled off his shirt and breeches. When he came back to the sofa and stood in front of her he did not have to guide her hands and she reached for him naturally. She gazed at his sex as she slid back the loose skin to reveal the shiny plum-coloured head, as he had taught her. Then he reached down, removed her hands and sank to the floor in front of her. He pushed apart her knees and laid her back on the velvet-covered sofa. He lowered his face and she felt his moustaches tickling the inside of her thighs, then moving higher.

'What are you doing?' she cried, with alarm. He had not done this before, and she tried to sit up. He held her down and suddenly she cried out and sank her fingernails into his shoulders. His mouth had settled on her most secret parts. The sensation was so intense that she feared for a moment she might faint.

It was not every night that he came down the spiral staircase to fetch her. On many nights there was the rumble of carriage wheels on the cobbled streets below Louisa's window. She blew out her candle and peeped through the curtains to watch Mijnheer van Ritters' guests arriving for another banquet or fashionable soirée. Long after they had left she lay awake, hoping to hear his footstep on the staircase, but she was usually disappointed.

For weeks or even months at a time he was gone, sailing on one of his fine ships to places with strange and evocative names. While he was gone she was restless and bored. She found that she was even impatient with Gertruda, and unhappy with herself.

When he came back his presence filled the great house, and even the other servants were enlivened and excited by it. Suddenly all the waiting and pining were as if they had never happened as she heard him descending the staircase and leaped from her bed to meet him as he stepped through the secret door in the panelling. After that he devised a signal to summon her to his chamber so that he no longer had to come down to fetch her. At dinner time he would send a footman to deliver a red rose to Gertruda. None of the servants who delivered the bloom thought it odd: they all knew that Mijnheer had an inexplicable affection for his ugly slow-witted daughter. But on those nights the door at the top of the spiral staircase was unlocked, and when Louisa stepped through he was waiting for her.

These meetings were never the same. Every time he invented some new game for them to act out. He made her dress in fantastic costumes, play the role of milkmaid, stable-boy or princess. Sometimes he made her wear masks, the heads of demons and wild animals.

On other evenings they would study the pictures in the green book, and then enact the scenes they depicted. The first time he showed her the picture of the girl lying under the boy and his shaft buried in her to the hilt, she did not believe it was possible. But he was gentle, patient and considerate, so that when it happened there was little pain and only a few drops of her virgin blood on the sheets of the wide bed. Afterwards she felt a great sense of accomplishment and when she was alone she studied her lower body with awe. It amazed her that the parts she had been taught were unclean and sinful could be the seat of such delights. She was convinced now that there was nothing more that he could teach her. She believed that she had been able to pleasure him, and herself, in every conceivable way. But she was wrong.

He went away on one of his seemingly interminable voyages, this time to a place called St Petersburg in Russia to visit the court of Pyotr Alekseyevich, whom other men called Peter the Great, and to expand his interests in the trade in precious furs. When he returned Louisa was in a fever of excitement, and this time she did not have long to wait for his summons. That evening a footman delivered a single red rose to Gertruda while Louisa was cutting up her roasted chicken.

'Why are you so happy, Louisa?' Gertruda demanded, as she danced around the bedroom.

'Because I love you, Gertie, and I love everybody in the world,' Louisa sang.

Gertruda clapped her hands. 'And I love you too, Louisa.'

'Now it's time for your bed, and here is a cup of hot milk to make you sleep tight.'

That evening when Louisa stepped through the secret

doorway into Mijnheer van Ritters' bedchamber, she stopped dead in astonishment. This was a new game and she was at once confused and frightened. This was too real, too terrifying.

Mijnheer van Ritters' head was concealed with a tight-fitting black leather hood with round cutout eyeholes and a crude gash for a mouth. He wore a black leather apron and shiny black boots that reached to the top of his thighs. His arms were folded across his chest, and his hands were covered with black gloves. She could barely tear her gaze away from him to look at the sinister structure that stood in the centre of the floor. It was identical to the flogging tripod on which miscreants received public punishment in the square outside the law courts. However, in place of the usual chains, silk ropes dangled from the top of the tripod.

She smiled at him with trembling lips, but he stared back at her impassively through the eyeholes in the black hood. She wanted to run, but he seemed to anticipate her intentions. He strode to the door and locked it. Then he placed the key in the front pocket of his apron. Her legs gave way under her, and she sank to the floor. 'I am sorry,' she whispered. 'Please don't hurt me.'

'You have been sentenced for the sin of harlotry to twenty strokes of the whip.' His voice was stern and harsh.

'Please let me go. I don't want to play this game.'

'This is no game.' He came to her, and though she pleaded with him for mercy he lifted her and led her to the tripod. He tied her hands high above her head with the silken ropes, and she peered back at him over her shoulder with her long yellow hair hanging over her face. 'What are you going to do to me?'

He went to the table against the far wall and, with his back turned to her, picked up something. Then, with theatrical slowness, he turned back with the whip in his hand. She whimpered and tried to free herself from the silken bonds that pinioned her wrists, twisting and turning as she hung on the tripod. He came to her and placed one finger into the opening of her nightdress, and ripped it down to the hem. He stripped away the tatters and she was naked. He came to stand in front of her, and she saw a huge bulge under his leather apron, evidence of his arousal.

'Twenty strokes,' he repeated, in the cold, hard voice of a stranger, 'and you will count each one as it falls. Do you understand, you wanton little whore?' She winced at the word. Nobody had ever called her that before.

'I did not know I was doing wrong. I thought I was pleasing you.'

He cut the whip through the air, and the lash hissed close to her face. Then he went behind her, and she closed her eyes and tensed every muscle in her back, but still the pain of the stroke defied her belief and she shrieked aloud.

'Count!' he ordered, and through white, quivering lips she obeyed.

'One!' she screamed.

It went on and on without pity or respite, until she fainted. He held a small green bottle under her nose and the pungent fumes revived her. Then it started again.

'Count!' he ordered.

At last she was able to whisper, 'Twenty,' and he laid the whip back on the table. He was loosening the strings of his leather apron as he came back to her. She hung on the silk ropes, unable to lift her head or support herself. Her back, her buttocks and the tops of her legs felt as though they were on fire.

He came up behind her, and she felt his hands on her lower body, drawing her red, throbbing buttocks apart. Then there was a pain more dreadful than any that had gone before it. She was being impaled in the most unnatural way, ripped apart. Agony tore through her bowels, and she found fresh strength to scream and scream again.

At last he cut her down from the tripod, wrapped her in a blanket and carried her down the staircase. Without another word he left her sobbing on the bed. In the morning when she tottered to the cubicle and sat on the commode she found that she was still bleeding. Seven days later she had still not healed completely, and another red rose was delivered to

73

Gertruda. Trembling and weeping quietly, she climbed the staircase to answer his summons. When she entered his chamber the tripod stood in the middle of the floor and, once again, he wore the hood and apron of the executioner.

It took months for her to gather her courage, but at last she went to Elise and told her how Mijnheer was treating her. She lifted her dress and turned to show the welts and stripes across her back. Then she bent over and showed her the torn, festering opening.

'Cover yourself, you shameless strumpet,' Elise shouted, and slapped her cheek. 'How dare you make up filthy lies about such a great and good man? I shall have to report you to Mijnheer for this, but in the meantime I will tell Stals to lock you in the wine cellar.'

For two days Louisa crouched on the stone floor in a dark corner of the cellar. The agony in her lower belly was a fire that threatened to consume her very soul. On the third day a sergeant and three men of the city watch came to fetch her. As they led her up the stairs to the kitchen yard she looked for Gertruda, Elise or Stals but there was no sign of them or any of the other servants.

'Thank you for coming to rescue me,' she told the sergeant. 'I could not have borne it another day.' He gave her an odd enigmatic glance.

'We searched your room and found the jewellery you had stolen,' he said. 'What terrible ingratitude to a gentleman who treated you so kindly. We shall see what the magistrate has to say to you.'

The magistrate was suffering from the effects of the previous evening's overindulgence. He had been one of fifty dinner guests at Huis Brabant whose cellars and table were famous throughout the Low Countries. Koen van Ritters was an old friend, and the magistrate glowered at the young female prisoner arraigned before him. Koen had spoken to him about this hussy after last night's dinner, while they puffed on their cheroots and finished off a bottle of fine old cognac. He listened impatiently as the sergeant of the watch gave evidence

74

against her, and laid before the magistrate the package of stolen jewellery that they had found in her room.

'Prisoner is to be transported to the penal colony in Batavia for life,' the magistrate ordered.

Het Gelukkige Meeuw was lying in the harbour, almost ready to sail. They marched Louisa from the court room directly to the docks. At the top of the gangplank she was met by the head gaoler. He entered her name in the register, then two of his men locked leg irons on her ankles and shoved her down the hatchway to the gundeck.

Now almost a year later the *Meeuw* lay at anchor in Table Bay. Even through the thick oaken planking Louisa heard the hail, 'Longboat with supplies. Permission to hook on?'

She roused herself from her long reverie, and peeped through the chink in the joint of the port-lid. She saw the longboat being rowed towards the ship by a mixed crew of a dozen black and white men. There was a big, broad-shouldered ruffian standing in the bows, and she started as she recognized the man at the tiller. It was the young one who had asked her name and thrown the fish to her. She had fought for possession of that precious gift, then divided it with her little blade and shared it with three other women. They were not her friends, for there were no friends aboard this ship, but early in the voyage the four had forged a pact of mutual protection for survival. They had gobbled down the fish raw, watchful of the other starving women who crowded round them, waiting for an opportunity to snatch a scrap.

She remembered, with longing, the sweet taste of the raw fish now as she watched the heavily laden longboat moor against the side of the ship. There was a hubbub of banging and shouting, the squeal of sheave blocks and more shouted orders. Through the chink she watched the baskets and boxes of fresh produce being swung on board. She could smell the

75

fruit and the newly picked tomatoes. Saliva flooded her mouth, but she knew that most of this bounty would go to the officers' mess, and what remained to the gunroom and the common seamen's kitchen. None of it would find its way down to the prison decks. The convicts would subsist on the weevily hard biscuit and the rotten salt pork, crawling with maggots.

Suddenly she heard someone banging on one of the other gunports further down the deck, and a masculine voice from outside called softly but urgently, 'Louisa! Is Louisa there?'

Before she could answer, some of the other women howled and shouted back, '*Ja*, my *dottie*. I am Louisa. Do you want a taste of my honey-pot?' Then there were shrieks of laughter. Louisa recognized the man's voice. She tried to shout to him above the chorus of filth and invective, but her enemies swamped her with malicious glee and she knew he would not hear her. With rising despair she peered through her peephole, but the view was restricted.

'I am here,' she shouted in Dutch. 'I am Louisa.'

Abruptly his face rose into her view. He must have been standing on one of the thwarts of the longboat that was moored below her gunport.

'Louisa?' He put his eye to the other side of the chink and they stared at each other from a range of a few inches, 'Yes.' He laughed unexpectedly. 'Blue eyes! Bright blue eyes.'

'Who are you? What is your name?' On impulse she spoke in English, and he gaped at her.

'You speak English?'

'No, you weak-wit, it was Chinese,' she snapped back at him, and he laughed again. By the sound of him he was overbearing and cocky, but his was the only friendly voice she had heard in over a year.

'It's a saucy one you are! I have something else for you. Can you get this port-lid open?' he asked.

'Are any of the guards watching from the deck?' she asked. 'They will have me flogged if they see us talking.'

'No, we are hidden by the tumble-home of the ship's side.'

'Wait!' she said, and drew the blade from her pouch. Quickly she prised out the single shackle that still held the lock in place. Then she leaned back, placed both bare feet against the port-lid and pushed with all her might. The hinges creaked, then gave a few inches. She saw his fingers at the edge and he helped to pull it open a little wider.

Then he thrust a small canvas bag through the opening. 'There is a letter for you,' he whispered, his face close to hers. 'Read it.' And then he was gone.

'Wait!' she pleaded, and his face appeared in the opening again. 'You did not tell me. What's your name?'

'Jim. Jim Courtney.'

'Thank you, Jim Courtney,' she said, and let the port-lid thump shut.

The three women crowded round her in a tight circle of protection as she opened the bag. Quickly they divided up the dried meat and the packets of hard biscuit, and gnawed at the unappetizing fare with desperate hunger. When she found the comb tears came to Louisa's eyes. It was carved from dappled honey-coloured tortoiseshell. She stroked it through her hair, and it glided smoothly, not pulling painfully like the ugly hand-whittled thing she had been reduced to. Then she found the file and the knife wrapped together in a scrap of canvas. The knife was horn-handled, and the blade, when she tested it on her thumb, was keen, a fine weapon. The sturdy little file had three cutting edges. She felt a lift of hope, the first in all those long months. She looked down at the irons on her ankles. The skin beneath the cruel bonds was calloused.

Knife and file were invaluable gifts, but it was the comb that touched her deepest. It was an affirmation that he had seen her as a woman, not as gaol dregs from the slums and the gutter. She rummaged in the bottom of the bag for the letter he had promised. It was a single sheet of cheap paper, folded cunningly to form its own envelope. It was addressed to 'Louisa' in a bold but fair hand. She unfolded it, careful not to tear it. It was in poorly spelt Dutch, but she was able to make out the gist of it.

Use the file on your chains. I will have a boat under the stern tomorrow night. When you hear the ship's bell strike two bells in the middle watch, jump. I will hear the splash. Have courage.

Her pulse raced. At once she knew that the chances of success were negligible. A hundred things could go wrong, not least a musket ball or a shark. What mattered was that she had found a friend and with it new hope of salvation, no matter how remote. She tore the note into shreds and dropped them into the reeking latrine bucket. None of the guards would try to retrieve it from there. Then she crept back under the cannon, into the darkness that was her only privacy, and sat with her legs folded under her so she could easily reach the links of her leg irons. With the first stroke of the little file she cut a shallow but bright notch and a few grains of iron filtered down to the deck. The shackles had been forged from untempered steel of poor quality but it would take time and heartbreaking perseverance to cut through a single link.

'I have a day and a night. Until two bells in the middle watch tomorrow night,' she encouraged herself, and laid the file into the notch she had already cut. At the next stroke more iron filings dusted the deck.

The longboat had been relieved of the heavy load of produce and now she rode lightly. Mansur was at the tiller, and Jim gazed back over the stern as he rowed. Every now and again he grinned as he went over in his mind the brief meeting with Louisa. She spoke English, good English, with only a touch of a Dutch accent, and she was spirited and quick-witted. She had responded swiftly to the circumstances. This was no dull-witted lump of gaol-bait. He had seen her bare legs through the chink in the port-lid as she helped him prise it open. They were starved painfully thin, and galled by her chains, but they were long and straight, not twisted and deformed by rickets. 'Good breeding there!' as his father would say of a blood filly. The hand that had taken the canvas bag from his was grubby, and the nails were cracked and broken, but it was beautifully shaped, with gracefully tapered fingers. The hands of a lady, not a slave or scullerymaid. 'She does not smell like a posy of lavender. But she's been locked up in that filthy tub for Lord alone knows how long. What do you expect?' He made excuses for her. Then he thought about her eyes, those wondrous blue eyes, and his expression was soft and dreamy. 'In all my life, I have never laid eyes on a girl like that. And she speaks English.'

'Hey, coz!' Mansur shouted. 'Keep the stroke. You will have us on Robben Island if you're not more careful.' Jim started out of his day-dream just in time to meet the next swell that lifted the stern high.

'Sea's getting up,' his father grunted. 'Like as not it will be blowing a gale by tomorrow. We'll have to try to take out the last load before it gets too rough.'

Jim took his eyes off the receding shape of the ship, and looked beyond her. His spirits sank. The stormclouds were piling up high and heavy as mountains upon the horizon.

I have to think up an excuse to stay ashore when they take out the next load to the *Meeuw*, he decided. There is not going to be another chance to make ready.

As the mules dragged the longboat up the beach, Jim told his father, 'I have to take Captain Hugo his cut. He might scotch us if he doesn't have some coin in his fat fist.'

'Let him wait for it, the old sheep thief. I need you to help with the next shipment.'

'I promised Hugo and, anyway, you have a full crew for the next trip out to the ship.'

Tom Courtney studied his son with a searching gaze. He knew him well. He was up to something. It was not like Jim to shirk. On the contrary, he was a rock on which Tom could depend. It was he who had established good terms with the purser on the convict ship, he had obtained the licence to trade from Hugo, and he had supervised the loading of the first shipment. He could be trusted.

'Well, I don't know . . .' Tom stroked his chin dubiously.

Mansur stepped in quickly. 'Let Jim go, Uncle Tom. I can take over from him for the time being.'

'Very well, Jim. Go and visit your friend Hugo,' Tom acquiesced, 'but be back on the beach to help with the boats when we return.'

Later, from the top of the dunes, Jim watched the longboats rowing back towards the *Meeuw* with the final load of produce. It seemed to him that the swells were higher than they had been that morning, and the wind was starting to claw off the tops in a parade of leaping white horses.

'God spare us!' he said aloud. 'If the storm comes up I will not be able to get the girl off until it passes.' Then he remembered his instructions to her. He had told her to jump overboard at precisely two bells in the middle watch. He could not get another message to her to stop her doing that. Would she have the good sense to stay on board if there was a full gale blowing, realizing that he had not been able to keep the rendezvous, or would she throw herself overboard regardless and perish in the darkness? The thought of her drowning in the dark waters struck him like a fist in his belly, and he felt nauseous. He turned Drumfire's head towards the castle and pressed his heels into the horse's sides.

Captain Hugo was surprised but pleased to have his commission paid so promptly. Jim left him without ceremony, refusing even a mug of coffee, and galloped back along the beach. He was thinking furiously as he rode.

There had been so little time to lay his plans. It was only in the last few hours that he had been sure the girl had the spirit to chance such a hazardous escape. The first consideration, if he succeeded in getting her ashore, would be to find a safe hiding-place for her. As soon as her escape was discovered the entire castle garrison would be sent out to find her, a hundred infantry and a squadron of cavalry. The Company troops in the castle had little enough employment, and a manhunt or, better still, a woman-hunt would be one of the most exciting events in years. Colonel Keyser, the garrison commander, would be hot for the honour of capturing an escaped convict.

For the first time he allowed himself to consider the consequences if this hare-brained scheme fell to pieces. He worried that he might be making trouble for his family. The strict law laid down by the directors of the VOC, the almighty Zeventien in Amsterdam, was that no foreigner was permitted to reside or carry on a business in the colony. However, like so many other strict laws of the directors in Amsterdam, there were special circumstances by which they could be circumvented. Those special circumstances always involved a monetary token of esteem to His Excellency Governor van de Witten. It had cost the Courtney brothers twenty thousand guilders to obtain a licence to reside and trade in the Colony of Good Hope. Van de Witten was unlikely to revoke that licence. He and Tom Courtney were on friendly terms, and Tom contributed generously to van de Witten's unofficial pension fund.

Jim hoped that if he and the girl simply disappeared from the colony, there would be nothing to implicate the rest of his family. There might be suspicions, and at the worst it might cost his father another gift to van de Witten, but in the end it would blow over, just as long as he never returned.

There were only two avenues of escape from the colony. The natural and best was the sea. But that meant a boat. The Courtney brothers owned two armed traders, handy and fleet schooners with which they traded as far as Arabia and Bombay. However, at the present time both these vessels were at sea and were not expected back until the monsoon changed, which would not be for several months yet.

Jim had saved up a little money, perhaps enough to pay for a passage for the girl and himself on one of the ships lying in Table Bay at the moment. But the first thing Colonel Keyser would do as soon as the girl was reported missing was to send search parties aboard every ship. He could try to steal a small boat, a pinnace perhaps, something seaworthy enough in which he and the girl could reach the Portuguese ports on the Mozambique coast, but every captain was alert for piracy. The most likely reward for his efforts would be a musket ball in the belly.

Even in his most optimistic expectations he had to face the fact that the sea route was closed to them. There was only one other still open, and he turned and looked northwards at the far mountains on which the last of the winter snows had not yet thawed. He pulled up Drumfire and thought about what lay out there. Jim had not travelled more than fifty leagues beyond those peaks, but he had heard of others who had gone further into the hinterland and returned with a great store of ivory. There was even a rumour of the old hunter who had picked a shiny pebble out of a sandbank of a nameless river far to the north, and had sold the diamond in Amsterdam for a hundred thousand guilders. He felt his skin prickle with excitement. On countless nights he had dreamed of what lay beyond that blue horizon. He had discussed it with Mansur and Zama, and they had promised each other that one day they would make the journey. Had the gods of adventure overheard his boasts, and were they conspiring now to drive him out there into the wilderness? Would he have a girl with golden hair and blue eyes riding at his side? He laughed at the thought, and urged Drumfire on.

With his father, his uncle Dorian and almost all the servants and freed slaves out of the way for the next few hours, he had to work quickly. He knew where his father kept the keys to both the strongroom and the armoury. He selected six strong mules out of the herd in the kraal, pack-saddled them and took them on a lead rein up to the rear doors of the godown. He had to choose carefully as he selected goods from the warehouse to make up the loads. A dozen best Tower muskets and canvas ball-pouches, kegs of black powder, and lead bars and moulds to cast more ball; axes, knives and blankets; beads and cloth to trade with the wild tribes they might meet; basic medicines, pots and water bottles; needles and thread, and all the other necessities of existence in the wilderness, but no luxuries. Coffee was not a luxury, he consoled himself, as he added a sack of beans.

When they were loaded he led the string of mules away to a quiet place beside a stream in the forest almost two miles from High Weald. He relieved the animals of their packs so they could rest, and left them with knee-halters to allow them to graze on the lush grass on the stream bank.

By the time he returned to High Weald the longboats were on their way back from the *Meeuw*. He went down to meet his father, Mansur and the returning crews as they came back over the dunes. He rode along with them, and listened to their desultory conversation. They were all drenched with seawater and almost exhausted, for it had been a long haul back from the Dutch ship in the heavy seas.

Mansur described it to him succinctly: 'You were lucky to get out of it. The waves were breaking over us like a waterfall.'

'Did you see the girl?' Jim whispered, so his father would not overhear.

'What girl?' Mansur gave him a knowing glance.

'You know what girl.' Jim punched his arm.

Mansur's expression turned serious. 'They had all the convicts locked up and battened down. One of the officers told Uncle Tom that the captain is anxious to sail as soon as he can finish reprovisioning and filling his water butts. By tomorrow at the very latest. He does not want to be pinned down by the storm on this lee shore.' He saw Jim's despairing expression, and went on sympathetically, 'Sorry, coz, but like as not the ship will be gone by noon tomorrow. She would have been no good for you anyway, a convict woman. You know nothing about her, you don't know what crimes she has committed. Murder, perhaps. Let her go, Jim. Forget about her. There is more than one bird in the blue sky, more than a single blade of grass on the plains of Camdeboo.'

Jim felt anger flare and bitter words rose to his lips, but he held them back. He left the others and turned Drumfire towards the top of the dunes. From the height he looked out across the bay. The storm was mounting even as he watched, bringing on the darkness prematurely. The wind moaned and ruffled his hair, and whipped Drumfire's mane into a tangle. He had to shield his eyes against the sting of flying sand and spume. The surface of the sea was a welter of breaking white spray, and tall, heaving swells that rose up and crashed down on the beach. It was a wonder that his father had been able to bring the boats in through that turmoil of wind and water, but Tom Courtney was a master mariner.

Almost two miles out the *Meeuw* was an indistinct grey shape that rolled and pitched with swinging bare masts, and disappeared as each fresh squall swept across the bay. Jim watched until the darkness hid her completely. Then he galloped down the back of the dune towards High Weald. He found Zama still working in the stables, bedding down the horses. 'Come with me,' he ordered, and obediently Zama followed him out into the orchard. When they were out of sight of the house they squatted down side by side. They were silent for a while, then Jim spoke in Lozi, the language of the forests, so that Zama would know there were deadly serious matters to discuss.

'I'm going,' he said.

Zama stared into his face, but his eyes were hidden by the darkness. 'Where, Somoya?' he asked. Jim pointed with his chin towards the north. 'When will you return?'

'I do not know, perhaps never,' said Jim.

'Then I must take leave of my father.'

'You're coming with me?' Jim asked.

Zama glanced at him pityingly. No answer was needed to such a fatuous question.

'Aboli was a father to me also.' Jim stood up and placed an arm around his shoulder. 'Let us go to his grave.'

They climbed the hill in the intermittent lightning flashes, but they both had the night-vision of youth so they went swiftly. The grave was on the eastern slope, sited deliberately to face each morning's sunrise. Jim remembered every detail of the funeral. Tom Courtney had slaughtered a black bull and Aboli's wives had stitched the old man's corpse into the wet hide. Then, Tom had carried Aboli's once great body, shrunken now with age, like a sleeping child, down into the deep shaft. He had sat him upright, then laid out all his weapons and his most treasured possessions around him. Lastly the entrance to the shaft was sealed with a round boulder. It had taken two full spans of oxen to drag it into position.

Now, in the darkness, Jim and Zama knelt before it and prayed to the tribal gods of the Lozi, and to Aboli, who in death had joined that dark pantheon. The rolling thunder counterpointed their prayers. Zama asked his father for his blessing on the journey that lay ahead of them, then Jim thanked him for teaching him the way of the musket and the sword, and reminded Aboli of when he had taken him to hunt his first lion. 'Protect us your sons as you shielded us that day,' he asked, 'for we go upon a journey we know not where.'

Then the two sat with their backs against the gravestone, and Jim explained to Zama what he must do. 'I have loaded a string of mules. They are tethered by the stream. Take them up into the mountains, to Majuba, the Place of Doves, and wait for me there.'

Majuba was the rude hut, hidden in the foothills, that was used by the shepherds who took the Courtney flocks up to the high pastures in the summer, and by the men of the Courtney family when they went out to hunt the quagga, the eland and the bluebuck. It was deserted at this season of the year. They said their last farewells to the old warrior who sat eternally in the darkness behind the boulder, and went down to the clearing beside the stream in the forest. Jim took a lantern from one of the packs and, by its light, helped Zama load the mules with the heavy packs. Then he set him on the path that led northwards into the mountains.

'I will come in two days, whatever happens. Wait for me!' Jim shouted as they parted, and Zama rode on alone.

By the time Jim arrived back at High Weald the household was asleep. But Sarah, his mother, had kept his dinner warm for him on the back of the stove. When she heard him clattering the pots, she came down in her nightgown and sat to watch him eat. She said little but her eyes were sad, and there was a droop at the corners of her mouth. 'God bless you, my son, my only son,' she whispered, as she kissed him goodnight. Earlier that day she had seen him lead away the mule train into the forest and, with a mother's instinct, she had known he was leaving. She picked up the candle and climbed the stairs to the bedroom where Tom snored peacefully.

Jim slept little that night, while the wind buffeted the house and rattled the window-frames. He was up long before the rest of the household. In the kitchen he poured a mug of bitter black coffee from the enamel kettle that always stood on the back of the stove. It was still dark as he went down to the stables, and led out Drumfire. He rode down to the seashore, and as he and the horse topped the dunes the full force of the wind came at them out of the darkness like a ravening monster. He took Drumfire back behind the shelter of the dune and tethered him to a low saltbush, then climbed again on foot to the crest. He wrapped his cloak closer round his shoulders and pulled his wide-brimmed hat low over his eyes as he squatted and waited for the first show of dawn. He thought about the girl. She had shown herself to be quick-witted but was she sensible enough to realize that no small boat could come out to the anchorage in the bay until this storm abated? Would she understand that he was not deserting her?

The low, scudding clouds delayed the dawn, and even when it broke it could hardly illuminate the wild scene before him. He stood up, and had to lean into the wind as though he were crossing a fast-flowing river. He held onto his hat with both hands and searched for a glimpse of the Dutch ship. Then, far out, he saw a flash of something not as evanescent as the leaping foam and spray that strove to extinguish it. He watched it avidly, and it persisted, constant in this raging seascape.

'A sail!' he cried, and the wind tore the words from his lips. However, it was not where he had expected to find the

Meeuw. This was a ship under sail, not lying at anchor. He must know if this was the *Meeuw*, trying to fight her way out of the bay, or if it was one of the other ships that had been anchored there. His small hunting telescope was in his saddle-bag. He turned and ran back through the soft sand to where he had left Drumfire out of the wind.

When he reached the crest again he searched for the ship. It took him minutes to find her, but then her sails flashed at him again. He sat flat in the sand and, using his knees and elbows like a tripod to steady himself against the buffeting of the wind, he trained the lens on the distant ship. He picked up her sails, but the swells obscured the hull until suddenly a freak combination of wave and wind lifted her high.

'It's her!' There was no doubt left. '*Het Gelukkige Meeuw.*' He was swamped by an enervating sense of doom. Before his eyes Louisa was being carried away to some foul prison at the far ends of the earth and there was nothing he could do to prevent it happening.

'Please, God, don't take her from me so soon,' he prayed, in despair, but the distant ship battled on through the storm, close-hauled, her captain trying to get clear of the deadly lee shore. Through the lens Jim watched her with a seaman's eye. Tom had taught him well, and he understood all the forces and counter-forces of wind, keel and sail. He saw how close to disaster she was hovering.

The light strengthened and, even with the naked eye, he could make out the detail of this dreadful contest of ship against storm. After another hour she was still locked in the bay and Jim trained the telescope from the ship on to the black, sharklike shape of Robben Island that guarded the exit. Every minute that passed made it more apparent that the *Meeuw* could not break out into the open sea on this tack. The captain would have to come about. He had no alternative: the bottom under him was already too deep for him to drop anchor again, and the storm was pushing him down inexorably on to the rocks of the island. If he went aground there, the hull would be smashed to splinters.

'Go about!' Jim jumped to his feet. 'Tack now! You're going

to murder them, you idiot!' He meant both the ship and the girl. He knew that Louisa would still be battened down below, and even if by some miracle she escaped from the gundeck the chains around her ankles would drag her under as soon as she went over the side.

Doggedly the ship held her course. The manoeuvre of bringing such an ungainly ship about in the weather would entail terrible risk, but soon the captain must realize that no other course lay open to him.

'It's too late!' Jim agonized. 'It's already too late.' Then he saw it begin to happen, the sails slanting and their silhouette altering as she turned her head to the storm. He watched her through the lens, his hand shaking as her turn slowed. At last she hung there, caught in stays, with all her sails flogging and hammering, unable to complete the turn on to the other tack. Then Jim saw the next squall bearing down on her. The sea boiled at the foot of the racing curtain of rain and wind, which caught her and laid the ship over until her bottom planking showed, thick and filthy with weed and barnacles. Then the squall smothered her. She was gone as though she had never existed. In anguish Jim watched for her to reappear. She might have turned turtle to float keel uppermost, or she might even have been trodden right under – there was no way for him to know. His eye burned and his vision blurred with the intensity of his stare through the lens of the telescope. It seemed to take an age for the squall to pass. Then, abruptly, the ship appeared again, but it seemed that it could not be the same vessel, so drastically had her silhouette altered.

'Dismasted!' Jim groaned. Though tears brought on by strain and wind ran down his cheeks, he could not take his eye from the lens. 'Main and fore! She's lost both masts.' Only the mizzen poked up from the rolling hull and the tangle of sails and masts hanging over her side barely slowed her as she paid off before the wind. It swept her back into the bay, clear of the rocks of Robben Island but straight towards the thundering surf on the beach below where Jim stood.

Swiftly Jim calculated the distance, angles and speed. 'She will be on the beach in less than an hour,' he whispered to himself. 'God help all those on board when she strikes.' He lowered the telescope and, with the back of his arm, wiped the wind-tears from his cheek. 'And, most of all, God help Louisa.' He tried to imagine the conditions on the gundeck of the *Meeuw* at that moment, but his imagination baulked.

Louisa had not slept all that night. For hour after hour, while the *Meeuw* rolled and surged and snubbed against her anchor cable, and the storm howled relentlessly through the rigging, she had crouched under the gun carriage, working away with the file. She had padded the chain links with the canvas bag to deaden the scraping sound of metal against metal. But the file handle had raised a blister in her palm. When it burst she had to use the bag to cushion the raw flesh. The first pale light of dawn showed through the chink in the port-lid, and there was only a thin sliver of metal holding the chain link when she lifted her head and heard the unmistakable sounds of the anchor cable being hauled in, the stamp of the bare feet of the sailors working at the windlass on the deck above her. Then, faintly, she heard the shouted orders of the officers on the main deck, and the rush of feet to the masts as men went aloft in the storm.

'We're sailing!' The word was passed along the gundeck and women cursed their misfortune, or shouted abuse at the captain and his crew on the deck above or at God as their mood dictated. The respite was over. All the tribulations of making passage in this hell-ship were about to begin again. They felt the altered motion of the hull as the anchor flukes broke out of the mud bottom, and the ship came alive to begin her struggle with the raging elements.

A dark, bitter anger swept over Louisa. Salvation had seemed so close. She crept to the chink in the port-lid. The light was too poor and the spray and rain were too thick to allow her more than a dim glimpse of the distant land. 'It is still close,' she told herself. 'By God's grace, I might reach it.' But in her heart she knew that across those miles of storm-driven sea the shore was far beyond her reach. Even if she managed to shed her leg irons, climb out through the gunport and leap overboard, there was no chance of her surviving more than a few minutes before she was driven under. She knew that Jim Courtney could not be there to rescue her.

'Better to go quickly by drowning,' she told herself, 'than to rot away in this lice-infested hell.' Frenziedly she sawed at the last sliver of steel that held the chain link closed. Around her the other prisoners were screaming and howling as they were thrown about mercilessly. Close-hauled against the gale the ship pitched and rolled wildly. Louisa forced herself not to look up from her work. Just a few strokes more of the file, the link parted and her chains fell to the deck. Louisa wasted only a minute to massage her swollen, galled ankles. Then she crawled back under the cannon and took out the horn-handled knife from where she had hidden it. 'Nobody must try to stop me,' she whispered grimly. She crawled back to the gunport, and prised loose the shackle of the lock. Then she tucked the knife into the pouch under her skirt. She wedged her back against the gun carriage and tried to force open the port-lid. The ship was on the starboard tack, and the heel of the deck was against her. With all her strength behind it she could push the heavy port-lid open only a few inches, and when she achieved this a solid jet of salt water spurted through the crack. She had to let it slam closed again.

'Help me! Help me get the port-lid open,' she called desperately to her three allies among the prisoners. They stared back at her with dull, bovine expressions. They would rouse themselves to help her only if their own survival depended on it. Between waves Louisa stole another quick glance through the chink of the port-lid, and saw the dark shape of the island not far ahead.

We will be forced to tack now, she thought, or we will be driven aground. Over the months aboard she had picked up a working knowledge and understanding of the ship's navigation and handling. On the other tack, I will have the heel of the hull to help me get it open. She crouched ready, and at last felt the bows coming up into the wind, the motion of the hull changing under her. Even above the keening of the wind she heard, from the deck above, the faint bellowing of orders and the running of frantic feet. She braced herself for the heel of the deck on to the opposite tack. But it did not happen, and the ship rolled with a heavy, slack motion, dead in the water.

One of the other prisoners, whose putative husband had been a boatswain on a VOC Indiaman shouted, with rising panic, 'Stupid pig of a captain has missed stays. Sweet Jesus, we're in irons!' Louisa knew what that meant. Head to the wind, the ship had lost her way through the water and now she could not pay off on the other tack. She was pinned down helplessly before the storm.

'Listen!' the woman screamed. Then, above the din of the storm, they all heard it coming. 'Squall! She's going to lay us over!' They crouched helplessly in their chains, and listened to it grow louder. The shriek of the approaching squall deafened them, and when it seemed that it could not rise higher, it struck the ship. She reeled and staggered and went over like a bull elephant shot through the heart. They were stunned by the crackling uproar of breaking rigging, then the cannon shot of the mainstay parting under the strain. The hull went on over, until the gundeck was vertical, and tackle, gear and human beings slid down the slope until they piled up against the hull. Loose iron cannon-balls slammed into the piles of struggling prisoners. Women were shrieking with pain and terror. One of the iron balls came rolling down the slanting deck towards where Louisa clung to her gun carriage. At the last moment she threw herself aside, and the cannon-ball hit the woman who crouched beside her. Louisa heard the bones in both her legs shatter. The woman sat and stared at the tangle of her own limbs with an expression of astonishment.

One of the great guns, nine tons of cast bronze, broke out of its tackle and came hurtling down the deck. It crushed the struggling women who lay in its path as though they were rabbits under the wheels of a chariot. Then it struck the hull. Even the massive oaken planking could not check its charge. It burst through and was gone. The sea poured through the splintered opening, and swamped the gundeck under an icy green wave. Louisa held her breath and clung to the gun carriage as she was engulfed. Then she felt the hull begin to right itself as the squall raced past and relinquished its grip on the ship. The water poured out through the gaping hole in the side of the hull, and sucked out a struggling, screaming knot of women. As they dropped into the sea their chains dragged them under instantly.

Still clinging to her gun carriage Louisa could look out of the gaping wound in the ship's side as though it were an open doorway. She saw the broken mast, the tangled ropes and canvas hanging down into the churning water from the deck above. She saw the bobbing heads of the seamen who had been swept over the side with the wreckage. Then, beyond it, she saw the shore of Africa, and the high surf bursting upon its beaches like volleys of cannonfire. The crippled ship was drifting down upon it, driven on by the gale. She watched the inexorable progress, terror mingled with burgeoning hope. With every second that passed the shore was drawing closer, and the runaway cannon had smashed open an escape hatch for her. Even through the driving rain and spray she could make out features on the shore, trees bending and dancing in the wind, a scattering of whitewashed buildings set back from the beach.

Closer and closer the stricken ship drifted in, and now she could make out tiny human figures. They were coming from the town, scurrying along the edge of the beach, some waving their arms, but if they were shouting their voices could not carry against that terrible wind. Now the ship was close enough for Louisa to tell the difference between man, woman and child in the gathering throng of spectators.

It took an immense effort for her to force herself to leave her place of safety behind the gun carriage, but she began to crawl along the heaving deck, over the shattered human bodies and sodden equipment. Cannon-balls still rolled aimlessly back and forth, heavy enough to crush her bones and she dodged those that trundled towards her. She reached the hole in the hull. It was wide enough for a horse to gallop through. She clung to the splintered planks, and peered through the spray and the breaking surf at the beach. Her father had taught her to tread water and to swim in a dog-paddle in the lake at Mooi Uitsig. With his encouragement, as he swam beside her, she had once succeeded in crossing from one side of the lake to the other. This was different. She knew she could keep afloat only for a few seconds in this maelstrom of crazed surf.

The shore was so close now that she could make out the expressions of the spectators who waited for the ship to strike. Some were laughing with excitement, two or three children were dancing and waving their arms above their heads. None showed any compassion or pity for the death struggle of a great ship and the mortal predicament of those aboard her. For them this was a Roman circus, with the prospect of profit from salvaging the wreckage as it washed ashore.

From the direction of the castle she saw a file of soldiers come down the beach at a dog-trot. A mounted officer in a fine uniform was leading them – she could see his insignia glinting on his green and yellow jacket even in this dull light. She knew that, even if she succeeded in reaching the shore, the soldiers would be waiting for her.

There was a fresh chorus of screams and heart-stopping cries from the women around her as they felt the vessel touch the bottom. The ship tore herself free and drifted on, only to touch again, the impact shivering the timbers of the hull. This time she stuck fast, pinned down on the sands, and the waves charged at her like rank after rank of a monstrous cavalry. The ship could not yield to their assault, and each wave struck with a malicious boom and a high white fountain of foam. Slowly the hull rolled over, and her starboard side came uppermost. Louisa scrambled out through the jagged opening. She stood upright on the high side of the heavily canted hull. The wind flung out her long yellow hair in a tangle, and flattened the threadbare canvas shift against her thin body. The wet cloth emphasized the thrust of her breasts, which were full and round.

She gazed towards the beach, saw the heads of the sailors

who had abandoned the ship bobbing in the wild waters. One reached the shallows and stood up only to be knocked flat by the next wave. Through the hole in the hull three other convicts followed her out, but as they clung to the planking their leg irons slowed their movements. Another wave swept the hull and Louisa grabbed one of the shrouds from the mainmast, which dangled close by. The waters swirled round her waist but she clung on. When the wave receded all three of the other women were gone, drawn instantly under the green water by their chains.

Using the shroud Louisa pulled herself to her feet again. The spectators were galvanized by the sight of her, seemingly rising like Aphrodite from the waves. She was so young and lovely, and in such mortal danger. This was better than any flogging or execution on the parade-ground of the castle. They danced and waved and shouted. Their voices were faint but in the lull in the wind she could make out their cries.

'Jump, Meisje.'

'Swim, let's see you swim!'

'Better than a gaol cell, Poesje?'

She could see the sadistic excitement on their faces, and hear the cruelty in their voices. She knew that there was no promise of help to be had from them. She raised her face to the sky and, at that moment, a movement caught her eye.

A horse and rider had appeared on the crest of the dune overlooking the stricken ship. The horse was a magnificent bay stallion. The rider sat astride the bare back. He had stripped off all his clothing except a breech clout knotted round his waist. His torso was pale as porcelain, but his strong young arms were tanned by the sun to the colour of fine leather and his dense dark curls danced in the wind. He gazed back at her across the beach and the booming surf, and suddenly he raised his arm above his head and waved at her. Then she recognized him.

Wildly she waved back, and screamed his name. 'Jim! Jim Courtney!'

With mounting horror Jim had watched the final moment of *Het Gelukkige Meeuw*'s agony. A few of the crew still huddled on the capsized hull, then some of the female convicts were creeping out of the open gunports and shattered hatches. The crowds on the beach taunted them as they clustered on the wave-swept hull. When a woman was washed overboard, and her chains pulled her under, there was an ironic chorus of laughter and cheers from the spectators. Then the ship's keel struck the sand and the impact hurled most of the convicts over the side.

As the ship was rolled and pummelled on to the beach by the waves, the crew leaped from the heavily listing deck into the sea. The water overpowered most of them. One or two drowned bodies were washed up on the beach and the spectators dragged them up above the high-water mark. As soon as it was evident there was no life in them they threw them into an untidy pile, and ran back to join the sport. The first of the survivors waded out through the surf and fell to his knees in prayerful gratitude for his escape. Three convict women were thrown ashore, clinging to a spar from the shattered rigging; it had supported them despite the weight of their chains. The soldiers from the castle rushed waist deep into the creaming surf to drag them out on to the beach and arrest them. Jim saw that one was an obese creature with flaxen hair. White breasts the size of a pair of Zeelander cheeses bulged out of her torn shift. Struggling with her captors she screamed an obscenity at Colonel Keyser as he rode up. Keyser leaned out of the saddle, lifted his sheathed sword and struck her a blow with the scabbard that knocked her to her knees. But she was still shrieking as she looked up at him. There was a livid purple scar down her fat cheek.

The next blow with the steel scabbard dropped her face down into the sand, and the soldiers dragged her away.

Desperately Jim searched the open deck for a glimpse of Louisa, but he could not find her. The hull dragged itself free of the sand and began once more to drift closer. Then she struck again solidly, and began to roll over. The surviving women slid down the listing deck, and one after another dropped over the side and splashed into the green water. The ship now lay on her side. There were no living souls clinging to the wreck. For the first time Jim saw the gaping hole through which the loose cannon had burst out. This opening was pointed to the sky, and suddenly a slim feminine form crawled out of it, and came to her feet shakily on the rounded hull. Her long yellow hair was streaming with seawater, and flapped heavily in the gale. Her tattered shift barely covered her coltish limbs. She might have been a boy, were it not for the full bosom under the rags. She gazed imploringly towards the crowds on the beach, who jeered and mocked her.

'Jump, gallows-bait,' they hooted.

'Swim. Swim for us, little fish.'

Jim focused the telescope on her face, and it did not need the sapphire flash of blue from the eyes in her gaunt and pale face for him to recognize her. He sprang to his feet and ran down the back slope of the dune to where Drumfire stood patiently. He lifted his head and whinnied when he saw Jim coming. As he ran Jim stripped off his clothing and left it strewn behind him. Hopping first on one leg and then the other he pulled off his boots, until he wore only his cotton breech clout. He reached the stallion's side, undid the girth and let the saddle drop into the sand. Then he swung himself on to Drumfire's bare back, urged him up the slope and halted him on the crest.

He looked out with dread that he might find that the girl had been washed off the wallowing hull. His spirits surged when he saw that Louisa was still perched there, as he had last seen her, but the ship was breaking up under the brutal hammer blows of the surf. He lifted his right arm high and waved at her. Her head jerked as she looked towards him, and he saw the moment that she recognized him. She waved back at him wildly, and although the wind smothered the sound she mouthed his name: 'Jim! Jim Courtney!'

'Ha! Ha!' he called to Drumfire, and the stallion leaped

forward down the slope of loose white sand, going back on his haunches to balance as they slid down the dune. They hit the beach at a gallop, and the crowd of onlookers scattered in front of Drumfire's flying hoofs. Keyser spurred his horse forward as if to intercept them. His plump, clean-shaven face was stern and the ostrich feathers in his hat were blowing like the white surf. Jim touched Drumfire's flank with his toe and the stallion swerved past the other horse and they raced down towards the sea.

A broken wave came tumbling to meet them, but its main force was spent. Without hesitation Drumfire gathered his forefeet under his chest and leapt over the leading edge of white water as though he were jumping a fence. When he splashed in on the other side, it was already too deep for his hoofs to find the bottom. He began to swim, and Jim slid off his back and wove his fingers into the horse's mane. With his free hand on the stallion's neck he guided him towards the wallowing wreck.

Drumfire swam like an otter, his legs pumping in a mighty rhythm beneath the surface. He had gone twenty yards before the next tall wave struck, and burst over them, submerging them.

The girl on the wreck stared in horrified fascination, and even the watchers on the beach were silenced as they searched for a sign of them in the swirling aftermath of the wave's passage. Then a shout went up as their heads appeared through the foam. They had been washed back half the distance gained, but the stallion was swimming strongly – and the girl could hear him snorting the seawater from his nostrils with each breath. Jim's long black hair was sleeked down his face and shoulders. She could hear his cries faint in the thunder of waters: 'Come, Drumfire. Ha! Ha!'

They swam on through the icy green seas, swiftly making up the distance lost. Another wave came in but they swam up and over the crest, and now they were almost half-way across the gap between shore and ship. The girl stood up and balanced precariously on the heaving hull, gathering herself for the leap over the side.

'No!' Jim yelled up at her. 'Not yet! Wait!' He had seen the next wave humping up against the horizon. This one dwarfed all those that had come before it. Its cliff-like face seemed to be carved from solid green malachite, laced with white spume. As it came on in ponderous majesty it blocked out half of the sky.

'Hold hard, Louisa!' Jim shouted, as the mighty wave crashed into the ship, and smothered her. It left her submerged in its wake. Then it gathered itself again like a predator pouncing on its prey. For long seconds horse and rider swam up its curling front. They were a pair of insects trapped on a wall of green glass. Then the face of the wave toppled forward, curling over them and falling in a solid avalanche as it crashed down on itself with such weight and power that the men on the beach felt the earth jump beneath their feet. Horse and rider were gone, driven so deeply under that surely they could never surface again.

The watchers who, only seconds before, had clamoured to see the storm prevail and its victims perish, now stood smitten with dread, waiting for the impossible to happen, for the heads of that gallant horse and his rider to reappear through the wild surf. Then the water subsided around the ship and as it poured away they saw the girl still lying on the hull, the loose ropes of the rigging holding her from being sucked over the side. She lifted her head and, with the water streaming from her long hair, searched desperately for any sign of horse and man. The seconds drew on and became minutes. Another wave crashed in, then another, but they were not as high and powerful as the one that had buried horse and rider.

Louisa felt despair settle on her. It was not for herself that she feared. She knew she was about to die, but her own life did not seem to matter any more. Instead she grieved for the young stranger who had given his own trying to save her. 'Jim!' she pleaded. 'Please don't die.'

As if in response to her call, the two heads burst out

through the surface. The undertow of the great wave that had pinned them under had also sucked them back almost to where they had disappeared.

'Jim!' she screamed, and leaped to her feet. He was so close that she could see the agony that contorted his face in the effort to draw breath, but he looked up at her, and tried to say something. Perhaps it was a farewell, but then she knew in her heart that this was not a man who would ever surrender, not even to death. He was trying to shout a command, but his breath only whistled and gurgled in his throat. The horse was swimming again, but when it tried to turn its head back towards the beach she saw Jim's hand in its mane guide it back towards her. Jim was still choking and could not use his voice, but he made a gesture with his free hand, and now he was close enough for her to see the determination in his eyes.

'Jump?' she shouted, against the wind. 'Shall I jump?'

He nodded his sodden curls emphatically, and she could just make out the hoarse croak of his voice: 'Come!'

She glanced over her shoulder and saw that, even in his distress, he had picked the slack between the waves to call her on. She threw aside the piece of rope that had saved her, took three running strides across the shattered deck and leaped over the side with her shift ballooning round her waist and her arms windmilling. She hit the water and went under, to reappear almost immediately. She struck out the way her father had taught her and swam to meet them.

Jim reached out and seized her wrist. His grip was so powerful that she thought it might crush her bones. And after what she had suffered at Huis Brabant she had thought that she would never allow a man to touch her again. But there was no time to think of that now. The next wave broke over her head, but his grip never slackened. They came up again and she was spluttering and gasping for breath, yet she seemed to feel strength flowing into her through his fingers. He guided her hand to the horse's mane, and now he had recovered some of his voice.

'Don't hamper him.' She understood what he meant for she knew horses, and she tried not to put her weight on the stallion's back but to swim beside him. Now they were heading towards the beach and each wave that came up behind them carried them forward. Louisa heard voices, faint at first but growing louder every second. The spectators on the beach were caught up in the excitement of the rescue and, fickle as any mob, they were cheering them on. They all knew this horse – most of them had seen him win on Christmas Day. Jim Courtney was a well-known figure in the town: some envied him as the son of a rich man, some thought him too brash, but they all were forced to pay him respect. This was a famous battle he was waging against the sea, and most of them were sailors. Their hearts went out to him.

'Courage, Jim!'

'Power to you, lad.'

'Good on you! Swim, Jim boy, swim.'

Drumfire had felt the shore shelving under his hoofs, and lunged forward powerfully. By now Jim had recovered his breath and coughed most of the water out of his lungs. He threw one leg over the stallion's back. As soon as he was astride he reached down and pulled Louisa up behind him. She wrapped both arms round his waist and hung on with all her strength. Drumfire burst out of the shallows, water exploding before his charge, and then they were out on the beach.

Jim saw Colonel Keyser galloping to intercept them, and urged Drumfire into full stride, swinging his head away until Keyser was trailng twenty strides behind.

'*Wag, jou donder!* Wait! She's an escaped prisoner. Hand the cow over to the law.'

'I will deliver her to the castle myself,' Jim yelled, without looking back.

'No, you don't! She's mine. Bring the bitch back!' Keyser's voice was thick with fury. As Jim urged Drumfire on down the beach he was determined on one thing only. He had already chanced too much ever to turn this girl over to anyone in the garrison, and in particular to Keyser. He had watched too many of the floggings and executions on the parade-ground outside the castle walls over which Keyser had presided. Jim's own great-grandfather had been tortured and executed on that very ground after being falsely convicted of piracy on the high seas.

'They aren't going to get this one,' he swore grimly. Her thin arms were clasped round his waist and he could feel the length of her body pressed against his naked back. Although she was half starved, wet and shivering with the cold of the green waters and the wind of Drumfire's speed, he could sense the courage and determination in her, which matched his own.

She's a fighter, this one. I can never let her down, he thought, and called back to her, 'Hold tight, Louisa. We're going to run the fat colonel into the dirt.' Though she did not answer and he could hear her teeth chattering, she tightened her grip round him and crouched low. He could feel by her balance and the way she adjusted to Drumfire's motion that she was a horsewoman.

He glanced back under his arm, and saw that they had opened the gap on Keyser. Jim had raced against Trouwhart before and he knew the mare's best points and her weaknesses. She was quick and game as her name, Trueheart, suggested, but Keyser overburdened her light frame. On firm, smooth going she was in her element and she probably had the legs of Drumfire out in the open, but on this soft beach sand or over rock and other heavy going, Drumfire's great strength gave him the advantage. Although the stallion was carrying a double load, Louisa was light as a sparrow and Jim was not as heavily built as the colonel. Yet Jim knew better than to underestimate the mare. He knew she had the heart of a lioness and had almost run Drumfire down over the last half-mile of the Christmas racing.

I must pick the course to our advantage, he decided. He had ridden every inch of the ground between here and the foothills, and knew every hill and marsh, salt pan and patch of forest where Trueheart would be at a disadvantage.

'Stop, *jongen*, or I will shoot.' There was another shout

101

behind and when Jim looked back, Keyser had drawn the pistol from the holster on the front of his saddle and was leaning out to avoid hitting his own horse. In that swift glance Jim saw that it was a single-barrelled weapon, and there was not a second in the holster. Jim swerved Drumfire to the left without a break in his stride, cutting sharply across the mare's nose. In an instant he had changed Keyser's target from a steady going-away shot to one with a sharp angle of deflection. Even an experienced soldier like the colonel, shooting from a galloping horse, would have difficulty judging the forward allowance.

Jim reached back, seized Louisa round the waist and swung her round on his off-side, tucking her under his armpit and shielding her with his own body. The pistol shot boomed out, and he felt the strike of the heavy ball. It was high in his back across his shoulders, but after the numbing shock his arms were still strong and his senses alert. He knew he was not badly wounded.

Only pricked me, he thought, and then he spoke: 'That's his one and only shot.' He said it to encourage Louisa, and swung her back into her place behind him.

'Mercy! You're hit,' she exclaimed fearfully. Blood was streaming down his back.

'We'll worry about that later,' he sang out. 'Now Drumfire and I are going to show you a few of our tricks.' He was enjoying himself. He had just been half drowned and shot, but he was still cocky. Louisa had found herself an indomitable champion, and her spirits soared.

But they had lost ground with that evasive turn, and close behind they heard Trueheart's hoofs slapping into the sand, and the scraping of steel in the scabbard as Keyser drew his sabre. Louisa glanced back and saw him rise up over her, standing in the stirrups with his blade held high, but the change of his balance wrong-footed the mare and she stumbled. Keyser swayed and grabbed at the pommel of his saddle to regain balance and Drumfire pulled ahead. Jim put him at the slope of the high dune, and here the stallion's great strength came into play. He went up in a series of violent lunges with the sand spurting out from under his hoofs. Trueheart dropped back sharply as she carried the colonel's weight up the slope.

They went over the top and slid down the far side. From the foot of the dune there was open ground and firm going to the edge of the lagoon. Louisa looked back. 'They're gaining again,' she warned Jim. Trueheart was striding out gracefully. Even though she was carrying the weight of the colonel, and all his weapons and accoutrements, she seemed to flirt with the earth.

'He's reloading his pistol.' There was an edge of alarm in her voice. Keyser was ramming a ball into the muzzle.

'Let's see if we can wet his powder for him,' Jim said, and they reached the edge of the lagoon and plunged in without a check.

'Swim again,' Jim ordered, and Louisa slipped into the water on Drumfire's other flank. They both looked back as Trueheart reached the edge of the lagoon and Keyser pulled her up. He jumped down and primed the pan of his pistol. Then he cocked the hammer, and aimed at them across the open water. There was a puff of white gunsmoke. A fountain of water jumped from the surface an arm's length behind them and, with a hum, the heavy ball ricocheted over their heads.

'Now throw your boots at us.' Jim laughed, and Keyser stamped with rage. Jim hoped that he would give up now. Surely, even in his anger, he must consider the fact that Trueheart was so heavily burdened, while they were almost naked and Drumfire's back was bare. Keyser made the decision, and swung up on to the mare's back. He pushed her into the water, just as Drumfire emerged on to the muddy bank on the far side. Immediately Jim turned him parallel to the shore and, keeping to the soft ground, led him along the shore at a trot.

'We must give Drumfire a chance to breathe,' he told Louisa as she ran behind him. 'That swim out to the ship would have drowned any other horse.' He was watching their pursuers. Trueheart was only half-way across the lagoon. 'Keyser wasted time with his pistol practice. One thing is certain, there will be no more of that. His powder is well and truly soaked by now.'

'The water washed the blood from your wound,' she told him, reaching out to touch his back lightly. 'I can see now it's a graze, not deep, thank the good Lord.'

'It's you we have to worry about,' he said. 'You're skin and bones, not a pound of meat on you. How long can you run on those skinny legs?'

'As long as you can,' she flared at him, and angry red spots appeared on her pale cheeks.

He grinned at her unrepentantly. 'You may have to prove that boast before this day is done. Keyser is across.'

Far behind them Trueheart came out on to the bank and, streaming water from his tunic, breeches and boots, Keyser mounted her and set out along the bank after them. He urged the mare into a gallop, but heavy clods of mud flew from her hoofs and it was immediately obvious that she was making heavy work of it. Jim had kept to the mud flats for just that reason, to test Trueheart's strength.

'Up you get.' Jim seized Louisa, threw her up on to the stallion's back and broke into a run. He kept a firm grip on Drumfire's mane so he was pulled along, keeping pace with horse's easy canter while saving the animal's strength. He kept glancing back to judge their relative speeds. He could afford to let Keyser gain a little ground now. Carrying only Louisa's weight Drumfire was going easily, while the mare was burning up her strength in this reckless pursuit.

Within half a mile Keyser's weight began to tell, and Trueheart slowed to a walk. She was still trailing by a half pistol-shot. Jim slowed to her speed to keep the gap constant.

'Come down, if you please, your ladyship,' he told Louisa. 'Give Drumfire another breather.'

She jumped down lightly, but flashed at him, 'Don't call me that.' It was a bitter reminder of the taunts she had endured from her fellow convicts.

'Perhaps we should rather call you Hedgehog?' he asked. 'The Lord knows, you have prickles enough to warrant it.'

Keyser must be almost exhausted by now, Jim thought, for he stayed in the saddle, not taking his weight off his mount. 'They are almost done in,' he told Louisa. He knew that not far ahead and still on the Courtney estate lay a salt pan that they called Groot Wit – Big White. That was where he was leading Keyser.

'He's coming on again,' Louisa warned him, and he saw that Keyser was pushing the mare into a canter. She was a game little filly, and she was responding to the whip.

'Mount!' he ordered.

'I can run as far as you can.' She shook the salt-crusted tangle of her long hair at him defiantly.

'In Jesus's name, woman, must you always argue?'

'Must you always blaspheme?' she riposted, but she allowed him to hoist her on to the stallion's back. They ran on. Within the mile Trueheart had slowed to a walk, and they could do the same.

'There is the beginning of the salt.' Jim pointed ahead and even under the low stormclouds and in the gathering dusk, it shone like a vast mirror.

'It looks flat and hard.' She shaded her eyes against the glare.

'It looks that way, but under the crust it's porridge. With that great fat Dutchman and all his equipment upon her back the mare will break through every few paces. It's almost three miles across the pan. They will be completely finished before they reach the other side and . . .' he looked at the sky '. . . by then it will be dark.'

Although it was hidden by the lowering blanket of cloud the sun must have been close to the horizon and the darkness was coming on apace as Jim led Drumfire, the girl staggering beside him, off the treacherous white plain. He paused at the edge of the forest, and they both looked back.

Like a long string of black pearls Drumfire's hoofprints were deeply scored into the smooth white surface. Even for him the crossing had been a terrible ordeal. Far behind they could just make out the small dark shape of the mare. Two hours earlier, with Keyser on her back, Trueheart had broken through the salt crust and into the quicksand beneath. Jim had stopped and watched Keyser struggle to free her. He had been tempted to turn back and help them. She was such a game, beautiful animal that he could not bear to watch her bogged down and exhausted. Then he remembered that he was unarmed and almost naked, while Keyser had his sabre and was a swordsman to be reckoned with. Jim had watched him leading his cavalry troop through their evolutions on the parade-ground outside the castle. While he hesitated Keyser had managed, by force, to drag the mare free of the mud and continue plodding in pursuit.

Now he was still following and Jim frowned. 'If there were ever a time to meet Keyser it would be when he comes off the salt. He will be exhausted and in the dark I would have the benefit of surprise. But he has his sabre and I have nothing,' he murmured. Louisa looked at him for a moment, then turned her back to him modestly, and reached under the skirt of her shift. She found the horn-handled clasp knife in the pouch she wore strapped round her waist and handed it to him without a word. He stared at it in astonishment, then burst out laughing as he recognized it.

'I withdraw everything I said about you. You look like a Viking maid and, by Jesus, you act like one too.'

'Watch your blaspheming tongue, Jim Courtney,' she said, but there was no fire in the rebuke. She was too tired to argue further, and the compliment had been a pretty one. As she turned away her head there was a weary half smile on her lips. Jim led Drumfire into the trees, and she followed them. After a few hundred paces, in a spot where the forest was thickest, he tethered the stallion and told Louisa, 'Now you can rest a while.'

This time she did not protest but sank down on the thick leaf mould on the forest floor, curled up, closed her eyes. In her weakened state she felt that she might never have the strength to stand up again. Hardly had the thought flashed through her mind than she was asleep.

Jim wasted a few moments admiring her suddenly serene

features. Until then he had not realized how young she was. Now she looked like a sleeping child. While he watched her he opened the blade of the knife and tested the point on the ball of his thumb. At last he tore himself away, and ran back to the edge of the forest. Keeping well hidden he peered out across the darkening salt pan. Keyser was still coming on doggedly, leading the mare.

Will he never give up? Jim wondered, and felt a twinge of admiration for him. Then he looked around for the best place to hide beside the tracks that Drumfire had left. He picked a patch of dense bush, crept into it and squatted there with the knife in his hand.

Keyser reached the edge of the pan, and staggered out on to the firm footing. By this time it was so dark that, although Jim could hear him panting for breath, he was just a dark shape. He came on slowly, leading the mare, and Jim let him pass his hiding-place. Then he slipped out of the bush and crept up behind him. Any sound he might have made was covered by the hoof-falls of the mare. From behind he locked his left arm around Keyser's throat and, at the same time, pressed the point of the knife into the soft skin under his ear. 'I will kill you if you force me to it,' he snarled, making his tone ferocious.

Keyser froze with shock. Then he regained his own voice. 'You can't hope to get away with this, Courtney. There is no place for you to run. Give me the woman, and I will settle things with your father and Governor van de Witten.'

Jim reached down and drew the sabre from the scabbard on the colonel's belt. Then he released his lock around the man's throat and stepped back, but he held the point of the sabre to Keyser's chest. 'Take off your clothes,' he ordered.

'You are young and stupid, Courtney,' Keyser replied coldly. 'I will try to make allowances for that.'

'Tunic first,' Jim ordered. 'Then breeches and boots.'

Keyser did not move. Jim pricked his chest, and at last, reluctantly, the colonel reached up and began to unbutton his tunic.

'What do you hope to achieve?' he asked, as he shrugged out of it. 'Is this some boyish notion of chivalry? The woman is a convicted felon. She is probably a whore and a murderess.'

'Say that again, Colonel, and I will spit you like a sucking pig.' This time Jim drew blood with the point. Keyser sat down to pull off his boots and his breeches. Jim stuffed them into Trueheart's saddlebags. Then, with the point of the sabre at the man's back, he escorted Keyser, barefoot and wearing only his undershirt, to the edge of the salt pan.

'Follow your own tracks, Colonel,' he told him, 'and you should be back at the castle in time for breakfast.'

'Listen to me, *jongen*,' Keyser said, in a thin tight voice. 'I will come after you. I will see you hanged on the parade, and I promise you it will be slow – very slow.'

'If you stand here talking, Colonel, you're going to miss your breakfast.' Jim smiled at him. 'You had far better start walking.'

He watched Keyser trudge away across the salt pan. Suddenly the heavy clouds were stripped away by the wind and the full moon burst through to light the pale surface as though it were day. It was bright enough to throw a shadow at Keyser's feet. Jim watched him until he was only a dark blob in the distance, and knew that he was not coming back. Not tonight, at least. But it's not the last we've seen of the gallant colonel, he thought, we can be sure of that. Then he ran back to Trueheart, and led her into the forest. He shook Louisa awake. 'Wake up, Hedgehog. We have a long journey ahead of us,' he told her. 'And by this time tomorrow we are going to have Keyser and a squadron of cavalry in full cry after us.'

When she sat up groggily he went to Trueheart. A rolled woollen cavalry cloak was strapped on top of Keyser's saddlebags.

'It will be cold when we get into the mountains,' he warned her. She was still half asleep and did not protest as he wrapped the cloak round her shoulders. Then he found the colonel's food bag. It held a loaf of bread, a wedge of cheese, a few apples and a flask of wine. 'The colonel dearly loves his food.' He tossed her an apple and she wolfed it down core and all.

'Sweeter than honey,' she said, through a mouthful. 'I never tasted anything like it before.'

'Greedy little Hedgehog,' he teased her and this time she gave him an urchin smile. Most people found it hard to be angry with Jim for long. He squatted on his haunches in front of her and, with the clasp knife, cut a hunk of bread and slapped a thick slice of cheese on top of it. She ate with ferocious intensity. He watched her pale face in the moonlight. She looked like a pixie.

'And you?' she asked. 'Aren't you eating?' He shook his head. He had decided that there would not be enough for both of them: this girl was starving.

'How did you learn to speak such good English?'

'My mother came from Devon.'

'My oath! That's where we're from. My great-great-grandfather was a duke, or something of that ilk.'

'So, shall I call you Duke?'

'That will do until I think of something better, Hedgehog.' She took another bite of bread and cheese so she could not reply. While she ate he sorted through the rest of Keyser's possessions. He tried on the gold-frogged tunic, and held the lapels together.

'Space for two of us in here, but it's warm.' The front flaps of the colonel's breeches went half-way again round Jim's middle but he belted them with one of the straps from the saddlebags. Then he tried the boots. 'At least these are a good fit.'

'In London I saw a play called *The Tin Soldier*,' she said. 'That's who you look like now.'

'You were in London?' Despite himself he was impressed. London was the centre of the world. 'You must tell me about it as soon as we have an opportunity.'

Then he led the horses to the well on the edge of the pan where the cattle were watered. He and Mansur had dug it themselves two years ago. The water in it was sweet, and the horses drank thirstily. When he led them back he found Louisa had fallen asleep again under the cloak. He squatted beside her and studied her face in the moonlight, and there was a strange hollow feeling under his ribs. He left her to sleep a little longer and went to feed the horses from the colonel's grain bag.

Then he selected what he needed from Keyser's equipment. The pistol was a lovely weapon, and tucked into the leather holster was a small canvas roll that contained the ramrod and all the accessories. The sabre was of the finest steel. In the tunic he found a gold watch and a purse filled with silver guilders and a few gold ducats. In the back pocket there was a small brass box that contained a flint and steel, and cotton kindling.

'If I steal his horse I might as well take the money too,' he told himself. However, he drew the line at filching Keyser's more personal possessions, so he placed the gold watch and the medals in one of the saddlebags, and left it lying conspicuously in the centre of the clearing. He knew that Keyser would return here tomorrow with his Bushman trackers, and would find his personal treasures. 'I wonder how grateful he will be for my generosity?' He smiled bleakly. He was carried along by a sense of reckless inevitability. He knew that there was no turning back. He was committed. He went to resaddle Trueheart, then squatted beside Louisa. She was curled into a ball under the cloak. He stroked her hair to wake her gently.

She opened her eyes and looked up at him. 'Don't touch me like that,' she whispered. 'Don't ever touch me like that again.'

Her voice was filled with such bitter loathing that he recoiled. Years ago Jim had captured a wild-cat kitten. Despite all his loving patience he had never been able to tame the creature. It snarled and bit and scratched. In the end he had taken it out into the veld and set it free. Perhaps this girl was like that. 'I had to wake you,' he said. 'We must go on.' She stood up immediately.

'Take the mare,' he said. 'She has a soft mouth and a gentle nature, yet she is fast as the wind. Her name is Trueheart.' He boosted her into the saddle, and she took the reins and wrapped the cloak tightly around her shoulders. He handed her the last of the bread and cheese. 'You can eat as we go.'

She ate as though she were still famished, and he wondered what terrible privations she had been forced to endure that had turned her into this starved, abused wild creature. He felt a fleeting doubt at his own ability to help or redeem her. He thrust it aside and smiled at her in what he imagined was a placatory way, but which to her seemed merely supercilious. 'When we get to Majuba, Zama will have the hunter's pot going. I hope he has filled it to the brim. I would place money on you in an eating contest with the good colonel.' He sprang up on Drumfire's back. 'First, though, we have something else to do here.'

He set off at a trot in the direction of High Weald, but he circled well clear of the homestead. By now it was after midnight, but still he did not want to chance running into his father or Uncle Dorian. The news of his escapade would have reached their ears almost as soon as he had plucked the girl out of the sea. He had seen many of the family freed slaves and servants among the spectators on the beach. He could not face his father now. We will get no sympathy there, he thought. He will try to force me to turn Louisa over to the colonel. He rode instead to a cluster of huts at the east side of the paddock. He dismounted in a stand of trees and handed Drumfire's reins to Louisa. 'Stay here. I won't be long.'

He approached the largest mud-walled hut in the village carefully and whistled. There was a long pause, then a lantern flared behind the uncured sheepskin that covered the single window in place of a curtain. The reeking fleece was drawn aside, and a dark head poked out suspiciously. 'Who's there?'

'Bakkat, it's me.'

'Somoya!' He came out into the moonlight with a greasy blanket tucked around his waist. He was as tiny as a child, his skin amber in the moonlight. His features were flattened and his eyes had a curious Asiatic slant. He was a Bushman, and he could track a lost beast for fifty leagues over desert and mountain, through blizzard and storm. He smiled up at Jim, and his eyes were almost hidden in a web of wrinkles. 'May the Kulu Kulu smile upon you, Somoya.'

'And on you also, old friend. Call out all the other

shepherds. Gather up the herds and drive them over every road. Especially all the paths heading towards the east and north. I want them to chop up the ground until it looks like a ploughed field. Nobody must be able to follow my tracks when I leave here, not even you. Do you understand?'

Bakkat cackled with laughter. 'Oh, *ja*, Somoya! I understand very well. We all saw the fat soldier chasing you when you ran off with that pretty little girl. Don't worry! By morning there won't be a single one of your tracks left for him to follow.'

'Good fellow!' Jim clapped him on the back. 'I am off.'

'I know where you are going. You are taking the Robbers' Road?' The Robbers' Road was the legendary escape route out of the colony, travelled only by fugitives and outlaws. 'Nobody knows where it leads, because nobody ever comes back. The spirits of my ancestors whisper to me in the night, and my soul pines for the wild places. Do you have a place for me at your side?'

Jim laughed. 'Follow and be welcome, Bakkat. I know that you'll be able to find me wherever I go. You could follow the tracks of a ghost over the burning rocks of hell. But, first, do what you must do here. Tell my father I am well. Tell my mother I love her,' he said, and ran back to where Louisa and the horses were still waiting.

They went on. The storm had blown itself out, the wind had dropped, and the moon was low in the west before they reached the foothills. He stopped beside a stream that ran down from the hills. 'We will rest and water the horses,' he told her. He did not offer to help her dismount, but she dropped to the ground as lithely as a cat, and took Trueheart to drink at the pool. She and the mare seemed already to have established an accord. Then she went into the bushes on her own. He wanted to call after her and warn her not to go far, but he held back the words.

The colonel's wine flask was half-empty. Jim smiled as he shook it. Keyser must have been nipping at it since breakfast time yesterday, he thought and went to the pool to dilute what remained with the sweet mountain water. He heard the girl come back through the bushes and, still hidden from him by a pile of tall rocks, go down to the water. There was a splash.

'Damn me if the mad woman is not taking a bath.' He shook his head, and shivered at the thought. There was still snow on the mountains, and the night air was chill. When Louisa returned she sat on one of the rocks at the edge of the pool, not too close to him nor again too far away. Her hair was wet and she combed it out. He recognized the tortoiseshell comb. He went over to her and passed her the wine flask. She paused long enough to drink from it.

'That's good.' She said it like a peace-offering, then went on combing the pale hair that reached almost to her waist. He watched her quietly but she did not look in his direction again.

A fishing owl darted down on the pool on silent wings like a gigantic moth. Hunting only by the last rays of the moon it snatched a small yellowfish from the waters and flew with it to a branch of the dead tree on the far bank. The fish flapped in its talons as the owl tore chunks of meat out of its back.

Louisa looked away. When she spoke again her voice was soft and the faint accent appealing. 'Don't think I'm not grateful for what you have done for me. I know you have risked your life and maybe more than that to help me.'

'Well, you must understand that I keep a menagerie of pets.' He spoke lightly. 'I needed only one more to add to it. A small hedgehog.'

'Perhaps you have the right to call me that,' she said, and sipped from the flask again. 'You know nothing about me. Things have happened to me. Things that you could never understand.'

'I know a little about you. I have seen your courage and your determination. I saw what it was like and how it smelt on board the *Meeuw*. Perhaps I might understand,' he replied. 'At least, I would try.'

He turned to her, then felt his heart break as he saw the

tears running down her cheeks, silver in the moonlight. He wanted to rush to her and hold her tightly, but he remembered what she had said: 'Never touch me like that again.'

Instead he said, 'Whether you like it or not, I'm your friend. I want to understand.'

She wiped her cheeks with the palm of one small dainty hand, and sat huddled, thin, pale and disconsolate in the cloak.

'There is just one thing I must know,' Jim said. 'I have a cousin called Mansur. He is closer to me than a brother could be. He said that perhaps you are a murderess. That burns my soul. I must know. Are you? Is that why you were on the *Meeuw*?'

She turned slowly towards him and, with both hands, parted the curtain of her damp hair so that he could see her face. 'My father and mother died of the plague. I dug their graves with my own hands. I swear to you, Jim Courtney, on my love for them and on the graves in which they lie, that I am no murderess.'

He heaved a great sigh of relief. 'I believe you. You don't have to tell me anything else.'

She drank again from the flask, then handed it back to him. 'Don't let me have more. It softens my heart when I need to be strong,' she said. They sat on in silence. He was just about to tell her that they must go on deeper into the mountains when she whispered, so quietly that he was not sure that she had spoken, 'There was a man. A rich and powerful man whom I trusted as once I trusted my dead father. He did things to me that he did not want other people to know about.'

'No, Louisa.' He held up his hand to stop her. 'Don't tell me this.'

'I owe you my life and my freedom. You have a right to know.'

'Please stop.' He wanted to jump to his feet and run into the bushes to escape her words. But he could not move. He was held mesmerized by them, as a mouse by the swaying dance of the cobra.

114

She went on in the same sweet, childlike tones. 'I will not tell you what he did to me. I will never tell anyone that. But I cannot let any man touch me again. When I tried to escape from him, he had his servants hide a packet of jewellery in my room. Then they called the watch to find it. They took me before the magistrate in Amsterdam. My accuser was not even in the court room when I was condemned to be transported for life.' They were both silent for a long time. Then she spoke again. 'Now you know about me, Jim Courtney. Now you know that I am a soiled and discarded plaything. What do you want to do now?'

'I want to kill him,' said Jim at last. 'If ever I meet this man I will kill him.'

'I have spoken honestly to you. Now you must speak honestly to me. Be sure of what you want. I have told you that I will let no man touch me again. I have told you what I am. Do you want to take me back to Good Hope and hand me over to Colonel Keyser? If you do, I am ready to go back with you.'

He did not want her to see his face. Not since he was a child had anyone seen him weep. He jumped to his feet and went to saddle Trueheart. 'Come, Hedgehog. It's a long ride to Majuba. We have no more time to waste in idle chatter.' She came to him obediently and mounted the horse. He led her into the deep defile in the mountains and up the steep gorge. It grew colder as they climbed, and in the dawn, the sun lit the mountain tops with a weird pink light. Patches of old unmelted snow gleamed among the rocks.

It was late in the morning before they paused on the crest at the limit of the treeline and looked down into a hidden valley. There was a tumbledown building among the rocks of the scree slope. She might not have noticed it, were it not for the thin column of smoke rising from the hole in the tattered thatch roof, and the small herd of mules in the stone-walled kraal.

'Majuba,' he told her, as he reined in, 'the Place of the Doves, and that is Zama.' A tall young man dressed in a loincloth had come out into the sunlight and was staring up at them. 'We have been together all our lives. I think you will like him.'

Zama waved and bounded up the slope to meet them. Jim slipped down from Drumfire's back to greet him. 'Have you got the coffee-pot on?' he asked.

Zama looked up at the girl on the horse. They studied each other for a moment. He was tall and well formed, with a broad, strong face, and very white teeth. 'I see you, Miss Louisa,' he said at last.

'I see you also, Zama, but how did you know my name?'

'Somoya told me. How did you know mine?'

'He told me also. He is a great chatterbox, is he not?' she said, and they laughed together. 'But why do you call him Somoya?' she asked.

'It is the name my father gave him. It means the Wild Wind,' Zama replied. 'He blows as he pleases, like the wind.'

'Which way will he blow now?' she asked, but she was looking at Jim with a small, quizzical smile.

'We shall see.' Zama laughed. 'But it will be the way we least expect.'

Colonel Keyser led ten mounted troopers clattering into the courtyard of High Weald. His Bushman tracker ran at his horse's head. Keyser stood in the stirrups and shouted towards the main doors of the godown: 'Mijnheer Tom Courtney! Come out at once!'

From every window and doorway white and black heads appeared, children and freed slaves gawked at him in round-eyed amazement.

'I am on dire Company business,' Keyser shouted again. 'Do not trifle with me, Tom Courtney.'

Tom came out through the tall doors of the warehouse. 'Stephanus Keyser, my dear friend!' he called, in jovial tones, as he pushed his steel-rimmed spectacles on to the top of his head. 'You are welcome indeed.'

The two had spent many evenings together in the Mermaid tavern. Over the years they had done each other many favours. Only last month Tom had found a string of pearls for Keyser's mistress at a favourable price, and Keyser had seen to it that the charges of public drunkenness and brawling laid against one of Tom's servants were quashed.

'Come in! Come in!' Tom spread his arms in invitation. 'My wife will bring us a pot of coffee, or do you prefer the fruit of the vine?' He called across the courtyard to the kitchens, 'Sarah Courtney! We have an honoured guest.'

She came out on to the terrace. 'Why, Colonel! This is a delightful surprise.'

'A surprise maybe,' he said sternly, 'but delightful, I doubt it, Mevrouw. Your son James is in serious trouble with the law.'

Sarah untied her apron and went to stand beside her husband. He put one thick arm around her waist. At that moment Dorian Courtney, slim and elegant, his dark red hair bound up in a green turban, stepped out of the shadows of the godown and stood at Tom's other hand. Together, the three presented a united and formidable front.

'Come inside, Stephanus,' Tom repeated. 'We cannot talk here.'

Keyser shook his head firmly. 'You must tell me where your son, James Courtney, is hiding.'

'I thought *you* might be able to tell *me* that. Yesterday evening all the world and his brothers saw you racing Jim over the dunes. Did he beat you again, Stephanus?'

Keyser flushed and fidgeted on his borrowed saddle. His spare tunic was too tight under the armpits. Only hours ago he had recovered his medals and the star of St Nicholas from the abandoned saddlebags his Bushman tracker had found on the edge of the salt pan. He had pinned these decorations on awry. He touched his pockets to reassure himself that his gold watch was still in place. His breeches were fit to burst their seams. His feet were raw and blistered from the long walk home in the darkness; his new boots pinched the sore spots.

He usually took pride in his appearance, and his present disarray and discomfort compounded the humiliation he had suffered at the hands of Jim Courtney.

'Your son has absconded with an escaped convict. He has stolen a horse and other valuable items. All these are hanging matters, I warn you. I have reason to believe that the fugitive is hiding here at High Weald. We have followed his tracks here from the salt pan. I am going to search every building.'

'Good!' Tom nodded. 'And when you are finished my wife will have refreshments ready for you and your men.' As Keyser's troopers dismounted and drew their sabres, Tom went on, 'But, Stephanus, you warn those ruffians of yours to leave my serving girls alone, otherwise it will really be a hanging matter.'

The three Courtneys withdrew into the cool shade of the godown, and crossed the wide, cluttered floor to the counting-house on the far side. Tom slumped into the leather-covered armchair beside the cold fireplace. Dorian sat cross-legged on a leather cushion on the far side of the room. With his green turban and embroidered waistcoat he looked like the Oriental potentate he had once been. Sarah closed the door but remained standing beside it to keep watch for any possible eavesdroppers. She studied the pair while she waited for Tom to speak. Brothers could scarcely have been more different: Dorian slim, elegant, marvellously handsome and Tom so big, solid and bluff. The strength of her feelings for him, even after all these years, still surprised her.

'I could happily wring the young puppy's neck.' Tom's genial smile had given way to a furious scowl. 'We can't be sure what he has got us all into.'

'You were young once, Tom Courtney, and you were always in hot water up to your neck.' Sarah gave him the smile of a loving wife. 'Why do you think I fell in love with you? It could never have been your looks.'

Tom tried not to let his smile reappear. 'That was different,' he declared. 'I never asked for trouble.'

'You never asked,' she agreed. 'You simply grabbed it with both hands.'

Tom winked at her and turned to Dorian. 'It must be wonderful to have a dutiful, respectful wife like Yasmini.' Then he was serious again.

'Has Bakkat returned yet?' The herder had sent one of his sons to Tom to tell him of Jim's nocturnal visit. Tom had felt a sneaking admiration for Jim's ruse in covering his tracks. 'It's the sort of thing I would have done. He may be wild as the wind but he's no fool,' he had told Sarah.

'No,' Dorian answered. 'Bakkat and the other herders are still moving all of the cattle and sheep over every path and road this side of the mountains. Even Keyser's Bushman will not be able to work out Jim's tracks. I think we can be sure that Jim has got clean away. But where did he go?' Both of them looked at Sarah for the answer.

'He planned it carefully,' she answered. 'I saw him with the mules a day or so ago. The shipwreck might have been a stroke of luck as far as he was concerned, but he was planning to get the girl off the ship one way or the other.'

'That damned woman! Why is it always a woman?' Tom lamented.

'You, of all people, should not have to ask that,' Sarah told him. 'You stole me away from my family with musket balls whizzing around our heads. Don't try to play the Pope with me, Tom Courtney!'

'Sweet heavens, yes! I'd almost forgotten about that. It was fun, though, wasn't it, my beauty?' He leaned across and pinched her bottom. She slapped his hand, and he went on unperturbed, 'But this woman Jim is with. What is she? A prison drab. A poisoner? A cutpurse? A whore mistress? Who knows what the idiot has picked for himself.'

Dorian had been watching this exchange with a fond expression while he got his hookah pipe to draw properly. It was a habit he had brought back from Arabia. Now he took out the ivory mouthpiece and remarked drily, 'I have spoken to at least a dozen of our people who were on the beach and saw it all. She may be all the other things you suggest, but she is no drab.' He blew a long feather of fragrant smoke. 'Reports of her vary. Kateng says she is an angel of beauty, Litila says she is a golden princess. Bakkat says she is as lovely as the spirit of the rain goddess.'

Tom snorted with derision. 'A rain goddess out of a stinking convict ship? A sunbird hatching from a turkey buzzard's egg is more likely. But where has Jim taken her?'

'Zama has been missing since the day before yesterday. I didn't see him go, but my guess is that Jim sent him off with the mules to wait for him somewhere,' Sarah suggested. 'Zama will do whatever Jim asks.'

'And Jim spoke to Bakkat about the Robbers' Road,' Dorian added, 'and told him to sweep his tracks from the road to the east and the north of here.'

'The Robbers' Road is a myth,' said Tom firmly. 'There are no roads into the wilderness.'

'But Jim believes in it. I heard him and Mansur discussing it,' Sarah said.

Tom looked worried. 'It's madness. A babe and a prison drab going off empty-handed into the wilderness? They won't last a week.'

'They have Zama, and they are hardly empty-handed. Jim took six mule-loads of goods,' said Dorian. 'I've been checking what is missing from the stores, and he chose well. They are well set-up and provisioned for a long journey.'

'He didn't even say goodbye.' Tom shook his head. 'He's my son, my only son, and he didn't even say goodbye.'

'He was in somewhat of a hurry, brother,' Dorian pointed out.

Sarah rallied to her son's defence: 'He sent us a message through Bakkat. He didn't forget us.'

'It's not the same,' said Tom heavily. 'You know he might never come back. He has closed this door behind him. Keyser will catch him and hang him if he ever sets foot in the colony again. No, damn my eyes, I must see him again. Just once more. He is so headstrong and wild. I have to give him my counsel.'

'You have been giving him your counsel for the last nineteen years,' Dorian said wryly. 'Look where it has got us now.'

120

'Where was his rendezvous with Zama?' Sarah asked. 'That is where they will be.'

Tom thought about it for a moment, then grinned. 'Only one place it could be,' he said firmly.

Dorian nodded. 'I know what you're thinking,' he told Tom. 'Majuba is the obvious place for them to hide out. But we dare not follow them there. Keyser will be watching us like a leopard at the water-hole. If one of us leaves High Weald he will put that little yellow bloodhound of his on to us, and we will lead him straight to Majuba, and Jim.'

'If we're going to find him it must be soon, otherwise Jim will be gone from Majuba. They are well mounted. They have Drumfire and Keyser's mare. Jim will be half-way to Timbuktu before we can catch up with him.'

At that moment the tramp of boots and loud masculine voices echoed through the main storeroom of the godown.

'Keyser's men have searched the house.' Sarah glanced out of the door. 'Now they're starting on the warehouse and the outbuildings.'

'We'd better go out to keep an eye on those rogues,' Dorian stood up, 'before they start helping themselves.'

'We'll decide what to do about Jim once we've seen Keyser off,' Tom said, as they went through on to the main floor of the godown.

Four of the troopers were poking about aimlessly among the clutter. They were obviously tiring of their fruitless hunt. The long storeroom was piled to the high yellow-wood rafters. If they were to search it thoroughly they would need to clear the tons of goods with which the warehouse was congested. There were bales of silk from China, and cottons from the Indies; sacks of coffee beans and gum arabic from Zanzibar and other ports beyond the Horn of Hormuz; balks of sawn teak, sandalwood and ebony; mounds of pure gleaming copper cast into huge wheels so that armies of slaves could trundle them down the mountain tracks from the far interior of Ethiopia to the coast. There were bundles of the dried skins of exotic animals, tigers and zebras, and the furs of monkeys and seals, and the long curved horns of the rhinoceros, famous through China and the Orient for its aphrodisiac powers.

The Cape of Good Hope sat across the trade routes between Europe and the Orient. In former times the ships from the north had made the long voyage down the Atlantic. Even when they anchored in Table Bay they still faced another seemingly endless passage to the Indies and China, then even further north again to far Japan. A ship might be at sea for three or four years before it could return to Amsterdam, or the Pool of London.

Tom and Dorian had gradually evolved another network of trade. They had convinced a syndicate of ship-owners in Europe to send their ships only as far as the Cape. From the Courtney Brothers' warehouse they could fill their holds with choice goods, turn round in Table Bay and, with favourable winds, be back in their home ports in under a year. The profit the Courtneys exacted more than compensated for the additional years that the ships would be forced to spend at sea if they went further afield. In the same way ships coming from the east could discharge in Table Bay into the godown of the Courtney Brothers and be back in Batavia, Rangoon or Bombay in less than half the time it would have taken to make the journey across two great oceans.

This innovation was the foundation on which they had built their fortune. Added to this, they had their own trading schooners, which plied the African coast and were captained by Dorian's trusted Arab followers. As Muslims they could travel into waters forbidden to Christian captains, and venture as far as Muscat and Medina, the Luminous City of the Prophet of God. Although these vessels lacked the large holds in which to carry bulky cargoes, they dealt in the goods of higher value: copper and gum arabic, pearls and mother-of-pearl shells from the Red Sea, ivory from the markets of Zanzibar, sapphires from the mines of Kandy, yellow diamonds from the alluvial field along the great rivers of the empire of the Moguls, and cakes of black opium from the mountains of the Pathans.

There was only one commodity in which the Courtney

brothers refused to trade: human slaves. They had intimate knowledge of the barbaric practice. Dorian had spent most of his boyhood in slavery, until his owner, Sultan Abd Muhammad al-Malik, the ruler of Muscat, had adopted him as a son. In his younger days Tom had waged a bitter war against the Arab slave-traders of the East African coast, and had been a witness at first hand of the heartless cruelty of the trade. Many of the Courtney servants and sailors were former slaves who had come into their possession and whom they had manumitted at once. The means by which some of these unfortunates had been brought under the wing of the family varied – sometimes by force of arms, for Tom dearly loved a good fight, or by shipwreck, or in payment of debts, or even by outright purchase. Sarah could seldom bring herself to walk past a weeping orphan on the auction block without importuning her husband to buy the child and give it into her care. She had reared half of her house servants from infancy.

Sarah went out to the kitchens and came back almost immediately with her sister-in-law Yasmini, and a chattering, giggling train of housemaids all bearing jugs of freshly squeezed lime juice, trays of Cornish pasties, pork pies and samosas filled with spicy lamb curry. The bored, hungry troopers sheathed their blades and fell upon the fare with a will. Between bites they ogled and flirted with the maids. The soldiers who were supposed to be searching the coach-house and the stables saw the women carrying the provender out of the kitchens and found an excuse to follow them.

Colonel Keyser interrupted the feast and ordered his men back to work, but Tom and Dorian placated him and inveigled him into the counting house.

'I hope that now you will accept my word of honour, Colonel, that my son Jim is not anywhere on High Weald.' Tom poured him a glass of *jonge jenever* from a stone bottle; Sarah cut him a thick wedge of steaming Cornish pasty.

'*Ja*, very well, I accept that he is not here now, Tom. He has had enough time to get clean away – for the moment, that is. But I think you know where he is hiding.' He glared at Tom as he accepted the long-stemmed glass.

Tom assumed the expression of a choirboy about to receive the sacrament. 'You can trust me, Stephanus.'

'That I doubt.' Keyser washed down a mouthful of the pasty with a swallow of gin. 'But I warn you, I am not going to let that bumptious puppy of yours get away with what he has done. Do not try to soften my resolve.'

'Of course not! You have your duty to perform,' Tom agreed. 'I offer you only common hospitality and I am not attempting to influence you. The minute that Jim returns to High Weald I myself will frogmarch him up to the castle to account to you and His Excellency. You have my word on it as a gentleman.'

Only slightly mollified, Keyser allowed them to usher him out to where a groom was holding his horse. Tom slipped two more bottles of the young Hollands gin into his saddlebags and waved to him as he led his squadron out through the gates.

As they watched them go, Tom said quietly to his brother, 'I have to get a message to Jim. He must stay at Majuba until I can reach him. Keyser will be watching for me to ride into the mountains and show him the way, but I'll send Bakkat. He leaves no tracks.'

Dorian threw the tail of his turban over his shoulder. 'Listen to me well, Tom. Don't take Keyser too lightly. He is not the clown he pretends to be. If he gets his hands on Jim it will be a tragic day for this family. Never forget that our own grandfather died on the gallows of the castle parade.'

The rutted road from High Weald back to the town led through a forest of tall yellow-wood trees with trunks as thick as cathedral columns. Keyser halted his troop as soon as they were hidden from the homestead. He looked down at the little Bushman at his stirrup, who gazed back at him with the eager expression of a hunting dog.

'Xhia!' He pronounced the name with the explosive sound of a sneeze. 'Soon they will send someone with a message to wherever the young rogue is hiding. Watch for the messenger. Follow him. Do not let yourself be seen. When you have found the hiding-place, return to me swiftly. Do you understand?'

'I understand, Gwenyama.' He used the term of utmost respect, which meant He Who Devours His Enemies. He knew that Keyser enjoyed the title. 'I know who they will send. Bakkat is an old rival and enemy of mine. It will give me pleasure to bring him down.'

'Go, then. Keep watch.'

Xhia slipped away into the yellow-wood forest, silent as a shadow, and Keyser led the troop of horsemen back towards the castle.

The lodge at Majuba was a single long room. The low roof was thatched with reeds from the banks of the stream that flowed close by the door. The windows were slits in the stonework, curtained by the dried skins of eland and bluebuck. There was an open fireplace in the centre of the earthen floor, with a hole in the roof above to let the smoke escape. The far corner of the hut was screened off by a hanging curtain of rawhide.

'We put my father behind that curtain when we came hunting up here. We thought it might deaden the sound of his snores,' Jim told Louisa. 'Of course it didn't work. Nothing could deaden his snores.' He laughed. 'But now we will put you there.'

'I don't snore,' she protested.

'Even if you do, it won't be for long. We're going to move on as soon as I have rested the horses, repacked the loads and put some decent clothes on you.'

'How long will that be?'

'We will go on before they can send soldiers after us from the castle.'

'To where?'

'I don't know.' He smiled at her. 'But I will tell you when

we get there.' He gave her an appraising glance. Her tattered shift left her almost naked and she drew the cloak around herself. 'You are hardly dressed for dinner with the governor at the castle.' He went to one of the mule packs, which Zama had stacked against the wall. He rummaged in it and pulled out a roll of trade cloth, and a canvas housewife roll, which contained scissors, needles and thread. 'I hope you can sew?' he asked, as brought them to her.

'My mother taught me to make my own clothes.'

'Good,' he said. 'But we will sup first. I haven't eaten since breakfast two days ago.'

Zama ladled out venison stew from the three-legged hunter's pot standing on the coals. On top of it he placed a chunk of stiff maize cake. Jim took a spoonful. With his mouth full he asked Louisa, 'Did your mother teach you to cook also?'

Louisa nodded. 'She was a famous cook. She cooked for the Stadholder of Amsterdam, and the Prince of the House of Orange.'

'Then you have much employment here. You shall take over the cooking,' he said. 'Zama once poisoned a chief of the Hottentots, without even exerting himself. You may not think this a great accomplishment, but let me tell you that a Hottentot will grow fat on what kills the hyenas.'

She glanced at Zama uncertainly, her spoon half-way to her mouth. 'Is that true?'

'The Hottentots are the greatest liars in all Africa,' Zama answered, 'but none can match Somoya.'

'So it is a joke?' she asked.

'Yes, it is a joke,' Zama agreed. 'A bad English joke. It takes many years to learn to understand English jokes. Some people never succeed.'

When they had eaten, Louisa spread out the roll of cloth and began to measure and cut. Jim and Zama unpacked the mule loads that Jim had thrown together in such haste, and they noted and rearranged the contents. With relief Jim donned his own familiar boots and clothing, and gave Keyser's tunic and breeches to Zama. 'If we ever get into a battle with the wild tribes of the north, you can impress them with the uniform of a Company colonel,' he told him.

They cleaned and oiled the muskets, then replaced the flints in the locks. They placed the lead pot on the fire and melted lead to cast additional balls for the pistol Jim had captured from Colonel Keyser. The shot bags for the muskets were still full.

'You should have brought at least another five kegs of powder,' Zama told Jim, as he filled the powder flasks. 'If we meet hostile tribes when we start hunting, this will not last long.'

'I would have brought another fifty kegs, if I had found another twenty mules to carry them,' Jim said acidly. Then he called across the hut to where Louisa was kneeling over the bolt of material she had spread on the floor. She was using a stick of charcoal from the fireplace to mark her pattern before cutting it. 'Can you load and fire a musket?'

She looked abashed, and shook her head.

'Then I shall have to teach you.' He pointed to the material she was working on. 'What is that you are making?'

'A skirt.'

'A stout pair of trousers would be more useful, and would take less cloth.'

Her cheeks turned an intriguing shade of pink. 'Women don't wear trousers.'

'If they are going to ride astride, walk and run, as you are, then they should.' He nodded at her bare feet. 'Zama will make you a fine pair of *velskoen* boots from eland skin to go with your new trousers.'

Louisa cut the legs of her trousers very full, which made her appear even more boyish. She trimmed the tattered hem of her convict shift into a long shirt that she wore over the top and it hung half-way down her thighs. She gathered this in at the waist with a rawhide belt that Zama made for her. She learned that he was an expert sailmaker and leather-worker. The boots he made fitted her well. They reached half-way up her calves, and he turned the fur on the outside, which gave them a dashing appearance and enhanced the length of her legs. Lastly, she made herself a canvas bonnet to cover her hair and keep off the sun.

Early the next morning Jim whistled for Drumfire. He charged up from the bank of the stream where he had been cropping the young spring grass. In his usual display of affection, he pretended he was going to run his master down. Jim bestowed on him a few affectionate insults while he slipped the bridle over his head.

Louisa appeared in the door of the hut. 'Where are you going?'

'To sweep the back trail,' he told her.

'What does that mean?'

'I must go back the way we came to make certain we are not being followed,' he explained.

'I would like to come with you, for the ride.' She looked out at Trueheart. 'Both the horses are well rested.'

'Saddle up!' Jim invited her.

Louisa had hidden a large chunk of maize bread in the pouch on her belt, but Trueheart smelt it as soon as she stepped out of the door of the hut. The mare came to her at once, and while she ate the bread Louisa settled the saddle on her back. Jim watched her buckle the girth and mount. She moved easily in her new breeches.

'She must be the luckiest horse in Africa,' Jim commented, 'to have exchanged the colonel for you. An elephant for a hedgehog.'

Jim had saddled Drumfire: he slid a long musket into the sheath, slung a powder horn over his shoulder then sprang on to Drumfire's back. 'Lead the way,' he told her.

'Back the way we came?' she asked, and without waiting for his reply she started up the slope. Louisa had a light hand on the reins, and a natural seat. The mare seemed not to notice her weight, and flew up the steep mountainside.

From behind Jim appraised her style. If she was accustomed

to the side-saddle, she had adapted readily to riding astride. He remembered how she had endured during the long night ride, and was amazed at how quickly she had recovered. He knew that she would be able to keep up, no matter how gruelling the pace he set.

When they reached the crest, he moved into the lead. Unerringly he found his way back through the labyrinth of valleys and defiles. To Louisa each sheer cliff and hillside seemed the same as the one before it, but he twisted and turned through the maze without hesitation.

Whenever a new stretch of ground opened before them he dismounted and climbed to a vantage-point to scan the terrain ahead through the lens of his telescope. These halts gave her respite to enjoy the grand scenery that surrounded them. After the flat country of her native land, these mountain tops seemed to reach to the heavens. The cliff walls were umber, red and purple. The scree slopes were densely clad with shrubs: some of their flowers looked like huge pincushions, and the colours were daffodil yellow and brilliant orange. Flocks of long-tailed birds swarmed over them, probing their curved beaks deeply into the flowers.

'*Suiker-bekkies* – sugar-beaks,' Jim told her, when she pointed them out. 'They are drinking the nectar from the protea bushes.'

It was the first time since the shipwreck that she had been able to look around her, and she felt drawn by the beauty of this strange new land. The horrors of the *Meeuw*'s gundeck were already fading, seemed now to belong to an old nightmare. The path they were following climbed another steep slope, and Jim stopped below the skyline and handed her Drumfire's reins to hold, while he climbed to the crest to observe the far side of the mountain.

She watched him idly. Suddenly his manner changed abruptly. He ducked down, doubled over, and scrambled back to where she waited. She was alarmed, and her voice shook: 'Are we being followed? Is it the colonel's men?'

'No, it's much better than that. It's meat.'

'I don't understand.'

'Eland. Herd of twenty or more. Coming straight up the far side towards us.'

'Eland?' she asked.

'The largest antelope in Africa. As big as an ox,' he explained, as he checked the priming in the pan of the musket. 'The flesh is rich with fat and closer to the taste of beef than any other antelope's. Salted and dried or smoked the flesh of a single eland will last us many weeks.'

'Are you going to kill one? What if the colonel is following us? Won't he hear the shot?'

'In these mountains the echoes will break up the sound and confuse the direction. In any event, I cannot miss this opportunity. We are already short of meat. I must take the chance if we are not to starve.'

He took hold of the bridles of both horses and led them off the path, then stopped behind an outcrop of raw red rock.

'Dismount. Hold the horses' heads, but try to stay out of sight. Don't move until I call you,' he ordered Louisa, and then, carrying the musket, he ran back up the slope. Just before he reached the crest he dropped into the grass. He glanced back and saw that she had followed his instructions. She was squatting down so that only her head was visible.

'The horses will not alarm the eland,' he told himself. The eland would take them for other wild game.

With his hat he wiped the sweat out of his eyes, and wriggled down more comfortably behind a small rock. He was sitting, not lying flat. Fired from the prone position the recoil of the heavy musket might break his collar-bone. He used his hat as a cushion and laid the stock of the musket on it, aiming up the slope.

The profound silence of the mountains settled over the valley; the soft hum of insects in the protea blossoms and the lonely, plaintive whistle of a red-winged mountain starling sounded abnormally loud.

The minutes passed as slowly as honey dripping, then Jim lifted his head. He had heard another sound that made his heartbeat trip. It was a faint clicking, like dry sticks being tapped together. Jim recognized it instantly. The eland antelope has a peculiar characteristic, unique in the African wild: the mighty sinews in its legs make a strange click with each step it takes.

Bakkat, the little yellow Bushman, had explained to Jim when he was a child how this had come about. One day in that far-off time when the sun had risen on the first day and the world was new with the dew still fresh upon it, Xtog who was the father of all the Khoisan, the Bushmen, caught in his cunning snare Impisi, the hyena. As all the world knows, Impisi was and still is a powerful magician. As Xtog was sharpening his flint knife to cut his throat, Impisi said to him, 'Xtog, if you set me free, I will make a magic for you. Instead of my flesh, which stinks of the carrion I eat, you will have hills of white fat and mountains of the sweet meat of the eland roasting on your fire every night of your life.'

'How can this be, O Hyena?' Xtog had wondered, although he was beginning to drown in his own saliva at the thought of the eland meat. But the eland was a cunning animal and difficult to find.

'I will place a spell on the eland so that wherever he roams over desert and mountain he will make a sound that will guide you to him.'

Thus Xtog had set Impisi free, and from that day onwards the eland has clicked as he walks to warn the hunter of his approach.

Jim grinned as he remembered Bakkat's story. Gently he drew back the heavy hammer of the musket to full cock, and settled the brassbound butt into his shoulder. The clicking sounds grew louder, stopping as the animals that made them paused, then coming on again. Jim watched the skyline just ahead of where he lay and suddenly a massive pair of horns rose against the blue. They were as long and thick as a strongman's arm, spiralled like the horn of the narwhal, polished black so the sun glinted upon them.

The clicking sound ceased and the horns turned slowly from side to side, as if the animal that carried them was listening. Jim heard his breath whistling in his ears, and his nerves tightened like the string of a crossbow. Then the clicking sound began again and the horns rose higher, until two trumpet-shaped ears and a pair of huge eyes appeared beneath them. The eyes were dark and gentle, seeming to swim with tears. Long curling lashes veiled them. They stared directly into Jim's soul, and his breath stopped. The beast was so close that he could see it blink, and he dared not move.

Then the eland looked away, swinging its great head to stare down the slope up which it had come. Then it started forward towards Jim, and the rest of its body came into view. He could not have circled that thick neck with his arms: a heavy dewlap hung beneath it, swinging ponderously with each pace. Its back and shoulders were blue with age, and it stood as tall as Jim himself.

Only a dozen paces from where he sat it stopped and lowered its head to pull the new spring leaves from a cripple-wood bush. Over the ridge behind the bull, the rest of the herd came into view. The cows were a soft creamy brown, and although they carried the long spiral horns, their heads were more graceful and feminine. The calves were a ruddy chestnut, the younger ones hornless. One dropped its head and butted its twin playfully, then they bucked and chased each other in a circle. The mother watched with mild disinterest.

The hunter's instinct drew Jim's eyes back to the great bull. It was still chewing the cripplewood. It was an effort for Jim to reject this old animal. Despite the mighty trophy it carried, its flesh would be tough and gamy, its fat sparse.

Bakkat's philosophy came back to him: 'Leave the old bull to breed, and the cow to suckle her young.' Slowly Jim turned his head to examine the rest of the herd. At that moment the perfect quarry came up over the ridge.

This was a much younger bull, not more than four years old, his hindquarters so plump they seemed to be bursting from his glossy golden-brown hide. He turned aside, attracted by the shiny green leaves of a gwarrie tree. The branches were laden with ripe purple berries, and the young bull moved round until he was facing Jim. Then he stretched up to nibble at the berries, exposing the creamy curve of his throat.

Jim traversed the barrel of the musket towards him. His

movements were as slow as the advance of a chameleon on a fly. The frolicking calves kicked up dust and distracted the usually watchful gaze of the cows. Carefully Jim laid the bead of the foresight on the base of the bull's throat, on the crease of skin that encircled it like a necklace. He knew that even at such close range either of the beast's massive shoulder-blades would flatten and stop the musket ball. He had to find the gap in the animal's brisket through which he could drive the ball deep into the vitals to tear through the heart, lungs and pulsing arteries.

He took up the slack in the trigger and felt the resistance of the sear. Steadily he increased the pressure, staring hard at his aiming point on the throat, resisting any impulse to jerk the trigger that final hair-breadth. The hammer fell with a loud snap, and the flint struck a shower of sparks off the frizzen, the powder in the pan ignited in a puff of white smoke, and with a bass roar the butt slammed back into his shoulder. Before he could be unsighted by the heavy recoil and the gush of powder smoke, Jim saw the eland hump its back in a mighty spasm. He knew from this that the ball had sliced through its heart. He sprang to his feet to see over the bank of smoke. The young bull was still frozen in agony, its mouth gaping. Jim could see the bullet wound, a dark, bloodless hole in the smooth hide of the throat.

All around him the rest of the herd burst into flight, scattering away down the rocky hillside in a mad gallop, loose stones and dust flying from under their hoofs. The stricken bull backed away, racked in a gigantic contortion. Its legs shook and quivered, and it sank back on its haunches. It lifted its head to the sky and the bright lung blood sprayed from its gaping jaws. Then it twisted over and fell on its back, all four legs kicking spasmodically in the air. Jim stood and watched the beast's last throes.

His jubilation was gradually replaced by the melancholy of the true hunter, caught up in the beauty and tragedy of the kill. As the eland subsided and was still, he laid aside the musket and drew the knife from its sheath on his belt. Using the horns as a lever he pulled back the beast's head and, with two expert incisions, he laid open the arteries on each side of the throat and watched the bright blood flow out. Then he lifted one of the massive back legs and cut away the scrotum.

Louisa rode up as he straightened with the furry white pouch in his hand. He felt bound to explain: 'It would taint the flesh if we left it.'

She looked away. 'What a magnificent animal. So big.' She seemed subdued by the enormity of what he had done. Then she sat up straighter in the saddle. 'What must I do to help you?'

'Tether the horses first,' he told her and she swung down from Trueheart's back and led the horses to the gwarrie tree. She hitched them to the trunk, then came back.

'Hold one of the back legs,' he said. 'If we leave the guts inside, the meat will sour and spoil in a few hours.'

It was heavy work, but she did not flinch from it. When he made the paunching stroke from the crotch to the ribs the bowels and entrails came ballooning out of the opening.

'This is when you get your hands messy,' he warned her, but before he could go on, another voice spoke near at hand, a piping, childlike voice.

'I taught you well, Somoya.'

Jim spun round, the knife held instinctively in the underhand defensive grip, and stared at the little yellow man who sat on a rock watching them.

'Bakkat, you little *shaitan*,' Jim shouted, more in fright than anger. 'Don't ever do that again. Where in the name of the Kulu Kulu did you come from?'

'Did I startle you, Somoya?' Bakkat looked uncomfortable, and Jim remembered his manners. He had come close to giving offence to his friend.

'No, of course not. I saw you from afar.' You must never tell a Bushman that you had overlooked him: he will take it as an insulting reference to his tiny stature. 'You stand taller than the trees.'

Bakkat's face lit up at the compliment. 'I watched you from the beginning of the hunt. It was a fair stalk and a clean kill,

134

Somoya. But I think you need more than a young girl to help you dress the meat.' He hopped down from the rock. He paused in front of Louisa and crouched down, clapping his hands in greeting.

'What is he saying?' she asked Jim.

'He says that he sees you, and that your hair is like sunlight,' he told her. 'I think you have just been given your African name, Welanga, Girl of Sunlight.'

'Please tell him that I see him also, and that he does me great honour.' She smiled down at him and Bakkat cackled with delighted laughter.

Bakkat carried a native axe hooked over one shoulder, and his hunting bow over the other. He laid aside the bow and quiver, and hefted the axe as he came to help Jim with the huge carcass.

Louisa was amazed at how quickly the two of them worked. Each knew his job and did it without hesitation or argument. Bloody to the elbows they drew out the entrails and the bulging sac of the stomach. With barely a check in the work Bakkat cut a strip of the raw tripes. He slapped it against a rock to knock off the half-digested vegetation, then stuffed it into his mouth and chewed with unfeigned relish. When they pulled out the steaming liver, even Jim joined in the feast.

Louisa stared in horror. 'It's raw!' she protested.

'In Holland you eat raw herring,' he said, and offered her a sliver of the purple liver. She was about to refuse, then saw from his expression that this was a challenge. She hesitated still until she realized that Bakkat also was watching her with a sly smile, his eyes slitted between leathery wrinkles.

She took the slice of liver, gathered her courage and placed it in her mouth. She felt her gorge rise but forced herself to chew. After the first shock of the strong taste, it was not unpleasant. She ate slowly, and swallowed it. To her deep satisfaction Jim looked crestfallen. She took another slice from his bloody hand and began to chew at it.

Bakkat let out a squeal of laughter, and dug his elbow into Jim's ribs. He shook his head with delight, mocking Jim, and miming the way she had won the silent contest, staggering around in a circle as he crammed imaginary lumps of liver into his mouth with both hands, weak with mirth.

'If you were half as funny as you think you are,' Jim told him sourly, 'you would be the wit of all the fifty tribes of the Khoisan. Now let's get back to work.'

They divided up the meat into loads for both the horses, and Bakkat made a sack of the wet skin into which he stuffed all the titbits of kidneys, tripes and liver. It weighed almost as much as he did, but he shouldered it and set off at a trot. Jim carried a shoulder of the eland, which almost buckled his knees, and Louisa led the horses. They covered the last mile down the gorge to Majuba in darkness.

Xhia trotted with the rapid bow-legged gait that the Bushmen call 'drinking the wind'. He could keep it up from first light in the morning until nightfall. As he went he talked to himself as if to a companion, replying to his own questions, chuckling at his jokes. Still on the run, he drank from his horn bottle and ate from the leather food bag slung over his shoulder.

He was reminding himself of how cunning and brave he was. 'I am Xhia the mighty hunter,' he said, and gave a little jump in the air. 'I have killed the great bull elephant with the poison that tips my arrow.' He remembered how he had followed it along the banks of the great river. Doggedly, he had kept up the hunt during the time that it had taken the new moon to wax to the full, then wane again. 'Not once did I lose the spoor. Could any other man do that?' He shook his head. 'No! Could Bakkat perform such a feat? Never! Could Bakkat have fired the arrow into the vein behind the ear so that the poison was taken straight to the heart of the bull? He could not have done it!' The frail reed arrow could barely pierce the thick pachyderm hide – it would never penetrate to heart or lung: he had had to find one of the great blood vessels close to the surface to carry the poison. It had taken the poison five days to bring the bull down. 'But I followed him all that time and I danced and sang the hunter's song when, at last, he fell like a mountain and raised the dust as high as the treetops. Could Bakkat have performed such a feat?' he asked the high peaks around him. 'Never!' he replied. 'Never!'

Xhia and Bakkat were members of the same tribe, but they were not brothers. 'We are not brothers!' Xhia shouted aloud, and he became angry.

Once there had been a girl, with skin as bright as the plumage of a weaver bird and a face shaped like a heart. Her lips were as full as the fruit of the ripe marula, her buttocks were like ostrich eggs and her breasts as round as two yellow Tsama melons warming in the Kalahari sun. 'She was born to be my woman,' Xhia cried. 'The Kulu Kulu took a piece of my heart while I slept and moulded it into that woman.' He could not bring himself to say her name. He had shot her with the tiny love arrow tipped with the feathers of the mourning dove to demonstrate to her how much he wanted her.

'But she went away. She would not come to lie on the sleeping mat of Xhia the hunter. She went instead with the despicable Bakkat and bore him three sons. But I am cunning. The woman died from the bite of the mamba.' Xhia had captured the snake himself. He had found its hiding-place under a flat rock. He had tethered a live dove as bait beside it and when the snake slid out from under the rock, he had pinned it behind the head. It was not a large mamba, only as long as one of his arms, but its venom was virulent enough to kill a bull buffalo. He placed it in the girl's harvesting bag while she and Bakkat slept. The next morning when she opened the mouth of the bag to place a tuber inside, the snake had bitten her three times, once on the finger and twice on the wrist. Her death, though swift, was terrible to behold. Bakkat wept as he held her in his arms. Concealed among the rocks, Xhia had watched it all. Now the memory of her death and Bakkat's grief was so sweet that Xhia jumped with both feet together like a grasshopper.

'There is no animal who can elude me. There is no man who can prevail against my guile. For I am Xhia!' he shouted, and the echo came back from the cliffs above. 'Xhia, Xhia, Xhia.'

After Colonel Keyser left him, he had waited two days and a night on the hills and in the forests of High Weald, watching for Bakkat. On the first morning he saw him come out of his hut in the dawn, yawn, scratch himself and laugh at the squeal of gas from between his buttocks. For the Bushmen a flourish of flatus was always a propitious sign of good health. He watched him let the herd out of the kraal and drive them down to the water. Lying like a partridge concealed in the grass Xhia saw the big white man with the black beard that they called Klebe, the hawk, ride down from the homestead. He was Bakkat's master and the two squatted in the middle of the open field with their heads close together and they spoke in whispers for a long time so that no one could overhear them. Even Xhia was not able to creep close enough to pick up their words.

Xhia grinned to watch their secret counsel. 'I know what you are saying, Klebe. I know you are sending Bakkat to find your son. I know you are telling him to take care that he is not followed but, like the spirit of the wind I, Xhia, will be watching when they meet.'

He watched Bakkat close the door of his hut at nightfall, and saw the glow of his cooking fire, but Bakkat did not come out again until the dawn.

'You try to lull me, Bakkat, but will it be tonight or tomorrow?' he asked, as he watched from the hilltop. 'Is your patience greater than mine? We shall see.' He watched Bakkat circle around his hut in the early light, searching the earth for the sign of an enemy, for someone who had come to spy upon him.

Xhia embraced himself with glee, and rubbed his back with both hands. 'Do you think I am such a fool as to come in close, Bakkat?' This was the reason he had sat all night upon the hilltop. 'I am Xhia and I leave no sign. Not even the high-flying vulture can discover my hiding-place.'

All that day he had watched Bakkat go about his business, tending his master's herds. At nightfall Bakkat went into his hut again. Xhia worked a charm in the darkness. He took a pinch of powder from one of the stoppered duiker-horn flasks on his beaded belt and placed it on his tongue. It was the ash of a leopard's whiskers, mixed with the dry, powdered dung of a lion and other secret ingredients. Xhia mumbled an incantation as it dissolved in his own saliva. It was the spell for outwitting prey. Then he spat three times in the direction of the hut in which Bakkat lived.

'This is a charm of great power, Bakkat,' he warned his enemy. 'No animal or man can resist its spell.' This was not always true, but whenever it failed there was always good reason for it. Sometimes it was because the wind had changed direction, or because a black crow flew overhead, or because the sore-eye lily was in bloom. Apart from these and similar circumstances it was an infallible charm.

Having cast the spell he settled down to wait. He had not eaten since the day before, so now he swallowed a few fragments of smoked meat from his food bag. Neither hunger nor the cold wind off the snows of the mountain deterred him. Like all his tribe he was inured to pain and hardship. The night was still, proof that his spell was efficacious. Even a small breeze would have covered the sounds for which he was listening.

It was soon after the moon had set that he heard a nightbird utter its alarm call in the forest behind Bakkat's home. He nodded to himself. 'Something moves there.'

A few minutes later he heard the nightjar's mate whirl up from the forest floor, and by correlating the two clues he guessed the direction in which his quarry was moving. He went down the hill, silent as shadow, testing each footfall with his bare toe for twigs or dry leaves that might crackle and disclose his presence. He stopped to listen at every second step, and heard, down by the stream, the dry rustle of a porcupine erecting its quills as a warning to a predator who had ventured too close. The porcupine might have seen a leopard, but Xhia knew it had not. The leopard would have lingered to harass its natural prey, but a man moved on immediately. Not even an adept of the San, such as Bakkat or even Xhia himself, could have avoided encountering the nightjar or the prowling porcupine in the darkness of the forest. Those little signs had been all that Xhia needed to work out how Bakkat was moving, and the direction he was taking.

Another hunter might have made the mistake of closing in too swiftly, but Xhia hung back. He knew that Bakkat would backtrack and circle to make certain he was not followed.

'He is almost as cunning in the lore of the wild as I am. But I am Xhia and there is no other like me.' Telling himself this made him feel strong and brave. He found where Bakkat had crossed the stream and, in the last rays of the waning moon he picked out a single wet footprint gleaming on the top of one of the river boulders. It was the size of a child's, but broader, and there was no arch.

'Bakkat!' He gave a little hop. 'I will remember the shape of your foot all the days of my life. Have I not seen it a hundred times running beside the track of the woman who should have been my wife?' He remembered how he had followed their tracks into the bush so that he could creep up on them and watch them as they coupled, writhing together in the grass. The memory made him hate Bakkat with a fresh, corroding passion. 'But you will never savour those melon breasts again. Xhia and the snake have seen to that.'

Now that he had clearly established the direction and run of the spoor, he could hang back to avoid, in the dark, the traps that Bakkat would surely set for him. 'Because he moves in darkness he will not be able to cover his sign as completely as he would in daylight. I will wait for the coming of the sun to read more clearly the sign he has left for me.'

In the first flush of the dawn he picked up the spoor again. The wet footprint had dried leaving no trace, but within a hundred paces he found a dislodged pebble. Another hundred paces and there was a broken blade of grass, dangling and beginning to wither. Xhia did not stop to pore over these clues. A quick darting glance confirmed his instinct and enabled him to make minute adjustments to his direction. He smiled and shook his head when he found where Bakkat had lain in wait beside his spoor. Because he had squatted unmoving for so long, his bare heels had left indentations in the earth. Then, much further on, he found where Bakkat had made a wide circle to wait again beside his own spoor, the same way as a wounded buffalo circles back to wait for the hunter who pursues him.

Xhia was so pleased with himself that he took a little snuff, sneezed softly and said, 'Know, Bakkat, that it is Xhia who follows, that Xhia is your master in all things!' He tried not to think of the honey-yellow girl, the one thing in which Bakkat had prevailed.

Once the spoor led into the mountains it became even more elusive. Up one long narrow valley he found where Bakkat had hopped from rock to rock, never touching soft earth or disturbing a blade of grass or other growing thing, except for the grey lichen that grew sparsely on the rocks. This plant was so dry and tough, and Bakkat so light, his sole so small and pliant, that he passed over it almost as softly as the mountain breeze. Xhia squinted to pick out the slightly different shade of lichen grey where his foot had touched. Xhia kept carefully to the side of the tracks furthest from the rising sun, to highlight the faint spoor and not to disturb it in case he was forced to come back to rework it.

Then even Xhia was confounded. The tracks climbed a scree slope, again moving from rock to rock. Then abruptly, half-way up the scree, the tracks ended. It was as though Bakkat had been plucked into the sky in the talons of an eagle. Xhia went on in the established line of the spoor until he reached the head of the valley, but he found nothing more. He went back to where the sign ended, squatted down and turned his head one way then the other to contemplate the faint smears on the lichen coating of the rocks.

As a last resort he took another pinch of the magical powder from the duiker horn and let it dissolve in his saliva. He closed his eyes to rest them, and swallowed the mixture. He half opened his eyes and, through the veil of his own lashes, he had a fleeting glimpse of movement, faint shadows like the flicker of bat's wings in the gloaming. When he looked directly at them they disappeared as though they had never existed. The saliva dried in his mouth and the skin on his arms prickled. He knew that one of the spirits of the wilderness had touched him, and what he had seen was the memory of Bakkat's feet running across the rocks. They were running not upwards but back down the scree.

In that moment of heightened awareness, he realized, from the colour of the lichen, that Bakkat's feet had touched it twice, going up and coming back. He laughed out loud. 'Bakkat, you would have deceived any other man, but not Xhia.' He moved back down the scree and saw how he had done it. How he had run up the slope, bouncing from rock to rock and then, in mid-stride, he had reversed direction and run backwards, his tiny feet falling exactly in the same spoor. The only tell-tale sign was the slight colour difference of the double tracks.

Near the bottom of the slope the spoor passed under the low branch of a Boer bean tree. Lying on the earth beside the tracks was a fragment of dried bark no bigger than a thumbnail. It had recently fallen or been dislodged from the branch above. At this point the double tracks on the lichen-coated rocks suddenly became single tracks again. Xhia laughed out loud.

'Bakkat has taken to the trees like the baboon that was his mother.' Xhia went to stand under the outspread branch, jumped, caught a hold and drew himself up until he stood upright, balancing on the narrow branch. He saw the marks Bakkat's feet had made on the bark. He ran along them to the main trunk of the tree, slid down to the earth, picked up the spoor again and ran along it.

Twice more Bakkat had set him puzzles to solve. The first of these was at the base of a red cliff and cost him more time. But after the Boer bean tree he had learned to look upwards and found the place where Bakkat had reached up high and traversed hand over hand along a ledge so that his feet had not touched the earth.

The sun had started down the sky by the time he reached the place where Bakkat had laid the second puzzle. This one

142

seemed to defy even his powers of solution. After a while he felt a superstitious tingle of his nerves that Bakkat had worked some counter-charm and grown wings like a bird. He swallowed another dose of the hunter's powder, but the spirits did not touch him again. Instead his head began to ache.

'I am Xhia. No man can deceive me,' he told himself, but even though he said it loudly he could not dispel the sense of failure that slowly overwhelmed him.

Then he heard a sound, dulled by distance but unmistakable. The echoes from the cliffs confirmed it, but at the same time muddled the direction so that Xhia turned his head from side to side to try to pinpoint it. 'Musket shot,' he whispered. 'My spirits have not deserted me. They lead me on.'

He left the spoor and climbed the nearest peak, squatted there and watched the sky. It was not long before he picked out a tiny black speck high against the blue. 'Where there is gunfire, there is Death. And Death has his faithful minions.'

Another speck appeared, then many more. They coalesced into a slow-turning wheel in the sky. Xhia sprang to his feet and trotted in that direction. As he approached, the specks resolved themselves into carrion birds, soaring on fixed wings, turning their repulsive naked heads to peer down at one spot among the mountains below them.

Xhia knew well all the five varieties of vulture, from the common tawny bird of the Cape to the huge bearded vulture with its patterned throat and triangular fan of tail feathers.

'Thank you, old friends,' Xhia called up to them. Since time beyond memory these birds had led him and his tribe to the feast. As he came closer to the centre of the spinning circle, he became more furtive, creeping from rock to rock, peering all around with those sharp bright eyes. Then he heard human voices coming from the far side of the ridge ahead of him and, like a puff of smoke, Xhia seemed simply to dissolve in the air.

From his place of concealment he watched the trio loading the butchered meat on to the horses. Somoya, he knew well. His was a familiar face in the colony. Xhia had watched him win the Christmas Day races from his own master. However, the woman was a stranger. 'This must be the one that Gwenyama seeks. The woman who escaped from the sinking ship.'

He chuckled when he recognized Trueheart tethered beside Drumfire. 'Soon you will return to our master,' he promised the mare. Then he concentrated all his attention on the dainty figure of Bakkat and his eyes slitted with hatred.

He watched the little band finish loading the horses, and move off out of sight along the game trail that meandered down the valley. As soon as they had gone Xhia ran down to dispute what remained of the eland carcass with the vultures. There was a puddle of blood lying where Jim had cut the eland's throat. It had coagulated to a black jelly, and Xhia scooped it up in his cupped hands, and dribbled it into his open mouth. Over the past two days he had eaten only sparingly from his food bag, and he was famished. He licked every last sticky clot from his fingers. He could not afford to spend much time on the carcass, for if Bakkat looked back he would notice that the vultures had not settled immediately, and know that something or someone was keeping them in the air. The hunters had not left much for him. There was the long rubbery tube of the small intestines, which they had not been able to carry away. He drew it through his fingers to squeeze out the liquid dung. The coating of excrement that remained gave it a pungent relish, which he savoured as he chewed. He was tempted to use a rock to crack open the massive leg bones and suck out the rich yellow marrow, but he knew that Bakkat would return to the kill, and he would not overlook such an obvious clue. Instead he used his knife to scrape off the shreds and strips of flesh that still adhered to the bones and ribcage. He stuffed these fragments into his food bag, then used a switch of dried grass to brush away his footprints. The birds would soon obliterate any small traces of his presence that he had overlooked. When Bakkat returned to sweep his back trail there would be nothing to alert him.

Chewing happily on strips of the reeking intestines, he left the carcass and went on after Bakkat and the white couple. He did not follow directly in their tracks but kept well out on the slope above the valley. At three places he anticipated the twists and turns of the valleys ahead, cut across the high ground where the horses could not go and intercepted them on the far side. From a distance he picked out the smoke from the camp at Majuba and hurried ahead. He was watching from the peak when they arrived with the horses. He knew that he should go back at once to report to his master his success in discovering the hiding-place of the fugitives, but the temptation to linger and gloat over his old enemy, Bakkat, was too great to resist.

The three men, white, black and yellow, cut the raw eland meat into thick strips, and the woman sprinkled coarse sea salt from a leather bag on to them then rubbed it in with her palms and spread out the strips on the rocks to cure. In the meantime the men threw the lumps of white fat they trimmed from the meat into a three-legged pot on the fire to render it down for cooking or making soap.

Whenever Bakkat stood up or moved apart from the others, Xhia's eyes followed him with the malevolent gaze of a cobra. He fingered one of the arrows in his little bark quiver and dreamed of the day when he would sink the poisoned tip deep into Bakkat's flesh.

When the butcher's work was done, and the men were tending the horses and the mules, the white woman laid out the last strips of meat to dry. Then she left the camp and picked her way along the bank of the stream until she reached a green pool screened by the bend from the camp. She took off her bonnet and shook out her hair in a glowing cloud. Xhia was taken aback. He had never seen hair that colour and length. It was unnatural and repellent. The scalps of the women of his tribe were covered by crisp, furry peppercorns, pleasant to touch and look upon. Only a witch or some other disgusting creature would have hair like this one. He spat to ward away any evil influence she might emit.

The woman looked about her carefully, but no human eye could discover Xhia when he wished to remain concealed. Then she undressed, stepping out of the baggy clothes that covered her lower body, and stood naked at the edge of the pool. Again Xhia was repelled by her appearance. This was no female but some hermaphroditic thing. Her body was misshapen: her legs were elongated, her hips narrow, her belly concave and she had the buttocks of a starving boy. The San women gloried in their steatopygia. There was another puff of hair at the juncture of her thighs. It was the colour of the Kalahari desert sands and so fine that it did not completely screen her genitals. Her slit was like a tightly pursed mouth. There was no sign of the inner lips. The mothers of Xhia's tribe pierced their daughters' labia in infancy and hung stones upon them to stretch them and make them protrude attractively. In Xhia's estimation monumental buttocks and dangling labia were signs of true feminine beauty. Only her breasts proclaimed this woman's sex, yet they, too, were strangely shaped. They thrust out pointedly and the pale nipples pricked upwards like the ears of a startled dik-dik. Xhia covered his mouth and giggled at his own simile. 'What man could want a creature like that?' he asked himself.

The woman waded out into the pool until the water reached her chin. Xhia had seen enough and the sun was sinking. He slipped back over the skyline and set off at a trot towards the flat-topped mountain, blue and ethereal in the distance, that showed above the southern horizon. He would travel on through the night to bring the news to his master.

They sat close to the small fire in the centre of the hut, for the nights were still chill. They feasted on thick steaks cut from the long back strips of the eland, and kebabs of kidney, liver and fat grilled over the coals. The rich juices greased Bakkat's chin. When Jim sat back with a sigh of contentment, Louisa poured a mug of coffee for him. He nodded his thanks. 'Won't you take some?' he invited, but she shook her head.

'I do not like it.' This was untrue. She had developed a taste for it while she lived in Huis Brabant, but she knew how rare and expensive it was. She had seen how he treasured the small bag of beans, which would not last much longer. Her gratitude towards him, as her saviour and protector, was so strong that she did not want to deprive him of something that gave him so much pleasure. 'It's harsh and bitter,' she explained.

She went back to her place on the opposite side of the fire and watched the men's faces in the firelight as they talked. She did not understand what they were saying for the language was strange, but the sound was melodious and lulling. She was drowsy and well fed, and had not felt as safe and contented since she had left Amsterdam.

'I gave your message to Klebe, your father,' Bakkat told Jim. This was the first time they had mentioned the subject uppermost in both their minds. It was callow and ill-mannered to speak of important matters until the right moment for serious discussion.

'What was his reply?' Jim demanded anxiously.

'He told me to greet you in his name and in the name of your mother. He said that although you would leave a hole in their hearts that would never be filled, you must not return to High Weald. He said that the fat soldier from the castle would wait for your return with the patience of a crocodile buried in the mud of the water-hole.'

Jim nodded sadly. He had known what the consequences must be from the moment he had decided he must rescue the girl. Yet now that he heard his father confirm it, the enormity of his exile from the colony weighed like a stone. He was truly an outcast.

In the firelight Louisa saw his expression and instinctively she knew she was the cause of his grief. She looked down into the wavering flames, and her guilt was a knife under her ribs.

'What else did he say?' Jim asked softly.

'He said that the pain of parting from his only son would be too great to bear, unless he could hold you in his eye once more before you go.' Jim opened his mouth to speak, then closed it again. Bakkat went on, 'He knows that you intend to follow the Robbers' Road northwards into the wilderness. He said that you will not be able to survive with such meagre

147

stores as you were able to take with you. He intends to bring you more. He said that would be your inheritance.'

'How is that possible? I cannot go to him and he cannot come to me. The risk is too great.'

'He has already sent Bomvu, your uncle Dorian, and Mansur with two wagons laden with sacks of sand and chests filled with stones along the west coast road. This will draw Keyser away so that your father can come to meet you at an arranged place. He will have with him other wagons carrying his parting gifts to you.'

'Where is the place of meeting?' Jim asked. He felt a deep sense of relief and excitement that he might see his father. He had thought they were parted for ever. 'He cannot come here to Majuba. The road through the mountains is too steep and treacherous for wagons to pass.'

'No, he will not come here.'

'Where then?' Jim asked.

'Do you remember two years ago when we travelled together to the frontiers of the colony?' Jim nodded. 'We went through the mountains by the secret pass of the Gariep river.'

'I remember.' That journey had been the adventure of Jim's life.

'Klebe will take the wagons out through that pass and meet you on the edge of the unknown lands, by the *kopje* shaped like the head of a baboon.'

'Yes, that was where we hunted and killed the old gemsbuck bull. It was the last camp before we returned to the colony.' The disappointment he had felt when they turned back came to him vividly. 'I wanted to go on to the next horizon, and the next, until I reached the last.'

Bakkat laughed. 'You were always an impatient boy, and you still are. But your father will meet you at the Hill of the Baboon's Head. Can you find it without me to lead you, Somoya?' He mocked Jim lightly, but for once he could not draw him. 'Your father will only leave High Weald when he is sure that Keyser is following Bomvu and Mansur, and when I have returned with your reply.'

'Tell my father I will meet him there.'

Bakkat stood up and reached for his quiver and bow.

'You cannot leave yet,' Jim told him. 'It is still dark, and you have not rested since you left High Weald.'

'I have the stars to guide me,' Bakkat went to the door of the hut, 'and Klebe told me to return at once. We will meet again at the Hill of the Baboon's Head.' He crossed to the door of the hut, and smiled back at Jim. 'Until that day go in peace, Somoya. Keep Welanga beside you always, for it seems to me that, although she is young, she will grow to be a fine woman, like your own mother.' Then he was gone into the night.

Bakkat moved as swiftly through the darkness as any of the other night creatures, but it had been late when he left Majuba, and the dawn light was already strengthening when he reached the remains of the eland carcass. He squatted beside it and searched for clues as to who and what had visited it since the previous day. The vultures were roosting, humpbacked, on the surrounding cliffs and kranzes. The ground around the carcass was littered with their feathers where they had squabbled over the scraps, and white streaks of their liquid dung painted the rocks around the kill. Their talons had raked the earth, but he was able to pick out the tracks of a number of jackal and other small wild cats and scavengers in the softened earth. There were no signs of hyena, but that was not surprising: the mountains were too high and cold for them at this season of the year. Although picked bare, the skeleton of the eland was intact. Hyena would have chewed the bones to splinters.

If there had been a human visitor, any sign of him had been obliterated. However, Bakkat was confident that he had not been followed. Few men could have untangled the trail he had laid. Then his eyes fell on the ribcage of the eland. The bones were smooth and white. Suddenly he gave a soft whistle of alarm, and his confidence wavered. He touched the bare ribs, running his finger down them one after another. The marks on them were so light that they might have been natural or the toothmarks of one of the scavengers. But Bakkat felt a sick spasm of doubt tighten his stomach muscles. The marks were too smooth and regular, not those of teeth but of a tool. Someone had scraped the flesh off the bone with a blade.

If it were a man, he would have left the mark of boot or sandal, he thought, and made a quick cast around the carcass, wide enough to avoid the chaos created by the scavengers. Nothing! He returned to the skeleton and studied it again. Perhaps he was barefoot? he wondered. But the Hottentot wear sandals, and what would one of them be doing in the mountains in this season? They will be with their herds down in the plains. Perhaps, after all, I was followed? But only an adept could have read my sign. An adept who goes unshod? A San? One of my own kind? As he pondered it he became more anxious. Should I go on to High Weald, or should I go back to warn Somoya? He hesitated, then made his decision. I cannot go in both directions at the same time. I must go on. That is my duty. I must take my news to Klebe.

Now in the morning light he could move faster. As he ran, his dark eyes were never still and no sound or smell, however faint, eluded him. As he skirted a stand of cripplewood, whose stems were hung with beards of grey moss, his nostrils flared as he caught a whiff of faecal odour. He turned off the path to trace the source, and found it within a few paces. A single glance told him that these were the droppings of a carnivore, who had gorged recently on blood and meat: they were black, loose and foetid.

Jackal? he thought, then immediately knew that it was not. It must be human, for close by were the stained leaves with which he had cleaned himself. Only the San used the leaves of the wash-hand bush for that purpose: they were succulent and soft, and when rubbed between the palms of the hand they burst open and ran with herbal-scented juice. He knew then that the same man who had eaten at the eland carcass had defecated here, close to the path that led from Majuba down the mountains, and that the man was of the

San. Apart from himself how many adepts of the San lived within the borders of the colony? His people were of the deserts and the wilderness. Then his instincts told him who it must be.

'Xhia!' he whispered. 'Xhia, who is my enemy has followed me and learned my secrets. Now he runs back to his master in the castle. Soon they will ride out to Majuba with many horsemen to run down Somoya and Welanga.' He was immediately stricken by the same dreadful uncertainty. 'Must I go back to warn Somoya, or go on to High Weald? How far is Xhia ahead of me?' Then he reached the same decision. 'Somoya will already have left Majuba. Keyser and his troopers will move slower than Somoya. If I drink the wind, I might be able to warn both Klebe and Somoya before Keyser catches up with them.'

He began to run as he had seldom run before, as though he were following a wounded gemsbuck, or being chased by a hungry lion.

It was late at night when Xhia reached the colony. The gates of the castle were closed and would not open again until reveille and the hoisting of the VOC flag at daybreak. But Xhia knew that, these days, Gwenyama, his master, seldom slept in his sumptuous quarters within the high stone walls. There was a fresh and irresistible attraction for him in the town.

It was the decree of the VOC council in Amsterdam that the burghers of the colony, and more especially the servants of the Company, should not have congress with the natives of the country. Like many of the other decrees of the Zeventien they were written only on paper, and Colonel Keyser kept a discreet little cottage on the far side of the Company gardens. It was situated down an unpaved lane and was screened by a tall, flowering lantana hedge. Xhia knew better than to waste time arguing with the sentries at the gates of the castle. He went directly to the colonel's love nest, and slipped through the opening in the lantana hedge. A lamp was burning in the kitchen at the rear of the cottage, and he tapped on the window. A shadow passed between the lamp and the pane, and a female voice he recognized called, 'Who is there?' Her tone was sharp and nervous.

'Shala! It is Xhia,' he called back, in the Hottentot tongue, and heard her lift the locking bar on the door. She swung it open and peered out. She was only a little taller than Xhia and looked childlike, but she was not.

'Is Gwenyama here?' Xhia asked. She shook her head. He looked at her with pleasure: the Hottentot were cousins of the San and Shala was Xhia's ideal of a beautiful woman. Her skin glowed like amber in the lamplight, her dark eyes slanted up at the corners, her cheekbones were high and wide, and her chin was narrow so that her face was the shape of an inverted arrowhead. The dome of her head was perfectly rounded, and covered with a pelt of peppercorn curls.

'No! He has gone away,' she repeated, and held open the door in invitation.

Xhia hesitated. From their previous encounters he had a clear picture of her sex in his mind. It resembled one of the succulent desert cactus flowers, with fleshy petals of a pouting purple texture. Added to that, there was an intense pleasure to be had from stirring his master's porridge pot. Shala had once described the colonel's manly part to Xhia. 'It is like the beak of a sugar-bird. Thin and curved. It sips my nectar only lightly, then flits away.'

The men of the San were famous for their priapism, and for penile dimensions unrelated to their diminutive stature. Shala, who had much first-hand experience in these matters, considered Xhia to be gifted beyond all his tribe.

'Where is he?' Xhia was torn between duty and temptation.

'He rode away yesterday with ten of his men.' She took Xhia's hand and drew him into the kitchen, closed the door behind him and replaced the locking bar.

'Where did they go?' he asked, as she stood before him and unwrapped her robe. Keyser delighted in dressing her in the gaudy silks of the Indies, and in pearls and other finery that he

152

purchased at great expense from the godown of the Courtney brothers.

'He said they were following the wagons of Bomvu, the red-haired one,' she said, and let the robe slide down her body to the floor. He drew in his breath sharply. No matter how often he saw those breasts it was always with a shock of delight.

'Why is he following those wagons?' He reached out, took one of her breasts and squeezed it.

She smiled dreamily and swayed closer to him. 'He said they would lead him to the runaways, to Somoya, the son of the Courtneys, and the woman he stole from the shipwreck,' she answered, her voice husky. She lifted the front of his kilt and reached under it. Her eyes slanted lasciviously and she showed small white teeth as she smiled.

'I do not have much time,' he warned her.

'Then let us be quick,' she said, and sank to her knees in front of him.

'Which way did he go?'

'I watched them from the top of Signal Hill,' she replied. 'They went along the coastal road towards the west.'

She placed her elbows on the floor to brace herself and leaned forward until her extraordinary golden buttocks were raised towards the thatched ceiling. He went behind her, moved her knees apart, knelt between them and, both hands on her hips, pulled her back towards him. She gave a soft little squeal as he forced apart her fleshy petals and went in deeply.

At the end she squealed again, but this time as though in mortal agony and then she flopped forward on to her face and lay there in the centre of the kitchen floor writhing weakly.

Xhia stood up and adjusted his leather skirt. He picked up his quiver and bow and slung them over his shoulder.

'When will you come back?' She sat up shakily.

'When I can,' he promised, and went out into the night.

As Bakkat topped the hills above High Weald, he saw that the entire estate was bustling with unusual activity. Every one of the servants seemed frantically employed. The wagon drivers and the *voorlopers*, the lead boys, were bringing up the trek oxen from the kraals at the far end of the main paddock. They had inspanned four full teams of twelve bullocks each, which were trudging up the road to the homestead. Another group of herders had assembled small herds of fat-tailed sheep, milking cows with their unweaned calves, and spare trek bullocks, and were driving them slowly towards the north. They were already strung out over such a distance that the furthest of the small herds were specks almost obscured by their own dust.

'Already they are heading for the Gariep river pass to meet Somoya.' Bakkat nodded with satisfaction, and started down the hill towards the homestead.

As soon as he entered the courtyard he saw that the preparations for departure were well advanced. On the loading ramp of the warehouse Tom Courtney was in his shirt-sleeves giving orders to the men who were packing the last chests of goods into the wagon beds.

'What is in that chest?' he demanded of one. 'I don't recognize it.'

'The mistress told me to load it. I do not know what is in it.' The man shrugged. 'Woman's things, perhaps.'

'Put it into the second wagon.' Tom turned, and spotted Bakkat as he entered the yard. 'I saw you as soon as you came over the hill. You grow taller every day, Bakkat.'

Bakkat grinned with pleasure, squared his shoulders and puffed out his chest a little. 'I see your plan has worked, Klebe?' It was more a question than a statement.

'Within a few hours of Bomvu taking the wagons out along the west coast, Keyser and all his men were after them.' Tom laughed. 'But I don't know how soon he will realize that he is following the wrong game, and come rushing back. We have to get clear as soon as we can.'

'Klebe, I bring evil tidings.'

Tom saw the little man's expression and his own smile faded. 'Come! We will go where we can talk privately.' He led Bakkat into the warehouse, and listened seriously as the little man related all that had happened during his foray into the mountains. He exclaimed with relief when he heard that their guess had proved correct and Bakkat had found Jim at Majuba.

'So Somoya, Zama and the girl will already have left Majuba, and will be riding to the meeting place on the frontier at the Hill of the Baboon's Head,' Bakkat went on.

'This is good news,' Tom declared. 'So why do you wear such a gloomy countenance?'

'I was followed,' Bakkat admitted. 'Somebody followed me to Majuba.'

'Who was it?' Tom could not disguise his alarm.

'A San,' said Bakkat. 'An adept of my tribe, one who could unravel my spoor. One who was watching for me to leave High Weald.'

'Keyser's hunting dog!' Tom exclaimed furiously.

'Xhia,' Bakkat agreed. 'He tricked me and even now he must be hurrying back to his master. Within the next day he will lead Keyser to Majuba.'

'Does Somoya know he has been discovered by Xhia?'

'I only discovered Xhia's sign when I was half-way back from Majuba. I came on to warn you first,' Bakkat said. 'Now I can go back to find Somoya, warn him also, and lead him out of danger.'

'You must reach him before Keyser catches up with him.' Tom's bluff features were twisted with anxiety.

'Xhia must return to Majuba again before he can pick up Somoya's outgoing tracks. Keyser and his men will travel slowly for they are unaccustomed to the mountain paths,' Bakkat explained. 'He will be forced to make a wide loop to the south. On the other hand, I can cut through the mountains further north, get ahead of them and find Somoya before they do.'

'Go swiftly, old friend,' Tom told him. 'I place the life of my son in your hands.'

Bakkat bobbed his head in farewell. 'Somoya and I will be waiting for you at the Hill of the Baboon's Head.'

Bakkat turned to leave, but Tom called him back. 'The woman—' He broke off, unable to look at the little man's face. 'Is she still with him?' he asked gruffly, and Bakkat nodded.

'What is she—' Tom stopped, then tried to rephrase his question. 'Is she . . . ?'

Bakkat took pity on him. 'I have named her Welanga, for her hair is like sunlight.'

'That is not what I wanted to know.'

'I think that Welanga will walk beside him for a long, long time. Perhaps for the rest of his life. Is that what you wanted to know?'

'Yes, Bakkat, that is exactly what I wanted to know.'

From the loading ramp he watched Bakkat trot out of the gateway, and take the path back towards the mountains. He wondered when last the little man had rested or slept, but the question was irrelevant. Bakkat would keep on as long as his duty beckoned him.

'Tom!' He heard Sarah call his name, and turned to see her hurrying towards him from the kitchens. To his surprise he saw that she was wearing breeches, riding boots and a wide brimmed straw hat tied down with a red bandanna under her chin. 'What was Bakkat doing here?'

'He has found Jim.'

'And the girl?'

'Yes.' He nodded reluctantly. 'The girl also.'

'Then why aren't we ready to leave yet?' she demanded.

'We?' he asked. 'We are going nowhere. But I will be ready to leave within the next hour.'

Sarah placed her clenched fists on her hips. He knew that that was the equivalent of the first rumbling of an active volcano about to erupt. 'Thomas Courtney,' she said coolly, but the light of battle shone in her eyes, 'James is my son. My only child. Do you think for one moment that I will sit here in my kitchen while you ride off to bid him farewell, possibly for ever?'

'I will give him your maternal love,' he offered, 'and when I return, I will describe the girl to you in minute detail.'

He argued a little longer, but when he rode out through the gates of High Weald Sarah rode at his side. Her chin was up, and she was trying not to smile triumphantly. She glanced sideways at him and said sweetly, 'Tom Courtney, you are still the most handsome man I have ever laid eyes upon, except when you are sulking.'

'I am not sulking. I never sulk,' he said sulkily.

'I will race you to the ford,' she said. 'Winner may claim a kiss.' She tickled the mare's rump with the switch she carried, and bounded forward. Tom tried to hold the stallion, but he danced in a circle, eager to be after them.

'Damn it! All right then.' Tom let him have his head. He had given the mare too much of a start, and Sarah was an expert horsewoman.

She was waiting for him at the ford, with flushed cheeks and sparkling eyes. 'Where is my kiss?' she asked. He leaned out of the saddle to take her in a bear-hug. 'That is just an instalment,' he promised, as he set her back in the saddle. 'You will get the main payment tonight.'

Jim had a well-developed sense of direction, but Bakkat knew it was not infallible. He remembered the time when Jim had slipped away from camp while everyone else was sleeping in the heat of noon. Jim had seen a small herd of gemsbuck on the horizon, and as they were short of meat he had ridden after them. Three days later, Bakkat had found him wandering in circles through the trackless hills, leading a lame horse, and half crazed with thirst.

Jim hated to be reminded of that episode, and before they parted at Majuba he had listened with full attention while Bakkat gave him detailed directions on how to find his way through the mountains, following the well-defined game trails used for centuries past by the elephant and eland herds. One of these would lead him to a ford on the Gariep river where it debouched on to the plains at the frontier where the wilderness began. From that point the Hill of the Baboon's Head stood out clearly on the horizon to the east. Bakkat could rely on Jim to follow those directions accurately, so he had a clear picture in his mind of where Jim might be now, and what route he must take to intercept him.

Bakkat cut through the foothills and was well out to the north before he turned back into the main range, and went up between tall umber-coloured cliffs into the high valleys. On the fifth day after leaving High Weald he cut their sign. With two steel-shod horses and six heavily laden mules they had left a well-trodden spoor. Before noon he had caught up with Jim's party. He did not announce himself, but instead circled out ahead of them to wait beside the path they must follow.

Bakkat watched Jim coming down the path at the head of the file. As Drumfire came level with his hiding-place, he popped up from behind his boulder like the *ajinni* from the lamp and shouted shrilly, 'I see you, Somoya!' Drumfire was so startled that he shied wildly. Jim, also taken by surprise, was thrown on to his neck, and Bakkat shrieked with laughter at the joke. Jim recovered his balance instantly and rode after him as Bakkat darted away down the game path, still hooting with laughter. Jim snatched off his hat, leaned out of the saddle and slapped him with it round the head and shoulders.

'You horrible little man! You are so small, so tiny, so minute that I did not even see you.' These insults sent Bakkat into such paroxysms of mirth that he fell and rolled on the earth.

When Bakkat had recovered sufficiently to stand up again, Jim looked him over carefully while they greeted each other with a little more formality. Now it was apparent how finely drawn Bakkat was. Even though his tribe were famous for their fortitude and endurance, over the past week Bakkat had run over a hundred leagues through mountainous terrain, without allowing himself time to eat or drink adequately, or to sleep for more than a few hours. Instead of being golden and glossy, his skin was as grey and dusty as the ashes of last night's campfire. His head looked like a skull, and his gaunt cheek-bones stood proud. His eyes had sunk deeply into their sockets. A Bushman's buttocks are like the camel's hump: when he is well-fed and rested they are majestic, and sway independently as he walks. Bakkat's backside had collapsed into folds of loose skin that dangled out of the back of his kilt. His legs and arms were as thin as the limbs of a praying mantis.

'Zama,' Jim called as he brought up the string of mules. 'Unload one of the *chagga* bags.'

When Bakkat started to make his report, Jim silenced him. 'Eat and drink first,' he ordered, 'and then sleep. We can talk later.'

Zama dragged up one of the leather bags filled with *chagga* made from the eland meat. The salted strips had been half dried in the sun, then packed so tightly into the bag that the air and the flies could not get to them. The first African travellers had probably taken the idea from the pemmican of the North American Indians. Treated like this the meat would not putrefy, but keep indefinitely. It retained much of its moisture, and though the taste was high and gamy, the salt disguised the tang of rot. It was a taste that, in circumstances of need, could be readily acquired.

Bakkat sat in the shade by the mountain stream and, with a heap of the black *chagga* sticks in front of him, began to eat. After Louisa had bathed in one of the pools further down-stream she came to sit beside Jim and they watched Bakkat eat.

After a while she asked, 'How much more can he take in?'

'He is only now starting to get the taste for it,' Jim said.

Much later she said, 'Look at his stomach. It's beginning to swell.'

Bakkat stood up and went to kneel at the pool. 'He has finished!' Louisa said. 'I thought he would go on until he burst.'

'No.' Jim shook his head. 'He just needs to wash it down to make room for the next course.'

Bakkat returned from the pool, water dripping from his

chin, and fell on the pile of *chagga* with undiminished appetite. Louisa clapped her hands and laughed with amazement. 'He is so tiny, it does not seem possible! He is never going to stop.'

But at last he did. With an apparent effort he forced down one last mouthful. Then he sat cross-legged and glassy eyed and hiccuped loudly.

'He looks as though he is eight months along with child.' Jim pointed out his bulging stomach. Louisa blushed at such an intimate and improper reference, but she could not hold back her smile. It was an apt description. Bakkat smiled at her, then collapsed sideways, curled himself into a ball and began to snore.

In the morning his cheeks had filled out miraculously and his buttocks, although not yet restored to their former grandeur, showed a distinct bulge under his kilt. He set upon a breakfast of *chagga* with renewed gusto and, thus fortified, was ready to make his report to Jim.

Jim listened mostly in silence. When Bakkat told him of discovering the evidence that Xhia had followed them into the mountains, that he would certainly bring Keyser to Majuba, that they would follow their spoor from there, Jim looked worried. But then Bakkat gave him his father's message of love and support. The dark clouds around Jim seemed to lift, and his face lit with the familiar smile. When Bakkat had finished, they were both silent for a while. Then Jim stood up and went down to the pool. He sat on a rotten tree stump, and brooded heavily. He broke off a lump of rotten bark, picked out the white wood maggots he had exposed and flicked them into the water. A large yellow fish rose to the surface and, in a swirl of water, gobbled them down. At last he came back to where Bakkat waited patiently, and squatted, facing him. 'We cannot go on to the Gariep with Keyser following us. We will lead him straight to my father and the wagons.' Bakkat nodded. 'We must lead him away, and throw him off the spoor.'

'You have wisdom and understanding far beyond your tender years, Somoya.'

Jim picked up the sarcasm in his voice. He leaned across

and gave Bakkat an affectionate cuff. 'Tell me then, Prince of the Polecat Clan of the San, what must we do?'

Bakkat led them in a wide, meandering circle, away from the Gariep, back the way they had come, following game trails and crossing from one valley to the other until they arrived back above the Majuba camp. They did not approach within half a league of the stone and thatch hut, but camped instead behind the eastern watershed of the valley. They made no fire but ate their food cold and slept wrapped in jackal-skin karosses. During the day the men took turns to climb to the high ground with Jim's telescope and watch the camp at Majuba for Xhia, Keyser and his troopers to arrive.

'They cannot match my speed through these mountains,' Bakkat boasted. 'They will not arrive until the day after tomorrow. But until then we must keep well hidden for Xhia has the eyes of a vulture and the instincts of a hyena.'

Jim and Bakkat built a hide of dead cripplewood branches and grass below the crest. Bakkat examined it from all angles to make certain that it was invisible. When he was satisfied, he cautioned Jim and Zama not to use the telescope when the sun was at an angle to reflect from the lens. Jim set himself the first morning shift in the lookout hide.

He had settled down comfortably and sunk softly into a pleasant reverie. He thought about his father's promise of wagons and supplies. With this help, his dreams of a journey to the ends of this vast land might become reality. He thought about the adventures he and Louisa would experience, and the wonders they would find in that unexplored wilderness. He remembered the legends of riverbeds lined with gold nuggets, of the vast ivory herds, the deserts paved with glittering diamonds.

Suddenly he was startled to reality by the sound of a loose pebble rattling down the hillside behind him. He reached instinctively for the pistol on his belt. But he could not risk a shot. Bakkat had chided him none too gently about the musket shot that had brought down the eland and had led Xhia to them.

'Xhia would never have unravelled my spoor if you had not led him on, Somoya. That shot you fired confounded us.'

'Forgive me, Bakkat,' Jim had apologized ironically. 'And I know how you hate the taste of eland *chagga*. It would have been far better for us to starve.'

Now he dropped his hand from the pistol, and reached for the handle of his knife. The blade was long and sharp, and he held it poised for a defensive stroke, but at that moment Louisa whispered softly outside the back wall of the hide, 'Jim?'

The alarm he had felt at her approach was replaced with a lift of pleasure at the sound of her voice.

'Come in quickly, Hedgehog. Don't show yourself.' She crawled in through the low entrance. There was barely room inside the lookout for both of them. They sat side by side, only inches between them. The silence was heavy and awkward. He broke it at last. 'Is everything well with the others?'

'They are sleeping.' She did not look at him, but it was impossible for her not to be intensely aware of him. He was so close, and he smelt of sweat, leather and horses. He was so powerful and masculine that she felt confused and flustered. Dark memories mixed with new conflicting emotions, and she drew as far away from him as the space allowed. Immediately he did the same.

'Crowded in here,' he said. 'Bakkat built it to fit himself.'

'I didn't mean—' she started.

'I understand, Hedgehog,' he said. 'You explained to me once.' She shot him a glance from the corner of her eye, but saw with relief that his smile was unfeigned. She had learned over the past days that the name 'Hedgehog' was not a rebuke or an insult, but friendly teasing.

'You said you once wanted one as a pet.' She followed her thoughts.

'What?' He looked puzzled.

'A hedgehog. Why didn't you find yourself one?'

'Not easy. There aren't any in Africa.' He grinned. 'I've

162

seen them in books. You are the first in the flesh. You don't mind when I call you that?'

She thought about it, and realized that now he was not even teasing her, but using it as an endearment. 'I did at first, but now I am accustomed to it,' she said, and added softly, 'Let me tell you that hedgehogs are sweet little creatures. No, I don't mind too much.'

They were silent again, but it was no longer tense and awkward. After a while she made a peephole for herself in the grass of the front wall. He handed her the telescope and showed her how to focus it.

'You told me you are an orphan. Tell me about your parents,' he said. The question shocked her, and her temper flared. He had no right to ask that. She concentrated on her view through the telescope, but saw nothing. Then the anger subsided. She recognized a deep need to speak of her loss. She had never been able to before, not even to Elise while she still trusted the old woman.

'My father was a teacher, gentle and kind. He loved books and learning.' Her voice was almost inaudible but became stronger and surer as she remembered all the wonderful things about her mother and father, the love and kindness.

He sat beside her quietly, asking a question as her words faltered, leading her on. It was as though he had lanced an abscess in her soul, and let all the poison and the pain escape. She felt a growing trust in him, as though she could tell him everything and he would somehow understand. She seemed to lose track of time, until she was jerked into the present by a soft scratching sound at the back wall of the hide. Bakkat's voice whispered a question. Jim replied and Bakkat went again as silently as he had come.

'What did he say?' she asked.

'He came to take over the watch, but I sent him away.'

'I have been talking too much. What time is it?'

'Out here, time matters little. Go on with what you were saying. I like to listen to you.'

When she had told him everything she could remember of her parents, they went on to discuss other things, anything

163

that came into her head, or wherever his questions led her. It was such a joy for her to talk freely to someone again.

Now that she was at her ease, and her defences were lowered, Jim found, to his delight, that she had a dry, quirky sense of humour: she could be funny and self-deprecating, sometimes sharply observant or wickedly ironic. Her English was excellent, far surpassing the quality of his Dutch, but her accent made things sound fresh, and her occasional lapses and solecisms were enchanting.

The education she had received from her father had armed her with wide knowledge and understanding of a surprising range of subjects, and she had travelled to places that fascinated him. England was his ancestral and spiritual home, but he had never been there, and she described scenes and places he had heard of from his parents but seen only in books.

The hours sped away, and it was only when the long mountain shadows fell over the little hut that he saw the day was almost gone. Guiltily he realized that he had neglected his watch, had not so much as glanced out of his peephole for several hours.

He leaned forward and peered down the mountainside. Louisa jumped with surprise as his hand fell on her shoulder. 'They are here!' His voice was sharp and urgent, but for a moment she did not understand. 'Keyser and his men.'

Her pulse raced and the fine pale hair on her forearms rose. She peered out with trepidation, and saw movement in the valley far below. A column of horsemen was crossing the stream, but at this range it was not possible to identify the individual riders. Jim snatched the telescope out of her lap. He checked the angle of the sun with a glance, but the hut was already in shadow so there was no danger of a reflection from the lens. He refocused it swiftly.

'Xhia the Bushman is leading them. I know that little swine of old. He is as cunning as a baboon and as dangerous as a wounded leopard. He and Bakkat are mortal enemies. Bakkat swears he killed his wife with wizard craft. He says Xhia charmed a mamba to sting her.'

He traversed the telescope, and went on to describe what

164

he was seeing: 'Keyser is close behind Xhia. He is riding his grey. That's another good horse. Keyser is a wealthy man, from the bribes he has taken and with what he has stolen from the VOC. He has one of the finest stables in Africa. He is not as soft as his big belly would suggest. They have arrived a full day sooner than Bakkat expected them.'

Louisa shrank a little closer to him. She felt the cold reptiles of fear slither down her back. She knew what would happen to her if she fell into Keyser's hands.

Jim moved the glass on. 'That's Captain Herminius Koots following Keyser. Sweet Mother Mary, there's a naughty fellow for you! There are stories about Koots that would make you blush or faint. That's Sergeant Oudeman, behind him. He is Koots' boon companion, and they share the same tastes. What interests them mostly is gold and blood and what's under a skirt.'

'Jim Courtney, I'll thank you not to talk like that. Remember, I am a woman.'

'Then I'll not have to explain it to you, will I, Hedgehog?' He grinned, and she tried to look severe, but he ignored her disapproval and reeled off the names of the other troopers following Keyser.

'Corporals Richter and Le Riche are in the rear, bringing up the spare horses.' He counted ten in the little herd that followed the troop. 'No wonder they've made such good time. With all those spares, they'll be able to push us hard.'

Then he snapped the telescope shut. 'I'm going to explain what we have to do now. We have to lead Keyser away from the Gariep river where my father will be waiting for us with wagons and supplies. I'm sorry, but it's going to mean running away like this for days and even weeks more. It will mean much more hard living, no tents or time to build a shelter, short rations once the eland meat runs out – unless we can kill more, but at this season most of the game herds are down on the plains. With Keyser close behind us we won't be able to hunt. It's not going to be easy.'

She hid her fears behind a smile, and a cheerful tone: 'After the gundeck of the *Meeuw* it will seem like Paradise.'

She rubbed the chain galls on her ankles. These injuries were healing: the scabs were peeling away, leaving fresh pink skin underneath. Bakkat had concocted a balm of eland fat and wild herbs for her that was proving almost miraculously efficacious.

'I thought about sending you off to the Gariep with Zama to protect you and take you to the rendezvous with my father, while Bakkat and I led Keyser away, but when I discussed it with Bakkat we decided we could not take the risk. Keyser's Bushman tracker is a magician. You and Zama could never elude him, even with Bakkat playing all the tricks he knows. Xhia would pick up your spoor at the place where we parted and Keyser wants you almost as much as he wants me.' His face darkened as he thought of her left without protection to the mercy of Keyser and Koots and Oudeman. 'No, we will stay together.'

She was surprised at how relieved she felt that he would not leave her.

They watched as Keyser's men searched the deserted hut, then remounted and set off up the valley following the cold trail they had left. They disappeared into the mountains.

'They will return soon enough,' Jim predicted.

It took Xhia three days to lead Keyser round the wide circuit of the spoor and return to the hills above Majuba. Jim had used this respite to graze and rest the horses and mules. While they waited Bakkat recovered his strength. His backside grew full and fat again while they watched the trail. At a little after noon on the third day, Keyser's column appeared again, doggedly following the old spoor. As soon as Bakkat had them in sight, Jim and his party began to retreat further and further into the mountain fastness. He adjusted their pace to that of the pursuit: they kept far enough ahead of Keyser to keep him under observation and be alert to any sudden dash he might make, or to any other stratagem he and Xhia might conceive to take them unawares.

Their order of march was to send Zama and Louisa ahead with the mules and the baggage. Zama set the best pace that the animals could sustain. They had to be allowed to graze and rest or they would soon weaken and break down. Fortunately the same restrictions on the rapidity of march applied to Keyser's animals, although he had spare horses. Even so, Zama and Louisa were able to keep well out in front.

Bakkat and Jim stayed under Keyser's nose, shadowing him, keeping loose contact, but trying to make certain of his exact whereabouts at all times. Whenever the trail led over a ridge or crossed a watershed they waited on the high ground until Keyser's troop came in sight. Before they moved on Jim counted horses and men through the telescope and made certain that none had detached.

When night fell Bakkat would creep back to watch Keyser's camp from the shadows in case he was planning mischief. He could not take Jim with him. Xhia was a constant danger and, skilled in bush lore as Jim might be, he was no match for Xhia in the darkness. With Louisa and Zama far ahead, Jim would eat alone at his own campfire, then leave it burning to mislead any watcher and slip away into the night, following the other two, guarding their back trail against a surprise attack.

Before it was light Bakkat would break off his vigil over the enemy camp and hurry back to Jim. Then, all that day, they would resume the same order of retreat.

Next morning Xhia was able to read all their movements when he studied the sign they had left. On the third night Keyser ordered a surprise attack. He set up camp at nightfall. His troopers secured the horses, ate their dinners and posted sentries, then the others rolled into their blankets and let the fires die down. They knew from Xhia's observations that Bakkat must be spying on them. As soon as it was dark, Xhia led Koots and Oudeman silently and secretly out of camp. They circled out to try to slip past Bakkat, and surprise Jim at his campfire. But the two white men, even though they had removed their spurs and wrapped rags around their boots to deaden the sound, were no match for Bakkat. He heard every blundering step they took in the darkness. When Xhia and the two white men reached Jim's campfire it was long deserted and the flames had burned down to embers.

Two nights later Koots and Oudeman lay in wait for Bakkat well outside the perimeter of their camp. Bakkat had an animal instinct for survival. He smelt Koots from twenty paces: a white man's sweat and stale cigar smoke have a distinctive aroma. Bakkat rolled a small boulder down the hillside on top of him. Both Koots and Oudeman blazed away with their muskets at the sound. The camp erupted with shouting and gunfire, and neither Keyser nor any of his men got much sleep for the rest of the night.

The next day Jim and Bakkat were watching when the enemy mounted up and came after them again. 'When will Keyser give up, and turn back to the colony?' Jim wondered.

Running beside him, hanging on to a stirrup leather, Bakkat chuckled. 'You should not have stolen his horse, Somoya. I think you have angered him, and made it a matter of pride. We will either have to kill him or give him the slip. But he will not give up before that.'

'No killing, you bloodthirsty little devil. Abduction of a VOC convict and horse theft are bad enough. But even Governor van de Witten could not overlook the murder of his military commander. He would take it out on my family. My father—' Jim broke off. The consequences were too terrible to think about.

'Keyser is no dumbhead,' Bakkat went on. 'He knows by now that we are going to a meeting with your father. If he does not know where, all he has to do is follow us. If you are not going to kill him, you will need help from the Kulu Kulu himself to throw Xhia off our spoor. I could not be certain of doing it even if I were travelling alone. But now we are three men, a girl who has never been in the wilderness before, two horses and six loaded mules. What hope do we have against the eyes, nose and magic of Xhia?'

They reached another ridgeline where they stopped to rest Drumfire and let the pursuit come in sight once again.

'Where are we, Bakkat?' Jim rose in the stirrups and gazed around at the awe-inspiring chaos of mountain and valley that surrounded them.

'This place has no name for ordinary men do not come here, unless they are lost or mad.'

'Then which way are the sea and the colony?' He found it difficult to keep a sense of direction in the maze of the mountains.

Bakkat pointed without hesitation, and Jim squinted at the sun to check his bearings, but he did not question Bakkat's infallibility. 'How far?'

'Not far if you ride on an eagle's back.' Bakkat shrugged. 'Perhaps eight days if you know the road, and travel fast.'

'Keyser must be running out of supplies by now. Even we are down to the last bag of *chagga*, and twenty pounds of maize meal.'

'He will eat his spare horses before he gives up and lets you go to the meeting with your father,' Bakkat predicted.

Late that afternoon they watched, from a safe distance, as Sergeant Oudeman selected one of the horses from the remount herd and led it into a ravine near where Keyser's troop were camped. While Oudeman held its head, and Richter and Le Riche stropped their knives on a rock, Koots checked the flint and priming in his pistol. Then he walked up to the animal and placed the muzzle against the white blaze on its forehead. The shot was muted but the horse dropped instantly and kicked convulsively.

'Horse steaks for dinner,' Jim murmured. 'and Keyser has food for another week at the least.' He lowered his telescope. 'Bakkat, we cannot go on like this much longer. My father will not wait for ever at the Gariep.'

'How many horses do they have left?' Bakkat asked as he picked his nose thoughtfully, and examined what he had excavated.

Jim lifted the glass again and ran it over the distant herd.

'. . . sixteen, seventeen, eighteen,' he counted. 'Eighteen, including Keyser's grey.' He studied Bakkat's face, but it was innocent. 'The horses? Yes, of course!' he exclaimed. Bakkat's studied expression broke and his face creased into an impish grin. 'Yes. Their horses are the only way for us to attack them.'

The pursuit drove them on relentlessly into wild country where not even Bakkat had ventured before. Twice they saw game – once a herd of four eland crossing the skyline, then fifty beautiful bluebuck in a single herd together. But if they had turned aside to pursue the animals they would have lost ground and the gunfire would have brought Keyser and his troopers on at full tilt – he would be with them before they could butcher their kill. If they shot one of the mules, the same thing would happen. They rode on with the last of their provisions almost gone. Jim hoarded the last handful of coffee beans.

Gradually the pace Zama could maintain with Louisa and the mules fell off. The gap between the two parties dwindled until Jim and Bakkat caught up with them. Still Keyser's troopers came on apace, so that Jim's little band had more and more difficulty holding them off. Fresh horse steaks grilled over the fire seemed to have restored the strength and determination of Keyser's troopers. Louisa was flagging. She had been emaciated before the chase began, and now, with little food and rest, she was nearing the limit of her endurance.

To add to Jim's worries other hunters had joined the chase. Sleeping fitfully in the darkness, cold and hungry, unable to afford time during daylight even to collect firewood, expecting at any moment that Keyser's men might creep up on them, they were startled awake by a terrible sound. Louisa screamed before she could stop herself.

'What is that?'

Jim leaped out of his fur kaross and went to her. He put an arm round her shoulders. She was so terrified that she did not pull away. The sound came again: a series of deep grunts, each louder than the last, crescendoing into a thunder that echoed and rolled off the dark mountains.

'What is it?' Louisa's voice shook.

'Lions,' Jim told her. There was no point in trying to deceive her so, instead, he tried to distract her. 'Even the bravest of men is frightened by a lion three times – when first he sees its spoor, when first he hears its roar, when first he meets it face to face.'

'Once is enough for me,' she said, and although her voice quavered, she gave a small, uncertain laugh. Jim felt a lift of pride at her courage. Then he dropped his arm from her shoulders as he felt her shift uncomfortably in his embrace. She still could not bear a masculine touch. 'They are after the horses,' he told her. 'If fortune favours us, they might go after Keyser's animals instead of ours.' As if in answer to his wish, a few minutes later they heard a fusillade of musket fire further back down the valley where they had seen the enemy set up camp at nightfall.

'The lions must be on our side.' Louisa laughed again, a little more convincingly. At intervals during the rest of the night there came the clap of a distant musket shot.

'The lions are still harassing Keyser's camp,' Jim said. 'With luck they will lose some horses.'

At dawn as they began their flight again, Jim looked back through the telescope and saw that Keyser had lost none of his horses. 'They were able to drive off the lions, more's the pity,' he told Louisa.

'Let's hope they try again tonight,' she said.

It was the hardest day they had so far been forced to endure. During the afternoon a thunderstorm swept down from the north-west and drenched them with cold, driving rain. It blew over just as the sun was setting, and in the last light of the day they saw the enemy less than a league behind them, coming on steadily. Jim continued the retreat long after dark. It was a nightmare march over wet and treacherous ground, through rills that had swollen dangerously with rain. Jim knew in his heart that they could not carry on like this much longer.

When at last they halted Louisa almost fell from True-heart's back. Jim wrapped her in a sodden fur kaross and gave her a small stick of *chagga*, almost the last of their food.

'You have it. I am not hungry,' she protested.

'Eat it,' he commanded. 'No time for heroics now.'

She slumped and fell asleep before she had taken more than a few mouthfuls. Jim went to where Zama and Bakkat were sitting together. 'This is just about the end,' he said grimly. 'We have to do it tonight, or not at all. We have to get at their horses.' They had been planning all that day, but it would be a forlorn attempt. Although he kept a bold face, Jim knew it was almost certainly doomed.

Bakkat was the only one of them who had any chance at all of thwarting Xhia's vigilance and getting into the enemy camp undiscovered, and he could not untether all eighteen horses and bring them out on his own.

'One or two, yes,' he told Jim, 'but not eighteen.'

'We must take all of them.' He looked up at the sky. A sickle moon sailed through the streaming remnants of the rainclouds. 'Just enough light to do the job.'

'Bakkat could get into the horselines and cripple them, hamstring them,' Zama suggested.

Jim shifted uneasily: the idea of mutilating a horse was distasteful. 'The first animal would scream so loudly Bakkat would have the whole camp down on him. No, that won't work.'

At that moment Bakkat sprang to his feet and sniffed loudly. 'Hold the horses!' he cried. 'Quickly! The lions are here.'

Zama ran to Trueheart and seized her halter rope. Bakkat darted to the mules to control them. They would be more docile than the two thoroughbreds.

Jim was only just in time. He grabbed Drumfire's head as the stallion reared on his hind legs and whinnied shrilly with terror. Jim was lifted off his feet but he managed to throw an arm around Drumfire's neck, and hold him down. 'Steady, my darling. Whoa now! Easy! Easy!' he soothed him. But still the horse stamped and reared and tried to break away. Jim shouted across at Bakkat, 'What is it? What's happening?'

'It's the lion,' Bakkat panted. 'Foul demon! He has circled upwind, and squirted his stinking piss for the horses to smell. The lioness will be waiting down wind to catch any that break away.'

'Sweet Christ!' Jim exclaimed. 'Even I can smell it!' It was a rank feline stench in the back of his throat, more repulsive than the spray of a tomcat. Drumfire reared again. The odour was driving him crazy. He was beyond control. This time Jim knew he could not hold him. He still had both arms around the stallion's neck but his feet barely touched the ground. Drumfire broke into a gallop dragging Jim along with him.

'The lioness!' Bakkat yelled. 'Beware! The lioness is waiting for you.'

Drumfire's hoofs thundered over the rocky ground, and Jim felt as though his arms were being wrenched out of their sockets.

'Let him go, Somoya. You cannot stop him!' Bakkat screamed after him. 'The lioness will get you too!'

Jim jackknifed his body forward and as his feet struck the earth he used the power of both legs to boost himself high and swing one leg over Drumfire's back. Balancing easily to the stallion's run, he snatch Keyser's pistol from his belt and cocked the hammer with a single movement.

'To your right, Somoya!' Bakkat's voice receded behind him, but he picked up the warning just in time. He saw the movement as the lioness broke from cover and streaked in from his right. She was ghostly pale in the faint moonlight, silent, huge and terrible.

He lifted the pistol and leaned forward. He tried to steer Drumfire with the pressure of his knees, but the horse was far beyond any restraint. He saw the lioness get ahead of them and crouch down, gathering herself to spring. Then she rose from the earth, launching herself straight at Jim. There was no time to aim. Instinctively he pointed the muzzle into her face. She was so close that he could see both her front paws, reaching for him with great curved claws. Her open jaws were a black pit. Her teeth shone like porcelain in the moonlight, and the graveyard stench of her breath blew hot into his face as she roared.

He fired the pistol at the full reach of his right arm, and the muzzle flash blinded him. The weight of the lioness's body crashed into them. Even Drumfire reeled at the weight, but then he gathered himself and galloped on. Jim felt the lioness's claws rip into his boot, but they did not hold. The huge carcass dropped away, tumbled slackly across the hard ground, then lay in an inert pile.

It took seconds for Jim to realize that he had come through the attack unscathed. Then his next care was for Drumfire. He leaned forward and clasped him around the neck, calling to him soothingly, 'It's all over, my sweetheart. Whoa! There's a good boy.'

Drumfire's ears twitched back as he listened to Jim's voice. He slowed down to an easy trot, and at last to a walk. Jim steered him back up the slope. But as soon as he smelt the lioness's blood, he started mincing and dancing, throwing his head nervously.

'Lioness is dead,' Bakkat called out of the darkness. 'Shot through the mouth and out the back of her skull.'

'Where is the lion?' Jim shouted back.

As if in reply they heard the lion roar near the top of the mountain, a good mile off. 'Now she is of no further use to him, he has deserted his wife,' Bakkat sneered. 'Cowardly and thieving beast.'

It was with difficulty that Jim coaxed Drumfire back to where Bakkat stood beside the dead lioness. He was still skittish and nervous. 'I've never seen him so terrified,' Jim exclaimed.

'No animal can stay calm and brave with the smell of lion's piss or blood in his nostrils,' Bakkat told him. Then they exclaimed in the same voice: 'That's it! We have it!'

It was long after midnight by the time they reached the ridge overlooking the enemy camp. Keyser's watchfires had burned low, but they could see that the sentries were still awake.

'Just a small breeze from the east.' Jim held Drumfire's head to calm him. The stallion was still shivering and sweating with terror. Not even Jim's hand and voice could soothe him. Every time the carcass he was towing behind him slithered forward, he rolled his eyes until the whites glared in the moonlight.

'We must keep below the wind,' Bakkat murmured. 'The other horses must not catch the scent until we are ready.'

They had muffled Drumfire's hoofs with leather booties, and wrapped all the metal pieces of his tack. Bakkat went ahead to make sure that the way was clear as they circled out round the western perimeter of the enemy camp.

'Even Xhia has to sleep sometime,' Jim whispered to Bakkat, but he was unconvinced. They closed in slowly and were within half a pistol shot of the perimeter where they could see the enemy sentries outlined against the faint glow of their fire.

'Give me your knife, Somoya,' whispered Bakkat. 'It is sharper than mine.'

'If you lose it, I will have both your ears in exchange,' Jim muttered, as he handed it over.

'Wait for my signal.' Bakkat left him, in his disconcertingly abrupt fashion, seeming to vanish into the air. Jim stood at Drumfire's head, holding his nostrils closed to prevent him whickering at the smell of the other horses so close to him.

Like a wraith Bakkat drifted closer to the fires and his heart leaped as he saw Xhia. His enemy sat on the opposite side of the second fire, his kaross wrapped about his shoulders. Bakkat could see that his eyes were closed and his head nodded on the verge of sleep.

Somoya was right. Bakkat smiled to himself. He does sleep sometimes.

Nevertheless he kept well clear of Xhia, but he slipped almost contemptuously within touching distance past Corporal

Richter who was guarding the horselines. Keyser's grey was the first animal he came to. As Bakkat crept up to it, he began to hum in his throat, a lulling sound. The grey shifted slightly and pricked its ears, but made no other sound. Bakkat took only a moment to sever three strands of its halter rope. Then he moved on to the next horse in the line, still humming his lullaby, and drew the blade carefully across the rope that held it.

He was half-way down the line when behind him he heard Corporal Richter cough, hawk and spit. Bakkat sank to the earth and lay still. He heard Richter's booted footsteps coming down the line and watched him pause beside the grey's head to check the halter. In the darkness he overlooked the unravelling strands of the fraying rope. Then he came on and almost stepped on Bakkat. When he reached the end of the line he unfastened the fly of his breeches and urinated noisily on the earth. When he came back, Bakkat had crawled under the belly of one of the horses, and Richter passed without glancing in his direction. He went back to his place by the fire, and said something to Xhia who grunted a reply.

Bakkat gave them a few minutes to settle again, then crept on down the line of horses, and dealt with each of their halter ropes.

Jim heard the signal, the soft liquid call of a nightbird, so convincing that he hoped that it was indeed the little man and not a real bird that had uttered it.

'No going back now!' He swung up on to Drumfire's back. The stallion needed no urging, his nerves were raw, and as he felt Jim's heels he started forward. The carcass of the lioness, half disembowelled, her reeking guts hanging out of the cavity, slithered after him and Drumfire could stand it no longer. At full tilt he tore into the sleeping camp, and on his back Jim was howling, gibbering and waving his hat over his head.

Bakkat leaped out of the darkness on the far side grunting

and roaring at an incredible volume for such a small frame. It was a perfect imitation of the beast.

Corporal Richter, half asleep, staggered to his feet and fired his musket at Jim as he charged past. The ball missed Drumfire but hit one of the horses tethered in the lines, shattering its front leg. The animal screamed and plunged, snapping its weakened halter rope, then fell and rolled on its back kicking in the air. The other troopers woke and snatched up their muskets. The panic was contagious and they blazed away at imaginary lions and attackers, shouting challenges and orders.

'It's the Courtney bastard!' Keyser bellowed. 'There he is! Shoot him! Don't let him get away!'

The horses were bombarded with shouts and screams and roars, by blasts of gunfire and, finally, by the terrifying scent of lion blood and guts. On the previous night they had been attacked repeatedly by the lion pride, and that memory was still vivid. They could stand no more. They fought their head ropes, kicking, rearing and whinnying with terror. One after another the ropes snapped and the horses were free. They wheeled away and thundered out of the camp in a solid bunch, heading downwind. Close behind them rode Jim on Drumfire. Bakkat darted out of the shadows and seized one of his stirrup leathers. While Drumfire carried him along, Bakkat was still roaring like a ravening lion. In their dust ran Keyser and his troopers, bellowing with rage and firing as fast as they were able to reload.

'Stop them!' Keyser howled. 'They have got the horses! Stop them!' He tripped over a rock and fell to his knees, gasping for breath, his heart pounding as though it were about to burst. He stared after the vanishing herd, and the import of his predicament struck him with full force. He and his men were stranded in tractless, mountainous terrain, at least ten days' march from civilization. Their supplies were severely depleted even those they would not be able to carry with them.

'Swine!' he shouted. 'I will get you, Jim Courtney. I will

not rest until I see you swinging on the gibbet, until I see the maggots filling your skull and dribbling out of your eye-sockets. I swear by all that is holy, and may God be my witness.'

The runaway horses kept bunched together, and Jim herded them along. He cut the rope on which he was towing the lioness, and left her carcass behind. Glad to be rid of his odorous burden, Drumfire calmed down at once. Within a mile the running herd dropped from a gallop to a canter, but Jim kept them moving steadily. Within an hour he knew that none of the troopers, shod as they were and carrying their weapons and equipment, could overhaul them. He slowed down to a steady trot, a pace they could keep up for hours.

Before the attack on Keyser's camp, Jim had sent Zama and Louisa on ahead with Trueheart and the mules. They had had several hours' start, but Jim caught up with them an hour after sunrise. The meeting was emotional.

'We heard the gunfire in the night,' Louisa told Jim, 'and feared the worst, but I prayed for you. I didn't stop until a minute ago when I heard you shout behind us.'

'That's what did it, then, Hedgehog. You must be a champion prayer-maker.' Although he grinned, Jim felt an almost irresistible urge to lift her down from Trueheart's back and hold her close, to protect her and cherish her. She looked so thin, pale and exhausted. Instead he swung down from his own saddle. 'Make a fire, Zama,' he ordered. 'We can warm up and rest. Damn me, if we won't eat the last mouthful of the food, drink the last mug of coffee, then sleep until we wake up.' He laughed. 'Keyser is on his way back to the colony on Shanks's pony and we won't have any more trouble from him for a while.'

This time Jim would not allow Louisa to refuse a mug of coffee, and once she had tasted the bitter liquid she could no longer deny herself, and drank the rest thankfully. It revived her almost immediately. She stopped shivering and a little colour returned to her cheeks. She even raised a wan smile at a few of Jim's worst jokes. He refilled the canteen with boiling water every time it was emptied. Each brew of coffee became progressively weaker but it restored his spirits and he was cheerful and ebullient again. He described to Louisa how Keyser had reacted to the surprise raid, and imitated him staggering about barefoot, waving his sword over his head, bellowing threats and tripping over his own feet in the dark. Louisa laughed until tears ran down her cheeks.

Jim and Zama examined the horses they had captured. They were in good condition, considering the long, gruelling journey that had been forced on them. Keyser's grey gelding was the pick of the herd. Keyser had named him Zehn, but Jim translated that to the English, Frost.

Now that they had remounts they would be able to push on at speed towards the rendezvous on the Gariep. But first Jim rested and grazed the horses knowing that Keyser could not harass them. Louisa took full advantage of this respite. She curled under her kaross and slept. She lay so still that Jim was worried. Quietly he lifted a corner of the fur to make sure she was still breathing.

That morning, just before they had caught up with Zama and Louisa, Jim had spotted a small herd of four or five mountain rhebuck grazing among the rocks higher up the slope from the valley. Now he saddled Frost and Bakkat rode bareback on another of the captured horses. Jim left Louisa to sleep with Zama to guard her, and they rode back to where they had seen the rhebuck. They found that the herd had moved on and the slope was empty, but Jim knew they were unlikely to have gone far. They knee-haltered the horses and left them to graze on a patch of sweet grass with fluffy pink seedheads ripening in the spring sunshine. They climbed the slope.

Bakkat picked up the rhebuck spoor just below the crest, and worked it swiftly, trotting along over rocky ground with Jim striding after him. On the far side of the ridge they found the herd already bedded down in the lee of a cluster of large boulders that sheltered them from the cold wind. Bakkat led Jim in close, leopard-crawling with the musket cradled in the crook of his elbow. At seventy paces Jim knew they could not get closer without bolting the herd. He picked a fat dun-coloured ewe who was lying facing away from him, chewing the cud contentedly. He knew that the musket threw three inches to the right at a hundred paces, so he propped his elbows on his knees for a steady shot and laid off his aim a thumb's width. The ball struck at the base of the ewe's skull with a sound like a ripe melon dropped on a stone floor. She did not move again, except to drop her head flat against the earth. The rest of the herd bounded away, flashing their bushy white tails and whistling with alarm.

They skinned the ewe and gralloched her, feasting on raw liver as they worked. She was only a medium-sized antelope, but young and plump. They left the skin and head and entrails and between them carried the rest of the carcass back to the horses.

Once they had loaded it on to Frost's back, Bakkat stuffed his food bag with strips of fresh raw meat, and they parted. Armed with Jim's telescope, he rode back to spy on Keyser and his troopers. Jim wanted him to make certain that they had abandoned the chase, now that they had lost their horses, and that they were starting on the long, bitter march back through the mountains to the distant colony. Jim would not trust Keyser to do what was expected of him: he was learning to respect the colonel's tenacity, and the strength of his hatred.

By the time Jim reached the camp where he had left Louisa it was after noon, and she was still sleeping. The aroma of roasting rhebuck steaks roused her. Jim managed to brew one more watery canteen of coffee with the old beans, and Louisa ate with obvious relish.

In the late afternoon, just as the sun was settling on the peaks, painting them bloody and fiery, Bakkat rode back into camp. 'I found them about five miles from where we attacked them last night,' he told Jim. 'They have given up the chase. They have abandoned all of the supplies and equipment they could not carry on their backs – they did not even take the time to burn it. I brought back everything I thought we could use.'

While Zama helped him unload the booty, Jim asked, 'Which way are they heading?'

'As you hoped, Xhia is leading them back west again, straight towards the colony. But they are travelling slowly. Most of the white men are suffering. Their boots are better suited to riding than walking. The fat colonel is already limping, and using a stick. It does not seem as though he will be able to carry on much longer, not for the ten days' travel it will take them to reach the colony.' Bakkat looked at Jim. 'You said that you did not want to kill him. The mountains might kill him for you.'

Jim shook his head. 'Stephanus Keyser is no fool. He will send Xhia ahead to fetch fresh horses from the Cape. He might lose some of his belly, but he won't die,' he declared, with assurance he did not feel. He added silently, Or, at least, I hope not. He did not want Keyser's murder laid at the door of his family.

For the first time in weeks they did not have to run to keep ahead of their pursuers. Bakkat had found a small bag of flour and a bottle of wine in one of the saddlebags Keyser had abandoned. Louisa cooked flat unleavened breadcakes over the coals, and kebabs of rhebuck meat and liver, and they washed it down with Keyser's fine old claret. Alcohol is poison to the San, and Bakkat, giggling tipsily, almost fell into the fire when he tried to stand. The fur karosses had dried out after the soaking in the previous day's thunderstorm, and they collected armfuls of cedarwood to feed a fragrant campfire, so they enjoyed their first unbroken sleep for many a night.

Early the next morning they rode on, well fed, rested and mounted, towards the meeting place at the Hill of the Baboon's Head. Only Bakkat was still suffering the ill-effects of the three mouthfuls of wine he had drunk the night before. 'I am poisoned,' he muttered. 'I am going to die.'

'No, you won't,' Jim assured him. 'The ancestors will not take a rogue like you.'

For three days Colonel Stephanus Keyser limped along, leaning heavily on the staff that Captain Koots had cut for him, supported on the other side by Goffel, one of the Hottentot troopers. The trail was endless: steep descents followed by treacherous uphill stretches on which the loose round scree rubble rolled underfoot. An hour before noon on the third day of the march Keyser could go no further. He collapsed with a groan on a small boulder beside the game trail they were following.

'Goffel, you useless bastard, pull off my boots,' he shouted, and offered one of his feet. Goffel struggled with the large, scuffed, dusty boot, then staggered backwards as it came free in his hands. The others gathered around and stared in awe at the exposed foot. The stocking was in bloody ribbons. The blisters had burst and tatters of skin hung from the open wounds.

Captain Koots blinked his pale eyes. His eyelashes were colourless which gave him a perpetual bland stare. 'Colonel, sir, you cannot go on with your feet in that condition.'

'That's what I have been telling you for the last twenty miles, you gibbering idiot,' Keyser roared at him. 'Get your men to build me a carrying chair.'

The men exchanged glances. They were already heavily burdened with the equipment Keyser had insisted they carry back to the colony, including his English hunting saddle, his folding camp chair and bed, his canteen and bedroll. Now they were about to be accorded the honour of carrying the colonel himself.

'You heard the colonel.' Koots rounded on them. 'Richter! You and Le Riche find two cedarwood poles. Use your bayonets to trim them into shape. We will tie the colonel's saddle over them with strips of bark.' The troopers scattered to their tasks.

Keyser hobbled on bare, bleeding feet to the stream and sat on the bank. He soaked his feet in the cold clear water and sighed with relief. 'Koots!' he shouted, and the captain hurried to join him.

'Colonel, sir!' He stood to attention on the bank. He was a lean, hard man, with narrow hips and wide bony shoulders under the green baize tunic.

'How would you like to earn ten thousand guilders?' Keyser dropped his voice to a confidential tone. Koots thought about that sum of money. It represented almost five years' pay on his present level, and he had no illusions about climbing higher up the military ladder. 'It is a large sum of money, sir,' he said cautiously.

'I want that young bastard Courtney. I want him as much as anything I have ever wanted in my life.'

'I understand, Colonel.' Koots nodded. 'I would like to get my hands on him myself.' He smiled like a cobra at the thought, and clenched his fists instinctively at his sides.

'He is going to get away, Koots,' Keyser said heavily. 'Before we ever reach the castle he will be over the frontier of the colony and we will never see him again. He has made a jackass of me, and of the VOC.'

Koots showed no sign of distress at these trespasses. He could not prevent a bleak smile reaching his thin lips as he thought, That's no great feat. It doesn't take a genius to make a jackass of the colonel.

Keyser caught a glimmer of the smile. 'You, too, Koots. You will be the butt of every joke of every drunkard and whore in every tavern in the colony. You will be buying your own drinks for years to come.' Koots's face darkened into a murderous scowl. Keyser pressed the advantage. 'That is, Koots, unless you and I can see to it that he is captured and brought back to give a public performance of the rope dance on the parade outside the castle.'

'He is taking the Robbers' Road to the north,' Koots protested. 'The VOC cannot send troops after him. It's outside their suzerainty. Governor van de Witten would never allow it. He could not flout the orders in council of Het Zeventien.'

'I could arrange for you, my fine fellow, to take an indefinite leave of absence from the Company service. Paid leave, of

183

course. I would also arrange a travel pass for you to cross the frontier on a hunting expedition. I would give you Xhia and two or three other good men – Richter and Le Riche, perhaps? I would provide all the supplies you needed.'

'And if I succeed? If I capture Courtney and bring him back to the castle?'

'I will see to it that Governor van de Witten and the VOC place a bounty on him of ten thousand guilders in gold. I would even settle for his head pickled in a vat of *brandewijn*.'

Koots's eyes widened as he thought about it. With ten thousand guilders he could leave this God-forsaken land for ever. Of course, he could never return to Holland. He was known by a name other than Koots in the old country, and he had unfinished business there that might end on the gallows. However, Batavia was Paradise compared to this backward colony on the tip of a barbaric continent. Koots allowed himself a fleeting erotic fantasy. The Javanese women were famous for their beauty. He had never developed a taste for the simian-featured Hottentots of the Cape. Moreover, there were opportunities in the east for a man who was good with a sword and gun, who did not flinch at the sight of blood, and even more so if he had a purse of gold guilders on his belt.

'What do you say to that, Koots?' Keyser interrupted his day-dreams.

'I say fifteen thousand.'

'You are a greedy fellow, Koots. Fifteen thousand is a fortune.'

'You are a wealthy man, Colonel,' Koots pointed out. 'I know that you paid two thousand each for Trueheart and Frost. I would bring back your two horses, along with Courtney's head.'

At the mention of his stolen horses Keyser's sense of outrage, which he had managed to hold under tenuous control, returned in full force. They were two of the finest animals outside Europe. He looked down at his ruined feet, the pain in them almost as bitter as the loss of his horses. Yet fifteen thousand guilders out of his own purse was indeed a fortune.

Koots saw him wavering. He needed only a gentle push. 'Then there is the stallion,' he said.

'What stallion?' Keyser looked up from his feet.

'The one who beat you at Christmas. Drumfire. Jim Courtney's stallion. I would throw him into the bargain.'

Keyser was weakening, but he set one last condition. 'The girl. The convict girl, I want her also.'

'I will have a little fun with her first.' Although his lean, hard features were impassive, Koots was enjoying the bargaining. 'I will bring her to you damaged but alive.'

'She is probably damaged already.' Keyser laughed. 'And will be more so when that young Courtney ram is finished with her. I want her only to make a good show on the gallows. The crowds always love to see a young girl on the rope. I don't mind what you do to her before that.'

'We have an agreement, then?' Koots asked.

'The man, the girl and the three horses.' Keyser nodded. 'Three thousand each, or fifteen thousand for all of them.'

There were ten men to share the labour of carrying the colonel. A team of four was changed every hour, timed with Keyser's gold watch. The saddle was in the English style, but the work of one of Holland's finest saddle-makers. They secured it in the centre of the carrying poles. Keyser sat at ease with his feet in the stirrups, while two men at each end lifted the poles on to their shoulders and walked away with them. It took them nine days to reach the colony, the last two without food. The shoulders of the men were sadly galled by the weight of the poles, but Keyser's feet had almost healed, and the enforced diet had slimmed down his belly and bulk; he looked ten years younger.

Keyser's first duty was to report to Governor Paulus Pieterzoon van de Witten. They were old comrades, and shared many secrets. Van de Witten was a tall dyspeptic-looking man of not yet forty. His father and grandfather before him had been members of Het Zeventien in Amsterdam, and his wealth and power were considerable. Very soon he would return to Holland and take his seat on the board of the VOC, as long as there were no blemishes on his career or reputation. The activities of this English bandit might conceivably leave such a stain on his reputation. Colonel Keyser described in detail the crimes against the property and dignity of the VOC perpetrated by the youngest Courtney. Slowly he stoked the flames of the governor's outrage, repeatedly hinting at van de Witten's own responsibility in the affair. Their discussion lasted several hours, helped along by the consumption of quantities of Hollands gin and French claret. Finally van de Witten capitulated and agreed that the VOC would offer a reward of fifteen thousand guilders for the capture of Louisa Leuven and James Archibald Courtney, or for positive proof of their execution.

The placing of rewards on the heads of criminals who had fled the colony was a long-established practice. Many of the hunters and traders who had licences to leave the colony supplemented their profits with bounty money for the VOC.

Keyser was well pleased with this result. It meant that he was not obliged to risk a single guilder of his own carefully accumulated fortune to contribute to the bounty he had agreed with Captain Koots.

That same night Koots visited him in the little cottage in the lane behind the Company gardens. Keyser advanced him four hundred guilders to cover the costs of provisioning the expeditionary force that was to pursue Jim Courtney. Five days later a small party of travellers assembled on the banks of the Eerste river, the first river after leaving the colony. They had come separately to the meeting place. There were four white men: Captain Koots, with his pale eyes and colourless hair, his skin reddened by the sun; Sergeant Oudeman, bald, but with heavy drooping moustaches, Koots's right-hand man and accomplice; Corporals Richter and Le Riche, who hunted together like a pair of wild dogs. Then there were five Hottentot troopers, including the notorious Goffel, who was the interpreter, and Xhia, the Bushman tracker. None of them wore VOC military uniform: they were dressed in the coarse homespun and leather of the Cape burghers. Xhia's loincloth was made of tanned springbuck skin decorated with beads of ostrich eggshell and Venetian trade beads. Over his shoulders he carried his bow and bark quiver of poisoned arrows, and round his waist a belt hung with an array of charms and buck horns filled with magical and medical potions, powders and unguents.

Koots swung up into the saddle and looked down at Xhia, the Bushman. 'Take the spoor, you little yellow devil, and drink the wind.' They followed Xhia in single file, each trooper leading a spare horse that carried a pack-saddle.

'Courtney's spoor will be many weeks old before we cut it again,' Koots watched Xhia's bare back and peppercorned head bobbing along ahead of his horse's nose, 'but this hunting dog is a *shaitan*. He could follow a snowball through the fires of hell.' Then he let himself savour the thought of the warrant in his saddlebag signed by Governor van de Witten, and the prospect of fifteen thousand guilders in gold. He smiled. It was not a pretty smile.

Bakkat knew that this was only a respite, and that Keyser would not allow them to escape so easily: sooner rather than later Xhia would be following their spoor again. He scouted well ahead and on the sixth day after the capture of Keyser's horses he found the place ideally suited to his purpose. Here, a stratum of black igneous rock cut diagonally across the floor of a wide valley, through the bed of a fast-flowing river, then climbed the steep far side of the valley. The stratum ran straight and stood out as clearly as a paved Roman road, for no grass or other vegetation grew upon it. Where it crossed the river it was so resistant to the erosion of the waters that it formed a natural weir. The river dropped over the far side, a thundering waterfall, into a whirlpool twenty feet below. The black rock was so hard that not even the steel-shod hoofs of the horses left a scratch upon the surface.

'Keyser will come back,' Bakkat told Jim, as they squatted on the shiny black floor. 'He is a stubborn man, and you have made it a matter of his pride and honour. He will not give up. Even if he does not come himself he will send others to follow you, and Xhia will guide them.'

'It will take even Xhia many days and weeks to reach the Cape and then return,' Jim demurred. 'By then we will be hundreds of leagues away.'

'Xhia can follow a spoor that is a year old, unless it has been carefully wiped clean.'

'How will you wipe our spoor, Bakkat?' Jim asked.

'We have many horses,' Bakkat pointed out, and Jim nodded. 'Perhaps too many,' Bakkat persisted.

Jim looked over the herd of mules and captured horses. There were over thirty. 'We do not need so many,' he agreed.

'How many do you need?' Bakkat asked.

Jim considered. 'Drumfire and Trueheart, Frost and Crow to ride, Stag and Lemon as spares and to carry the packs.'

'I will use the rest, horses and mules, to wipe our spoor and act as a decoy to lead Xhia away,' Bakkat declared.

'Show me!' Jim ordered, and Bakkat set about the preparations. While Zama watered the herd above the black rock weir, Louisa and Jim fashioned leather booties from the captured saddlebags and the skins of the eland and rhebuck. These would muffle the hoofs of the six horses they were taking with them. While they were busy with this task, Bakkat scouted downstream. He kept well up on the slope of the valley and never approached the river bank. When he returned they cut out the six chosen horses and strapped the booties over their hoofs. It would not take long for the steel shoes to bite through the leather, but it was only a few hundred yards to the river bank.

They secured the equipment to the backs of the six horses. Then, when all was in readiness, they assembled the entire herd of horses and mules into a tight bunch and walked them easily across the black rock. Half-way across they held the six loaded horses, and let the rest go on and start grazing on the far slope of the valley.

Jim, Louisa and Zama removed their own boots, strapped them on to the backs of their mounts, then led them barefoot along the black stone pathway. Bakkat came behind them, examining each inch of the ground they had covered. Even to his eye they left no sign. The leather booties had padded the hoofs, the bare human feet were soft and pliant, and they had walked slowly, not adding their weight to that of the horses. The hoofs had neither scored nor scratched the rock.

When they reached the river bank Jim told Zama, 'You go first. Once they hit the water the horses will want to swim straight to the bank. Your job will be to prevent them doing that.'

They watched anxiously as Zama waded out along the natural causeway, with the water reaching first to his knees, then to his waist. In the end he did not have to dive over the edge, the racing waters simply carried him away. He struck the surface of the pool twenty feet below and disappeared for what seemed to the watchers an age. Then his head broke out and he lifted one arm and waved up at them. Jim turned to Louisa.

'Are you ready?' he asked. She lifted her chin and nodded. She did not speak, but he saw the fear in her eyes. She walked firmly to the river's edge, but he could not let her go alone. He took her arm, and for once she made no move to pull away from him. They waded out side by side until the water reached over their knees. Then they stopped and teetered slightly, Jim bracing himself to hold her. 'I know you swim like a fish. I have seen you,' he said. She looked up and smiled at him, but her eyes were huge and dark blue with terror. He released his grip on her arm, and she did not hesitate but dived forward and instantly disappeared in the spray and thunder. Jim felt his heart go with her, and was frozen with dread as he peered down.

Then her head burst out of the creaming foam. She had tucked her hat under her belt, and her hair had come down. It streamed over her face like a sheet of shining silk. She looked up at him and, incredulously, he saw that she was laughing. The sound of the waterfall smothered her voice, but he could read her lips: 'Don't be afraid. I'll catch you.'

He guffawed with relief. 'Saucy wench!' he shouted back, and returned to the bank where Bakkat was holding the horses. He led them out one at a time, Trueheart first because she was the most tractable. The mare had watched Louisa take the leap and she went readily enough. She landed with a tall splash. As soon as she came up she tried to head for the bank, but Louisa swam to her head and turned her downstream. When they reached the tail of the pool the bottom shelved and they were able to stand. Louisa waved up at Jim again to signal that they were all right. She had replaced her hat on her head.

Jim brought out the other horses. Crow and Lemon, the two mares, went over without any ado. The geldings Stag and Frost were more difficult, but in the end Jim forced them to take the plunge. As soon as they hit the water Zama swam to them and steered them downstream to where Louisa waited to hold them, belly deep in the middle of the river.

Drumfire had watched the other horses jump, and when his turn came he decided he wanted no part of such madness. In the middle of the stone weir, with turbulent waters booming around them, he staged a battle of wills with Jim. He reared and plunged, losing his footing, then regaining it, backing away and throwing his head around. Jim hung on as he was tossed about, reciting a string of insults and threats in a tone that was meant to sound endearing and soothing. 'You demented creature, I'll use you as lion bait.' In the end he managed to wrestle Drumfire's head around into a position where he could make a flying mount. Once he was astride, he had the upper hand and he forced Drumfire to the edge, where the current did the rest. They went over together, and during the long drop Jim twisted free. If Drumfire had landed on top of him he would have been crushed, but he threw himself clear and as soon as Drumfire's head broke the surface he was ready to seize a handful of his mane, and swim him down to where Louisa and the rest of the horses stood.

Bakkat alone was still at the top of the waterfall. He gave Jim a brief hand signal to urge him on downstream, then went back along the black rock stratum, for a second time scrutinizing the surface for any sign he might have overlooked.

Satisfied at last, he reached the point where the rest of the herd had crossed the black rock. There he worked the masking spell for blinding the enemy. He lifted his leather skirt and urinated, intermittently pinching off the stream between thumb and forefinger as he turned in a circle.

'Xhia, you murderer of innocent women, with this spell I close your eyes so you cannot see the sun above you at noon.' He let fly a mighty squirt.

'Xhia, beloved of the darkest spirits, with this spell I seal your ears so that you might not hear the trumpeting of wild elephants.' He farted with the effort of expelling the next spurt, jumped in the air and laughed.

'Xhia, you stranger to the customs and traditions of your own tribe, with this spell I seal your nostrils so that you might not even smell your own dung.'

His bladder empty, he unstoppered one of the duiker horns on his belt, shook out the grey powder and let it blow away on the breeze. 'Xhia, you who are my enemy unto the death, I dull all your senses so that you will pass this place without divining the parting of the spoors.'

Then, at last, he lit a dried twig of the tong tree from his clay fire-pot and waved it over the spoor. 'Xhia, you nameless filth and excrement, with this smoke I mask my spoor that you may not follow.'

Satisfied at last, he looked down the valley and, in the distance, saw Jim and the others leading the horses away, keeping to the middle of the fast-flowing stream. They would not leave the water until they reached the place he had picked out for them almost a league downstream. Bakkat watched them disappear round the bend of the river.

The horses and mules they were leaving behind as decoys were already spread out down the valley, grazing quietly. Bakkat followed them, picked out a horse and mounted it. In an unhurried manner, not alarming the herd, he gathered it up and began to move it away from the river, crossing the divide into the next steep valley.

He went on for another five days, an aimless meandering through the mountainous terrain, making no effort to hide the spoor. On the evening of the fifth day he strapped the hoofs of the dead rhebuck back-to-front on his own feet. Then he abandoned the herd of remaining horses and mules, and minced away imitating the gait and the length of stride of the living rhebuck. Once he was well clear he laid another magical spell to blind Xhia, in the unlikely event that his enemy had been able to unravel the spoor this far.

He was confident at last that Xhia would not find where the party had split on the rock, and that he would follow the more numerous, undisguised spoor of the herd. When he caught up with it, he would find a dead end.

Now, at last, he could circle back towards the riverine valley where he had parted from Jim and the others. When he reached it, he was not surprised to find that Jim had followed his instructions exactly. He had left the river on the rocky stretch of the bank that Bakkat had selected and doubled back towards the east. Bakkat followed, carefully wiping clean the light spoor the party had left. He used a broom made from a branch of the magical tong tree. When he was well clear of the river, he cast a third magical spell to confuse any pursuit, then followed at a faster pace. By this time he was almost ten days behind Jim, but he travelled so swiftly that even on foot he caught up with them four days later.

He smelt their campfire long before he reached it. He was pleased to find that, once they had eaten the evening meal, Jim had doused the fire under a heavy blanket of sand, then moved on in the dark to spend the night in another better-protected place.

Bakkat nodded his approval: only a fool sleeps beside his own campfire when he knows he may be followed. When he crept up to the camp he found Zama was the sentry. Bakkat bypassed him effortlessly, and when Jim woke in the first light of dawn he was sitting close beside him.

'Somoya, when you snore you shame the lions,' he greeted him.

When Jim recovered from the shock, he embraced him. 'I swear to the Kulu Kulu, Bakkat, that you have grown even

192

smaller since last I saw you. Soon I will be able to carry you in my pocket.'

Bakkat rode ahead on the gelding, Frost. He led them straight towards the cliff that blocked off the head of the valley like a mighty fortress. Jim pushed his hat to the back of his head and gazed up at the wall of rock.

'There is no way through.' He shook his head. High above them the vultures sailed across the rockface on wide wings, coming in to land on the ledges beside their bulky nests of sticks and twigs.

'Bakkat will find the way,' Louisa contradicted him. Already she had complete confidence and trust in the little Bushman. They shared not a single word of a common language, but in the evenings at the campfire the two often sat close together, communicating with hand signs and facial expressions, laughing at jokes that they both seemed to understand perfectly. Jim wondered how he could be jealous of Bakkat, but Louisa was not as at ease with him as she was with the Bushman.

They climbed on upwards, straight towards the solid wall of rock. Louisa had dropped back to ride with Zama, who was bringing up the two spare horses at the rear of the column. Zama had been her protector and constant companion during all the long, hard days of the flight from Keyser, while Jim had been occupied with guarding the back trail and keeping the pursuit at bay. They had developed a rapport too. Zama was teaching her the language of the forests, and as she had an ear for the language she was learning swiftly.

Jim had come to realize that Louisa possessed some quality that drew others to her. He tried to fathom what it was. He cast his mind back to their first encounter on the deck of the convict ship. For him the attraction had been immediate and compelling. He tried to put it into words. Is it that she emanates a feeling of compassion and goodness? He was not sure. It seemed that she hid only from him behind the defensive armour he called her hedgehog prickles; to others she was open and friendly. It was confusing and at times he resented it. He wanted her to ride at his side, not with Zama.

She must have felt his gaze upon her for her head turned towards him. Even at that distance her eyes were an extraordinary blue. She smiled at him through the thin veil of dust kicked up by the hoofs of the horses.

Bakkat stopped half-way up the scree. 'Wait for me here, Somoya,' he said.

'Where are you going, old friend?' Jim asked.

'I go to speak to my fathers, and take them a gift.'

'What gift?'

'Something to eat, and something pretty.' Bakkat opened the pouch on his belt and brought out a stick of eland *chagga* half the length of his thumb that he had been hoarding, and the dried wing of a sunbird. The iridescent feathers gleamed like emeralds and rubies. He dismounted and handed Frost's reins to Jim. 'I have to ask permission to enter the sacred places,' he explained, and disappeared among the proteas and sugarbushes. Zama and Louisa came up and they unsaddled the horses and settled down to rest. Time passed and they were drowsing in the shade of the proteas when they heard the sound of a human voice, tiny with distance, but the echoes whispered along the cliff. Louisa scrambled to her feet and looked up the slope. 'I told you Bakkat knew the way,' she cried.

High above them he stood at the base of the cliff, and waved to them to follow. They saddled up quickly, and climbed up to meet him.

'Look! Oh, look!' Louisa pointed to the vertical gash that split the rockface from the base of the cliff to the crest. 'It is like a gateway, the entrance to a castle.'

Bakkat took Frost's reins from Jim and led the horse into the dark opening. They dismounted and, leading their own horses, they followed him. The passage was so narrow that they were forced to walk in single file with their stirrup irons almost scraping the rock walls on each side. On both sides of them the glassy smooth stone seemed to reach to the strip of blue high above them. The sky was so remote that it appeared thin as the blade of a rapier. Zama drove the spare horses into the opening behind them but their hoofbeats were muffled by the floor of soft white sand. Their voices echoed weirdly in the confined spaces as the passage twisted and turned through the depths of the rock.

'Oh, look! Look!' Louisa cried, with delight, and pointed to the paintings that covered the walls from the sandy floor to her eye-level. 'Who painted these? Surely they are not the work of men, but of fairies.'

The paintings depicted men and animals, herds of antelope that galloped wildly across the smooth stone, and dainty little men who pursued them with arrows nocked to their bows, ready to shoot. There were herds of giraffe, blotched with ochre and cream, long sinuous necks entwined like serpents. There were rhinoceros, dark and menacing, with nose horns longer than the little human hunters who surrounded them and fired arrows into them so that the red blood flowed and dribbled into pools beneath their hoofs. There were elephant, birds and snakes, all the profusion of creation.

'Who painted these, Bakkat?' Louisa asked again. Bakkat understood the sense of the question but not the language she spoke. He turned on Frost's back and answered her in a rush of clicking words that sounded like snapping twigs.

'What does he say?' Louisa turned to Jim.

'They were painted by his tribe, by his fathers and grand-fathers. They are the hunting dreams of his people – praise-pictures to the courage and beauty of the quarry and the cunning of the hunters.'

'It's like a cathedral,' Louisa's voice was hushed with awe.

'It is a cathedral.' Jim agreed. 'It is one of the holy places of the San.'

The paintings covered the walls on both sides. Some must have been ancient, for the paint had faded and crumbled and other artists had painted over them, but the ghostly images of the ages blended together and formed a tapestry of infinity. They were silent at last, for the sound of their voices seemed sacrilegious in this place.

At last the rock opened ahead of them and they rode towards the narrow vertical blade of sunlight at the end of the passage. Then they emerged through the rock cleft and the sunlight dazzled them. They found themselves high above the world, with a vulture's view across a vastness that left them silent and astonished. Great plains stretched away, dun and limitless, laced with veins of green where the rivers flowed, and dotted with patches of darker forest. Beyond the plains, almost at the reach of the eye, rose an infinity of hills, rank upon rank, like the serrated fangs of a monstrous shark, fading with distance, purple and blue, until they merged with the blue of the tall African sky.

Louisa had never imagined a sky so high or a land so wide, and gazed upon it with a rapt expression, silent until Jim could bear it no longer. This was his land and he wanted her to share it with him and love it the way he loved it.

'Is it not grand?'

'If I had never believed in God before, I would now,' she whispered.

They reached the Gariep river the next morning, at the point where it debouched from the mountains. Over the aeons its waters had cut this deep pass through the rock. The river was running wide and apple green with the thawing of the high snows.

After the mountains, the air here was warm and caressing. The banks of the river were lined with dense stands of sweet thorn and wild willows, carpeted with spring flowers. The saffron-plumed weaver birds were shrieking and fluttering as they wove their basket nests on to the drooping wands of the willows. Five kudu bulls were drinking at the water's edge. They threw up their massive spiralled horns and stared with astonishment at the cavalcade of horses coming down the far

bank to the ford. Then they fled into the sweet thorn with
their horns laid back and water dripping from their muzzles.

Jim was the first across the river, and let out a hoot of
triumph as he examined the deep tracks cut by steel-shod
wheels into the soft earth of the opposite bank. 'The wagons!'
he shouted. 'They passed through here less than a month ago!'

They rode on faster, Jim barely able to contain his eagerness. From a distance of many miles he picked out the single
kopje that stood upon the plain ahead. A forest of camel-thorn
trees surrounded the base of the hill, then the conical slopes
rose steeply to a buttress of grey rock. This formed a plinth for
the weird, wind-carved natural sculpture that surmounted it.
It was the shape of a squatting bull baboon, with domed pate
and low, beetling brows, his elongated muzzle pointed towards
the north, staring out across the lion-coloured plain over
which the springbuck herds drifted like puffs of cinnamon-
coloured smoke.

Jim kicked his feet out of the stirrups and stood erect on
Drumfire's back. Through the lens of the telescope he swept
the base of the distant *kopje*. He laughed with joy as he picked
out a flash of white in the sunlight, like the sail of a tall ship
seen from afar.

'The wagons! They are there, waiting for us.' He dropped
into the saddle and as his backside slapped against the leather
Drumfire jumped forward and bore him away at full gallop.

Tom Courtney was butchering the venison he had killed
that morning. Under the wagon tent one of the servants
was turning the handle, another feeding the strips of fresh
meat into the sausage-making machine. Sarah was working at
the nozzle from which the paste oozed, filling the long tubes
of pig's gut. Tom straightened up, glanced out across the veld
and spotted the distant dustcloud raised by flying hoofs. He
swept off his hat and used it to shade his eyes against the cruel
white glare. 'Rider!' he called to Sarah. 'Coming fast.'

She looked up but kept the long coils of sausage running

between her fingers. 'Who is it?' she demanded. Of course, with a mother's instinct, she knew who it was, but she did not want to jinx it by saying the name until she could see his face.

'It's himself!' Tom cried. 'Or if it is not, I will shave my beard. The little devil must have succeeded in showing Keyser a clean pair of heels.'

For weeks they had waited, worried and tried to cheer each other, insisting that Jim was safe, while hope eroded with the passage of the long days. Now their relief and joy were unbounded.

Tom seized a bridle from the rack on the tailboard of the wagon and ran to one of the horses tethered in the shade. He slipped the bit between its jaws and tightened the cheek-strap. Scorning a saddle he went up on its bare back and galloped out to meet his son.

Jim saw him coming and rose in the stirrups, waving his hat over his head, hooting and bellowing like an escaped maniac. They raced towards each other and then as they came level, dismounted on the run, hurled by the momentum of their mounts into each other's arms. They hugged each other, beat each other on the back and danced in a circle trying to swing each other off their feet. Tom ruffled Jim's long hair and pulled and twisted his ears painfully.

'I should thrash you within an inch of your life, you little *skellum*,' he scolded. 'You have given your mother and me the worst days of our lives.' He held him at arm's length and glared at him lovingly. 'I don't know why we bothered. We should have let Keyser have you, and good riddance.' His voice choked, and he hugged Jim again. 'Come on, boy! Your mother is waiting for you. I hope she gives you a royal slice of her tongue.'

Jim's reunion with Sarah was less boisterous but if anything even more loving than it had been with his father. 'We were so worried about you,' she said. 'I thank God with all my heart for your deliverance.'

Then her first instinct was to feed him. Through mouthfuls of jam roly-poly and milk tart he gave his parents a colourful, if expurgated, account of his exploits since he had last seen them. He did not mention Louisa, and they were all aware of the omission.

At last Sarah could contain herself no longer. She stood over him and placed her fists on her hips. 'That's all very well and good, James Archibald Courtney, but what about the girl?' Jim choked on the tart, then looked shamefaced and at a loss for words.

'Out with it, boy!' Tom said, in support of his wife. 'What about the girl – or woman or whatever she may be?'

'You will meet her. She's coming now,' Jim said, in a subdued voice, and pointed to the horses and riders coming towards them across the plain in a cloud of their own dust. Tom and Sarah stood together and watched it drawing closer.

Tom spoke first. 'An't no girl there that I can see,' he said, with finality. 'Zama and Bakkat, yes, but no girl.'

Jim jumped up from the trestle table and came to join them. 'She must be . . .' His voice trailed off as he realized that his father was right. Louisa was not with them. He ran to meet Zama and Bakkat as they rode into camp. 'Where is Welanga? What have you done with her?'

Zama and Bakkat looked at each other, both waiting for the other to answer. At times such as these Bakkat could be conveniently mute. Zama shrugged and took the responsibility of replying. 'She will not come,' he said.

'Why not?' Jim shouted.

'She is afraid.'

'Afraid?' Jim was puzzled. 'What has she got to be afraid of?'

Zama did not reply but glanced significantly at Tom and Sarah.

'What a time for her to start jibbing!' Jim strode towards where Drumfire was enjoying a nosebag of oats. 'I will go and fetch her.'

'No, Jim!' Sarah called softly, but in a tone that stopped him in his tracks. He stared at his mother. 'Saddle Sugarbush for me,' she told him. 'I will go to her.'

From the saddle she looked down at Jim. 'What's her name?'

'Louisa,' he answered. 'Louisa Leuven. She speaks good English.'

Sarah nodded. 'I may be some time,' she said to her husband. 'Now, don't come looking for me, do you hear?' She had known Tom from girlhood, and loved him past the power of words to describe, but she knew that at times he had the tact of a wounded bull buffalo. She flicked the reins and Sugarbush cantered out of camp.

She saw the girl half a mile ahead, sitting under a camel-thorn tree on one of the fallen dead branches with Trueheart tethered beside her. Louisa scrambled to her feet when she saw Sarah riding towards her. On the vast plain she was a tiny forlorn figure. Sarah rode up to her and reined in Sugarbush. 'You are Louisa? Louisa Leuven?'

'Yes, Mistress Courtney.' Louisa took off her hat and her hair tumbled down. Sarah blinked at its golden profusion. Louisa bobbed a small curtsy and waited respectfully for her to speak again.

'How do you know who I am?' Sarah asked.

'He looks just like you, mistress,' Louisa explained, 'and he told me all about you and his father.' Her voice was low but sweet, and trembled on the verge of tears.

Sarah was taken aback. This was not at all what she had expected. But what *had* she expected of an escaped convict? Hard-boiled defiance? World-weariness? Corruption and depravity? She looked into those blue eyes and could find no vice in them.

'You're very young, Louisa.'

'Yes, mistress.' Her voice broke. 'I am so sorry. I didn't mean to get Jim into trouble. I didn't mean to take him away from you.' She was weeping slow, silent tears, which sparkled like jewels in the sunlight. 'We haven't done anything bad together, I promise you.'

Sarah stepped down from Sugarbush's back and went to her. She placed one arm round her shoulders and Louisa clung

200

to her. Sarah knew that what she was doing was dangerous, but her maternal instincts were strong, and the girl was so young. The aura of innocence that surrounded her was almost palpable. Sarah found herself drawn irresistibly to her.

'Come, child.' Gently Sarah led her into the shade, and they sat side by side on the dead branch.

They talked while the sun climbed to its zenith, then began its slow slide down the sky. At first Sarah's questions were probing, and she fought her inclination to let down all her defences and allow this stranger into her inner keep, into the place of trust. From bitter experience she knew that the devil often conceals his true nature behind a beautiful exterior.

Louisa's replies were open, unstinted, almost disconcertingly honest. She never avoided Sarah's searching gaze. She seemed pathetically eager to please, and Sarah felt her reservations crumbling.

At last she took the girl's hand. 'Why do you tell me all this, Louisa?' she asked.

'Because Jim risked his life to save me, and you are Jim's mother. I owe you that at least.' Sarah felt her own tears rising to the surface. She was silent while she brought herself under control.

At last Louisa broke the quiet. 'I know what you are thinking, Mistress Courtney. You are wondering why I was on a convict ship. You wish to know what crime I am guilty of.' Sarah could not trust her voice to deny it. Of course, she wanted to know the answer. Her only son was in love with this girl, and she had to know.

'I will tell you,' Louisa said. 'I have told no one except Jim, but now I will tell you.'

And she did. When she had finished Sarah was weeping with her. 'It is late.' She glanced at the height of the sun, and stood up. 'Come, Louisa, we will go home now.'

Tom Courtney was astonished to see that his wife had been weeping. Her eyes were swollen and red. He could not remember the last time that had happened, for Sarah was not much given to tears. She did not dismount, or make any move to introduce him to the pale girl who rode beside her into the camp.

'We need to be alone for a while, before Louisa is ready to meet you,' she told him firmly, and the girl kept her head down and her eyes averted as they rode past and went to the last wagon in the line. The two women disappeared behind the afterclap, the canvas screen at the back of the wagon, and Sarah called for the servants to bring the copper hipbath and buckets of hot water from the cooking fire. The mysterious chest that she had ordered to be loaded on to the wagon, which they had carried with them from High Weald, contained everything that a girl might need.

The two men were sitting beside the fire on the *riempie* camp chairs, the backs and seats laced with the criss-crossed rawhide strips that gave the chairs the name. They were drinking coffee, and Tom had laced their mugs with a liberal dram of Hollands gin. They were still discussing everything that had overtaken the family since their last meeting, and were making plans on how to proceed. They both skirted tactfully around the subject of Louisa and how she fitted into these plans. The nearest Tom had come to it was to say, 'That is women's business. We will have to let your mother decide.'

Night had fallen and out on the plain the jackals were wailing. 'What is your mother doing?' Tom complained. 'It's long past my dinner time, and I'm hungry.' As if she had heard, Sarah came up from the last wagon carrying a lantern, and leading Louisa by the hand. As they stepped into the firelight, both men stared bemusedly at the girl. Jim was as amazed as his father.

Sarah had washed Louisa's hair with lavender-scented soap

from England, then rubbed it dry, brushed it, trimmed the ragged ends and caught it up with a satin ribbon. It hung down her back in a lustrous wave. Her blouse was buttoned demurely at the throat and the sleeves at the wrists. The full skirt just allowed her ankles to peep out from under the hem. White stockings hid the faint scars of the leg irons.

The firelight emphasized the smooth perfection of her skin, and the size of her eyes. Tom stared at her, and Sarah pre-empted any humorous remark he might come up with. 'This is Jim's friend, Louisa Leuven. She may be staying with us for a while.' It was an understatement. 'Louisa, this is my husband Mr Thomas Courtney.' Louisa made one of her graceful curtsies.

'You are welcome, Louisa.' Tom bowed.

Sarah smiled. She hadn't seen him do that for a while – her husband was not the courtly kind. So much for your prison drab, Tom Courtney, she thought complacently, I give you instead a golden Dutch daffodil.

She glanced at her only son, and saw his expression. No doubt about where Jim stands either. It seems that Louisa has been unanimously elected to the Courtney clan.

Later that night Sarah and Tom settled under the blankets in their nightclothes: even down here on the plains the nights were chilly. For twenty years they had slept like spoons, one body fitted into the curve of the other, changing places when one rolled over without waking or losing contact. That night they lay in poignant silence, neither wanting to be the first to speak.

Tom gave in first.

'She is rather pretty,' he ventured.

'You might say so,' Sarah agreed. 'You might even go so far as to say she's no prison drab.'

'I never said that.' Tom sat up indignantly, but she pulled him down again, and cuddled comfortably into the warm bulge of his belly. 'Well, if I did say it, I take it back now.'

She knew how much it cost him to admit that he was wrong, and her heart went out to him. 'I have spoken to her,' she said. 'She's a good girl.'

'Well, if you say so, that's all right, then.' He closed the subject. They began drifting towards sleep.

'I love you, Tom Courtney,' she murmured drowsily.

'I love you, Sarah Courtney,' he replied. 'Young Jim will be a lucky lad if she ever makes him half as happy as you make me.' Usually he scorned what he called mawkishness. This was a rare pronouncement.

'Why, Tom Courtney! Sometimes you can still surprise me,' she whispered.

They were all up before dawn. Louisa emerged from her wagon, which was parked close alongside Tom and Sarah's. Sarah had placed her there deliberately, and sequestered Jim in the furthest. If there had been any nocturnal shenanigans she would have heard every last whisper.

Poor child, Sarah thought with an inward smile. She had to listen to my Tom's snores all night long. In the event her precautions had proved unnecessary: Tom and the jackals had provided all the vocal entertainment and there had been not so much as a whisper from Louisa's wagon.

When Louisa saw Sarah already at the cooking fire she ran to help her with the breakfast, and soon the two were chatting like friends. While Louisa laid rows of sausages to splutter and hiss on the grill, Sarah poured batter on to the flat iron griddle and watched it brown into pancakes.

Tom and Jim were already inspecting the wagons Tom had brought up from the Cape. These were large, powerful vehicles, built in the colony to a design that was constantly being modified to suit the rough African conditions. They ran on four wheels, the front pair of which were used to steer. The pivoted front axle was connected to the *disselboom*, the long, sturdy main drag pole. The team of twelve oxen were inspanned in pairs by a simple system of yokes, yoke-pins and rawhide ropes. The main harness, or *trek-tow*, was connected to the front end of the *disselboom*. The rear wheels were much larger in diameter than the front pair.

The body of the vehicle was a capacious eighteen feet in length, with a breadth of four feet. At the bow the wooden sides were two feet high, rising to over three at the stern. Along both sides of the body, iron staples were riveted to hold the arched greenwood boughs over which was spread the tent. The interior was about five feet high, so a tall man had to stoop beneath it. The awning was double-layered. A strong canvas outer sail rendered it waterproof, or at least deterred the ingress of large quantities of rainwater. A mat of coarse coir fibre, woven from the husk of the coconut, insulated the interior from the worst heat of the sun. The long sail curtains at front and back were called the foreclap and afterclap. The driver's seat was a large chest that stretched the full breadth of the wagon, and there was a similar chest at the rear, the forechest and the afterchest. Along the outsides of the body and under the floorboards were rows of iron hooks from which were suspended pots and pans, tools, canvas bags, powder kegs and other heavy paraphernalia.

Within the wagon another row of hooks held the square-cut canvas side pockets into which were stuffed spare clothing, combs, brushes, soap and towels, tobacco and pipes, pistols, knives, and anything that might be needed urgently. There were also adjustable pegs to support the cardell, the comfort-able and spacious bed upon which the traveller slept. By means of the pegs, this could be raised or lowered to make room for the bags, boxes, chests and kegs stored beneath it. Like the camp chairs, the bed was also strung with rawhide *riempies*, criss-crossed like the catgut strings of the racquets used in the royal game of tennis.

Tom had brought four of these enormous vehicles and the oxen to pull them. Each vehicle required a skilled driver, and a *voorloper*, a lad to lead the front oxen by a halter of kudu skin looped about the base of their horns.

All four wagons were heavily laden, and after breakfast Sarah and Louisa were summoned to help take an inventory of the contents. For this purpose the wagons had to be unloaded, and all the goods checked. Tom, as an old ship's captain, had made out an itemized bill-of-lading, and Jim had to know exactly where each item was stowed. It would be wasted and frustrating labour if somewhere out in the wilderness they had to unload and search all four wagons to find a lynch-pin, horse-shoes or a hank of sail twine.

Even Jim was amazed at what his father had provided for them. 'It's all your inheritance, my boy, and there's no more coming to you. Use it wisely.'

The huge yellow-wood chest that Sarah had packed for Louisa was placed in the bows of the wagon that would be Louisa's home over the months, perhaps years to come. It contained combs and brushes, needles and thread, a complete wardrobe of clothing and rolls of cloth to make more, gloves and bonnets to protect delicate skin from the sun, scissors and nail files, scented English soaps and medicines. Then there was a thick book of recipes and prescriptions written in Sarah's own hand, invaluable empirical knowledge gathered at first hand: instructions for cooking everything from an elephant's trunk to wild mushrooms, for making soap and tanning leather; lists of medicinal wild herbs and edible plants and tubers; cures for sunstroke, stomach upsets and a baby's teething problems. Then there was a small library of other books, including a medical lexicon published in London and an almanac beginning at the year 1731, the Holy Bible, ink, pens and writing paper, a box of watercolours and brushes, reams of fine-quality drawing paper, knitting needles and wool, a roll of soft tanned leather from which to make the uppers for footwear – the soles would be cut from buffalo rawhide. Then there was bed-linen, blankets, pillows stuffed with wild-goose down, shawls and knitted stockings, a beautiful kaross of jackal fur, a long coat of sheepskin, and a waterproof cape of tarpaulin with an attached hood. That was but the half of it.

Jim's chest was smaller and contained all his old and wellworn clothing, his razor and strop, his hunting and skinning knives, fishing line and hooks, the tinder box that held his flint and steel, a magnifying glass, a spare telescope, and other items that he would never have considered. They bespoke his mother's concern for his well-being: a long tarpaulin waterproof coat and a wide-brimmed hat of the same material, scarves and gloves, neckerchiefs and woollen socks, a dozen bottles of extract-of-lettuce cough mixture and another dozen of Dr Chamberlain's sovereign diarrhoea remedy.

When they came to the list of general stores and provisions, this seemed endless. At the head of it were eight quarter-chests of coffee beans, totalling six hundred pounds in weight, and three hundred pounds of sugar. Jim was overjoyed to see them. Then there were two hundred pounds of salt for preserving venison, ten pounds of pepper, a large box of strong curry powder, sacks of rice, flour and maize meal, bags of spices and bottles of flavouring essences for stews and cakes, bottles of jam and kegs of pickles from the kitchens of High Weald. Cheeses and hams hung from the hooks inside the wagons. There were pumpkins and sun-dried maize on the cob, and packets and boxes of vegetable seeds to be planted wherever they camped long enough to raise a crop.

For cooking and eating there were three-legged pots, baking, stewing and frying pans, saucepans, gridirons and kettles, water buckets, plates and mugs, forks, spoons and soup ladles. Each wagon was equipped with two fifty-gallon Fagies, or water casks. Then there were canteens and water bottles of military design to carry on horseback. There was fifty pounds of yellow soap, and when this was expended Jim could make more with hippopotamus fat and wood ash.

For the maintenance of the wagons there were two drums of tar to be mixed with animal fat to grease the wheel hubs, heavy coils of rawhide trek ropes, *riems* and straps, yokes and yoke-pins, lynch-pins for the wheel hubs, rolls of canvas and coir matting to repair the tents. One of the afterchests contained a selection of tools such as augers, brace and bits, wood planes and spoke shaves, chisels, a heavy vice, blacksmith's tongs and hammers, and a huge selection of other carpenter's and blacksmith's equipment stores, including two hundred horseshoes, bags of nails and drawing knives to trim hoofs.

'Now, these are important, Jim.' Tom showed him the iron pestle and mortar for crushing rock samples, and a nest of gold pans, each a broad flat dish with a groove around the circumference. The groove would capture the heavy flakes of gold when the ore or river-sands were washed.

'Old Humbert showed you how to use them.' Humbert had been Tom's gold-finder until his liver had succumbed to a steady diet of Hollands gin and cheap Cape brandy. 'There is also a tub of slow-match – two hundred yards of fuse for blasting open the reef when you find gold.'

As trade goods and gifts to African chieftains and potentates, Tom had selected stores that he knew were highly valued by all the wild tribes they might meet in the far interior: two hundred cheap knives, axe heads, bags of Venetian trade beads in fifty different patterns and colours, hand mirrors, tinder boxes, coils of thin copper and brass wire to be converted into bracelets, anklets and other ornaments by the indigenes who received them.

There were two fine English hunting-saddles and tack, common saddles for the servants, two pack-saddles for bringing in venison from the veld, a large bell tent for a kitchen and dining room, folding chairs and tables to furnish it.

For hunting and defence against attack by the more warlike tribes Tom had provided twenty naval cutlasses and thirty smooth-bore Brown Bess muskets, which most of the servants could load and fire with some proficiency, two heavy German elephant guns that threw four to the pound and could drive to the heart of an elephant or a rhinoceros, and a pair of iniquitously expensive London-made two-grooved double-barrelled rifles so accurate that Jim knew from experience that with the conical bullet he could bring down an oryx or kudu at four hundred paces. There was one other rifle, a lovely little lady's gun made in France. Its provenance was noble for the lock was gold inlaid with the coat of arms of the dukes of d'Ademas. Tom had given it to Sarah when Jim was born. It was light and accurate and there was a pink velvet cheek pad on the walnut stock. Although nowadays she seldom hunted, Jim had once seen his mother drop a running springbuck at two hundred paces with this weapon. Now she was giving it to Louisa. 'It may be useful.'

Sarah dismissed Louisa's thanks, but impulsively Louisa threw both arms round her and whispered, 'I shall treasure your gifts, and always remember your kindness to me.'

To serve this battery of guns there was an assortment of lead ladles, bullet moulds, loading ramrods, shot-belts and powder flasks. To manufacture ammunition there were five hundredweight of lead in bars, fifty pounds of pewter to harden the balls to be used against heavy game, twenty thousand prepared lead musket balls, twenty kegs of first-class sporting gunpowder for the rifles and a hundred kegs of coarse black powder for the Brown Bess muskets, two thousand gunflints, greased patches to ensure a tight fit of the conical bullets in the rifle bore, fine cotton cloth to be cut into more patches, and a large keg of rendered hippopotamus fat to grease them.

So great was this store of goods that by nightfall on the second day they had not finished reloading the wagons. 'That can wait until tomorrow,' Tom said expansively, 'but now the ladies are free to make supper for us.'

The last meal together was marred by melancholy silences when they were reminded of their imminent parting. These were followed by bursts of forced jollity. In the end Tom brought it to its conclusion with typical directness. 'Early start tomorrow.' He stood up and took Sarah's hand. As he led her to their quarters in the first wagon he whispered, 'Can we leave them alone? Should we not chaperone them?'

Sarah laughed gaily at him. 'Tom Courtney, what a time for you to turn prissy on me! They have already spent weeks alone in the wilderness together, and it seems they are about to spend several years more. What good could you do now?'

Tom grinned ruefully, picked her up in his arms and boosted her into the wagon. Later as they settled in the cardell bed Sarah murmured, 'Don't worry about Louisa. I have told you already that she is a good girl, and we have brought up Jim to behave like a gentleman. Nothing has happened between them yet, and nothing will until the time is ripe. Then herds of wild buffalo could not prevent it. If things have changed when next we all meet we can think of a wedding. As I recall, Tom Courtney, you showed less restraint when we first met, and there was some delay before we celebrated our own nuptials.'

'In these matters, at least, you are wiser than me,' Tom admitted and pulled her closer. 'Mind you, Mistress Courtney, there are no herds of wild buffalo present to prevent anything happening here tonight, between you and me.'

'Indeed, Mr Courtney, how perceptive of you,' she said, and giggled like a girl.

They had taken breakfast and completed the rest of the loading before the sun had fully dispersed the last of the night's chill. With a single stroke of his trek whip Smallboy, the huge head driver, gave the signal to begin inspanning the oxen. This formidable instrument was a bamboo pole twenty-two feet in length, with a whip thong even longer. Without leaving his seat on the wagon or removing his clay pipe from his mouth, Smallboy could kill a fly on the rump of the lead ox in his team with the tapered forelash of kudu hide and not disturb a hair on the beast's back.

Now as he cracked the long whip with a report like a double-shotted pistol that could be heard a mile away across the plain, the lead boys ran to yoke the oxen in pairs and bring them in from the veld where they had been grazing. They drove them in with shouted insults and well-aimed pebbles.

'Come, Scotland, you snake with twenty-two fathers and only one mother.'

'Hey! Squint Eye, look this way or you will fetch another stone.'

'Wake up, Lizard, you lazy *skellum*!'

'Move along, Blackheart, don't try any of your tricks today.'

Pair after pair the beasts were linked into the span. Then the leaders, the strongest and most tractable animals, were led to their places. Smallboy fired his great whip again and, without apparent strain, the oxen walked away and the heavily loaded wagon rolled smoothly after them. At intervals of a few hundred paces the other three wagons fell into caravan behind the leader. They maintained the wide spacing to avoid the dust raised by the hoofs of the leading oxen and the iron-rimmed wheels of the vehicles they pulled. Behind the wagons followed a loose herd of horses, spare oxen, milk cows and sheep and goats for slaughter. Although they spread out to graze, they were kept in a loose formation and brought along at a leisurely pace by four herd-boys. None of these lads was older than thirteen or younger than ten. They were some of the orphans Sarah had gathered over the years, and who had pleaded to be allowed to join in the great adventure with Somoya, whom they revered. At their heels ran a motley pack of mongrel hounds, who would earn their keep by hunting and finding wounded game or stray animals.

Soon only one small dog-cart remained in the encampment below the Baboon's Head *kopje*, but it was packed and the horses were grazing nearby, ready to take Tom and Sarah back to High Weald. The family were reluctant to part. They drew out the last hour together, drinking a final mug of coffee around the smouldering fire, remembering all the things they had forgotten to say over the last few days, and repeating all those that had been said many times already.

Tom had kept one of the most serious matters to the last. Now he fetched a mariner's tarpaulin chart case from the dog-cart and came back to sit beside Jim again. He opened the flat case, and drew out a chart. 'This is a copy of a chart I've been drawing up over the past fifteen years. I have kept the original, and this is the only copy. It's a valuable document,' he told Jim.

'I will keep it safe,' his son promised.

Tom spread the sheet of heavy parchment on the ground in front of them, and placed small stones on each corner to hold it down in the light morning breeze. Jim studied the finely drawn and coloured topography of the south continent. 'I had no idea, Father, that you were a talented artist.'

His father looked mildly uncomfortable and glanced at Sarah. 'Well,' he drawled, 'I had a little help.'

'You are too modest, Tom.' Sarah smiled. 'You did all the supervision.'

'Of course,' Tom chuckled, 'that was the difficult part.' Then he was serious again. 'The outline of the coast is accurate, more accurate than any other map I have seen. Your uncle Dorian and I made the observations as we sailed and traded along both the western and eastern coastlines over the last twenty years. You have been on one of these voyages with me, Jim, so you will remember these places.' He named them as he pointed them out. 'On the west coast the Bay of Whales and New Devon Harbour – I named it for the old country. On the east coast this is Frank's Lagoon, where your great-grandfather buried the treasure he captured from the Dutch galleon the *Standvastigheid*. It's a fine anchorage guarded from the open sea by an entrance protected by rocky headlands. Here much further north is another great bay, which the Portuguese call Nativity Bay, or Natal.'

'But you don't have godowns built at these ports, Father,' Jim interjected. 'I know that they are desolate, deserted places, all of them.'

'You're right, of course, Jim. But one of our schooners calls in at these places every six months or so, depending on the season and the winds. The natives know that we come regularly, and they wait for us there with hides, gum arabic, ivory and other goods to trade.'

Jim nodded.

Tom went on, 'Because you have already been there, you will recognize any of those places on the coast when you reach it. You know where the mail stones are.' These were large brightly painted flat stones set at prominent places on shore under which visiting sailors could leave letters in waterproof tarpaulin packets to be found by other ships and carried on to the person to whom they were addressed. 'If you leave a letter there you know that I or your uncle will find it in time. We also will leave them for you, on the off-chance.'

'Or I could wait there for the next visit of one of our ships.'

'Yes, Jim, you could do that. But make sure it's not a VOC

ship that you meet. By now Governor van de Witten will have a large bounty on your head and Louisa's too.'

They all looked serious as they considered the predicament in which the young couple now stood. Tom went on quickly to cover the pause: 'Before you reach the coast, however, you will have to cross hundreds, even thousands of leagues of virtually unexplored wilderness.' Tom spread his big scarred hand across the map. 'Just look what lies ahead of your wagons. It's an opportunity I've been hankering for all my life. This place where we are sitting now is as far into the interior as I have ever been able to travel.'

'You have nobody to blame for that but yourself, Thomas Courtney,' Sarah told him. 'I never stopped you, but you were always too busy making money.'

'And now it's too late. I'm getting old and fat.' Tom put on a lugubrious expression. 'But Jim here is going in my place.' He stared longingly at the map, then lifted his gaze across the plain to where the wagon train was rolling away in its own yellow dustcloud, and murmured, 'You lucky devil, you are going to see places never before looked upon by civilized eyes.'

Then he returned his attention to the map. 'Over the years I have sought out every man, black, white and yellow, who was ever reputed to have travelled beyond the borders of the Cape colony. I questioned them exhaustively. When Dorian and I went ashore on our trading expeditions we interrogated the natives we traded with. I have written everything that I ever learned from these sources on to this map. I have spelled the names as they sounded in my ear. Here, in the margins and on the reverse side, I have made notes of every story and legend I was told, the names of the different tribes, their villages, kings and chiefs. Then I have tried to mark in the rivers, lakes and water-holes, but there was no way of telling the distances between them and their compass bearings from each other. You, Bakkat, Zama and Smallboy between you speak a dozen or so native dialects. You will be able to hire guides and translators as you travel on and come in contact with new and unknown tribes.' Tom folded the map again and placed it back with reverential care in the tarpaulin case. He handed it to Jim. 'Guard it well, my boy. It will guide you on your journey.'

Then he went back to the dog-cart and brought out a hard leather case. He opened it and showed Jim what it contained. 'I would have liked you to have one of those new-fangled chronometers that Harrison in London has so recently perfected, so that you could more accurately determine your latitude and longitude as you travel, but I have never even laid eyes on one, and they do say that even if you find one they cost five hundred pounds each. The same goes for one of John Hadley's reflecting quadrants. But here are my trusty old compass and octant. They belonged to your grandfather, but you know well how to use them, and with this copy of the Admiralty tables you will always be pretty sure at least of your latitude any time you can see the sun. You should be able to navigate to any of the places I have marked on the chart.'

Jim took the leather case from his father, opened it and lifted out the beautiful, complex instrument. It was of Italian manufacture. On top was the brass ring from which it could be suspended to establish its own level, then the rotating brass rings lovingly engraved with star charts, circles of latitude and a marginal circle of hours. The alidade, or diametral rule, which served as a sun sight, could pick up the sun's shadow, and throw it across the coinciding circles of time and latitude.

Jim fondled it, then looked up at his father. 'I shall never be able to repay you for all these wonderful gifts and for all you have done for me. I do not deserve such love and generosity.'

'Let your mother and me be the judge of that,' Tom said gruffly. 'And now we must start for home.' He called to the two servants who were returning to the colony with them. They ran to inspan the draught horses to the dog-cart, and to saddle Tom's big bay gelding.

Up on Drumfire and Trueheart, Jim and Louisa rode beside the dog-cart for almost a league, taking this last chance to repeat their farewells. When at last they knew they should go no further if they wanted to catch up with their own wagons before sunset, they lingered and watched the dog-cart dwindling across the dusty veld.

'He's coming back,' Louisa exclaimed, as she spotted Tom returning at a gallop. He reined in beside them again.

'Listen to me, Jim, my lad, don't you forget to keep a journal. I want you to record all your navigational notes. Don't forget the names of the native chiefs and their towns. Keep a lookout for any goods we might be able to trade with them in future.'

'Yes, Father. We have spoken about this already,' Jim reminded him.

'And the gold pans,' Tom went on.

'I will pan the sands of every riverbed we cross.' Jim laughed. 'I won't forget.'

'You remind him, Louisa. He is a scatterbrain, this son of mine. I don't know where he gets it from. Must be his mother.'

'I promise, Mr Courtney.' Louisa nodded seriously.

Tom turned back to Jim. 'James Archibald, you look after this young lady. She is obviously a sensible girl, and much too good for you.'

At last Tom left them and rode off after the dog-cart, turning in the saddle every few minutes to wave back at them. They saw him rejoin the distant cart, and then suddenly Jim exclaimed, 'Name of the devil, I forgot to send my respects and farewells to Mansur and Uncle Dorian. Come on!' They galloped in pursuit of the cart. When they caught up with it they all dismounted and embraced again.

'This time we really are leaving,' Jim said at last, but his father rode back with them a mile before he could bring himself to let them go, and he waved them out of sight.

The wagons had long ago disappeared into the distance, but the tracks of their iron-rimmed wheels were scored into the earth, and as easy to follow as a signposted road. As the two of them rode along it the herds of springbuck were driven ahead of them like flocks of sheep, the smaller herds mingling with those ahead, until the land seemed to seethe and the grass was hidden beneath this living sea.

Other larger wild animals became part of this tide of life.

Dark troops of gnu pranced and cavorted, shaking their shaggy manes, arching their necks like thoroughbreds and kicking their hind legs to the sky as they chased each other in circles. Squadrons of quagga galloped away in ranks, barking like packs of hounds. These wild horses of the Cape, striped like the zebra except for their plain brown legs, were so numerous that the Cape burghers killed them in thousands for their hides. They sewed them into grain bags and left the carcasses for the vultures and the hyenas.

Louisa looked upon this host with amazement. 'I have never seen such a marvellous sight,' she cried.

'In this land we are blessed with such multitudes that no man need stint himself or put up his gun until his arms are too exhausted to lift it,' Jim agreed. 'I know of one great hunter who lives in the colony. He destroyed three hundred head of big game in a single day, and rode four horses to a standstill to achieve it. What a feat that was.' Jim shook his head in admiration.

The campfires guided them to the laagered wagons in the last mile of darkness, where Zama had the black iron kettle boiling and coffee beans freshly ground in the mortar.

Relying on his father's chart and navigational instruments, Jim steered the wagons north by east. The days fell into a natural rhythm, and became weeks, which in their turn became months. Each morning Jim rode out with Bakkat to spy out the land that lay ahead, and to find the next water-hole or river. He took his breakfast with him in the canteen slung with his bedroll on the back of his saddle, and Bakkat led a pack-horse to bring in any game they bagged.

Often Louisa was busy around the wagons, mending and cleaning, directing the servants in running her movable home the way she wanted, but most days she was free to ride out with Jim on Trueheart. From the beginning she was enchanted by the animals and birds that teemed in every direction she cast her eye. Jim taught her the names of all of them and they discussed their habits in detail. Bakkat joined in with an endless fund of facts and magical stories.

When they halted at midday to rest and graze the horses, Louisa brought out of her saddlebag one of the pads Sarah had given her and sketched the interesting things they had seen that day. Jim lounged nearby and advised on how she might improve each portrait, though secretly he was amazed at her artistic skills.

He insisted she always carry the little French rifle in the gun sheath under her right knee. 'When you need a gun you need it in a hurry,' he told her, 'and you had better be sure you know how to use it.' He rehearsed her in loading, priming and firing the weapon. With the report and recoil of her first shot she cried out with alarm and would have dropped the rifle, had not Jim been ready to snatch it out of her hands. After much reassurance and encouragement he convinced her that it had not been as fearful an experience as her reaction had indicated, and Louisa expressed herself ready for a second attempt. To encourage her, Jim placed his own hat on a low thornbush twenty paces away.

'I tell you now, Hedgehog, you'll not come within ten feet of it.' It was a calculated challenge. Louisa's eyes narrowed into blue diamond chips of determination. This time her hand was steady. When the gunsmoke cleared after the shot, Jim's hat was spinning high in the air. It was his favourite hat, and he raced after it. When he stuck his forefinger through the hole in the brim his expression was of such disbelief and dismay that Bakkat dissolved into hoots of mirth. He staggered in circles demonstrating with hand signals how the hat had sailed into the air. Then his legs gave way under him, and he collapsed in the dust and beat his belly with both hands, shrieking with laughter.

His mirth was infectious and Louisa broke into peals of laughter. Up to that time Jim had not heard her laugh so naturally and so wholeheartedly. He placed the riddled hat on his head, and joined in the merriment. Later he stuck an eagle feather in the hole and wore it proudly.

They sat in the shade of a sweet thorn tree and ate the

lunch of cold venison and pickles that Louisa had packed into his canteen. Every few minutes one of them would start laughing again and set off the other two.

'Let Welanga shoot your hat again,' Bakkat pleaded. 'It was the greatest joke of my life.'

Jim declined, and instead he blazed the trunk of the sweet thorn tree with his hunting knife. The bright white patch formed an idle target. He was learning that when Louisa set her mind on something she was determined and tenacious. She swiftly mastered the art of loading the rifle: measuring the powder charge from the flask, ramming the wad down upon it, selecting a symmetrical ball from the bag on her belt, wrapping it in the greased patch, and rodding it down the bore, tapping it home with the little wooden mallet until it seated on the wad, then priming the pan and closing the frizzen over it to prevent it spilling.

By the second day of instruction she could load and fire the weapon unaided, and soon she was able to hit the sap-oozing blaze on a tree with four balls out of five.

'This is becoming too easy for you now, Hedgehog. Time for your first real hunt.'

Early the next morning she loaded the rifle in the way he had trained her, and they rode out together. As they approached the first herds of grazing game Jim showed her how to use Trueheart as a stalking horse. They both dismounted and Jim led Drumfire, while she followed in his tracks leading the mare and staying close to her flank. Screened by the bodies of the horses they angled across the front of a small bachelor herd of springbuck rams. These animals had never seen human beings or horses before and they stood and stared with innocent amazement at the strange creatures passing by. Jim approached them on the diagonal, not heading directly towards the herd, which might have alarmed them and set them to flight.

At the point of closest approach, less than a hundred paces from the nearest animals in the herd, Jim halted Drumfire and whistled softly. Louisa dropped Trueheart's reins. The mare stopped and stood obediently, trembling in anticipation of the shot she knew was coming. Louisa sank down and, from a seated position, took careful aim at a ram who was standing broadside to her and slightly separated from the rest of the herd. Jim had drummed into her the point of aiming behind the shoulder, showing it to her on a drawing of the animal, and on carcasses that he had shot and brought into camp.

Nevertheless, she found this different from aiming at a blaze on a tree. Her heart was racing, her hands shook almost uncontrollably and her aim danced up and down and across.

Softly Jim called to her, 'Remember what I told you.'

In the excitement of the hunt she had forgotten his advice. 'Take a deep breath. Swing it up smoothly. Let half of your breath out. Don't hang on the trigger. Squeeze it off as your sights bear.'

She lowered the rifle, gathered herself and did it just the way he had taught her. The little rifle felt light as thistledown as it floated up, and fired of its own accord, so unexpectedly that she was startled by the crash of the shot and long spurt of gunsmoke.

There was a thud of the ball striking, the ram leaped high in the air, and came down in a graceful pirouette. Then its legs collapsed under it, it rolled like a ball across the sun-baked earth, and at last stretched out and lay still. Jim let out a whoop of triumph and raced out to where it lay. With the smoking rifle in her hand Louisa ran after him.

'Shot cleanly through the heart,' Jim cried. 'I could not have done it better myself.' He turned to meet her as she came running up. Her cheeks were flushed, her hair had escaped in glorious disarray from under her hat and her eyes sparkled. Despite her efforts to avoid the sun, her skin had taken on the colour of a ripe peach. Her excitement matched his own, and he thought he had never seen anything as beautiful as she was at that moment.

He reached out with both arms to take her into his embrace. She came up short, just out of his reach and backed away from him. With a mighty effort, he checked his impulse. They stared at each other, and he saw the horror replace the sparkle in her eyes, her revulsion at a masculine touch. It was only a fleeting moment, but he knew how close he had come to disaster. All these months spent in building her trust, in showing her how he respected her, and cared for her well-being, how he wanted to protect and cherish her, all of that so nearly lost in a boisterously impulsive gesture.

He turned away quickly, giving her time to recover from her fright. 'It's a magnificent buck, fat as butter.'

As the animal relaxed in death, the long fold of skin that ran down the centre of its back opened, and it displayed the dorsal plume of snowy white hair. Jim stooped and ran one finger down the fold of skin, then raised the finger to his nose. 'It's the only animal that smells like a flower.' A pale yellow wax from the animal's sebaceous glands coated his finger. He did not look at her. 'Try it,' he suggested.

She averted her eyes from his as she combed her fingers through the animal's dorsal plume, then held them to her own nose. 'Perfumed!' she exclaimed, with surprise. He called Bakkat and between them they gralloched the springbuck and hoisted the carcass on to the pack-saddle. The wagons were tiny specks across the plain. They rode towards them, but the joyous mood of the morning was spoilt, and they were silent. Jim was consumed with despair. It seemed that he and Louisa had lost all the ground they had travelled together, and were back at the starting point of their relationship.

Fortunately, when they reached the wagons there was something to distract him. Smallboy had driven the lead wagon over the underground burrow of an antbear, and the earth had collapsed. The heavily laden vehicle had crashed into the excavation as far as its floorboards. A number of spokes in the offside front wheel were shattered, and the vehicle was firmly stuck. They had to unload it before it was light enough for a double span of oxen to heave it out. Darkness had fallen before they had freed the wagon. It was too late to start repairs to the broken front wheel. The shattered spokes would have to be replaced, and the work of shaving the new parts to fit was finicky and might take days.

Tired and sweat-drenched, Jim went to his own wagon. 'Bath! Hot water!' he shouted at Zama.

'Welanga has already ordered it,' Zama told him disapprovingly.

Well, at least, we know whose side you're on, Jim thought bitterly, but his mood lifted when he found the galvanized-iron bath filled with hot water waiting for him, a bar of soap and a clean towel laid out beside it. After he had bathed he went to the kitchen tent.

Louisa was working at the cooking fire. He was still feeling too affronted by her rejection to thank her or acknowledge her gesture of contrition in preparing his bath. When he entered the tent she glanced up then looked away again quickly.

'I thought you might like a dram of the Hollands that your father gave you.' The gin bottle stood on the camp table ready for him. This was the first time he had seen it since he had parted from his family. He did not know how to decline her offer gracefully, and tell her that he did not like to fuddle his senses with alcohol. He had been drunk only once in his life and regretted the experience. However, he did not wish to spoil this delicate mood, so he poured half a dram and drank it reluctantly.

Louisa had grilled fresh springbuck cutlets for dinner, and she served them with caramelized onions and herbs, a recipe Sarah had given her. This he fell on with great appetite, and his mood improved sufficiently to compliment her. 'Not only well shot, but perfectly cooked.' Yet after that their conversation was stilted and interspersed with awkward silences. They had come so close to being friends, he lamented silently, as he drank a mug of coffee.

'I am off to bed.' He stood up sooner than he usually did. 'How about you?'

'I want to write up my journal,' she answered. 'For me it has been a special day. My first hunt. And, what is more, I promised your father not to miss a day. I will come later.' He left her and made his way to his own wagon.

Each night the wagons were drawn up in a square, and the spaces between them filled with branches of thorn trees, to pen the domestic animals and keep out the predators. Louisa's wagon was always parked alongside Jim's, so that there was only the thickness of the two wagon tents between them. This ensured that Jim was always on hand if she needed him, and during the night, without leaving their separate beds, they were able to speak to each other.

That evening Jim lay awake, until he heard her footsteps coming from the kitchen tent, and saw the glow of her lantern pass along the wall of his tent. Later he heard her changing into her nightdress. The rustle of her clothing conjured up disturbing images of her, and he tried unsuccessfully to banish them. Then he heard her brushing her hair, every stroke of the brush a soft whisper like the wind in a field of ripe wheat. He could imagine the way it rippled and glowed in the lamplight. At last he heard the creak of the cardell bed as it took her weight. Then there was a long silence.

'Jim.' Her voice was low, almost a whisper. It shocked and thrilled him. 'Jim, are you awake?'

'Yes.' His voice sounded loud in his own ears.

'Thank you,' she said. 'I cannot remember when last I enjoyed a day so much.'

'I have enjoyed it also.' He almost added, 'Except—' but he bit back the word.

They were silent for so long that he thought she had fallen asleep, but she whispered again: 'Thank you also for your gentleness.'

He said nothing, for there was nothing to say. He lay long awake, and his hurt slowly gave way to anger. I do not deserve to be treated like this. I have given up everything for her, my home and my family. I have become an outlaw to save her, yet she treats me like some repulsive and poisonous reptile. Then she goes off to sleep as though nothing has happened. I hate her. I wish I had never laid eyes upon her.

Louisa lay rigid and wakeful on her bed. She knew he could hear any movement she made and she did not want him to know that she was unable to sleep. She was racked by guilt and remorse. She felt a deep sense of obligation to Jim. She knew only too well what he had sacrificed for her.

Added to this she liked him. It was impossible not to. He was so outgoing and cheerful, so strong, dependable and resourceful. She felt safe when he was near at hand. She liked the way he looked, big and strong, with an open, honest face. He could make her laugh. She smiled as she thought of the way he had reacted when she shot a hole through his hat. He had a quirky sense of humour that she was at last coming to understand. He could retell the day's events in a way that made her laugh with surprise, even though she had witnessed them. She felt that he was her friend when he called her Hedgehog, and teased her in that rude, almost incomprehensible English way.

Even now that he was sulking it was good to know that he was within call. Often in the night when she heard strange wild sounds, the gibbering of hyena or the roaring of a pride of lions, she was mortally afraid. Then he would speak to her quietly through the wall of the tent. His voice reassured her, calmed her fears, and she could sleep again.

Then there were the nightmares. Often she dreamed that she was at Huis Brabant again; she saw the tripod and the silk ropes and, in the candlelight, the dark figure dressed in the costume of the executioner, the black gloves and the leather mask with the eye slits. When the nightmares came upon her she was trapped in those dark fantasies, unable to escape, until his voice woke her, rescued her from the terror.

'Hedgehog! Wake up! It's all right. It's only a dream. I'm here. I won't let anything happen to you.' She always woke to a deep sense of gratitude.

She liked him a little more each day, and she trusted him. But she could not let him touch her. At even the most casual contact – if he adjusted her stirrup leather and touched her ankle, if he handed her some ordinary object like a spoon or a coffee mug and their fingers brushed – she felt afraid and repelled.

Strangely, from a distance she found him attractive. When he rode beside her and she smelt his warm man smell and listened to his voice and his laughter, it made her happy.

Once she had come upon Jim unexpectedly while he was washing in the river. He had still been wearing his breeches, but he had thrown his shirt and leather jacket on the bank; he was scooping handfuls of water and dashing them over his head. His back had been towards her so he had not seen her. For a long moment, before she turned away, she had stared at the smooth, unblemished skin of his bare back. It was in sharp contrast to his sun-browned arms. The muscles were strongly defined below the pale skin and changed shape as he lifted his arms.

She had felt again that wicked stirring of her senses, that shortness of breath, the melting heaviness of her loins, and the unfocused but lascivious longing that Koen van Ritters had awakened in her, before he plunged her into the horrors of his evil fantasy.

I don't want that ever again, she thought as she lay in darkness. I cannot let another man touch me. Not even Jim. I want him to be my friend, but I don't want *that*. I should go into the Church, a nunnery. That is the only escape for me.

But there was no nunnery in the wilderness, and at last she slept.

Xhia led Koots and his band of bounty-hunters back to the camp where Jim Courtney had stampeded their horses, the camp from which they had begun the long march back to the colony. Many weeks had passed since that night, and in the meantime there had been high winds and heavy rainfall in the mountains. To any other eye than Xhia's the elements had washed away every last vestige of the sign.

Xhia worked outwards from the old campsite, following the direction of the stampede, then instinctively divining the direction in which Jim would have driven the stolen herd once he had it under control again. A quarter of a league from the old camp he picked out the faintest trace of the spoor, the scrape of a steel horseshoe on shale that could not have been made by the hoof of an eland bull or any other wild game. He aged the sign, it was not too fresh, nor too old. This was the first peg upon which he began to build the picture of the chase.

He worked away from it searching in the sheltered places, between two rocks, in the lee of fallen trees, in the malleable clay of a donga bottom, in the stratas of shale soft enough to bear an imprint and hard enough to retain it.

Koots and his men followed at a distance, careful not to over-tread and spoil the ancient sign. Often when the spoor was so ethereal as to be obscured from even Xhia's sorcery, they unsaddled their horses and waited, smoking and bickering, playing dice, gambling for the reward money they would win with the capture of the fugitives. At last Xhia, with infinite patience, would unravel that part of the puzzle. He would call them, and they would mount up and follow him on through the mountains.

Gradually the sign became fresher as he narrowed the gap between them and their quarry, and Xhia moved along it with more confidence. None the less, it was three weeks after picking up that first faint hoofprint that Xhia caught up with the wandering herd of mules and horses that Jim and Bakkat had used to lure them on, then abandoned.

At first Koots could not understand how they had been gulled. Here were their horses but no human beings with them. Since the first day he had encountered great difficulty communicating with Xhia, for the Bushman's Dutch was rudimentary and hand signs were not adequate for explaining the complicated nature of the deceit that Bakkat had played upon them. Then it dawned upon Koots that the best horses were missing from this herd of strays: Frost, Crow, Lemon, Stag and, of course, Drumfire and Trueheart.

'They split off, and left this bunch of animals to lead us away.' Koots had understood at last and he blanched with fury. 'For all this time we have been wandering in circles, while those criminals got clear away in another direction.'

His anger needed a focus, and that was Xhia. 'Catch that yellow rat!' he shouted at Richter and Le Riche. 'I want some skin from this stinking little *swartze*.' They grabbed the Bushman before he realized their intention.

'Tie him to that tree.' Koots pointed out a large cripplewood. They were enjoying this. Their anger with the Bushman was every bit as intense as Koots's: he was directly responsible for their hardship and discomfort over the past months, and retribution would be sweet. They bound him with leather thongs at ankles and wrists. Koots tore off Xhia's leather breech cloth and left him naked.

'Goffel!' Koots shouted at the Hottentot trooper. 'Cut me a bundle of thorn branches this thick.' He made a circle of thumb and forefinger. 'Leave the thorns on them.'

Koots shrugged off his leather coat, and windmilled his right arm, loosening the muscles. Goffel came up from the bank of the stream with an armful of thorn branches, and Koots took his time selecting one that had a pleasing whip and rigidity. Xhia watched him with huge eyes as he strained at his bonds. Koots chopped the thorns off the butt end of the stick of his choice so they would not prick his own fingers, but the rest of the limber wand bristled with the red-tipped spikes. He flourished the scourge as he advanced on Xhia. 'Now, you little reptile, you have led me a fine fandango, but it's your turn to dance now.'

He swung the first cut across Xhia's shoulder-blades. The cane raised a welt upon it, studded with an irregular rash of thorn punctures, from each of which oozed a drop of blood. Xhia howled with pain and outrage.

'Sing, you bastard mating of baboons,' Koots told him, with grim satisfaction. 'You must learn that you cannot take Herminius Koots for a fool.' He swung again. The green branch began to disintegrate with the force of the blows, and the thorns broke off and embedded themselves in Xhia's flesh.

Xhia twisted and fought against his bonds until his wrists were rubbed bloody and raw by the leather loops. In a voice too loud for his little frame he screamed his fury and his vows of revenge in a language that the white man could not understand.

'You will die for this, you white hyena! You eater of dung! You copulater with corpses! I shall kill you with the slowest of my poisons, you drinker of snake's piss and monkey sperm.'

Koots discarded the broken branch and selected another. He wiped the sweat off his face with the sleeve of his shirt and began again. He kept it up until both he and Xhia were exhausted. His shirt was sodden and his breathing hoarse. Xhia hung silently on the leather thongs and the blood ran in dark snakes down his back and buttocks to drip into the dust between his feet. Only then did Koots step back. 'Leave him hanging there tonight,' he ordered. 'He should be in a more willing mood by the morning. Nothing like a good thrashing to get these *zwartes* working properly.'

Slowly Xhia turned his head and looked into Koots's face. He spoke softly. 'I will give you the death of twenty days. You will plead with me to kill you at the end.'

Koots did not understand the words but when he saw the hatred in Xhia's beady black eyes he understood the sense, and stepped back involuntarily. 'Corporal Richter,' he said, 'we will have to keep him tied up until he gets over his sore back and his murderous temper.' He picked up Xhia's quiver of poisoned arrows and tossed it on to the fire. 'Don't let him have any weapon until he's learned his lesson. I don't want it between my shoulder-blades. They are treacherous bastards, these little apes.'

In the morning Goffel used the point of his bayonet to dig the thorns out of the punctures that covered Xhia's back, but some had been driven in too deeply. Over the following days they festered and suppurated, before they sloughed to the surface. With the fortitude of a wild thing Xhia recovered his strength and agility swiftly. His expression was inscrutable, and only when he looked at Koots did the hatred gleam out of those anthracite dark eyes.

'Drink the wind, Xhia,' Koots cuffed him casually as he would a recalcitrant dog, 'and don't look at me like that, or I'll waste another thorn tree on your stinking hide.' He pointed back along the trail that had led them to this place. 'Now go back and find where Jim Courtney split his spoor.'

They retraced their footsteps over the ground they had covered during the last ten days. They followed Xhia. Gradually his torn back clotted with festering scabs as his injuries started to heal. However, it seemed that the beating had indeed been beneficial for he worked hard. He seldom lifted his eyes from the ground, except to study the lie of the terrain ahead. They went swiftly for he had their own tracks to use as a marker. Sometimes he followed a spur for a short way until it proved false or illusory, then returned to the main trail.

At last they reached the stratum of black igneous rock beside the waterfall. On the way out they had passed this spot with only a brief pause. Even though this seemed an ideal location for Bakkat to stage a deception, Xhia's suspicions had been only mildly excited. Almost immediately he had picked up the strong clear spoor on the further side of the stratum, and followed it away.

Now he shook his head as he returned to the spot. 'I was a fool. Now I can smell Bakkat's treachery in the air.' He sniffed like a dog getting a whiff of the chase. He reached the place where Bakkat had cast the masking spell, and he picked up a fragment of black ash. He examined it carefully and saw it was the ash of the tong tree, the wizard's tree.

'Here he burned the tong and cast his spell to cheat me. I walked past this place with my eyes blinded.' He was angry at having been so easily deluded by a man he considered his inferior in cunning and wizard-craft. He went down on his hands and knees and snuffled the earth. 'This is where he would have pissed to cover his scent.' But the traces were months old and even his nose could distinguish no residual ammoniac odour of Bakkat's urine.

He stood up again and made a sign of separation to Koots, laying the palms of his hands together, then parting them with a swimming motion. 'This is the place,' he said in execrable

Dutch, pointing left and right. 'Horses go that way. Man go that way.'

'By the blood of the crucifixion, this time you had better be right or I will have your balls. Do you understand?'

'No understand.' Xhia shook his head.

Koots reached down and seized a handful of Xhia's genitalia, and with his other hand drew his dagger. He lifted Xhia on tiptoe by his scrotum, then made the gesture of drawing the blade across the stretched sac, almost touching the skin, but shaving past it by a hair's breadth.

'Cut your balls,' he repeated. '*Verstaan?*'

Xhia nodded soundlessly and Koots pushed him away. 'Get on with it, then.'

They camped on the bank above the waterfall, and Xhia worked both banks of the river for three miles upstream and down. First he covered the water's edge, but in the last ten days or so the river had come down in spate, then subsided again. At the high-water mark dry grass and debris were stranded in the branches of the trees that grew along the banks. Not even the heaviest trodden spoor could have survived the inundation.

Next Xhia moved out from the river bank, climbing up the slopes to the highest point that the flood waters had reached. He worked the ground painstakingly, scrutinizing every inch. All his experience and magic yielded nothing. The trail was gone, washed away. He had no way of knowing whether Bakkat had gone upstream or down. He had come up against an impenetrable wall.

Koots's nerves were already raw, and when he realized that Xhia had failed again he flew into a fit of fury more vicious than the last. He had Xhia bound again, but this time they hung him by his heels over a smouldering fire which Koots stoked carefully with green leaves. Xhia's peppercorn hair frizzled in the heat and he coughed, choked and retched in the smoke as he writhed and swung on the rope's end.

The rest of the band broke off their dice game to watch. They were all thoroughly bored and dispirited by this time, and the lure of the reward was waning as the trail grew colder each day. Richter and Le Riche had already started muttering threats of mutiny, of abandoning the pursuit, escaping from these harsh and merciless mountains and heading back to the colony.

'Kill the little monkey,' said Le Riche in a tone of disinterest. 'Have done with him, and let's go home.'

Instead Koots stood up and drew his knife, slashed the rope that held Xhia suspended, and the little man dropped headlong into the coals. He let out another shriek and rolled out of the fire, only slightly more singed than he had been already. Koots grabbed the end of the rope that was still round his ankles and dragged Xhia to the nearest tree. He tied him there, and left him while he went back to eat the midday meal.

Xhia crouched against the trunk of the tree, muttering to himself and examining his injuries. When Koots had finished eating he flicked the coffee grounds out of his mug, and shouted for Goffel. The Hottentot went with him to the tree and they both looked down at Xhia. 'I want you to tell this little bastard in his own language, that I am going to keep him tied up. He will receive no water or food and I will beat him every day until he does his job and finds the spoor again.'

Goffel translated this threat. Xhia hissed angrily and covered his face, to show how the sight of Koots offended him.

'Tell him I am in no hurry,' Koots instructed. 'Tell him I can wait until he shrivels up and dries in the sun like the baboon turd that he is.'

In the morning Xhia was still tied to the tree, but while Koots and his troopers were eating a breakfast of grilled corncakes and smoked Dutch sausage Xhia called out to Goffel in the language of the San. The Hottentot went to squat in front of him and they spoke together quietly for a long time. Then Goffel came back to Koots. 'Xhia says that he can find Somoya for you.'

'Well, he hasn't done a good job of it so far.' Koots spat a piece of sausage skin into the fire.

230

'He says that the only way to find the spoor now is to work a solemn magic.'

Le Riche and Richter guffawed scornfully, and Le Riche said, 'If we have come to witchcraft then I'm spending no more time here. I am going back to the Cape, and Keyser can stick his reward up his arsehole.'

'Shut your fat face,' Koots told him, and turned back to Goffel. 'What kind of solemn magic is this?'

'There is a sacred place in the mountains where the spirits of the San have their abode. There, their power is strongest. Xhia says that if we go to this place and sacrifice to the spirits Somoya's tracks will be revealed.'

Le Riche stood up. 'I have heard enough of this mumbo-jumbo. I have listened to it for almost three months and we are still no nearer having the gold guilders in hand.' He picked up his saddle and began to walk towards where his horse was grazing.

'Where are you going?' Koots asked.

'Are you deaf or just stupid?' Le Riche asked belligerently, and placed his right hand on the hilt of his sabre. 'I told you once, but I will tell you again. I am going back to the Cape.'

'It is called desertion and dereliction of duty, but I can understand why you want to go,' Koots said, in such a mild tone that Le Riche looked surprised. Koots went on, 'If anyone else wants to go with Le Riche, I will not stop them.'

Richter stood up slowly. 'I think I will,' he said.

'Good!' said Koots. 'But leave any VOC property when you go.'

'What do you mean, Koots?' Le Riche demanded.

'The saddle and bridle,' Koots said, 'the musket and your sabre are all Company issue. The horse and, of course, your boots and uniform, not to mention your water bottle and blanket.' Koots smiled. 'Just leave all that over there, and you can say goodbye.'

Richter had not yet committed himself, so he sat down again hurriedly. Le Riche stood uncertainly, looking from Koots to his grazing horse. Then, with a visible effort, he steeled himself. 'Koots,' he said, 'the first thing I will do when I get back to the Cape, even if it costs me five guilders, is fuck your wife.' Koots had recently married a beautiful young Hottentot girl. Her name was Nella, and she had been one of the most famous *filles de joie* in the colony. Koots had married her in an attempt to gain exclusive rights to her bountiful charms. That ruse had not been entirely successful, and he had already killed one man who had not understood the niceties of holy wedlock.

Koots glanced at Sergeant Oudeman, his old comrade in arms. Oudeman was bald as an ostrich egg, but he had a fine dark moustache. He understood Koots's unspoken orders, and he let one eyelid droop in acknowledgement. Koots stood up, and stretched like a leopard. He was tall and lean, and his pale eyes were dangerous beneath the colourless lashes. 'One other item I forgot to mention,' he said ominously. 'You can leave your testicles here also. I am coming to get them from you.' With a metallic scraping he drew his own sabre, and walked towards Le Riche. Le Riche dropped his saddle and spun to face him, his blade leaping from the scabbard in a flash of sunlight.

'A long time I have waited for a chance at you, Koots.'

'Now you have it,' Koots said, and lifted his point. He drifted in closer and Le Riche raised his own blade. Steel tapped lightly on steel as they measured each other. They knew one another well: they had trained and practised together over the years. They drew apart and circled.

'You are guilty of desertion,' said Koots. 'It is my duty to arrest you, or to kill you.' He smiled. 'I prefer the second option.'

Le Riche scowled and ducked his head aggressively. He was not as tall as Koots, but he had long simian arms and powerful shoulders. He attacked with a series of lunges, driving in hard and fast. Koots had been expecting this. Le Riche lacked finesse. Koots faded away before him, and when he reached the limit of his extension, Koots riposted with the strike of a puff adder. Le Riche jumped back only just in time but his sleeve was split and a few drops of blood dripped from the scratch on his forearm.

They engaged again, steel scraping and thrilling on steel, but they were neatly matched. They broke and circled, Koots trying to move him towards where Oudeman lounged against the trunk of a thorn tree. Over the years Koots and Oudeman had developed an understanding. Twice Koots almost had Le Riche in position for Oudeman to deal with him, but each time he moved out of the trap.

Oudeman left the thorn tree and moved out towards the cooking fire, as if to refill his coffee mug, but he kept his right hand behind his back. He usually went for the kidneys. A blade in the small of the back would paralyse the victim, and Koots would finish off Le Riche with a thrust through the throat.

Koots changed the direction and angle of his attack, squeezing Le Riche back towards where Oudeman waited. Le Riche jumped back and whirled suddenly, nimble as a ballerina. In the same instant, he slashed his blade across the knuckles of Oudeman's hand, which held the dagger. The knife flew out of his nerveless fingers, and Le Riche spun back to face Koots. He was still smiling. 'Why don't you teach your dog a new trick, Koots? I have seen that one too many times before, and it's becoming boring.'

Oudeman was swearing and clutching his injured hand, and Koots was clearly disconcerted by Le Riche's unexpected ploy. He glanced at his accomplice, and as his eyes left Le Riche's face, Le Riche attacked *en flèche*, the attack of the arrow: he went straight for Koots's throat. Koots stumbled back, and lost his footing. He went down on one knee, and Le Riche pressed home to end it. At the last moment he saw the flare of triumph in Koots's pale eyes and tried to turn aside, but his right foot was leading and Koots went in low, cutting under his guard. The razor steel sliced through the back of Le Riche's boot, and there was an audible pop as it severed his Achilles tendon. Koots was on his feet again in the same instant, and sprang back outside even Le Riche's long reach.

233

'There is a new trick for you, Corporal, and how do you like it?' he asked. 'Now, pray tell me, who has fucked whom?'

Blood was spurting from the gash in the back of Le Riche's boot, and he hopped back on his good leg, dragging his crippled foot behind him. His expression was desperate as Koots came in again fast, cutting and thrusting at his face. On one leg Le Riche could not hope to hold him off and he toppled over backwards. As he sprawled, Koots made the next cut with the precision of a surgeon. He slashed through the back of Le Riche's left boot and his other tendon parted cleanly. Koots ran his sabre back into its scabbard and walked away from him contemptuously. Le Riche sat up and, with shaking hands and pale sweating face, drew off his boots one at a time. He stared silently at the terrible crippling injuries. Then he tore the hem off his shirt and tried to bind up the wounds, but the blood soaked swiftly through the grubby cloth.

'Break camp, Sergeant,' Koots called to Oudeman. 'Everyone mounted and ready to leave in five minutes. The Bushman is taking us to this sacred place of his.'

The troop rode out of the camp in single file following Xhia. Oudeman was leading Le Riche's horse, and his musket, water bottle and all his other equipment were tied to the empty saddle.

Le Riche crawled after them. 'Wait! You can't leave me here.' He tried to stand, but he had no control of his feet, and he toppled over again. 'Please, Captain Koots, have mercy. In the name of Jesus, at least leave me my musket and water bottle.'

Koots turned his horse back and looked down at Le Riche from the saddle. 'Why should I waste valuable equipment? Soon you will have no further use for it.'

Le Riche crawled towards him on his hands and knees, his crippled feet flopping and dragging behind him like stranded fish. Koots backed his horse away, keeping just out of his reach.

'I can't walk, and you have taken my horse,' he pleaded.

'It's not your horse, Corporal. It belongs to the VOC,' Koots pointed out. 'But I have left you your boots and your testicles. That is enough generosity for one day.' He turned his horse's head and rode after the rest of his troop.

'Please!' Le Riche screamed after him. 'If you leave me here I will die.'

'Yes,' Koots agreed over his shoulder, 'but probably not until the vultures and the hyenas find you.' He rode away. The sound of the horses' hoofs faded, and the silence of the mountains pressed down upon Le Riche with such weight that he felt the last shreds of his courage and resolve crushed beneath it.

It did not take long before the first vulture planed overhead on widespread wings. It twisted its head on its long naked red neck and peered down at Le Riche. Then, satisfied that he was crippled and moribund, and unable to protect himself, it circled in for a landing on the rocky pinnacle above him. It flared its massive wings and stretched out its talons to find purchase on the rock. Then it settled, hump-backed, folded away the long wings, and watched him impassively. It was an enormous bird, black and lappet-faced.

Le Riche crawled to the nearest tree, and leaned against the trunk. He gathered every stone within reach, but they made a pathetically small pile. He hurled one at the crouching vulture, but the range was long, and from a sitting position his throw lacked power. The great bird blinked its eyes but made no other movement. A dead branch had fallen from the tree and lay just within Le Riche's reach. It was too heavy and too awkwardly shaped to wield effectively, nevertheless he placed it across his lap. It was his weapon of last resort, but when he studied the great bird, he knew just how puny it was.

They watched each other for the rest of that day. Once the vulture ruffled out its feathers, then preened them carefully and settled into immobility again. By nightfall Le Riche was thirsty, and the pain in his feet was almost unbearable. The brooding silhouette of the bird was satanic black against the background of stars. Le Riche thought about creeping up upon it as it slept and strangling it with his bare hands, but when he tried to move the pain in his feet held him as effectively as leg irons.

235

The midnight cold drained his vital force, and he sank into a delirious sleep. The faint warmth of the sun on his face and the dazzle of it in his eyes roused him. For many seconds he did not know where he was, but when he tried to move, the pain in his feet held him fast and brought back the horrors of his predicament in full force.

He groaned and turned his head, then screamed wildly with shock. The vulture had come down from its perch on the rocky pinnacle. It sat close by, just out of his reach. He had not realized the size of the creature. It seemed to tower over him as he sat. Close up it was even more hideous. Its naked head and neck were raw scaly red, and it reeked of carrion.

He snatched up a stone from the pile at his side and hurled it with all his strength. It glanced off the vulture's gleaming funereal plumage. The creature spread its huge wings, wider than he was tall, and hopped back a little, then folded them again.

'Leave me, you foul beast!' he sobbed with terror. At the sound of his voice, it raised its feathers, and ducked the monstrous head on its shoulders, but that was its only reaction. The day drew on and the heat of the sun rose until Le Riche felt that he was trapped in a bread oven, barely able to breathe, and his thirst became a terrible torment.

The vulture sat like a carved cathedral gargoyle and watched him. His senses reeled and the darkness drew in on him. The bird must have sensed it also, for suddenly it spread its wings like a black canopy. It uttered a guttural squawk and bounded towards him, hopping on spread talons. Its hooked beak gaped wide open. Le Riche howled with terror, snatched up the stick from his lap and struck out wildly. He fetched the vulture a blow along its naked neck, with just enough force to knock it off-balance. But it used its wings to recover and hopped back out of his reach again. It folded its wings and resumed its inscrutable vigil.

It was the vulture's indefatigable patience that drove him beyond the bounds of sanity. He raved at it through lips swollen with thirst and cracked by the baking sun until the blood dripped from his chin. The vulture never moved, except to blink its glittering eyes. In his madness he threw his precious stick at its head, his weapon of last resort. The vulture lifted its wings and croaked as the stick glanced off its armoured plumage. Then it settled down again to wait.

The sun reached its zenith, and Le Riche raved and shouted, challenging God and the devil, swearing at the patient bird. He scratched up handfuls of dust and sand to throw at it, until his fingernails were broken off to the quick. He sucked his bleeding fingers to find moisture to slake his thirst, but the dirt clogged his swollen tongue.

He thought about the stream they had crossed on their way here, but it was at least half a mile back down the valley. The picture of the cold tumbling waters excited his dementia. He left the illusionary shelter of the thorn tree, and started crawling slowly back along the rocky pathway towards the river. His feet flopped along behind him, and the crusted sabre cuts burst open and started bleeding again. The vulture smelt the blood, squawked hoarsely and hopped along behind him. Le Riche covered less than a hundred paces, and told himself, 'I will rest for a while.' He lowered his face on to his arm, and lapsed into unconsciousness. The pain woke him. It was as though a dozen spear-heads were being driven into his back.

The vulture was perched between his shoulder-blades, its curved talons locked deeply in his flesh. It was flapping its wings to maintain its balance as it lowered its head and, with a slash of its beak, tore away his shirt. Then it stuck in the hooked, pointed tip and ripped away a long strip of his flesh.

Le Riche screamed hysterically, and rolled over trying to crush the bird under his own body, but with a flap of its wings it rose and settled again close by.

Although his eyesight was blurring and wavering he watched it swallow his flesh, stretching its neck and gulping to force it down. Then it lifted its head and turned its eyes upon him again, holding his gaze unflinchingly.

He knew that it was waiting for him to slip once more into unconsciousness. He sat up and tried to remain alert, singing and shouting at it and clapping his hands, but slowly his voice became an incoherent mumble, his arms fell to his sides and his eyes closed.

This time when he came awake he could not believe the intensity of the pain that overwhelmed him. There was a battering whirlwind of wings around his head and it felt as though a steel hook had been driven through his eye-socket, that his brains were being drawn out of his skull.

He thrashed around weakly on his back, no longer with the strength to cry out, and tried to open his eyes, but he was blind and he could feel sheets of hot blood pouring down his face, filling his good eye, mouth and nostrils so that he was drowning in it.

He reached up with both hands, clutching at the bird's scaly neck, and realized that the bird had driven its beak deep into one of his eye-sockets. It was pulling out his eyeball on the long rubbery string that contained the optic nerve.

They always go for the eyes, he thought, with final resignation, past any further resistance. Blinded and now too weak to lift his hands he listened to the bird somewhere close at hand, gulping down his eyeball. He tried to peer at it through his remaining eye, but it was obscured by a streaming river of blood, too copious for him to blink away. Then the buffeting of heavy wing strokes burst around his head again. The last thing he felt was the point of the beak being driven deeply into his other eye.

Oudeman rode close behind Xhia, holding him on a long rope like a hunting dog on a leash. They all knew that if Xhia left them, perhaps slipping away into the night, none of them was likely to find his way out of this wilderness and back to the distant colony. After the treatment he had received from Koots, this eventuality was more than just a possibility, so they took turns to guard Xhia, keeping him on the rope night and day.

They crossed another small clear stream and turned a corner in the valley between two tall pinnacles of stone. An

238

extraordinary vista opened before them. Their senses had become dulled by the wild grandeur of these mountains, but now they reined in their horses and stared in astonishment.

Xhia began to sing, a plaintive, repetitive chant, shuffling and dancing, as he looked up at the sacred cliffs that rose in front of them. Even Koots was awed. The riven walls of rock seemed to reach to the very sky, and the clouds rolled over the summit, like spilled milk.

Suddenly Xhia leaped high in the air and uttered a dreadful shriek, which startled Koots and raised the fine hair on his forearms. Xhia's cry was picked up in the great basin of stone, and flung back in a glissando of descending echoes.

'Hear the voices of my ancestors answer me!' Xhia cried, and jumped again. 'O holy ones, O wise ones, give me leave to enter.'

'Enter! Enter!' the echoes answered him and, still dancing and singing, Xhia led them up the scree to the foot of the cliffs. The walls of lichen-covered stone seemed to hang over them, and the clouds flying over the tops gave the illusion that the cliff was toppling down on them. The wind thrummed through the turrets and towers of stone like the voices of the long-dead, and the troopers were silent, their horses fidgeting nervously.

Half-way up the scree a massive boulder blocked their way. In ancient time it had fallen out of the cliff face and tumbled down to this resting place. It was the size of a cottage and so almost perfectly rectangular that it might have been shaped by human hand. Koots saw that in the near side of the block there was a small natural shrine. A strange collection of objects was laid in the niche: horns of bluebuck and rhebuck so old they were encrusted with the cocoons of the bacon beetle, the skull of a baboon and the wings of a heron, dry and brittle with age, a calabash half filled with pretty agate and quartz pebbles, water-worn and polished, a necklace of beads chipped from ostrich egg, flint arrow-heads and a quiver that was rotted and cracked.

'We must leave gifts here for the Old People,' Xhia said, and Goffel translated.

Koots looked uncomfortable. 'What gifts?' he asked.

'Something to eat or drink, and something pretty,' Xhia told him. 'Your little shiny bottle.'

'No!' Koots said, but without conviction. He had been saving the last few inches of Hollands gin in his silver flask, rationing himself to an occasional sip.

'The Old People will be angry,' Xhia warned. 'They will conceal the sign from us.'

Koots wavered, then reluctantly unfastened the flap of his saddlebag and brought out the silver flask. Xhia reached up for it, but Koots kept his grip. 'If you fail me again, I will have no further use for you, except to fatten the jackals.' He gave up the flask.

Chanting softly Xhia approached the shrine and poured a few drops of the gin down the face of the rock. Then he picked up a fist-sized stone and battered the metal flask. Koots winced, but kept silent. Xhia placed the flask with the other offerings in the niche, then backed away, still singing softly.

'Now what do we do?' Koots demanded. This place made him nervous. He wanted to be gone. 'What about the spoor?'

'If the Old People are pleased with your gift they will reveal it to us. We must go on into the sacred places,' Xhia told him. 'First you must take this rope from my neck, or the Old People will be angered that you treat one of their own tribe in this manner.'

Koots looked doubtful, but Xhia's plea made good sense. He reached a decision. He drew his musket from its sheath and cocked the hammer. 'Tell him that he must stay close. If he tries to run, I will ride him down and shoot him like a rabid dog. This gun is loaded with goose-shot and he has seen me shoot. He knows I don't miss,' he ordered Goffel, and waited while he translated for the little Bushman.

'Turn him loose.' He nodded to Oudeman. Xhia made no attempt to escape, and they followed him up to the base of the cliff. Abruptly Xhia vanished, as though by the magic of his forefathers.

With a shout of anger, Koots spurred his horse forward, his musket at the ready. Suddenly he reined in and stared with amazement into the narrow gateway in the rock that opened in front of him.

Xhia had disappeared into the dim depths of the passage. Koots hesitated to follow him in there. He could see that once he was inside it the passage was too narrow for him to turn his horse. The other troopers hung back behind him.

'Goffel!' Koots shouted. 'Go in there and pull the little bastard out.'

Goffel looked behind him, back down the slope, but Koots turned the cocked musket on him.

'If I can't have Xhia, then by God you will have to do.'

At that moment they heard Xhia's voice issue from the mouth of the passage, and he was singing.

'What is he saying?' Koots demanded, and Goffel looked mightily relieved.

'It is his song of victory. He is thanking his gods for their kindness in revealing the spoor to him.'

Koots's misgivings evaporated. He swung down from the saddle and strode into the passage. He found Xhia around the first bend, singing, clapping and giggling with triumph. 'What have you found?'

'Look under your feet, you white baboon,' Xhia told him, making sure he would not understand the insult, but pointing at the trampled white sand. Koots understood the gesture, but still he was uncertain. Any definition of the spoor was long ago obliterated: it was merely a dimpling of the surface.

'How can he be sure that this is our quarry?' Koots demanded of Goffel as he came up. 'It could be anything – a herd of quagga or eland.'

Xhia answered this objection with a rapid fire of denials, and Goffel spoke for him: 'Xhia says that this is a sacred place. No wild animal ever passes through here.'

'I don't believe that!' Koots scoffed. 'How would an animal know?'

'If you cannot feel the magic here, your eyes are blind and your ears are deaf indeed,' Xhia told him, but he went to the nearest wall of the passage and peered minutely at it. Then he began to pick things off the rock, the way a baboon picks nits

241

from a companion's scalp. He gathered whatever it was in the palm of his hand, then came back to Koots. Between forefinger and thumb he offered him something. Koots had to look closely to see that it was a hair.

'Behold, with your pale and disgusting eyes, O eater of dung!' he said, so Koots could not understand. 'This white hair came from the shoulder of the gelding, Frost. This brown and silky one from Trueheart when she touched the rock, and this yellow one from Lemon. This dark one is from Somoya's horse, Drumfire.' He hooted scornfully. 'And now do you believe that Xhia is the mightiest hunter of all the San, and that he has worked a great and solemn magic and revealed the spoor to you?'

'Tell the little yellow ape to stop chattering, and take us after them.' Koots tried, unsuccessfully, to disguise his elation.

'What river is that?' Koots asked. They stood on the peak and looked down from the mountains, over endless plains and vistas of rolling grassland, to another range of hills, pale against the milky blue of the tall African sky at noon day.

'It is called the river Gariep,' Goffel translated. 'Or, in the language of the San, Gariep Che Tabong, the River Where the Elephant Died.'

'Why is it called that?' Koots wanted to know.

'It was on the banks of this river when he was a young man that Xhia slew the great elephant he had followed for many days.'

Koots grunted. Since the Bushman had found the spoor again Koots was more kindly disposed towards him. He had treated his burns and other injuries from the field chest of medicines he carried on the pack-horse. Xhia healed quickly, the way a wild animal does.

'Tell him that if he can find where Somoya crossed this river, I will give him a fine cow as his own animal when we return to the colony. Then, if he can lead me to the capture or the killing of Somoya, I will give him five more fat cows.'

Koots was now regretting his previous harsh treatment of the Bushman. He knew that if he wanted to catch up with the fugitives, he must make amends and buy back Xhia's loyalty.

Xhia received this promise of wealth joyfully. Few men of the San owned a sheep, let alone a single head of kine. Childlike, his memory of abuse faded with the offer of reward. He started down the mountain slopes towards the plains and the river with such alacrity that even on horseback Koots was hard-pressed to keep him in sight. When they reached the river they found wild game concentrated on these waters in numbers that Koots had not imagined possible. The herds within the colony had been hunted extensively since the first Dutch colonists, under Governor van Riebeeck, had set foot ashore almost eighty years before. The burghers were all enthusiastic hunters, indulging in the pastime not only for the thrill of the chase but also for the meat, hides and ivory it yielded. Within the borders of the colony at any time of day one could hear the boom of their long *roers*, and in the season of the great animal migrations across the plains they had organized themselves into large mounted parties to hunt the wild horses, the quagga, for their hides, the springbuck and eland for their meat. After one of these great *jags* the vultures darkened the sky with their wings and the stench of death hung in the air for months thereafter. The bleached bones lay like banks of snowy arum lilies, gleaming in the sunlight.

As a consequence of these predations the game had been severely reduced in numbers, and even the quagga had become something of a rarity within the immediate environs of the town and castle. The last elephant herds had been driven far from the frontiers of the colony almost forty years before, and only a few hardy souls occasionally made the journey of months and even years into the remote wilderness to pursue them. In fact, not many white men had ventured even thus far from the safety and security of the colony, which was why this mighty gathering of wild beasts was a revelation to Koots.

Game had been scarce in the mountains, and they were hungry for fresh meat so Koots and Oudeman spurred ahead of the rest of the troop. Riding hard they caught up with a herd of giraffe who had been grazing on the top branches of an isolated clump of acacia trees. These gigantic creatures ran with a ponderous, swaying motion, twisting their bushy tails up on to their haunches. They thrust their long, sinuous necks forward as though to counterbalance their massive bodies. Koots and Oudeman cut a young cow out of the herd of a dozen and, riding hard at her heels, with the stones and pebbles flung up by her hoofs whizzing past their ears they fired into her rump, trying to send a ball through the ridge of her spine, which showed clearly under her dappled brown and yellow skin. At last Koots pressed in so close to her that he almost touched her with the muzzle of his musket, and this time the ball flew true. It severed her spinal column and she collapsed in a cloud of dust and debris. Koots dismounted to reload and as soon as his weapon was recharged he ran close to her. She was thrashing about weakly, but he avoided the convulsive kicks of her long front legs, which could snap the spine of an attacking lion. Then he fired another ball into the back of her skull.

That night while the hyena squalled and squabbled with a pride of lions for possession of what remained of the colossal carcass, Koots and his men feasted around their campfire on marrow from the giraffe's thigh-bones. They cracked the roasted bones between two rocks, and out slid long cylindrical lumps of the rich yellow marrow, as thick as a man's arm and twice as long.

In the dawn when Koots awoke, he found Goffel, who was on sentry duty, fast asleep. Xhia was gone. Raging, Koots booted Goffel in the stomach and crotch, then laid into him with a bridle, swinging the bit end and the metal cheek buckles across his shoulders and close-cropped scalp. At last he stepped back and snarled, 'Now, take the spoor and catch that little yellow ape, or there'll be another helping of ginger for you.'

Xhia had made no attempt to cover his tracks so even Goffel could read them easily. Without breakfast they mounted up and rode after Xhia before he could make good his escape. On the open plain Koots hoped to spot him at a distance, and even a Bushman could not hope to outdistance a good horse.

Xhia's tracks led straight towards the dark green ribbon of riverine bush on the horizon that marked the course of the Gariep river. They were only half-way there when Koots saw the springbuck herds ahead pronking, leaping high in the air with all four feet together and noses almost touching their front hoofs, the snowy dorsal plumes flashing in full display.

'Something's alarming them,' Goffel said. 'Maybe it is the Bushman.' Koots spurred forward. Then, through the dust kicked up by the antics of the springbuck herds, he saw a tiny familiar figure trotting towards them.

'By the breath of Satan!' Koots swore. 'It's him. It's Xhia and he's coming back!'

As he came towards them Xhia broke into a dance and a litany of triumph and self-congratulation. 'I am Xhia, the greatest hunter of all my tribe. I am Xhia, the beloved of the ancestors. My eyes are like the moon for they see all, even in the night. My arrows are swift as swallows in flight, and no animal may run from them. My magic is so powerful that no man may avoid it.'

That same day Xhia led them to the Gariep river, and he showed Koots the wheel ruts of many wagons scored deeply into the soft alluvial earth along its banks.

'Four great wagons and one small one passed this way.' Through Goffel he explained the sign to Koots. 'With the wagons were many animals, horses and cattle and some sheep. See here! The small wagon has returned towards the colony, but the four great wagons have gone on into the wilderness.'

'Whose wagons are these?' Koots asked him.

'In all the colony there are few burghers rich enough to boast five wagons. One of those is Klebe, the father of Somoya.'

'I do not understand.' Koots shook his head.

Goffel explained: 'It seems that while Bakkat and Somoya led us on a chase through the mountains, Klebe came here to the Gariep with these wagons. When Somoya had stolen our horses and knew we could follow him no further, he came back here to meet his father.'

'What of the small wagon that went back towards the colony?' Koots wanted to know.

Xhia shrugged. 'Perhaps after he had given the great wagons to his son, Klebe returned to the Cape.' Xhia touched the wheel marks with his toe. 'See how deeply the wheels have bitten into the earth. They are heavily laden with goods.'

'How does Xhia know all this?' Koots demanded.

'Because I am Xhia, with eyes like the moon, that sees all.'

'That means the little bastard is guessing.' Koots lifted his hat and wiped the sweat from his balding pate.

'If we follow the wagons Xhia will give you proof,' Goffel suggested. 'Or if he does not, you will shoot him and save yourself the cattle you promised him.'

Koots replaced his hat. Despite his forbidding expression he felt more confident of eventual success than at any time since they had left the colony.

It is plain to see that they are carrying much cargo, Koots thought. It may be that those wagons are worth almost as much as the bounty money itself. He looked towards the heat-shimmering horizon where the tracks led. Out there, there is no civilized law. Head money or cargoes, one way or the other I smell a sweet profit in this.

He dismounted and inspected the wagon tracks more closely, giving himself time to think. 'How long since the wagons passed this way?'

Goffel referred the question to Xhia.

'Some months. It is not possible to say more than that. But wagons travel slowly, while horsemen travel fast.'

Koots nodded to Goffel. 'Good, very good! Tell him to follow, and find proof of who these wagons belong to.'

They found proof a hundred leagues further and twelve days later. They came to a place where one of the wagons had run into an antbear hole and been badly damaged. A number of the spokes in one of the front wheels had been shattered. The travellers had camped for some days at the site of the accident, making repairs to the wagon. They had whittled and shaved new spokes, and discarded the damaged ones.

Xhia retrieved one of the broken pieces from where it had been thrown into the grass. He cackled with triumph. 'Did not Xhia tell you this truth and that truth? Did you believe him? No! You did not believe him, you stupid white maggot.' He brandished the broken spar. 'Know now, once and for all time, white man, that Xhia sees all and knows all.' He brought the fragment of the spoke to Koots and showed him the design that had been burnt into the wood with a branding iron. 'Do you know this picture?' he demanded.

Koots grinned wolfishly and nodded with recognition.

It was the stylized picture of a cannon, a long nine-pounder on its carriage. In the ribbon below it were the letters CBTC. Koots had seen the same design on the flag that flew above the godown at High Weald, and on the pediment above the front wall of the main building. He knew that the initials stood for Courtney Brothers Trading Company.

He called his troopers and showed them the fragment of wood. They passed it from hand to hand. They all knew the design. The entire population of the colony was less than three thousand souls, and within its boundaries everyone knew everything about everyone else. After Governor van de Witten himself, the Courtney brothers were the richest, most influential men in the colony. Their coat-of-arms was almost as well known as that of the VOC. The brothers emblazoned it on all their possessions, their buildings, ships, wagons. It was the seal they used on their documents and the brand on their horses and livestock. There was no longer any doubt of the identity of the wagon train they were following.

Koots looked over his band, and picked out Richter. He tossed him the broken spoke. 'Corporal, do you know what that is you are holding?'

'Yes, Captain, sir. It's a wheel spoke.'

'No, Corporal!' Koots told him. 'That is thousands of guilders in gold coin in your hand.' He looked from the two white faces, Oudeman and Richter's, to the yellow and chocolate ones of Xhia and Goffel and the other Hottentots. 'Do any of you still want to go home? Unlike that miserable bastard Le Riche, this time I will let you take your horse when you leave. The reward money is not all that we will win. There are four wagons also, and a herd of domestic animals. Even Xhia will win more than the six head of cattle I promised him. The rest of you? Do any of you want to go home, yes or no?'

They grinned at each other, like a pack of wild hunting dogs with the smell of a wounded quarry in their nostrils, and shook their heads.

'Then there is the girl. Would any of you black bastards like to play with a white girl with golden hair?'

They burst into laughter at the suggestion, lewd and loud.

'I must apologize, but one of you will not have that pleasure.' He looked them over thoughtfully. There was one Hottentot trooper whom he would be pleased to see the back of. His name was Minna, and he had a squint. This gave him a sly, villainous expression, which Koots had realized reflected accurately his true nature. Minna had sulked and whined ever since leaving the colony, and he was the only one of the troop who was exhibiting no enthusiasm for following the tracks of Jim Courtney's wagons.

'Minna, you and I are brothers of the warrior blood,' Koots placed his arm around the man's shoulders, 'so it grieves me sorely that we must part. However, I need a good man and true to carry a message back to Colonel Keyser at the castle. I have to let him know of the success of our expedition. You, my dear and stalwart Minna, are the man for that job. I shall ask the colonel to reward you handsomely. Who knows? You may have some gold braid upon your sleeve, and gold in your pocket from this day's work.'

Koots hunched over his grubby notebook for almost an hour as he composed the message. He knew that Minna was illiterate. After extolling his own achievements in the conduct of the expedition the final paragraph of his report to Colonel Keyser read, 'The trooper who carries this message, Johannes Minna, lacks any soldierly virtues. It is my respectful recommendation that he be stripped of rank and privilege and discharged from the Company service without benefit of pension.'

And that, he thought, with satisfaction, when he folded the message, takes care of any obligation I might have to share the bounty with Minna when I bring Jim Courtney's head back to the colony. 'You have only to follow the wagon tracks, and they will lead you back to the Cape of Good Hope,' he told Minna. 'Xhia says it is less than ten days' ride.' He handed the message and the broken wagon spoke to Minna. 'Give these both to Colonel Keyser in person.'

Minna leered and went with alacrity to saddle his horse. He could hardly believe his good fortune in escaping this dreadful journey, and being offered a reward for doing so.

The days sped by much faster than the slow turning of the wagon wheels. It seemed that the hours were too short for them to enjoy in full measure all the wonders they saw, or to savour the adventures, great and small, that they encountered each day. Were it not for the journal that Louisa kept with such dedication they would soon have lost track of those golden days. She had to nag at Jim to keep his promise to his father. He made the solar observations of their position only when she insisted that he do so, and she recorded the results.

Jim was more reliable with the gold pans and he tested the sands of every river they crossed for the precious metal. On many occasions he found a bright yellow tail of metallic dust around the rim of the pan, but his excitement was short-lived when he tested it with hydrochloric acid from the gold-finder's chest, and the yellow metal bubbled and dissolved. 'Iron pyrites! Fool's gold!' he told Louisa bitterly. 'How old Humbert would laugh at me as a dupe.' But the disappointment and bitterness did not last long, and within hours Jim's enthusiasm would have fully regenerated. His boyish optimism was one of the things Louisa found endearing about him.

Jim looked for signs of other human presence, but there was little evidence of this. Once they found the tracks of

249

wagon wheels preserved in the sterile crust of a salt pan, but Bakkat declared them to be very old indeed. Bakkat's concept of the passage of time was different from that of the European mind, so Jim pressed him further. 'How old is very old, Bakkat?'

'These tracks were made before you were born, Somoya,' he told Jim. 'The man whose wagon made them is probably dead of old age.'

There were other, fresher signs of human existence. These were of Bakkat's own people. Wherever they found a rock shelter or cave in the side of a hill or *kopje*, there were usually whimsical, vividly coloured paintings decorating the rock walls, and fairly recent hearths on which charcoal fragments showed how the little people had cooked their quarry, and discarded the bones on the midden piles nearby. Bakkat was able to recognize which clans of the tribe had passed this way by the symbols and styles of the paintings. Often when they were examining these artistic tributes to strange gods and quaint custom, Louisa sensed the deep longing and nostalgia that Bakkat felt for his people, who were living the free, careless existence that nature had decreed for them.

The land changed as they travelled across it, the plains giving way to forests and hills with rivers running through wide green valleys and straths. In places, the bush was so dense and thorny that they could not force a way through it. Even attempts to cut a roadway for the wagons failed. The tangled branches were iron hard and defied the sharpest axes. They were obliged to make detours of many days to pass around these jungles. In other places the veld was like English parkland, open and fertile, with great trees as tall as cathedral columns and widespread canopies of green leaf. Birds and monkeys shrieked and chattered in the treetops as they competed for fruit.

It seemed that there were animals and birds wherever they cast their eyes. The numbers and varieties never palled. They ranged in size from tiny sunbirds to ostriches taller than a mounted man with white plumes in their wings and tail tufts, from shrews not much bigger than Jim's thumb to hippopotamus as heavy as their largest oxen. These behemoths seemed to inhabit every pool and river, their huge bodies crowded so close together that they formed massive rafts on which the white egrets perched as though they were rocks.

Jim sent a hardened ball between the eyes of one old bull. Although he plunged below the surface in his death throes and disappeared from their sight, on the second day the gases in his belly brought him to the surface and he floated like a balloon with his stubby legs sticking into the air. With a span of oxen they dragged the carcass to the bank. The pure white fat that filled his body cavity filled a fifty-gallon water keg when rendered down. It was perfect for cooking and sausage-making, for the manufacture of soap, for lubricating the wheel hubs of the wagons, or for greasing the rifle patches.

There were so many kinds of antelope, each with flesh of different taste and texture: Louisa was able to order her favourites from Jim's rifle, like a housewife from her butcher. Herds of dun-coloured reedbuck lived on the grassland under the tall trees. Fantastically striped zebra galloped together in herds. They came across other horse-like antelope, with backs and limbs of ebony black, bellies of frosty white, and huge back-swept scimitar-shaped horns. In every thicket and thorn forest they found nervous kudu with spiral horns, and herds of bovine black buffalo, so numerous that they flattened the tangled bush when they stampeded.

Always Jim longed for his first sighting of elephant, and at night spoke of them with almost religious awe. He had never laid eyes on a living beast, but their tusks were piled high in the Company godown at High Weald. In his youth Jim's father had hunted the elephant in the eastern lands of Africa, a thousand miles and more from where Louisa and he now found themselves. Jim had been reared on tales of his father's chases after these legendary animals, and the thought of his first encounter with them became an obsession to him. 'We have travelled almost a thousand leagues since we left the Gariep,' he told Louisa. 'Surely no other man has travelled further from the colony. We must come up with the elephant herds very soon.'

Then his dreams had something to feed upon. They came upon a whole forest whose trunks had been thrown to earth as though by a hurricane of wind, and shattered to splinters. Those trees left standing had been stripped of their bark by the mighty pachyderms.

'See how they have chewed the juice out of the bark.' Bakkat showed Jim the huge balls of desiccated bark the animals had spat out. 'See how they have torn down this tree, which once stood higher than the mainmast of your father's ship – and they ate only the tender top leaves. Hau! They are truly wondrous beasts.'

'Follow them, Bakkat!' Jim pleaded. 'Show these beasts to me.'

'These signs were made a full season ago. See how the marks of the pads that they left in the mud of the last rains have dried hard as stone.'

'When will we find them?' Jim demanded. 'Will we ever find them?'

'We will find them,' Bakkat promised. 'And when we do, perchance you will wish we had not.' With a thrust of his chin he indicated one of the fallen trees: 'If they can do that to such a tree, what might they do to a man?'

Each day they rode out to explore the land ahead, to look for fresher elephant sign, and blaze a road for Smallboy and the wagons to follow. Always they had to make certain of sources of potable water and good fodder for the oxen and other domestic animals, and to refill the fagies against the times when their search for fresh water-holes might prove unsuccessful. Bakkat showed Jim how to watch the flight of flocks of sandgrouse and other birds, and the direction of travel of the thirsty game herds to the nearest water-holes. The horses were also good guides – they could smell it on the wind from many miles off.

Often they reached so far ahead of the wagon train that they were unable to return to its security and comfort before the setting of the sun, and they were forced to pitch a fly-camp wherever darkness and exhaustion overtook them. However, on those nights that they returned to the wagons it was always with a sense of joyous homecoming when they saw the campfires from a distance, or heard the lowing of the oxen. Then the dogs rushed out, barking with excitement, and Smallboy and the other drivers shouted greetings.

Louisa marked the calendar religiously, and she never missed the Sabbath. She insisted that she and Jim stay in camp for that day. They slept late on Sunday mornings, hearing each other wake as the sun shone through the chinks in the afterclap. Then they lay on their own cardell beds and chatted drowsily through the canvas of the wagon tents, until Louisa argued with Jim that it was time to be up and about. The smell of Zama brewing coffee at the campfire would convince him that she was right.

Louisa always cooked a special Sunday dinner, usually with some new recipe from the cookbook Sarah had given to her. In the meantime Jim saw to the small jobs around the camp that had been neglected during the week, from shoeing a horse to repairing a tear in the wagon tent or greasing the wheel hubs.

After lunch they often slung hammocks in the shade of the trees and read to each other from their small library of books. Then they discussed the events of the past week, and made plans for the week ahead. As a surprise for Jim on the first of his birthdays they spent together, Louisa secretly carved a set of chessmen and a board, using woods of different colours. Although he tried to look enthusiastic, Jim was not entirely enchanted by the gift for he had never played the game before. But she read him the rules from the back pages of the almanac, then set up the board under the spreading branches of a mighty camel-thorn tree.

'You can play white,' she told him magnanimously, 'which means you move first.'

'Is that good?' he demanded.

'It is of the utmost advantage,' she assured him. With a laugh he advanced a rook's pawn three squares. She made him correct this, then proceeded to give him a thorough and merciless drubbing. 'Checkmate!' she said and he looked startled.

Humiliated by the ease with which she had accomplished this feat, he examined the board minutely and argued the legitimacy of each move that had led to his defeat. When it became apparent that she had not cheated, he sat back and stared morosely at the board. Then, slowly, the light of battle dawned in his eyes, and he squared his shoulders. 'We will play again,' he announced ominously. But the result of their second game was no less humiliating. Perhaps for this reason Jim became captivated by it, and it soon became a major, binding force in their shared existence. With Louisa's tactful tuition he made such rapid progress that soon they were almost evenly matched. They fought many memorable, epic battles across the chequered board but, strangely, these encounters brought them closer together.

In one endeavour she could not match him, although she tried with all her determination and often came close to doing so. This was in shooting. On Sunday afternoons after dinner, Jim set up targets at fifty, a hundred and a hundred and fifty paces. Louisa shot with her little French rifle, while he used one of the pair of heavier London guns. The trophy was the bushy tail of a giraffe, and the winner of this weekly competition was entitled to hang the tail on the front of his or her wagon for the rest of the week. During the rare weeks that Louisa had that honour, Smallboy, the driver of her wagon, strutted, preened and fired his great whip more often, and with more force, than was necessary for the encouragement of the ox team.

Gradually Louisa developed such a sense of pride and fulfilment in the running of the camp and the ordering of their existence, and came to derive so much pleasure from Jim's companionship, that the dark memories of her old life began to recede. The nightmares became less frequent and terrifying. Slowly she regained the sense of fun and the enjoyment of life that more suited her age than defensiveness and suspicion.

Riding out together one afternoon they came upon a tsama vine in full fruit. The green and yellow striped melons were the size of a man's head. Jim filled his saddlebags with them, and when they returned to the wagons he cut one into thick wedges. 'One of the delicacies of the wilderness.' He handed her a piece, and she tasted it gingerly. It was running with juice, but the flavour was bland and only slightly sugary. To please him, Louisa pretended to enjoy it.

'My father says that one of these saved his life. He had been lost for days in the desert, and would have died of thirst had he not chanced upon a tsama vine like this one. Isn't it tasty?'

She looked at the pale yellow pith that filled the shell, then up at him. Unexpectedly she was filled with a girlish mischief she had not known since before the death of her parents.

'What are you grinning at?' Jim demanded.

'This!' she said, leaned across the camp table and mashed the soft wet fruit into his face. He gaped at her in astonishment as juice and the yellow flesh dripped off his nose and chin. 'Isn't it tasty?' she asked, and dissolved into peals of laughter. 'You look so silly!'

'We shall see who looks even more silly.' Jim recovered, and snatched up the remains of the melon. She squealed with alarm, leaped up from the table and ran. Jim pursued her through the camp brandishing the melon, with pips in his hair and juice down his shirt.

The servants were astounded as Louisa dodged and ducked around the wagons. But she was weak with laughter and at last Jim caught her, pinned her against the side of a wagon with one hand and took aim with the other.

'I am mortally sorry,' she gasped. 'Please forgive me. I am abject. It will not happen again.'

'No! It will never happen again,' he agreed. 'I'll show you what will happen if it does.' He gave her the same treatment, and by the time he had finished she had yellow melon in her hair and eyelashes, and in her ears.

'You are a beast, James Archibald!' She knew how he hated that name. 'I hate you.' She tried to glare at him, but burst into laughter again. She raised one hand to strike him, but he caught her wrist and she stumbled against him.

Suddenly neither of them was laughing. Their mouths were so close that their breath mingled and there was something in her eyes that he had not seen before. Then she began to tremble and her lips quivered. The emotion he had seen faded and was replaced with terror. He knew that all the servants were watching them.

With an effort he released her wrist and stepped back, but now his laughter was breathless. 'Beware, wench. Next time it will be a cold slimy lump of melon down the back of your neck.'

The moment hung precariously, for she was on the edge of tears. Bakkat saved them by breaking into a pantomime of their contest. He picked up the remains of the melon and hurled it at Zama. The drivers and *voorlopers* joined in, and melon rind flew in all directions. In the uproar Louisa slipped away to her wagon. When she emerged later she was demure in a fresh frock, her hair in long plaits. 'Would you like a game of chess?' she asked, not looking into his eyes.

He checkmated her in twenty moves, then doubted the merit of his victory. He wondered if she had purposely allowed him to win, or whether she had merely been distracted.

The next morning Jim and Louisa, with Bakkat, rode out before dawn, taking their breakfast with them tied in the canteens behind their saddles. Only an hour ahead of the wagons, they stopped to water the horses and eat their breakfast beside a small stream that meandered down from the line of lightly forested hills that lay across their path.

They sat opposite each other on fallen logs. They were shy and subdued, unable to meet each other's eyes. The memory of the moment from the previous day was still vivid in their minds, and their conversation was stilted and overly polite. After they had eaten Louisa took the canteens down to the stream to wash them while Jim resaddled the horses. When she came back he hesitated before helping her to step up into

Trueheart's saddle. She thanked him more profusely than the small act called for.

They rode up the hill, Bakkat leading the way on Frost. As he reached the crest he wheeled Frost back off the skyline, and raced towards them, his face contorted with some strong emotion, his voice reduced to an unintelligible squeak.

'What is it?' Jim shouted at him. 'What have you seen?' He seized Bakkar's arm and almost yanked him out of the saddle.

Bakkat found his voice at last. '*Dhlovu!*' he cried, as though in pain. 'Many, many.'

Jim threw his reins to Bakkat, jerked the small-bore rifle from its sheath and sprang out of the saddle. He knew better than to show himself on the skyline and stopped below the crest to gather himself. Excitement had clamped down on his chest and he could hardly breathe. His heart seemed on the point of leaping out of his mouth. Yet he still had the good sense to check the direction of the breeze: he picked a few blades of dry grass, shredded them between his fingers, and studied the drift of the tiny fragments. It was favourable.

Suddenly he felt Louisa's presence close beside him. 'What is it, Jim?' She had not understood the word Bakkat had used.

'Elephant!' Jim could barely enunciate the magical word.

She stared at him for only a moment, then her eyes flared like sunlight in blue sapphire. 'Oh, Jim! Show me!'

Even in the turmoil that had overwhelmed him, he was grateful she was there to share something he knew, deep in his heart, would stay with him all his days. 'Come!' he said, and, quite naturally, she took his hand. Despite all that had gone between them, this trusting gesture came as no surprise to him. Hand in hand they went to the crest of the hill and looked over.

Below them lay a vast bowl of land hemmed about with hills. It was carpeted with new growth, freshly sprung after the recent rains on ground that had been burned by grass-fires during the dry season. It was green as an English meadow, and scattered with clumps of tall mahoba-hoba trees, and copses of thornbush.

Spread out in the bottom of the bowl, alone or in small herds, were hundreds of elephant. For Jim, who had imagined this first encounter so many times and in so many ways, the reality far outweighed all his fantasy. 'Oh, sweet Mary!' he whispered. 'Oh, God, oh, beloved God!'

She felt his hand shaking in hers and tightened her grip. She recognized this as a seminal moment in his life and suddenly she was proud to be beside him, to share it with him. It seemed that this was her place: as though she had at last found where she belonged.

He could see at once from their relative size that most of the elephant herds consisted of females and their young. They formed grey agglomerations like reefs of granite, and the shapes of the herds changed only slowly, coming together, then flowing apart again. In all this mass of animals the great bulls stood apart and aloof, massive dark shapes, even at this remove dominating the herds that surrounded them, unmistakable in their majesty.

Close below where Jim and Louisa stood one particular animal made all the others seem insignificant. Perhaps it was merely the way the sunlight played upon him, but he was darker than any other. His ears were spread like the mainsail of a ship, and he fanned them with a lazy, flapping motion. With each movement the sun caught the curve of a huge tusk, and shot a ray towards them like the reflection of a mirror. Once the bull reached down with his trunk, and gathered up the dust at his feet and threw it back over his head and shoulders in a pale cloud.

'He is so big!' Louisa whispered. 'I never expected them to be that size.'

Her voice roused Jim from his trance of wonder, and he looked back to see Bakkat hovering close behind him.

'I have only this small-bore gun with me.' Jim had left the two big German four-to-the-pounders with the wagons. They were awkward weapons to carry and handle and, having been so often disappointed, he had not expected to run into elephant today, and certainly not in such numbers. He regretted the oversight now, but he knew it would be folly to use the little London rifle he had with him against a creature endowed with such bulk of muscle and sinew, such massive bone structure. Only with great luck could he hope to send such a light ball into its vitals.

'Ride back, Bakkat, as fast as Frost will carry you, and bring the two big guns to me with the powder flask and shotbelt.' No sooner had Jim finished speaking than Bakkat was up on Frost and going back down the hill at a mad gallop. They did not watch him go, but Jim and Louisa crept forward, using a small bush to break up their silhouette as they crossed the skyline. On the far slope they found a clump of thorny acacia that offered concealment, and settled among the fluffy branches and yellow blossom, sitting side by side while Jim focused his telescope on the great bull below them.

He gasped aloud, amazed at the animal's enhanced size when seen through the lens, and he stared in awe at the length and thickness of those shafts of ivory. Although he had not yet had his fill of such a magnificent sight he passed the glass to Louisa. By now she had learned to use it with expertise, and she trained it on the great animal. But after only a few minutes her attention was diverted to the playful antics of a group of calves further on: they were squealing and chasing each other through the forest.

When Jim saw the direction of the telescope wandering away from the patriarch he was strongly inclined to take it out of Louisa's hands and continue his study of the bull. Then he saw the tender smile on her face as she watched the calves at play, and he restrained himself. This in itself was a mark of his feelings for her: he was almost consumed by the hunter's passion and his heart beat hotly for the chase.

Then, to his delight, the bull left the shade of the mahoba-hoba tree and started ambling up the slope directly towards where they sat. He placed his hand on Louisa's shoulder to warn her. When she lowered the telescope he put a finger to his lips and pointed at the approaching bull.

Louisa's expression changed to awe as it drew closer, and loomed larger. Even in broad daylight there was something ghostly and unnerving about the utter silence of its walk: it placed its feet with a precision and grace disproportionate to its size, and the huge spongy pads absorbed all sound. The trunk hung slackly, almost to the ground and only the tip unrolled and touched the earth, picking up a leaf or a seed pod with an extraordinary dexterity that matched human fingers, toying with it then tossing it aside.

Closer still, they could see clearly that its one visible eye was set in a web of deep grey wrinkles, like the concentric rings of a spider's web. A wet stain of tears ran from one corner down its weathered cheek, but the eye gleamed with a sheen of intelligence and sagacity. With every few slow strides the tip of one of those long tusks touched the ground and left a tiny furrow in the earth.

Closer it came until it seemed to fill the sky above them, and they held their breath, expecting to be trodden on or at least stabbed through by a thrust from one of those gleaming ivory shafts. Louisa stirred, ready to spring up and run, but Jim tightened his grip on her shoulder and restrained her.

The bull was making a deep rumble in his throat and belly, which sounded like distant thunder. Louisa trembled in sympathy, excitement mingling with dread. Slowly, so as not to alarm the animal, Jim raised the little rifle to his shoulder and looked over the sights at the great grey head. Beside him he felt Louisa stiffen in anticipation of the shot. Then he remembered all that his father had told him, where to aim for a shot to the brain.

'But only a fool and a braggart tries that shot,' Tom had told him. ''Tis such a tiny mark to hit in the huge bony castle of the skull. The true hunter makes certain of the kill. He uses a heavy bore that throws a weighty ball, and he shoots for the shoulder, for the heart and the lungs.'

Jim lowered the rifle, and beside him Louisa relaxed. The elephant passed their hiding-place with its stately stride, and fifty paces further on it reached a small gwarrie tree, began to strip its purple berries and lift them fastidiously to its mouth. When the withered, baggy rump was turned towards them, Jim rose cautiously and led Louisa back over the ridge. He picked out the feather of dust coming towards them from the direction of the wagons, and the pale shape of Frost at full gallop.

As Bakkat came up, Jim said, 'That was quick work, and well done.' He snatched one of the great guns from his hand before Bakkat had a chance to dismount. Quickly he examined the weapon. It was unloaded and thick with grease, but the flint was new and well shaped. Quickly he set about loading. He rammed the huge, glistening ball down the barrel. At four ounces, it was almost twice the size of a ripe grape. It had been rendered adamantine by the addition of pewter to the molten lead. When it was seated firmly on the wad and the heavy charge of black powder, he looked to the priming, then exchanged the weapon for the second of the pair Bakkat held out to him. When both were loaded, he said, 'There is a magnificent bull feeding close by, just over yonder ridge. I will attack him on foot but as soon as you hear my shot, bring up Drumfire and the second gun with all speed.'

'What must I do?' Louisa asked, and he hesitated. His instinct was to send her back to the wagons, but he knew that would be unfair. She should not be deprived of the excitement and adventure of this first chase after the mighty beasts. More importantly, she would probably refuse to obey him, and he did not have time now for an argument he would almost certainly lose. On the other hand he could not leave her here. He knew, from vivid accounts that his father had given him, that once the first shot was fired the bush would be swarming with panic-stricken beasts running in all directions. If one came upon her when she was unprotected she would be in mortal danger. 'Follow us, but not too closely. You must keep me or Bakkat in sight at all times, but you must also keep a watchful eye all around you. Elephant might come from any direction, even from behind. But you can rely on Trueheart to carry you out of danger.'

He drew back the hammer of the big gun to half-cock, ran to the crest of the ridge, and peered over. Nothing had changed in the time since he had last seen the bull. He was still feeding quietly on the gwarrie tree, facing away from Jim.

The herds below were resting, or feeding quietly, and the young calves were still frolicking around the legs of their dams.

Jim paused only to check the direction of the breeze once more. He felt its cool, light touch on his sweaty face, but he took a few moments to dribble a handful of dust through his fingers. The breeze was still steady and in his favour. He knew that there was little reason for concealment now. The eyesight of the elephant is poor, and they are unable to distinguish the form of a man at fifty paces, as long as he remains motionless. On the other hand, their sense of smell is phenomenal.

With the breeze in his favour, and stepping lightly, Jim crept up behind the feeding bull. His father's words came back to him: 'Close. Always get as close as you can. Every yard you close with the quarry makes the kill more certain. Thirty paces is too far. Twenty is not as good as ten. Five paces is perfect. From that range your ball will drive to the heart.'

As he drew in closer Jim's steps slowed. It was as though his legs were filling with molten lead. His breath became laboured, and he felt as though he was suffocating. The gun in his hands was becoming heavier. He had not expected to be afraid. I have never been scared before, he thought, and then, well, perhaps just a little, sometimes.

Closer and still closer. Then he remembered he had forgotten to fully cock the hammer of the big gun. He was so close that the bull would hear the click of the mechanism, and take fright. He hesitated, and the animal moved. With that ponderous, deliberate stride it began to circle the gwarrie tree. Jim's heart jumped against his ribs as its flank was exposed to him, and he could make out the outline of the massive shoulder-blade beneath the riven, creased hide. It was just as his father had drawn it for him. He knew exactly where to aim. He lifted the butt to his shoulder, but the bull kept moving round the tree, until its shoulder was covered by the twisted branches and thick, shiny green foliage. It stopped on the far side of the bush from him, and began to feed again. It was so close that Jim could see the individual bristles in its ear, and the thick, matted eyelashes surrounding the knowing

262

little eye that seemed so incongruous in the ancient, mountainous head.

'Only a fool and a braggart shoots for the brain,' his father had warned him, but the shoulder was covered and he was so close. Surely he could not miss from this range. First he had to fully cock the rifle. He placed his hand over the action, trying to muffle it, and he inched back the engraved steel hammer. He felt the moment when the sear was about to engage and bit his tongue as he concentrated on easing it through that last fraction of the arc.

He was watching the bull, trying by the force of his will to lull it to the sound of metal on metal. The elephant was chewing with evident satisfaction, stuffing the ripe berries into its mouth; the inside of its lips was stained purple.

Click! To Jim the sound was deafening in the great silence of the wilderness. The elephant stopped chewing and froze in monumental stillness. It had heard that alien sound, and Jim knew that it was poised on the edge of flight.

Jim stared hard at the dark slit of the earhole, and slowly lifted the butt to his shoulder. The iron sights did not impinge upon his vision: he seemed to look through them. All his being was concentrated on that spot half a finger's length in front of the ear. He knew the pull and feel of the trigger intimately, but so intense was his concentration that the thunder of the shot surprised him.

The butt of the weapon pounded into his shoulder, driving him back two paces before he regained his balance. The long bluish plume of powder smoke gushed out from the muzzle and seemed to stroke the wrinkled grey skin of the bull's temple. Jim was unsighted by the recoil and by the cloud of smoke, so he did not see the strike of the ball, but he heard it crack against the skull like an axe blade against the trunk of an ironwood tree.

The bull threw back its great head and dropped with almost miraculous suddenness, hitting the earth with such force that he raised a cloud of dust. The ground under Jim's feet seemed to jump with the impact. Jim regained his balance and gaped with astonishment at what he had achieved. Then his heart soared and he whooped with triumph. 'He's down! With a single shot I have slain him.' He started forward to gloat over his kill, but there came the pounding of hoofs from behind.

When he glanced round Bakkat was galloping up on Frost, waving the second gun and leading Drumfire. 'Change guns, Somoya!' he shouted. 'Behold! There are *dhlovu* all about us. We may kill ten more if we ride hard.'

'I must see the bull I have killed,' Jim protested. 'I must cut off his tail.' This was the trophy his father had always taken from a downed beast, even in the heat of the chase.

'If he is dead he will stay dead.' Bakkat reined in, snatched the empty gun from his hand and thrust the loaded one towards him. 'The others will be gone before you have a chance to cut off the tail. Once they are gone you will never see them again.' Still Jim hesitated, looking longingly to where the fallen bull lay concealed behind the gwarrie tree. 'Come, Somoya! See the dust they raise as they run. Soon it will be too late.'

Jim looked down the slope and saw that his shot had startled the herds, and in the basin below them the elephant were scattering and fleeing in every direction. His father had told him of the peculiar instinctive horror that the elephant entertains towards man: even if they have never before encountered his cruel, warlike behaviour they will run a hundred leagues from their first contact with him. Still he hesitated, and Bakkat told him urgently, 'Somoya, the moment passes.' He pointed at two more great bulls charging past, less than a pistol shot from where they stood. Their ears were folded back against their shoulders and they were at full run. 'They will be gone before you can draw three more breaths. Follow! Follow with all speed!'

The bulls were already disappearing into the forest, but Jim knew he could catch up within a mile of hard riding. He hesitated no longer. With the loaded rifle in hand he leaped into Drumfire's saddle and booted him in the ribs. 'Ha! Ha! Drumfire! After them, my darling.' He turned the stallion's head down the slope and they tore off in pursuit. Drumfire caught the contagious excitement of his rider, and his eyes rolled wildly as he drove his head into each stride like a sledgehammer. They swung in behind the running bulls, closing swiftly. Jim slitted his eyes against the dust storm they were throwing up with the huge pads of their feet, and the thorn branches that whipped back into his face. He picked out the larger of the two great bulls. Even from his station dead astern he could see the wide curves of its tusks showing on each side of its heaving flanks.

'I will sup with the devil if he's not bigger than the first one I downed,' he exulted, and steered Drumfire out to one side, trying to come level with the bull, seeking to open his flank for a shot at the shoulder. He held the rifle across the pommel of his saddle and eased the hammer back into the half-cock position.

Then, from behind him, he heard the wild trumpeting of an enraged elephant, followed, almost immediately, by Louisa's scream.

The two dreadful sounds were almost drowned by distance and the thunder of Drumfire's hoofs. But there was a timbre to Louisa's cry that raked every nerve in his body and cut him to the heart. It was the wild ringing screech of abject terror. He swivelled in the saddle and looked back and saw her mortal predicament.

Obedient to Jim's instructions, Louisa had hung back, keeping Trueheart behind Frost as they crossed the ridge at a walk. She saw Jim two hundred paces ahead. His back was turned towards her, and he was moving forward deliberately, half crouched over the weapon he carried level with his waist.

For a moment she failed to see the bull. With its grey colour it seemed to blend like smoke into the bush around him. Then she gasped as her eyes picked out its form. It seemed mountainous, and Jim was so close to the beast that she was terrified for his safety. She stopped Trueheart and watched, with dreadful fascination, as Jim crept closer still.

She saw the bull change its position, move behind the gwarrie tree, and for a moment she thought it had eluded Jim's stalk. Then she saw Jim rise from his crouch and lift the long barrel of his rifle. When he aimed, the muzzle seemed to touch the bull's head, and then came the thunderous clap of the discharge, like the mainsail of the *Meeuw* filling with wind as she tacked into the storm.

The blue powder smoke boiled and churned in the breeze, and the bull went down as though struck by an avalanche. Then all was shouting and commotion as Bakkat spurred forward from beside her, and raced to where Jim stood, dragging Drumfire on the lead rein after him. Jim went up on Drumfire and, leaving the downed bull lying where it had fallen, he and Bakkat raced down the slope, chasing two more huge elephant that she had not noticed until that moment.

Louisa let them go. Without conscious volition, she found that Trueheart had responded to a slight pressure of her knees and was walking forward towards the gwarrie tree behind which the bull had fallen. She did not try to stop the mare and as they approached her curiosity increased. She raised herself in the stirrups to see over the tree, trying to catch a glimpse of the mighty creature she had seen fall there.

She was almost up to the tree when she saw a small flirt of movement, too insignificant to have been made by such a large beast. She rode closer, and this time she realized that what she had seen was a flick of the elephant's stubby tail. The clump of bristles at the end was worn and ragged as an old paintbrush.

She was about to dismount and lead Trueheart forward for a better view of the carcass and the curved, magnificent yellow tusks that intrigued her. Then, to her horrified disbelief, the bull stood up. It came to its feet in one swift motion, alert and agile as though waking from a light sleep. It stood for a moment, as though listening. A rivulet of bright scarlet blood poured from the wound in its temple, and down its grey, wrinkled cheek. Trueheart snorted with fright and shied away. In the act of dismounting, Louisa had only one foot in the stirrup and she was nearly thrown, but with an effort she regained her seat.

The bull had heard Trueheart snort, and turned towards them. Its huge ears flared out: it saw them as his tormentors. The horse and human scent filled its head, an alien odour it had never smelt before, but which reeked of danger.

The bull shook its head, the huge ears snapping and clattering with the strength of the movement, and it squealed its fury and affront. Blood splattered from the bullet wound, and the droplets pelted into Louisa's face, warm as monsoon rain, and she screamed with all her breath and all the strength of her lungs. 'Jim! Save me!'

The bull rolled its trunk up against its chest, and half cocked its ears back with the ends curled, the attitude of ultimate aggression. Then it charged straight at them. Trueheart wheeled away, laid her ears flat and burst into full gallop. She seemed to take flight, to skim lightly over the rough surface, but the bull stayed close at her tail, squealing again and again with fury, a pink feather of blood blowing back from its head wound.

With a burst of speed Trueheart opened the gap, pulling ahead, but suddenly there was a hedge of thorn bush in front of her and she was forced to check, and change direction to swerve round the obstacle. The bull did not hesitate, but burst through the thorn thicket as though it did not exist, regaining all the ground it had lost. It was now closer still.

With horror Louisa saw that there was rocky ground ahead and denser thickets of thorn bush blocking their path. The bull was driving them into a trap, in which even Trueheart's speed would be of little avail. Louisa remembered the small French rifle under her right leg. In her terror she had forgotten its existence, but now she knew it was all she had to stop the bull snatching her from the saddle. She glanced back and saw that the long ophidian trunk was already reaching out for her.

She drew the rifle from its leather sheath, swivelled round and cocked the weapon in the same movement. Again she screamed involuntarily as she saw the grasping trunk waving

267

in her face, and threw up the rifle. The enormous head filled all her vision and she did not aim but fired blindly into the bull's face.

The light ball could never have penetrated the thick hide and the bony casket of the skull, but the bull was vulnerable in one place. By the wildest chance the ball found that mark. It entered the eye-socket at a raking angle, and burst the eyeball, blinding the bull instantly on the same side of its head as the wound Jim had inflicted.

The elephant reeled and staggered, losing ground on Trueheart, but it recovered almost immediately and started forward again. All of Louisa's attention was fastened on the task of reloading the rifle, but she had never done this on horseback at full gallop, and the gunpowder spewed from the flask and blew away in the wind. She glanced back and saw that the bull still had them in the focus of its right eye and was reaching for her again. She knew that this time it would have her.

So complete was her fascination with her fate that she did not see the thicket looming ahead. Trueheart swerved to avoid running full into it, and Louisa was thrown off balance teetering in the saddle. She dropped the rifle as she clutched at the pommel. The weapon clattered on the rocky ground.

Hanging half out of the saddle she was dragged down the length of the thicket. The hooked thorns were tipped with crimson and needle sharp. They bit into her clothing and into her flesh like myriad cats' claws. Their combined grip was irresistible and Louisa was jerked cleanly from Trueheart's back. The mare galloped on with an empty saddle, leaving Louisa dangling and struggling in the tenacious grip of the thorns.

The elephant had lost sight of her on his blind side, but it smelled her: the odour of the fresh blood from the tiny wounds inflicted by the thorns was strong. It let Trueheart run on unmolested and turned back. It began to search for Louisa with outstretched trunk, pushing its way into the thicket, its thick grey hide impervious to the hooked thorns, guided by the sound of Louisa's struggles and her scent. It closed in on her swiftly. She realized her danger and froze into stillness.

She lay quietly in the grip of the thorns and watched with resignation as the questing tip of the trunk groped towards her. It touched her boot, then locked round her ankle. With unimaginable strength she was torn out of the thicket, the clinging thorns breaking off in the folds of her clothing or in her skin.

She hung upside down, dangling by one leg from the trunk of the elephant. Its grip on her ankle tightened and she feared that at any moment the bone would crush to splinters. From all Jim had told her, she knew what would happen next. The bull would lift her high in the air and then, with all its monstrous power, would dash her head first against the rocky ground. It would beat her against the earth again and again, until almost every bone in her body was shattered and then it would kneel on her and crush her to pulp, driving the points of its tusks through and through.

Jim turned at the sound of her first scream and the shrill trumpeting of the huge bull. He broke off the chase after the two other elephants, and reined Drumfire hard down on his haunches. Then he stared back in horror and disbelief. 'I killed it!' he gasped. 'I left it dead.' But at the same time he remembered his father's warning. 'The brain is so small, and is not placed where you would expect it to be. If you miss it by even the breadth of your little finger, the animal will drop as though stone-dead, but it is stunned only. When it comes round, it will be unimpaired and many times more dangerous than before. I have seen good men killed that way. Never chance that shot, Jim, my boy, or you will live to regret it.'

'Bakkat!' Jim yelled. 'Stay close with the second gun!' He gave Drumfire the spurs, and sent him back at full gallop. Louisa and the bull were running directly away from him, and he overhauled them only gradually. He was seized by a feeling

269

of debilitating impotence: he could see that Louisa would be killed before he could reach her, and it was his fault: he had left the enraged animal in a position where it could attack her.

'I'm coming!' he yelled. 'Hold hard!' He tried to give her courage but in the thunder of hoofs and the ringing trumpeting of the bull she showed no sign of having heard him. He watched her turn in the saddle and fire the little lady's rifle, but though the bull staggered slightly to the shot it did not leave her.

Then he watched in despair as Louisa ran into the bushes and was plucked from the saddle. The elephant turned back to hunt for her, as she was held powerless in the grip of the thorns. However, this check enabled Jim to push in so close that Drumfire baulked and shied at the gamy stench of the elephant, and at its threatening presence. Using his spurs without mercy, Jim drove him in closer still, watching for an opportunity to send in a telling shot. He knew that his ball must break bone or hit the vitals to distract the bull. However, all was confused movement, noise and flying dust. The elephant was wading through the thorn bush, and the waving branches protected his vulnerable parts and frustrated Jim's aim. Drumfire was skittering under him, throwing his head and trying to back away from the terrible menace of the elephant.

He saw Louisa tangled in the thorns. She showed no sign of life. He thought that her neck might have snapped in the fall or that her skull was crushed in. The idea of losing her was too agonizing to be borne, and he forced Drumfire forward with all his strength and will. Suddenly the bull found Louisa's limp body and hauled her out of the thicket. Jim dared not fire at its head for fear of hitting Louisa. He was forced to wait until the beast backed and turned broadside to him, at last exposing its flank. Jim leaned far out of the saddle, reaching up until the muzzle of the heavy gun almost touched the rough and baggy skin, and he fired.

The ball struck the point of the bull's shoulder, on the

heavy joint of humerus and scapula, shattering the bone. The elephant reeled back from the shot, and threw out its trunk to balance itself on three legs. It released its grip on Louisa's leg, and she fell back into the thicket where the branches cushioned her from the hard earth.

The elephant turned towards Jim, ears flaring, shrilling with pain and rage, then reached out with its trunk to pull him from the saddle. But it was pinned by its broken front leg, and Jim turned Drumfire away, swinging out of reach, and rode back to meet Bakkat who was coming up with the second gun. With expertise born of long practice they exchanged guns. 'Reload! As quick as you like!' Jim shouted, and with the second weapon in his hand he spurred back to confront the bull, which was dragging itself to meet him, hobbling on three legs, the crippled front leg twisted and useless.

Jim could see now that Louisa's shot had blinded one eye, for blood and eye jelly poured down its cheek. He changed direction, coming in from the bull's blind side, so close that the tip of one tusk grazed his shoulder, and as he went by he fired into its chest without checking Drumfire's gallop. The bull staggered. This time the heavy four-ounce ball had gone in deeply, cutting through the vital organs, the tangled arteries and veins deep in the chest cavity. It was a fatal wound but it would take time for the beast to fall.

He reckoned that Louisa was out of harm's way, as long as she stayed where she was, deeply hidden in the thicket. In the utmost haste Jim rode back to where Bakkat had dropped down from Frost's back, the better and swifter to reload the other gun. It took courage to dismount in the face of a wounded elephant.

Courage is one thing he lacks not! Jim thought, as he watched for him to finish the complicated business of reloading the heavy gun. Drumfire danced in nervous circles, and Jim glanced back to watch the bull. Then he shouted with alarm as he saw Louisa crawling out of the thorn bush on hands and knees, almost under the bull's trampling feet. Exposed as she now was, she was once again in terrible danger. He dropped

271

the empty gun and, not waiting for Bakkat to finish reloading, galloped back. Again he swerved in from the bull's blind side so that he could risk a much closer pass.

Obviously half stunned, Louisa came to her feet, favouring her injured leg where the bull's trunk had seized her. She saw Jim riding towards her, hopped towards him and lifted her arms. She was a dreadful sight, her clothing torn by thorns and stained with blood. She was covered with scratches and dust, her long hair tumbling down over her face.

Drumfire brushed so closely along the bull's blind side that the blood that flowed down from the wound in its shoulder stained Jim's breeches at the knee, but when the elephant swung its trunk to swat him like a fly, Jim flattened himself along Drumfire's neck and ducked under the blow. They galloped up to Louisa and, without pausing, Jim leaned far out of the saddle, gripping only with his knees, flung one arm round Louisa and swung her up behind him. As soon as she was astride she locked both her arms around his waist and pressed her face into his sweaty shirt between his shoulder-blades. She was sobbing with pain and fright, unable to utter a word. He carried her to the crest of the hill, swung himself to the ground, and reached up to lift her down from Drumfire's back.

She was still unable to speak, but words were unnecessary and inadequate. Her eyes, close to his, expressed all her gratitude and gave him a glimpse of her other emotions, still too complex and confused for her to express.

Jim set her carefully on the ground. 'Where are you hurt?' he asked. His voice was choked with concern for her. The toll that their brush with death had exacted was clear to see on his face, and this rallied her. She clung to him still as he knelt over her.

'My ankle, but 'tis almost nothing,' she whispered.

'Let me see it,' he said, and she let her arms slip away from his neck. 'Which one?' he asked, and she showed him. He eased the boot from her foot and tested her leg gently. 'It's not broken,' he said.

'No.' She sat up. 'And 'tis only a little sore.' She brushed the golden hair off her dusty face and he saw that a thorn was stuck into her cheek. He plucked it out, and she winced but held his gaze. 'Jim!' she whispered.

'Yes, my little hedgehog?'

'No, 'tis nothing, except—' She broke off, unable to finish, then went on lamely, 'I like it well enough when you call me that.'

'I'm glad to have you back,' Jim said. 'For a moment I thought you had taken leave of us.'

'I must be a sight to give children nightmares.' She could look no longer into his eyes, and tried to wipe the dust from her face.

Only a woman could consider her appearance at such a time, Jim thought, but he did not say it. 'You are such a sight as I have dreamed on,' he said instead, and she blushed under the dirt.

Then Bakkat rode up on Frost with both the great guns loaded and primed. 'The bull will escape us yet, if you let him, Somoya.'

Jim roused himself to what was happening around them. He saw the old bull walking away slowly downhill, dragging one front leg and shaking its huge head as the agony of the burst eyeball raged through its skull.

'Oh, Jim,' Louisa whispered. 'The poor beast is in terrible extremes. You must not let him suffer so.'

'It will not take long,' he promised her. He stepped up into Drumfire's saddle and took the gun Bakkat handed up to him. Then he rode down the slope, circled out ahead of the maimed animal and stopped Drumfire squarely in its path. He cocked the hammer and waited.

The bull seemed not to notice them and came on slowly, painfully. At ten paces Jim fired into the front of its chest. As the ball socked heavily into the wrinkled hide, he spun Drumfire away like a dancer. The bull made no move to follow them. It stood still as a monument, and the heart blood pumped from the fresh bullet hole, bright as a fountain in the sunlight.

Jim changed guns with Bakkat, then brought Drumfire back

towards where the bull still stood. He came in on its blind side at a steady walk. The bull began to rock gently on its feet, once again making a soft rumbling sound deep in its chest. Jim felt all his warlike passions abating, to be replaced by a feeling of sadness and aching remorse. With this most noble of all quarry, he felt more intensely than ever the eternal tragedy of the kill. It was an effort to raise the gun and fire again. The bull shuddered when it received the ball, and began to back away, but its movements were slow and unsteady. Then, at last, it sighed, a laboured, gusty sound.

It fell the way a great tree goes down before the axe and cross-saw, slowly at first, then faster until it hit the earth with a crash that echoed from the hills across the valley.

Bakkat slipped off Frost's back, and went forward. The elephant's good eye was wide open, and Bakkat ran his finger lightly along the fringe of its lashes. It did not blink. 'It is over, Somoya. He belongs to you for ever.'

Despite her protests that her injuries were of no consequence, Jim would not let Louisa ride back to the wagons. He and Bakkat cut two long, supple poles and with a framework of lighter sticks fastened between them, the whole covered by the canvas ground sheets from their blanket rolls, they contrived a travois for Trueheart to drag behind her. Jim laid Louisa tenderly on it and picked the smoothest path to lead Trueheart back to the wagons.

Although Louisa laughed from this comfortable bed, and declared it the easiest journey she had ever made, by the time they reached the wagons her injuries had stiffened. When she rose from the travois she hobbled to her wagon like a very old lady.

Jim hovered around her anxiously, aware that any uninvited help he might offer would be rejected. He was surprised and delighted when she placed a hand on his shoulder as she climbed the wagon steps. He left her to take off her torn, soiled clothing while he supervised the heating of the water cauldron and the preparation of the copper hip-bath. Zama and the other servants removed the afterchest from her wagon and set up the bath in its place. Then they filled it with steaming water. When all was ready, Jim retired and listened through the canvas tent to her splashes, and winced in sympathy at her small cries and exclamations of pain as the water stung her abrasions and thorn pricks. When at last he judged that she had finished he asked permission to enter her wagon tent. 'Yes, you may come in, for I am as chastely attired as a nun.'

She was wearing the dressing-robe Sarah Courtney had given her. It reached from her chin to her ankles, and down to her wrists.

'Is there aught I can do to ease your discomfort?' he asked.

'I have rubbed your aunt Yasmini's sovereign balm and ointment upon my ankle and on most of my other afflictions.' She lifted the hem of the robe a few inches to show her ankle tightly wrapped in bandages. Dorian Courtney's wife was an adept of Arabian and Oriental medicine. Her famous ointment was the family cure-all. Sarah had packed a dozen large jars of it into the medical chest she had given them. There was an open jar beside Louisa's cardell bed, and the strong but pleasant herbal smell permeated the interior of the tent.

Jim was not sure where these remarks were leading, but he nodded wisely. Then she blushed again, and, without looking at him, murmured, 'However, I have thorns in places that I cannot reach. And bruises sufficient for two persons to share.'

It did not occur to him that she was asking for his help, and she had to make it more apparent. She reached over one shoulder and touched her back as far down as she could reach. 'It feels as though I have an entire forest of thorns embedded down there.' Still he stared at her, and she had to eschew all attempts at subtlety and modesty.

'In the chest you will find a pair of tweezers and a selection of needles you can use,' she said, turned her back to him and slipped the robe off her shoulder. 'There is one particular thorn here, just below my shoulderblade.' She touched the spot. 'It feels like a crucifixion nail.'

He gulped as he grasped her meaning, and reached for the tweezers. 'I shall try not to hurt you, but cry out if I do,' he said, but he was well practised in caring for sick and wounded animals, and his touch was firm but gentle.

She stretched out face down upon the sheepskin mattress, and gave herself over to his ministrations. Although her back was scratched and punctured in many places, and pale lymph and watery blood wept from the injuries, her skin was marble smooth and lustrously pale where it was undamaged. Although when he had first met her she had been a skinny waif, since then an abundance of good food and months of riding and walking had firmed and shaped her muscles. Even in her present straits, her body was the loveliest thing he had ever laid eyes on. He worked in silence, not trusting his voice, and except for the occasional gasp or small whimper Louisa said nothing.

When he folded back the hem of her robe to reach another hidden thorn, she moved slightly to make it easier for him. When he peeled back the silk a little further it revealed the beginning of the delicate cleft that separated her buttocks and down so fine and pale that it was invisible until the light fell upon it from a certain angle. Jim stood back and averted his eyes, although the effort required to do so was almost beyond him. 'I cannot go further,' he blurted.

'Pray, why not?' she asked, without lifting her face from the pillow. 'I can feel there are thorns that still demand your attention.'

'Modesty forbids it.'

'So you will not care if my injuries mortify, and I die of blood poisoning to save your precious modesty?'

'Do not jest so,' he exclaimed. The thought of her death struck deep into his soul. She had come so close to it this very morning.

'I jest not, James Archibald.' She raised her head from the pillow and regarded him frostily. 'I have no one else to whom I may turn. Think of yourself as a surgeon, and me as your patient.'

The lines of her naked bottom were pure and symmetrical beyond any geometrical or navigational diagram he had studied. Under his fingers her skin was warm and silken. When he had removed the thorns and anointed her various wounds with the balm, he measured a dose of laudanum to ease her discomfort. Then, at last, he was free to leave her wagon tent. But his legs seemed almost too weak to carry him.

Jim ate dinner alone at the campfire. Zama had roasted a large slice of the elephant's trunk, considered by his father and other connoisseurs to be one of the great delicacies of the African bush. But Jim's jaw ached from the effort of chewing it and it had all the flavour of boiled woodchips. When the flames of the campfire died down, exhaustion overtook him. He had just sufficient energy to peep through the chink in the afterclap of Louisa's wagon tent. She was stretched out, face down under the kaross, and sleeping so soundly that he had to listen intently for the faint sound of her breathing. Then he left her and tottered to his own bed. He stripped off his clothing and dropped it on the floor, then collapsed on the sheepskin.

He woke in confusion not sure if what he was hearing was a dream or reality. It was Louisa's voice, shrill with terror: 'Jim, Jim! Help me!'

He sprang from his bed to go to her, then remembered he was naked. While he groped for his breeches she cried out again. He did not have time to don his breeches, but holding them before him, he went to her rescue. He skinned his knee on the tailboard of the wagon as he jumped down, then ran to hers and dived through the curtains of the afterclap. 'Louisa! Are you safe? What troubles you?'

'Ride! Oh, ride with all haste! Don't let it catch me!' she screamed. He realized that she was locked in a nightmare. This time it was difficult to wake her. He had to seize both of her shoulders and shake her.

'Jim, is it you?' At last she came back from the land of shadows. 'Oh, I had such a terrible dream. It was the elephant again.'

She clung to him, and he waited for her to calm. She was hot and flushed, but after a while he laid her back and pulled the fur kaross over her. 'Sleep now, little hedgehog,' he whispered. 'I will not be far away.'

'Don't leave me, Jim. Stay with me for a while.'

'Until you sleep,' he agreed.

But he fell asleep before she did. She felt him topple over slowly and lie full length beside her. Then his breathing became slow and even. He was not touching her, but his presence was reassuring and she let herself slip back into sleep. This time there were no dark fantasies to haunt her rest.

When she awoke in the dawn to the sounds of the camp stirring around her she reached out to touch him, but he was gone. She felt a sharp sense of loss.

She dressed and climbed painfully down from the wagon. Jim and Bakkat were busy at the horselines, washing the scratches and small injuries that Drumfire and Trueheart had received in yesterday's battle with the elephant, and feeding them a little of the precious oats and bran moistened with black molasses as a reward for their courage. When he looked up and saw Louisa struggling down from her wagon, Jim exclaimed with alarm and ran to her. 'You should keep to your bed. What are you doing here?'

'I am going to see to breakfast.'

'What madness is this? Zama can do without your instruction for a day. You must rest.'

'Do not treat me like a child,' she told him, but the reprimand lacked fire and she smiled at him as she limped to the cooking fire. He did not argue. It was a gorgeous morning, bright and cool, and this put them both in a sunny mood. They ate under the trees to the sound of birdsong from the branches above them, and the meal became a small cel-

278

ebration of the previous day's events. With animation they discussed every detail of the hunt and relived all the excitement and terror, but neither mentioned the events of the night, although they were uppermost in their minds.

'Now I must go back to the carcass to remove the tusks. It is not a task I can leave to others. A careless slip of the axe will damage the ivory irrevocably,' he told her, as he mopped his plate with a piece of unleavened pot bread. 'I will rest Drumfire today, he worked hard yesterday, and I will take Crow. Trueheart will stay in camp, for she is as lame as you are.'

'Then I shall ride Stag,' she said. 'It will not take me long to don my boots.' Stag was a strong but gentle gelding they had taken from Colonel Keyser.

'You should stay in camp to recuperate fully.'

'I must go with you to retrieve my rifle, which I dropped in the thorn thickets.'

'That is a feeble pretext. I can do that for you.'

'You do not truly believe that I shall not attend the removal of the tusks for which we risked our very lives?'

He opened his mouth to protest, but saw from her expression that it would be wasted effort. 'I shall tell Bakkat to saddle Stag.'

There were two traditional methods of withdrawing the tusks. The carcass could be left to decompose, and when the cartilage that held the tusks in their sockets had softened and disintegrated they could be pulled forcibly from the skull. This was a lengthy and malodorous business, and Jim was impatient to see his trophies revealed in all their magnificence. So was Louisa.

When they rode back they found a canopy of circling carrion birds darkening the sky above the body of the dead bull. In this vast assembly there was every species of vulture and eagle, as well as the undertaker storks with their monstrous beaks and bald pink heads, which seemed to have been parboiled. The branches of the trees around the dead bull groaned under the weight of this feathered horde. As Jim and Louisa rode up to the carcass, packs of hyena slunk away, and little red jackals peered at them from the cover of the thornbushes with pricked ears and bright eyes. These scavengers had picked out the eyes of the bull and burrowed in through his anus, but they had not been able to tear open the tough grey hide to reach the flesh. Where the vultures had perched upon the carcass their excrement had left white stains down its sides. Jim felt a sense of outrage at this desecration of such a noble beast. Angrily he drew his rifle from its sheath and fired at one of the black vultures on the top branches of the nearest tree. Struck squarely by the leaden ball, the hideous bird came tumbling down in a welter of feathers and flapping wings. The rest of the roosting flock rose and climbed to join their peers in the sky above.

When Louisa retrieved her rifle, she found that the woodwork was only lightly scratched. She came back and selected a vantage-point in the shade. Seated on a saddle blanket she sketched the proceedings, and made notes in the margins of the page.

Jim's first task was to sever the bull's immense head from the neck. This had to be done to make it easier to handle – it would have taken fifty men or more to roll the massive carcass from one side to the other. As it was, the decapitation took half the morning. Stripped to the waist the men were sweating in the noonday sun before it was accomplished.

Then came the painstaking work of removing the skin and chipping away the bone from around the roots of the tusks, with meticulous axe strokes. Jim, Bakkat and Zama took turns, not trusting the clumsy touch of the wagon drivers and servants on the precious ivory. First one and then the other tusk was lifted out of its bony canal and laid upon a mattress of cut grass. With quick strokes of her brush Louisa recorded the moment when Jim stooped over the tusks and, with the point of his knife, freed the long cone-shaped nerve from the hollow butt end of each one. They slithered out, white and glutinous as jelly.

They wrapped the tusks in cushions of cut grass, loaded them on to the backs of the pack-horses and bore them back to the wagons in triumph. Jim unpacked the scale his father had given him for this purpose and suspended it from the branch of a tree. Then, surrounded by everyone, he weighed the tusks one at a time. The right-hand shaft of ivory, the bull's working tusk, was more worn and weighed 143 pounds. The larger tusk weighed 150 pounds precisely. Both were stained brown by vegetable juices where they had been exposed, but the butts were a lovely cream colour, glossy as precious porcelain where they had been protected in the sheath of bone and cartilage. 'In all the hundreds of traded tusks I have seen pass through the godown at High Weald I have never seen one larger,' he told Louisa proudly.

They sat late beside the campfire that night for there seemed so much still to say. Bakkat, Zama and the other servants had all rolled themselves in their blankets and were sleeping beside their fires when Jim walked Louisa back to her wagon.

Afterwards he lay on his own bed, naked in the balmy night. As he drifted off he listened to the weird sobbing and laughter of the hyena patrolling the outskirts of the camp, attracted by the scent of the raw elephant meat curing on the smoking racks. His last thought was to wonder if Smallboy and the other drivers had placed the leather ropes and tackle of the wagon harness out of reach of those scavengers. With their formidable jaws the hyena could chew and swallow the toughest tanned leather as easily as he could devour a luscious oyster. But he knew that the safety and condition of the wagon harness was always Smallboy's first concern, and let himself drop into a sound sleep.

He woke suddenly, aware that the wagon had rocked lightly under him. His first thought was a continuation of the last: perhaps a hyena was raiding the camp. He sat up and reached for the loaded musket that always lay beside his bed, but before his hand could fall upon the stock he froze and stared towards the afterclap.

The moon still lacked two nights of full, and he could tell by its angle that it must be after midnight. Its light threw a soft glow through the canvas curtain of the afterclap. Louisa was silhouetted against it, an ethereal fairy figure. He could

281

not see her face, for it was in shadow, but her hair came down in a pale cascade around her shoulders.

She took a hesitant pace towards his bed. Then she stopped again. He could see by the way in which she held her head that she was shy or afraid, maybe both. 'Louisa? What ails you?'

'I could not sleep,' she whispered.

'Is there anything I can do?'

She did not reply at once, but instead she came forward slowly and lay down at his side. 'Please, Jim, be kind to me. Be patient with me.'

They lay in silence, without touching, their bodies rigid. Neither knew what to do next.

Louisa broke the silence. 'Speak to me, Jim. Do you want me to go back to my own wagon?' It irked her that he who was usually so bold was timid now.

'No. Oh, please, no,' he blurted out.

'Then speak to me.'

'I'm not sure what you want me to say, but I will tell you all that is in my mind and heart,' he said. He thought for a while, and his voice sank to a whisper. 'When first I saw you on the deck of the ship, it seemed that I had been waiting all my life for that moment.'

She sighed softly, and he felt her relax beside him, like a cat spreading herself out in the warmth of the sun. Encouraged, he went on, 'I have often thought when I watch my father and mother together that for every man born God fashions a woman.'

'Adam's rib,' she murmured.

'I believe that you are my rib,' he said. 'I cannot find happiness and fulfilment without you.'

'Go on, Jim. Please don't stop.'

'I believe that all the terrible things that happened to you before we met, and all the hardships and dangers we have endured since then, have had but one purpose. That is to test and temper us, like steel in the furnace.'

'I had not thought of that,' she said, 'but now I see it is true.'

He reached out and touched her hand. It seemed to him that a spark passed between their fingertips like the crackling discharge of gunpowder in the pan. She jerked away her hand. He sensed that their moment, although close, had not yet arrived. He took back his own hand and she relaxed again.

His uncle Dorian had once given him a filly that no one else could break to the bit and saddle. It had been very much like this, weeks and months of slow progress, of advance and retreat, but in the end she had become his, as beautiful and wondrous a creature as it was possible to imagine. He had called her Windsong and had held her head as she died of the horse-sickness.

On an inspiration he told Louisa about Windsong, how he had loved her and how she had died. She lay beside him in the darkness and listened, captivated. When he came to the end of the story she wept like a child, but they were good tears, not the bitter hurting tears that had so often gone before.

Then she slept at last, still lying beside him, still not quite touching. He listened to her gentle breathing, and at last slept also.

They followed the elephant herds northwards for almost another month. It was as his father had warned him: when disturbed by man the great beasts moved hundreds of leagues to new country. They travelled at that long, striding walk that even a good horse could not match over a long distance. The entire southern continent was their domain, and the old matriarchs of the herds knew every mountain pass and every lake, river and water-hole along the way; they knew how to avoid the deserts and the desolate lands. They knew the forests that were rich in fruits and luxuriant growth, and they knew the fastness where they were safe from attack.

However, they left tracks that were clear to Bakkat's eye, and he followed them into wilderness where even he had never ventured. The tracks led them to good water, and to the easy passes through the mountains.

Thus, they came at last to a river set in a strath of grassy veld, and the waters were sweet and clear. Jim took his sights of the noon passage of the sun on five consecutive days until he was certain he had accurately fixed their position on his father's chart. Both he and Louisa were amazed at the great distance the leisurely turning wheels of the wagons had covered to bring them here.

They left the camp on the river bank each day and rode out to explore the country in all directions. On the sixth day they climbed to the top of a tall, rounded hill that overlooked the plains beyond the river.

'Since we left the frontier of the colony we have seen no sign of our fellow men,' Louisa remarked, 'just that one wagon track almost three months ago, and the paintings of Bakkat's tribe in the caves of the mountains.'

'It is an empty land,' Jim agreed, 'and I love it so, for it and everything in it belongs to me. It makes me feel like a god.'

She smiled as she watched his enthusiasm. To her he looked indeed like a young god. The sun had burned him brown, and his arms and legs were carved from granite muscle. Despite her frequent clipping with the sheep shears, his hair had grown down to his shoulders. Accustomed to staring at far horizons, his gaze was calm and steady. His bearing displayed his confidence and authority.

She could not much longer try to deceive herself, or deny how her feelings had changed towards him in these last months. He had proved his worth a hundred times. He now stood at the centre of her existence. However, she must first throw off the brake and burden of her past – even now when she closed her eyes she could see the sinister head in the black leather mask, and the cold eyes behind the slits. Van Ritters, the master of Huis Brabant, was with her still.

Jim turned back to face her, and she averted her eyes: surely her dark thoughts must be clear for him to see in them. 'Look!' she cried, and pointed across the river. 'There is a field of wild daisies growing there.'

He shaded his eyes and followed the direction of her out-thrust hand. 'I doubt that they are flowers.' He shook his head. 'They shine too bright. I think what you see is a bed of chalk stone or white quartz pebbles.'

'I am sure they are daisies, like those that grew beside the Gariep river.' Louisa pushed Trueheart forward. 'Come, let's cross to look at them. I wish to draw them.' She was already well down the hill, leaving him little choice but to follow her, although he had no great interest in flowers.

A well-trodden game path led them through a grove of wild willows to a shallow ford. They splashed through the green waters belly deep and rode up the steep cut of the far bank. They saw the mysterious white field not far ahead, glaring in the sunlight, and raced each other to it.

Louisa was a few lengths ahead, but suddenly she reined in and the laughter died on her lips. She stared down at the ground, speechless with horror. Jim stepped down from the stirrup and, leading Drumfire, walked forward slowly. The ground beneath his feet was thickly strewn with human bones. He stooped and picked up a skull from the macabre display. 'A child,' he said, and turned the tiny relic in his hands. 'Its head was staved in.'

'What has happened here, Jim?'

'There has been a massacre,' he answered, 'and not too long ago, for although the birds have picked the skeletons clean, the hyena have not yet devoured them.'

'How did it happen?' The tragic remains had moved her, and her eyes swam with tears.

He brought the child's skull to her, and held it up so she might examine it more closely. 'The imprint of a war club. A single blow to the back of the head. 'Tis how the Nguni despatch their enemies.'

'Children also?'

'It is said that they kill for the thrill and prestige.'

'How many have died here?' Louisa averted her gaze from the tiny skull, and looked instead to the piled skeletons, which lay in snowdrifts and windrows. 'How many?'

'We shall never know, but it seems that this was an entire

tribe.' Jim laid the little skull down on the spot where he had found it.

'No wonder we found no living man on all our long journey,' she whispered. 'These monsters have slain every one, and laid waste to the land.'

Jim fetched Bakkat from the wagons and he confirmed Jim's first estimate. He picked out from among the bones evidence to paint a broader picture of the slaughter. He found the broken head and the shaft of a war club, which he called a *kerrie*. It had been skilfully carved from a shoot of a knobthorn bush: the bulbous root section formed a natural head for the vicious club. The weapon must have snapped in the hand of the warrior who had wielded it. He also found a handful of glass trade beads scattered in the grass. They might once have been part of a necklace. They were cylindrical in shape, red and white.

Jim knew them well: identical beads were among the goods they carried in their own wagons. He showed them to Louisa. 'Beads like these have been common currency in Africa for a hundred years or more. Originally they were probably traded by the Portuguese to the northern tribes.'

Bakkat rubbed one between his fingers. 'They are highly prized by the Nguni. One of the warriors might have had a string of these torn from his neck, perhaps by the dying fingers of one of his victims.'

'Who were the victims?' Louisa asked, and spread her hands to indicate the bones that lay so thickly around them.

Bakkat shrugged. 'In this land men come from nowhere and depart again leaving no trace of their passing.' He tucked the beads into the pouch on his belt, which was made from the scrotum of a bull buffalo. 'Except my people. We leave our pictures on the rocks so that the spirits will remember us.'

'I would like to know who they were,' Louisa said. 'It is so tragic to think of the little ones who were snuffed out here, with no one to bury them or mourn their passing.'

She did not have to wait long to find out who the victims were.

The next day as the wagon train rolled northwards they saw, at a distance, the herds of wild antelope parting like the bow wave of an ocean-going vessel. Jim recognized that this was how animals reacted to the presence of human beings. He had no way of knowing what lay ahead, so he ordered Smallboy to form the wagons into a defensive square and issue a musket to each man. Then, taking Bakkat and Zama with them, he and Louisa rode out to scout the land ahead.

The grassy plain undulated like the swells of the ocean, and when they reached the next crest of higher ground and could see ahead, they reined in spontaneously and stared in silence at the strange sight that was revealed to them.

Tiny with distance a column of forlorn human figures toiled across the plain, moving so painfully slowly that they raised almost no dust. They had no domestic animals with them, and as they drew closer Jim could see through the telescope that they were carrying their meagre possessions on their heads: clay pots and calabashes, or bundles wrapped in animal skins. There was nothing hostile in their appearance, and Jim rode to meet them. As the distance narrowed more details became apparent.

The straggling file was made up almost entirely of women and their children. The infants were being carried in leather pouches slung on the backs or across the hips of their mothers. They were all wasted and thin, with legs like dried sticks. They walked with the slack, dragging gait of exhaustion. As Jim and Louisa watched, one of the skeletal women sagged to the ground. The bundle and the two small children she carried on her back were too great a burden. Her companions stopped to help her back to her feet. One held a water gourd to her mouth to allow her to drink.

It was a touching gesture. 'These people are dying on their feet,' Louisa said softly. As they rode closer she counted their heads: 'There are sixty-eight of them, but I may have missed some of the children.'

When they were within hail of the head of this sorry file, they stopped the horses and Jim rose in the stirrups. 'Who are you, and where do you come from?'

It seemed that they were so far gone they had not seen the party until then, for Jim's voice caused confusion and despair among them. Many of the women threw down their bundles and seized their children. They scattered back the way they had come, but their efforts at escape were pathetic, and one after another they staggered to a halt and collapsed in the grass, unable to run further. They tried to escape attention by lying flat and pulling their leather capes over their heads.

Only one had not run, an old man. He, too, was stick-thin and frail, but he straightened and stood with dignity. He let the shawl drop from his shoulders, let out a shrill, quavering war-cry and charged straight at Jim, brandishing a throwing spear. From fifty paces, out of range of his old arm, he hurled the spear, which pegged into the earth half-way between him and Jim. Then he sagged to his knees. Jim rode warily closer, alert for another warlike attack from the silver-headed ancient.

'Who are you, old father?' he repeated. He had to ask the same question in three different dialects before the man started with recognition, and answered: 'I know who you are, you who ride upon the back of wild animals and speak in tongues. I know you are one of the white crocodile wizards that come out of the great waters to devour men. How else would you know the language of my people? Yet I fear you not, foul demon, for I am old and ready to die. But I will die fighting against you who would devour my daughters and my grand-children.' He staggered to his feet and drew the axe from his belt. 'Come, and we will see if you have blood in your veins like other men.'

The dialect he spoke was of the northern Lozi, which old Aboli had taught Jim. 'You terrify me, bold warrior,' he told the old man gravely, 'but let us put aside our weapons and talk for a while before we do battle.'

'He looks confused and terrified,' Louisa said. 'The poor old man.'

'It may be that he is not accustomed to discourse with

wizards and demons,' Bakkat remarked drily, 'but one thing I know, if he is not fed soon the wind will blow him away.'

The old man was swaying on his bony legs. 'When did you last eat, great chieftain?' Jim asked.

'I do not parley with wizards or crocodile spirits,' announced the old man, with disdain.

'If you are not hungry, then tell me, chieftain, when did your daughters and your grandchildren last eat?'

The old man's defiance wavered. He looked back at his people, and his voice was low as he replied with simple dignity, 'They are starving.'

'I can see that,' Jim said grimly.

'Jim, we must fetch food for them from the wagons,' Louisa burst out.

'It will need more than our few fish and loaves to feed this multitude. Then, when they have eaten our pantry bare, we will starve with them,' Jim answered, and turned in the saddle to survey the herds of game that were scattered across the plains in every direction. 'They are starving in the midst of plenty. Their hunting skills and crude weapons will not bring down a single head of game from all this multitude,' he said, then looked back at the old man. 'I will use my witchcraft not to destroy your people but to feed them.'

They left him standing and rode out across the plain. Jim picked out a herd of cow-like wildebeest, strange-looking creatures with fringes of dark mane and lunate horns, their legs too thin for their robust bodies. These were the fools of the veld, and they gambolled ahead of Bakkat and Zama as they rode in a wide circle to surround them and drive them back towards Jim and Louisa. When the herd leaders were almost within gunshot, they sensed the danger and put down their ugly heads. Snorting and kicking up their heels they ran in earnest. Drumfire and Trueheart came up on them easily. Riding in close and shooting from the saddle Jim dropped a beast with a shot from each of his guns, and Louisa brought down another with the little French rifle. They roped the carcasses by the heels and dragged them behind the horses to where the old man was squatting in the grass.

He rose to his feet. When he realized what they had brought him, he cried out to his followers, in a quavering voice, 'Meat! The devils have brought us meat! Come quickly, and bring the children.'

Timidly one old woman crept forward, while the others hung back. The two old people started work on the carcasses, using the blade of the throwing spear as a butcher's knife. When the rest of the band saw that they were not being molested by the white devils they came swarming forward to the feast.

Louisa laughed aloud to see mothers hacking off lumps of raw meat, and chewing it to a pulp before spitting it into the mouths of their children, like mother birds feeding their chicks. When their first hunger was appeased, they built fires to roast and smoke the rest of the kill. Jim and Louisa hunted again, bringing in more prime game to provide enough smoked meat to feed even this number of mouths for some months.

Very soon the little tribe lost all fear and became so trusting that they no longer skittered away when Louisa walked among them. They even allowed her to pick up and dandle the little ones. Then the women clustered around her, touched her hair and stroked her pale skin with awe.

Jim and Bakkat sat with the old man and questioned him. 'What people are you?'

'We are of the Lozi, but our totem is the Bakwato.'

'How are you called, great chieftain of the Bakwato?' Jim asked.

'Tegwane, and in truth I am but a very small chief,' he replied. The tegwane was the little fish-eating brown stork with a feathered topknot that frequented every stream and river pool.

'Where do you come from?' The old man pointed to the north. 'Where are the young warriors of your tribe?'

'Slain by the Nguni,' Tegwane said, 'fighting to save their families. Now I am trying to find a place where the women and children will be safe, but I fear the killers are not far behind us.'

'Tell me about these Nguni,' Jim invited. 'I have heard the

name spoken with fear and awe, but I have never seen them, nor met any man who has.'

'They are killer devils,' Tegwane replied. 'They come swiftly as cloud shadows the plain, and they slaughter every living soul in their path.'

'Tell me all you know of them. What do they look like?'

'The warriors are big men built like ironwood trees. They wear black vulture feathers in their headdress. They have rattles on their wrists and ankles so their legions make the sound of the wind when they come.'

'What of their weapons?'

'They carry black shields of dried ox-hide, and they scorn the throwing spear. They like to come close with the short stabbing *assegai*. The wound from that blade is so wide and deep that it sucks the blood from the victim like a river as they pluck out the steel.'

'Where do they come from?'

'No man knows, but some say from a land far to the north. They travel with great herds of plundered cattle, and they send their cohorts ahead to slaughter all in their path.'

'Who is their king?'

'They have no king, but a queen. Her name is Manatasee. I have never seen her, but they say she is crueller and more warlike than any of her warriors.' He looked fearfully to the horizon. 'I must take my people on to escape her. Her warriors cannot be far behind us now. Perhaps if we cross the river they may not follow us.'

They left Tegwane and his women working over the fires to smoke the rest of the meat, and rode back to the wagons. That night, as they ate their dinner by the glow of the campfire under a canopy of glittering stars, they discussed the predicament of the little tribe of refugees. Louisa proposed to return next morning with their meagre chest of medicines, and bags of flour and salt.

'If you give them all we have, what will happen to us?' Jim asked reasonably.

'Just for the children?' she tried again, although she knew he was right and it was a forlorn hope that he might agree.

'Child or grown, we cannot take an entire tribe under our wing. We have provided them with food sufficient to see them to the river and beyond. This is a cruel land. Like us, they have to fend for themselves or perish.'

She did not come to his wagon that night, and he missed her. Although they were still as chaste as brother and sister, he had become accustomed to her presence in the night. When he woke she was already working at the campfire. During this hiatus on the river bank, their hens had been allowed out of their coop on the back of the wagon to forage. In gratitude they had produced half a dozen eggs. Louisa made an omelette for his breakfast, and served it without a smile, making her disapproval obvious.

'I had a dream last night,' she told him.

He suppressed a sigh. He was learning to make room in his life for her dreams. 'Tell me.'

'I dreamed that something terrible happened to our friends, the Bakwato.'

'You do not yield without a fight, do you?' he asked. She only smiled at him once they were riding back towards where they had left the small group of fugitives. During the ride he tried to think of other good reasons to dissuade her from taking on the role of benefactor and protector of the seventy starvelings, but he bided his time before he returned to the contest of wills.

The drifting smoke from the fires on which the meat was curing guided them the last league. As they crested the rise they reined in with surprise. Tegwane's encampment was not as they had last seen it. Dust mingled with the smoke of the fires to veil the scene, but many tiny figures were scurrying in and out of the low cloud. Jim pulled his telescope out of its case. After one glance through the lens he exclaimed, 'Sweet Jesus, the Nguni have found them already!'

'I knew it!' Louisa cried. 'I told you something terrible had happened, didn't I?'

She spurred forward and he had to ride hard to catch her. He grabbed Trueheart's rein and brought them to a halt.

'Wait! We must have a care. We don't know what we are riding into.'

'They are killing our friends!'

'The old man and his tribe are probably dead already and we do not want to join them.' Quickly he explained to Bakkat and Zama what he planned.

Fortunately the wagons were not far behind them. He gave orders to Zama to ride back and warn Smallboy and his men to stand on guard, and to bring all the oxen, spare horses and other animals into the centre of the laager.

'When they have secured the camp bring Smallboy and two of the other drivers back here, fast as you like! Bring two muskets for each man. Fill the bullet bags with goose-shot, and bring extra powder flasks.'

The smooth bores were quicker to reload than the rifles. A handful of goose-shot fired at close range would spread widely and might bring down more than one enemy with each discharge.

Although Louisa fretted and argued to go immediately to the rescue of the little band of refugees, he made her wait until Zama brought up the reinforcements of men and weapons. 'They will be here within the hour,' he assured her.

'By then the Bakwato will all be wiped out.'

She wanted to take the telescope from his hand, but he would not give it to her. 'It's better that you do not watch this.'

Through the lens he could see the sparkle of steel blades in the sunlight, waving war-shields and dancing feathered head-dresses. Even his flesh crawled with horror as he saw a naked Bakwato woman run out of the dustclouds, clutching an infant to her breast. She was pursued by a tall plumed warrior. He came up behind her and stabbed her in the back. The point of the *assegai* came out between her breasts. Jim saw the steel flash pink with her blood, like the shine of a salmon's flank turning below the surface. She fell forward into the grass. The warrior stooped over her, then straightened up with her infant dangling from one hand. He threw the child high into the air, and as it fell he caught it, neatly skewered on the point of the *assegai*. Then, brandishing the little corpse like a standard, he rushed back into the dust and smoke.

At last, but not too soon for Louisa, Zama galloped back with Smallboy, Klaas and Muntu, the other drivers. Swiftly Jim checked to see that their muskets were primed and loaded. They were all well versed in the use of the guns, but Jim had never seen their temper tested in a hard fight. He formed them into an extended line, and then, keeping the horses to a walk to save their strength, they rode towards the embattled encampment. Jim kept Louisa close to him. He would have preferred to send her back to the safety of the wagons, but he knew better than to suggest it.

As they closed in they could hear the outcry coming from the encampment, the screams and the wailing, the wild, triumphant ululations of the Nguni as they plied the *assegai* and the *kerrie*. Under the cloud of dust and smoke the grassland was littered with the broken bodies of the dead women and children, like flotsam thrown on a storm-swept beach.

They are all killed, Jim thought, and his anger became murderous. He glanced across at Louisa. Her face was blanched with horror as she looked upon the carnage. Then, incredibly, he saw that one, at least, of the Bakwato was still alive.

In the centre of the encampment there was a low outcrop of granite. It formed a natural strongpoint, a *zareeba* walled with rock. Here stood the gaunt figure of Tegwane, a club in one hand and a spear in the other. His body was painted with his own blood and that of his enemies. He was surrounded by Nguni warriors. They seemed to be toying with the old man, amused by his courage. Cats with a doomed mouse, they danced about him, mocking him and laughing at his warlike antics. Tegwane had regained a little of the strength and ferocity of his lost youth. His shrill war-cry and his shouts of defiance rang out, and Jim saw one of his attackers stagger back from a spear thrust into his face. He clutched the wound and blood spurted out between his fingers. This success sealed Tegwane's fate, and the Nguni moved in with purpose.

By now the thin line of horsemen was within a hundred paces of the periphery of the camp. So immersed were the Nguni in the joy of killing that none was aware as yet of their approach.

'How many of them are there?' Jim called to Louisa.

'I see not more than twenty or so,' she answered.

'A small scouting party,' Jim guessed. Then he shouted to his men, 'Have at them! Take them! Shoot them down like rabid jackals.'

They pushed the horses into a canter and charged down on the camp. Just ahead of the line a Nguni was prodding one of the younger women with his *assegai*, goading her into position for a thrust to her belly, but she was rolling and writhing on the ground like an eel, avoiding the bright steel point. He was so preoccupied with his cruel game that Louisa was almost on him before he looked up. Jim was not sure what she intended, but it took him by surprise when she raised the musket and fired. The charge of goose-shot slammed into the Nguni's sweat-glazed chest, and he was flung backwards by the force of it.

Louisa pulled the second musket from its sheath and kept her station at Jim's side, as they charged the knot of warriors that surrounded Tegwane. She fired again and another man dropped. Even in the exigency of the moment, Jim felt awed by her ruthlessness. This was not the girl he had thought he knew. She had just killed two men, coldly and efficiently, allowing none of the emotions that raged within her to show.

The warriors attacking Tegwane heard the gunfire behind them. The heavy reports were sounds alien to them, and when they turned to face the line of horsemen their astonishment and bewilderment showed clearly on their faces, which were speckled with the blood of their victims. Jim fired only seconds after Louisa. The heavy lead goose-shot tore into one naked belly, felling the man instantly, and shattered the arm of the warrior beside him. His *assegai* dropped from his grip and the arm hung uselessly at his side, half severed above the elbow.

The wounded man looked down at his dangling arm, then reached down and picked up his fallen *assegai* with his left hand and ran straight at Jim, who was astonished by his courage. Both his muskets were empty, and he was forced to draw the pistol from the holster on the front of his saddle. The ball hit the charging Nguni full in the throat. He made a gargling noise and blood sprayed from his severed windpipe, but his example was an inspiration to his comrades. They recovered from their surprise, left Tegwane and launched themselves at the horsemen, keening with eagerness, their faces alight with bloodlust, the rattles at their ankles buzzing with every stamp of their bare feet and thrust of their stabbing arms.

Zama and Bakkat fired together and each killed one. Two more were struck by the volley from Smallboy and the other drivers, but their aim was wild, and even the wounded Nguni came on strongly, almost closing within range of their short *assegais*.

'Back! Back to reload!' Jim shouted. The line of horsemen broke and wheeled away, galloping out of the encampment. The charge of the Nguni faltered and halted when they could not overtake the horses. Well out in the veld, Jim stopped his men and brought them under control again. 'Dismount and reload!' he ordered. 'Keep your mounts on the rein. You don't want to lose them now!'

They obeyed with alacrity. With the reins secured round their shoulders they poured powder and shot into the muzzles, and rodded a handful of goose-shot down on top.

'Smallboy and his lads may shoot like rabbits,' Jim muttered to Louisa, as he primed the pan of his second musket, 'but at least they are still under control.'

Louisa worked almost as quickly and neatly as he did and she finished loading both her weapons only a little after him. The Nguni were encouraged to see them halted. With savage shouts they broke into a run again, swiftly covering the open grassland towards the group of dismounted riders.

'At least we have drawn them away from their victims,' Louisa said, as she stepped into the saddle. Jim went up on Drumfire, but the rest of the men were still busy reloading. Jim saw that Louisa was right. All of the remaining enemy warriors had joined in the chase, and were streaming towards them across the grassland. At the granite outcrop old Tegwane stood alone, obviously badly hurt but still alive.

Bakkat finished priming the pan of his musket and, with the agility of a monkey, leaped into the saddle. He fell in beside Jim, but the others were still busy.

'Follow us when you're loaded,' Jim shouted, 'but hurry!' Then, to Louisa and Bakkat, 'Come on! We will give them a whiff of gunsmoke to blunt their appetite.' The three trotted out to meet the advancing band of warriors.

'They show no fear!' Louisa said, with reluctant admiration, as the Nguni bayed like a pack of hunting dogs and burst into a headlong charge, straight at them.

When only a hundred paces separated them, Jim halted. From the saddle they fired deliberately. Two of the attackers collapsed; a third fell to his knees and clutched his belly. They changed muskets and fired again. Both Jim and Bakkat brought down another man each, but the strain was telling on Louisa. The muskets were far too heavy for her, and she flinched instinctively at the painful recoil. Her second shot flew high. The other Nguni closed in howling savagely. Only a few were still on their feet, but their faces were lit with battle fever, and they held their black war-shields high.

'Back!' Jim ordered, and they turned away, almost under the shadow of the shields, and galloped towards where Zama, Smallboy and the rest of the company were at last reloaded and mounting. As they passed each other Jim shouted across at Smallboy, 'Don't let them get too close. Stand off and shoot them down. We'll reload and come after you.'

While Jim's party reloaded, he saw that Smallboy was obeying his orders. He and his men were keeping their horses just ahead of the charge of the Nguni, baiting them on, stopping to fire when they were in killing range, then spurring ahead again. They were doing better now: two more of the warriors were lying lifeless in the grass. When their muskets were empty Smallboy broke off his attack and led his men back.

By this time Jim's party had reloaded and were in the saddle again. The ranks of horsemen passed through each other as one retreated and the other went forward.

'Pretty shooting!' Jim encouraged Smallboy. 'Now it's our turn.'

The Nguni warriors saw them coming and stopped. For a moment, they stood in a small, uncertain group. By now, they had realized the futility of charging to meet these strangers mounted on the back of fleet, alien animals whose speed no man on foot could match. They had swiftly learned the menace of the weapons that boomed out smoke and struck men down from afar with the force of witchcraft. One broke away and fled. However, Jim noted that he did not discard his shield and *assegai*. It was clear he meant not to yield but to fight again. His companions seemed infected by his example. They turned and ran.

'Steady!' Jim cautioned his own men. 'Don't let them draw you in.' Tegwane had warned him that it was a favoured tactic of the Nguni to pretend flight, or even to feign death, to lure their enemy on.

One of them, the slowest runner, had fallen far behind the others. Jim went after him and caught him up swiftly. As he raised the musket the warrior turned at bay. Jim saw that he was no stripling: there were silver strands in his short, curling beard, and he wore a headdress of ostrich feathers and the cow tails of honour and courage around his spear arm. He displayed a sudden burst of speed and darted towards Jim. He might have driven his *assegai* blade into Drumfire's flank but Jim hit him full in the face with a load of goose-shot.

When he looked round he saw that Louisa had obeyed his order. She had not taken up the pursuit, and Bakkat and Zama had also turned back. Jim was pleased with this show of discipline and good sense: it might have been fatal to have his small force scattered across the veld. He rode back to where Louisa waited.

As he reached her side Jim saw from her face that her rage had vanished as swiftly as it had arisen. She was looking down at one of the dead Nguni with sadness and remorse in her eyes.

'We have driven them off, but they will return, I'm sure of that,' Jim told her, and she watched the distant figures of the surviving Nguni dwindle into the golden grassland, and disappear at last over the fold of the ground.

'It was enough,' she said. 'I'm glad you let them go.'

'Where did you learn to fight?' he asked.

'If you had spent a year on the gundeck of the *Meeuw*, you would understand.'

At that moment Smallboy and the other drivers rode up with their muskets recharged. 'We will follow them, Somoya,' he cried eagerly. It was clear that he was still gripped by the ecstasy of battle.

'No! Leave them!' Jim ordered sharply. 'Manatasee and all her army are probably waiting for you over the next hill. Your place is back at the wagons. Go there now, protect the cattle, and make ready to meet another attack.'

While Smallboy and the drivers rode off, Jim led the others back to the grisly encampment. Old Tegwane was sitting on a lump of granite, nursing his injuries and crooning a soft lament for his family and the other women and children of his tribe, whose corpses were scattered around him.

While Louisa gave him water from her flask, then washed his wounds and bound them up to staunch the bleeding, Jim went through the encampment. He approached the bodies of the fallen Nguni warily, loaded pistol at the ready. But all of them were dead: the goose-shot had inflicted terrible wounds. They were mostly big, handsome men, young and powerfully built. Their weapons were the work of skilled blacksmiths. Jim picked up one of the *assegais*. It had a marvellous balance in his hand and both edges were sharp enough to shave the hair from his forearm. The dead warriors all wore necklaces and bangles of carved ivory. Jim took one of these ornaments from the neck of the Nguni elder he had killed with his last shot. By the ostrich feathers in his headdress, and the white cow tails round his upper arms Jim judged that he must have been senior in the band. The ivory necklace was beautifully carved, tiny human figures threaded on to a leather thong.

'Each figure represents a man he has killed in battle,' Jim

guessed. It was obvious that the Nguni placed a high value on ivory. This intrigued Jim, and he slipped the necklace into his pocket.

As he went on through the camp he found that the Nguni had done their gruesome work thoroughly. The children had all been despatched with merciless efficiency. For most a single blow with a war club was all it had taken. Apart from Tegwane, they found only one other Bakwato still alive, the girl Louisa had saved with her first shot. She had a deep spear wound in her shoulder, but she was able to walk when Zama lifted her to her feet. Louisa saw that she was too young to have given birth to her first child, for her belly was flat and smooth, her breasts like unripe fruit. Tegwane let out a joyous cry when he saw she was still alive, and hobbled to embrace her.

'This is Intepe, the lily of my heart, my granddaughter,' he cried.

Louisa had noticed her at their first meeting with the tribe, for she was the prettiest of all the women. Intepe came to her trustingly and sat patiently as Louisa washed and dressed her wound. When Louisa had finished tending Tegwane and his granddaughter, she looked around at the dead who lay half hidden in the grass.

'What must we do with all these others?' she called to Jim.

'We have finished here,' Jim replied, then glanced up at the cloudless sky where, high above, the vultures were gathering. 'We will leave the rest of the work to them. Now we must hurry back to the wagons. We have much to do there before the Nguni return.'

Jim picked out the best defensive position along the river bank. Here a small tributary stream flowed down from the hills to join the main flow. It came in at an acute angle, forming a narrow wedge of ground bounded on one side by a pool of the main river. Jim plumbed the depth of the pool and found that it was deeper than a man was tall.

'The Nguni will never swim,' Tegwane assured him. 'Water is perhaps the only thing they fear. They will eat neither fish nor hippopotamus, for they have an abhorrence of anything that comes from water.'

'So the pool will protect our flank and rear.' Jim was relieved. Tegwane was proving a useful source of information. He boasted that he could speak the Nguni language fluently, and that he knew their customs. If this was true, he was well worth his keep.

Jim walked along the top of the steep bank of the tributary stream. The drop was over ten feet, a wall of greasy clay that would be difficult to scale without a ladder.

'This will protect the other flank. We have only to draw up the wagons across the neck between river and stream.'

They rolled them into position, and roped the wheels together with rawhide *riems*, to prevent the Nguni pushing them aside and forcing a breach. In the gaps between the wagon bodies, and under the wagon beds they packed thorn-branches, leaving no space for the warriors to crawl through. In the centre of the wagon line they left a narrow gate.

Jim ordered that the horses and the other domestic animals were to be herded and grazed close by, so that within minutes they could be driven into the protection of the laager and the gateway sealed off against attack with faggots of thornbush placed ready to hand.

'Do you truly believe that the Nguni will return?' Louisa tried to hide her fear as she asked the question. 'Don't you think they might have learned by hard experience and that they will pass us by?'

'Old Tegwane knows them well. He has no doubt that they will come if only because they dearly love a fight,' Jim replied.

'How many more of them are there?' she asked. 'Does Tegwane know?'

'The old man cannot count. He says only that they are many.'

Jim carefully measured and selected a spot well out in front of the wagons, where he made Smallboy and his drivers dig a shallow hole. In it he placed a fifty-pound keg of coarse black gunpowder, set a fuse of slow-match in the bung-hole and ran it back between the wheels of the centre wagon. He covered the keg with sacks of pebbles from the river bed which he hoped would scatter like musket balls when the keg exploded.

He had the men cut firing loopholes into the wall of thorns through which they could lay down enfilading fire along the front of the defences. With the grindstone Smallboy sharpened the naval cutlasses and placed them ready to hand. Then the loaded muskets were stacked beside the cutlasses, with powder kegs and shot bags and spare ramrods close by. Louisa instructed and rehearsed the *voorlopers* and herd-boys in loading and priming the weapons. She had some difficulty in persuading them that if one handful of gunpowder resulted in such a satisfactory explosion, two would be no improvement; it might result in a burst gun barrel and even the decapitation of whoever pulled the trigger.

The water fagies were refilled from the river pool and made ready, either to slake the thirst of fighting men or to quench the flames if the Nguni latched on to the old trick of hurling lighted torches into the laager.

Two herd-boys were placed as lookouts on the crest of the low hill from which Louisa had first spied the charnel field. Jim gave them a clay fire-pot, and ordered them to light a fire of green leaves if they saw the main Nguni *impi*, or warrior band, approaching. The smoke would warn the camp and, when it was lit, they could race down the hill into the laager to spread the alarm. Jim made certain that the boys came down from the hilltop and were safely in the laager each evening before nightfall. It would have been heartless to leave them out there in the dark at the mercy of wild beasts and Nguni scouts.

'The Nguni never attack at night,' Tegwane told Jim. 'They say that the darkness is for cowards. A true warrior should die only in the sunlight.' Nevertheless Jim brought in his pickets and placed sentries around the periphery of the laager at nightfall, and inspected them regularly during the night to make certain that they stayed awake.

'They will come singing and beating their shields,' Tegwane

302

said. 'They wish to warn their enemy. They know that their fame precedes them, and that the sound of their voices and sight of their black headdresses fills the bellies of their enemy with fear.'

'Then we must prepare a fitting greeting for them,' Jim said.

They cleared the trees and underbrush for a hundred paces in front of the wagons, and the spans of trek oxen dragged away the felled trees. The ground was left open and bare. The attacking *impi* would have to cross this killing ground to reach the wagons. Then Jim paced out the distances in front of the defences, and laid a line of white river stones to mark the most effective range and spread patterns of the goose-shot. He impressed on his men that they must not open fire until the first rank of the attackers crossed this line.

When he had completed all his preparations, they settled down to wait. This was the worst time, and the slow drag of the hours was corrosive to their spirits. Jim took advantage of this delay by spending time with Tegwane, learning more about the enemy from him.

'Where do they keep their women and children?'

'They do not bring them to war. Perhaps they leave them in their homeland.'

'Do they have a great store of plunder and riches?'

'They have many cattle, and they love the ivory teeth of the elephant and the hippopotamus.'

'Tell me of their cattle.'

'They have huge herds. The Nguni love their cattle like their own children. They do not slaughter them to eat their meat. Instead they tap off their blood and mix it with the milk. This is their main food.'

A calculating look came into Jim's eyes as he listened. A prime ox fetched a hundred guilders in the colony.

'Tell me of their ivory.'

'They love ivory very much,' Tegwane replied. 'Perhaps they need it for trade with the Arabs of the north or with the Bulamatari.' The name meant Breakers of Rock, a reference to the Portuguese, whose prospectors chipped the reef for traces of gold. Jim was surprised that here, in the deep interior,

Tegwane had heard of these nations. He questioned him on this, and Tegwane smiled. 'My father's father knew of you crocodile wizards, and his father before him.'

Jim nodded. It was naïve of him. The Omani Arabs had been trading and slaving in Africa since the fifth century. It was a hundred and fifty years ago that Vasco da Gama landed at Mozambique island and the Portuguese had begun building their forts and trading stations on the mainland. Of course rumours of these events must have penetrated even to the most primitive tribes in the remotest corners of this vast land.

Jim showed the old man the tusks of the bull he had killed, and Tegwane was amazed. 'I have never seen teeth of this size before.'

'Where do the Nguni find the ivory? Do they hunt the elephant?'

Tegwane shook his head. 'The elephant is a mighty beast, and even the Nguni cannot kill him with their *assegais*.'

'Where, then, does the ivory come from?'

'I have heard that there are some tribes who dig pits to trap them, or hang a spear weighted with stones in a tree over the pathway they frequent. When the elephant touches the trip-rope the spear drops and pierces him to the heart.' Tegwane paused and glanced at Bakkat who was asleep under one of the wagons. 'I have also heard that those little yellow monkeys of the San sometimes kill them with their poisoned arrows. But they can kill few by these methods.'

'Then where do the Nguni get their ivory?' Jim persisted.

'Each season, especially in the time of the rains, some of the great beasts die of age or sickness or they flounder in mudholes or fall from the mountain passes. The ivory tusks lie there for any man to gather up. During my lifetime my own tribe has gathered up many.'

'What happened to the tusks of your tribe?' Jim leaned forward eagerly.

'When they slaughtered our young men, the Nguni stole them from us, as they steal them from every tribe they attack and massacre.'

304

'They must have a great store of ivory,' Jim said. 'Where do they keep it?'

'They carry it with them,' Tegwane replied. 'When they move they load the tusks onto the backs of their cattle. They have as much ivory as they have cattle to carry it. They have many cattle.'

Jim repeated the story to Louisa. 'I should like to find one of these herds, each beast with a fortune in ivory strapped to its back.'

'Would it belong to you?' she asked innocently.

'The spoils of war!' he said, with righteous indignation. 'Of course it would be mine.' He looked to the hills over which he expected the *impis* of the Nguni to appear. 'When will they come?' he wondered.

The longer they had to wait, the more it played on all their nerves. Jim and Louisa passed much of the time over the chessboard, but when that palled she painted his portrait again. While he posed for her, he read aloud *Robinson Crusoe*. It was his favourite book. Secretly he saw himself as the resourceful hero. Although he had read it many times, he still chuckled and exclaimed at Crusoe's adventures, and bewailed his misfortunes.

Two or three times during the day they rode out to inspect the lookouts on the hilltop and make sure the herd-boys were awake and alert, and had not wandered off in search of honey or some other childish distraction. Then they scouted the lie of the land around the laager to make certain the Nguni pickets were not creeping up on them through the gullies and the light forests that were interspersed in the grassy veld.

On the twelfth day after the massacre of the Bakwato, Jim and Louisa rode out alone. The herd-boys on the hilltop were bored and disgruntled, and Jim had to speak to them sternly to make them stay at their posts.

They came back down the hill and crossed the river at the ford. They rode out almost to the site of the massacre, but turned back before they reached it. Jim wanted to spare Louisa the harrowing memories associated with that place.

They returned to within sight of the laager, and Jim stopped to examine the defences through the lens of the telescope to see if he could pick out any weak spot he had overlooked. While he was preoccupied Louisa dismounted and looked around for some place where she could go about her private business. The ground was open here, and the grass had been grazed down by the game herds until it reached only half-way to her knees. However, she saw that close by ran a *donga*, a natural gully cut out by the rainwaters draining towards the river. She handed Trueheart's reins to Jim.

'I will not be gone long,' she said, and started towards the gully. Jim opened his mouth to caution her, then thought better of it and looked away to preserve her modesty.

As Louisa approached the lip of the gully she became aware of a strange sound, a whisper, a susurration, that seemed to tremble in the air. She kept on walking, but more slowly, puzzled but not alarmed. The sound grew louder, like running water or the hum of insects. She was not certain from which direction it came.

She glanced back at Jim, but he was gazing through the lens, not looking in her direction. It was clear that he had not heard the sound. She hesitated then stepped to the lip of the *donga* and looked down into it. As she did so, the sound rose to an angry buzz as though she had disturbed a nest of hornets.

The gully below her was closely packed with rank upon rank of Nguni warriors. They were sitting on their shields, but each man had his stabbing *assegai* in his right hand and they were pointing the blades at her, and at the same time shaking the weapons, a slight trembling movement that agitated the war rattles on each wrist. This gave off the buzzing sound that had troubled her. The small movement also set the glossy black feathers in their headdresses dancing. Their naked torsos were anointed with fat so that they shone like washed coal. The whites of their eyes staring up at her were the only contrast in this seething expanse of black. It seemed to Louisa that she was gazing down on an enormous dragon coiled in its lair, black scales glittering, angry and venomous, poised to strike.

She whirled and ran. 'Jim! Beware! They are here!'

Jim looked back, startled by her cry. He saw no sign of danger, only Louisa racing towards him with her face working with terror.

'What is it?' he called, and at that moment the ground seemed to open behind the running girl and from it erupted a mass of warriors. Their bare feet beat upon the hard earth and the war rattles on their ankles crashed in unison. They drummed on their black war-shields with the *assegais*, a deafening roar, and they shouted, *'Bulala! Bulala amathagati!* Kill! Kill the wizards!'

Louisa fled before this rolling tide. She ran like a whippet, nimble and quick, but one of her pursuers was quicker still. He was tall and lean, made taller by the headdress. The muscle started proud in his belly and shoulders, as he bounded after her. He threw aside his shield to unburden himself. Although Louisa had a lead of twenty paces or more, he was overhauling her swiftly. The haft of his *assegai* rested lightly on his shoulder, but the long blade was pointed forward, poised for the thrust between her shoulder-blades. Jim had a fleeting memory of the Bakwato girl run through in this way, the blade appearing magically out of the middle of her breast, smeared pink with her heart's blood.

He sent Drumfire into full gallop and, dragging Trueheart on the rein behind him, raced to meet Louisa. But he saw that the leading warrior was already too close. She would not have time to mount before he was on her, his blade transfixed through her body. He did not slow or check Drumfire's charge. They brushed past Louisa so closely that her hair fluttered in the wind of their passing. Jim tossed her Trueheart's reins.

'Get up and away!' he shouted as he went by. He had only one musket with him, for he had not expected a fight. He could not afford to waste that single shot. The light ball of the pistol might only wound and not kill cleanly. There was no latitude for error here. He had seen the warrior throw aside his shield. He jerked the naval cutlass from its scabbard. Under the eye of Aboli and his father he had practised with this weapon until he mastered the Manual of Arms. He did not brandish the blade to warn his man. He charged Drumfire straight at the Nguni, and saw him check and change his grip on the *assegai*. His dark eyes locked on Jim's face. Jim knew by his haughty expression that he would not deign to wound the horse under him, but would take him on man to man. He watched for the *assegai* thrust, leaning forward to meet it. The Nguni struck, and Jim dropped the cutlass into the classic counter, sweeping aside the point of the *assegai*, then reversed and, as he passed, he swung the cutlass back-handed. Smallboy had put a fine edge on the steel and it was sharp as a butcher's cleaver. Jim swept it across the back of the warrior's neck, and felt the hilt jar in his hand as it sheared cleanly through his vertebrae. The man dropped as though a gallow's trap had opened under him.

At the pressure of his knees Drumfire spun round like a weathercock in a fluke of wind. He saw that Louisa was having difficulty trying to mount Trueheart. The mare had smelt the Nguni and seen the ranks racing towards them. She was skittering sideways and throwing her head wildly. Holding on to the reins Louisa was being pulled off her feet.

Jim sheathed the bloody cutlass, and turned Drumfire in behind her. Leaning from the saddle he grabbed a handful of the baggy seat of her breeches and boosted her up into the saddle. Then he steadied her with a hand on her arm as they galloped back knee to knee. As soon as they were clear he drew his pistol and fired a shot into the air, to alert the sentries at the laager. As soon as he saw that they had heard it, he told Louisa, 'Ride back! Warn them to get the animals into the laager. Send Bakkat and Smallboy to help me delay them.'

To his relief she had the good sense not to argue, and raced away, pushing Trueheart to the top of her speed. He turned back to face the charging warriors, drew the musket from its sheath and walked Drumfire towards them. He picked out the *induna* in the front rank who was leading them. Tegwane had told him how to recognize the captains. 'They are always older men, and they wear ostrich plumes in their headdress and white cow tails on their arms.'

He touched Drumfire with his toes and broke into a trot,

heading directly for the *induna*. By now the Nguni must have understood the terrible menace of the firearms, but the man showed no fear: he increased the speed of his charge, and lifted his shield to clear his spear arm, his face twisted with the ferocity of his war-cry.

'*Bulala*! Kill! Kill!' Behind him his men surged forward. Jim let him come in close, then fired. Still at full run the *induna* went down, the *assegai* flew from his hand and he rolled in the grass. The spread of shot caught the two men directly behind him, and sent them tumbling too.

An angry roar went up from the black mass of the *impi* to see their captain and their comrades shot down, but Jim had wheeled away and was already galloping back to reload. The Nguni could not keep up the pace, and they slowed to a trot. But still they came on.

With the musket reloaded, Jim mounted again and rode to meet them. He wondered how many there were in that dark mass, but it was impossible to guess. He crossed their front at less than twenty paces and fired into them. He saw men stumble and fall, but their comrades swept over them so their bodies were hidden almost immediately. This time there was no angry shout to acknowledge the damage he had inflicted.

The *impi* slowed to a smooth, swinging trot, and began to sing. The deep African voices were beautiful, but the sound made the hair rise on the back of Jim's neck, and seemed to reverberate deep in his guts. They moved inexorably towards the fortified walls of the laager.

As Jim finished reloading again, he heard the sound of hoofs and looked up to see Bakkat and Louisa leading Zama and the other drivers out through the gateway between the wagons.

'Lord give me strength! I meant her to stay safely in the laager,' he muttered, but then he made the best of it. As she rode up and handed him his second musket, he said, 'The same drill as before, Hedgehog. You take command of the second section, Zama, Bakkat and Muntu with you. Smallboy and Klaas with me.'

He led his section in, right under the *assegais* of the front

309

rank of warriors, and they fired the first guns, then changed, came back and fired the second volley before breaking off and galloping back with empty guns.

'Pick out the *indunas*,' Jim called, 'kill their captains,' as Louisa led her section forward. Again and again the two sections changed places smoothly, and the steady volleys never faltered. Jim saw with grim satisfaction that most of the *indunas* at the front of the attack had fallen under the onslaught.

The Nguni wilted before this fearsome unrelenting attack. Their pace slowed, the singing sank away to an angry, frustrated hissing. At last they stopped only three hundred paces short of the laager. The horsemen kept up the steady attack.

Jim rode in once again at the head of his section, and saw the change. Some of the warriors in the front rank lowered their shields and glanced behind them. Jim and his men fired a volley with their first guns, then turned and rode back along the front with their second guns at the ready. The headdresses waved, the feathers fluttered like the wind in the grass. The next volley crashed into them, and the lead-shot clapped into living flesh. Men reeled and fell.

The echoes of the volley were still booming back from the hills when Louisa galloped forward with Zama, Bakkat and Muntu close behind her. The front rank of the Nguni saw them coming and broke. They turned back and shoved with their shields into the men behind them shouting, '*Emuva!* Back, go back!' but those behind shouted, '*Shikelela!* Forward! Push forward!'

The entire *impi* wavered, swaying back and forth, men struggling, their shields tangling and blocking each other's spear arms. Louisa and her men charged in close and they fired a rolling volley into the struggling mass. A groan of despair went up and the rear rank gave way. They turned and streamed back across the grassland, leaving their dead and wounded lying where they had fallen, their shields, spears and *kerries* strewn about them. Louisa's party galloped after them, firing their second guns into the ruck.

Jim saw the danger of them being drawn into a trap, and raced after them. Drumfire swiftly overhauled them. 'Stop!

Break off the chase!' Louisa obeyed at once and called off her men. All of them rode back. As soon as they were safely into the laager, a span of oxen dragged the faggots of thornbush into the gap in the defences to seal it off.

It seemed impossible that such a mass of humanity could disappear so swiftly, but by the time the gate was secured the *impi* were gone, and the only signs of the fighting were the dead and the trampled, bloodstained grass in front of the laager.

'We hurt them grievously. Will they come back?' Louisa asked anxiously.

'As surely as the sun will set and rise again tomorrow,' Jim said grimly, and nodded to where it was already sinking towards the horizon. 'That was probably only the scouting party, sent by Manatasee to test our mettle.'

He called for Tegwane, and the old man came at once, trying not to favour his wounds. 'The *impi* were lying up close to the laager. If Welanga had not come across them, they would have waited for nightfall to attack us. You were wrong, old man. They do fight at night.'

'Only the Kulu Kulu is never wrong,' Tegwane answered, with an unconvincing attempt at nonchalance.

'You can redeem yourself,' Jim told him sternly.

'I will do whatever you say.' Tegwane nodded.

'Some of the Nguni are not dead. As we rode back, I saw at least one still moving. Go out with Bakkat to guard you. Find one of the Nguni who still lives. I want to know the whereabouts of their queen. I also want to know where their baggage train is camped, the cattle and the ivory.'

Tegwane nodded, and loosened his skinning knife in its sheath. Jim was about to order him to leave his knife in the laager, but then he remembered the women and children of the old man's tribe, and the manner of their deaths.

'Go at once, great chief. Go before the coming of darkness and before the hyena find the wounded Nguni.' Then he turned to Bakkat. 'Have your musket ready. Never trust a Nguni, especially a dead one.'

Three times Jim looked up from inspecting the defences of

the laager at the sound of Bakkat's musket booming out across the battlefield. He knew that the little Bushman was finishing off the wounded enemy. Just as the light was fading, Bakkat and Tegwane returned to the laager. Both were carrying *assegais* and looted ivory ornaments. Tegwane had fresh blood on his hands.

'I spoke to a wounded *induna*, before he died. You were right. This was only a scouting party. However, Manatasee is very close, with the rest of her *impis* and the cattle. She will be here within two days.'

'What did you do with the man who told you this?'

'I recognized him,' Tegwane replied. 'He was the one who led the first attack on our village. Two of my sons died that day.' Tegwane was silent for a while, then smiled thinly. 'It would have been heartless to leave a fine warrior, such as he was, to the hyenas. I am a man of compassion.'

After dinner, the drivers and other servants drifted across from their fires and gathered at a respectful distance around Jim and Louisa. The drivers smoked their long-stemmed clay pipes. The smell of the strong Turkish tobacco was rank on the sweet night air. This was one of the informal councils, which they called *indaba*, that had become a tradition of camp life over the months. Although most of them listened more than they spoke, every man present – from Smallboy, the head driver, to Izeze, the youngest herd-boy – knew that he was entitled to state his views as strongly as he felt inclined.

They were all nervous. At even the most ordinary night sounds they started and peered out into the darkness beyond the walls of the laager. The yipping of a jackal might be the rallying call of the Nguni pickets. The whisper of the night wind in the thorn trees along the river bank might be the sound of their war rattles. The rumbling hoofs of a stampeding herd of wildebeest, frightened by a marauding pride of lions, might be the sound of *assegais* drumming on rawhide shields. Jim knew that his men had come to him to seek reassurance.

Though he was younger than any of the adults except Zama, he spoke to them like a father. He told them of the battles they had fought already, and singled them out one by one to praise their feats, their steadiness in the heat of the action, and the terrible losses they had inflicted on the enemy. He did not forget the part played by the herders and the *voorlopers*, and the boys grinned with pride. 'You have proved to me, and yourselves, that the Nguni cannot prevail against our horses and muskets – as long as we stand firm and hold hard.'

When they drifted away at last from the campfire to their own mattresses their mood had changed. They chatted cheerfully among themselves, and their laughter was unfeigned.

'They trust you,' Louisa said quietly. 'They will follow where you lead them.' She was silent a moment and then she said, so softly that he barely caught the words, 'And so will I.' She paused, then 'Come!' she said, took his hand and pulled him to his feet. Her voice was firm and decided. Before this she had always come to him surreptitiously once the rest of the camp was asleep. Now she went openly with him to his wagon. She could hear the murmur of other voices in the darkness and knew that the servants were watching them. It did not deter her.

'Hand me up,' she said when they reached the rear steps of the wagon. He stooped and lifted her in his arms. She placed both her arms round his neck and pressed her face into its curve. He made her feel as small and light as a child as he carried her up the ladder and brushed through the curtain of the afterclap. 'I am your woman,' she told him.

'Yes.' He laid her on the cardell bed. 'And I am your man.'

He stood over her and stripped off his clothing. His body was pale and strong in the lamplight. She saw that he was fully aroused, and felt no revulsion. She reached out unashamedly and took him in her hand, her thumb and fingers barely encompassing his girth. He was as hard as if he had been carved from a branch of ironwood. The tips of her breasts ached with wanting him. She sat up and unlaced the front of her tunic.

'I need you, Jim. Oh, how I need you,' she said, still staring at him. He was rough with haste, his need surpassing hers. He pulled off her boots, then stripped off her breeches. Then he stopped and stared in awe at the pale golden cluster of curls in the fork of her thighs.

'Touch me,' she said, her voice husky. For the first time he laid his hand upon the entry-port to her body and soul. She let her thighs fall apart, and he felt the heat almost scald his fingertips. Gently he parted the fleshy lips, and slippery beads of moisture anointed him.

'Hurry, Jim,' she whispered, and clasped him again. 'I can bear it no longer.' She tugged at him insistently, and he fell forward on top of her.

'Oh, God, my little hedgehog, how I love you.' His words were choked.

Clasping him in both her hands, she tried to guide him into herself, but there was a moment when she thought she was too small for him. 'Help me!' she cried again, and placed both hands upon his buttocks. She pulled him towards her desperately, and felt the hard round muscles convulse under her hands as he thrust forward with his hips. She cried out incoherently, for he was cleaving her apart. It was pleasure driven to the frontiers of agony. Then, suddenly, he forced his way past all resistance, and she felt the full slithering length of him. She screamed, but when he tried to pull back she locked both legs over his back to hold him. 'Don't leave me,' she cried. 'Don't ever leave. Stay with me for ever.'

When he woke, the first light of dawn was pearling the canvas curtain of the afterclap. She was awake and watching him, lying quietly with her head on his bare chest. When she saw his eyes open she traced with her forefinger the shape of his mouth. 'When you sleep you look like a little boy,' she whispered.

'I will prove to you that I am a big boy,' he whispered back.

'I want you to know, James Archibald, that I am always open to proof.' She smiled, then sat up and placed her hands on his shoulders to pin him down. In one lithe movement, as though she were mounting Trueheart, she straddled his lower body.

Their joy was so incandescent that it seemed to light the whole encampment, and changed the mood of all those around them. Even the herd-boys were aware that something monumental had taken place, and they giggled and nudged each other when they watched Jim and Louisa together. It gave them all something to gossip about, and even the threat of Manatasee and her *impis* seemed to recede in the face of this new fascination.

Jim sensed the lackadaisical mood that was spreading through the laager, and did all he could to keep them alert and vigilant. He exercised the mounted musketeers every morning, honing the tactics of the fighting withdrawal they had struck upon almost by chance.

Then he reviewed the defence of the laager. Each of the musketeers was allotted his station on the perimeter, and given two boys to load for him. Jim and Louisa together drilled the *voorlopers* and herd-boys at reloading the muskets. Jim nailed a gold guilder coin to the tailboard of his wagon. 'On Sunday, after Welanga reads to you from the Bible, we will hold a competition for the fastest gun team,' he promised, and hauled from his pocket the big chiming watch on its gold chain that Tom and Sarah had given him on his last birthday. 'I will time you with this, and the gold guilder goes to the champions.'

A gold coin was a fortune beyond the imagining of the boys, and the promise spurred them on until soon they were almost as quick as Louisa. Although some were so small that they had to stand on tiptoe to rod the charge down the long barrels, they learned to cant the weapon so they could reach the muzzle more readily. They weighed the powder charge by scooping a handful from the kegs, rather than fumbling with the flask, and stuffed the shot into their mouths to spit it into the muzzle. Within days they were able to keep a ripple of gunfire running up and down the barricade, handing the recharged muskets to the front almost as fast as the men could fire them. Jim felt that the expenditure of gunpowder and shot was worthwhile. The boys were inflamed with excitement as the day of the loading competition drew nearer, and the men gambled heavily on the outcome.

On Sunday Jim woke while it was still dark. He was immediately aware that something was amiss. He could not place it, but then he heard the horses moving restlessly in the lines, and the cattle milling about in the laager.

'Lions?' he wondered, and sat up. At that moment one of the dogs barked, and the others joined in. He jumped out of bed and reached for his breeches.

'What is it, Jim?' Louisa asked, and he could hear that she was still half asleep.

'The dogs. The horses. I'm not sure.' He pulled on his boots, sprang down from the wagon, and saw that most of the camp was already astir. Smallboy was throwing wood on to the fire and Bakkat and Zama were in the horselines trying to soothe the agitated animals with words and caresses. Jim strode to the barricade and spoke softly to the two boys who were crouched there, shivering in the dawn chill.

'Have you seen or heard anything out there?' They shook their heads and peered out into the darkness. It was still too dark to make out the tops of the thorn trees against the sky. He listened intently, but the only sound he heard was the dawn breeze in the grass. Nevertheless, he was as restless as the horses, and relieved that he had ordered all the livestock to be brought in from the veld at sunset the previous evening. The laager was sealed off and barricaded.

Louisa came to stand beside him. She was fully dressed with a shawl over her shoulders, and she had bound up her hair with a headcloth. They stood close together, waiting and listening. Trueheart whickered and the other horses stamped and jingled the chains of their halters. Every person in the laager was awake now, but their voices were strained and subdued.

Suddenly Louisa seized Jim's hand and squeezed it hard. She heard the singing before he did. The voices were faint, but bass and deep on the soft dawn breeze.

Tegwane came from the fire, still limping from his wounds. He stood by Jim's other side and they listened to the singing. 'It is the Death Song,' Tegwane said softly. 'The Nguni are asking the spirits of their fathers to prepare a feast to welcome them in the land of shades. They are singing that this day they will die in battle or bring great honour to the tribe.' They listened in silence for a while.

'They are singing now that tonight their women will weep or rejoice for them, and their sons will be proud.'

'When will they come?' Louisa asked softly.

'As soon as it is light,' Tegwane told her.

Louisa was still clinging to Jim's hand. Now she lifted her face to his. 'I have not said it before, but I must say it now. I love you, my man.'

'I have said it many times before, but I say it again,' he replied. 'I love you, my little hedgehog.'

'Kiss me,' she said, and their embrace was long and fierce. Then they drew apart.

'Go to your places now,' Jim called to the men. 'Manatasee has come.'

The herd-boys brought them their breakfast from the cooking fires, and they ate their salted porridge in darkness, standing by the guns. When daylight came, it came swiftly. First the tops of the trees showed against the brightening sky, then they could make out the vague shape of the hills beyond. Suddenly Jim drew breath sharply, and Louisa started next to him.

'The hills are dark,' she whispered. The light strengthened and the singing grew with it, rising in majestic chorus. Now they could make out the mass of the regiments that lay like a deep shadow upon the pale grassland. Jim studied them through the lens of the telescope.

'How many are there?' Louisa asked softly.

'As Tegwane has said, they are many. It is not possible to count their numbers.'

'And we are only eight.' Her voice faltered.

'You have not counted the boys.' He laughed. 'Don't forget the boys.'

Jim went back to where the boys waited beside the gun racks, and spoke to each of them. Their cheeks were stuffed with goose-shot, and they held the ramrods ready, but they grinned and bobbed their heads. Children make fine soldiers, he thought. They have no fear for they think it is a game, and they obey orders.

Then he walked along the line of men who stood behind the barricades. To Bakkat he said, 'The Nguni will have seen you from afar, for you stand tall as a granite hill in their path and strike terror into their hearts.'

'Have your long whips ready,' he told Smallboy and the drivers. 'After this little fight you will have a thousand head of cattle to drive down to the coast.'

He clasped Zama's shoulder. 'I am glad that you stand beside me as you have always done. You are my right hand, old friend.'

As he returned to Louisa's side the singing of the *impis* swelled to a crescendo, then ended with the stamp of hundreds of horny bare feet that rang out like a salvo of artillery. The silence after it was shocking.

'Now it begins,' Jim said and lifted the telescope.

The black ranks stood like a petrified forest. The only movement was the rising dawn wind ruffling the vulture feathers in their headdresses. Then Jim saw that the centre of the line was opening like the petals of a night orchid, and a column of men came through, winding like a serpent down the grassy hillside towards the laager. In stark contrast to the massed *impis* they wore kilts made of strips of white oxhide, and tall headdresses of snowy egret feathers. Twenty men led the column. On their hips were slung war drums made from hollowed-out logs. The rank behind them carried trumpets of kudu horn. In the centre of the column there was a massive litter whose interior was screened by leather curtains. Twenty men carried it on their shoulders, shuffling and swaying, dipping and turning.

One of the drummers began to tap out a tattoo, which throbbed like the pulse of all the world, and the *impis* swayed to the rhythm. One by one the other drummers joined in and the music swelled. Then the trumpeters lifted their kudu horns, and blew a warlike fanfare. The column opened into a single file with the great litter in the centre, and halted just out of range of the barricade of the laager. The trumpets sounded a second blast that rang against the hills, then another eerie silence fell.

By now the first rays of the rising sun played over the massed regiments. It struck sparks of light from the blades of the *assegais*.

'We should strike now,' Louisa said. 'We should sortie on horseback, and attack them first.'

'They are already too close. We would only get in two or three volleys before they drove us back into the laager,' Jim told her gently. 'Let them expend themselves on the barricades. I want to save the horses for what will come later.'

Again the trumpets sang out and the bearers lowered the litter to the ground. There was another trumpet blast, and from the litter emerged a single dark shape like a hornet from its nest.

'*Bayete!*' thundered the regiments. '*Bayete!*' The royal salute drowned the drums and trumpets. Hurriedly Jim snatched up the telescope and stared at the macabre figure.

The woman was slim and sinuous, taller than her body-guards in their egret headdresses. She was stark naked, but her entire body was painted in fantastic patterns. There were glaring white circles around her eyes. A straight white line ran up her throat, over her chin and nose, between her eyes and over her shaven scalp, dividing her head into hemispheres. One half was painted blue as the sky, the other half blood red. She carried a small ceremonial *assegai* in her right hand, the haft covered with fine designs of beadwork and tassels of lion's mane hair.

Whorls and swirls of white paint highlighted her breasts and her mons Veneris. Diamond and arrowhead patterns enhanced the length of her slim arms and legs.

'Manatasee!' Tegwane said softly. 'The queen of death.'

Manatasee began to dance, a slow, mesmeric movement like that of an erect cobra. She came down the hillside towards the laager, graceful and deadly. None of the men in the laager moved or spoke and stared in dread fascination.

The *impis* moved forward behind her, as though she were the head of the dragon and they the monstrous body. Their weapons sparkled like reptilian scales in the low sun.

Manatasee stopped just short of the cut line that Jim had cleared in front of the wagons. She stood with her legs apart and her back arched, thrusting her hips towards them. Behind her the drums crashed out again and the kudu-horn trumpets shrilled.

'Now she will mark us for death.' Tegwane spoke loud enough for them all to hear, but Jim was not certain what he meant until from between her long painted legs Manatasee sent a powerful gush of urine arcing towards them.

'She pisses upon us,' Tegwane said.

Manatasee's stream dwindled and as the last yellow drops fell to earth she let out a wild scream and leaped high in the air. As she landed again she aimed the point of her *assegai* at the laager.

'*Bulala*!' she screeched. 'Kill them all!' A deafening roar went up from the *impis* and they surged forward.

Jim snatched up one of his London rifles, and tried to pick up the queen in the sights, but he had left it too late. As with all the others, Manatasee had held him enthralled. Before he could fire she was screened by the advancing wall of her warriors. A plumed *induna* had stepped in front of her, and in frustration Jim almost shot him down, but checked his trigger finger at the last instant. He knew that the sound of the shot would be echoed by his own men, and the first carefully aimed volley would be wasted before the enemy were in effective range. He lowered the rifle and strode down the barricades, calling to them: 'Steady now! Let them come in close. Don't be greedy. There will be enough for all of you.' Only Smallboy laughed at his joke. The sound was raucous and forced.

Jim moved back to his place beside Louisa, nonchalant and unhurried, setting an example to the musketeers and to the boys. The front rank of the *impi* was sweeping up to the line of white stones. They came dancing and singing, stamping their bare feet and shaking their war rattles, beating with the bright blades upon their shields. There were no gaps between the black shields.

I have let them come too close, Jim thought. To his fevered gaze, they seemed already within range with those deadly stabbing blades. Then he saw that they had not yet reached the stones. He steeled his nerve and shouted down the line, 'Wait! Hold your fire!'

He picked out the *induna* who was still in the front rank. He was horribly scarred. An axe cut ran from his scalp through his eye and down his cheek. The healed cicatrice was smooth and shiny, and over the top edge of his black shield the empty eye socket seemed to glare straight at Jim.

'Wait!' Jim called. 'Let them come.' Now he could see the separate drops of sweat sliding down the *induna*'s cheeks like grey seed pearls. The man's bare feet kicked over one of the cairns of white river stones.

'Now, fire!' Jim shouted, and the first volley was a single clap of thunder. The gunsmoke spurted out in a grey cloudbank.

From such close quarters the rawhide shields were no protection at all. The goose-shot cut through, and the destruction was terrible. The front rank seemed to dissolve in the wash of smoke. The heavy lead pellets drove clean through flesh and bone, going on to rattle against the shields and bodies of those behind. The second rank stumbled over the dead and dying. Those warriors coming up behind were impatient to get within *assegai* range. They shoved forward with their shields, knocking off-balance the stunned survivors in the front rank.

The smoking gun was snatched from Jim's grip and a loaded musket thrust into his hands by one of the herd-boys. The second volley bellowed out with almost the same precision as the first, but then each successive volley became more ragged as some of the musketeers fired faster, served more quickly by their boys.

Mounds of dead and wounded piled up in front of the barricades, and the warriors coming up from the rear ranks had to clamber over them. The limp corpses were treacherous footing, and slowed them down, while the muskets were changed swiftly and a continuous rolling fire thundered down the line of wagons.

When the most determined Nguni reached the barricades they tried to tear away the thorn branches with their bare hands, but the musket fire never slackened. They climbed over their own dead and tried to scale the sides of the wagons. The relentless fire from the redoubts caught them in enfilade, and they tumbled back on to those below them.

The narrow wedge of land between the pool of the river and the high clay bank of the stream compressed the *impi* as they advanced in a solid mass. Like the sweep of a scythe, every blast of shot from the muskets cut swathes through them.

The wind was blowing from the direction of the river, into the faces of the attackers, and the gunsmoke rolled over them in a dense fog, half blinding them and confusing their attack. The same wind cleared the range for the defenders.

One of the warriors used the spokes of a wagon wheel as a ladder and succeeded in clambering over the tailboard of the central wagon. Jim was occupied with the Nguni storming the barricade directly in front of him when Louisa's scream alerted him. As he turned, the warrior stabbed at Louisa over the side of the wagon. She jumped back but the steel point slit the front of her tunic.

Jim dropped his empty musket and grabbed the cutlass he had pegged into the wood of the wagon, ready to hand. He sent a thrust deep into the man's chest, under his raised right arm. As he fell back, Jim jerked his blade clear and pegged the point back into the wagon, then reached back to take the loaded musket from the boy behind him.

'Good lad!' he grunted, and shot down the next attacker as he tried to pull himself up the side of the wagon. Jim glanced to his right and saw that Louisa had returned to her place by his side. The front of her tunic flapped open where the *assegai* had ripped it and a flash of her tender white skin showed in the tear.

'You're not hurt?' He smiled encouragement at her. Her face and arms were already blackened with the soot of gunsmoke, and her eyes were misty blue in contrast. She nodded without smiling, and took the next gun her loader handed her. She paused, let the oncoming warrior reach up to start scaling the barricade and then she fired. The recoil rocked her back on her feet, but the man cried out as the shot whipped into his face and throat and he slumped back onto the man beneath him.

Jim lost track of the passage of time. It all became a blur of smoke, sweat and gunfire. The smoke choked them, the sweat ran into their eyes, and the gunfire deafened and dazed them. Then, abruptly, the warriors who, a moment before, had been swarming like hiving bees upon the barricades were gone.

The defenders gazed about them in astonishment, seeking another target to fire at. The bank of gunsmoke drifted away, and it came as a shock to see the shattered *impis* running and staggering back up the hillside, dragging their wounded with them.

'To horse! We must mount and pursue them,' Louisa called to Jim.

He was amazed by her aggressive spirit, and that her grasp of tactics was so astute. 'Wait! They are not beaten yet.' He pointed beyond the retreating *impis*. 'Look! Manatasee still has half her forces in reserve.' Louisa shaded her eyes. Just below the crest of the high ground she saw the orderly ranks of warriors sitting on their shields, waiting for the order to attack.

The herd-boys ran up with the water bottles. They swallowed and gasped, and drank again, spluttering in their eagerness. Jim hurried down the line, anxiously questioning each of his men.

'Are you hurt? Are you all right?' It seemed impossible, but not one had been touched. Louisa had come closest, with the *assegai* thrust that had split open her tunic.

She scrambled through the afterclap of her own wagon and, within a short while, emerged again. Her face and arms were scrubbed pink. She wore a fresh tunic, and a starched, ironed headcloth bound about her hair. She hurried to help Zama relight the cooking fires and prepare a hasty meal for the defenders. She brought Jim a pewter plate piled with hunks of bread, and cuts of grilled venison and pickles.

'We have been fortunate,' she said, as she watched him wolf down the food. 'More than once I was certain they were going to overwhelm us.'

Jim shook his head and replied, with his mouth half full, 'Even the bravest men cannot prevail against firearms. Have no fear, Hedgehog, it's hard but in the end we will survive.'

She saw that he spoke to encourage her rather than out of conviction, and smiled. 'Whatever comes we will face it side by side.'

As she spoke the singing started again on the hillside. The defenders, who had been stretched out in the shade of the wagons, pulled themselves to their feet, and went back to their places at the barricade. The fresh *impis* were moving forward through the wounded and exhausted stragglers, who were scattered back from the battlefield. Manatasee danced ahead of the advancing cohorts, surrounded by her drummers.

Jim picked his best London rifle from the rack. He checked the priming. Louisa was watching him.

'If I can kill the she-wolf, her pack will lose heart,' he told her.

He stepped to the side of the wagon, and measured the shot. The range was long even for the rifle. The wind had risen and was swirling and gusting – it could blow even the heavy lead ball off its trajectory. Dust obscured the range, and Manatasee was dancing and twisting like a serpent. Jim handed the telescope to Louisa.

'Call the strike of my shot,' he told her, and braced himself, holding the rifle at high port, waiting for the moment. The wind gusted coolly against his sweaty cheek, then dropped. At the same time a gap opened in the curtain of dust, and Manatasee raised both arms above her head, and posed in this dramatic attitude. Jim swung up the rifle and picked up her tall shape in the notch of the rear sight. He did not try to hold the picture, but let the pip of the foresight ride smoothly up her painted body. At the same time his forefinger took up the slack of the trigger, and the shot crashed out as it came level with her eyes, aiming high to allow for the drop of the ball over the range.

For an instant Jim was unsighted by the recoil and the smoke, then he focused again. It took the heavy ball a heartbeat to cover the distance, and he saw Manatasee spin round and fall.

'You have struck her!' Louisa screamed with excitement. 'She is down.'

A growl went up from the *impis*, the voice of an angry beast.

'That will break their spirit,' Jim exulted. Then he grunted with surprise. 'Sweet Jesus, I do not believe my eyes!'

Manatasee had risen to her feet again. Even at this range Jim could see the tint of crimson on her painted skin, a rose petal of blood that ran down her flank.

'It has grazed across her ribs.' Louisa stared through the lens. 'She is only lightly wounded.'

Manatasee pirouetted before her *impis* showing herself to them, proving that she was still alive. They responded with a joyous shout and lifted their shields to salute her.

'*Bayete!*' they bellowed.

'*Zee!*' the queen screeched. '*Zee, Amadoda!*' and she began to ululate. The sound drove her *impis* into frenzy.

'*Zee!*' they exhorted themselves and those about them, and they came down to the wagons like lava pouring from the mouth of the volcano. Manatasee still pranced at the head of the charge.

Jim snatched up the second rifle of the pair, and fired again, trying to pick out her slender weaving figure from the flowing tide of blackness. The plumed *induna* at her side threw up his

arms and went down, struck squarely by the ball, but Manatasee danced on. Fortified by her rage, she seemed at every
instant to grow stronger.

'Stand firm, and wait your chance,' Jim called to his men.

The first ranks of the attackers poured across the open
ground, and clambered over the mounds of the dead and
wounded.

'Now!' Jim yelled. 'Hit them! Hit them hard!'

The fusillade struck them as though they had run into a
wall of stone, but those behind dragged the dead and wounded
from the pile and scrambled up into the hellstorm of shot.
The barrels of the muskets blistered the fingers of the musketeers when they touched them. The steel was so hot that it
could have set off the gunpowder as it was poured into the
muzzle. The gun barrels hissed and sizzled when the boys
plunged them into the water kegs to quench them. Even in
their haste they were careful not to immerse the locks and
soak the flints.

The need to cool the guns slowed up the rate of reloading,
the fire slackened as the defenders at the barricades shouted
desperately for fresh muskets. Some of the smaller boys were
almost exhausted by the gruelling work and were beginning to
panic. Louisa left her place at the barricade and ran back to
steady and encourage them. 'Remember your drill! Steady
now, don't try to hurry!'

Through the haze of gunsmoke and over the heads of the
attackers Jim glimpsed Manatasee again. She was close behind
her *impi*, waving them forward to the attack. Her wild screams
and ululation goaded them to mightier efforts. Many more of
the warriors were swarming over the piles of corpses and
reaching the barricade below where Jim stood. The smell of
blood was in their nostrils and their expressions were wolfish.
Their baying chilled the soul and weakened the arms of the
defenders.

Unable to climb the barricades in the face of the steady
volleys, the warriors began to rock the central wagon on its
wheels. Fifty of them heaved together, and the wagon swayed

dangerously back and forth. Jim realized that soon it would reach the critical point of balance and capsize. The warriors would swarm through the breach it left. The *assegais* would drink deeply of blood, and the fight would be over in minutes.

Manatasee had seen the opportunity, and sensed victory almost within her grasp. She pranced in close behind the rear rank of the attackers and climbed on to a mound of rocks to see over their heads.

'Zee!' she screamed. 'Zee!' Her warriors answered her and thrust with their shoulders against the wagon truck. It teetered at the limit of its balance, seemed at any moment to be going over, then fell back on to all four wheels.

'*Shikelela*!' shouted the *indunas*. 'Again!' The warriors gathered themselves, and bent to take their grip on the axles and the chassis of the wagon.

Jim looked back at Manatasee. The mound of rocks on which she stood was the one Jim had built to cover the keg of gunpowder. He glanced under the front wheels of the wagon. The end of the slow match was still lashed to one of the spokes, and the rest of the long fuse ran back under the chassis, under the heaps of the Nguni corpses to the mound on which Manatasee stood. He had buried the fuse under only a light layer of earth. He could see that in places it had been trampled and exposed by the feet of the attackers. Perhaps the other end of the fuse had been plucked from the bung-hole of the powder keg.

'Only one way to find out!' he told himself grimly. He snatched the next loaded musket that one of his gunboys handed him, and cocked the hammer, then ducked under the swaying body of the wagon.

If the wagon goes over now, I'll be crushed like a frog under the wheels, he thought, but he found the end of the fuse and laid it over the pan of the musket lock. He held it there with one hand and pulled the trigger. The falling flint struck a shower of sparks from the frizzen and the powder in the pan flared up in a puff of smoke. The musket jumped in his grip and the shot ploughed into the ground at his feet. The flash in the pan had ignited the fuse. It hissed and blackened, then the flame shot along its length, and disappeared into the earth, like a snake into its hole.

Jim sprang back on to the truck of the violently rocking wagon, and stared across at Manatasee. A fine slick of blood was running down her flank from the flesh wound his ball had inflicted. She saw him and pointed her *assegai* at his face. Her grotesquely painted features contorted with hatred, and spittle flew from her lips in a cloud and sparkled in the sunlight, as she screamed her death curses at him.

Then he saw the length of slow-match had been exposed across the last yard of trampled earth below the mound on which the queen stood. The swift flame shot along it, leaving the fuse blackened and twisted as it burned. Jim clenched his jaws and waited for the explosion. It hung fire for a terrible moment and in that pause the wagon finally toppled over, ripping a fatal gap in the barricade. Jim was thrown from his platform, and sprawled half under the wagon body. The attacking warriors shouted triumphantly and surged forward.

'*Bulala!*' they bellowed. 'Kill!'

Then the powder keg exploded beneath Manatasee's feet. A mighty tower of dust and stones shot higher than the treetops. The explosion tore the queen's body into three separate parts. One of her legs cartwheeled high into the air. The other, still attached to her torso, was thrown back into the ranks of her oncoming warriors, splattering them with her blood. Her head sailed like a cannon ball over the barricade and rolled across the open ground within the laager.

The blast swept over the Nguni who had overturned the wagon, and who were crowded into the gap they had opened. It cut them down, killing and maiming them and piling their corpses on to those of their comrades who had already fallen.

Jim was protected from the full force of the explosion by the body of the overturned wagon. Half dazed he came to his feet; his first concern for Louisa. She had been with the herd-boys, and the blast had knocked her to her knees, but she jumped up again and ran to him.

'Jim, you are hurt!' she cried, and he felt something warm

and wet running down from his nose into his mouth. It tasted metallic and salty. A flying splinter of rock had sliced across the bridge of his nose.

'A scratch!' he said, and hugged her to his chest. 'But thank God you are unhurt.' Still clinging together they gazed through the gap in the barricade at the carnage the explosion had wrought. The Nguni dead were lying waist deep, piled upon each other. Manatasee's *impis* were in full flight, back up the grassy hillside. Most had thrown aside their shields and weapons. Their terrified voices were filled with superstitious dread as they screamed to each other, 'The wizards are immortal.'

'Manatasee is dead.'

'She is slain by the lightning of the wizards.'

'The great black cow is devoured by witchcraft.'

'Flee! We cannot prevail against them.'

'They are ghosts, and the spirits of crocodiles.'

Jim looked along the wall of the laager. Smallboy was leaning on the ramparts, staring after the routed enemy, in a stupor of exhaustion. The other men had slumped down, some in attitudes of prayer, still holding their hot, smoking muskets. Only Bakkat was indefatigable. He had climbed on to the top of one of the wagons, and was shrieking insults at the routed *impis* as they fled.

'I defecate on your heads, I piss on your seed. May your sons be born with two heads. May your wives grow beards, and fire-ants eat your testicles.'

'What is the little devil telling them?' Louisa asked.

'He wishes them a fond farewell and lifelong happiness,' Jim said, and the sound of her laughter revived him.

'To horse!' he shouted at his men. 'Mount! Our hour has come.'

They stared at him dully, and he thought they might not have heard him, for his own ears still hummed with the memory of the guns.

'Come on!' he told Louisa. 'We must lead them out.' The two ran to the horselines. Bakkat jumped down from his perch and followed them. The horses were already saddled. They

329

had been held ready for this moment. Jim and Louisa mounted, and the others came running.

Bakkat retrieved Manatasee's painted head, and spiked it on the point of a Nguni *assegai*. He carried it high as a Roman eagle standard. The queen's purple tongue lolled out of the corner of her mouth, and one eye was closed while the other glared white and malicious.

As the band of horsemen sallied forth through the gap the Nguni had torn in the laager wall, each carried two muskets, one in hand and the other in the gun sheath. They had shot-belts slung over each shoulder and powder flasks tied to the pommel. Behind them came the boys, riding bareback, each leading a spare horse loaded with powder kegs, shot-bags and water bottles.

'Keep together!' Jim exhorted them. 'Don't get cut off. Like cornered jackals the Nguni are still dangerous.'

They trampled the corpses and the fallen shields under their hoofs before they reached the open grassland and spurred forward, but Jim called again: 'Steady! Keep to a trot. There are still many hours of daylight ahead of us. Don't burn up the horses!'

In a wide line abreast they swept the veld, and the muskets began to boom out as they overtook the running warriors. Most of the Nguni had thrown away their weapons and lost their headdresses. When they heard the steady pounding of the hoofs coming up behind them, they ran until their legs gave way. Then they knelt in the grass and waited like dumb animals for the blast of goose-shot.

'I cannot do this,' Louisa called desperately to Jim.

'Then tomorrow they will return and do it to you,' he warned her.

Smallboy and his men revelled and rejoiced in the slaughter. The herd-boys had to replenish their powder flasks, and refill the shot-bags. Bakkat waved the head of Manatasee on high, and shrieked with excitement as he rode down on another isolated bunch of demoralized warriors.

'He's a bloodthirsty hobgoblin,' Louisa muttered, as they followed him. But when the Nguni saw the head of their queen they wailed with despair and threw themselves down in attitudes of surrender.

Ahead of the line of avenging riders rose another series of low, rolling hills, and it was towards these that the remnants of the broken *impis* were flying. Jim would not allow his men to increase their pace, and as they rode up towards the crest at a steady trot the musket fire had dwindled: the *impis* were scattering away to the horizon, and offered few targets.

Jim and Louisa reined in on the crest and looked down into a wide strath, a gently sloping valley through which another river meandered. Its banks were forested with magnificent trees, and open grass meadows lay beneath them. The air was blue with smoke from the fires of a vast encampment. Hundreds of small thatched huts were laid out on the grassland with military precision. They were deserted. What remained of the *impis* had fled: the tail end of the army disappearing over the far rise of the valley.

'Manatasee's camp!' Louisa exclaimed. 'This is where she mustered her *impis* before she attacked us.'

'And, by the love of all that is holy, there are her herds!' Jim pointed. Beneath the trees, along both banks of the river and spread out widely over the grassy saucer, were the dappled herds of cattle.

'They are Manatasee's treasury. The wealth of her nation. We have only to ride down and gather them up.' Jim's eyes sparkled as he surveyed them. Each herd was composed of animals of the same colour. The black cattle formed a dark stain on the golden veld, well separated from the red-brown herds and the dappled beasts.

'There are too many of them.' Louisa shook her head. 'We will not be able to manage such numbers.'

'My sweet hedgehog, there are some things of which a man can never have too much: love, money and cattle to name just a few.' He rose in his stirrups and ran the lens of his telescope over the multicoloured masses of animals, then over the last of the fleeing Nguni. He lowered the telescope. 'The *impis* are beaten and broken. We can call off the pursuit and count our winnings.'

Although the Nguni dead littered the grassland, not a single one of Jim's men had been wounded, apart from little Izeze who had caught his finger in the lock of a musket he was reloading and lost the first joint. Louisa had dressed it and Jim told him it was a wound of honour. Izeze held the finger aloft proudly and showed off the turban of white bandage to anyone who would look.

With the eye of a stockman born and raised, Jim appraised the booty as he rode among the captured herds. These were tough, hardy animals, with massive shoulder humps and a wide rack of horns. They were tame and trusting and showed no alarm as Jim rode within arm's length. All were in prime condition, glossy hides and rumps bulging with fat. At this first inspection Jim saw no evidence of the maggot-infested wounds of screw-worm, or the wall eyes of fly-borne ophthalmia. But he did notice with satisfaction the healed scars of sweat sickness on the glands of the throat, which proclaimed their immunity from further infection. For them to have survived in such fine condition he was sure they must also be salted against the disease of the tsetse fly.

'These are more valuable than any cattle brought from Europe,' he told Louisa. 'They have immunity to the diseases of Africa, and have been lovingly raised by the Nguni. As Tegwane told us, they love their cattle more than their own children.'

Zama had left the band of horsemen and disappeared into the encampment of thatched huts. Suddenly he rode back, his face working with agitation. He was speechless with excitement, and gesticulated for Jim to follow him.

He led Jim to a stockade of freshly hewn tree-trunks. They lifted the logs out of the gateway and Jim went through, then stopped to stare in wonder. Before him lay Manatasee's treasure house. The ivory was piled in stacks as high as a man could reach. The tusks had been graded by length and thickness. The immature ivory, some of which was no thicker than a human wrist, had been bound with strips of bark rope into fascicles, each making up a load that an ox could carry comfortably. The larger tusks were also bound with bark rope so that they could be secured to a pack-saddle for transportation. Some of the tusks were huge, but Jim saw none to match the pair he had taken from his own great bull.

While Smallboy and the other driver unsaddled the horses and took them down to the river to drink, Jim and Louisa wandered around the ivory storeroom. She watched his face as he gloated on this mass of treasure. He is like a little boy at Christmas time, she thought, as he came back to her and took her hand.

'Louisa Leuven,' he said, with solemn formality, 'I am at last a rich man.'

'Yes.' She tried to wipe the smile from her lips. 'I can see that you are. But, despite all your wealth, you are really quite a lovable lad.'

'I am pleased you have noticed that. That being agreed between us, will you marry me, and share my riches and my abundant charms?'

The laughter died on her lips. 'Oh, Jim!' she whispered, and then the strain of the battle and the pursuit of the *impis* caught up with her, and she began to weep. Her tears cut runnels through the gun-soot and dust that coated her cheeks. 'Oh, yes, Jim! I can think of nothing that would please me better than to become your wife.'

He caught her up and hugged her. 'Then this is the happiest day of my life.' He bussed her heartily. 'Now, dry your tears, Hedgehog. I'm sure we will find a priest somewhere, if not this year then next.'

With Louisa held in the crook of one arm, and his other hand laid possessively on one of the stacks of ivory, he looked over his newly acquired herds, which filled half of the valley with their abundance. Slowly his expression changed as he was struck by the age-old dilemma of the rich man.

How, in the name of Satan himself, do we keep our hands on what we have won, for every man and beast in Africa will be eager to take it from us? he wondered.

It was sunset before Jim could tear himself away from the captured encampment. Leaving Zama and half of his tiny force to guard the ivory and the herds, they set off back to the laager. The dazzling panoply of stars lit their way. As the group passed the corpses of the Nguni who had died that day, hyena and jackals scattered before the horses.

When they were almost within sight of the wagon laager they reined in their horses and stared at the night sky with awe. A mystic glow rose over the eastern horizon, and lit the world so clearly that they could see each other's startled faces turned upwards. It was as though the sun was rising from the wrong direction. They watched in awe as an enormous fireball climbed over the horizon and hurtled silently overhead. Some of the herd-boys whimpered and pulled their blankets over their heads.

''Tis nothing but a shooting star.' Jim reached across to take Louisa's hand and reassure her. 'They are common visitors in these African skies. This one is a little larger than most.'

'It is the spirit of Manatasee,' Smallboy cried. 'She begins her journey to the land of shades.'

'The death of kings,' Bakkat whimpered. 'The fall of tribes. War and death.'

'An omen of the worst kind.' Zama shook his head.

'I thought I had civilized you,' Jim laughed, 'but you are still a crew of superstitious savages at heart.'

The gigantic heavenly body swept down into the west, leaving its fiery trail clear across the sky behind it as it disappeared below the horizon. It lit the sky for the rest of that night, and the next, and for many nights thereafter.

By its ghostly light they reached the wagon laager. They found old Tegwane, spear in hand, his beautiful granddaughter at his side, guarding it like a pair of faithful watchdogs.

Although they were all nearly at the end of their tether, Jim roused the camp again before dawn. Using a span of oxen, and with much shouting and cracking of long whips, they heaved the overturned wagon back on to its wheels. The robust vehicle had suffered little damage, and within a few hours they had repacked its scattered load. Jim knew that they must leave the battlefield at once. In the heat of the sun the corpses would very soon putrefy, and, with the stench of their rotting, sickness and disease would come.

At his orders they inspanned every other wagon in the train. Then Smallboy and the other drivers fired the long whips and the oxen trundled the vehicles out of the gruesome laager and into the open grassland.

They set up camp that evening among the deserted thatched huts of the Nguni town, surrounded by the vast herds of humpbacked cattle, with the piles of ivory securely enclosed within the wagon laager.

The next morning, after breakfast, Jim summoned all his men to the *indaba*. He wanted to explain to them his future plans, and to tell them where he would lead them next. First he asked Tegwane to explain how the Nguni used their cattle to carry the ivory when they were on the march.

'Tell us how they place the loads, and secure them to the backs of the animals,' Jim ordered.

'That I do not know,' Tegwane admitted. 'I have only watched their advance from afar.'

'Smallboy will be able to work out the harness for himself,' Jim decided, 'but it would have been better to use a method to which the cattle are accustomed.' Then he turned to the small group of herd-boys and said, 'Can you men' – they liked to be called men and they had earned the right at the barricades – 'can you men take care of so many?'

They considered the vast herds of cattle that were scattered down the full length of the valley.

'They are not so very many,' said the eldest, who was the spokesman.

'We can herd many more than that,' said another.

'We have vanquished the Nguni in battle,' squeaked Izeze, smallest and cheekiest of the boys, his voice not yet broken. 'We can take care of their cattle, and their women also, when we capture them.'

'It may be, Izeze,' the name Jim had given him meant Little Flea, 'it may be that neither your whip nor your whistle are yet large enough for those tasks.'

Izeze's companions shrieked with laughter. 'Show it to us!' they cried, and tried to catch him, but like the insect that was his namesake he was quick and agile. 'Show us the weapon that will terrify the women of the Nguni.' Clinging to his loincloth to preserve his modesty and dignity Izeze fled, pursued by his peers.

'All of which brings us no closer to a solution of the problem,' Jim remarked as he and Louisa made the final inspection of the laager's defences before turning in for the night.

Although it seemed apparent that the Nguni *impis* had been shattered and would not return, Jim was taking no chances. He set his sentries at nightfall and the next morning they stood to their guns in the dawn.

'Sweet heavens!' Jim exclaimed, as the light strengthened. 'They have returned!' He seized Louisa's arm and pointed out to her the rows of shadowy figures squatting just out of musket shot beyond the barricades of the laager.

'Who are they?' she whispered, though in her heart she knew the answer well.

'Who else but the Nguni?' he told her grimly.

'I had thought it was over, the killing and the fighting. God grant that it was enough.'

'We shall soon find out,' he said, and called for Tegwane. 'Hail them!' he ordered the old man. 'Tell them that I will send our lightning down upon them as I did to Manatasee.'

Tegwane climbed shakily on to the side of the wagon, and called across the open grassland. A voice answered him from among the gathered Nguni, and a long shouted exchange followed.

'What do they want?' Jim demanded impatiently. 'Do they not know that their queen is dead and their *impis* shattered?'

'They know it well,' Tegwane said. 'They have seen her head carried upon the *assegai* as they fled the battlefield, and her fiery spirit passing in the night sky as she travelled to meet her forefathers.'

'Then what is it they want?'

'They want to speak with the wizard who struck down their queen with his lightning.'

'A parley,' Jim explained to Louisa. 'It seems that these are some of the survivors of the battle.'

'Talk to them, Jim,' she urged. 'Perhaps you can prevent any more bloodshed. Anything is better than that.'

Jim turned back to Tegwane. 'Tell their *induna*, their leader, that he must come into the laager alone and unarmed. I will not harm him.'

He came dressed in a simple kilt of leather strips, without headdress or weapons. He was a fine-looking man in his middle years, with the body and limbs of a warrior and a handsome moon face the chocolate colour of freshly hewn mabanga wood. As soon as he entered the laager he recognized Jim. He must have seen him upon the battlefield. He went down on one knee, an attitude of respect, clapping his hands and chanting praises: 'Mightiest of warriors! Invincible wizard who comes out of the great waters! Devourer of *impis*! Slayer of Manatasee! Greater than all of her fathers!'

'Tell him that I see him, and that he may approach me,' Jim ordered. He realized the significance and importance of this delegation, and assumed a dignified manner and haughty expression. The *induna* went down on all fours and crawled towards him. He took Jim's right foot and placed it on his own bowed head. Jim was taken by surprise and almost lost his balance, but he recovered swiftly.

'Great white bull elephant,' the *induna* chanted, 'young in years but mighty in power and wisdom, grant me mercy.'

From his father and his uncle Jim had learned enough of African protocol to know how to conduct himself. 'Your worthless life is mine,' he said. 'Mine to take or spare. Why should I not send you on the same road through the sky as the one on which I sent Manatasee?'

'I am a child without a father or mother. I am an orphan. You have taken my children from me.'

'What is he talking about?' Jim demanded angrily of Teg-wane. 'We killed no children.'

The *induna* heard his tone and realized he had given offence. He pressed his face into the dirt. When he answered Tegwane's questions his voice was hoarse with dust. Jim used the opportunity to remove his foot from the *induna*'s head: standing on one leg was uncomfortable and undignified.

At last Tegwane turned back to Jim. 'He was Manatasee's keeper of the royal herds. He calls the cattle his children. He begs you either to kill him, or to allow him the honour of becoming your keeper of the herds.'

Jim stared at the man in astonishment. 'He wants to work for me as my chief herdsman?'

'He says he has lived with the herds since he was a child. He knows each animal by name, which bull covered their dams. He knows each one's age and temper. He knows the remedy and the treatment for every disease to which the herds are prone. With his own *assegai* he has killed five lions who were attacking the animals. What is more . . .' Tegwane paused to draw breath.

'Enough.' Jim stopped him hastily. 'I believe what he says, but what of these others?' He pointed at the other files of squatting figures outside the laager. 'Who are they?'

'They are his herders. Like him they have been dedicated to the care of the royal cattle since childhood. Without the herds their lives are without purpose.'

'They, too, are offering themselves?' Jim was having diffi-culty grasping the extent of his good fortune.

'Every one of them wishes to become your man.'

'What do they expect from me?'

'They expect you to kill them if they err or fail in their duties,' Tegwane assured him. 'Manatasee would have done so.'

'That is not exactly what I meant,' Jim said in English, and Tegwane looked baffled. He went on quickly: 'What do they expect in return for their work?'

'The sunshine of your pleasure,' said Tegwane. 'As I do.'

Jim pulled his ear thoughtfully, and the *induna* rolled his head to watch his face, worried that their request would be denied and that the white wizard would strike him down as he had the queen. Jim was considering the expense of adding the *induna* and fifty or sixty of his comrades to the strength of his already numerous crew. However, there seemed to be no additional cost that he could fathom. From what Tegwane had told him he knew these herders would live on the blood and milk of the herds, and the venison that fell to his gun. He was sure he could expect a most extraordinary level of loyalty and dedication in return. These were skilled cattlemen and fearless spearmen. He would find himself at the head of his own tribe of warriors. With the Hottentot musketeers and the Nguni spearmen he need fear nothing in this wild and savage land. He would be a king. 'What is this man's name?' he asked Tegwane.

'He is called Inkunzi, for he is the bull of all the royal herds.'

'Tell Inkunzi that I look with favour on his request. He and his men are now my men. Their lives are in my hands.'

'*Bayete!*' Inkunzi shouted with joy when he heard this. 'You are my master and my sun.' Once again he placed Jim's right foot upon his head, and his men seeing this, knew they had been accepted.

They rose to their feet, drummed on their shields with their *assegais*, and shouted together, '*Bayete*! We are your men! You are our sun!'

'Tell them that the sun can warm a man, but it can also burn him to death,' Jim warned them solemnly. Then he turned to Louisa and explained to her what had just taken place.

Louisa looked upon this fearsome band of warriors, and remembered how, only days before, they had come singing to the laager. 'Can you trust them, Jim? Should you not disarm them?'

'I know the traditions of these people. Once they have sworn their allegiance I will trust them with my life.'

'And mine,' she pointed out softly.

The next day Jim made an observation of the noon passage of the sun, and plotted their position on his father's chart. 'According to my reckoning we are only a few degrees south of the latitude of the Courtney trading post at Nativity Bay. By my calculations, it should be less than a thousand leagues to the east, three months' travel. It is possible that we might encounter one of our ships there, or at least find a message from my family under the mail stones.'

'Is that where we are going next, Jim?' Louisa asked. He looked up from the parchment of the chart and raised an eyebrow. 'Unless you have a better suggestion?'

'No.' She shook her head. 'That will suit me as well as any other.'

The following morning they broke camp. Inkunzi and his herders brought in the captured royal herds, and Jim watched with interest as they loaded the ivory. The rawhide harness they used was simple, but had obviously been perfected by the Nguni to fit over the heavy hump and be secured behind the front legs. The loads of ivory were counterbalanced to hang comfortably but securely on each side of the beast's back, allowing it freedom of movement. Inkunzi and his men matched the weight of each load to the size and strength of the animal that would carry it. The cattle seemed unaware of their burden as they moved along at the leisurely pace set by the herders, grazing contentedly as they spread out like a river in flood across the veld. By the time the entire herd was on the move they covered several leagues.

Jim took a compass bearing along the line of march, and pointed out to Inkunzi a landmark on the horizon to head for. Inkunzi himself stalked along at the head of his herds, wrapped in his leather cloak with his *assegai* and his black war shield slung on his back. He played on a reed flute as he went, a sweet but monotonous tune, and the cattle followed him like faithful hounds. The wagon train brought up the rearguard.

Each morning Jim and Louisa rode out with Bakkat to

break trail and search ahead for any lurking danger or for fresh sign of the elephant herds. They scouted far ahead of the slowly moving caravan, picking out the passes through the hills, the fords and drifts across the rivers. The herds of wild game astonished them, but they found that the Nguni had swept the land bare of human presence. Villages had been burnt to the ground, only the smoke-blackened patterns of the foundation stones still standing, and the veld around was strewn with the white fields of human bones. There was no living soul.

'The *mefecane*,' Tegwane called this great slaughter. 'The pounding of the tribes, like corn between the grinding stones of the *impis*.'

Once Inkunzi had proved his worth and established his place high in the hierarchy of the band, he joined quite naturally in the *indabas* around the campfire. He was able from his own life to paint for them a picture of these terrible events. He told them how his people had their origins far to the north, along some mythical valley, a place he called the Beginning of All Things.

Generations before, his tribe had been overtaken by some cataclysmic event, another *mefecane*, and the famine that naturally followed. They and their herds had begun the long migration southwards plundering and killing all the other tribes that stood in their path. As pastoralists and nomads they always moved on, seeking grazing for their herds, more plunder and women. It was a tragic saga.

'We will never know how many human souls have perished on these lovely wild fields,' Louisa said softly.

Even Jim was subdued by the extent of the tragedy that had swept like the black plague across the continent. 'This is a savage land. To flourish it needs to be watered by the blood of man and beast,' he agreed with her.

When they scouted ahead of the wagons Jim was always on the lookout for signs of the rest of the Nguni, and drilled his small band in the defensive tactics they would adopt if they were attacked.

He was searching also for the elusive elephant herds, but as the weeks passed, and mile after mile of this grand and tractless land fell behind the turning wagon wheels, they discovered neither Nguni nor elephant.

Almost three months after they had turned east, they came abruptly upon a steep, broken escarpment where the land fell away before them into a sheer abyss.

'This seems to be the end of the world,' Louisa breathed. They stood together and stared in wonder. In the clear air and bright sunshine it seemed they could indeed see to the ends of the earth. Staring through the lens of his telescope Jim saw that as it blended with the distant horizon the sky shaded to an unearthly blue, bright and translucent as polished lapis-lazuli.

It took him some time to realize what he was looking at. Then the angle of the sunlight changed subtly and he exclaimed, 'In the name of all that is holy and beautiful, Hedgehog, 'tis the ocean at last.' He handed her the telescope. 'You shall now see what a famous navigator I am, for I shall lead you unerringly to the beach at Nativity Bay in the land of the elephants.'

Tom and Dorian Courtney rode up to the main gates of the castle. They were expected and the sergeant of the guard saluted and waved them through into the courtyard. Grooms came running to take their horses as they dismounted.

The Courtney brothers were accustomed to such respect. As two of the leading burghers of the colony and its most prosperous merchants, they were often guests of Governor van de Witten. The governor's secretary, himself an important VOC official, came scurrying out of his office to greet them and usher them through into the governor's private quarters.

They were not kept waiting in the anteroom, but taken immediately into the spacious council chamber. The long central table and all the twenty chairs around it were of stinkwood, one of the most beautifully grained timbers of Africa, lovingly carved by the skilled Malay slave cabinetmakers. The floors were of lustrous yellow-wood planks polished with beeswax until they shone like glass. The panes of the bay windows at the far end of the room were of jewel-like stained glass shipped down the length of the Atlantic from Holland. They looked out over the vista of Table Bay, with the monumental bulk of Lion's Head mountain beyond. The bay was cluttered with shipping, and whipped by the south-easter into a froth of prancing white horses.

The panelled walls were hung with the seventeen portraits of the council members of the VOC in Amsterdam: serious bulldog-faced men in black hats with lace collars, paper white on their high-buttoned black coats.

Two men rose from their seats at the council table to greet the brothers. Colonel Keyser was in the dress uniform he had designed for himself. It was of scarlet brocade, with sashes over both shoulders, one blue, the other gold. His ample girth was encircled by a sword belt embossed with gold medallions, and the hilt of his rapier was inlaid with semi-precious stones. There were three large enamelled diamanté stars pinned on his chest. The largest of these was the Order of St Nicholas. The tops of his glossy boots reached above his knees. His hat was wide-brimmed, crowned with a large bunch of ostrich feathers.

In contrast, Governor van de Witten wore the sombre dress that was almost the uniform of the most senior officials of the VOC: a black velvet skull-cap, a Flemish lace collar, and a black high-buttoned jacket. His thin legs were clad in black silk hose, and his square-toed shoes were buckled with solid silver.

'Mijnheeren, you do us honour by your presence,' he said, his face pale and lugubrious.

'The honour is ours alone. We came as soon as we received your invitation,' Tom said, and the brothers bowed together. Tom was dressed in dark broadcloth, but of first quality and London cut. Dorian wore a green silk jacket and voluminous breeches. His sandals were camel-skin, and his turban matched his jacket and was secured with an emerald pin. His short red beard was neatly trimmed and curled. It was in sharp contrast to Tom's more luxuriant, silver-shot growth. Looking at them together nobody would have guessed they were brothers. Colonel Keyser came forward to greet them, and they bowed again.

'Your servant, Colonel, as ever,' Tom said.

'*Salaam aleikum*, Colonel,' Dorian murmured. Although when he was at High Weald and in the bosom of his own family he often forgot it, when he went abroad, and especially in these formal surroundings, he liked to remind the world that he was the adopted son of Sultan Abd Muhammad al-Malik, the Caliph of Muscat. 'Peace be unto you, Colonel.' Then he added in Arabic, making it sound like part of the greeting, 'I like not the fat one's expression. The tiger shark smiles in the same way.' This was entirely for Tom's benefit: he knew that the others in the room understood not a word of what he had said.

Governor van de Witten indicated the chairs facing his own across the glistening expanse of the table. 'Gentlemen, please be seated.' He clapped his hands, and immediately a small procession of Malay slaves appeared carrying silver salvers of choice morsels of food, and decanters of wine and spirits.

While they were being served the governor and his guests continued the customary exchange of compliments and small talk. Both Tom and Dorian refrained from more than a single glance at the mysterious object that lay in the centre of the stinkwood table between them. It was covered with a velvet cloth, beaded around the edges. Tom pressed his knee lightly against Dorian's. Dorian did not look at him, but touched the side of his nose, a signal that he had also noticed the object. Over the years they had grown so close that they could read each other's minds with accuracy.

The slaves at last backed out of the council chamber, and the governor turned to Tom. 'Mijnheer Courtney, you have already discussed with Colonel Keyser the distressing and reprehensible behaviour of your son, James Archibald Courtney.'

Tom stiffened. Although he had been expecting this, he

braced himself for what would follow. What new trick has Keyser come up with now? he wondered. As Dorian had pointed out, Keyser's expression was smug and gloating. Aloud he said, 'Indeed, Governor, I well recall our conversation.'

'You assured me that you disapproved of your son's behaviour, his interference with the course of justice, the abduction of a female prisoner, the theft of VOC property.'

'I remember it well,' Tom assured him hastily, anxious to cut short the list of Jim's transgressions.

However, van de Witten went on remorselessly: 'You gave me your assurance that you would keep me informed of your son's whereabouts as soon as you obtained knowledge of his movements. You promised that you would do all in your power to see to it that he and this female criminal, Louisa Leuven, were brought to the castle at the first opportunity to answer to me personally for their crimes. Did we not agree on this?'

'Yes, we did, Your Excellency. I also recall that, as an earnest of my good faith and intentions and to compensate the VOC for its losses, I made a payment to you of twenty thousand guilders in gold.'

Van de Witten ignored this solecism. He had never issued an official receipt for that payment, ten per cent of which had gone to Colonel Keyser and the balance into his own purse. As he went on speaking his expression became increasingly sorrowful: 'I have reason to believe, Mijnheer Courtney, that you have not kept your side of our bargain.'

Tom threw up his hands, and made theatrical sounds of amazement and denial, but did not go so far as to deny the charge outright.

'You would like me to substantiate what I have just said?' van de Witten asked, and Tom nodded warily. 'As Colonel Keyser is the officer responsible to me for the conduct of this case, I will ask him to explain what he has discovered.' He looked at the colonel. 'Would you please be kind enough to enlighten these gentlemen?'

'Certainly, Your Excellency, it will be my duty and privilege.' Keyser leaned across the table and touched the mysterious object under the beaded velvet cloth. All their eyes went to it. Teasingly, Keyser removed his hand and leaned back in his chair again.

'Let me first ask you, Mijnheer Courtney, if at any time during the last three months any of the wagons belonging to you and your brother,' he nodded at Dorian, 'left the colony.'

Tom pondered a moment, then turned to his brother. 'I don't remember that happening, do you, Dorry?'

'None of our vehicles received VOC permission to leave the colony.' Dorian begged the question neatly.

Once again Keyser leaned forward, but this time he whipped away the velvet cloth and they all stared at the broken stub of the wheel spoke. 'Is that your company cypher branded into the wood?'

'Where did you find it?' Tom asked ingenuously.

'An officer of the VOC found it lying beside the tracks of four wagons that left the colony near the headwaters of the Gariep river and headed north into the wilderness.'

Tom shook his head. 'I cannot explain it.' He tugged his beard. 'Can you, Dorian?'

'In March last year we sold one of the old lumber wagons to that Hottentot hunter, what was his name? Oompie? He said he was going to find ivory in the desert lands.'

'My sacred oath!' Tom exclaimed. 'I had forgotten that.'

'Did you get a receipt for the sale?' Keyser looked frustrated.

'Old Oompie cannot write,' Dorian murmured.

'So, then, let us get this clear. You never travelled with four heavily laden wagons to the borders of the colony, and you did not hand these wagons over to the fugitive from justice, James Courtney. And you never encouraged and abetted this runaway to flee the borders of the colony without VOC sanction. Is that what you are telling me?'

'That is correct.' Tom looked him steadily in the eyes across the table. Keyser grinned with triumph and glanced at Governor van de Witten for permission to continue. He nodded his agreement, and Keyser clapped his hands again. The double doors swung open and two uniformed VOC corporals entered, dragging between them a human figure.

For a moment neither Tom nor Dorian recognized him. He

wore only a pair of breeches that were filthy with dried blood and his own excrement. The nails had been plucked from his toes and fingers with blacksmith's tongs. His back had taken the lash until it was a bloody pulp. His face was swollen grotesquely. One eye was closed completely, and the other a mere slit in the bloated purple flesh.

'A pretty sight.' Keyser smiled. Governor van de Witten held a small sachet of dried herbs and flower petals to his nose. 'I beg your pardon, Your Excellency.' Keyser noticed the gesture. 'Animals must be treated as such.' He turned back to Tom. 'You know this man, of course. He is one of your wagon drivers.'

'Sonnie!' Tom started up, then thought better of it and sank back into his chair. Dorian looked distressed. Sonnie was one of their best men, when he was sober. He had been missing from High Weald for over a week, and they had presumed that he had gone off on one of his periodic binges, from which he always returned reeking of bhang, cheap brandy and even cheaper women, but chastened, apologetic and swearing on the grave of his father that it would not happen again.

'Ah, yes!' Keyser said. 'You do know him. He has been telling us interesting details of your movements, and those of your family. He says that last September two of your wagons led by Mijnheer Dorian Courtney's son, Mansur, set off along the coastal road to the north. This I can substantiate, because I led a full troop of my own men to follow those wagons. I now know that this was a diversion to draw my attention away from the other matters of more consequence.' Keyser looked at Dorian. 'I am sad that a fine lad like Mansur should have become embroiled in this sordid affair. He also must face the consequence of his actions.' It was said lightly, but the threat was undisguised.

Both Courtney brothers remained silent. Tom could not look at Sonnie, lest he lose his temper and self-control. Sonnie was a free spirit who, despite his multitudinous failings, stood high in his affections, and Tom felt paternally responsible for him.

Keyser turned his attention back to Tom. 'This man has also told us that soon after the two decoy wagons left High Weald, and when you were sure that my troops had followed them, you and Mevrouw Courtney slipped away with four other heavily loaded wagons, a large number of horses and other animals to the Gariep river. You waited there for some weeks, and eventually your son, James Courtney, and the escaped female prisoner came out of the mountains to join you. You handed over the wagons and the animals to them. They made good their escape into the wilderness, and you returned with assumed innocence to the colony.'

Keyser leaned back in his chair and clasped his hands over the buckle of his sword belt. The room was silent, until Sonnie blurted out, 'I am sorry, Klebe.' His voice was indistinct for his lips were cut and crusted with half-healed scabs, and there were black holes in the front of his mouth where two of his front teeth had been knocked out. 'I did not want to tell them, but they beat me. They said they would kill me, then do the same to my children.'

'It is not your fault, Sonnie. You only did what any man would do.'

Keyser smiled and inclined his head towards Tom. 'You are magnanimous, Mijnheer. If I were in your place I would not be so understanding.'

Governor van de Witten intervened: 'Can we be rid of this fellow now, Colonel?' he asked irritably. 'His stink is atrocious, and he is dripping blood and other less salubrious fluids on to my floor.'

'I beg your pardon, Your Excellency. He has served his purpose.' He nodded at the uniformed warders and waved them away. They dragged Sonnie out through the doors, and closed them as they left.

'If you set bail for him, I will pay it and take that poor wretch back to High Weald with me,' Tom said.

'That presupposes that the two of you are going back to High Weald,' Keyser pointed out. 'But, alas, even if you were, I could not allow you to take the witness with you. He must remain in the castle dungeons until your son James and the

escaped prisoner are brought to trial in front of the governor.'
He unclasped his fingers and leaned forward. The smile faded
and his expression became hard, his eyes cold and fierce. 'And
until your own part in these matters has been made clear.'

'Are you arresting us?' Tom asked. 'On the unsubstantiated
testimony of a Hottentot wagon driver?' Tom looked at
Governor van de Witten. 'Your Excellency, under article 152
of the Criminal Procedure Act, laid down by the governors in
Amsterdam, no slave or native may give evidence against a
free burgher of the colony.'

'You have missed your vocation, Mijnheer. Your grasp of
the law is impressive.' Van de Witten nodded. 'Thank you for
bringing the Act to my attention.' He stood up and walked on
those thin black-hosed legs to the stained-glass windows. He
folded his arms over his pigeon chest and stared out at the
bay. 'I see both your ships have returned to port.'

Neither brother answered this remark. It was superfluous.
The two Courtney vessels were clearly visible from where he
stood, lying at anchor off the foreshore. They had come into
the bay in convoy two days previously, and had not yet
offloaded. The *Maid of York* and the *Gift of Allah* were lovely
schooners. They had been built in the yards at Trincomalee
to Tom's own design. They were fast and handy, with shallow
draught and well armed, perfect for inshore work, trading
into estuaries and the shallows of a dangerous and hostile
coast.

Sarah had been born in York and Tom had named one
vessel for her. Dorian and Yasmini had chosen the name for
the other ship.

'A lucrative voyage?' van de Witten asked. 'Or so I hear.'

Tom smiled thinly. 'We thank the Lord for what we have
had, but for a little more we would be glad.'

Van de Witten acknowledged the witticism with an acidic
smile, and returned to his chair. 'You ask if you are under
arrest. The answer, Mijnheer Courtney, is no.' He shook his
head. 'You are a pillar of our small society, a gentleman of the
highest reputation, industrious and hard-working. You pay
your taxes. Technically you are not a free Dutch burgher, but

349

a citizen of a foreign nation. However, you pay your residence-licence fees and, as such, you are entitled to the equivalent rights of a burgher. I would not even think of arresting you.' It was clear from Colonel Keyser's expression that in fact deep consideration had been given to the possibility.

'Thank you, Your Excellency.' Tom rose to his feet, and Dorian followed his example. 'Your good opinion means a great deal to us.'

'Please, Mijnheeren!' Van de Witten held up his hand to delay them. 'There are some other small matters that we should discuss before you go.' They sat down again.

'I would not want either of you, or any member of your family, to leave the colony without my express permission until this matter is fully resolved. That includes your son, Mansur Courtney, who was responsible for deliberately drawing out a troop of the VOC cavalry on a fruitless expedition to the northern borders of the colony.' He stared at Dorian. 'Do I make myself clear?' Dorian nodded.

'Is that all, Your Excellency?' Tom asked, with exaggerated politeness.

'No, Mijnheer. Not quite all. I have determined that you should place with me a nominal surety to ensure that you and your family abide by the conditions I have imposed.'

'Just how nominal?' Tom braced himself to hear the response.

'One hundred thousand guilders.' Van de Witten picked up the decanter of honey-golden Madeira wine. He came round the table to refill their spiral-stemmed glasses. A heavy silence hung over the room. 'I will make allowance for the fact you are foreigners and perhaps you did not understand me.' Van de Witten resumed his seat. 'I will repeat myself. I require a surety of one hundred thousand guilders from you.'

'That is a great deal of money,' Tom said at last.

'Yes, I would think it should be sufficient.' The governor nodded. 'But a relatively modest sum when we take into consideration the profits of your last trading voyage.'

'I will need some time to raise that amount in cash,' Tom

said. His face was almost impassive; a slight tic of one eyelid was all that betrayed his agitation.

'Yes, I understand that,' van de Witten agreed. 'However, while you are making provision for the surety, you should take into consideration that your residence-licence renewal fee is also due for payment within a few weeks. It would be just as well if you paid both amounts at the same time.'

'An additional fifty thousand guilders,' Tom said, trying to hide his dismay.

'No, Mijnheer. On account of these unforeseen circumstances I have had to reconsider the amount of the residence licence. It has been increased to one hundred thousand guilders.'

'That is piracy,' Tom snapped, losing his temper for the instant, then recovering it at once. 'I beg you pardon, Your Excellency. I withdraw that remark.'

'You should know about pirates, Mijnheer Courtney.' Van de Witten sighed mournfully. 'Your own grandfather was executed for that crime.' He pointed through the bay windows. 'Out there on the parade-ground within sight of this very room. We must pray that no other member of your family meets the same tragic end.' The threat was implicit, but it lay across the quiet room like the shadow of the gallows.

Dorian intervened for the first time: 'A fee of one hundred thousand on top of the surety deposit will beggar our company.'

Van de Witten turned to him. 'I think that you still misunderstand me,' he said sadly. 'The fee for your brother's family residence is one hundred thousand and for your family an additional one hundred thousand. Then you must add to that the surety for good behaviour.'

'Three hundred thousand!' Tom exclaimed. 'That is not possible.'

'I am sure it is!' van de Witten contradicted him. 'As a last resort you could always sell your ships and the contents of your warehouse. That will surely bring in the full amount.'

'Sell the ships?' Tom leaped to his feet. 'What madness is this? They are the blood and bones of our company.'

'I assure you it is not madness.' Van de Witten shook his head and smiled at Colonel Keyser. 'I think you should explain the position to these gentlemen.'

'Certainly, Your Excellency.' Keyser hoisted himself out of his chair and swaggered to the window. 'Ah, good! Just in time to illustrate the point.'

On the beach below the ramparts of the castle two platoons of VOC soldiers were drawn up. The bayonets were fixed on their muskets, and they carried full packs. Their green uniform jackets stood out sharply against the white sands. As Tom and Dorian watched they began to embark in two open lighters at the edge of the water, wading out knee-deep to reach them.

'I am taking the precaution of placing guards on board both your ships,' Keyser announced, 'merely to ensure your compliance with Governor van de Witten's edict.' Keyser settled back in his chair again. 'Until further notice, both of you will report every day before the noon gun to my headquarters to reassure me that you have not left the colony. Of course, as soon as you can produce a receipt from the treasury for the full amount you owe, and a passport from Governor van de Witten, you will be free to leave. I fear, however, that it might not be so easy to return next time.'

'Well, perhaps we have overstayed our welcome,' Tom said, and beamed round the room. The family was seated in the counting-house of the High Weald godown.

Sarah Courtney tried to show her disapproval in sternness, but an expression of resignation was not entirely hidden by her lowered lids. He will never cease to amaze me, this husband of mine, she thought. He revels in circumstances that would devastate other men.

'I think Tom is right.' Dorian joined in between puffs on his hookah. 'We Courtneys have always been voyagers on the oceans and wanderers on the continents. Twenty years in one spot on this earth is too long.'

'You are talking about my home,' Yasmini protested, 'the

place where I have spent half my life, and where my only son was born.'

'We will find both you and Sarah another home, and give you both more sons, if that is what will make you happy,' Dorian promised.

'You are as bad as your brother,' Sarah rounded on him. 'You don't understand a woman's heart.'

'Or her mind.' Tom chuckled. 'Come now, my sweeting, we cannot stay here to be beggared by van de Witten. You have been forced to up sticks and run before. Don't you remember how we had to clear out of Fort Providence at five minutes' notice when Zayn al-Din's men came calling?'

'I shall never forget it. You threw my harpsichord overboard to lighten the ship so we could clear the sandbars at the mouth of the river.'

'Ah, but I bought you another,' Tom said, and they all glanced across the room to the triangular instrument standing against the inner wall. Sarah stood up and crossed to it. She opened the lid of the keyboard, took her seat on the stool and played the opening bars of 'Spanish Ladies'. Tom hummed the chorus.

Abruptly Sarah closed the lid, and stood up. There were tears in her eyes. 'That was long ago, Tom Courtney, when I was a silly young girl.'

'Young? Yes. Silly? Never!' Tom went to her quickly and placed an arm round her shoulders.

'Tom, I am too old to start all over again,' she whispered.

'Nonsense, you are as young and strong as you ever were.'

'We will be destitute,' Sarah mourned. 'Beggars and homeless wanderers.'

'If you think that, you do not know me as well as you think you do.' Still holding her fondly he looked at his brother. 'Shall we show them, Dorry?'

'There will be no peace for us if we do not.' Dorian shrugged. 'They are scolds and martinets, these women of ours.'

Yasmini leaned over and tugged his curling red beard. 'I have always been a dutiful Muslim wife to you, al-Salil.' She used his Arabic name, the Drawn Sword. 'How dare you accuse me of disrespect? Recant at once or you shall be deprived of all favours and privileges until next Ramadan comes round.'

'You are so lovely, full moon on my life. You grow sweeter and more docile with each day that passes.'

'I shall take that as a recantation.' She smiled and her great dark eyes glowed at him.

'Enough!' cried Tom. 'This dispute tears apart our family and our hearts.' They all laughed, even the women, and Tom seized the advantage. 'You know that Dorian and I were never such fools as to trust that gang of footpads and cutpurses who make up the board of governors of the VOC,' he said.

'We always knew that we were in this colony under sufferance,' Dorian went on. 'The Dutch looked upon us as milch cows. For the last twenty years they have been sucking our udders dry.'

'Well, not entirely dry,' Tom demurred, and went to the bookcase at the far end of the room, which reached from floor to ceiling. 'Lend a hand here, brother,' he said, and Dorian went to help him. The bookcase, filled with heavy leatherbound tomes, was set on steel rollers cunningly concealed beneath the dark wooden skirting-board. With both of them shoving at one end, it slid aside, with squealing protest from the rollers, to reveal a small door in the back wall, barred with iron crossbolts and locked with an enormous bronze padlock.

Tom lifted down a book, whose spine was embossed in gold leaf *Monsters of the Southern Oceans*. He opened the covers; in the hollowed-out interior lay a key.

'Bring the lantern,' he told Sarah, as he turned the key in the padlock, shot back the bolts and opened the door.

'How did you keep this from us over all these years?' Sarah demanded.

'With the greatest difficulty.' Tom took her hand, and led her into a tiny room, not much bigger than a cupboard. Dorian and Yasmini followed. There was barely enough space for them all and the stack of small wooden chests piled neatly against the far wall.

'The family fortune,' Tom explained. 'The profits of twenty years. We did not have the reckless courage or the lack of good sense to entrust it to the Bank of Batavia, which is owned by our old friends in Amsterdam, the VOC.' He opened the top chest, which was packed to the brim with small canvas bags. Tom handed one of the bags to each of the women.

'So heavy!' Yasmini exclaimed, and nearly dropped hers.

'An't nothing heavier,' Tom agreed.

When Sarah opened the mouth of the bag she held she gasped. 'Gold coins? All three chests filled with gold?'

'Naturally, my sweeting. We pay our expenses in silver, and keep the profits in gold.'

'Tom Courtney, you are a dark horse. Why did you never tell us of this hoard?'

'There was never a reason until now.' He laughed. 'The knowledge would have made you discontent, but now it has taken a weight off your heart.'

'How much have you and Dorry squirrelled away in here?' Yasmini asked, in wonder.

Tom knocked with his knuckles on each of the three chests in turn. 'Seems all three are still full. This is the most part of our savings. In addition we have an ample collection of sapphires from Ceylon and diamonds from the fabulous Kollur mine on the Krishna river in India. They are all large stones of the first water. If not quite a king's ransom, then at least a rajah's.' He chuckled richly. 'In truth, that is not quite all. Both our ships lying in the bay have their weighty cargoes still intact.'

'To say nothing of two platoons of VOC soldiers on board as well,' Sarah pointed out spicily, as she backed out of the concealed strongroom.

'That presents an interesting problem,' Tom admitted, as he locked the door and Dorian helped him push the bookcase back into position to cover it. 'But one that is not insoluble.' He went to take his seat again, and patted the chair next to him. 'Come sit beside me, Sarah Courtney. I am going to need the benefit of your sharp wit and famous erudition now.'

'I think it is time that we invited Mansur to join the family deliberations,' Dorian suggested. 'He is old enough at last and, what is more, his life will be changed as profoundly as ours when we sail out of Table Bay. He will probably be distraught to be taken from his childhood home.'

'Quite right!' Tom agreed. 'But now speed is everything. Our exodus must take van de Witten and Keyser by surprise. They cannot be expecting us to abandon High Weald and all its contents. There is a great deal to be seen to, but we must set ourselves a limit.' He looked up at Dorian. 'Three days?'

'It will be a close-run thing.' Dorian frowned as he considered it. 'But, yes, we can be ready to sail in three days.'

Those three days were filled with frenzied activity, carefully concealed from the rest of the world. It was essential that even the most trusted of their servants had no inkling of their true intentions. Loyalty did not presuppose discretion: the serving girls were notorious chatterboxes, and the chambermaids even worse. Many had romantic attachments to men in the town and a few consorted with the soldiers and petty officers in the castle. To allay any suspicions, Sarah and Yasmini put it about that the sorting and packing of clothes and furniture was merely a seasonal reordering and cleaning of the rambling homestead. In the godown Tom and Dorian conducted their annual stock-taking three months earlier than was their usual custom.

An English East Indiaman was lying at anchor in the bay, and the captain was an old and trusted friend of Tom. They had dealt with each other over the last twenty years. Tom sent him an invitation to dinner and, during the meal, swore him to secrecy and informed him of their plans to leave Good Hope. Then he sold him the entire contents of the godown at High Weald for a fraction of its real value. In return Captain Welles promised not to take possession until after the two Courtney ships had sailed from the bay. He undertook to make payment for the goods directly into the CBTC account at Mr

Coutts's bank in Piccadilly immediately on his return to London.

The land and buildings of High Weald were held under perpetual quit-rent to the VOC. Mijnheer van de Velde, another prosperous burgher of the colony, had been importuning Tom and Dorian for years to sell the estate to him.

After midnight the brothers, dressed in black, their faces covered by the brims of their hats and the collars of their greatcoats, rode across to his homestead on the banks of the Black river, and knocked on the shutters of van de Velde's bedroom. After his initial alarm, angry shouts and threats, he came out in his nightshirt brandishing a bell-mouthed blunderbuss. He shone his lantern into their faces.

'Name of a dog, it is you!' he exclaimed, and led them into his counting-house. As the first light of dawn paled the sky and the doves cooed in the oaks outside the windows they shook hands on the bargain. Tom and Dorian signed the deed of transfer of High Weald and, grinning triumphantly, van de Velde handed over an irrevocable letter of credit drawn on the Bank of Batavia for an amount less than half of what he had been prepared to pay for it only a few months before.

On the planned evening of departure, as the sun set and the light faded, when they could not be observed from the beach or the castle walls, Mansur and a small crew rowed out to the anchored ships. Keyser had placed six Hottentot troopers under a corporal on board each. After five days at anchor, with the vessels pitching and rolling in the steep swells kicked up by the south-easter, those soldiers who were not prostrated with seasickness were bored and disenchanted with this duty. To add to their misery they could see the lights of the taverns along the beachfront and hear snatches of song and revelry drifting across the dark, wind-churned surface from the shore.

Mansur's arrival alongside was a pleasant distraction, and they crowded the rail to exchange jests and friendly insults with him and his rowers. Mansur was a favourite of the Hottentot community in the colony. The nickname they had bestowed upon him was Specht, Woodpecker, for his fiery topknot.

'You are not allowed on board, Specht,' the corporal told him sternly. 'Colonel Keyser's orders. No visitors allowed.'

'Do not fuss yourself. I am not coming on board. I would not want to be seen in the company of such rogues and ruffians,' Mansur shouted back.

'So you say, old Specht, but then what are you doing here? You should be giving the girls in the village sewing lessons.' The corporal shouted with laughter at his own wit. The word *naai* had a double meaning: not only to sew but also to fornicate. Mansur's red hair and startling good looks rendered him almost irresistible to the members of the fair sex.

'It's my birthday,' Mansur told them, 'and I have brought a present for you.' He kicked the keg of Cape *brandewijn* that lay in the bottom of the boat. 'Send down a cargo net.' They jumped to obey, and the keg swayed up on to the deck.

The Muslim captain of the *Gift of Allah* came up from his cabin to protest at this devil's brew, forbidden by the Prophet, coming on board.

'Peace be upon you, Batula,' Mansur called to him in Arabic. 'These men are my friends.' Batula had been Dorian's lance-bearer in the early days in the deserts, they had spent most of their lives together and the links between them were of iron. Batula had known Mansur from the day of his birth. He recognized Mansur's voice and his anger abated a little. He consoled himself that all his men were believers and they would not be tempted by Satan's liquor, unlike the *kaffir* soldiers.

The Hottentot corporal knocked the bung out of the brandy keg and filled a pewter mug. He took a mouthful of the neat spirits, gasped and exhaled the fumes noisily. '*Yis maar!*' he exclaimed. '*Dis lekker!* It's so good!'

Mugs in hand his men crowded round him for their turn at the keg, but the corporal relented his former strictures and called down to Mansur, 'Hey, Specht! Come on board and share a cup.'

Mansur waved an apology as they pulled away and headed for the other ship. 'Not now, perhaps later. I have another present for your men on the *Maid of York*.'

Sarah and Yasmini had been strictly charged by their husbands to restrict their luggage to two large travelling trunks each. Tom absolutely forbade Sarah to try to smuggle her harpsichord on to the ship. As soon as the men were occupied elsewhere, the two goodwives had the servants load their ten large chests on to the waiting cart, and the harpsichord sat four-square on top of this abundant cargo. The wheels of the cart were splayed under the weight.

'Sarah Courtney, you astound me. I know not what to say.' Tom glared at the offending instrument when he returned.

'Then say naught, Tom, you big booby. And I shall play you the sweetest rendition of "Spanish Ladies" you have ever heard when we reach the new home you shall build me.' That was his favourite song, and he stumped off in defeat to oversee the loading of the other wagons.

At this last hour it was not possible that word of their departure might reach Colonel Keyser's ear in time for him to intervene, so the servants were assembled and Tom and Dorian told them that the family was leaving High Weald for ever. There was not space on board the two ships for all of the servants and freed slaves that made up the High Weald household. Those who had been chosen to go with the family were given the right to refuse and stay in the colony. Not one took up that option. They were given an hour to pack. Those who were being left behind huddled in a forlorn group at the end of the wide veranda. The women were weeping softly. All the members of the Courtney family went down the line of familiar, well-beloved faces, talking to each in turn and embracing them. Tom and Dorian handed each a canvas purse, and a deed of manumission and release from service, with a glowing letter of character reference.

'Where is Susie?' Sarah asked, when she reached the end of the line, and looked around for one of her older housemaids. Susie was married to the wagon driver Sonnie, who was still a prisoner in the castle dungeons.

The other servants looked around with surprise. 'Susie was here,' one answered. 'I saw her at the end of the veranda.'

'She was probably overcome by the shock of hearing that we are leaving,' Yasmini suggested. 'When she has recovered I'm sure she will come back to take her leave.'

There was so much still to be done that Sarah was forced to put Susie's absence to the back of her mind. 'I'm sure she would never let us go without a word,' she said, and hurried down to make sure that the cart carrying her special treasures was ready to leave for the beach.

By the time the wagons were ready to leave the homestead the moon had risen, and by its light Susie was hurrying along the road to the castle. She had her shawl over her head, the tail of it wrapped round the lower half of her face. Her face was wet with tears, and she muttered to herself as she ran: 'They don't think about me and Sonnie. No, they leave my husband in the hands of the Boers, to be beaten and killed. They leave me here with three little ones to starve while they sail away.' The twenty years of kindness she had received from Sarah Courtney were swept from her mind and she burst into sobs as she thought about the cruelty of her employer.

She quickened her pace. 'Well, if they don't care for me and Sonnie and the little ones, why should I care for them?' Her voice hardened with her resolve. 'I will make a bargain with the Boers. If they let Sonnie go from the dungeon, I will tell them what Klebe and his wife are up to tonight.'

Susie did not waste time going to the castle to find Colonel Keyser. She went directly to the little cottage behind the Company gardens. The Hottentot community was close-knit and Shala, Colonel Keyser's paramour, was the youngest daughter of Susie's sister. Her liaison with the colonel gave Shala great prestige in the family.

Susie knocked on the shutters of the back room of the cottage. After some fumbling and grumbling in the darkened bedroom, lantern light flared behind the shutters and Shala's voice demanded sleepily, 'Who is it?'

'Shala, it's me. Tannie Susie.'

Shala opened the shutters. She stood naked in the light of her own lantern, and her fat honey-coloured breasts joggled together as she leaned over the window-sill. 'Auntie? How late is it? What do you want at this hour?'

'Is he here, child?' Susie's question was redundant. Keyser's snores rumbled from the darkened bedroom like distant thunder. 'Wake him up.'

'He will beat me if I do,' Shala protested. 'You also, he will thrash you.'

'I have important news for him,' Susie snapped. 'He will reward us both when he hears it. Your uncle Sonnie's life depends on it. Wake him at once.'

When the line of wagons set off from High Weald towards the seafront even those who were not sailing with the family walked alongside. When they reached the beach they helped load the cargo into the lighters that were already waiting at the edge of the surf. Before all the wagons had made their way down through the dunes both boats were fully loaded.

'In this surf we will risk a capsize if we burden them any more,' Tom decided. 'Dorian and I will take this load out to the ships and secure the guards.' He turned to Sarah and Yasmini. 'If they are not sufficiently lulled with Mansur's brandy, there may be a rumpus on board. I don't want you mixed up in that. You two must wait here and I will bring you out to the ships on the next trip.'

'The cart with our luggage has not arrived yet.' Sarah peered back worriedly into the darkness of the dunes.

'It will be here in short order,' Tom assured her. 'Now, please wait here and do not take Yassie and go wandering off to heaven knows where.' He embraced her and whispered in

361

her ear, 'And I would be mightily obliged if you do as I ask just this once.'

'How can you think so poorly of your own wife?' she whispered back. 'Off you go. When you return I shall be here, as good as gold.'

'And twice as beautiful,' he added.

The men scrambled aboard the lighters and seized the oars. The pull out to the ships was rough and wet, for the laden vessels were low in the water. The spray came over the bows, soaking them to the skin. When at last they rowed into the calmer water in the lee of the *Gift of Allah* there was no challenge from the ship. Tom swarmed up the rope-ladder with Dorian and Mansur not far behind him. They drew their blades, ready to meet an attack from the VOC troops, but instead they found Captain Batula waiting at the entry-port.

'May the peace of God be upon you.' He greeted his ship's owners with the deepest respect. Dorian embraced Batula warmly. They had ridden thousands of leagues together and sailed even further. They had fought side by side in the battles that had won a kingdom. They had shared bread and salt. Their friendship was a rock.

'Where are the guards, Batula?' Tom cut short their greetings.

'The forecastle,' Batula told him. 'They are sodden with drink.'

Tom ran to the open companionway and jumped down. The cabin stank of brandy fumes and other less attractive odours. The VOC troopers and their corporal were lying comatose in puddles of their own vomit.

Tom sheathed his sword. 'These gentlemen are quite happy for a while. Tie them up and let them enjoy their rest until we are ready to leave. Let's get the gold chests and the rest of the cargo on board.'

Once the chests of gold coins were safely stowed in the main cabin, Tom left Dorian and Mansur to supervise the loading of the rest of the cargo. He took charge of the second lighter and they rowed across to the *Maid of York*. They found the VOC guards there in no better condition than their comrades on the *Gift of Allah*.

'Sunrise in eight hours, and we must be out of sight of land by then,' Tom told Kumrah, the Arab captain. 'Get this cargo on board as soon as you like.' The crew flew at the task and as the last bale of goods came on board, Tom looked across at the other ship and saw that Dorian had sent a single lantern to the masthead of the *Gift*, the signal that the first lighter was unloaded and returning to the beach to pick up the women and the remaining cargo.

As soon as the bales were lashed down, Tom had his crew carry the VOC soldiers up from the forecastle and dump them, trussed like chickens, into the lighter lying alongside. By then some were regaining consciousness, but on account of their gags and bonds they were unable to express their indignation except by grunting and rolling their eyes.

They pushed off from the ship's side and Tom took the tiller and steered back towards the shore following Dorian's lighter. As they came on to the sand Tom saw Dorian's boat was already on the beach, but nobody was at work loading it. Instead an agitated knot of servants and crew was gathered at the foot of the dunes. Tom jumped down into the shallow water and waded to the shore. He ran up the beach and saw Dorian arguing with the head driver.

'What has happened?' Then he saw that Sarah and Yasmini were missing. 'Where are the women?' Tom called.

'This idiot has let them go back.' Dorian's tone was edged with desperation.

'Go back?' Tom stopped dead and stared at him. 'What do you mean, go back?'

'The cart with their luggage broke down in the dunes. The axle snapped. Sarah and Yasmini have taken one of the empty wagons to fetch the load.'

'Those mad women!' Tom exploded, and then, with a great effort, brought his temper under control. 'Very well, we must make the best of it. Mansur, take the prisoners up above the high-water mark. Do not untie them. Leave them there for

Keyser to find in the morning. Then load these goods into the first lighter.' He pointed at the remaining boxes and crates piled on the beach. 'Send them out to the ships with the crew from the *Maid of York*. Thank the good Lord we have the gold chests on board already.'

'What shall I do after that?' asked Mansur.

'You have charge here at the landing. Wait with the second boat. Be ready to load up and launch as soon as we return with the women.' Mansur ran to obey, and Tom turned back to Dorian. 'Come, brother, you and I will go to fetch the sweet chickens that have flown the coop.'

They hurried to the horses. 'Loosen your blade in its scabbard, and make sure both your pistols are charged, Dorry. I like this turn in the road not at all,' Tom muttered, as they mounted. He took his own advice, loosened the blue sword in its scabbard, drew the pistols from the holsters on the front of his saddle, checked them, then thrust them back again.

'Come!' he said, and the two galloped back along the sandy track. Tom was expecting at any moment to come across the stranded cart, but when they rode down out of the dunes and started up through the paddocks towards the homestead they had still not found it.

'If the cart did not get very far,' Dorian muttered, 'you cannot place much blame on the driver. It collapsed under that great mountain of female baggage.'

'We should have packed it on the larger wagon.'

'The ladies would not have it so,' Dorian reminded him. 'They did not want their treasures contaminated by sharing the ride with common goods.'

'I see no call for levity in this, brother. Time runs us short.' Tom looked up at the eastern sky, but there was no sign of the dawn.

'There they are!' Ahead they saw the gleam of a lantern, and the dark shape of a wagon beside the lesser bulk of the capsized cart. They urged the horses to the top of their speed. As they came up Sarah stepped into the road, holding up the lantern, with Yasmini beside her.

364

'You are just in time to be too late, husband of mine.' Sarah laughed. 'Everything is safely repacked on board the wagon.'

At that moment Tom saw the driver behind her brandish his long whip, flicking out the lash to fire it over the backs of the oxen. 'Stay your hand, Henny, you damned fool. They will hear your whiplash down in the castle. You will bring the colonel and all his men upon us like a pride of lions!'

Guiltily Henny lowered the great whip, and instead he and his *voorloper* ran alongside the oxen slapping their rumps and urging them to pull away. The wagon began lumbering along towards the start of the dunes. The harpsichord swayed and rocked on top of the load. Tom spared it one bitter glance. 'May it fall and burst into a thousand pieces!' he grumbled.

'I choose to ignore that remark,' Sarah said primly, 'for I know you did not mean it.'

'Come up behind me, my sweeting.' Tom leaned out of the saddle to lift her up. 'I shall whisk you back to the beach and have you on board before you can blink an eye.'

'I thank you, no, my own true heart. I prefer to stay with the wagon, to see that no further mishaps befall my baggage.' In frustration Tom slapped the lead ox across its rump with the heavy sword scabbard.

They reached the first slope of the dunes and Tom looked back, and felt the first flare of alarm. There were lights showing around the homestead, which only minutes before had been in complete darkness.

'Look at that, brother,' he muttered to Dorian, keeping his voice low. 'What do you make of it?'

Dorian turned in the saddle. 'Mounted men carrying lighted torches,' Dorian exclaimed. 'They are coming up the hill from the direction of the colony. A large troop, riding in column. They must be cavalry.'

'Keyser!' Tom agreed. 'Stephanus Keyser! It can be no other. Somehow he has got wind of what we are about.'

'When he finds that we have left the homestead, he will come straight on to the landing on the shore.'

'He will catch us before we can load this baggage into the

boats,' Tom agreed. 'We must abandon the wagon, and run for the beach.'

He spurred back to where Sarah and Yasmini were walking alongside the span of oxen. They had cut sticks from the side of the road and were helping to drive the span onwards.

'Douse that lantern. Keyser has come,' Tom shouted at Sarah and pointed back. 'He will be after us in no time at all.'

'Leave the wagon. We must run.' Dorian was at Tom's side.

Sarah cupped her hand around the glass chimney of the lantern, blew out the flame. Then she turned on her husband. 'You cannot be sure it is Keyser,' she challenged him.

'Who else would be leading a troop of cavalry to High Weald at this time of the night?'

'He will not know that we are heading for the beach.'

'He may be fat, but that does not make him blind or stupid. Of course he will come after us.'

Sarah looked ahead. 'It's not far now. We can reach the shore before him.'

'A loaded ox-wagon against a troop of cavalry? Don't be daft, woman.'

'Then you must think of something,' she said, with simple faith. 'You always do.'

'Yes, I have already thought of something. Get up behind me, and we will run as though the devil is breathing fire down our necks.'

'Which he is!' said Dorian, and then to Yasmini, 'Come, my darling, let us go at once.'

'You may go, Yassie,' Sarah said, 'but I am staying.'

'I cannot leave you, Sarah, we have been together too long. I will stay with you,' said Yasmini, and moved closer to her side. They presented the men with an unassailable front. Tom hesitated just a moment longer. Then he turned back to Dorian.

'If I have learned nothing else in my life, this I know. They will not be moved.' He drew one of the pistols from its holster on the pommel of his saddle. 'Look to your priming, Dorry.' He turned back to Sarah and told her sternly, 'You will get us all killed. Perhaps then you will be satisfied. Make all haste.

When you reach the beach Mansur will be waiting with the lighter. Have it loaded and ready to shove off. When next you see us Dorry and I might be in somewhat of a hurry.' He was about to ride off when a sudden thought occurred to him. He leaned over and lifted the spare trek chain from its bracket at the back end of the wagon. Every wagon carried this piece of equipment: it was there for use when the teams had to be double spanned.

'What do you mean to do with that?' Dorian demanded. 'It will weigh down your mount.'

'Perhaps nothing.' Tom lashed the chain to the pommel of his saddle. 'But then again, perhaps a great deal.'

They left their two wives and the wagon after one last exhortation to make for the beach at their best speed, and galloped back up the hill. As they approached, the lights of the torches became brighter and the scene clearer. They reined in at the edge of the paddock, just below the homestead, and walked the horses into the deeper darkness below the out-spread branches of the trees. They saw at once that these visitors were uniformed troopers. Many were dismounted and running in and out of the buildings, their sabres drawn, searching the rooms. Tom and Dorian could clearly make out their faces and features.

'There is Keyser,' Dorian exclaimed, 'and, by the beard of the Prophet, that is Susie with him.'

'So, she is our Judas!' Tom's tone was grim. 'What possible reason would she have to betray us?'

'Sometimes there is no accounting for the treacherous spite of those we have loved and trusted most,' Dorian replied.

'Keyser won't waste much time searching for us in the homestead,' Tom grunted, as he untied the *riempie* that secured the heavy trek chain to the front of his saddle. 'Here is what you must do, Dorry.'

Quickly he outlined his plan. Almost as soon as he started talking Dorian had grasped it all.

'The gate above the main kraal,' Dorian agreed.

'When you have done, leave it open,' Tom warned him.

'You do have a hellish mind, brother Tom.' Dorian

367

chuckled. 'At times such as these, I am pleased that I am for you, not against.'

'Go quickly,' Tom said. 'Keyser has already discovered that the stable is empty and the birds have flown.' Tom mixed his metaphors cruelly.

Dorian left Tom under the trees and took the fork of the road that led down to the main cattle stockades above the lagoon. Tom noted that he had the good sense to keep to the verge so that the grass muffled his horse's hoofbeats. He watched until Dorian disappeared into the darkness, then switched his attention to what was happening around the buildings of High Weald.

The troopers had at last abandoned the search and were hurrying back to their horses. On the front *stoep* of the homestead Susie was cowering in front of Keyser, who was shouting at her. His angry tone carried to where Tom waited, but he was too distant to catch the words.

Perhaps Susie has been stricken by an attack of conscience, Tom thought, and watched Keyser lash the woman across the face with his riding crop. Susie fell to her knees. Keyser struck her again across her shoulders with a full overhead stroke of the whip. Susie screamed shrilly and pointed down the road to the dunes.

The cavalry troopers mounted hastily and fell in behind Keyser as he rode at the head of the column. By the light of the torches they carried, Tom watched them come down towards the paddock. The jingle of the harness and the clatter of the carbines and sabres in the scabbards grew louder. When they were so close that he could hear the breathing of their horses, Tom spurred his own horse out of the darkness into the middle of the road in front of them.

'Keyser, you treacherous bag of pig's lard! A curse on your black heart and a pox on your shrivelled genitals!' he shouted. Keyser was so taken aback that he reined in his horse. The troopers behind him bumped into each other. For a moment there was confusion in the column as the horses milled about.

'You will never take me, Keyser, you great round of cheese! Not on that donkey you call a horse.'

Tom lifted the double-barrelled pistol and aimed as close over the top of the ostrich plumes in Keyser's hat as he dared. Keyser ducked as the ball buzzed past his ear.

Tom spun his horse and sent him racing down the road towards the kraal. Behind him he heard the thud of answering pistol shots, and Keyser's furious bellows: 'Catch that man! After him! Alive if you can, but dead if you must. Either way, I want him!'

The troop of cavalry pounded after Tom. A blast of pellets from a cavalry carbine whirred around him like a covey of partridge rising from cover, and he lay flat on his horse's mane and lashed the loose end of the reins across its neck.

He looked back under his arm to judge the gap between himself and the pursuit, and when he saw that he was drawing ahead he slowed down a little into a firm gallop and let Keyser close in. The excited shouts and halloos of the troopers reassured Tom that they had him well in sight. Every few seconds there came the bang and thud of a pistol or carbine, and a few balls flew close enough for him to hear them pass. One struck his saddle only inches from his buttocks and went whining off into the night. If it had hit him, it would certainly have inflicted a wound that would have ended it all there and then.

Although he knew exactly where the gate was and he was looking ahead to find it, it still surprised him when it appeared suddenly out of the darkness ahead of him. He saw instantly that Dorian had done as he had asked and left it wide open. The hedge on each side of the opening was shoulder high, thick and dark with matted thorn. Tom had only a moment to steer away from the gateway, and aim at the hedge. As he gathered his mount for the jump with the pressure of his knees and his hands on the reins, from the corner of his eye he saw the glint of steel. Dorian had wrapped each end of the chain around the heavy wooden gate-posts and the links were stretched at waist height across the opening.

Tom let the horse under him judge the moment of take-off, moved his weight forward and helped him surge upwards. They brushed over the top of the hedge and landed well in hand on the far side. The instant Tom recovered his balance and steadied his mount he turned and looked back. One of the troopers had pulled well ahead of his comrades, and tried to follow Tom over the hedge. His horse shied and refused at the last moment, running out while his rider flew off his back and came sailing over the hedge, flying free. He struck the ground in a tangle of limbs and equipment and lay like a sack of beans.

Colonel Keyser saw his man unhorsed, waved his sword over his head and shouted, 'Follow me! Through the gate!'

His squadron bunched up close behind him and he charged into the gateway. With a metallic clash the chain sprang tight as the combined weight of animals and men crashed into it. In an instant the entire column was cut down, horses piling into each other as they fell. The bones of their legs snapped like dry firewood as they hit the chain. Their bodies filled the gateway in a struggling, kicking, screaming mass. Men were caught under the animals and their cries swelled the tumult.

Even Tom, who had engineered it, was appalled by the shambles. Instinctively he turned back his horse, tempted for a fleeting moment to try to render assistance to his victims. Dorian rode out from behind the wall of the kraal where he had been concealed and stopped beside Tom. The two stared in horror. Then Keyser struggled to his feet almost under the noses of their horses.

As the first into the trap, Keyser's mount had struck the chain cleanly, and as they went down Keyser was hurled from the saddle like a stone from a sling. He struck and rolled across the earth, but somehow retained his grip on his sabre. Now he stood up unsteadily and gazed back in disbelief at the pile of struggling men and horses. Then he let out a cry of rage and despair mingled. He raised his sword and rushed at Tom.

'For this I shall have your hide and heart!' he bellowed. With a flick of his sword Tom sent the sabre spinning from his grip to peg into the earth ten paces away. 'Don't be an idiot, man. There has been enough damage done for one day. See to your men.' Tom glanced at Dorian. 'Come, Dorry, let's go on.'

They turned their horses. Still half stunned Keyser staggered to retrieve his sword and as they rode away he shouted after them, 'This is not the end of the business, Tom Courtney. I shall come after you with all the might and authority of the VOC. You shall not escape my wrath.' Neither Tom nor Dorian looked back and he ran after them shouting threats, until they had pulled away and he had run out of breath. He stopped, panting, and hurled his sabre after them. 'I shall hunt you down and root you out, you and all your seed.'

Just as they were disappearing into the night, Keyser bellowed his last taunt: 'Koots has already captured your bitch-born bastard. He is bringing back Jim Courtney's head, and the head of his convict whore, pickled in a keg of brandy.'

Tom stopped and stared back at him.

'Yes, Koots has caught him,' Keyser shouted, with wild laughter.

'He is lying, brother. He says it to wound you.' Dorian laid a hand on Tom's arm. 'How could he know what has happened out there?'

'You are right, of course,' Tom whispered. 'Jim has got clean away.'

'We must get back to the women, and see them safely aboard,' Dorian insisted. They rode on and Keyser's shouts receded behind them.

Struggling for breath, Keyser tottered back to the tangle of men and horses. A few of his troopers were crawling to their feet, or sitting holding their heads or nursing other injuries.

'Find me a horse,' Keyser yelled.

His own horse, like most of the others, had broken its legs when it struck the chain, but a few animals, who had been in the rear rank of the charge, had been able to heave themselves upright and were standing, shivering and shaken. Keyser ran from one to another, checking their legs. He selected the one that seemed strongest, hoisted himself into the saddle and

371

shouted to his men who could still walk, 'Come on! Find yourselves a mount and follow me. We can still catch them on the beach.'

Tom and Dorian found the last wagon descending the final slope of the dunes. The women were walking beside it. Sarah had relit the lantern and held it high when she heard the horses galloping up.

'Will you not hurry, woman?' Tom was so agitated that he shouted at her from a distance.

'We *are* hurrying,' she replied, 'and your rough seaman's language will make us go no faster.'

'We have delayed Keyser for the moment, but he will be after us again soon enough.' Tom realized his mistake in adopting that brusque approach to his wife and, despite his agitation, tried to ameliorate his tone. 'We are in sight of the beach, and all your possessions are safe.' He pointed ahead. 'Will you now let me take you to the boat, my sweeting.'

She looked up at him and, even in the poor light of her lantern, could see the strain on his face. She relented. 'Lift me up, then, Tom.' She raised her arms to him like a small girl to her father. When he swung her up and placed her behind him she hugged him close, and whispered into the thick curls that bushed down the back of his neck, 'You are the finest husband God ever placed upon this earth, and I am the most fortunate of wives.'

Dorian gathered up Yasmini and they followed Tom down to where Mansur waited with the lighter at the water's edge. They placed the two women firmly on board. The wagon came trundling down, and as it reached the lighter it sank axle deep into the wet sand. But this made it easier to transfer the last of their possessions into the boat. Once the wagon was empty the oxen were able to haul it away.

While this was going on, Tom and Dorian kept glancing back into the darkness of the dunes, expecting the worst of Keyser's threats to materialize, but the harpsichord was at last lashed down and covered with a tarpaulin to protect it from the spray.

Mansur and the crewmen who were shoving out the boat were still waist deep, when there was an angry shout from the dunes and the flash and clap of a carbine shot. The ball slammed into the transom of the boat, and Mansur leaped in.

There was another shot and again the ball struck the hull. Tom pushed the women down until they were sitting on the deck, in an inch or more of bilge water, protected by the pile of hastily loaded cargo.

'I entreat you now to keep your heads well down. We can argue the merits of this suggestion later. However, I assure you those are real musket balls.'

He looked back and could just make out Keyser's distinctive outline against the pale sand, but his stentorian bellows carried clearly: 'You will not escape me, Tom Courtney. I shall see you hanged, drawn and quartered on the same scaffold as that bloody pirate, your grandfather. Every Dutch port in this world will be closed to you.'

'Take no notice of what he says,' Tom told Sarah, dreading that Keyser would repeat his gruesome description of Jim's fate and torment her beyond bearing. 'In his pique he utters only monstrous lies. Come, let us give him a farewell tune.'

To drown Keyser's threats, he launched into a hearty but off-key rendition of 'Spanish Ladies', and the others all joined in. Dorian's voice was as magnificent as ever and Mansur had inherited his ringing tenor. Yasmini's soprano lisped sweetly. Sarah leaned against Tom's reassuring bulk and sang with him.

'Farewell and adieu to you, fair Spanish ladies,
Farewell and adieu to you,' ladies of Spain
For we've received orders to sail for old England,
But we hope in a short time to see you again . . .

Then let every man here toss off a full bumper,
Then let every man here toss off his full bowl,
For we will be jolly and drown melancholy,
With a health to each jovial and true-hearted soul . . .'

Yasmini laughed and clapped her hands. 'That's the first naughty song Dorry ever taught me. Do you remember when first I sang it to you, Tom?'

'My oath on it, I will never forget it.' Tom chuckled as he steered for the *Maid of York*. ''Twas the day you brought Dorrie back to me after I had lost him for all those years.'

As Tom clambered aboard the *Maid of York* he gave orders to his captain: 'Captain Kumrah, in God's name, get this last load on board as quick as you like.' He went back to the rail and looked down at Dorian, who was still in the lighter. He called to him, 'As soon as you're on board the *Gift of Allah* douse all lights and hoist anchor, we must be clear of the land before first light. I don't want Keyser and the Dutch lookouts in the castle to spy out in which direction we are headed. Let them guess whether it be east or west, or even south to the Pole.'

The last of the baggage to come on board from the lighter was Sarah's harpsichord. As it dangled over the side, Tom called to the men on the fall of the tackle, 'A guinea for the man who lets that damn thing drop down to Davy Jones.'

Sarah prodded him sharply in the ribs, and the crewmen paused and looked at each other. They were never sure what to make of Tom's sense of humour. Tom put his arm around Sarah and went on, 'Of course, once you have your guinea, out of deference to the feeling of my wife, I shall be obliged to throw you in after it.'

They laughed uncertainly and swung the harpsichord on board. Tom strode back to the side. 'Be away with you then, brother,' he called to Dorian.

The crew of the lighter shoved off and Dorian hailed back, 'If we become separated in the dark, then the rendezvous will be off Cape Hangklip, as always?'

'As always, Dorry.'

The two ships sailed within minutes of each other, and for the first hour they were able to keep station. Then the wind increased to near gale force and the last sliver of moon went behind the clouds. In the darkness they lost contact with each other.

When dawn broke the *Maid* found herself alone, with the south-easter howling through her rigging. The land was a blue smear, low on the northern horizon, almost obscured by the breaking waves and the swirling sea fret.

'Fat chance that the Dutch will make us out in this weather,' Tom shouted at Kumrah, as the tails of his tarpaulin coat flapped around his legs, and the ship heeled over to the push of the storm. 'Make this your offing, and come about for Cape Hangklip.'

Close-hauled against the storm they raised the Cape the next morning, and found the *Gift* there before them, beating back and forth on the rendezvous. Once more in convoy they set out eastwards to round Cape Agulhas, the southernmost tip of Africa. The wind held steadily out of the east. They spent many weary days tacking back and forth, steering clear of the treacherous shoals that guarded Agulhas and clawing their way into their eastings. At last they were able to double the Cape and turn northwards along that rugged and inhospitable coast.

Three weeks after leaving High Weald they finally passed through the heads of grey rock that guarded the great Lagoon of the Elephants. They dropped anchor in the blessedly calm waters, clear as good Hollands gin and teaming with shoals of fish.

'This is where my grandfather Frankie Courtney fought his last battle with the Dutch. Here, they made him prisoner and took him down to Good Hope to perish on the gallows,' he told Sarah. 'My sacred oath, they were tough old devils those ancestors of mine,' he said with pride.

Sarah smiled at him. 'Are you suggesting that you are a milktoast and a caitiff when compared with them?' Then she shaded her eyes and peered up at the hillside that rose above the lagoon. 'Is that your famous post stone?'

Half-way up the hill a prominent lump of grey stone the size of a hayrick had been painted with a large, lop-sided letter P in scarlet paint, so that it was visible to any ship anchored in the lagoon.

'Oh, take me ashore immediately. I feel certain that there is a letter from Jim awaiting us.'

Tom was certain that her hopes were doomed to disappointment, but they rowed to the beach in the longboat. Sarah was first over the side with the water reaching to her thighs and soaking her skirts. Tom had difficulty keeping up with her as she lifted the sodden cloth to her knees and scrambled up the hillside. 'Look!' she cried. 'Someone has placed a cairn of stones on the summit. That surely is a sign that a letter is waiting for us.'

A hollow space had been burrowed out beneath the post stone, and the entrance to it was blocked with smaller ones. She pulled these apart and beyond them she found a bulky parcel. It was stitched up in a wrapper of heavy tarpaulin and sealed with tar.

'I knew it! Oh, yes, I knew it,' Sarah sang, as she dragged the parcel from its hiding-place. But when she read the inscription on it her face fell. Without another word she handed the packet to Tom and started back down the hill.

Tom read the inscription. It was in an ill-formed hand, misspelled and crude: 'Hail, you tru and worfy sole who doth this missif find. Tak it with you to London Town and gif it over to Nicolas Whatt Esquire at 51 Wacker Street close by the East Hindia Dok. He shall gif you a giny for it. Opun not this paket! Fayle me nefer! If you do so, then I do rot your balls and dam your eyes! May your mannikin never rise, you God forsaken boger!' The message was signed, 'Cpt Noah Calder abord the Brig *Larkspur* out bound for Bombay, 21 May in the yer of ow Lord Jassus 1731.'

'Words well chosen, and sentiments sweetly expressed.' Tom smiled as he replaced the packet in the recess and covered it with the stones. 'I am not headed for old London Town, so I will not risk the dire consequences of failure. It must wait for a bolder soul heading in the right direction.'

He went down the hill, and half-way to the beach he found Sarah sitting forlornly upon a rock. She turned away as he sat down beside her, and tried to stifle her sobs. He took her face between his big hands and turned it towards him. 'No, no, my love. You must not take on so. Our Jim is safe.'

'Oh, Tom, I was so sure it was his letter to us, and not that of some oaf of a sailor.'

'It was most unlikely that he would come here. Surely he will be heading further north. I do believe he had set upon Nativity. We shall find him there, and little Louisa with him. Mark my words. Nothing can befall our Jim. He is a Courtney, ten feet tall and made from billets of cast iron covered with elephant hide.'

She laughed through her tears. 'Tom, you silly man, you should be upon the stage.'

'Even Master Garrick could not afford my fee.' He laughed with her. 'Come along now, my own sweet girl. There is no profit in pining, and there is work to do if we purpose to sleep ashore this night.'

They went back down to the beach, and found that Dorian and his party from the *Gift* had already come ashore. Mansur was unloading the water casks into the longboat. He would refill them from the sweet-water stream that flowed into the top end of the lagoon. Dorian and his men were building shelters on the edge of the forest, weaving frameworks of saplings. They were thatching these with new reeds, fresh cut from the edge of the water. The smell of sweet sap perfumed the air.

After the trying weeks at sea in rough weather the women needed comfortable quarters on dry land in which to recuperate. It was over a year since the brothers had visited the lagoon on their last trading expedition along the coast. The huts they had built then they had burned to the ground when they sailed, for by now they would have been infested by scorpions, hornets and other unpleasant flying insects and crawling creatures.

There was a brief alarum when they heard a succession of musket shots banging out from the top end of the lagoon, but Dorian reassured them quickly: 'I told Mansur to bring us in fresh meat. He must have found game.'

When Mansur returned with the refilled water casks, he brought with him the carcass of a half-grown buffalo. Despite its tender age the beast was the size of an ox, enough to feed them all for weeks once it was salted and smoked. Then the other longboat returned from the edge of the channel where Tom had sent five of the crew to catch fish. The bins amidship were filled with sparkling silver mounds, still quivering and twitching.

Sarah and Yasmini set to work at once with their servants to prepare a suitable feast to celebrate their arrival. They ate under the stars, with sparks from the campfire rising into the dark sky in a torrent. After they had eaten their fill, Tom sent for Batula and Kumrah. They came ashore from the anchored ships and took their places, sitting cross-legged on their prayer mats in the circle around the fire.

'I ask your forgiveness for any disrespect,' Tom greeted the two captains. 'We should have heard the news you bring sooner than this. However, with the need to sail from Good Hope with such despatch, and the gale that assailed us since then, there has been no opportunity.'

'It is as you say, *effendi*,' Batula, the senior captain, replied. 'We are your men and there was never any disrespect.'

The servants brought coffee from the fire in brass kettles, and Dorian and the Arabs lit their hookahs. The water in the bowls bubbled with each breath of the perfumed Turkish tobacco smoke they drew.

First they discussed the trade and the goods that the captains had gathered during their last voyage along this coast. As Arabs they were able to travel where no Christian ship was allowed to pass. They had even sailed on past the Horn of Hormuz into the Red Sea as far as holy Medina, the luminous city of the Prophet.

On their return journey they had parted company, Kumrah in the *Maid* turning eastwards to call in at the ports of the empire of the Moguls, there to deal with the diamond merchants from the Kollur mines, and to buy bales of silken rugs from the souks of Bombay and Delhi. Meanwhile, Batula sailed along the Coromandel coast and loaded his ship with tea and spices. The two ships met again in the harbour of Trincomalee in Ceylon. There, they took on board cloves, saffron, coffee beans and choice packets of blue star sapphires. Then, in company, they had returned to Good Hope, to the anchorage off the beach of High Weald.

Batula was able to recite from memory the quantities of each commodity they had purchased, the prices they had paid, and the state of the various markets they had visited.

Tom and Dorian questioned them carefully and exhaustively, while Mansur wrote everything in the CBTC journal. This information was vital to their prosperity: any change in the state and condition of the markets and the supply of goods could spell great profit or, perhaps, even greater disaster to their enterprise.

'The largest profits still lie in the commerce of slaves,' Kumrah summed up delicately, and neither captain could meet Tom's eye as he said it. They knew his views on their trade, which he called 'an abomination in the face of God and man'.

Predictably Tom rounded on Kumrah. 'The only piece of human flesh I will ever sell is your hairy buttocks to the first man who will pay the five rupees I ask for them.'

'Effendi!' cried Kumrah, his expression a Thespian masterpiece: an unlikely mixture of contrition and pained sensibility. 'I would rather shave off my beard and feast on pig flesh than buy a single human soul from the slave block.'

Tom was about to remind him that slaving had been his chief enterprise before he entered the service of the Courtney brothers, when Dorian, playing the peace-maker, intervened smoothly: 'I hunger for news of my old home. Tell me what you have learned of Omani and Muscat, of Lamu and Zanzibar.'

'We knew that you would ask us this, so we have saved this news for the last. Those lands have been overtaken by momentous events, al-Salil.' They turned to Dorian eagerly, grateful to him for having diverted Tom's wrath.

'Good captains, tell us all you have learned,' Yasmini demanded. Until now she had sat behind her husband and held her peace as a dutiful Muslim wife should. Now, however, she could restrain herself no longer, for they were speaking of her homeland and her family. Although she and Dorian had fled the Zanzibar coast almost twenty years ago, her thoughts often returned there and her heart hankered for the lost years of her childhood.

It was true indeed that not all of her memories were happy ones. There had been times of loneliness in the isolation of the women's zenana, although she had been born a princess, daughter of Sultan Abd Muhammad al-Malik, the Caliph of Muscat. Her father had possessed more than fifty wives. He showed interest only in his sons, and could never bother himself to keep track of his daughters. She knew that he was barely aware of her existence, and could not remember any word he had spoken to her, or even a touch of his hand or a kindly glance. In all truth, she had laid eyes on him only on state occasions or when he visited his women in the zenana. Then it had been only at a distance, and she had trembled and covered her face in terror of his magnificence and his godlike presence. Even so she mourned and fasted the full forty days and nights stipulated by the Prophet when news of his death reached her in the African wilderness whence she had fled with Dorian.

Her mother had died in Yasmini's infancy, and she could not remember a single detail about her. As she grew older she learned that she had inherited from her the startling streak of silver hair that divided her own thick midnight black tresses. Yasmini had spent all her childhood in the zenana on Lamu island. The only maternal love she had known was given to her unstintingly by Tahi, the old slave woman who had nursed her and Dorian.

In the beginning Dorian, the adopted son of her own father, was with her in the zenana. This was before he reached his puberty and underwent the ordeal of the circumcision knife. As her adopted elder brother, he protected her, often with his fists and feet from the malice of her blood brothers. Her particular tormentor was Zayn al-Din. When Dorian defended her, he had made a mortal enemy of him; the rancour would persist througout their lives. To this day Yasmini remembered that dire confrontation between the two boys in every detail.

Dorian and Zayn had been only a few months short of puberty, and their departure from the zenana and entry into manhood and military service was looming large. That day Yasmini was playing alone on the terrace of the old saint's tomb, at the end of the zenana gardens. This was one of her secret places where she could escape from the bullying of their peers, and find solace in daydreams and childish games of fantasy. With Yasmini was her pet vervet monkey, Jinni. Zayn al-Din and Abubaker, both her half-brothers, had discovered her there.

Plump, sly and vicious, Zayn was bravest when he had one of his toadies with him. He wrested the little monkey from Yasmini and threw him into the open rainwater cistern. Though Yasmini screamed at the top of her lungs and jumped on his back, pummelling his head and trying to scratch lumps out of his skin, he ignored her and began systematically to drown Jinni, ducking the monkey's head each time he surfaced.

Summoned by Yasmini's screams Dorian came racing up the staircase from the garden. He took in the scene at a glance, then launched himself at the two bigger boys. Before his capture by the Arabs, his brother Tom had coached Dorian in the art of boxing, but Zayn and Abubaker had never before come into contact with bunched, flying fists. Abubaker fled from this terrible attack, but Zayn's nose burst in a spray of scarlet at the first punch, while the second sent him somersaulting down the steep staircase. When he struck the bottom, one of the bones in his right foot snapped. The bone set ill, and he would limp for the rest of his life.

In the years after he had left behind his childhood and the zenana, Dorian had become a prince in his own right and a famous warrior. Yasmini, however, was forced to remain behind, at the mercy of Kush, the head eunuch. Even after all these years, his monstrous cruelty lived vividly in her memory. Yasmini grew to lovely womanhood while Dorian fought his adopted father's enemies in the Arabian deserts far to the north. Covered in glory he had returned at last to Lamu, but he had almost forgotten his adopted sister and childhood sweetheart. Then Tahi, his ancient slave nurse, had come to him in the palace and reminded him that Yasmini was still languishing in the zenana.

With Tahi as a go-between they had arranged a dangerous tryst. When they became lovers they were committing a double sin from the consequences of which not even Dorian's exalted position could protect them. They were adopted brother and sister and, in the eyes of God, the Caliph and the council of mullahs, their union was both fornication and incest.

Kush had discovered their secret, and planned a punishment for Yasmini so unspeakably cruel that she still shuddered when she thought about it, but Dorian had intervened to save her. He killed Kush and buried him in the grave the eunuch had dug for Yasmini. Then Dorian disguised her as a boy and smuggled her out of the harem. Together they escaped from Lamu.

Many years later, after his father Abd Muhammad al-Malik had died of poisoning, Zayn – still limping from the injury Dorian had inflicted – ascended the Elephant Throne of Oman. One of his first acts as caliph was to send Abubaker to find and capture Dorian and Yasmini. When Abubaker caught up with the lovers there had been a terrible battle in which Dorian had killed him. Yasmini and Dorian had escaped once again from Zayn's vengeance and been reunited with Tom. However, Zayn al-Din sat on the mighty Elephant Throne to this day, and was still Caliph of Oman. They knew they were never entirely safe from his hatred.

Now, sitting by the campfire on this wild and savage shore, she reached out to touch Dorian. It was almost as though he had read her thoughts, for he took her hand and held it firmly. She felt strength and courage flowing from him into her like the balmy influence of the *kusi*, the trade wind of the Indian Ocean.

'Recount!' Dorian ordered his captains. 'Tell me these momentous tidings you bring from Muscat. Did you hear aught of the Caliph, Zayn al-Din?'

'Our tidings are all of Zayn al-Din. As Allah bears witness, he is Caliph in Muscat no longer.'

'What is this you say?' Dorian started up. 'Is Zayn dead at last?'

'Nay, my Prince. A *shaitan* is hard to kill. Zayn al-Din lives on.'

'Where is he, then? We must know all of this affair.'

'Forgive me, *effendi*.' Batula made a gesture of deep respect, touching his lips and his heart. 'There is one in our present company who knows all this far better than I do. He comes from the bosom of Zayn al-Din, and was once one of his trusted ministers and confidants.'

'Then he is no friend of mine. His master has tried on many occasions to kill me and my wife. It was Zayn who drove us into exile. He is my mortal enemy, and he has sworn a blood feud against us.'

'All this I know well, lord,' Batula replied, 'for I have been with you since that happy day when the man who then was Caliph, your sainted adoptive father al-Malik, made me your lance-bearer. Do you forget that I was at your side when you captured Zayn al-Din at the battle of Muscat and you roped him behind your camel and dragged him as a traitor to face the wrath and justice of al-Malik?'

'That I will never forget, as I will not forget your loyalty and service to me over all these years.' Dorian's expression became sad. 'Pity it is that my father's wrath was so short-lived, and his justice too heavily tempered with mercy. For he pardoned Zayn al-Din and clasped him once again to his bosom.'

'By God's Holy Name!' Batula's anger matched that of his master. 'Your father died from that show of mercy. It was Zayn's effeminate hand that held the poisoned cup to his lips.'

'And Zayn's fat buttocks that sat on the Elephant Throne when my father was gone.' Dorian's handsome features were marred by an expression of ferocity. 'Now you ask me to accept into my camp the minion and minister of this monster?'

'Not so, Highness. I said that this man was once all those

383

things to Zayn al-Din. But no longer. Like all who know him well, he became sickened to the heart by the monstrous cruelty of Zayn al-Din. He watched while Zayn tore the sinews and the heart of the nation to shreds. He watched helplessly while Zayn fed his pet sharks with the flesh of good and noble men, until they were almost too bloated to swim. He tried to protest when Zayn sold his birthright to the Sublime Porte, to the Turkish tyrants in Constantinople. In the end he was one of the chief conspirators in the plot against Zayn that overturned his throne and drove him out through the gates of Muscat.'

'Zayn is overthrown?' Dorian stared at Batula in astonishment. 'He was Caliph for twenty years. I thought he would stay in power until he died of old age.'

'Some men of great evil possess not only the savagery of the wolf but also that beast's instincts of survival. This man, Kadem al-Jurf, will tell you the rest of the story if you will allow it.'

Dorian glanced at Tom, who had been following every word with intense interest. 'What do you think, brother?'

'Let us hear the man's story,' Tom said.

Kadem al-Jurf must have been awaiting their summons for he came within minutes from the crew's encampment at the edge of the forest. They all realized that they had seen him often during the stormy voyage up from Good Hope. Although they had not known his name, they had understood that he was Batula's newly hired writer and purser.

'Kadem al-Jurf?' Dorian greeted him. 'You are a guest in my camp. You are under my protection.'

'Your beneficence lights my life like the sunrise, Prince al-Salil ibn al-Malik.' Kadem prostrated himself before Dorian. 'May the peace of God and the love of his last true Prophet follow you all the days of your long and illustrious life.'

'It is many years since any man has called me by that title.' Dorian nodded, gratified. 'Rise up, Kadem, and take a place in our council.' Kadem sat beside Batula, his sponsor. The servants brought him coffee in a silver cup and Batula passed him the ivory mouthpiece of his pipe. Both Dorian and Tom studied

384

the new man carefully while he enjoyed these expressions of hospitality and favour.

Kadem al-Jurf was young, no more than a few years older than Mansur. He had a noble face. His features reminded Dorian of his own adoptive father. Of course, it was not impossible that he was a royal bastard. The Caliph had been a man indeed, and prolific with his seed. He had ploughed and sowed wherever the ground pleased him.

Dorian smiled faintly, then put aside the thought, and once more regarded Kadem with his full attention. His skin was the colour of fine polished teak. His brow was deep and wide, his eyes clear, dark and penetrating. He returned Dorian's scrutiny calmly and, despite his protestations of loyalty and respect, Dorian thought he recognized in his gaze the disconcerting gleam of the zealot. This is a man who lives by the Word of Allah alone, he thought. Here is one who places scant value in the law and opinions of men. He knew well how dangerous such men could be. While he composed his next question he looked at Kadem's hands. There were telltale calluses on his fingers and his right palm. He recognized these as the stigmata of the warrior, the gall of bowstring and sword hilt. He looked again at his shoulders and arms and saw the development of muscle and sinew that could only have been built up during long hours of practice with bow and blade. Dorian let none of these thoughts show in his own eyes as he asked gravely, 'You were in the service of Caliph Zayn al-Din?'

'Since childhood, Lord. I was an orphan and he took me under his protection.'

'You swore a blood oath of loyalty to him,' Dorian insisted. For the first time Kadem's steady gaze shifted slightly. He did not reply. 'Yet you have reneged on this oath,' Dorian persisted. 'Batula tells me you are no longer the Caliph's man. Is that true?'

'Your Highness, I swore that oath nearly twelve years ago, on the day of my circumcision. In those days I was a man in name only, but in reality I was a mere child and a stranger to the truth.'

'And now I can see that you have become a man.' Dorian went on appraising him. Kadem was supposedly a writer, a man of papers and ink, but he did not have that look. There was a latent fierceness about him, like a falcon at roost. Dorian was intrigued. He went on, 'But, Kadem al-Jurf, does this release you from a blood oath of fealty?'

'My lord, I believe that fealty is a dagger with two edges. He who accepts it has a responsibility towards he who offers it. If he neglects that duty and responsibility, then the debt is cancelled.'

'These are devious semantics, Kadem. I find them too convoluted to fathom. To me an oath is an oath.'

'My lord condemns me?' Kadem's voice was silky, but his eyes were cold as obsidian.

'Nay, Kadem al-Jurf. I leave judgement and condemnation to God.'

'*Bismallah!*' Kadem intoned, and Batula and Kumrah stirred.

'There is no God, but God,' said Batula.

'God's wisdom surpasses all understanding,' said Kumrah.

Kadem whispered, 'Yet I know that Zayn al-Din is your blood enemy. That is why I come to you, al-Salil.'

'Yes, Zayn is my adopted brother and my enemy. Many years ago he swore to kill me. Many times since then I have felt his baleful influence touch my life,' Dorian agreed.

'I have heard him relate to his courtiers how he owes his crippled foot to you,' Kadem went on.

'He owes me much else besides.' Dorian smiled. 'I had the great pleasure of placing a rope around his neck and dragging him before our father to face the Caliph's wrath.'

'Posterity and Zayn al-Din remember this deed of yours well.' Kadem nodded. 'This is part of the reason that we chose to come to you.'

'Before it was "I", but now it is "we"?'

'There are others who have repudiated their oaths of fealty to Zayn al-Din. We turn to you, for you are the last of the line of Abd Muhammad al-Malik.'

'How is that possible?' Dorian demanded, and suddenly he

was angry. 'My father had countless wives who bore him sons, and they in turn had sons and grandsons. My father's seed was fruitful.'

'Fruitful no longer. Zayn has harvested all his father's fruits. On the first day of Ramadan there was such a slaughter as to shame the Face of God and astound all Islam. Two hundred of your brothers and nephews were gathered up by Zayn al-Din's reapers. They died by poison, that coward's tool, and they died by steel and rope and water. Their blood soaked the desert sands and tinted the sea to rose. Every person who had a blood claim to the Elephant Throne in Muscat perished in that holy month. Murder was compounded ten thousand times by sacrilege.'

Dorian stared at him in horrified disbelief, and Yasmini choked back her sobs: her brothers and other kin must be among the dead. Dorian put aside his own shocked grief to comfort her. He stroked the silver blaze that shone like a diadem in her sable locks, and whispered softly to her before he turned back to Kadem. 'This is hard news and bitter,' he said. 'It takes great effort for the mind to encompass such evil.'

'My lord, neither were we able to treat with such monstrous evil. That is why we repudiated our vows and rose up against Zayn al-Din.'

'There has been a rising?' Although Batula had already warned him of this, Dorian wanted Kadem to confirm it: all this seemed too far beyond the frontiers of possibility.

'A battle raged within the walls of the city for many days. Zayn al Din and his adherents were driven into the keep of the fort. We believed that they would perish there but, alas, there was a secret tunnel under the walls that led down to the old harbour. Zayn escaped by this route, and his ships bore him away.'

'Whither did he flee?' Dorian demanded.

'He sailed back to his birthplace on Lamu island. With the help of the Portuguese and the collusion of the minions of the English East India Company at Zanzibar, he has seized the great fort and all the Omani settlements and possessions along the Fever Coast. Under the threat of the English guns his forces in those possessions have remained loyal to him, and have resisted our efforts to cast down the tyrant.'

'In God's name, you and your junta in Muscat must be preparing your fleet to exploit these successes and to attack Zayn in Zanzibar and Lamu, is that not so?' Dorian demanded.

'My lord prince, our ranks are riven by dissent. There is no successor of royal blood to head our junta. Thus we lack loyal support from the Omani nation. In particular the desert tribes are hesitating to declare against Zayn and join our standard.'

Dorian's expression became wooden and remote as he realized where Kadem's protestations were heading.

'Without a leader our cause grows weaker and more divided each day, while each day Zayn regains his stature and strength. He commands the Zanzibar coast. We have learned that he has sent envoys to the Great Mogul, the Supreme Emperor in Delhi, and to the Sublime Porte in Constantinople. His old allies are rallying to support him. Soon all of Islam and Christendom will unite against us. Our victory will drain away into the sands, like the ebb of the spring tide.'

'What do you want from me, Kadem al-Jurf?' Dorian asked softly.

'We need a leader with a rightful claim to the Elephant Throne,' Kadem replied. 'We need a tried warrior who has commanded the desert tribes in battle: the Saar, the Dahm and the Karab, the Bait Kathir and the Awamir, but most of all the Harasis who hold within their sway the plains of Muscat. Without these there can be no ultimate victory.'

Dorian sat quietly but his heart had beaten faster as Kadem recited those illustrious names. In his mind's eye he saw again the battle array, the glint of steel in the dustclouds and the banners unfurled. He heard the war-cries of the riders, 'Allah Akbar! God is great!' and the roaring of the ranks of camels racing onwards across the sands of Oman.

Yasmini felt his arm tremble under her hand, and her heart quailed. I believed in my heart that the dark days were past for ever, she thought, that I might never again hear the beat of the war drums. I hoped that my husband would always stay beside me and never again ride away to war.

The company was silent, each of them thinking their own thoughts. Kadem was watching Dorian with that glittering, compulsive stare.

Dorian shook himself back to the present. 'Do you know these things are true?' he asked. 'Or are they merely the dreams born of desire?'

Kadem answered straight, without lowering his eyes: 'We have been in council with the desert sheikhs. They who are often divided all speak with a single voice. They say, "Let al-Salil take his place at the head of our armies, and we will follow wherever he leads."'

Dorian stood up abruptly and left the circle around the campfire. None of the others followed him, neither Tom nor Yasmini. He paced along the edge of the water, a romantic figure in his robes, tall and shining in the moonlight.

Tom and Sarah whispered together, but the others were silent.

'You must not let him go,' Sarah told Tom quietly, 'for Yasmini's sake and ours. You lost him once. You cannot let him go again.'

'And yet I cannot stop him. This is between Dorian and his God.'

Batula packed fresh tobacco in the bowl of the hookah, and it was almost consumed to ash before Dorian came back to the fire. He sat cross-legged with his elbows on his knees and his chin cupped in both hands, staring into the leaping flames.

'My lord,' Kadem whispered, 'give me your answer. With the trade winds standing fair, if you sail at once you can mount the Elephant Throne in Muscat at the beginning of the Feast of Lights. There can be no more propitious day than that to begin your reign as Caliph.'

Dorian was silent still, and Kadem went on – his tone was not wheedling, but strong and sure of his purpose: 'Your Highness, if you return to Muscat, the mullahs will declare *jihad*, a holy war, against the tyrant. God and all of Oman will be at your back. You cannot turn aside from your destiny.'

Dorian raised his head slowly. Yasmini drew a long slow breath and held it. Her nails sank into the hard muscles of his forearm.

'Kadem al-Jurf,' Dorian replied, 'this is a terrible decision. I cannot make it alone. I must pray for guidance.'

Kadem fell forward, prostrating himself on the sand before Dorian. His arms and legs were spread wide. 'God is great!' he said. 'There can be no victory without His benevolence. I shall wait for your answer.'

'I will give it to you tomorrow night at this same time and place.'

Yasmini let out her breath slowly. She knew that this was only a reprieve, and not a pardon.

Early the next day Tom and Sarah climbed to the top of the grey rocks that guarded the entrance to the lagoon, and found a sheltered nook out of the wind but full in the sun.

The Ocean of the Indies was spread beneath them, raked with creamy furrows. A sea bird used the wind to hang like a kite above the green waters. Suddenly it folded its wings and plunged from on high, hitting the surface with a tiny splash, rising again almost immediately with a silver fish wriggling in its beak. On the rocks above where they lay, the hyrax sat in the sun, rabbity brown balls of fluff watching them with huge, curious eyes.

'I want to have serious speech with you,' Sarah said.

Tom rolled on to his back and locked his fingers behind his head, grinning at her. 'Fool that I am, I thought you had brought me here to have your wicked way with me, to ravish my tender flesh.'

'Tom Courtney, will you never be serious?'

'Aye, lass, that I will, and I thank you for the invitation.' He reached for her, but she struck away his hand.

'I warn you, I shall scream.'

'I will cease and desist, for the moment at least. What is it that you wanted to discuss with me?'

''Tis Dorry and Yassie.'

'Why does this not come as any great surprise to me?'

'Yassie is sure that he will sail to Muscat to take up the offer of the throne.'

'I am sure she would not hate the thought of becoming a queen. What woman would?'

'It will destroy her life. She explained it all to me. You can have no conception of the intrigues and conspiracies that surround an Oriental court.'

'Can I not?' He raised an eyebrow. 'I have lived twenty years with you, my heart, which has given me good training.'

She went on as though he had not spoken: 'You are the elder brother. You must forbid him to leave. This offer of the Elephant Throne is a poisoned gift, which will destroy them and us also.'

'Sarah Courtney, you do not truly believe that I would forbid Dorian anything? It is a decision that only he can make.'

'You will lose him again, Tom. Do you not remember how it was when he was sold into slavery? How you thought he was dead, and part of you died with him?'

'I remember it well. But this is not slavery and death. It's a crown and power unbounded.'

'I think you begin to relish the thought of him going,' she accused him.

Tom sat up quickly. 'No, woman! He is blood of my blood. I want only what is best for him.'

'You think this may be best?'

'It was the life and the destiny for which he was trained. He has become a trader with me, but I have known all along that his heart is not truly in our enterprise. For me it is meat and wine, but Dorry hankers after more than we have here. Have you not heard him speak of his adoptive father and the days when he commanded the army of Oman? Do you not sometimes see the regret and longing in his eyes?'

'Tom, you look for signs that are not there,' Sarah protested.

'You know me well, my love.' He paused, then went on, 'It is my nature to dominate those around me. Even you.'

She laughed, a gay pretty sound. 'You do try, I grant you that.'

'I try with Dorry too, and with him I succeed better than I do with you. He is my dutiful younger brother, and over all these years I have treated him like that. Perhaps this summons to Muscat is what he has been waiting for.'

'You will lose him again,' she repeated.

'No, there will be only a little water between us, and I have a fast ship.' He lay back in the grass and pulled his hat down over his eyes to shield them from the sun. 'Besides, it will not be bad for business to have a brother able to issue licences for my ships to trade in all the forbidden ports of the Orient.'

'Tom Courtney, you mercenary monster. I do truly hate you.' She leaped on him and pummelled his chest with clenched fists. He rolled her easily on to her back in the grass and lifted her skirts away from her legs. They were still strong and shapely as those of a girl. She crossed them firmly.

'Sarah Courtney, show me how much you really hate me.' He held her down with one hand while he unbuckled his belt.

'Stop this at once, you lecherous knave. They're watching us.' She struggled but not too hard.

'Who?' he asked.

'Them!' She pointed at the ring of staring rock rabbits.

'Boo!' Tom shouted at them, and they shot down the entrances to their burrows. 'They aren't watching now!' said he.

Sarah uncrossed her legs.

The gathering at the campfire that night was solemn and fraught with uncertainty and anxiety. No one in the family knew what Dorian had decided. Yasmini, sitting beside

392

her husband, answered the silent question that Sarah flashed to her across the firelit circle with a resigned lift of her shoulders.

Tom alone was determinedly cheerful. While they ate grilled fish with chunks of new baked bread, he retold the story of their grandfather Francis Courtney, and the capture of the Dutch East India galleon off Cape Agulhas nearly sixty years before. He explained to them where Francis had hidden his booty, in a cave up at the head waters of the stream that ran into the lagoon, near where Mansur had shot the buffalo the previous day. Then he laughed as he pointed out the trenches and overgrown excavations all around their encampment that the Dutch had dug in their efforts to find and retrieve the plundered treasure. 'While they sweated and swore, our own father, Hal Courtney, had spirited away the booty long before,' he told them, but they had heard the story often enough not to be amazed by it. In the end even Tom was defeated by the silence, and instead of regaling them further he addressed himself to the bowl of spiced buffalo stew that the women had served after the fish.

Dorian ate little. Before the silver coffee-pot was brought from its cradle over the coals he told Tom, 'If you agree, brother, I will speak to Kadem now and give him my decision.'

'Aye, Dorry,' Tom agreed. ''Twould be best to have done with the whole business. The ladies have been sitting on a nest of ants since yesterday.' He shouted for Batula. 'Tell Kadem he might join our council, if he has a mind.'

Kadem came striding down the beach. He walked like a desert warrior, lithe and long-limbed, and prostrated himself before Dorian.

Mansur leaned forward eagerly. He and Dorian had left the camp earlier that day and passed many hours alone together in the forest. Only they knew what they had discussed. Yasmini looked at her son's shining face and her heart sank. He is so young and beautiful, she thought, so bright and strong. Of course he pines for such an adventure as he sees here. He knows only the ballad singers' romantic vision of battle. He dreams of glory, power and a throne. For, depending on the choice Dorian makes this evening, the Elephant Throne of Oman might one day be his.

She drew the veil over her face to hide her fears. My son does not understand what pain and suffering the crown will bring him all the days of his life. He knows nothing of the poison cup and the assassin's blade. He does not understand that the caliphate is a slavery more oppressive than the chains of the galley slave or those of the worker in the copper mines of Monomatapa.

Her thoughts were interrupted when Kadem greeted Dorian. 'The Prophet's blessing upon you, Majesty, and the peace of God. May he bless our undertakings.'

'It is early to speak of Majesty, Kadem al-Jurf,' Dorian cautioned him. 'Wait rather until you have heard my decision.'

'Your decision has already been made for you by the prophet and saint Mullah al-Allama. He died in his ninety-ninth year, in the mosque on Lamu island, praising God with his last breath.'

'I did not know he was dead,' Dorian said sadly, 'though, in all truth, at that venerable age it could not have been otherwise. He was a holy man indeed. I knew him well. It was his hand that circumcized me. He was my wise councillor, and a second father to me.'

'In his last days he thought of you, and made a prophecy.'

Dorian inclined his head. 'You may recite the words of the holy mullah.'

Kadem had the gift of rhetoric, and his voice was strong but pleasing. 'The orphan from the sea, he who won the Elephant for his father, shall sit upon its back when the father has passed, and he shall wear a crown of red gold.' Kadem spread his arms. 'Majesty, the orphan of the prophecy can mean no other than you. For you are crowned now in red gold, and you were the victor of the battle that gave the Elephant Throne to your adoptive father, Caliph Abd Muhammad al-Malik.'

A long silence followed his ringing speech, and Kadem stood with arms outspread like the Prophet himself.

Dorian broke the silence at last. 'I have heard your pleas, and I will give you my decision that you must take back to the sheikhs of Oman. But first I must tell you how I have reached it.'

Dorian placed his hand upon Mansur's shoulder. 'This is my son, my only son. My decision touches him deeply. He and I have discussed it in every detail. His fierce young heart is hot for the enterprise, just as mine was at the same age. He has urged me to accept the invitation of the sheikhs.'

'Your son is wise far beyond his years,' said Kadem. 'If it please Allah, he shall rule in Muscat after you.'

'*Bismallah!*' cried Batula and Kumrah together.

'If God pleases!' cried Mansur in Arabic, his expression rapt with joy.

Dorian held up his right hand, and they fell silent again. 'There is another who is touched deeply by my decision.' He took Yasmini's hand. 'The Princess Yasmini has been my companion and my wife all these years, from childhood to this day. I swore an oath to her long ago, a blood oath.' He turned to her. 'Do you remember my marriage vows to you?'

'I remember, my lord husband,' she said softly, 'but I thought you might have forgotten.'

'I swore two vows to you. The first was that, even though the law and the prophets allow it, I would take no other wife than you. I have kept that vow.'

Yasmini was not able to speak, but she nodded. At the movement a tear that trembled on her long eyelashes detached itself and splashed upon the silk that covered her bosom, leaving a wet stain.

'The second oath I swore that day was that I would not cause you pain if it was in my power to prevent it.' Yasmini nodded again.

'Let all of you here present know that if I were to take up the invitation of the sheikhs to the Elephant Throne, it would cause the Princess Yasmini pain more poignant than the pain of death itself.'

The silence drew out, tingling, in the night, like the threat of summer thunder. Dorian stood up and spread his arms. 'This is my reply. May God hear my words. May the holy prophets of Islam bear witness to my oath.'

Tom was amazed by the transformation that had overtaken his younger brother. Now he looked like a king indeed. But Dorian's next words shattered that illusion. 'Tell them that my love and admiration is with them still, as it was at the battle of Muscat and every day since then. Despite this, the burden they would place upon me is too heavy for my heart and my shoulders. They must find another for the Elephant Throne. I cannot take up the caliphate and keep true to my oath to the Princess Yasmini.'

Mansur gave a small involuntary cry of distress. He leaped to his feet and ran into the night. Tom jumped up and might have chased after him had not Dorian shaken his head. 'Let him go, brother. His disappointment is sharp, but it will pass.' He sat down again and turned to smile at Yasmini. An expression of adoration shone upon her lovely face. 'I have kept both my oaths to you,' Dorian said.

'My lord!' she whispered. 'My own heart.'

Kadem stood up again, his face expressionless. He bowed deeply to Dorian. 'As my prince commands,' he agreed softly. 'Would that I could call you "Majesty". It saddens me, but that is not to be. God's will be done.' He turned and strode away into the darkness, heading in the opposite direction to that taken by Mansur.

It was the time of the evening prayers and the man who called himself Kadem al-Jurf performed his ritual ablutions in the salt waters of the lagoon. Once he was cleansed, he climbed to a high place on the rocks above the ocean. He spread his prayer mat, recited the first prayer and made the first prostration.

For once neither the act of worship nor submission to the will of God could calm the anger that seethed within him. It required all his self-discipline and dedication to complete the prayers without letting his unruly emotions mar them. When he had finished, he built a small fire from the faggot of wood he had gathered on the way up the hill. When it was burning brightly Kadem sat cross-legged on the mat in front of it and gazed through the curtain of shimmering heat at the glowing wood.

Rocking slightly, as though he were riding a racing camel across the desert, he recited the twelve mystical *sura* of the Qur'an, and waited for the voices. They had been with him since childhood, since the day of his circumcision. Always they came to him clearly after praying or fasting. He knew they were the voices of God's angels and of his prophets. The first to speak was the one he dreaded most.

'You have failed in your task.' He recognized the voice of Gabriel, the avenging archangel, and quailed before the accusation.

'Highest of the high, it was not possible that al-Salil could spurn the bait that was so carefully prepared for him,' he murmured.

'Hear me, Kadem ibn Abubaker,' said the angel. 'It was your overweening pride that led you into failure. You were too certain of your own powers.'

The angel used his true name, for Kadem was the son of Pasha Abubaker, the general Dorian had slain in the battle on the banks of the river Lunga twenty years before.

Pasha Abubaker had been the half-brother and boon companion of Zayn al-Din, the Caliph of Oman. They had grown up together in the zenana on Lamu island, and it was there that their destinies had first become entangled with those of Dorian and Yasmini.

Much later, in the palace at Muscat, when their royal father was dead and Zayn al-Din was caliph, he had appointed Abubaker supreme military commander and a Pasha in the service of the caliphate. Then he had sent Abubaker with his army to Africa to hunt down and capture Dorian and Yasmini, the incestuous runaway couple.

At the head of his cavalry squadrons Abubaker had caught up with them as they were trying to escape down the river Lunga and reach the open sea in Tom's tiny ship, the *Swallow*.

Abubaker had attacked them while they were stranded on the sandbar at the mouth of the river. The battle was fierce and bloody, with Abubaker's cavalry squadrons charging through the shallows. But the ship had been armed with cannon and Dorian had touched off the blast of grape-shot that blew off Pasha Abubaker's head and drove off his troops in disarray.

Although Kadem had been an infant at the time of his father's death, Zayn al-Din had taken him under his protection and shown him the favour and preference he offered his own sons rather than treating him as a nephew. In doing so he made Kadem his liege man, his blood bondsman. He fettered him with chains of steel that could never be broken. Despite what Kadem had told Dorian at the campfire, the strength of his oath to Zayn al-Din was matched only by his awareness of his duty to take vengeance on the man who had slain his father. This was a holy duty, a blood feud imposed on him by God and his own conscience.

Zayn al-Din, who loved few men, loved Kadem, his nephew. He kept him close, and when he became a true warrior he made him the commander of the royal bodyguard. Only Kadem, of the possible heirs to the caliphate, was spared from the Ramadan massacre. During the uprising that followed, Kadem had fought like a lion to protect his caliph, and in the end it was Kadem who had led Zayn al-Din through the maze of underground passages, under the palace walls to the ship waiting in the harbour of Muscat. He had carried his master safely to the palace on Lamu island off the Fever Coast.

Kadem was the general who had overwhelmed the forts along the coast that attempted to rise in support of the revolutionary junta in Muscat. Kadem had negotiated the alliance with the English consul in Zanzibar, and Kadem had urged his master to send envoys to Constantinople and Delhi to garner support. During these campaigns along the Fever Coast, Kadem had captured most of the leaders of the factions who opposed Zayn. As a matter of course, the prisoners were handed over to his inquisitors so that they could extract from them all the information and intelligence they could.

In this way, by the intelligent and judicious application of the bastinado, the screw and the garotte, the inquisitors dredged up a precious gem: the whereabouts of al-Salil, the murderer of Pasha Abubaker and the sworn blood enemy of the Caliph.

Armed with this knowledge, Kadem pleaded with Zayn al-Din to allow him to be the instrument of retribution. Zayn consented, and Kadem would entrust his sacred duty to none of his underlings. He alone devised the stratagem of luring al-Salil into the Caliph's realm and power by impersonating an envoy of the rebel junta who still held the capital city of Muscat.

When Kadem revealed his plan to Zayn al-Din, the Caliph was delighted and gave the enterprise his blessing. He promised Kadem the title of pasha, like his father before him, and any other reward Kadem could ask for, if he succeeded in bringing al-Salil and his incestuous wife Yasmini back to Lamu island to face his wrath and retribution. Kadem asked only one reward; that when the time came for al-Salil to die, Kadem should be given the honour of strangling him with his own hands. He promised Zayn that the garotting would be slow and agonizing. Zayn smiled and granted this boon also.

Kadem had learned from the inquisitors that the trading ship, *Gift of Allah*, which called often at the ports of the Fever Coast, belonged to al-Salil. When next it arrived in the port of Zanzibar Kadem inveigled himself into the confidences of Batula, al-Salil's old lance-bearer. Kadem's plot had unfurled smoothly, until now, with the prize almost within his grasp, when he had been thwarted by al-Salil's unfathomable refusal to accept the lure. Now Kadem had to answer the accusation of God's angel.

'Highest of the high, I have indeed committed the sin of pride.' Kadem made the sign of penitence by wiping his face with open hands, as though washing away the sin.

'You believed that without divine intervention, you alone could bring the sinner to justice. This was vanity and foolishness.'

The accusations thundered in his head until it felt that his eardrums must burst. Kadem bore the pain stoically. 'Merciful one, it did not seem possible that any mortal man could spurn the offer of a throne.' Kadem prostrated himself before the fire and the angel. 'Tell me what I should do to make amends for my arrogance and stupidity. Command me, O highest of the high.'

There was no reply. The only sounds were the crashing of the high surf on the rocks below and the mewing of the gulls as they circled overhead.

'Speak to me, holy Gabriel,' Kadem pleaded. 'Do not desert me now, not after all these years when I have done as you commanded.' He drew the curved dagger from his belt. It was a magnificent weapon. The blade was of Damascus steel and the hilt was rhinoceros horn covered with pure gold filigree. Kadem pressed the point of the blade into the ball of his own thumb, and blood flowed out.

'Allah! Allah!' he cried. 'With this blood I entreat you, give me guidance.'

Only then, through his pain, the other voice spoke, not the thunder of Gabriel but calm and measured, melodious. Kadem knew that this was the very voice of the Prophet, terrible in its quiet simplicity. He trembled and listened.

'You are fortunate, Kadem ibn Abubaker,' said the Prophet, 'for I have listened to your confession and been moved by your cries. I will allow you one last chance of redemption.'

Kadem threw himself down on his face, not daring to answer that voice. It spoke again. 'Kadem ibn Abubaker! You must wash your hands in the heart blood of the murderer of your father, the traitor and heretic, the sinner who wallows in incest, al-Salil.'

Kadem beat his head against the earth, weeping for joy at the mercy the Prophet had shown him. Then he sat back on his heels and held up his hand with fingers and thumb spread. The blood still dribbled from the self-inflicted wound. 'God is great,' he whispered. 'Show me a mark of your favour, I beseech you.' He stretched out his hand and held it in the leaping flames, which engulfed it. 'Allah!' he chanted. 'The One! The Only!'

In the flames the flow of bright blood shrivelled and dried.

Then miraculously the wound closed like the tentacled mouth of a sea anemone. His flesh healed before his eyes.

He lifted his hand out of the flames, still chanting God's praises, and held it aloft. There was no mark where the wound had been. There was no redness or blistering from the flames. His skin was smooth and flawless. It was the sign he had asked for.

'God is great!' he exulted. 'There is no God but God, and Muhammad is his last true Prophet!'

After they had eaten the evening meal with the rest of the family, Dorian and Yasmini took their leave. Yasmini embraced Sarah first, then her own son, Mansur. She kissed his eyes and stroked his hair, which gleamed in the firelight like molten copper poured from the melting pot.

Tom hugged Dorian so hard that his ribs creaked. 'Damn my eyes, Dorian Courtney, I thought we had got rid of you at last, and could pack you off to Oman.'

Dorian hugged him back. 'Are you not the unlucky one? I will be here to plague you for a while yet.'

Though Mansur embraced his father briefly, he did not speak or look into his eyes, and the line of his lips was hard with bitter disappointment. Dorian shook his head sadly. He knew that Mansur had set his heart on glory, and his own father had snatched it from him. The pain was still too intense to be assuaged by words. Dorian would console him later.

Dorian and Yasmini left the campfire, and started down the beach together. As soon as they were out of the ruddy light of the flames Dorian placed his arm round her. They did not speak, for they had said it all. The physical contact expressed their love more than words ever could. At the turning of the sandbar, where the deeper channel ran close in to the beach, Dorian stripped off his robes and unwound his turban. He handed his clothing to Yasmini and waded naked into the water. The tide was flowing strongly between the rocky heads and the water was chilled with the memory of the open ocean.

Dorian dived into the deep channel and surfaced again, gasping and snorting with the cold.

Yasmini sat on the sandbar and watched him. She did not share his love of cold water. She held his clothes in a bundle, then almost stealthily buried her face in them. She inhaled the masculine odour of her husband and delighted in it. Even after all these years she had never tired of it. The smell of him made her feel safe and secure. Dorian always smiled when she picked up the discarded robe he had worn all day and donned it in preference to her nightdress.

'I would wear your skin if it were possible,' she replied seriously to his gentle teasing. 'This way I can be close to you, part of your raiment, part of your body.'

At last Dorian waded ashore. The phosphorescence of the tiny plankton in the lagoon sparkled upon his body, and Yasmini exclaimed with delight. 'Even nature decks you in diamonds. God loves you, al-Salil, but not as much as I do.'

He stooped over her, kissed her with salty lips, took his turban from her and used it to dry himself. Then he wound it round his waist as a loincloth, and let his long wet hair hang down his back.

'This night breeze will finish the job before we reach our hut,' he told her, and they walked back along the sand to the encampment. The sentry greeted them and called a blessing as they passed the watchfire. Their own hut was well separated from that of Tom and Sarah. Mansur preferred to sleep with the ship's officers and the men.

Dorian lit the lanterns, and Yasmini carried one when she went behind the screen at the far end of the room. She had furnished the hut with Persian carpets, silk draperies, silk mattresses and cushions filled with wild-goose down. Dorian heard the purl of water from the jug into the basin, and Yasmini hummed and sang softly as she washed. Dorian felt his loins stir: this was Yasmini's prelude to lovemaking. He threw his robe and damp turban aside and stretched out on the mattress. He watched her silhouette, thrown by the lamp-light on to the design of birds and flowers that decorated the

Chinese screen. She had placed the lamp artfully and knew he was watching her. When she stood in the basin and bent over to wash her intimate parts, she turned so that he could watch the shadow show, and see how she was sweetening and preparing the way for him.

When at last she came out from behind the screen she hung her head demurely, allowing her hair to hang forward over her face like a dark silver-shot curtain. She covered her pudenda with both hands, then tilted her head and peeped at him with one eye through the veil. It was huge and luminous with the light of passion.

'You succulent, salacious little houri,' he said, and stiffened into full arousal. She saw what she had done to him, and tinkled with laughter. She let her hands fall to her sides, and her own sex was meticulously plucked free of hair. It was a plump and naked cleft below the ivory smooth curve of her belly. Her breasts were small and pert, so her body seemed that of a young girl.

'Come to me!' he commanded, and she obeyed with joy.

Much later in the night Yasmini felt him stir beside her and came fully awake immediately. She was always sensitive to his moods or needs. 'Are you well?' she whispered. 'Is there anything you need?'

'Sleep on, little one,' he whispered back. ''Tis only your friend and fervent admirer who demands to be taken in hand.' He stood up from the mattress.

'Please convey to the friend my respectful salaams and my wifely duty,' she whispered. He chuckled sleepily and kissed her lightly before he rose from their mattress. Dorian would only use the chamber-pot in the gravest emergency. Squatting was the woman's way. He slipped out through the back door, to the pit latrine which stood fifty yards from their hut, screened by the trees of the forest verge. The sand was cool under his bare feet, the night air soft and perfumed by forest flowers and the fret off the ocean. When Dorian had relieved himself, he started back. But he stopped before he reached the rear door of the hut. The night was so beautiful and the blaze of the stars so dazzling that they mesmerized him. He stared up at them and, slowly, he found himself transported into a deep sense of peace.

Until this moment he had been storm-tossed by doubts. Had his decision to turn his back on the Elephant Throne been selfish, and unfair to Mansur? Had he failed in his duty to the peoples of Oman who were grinding under the cruel yoke of Zayn al-Din? He knew deep in his heart that Zayn had murdered their father. Did not the laws of man and God also place upon him the blood duty of retribution for the terrible crime of patricide?

All these doubts receded as he stood now under the stars. Even though the night was chilly and he was naked as a newborn, he was still warm from the arms of the only woman he had ever loved. He sighed with contentment. *Even if I have sinned, it was the sin of omission. My first duty is to the living, not the dead, and Yasmini needs me as much if not more than all the others.*

He started back towards the hut and at that moment he heard Yasmini scream. It was a shocking sound, terror and mortal agony blending.

As Dorian left the hut Yasmini sat up and shivered. The night had turned cold, much colder than it should have been. She wondered if it was a natural cold or the cold of evil. Perhaps some baleful spirit hovered over them. She believed implicitly in the other world, which overlapped their own so intimately, the realm in which the angels, the *djinni* and the *shaitans* existed. She shivered again, this time more in dread than with cold. She made the sign to avert the evil eye with thumb and forefinger. Then she stood up from the mattress and turned up the wick of the lantern, so that Dorian would have light when he returned. She went to where Dorian's robe hung over the screen and slipped it over her naked body. Sitting on the mattress, she wound his turban round her head.

It had dried but it still smelt of his hair. She lifted a fold of his robe to her nose, and smelt the odour of his sweat floating up from the cloth. She inhaled it with pleasure, and the comfort it imparted to her forced back the premonition of lurking evil. Just the faintest twinge of unease lingered.

'Where is Dorry?' she whispered. 'He should not take so long.' She was about to call out to him through the thatched wall when she heard a stealthy sound behind her. She turned and was confronted by a tall figure clad in black, a black headcloth swaddling its face. It seemed to be some evil manifestation, a *djinni* or a *shaitan*, rather than a human. It must have entered through the other door, and its ghastly influence seemed to fill the room with a choking, cloying emanation of pure evil. In its right hand a long curved blade glinted, reflecting the dim lantern light.

Yasmini screamed with all her strength and tried to rise, but the thing sprang towards her and she did not see the knife stroke for it was so swift as to cheat her eye. She felt the blade go in, so sharp that her tender flesh offered little resistance to its entry. There was only a stinging sensation deep in her bosom.

The assassin stood over her as she sagged down on legs that were suddenly without strength. He made no effort to pull out the long blade. Instead he cocked his wrist and held it rigid, so the blade was angled upwards. He allowed the razor edge to slice its own way out, enlarging the wound, cutting through muscle, vein and artery. When at last the blade came free, Yasmini fell back upon the mattress. The dark figure looked about, seeking the man who should have been present, but was not there. He had only realized that his victim was a woman when she screamed – but by then it was too late. He stooped and pulled the turban loose from Yasmini's face. He stared at her lovely features, now so pale and still in the lantern-light that they seemed carved from ivory.

'In God's Holy name, only half my work is done,' he whispered. 'I have killed the vixen but missed the fox.'

He whirled and ran for the door through which he had

entered the hut. At that moment Dorian burst naked into the room behind him. 'Guards!' Dorian shouted. 'Succour! On me! Here!'

Kadem ibn Abubaker recognized the voice and turned back on the instant. This was the victim he was seeking, this man and not his woman dressed in his robes. He leaped at Dorian who was slow to react, but threw up his right arm to deflect the blow. The blade raked him from shoulder to elbow. His blood sprang darkly in the lamplight and he yelled again, then dropped to his knees. His arms dangling at his sides, he looked up with a piteous expression at the man who was killing him.

Kadem knew that his victim was twice his age, and from his first reaction that the years had slowed him, that now he was helpless. This was his chance to end it swiftly and he sprang forward eagerly. But he should have been warned by the warlike reputation of al-Salil. As he stabbed down, going once more for the heart, two steely arms shot out, swiftly as striking adders. He found his knife arm trapped in a classic wrist block.

Dorian came to his feet, splattering blood from the long wound down his arm, and they whirled together. Kadem was intent on breaking the lock, so that he could stab again. Dorian was trying even more desperately to hold him, as he shouted for help. 'Tom!' he screamed. 'Tom! On me! On me!'

Kadem hooked his heel behind Dorian's foot and lunged against him to trip him and throw him over, but Dorian changed his weight smoothly to the other foot, and turned inside him, twisting the wrist of his knife hand back against the joint, straining the sinews and tendons. Kadem grunted with pain, and fell back a pace against the unbearable pressure. Dorian pressed forward. 'Tom!' he yelled. 'Tom, in God's Name.'

Kadem yielded to the pressure on his wrist. The release gave him just enough latitude to turn his hip into Dorian, and throw him across it. He broke Dorian's grip and sent him cartwheeling across the floor of the hut. Like a ferret on a rabbit, he went at him, and Dorian was only just able to catch his knife wrist again as he fell back. Once more they were chest to chest, but now Kadem was on top of him, and the difference in their ages and their state of martial fitness began to tell. Remorselessly Kadem forced the point of the curved blade down towards Dorian's chest. The assassin's face was still covered by the headcloth. Only his eyes glittered above the black folds, just inches from Dorian's.

'For my father's memory,' grated Kadem, his breath coming hard with the effort, 'I perform my duty.'

All Kadem's weight was behind his knife arm. Dorian could not hold it longer. His own arm buckled slowly. The knife point pricked the bare skin of his chest and slid on, deeper and still deeper, up to the hilt.

'Justice is mine!' Kadem cried in triumph.

Before the cry had died in Kadem's throat, Tom charged through the doorway behind him, furious and powerful as a black-maned lion. He took it all in at a glance, and swung the heavy pistol he carried in his right hand, not daring to fire it for fear of hitting his brother. The steel barrel crunched across the back of Kadem's skull. Without another sound he collapsed on top of Dorian.

As Tom stooped to drag the Arab off his brother's inert body, Mansur dashed into the hut. 'For the love of God, what's amiss?'

'This swine set upon Dorry.'

Mansur helped Tom to lift Dorian into a sitting position. 'Father, are you hurt?' Then they both saw the terrible knife wound in his bare chest. They stared at it in horror.

'Yassie!' Dorian wheezed. 'Look to her.'

Tom and Mansur turned towards the small figure curled on the mattress. Neither of them had noticed her until then.

'Yassie is all right, Dorry. She's sleeping,' Tom said.

'No, Tom, she is mortal hurt.' Dorian tried to shrug off their restraining hands. 'Help me. I must attend to her.'

'I will see to Mother.' Mansur jumped up and ran to the mattress. 'Mother!' he cried, and tried to lift her. Then he reeled back, staring at his hands, which were shining with Yasmini's blood.

Dorian crawled across the floor, dragged himself on to the

mattress and lifted Yasmini in his arms. Her head lolled lifelessly. 'Yassie, please don't leave me.' He wept tears of utter desolation. 'Don't go, my darling.'

His entreaties were in vain for Yasmini's elfin spirit was already well sped along the fatal way.

Sarah had been awakened by the uproar. She came swiftly to join Tom. A quick examination showed her that Yasmini's heartbeat had stilled, and she was past any help. She stifled her grief, and turned to Dorian for he was still alive, if only just.

At Tom's curt order, Batula and Kumrah dragged Kadem out of the hut. Using rawhide thongs, they tied his elbows and wrists behind his back. Then they pulled his ankles to his wrists and bound them together. His spine arched painfully as they riveted a steel slave collar round his neck and chained him to a tree in the centre of the encampment. As soon as the dreadful tidings of the assassination flashed through the camp, the women gathered around Kadem to curse and spit at him in anger and revulsion: they had all loved Yasmini.

'Keep him secure. Do not let them kill him, not yet, not until I order it,' Tom told Batula grimly. 'You sponsored this murderous swine. The duty is with you, on your own life.'

He went back into the hut to give what help he could. This was not much, for Sarah had taken charge. She was highly skilled in the medical arts. She had spent much of her life tending broken bodies and dying men. She only needed his strength to pull the compression bandages tightly enough to stem the bleeding. For the remainder of the time Tom hovered in the background, cursing his own stupidity for not anticipating the danger and taking precautions to forestall it.

'I am not an innocent child. I should have known.' His lamentations hampered rather than helped, and Sarah ordered him out of the hut.

When she had dressed Dorian's wound and he was lying more comfortably Sarah relented and allowed Tom to return.

She told him that although his brother was gravely injured, the blade had missed his heart – as far as she could divine. She thought it had pierced the left lung, for there was bloody froth on his lips.

'I have seen men less robust than Dorry recover from worse wounds. Now it is up to God and time.' That was the best reassurance she had for Tom. She gave Dorian a double spoonful of laudanum, and, once the drug had taken effect, left him with Tom and Mansur to tend him. Then she went to start the heartbreaking process of laying out Yasmini's body for burial.

The Malay servant girls, also Muslim, helped her. They carried Yasmini to Sarah's own hut at the far end of the encampment, laid her on the low table, and placed a screen round her. They took away the bloodied robe and burned it to ash on the watchfire. They closed the lids of those magnificent dark eyes, from which the luminosity had faded. They bathed Yasmini's childlike body and anointed her with perfumed oils. They bandaged the single dreadful wound that had stabbed through to her heart. They combed and brushed her hair, and the silver blaze shone as brightly as ever. They dressed her in a clean white robe and laid her on the funeral bier. She looked like a child asleep.

Mansur and Sarah, who after Dorian had loved her best, chose a burial site in the forest. With the crew of the *Gift*, Mansur stayed to help dig the grave, for the law of Islam decreed that Yasmini should be buried before sunset on the day of her death.

When they lifted Yasmini's bier and carried her from the hut, the lamentations of the women roused Dorian from the sleep of the poppy and he called weakly for Tom, who came at the run. 'You must bring Yassie to me,' Dorian whispered.

'No, brother, you must not move. Any movement could do you terrible ill.'

'If you will not bring her, then I will go to her.' Dorian tried to sit up, but Tom held him down gently, and shouted for Mansur to bring the funeral bier to Dorian's bedside.

At his insistence, Tom and Mansur supported Dorian so he

could kiss his wife's lips for the last time. Then Dorian worked free from his own finger the gold ring over which he had spoken his wedding vows. It came off with difficulty for he had never before removed it. Mansur guided his father's hand as he placed it on Yasmini's slim tapered finger. It was far too large for her, but Dorian folded her fingers around it so that it would not slip off.

'Go in peace, my love. And may Allah take you to His bosom.'

As Tom had warned, the effort and sorrow exhausted Dorian and he sank back on to the mattress. Bright new blood soaked into the bandages about his chest.

They carried Yassie out to the grave, and lowered her into it gently. Sarah placed a silk shawl over her face, and stood to one side. Tom and Mansur would let no one else undertake the harrowing task of covering her with earth. Sarah watched until they had finished. Then she took Tom's hand on one side and Mansur's on the other and led them back to the camp.

Tom and Mansur went directly to the tree where Kadem was chained. Tom was scowling darkly as he stood over the captive, arms akimbo. There was a large swelling on the back of Kadem's head from the blow with the pistol barrel. His scalp was split and the blood was already congealing into a black scab over the laceration. However, Kadem had recovered consciousness and he was once more alert. He stared up at Tom with a steely, fanatical gaze.

Batula came and prostrated himself before Tom. 'Lord Klebe, I deserve all your wrath. Your accusation is just. It was I who sponsored this creature and brought him into your camp.'

'Yes, Batula. The blame is indeed yours. It will take you the rest of your life to redeem yourself. In the end it may even cost you your own life.'

'As my lord says. I am ready to repay the debt I owe,' Batula said humbly. 'Shall I kill this eater of pig flesh now?'

'No, Batula. First he must tell us who he truly is and who was the master who sent him to carry out this vile deed. It may be difficult to make him tell us. I see by his eyes that this man lives not on an earthly plane, as other men.'

'He is ruled by demons,' Batula agreed.

'Make him speak, but make certain he does not die before he has done so,' Tom reiterated.

'As you say, lord.'

'Take him to some place where his cries will not affright the women.'

'I will go with Batula,' said Mansur.

'No, lad. It will be grisly work. You will not want to watch it.'

'The Princess Yasmini was my mother,' Mansur said. 'Not only will I watch but I shall delight in every scream he utters, and glory in every drop of his blood that flows.'

Tom stared at him in astonishment. This was not the winsome child he had known from birth. This was a hard man grown to full maturity in a single hour. 'Go with Batula and Kumrah then,' he agreed at last, 'and note well the replies of Kadem al-Jurf.'

They took Kadem in the longboat to the head-waters of the stream over a mile from the camp and found another tree to which to chain him. They tied a leather strap round his forehead, then back around the bole of the tree, twisting it tightly so that it cut into his flesh and he could not move his head. Mansur asked him his real name, and Kadem spat at him. Mansur looked at Batula and Kumrah.

'The work we must do now is just. In God's Name, let us begin,' said Mansur.

'*Bismallah!*' said Batula.

While Mansur guarded the prisoner, Batula and Kumrah went into the forest. They knew where to search, and within the hour they had found a nest of the fierce soldier ants. These insects were bright red in colour, and not much bigger than a rice grain. The glistening head was armed with a pair of poisonous pincers. Careful not to injure them and even more careful to avoid their stings, Batula picked the ants out of the nest with a pair of bamboo tweezers.

When they returned Kumrah cut a hollow reed from the stream verge, and carefully worked one end of the tube as far as it would go into the opening of Kadem's ear.

'Regard this tiny insect.' In the jaws of the tweezers Batula held up an ant. 'The venom of his sting will make a lion roll on the ground roaring with agony. Tell me, you who call yourself Kadem, who are you and who sent you to commit this deed?'

Kadem looked at the wriggling insect. A clear drop of venom oozed out between the serrated jaws of its mandibles. It had a sharp, chemical odour that would drive any other ant that smelt it into an aggressive frenzy.

'I am a true follower of the Prophet,' Kadem replied, 'and I was sent by God to carry out His divine purpose.'

Mansur nodded to Batula. 'Let the ant whisper the question more clearly in the ear of this true follower of the Prophet.'

Kadem's eyes swivelled towards Mansur and he tried to spit again, but his mouth had dried. Batula placed the ant in the opening of the reed tube in his ear and closed the end with a plug of whittled soft wood.

'You will hear the ant as it comes down the tube,' Batula told Kadem. 'Its footsteps will sound like the hoofs of a horse. Then you will feel it walking in your eardrum. It will stroke the membrane of your inner ear with the sharp tips of its feelers. Then it will sting you.'

They watched Kadem's face. His lips twitched, then his eyes rolled back in their sockets until the whites showed and his whole face worked furiously.

'Allah!' he whispered. 'Arm me against the blasphemers!'

The sweat burst out from the pores of his skin like the first drops of monsoon rain, and he tried to shake his head as the footfalls of the ant in his eardrum were magnified a thousand times. But the thong held his head in a vice-like grip.

'Answer, Kadem,' Batula urged him. 'I can still wash out the ant before it stings. But you must answer swiftly.' Kadem closed his eyes to shut out Batula's face.

'Who are you? Who sent you?' Batula came closer and whispered in his open ear. 'Swiftly, Kadem, or the pain will be beyond even your crazed imagining.'

Then, deep in the recesses of the eardrum the ant humped its back and a fresh globule of venom oozed out between its curved mandibles. It sank the barbed points into the soft tissue at the spot where the auditory nerve was closest to the surface.

Kadem al-Jurf was consumed by waves of agony, and they were fiercer than Batula had warned him. He screamed once, a sound that was not human but something from a nightmare. Then the pain froze the muscles and vocal cords in his throat, his jaws clamped together in such a rock-hard spasm that one of the rotten teeth at the back of his mouth burst, filling his mouth with splinters and bitter pus. His eyes rolled back in his skull like those of a blind man. His back arched until Mansur feared that his spine would crack, and his body juddered so that his bonds cut deeply into his flesh.

'He will die,' Mansur asked anxiously.

'A *shaitan* is hard to kill,' Batula answered. The three squatted in a half-circle in front of Kadem and studied his suffering. Although it was dreadful to behold, none of them felt the slightest twinge of compassion.

'Regard, lord!' said Kumrah. 'The first spasm passes.' He was right. Kadem's spine slowly relaxed, and although a series of convulsions still shook him, each was less violent than the one before.

'It is finished,' Mansur said.

'No, lord. If God is just, soon the ant will sting again,' Batula said softly. 'It will not finish so swiftly.' As he said it, so it happened: the tiny insect struck again.

This time Kadem's tongue was caught between his teeth as they snapped closed. He bit through it, and the blood streamed down his chin. He shuddered and leaped against the chain. His bowels loosened with a spluttering rush, and even Mansur's lust

413

for vengeance faltered. The dark veils of hatred and grief parted and his instinct for humanity shone through. 'Enough, Batula. End it now. Wash out the ant.'

Batula withdrew the wood plug from the end of the reed and filled his mouth with water. Through the hollow reed he spurted a jet into Kadem's eardrum, and in the overflow the drowned red body of the insect was washed down Kadem's straining neck.

Slowly Kadem's tortured body relaxed, and he hung inert in his bonds. His breathing was rapid and shallow, and every few minutes he let out a harsh, ragged exhalation, half sigh and half groan.

Once again, his captors squatted in a semi-circle in front of him and watched him carefully. Late in the afternoon, as the sun touched the tops of the forest trees Kadem groaned again. His eyes opened and focused slowly on Mansur.

'Batula, give him water,' Mansur ordered. Kadem's mouth was black and crusted with the blood. His torn tongue protruded between his lips like a lump of rotten liver. Batula held the waterskin to his mouth, and Kadem choked and gasped as he drank. Once he vomited up a gush of the jellied black blood he had swallowed, but then he drank again.

Mansur let him rest until sunset, then ordered Batula to let him drink again. Kadem was stronger now, and followed their movements with his eyes. Mansur ordered Batula and Kumrah to relax his bonds to allow the blood to flow back, and to chafe his hands and feet before gangrene killed off the living flesh. The pain of the returning blood must have been agonizing but Kadem bore it stoically. After a while they tightened the leather thongs again.

Mansur came to stand over him. 'You know well that I am the son of the Princess Yasmini whom you murdered,' he said. 'In the eyes of God and of men, vengeance is mine. Your life belongs to me.'

Kadem stared back at him.

'If you do not reply to me, I will order Batula to place another insect in your good ear.'

Kadem blinked, but his face remained impassive.

'Answer my question,' Mansur demanded. 'Who are you and who sent you to our home?'

Kadem's swollen tongue filled his mouth, so his reply was slurred and barely intelligible. 'I am a true follower of the Prophet,' he said, 'and I was sent by God to carry out His divine purpose.'

'That is the same answer, but it is not the one I wait for,' Mansur said. 'Batula, select another insect. Kumrah, place another reed in Kadem's ear.' When they had done as he ordered, Mansur asked Kadem, 'This time the pain may kill you. Are you ready for death?'

'Blessed is the martyr,' Kadem replied. 'I long with all my heart to be welcomed by Allah into Paradise.'

Mansur took Batula aside. 'He will not yield,' he said.

Batula looked dubious. His tone was uncertain as he replied, 'Lord, there is no other way.'

'I think there is.' Mansur turned to Kumrah. 'We do not need the reed.' Then, to both of them, 'Stay with him. I shall return.'

He rowed back down the stream. It was almost dark by the time he reached the encampment, but the full moon was already lighting the eastern sky with a marvellous golden glow as it pushed over the tops of the trees. 'Even the moon hastens to assist our enterprise,' Mansur murmured, as he went ashore on the beach below the camp. He saw the lamplight shine in chinks through the thatched wall of his father's hut and he hurried there.

His uncle Tom and aunt Sarah sat by the mattress on which Dorian lay. Mansur knelt beside his father and kissed his forehead. He stirred but did not open his eyes.

Mansur leaned close to Tom and whispered low, 'Uncle, the assassin will not yield. Now I need your help.'

Tom rose to his feet and jerked his head for Mansur to follow him outside. Swiftly Mansur told him what he wanted, and at the end said simply, 'This is something that I would do myself, but Islam forbids it.'

'I understand.' Tom nodded and looked up at the moon. ''Tis favourable. I saw a place in the forest close by here where they feed each night on the tubers of the arum lily plant. Tell your aunt Sarah what I am about, and that she is not to fret. I shall not be too long gone.'

Tom went to the armoury and selected his big double-barrelled German four to the pound musket. He drew the charge and reloaded the weapon with a handful of Big Looper, the formidable lion shot. Then he checked the flint and the priming, made sure that his knife was on his belt and loosened the blade in its sheath.

He selected ten of his men and told them to wait for his call, but he left the camp alone: silence and stealth were vital to success. When he waded across the stream he stooped to take up a handful of black clay and smear it over his face, for pale skin shines in the moonlight and his quarry was stealthy and cunning. Although it was a huge creature he was hunting it was nocturnal in its habits, and for that reason few men ever laid eyes on it.

Tom followed the far bank of the stream for almost a mile. As he came closer to the swamp in which the arum lilies grew his steps slowed and he paused every fifty paces to listen intently. At the edge of the swamp he squatted and held the big gun across his lap. He waited patiently, never moving even to flick away the mosquitoes that whined around his head. The moon rose higher and its light grew stronger so that the shadows thrown by each tree and shrub had sharp edges.

Abruptly there came a grunt and a squeal from close at hand, and his pulse tripped. He waited, as still as one of the dead tree stumps, as the silence fell again. Then he heard the squelch of hoofs in the mud, more grunts, the sound of hog-like rooting and the champing of tusked jaws.

Tom eased forward towards the sounds. Without warning they ceased as abruptly as they had begun, and he froze. He knew that this was the customary behaviour of the bush pigs. The entire sounder would freeze together and listen for predators. Although Tom was on one leg, he froze in that attitude, still as an ungainly statue as the silence drew out. Then the grunting and feeding started again.

With relief he lowered his foot, his thigh muscles burning,

416

and crept forward again. Then he saw the sounder just ahead of him: there were several dozen, dark hump-backed sows, with their piglets underfoot, rooting and wallowing. None was large enough to be a mature boar.

Tom moved with infinite care to a mound of harder earth at the edge of the swamp and crouched there, waiting for the big boars to come out of the forest. A cloud blew across the moon, and suddenly, in the utter darkness, he sensed a presence close by. He turned all his attention upon it and vaguely made out massive movement so close that he felt he could touch it with the muzzle of his musket. He inched the butt-stock to his shoulder, but dared not cock the hammers. The beast was too close. It would hear the click as the sear engaged. He stared into the darkness, not sure if it was real or his imagination. Then the clouds overhead blew open and the moonlight burst through.

In front of him loomed a gigantic hog. Along its mountain-ous back rose a mane of coarse bristles, shaggy and black in the moonlight. Its jaws were armed with curved tusks, sharp enough to rip the belly out of a man or to slice through the femoral artery in his groin and bleed him white within minutes.

Tom and the boar saw each other in the same moment. Tom swept back the hammers of the musket to full cock, and the boar squealed and charged straight at him. Tom fired the first barrel into its chest, and the heavy leaden loopers thudded into flesh and bone. The boar staggered and dropped on to its front knees but in an instant it bounded to its feet and came straight in. Tom fired the second barrel, then smashed the empty musket into the pig's face and dived to one side. One tusk hooked into his coat and split it like a razor, but the point missed his flesh. The beast's heavy shoulder struck him a glancing blow, which was powerful enough nevertheless to send him rolling into the mud.

Tom struggled to his feet with his knife clutched in his right hand, ready to meet the next attack. All around him there was the rush of dark bodies and squeals of alarm as the pigs scattered back into the forest.

Silence fell almost immediately after they were gone. Then

Tom heard a much softer sound: laboured gasping and snuffling and the convulsive thrashing of back legs in the reeds of the swamp. Cautiously he went towards the sounds, and found the boar down, kicking his last in the mud.

Tom hurried back to the camp and found his ten chosen men where he had left them, waiting his summons. None of them was a Muslim, so they had no religious qualms about touching a pig. Tom led them back to the swamp and they lashed the huge evil-smelling carcass to a carrying pole. It took all ten to stagger with this burden along the bank of the river to where Kadem was still tied to the tree and Mansur was waiting beside him with Batula and Kumrah.

By this time the dawn was breaking, and Kadem stared at the pig carcass as they dropped it in front of him. He said nothing but his expression clearly showed his horror and repugnance.

The bearers of the carcass had brought spades with them. Mansur put them to work at once digging a grave beside the carcass. None of them spoke to Kadem, and they barely glanced in his direction while they worked. However, Kadem's agitation increased as he watched them. He was again sweating and shivering, but this was not only the effects of the shock and agony of the ant stings. He had begun to understand the fate that Mansur was preparing for him.

When the grave was deep enough, the men laid aside their spades at Tom's order, and gathered around the carcass of the boar. Two stropped the blades of their skinning knives while the others rolled the boar on to its back and held all four legs widely separated to make the job of the skinners easier. They were expert, and the thick bristly hide was soon flayed away from pink and purple muscle and the white fat of the belly. At last it was free and the skinners stretched it open on the ground.

Mansur and the two sea captains kept well clear, careful not to let a drop of the vile creature's blood splatter them. Their revulsion was as evident as that of their captive. The stench of the old boar's fatty flesh was rank in the early-morning air, and Mansur spat the taste of it out of his mouth before he spoke to Kadem for the first time since they had brought in the carcass.

'O nameless one who calls himself a true follower of the Prophet, sent by God to carry out His divine purpose, we have no further need of you and your treachery. Your life on this earth has come to an end.' Kadem began to exhibit more distress than the agony that the insect's sting had inflicted upon him. He gibbered like an idiot, and his eyes rolled from side to side. Mansur ignored his protests and went on mercilessly, 'At my command, you will be stitched into this wet and reeking skin of the pig, and buried alive in the grave we have prepared for you. We will place the flayed carcass of this beast on top of you so that as you suffocate its blood and fat will drip into your face. As you and the pig rot your stinking bodily juices will mingle and you will become one. You will be fouled, *harom* for ever. The faces of God and all his prophets will be turned away from you for all eternity.'

Mansur gestured to the men who were waiting ready, and they came forward. Mansur unlocked Kadem's chains, but left him pinioned at wrists to ankles. The men carried him to the open pigskin and laid him upon it. The ship's sailmaker threaded his needle and donned his leather palm to sew Kadem into the winding sheet formed by the skin.

As Kadem felt the wet and greasy folds embrace him, he screeched like a condemned soul cast into eternal darkness. 'My name is Kadem ibn Abubaker, eldest son of Pasha Suleiman Abubaker. I came here to seek vengeance for the murder of my father and to carry out the will of my master Caliph Zayn al-Din ibn al-Malik.'

'What was the will of your master?' Mansur insisted.

'The execution of the Princess Yasmini and of her incestuous lover, al-Salil.'

Mansur turned to Tom who was squatting close by. 'That is all we need to know. May I kill him now, Uncle?'

Tom rose to his feet and shook his head. 'His life belongs not to me but to your father. Besides, we may have further need of this assassin yet, if we are to avenge your mother.'

With his damaged eardrum Kadem was unable to keep his

balance and he staggered and toppled over when they lifted him out of the folds of pigskin, cut loose his bonds and placed him on his feet. Tom ordered him to be strapped to the carrying pole on which they had brought in the pig's carcass. The bearers carried him like dead game back to the beach of the lagoon.

'It will be more difficult for him to escape from the ship. Take him out to the *Gift*,' Tom told Batula. 'Chain him in the orlop, and see to it that he is guarded day and night by your most reliable men.'

They stayed on in the encampment beside the lagoon during the forty days of mourning for Yasmini. For the first ten Dorian hung suspended over the black void of death, drifting from delirium into coma, then rallying again. Tom, Sarah and Mansur took turns to wait by his bedside.

On the tenth morning Dorian opened his eyes and looked at Mansur. He spoke weakly but clearly: 'Is your mother buried? Have you said the prayers?'

'She is buried and I have prayed over her grave, for you and for myself.'

'That is good, my son.' Dorian sank away, but within an hour he woke again and asked for food and drink.

'You will live,' Sarah told him as she brought a bowl of broth. 'You ran it very fine, Dorian Courtney, but now you will live.'

Relieved of the terrible anxiety over Dorian's condition, Tom let Sarah and the women servants take over his share of the vigil at the bedside, and he and Mansur devoted themselves to other business.

Every day Tom ordered Kadem to be brought up from the orlop deck, and exercised in the sunlight and open air. He made sure he was well fed, and that the gash in his scalp healed cleanly. He felt no compassion for the prisoner, but he wanted to ensure his survival in good condition: he was an important part of Tom's plans for the future.

Tom had ordered the bush-pigskin to be salted and hung in the *Gift*'s rigging. He questioned Kadem almost every day in fluent Arabic, forcing him to squat in the shadow of the pigskin that flapped over his head, a constant reminder of the fate that awaited him if he refused to answer.

'How did you learn that this ship belonged to me and my brother?' he demanded, and Kadem named the merchant in Zanzibar who had given him this information, before the life was choked out of him by the garotte.

Tom passed the information to Dorian, when he was strong enough to sit up unaided. 'So our identity is now known by the spies of Zayn al-Din at every anchorage along the coast from Good Hope to Hormuz and the Red Sea.'

'The Dutch know us also,' Dorian agreed. 'Keyser promised that every VOC port in the Orient would be closed to us. We must change the cut of our jibs.'

Tom set about altering the appearance of the two ships. One after the other they warped them to the beach. Tom used the rise and fall of the tide to careen them over. First they scraped away the heavy infestation of weed and treated the shipworm that had already taken firm hold in the hulls. Some of these loathsome creatures were as thick as a man's thumb and as long as his arm. They could riddle the timbers with holes until the ship was rotten as cheese and might easily break up in rough weather. They tarred the ship's bottom and renewed the copper sheathing where strips had been torn off, allowing the worm to enter. It was the only effective cure. Then Tom changed the masts and rigging. He stepped a mizzen on the *Gift*. This was something he and Dorian had discussed before: the additional mast altered the appearance and performance of the ship completely. When he took her out to sea for her trials, she sailed a full point closer to the wind and logged an additional two knots of speed through the water. Tom and Batula were delighted and reported the success gleefully to Dorian, who insisted on being allowed to hobble to the head of the beach to look at her.

'In God's name, she is as fresh as a virgin again.'

'She must have a new name, brother,' Tom agreed. 'What shall it be?'

Dorian barely hesitated. 'The *Revenge*.'

Tom saw by his expression what he was thinking, and gave him no argument. 'That is an illustrious name.' He nodded. 'Our great-great-grandfather sailed with Sir Richard Grenville on the old *Revenge*.'

They repainted the hull in sky blue, for that was the hue of the paint they had brought with them in abundance, and chequered the gunports in darker blue. It gave the *Revenge* a saucy air.

Then they began work on the *Maid of York*. She had always shown a flighty inclination to broach-to when driven hard before the wind. Tom took this opportunity to add an additional ten feet to the mainmast and give it five degrees more rake. He also lengthened the bowsprit and moved the jib stay and the staysail stay a touch forward. He repositioned the cradles of the water casks in the holds nearer to the stern to alter her trim. This not only changed her profile but made her more responsive to the helm and corrected her tendency to being down by the head.

Tom gave her the contrary colour scheme to the *Revenge*: a dark blue hull and sky blue gunports.

'She was named after you, the *Maid of York*,' Tom reminded Sarah. 'Fair is fair, you must rename her now.'

'*Water Sprite*,' she said immediately, and Tom blinked.

'How did you hit on that? 'Tis a quirky name.'

'And I am a quirky lady.' She laughed.

'That you are.' He laughed with her. 'But just plain *Sprite* might be better.'

'Are you naming her, or am I?' Sarah asked sweetly.

'Let's say rather, we are.' Sarah threw up both her hands in capitulation.

When the forty days of mourning for Yasmini had passed, Dorian was sufficiently recovered to walk unaided to the far end of the beach and swim back across the channel. Although he had recovered much of his strength, the loneliness and deep sadness had marked him. Whenever Mansur could find time from his duties he and Dorian spent it sitting together and talking quietly.

Each evening the entire family gathered around the camp-fire and discussed their plans. Soon it became obvious that none of them wished to make the lagoon their new home. As they were without horses Tom and Mansur's scouting expeditions on foot did not penetrate far inland, and they encountered none of the tribes that had once inhabited this country. The old villages were burned and deserted.

'There's no trade, unless you have someone to trade with,' Tom pointed out.

'It is a sickly place. Already we have lost one of our people to the fever.' Sarah supported him. 'I had hoped so much to meet our Jim Boy here, but in all this time there has been neither sign nor sight of him. He must have moved on further to the north.' There were a hundred other possible reasons why Jim had disappeared, but she put them out of her mind. 'We will find him there,' she said firmly.

'I, for another, cannot remain here,' Mansur said. In these last weeks he had taken his place quite naturally at the family councils. 'My father and I have a sacred obligation to find the man who ordered the death of my mother. I know who he is. My destiny lies to the north, in the kingdom of Oman.' He looked at his father enquiringly.

Slowly Dorian nodded agreement. 'Yasmini's murder has changed everything. I now share your sacred obligation of vengeance. We will go northwards together.'

'So, it's settled, then.' Tom spoke for all of them. 'When we reach Nativity Bay, we can decide again.'

'When can we sail?' Sarah asked eagerly. 'Name a day!'

'The ships are almost ready, and so are we. Ten days from now. The day after Good Friday,' Tom suggested. 'A propitious day.'

Sarah composed a letter to Jim. It ran to twelve pages of heavy parchment in her elegant close-written script. She stitched it into a canvas cover and painted the packet with sky blue ship's paint and sealed the seams with hot tar. She printed his name on it in white paint and block capitals: James

Archibald Courtney Esq. Then she carried it up the hill and, with her own hand, hid it in the recess below the post stone. She built a tall cairn on top to signal to Jim when he came that a letter was waiting for him.

Mansur hunted far up the valley and killed five more Cape buffalo. The women salted, pickled and dried the meat, then made spiced sausage for the voyage ahead. Mansur supervised the crews as they refilled all the water casks on both ships. When this was done, Tom and the Arab captains were rowed around the ships to check their trim. Though heavily laden, both vessels rode well. They looked wonderfully elegant in their new paint.

Chained and heavily guarded, Kadem al-Jurf was allowed on deck for a few hours each day. Tom and Dorian took turns to interrogate him. With the dried pigskin casting its shadow across the deck Kadem responded to their questions, if not willingly at least with some show of respect. However, that disconcerting stare never faded from his eyes. Though Tom and Dorian phrased the same questions in different guises, Kadem's replies were consistent and he avoided the traps they set for him. He must have known what his eventual fate would be. The law allowed Dorian and Mansur little discretion of mercy: when they stared at him Kadem saw death in their eyes, and all he could hope for was that when the time came they would grant him a swift, dignified execution, without the horror of dismemberment or the sacrilege of the pigskin.

Over the weeks, Kadem's incarceration in the orlop developed its own routine and rhythm. Three Arab seamen shared the duty of acting as his warders during the night, each taking a shift of four hours. They had been carefully chosen by Batula, and at first they were mindful of his orders. While themselves remaining mute, they reported Kadem's most casual remarks to Batula. However, the nights were long and the guard duty as dull as the need to remain awake was onerous. Kadem had been trained by the most famous mullahs of the Royal House of Oman in dialectic and religious debate. The things he whispered in the darkness to his warders while the rest of the crew were ashore or sleeping on the upper deck were compelling to those devout young men. The truths he spoke were too poignant and moving to report to Batula. They could not close their ears to him, and they listened at first with awe when he spoke of the truth and beauty of God's way. Then they began, against their own will, to respond to his whispers with their own. From the fire in his eyes they knew Kadem to be a holy man. By the fervour of his own devotion and the unassailable logic of his words they were convinced. Slowly they were held in thrall by Kadem ibn Abubaker.

Meanwhile, the excitement of impending departure built up in the rest of the company. The last sticks of furniture and goods were taken from the huts at the forest edge and ferried on board. On Good Friday Tom and Mansur applied torches to the empty huts. The thatch had dried out and they burned like bonfires. The day after Good Friday they sailed early in the morning watch, so that Tom had light enough to make out the channel. The wind stood fair offshore, and he led the little flotilla out through the heads into the open sea.

It was midday and the land was low and blue on the western horizon before one of the crew came up from below decks in a state of terrible agitation. Tom and Dorian were on the quarter-deck together, Dorian seated in the sling chair Tom had rigged for him. At first neither could understand the man's wild shouts.

'Kadem!' Tom caught the gist of it. He went bounding down the companionway to the orlop deck. Locked securely in the wooden cage that the carpenters had built for him, Kadem was curled in sleep upon the straw mattress. His chains were still secured to the ring bolts in the deck. Tom seized a corner of the single blanket that covered the prisoner from the top of his head to his feet, jerked it aside and then kicked the dummy that lay beneath it. It was cunningly made of two sacks filled with oakum and tied with short pieces of old rope to give it the outline of a human body beneath the blanket.

They searched the ship swiftly from stem to stern, Tom and Dorian with swords in hand raging through the holds and probing every corner and cranny.

'Three other men are missing,' Batula reported with a shamed face.

'Who are they?' Dorian demanded.

Batula hesitated before he could bring himself to answer. 'Rashood, Pinna and Habban,' he croaked, 'the same three men I set to guard him.'

Tom altered course and steered alongside the *Revenge*. Through the speaking tube, he hailed Mansur who had command of her. Both vessels went about and headed back towards the entrance of the lagoon, but the winds that had allowed them to clear the lagoon so handily now blocked them offshore. For days more they beat back and forth across the entrance. Twice they were almost piled up to the reef as Tom in frustration tried to force the passage.

It was six days after they had sailed that at last they dropped anchor off the beach of the lagoon once again. Since their departure it had rained heavily, and when they went ashore they found that any sign left by the fugitives had been washed away. 'Yet there is only one direction they would have taken.' Tom pointed up the valley. 'But they have almost nine days' start on us. If we are to catch up with them we must march at once.'

He ordered Batula and Kumrah to check the weapons lockers and the magazines. They came ashore with sorry expressions to report that four muskets were missing, with the same number of cutlasses, bullet bags and powder flasks. Tom stopped himself reviling the two captains further, for they had already suffered enough.

Dorian argued vehemently when Tom told him he must stay behind to take care of the ships and Sarah while they chased the fugitives. In the end, Sarah joined in to convince him that he was not yet strong enough for such an expedition, which would call for hard marches and perhaps even harder fighting. Tom selected ten of his best men to go with him, those who were proficient with sword, musket and pistol.

An hour after they had first stepped ashore all was ready. Tom kissed Sarah, and they left the beach heading inland. Tom and Mansur strode out at the head of the line of armed men.

'I would that little Bakkat were with us,' Tom muttered. 'He would follow them though they grew wings and flew ten feet above the ground.'

'You are a famous elephant hunter, Uncle Tom. I have heard you tell it since I was a child.'

'That was more than a year or two ago,' Tom smiled ruefully, 'and you must not remember all I tell you. Boasts and brags are like debts and childhood sweethearts – they often come back to plague the man who made them.'

At noon on the third day they stood on the crest of the range of mountains that ran in an unbroken rampart north and south. The slopes below them were covered with banks of purple heather. This was the dividing line between the littoral and the inland plateau of the continental shield. Behind, the forests lay like a green carpet down to the edge of the ocean. Ahead, the hills were harsh and rocky and the plains were endless, stretching for ever to the horizon, blue with distance. The tiny dustclouds kicked up by the moving herds of game drifted in the warm breezes.

'Any one of those might mark the path of the men we are hunting, but the hoofs of the herds will have wiped out their tracks,' Tom told Mansur. 'Still and all, I doubt they would have headed into that great emptiness. Kadem would have the sense at least to try to find human habitation.'

'The Cape colony?' Mansur looked southwards.

'More likely the Arab forts along the Fever Coast or the Portuguese territory of Mozambique.'

'The land is so big.' Mansur scowled. 'They could have gone anywhere.'

'We will wait for the scouts to come in before we decide what next to do.'

Tom had sent his best men to cast north and south, ordering them to try to cut Kadem's trail. He would not say so to Mansur, not yet at least, but he knew that their chances were remote. Kadem had too long a start on them and, as Mansur had remarked, the land was big.

The rendezvous Tom had set at which to meet the scouts was a distinctive peak shaped like a cocked hat that could be seen from twenty leagues in any direction. They camped on the southern slope at the edge of the treeline, and the scouts came dribbling back during the night. None had been able to cut human sign.

'They have got clean away, lad,' Tom told his nephew. 'I think we can do naught else but let them go, and turn back for the ships. But I would like your agreement. 'Tis your duty to your mother that dictates what we do next.'

'Kadem was only the messenger,' Mansur said. 'My blood feud is with his master in Lamu, Zayn al-Din. I agree, Uncle Tom. This is fruitless. Our energies may best be expended elsewhere.'

'Think on this also, lad. Kadem will fly straight back to his master, the pigeon to its loft. When we find Zayn, Kadem will be at his side, if the lions have not eaten him first.'

Mansur's face brightened and his shoulders straightened. 'In God's Name, Uncle, I had not considered that. Of course you are right. As for Kadem perishing in the wilderness, it seems to me that he has the animal tenacity and fanatical faith to survive. I feel sure we will meet him again. He will not escape my vengeance. Let's hurry back to the ships.'

Before first light Sarah left her bunk in the little cabin of the *Sprite*. Then, as she had done every morning since Tom left, she went ashore and climbed to the hilltop above the lagoon. From there she watched for Tom's return. From afar she recognized his tall, straight figure and his swinging walk at the head of his men. The image blurred as her eyes filled with tears of joy and relief.

'Thank you, God, that you paid heed to my prayers,' she cried aloud, and ran down the hillside straight into his arms. 'I was so worried that you would get yourself into trouble again, without me to look after you, Tom Courtney.'

'I had no chance for trouble, Sarah Courtney,' he hugged her hard, 'more's the pity.' He looked to Mansur. 'You are

428

faster than me, lad. Run ahead to warn your father that we are returning, and to have the ships ready to sail again as soon as I set foot aboard.' Mansur set off at once.

As soon as he was out of earshot Sarah said, 'You're the crafty one, aren't you, Thomas? You did not want to be the one who gave the bitter news to Dorry that Yassie's murder is unrevenged.'

''Tis Mansur's duty more than mine,' Tom replied breezily. 'Dorry would have it no other way. The only profit in this bloody business is that it might bring father and son closer than they have ever been before – and that was mighty close.'

They sailed with the ebb of the tide. The wind stood fair and they had made good their offing before darkness fell. The ships were within two cables' length of each other, with the wind fresh on the quarter, their best point of sailing. The *Revenge* showed her new turn of speed and began to pull ahead of the *Sprite*. Thus it was with reluctance that Tom gave the order to shorten sail for the night. It seemed a pity not to take full advantage of the wind that was bearing them so swiftly towards Nativity Bay.

'But I am a trader and not a man-o'-war,' Tom consoled himself. As he gave the order to shorten sail he saw Mansur in the *Revenge* furl his staysail and reef his mizzen and main. Both ships hoisted lanterns to their maintops, to enable them the better to keep night stations on each other.

Tom was ready to give over the quarter-deck to Kumrah and go down to the small saloon for the supper that he could smell Sarah was cooking: he recognized the rich aroma of one of her famous spiced bobooties and saliva flooded into his mouth. He spent a few more minutes checking the set of the sails and the pointing of the helmsman. Satisfied at last, he turned towards the head of the companionway, then stopped abruptly.

He stared at the dark eastern horizon and muttered, mystified, 'There is a great fire out there. Is it a ship ablaze? No, it's something greater than that. The fires of a volcano?'

The crew on deck had seen it too and crowded to the rail, gawking and gabbling. Then, to Tom's utter astonishment, there burst over the dark horizon a monstrous ball of celestial fire. It lit the dark surface of the sea. Across the water the sails of the *Revenge* glowed palely in this ghostly emanation.

'A comet, by God!' Tom shouted in wonder, and stamped on the deck above the saloon. 'Sarah Courtney, come up here at once. You have never seen aught such as this, nor will you ever again.'

Sarah came flying up the ladder with Dorian close behind her. They stopped and stared in wonder, struck speechless by the splendour of the sight. Then Sarah came to Tom and placed herself within the protective circle of his arms. 'It is a sign,' she whispered. 'It's a benediction from on high for the old life we have left behind at Good Hope, and a promise of the new life that lies ahead of us.'

Dorian left them, moved slowly down the deck until he reached the bows and sank to his knees. He turned his face up to the sky. 'All the days of mourning have passed,' he said. 'Your time here on earth with me is over. Go, Yasmini, my little darling, I commit you to the arms of God, but you must know that my heart and all my love go with you.'

Across the dark water Mansur Courtney saw the comet, and he ran to the main shrouds and leaped into them. He clambered swiftly upwards until he reached the maintop. He threw an arm around the top-gallant mast, balancing lithely against the roll and pitch of the hull, which were magnified by the sixty feet that separated him from the surface of the sea. He lifted his face to the sky and his long, thick hair streamed back in the wind. 'The death of kings!' he cried. 'The destruction of tyrants! All these portentous events heralded by God's finger writing in the heavens.' Then he filled his lungs and shouted into the wind, 'Hear me, Zayn al-Din! I am Nemesis, and I am coming for you.'

Night after night as the two little ships sailed northwards the comet climbed overhead, seeming to light their way, until at last they picked out a tall bluff of land that rose out of the dark waters ahead of their bows like the back of a monstrous whale. At the northern end of the promontory, the whale's mouth opened. They sailed through this entrance into a huge landlocked bay, far greater in extent than the Lagoon of the Elephants. On one side the land was steep-to, on the other it stretched in dense mangrove swamps, but between them lay the lovely embouchure of a river of sweet, clear water flanked by gently sloping beaches that offered a natural landing place.

'This is not our first visit to this place. Dorian and I have been here many times before. The natives hereabouts call this river Umbilo,' Tom told Sarah, as he steered for the beach and dropped his anchor in three fathoms. Looking over the side they could watch the steel flukes burying themselves in the pale, sandy bottom and the brilliant shoals of fish swirling as they feasted on the small crabs and shrimps disturbed from their burrows by the anchor.

When all the canvas was furled, the yards sent down and both ships at rest, Tom and Sarah stood by the rail and watched Mansur row ashore from the *Revenge*, eager to explore these new surroundings.

'The restlessness of youth,' Tom said.

'If restlessness is the sign of tender age, then you are an infant in arms, Master Tom,' she replied.

'That is most unfair to me,' he chuckled, 'but I shall let it pass.'

She shaded her eyes and studied the shoreline. 'Where is the mail stone?'

'There, at the foot of the bluff, but do not set your hopes too high.'

'Of course not!' she snapped at him, but she thought, he need not try to protect me from disappointment. I know, with a mother's sure instinct, that Jim is close. Even if he has not yet reached this spot, he soon will. I need only be patient, and my son will come back to me.

Tom offered an olive branch by changing the subject in a placatory tone: 'What do you think of this spot upon the globe, Sarah Courtney?'

'I like it well enough. Perhaps I will grow to like it even more if you allow me to rest here more than a day and a night.' She accepted his peace-offering with a smile.

'Then Dorian and I will begin to mark out the site for our

new fort and trading post immediately.' Tom lifted his glass to his eye. He and Dorian had done most of this work on their last visit to Nativity Bay. He ran the glass over the site they had chosen then. It was on a promontory in a meander of the river. Because the Umbilo waters enclosed three sides, it was easy to defend. A constant supply of fresh water was also assured, and there was a good field of fire in all directions. In addition, it was under the guns of the anchored ships and would benefit from their support in the event of an attack by savage tribesmen or other enemies.

'Yes!' He nodded with satisfaction. 'It will suit our purpose well enough. We will start work tomorrow at the latest, and you shall design our private quarters for me just as you did at Fort Providence twenty years ago.'

'That was our honeymoon,' she said, with awakening enthusiasm.

'Aye, lass.' Tom smiled down at her. 'And this shall be our second of that ilk.'

The small band of horsemen moved slowly across the veld, dwarfed by the infinite landscape that surrounded them. They led the pack-horses and let the small herd of remounts follow at their own pace. Animals and men were lean and hardened by the journey. Their clothing was ragged and patched, their boots long ago worn out and discarded, to be replaced by new ones crudely sewn from the skins of the kudu antelope. The tack of the horses was abraded by their passage through the thorn thickets, the seats of the saddles polished by the riders' sweaty backsides.

The faces and arms of the three Dutchmen were burned as dark as those of the Hottentot troopers. They rode in silence, strung out behind the tiny trotting figure of Xhia, the Bushman. Onwards, ever onwards, following the tracks of the wagon wheels that ran ahead like an endless serpent across the plains and the hills.

The troopers had long ago given up any thought of desertion. It was not only the implacable determination of their leader that prevented them but also the thousands of leagues of wilderness that had already unfurled behind them. They knew that a lone horseman would have little chance of ever reaching the colony. They were herd animals, forced to stay together to survive. They were not only the prisoners of Captain Herminius Koots's obsession, but also of the great empty distances.

Koots's worn leather jacket and breeches were patched and stained with sweat, rain and red dust. His lank hair hung down to his shoulders. It was bleached white by the sun, and the ends were raggedly trimmed with a hunting knife. With his gaunt sun-darkened features and his pale, staring eyes he seemed indeed a man possessed.

For Koots the lure of the reward had long ago faded: he was driven onwards by the need to quench his hatred in the blood of his quarry. He would allow nothing, neither man nor beast nor the burning distances, to cheat him of that ultimate fulfilment.

His chin was sunk on his chest, but now he lifted it and stared ahead, eyes narrowed behind the colourless lashes. There was a dark cloud across the horizon. He watched it climb higher into the sky and roll towards them across the plain. He reined in and called to Xhia: 'What is this that fills the sky? It is not dust or smoke.'

Xhia cackled with laughter and broke into a gleeful dance, shuffling and stamping. The distances and hardships of the journey had not wearied him: he had been born to this life. Enclosing walls and the company of hordes of his fellow men would have jaded him and chafed his spirit. The wilderness was his hearth, the open sky his roof.

He broke into another of his paeans of self-praise and vilification of his mad, cruel master that he alone of all the company could understand. 'Slimy white worm, you creature with skin the colour of pus and curdled milk, do you know nothing at all of this land? Must Xhia, the mighty hunter and slayer of elephants, nurse you like a blind, mewling infant?' Xhia jumped high and deliberately broke flatus, with such force that the wind stirred the back flap of his loincloth. He knew that this would drive Koots into a rage. 'Must Xhia, who stands so tall that his long shadow terrifies his enemies, Xhia beneath whose mighty prong women squeal with joy, must Xhia always lead you by the hand? You understand nothing that is written plain upon the earth, you understand nothing that is blazoned in the very heavens.'

'Stop that monkey chatter at once,' Koots shouted. He could not understand the words but he recognized the mockery in the tone, and knew that Xhia had farted only to provoke him. 'Shut your filthy mouth, and answer me straight.'

'I must shut my mouth but answer your questions, great master?' Xhia switched into the patois of the colony, a mixture of all the languages. 'Am I then a magician?' Over the months of their enforced companionship they had learned to understand each other much better than they had at the beginning, both in words and in intent.

Koots touched the hilt of the long hippopotamus-hide *sjambok* that hung by its thong from the pommel of his saddle. This was another gesture well understood by them both. Xhia changed his tone and expression again, and danced just beyond the reach of the whip. 'Lord, this a gift from the Kulu Kulu. Tonight we will sleep with full bellies.'

'Birds?' Koots asked, and watched the shadow of this cloud sweep across the plain towards them. He had been amazed by the flocks of the tiny quelea bird, but this was far greater in height and extent.

'Not birds,' Xhia told him. 'These are locusts.'

Koots forgot his anger, and leaned back in the saddle to take in the size of the approaching swarm. It filled half of the bowl of the sky from horizon to horizon. The sound of wings was like that of a gentle breeze in the high branches of the forest, but it mounted swiftly, becoming next a murmur, a rising roar and then a thunder. The great swarm of insects formed a moving curtain whose trailing skirts swept the earth. Koots's fascination turned to alarm as the first insects, buzzing low to earth, slammed into his chest and face. He ducked and cried out, for the locust's hind legs are barbed with sharp red spikes. One left a bloody welt across his cheek. His horse reared and plunged under him, and Koots threw himself from the saddle and seized the reins. He turned the horse's rump towards the approaching swarm, and shouted to his men to do the same. 'Hold the pack-horses and knee-halter the spares, lest they are driven away before this pestilence.'

They forced the animals to their knees, then shouted and jerked the reins until reluctantly they rolled flat on their sides and stretched out in the grass. Koots cowered behind the body of his own horse. He pulled his hat well down over his ears, and turned up the collar of his leather coat. Despite the partial protection afforded by the horse, the flying creatures slapped against any exposed parts of his body in a continuous hail-storm, each with the strength to sting painfully through the folds of his coat.

The rest of the band followed his example and lay behind their mounts, taking cover as though from enemy musket balls. Only Xhia seemed oblivious to the rain of hard bodies. He sat out in the open, snatching up the locusts that hit him and were stunned by the impact. He broke off their legs and goggle-eyed heads and stuffed the bodies into his mouth. The carapaces crunched as he chewed and the tobacco-coloured juices ran down his chin. 'Eat!' he called to them as he chewed. 'After the locust comes famine.'

From noon to sundown the locust swarm roared over them like the waters of a great river in flood. The sky was darkened by them so that the dusk came on them prematurely. Xhia's appetite seemed insatiable. He gobbled down the living bodies until his belly bulged, and Koots thought he must succumb to his own greed. However, Xhia was possessed of the same digestive tract as a wild animal. When his belly was stretched tight and shiny as a ball he staggered to his feet and tottered away a few paces. Then, still in full sight of Koots and with the breeze blowing directly to where Koots lay, Xhia lifted the tail flap of his loincloth and squatted again.

It seemed this abundance of food served only to lubricate

the action of his bowels. He defecated copiously and thunder-ously, and at the same time picked up more of the fluttering insects and stuffed them into his mouth.

'You disgusting animal,' Koots shouted at him, and drew his pistol, but Xhia knew that even if Koots thrashed him regularly, he could not kill him, not thousands of leagues from the colony and civilization.

'Good!' He grinned at Koots, and made the gesture of inviting him to join the feast.

Koots holstered his weapon and buried his nose in the crook of his arm. 'When he has served his purpose I will strangle the little ape with my own hands,' Koots promised himself, and gagged on the odours that wafted over him.

As darkness fell, the mighty locust swarm sank down out of the air and settled to roost wherever it came to earth. The deafening buzzing of their wings faded, and Koots rose to his feet at last and stared about.

For as far as he could see in every direction the earth was covered waist deep with a living carpet of bodies, reddish brown in the light of the sunset. The trees of the forest had changed shape as the swarms settled upon them. They were transformed into amorphous haystacks of living locusts, seething and growing larger as more insects settled upon those already at roost. With a crackle like volleys of musketry the main branches of the nearest trees gave way under the weight and came crashing down to earth, but still the locusts piled on to them and devoured the leaves.

From their burrows and lairs the carnivores emerged to feast upon this bounty. Koots watched in wonder as hyena, jackal and leopard became bold with greed and rushed upon the mounds of insects, gobbling them down.

Even a pride of eleven lions joined the banquet. They passed close to where Koots stood, but took not the slightest notice of the men or the horses, for they were preoccupied with the feast. Like grazing cattle they spread out across the plain, their noses to the earth, devouring the seething heaps of locusts, champing them between their great jaws. The lion cubs, their bellies stuffed full, stood up on their back legs and playfully batted the flying creatures out of the air as they were disturbed into flight again.

Koots's troopers swept a clear patch of earth, and built a fire on it. They used the blades of their spades as frying pans, and on these they roasted the locusts crisp and brown. Then they crunched them up with a relish almost as keen as Xhia's. Even Koots joined in and made a meal of these titbits. When night fell the men tried to compose themselves to rest, but the insects swarmed over them. They crawled into their faces, and their spiked feet rasped and scratched any exposed part of their skin and kept them from sleep.

The next morning when the sun rose it revealed a strange antediluvian landscape of dull featureless red-brown. Swiftly the sun warmed the motionless masses of locusts that had been chilled into a stupor during the night. They began to stir, to undulate and hum like a disturbed hive. Suddenly, as if at a signal, the entire horde rose into the air and roared away towards the east, borne on the morning breeze. For many hours the dark torrents streamed overhead, but as the sun reached its zenith the last had passed on. Once more the sky was brilliant blue and unsullied.

Yet the landscape they left behind was altered out of all recognition. It was bare earth and rock. The trees were denuded of their foliage, the bare branches snapped off to lie tangled below the stark boles and twisted trunks. It was as though a conflagration had consumed every leaf and green sprig. The golden grasses that had undulated in the breeze like the scend of the ocean were gone. In their place was this stony desolation.

The horses snuffled the bare earth and pebbles, then stood disconsolately, their empty bellies already rumbling with gases. Koots climbed to the top of the nearest bare hillock and played his telescope over the stony desert. The herds of antelope and quagga that had infested the land the previous day were gone. In the distance Koots made out a pale mist of drifting dust that might have been raised by the exodus of the last herds from this starvation veld. They were moving southwards to search for other grasslands that had not been devastated by the locusts.

He went back down the hill and his men, who had been arguing animatedly, fell silent as he walked into the camp. Koots studied their faces as he filled his mug with coffee from the black kettle. The last grain of sugar had been used up weeks before. He sipped from the mug, then snapped, '*Ja*, Oudeman? What is it that is worrying you? You have the same pained expression as an old woman with bleeding piles.'

'There is no grazing for the horses,' Oudeman blurted.

Koots made a show of amazement at this revelation. 'Sergeant Oudeman, I am grateful to you for pointing this out to me. Without your sharp sense of perception I might have overlooked it.'

Oudeman scowled at the laboured sarcasm. He was not sufficiently glib or well enough educated to match Koots in word-play. 'Xhia says that the herds of wild game will know which way to go to find grazing. If we follow them they will lead us to it.'

'Please go on, Sergeant. I never tire of gleaning these jewels of your wisdom.'

'Xhia says that since last night the game herds have started moving southwards.'

'Yes.' Koots nodded, and blew noisily into the mug of hot coffee. 'Xhia is right. I saw that from the hilltop up there.' He pointed with the mug.

'We must go southwards to find grazing for the horses,' Oudeman went on stubbornly.

'One question, Sergeant. Which way are the tracks of Jim Courtney's wagon heading?' Using the mug again, he pointed out the deep ruts, which were even more obvious now that the grass no longer screened them.

Oudeman lifted his hat and scratched his bald pate. 'Northeast,' he grunted.

'So, if we go southwards will we catch up with Courtney?' Koots asked, in a kindly tone.

'No, but . . .' Oudeman's voice trailed off.

'But what?'

'Captain, sir, without the horses we will never get back to the colony.'

Koots stood up and flicked the coffee grounds out of his mug. 'The reason we are here, Oudeman, is to catch Jim Courtney, not to return to the colony. Mount!' He looked at Xhia. 'Good, so! You, yellow baboon, take the spoor again and eat the wind.'

There was water in the streams and the rivers they crossed, but no grass on the veld. They rode for fifty and then a hundred leagues without finding grazing. In the larger rivers they found aquatic weeds and lily stems beneath the surface of the water. They waded out to harvest them with their bayonets, and fed them to the horses. In one steep, narrow valley the sweet-thorn trees had not been entirely stripped of their foliage. They climbed into the trees and cut down the branches that the locusts had not torn down with their weight. The horses ate the green leaves hungrily, but this was not their normal diet and they derived only small benefit from it.

By now the animals were showing all the signs of slow starvation, but Koots never wavered in his determination. He led them on across the desolation. The horses were so weakened that the riders were forced to dismount and lead them up any sharp incline to husband their strength.

The men were hungry too. The game had disappeared along with the grass. The once teeming veld was deserted. They ate the last few handfuls in the leather grain sacks, and then were reduced to any windfall that the ruined veld might provide.

With his slingshot Xhia knocked down the prehistoric blue-headed lizards that lived among the rocks, and they dug up the burrows of moles and spring-rats that were surviving on subterranean roots. They roasted them without skinning or cleaning the carcasses. This would have wasted precious nourishment. They simply threw them whole upon the coals, let the fur frizzle off, the skin blacken and burst open. Then they picked the half-cooked flesh off the tiny bones with their fingers. Xhia chewed the discarded bones like a hyena.

He discovered a treasure in an abandoned ostrich nest. There were seven ivory-coloured eggs in the rude scrape in the ground. Each egg was almost the size of his own head. He capered around the nest, screeching with excitement. 'This is another gift that clever Xhia brings to you. The ostrich, which is my totem, has left this for me.' He changed his totem with as little compunction as he would take a new woman. 'Without Xhia you would have perished long ago.'

He selected one of the ostrich eggs, set it on end in the sand, then looped his bowstring around the shaft of an arrow. He placed the point of the arrow on the top of the shell. By sawing the bow rapidly back and forth he spun the arrow. The point drilled neatly through the thick shell. As it broke through there was a sharp hiss of escaping gas and a yellow fountain erupted high in the air, like champagne from a bottle that had been shaken violently. Xhia clapped his open mouth over the hole and sucked out the contents of the egg.

The men around him leaped backwards, exclaiming with alarm and disgust as a sulphurous stench engulfed them.

'Mother of a mad dog!' Koots swore. 'The thing is rotten.'

Xhia rolled his eyes with relish, but did not remove his mouth from the hole, lest the rest of the yellow liquid spray out on to the dry earth and be lost. He gulped it down greedily.

'Those eggs have lain there since the last breeding season – six months in the hot sun. They are so badly addled that they would poison a dog hyena.' Oudeman choked and turned away.

Xhia sat beside the nest and drank two of the eggs without pause, except to belch or chuckle with pleasure. Then he packed those that remained into his leather bag. He slung it over his shoulder and set off again along the wheel ruts of Jim Courtney's wagon train.

The men and horses grew daily weaker and more emaciated. Only Xhia was plump and his skin shone with health and vigour. The addled ostrich eggs, the castings of owls, the dung of lions and jackals, bitter roots and herbs, the maggots of blow-flies, the larvae of wasps and hornets – food that only he could stomach – sustained him.

Wearily the band climbed another denuded hillside and came upon yet another of Jim Courtney's camps. This one was different from the hundreds they had found before. The wagon train had paused here long enough to build grass huts and set up long smoking racks of raw timber over beds of what was by now cold black ash, most of it scattered on the wind.

'Here Somoya killed his first elephant,' Xhia announced, after only a cursory examination of the abandoned campsite.

'How do you know that?' Koots demanded, as he dismounted stiffly. He stood with clenched fists pressed into his aching back, and gazed around him.

'I know it because I am clever and you are stupid,' Xhia said, in the language of his people.

'None of that monkey talk,' Koots snarled at him. But he was too tired to cuff him. 'Answer me straight!'

'They have smoked a mountain of meat on these racks, and these are the knucklebones of the elephant from which they have made a stew.' He picked a bone out of the grass. A few shreds of sinew adhered to it and Xhia gnawed at them before he went on: 'I will find the rest of the carcass nearby.'

He disappeared like a tiny puff of yellow smoke, a way he had that never failed to take Koots by surprise. One moment he was standing in plain sight, the next he was gone. Koots sank down in the meagre shade of a bare tree. He did not have long to wait. Xhia appeared again, as suddenly as he had vanished, with the huge white thigh bone of a bull elephant.

'A great elephant!' he confirmed. 'Somoya has become a mighty hunter, as his father was before him. He has cut the tusks from the skull. By the holes in the jawbone I can tell that each tusk was as long as two men, one standing on the shoulders of the other. They were as thick around as my chest.' He puffed it out to illustrate.

Koots had little interest in the subject, and jerked his head to indicate the abandoned huts. 'How long did Somoya camp here?'

441

Xhia glanced at the depth of the ash in the pits, at the midden heaps and the worn footpaths between the huts, and showed the fingers of both hands twice. 'Twenty days.'

'Then we have gained that much upon them,' Koots said, with grim satisfaction. 'Find something for us to eat before we go on.'

Under Xhia's direction the troopers dug up a spring-hare and a dozen blind golden moles. A pair of white-collared crows was attracted by this activity, and Oudeman brought them down with a single musket shot. The moles tasted like chicken but the flesh of the crows was disgusting, tainted with the carrion of their diet. Only Xhia ate it with relish.

They were sick with weariness, and saddle sore, and after they had eaten the scraps of flesh they rolled into their blankets just as the sun was setting. Xhia woke them with squeals of excitement, and Koots staggered to his feet with his pistol in one hand, drawn sword in the other. 'To arms! On me!' he shouted, before he was fully awake. 'Fix your bayonets!'

Then he stopped short and gazed into the eastern sky. It was alight with a weird glow. The Hottentots whimpered with superstitious awe and cowered in their kaross blankets. 'It is a warning,' they told each other, but softly so that Koots could not hear them. 'It is a warning that we should turn back to the colony, and abandon this mad chase.'

'It is the burning eye of the Kulu Kulu,' Xhia sang, and danced for the great shining deity in the sky above him. 'He is watching over us. He promises rain and the return of the herds. There will be sweet green grass, and rich red meat. Soon, very soon.'

Instinctively the three Dutchmen moved closer together.

'This is the star that guided the three wise men to Bethlehem.' Koots was an atheist, but he knew the other two were devout, so he turned the phenomenon deftly to his advantage. 'It is beckoning us on.'

Oudeman grunted, but he did not want to provoke his captain with argument. Richter crossed himself furtively, for he was a clandestine Catholic in the company of Lutherans and heathens.

Some in fear, others in joyous anticipation, they all watched the comet's stately progress across the heavens. The stars paled and then disappeared, obliterated by its splendour.

Before dawn the trail of the comet stretched in an arc from one horizon to the other. Then, abruptly, it was in turn obscured by dense banks of cloud that rolled in from the east, off the warm Ocean of the Indies. As a murky day broke, thunder rolled against the hills and a blade of vivid lightning ripped open the belly of the clouds. The rain came down. The horses turned their tails into the wind and the men huddled under their tarpaulins as icy squalls swept over them. Only Xhia threw off his loincloth and pranced naked in the rain, throwing back his head and letting the waters fill his open mouth.

It rained for a day and a night without ceasing. The earth dissolved under them, and each gully and *donga* became a raging river, every depression and hollow in the earth became a lake. Incessantly the rain raked them and the thunder bemused them, like a cannonade of heavy guns. Huddled in their blankets, they shivered with the wet and the cold, their guts cramped and churned with the sour fluids of starvation. At intervals the rain froze before it hit the ground, and hailstones as big as knucklebones rattled against their tarpaulins and drove the horses frantic. Some snapped their ropes and galloped away in front of the sweeping grey squall.

Then on the second day, the clouds broke up and streamed away in dirty grey tatters and the sun burst through, hot and bright. They roused themselves, mounted and sallied out to retrieve the missing horses, which were scattered away for leagues across the veld. One had been killed by a pair of young lions. The two big cats were still on the body, so Koots and Oudeman rode them down and shot both of them in furious retribution. It was another three days wasted before Koots could resume the chase. Though the rain had eroded and, in places, obliterated the wagon trail, Xhia never faltered and led them on without check.

The veld responded joyously to the rain and the hot sun that followed it. Within the first day a soft green fuzz covered the gaunt outlines of the hills, and the trees lifted their drooping bare branches. Before they had gone another hundred leagues the horses' bellies were distended with sweet new grass, and they encountered the first influx of returning wild game.

From afar Xhia spotted a herd of over fifty hartebeest, each animal the size of a pony, their red coats shining in the sunlight, their thick horns sweeping up then twisting back, tall as a bishop's mitre. The three Dutchmen spurred out to meet the herd. The strength of the horses was restored by the fresh grazing, and they ran them down swiftly. Musket fire boomed out across the plains.

They butchered the hartebeest where they fell, and built fires beside the carcasses. They threw bleeding hunks of flesh on to the coals and then, half crazed with hunger, they gorged on the roasted meat. Although he was sleek, well fed and only half the size of the troopers, Xhia ate more than any two of them, and for once not even Koots grudged it to him.

Kadem knelt behind a fallen log beside a rain-swollen rill of sweet water. He had laid the musket over the top of the log, with his turban folded into a cushion beneath it. Without this padding the weapon might bounce off the hardwood log at the discharge and the shot fly wide. The musket was one of those they had taken from the powder magazine in the *Revenge*. Rashood had only managed to steal four small powder bags. The mighty rainstorm that had drenched them for a day and a night had also soaked and caked most of the powder that remained. Kadem had crumbled and sorted the damaged remnants with his fingers, but in the end he had only been able to retrieve a single bag of the precious stuff. To conserve what remained, he had used only half a measure to charge the musket.

Through the riverine bush he watched a small herd of impala antelope feeding. They were the first game he had seen since the locust swarms had passed. They were nibbling the sprigs of new green growth that the rains had brought forth. Kadem picked out one of the rams from the herd, a velvety brown creature with lyre-shaped horns. He was an expert musketeer, but his weapon was half charged and he had loaded only a few lead pellets of goose-shot on top of the powder. For these to be effective he had to let the animal come in close. His moment came and Kadem fired. Through the whirling cloud of gunsmoke he saw the ram stagger, and then, bleating pitifully, it tottered in a circle with its front leg dangling from the shattered shoulder. Kadem dropped the musket and darted forward with the cutlass in his hand. He stunned the ram with a blow of the heavy brass pommel, then rolled it over swiftly and slit its throat while it still lived.

'In God's Name!' He blessed it and the flesh was halal, no longer profane, fit to be eaten by believers. He whistled softly and his three followers came up the bank of the rill, from where they had hidden. Swiftly they butchered the carcass, then roasted strips of meat from either side of the spine over the small fire Kadem allowed them to build. As soon as the meat was cooked he ordered them to extinguish it. Even in this vast, uninhabited wilderness he was always careful to remain hidden. This was a part of his desert training, where almost every tribe was in a blood feud with all its neighbours.

They ate quickly and sparingly, then rolled the remaining cold cooked meat in their turbans, draped them over their shoulders and knotted them round their waists.

'In God's Name, we go on.' Kadem stood up and led his three followers along the bank of the stream. It cut through a steep, rugged barrier of hills. By now their robes were stained and the hems so tattered that they seemed to have been nibbled away by rats, barely covering their knees. They had made sandals for themselves from the hides of game they had killed before the locusts came. The ground was harsh and stony underfoot. There were areas carpeted with the three-pointed devil thorns, which always presented one of their spikes uppermost. The auger points could pierce even the most leathery sole to the bone.

By now the rains had repaired most of the damage wreaked by the locust swarms. However, they had no horses and they had travelled hard on foot, from before dawn until sunset each day. Kadem had decided that they must head northwards, and try to reach one of the coastal Omani trading centres beyond the Pongola river before their powder ran out. They were still a thousand leagues or more short of their goal.

They halted again at midday, for even these indefatigable travellers must stop to pray at the appointed times. They had no prayer mats with them, but Kadem estimated the direction of Mecca from the position of the noon sun and they prostrated themselves on the rugged earth. Kadem led the prayers. They affirmed that God was one and Muhammad his last true Prophet. They asked no boon or favour in return for their faith. When their worship was completed in the pure, strict form, they squatted in the shade and ate a little more of the cold roasted venison. Kadem led the quiet conversation, then instructed them in religious and philosophical matters. At last he glanced up at the sun again. 'In God's Name, let us continue the journey.'

They rose and girded themselves, then froze together as they heard, faint but unmistakable, the sound of musket fire.

'Men! Civilized men, with muskets and powder!' Kadem whispered. 'To have ventured this far inland they must have horses. All the things we need to save ourselves from perishing in this dreadful place.'

The gunfire came again. He cocked his head and slitted his wild eyes as he tried to pinpoint the source of the sound. He turned in that direction. 'Follow me. Move like the wind, swift and unseen,' he said. 'They must not know we are here.'

In the middle of that afternoon, Kadem found the spoor of many horses moving towards the north-east. The hoofs were shod with steel and had left clear prints in the rain-damp earth. They followed them at a trot across the plains, which danced and wavered with mirage. In the late afternoon they saw the dark smear of smoke from a campfire ahead. They went forward more cautiously. In the gathering dusk they could make out the twinkle of red flames below the smoke. Closer still, Kadem saw the shapes of men moving in front of the fire. Then the wind of the day faded away, and the night breeze puffed from another direction. Kadem sniffed the air and caught the unmistakable ammoniac tang.

'Horses!' he whispered, with excitement.

Koots leaned back against the bole of the camel-thorn tree and carefully pressed shreds of crumbling dry shag into his clay pipe. His tobacco bag was made from the scrotum of a bull buffalo with a drawn string of sinew to close the mouth. It was less than half full, and he was rationing himself to this half-pipe a day. He lit it with a coal from the fire and coughed softly with pleasure as the first powerful inhalation filled his lungs.

His troopers were spread out under the surrounding trees; each man had picked his own spot to lay out his fur kaross. Their bellies were stuffed with the meat of the hartebeest, the first time in over a month that they had eaten their fill. So that they could better savour this feast, Koots had allowed an early halt to the day's march. There was almost an hour left of daylight. In the normal run of events they would have camped only when the dusk obscured the wagon ruts they were following.

From the corner of his eye Koots picked up a flicker of movement and he glanced around quickly, then relaxed again. It was only Xhia. Even as Koots watched him he vanished into the darkening veld. A Bushman, with every hand turned against him all his life, would never lie down to sleep until he had swept his back trail. Koots knew he would make a wide circle out across the ground that they had already travelled. If an enemy was following them, Xhia would have cut his tracks.

Koots smoked his pipe down to the last crumb, savouring every breath. Then, regretfully, he knocked out the ash. With

447

a sigh he settled down under his kaross and closed his eyes. He did not know how long he had slept, but he woke with a light touch on his cheek. As he started up Xhia made a soft, clucking sound to calm him.

'What is it?' Instinctively Koots kept his voice low.

'Strangers,' Xhia replied. 'They follow us.'

'Men?' Koots's wits were still fuddled with sleep. Xhia did not deign to answer such an inanity. 'Who? How many?' Koots insisted, as he sat up.

Quickly Xhia twisted a spill of dried grass. Before he lit it he held up a corner of Koots's kaross as a screen from watching eyes. Then he held the spill to the dying ash of the fire. He blew on the coals, and when the spill burst into flame he screened it with the kaross and his own body. He held something in his free hand. Koots peered at it. It was a scrap of soiled white cloth.

'Ripped from a man's clothing by thorns,' Xhia told him. Then he showed his next trophy, a single strand of black hair. Even Koots realized at once that it was a human hair, but it was too black and coarse to have come from the head of a northern European and it was too straight, free of kinks, to have come from the head of a Bushman or an African tribesman.

'This rag comes from a long robe such as Mussulmen wear. This hair from his head.'

'Mussulman?' Koots asked in surprise, and Xhia clicked in assent. Koots had learned better than to argue.

'How many?'

'Four.'

'Where are they now?'

'Lying close. They are watching us.' Xhia let the burning spill drop and rubbed out the last sparks in the dust with the palm of his childlike hand.

'Where have they left their horses?' Koots asked. 'If they had smelt ours they would have whinnied.'

'No horses. They come on foot.'

'Arabs on foot! Then, whoever they are, that is what they are after.' Koots pulled on his boots. 'They want our horses.'

Careful to keep a low profile, he crawled to where Oudeman was snoring softly and shook him. Once Oudeman was fully awake he grasped quickly what was happening, and understood Koots's orders.

'No gunfire!' Koots repeated. 'In the dark there is too much risk of hitting the horses. Take them with cold steel.'

Koots and Oudeman crept to each of the troopers, and whispered the orders. The men rolled out of their blankets, and slipped singly down to the horse pickets. With drawn sabres they lay up among shrub and low brush.

Koots placed himself on the southern perimeter furthest from the faint glow of the dying campfire. He lay flat against the earth, so that any man approaching the pickets would be silhouetted against the stars and the fading traces of the great comet, by now only an ethereal ghost in the western sky. Orion was no longer obliterated by its light: at this season of the year he was standing on his head below the dazzle of the Milky Way. Koots covered his eyes to enhance his night vision. He listened with all his attention, and opened his eyes only briefly, so that they would not be tricked by the light.

Time passed slowly. He measured it by the turning of the heavenly bodies. For any other man it might have been hard to keep his level of concentration screwed up to the main, but Koots was a warrior. He had to close his ears to the mundane sounds made by the horses as they shifted their weight or cropped a mouthful of grass.

The last glimmer of the great comet was low on the western horizon before Koots heard the click of two pebbles striking together. Every nerve in his body snapped taut. A minute later, and much closer, there came the slither of a leather sandal on the soft earth. He kept his head low, and saw a dark shape move against the stars.

He is closing in, he thought. Let him start to work on the ropes.

The intruder paused when he reached the head of the horselines. Koots saw his head turn slowly as he listened. He wore a turban and his beard bushed and curled. After a long minute he stooped over the running line to which the head halters of the horses were secured by steel rings. Two of the animals jerked their heads free as the line slipped through the rings.

As soon as Koots guessed that the intruder was absorbed in unravelling the next knot he rose to his feet and moved towards him. But he lost sight of him as he crouched below the skyline. He was no longer where Koots expected him to be, and abruptly Koots stumbled up against him in the darkness. Koots shouted to warn his men, then the two of them were struggling chest to chest, too close for Koots to use his blade.

Koots realized at once that the man he was wrestling was a formidable adversary. He twisted like an eel in his grip, and he felt all hard muscle and sinew. Koots tried to knee his groin, but his kneecap was almost torn loose as it struck the hard, rubbery muscle of the man's thigh instead of the soft bunch of his genitals. In an instantaneous riposte the man slammed the heel of his right hand up under Koots's jaw. His head snapped back and it felt as though his neck was broken as he went over backwards and sprawled on the ground. He saw the intruder rearing over him and the glint of his blade as it went up high for the forehand cut to his head. Koots threw up his own sabre in an instinctive parry, and steel thrilled on steel as the blades met.

The intruder broke off the attack and disappeared into the darkness. Koots crawled to his knees, still half stunned. There were shouts and the sound of blows from all around, and he heard both Oudeman and Richter bellowing orders and encouragement to the others. Then there was the bang and flash of a pistol shot. That galvanized Koots.

'Don't shoot, you fools! The horses! Have a care for the horses!' He pulled himself to his feet, and at that moment heard the clatter of shod hoofs behind him. He glanced around and saw the dark outline of a horseman bearing down upon him at full gallop. A sword glinted dully in the starlight and Koots ducked. The blade hissed past his cheek, and he glimpsed the turbaned head and beard of the rider as he raced by.

Wildly he looked about him. Nearby, the grey mare was a pale blob against the darker background. She was the fastest and strongest of the entire string. He sheathed his sword, and checked the pistol in the holster at his hip as he ran to her. As soon as he was astride her back he listened for the sound of hoofs, turned her with his knees and kicked her into a full gallop.

Every few minutes during the next hours he was forced to stop and listen for the fugitive's hoofbeats. Although the Arab often twisted and turned to throw off Koots's pursuit he always headed back towards the north. An hour before dawn Koots lost the sound of him altogether. Either he had turned again or he had slowed his mount to a walk.

North! He is set on north, he decided.

He placed the great Southern Cross squarely over his shoulder and rode into the north, keeping to a steady canter that would not burn up the mare. The dawn came up with startling rapidity. His horizon expanded as the darkness drew back, and his heart bounced as he made out the dark shape moving not a pistol shot ahead of him. He knew at once that it was not one of the larger species of antelope, for the shape of the rider upon its back was plain to see against the lightening veld. Koots pushed the mare harder and came up on him swiftly. The rider was not yet aware of him and was holding his horse to a walk. Koots recognized the bay gelding, a good strong mount, almost a match for his mare.

'Son of the great whore!' Koots laughed with triumph. 'The bay has gone lame. No wonder he had to slow down.' Even in this poor light it was plain to see that the gelding was favouring his off fore. He must have picked up a sharp stone or a thorn in the frog, and he was making heavy weather of it. Koots raced down upon them, and the fugitive swivelled round. Koots saw that he was a hawk-faced Arab, with a curling bush of beard. He took one quick look at Koots, then flogged the gelding into a laboured gallop.

Koots was close enough to risk a pistol shot and try to end it swiftly. He threw up his weapon and fired for the centre of the Arab's broad back. It must have been close for the Arab ducked and shouted, 'Swords, infidel! Man to man!'

As an ensign Koots had spent years with the VOC army in

the Orient. His Arabic was fluent and colloquial. 'Those are sweet words!' he shouted back. 'Stand and let me thrust them down your throat.'

Within two hundred yards the gelding was pulled up. The Arab slipped off his back, and turned to face Koots, flourishing the naval cutlass in his right hand. Koots realized he had no firearm: if he had carried a musket when he entered the camp, he had lost it somewhere along the way. He was dismounted, and had only the cutlass – and, of course, a dagger. An Arab always had a dagger. Koots had a great advantage, and no quixotic notions ever entered his calculations. He would exploit it to the full. He charged straight down on the Arab, leaning out to sabre him from horseback.

The Arab was quicker than he anticipated. As soon as he read Koots's intention, he feinted away from the charge and then, at the last moment, darted back under his sword arm, brushing down the flank of the running mare with the grace of a toreador leaning inside the horns of the charging bull. At the same time he reached up, grabbed a handful of the skirt of Koots's leather coat and threw all his weight on it. It was so sudden and unexpected that Koots was taken by surprise. He was leaning far out from his mount's bare back, without stirrups or reins to steady himself, and he was hauled bodily off the mare.

But Koots was a fighting man too, and, like a cat, he landed on his feet with his grip on the hilt of his sabre. The Arab went for the forehand cut to the head again. Then immediately he reversed and cut low for the Achilles tendon. Koots met the first stroke, deflecting it with a twist of the wrist, but the second was so fast that he had to jump over the swing of the cutlass. He was in balance when he landed and thrust straight at the Arab's dark glittering eyes. The Arab rolled his head and let the stroke fly over his shoulder, but so close that it razored a tuft of his beard from below his ear. They sprang apart and circled each other. Neither was even breathing hard: two warriors in peak condition.

'What is your name, son of the false prophet?' Koots asked easily. 'I like to know who I am killing.'

'My name is Kadem ibn Abubaker al-Jurf, infidel,' he said softly, but his eyes glittered at the insult. 'And, apart from Eater-of-Dung, what do men call you?'

'I am Captain Herminius Koots of the army of the VOC.'

'Ah!' said Kadem. 'Your fame goes ahead of you. You are married to the pretty little whore named Nella who has been fucked by every man who ever visited Good Hope. Even I had a few guilders' worth of her behind the hedge of the Company gardens when I was in the colony only a short while ago. I commend you. She knows her trade and enjoys her work.'

The insult was so barbed and unexpected that Koots gaped at him – the Arab even knew her name. His sword arm faltered with the shock. On the instant Kadem was at him again, and he had to scramble backwards to avoid the attack. They circled and came together, and this time Koots managed a touch high on his left shoulder. But it barely scratched the skin and no more than a few scarlet drops showed through the thin soiled cotton sleeve of Kadem's robe.

They essayed a dozen more passes without a hit, and then Kadem scored, slicing open Koots's hip, but only skin deep. The blood made it look worse than it was. Nevertheless Koots gave ground for the first time, and his sword arm ached. He regretted that wasted pistol shot. Kadem was smiling, a thin reptilian curl of the lips, and suddenly, as Koots had expected, a thin curved dagger appeared in his left hand.

Then Kadem came on again, very fast, leading with his right foot, his blade turning into a darting sunbeam, and Koots went back before it. His heel caught on a patch of thorns and he nearly fell, but recovered with a sideways twist that jarred his spine. Kadem broke off again and circled out left. He had read Koots accurately. Left was his weak side. Kadem was not to know that, years ago, during the fighting before Jaffna, he had taken a ball through that knee. It was aching now and he was panting for breath. Kadem came on again, steely and relentless.

By now Koots was flailing his blade a little, not thrusting straight and hard. His breath whistled in his own ears. He knew that it would not be much longer. The sweat burned his eyes, and Kadem's face blurred.

Then, abruptly, Kadem pulled back and lowered his cutlass. He was staring over Koots's shoulder. It might have been a ruse, and Koots refused to respond. He watched the dagger in Kadem's left hand, trying to steady and compose himself for the next pass.

Then he heard the sound of hoofs behind him. He turned slowly, and there were Oudeman and Richter mounted and fully armed, Xhia leading them. Kadem let both the dagger and the cutlass drop from his hand, but still he stood with his chin lifted and his shoulders squared.

'Shall I kill the swine-pig, Captain?' Oudeman asked, as he rode up. His carbine was resting across the saddle in front of him. Koots almost gave the order. He was shaken and angry. He knew how close he had come, and Kadem had called Nella a whore. It was the truth, but death to any man who uttered it in Koots's hearing. Then he checked himself. The man had spoken of Good Hope. There was something to learn from that, and later Koots would kill him with his own hands. That would give him more pleasure than letting Oudeman do it for him.

'I want to hear more from him. Tie him behind your horse.'

It was almost two leagues back to camp. They bound Kadem's wrists together and tied the other end of the rope to the snap-ring on the wing of Oudeman's saddle. He dragged Kadem at a trot. When he fell Oudeman jerked him to his feet again, but each time Kadem lost a piece of skin from where his elbows or his knees struck the hard ground. He was coated with a paste of dust, sweat and blood when Oudeman dragged him into the camp.

Koots swung down from the back of the grey mare, and went to inspect the other three Arab prisoners that Oudeman had captured.

'Names?' he demanded of the two who seemed uninjured.

'Rashood, *effendi*.'

'Habban, *effendi*.' They touched their foreheads and breasts in respect and submission. He went to the third prisoner, who was wounded. He lay groaning, curled like a foetus in the womb.

'Name?' Koots said, and kicked him in the belly. The wounded man groaned louder, and fresh blood trickled from between his fingers where he was clutching his stomach. Koots glanced at Oudeman.

'Stupid Goffel,' Oudeman explained. 'He was carried away with excitement. Forgot your orders and shot him. It's in the belly. He won't live until tomorrow.'

'So! Better this than one of the horses,' Koots said, and drew the pistol from the holster on his sword belt. He cocked it and held the muzzle to the back of the wounded man's head. At the shot the prisoner stiffened, his eyes rolled back in their sockets. His legs kicked spasmodically, then lay still.

'Waste of good powder,' said Oudeman. 'Should have let me use the knife.'

'I haven't had my breakfast yet, and you know how squeamish I can be.' Koots smiled at his own sense of humour and returned the smoking pistol to its holster. He waved his hand towards the other prisoners, 'Give them each ten with the *sjambok* across the soles of both feet to put them in a friendlier mood, and as soon as I have finished my breakfast I will speak to them again.'

Koots ate a bowl of stew made from the shanks of the hartebeest, and watched Oudeman and Richter lay on the *sjambok* to the bare feet of the Arab captives.

'Hard men.' Koots gave grudging approval when the only sound they made was a small grunt to the fall of each stroke. He knew what agony they were enduring. Koots wiped out the bowl with a finger and sucked it as he went back to squat in front of Kadem. Despite his torn and dusty robe, the cuts and abrasions that covered his limbs, Kadem was so obviously the leader that Koots wasted no time on the others. He glanced up at Oudeman and indicated Rashood and Habban. 'Take these pig-swine away.'

Oudeman knew that he wanted them out of earshot while he questioned Kadem so that they would not hear his replies. Later he would question them separately and compare their responses. Koots waited until the Hottentot troopers had dragged them, limping on their swollen feet, to a tree and tied them to its trunk. Then he turned back to Kadem. 'So you visited the Cape of Good Hope, Beloved of Allah?'

Kadem stared back at him with fanatical, glittering eyes in his dusty face. However, the mention of the place stirred something in Oudeman's sluggish mind. He fetched one of the muskets they had captured from the Arabs and handed it to his captain. Koots's first glance at the weapon was perfunctory.

'The butt-stock.' Oudeman directed his attention. 'See the emblem in the wood?'

Koots's eyes narrowed and his lips formed a thin, hard line as he traced the design that had been burned into the wood with a branding iron. It depicted a cannon, a long-barrelled nine-pounder on a two-wheeled carriage, and in the ribbon below it the initials CBTC.

'Good, so!' Koots looked up and stared at Kadem. 'You are one of Tom and Dorian Courtney's men.'

Koots saw something flare in the depths of those dark eyes, but it was so swiftly hidden again that he could not be certain of it, but the emotion the names had engendered was passionate. It might have been loyalty, dedication or something different. Koots sat and stared at him. 'You know my wife,' Koots reminded him, 'and I might have to castrate you for the way you spoke of her. But do you know the Courtney brothers, Tom and Dorian? If you do, it might just save your balls.'

Kadem stared back at him, and Koots spoke to Oudeman: 'Sergeant, lift his skirts that we can judge how big is the knife we must use for the job.'

Oudeman grinned and knelt beside Kadem, but before he could touch him Kadem spoke.

'I know Dorian Courtney, but his Arabic name is al-Salil.'

'The Red-headed One,' Koots agreed. 'Yes, I have heard him called that. What of his brother, Tom? The one whom men also call Klebe, the hawk.'

'I know them both,' Kadem affirmed.

'You are their hireling, their creature, their lackey, their lickspittle?' Koots chose his words with care to provoke him.

'I am their implacable enemy.' Kadem rushed into the trap, his pride bristling. 'If Allah is kind, then one day I will be their executioner.'

He said it with such fierce sincerity that Koots believed him. He said nothing, for often silence is the best form of interrogation.

Kadem was by now so agitated that he burst out: 'I am the bearer of the sacred *fatwa* entrusted to me by my master the ruler of Oman, Caliph Zayn al-Din ibn al-Malik.'

'Why would such a noble and mighty monarch entrust such a mission to a miserable slice of rancid pork fat such as you?' Koots gave a mocking laugh. Although Oudeman had not understood a word of the Arabic exchanges he laughed like an echo.

'I am a prince of the royal blood,' Kadem avowed angrily. 'My father was the Caliph's brother. I am his nephew. The Caliph trusts me because I command his legions and I have proven myself to him a hundred times over in war and in peace.'

'Yet you have failed to accomplish this sacred *fatwa* of yours,' Koots taunted him. 'Your enemies still flourish, and you are in rags, tied to a tree and covered with filth. Is that the Omani ideal of a mighty warrior?'

'I have slain the incestuous sister of the Caliph, which was part of the task I was given, and I have stabbed al-Salil so deeply and grievously that he might still perish of the wound. If he does not, I will not rest until my duty is accomplished.'

'All this is the raving of a madman.' Koots smirked at him. 'If you are driven by this sacred duty, why do I find you wandering like a beggar in the wilderness, dressed in filthy rags, carrying a musket with al-Salil's emblem branded on it, trying to steal a horse on which to escape?'

Skilfully Koots milked the information out of his captive. Kadem boasted of how he had inveigled himself on board the *Gift of Allah*. How he had waited his opportunity, and how he had struck. He described his assassination of the Princess Yasmini, and how he had come so close to killing al-Salil also. Then he described how, with the help of his three followers,

457

he had escaped from the Courtney ship while it lay in the lagoon, how they had avoided the pursuit and at last had stumbled on Koots's troop.

There was much in this account that was entirely new to Koots, especially the flight of the Courtneys from the colony of Good Hope. This must have taken place long after he had left in pursuit of Jim Courtney. However, all of it was logical and he could detect no weak spots in the story, nor any attempt to deceive him in Kadem's rendition of it. Everything seemed to fit neatly into what he knew of Keyser and his intentions. It was also the kind of resourceful enterprise that Tom and Dorian Courtney between them might devise.

He believed it, with reservations. There were always reservations. Yes! he gloated inwardly, without letting it show in his expression. This is an extraordinary stroke of fortune, he thought. I have been sent an ally I can bind to me by chains of steel, a religious *fatwa* and a burning hatred beside which even my own determination pales.

Koots stared hard at Kadem while he made his decision. He had lived among the Mussulmen, fought for and against them long enough to understand the teachings of Islam and the immutable codes of honour that bound them.

'I also am the sworn enemy of the Courtneys,' he said at last. He saw the naked passion in Kadem's eyes veiled immediately.

Have I made a fatal mistake? he wondered. Have I rushed too swiftly to my purpose, and startled my quarry? He watched Kadem's suspicion growing stronger. However, I have taken the plunge now, and I cannot go back. Koots turned to Oudeman. 'Loosen his bonds,' he ordered, 'and bring water for him to wash and drink. Give him food to eat and let him pray. But watch him carefully. I don't think he will try to escape, but do not give him the chance.'

Oudeman looked mystified by these orders. 'What about his men?' he asked uncertainly.

'Keep them tied up and under close guard,' Koots told him. 'Don't let Kadem speak to them. Don't let him go near them.'

Koots waited until after Kadem had bathed, eaten and

carried out the solemn ritual of the midday prayers. Only then did he send for him to continue their conversation.

Koots observed the polite form of greeting and, in so doing, changed Kadem's status from that of captive to guest, with all the responsibilities that that relationship placed on both of them. Then he went on. 'The reason why you find me here, in the wilderness so far from the civilized abodes of men, is that I am following the same quest as you. Behold these wagon tracks.' He pointed them out, and Kadem glanced at them. Of course he had noticed them while he had stalked the horses and closed in on the camp.

'Do you see them?' Koots insisted.

Kadem's face set in a stony expression. He was already regretting his previous indiscretions. He should never have let his emotions run away with his tongue and revealed so much to the infidel. By now he had recognized that Koots was a clever, dangerous man.

'These tracks were made by four wagons that are being driven by the only son of Tom Courtney, whom you know as Klebe.' Kadem blinked but showed no other expression. Koots let him think about that for a while. Then he explained why Jim Courtney had been forced to leave the colony.

Although Kadem listened in silence and his eyes showed no more emotion than those of a cobra, he was thinking furiously. While he had been masquerading as a lowly seaman aboard the *Gift of Allah* he had heard all this discussed by his companions. He knew about Jim Courtney's flight from Good Hope.

'If we follow these wagon tracks, we can be certain that they will lead us to the place somewhere on the coast where father and son have agreed to meet,' Koots finished, and again they were silent.

Kadem thought about what Koots had told him. He turned it over and back and forth in his mind, the way a jeweller examines a precious stone for impurities. He could detect no false notes in Koots's version of events. 'What do you want of me?' he asked, at last.

'We share the same purpose,' Koots answered. 'I propose a

pact, an alliance. Let us take the oath together in the sight of God and his Prophet. Let us dedicate ourselves to the total destruction of our mutual enemies.'

'I agree to that,' said Kadem, and the mad glitter he had so carefully masked returned to his eyes. Koots found it unsettling, more menacing than the cutlass and dagger in the Arab's hands when they had fought that morning.

They took the oath beneath the towering branches of a camel-thorn tree, in which new growth had already burgeoned to replace that which had been devoured by the locust swarms. They swore on the blade and the haft of Kadem's Damascus-steel dagger. Each placed a pinch of coarse salt on the other's tongue. They shared a slice of venison, swallowing a morsel each. With the razor-sharp Damascus blade they opened a vein in their right wrists, then massaged the arm until the blood was flowing bright and warm down into their cupped palms. Then they clasped hands so that their blood mingled, and maintained the grip while Kadem recited the wondrous names of God. At last they embraced.

'You are my brother in blood,' said Kadem, and his voice trembled in awe at the binding power of the oath.

'You are my brother in blood,' Koots said. Though his voice was firm and clear and his gaze into Kadem's eyes was steady, the oath sat lightly upon his conscience. Koots recognized no God, especially not the foreign deity of a dark-skinned, inferior race. The profit in the bargain was all his for he could turn away from it when the time came, even kill his new blood-brother with impunity if it were called for. He knew that Kadem was bound by his hope of salvation and the wrath of his God.

Deep in his heart Kadem recognized the fragility of the bond between them. That evening as they shared the campfire and ate meat together, he showed how astute he was. He gave Koots an undertaking more poignant than any religious oath. 'I have told you that I am the favourite of my uncle, the Caliph. You know also the power and riches of the Omani empire. Its realm encompasses a great ocean and the Red and Persian Seas. My uncle has promised me great reward if I carry his *fatwa* to a successful conclusion. You and I have sworn, as brothers in blood, to dedicate ourselves to that end. Once it is done we will return together to the Caliph's palace on Lamu island, and to his gratitude. You will embrace Islam. I will request my uncle to place you in command of all his armies on the African mainland. I will ask him to make you governor of the provinces of Monamatapa, the land from which come the gold and slaves of Opet. You will become a man of power and wealth uncountable.'

The spring tides of Herminius Koots's life were beginning to flow strongly.

Now they moved along the wagon trail with renewed determination. Even Xhia was infected with this enhanced sense of purpose. Twice they cut the trail of herds of elephant coming down out of the north lands. Perhaps in some mysterious way the elephant were aware of the bounty the rains had brought upon the land. From afar Koots surveyed the massed herds of these grey giants through the lens of his telescope, but he showed only a passing interest in them. He would not let a hunt for a few ivory tusks deter him from his main quest.

He ordered Xhia to detour round the herds and they went onwards, leaving them unmolested. Both Koots and Kadem grudged every hour of delay and they drove horses and men hard along the tracks of their quarry.

They passed out of the wide swath that the locusts had cut through the land and left the great plains behind them. They entered a lovely land of rivers and lush forests, and the air tasted as sweet as the perfume of wild flowers. Scenes of great beauty and grandeur surrounded them, and the promise of riches and glory led them onwards.

'We are not far behind the wagons now,' Xhia promised them, 'and each day we draw closer.'

Then they came to a confluence of two rivers, a wide, deep flow and a smaller tributary. Xhia was amazed by what he found there. He led Koots and Kadem through the field of rotting, sun-dried human remains, which had been chewed and scattered by the hyena and other scavengers. He did not have to point out to them the discarded spears and *assegais* and the rawhide shields, most of them shot through by musket fire. 'There was great battle here,' Xhia told them. 'These shields and weapons are those of the fierce Nguni tribes.'

Koots nodded. No man who had lived and travelled in Africa as he had could have been ignorant of the legend of the warrior tribes of the Nguni. 'Good, so!' he said. 'Tell us what else you see here.'

'The Nguni attacked the wagons Somoya had drawn up here, across the neck between the two rivers. That was a good place for him, his back and both his sides protected by the water. The Nguni had to come at him from the front. He killed them like chickens.' Xhia giggled and shook his head with admiration.

Koots walked across to the crater in the middle of the area of devastated ground in front of which the wagons had stood. 'What is this?' he asked. 'What happened here?'

Xhia picked a short length of charred slow-match out of the dirt, and brandished it. Even though he had seen fuse and explosives used before, he did not have the vocabulary to describe it. Instead he mimed the act of lighting the slow-match and made a sizzling sound as he ran along the path the flame must have taken. When he reached the crater he shouted, 'Ba-poof!' and leaped high into the air to illustrate the explosion. Then he fell on his back and kicked both legs, shrieking with laughter. It was so expressive that even Koots had to laugh.

'By the pox-ridden vagina of the great whore,' he guffawed, 'the Courtney puppy let off a mine under the *impis* as they stormed the wagons. We will have to take care when we catch up with him. He has grown as crafty as his father.'

It took Xhia the rest of the day to unravel all the secrets of the battlefield, spread out as it was over such a vast stretch of the veld. He showed Koots the path the routed *impis* had taken, and how Jim Courtney and his men had chased them on horseback and shot them down as they ran.

They came at last to the abandoned Nguni encampment, and Xhia became almost incoherent as he realized the extent of the cattle herds Jim had captured. 'Like the grass! Like the locusts!' he squeaked, as he pointed out the spoor the herds had trodden as they were driven away eastwards.

'A thousand?' Koots wondered. 'Five thousand, or maybe more?'

He tried to form a rough estimate of the value of these cattle if he could get them to Good Hope.

There are not enough guilders in the Bank of Batavia, he concluded. One thing is certain. When I catch up with them, Oudeman and these stinking Hottentots will not see a single centime. I will kill them first, before I hand over a guilder. By the time I am finished here I will make Governor van de Witten look like a pauper in comparison.

That was not the end of it. When they entered the camp Xhia led him to the far side of the encampment where a stockade stood, made of stout timber poles lashed together with strips of bark.

Koots had never seen such a sturdy construction, even in the permanent villages of the tribes. Is it a grain store? he wondered, as he dismounted and entered. He was further puzzled when he found that it contained what seemed to be drying or smoking racks. However, there was no sign of ash or scorched areas beneath them. As with the construction of the walls, the timber used seemed too massive for such a simple purpose. It was clear that the racks had been designed to support a much greater weight than strips of meat.

Xhia was trying to tell him something. He jumped up on the racks and repeated the word 'chicken'. Koots frowned irritably. This was no hen coop, nor even an ostrich coop. Koots shook his head. Xhia began another mime, holding one arm in front of his face like a long nose, and flapping his other hand from the side of his head like an ear. Koots puzzled over the meaning, then remembered that the San words for 'chicken' and 'elephant' were almost identical.

'Elephant?' he asked, and touched the elephant-hide belt at his waist.

'Yes! Yes! You stupid man.' Xhia nodded vigorously.

'Are you mad?' Koots asked in Dutch. 'An elephant would never fit through that doorway.'

Xhia leaped down from the rack and ferreted around under it. Then he crawled out again. He showed Koots what he had found. It was an immature tusk, taken from an elephant calf. It was only as long as Xhia's forearm and so slim that he could encircle it at the thickest point with thumb and finger. It must have been overlooked when the storeroom was emptied. Xhia waved it in Koots's face.

'Ivory?' Koots began to understand. Five years previously, when he was acting as aide-de-camp to the governor of Batavia, the governor had made an official visit to the Sultan of Zanzibar. The Sultan was proud of his collection of ivory tusks. He had invited the governor and his staff to tour his treasury and view the contents. The ivory had been laid out on racks much like these, to keep it off the damp floor.

'Ivory!' Koots breathed hard. 'These are ivory racks!' He imagined the tusks stacked high, and tried to estimate the value of such a treasure. 'In the name of the black angel, this is another great fortune to match the plundered herds of cattle.'

He turned and strode out of the shed. 'Sergeant!' he bellowed. 'Sergeant Oudeman, get the men mounted up. Kick the brown backsides of our Arab friends. We ride at once. We must catch Jim Courtney before he reaches the coast and comes under the protection of the guns on his father's ships.'

They rode eastwards along the spoor of the cattle herds, a beaten roadway almost a mile wide, along which the cattle had grazed and trodden down the grass.

'A blind man could follow this on a moonless night,' Koots told Kadem, who rode beside him.

'What a fine bait this piglet of the great hog will make for our trap,' Kadem agreed, with grim determination. They expected to come up with the wagons and the herds of plundered cattle at any moment. However, day succeeded day,

464

and although they rode hard and Koots took every opportunity to spy out the land ahead through his telescope they caught no glimpse of either cattle or wagons.

Each day Xhia assured them that they were gaining rapidly. From the sign he was able to tell Koots that Jim Courtney was hunting for elephant while his caravan was on the march.

'This is slowing him down?' Koots asked.

'No, no, he hunts far ahead of the wagons.'

'Then we can surprise the caravan while he is not with them to defend them.'

'We have to catch up with them first,' said Kadem, and Xhia cautioned Koots that if they approached Jim Courtney's caravan too closely before they were ready to attack it, Bakkat would immediately discover their presence. 'In just the same way as I discovered that these brown baboons,' he indicated Kadem and his Arabs disdainfully, 'were creeping up on us. Although Bakkat is no match for Xhia, the mighty hunter, in stealth and wizard-craft, neither is he a fool. I have seen his footprints and his sign where he swept his back trail every evening before the wagons went into camp.'

'How do you know it is Bakkat's sign?' Koots demanded.

'Bakkat is my enemy, and I can pick out his footprints from those of any other man that walks this land.' Then Xhia pointed out other circumstances that Koots had not taken into consideration before. The signs showed clearly that Jim Courtney had made other additions to his retinue apart from the herds of captured cattle: men, many men – Xhia thought there were at least fifty and that there might be as many as a hundred additional men to face them when they attacked the wagons. Xhia had employed all his genius and wizardry to determine the character and condition of these new men.

'They are big, proud men. That I can tell by the manner in which they carry themselves, by the size of their feet and the length of their stride,' he told Koots. 'They bear arms and are freemen, not captives or slaves. They follow Somoya willingly and they guard and care for his herds. It comes to me that these are Nguni who will fight like warriors.' Koots was learning from experience that it was best to accept the little

Bushman's opinion. So far he had never been wrong in such matters.

With such quantity and quality of reinforcements added to the hard core of mounted musketeers, Jim Courtney had now mustered a formidable force which Koots dared not underestimate.

'We are outnumbered many times over. It will be a hard fight.' Koots weighed these new odds.

'Surprise,' said Kadem. 'We have the element of surprise. We can choose our time and place to attack.'

'Yes,' Koots agreed. By this time his opinion of the Arab as a warrior had been much enhanced. 'We must not waste that advantage.'

Eleven days later they came to the brink of a deep escarpment. There were tall snow-capped mountain peaks to the south, but ahead the land dropped away steeply in a confusion of hills, valleys and forest. Koots dismounted and steadied his spyglass on Xhia's shoulder. Then, suddenly, he shouted aloud as he picked out in the blue distance the even bluer tint of the ocean. 'Yes!' he cried. 'I was right all along. Jim Courtney is headed for Nativity Bay to join up with his father's ships. That is the coast less than a hundred leagues ahead.' Before he could fully articulate his satisfaction at having pursued the quest so far, something even more compelling caught Koots's eye.

In the wide expanse of land and forest below him he descried drifts of pale dust dispersed over a wide area, and when he turned the glass on these clouds he saw beneath them the movement of the massed herds of cattle, slow and dark as spilled oil spreading on the carpet of the veld.

'Mother of Satan!' he cried. 'There they are! I have them at last.' With a mighty effort he checked his warlike instinct to ride down on them immediately. Instead he cautioned himself to consider all the circumstances and eventualities that he and Kadem had discussed so earnestly over the past days.

'They are moving slowly, at the speed of the grazing herds. We can afford the time to rest our own men and horses and

466

prepare ourselves for the attack. In the meantime I will send Xhia ahead to scout Jim Courtney's dispositions, to learn his line of march, the character of his new men, and the order of battle of his horsemen.'

Kadem nodded agreement as he surveyed the ground below them. 'We might circle out ahead and lie in ambush. Perhaps in a narrow pass through the hills or at a river crossing. Order Xhia to have an eye for a place such as that.'

'Whatever happens, we must not let them join up with the ships that might already be waiting for them in Nativity Bay,' said Koots. 'We must attack before that happens, or we will be facing cannon and grape-shot as well as muskets and spears.'

Koots lowered the telescope, and grabbed Xhia by the scruff of his neck to impress upon him the seriousness of his orders. Xhia listened earnestly, and understood at least every second word that Koots growled at him.

'I will find you here when I return,' Xhia agreed, when Koots ended his harangue. Then he trotted away down the escarpment wall without looking back. He did not have to make any further preparations for the task ahead of him, for Xhia carried upon his sturdy back every possession he owned.

It was a little before noon when he set out, and late afternoon before he was close enough to the cattle herds to hear their distant lowing. He was careful to cover his own sign, and not to approach any closer. Despite his braggadocio he held Bakkat's powers in high respect. He circled round the herds to find the exact position of Somoya's wagons. The cattle had trodden the tracks and confused the sign, so it was difficult even for him to read as much from them as he wanted.

He came up level with the wagons but a league out to the north of their line of march when suddenly he stopped. His heart began to pound like the hoofbeats of a galloping herd of zebra. He stared down at the dainty little footprint in the dust.

'Bakkat,' he whispered. 'My enemy. I would know your sign anywhere, for it is imprinted on my heart.'

All Koots's orders and exhortations were wiped from his mind and he concentrated all his powers on the spoor. 'He goes quickly and with purpose. In a straight line, not pausing

467

or hesitating. He shows no caution. If ever I can surprise him, this is the day.'

Without another thought he turned aside from his original purpose and followed the tracks of Bakkat, whom he hated above all else in his world.

I n the early morning Bakkat heard the honey-guide. It was fluttering in the treetops, chittering and uttering that particular whirring sound that could mean only one thing. His mouth watered.

'I greet you, my sweet friend,' he called, and ran to stand beneath the tree in which the drab little bird was performing its seductive gyrations. Its movements became more frenzied when it saw that it had attracted Bakkat's attention. It left the branch on which it was displaying and flitted to the next tree.

Bakkat hesitated, and glanced round at the square of wagons laagered at the edge of the forest on the far side of the glade, a mile away. If he were to take the time to run back merely to tell Somoya where he was going, the bird might become discouraged and fly away before he returned. Somoya might forbid him to follow it. Bakkat smacked his lips: he could almost taste the sweet, viscous honey on his tongue. He lusted for it. 'I will not be away long,' he consoled himself. 'Somoya will not even know that I am gone. He and Welanga are probably playing with their little wooden dolls.' This was Bakkat's opinion of the carved chessmen that so often occupied the couple to the exclusion of everything around them. Bakkat ran after the bird.

The honey-guide saw him coming and sang to him as it flitted on to the next tree, then the next. Bakkat sang as he followed: 'You lead me to sweetness, and I love you for it. You are more beautiful than the sunbird, wiser than the owl, greater than the eagle. You are the lord of all birds.' Which was not true, but the honey-guide would be flattered to hear it.

Bakkat ran through the forest for the rest of that morning,

and in the noonday when the forest sweltered in the heat, and all the animals and birds were silent and somnolent, the bird stopped at last in the top branches of a tambootie tree, and changed its melody.

Bakkat understood what it was telling him: 'We have arrived. This is the place of the hive, and it overflows with golden honey. Now you and I will eat our fill.'

Bakkat stood beneath the tambootie and threw back his head as he peered upwards. He saw the bees, highlighted by the low sunlight like golden dust motes, as they darted into the cleft in the tree trunk. Bakkat took from his shoulder his bow and quiver, his axe and leather carrying bag. He laid them carefully at the base of the tree. The honey-guide would understand that this was his guarantee that he would return. However, to make certain there was no misunderstanding, Bakkat explained it to the bird: 'Wait for me here, my little friend. I will not be gone long. I must gather the vine to lull the bees.'

He found the plant he needed growing on the bank of a nearby stream. It climbed the trunk of a lead-wood tree, wrapping round it like a slender serpent. The leaves were shaped like teardrops, and the tiny flowers were scarlet. Bakkat was gentle as he harvested the leaves he needed, careful not to damage the plant more than he had to for it was a precious thing. To kill it would be a sin against nature and his own people, the San.

With the wad of leaves in his pouch he moved on until he reached a grove of fever trees. He picked out one whose trunk was the right girth for his needs and ring-barked it. Then he peeled off a section and rolled it into a tube, which he secured with twists of bark string. He ran back to the honey tree. When the bird saw him return, it burst into hysterical chitterings of relief.

Bakkat squatted at the foot of the tree and made a tiny fire inside the bark tube. He blew into one end to create a draught, and the coals glowed hotly. He scattered a few of the flowers and the leaves of the vine on to them. As they smouldered they emitted clouds of pungent smoke. Bakkat stood up, hooked the blade of the axe over his shoulder and began to climb the tree. He went up as swiftly as a vervet monkey. Just below the cleft in the trunk he found a convenient branch and took a seat on it. He sniffed the waxy odour of the hive and listened for a moment to the deep murmurous voice of the swarm in the depths of the hollow trunk. He studied the entrance to the hive and marked his first cut, then placed one end of the bark tube into the opening and gently blew puffs of the smoke into it. After a while the humming of the swarm fell into silence as the bees were sedated and lulled.

Bakkat laid aside the smoke tube and braced himself, balancing easily on the narrow branch. He swung the axe. As the blow reverberated through the trunk a few bees came out and buzzed around his head, but the smoke of the vine leaves had dulled their warlike instincts. One or two stung him, but Bakkat ignored them. With quick, powerful axe strokes he cut a square hatchway in the hollow trunk, and exposed the serried ranks of honeycombs.

Then he climbed down to the ground and laid aside the axe. He returned to his perch on the branch with the leather bag over his shoulder. He scattered more vine leaves on the coals in the fire tube, and blew clouds of the thick, pungent smoke into the enlarged entrance. When the swarm was silent again he reached deep into the hive. With bees flowing over his arms and shoulders, he lifted out the combs one at a time and laid them gently in the bag. When the hive was empty he thanked the bees for their bounty, and apologized to them for his cruel treatment.

'Very soon you will recover from the smoke I have given you, and you will be able to repair your hive and fill it once again with honey. Bakkat will always be your friend, and he feels only great respect and gratitude towards you,' he told the bees.

He climbed down to the ground and cut a curl of bark from the trunk of the tambootie tree to form a tray on which he could lay out the honey-guide's share of the booty. He selected the choicest comb for his little friend and accomplice, one that was full of the yellow grubs, for he knew the bird loved these almost as much as he did.

He gathered up all his possessions and slung the bulging leather bag over his shoulder. For the last time he thanked the bird and bade it farewell. As soon as he stepped back the bird dropped down from the top of the tree, fell upon the fat golden comb and pecked out the juicy grubs at once. Bakkat smiled and watched it indulgently for a while. He knew it would eat it all, even the wax, for it was the only creature that was able to digest this part of the bounty.

He reminded the little bird of the legend of the greedy San who had cleaned out the hive and left nothing for the bird. The next time the bird had led him to a hole in the trunk of a tree in which was coiled a huge black mamba. The snake stung the cheating San to death.

'The next time we meet, remember that I treated you well and fairly,' Bakkat told the bird. 'I will look for you again. May the Kulu Kulu watch over you.' And he set off back towards the wagons. As he went, he reached into the bag, broke off pieces of comb and stuffed them into his mouth, humming with deep pleasure.

Within half a mile he stopped abruptly at a crossing place on the stream and stared in astonishment at the prints of human feet in the clay of the bank. The people who had passed this way recently had made no effort to hide their tracks. They were San.

Bakkat's heart leaped like a gazelle. Only when he saw the fresh footprints did he realize how he had pined for his own people. He examined the sign avidly. There were five of them, two men and three women. One man was old, and the other much younger. He divined this from the reach and alacrity of their separate strides. One of the women was ancient, and hobbled along on gnarled, twisted feet. Another was in her prime, with a strong, determined step. She led the Indian file of her family.

Then Bakkat's eyes fell on the fifth and last set of prints, and he felt a great longing squeeze his heart. They were dainty and as enchanting as any of the paintings of the artists of his tribe. Bakkat felt that he might weep with the beauty of them. He had to sit down for a while and stare at one until he could recover from the effect that they had had upon him. In his mind's eye he could see the girl who had left these signs for him to find. He divined with all his instincts that she was very young, but graceful, limber and nubile. Then he stood up again and followed her footprints into the forest.

On the far bank of the stream he came to the point where the two men had separated from the women and gone off among the trees to hunt. From that point the women had begun gathering the wild harvest of the veld. Bakkat saw where they had broken off the fruit from the branches, and dug out the edible tubers and roots with the sharp, pointed stakes that each carried.

He followed the tracks that the girl had left, and saw how swiftly and surely she worked. She made no false digs, wasting no effort, and it was clear to Bakkat that she knew every plant and tree she came upon. She passed by the poisonous and tasteless, and picked out the sweet and nourishing.

Bakkat giggled with admiration. 'This is a clever little one. She could feed her whole family with what she has gathered since she crossed the stream. What a wife she would make for a man.'

Then he heard voices in the forest ahead, feminine voices calling to each other as they worked. One was as musical and sweet as the call of the oriole, that golden songster of the high galleries of the forest.

It led him as irresistibly as the honey-guide had. Silent and unseen he crept towards the girl. She was working in a clump of thick scrub. He could hear her digging stick thudding into the earth. At last he was close enough to make out her movements, veiled by the latticework of branches and leaves. Then, suddenly, she moved into the open, directly in front of Bakkat. All the solitary years and loneliness were swept away like debris in the new, surging flow of his emotions.

She was exquisite, tiny and perfect. Her skin glowed in the noonday sunlight. Her face was a golden flower. Her lips were full and petal-shaped. She lifted one graceful hand and, with her thumb, wiped the clinging drops of perspiration from her arched eyebrow and flicked them away. They sparkled as they flew through the air. He was so close that one splashed on his dusty shin. She was oblivious of his presence, and began to walk away. Then one of the other women called to her from nearby, 'Are you thirsty, Letee? Shall we go back to the stream?' The girl stopped and looked back. She wore only a tiny leather apron in front, decorated with cowrie shells and beads made from chippings of ostrich-egg shell. The pattern of the shells and beads proclaimed that she was a virgin, and that no man had yet spoken for her.

'My mouth is as dry as a desert stone. Let us go.' Letee laughed as she replied to her mother. Her teeth were small and very white.

In that moment Bakkat's entire existence changed. As she walked away her little breasts joggled merrily and her plump, naked buttocks undulated. He made no attempt to stop or delay her. He knew that he could find her again anywhere and at any time.

When she had disappeared, he stood up slowly from his hiding-place. Suddenly he gave a leap of joy high into the air, and rushed away to make himself a love arrow. He selected a perfect reed from the edge of the stream, and lavished upon it all his talents as an artist. He painted it with mystic patterns and designs. The colours he chose from his paint horns were yellow, white, red and black. He fledged it with the purple feathers of the lourie, and padded the tip with a ball of tanned springbuck skin stuffed with sunbird feathers so that it would inflict no pain or injury on Letee.

'It is beautiful!' Bakkat admired his own handiwork when it was finished. 'But not as beautiful as Letee.'

That night he found the encampment of Letee's family. They were temporarily inhabiting a cave in the rocky cliff above the stream. He crept close in the darkness and listened to their banal inconsequential chatter. From it he learned that the old man and woman were her grandparents, and the other couple her mother and father. Her elder sister had recently found herself a fine husband and left the clan. The others were teasing Letee. She had seen her first menstrual moonrise fully three months previously, yet she was still a virgin and unmarried. Letee hung her head in shame at her failure to find herself a man.

Bakkat left the mouth of the cave and found a place to sleep further down the stream. But he was back before dawn, and when the women left the cave to go out into the forest he followed them at a discreet distance. When they started to forage they kept in touch with each other by calling and whistling, but after a while Letee became separated from them. Bakkat closed in on her with all his stalking skills.

She was digging for the fat tuber of the tiski plant, a variety of wild manioc. She kept her legs straight as she bent over and rocked to the rhythm of her digging stick. The protruding lips of her sex peeped out from between the backs of her thighs, and her plump little rear end was pointed to the sky.

Bakkat crept close. His hands shook as he raised the tiny ceremonial bow and aimed his love arrow. Yet his aim was true as ever and Letee squeaked with surprise, and sprang high in the air as the arrow smacked into her bottom. She wheeled round clutching herself with both hands, her expression betraying her astonishment and outrage. Then she saw the arrow lying at her feet and gazed around her at the silent bush. Bakkat had disappeared like a puff of smoke. The stinging in her bottom abated as she rubbed it. Then, slowly, she was overcome with shyness.

Suddenly Bakkat appeared, so close that she gasped with shock. She stared at him. His chest was broad and deep. His legs and arms were sturdy. She saw at an instant, by the easy way in which he bore his weapons, that he was a mighty hunter, and that he would provide well for a family. He carried the colour pots of the artist on his belt, which meant that he would have high standing and much prestige within all the tribes of the San. She dropped her eyes demurely and whispered, 'You are so tall. I saw you from afar.'

'I also saw you from afar,' Bakkat replied, 'for your beauty lights the forest like the rising of the sun.'

'I knew you would come,' she answered him, 'for your face was painted on my heart on the day of my birth.' Letee came forward timidly, took his hand and led him to her mother. In her other hand she carried the love arrow. 'This is Bakkat,' she told her mother, and held up the arrow. Her mother shrieked, which brought the grandmother running, cackling like a hen guinea-fowl. The two older women went ahead of them to the cave, singing, dancing and clapping. Bakkat and Letee followed them, still holding hands.

Bakkat gave Letee's grandfather the bag of wild honey. He could not have brought them a more acceptable gift. Not only were they all addicted to the sweetness, but it proved Bakkat's ability to provide for a wife and children. The family feasted on it, but Bakkat ate none because he was the giver. With every mouthful Letee smacked her lips and smiled at him. They talked until late in the light of the campfire. Bakkat told them who he was, the totem of his tribe and the list of his ancestors. The grandfather knew many of them, and clapped his hands as he recognized their names. Letee sat with the other women and they did not join in the talk of the men. At last, Letee stood up and crossed to where Bakkat sat between the other two men. She took his hand and led him to where she had laid out her sleeping mat at the back of the cave.

The two left early in the morning. All Letee's possessions were packed into the roll of her sleeping mat, and she carried it balanced effortlessly on her head. Bakkat went ahead of her. They moved at a trot, a pace they could keep up from morning until evening. Bakkat sang the hunting songs of his tribe as he ran, and Letee joined in the chorus in her sweet, childlike voice.

Xhia was concealed in the thickets across the stream from the mouth of the cave. He watched the couple emerge into the early sunlight. He had been spying on Bakkat during all the preceding days of his courtship. Despite his hatred for Bakkat, Xhia was intrigued by the ancient marriage ritual. He felt a lascivious thrill from watching the man and woman play out their appointed roles. He wanted to witness the final act of mating before he interceded, and exacted his revenge from Bakkat.

'Bakkat has plucked himself another pretty flower.' The fact that she was the woman of his enemy made her all the more desirable to Xhia. 'But he will not enjoy her long.'

Xhia hugged himself with glee, and let the couple trot off into the forest. He would not follow too closely for he knew that although Bakkat was distracted by his new companion he was still a formidable adversary. Xhia was in no hurry. He was a hunter and the first attribute of the hunter is patience. He knew there would be a time when Bakkat and the girl were separated, if only for a short time. That would be his chance.

A little before noon Bakkat came upon a small herd of buffalo. Xhia watched as he left his bag and accoutrements in Letee's care, and crept forward. He picked out a half-grown heifer whose flesh would be sweet and tender, not gamey and tough as that of an older beast. She was also much smaller in size so that the poison would work more swiftly. Keeping downwind, Bakkat manoeuvred skilfully into a position directly behind the heifer so that he could send an arrow into the thin skin surrounding her anus and genitals. The thicker hide of her body would resist the frail arrow. The network of veins around the heifer's body openings would convey the poison swiftly to her heart. His shot was true, and the animal galloped away in alarm with the rest of the herd. The shaft of the arrow broke off, but the barbed, poisoned head was buried deeply. She ran for only a short distance before the poison started to take effect, and she slowed to a walk.

Bakkat and Letee followed patiently. The sun had moved only a few fingers across the sky before the heifer halted and lay down. Bakkat and his little woman squatted nearby. At last the beast groaned and rolled over on to her side. Bakkat and Letee broke into a song of praise and thanks to the heifer for giving them her flesh to sustain them, and ran forward to butcher the carcass.

That evening while it was still light they made their camp

beside it. No matter that the flesh would soon turn in the heat, they would remain here until the entire cow was consumed, guarding it from the vultures and other scavengers. Letee made the fire and roasted strips of liver and the backstraps of meat. When they had finished eating, Bakkat led her to the sleeping mat and they coupled. Xhia crept closer to spy upon this final act of the courtship. In the end, when Bakkat and Letee writhed together as one and cried out in a single voice, he doubled over and, in a shuddering spasm, ejaculated in concert with them. Then, before Bakkat could recover, he slipped back into the bushes.

'It has been done,' Xhia whispered to himself, 'and now the time has come for Bakkat to die. He is lulled and softened by love. There will never be a better time than this.'

In the dawn Xhia was watching when Letee rose from the mat beside her husband and knelt before the ashes of the fire to blow life back into them. When the flames burned up brightly, she left the camp and came into the bushes close to where Xhia waited. She looked about her carefully, then untied the string of her beaded apron, laid it aside and squatted. While she was busy, Xhia crept up on her. As she stood again he sprang upon her from behind. Xhia was swift and powerful. She had no chance to cry out before he had covered her mouth and nose with her own apron. He held her down easily while he gagged and trussed her with the bark rope he had plaited the previous evening. Then he lifted her on to his shoulder and carried her away. He made no effort to cover his tracks. The girl was the bait. Bakkat would follow her and Xhia would be ready for him.

Xhia had scouted the ground the previous evening, and he knew exactly where to take the girl. He had chosen an isolated *kopje* not far from the campsite. The sides were sheer and rocky, so that from the heights he could keep a watch over the approaches. He had discovered only one path to the top, and its entire length was exposed to an archer on the summit.

The girl was small and light. Xhia ran with her easily. At first she kicked and struggled, but he chuckled and told her, 'Every time you do that I will punish you.' She took no heed of the warning and kicked wildly with both legs. She was moaning and mumbling into her gag.

'Xhia warned you to be still,' he told her, and pinched one of her nipples with his fingernails. They were sharp as flint knives, and blood oozed from the wounds they inflicted. She tried to scream, her face contorted with the effort. She writhed and fought, and tried to bump him in the face with her head. He took her other nipple and pinched it until his nails almost met in her tender flesh. She froze with agony and he started up the steep pathway to the top of the *kopje*. Just below the summit there was a cleft between two rocks. He laid her in it, then examined her bonds. He had tied them in haste. Now he retied the knots at ankles and wrists. Satisfied that they were tight, he removed the folds of her leather apron from between her jaws. Immediately she screamed with all the force of her lungs.

'Yes!' He laughed at her. 'Do that again. It will bring Bakkat to me even as the squeals of a wounded gazelle bring the leopard.'

She hissed and spat at him. 'My husband is a mighty hunter. He will kill you for this.'

'Your husband is a coward and a braggart. Before the sun sets today, I will make you a widow. Tonight you will share my sleeping mat. Tomorrow you will be married again.' He performed a few shuffling dance steps, and lifted his apron to show her that he was already tumescent.

Xhia had hidden his axe, bow and quiver among the rocks and he retrieved them. He tested his bowstring, flexing the bow to full draw. Then he removed the leather cover of his quiver and brought out his arrows. They were frail reeds, fletched with eagle feathers. Each of the arrowheads was carefully wrapped with a leather covering bound in place with twine. Xhia cut the twine and unwrapped the covers. He worked with great care. The arrowheads were carved from bone, barbed and needle sharp. They were blackened with poison made from the body juices of the larvae of a particular beetle boiled until they were thick and sticky as honey. A scratch from one of the poisoned arrows would inflict a death so certain and agonizing that Xhia kept the tips covered in case he accidentally scratched himself.

Letee knew these deadly weapons. She had seen her father and grandfather bring down the heaviest game with them. From infancy she had been warned that she must not touch even the quiver that contained them. She stared at them now in dread. Xhia held up one in front of her face. 'This is the one I have chosen for Bakkat.' He stabbed the deadly point at her face, stopping it only a finger's length before her eyes. She recoiled in horror against the rocks, and screamed again with all her strength.

'Bakkat, my husband! Danger! An enemy waits for you!'

Xhia stood up with his bow across his muscular shoulder and the unbarred arrows in his quiver, ready to hand. 'My name is Xhia,' he said to Letee. 'Tell him my name, so he will know who it is that waits for him.'

'Xhia!' she screamed. 'It is Xhia!' and the echoes flung the name back at her. 'Xhia! Xhia!'

'Xhia!' Bakkat heard the name, which only confirmed what he had already read in the sign. It was the sound of Letee's voice that cut him to the heart, with both joy and dread: joy that she was alive, and dread that she had fallen into the hands of such a terrible enemy. He looked up at the *kopje* from which her cries had come. He made out the one sure and easy route to the summit, and the urge to rush up it was almost too strong to resist. He dug the nails of his right hand into the palm so that the pain would steady him, then studied the bare cliffs of the hill.

'Xhia has chosen his ground well,' he said aloud. Once again he considered that single route to the summit and saw it was a deathtrap. Xhia would be perched above him, shooting his arrows down at him all the way.

Bakkat circled the *kopje*, and on the far side he picked out an alternative route. It was difficult – parts of it were so steep and dangerous that they might be impassable: a slip would mean he would plunge down on to the rocks below. However, most of the path was concealed from above by an overhang, jutting out just below the summit. Only the last part of the climb would be exposed to a watcher at the top of the *kopje*.

Bakkat ran back to the camp. He laid aside his bow and quiver. He would be on the summit and the range was too close for bow work before he and Xhia came together. He selected only his knife and the axe, both better suited to close fighting. Then he laid out the wet buffalo skin, and from it swiftly shaped and cut out a cape that would cover his head and shoulders. The thick hide had already begun to stink in the heat, but it would provide an effective armour against a reed arrow. He rolled the heavy cape and strapped it on to his back. Then he ran back to the *kopje*, but circled round to come directly to the protected route he had chosen. Stealthily he crept through the bush at the foot of the hill and reached the cliff under cover of the overhang, almost certain that Xhia had not spotted him. But with Xhia you could never be certain.

He rested for only a few moments, gathering himself for the climb, but before he could begin Letee's screams rang out again, high above him. Then Xhia's voice called down to him: 'Watch me, Bakkat. See what I am doing to this woman of yours. Ah, yes! There! My fingers are deep inside her. She is tight and slippery.'

Bakkat tried to close his ears to Xhia's taunts, but he could not. 'Listen to your woman, Bakkat. These are only my fingers, but next she will feel something much bigger. How she will squeal when she feels that.'

Letee was sobbing and shrieking, and Xhia was giggling. The stone cliffs of the *kopje* magnified and echoed the dreadful sounds. Bakkat had to force himself to remain silent. He knew that Xhia wanted him to voice his rage, and in so doing betray his position. Xhia could not be sure which path Bakkat would use to try to reach the summit.

Bakkat went to the wall of red rock and began to climb it. He went swiftly at first, running up the wall like a gecko lizard. Then he reached the overhang, and was hanging out backwards reaching for every finger- and toe-hold, dragging himself round by the strength of his arms. The axe and the roll of wet skin hampered his movements, and gradually his progress slowed. The drop gaped beneath his dangling feet.

He reached for another handhold, but as he placed his weight on it, it broke off. A lump of rock twice his own size came loose from the roof above him. It grazed his head, and hurtled down the cliff to crash against the wall lower down. The echoes boomed out across the valley as it bounded on, kicking up a storm of dust and rock splinters every time it struck.

For terrible seconds Bakkat hung by the fingers of one hand. He scrabbled desperately with the other, and at last found a hold. He hung there for a while, trying to gather himself.

There were no more taunts from Xhia. He knew now exactly where Bakkat was, and would be waiting for him at the top of the cliff, a poison arrow nocked to his bow. Bakkat had no choice. The slab that had broken away had altered the shape of the wall, and cut off his retreat. There was only one route open to him, and that was upwards, to where Xhia was waiting.

Painfully slowly, Bakkat worked his way over the last stretch, and round the outer angle of the overhang. At any instant he would have a view to the summit ridge, but Xhia would be able to see him. Then, with a rush of relief, Bakkat found a narrow ledge below the lip. It was only just wide enough for him to squeeze himself on to it. He crouched there for what seemed a lifetime, and slowly the strength returned to his numbed, shaking arms. Carefully he unrolled the buffalo-skin cape and draped it over his head and shoulders. He made certain that his knife and axe were still in his belt. He came gingerly to his feet on the tiny ledge and flattened his body against the wall to maintain his balance. He was standing on his toes, his heels hanging out over the drop. He reached up and ran both hands along the lip of the cliff as high as he could reach. He found a niche just wide and deep enough for him to insert both hands and take a firm grip. He pulled himself upwards and his toes left the ledge. For a long, terrible interlude his feet dabbed against the face without finding purchase. Then he pulled himself just high enough to throw one arm over the top of the cliff.

As his head came up he looked towards the summit ledge just above. Xhia was watching him: he was smiling and his eyes were slitted as he sighted over the arrow. His bow was at full draw, the arrowhead aimed at Bakkat's face. It was so close that Bakkat could see each of the carved barbs, as sharp as the eyetooth of the striped tigerfish: the dung-brown poison dried into a thick paste between each barb.

Xhia loosed his arrow. It came with a flitting sound as fast as a darting swallow, and Bakkat was unable to duck or dodge. It seemed that the point would find the opening in his hide cape and strike him in the throat, but at the last instant it drifted off course and struck his shoulder. He felt the jerk as the point of the arrowhead snagged in a fold of the tough buffalo hide. The shaft snapped off and fell away, but the head stayed buried in the cape. Bakkat was galvanized by the threat of horrible death. He threw himself upwards the last few feet but as he teetered on the brink of the cliff Xhia nocked another arrow and aimed from a distance of only a few paces.

Bakkat hurled himself forward, and Xhia loosed the second arrow. Once again Bakkat caught it in the heavy folds of his cape. Though the arrowhead was stuck in the tough hide, the shaft broke off. Xhia reached for another arrow from his quiver, but Bakkat charged into him, and sent him reeling backwards. He dropped the bow and clung to Bakkat, pinning his arms before Bakkat could draw the knife from his belt. Chest to chest they struggled, turning in tight circles as they tried to swing each other off their feet.

Letee lay where Xhia had thrown her after he heard the fall of loose rock that had marked Bakkat's position for him. She was still trussed at hand and foot, and she was bleeding where Xhia had forced his fingers into her and his ragged fingernails had torn her most tender flesh. She watched the two men wrestling each other, powerless to help her husband. Then she saw Xhia's axe lying nearby, where he had left it.

With two quick rolls she reached it. She used her bare toes to tilt the axe-head until the sharp blade was uppermost. Then, holding it securely between her feet, she laid the bark ropes that held her wrists across it and sawed at them with all her strength.

Every few seconds she glanced up. She saw Xhia manage to hook one foot behind Bakkat's heels and trip him over backwards. They both fell heavily on to the rocks, but Bakkat was pinned under Xhia's lithe, muscular body. He could not throw him off and, powerless to intervene, Letee watched Xhia reach for the knife on his belt. Then, suddenly, unaccountably, Xhia screamed and released his grip. He recoiled from Bakkat and stared down at his own chest.

It took Bakkat a moment to realize what had happened. The arrowhead that had broken off in the folds of his cape had come between them as they wrestled, and Xhia's weight had driven the poisoned barbs deeply into his own flesh.

Xhia sprang to his feet and tried with both hands to claw the arrowhead free of his flesh, but the barbs held fast. Each time he tore at them a bright trickle of blood snaked down his bare chest.

'You are a dead man, Xhia,' Bakkat croaked, as he came to his knees.

Xhia let out another scream, but this was rage not terror. 'I will take you with me to the land of shadows!' He drew the knife from the sheath on his belt and rushed at Bakkat who was still on his knees. He lifted the knife, but when Bakkat tried to dodge the blow his legs caught in the folds of the heavy cape and he toppled backwards.

'You will die with me,' Xhia screamed, as he stabbed at his adversary's chest. Bakkat flung himself aside and the knife point grazed his upper arm. Xhia poised for the next blow, but Letee came to her feet behind him. Her ankles were still tied but her hands were free, and she held the axe. She took one hop forward and swung the axe from overhead. The blade glanced off Xhia's skull, shaving away a thick slice of his scalp and one of his ears, then went on to bite deeply into the joint between his shoulder and knife arm. The knife dropped from his paralysed fingers and the arm dangled uselessly at his side. He whirled round to face the tiny girl, clutching his wounded scalp with one hand, blood springing from between his fingers in a fountain.

'Run!' Bakkat shouted at her and started to his feet. 'Run, Letee!'

Letee ignored him. Although her ankles were tied, she jumped straight at Xhia. Fearless as a honey badger, she flew at his face and swung the axe again. Xhia reeled backwards and lifted his other arm to protect himself. The axe blade crunched into his forearm just below the elbow and the bone snapped.

Xhia staggered back, both arms maimed and useless. Letee bent swiftly and hacked away the ropes that held her ankles. Before Bakkat could intervene, she rushed at Xhia again. He saw her coming, a small fury, naked and outraged. Grievously wounded, he was tottering on the edge of the cliff. As he tried to dodge her next attack he lost his balance and went over backwards. He had no arms to save himself and he rolled down to the lip of the overhang, his blood staining the rock. He reached the edge and went over, disappearing from their view. They heard his scream receding in volume until there was a meaty thump and silence.

Bakkat ran to Letee. She dropped the axe and threw herself into his embrace. They clung together for a long time, until Letee had stopped shaking and shivering. Then Bakkat asked, 'Shall we go down, woman?' She nodded vehemently.

He led her to the head of the pathway, and they climbed down to the bottom of the hill. They paused beside Xhia's corpse. He lay on his back, and his eyes were wide and staring. His own arrow-head still protruded from his chest, and his half-severed arm was twisted under his back at an impossible angle.

'This man is of the San, as we are. Why did he try to kill us?' Letee asked.

'I will tell you the story one day,' Bakkat promised her, 'but for now let us leave him to his totem, the hyenas.' They turned away, and neither looked back as they broke into the quick trot that eats the wind.

Bakkat was taking his new woman to meet Somoya and Welanga.

Jim Courtney woke slowly in the semi-darkness before sunrise, and stretched voluptuously on the cardell bed. Then, instinctively he reached for Louisa. She was still asleep but she rolled over and threw an arm across his chest. She mumbled something that might have been either an endearment or a protest at being awakened.

Jim grinned and held her closer, then opened his eyes fully and started up. 'Where in God's name do you think you have been?' he roared. Louisa shot bolt upright beside him and they both stared at the two tiny figures perched on the foot of the bed, like sparrows on a fence pole.

Bakkat laughed merrily. It was so good to be back and have Somoya bellowing at him again. 'I saw you and Welanga from afar,' he greeted them.

Jim's expression softened. 'I thought the lions had got you. I rode after you but I lost your spoor in the hills.'

'I have been able to teach you nothing about following tracks.' Bakkat shook his head sadly.

Both Jim and Louisa turned their attention to his companion. 'Who is this?' Jim demanded.

'This is Letee, and she is my woman,' Bakkat told them.

Letee heard her name mentioned and broke into a sunny golden smile.

'She is very beautiful, and so tall,' said Louisa. Since leaving the colony she had learned to speak the patois fluently. She knew all the expressions of San courtesy.

'No, Welanga,' Bakkat contradicted her. 'She is truly very small. For my sake, it is best that Letee is not encouraged to believe that she is tall. Where might such a notion lead us?'

'Is she not at least beautiful?' Louisa insisted.

Bakkat looked at his woman and nodded solemnly. 'Yes, she is as beautiful as a sunbird. I dread the day she looks into a mirror for the first time, and discovers just how beautiful she is. That day might mark the beginning of my woes.'

At that Letee piped up in her sweet treble.

'What does she say?' Louisa demanded.

'She says she has never seen such hair or skin as yours. She wants to know if you are a ghost. But enough of woman's talk.' Bakkat turned to Jim. 'Somoya, a strange and terrible thing has happened.'

'What is it?' Jim became deadly serious.

'Our enemies are here. They have found us out.'

'Tell me,' Jim ordered. 'We have many enemies. Which ones are these?'

'Xhia,' Bakkat answered. 'Xhia stalked Letee and me. He tried to kill us.'

'Xhia!' Jim looked grave. 'Keyser and Koots's hunting dog? Is it possible? We have come three thousand leagues since we last laid eyes on him. Could he have followed us that far?'

'He has followed us, and we can be sure that he has led Keyser and Koots to us.'

'Have you seen them, those two Dutchmen?'

'No, Somoya, but they cannot be far off. Xhia would never come so far if he were alone.'

'Where is Xhia now?'

'He is dead, Somoya. I killed him.'

Jim blinked with surprise, then said in English, 'So he will not be answering any questions, then.' Then he reverted to the patois: 'Take your beautiful little woman with you and let Welanga and me dress without the benefit of your eyes upon us. I will talk to you again as soon as I have my breeches on.'

Bakkat was waiting by the campfire when Jim emerged from his wagon a few minutes later. Jim called him and they walked away into the forest were no one would overhear them.

'Tell me everything that happened,' Jim ordered. 'Where and when did Xhia attack you?' He listened intently to Bakkat's account. By the time the little man had finished, Jim's complacency had been shaken. 'Bakkat, if Keyser's men

are after us, you must find them. Can you backtrack Xhia and
find where he came from?'

'That I know already. Yesterday, while Letee and I were on
our way back to you, I came upon Xhia's old spoor. He had
been following me for days. Ever since I left the wagons to
follow a honey-guide I found.'

'Before that?' Jim demanded. 'Where did he come from
before he began to follow you?'

'That way.' Bakkat pointed back at the escarpment, which
was now only a faint, hazy line against the sky. 'He came
along our wagon tracks, as though he had been shadowing us
all the way from the Gariep river.'

'Go back!' Jim ordered. 'Find out if Keyser and Koots were
with him. If they were, I want to know where they are now.'

'I t is eight days since Xhia left,' said Captain Herminius
Koots bitterly. 'I truly believe he has made a run for it.'

'Why would he do that?' Oudeman asked reasonably. 'Why
now, when we are on the very brink of success, after all these
hard and bitter months? The reward you promised him is
almost in his hands.' A crafty look came into Oudeman's eyes.
It was time to remind Koots about the reward once again. 'All
of us have earned our share of the reward. Surely Xhia would
not desert at this point, and forfeit his share?'

Koots frowned. He did not enjoy discussing the reward.
These last months he had been pondering every possible
expedient to avoid having to make good his promises in that
regard. He turned to Kadem. 'We cannot wait here longer.
The fugitives will get clean away from us. We must go on after
them without Xhia. Do you not agree?' Since their first
meeting the two had swiftly forged an alliance of convenience.
Koots had in the front of his mind Kadem's promise to open
the way for him into the favoured service of the Caliph of
Oman, the power and riches that would spring from that
position.

Kadem knew that Koots was his only chance of finding

Dorian Courtney again. 'I think you are right, Captain. We no longer need the little barbarian. We have found the enemy. Let us go forward and attack them.'

'Then we are in accord,' Koots said. 'We will ride hard and get well ahead of Jim Courtney. We will lay an ambush for them on ground where we have the advantage.'

It was a simple matter for Koots to keep track of Jim's caravan without closing in on him and disclosing his own presence. The dust kicked up by the cattle herds could be seen from leagues away. Having convinced himself that he no longer needed Xhia, Koots led his troop down the escarpment, then made a wide, cautious detour into the south to come out ten leagues ahead of the caravan. Now they started back to intercept it head-on. This way they would leave no tracks for Jim Courtney's Bushman tracker to pick up before they had a chance to spring their ambush.

The ground was favourable to them. It was evident that Jim Courtney was following a river valley down towards the ocean. There was grazing and good water for his herds along this way. However, at one point the river was pinched into a narrow gorge where it ran through a line of rugged hills. Koots and Kadem surveyed the bottleneck from the height of the hills above.

'They will have to come through here with the wagons,' Koots said, with satisfaction. 'The only other passage through these hills is four days' travel to the south.'

'It will take them days to traverse the gorge, which means that they must laager the wagons for at least one night in its confines,' Kadem agreed. 'We will be able to make a night attack. They will not be expecting that. The Nguni warriors they have with them will not fight in the dark. We will be the foxes in the hen coop, it will all be over before dawn breaks.'

They waited on the high ground, and at last watched the slow line of wagons enter the mouth of the gorge below them and follow the bank of the river deeper into the narrow way. Koots recognized Jim Courtney and his woman riding ahead of the lead wagon, and his smile was savage. He watched them make camp and outspan in the gut of the gorge. Koots was relieved to see that they made no attempt to laager the wagons, but merely parked them casually among the trees on the river bank, widely separated from each other. Behind the wagons the herds of cattle flowed into the mouth of the gorge. They watered at the river and the Nguni herders began to unload the ivory tusks each beast carried on its back.

This was the first time that Koots had been close enough to the caravan to see the quantity of the booty. He tried to count the cattle, but in the dust and confusion that was not possible. It was like trying to count the individual fish in a shoal of sardines. He turned his spyglass on the mounds of ivory piled up on the bank of the river. Here was a treasure greater than he had allowed himself to imagine.

He watched as the cattle settled down for the night, guarded by their Nguni herders. Then, as the sun sank and the light began to fade, Koots and Kadem left their hiding-place on the high ground and sneaked back from the skyline to where Sergeant Oudeman was holding the horses.

'Good, so, Oudeman,' Koots told him as he mounted. 'They are in a perfect position for the attack. We will go back now to join the others.'

They crossed the next ridgeline, then dropped down a steep game trail into the river gorge.

Bakkat watched them go. Even then he waited until the bottom limb of the sun touched the horizon before he stirred from his own place of concealment on the higher hilltop across the gorge. He was taking no chance on Koots doubling back. In the dusk he dropped swiftly and silently down the steep side of the gorge to report to Jim.

Jim listened until Bakkat had concluded. 'That does it,' he said, with satisfaction. 'Koots will attack tonight. Now that he has seen the cattle and the ivory, he will not be able to contain his greed. Follow them, Bakkat. Watch their every move. I will listen for your signals.'

As soon as it was dark enough to hide them from any

watcher on the hilltops, Jim inspanned the wagons again and moved them into a narrow re-entrant at the foot of the hills, with steep cliffs on three sides. They worked as silently as possible, without whipcracking or shouting. In this readily defensible position they laagered the wagons securely and lashed them wheel to wheel. They drove the herd of spare horses into the centre of the square. The horses they would ride tonight were hitched to the outside of the wagons, saddled and with muskets and cutlasses in the scabbards, ready for an instant sortie.

Then Jim went out to where Inkunzi, the head herdsman, and his Nguni waited. Under Jim's orders they bunched up the cattle and moved them quietly another three cables' length up the gorge from the bedding ground Koots had spied out at sundown. Jim spoke to the herders and explained exactly what he wanted of them. There was some muttered protest from these men, who looked upon the cattle as their children and were highly solicitous of their welfare, but Jim snarled at them and their protests subsided.

The cattle had sensed the mood of their herders, and they were restless and fretful. Inkunzi moved among them and played them a lullaby on his reed flute. They began to settle and some couched for the night. However, they kept bunched up together; in these nervous hours they needed the mutual assurance of the herd.

Jim went back to the wagons and made sure that all his men had eaten their dinner, and that they were booted and armed, ready to ride. Then he and Louisa climbed a short way up the cliff above the laager. From there they would be able to hear Bakkat's signals. They sat close together, sharing a woollen cape against the sudden night chill and talked quietly.

'They won't come before moonrise,' Jim predicted.

'When is that?' Louisa asked. Earlier in the evening they had consulted the almanac together, but she asked again mainly to hear his voice.

'A few minutes before ten of the clock. We are seven days from full moon. Just enough light for it.'

490

At last the moonrise lightened the eastern horizon. Jim stiffened and threw off the cape. On the hills on the far side of the gorge an eagle owl hooted twice. An eagle owl never hoots twice. 'That is Bakkat,' Jim said quietly. 'They are coming.'

'Which side of the river?' Louisa asked, as she stood up beside him.

'They will come to where they saw the wagons at sunset, on this side of the river.' The eagle owl hooted again, much closer.

'Koots is coming on fast.' Jim turned to the path down to the laager. 'Time to mount up.'

The men were waiting beside the horses, darkly muffled figures. Jim spoke a few words to each quietly. Some of the herd-boys had grown enough to be able to ride and handle a musket. The smallest, led by Izeze, the flea, would bring up the pack-horses with spare powder, shot and the waterbags, in case there was heavy fighting. Tegwane had twenty of the Nguni warriors under his command and he would stay to guard the wagons.

Intepe, Tegwane's granddaughter, was standing beside Zama, helping him secure his equipment on Crow's back. These days, the two spent much of their time together. Jim went to him now, and spoke low: 'Zama, you are my other arm. One of us must ride beside Welanga every minute. Do not become separated from her.'

'Welanga should stay in the laager with the other women,' Zama replied.

'You are right, old friend.' Jim grinned. 'She should do as I tell her, but I have never been able to find the words to convince her of that.'

The eagle owl hooted again, three times. 'They are close now.' Jim looked at the gibbous moon sailing above the hills.

'Mount!' he ordered. Every man knew what he had to do. Quietly they swung up on to the horses' backs. On Drumfire and Trueheart, Jim and Louisa led them to where Inkunzi waited with his warriors, guarding the bedded herds.

'Are you ready?' Jim asked, as he rode up. Inkunzi's shield was on his shoulder, and his *assegai* glinted in the moonlight. His men pressed up close behind him.

'I will lay a feast for your hungry blades tonight. Let them eat and drink their fill,' Jim told them. 'Now you know what you have to do. Let us begin.'

Quickly and silently, in an orderly, disciplined evolution, the warriors formed into an extended double rank across the breadth of the gorge, from river bank to cliff wall. The horsemen drew up behind them.

'We are ready, great lord!' Inkunzi sang out. Jim drew his pistol from the holster on the front of his saddle and fired a shot into the air. Immediately the still night was plunged into hubbub and uproar. The Nguni drummed on their shield with the blades of their *assegais* and shouted their war-cries. The horsemen fired their muskets and yelled like banshees. They surged forward down the gorge, and the cattle lumbered to their feet. The bulls bellowed in alarm for they were sensitive to the temper and mood of their herders. The breeding cows lowed plaintively, but when the ranks of yelling, drumming warriors bore down on them they panicked and whirled away before them.

These were all heavy beasts with great humps and swinging dewlaps. The span of their horns was twice the reach of a man's spread arms. Over the centuries the Nguni had bred them for this attribute, so that the cattle might better defend themselves against lions and other predators. They could run like wild antelope and when threatened they would defend themselves with those great racks of horn. In a dark and solid mass they stampeded down the valley. The running warriors and galloping horsemen pressed close behind them.

Koots was well satisfied that they had made a silent approach, and that they had not been detected by Jim Courtney's pickets. There was a good moon and, apart from the usual night sounds of birds and small nocturnal animals, all was silent and still.

Koots and Kadem were riding stirrup to stirrup. They knew that they had still more than a mile to cover before they reached the spot on the river bank where they had seen the wagons outspanned. All of the Hottentots and the three Arabs knew exactly what to do. Before the alarm went up, they must get among the wagons and shoot down Jim Courtney's people as they emerged. Then they could deal with the Ngunis. Even though they were greater in number, they were armed only with spears. They were the lesser threat.

'No quarter,' Koots had ordered. 'Kill them all.'

'What about the women?' Oudeman asked. 'I haven't had a taste of the honey-pot since we left the colony. You promised us a go at the blonde girl.'

'If you can catch yourself a bit of *poesje*, well and good. But make sure all of the men are dead before you drop your pants. If not, you might get a cutlass up your arse end to help you along while you're pumping cream.' They had all laughed. At times Koots could show the common touch and speak to them in the language they understood best.

Now the troopers pressed forward eagerly. Earlier that day, from the heights above the gorge, some had glimpsed the cattle, the ivory and the women. They had told their companions and all were fired by the promise of pillage and rape.

Suddenly a single musket shot thudded out in the darkness ahead and, without waiting for the order, the column reined in. They peered ahead uneasily.

'Son of the great whore!' Koots swore. 'What was that?' He did not have long to wait for his answer. Abruptly the night was filled with uproar and clamour. None of them had ever heard before the sound of drumming on war-shields, and that made it more alarming. Moments later there was a fusillade of musket fire, wild shouts and screams, the bellowing and lowing of hundreds of cattle, then the rising thunder of hoofs bearing down on them out of the night.

In the fallible light of the moon it seemed that the earth

was moving, a flowing mass like black lava bearing down on them, stretching across the full breadth of the gorge from wall to cliff wall. The sound of hoofs was deafening, and they saw the humped backs of the monstrous herd looming closer and faster, the moonlight glinting on their horns.

'Stampede!' Oudeman yelled in terror, and the others took up the cry. 'Stampede!'

The tight-knit group of riders whirled round, broke up and scattered away before the solid wall of great horned heads and pounding hoofs. Within a dozen strides Goffel's horse hit an antbear burrow with his off fore. The leg snapped as the horse went down. Goffel was thrown forward to hit the earth with one shoulder. In terror he dragged himself to his feet with his arm dangling from the shattered bones, just as the front rank of cattle swept over him. One of the lead bulls hooked at him as it passed. The point of the horn slid in under his ribs and out of the small of his back at the level of his kidneys. The bull tossed its head and Goffel was thrown high, to drop back under the hoofs of the herd, then trampled and kicked to a boneless pulp. Three other troopers were trapped against an angle of the cliff. When they tried to turn back the herd engulfed them, and their mounts were gored by the enraged bulls. The frenzied horses reared, kicked and threw their riders, and men and horses were overwhelmed by the thrusting of horns and went down under the pounding hoofs.

Habban and Rashood raced side by side, but when Habban's horse stepped in a hole and fell with a broken leg Rashood turned back and, right under the horns of the stampede, dragged him up behind his saddle. They rode on, but the double-loaded horse could not keep ahead of the cattle, and was swallowed up by a wave of swinging horns and bellowing beasts. Habban was gored deeply in the thigh and dragged from his perch behind his companion's saddle.

'Ride on!' he screamed at Rashood, as he hit the ground. 'I am lost. Save yourself!' But Rashood tried to turn back, and his horse was horned again and again until it also fell in a tangle of legs and loose equipment. On hands and knees Rashood crawled through the dust and flying hoofs. Though he was kicked repeatedly, felt muscle and sinew tear in his back and chest and his ribs snap, he reached his fallen comrade and dragged him behind the bole of one of the larger trees. They huddled there, choking and coughing in the dustclouds while the stampede thundered by.

Even after the stampede had passed they could not leave their hiding-place because a wave of howling Nguni spearmen followed hard on the heels of the herds. Just when it seemed that they would find the two Arabs, an unhorsed Hottentot trooper broke from cover and tried to make a run for it. Like hounds on the fox the Nguni went after him, and were drawn away from Rashood and Habban. They stabbed the trooper repeatedly, washing their blades in his blood.

Koots and Kadem spurred their horses at full gallop along the bank of the river to keep ahead of the stampede. Oudeman stuck close behind them. He knew that Koots had the animal instinct for survival, and trusted him to find an escape for them from this disaster. Suddenly the horses ran into stands of hook-thorn and were slowed by the dense thickets. The herd leaders coming on close behind them crashed through the thorn without check, and swiftly overhauled them.

'Into the river!' Koots bellowed. 'They'll not follow us in there.'

As he shouted he swerved his mount towards the bank and lashed him over the top. They dropped twelve feet and hit the surface of the water with a high splash. Kadem and Oudeman followed him over. They surfaced together and saw Koots already half-way across the river. Swimming beside the horses, they reached the south bank after Koots had landed.

They climbed out and stood in a sodden, exhausted group and watched the herd still careering by on the far bank. Then in the moonlight they saw Jim Courtney's horsemen galloping close on the heels of the herd, and heard the thud and saw the muzzle flashes of their muskets as they caught up with the surviving riders of Koots's troop and shot them down.

'Our powder is wet,' Koots gasped. 'We cannot stand and fight.'

'I have lost my musket,' said Oudeman.

'It is over,' Kadem agreed, 'but there will be another day and another place when we shall finish this business.' They mounted and rode on swiftly into the east, away from the river, the stampeding herd and the enemy musketeers.

'Where are we going?' Oudeman asked at last, but neither of the other two answered him.

It took the Nguni herdsmen many days to round up the scattered herds. They discovered that thirty-two of the great hump-backed beasts had died or been hopelessly maimed in the stampede. Some had fallen over precipices, run into holes, drowned in the rapids of the river or been killed by the lions when they had become separated from the herd. The Nguni mourned them. Lovingly they drove back those cattle that had survived the dreadful night. They moved among them, soothing and gentling them. They dressed their injuries, the horn wounds of their peers and the rips and contusions where they had run into trees or other objects.

Inkunzi, the head herdsman, was determined to express his outrage to Jim in the strongest terms he dared. 'I will demand that he suspend the march and rest in this place until all the cattle are recovered,' he assured his herders, and they all agreed staunchly with him. Despite his threats, the request when he made it to Jim was couched in much milder terms, and Jim agreed with him without quibble.

As soon as it was light, Jim and his men rode over the battlefield. They came upon four dead horses of Koots's troop with horn stabs, and two others so badly hurt that they had to be destroyed. However, they retrieved eleven more that were either unhurt or so little injured that they could be treated and added to Jim's own remount herd.

They also found the corpses of five of Koots's men. The features of three were so battered as to be unrecognizable, but from items of their clothing and equipment, and the pay books Jim found in the pockets of two, he could be certain that they were VOC cavalrymen, wearing mufti rather than military uniform. 'These are all Keyser's men. Although he did not come after us himself, Keyser sent them,' Jim assured Louisa.

Smallboy and Muntu recognized some of the corpses. The Cape colony was a small community where everyone knew his neighbours.

'Goffel! Now there was a truly bad *kerel*,' said Smallboy, as he prodded one of the battered corpses with his toe. His expression was stern and he shook his head. Smallboy himself was no angel of purity, and if he disapproved, thought Jim, Goffel must have been a veritable tower of vice.

'There are still five missing,' Bakkat told Jim. 'No sign yet of Koots and the bald sergeant, or of the three strange Arabs we saw with them yesterday. I must cast the far side of the river.' He waded across and Jim watched him scurry along the bank and peer at the ground as he read sign. Suddenly he stopped, like a pointer dog getting the scent of the bird.

'Bakkat! What have you found there?' Jim yelled across.

'Three horses, running hard,' Bakkat called back.

Jim, Louisa and Zama crossed the river to join him and they studied the tracks of galloping horses. 'Can you read who the riders were, Bakkat?' Jim asked. It seemed impossible but Bakkat responded to the question as though it were commonplace. He squatted by the tracks.

'These two are the horses that Koots and the bald one were riding yesterday. The other is one of the Arabs, the one with the green turban,' he declared, with finality.

'How can he tell?' Louisa asked, with wonder. 'They are all steel-shod horses. Surely the tracks are identical?'

'Not to Bakkat,' Jim assured her. 'He can tell from the uneven wear of the horseshoes, and dents and chips in the metal. To his eye each horse has a distinctive gait, and he can read it in the spoor.'

'So Koots and Oudeman have got away. What are you going to do now, Jim? Are you going to follow them?'

Jim did not reply at once. To delay the decision he ordered Bakkat to follow the spoor and make sure of the run of it.

After a mile the tracks turned determinedly towards the north. Jim ordered a halt and asked Bakkat and Zama for their opinion. It was a long debate.

'They are riding fast,' Bakkat pointed out. 'They have a start of almost half a night and a day. It will take many days to catch them, if you ever do. Let them go, Somoya.'

'I think they are beaten,' Zama said. 'Koots will not come back. But if you catch him, he will fight like a leopard in a trap. You will lose men.'

Louisa thought about that. Jim might be one of those wounded or killed. She thought of intervening, but she knew that might harden Jim's resolve. She had found a wide streak of contrariness in his nature. She bit back her pleas to make him stay, and instead said quietly, 'If you go after him, I shall go with you.'

Jim looked at her. The warlike gleam in his eye faded, and he smiled in defeat, but it was still a conditional surrender. 'I have a feeling that Bakkat is right, as usual. Koots has abandoned his hostile intentions towards us, for the present at least. Most of his men have been wiped out. But he still has a formidable force with him. There are five still unaccounted for: Koots, Oudeman and the three Arabs. They could make a bitter fight of it if we cornered them. Zama is also right. We can't hope to get away scot-free a second time. If we do catch up with them some of our people will be killed or hurt. On the other hand, what seems to be flight might be a trick to draw us away from the wagons. We know Koots is a crafty animal. If we follow, Koots might circle round and attack the wagons before we can get back to intervene.' He drew breath and conceded, 'We will keep on for the coast and see what we find at Nativity Bay.' They crossed the river and headed back down the narrow gut of the gorge along the path of the cattle stampede.

Now that she knew Jim would not ride off after Koots, Louisa was happy and chatted easily as they rode side by side. Zama was anxious to return to the wagons, and he drew steadily ahead, until he was almost obscured by the trees.

'In a hurry to get back to the lovely lily.' Louisa laughed.

'Who?' Jim was puzzled.

'Intepe.'

'Tegwane's granddaughter? Is Zama—'

'Yes, he is,' Louisa confirmed. 'Sometimes men are blind. How could you not have noticed?'

'You are the only thing in my eye, Hedgehog. I see nothing but you.'

'My love, that was neatly said.' Louisa leaned out of the saddle and offered her mouth. 'You shall have a kiss as a reward.'

But before he could claim it, there was a wild shout and the crash of a musket shot ahead. They saw Frost rear and shy under Zama as he reeled in the saddle.

'Zama's in trouble!' Jim shouted, and spurred forward. As he caught up he saw that Zama was wounded. He was hanging half out of the saddle, and blood was shining at the back of his coat. Before Jim could reach him he keeled over and fell to earth in a limp heap.

'Zama!' Jim shouted, and rode for him, but at that moment he saw a flash of movement to one side. There was danger there and Jim turned Drumfire to meet it. One of the Arabs, in a ragged robe stained with dirt and dried blood, was crouched behind the trunk of a fever tree. He was frantically reloading his long-barrelled musket, ramrodding a ball down the muzzle. He looked up as horse and rider charged down on him. Jim recognized him. 'Rashood!' he shouted. He was one of the crewmen from the family schooner, *Gift of Allah*, Jim had sailed with him more than once, and knew him well, yet here he was riding with a company of the enemy, treacherously attacking the Courtney wagons – and he had shot Zama.

At the same moment Rashood recognized Jim. He dropped the musket, sprang to his feet and ran. Jim unsheathed his cutlass, and steered Drumfire after him. When he realized he could not escape Rashood dropped to his knees and spread his arms in a gesture of surrender.

Jim rose over him in the stirrups.

'You treacherous, murderous bastard!' He was angry enough

to use the edge and split the man's skull, but at the last moment he controlled himself and swung the flat of the blade across Rashood's temple. The steel cracked against the bone with such force that Jim feared he might have killed him anyway. Rashood collapsed face forward on to the earth.

'Don't you dare die,' Jim threatened him, as he swung down from the saddle, 'not until you have answered my questions. Then I will give you a royal send-off.'

Louisa rode up, and Jim shouted, 'See to Zama. I think he is hard hit. I will come to you as soon as I have this swine secured.'

Louisa sent Bakkat to call for help from the men at the laager, and they carried Zama back on a litter. He had received a dangerous wound at an oblique angle through the chest and Louisa feared for his life, but she hid her anxiety. As soon as they reached the laager Intepe came running to help her nurse him.

'He is hurt, but he will live,' she told the weeping girl, as they laid Zama on the cardell bed in the spare wagon. With the help of the books and the medicine chest Sarah Courtney had given her, and by dint of much practice and experience, Louisa had become a proficient physician over the months since they had left the Gariep river. She made a more thorough examination of the wound, and exclaimed, with relief, 'The ball has gone clean through and out the other side. That's most propitious. We won't have to cut for it, and the danger of mortification and gangrene is much reduced.'

Jim left Zama to the women and took out his concern and anger on Rashood. With arms and legs spreadeagled like a starfish, they lashed him to the spokes of one of the big rear wagon wheels and jacked the rim clear of the ground. Jim waited for him to recover consciousness.

In the meantime Smallboy brought in the body of another Arab they had found lying close to where he had captured Rashood. This one had died from loss of blood: a horn wound in his groin had severed the big artery there. When they turned him face up, Jim recognized him as another of the sailors from the *Gift*. 'This one is Habban,' he said.

'It is indeed Habban,' agreed Smallboy.

'There is something going on here that stinks like rotten fish,' Jim said. 'I know not what it is, but this one can give us the answers.' He glared at Rashood, still hanging unconscious on the rear wheel of the wagon. 'Throw a bucket of water over him.' It needed not one but three buckets flung into his face to revive him.

'Salaam, Rashood,' Jim greeted him, as he opened his eyes. 'The beauty of your countenance lightens my heart. You are a servant of my family. Why did you attack our wagons and try to kill Zama, a man you know well as my friend?'

Rashood shook the water from his beard and long, lank hair. He stared back at Jim: he did not speak but the expression in his eyes was eloquent.

'We must loosen your tongue, Beloved of the Prophet.' Jim stepped back, and nodded to Smallboy. 'Give him a hundred turns of the wheel.'

Smallboy and Muntu spat on their hands and seized the rim. They began to spin it between them. Smallboy counted the turns. The speed built up swiftly until the image of Rashood's revolving body blurred before their eyes. Smallboy lost the count after fifty and had to start again. When at last he called the hundred and they braked the wheel, Rashood was writhing weakly against his bonds, his dirty robe drenched with sweat. His eyes were unfocused and he was heaving and gasping with vertigo.

'Rashood, why were you riding with Koots? When did you join his band? Who was the strange Arab with you, the man with the green turban?'

Despite his distress Rashood turned his eyes towards Jim and tried to focus on him. 'Infidel!' he blurted. '*Kaffir!* I act by virtue of the sacred *fatwa* of the Caliph Zayn al-Din of Muscat and at the command of his pasha, General Kadem ibn Abubaker. The Pasha is a great and holy man, a mighty warrior and beloved of God and the Prophet.'

'So the one in the green turban is a pasha? What are the terms of this *fatwa*?' Jim demanded.

'They are too sacred to be spoken into the ear of the profane.'

'Rashood has discovered religion.' Jim shook his head sadly. 'I have never heard him prate such bigoted and venomous nonsense before.' He nodded to Smallboy. 'Give him another hundred turns on the wheel to cool his ardour.'

The wheel blurred again, but before they reached the count of a hundred, Rashood vomited in a long, sustained jet. Smallboy grunted at Muntu: 'Don't stop!' Then Rashood's bowels loosed and his bodily excretions erupted simultaneously from both ends of his body, like a deck hose.

At the hundred count they braked the wheel, but Rashood's befuddled senses could not tell the difference. The sensation of violent movement seemed to become stronger and he moaned and vomited until his stomach was empty. Then he heaved and dry-retched painfully.

'What were the terms of the *fatwa*?' Jim insisted.

'Death to the adulterers.' Rashood's voice was barely audible and yellow bile ran down his chin into his beard. 'Death to al-Salil and Princess Yasmini.'

Jim recoiled at the mention of those two beloved names. 'My uncle and aunt? Are they dead? Tell me they are still alive or I shall spin your black soul loose from your foul body.'

Rashood recovered his scattered senses and once more tried to oppose Jim's questions, but gradually the wheel broke down his resistance, and he answered freely. 'The Princess Yasmini was executed by the Pasha. She died with a thrust through her adulterous heart.' Even in his extreme condition Rashood mouthed the words with relish. 'And al-Salil was wounded to the brink of death.'

Jim's anger and sorrow were overwhelming, so much so that he lost all stomach for further punishment that day. Rashood was cut down from the wheel but chained and guarded for the rest of the night. 'I will question him again in the morning,' Jim said and went to tell Louisa the terrible news.

'My aunt Yasmini was the essence of kindness and goodness. I only wish you could have met her,' he said that night, as they lay in each other's arms. His tears soaked her night-dress. 'Thank God my uncle Dorian seems to have survived the assassination attempt by this fanatic, Kadem ibn Abubaker.'

In the morning Jim ordered the wagon to be towed well away from the laager so that Louisa could not hear Rashood on the wheel. They lashed him to the spokes, but Rashood broke down before Jim had ordered a single spin. 'Pity, *effendi*. Enough, Somoya! I will tell you all you wish to know, only take me down from this accursed wheel.'

'You will stay on the wheel until you have answered all my questions straight and true. If you hesitate or lie, the wheel will turn. When did this creature Kadem murder the princess? Where did this happen? What of my uncle? Has he recovered? Where is my family now?'

Rashood answered each question as though his life depended on it. Which indeed it does, Jim thought grimly.

When he heard the whole story of how his family had fled from Good Hope in the two schooners, and that they had sailed north after leaving the Lagoon of the Elephants, Jim's sorrow for Yasmini was tempered with relief and his antici-pation of an imminent reunion.

'Now I know that we shall find my parents at Nativity Bay, and my uncle Dorian and Mansur with them. I count the days in my heart before I shall see them again. We must resume the journey again tomorrow at first light.'

Consumed with eagerness to reach Nativity Bay, Jim's hopes and longings ran ahead of the slow procession of wagons and grazing herds. He wanted to leave the caravan to ride for the coast at once. He urged Louisa to accompany him, but Zama's recovery from the bullet wound was slow. Louisa insisted that he still needed her care and she could not leave him.

'You go on ahead,' she told him. Even though he was sure she did not truly mean him to leave her, and that she expected him to refuse, he was sorely tempted to take her at her word. But then he recalled that Koots, Oudeman and the Arab assassin, Kadem, were still at large and might be in the offing. He could not leave Louisa alone. Each morning he and Bakkat rode out far ahead of the caravan to scout the road path, and he made certain that he returned before sunset each evening to be with Louisa.

They emerged from the bottom end of the narrow gorge into a country lush with grasslands and fair hills interspersed with green forests. Each day Bakkat found sign of the elephant herds but none fresh enough to follow up until the morning of the fifth day after leaving the gorge. As usual he was riding just ahead of Jim, breaking trail and scanning ahead for sign, when suddenly he turned Crow aside and reined him to a standstill. Jim came up beside him. 'What is it?' Bakkat pointed wordlessly at the damp earth and the tracks deeply trodden into it. Jim felt his pulse jump with excitement. 'Elephant!'

'Three big bulls,' Bakkat agreed, 'and very fresh. They passed this way in the dawn of this very morning, not long since.' Jim felt his anxiety to reach Nativity Bay abate as he stared at the spoor. 'They are very big,' he said.

'One is a king of all elephants,' Bakkat said. 'It may be as large as the first great beast you slew.'

'They cannot be too far ahead of us,' Jim suggested hopefully. There had been many successful hunts since the battle with Manatasee's *impis* on the river bank. Each time they caught up with the great ivory-bearing bulls Jim added to his fund of experience and knowledge of their habits. By now he had honed his skills as a hunter, and in so doing had become addicted to the dangers and the fascination of the chase after this most noble quarry.

'How long will it take to catch up with them?' he asked Bakkat.

'They are feeding as they go, moving slowly,' Bakkat pointed out the torn branches of the trees from which the bulls had fed, 'and they are heading down towards the coast, along our own line of march. We need not detour to follow them.' Bakkat spat thoughtfully and looked up at the sky. He held up his right hand and measured his spread fingers against the angle of the sun. 'If the gods of the hunt are kind, we might catch them before noon, and still be back at the wagons before nightfall.' These days Bakkat showed a reluctance equal to Jim's to spend a night away from the wagons, and the golden charms of Letee.

Jim was torn. Despite his passion for the chase, his love and concern for Louisa were stronger. He knew that the vagaries of the hunt were unpredictable. To follow the bulls might add a day or more to the journey to the coast. They might not be able to return to the wagons before the onset of night. On the other hand there had been no sign of Koots and his Arab ally since that disastrous night attack. Bakkat had swept the back trail for many leagues and it was clear. There seemed no longer to be a threat from that direction. Even so, dare he leave Louisa for so long?

He wanted desperately to follow the tracks. In the months of hunting he had learned to read the spoor so vividly that he could picture them in his mind's eye, and he knew that these were magnificent bulls. He vacillated for a while longer while Bakkat squatted patiently beside the huge oval pad marks, and waited for him to make up his mind.

Then Jim thought of the small army of men who were with the wagons, to guard and protect Louisa. Koots's force had been routed and decimated. Surely he would not return so soon. At last he convinced himself that Koots was heading either for Portuguese or Omani territory, that he would not double back to attack them again.

'Every minute I dither here the bulls are walking away from me.' He made up his mind. 'Bakkat, take the spoor, and eat the wind.'

They rode hard and closed the gap swiftly. The spoor headed steadily through the low hills and forest towards the coast. In places the raw trunks of the trees from which the elephant had stripped the bark shone like mirrors a cable's length ahead of them and they could push Drumfire and Crow into a canter. A little before noon they came upon a huge mound of spongy yellow dung, composed mostly of half-digested bark. It was lying in a puddle of urine that had not yet soaked away into the earth. The dung was covered by a swarm of butterflies with gorgeous white, yellow and orange wings.

Bakkat dismounted and thrust his bare toe into the moist pile to test the temperature. The butterflies rose around him in a cloud. 'The dung is still hot from his belly.' He grinned up at Jim. 'If you called his name the bull is so close he would hear your voice.'

The words were no sooner out of Bakkat's mouth than they both froze and their heads turned together. 'Ha!' Jim grunted. 'He heard you speak.'

In the forest not far ahead the elephant trumpeted again, high and clear as a bugle blast. Agile as a cricket Bakkat sprang into the saddle.

'What has alarmed them?' Jim asked, as he drew his big German four-to-the-pound gun from its sheath under his knee. 'Why did he trumpet? Did he catch our wind?'

'The wind is in our faces,' Bakkat replied. 'They have not smelt us, but something else has done it.'

'Sweet Mary!' Jim shouted with astonishment. 'That is musket fire!'

The heavy reports of the guns boomed out and the echoes were flung back by the surrounding hills.

'Is it Koots?' Jim demanded, then answered himself, 'It cannot be. Koots would never give himself away while he knows we're close. These are strangers, and they are attacking our herd.' Jim felt a flare of anger: these were his elephant – the interlopers had no right to intervene in his hunt. He felt a strong urge to rush forward, but he quelled that dangerous inclination. He did not know who these other hunters might be. Judging by the fusillade of gunfire he knew that there was more than one. Any stranger in the wilderness might be a deadly threat. Suddenly there was another sound, the crackle of breaking branches and the rush of an enormous body bearing down on them through the thick underbrush ahead.

'Be ready, Somoya!' Bakkat called urgently. 'They have driven one of the bulls back towards us. He may be wounded and dangerous.'

Jim had only time enough to swing Drumfire to face the sound, when the green forest wall ahead burst open and a bull elephant was upon him at full charge. In that moment of sudden danger, time seemed to slow as though he were caught in the coils of a nightmare. He saw curved tusks that seemed as massive as the main beams of a cathedral roof high above him, and the ears spread wide as the mainsail of a man-o'-war, tattered by shot after a close-fought battle. There was fresh blood smeared down the elephant's flank and fury in his tiny, gleaming eyes as they fastened on Jim.

Bakkat had guessed correctly: the gigantic animal was wounded and enraged. Jim realized that flight would be fatal for Drumfire would not be able to use his speed in the confines of the thorn underbrush while the bull would crash through it without check. Jim could not fire from the saddle. Drumfire was dancing in a circle under him and tossing his head. His antics would upset Jim's aim. Holding the heavy gun high above his head so that it would not hit him in the face as he landed, Jim threw one leg back over the cantle of the saddle and dropped to the ground, landing like a cat facing the charge.

He cocked the gun as his feet touched the earth. His fear was gone in that instant, replaced by a strange feeling of detachment, as though he stood outside himself and watched the gun come up.

Without conscious thought he knew that if he sent a ball through the beast's heart its stride would not even check. It would still rip him limb from limb as effortlessly as a butcher dismembers a chicken carcass, then walk another mile before it succumbed.

After his first near-fatal experience with the head shot, Jim had spent hours and days carefully dissecting and studying the skulls of all the other elephant he had killed since then. Now he could visualize the exact location of the brain in the massive casket of the skull as though it was not solid bone but clear glass. As the butt-stock came into his shoulder he seemed not to see the iron sights of the weapon, but he looked through them to his tiny concealed target.

The shot thundered out. He was instantly blinded by the dense fog of gunsmoke, and driven back on his heels by the recoil. Then, out of the smoke bank, a grey avalanche toppled down on him. He was struck by an enormous slack weight.

The heavy gun was wrenched from his grip and he was hurled backwards. He rolled twice head over heels until he hit a low bush, which brought him up short. He struggled up just as the light breeze blew aside the curtains of silver gunsmoke, and saw the bull elephant kneeling before him on its front legs with the curve of the huge tusks resting on the earth and the tips pointing up to the sky. It seemed to be in an attitude of submission, like a trained elephant waiting to be mounted by a mahout. It was as still and motionless as a granite boulder. There was a round dark hole low between its eyes. It was so close that he reached up and thrust his forefinger full length into it. The pewter-hardened ball, a quarter of a pound in weight, had cleaved the massive frontal bones of the skull and driven through to the brain. When he withdrew his finger it was smeared with custard-yellow brain tissue.

Jim stood up and leaned heavily on one of the tusks. Now that the danger was past his breathing came hard and ragged, and his legs shook under him so that they could scarcely bear his weight. While he clung to the great curve of ivory and swayed on his feet Bakkat rode in and seized Drumfire before he could bolt. He brought him back to Jim and handed him the reins.

'My teaching begins to bear fruit.' He giggled. 'Now you must give thanks and respect to your quarry.'

It was some minutes before Jim could gather himself to complete the ancient ritual of the hunt. Under Bakkat's approving eye he broke off a leafy twig of the sweet thorn and placed it between the bull's lips. 'Eat your last meal to sustain you on the journey to the shadow land. Take with you my respect,' he said. Then he cut off the tail like his father before him. Jim had not forgotten the other musket shots he had heard. But as he stooped to retrieve his fallen musket, he noticed again the thick coating of blood down the bull's flank, and saw a bullet wound high in its right shoulder.

'Bakkat, this animal has been wounded before my shot,' he called sharply. Before Bakkat could reply another human voice close at hand shouted a challenge or a question. It was so unexpected, yet so familiar, that Jim stood with the empty gun in his hand and gaped at the tall athletic figure striding towards him through the undergrowth. A white man, dressed in European-style breeches and jacket, boots and a wide-brimmed straw hat.

'Hey there, fellow. What the devil do you think you're playing at? I drew first blood. The kill is mine.' The voice rang as joyously as church bells in Jim's ears. Under the brim of the hat the interloper's beard curled red and wild as a bush fire.

Jim recovered his wits at once and shouted back just as belligerently, 'By God, you saucy knave!' It required an effort to keep the laughter out of his tone. 'You will have to fight me for it, and I will crack your pate as I have done fifty times before.'

The saucy knave stopped dead in his tracks and stared at Jim, then let out a wild hurrah and rushed at him. Jim dropped his musket and charged headlong to meet him. They came together with a violence that rattled their teeth.

'Jim! Oh, what joy! I thought we would never find you.'

'Mansur! I hardly recognized you with that fluffy red bush sprouting all over your face. Where in the name of the devil have you been?'

They gabbled incoherently as they hugged and buffeted each other, and tried to pull handfuls of hair from each other's heads and faces. Bakkat watched them, shaking his head and slapping his sides with amusement.

'And you, you little hooligan!' Mansur seized him, lifted him off his feet and tucked him under his arm, then embraced Jim again. It took some time for them to begin to behave like

509

sensible persons, but gradually they got themselves under a semblance of control. Mansur replaced Bakkat on his feet, and Jim released Mansur from the headlock in which he had pinned him.

They sat shoulder to shoulder, leaning against the dead elephant's side in the shadow cast by the massive carcass and talked, cutting in on each other, hardly waiting for the reply to one question before asking another. Every now and then Mansur would tug at Jim's beard and Jim would punch him affectionately in the chest or slap his hairy cheek. Though neither mentioned it, each of them was amazed at the changes that had taken place in the other during the time they had been apart. They had become men.

Then the retinue who had accompanied Mansur came looking for him. They were all servants from High Weald or sailors from the schooners. They were astonished to find Jim with their master. After Jim had greeted them affectionately, he set them to work under the supervision of Bakkat to cut out the tusks from the fallen bull. Then he and Mansur could continue their exchange of news, trying to cover in minutes all that had overtaken them and the family since their last meeting nearly two years ago.

'Where is Louisa, the girl you ran off with? Did she have the sense to send you packing?' Mansur demanded.

'By God, coz, I tell you that is a pearl of a lass. Presently I'll take you back to the wagons to be properly introduced to her. You will not credit your eyes when you see her, how lovely she has grown.' Then Jim broke off and his expression changed. 'I know not how best to tell you, coz, but only a few weeks past I fell in with a deserter from the *Gift of Allah*. You must remember the rogue. His name is Rashood. He had a strange and terrible tale to tell, once I could drag it out of him.'

The colour drained from Mansur's face and for a minute he could not speak. Then he blurted out, 'He must have been in the company of two other of our sailors, all three deserters, and there would have been a strange Arab with them.'

'One named Kadem ibn Abubaker al-Jurf.'

Mansur started up. 'Where is he? He murdered my mother, and almost killed my father.'

'I know it. I forced the whole story from Rashood.' Jim tried to calm him. 'My heart breaks for you. I loved Aunt Yassie almost as much as you did. But the assassin has escaped.'

'Tell me all of it,' Mansur demanded. 'Spare me not a single detail.'

There was so much to tell, and they sat so long telling it that the sun was low on the horizon before Jim stood up. 'We must get back to the wagons before nightfall. Louisa will be beside herself.'

Louisa had hung lighted lanterns in the trees to guide Jim home, and she rushed out of the wagon where she and Intepe were nursing Zama as soon as she heard the horses. At last she broke from Jim's embrace when she became aware that a stranger was with him, watching their uninhibited display of affection for each other.

'There is someone with you?' She tucked the loose strands of her silky hair under her bonnet, and straightened her clothing, which Jim had rumpled.

''Tis no one of consequence,' Jim assured her. ''Tis only my cousin Mansur, of whom I have spoken and whom you have seen before. Mansur, this is Louisa Leuven. She and I are affianced.'

'I thought you had over-extolled her virtues,' Mansur bowed to Louisa, then stared at her face in the lantern-light, 'but she is more lovely than you warned me.'

'Jim has told me much about you,' Louisa said shyly. 'He loves you better than a brother. When we saw each other before, on the deck of *Het Gelukkige Meeuw*, there was no opportunity for me to know you better. I hope that in the future we will be able to put that to rights.'

Louisa fed the two men, but as soon as they had eaten she left them to talk without interruption far into the night. It was after midnight when Jim came to join her in the wide cardell bed. 'Forgive me, Hedgehog, that I have neglected you this evening.'

'I would have it no other way, for I know what he means to you and how close you are to each other,' she whispered, as she held out her arms to him. 'But now is my time to be closer still.'

They were all astir before sunrise. While Louisa supervised the preparation of a celebratory breakfast to welcome Mansur to the laager, Mansur was at Zama's bedside. Jim joined them, and all three chatted and reminisced. Zama was so much encouraged by Mansur's arrival that he declared he was ready to leave his sickbed.

Smallboy and Muntu inspanned the wagons, and the caravan moved off. Louisa relinquished care of Zama to Intepe, and for the first time since Zama's wounding she saddled Trueheart and rode out with Jim and Mansur. They passed through the herds of cattle and Mansur was amazed by their numbers and by the weight of the ivory they carried on the pack-saddles strapped to their backs.

'Even though Uncle Tom and my father were able to escape from the colony with much of the family wealth, you have multiplied it many times over with what you have captured. Tell me how it happened. Tell me of the battle against this Nguni queen, Manatasee, and her legions.'

'I described it to you last night,' Jim protested.

'It is too good a tale to be told only once,' Mansur insisted. 'Tell it to me again.'

This time Jim embellished Louisa's role in the fighting, despite her protests that he was exaggerating. 'I warn you, coz, you must not anger this lady. She is a veritable Valkyrie once she is aroused. She is not feared far and wide as the Dreaded Hedgehog for no good reason.'

They rode to the crest of the next hill and looked down towards the ocean. It was so close that they could just make out the windswept white horses that danced on the horizon. 'How far are we from Nativity Bay?' Jim demanded.

'It took me less than three days on foot,' Mansur answered. 'Now that I have this good horse under me I could be there before nightfall.'

Jim looked at Louisa with a wistful air, and she smiled. 'I know what you are thinking, James Archibald,' she said.

'And what do you think about what I am thinking, Hedgehog?'

'I think we should leave Zama, the wagons and the cattle to come on at their best speed and that we should eat the wind.'

Jim let out a happy shout. 'Follow me, my love. This way for Nativity Bay.'

It took less time than Mansur had predicted and the sun was still above the horizon when they reined in on the hills above the wide, glittering bay. The two schooners were anchored off the mouth of the Umbilo river and Jim shaded his eyes with his hat against the sun's reflection off the water.

'Fort Auspice,' Mansur told them, and pointed out the newly erected buildings on the banks of the river. 'Your mother chose the name. She wanted to call it Fort Good Auspice, but Uncle Tom said, "That's a mouthful, and we all know that it an't a bad auspice, any which way you look at it." So that was it. Fort Auspice.'

As they rode closer they were able to make out the palisade of sharpened stakes that enclosed the high ground on which the fort was set. The earth was still raw around the gun emplacements that covered all the approaches to the fortifications.

'Our fathers have taken every precaution against attack by Keyser or other enemies. We have brought ashore most of the guns off the ships,' Mansur explained.

The roofs of the buildings it enclosed showed above the top of the palisade. 'There are barracks for the servants and each of our families have their own quarters.' Mansur pointed them out as they trotted down the hill. 'Those are the stables.

That is the warehouse, and there are the godown and the counting-house.'

All the roofs were still bright and unweathered with new-cut thatch.

'Father has the delusions of Nero.' Jim chuckled. 'He has built himself a city, not a trading post.'

'Aunt Sarah did little to dissuade him,' Mansur said. 'In fact you could say she was an active accomplice.' He snatched off his hat and waved it over his head. 'And there she is now!' A matronly figure had appeared in the gateway of the fort and was staring across at the little band of approaching riders. As soon as Jim waved she threw all dignity to the winds and came running down the path like a schoolgirl released from the classroom.

'Jim! Oh, Jim boy!' Her joyous cries echoed off the cliffs of the bluff. Jim sent Drumfire into a wild gallop to meet her. He jumped from the saddle while the stallion was still at full charge and gathered his mother into his arms.

When they heard Drumfire's hoofs Dorian and Tom Courtney came running out through the gates of the fort. Mansur and Louisa hung back to let the first frenzy of greeting abate.

It took another five days for the wagons and cattle to reach Fort Auspice. The entire family stood together on the firing platform of the palisade. The herd of spare horses led the way, and Tom and Dorian cheered as they galloped past. 'It will be good to have a horse under me again,' Tom exulted. 'I have felt that half of me was missing for lack of a good mount. Now we will be able to range through this land and claim it as our own.'

Then they gazed in awed silence as the dark mass of the cattle herds poured down the hills towards them. When Inkunzi and his Nguni herders began to offload the ivory on the open parade in front of the gates, Tom climbed down the ladder from the platform and walked among the tall stacks of tusks, marvelling at the quantity and size of some of them. Then he came back and scowled at Jim. 'For the love of all that's holy, lad! Have you no sense of moderation? Did you not give a thought to where we were going to store all this?

We shall have to build another warehouse, and you are solely to blame.' Tom's scowl faded and he laughed at his own wit, then folded his son in a bear-hug. 'After this haul, I think we will have no choice but to declare you a full partner in the company.'

Over the following months, there was employment for all, and much besides to plan and arrange. The main work on the fort was completed, including the extension to the warehouse to accommodate the abundance of captured ivory. Sarah was able at last to bring her furniture ashore. She set up her harpsichord in the hall, which was to serve as the dining and common room to both families. That night she played all their favourite tunes, while they joined in the choruses. Tone-deaf Tom made up in volume for what he lacked in tuneful-ness, until Sarah tactfully distracted him by asking him to turn the pages of her music book.

For lack of grazing, such a great number of cattle could not be held in the immediate vicinity of the fort. Jim split them into seven smaller herds, and ordered Inkunzi to move them out into the surrounding country, as far as twenty leagues distant from Fort Auspice, wherever good grazing and water could be found. The Nguni herders built their villages close to these new grazing grounds.

'They will form a buffer round the fort,' Jim pointed out to Tom and Dorian, 'and they will give us good warning of the approach of an enemy before they come within twenty leagues.' Then he added, as if in afterthought, 'Of course, I will have to ride out to inspect them at regular intervals.'

'And that will provide you with a fine excuse to run off hunting elephants.' Tom nodded sagely. 'Your devotion to company duty is moving, lad.'

However, after only a few such expeditions the elephant responded to Jim's attentions by moving out of this country and vanishing into the fastness of the deep interior.

Within a month of their arrival at Fort Auspice, Jim and

Louisa waylaid Sarah in her kitchen. After a long and emotional discussion, which left both women in tears of joy, Sarah went off immediately to speak to Tom.

'My oath, Sarah Courtney, I know not what to say,' said Tom, which she knew was his most forceful expression of amazement. 'There can be no mistake?'

'Louisa is certain. Women are seldom mistaken in such matters,' Sarah replied.

'We shall need somebody to splice the knot, and make it all shipshape and legal.' Tom looked worried.

'Well, you are a ship's captain,' Sarah pointed out tartly, 'so you have that power vested in you.'

The longer Tom thought about it, the more the idea of having a grandson appealed to him. 'Well, it seems Louisa has passed her trials fair enough,' he conceded, with a convincing show of nonchalance.

Sarah placed her fists on her hips, a storm warning. 'If that was meant as a jest, Thomas Courtney, it fell far short of the mark. As far as you and I, or anyone else in the world, is concerned, Louisa Leuven will be a virgin bride,' she said.

He gave ground rapidly. 'I am convinced of that, and I will fight any man who says different. As you and I are well aware, premature birth runs strongly on both sides of our family. On top of that, Louisa is a comely and likely lass. I daresay our Jim would have to sail a long way to find another better.'

'Does that mean you will do it?' Sarah demanded.

'I suspect I will not have much peace until I do.'

'For once you suspect correctly,' she said, and he picked her up and bussed her on both cheeks.

Tom married them on the quarter-deck of the *Sprite*. There was not space aboard for all the company so the overflow watched from the rigging of the *Revenge* or from the palisade walls of the fort. Jim and Louisa spoke their vows, then signed the ship's log. When Jim brought his bride ashore, Mansur and his men fired a salute of twenty-one guns from the cannons of the fort, which scattered the Nguni warriors in confusion, and reduced little Letee to hysteria until Bakkat could reassure her that the sky was not falling in upon them.

'Well!' said Tom, with satisfaction. 'That should hold them, until they can find a priest to do the job properly.' And he doffed his captain's cocked hat and exchanged the job of clergyman for that of bartender, by knocking the bung out of a cask of Cape brandy.

Smallboy slaughtered an ox, and they roasted it whole on a spit on the beach below the fort. The festivities went on until it was consumed and the brandy cask was at last drunk dry.

Jim and Louisa began work on the construction of their own private quarters within the walls of the fort. With so many willing hands to join in the work, it was less than a week before they vacated the wagon that for so long had been their home, and moved under a thatched roof between solid walls of sun-baked brick.

Then there were darker matters to address. Rashood was brought out in his chains from the cell in the fort, which had originally been intended as a cellar. Dorian and Mansur who were, by the law of Islam, the judges and the executioners, took him into the forest far out of sight and earshot of the fort. They were gone for only a few hours, but when they returned they were grim of countenance, and Rashood was no longer with them.

The next day Tom convened a session of the family council. For the first time Louisa Courtney attended as the newest addition to the clan. As the eldest, Tom explained the decisions that faced them. 'Thanks to Jim and Louisa we are heavily overstocked with ivory. The best markets are still Zanzibar, the factories on the Coromandel Coast or at Bombay in the realm of the Great Mogul. Zanzibar is in the hands of Caliph Zayn al-Din, so that port is closed to us. I will stay on here at Fort Auspice to conduct company business, and I will need Jim to help me. Dorian will take the ships north, laden with as much of the ivory as they can carry, though I doubt that will be even a quarter of our total stock. When it has been sold he has even more pressing business in Muscat.' He looked at his younger brother. 'I will ask Dorian to explain it to you.'

Dorian removed the ivory mouthpiece of his hookah from

between his teeth, which were still white, even and without gaps. He looked around the circle of well-beloved faces. 'We know that Zayn al-Din was ousted by a revolutionary junta in Muscat. Both Batula and Kumrah were able to obtain certain confirmation of that on their last voyage to Oman. Kadem ibn Abubaker,' Dorian's handsome features darkened as he pronounced the name of Yasmini's murderer, 'purported to bring me an invitation from the junta, to take Zayn al-Din's place on the Elephant Throne, and to lead the battle against him. We don't know if the junta are truly trying to find me, or if it was merely another lie to try to entice me into Zayn's clutches. In any event, I refused for the sake of Yasmini, but in attempting to protect her I condemned her to death.'

Dorian's voice faltered, and Tom cut in gruffly, 'You are too harsh on yourself, brother. No man living could have foreseen the consequences.'

'Nevertheless Yasmini is dead by Zayn's orders and by the bloody hands of Kadem. There is no surer way for me to avenge her death than by sailing to Oman and throwing in my lot with the revolutionaries in Muscat.'

Mansur got up from his stool at the foot of the long table and went to stand at Dorian's shoulder. 'If you will allow it, I will sail with you, Father, and take my place at your right hand.'

'Not only will I allow it, I will welcome you with all my heart.'

'That is settled, then,' said Tom briskly. 'Jim and his bride will be here to help Sarah and me, so we will not be short-handed and we can spare Mansur. When do you plan on sailing, brother?'

'The trade winds will give way to the monsoon within six weeks. The winds should stand fair towards the end of next month,' Dorian replied. 'That will give us time to make the preparations.'

'We will strip all the remaining cannon out of the ships to give you more burthen for the ivory,' Tom said. 'Besides, we can use them here in the fort to bolster our defences. We can never be certain that Keyser has not smelt us out. Then there are these marauding Nguni *impis* sweeping through the land. Jim has routed one group under Manatasee, but we know from the fugitives who have come in to us that there are others just as savage running amok out there. Once you have sold the ivory you will be able to buy new guns in India. There are handy armourers in the Punjab. I have seen their work, and they make excellent nine-pounders. Just the right weight and length of barrel for our hulls.'

When the guns had been lifted out of the schooners, and all the powder and shot with them, they were ferried ashore in the longboats, dragged up the hill by teams of oxen and set in the earth emplacements around the fort.

'Well, that should do nicely.' Tom eyed the new defences with satisfaction. 'It would take an army with siege machines to subdue us. I think we are safe from marauding tribes, or even from any force that Keyser might care to send against us once he gets wind of where we are.'

Relieved of the cannon, the schooners rode lightly at anchor, showing much of the copper sheeting on their bottoms. 'We will soon find ballast to restore their trim,' Dorian promised, and he ordered the loading of the ivory and the refilling of the water casks.

Since Yasmini's murder Dorian had been cast into sudden moods of deep melancholy. He seemed prematurely aged by grief. There were new strands of pure silver in his red-gold hair and beard, and fresh lines deeply etched in his brow. But now, with a definite goal in mind and Mansur beside him, he seemed rejuvenated, once more abounding in vigour and determination.

They began to load the ivory aboard the schooners, and to lay in fresh stores and top up the water casks for the voyage ahead. The pickle barrels were refilled with sides of beef from the captured herds, and the hulls of the two ships settled deeper in the water. Dorian and his captains, Batula and Kumrah, agonized over the trim to wring the best speed and handiness from them.

'Until we have new guns to defend ourselves, we will have to rely on speed to run from any enemy that we encounter.

Despite our father's and brother Tom's best intentions and effort twenty years ago, there are still pirates at work in the Ocean of the Indies.'

'Keep well offshore from the African coast. That's where they have their nests,' Tom advised, 'and with the monsoon in your sails you will be well able to outrun any pirate dhow.'

They were all so busily employed, the women ordering their new homes, Tom and Jim occupied with the cattle and horses, Dorian and Mansur making the ships ready, that the days sped by.

'It does not seem like six weeks,' Jim told Mansur, as they stood on the beach together and looked out at the two little schooners. The yards were crossed and the crews had gone aboard. All was ready for them to catch the tide on the morrow.

'It seems, these days, that we no sooner set eyes upon each other than it is time to part again,' Mansur agreed.

'I have a feeling that this time it will be for more than just a short while, coz,' Jim said sadly. 'I believe that an adventure and a new life await you over the blue horizon.'

'You also, Jim. You have your woman, soon you will have a son, and you have made this land your own. I am alone, and I still seek the country of my heart.'

'No matter how many leagues of sea or land come between us, I shall always feel close to you in spirit,' said Jim.

Mansur knew how great an effort it had taken him to make such a sentimental declaration. He seized his cousin and hugged him hard. Jim hugged him back just as fiercely.

The two schooners sailed with the dawn and the tide, and all the family was on board the *Revenge* as they cleared the mouth of the bay. A mile offshore Dorian hove to, and Tom and Sarah, Jim and Louisa went down into the longboat and watched the two ships sail on and grow tiny with distance. At last they disappeared over the horizon and Jim turned the longboat back for the bay.

The fort seemed strangely empty without Dorian and Mansur, and they missed their marvellous voices at the family singsongs around Sarah's harpsichord in the evenings.

The voyage across the Ocean of the Indies was swift and almost without incident. With Mansur commanding the *Sprite* and Dorian the *Revenge*, the two schooners sailed in close company and the monsoon wind was kind to them. They gave the island of Ceylon a wide berth, mindful of Keyser's threats to warn the Dutch governor in Trincomalee of their trespasses in the colony of Good Hope, and they sailed on to the Coromandel Coast of south-eastern India, to reach it before the change of season. They called in at the competing trading factories of the English, French and Portuguese, without admitting their true identity. Both Dorian and Mansur adopted Arabic dress and in public spoke only that language. In each port Dorian judged the demand for ivory precisely, and was at pains not to flood the market with abundance. They did much better than he and Tom had calculated. With the ships' coffers charged with silver rupees and gold mohurs, and still a quarter of their ivory unsold, they turned back southwards and rounded the southern tip of India, sailing through the Palk between Ceylon and the mainland, then northwards again along the western coast until they reached the territories of the Great Mogul. Here they sold the remainder of the ivory in Bombay where the English East India Company had its headquarters, and in the other markets of the western ports of the crumbling Mogul empire.

The once mighty empire, the richest and most glorious that had ever flourished in the great continent, was now in decay and dissolution as lesser emperors than Babur and Akbar struggled for dominance. Despite the political upheavals, the new Persian influence at the court of Delhi made for a favourable trading climate. The Persians were traders to the marrow of their bones, and the prices for ivory exceeded those that they had received in the factories of the Carnatic.

Dorian was now in a position to rearm the two schooners, fill their empty holds with powder and shot, and transform them from trading vessels into fighting ships. They sailed on northwards and anchored in the roads of Hyderabad, through which the Indus river ran to the Arabian Sea. Dorian and Mansur went ashore with an armed party under Batula. They hired a carriage in the main souk, and an interpreter, to take them to one of the outlying areas of the sprawling, bustling city. The iron foundry of one of the most famous gun manufacturers in all the Punjab and the Indus basin – which meant in all India – was located on this flat and featureless alluvial plain. The proprietor was a Sikh of imperial mien, one Pandit Singh.

Over the following weeks Dorian and Mansur selected from his stores a battery of guns, twelve for each ship. These were all long-barrelled, with a four-inch bore and an eleven-foot-long barrel that fired an iron ball of nine pounds weight. With such a narrow bore relative to the length of barrel it was an accurate, long-ranged weapon.

Dorian measured and bore-gauged each of the barrels so that he could be certain that the same size of round-shot would fit them all, and that there were no discrepancies in the casting. Then, much to the indignation of Pandit Singh who took it as a slur on his workmanship, he insisted on firing the selected guns, to satisfy himself that there were no flaws in the metal. Two barrels burst on the first discharge. Pandit Singh explained that this had nothing to do with his manufacture, but was indubitably caused by the malignant influence of a *goppa*, the most pernicious variety of *shaitan*.

Dorian ordered gun carriages to be built by local carpenters to his own design. Then the guns on their own carriages were towed by bullock teams to the harbour, and at last carried out to the ships in lighters. Pandit Singh cast several hundred rounds of iron shot to fit the new guns, as well as great quantities of grape- and chain-shot. He was also able to supply any amount of gunpowder, which he personally guaranteed to be of the best quality. Dorian opened and sampled every barrel, rejecting over half before sending the remainder on board the schooners.

Next he turned his attention to the appearance of his flotilla, which in these seas was a consideration almost as important as its armament. He sent Mansur ashore to bargain for bolts of the finest quality green and burgundy canvas in the souks of Hyderabad. The sailmakers made up resplendent suits of sails, to replace the faded and weather-stained articles. The tailors of the souk were also put to work fitting the crews of the schooners with wide-legged cotton breeches and jackets to match the new sails. The results were impressive.

Being so close to Oman, Hyderabad was a hothouse of political and military rumour. While they bargained with the merchants, Dorian and Mansur drank their coffee and listened to the gossip. Dorian learned that the revolutionary junta still held power in Muscat, but that Caliph Zayn al-Din had consolidated his hold on Lamu and Zanzibar and all the other ports of the Omani empire. On every hand he heard that Zayn was planning an attack on Muscat to overthrow the junta and to recover his lost throne. In this endeavour he would have the assistance of the English East India Company and the Sublime Porte in Constantinople, seat of the Ottoman Turkish empire.

Dorian was also able to learn the identity of the new rulers in Muscat. They were a council of ten, of whom Dorian recognized most by name. They were men with whom he had eaten bread and salt, and ridden into battle in years gone by. His spirits soared when at last he was ready for sea.

Even after they sailed he did not immediately set a course for Muscat, which lay less than seven hundred miles away, west along the Tropic of Cancer in the Gulf of Oman. Instead, they sailed back and forth just out of sight of land while he drilled the crews of both ships in serving the new guns. Dorian had spared no expense on powder and shot, and kept them hard at it until they were almost as swift and expert as the gun-crews of a British Royal Navy frigate.

The flotilla made an impressive show when at last it sailed into the harbour of Muscat with the pristine sails set to the royals and the crew manning the yards in their new uniforms. The schooners flew the gold and royal-blue colours of Oman at their masthead. Dorian ordered the top sails struck and the new guns fired as a salute to the palace and the fortress. The gun-crew had grown fond of the sound of their own fire. Once begun, the honours continued enthusiastically until, in the end, they were persuaded to stop wasting further powder and shot only by the strenuous application of the rope's end.

All this created a great stir on the shore. Through his telescope Dorian watched the scurrying of messengers along the waterfront, and the gunners running to man the batteries on the parapets of the fortress. He knew that there would be a long delay while the junta decided how to react to the arrival of this strange flotilla of warships, so he settled down to wait.

Mansur launched the cutter and had himself rowed across to join his father. The two stood by the rail and turned their attention to the other shipping anchored in the inner harbour. In particular they studied a handsome, well-appointed three-masted ship that flew the Union flag, together with the pennant of his Britannic Majesty's consul general at her maintop. At first he presumed that such a fine ship must belong to the English East India Company, but her defaced blue ensign showed she was a privately owned vessel, like his own.

'A wealthy owner. That plaything must have cost five thousand pounds at the very least.' He read her name on her stern: '*Arcturus*. Of course, we would not find a ship belonging to John Company here in Muscat, because the Company has openly allied itself with Zayn al-Din in Zanzibar,' he pointed out to his son.

The blue-jacketed officers on the deck of the *Arcturus* turned their telescopes on them with equal interest. For the most part they seemed to be Indian or Arab for they were dark-skinned and most were bearded. Dorian picked out the captain by his cocked hat and the gold frogging on his sleeves. He was the exception, a ruddy-faced, clean-shaven European. Mansur swept his glass from the quarter-deck towards the bows and stopped with surprise. 'They have white women on board.'

Two ladies were strolling along the deck, accompanied by a fashionably dressed gentleman in a frock coat and high white stock. He wore a tall black hat and carried a cane with a gold head with which he illustrated some point he was making to his female companions.

'That's your rich owner for you,' Mansur observed, 'dressed like a dandy and very much satisfied with himself.'

'You can tell so much from so far?' Dorian asked, with a smile, but he studied the man carefully. Of course, it was highly unlikely that he had ever seen him before, but there seemed something hauntingly familiar about him.

Mansur laughed lightly. 'Cannot you see how he struts along like a penguin with a lighted candle stuck up its arse? I can tell that the plum pudding waddling along beside him in all the frippery and furbelows is his wife. They make a splendid couple—' Mansur broke off abruptly. Dorian lowered his glass and glanced at him. Mansur's eyes had narrowed and his suntanned cheek was suddenly stained a darker bronze. Dorian had seldom seen his son blush, but that was what was happening to him now. He lifted his telescope and studied the second woman, who was clearly the cause of his son's change of mood. More a girl than a woman, he thought, though tall enough. Waist like an hourglass but, then, she can probably afford an expensive French corset. Graceful deportment and lithe walk. Then he spoke aloud: 'What do you make of the other one?'

'Which one is that?' Mansur feigned indifference.

'The skinny one in the cabbage-coloured dress.'

'She is not skinny, and it's emerald,' said Mansur furiously, and was cast into confusion as he realized he had been caught out. 'Well, not that I am in the least concerned.'

The man in the tall hat seemed to take offence at their bold appraisal for he glared across the water at them, then took the arm of his plump companion and led her across to the starboard rail of the *Arcturus*. The girl in the green dress hesitated and looked back towards them.

Mansur watched her avidly. The wide-brimmed straw hat must have protected her complexion from the tropical sun. Even so, it was tanned to a soft peach colour. Though he was too far away to make out detail, he could see that her features were regular and finely proportioned. Her light brown hair was

525

gathered up in a net on her shoulders. It was thick and lustrous. Her brow was wide and deep and her expression serene and intelligent. He felt strangely breathless, and wished he could tell the colour of her eyes. But then she tossed her head impatiently and gathered up her green skirts. She followed the older couple across the deck and out of Mansur's sight.

Mansur lowered the telescope, feeling oddly deprived.

'Well, the show is over for now,' Dorian said. 'I am going below. Call me if there is any change.'

An hour passed, then another, before Mansur hailed through the skylight of the stern cabin: 'Boat putting out from the palace jetty.'

It was a small lateen-rigged felucca with a crew of six, but there was a passenger in the stern sheets. He was dressed in snowy robes and turban, and at his waist was a scimitar in a gold scabbard. As they drew closer Dorian could make out the sparkle of a large ruby in his turban. This was a man of importance.

The felucca came in alongside and one of the crew hooked on to *Revenge*'s chains. After a short interval the visitor came up through the entry-port. He was probably a little older than Dorian. He had the sharp, hard features of one of the desert tribes, and the open, direct gaze of one who looked to far horizons. He crossed the deck towards Dorian with a long, supple stride.

'Peace unto you, bin-Shibam.' Dorian addressed him in the familiar form, as one comrade in arms might greet another. 'It is many years since you stood at my shoulder in the pass of the Bright Gazelle and let no enemy through.'

The tall warrior stopped in mid-stride and stared at Dorian in utter astonishment.

'I see that God has favoured you. You are as strong as you were when we were young. Do you still bear the lance against the tyrant and the patricide?' Dorian went on.

The warrior cried out and rushed forward to throw himself at Dorian's feet. 'Al-Salil! True prince of the royal house of

Caliph Abd Muhammad al-Malik. God has heard our fervent prayers. The prophecy of Mullah al-Allama is fulfilled. You have come back to your people in the time of their great sorrow, when most they need you.'

Dorian lifted bin-Shibam to his feet and embraced him. 'What are you, an old desert hawk, doing in the fleshpots of the city?' He held him at arm's length. 'You are dressed like a pasha. You who were once a fighting sheikh of the Saar, the fiercest of all the tribes of Oman.'

'My heart longs for the open desert, al-Salil, and to feel a racing camel under me,' bin-Shibam confessed, 'but instead I spend my time here in endless debate, when I should be riding free and wielding the long lance.'

'Come, old friend.' Dorian led him towards his cabin. 'Let us go where we can speak freely.'

In the cabin they reclined on the piled rugs and a servant brought them tiny brass cups of treacly coffee.

'To my sorrow and discomfort, I am now one of the war council of the junta. There are ten of us, one elected by each of the ten tribes of Oman. Ever since we toppled that murderous monster Zayn al-Din from the Elephant Throne, I have been sitting here in Muscat talking until my jaw aches and my gut grows slack.'

'Tell me the subject of these talks,' Dorian said, and over the next hours bin-Shibam confirmed almost everything that Dorian already knew.

He told of how Zayn al-Din had murdered all the heirs and descendants of Dorian's adoptive father Caliph al-Malik. He related many of his other unconscionable atrocities and the sufferings he had inflicted upon his people. 'In God's Name, the tribes rose up against his tyranny. We met his minions in battle and triumphed over them. Zayn al-Din fled the city and took refuge on the Fever Coast. We should have prosecuted our campaign against him to the end, but we were split by controversy over who should lead us. There were no heirs of the true Caliph left alive.' Here bin-Shibam bowed to Dorian. 'God forgive us, al-Salil, but we did not know your where-

527

abouts. It is only in the past few years that we heard whispers you were still alive. We have sent out messengers to every port in the Ocean of the Indies to seek you.'

'I have heard your pleas, though they were faint and far-off, and I have come to join your cause.'

'God's benevolence upon you, for we have been in grievous circumstances. Each of the ten tribes wants their own sheikh to take the caliphate. Zayn escaped with most of the fleet so we could not follow him to Zanzibar. While we talked end-lessly we grew weaker, and Zayn al-Din grew stronger. Seeing that we delayed, his minions, whom we had scattered, rallied and flocked back to him. He conquered the ports of the African mainland, and massacred those who supported us there.'

'It is the first principle of warfare that you should never give an enemy grace to gather his strength,' Dorian reminded him.

'Even as you say, al-Salil. Zayn has gathered powerful allies to his cause.' Bin-Shibam stood up and crossed to the porthole of the cabin. He drew aside the curtain. 'There is one of them who has come to us in all arrogance, purporting to act as a peace-maker, but in truth bringing an ultimatum and a deadly threat.' He pointed at the *Arcturus* anchored in the inner harbour.

'Tell me, who is aboard that ship? I see he flies the flag of a consul general.'

'He is the representative of the English monarch, his consul general to the Orient, one of the most powerful men in these seas. He comes purporting to mediate between us and Zayn al-Din, but we know this man well by reputation. As some merchants trade in rugs, he trades in nations, armies and all the weapons of war. He moves secretly from the conclaves of the English East India Company in Bombay to the court of the Great Mogul in Delhi, from the bosom of the Sublime Porte to the Emperor's cabinet in Peking. His wealth equals any of theirs. He has amassed it by dealing in power and war, and the lives of men.' Bin-Shibam spread his hands expressively. 'How can we children of the sands deal with such a one as this?'

'Have you heard his terms? Do you know what message he brings?'

'We have not yet met him. We have promised that we will do so on the first day of Ramadan. But we are afraid. We know that we will have the worst of any treaty we make with him.' He came back to kneel before Dorian. 'Perhaps in our hearts we were waiting for you to come to us, and to lead us into battle as you did so many times before. Give me your permission to go back to the council and tell them who you are, and why you have come.'

'Go, old friend. Tell them that al-Salil wishes to address the council.'

Bin-Shibam returned after nightfall. As soon as he entered the cabin he prostrated himself before Dorian. 'I would have come sooner but the council does not wish the English consul to see you come ashore. They bade me convey to you their deepest respect and, for your father's sake, they profess their loyalty to your family. They are waiting now in the throne room of the palace. I beg you, come with me and I will take you to them. From them you will learn more to your great profit and to ours.'

Dorian left Mansur in command of the flotilla. He threw a cloak of camel-hair over his head and shoulders and followed bin-Shibam down into the felucca. On the way to the palace jetty they passed close to the anchored *Arcturus*. The captain was on deck. Dorian saw his face in the light from the compass binnacle. He was giving orders to the officer of the watch. His was a fruity West Country accent, but it sounded strangely alien in Dorian's ears. I am already returning to the ties and loyalties of my childhood, he thought, and then his mind took another turning. If only Yasmini were with me now to share this homecoming.

Guards were waiting for them when they landed at the stone jetty, and they led Dorian through a heavy iron-grid door, and up a circular staircase into a maze of narrow passages.

The walls were of stone blocks and lit by torches guttering in wall brackets. It smelt of mould and rodents. At last they reached a heavily barred door. His escort beat upon it with the hilts of their lances, and when it swung open they went on down corridors that were wider and under high-domed ceilings. Now there were rushes on the floors and tapestries of silk and fine wool on the walls. They reached another doorway, with armoured sentries standing before it, who crossed their lance blades to deny them entrance.

'Who seeks admittance to the war council of Oman?'

'Prince al-Salil ibn al-Malik.'

The guards drew aside and made deep obeisance. 'Pass through, Your Highness. The council attends your arrival.'

The doors swung open slowly, creaking on their hinges, and Dorian stepped into the hall beyond. It was lit by hundreds of small ceramic lamps, the wicks floating in perfumed oil. But the light they shed was not sufficient to disperse the shadows that cloaked the far recesses, and left the high ceiling in darkness.

A circle of robed men was seated on cushions at a low table. The tabletop was cast from pure silver in the geometric patterns of Islamic religious art. The men rose as Dorian stood before them. One, who was clearly the elder and most senior of the council, came forward. His beard was shining white and he walked with the deliberate and venerable gait of age. He stared into Dorian's face.

'God's blessings on you, Mustapha Zindara,' Dorian greeted him, 'my father's trusted councillor.'

'It is him. In God's name, it is verily him,' cried the old man. He fell upon his face and kissed the hem of Dorian's robe. Dorian lifted him to his feet and embraced him.

One at a time the others came forward, and Dorian greeted most by name, asked after their families, and reminded them of desert crossings they had made together, battles they had fought as brothers in arms.

Then each took up a lamp. They all gathered around him and led him down the length of the long hall. As they approached the far end, something tall and massive glowed with a pearly lustre in the lamplight. Dorian knew what it was, for the last time he had seen it his father had been seated upon it.

They led Dorian up the steps and placed him on the piles of tigerskins and silken cushions embroidered with gold and silver thread that covered the summit platform of that tall structure. It had been carved three hundred years before from one hundred and fifty massive ivory tusks: the Elephant Throne of the Caliphate of Oman.

Over the following days and weeks, from before dawn until after midnight, Dorian sat in council with his councillors and ministers. They reported to him on every facet of the affairs of the kingdom, from the mood of the populace and the desert tribes to the coffers of the treasury, the condition of the fleet and the strength of the army. They told him of the virtual breakdown in trade, and explained the diplomatic and political dilemmas that confronted them.

Swiftly Dorian grasped the desperate straits to which their cause had been reduced. What remained of the fleet that had made Oman a great seafaring nation had sailed with Zayn al-Din to the Fever Coast. Many tribes had become disheartened by the endless procrastination of the council, and most of their squadrons had disappeared like mist into desert fastness. The treasury was almost bare, for Zayn had ransacked it before he fled.

Dorian listened, then gave his orders. They were succinct and direct. It all seemed so natural and familiar, as though he had never ceased to command. His reputation for political and military genius was multiplied tenfold as it was repeated in the streets and souks of the city. His appearance was handsome and noble. He had the air of command. His sure manner and confidence were infectious. He froze what remained of the contents of the treasury, and issued bills backed by his own authority to meet long-overdue expenses. He took charge of the granaries, rationed the food supplies and prepared the city for siege.

He sent messages by swift camel to the sheikhs of the desert tribes, and rode out into the desert to meet them when they came to him to swear their allegiance. He sent them back into the interior to summon their battle array.

Inspired by his example, his military captains plunged with fresh vigour into planning the defence of the city. He replaced those who were clearly incompetent with men he knew from experience that he could trust.

When he toured the defences and ordered immediate repairs, the populace thronged about him joyously. They held up their children for a glimpse of the legendary al-Salil, and touched his robes as he passed.

Three times Dorian sent messages to the *Arcturus*, begging the consul general's indulgence, pleading the excuse that he was so recently elevated to the caliphate that he had not been able to acquaint himself with all the affairs of state. He fobbed off the inevitable meeting for as long as possible. Every day he could delay made his position that much stronger.

Finally, a boat came from the *Arcturus* to the palace jetty, bearing a letter from the English consul general. It was written in beautiful flowing Arabic script, and Mansur thought he recognized a feminine touch, and that he knew who had penned it. It was addressed not to the Caliph but to the President for the Time Being of the Revolutionary Council of Oman, and pointedly made no acknowledgement of Dorian's existence or of his title, Caliph al-Salil ibn al-Malik, although by now the English consul, through his spies, must certainly have been aware of all that was taking place.

The letter was brusque, and eschewed any attempt at flowery diplomacy. His Britannic Majesty's consul general to the Orient regretted that the council had been unable to grant him audience. Other more pressing matters made it necessary for the consul general to sail from Muscat to Zanzibar in the near future, and it was uncertain as to when he would return to Muscat.

Dorian was untroubled by the veiled threat the letter contained, but he was flabbergasted when he read the signature appended to it. Wordlessly he handed the letter back to Mansur and pointed out the name and signature that had been written in English.

'He has the same name as us.' Mansur was puzzled. 'Sir Guy Courtney.'

'The same name, yes,' Dorian's face was still pale and tight with the shock, 'and the same blood too. The moment I set eyes on him, I thought there was something familiar about him. He is your uncle Tom's twin brother, and my half-brother. That makes him another uncle of yours into the bargain.'

'I have never heard his name mentioned before this day,' Mansur protested, 'and I do not understand it at all.'

'There is every good reason that you have not heard Guy Courtney's name. Dark deeds and bad blood run deep.'

'Might I not know now?' Mansur asked.

Dorian was silent for a while before he sighed. 'It is a sad and sorry tale of treachery and deceit, jealousy and bitter hatred.'

'Tell me, Father,' Mansur insisted quietly.

Dorian nodded. 'Yes, I must, though it gives me no pleasure to relive these dire affairs. It is only fair that you should know.' He reached for the comfort of his hookah and did not speak again until the fire glowed in the bowl, and the blue smoke bubbled through the scented water of the glass reservoir.

'It's over thirty years ago now that Tom, Guy and I, all brothers together, sailed from Plymouth bound for Good Hope. We were with your grandfather Hal in the old *Seraph*. I was the baby, scarcely ten years of age, but Tom and Guy were almost grown men. There was another family on board. We were giving them passage to Bombay where Mr Beatty was to take up a high appointment with John Company. He had with him his daughters. The eldest girl was Caroline, sixteen and a beautiful vixen.'

'Surely you do not speak of the plum pudding we saw on the deck of the *Arcturus* in the harbour?' Mansur exclaimed.

'It seems so.' Dorian nodded. 'I assure you she was once lovely. Time changes all things.'

'Forgive me, Father, I should not have interrupted you. You were about to tell me of the other daughters.'

'The youngest was Sarah, and she was sweet and lovable.'

'Sarah?' Mansur looked askance.

'I know what you are thinking and you are correct in your assumption. Yes, she is now your aunt Sarah, but wait, I shall come to it – if you give me half a chance to get in a word edgewise.' Mansur looked repentant, and Dorian went on: 'Hardly had the *Seraph* cleared Plymouth harbour when Guy fell hopelessly in love with Caroline. She, on the other hand, had sheep's eyes for Tom. Your uncle Tom being Tom obliged her. He double-shotted her dainty cannon, stoked her fireplace, rattled her timbers and finally placed a large fruit cake to bake in her hot little oven.'

Mansur smiled, despite the seriousness of the subject. 'I am aghast that my own father should be familiar with such vulgar terms.'

'Forgive me for offending your sensitive feelings – but to continue. Guy was infuriated that his brother had so treated the object of his love and devotion and challenged Tom to a duel. Even in those early days Tom was a fine swordsman. Guy was not. Tom did not want to kill his brother, but on the other hand he wanted nothing further to do with the fruit cake Caroline was baking. For Tom it had been nothing more than a bit of fun. I was only a child at the time, and not certain as to what was happening, but I can still remember the storm that rocked and split the family. Our father forbade the duel, luckily for Guy.'

Mansur could see how Dorian was suffering at the memory, although he tried to cover his distress with a flippant air. He remained silent, respecting his father's feelings.

At last Dorian continued: 'In the end Guy broke away from us. When we reached Good Hope, he married Caroline and took on board Tom's bastard as his own. Then he left us and went on with the Beatty family to India. I never saw him again until now when we spied him and Caroline on the deck of the *Arcturus*.' He was silent again, brooding in the blue clouds of tobacco smoke.

'That was not the end of it. In Bombay, with his father-in-law's patronage, Guy rose swiftly to consular rank. When I was abducted at the age of twelve and fell into the hands of the slavers, Tom went to Guy and asked for his help to find me and rescue me. Guy refused, and tried to have Tom arrested for murder and other crimes he had not committed. Tom made a run for it, but not before he had swept up Sarah and eloped with her. This only fanned the flames of Guy's hatred. Sir Guy Courtney, his Britannic Majesty's consul general to the Orient, is a fine hater. My brother he may be, but in name alone. In fact, he is a bitter enemy and the ally of Zayn al-Din. But now I need your help in composing a letter to him.'

They took great pains with it. It was in Arabic style, filled with flowery compliments and protestations of goodwill. It went on to offer profuse apologies for any unintended offence that had been given. It expressed the greatest respect for the power and dignity of the consul general's office. Finally it went on to beg the consul general to attend an audience with the Caliph at a date and time of his own choice, but preferably at the first convenient opportunity.

'I would go out to the *Arcturus* myself but, of course, that would not be diplomatically correct. You must deliver the message. Whatever you do, do not let him suspect that we are blood relatives, nor that you speak English. I want you to assess his mood and intentions. Ask him if we can supply his ship with water, meat or fresh produce. Offer him and his crew the freedom and hospitality of the city. If they come ashore our spies will be able to milk news and intelligence from them. We must try to delay him here as long as possible, until we are ready to confront Zayn al-Din.'

Mansur dressed carefully for the visit, in the style befitting the eldest son of the Caliph of Oman. He wore the green turban of the believer with an emerald pin, one of the few notable gems that remained in the palace treasury after Zayn al-Din's depredations. Over his white robes, his waistcoat was of tanned camelskin embroidered with gold thread. His sandals, sword-belt and scabbard were all worked with filigree by the skilled goldsmiths of the city.

When Mansur mounted the ladder to the deck of the *Arcturus* with his red beard glowing in the sunlight, he cut such a magnificent figure that the captain and his officers gaped at him, and took a minute to recover.

'My compliments, sir, I am William Cornish, captain of this vessel.' The English captain's Arabic was poor and heavily accented. 'May I enquire who I have the honour of addressing?' His large red face, which had earned him the name 'Ruby' Cornish in the fleet of the English East India Company, glowed in the sunlight.

'I am Prince Mansur ibn al-Salil al-Malik,' Mansur replied, in flowing Arabic, touching his heart and lips in greeting. 'I come as an emissary of my father, Caliph al-Salil ibn al-Malik. I have the honour to bear a message for His Excellency the Consul General of His Britannic Majesty.'

Ruby Cornish looked uncomfortable. He followed what Mansur had said only with difficulty, and he had been severely enjoined not to acknowledge any titles of royalty to which these Omani rebels might lay claim.

'Please ask your retainers to remain in the barge,' he said. Mansur dismissed them with a gesture, and Cornish went on, 'If you will come this way, sir.' He led Mansur to where a sail had been rigged over the midships section of the upper-deck as a sun shade.

Sir Guy Courtney sat in a comfortable armchair covered with a leopardskin. His cocked hat was laid on the table beside him, and his sword was between his knees. He made no effort to rise from his chair as Mansur approached. He wore a burgundy-coloured jacket of fine broadcloth with solid gold buttons, and a high stock. His shoes were square-toed with silver buckles, and his white silk hose reached to his knees, and were held by garters that exactly matched the colour of his jacket. His tight-fitting trousers were also white, with a codpiece that flattered his masculinity. He wore the ribbons and stars of the Order of the Garter and some Oriental decorations.

Mansur made the polite gesture of greeting: 'I am honoured by your condescension, Your Excellency.'

Guy Courtney shook his head irritably. Mansur knew now that he was Tom's twin and must therefore be in his late forties, but he looked younger. Although his hair was thinning and receding, his figure was slim and his belly flat. But there were liver-coloured bags under his eyes, and one of his front teeth was discoloured. His expression was sour and unfriendly. 'My daughter will translate,' he said in English, and indicated the girl who stood behind his chair. Mansur pretended not to understand. He had been acutely aware of her presence since the moment he had stepped aboard the yacht, but now he looked directly at her for the first time.

He had the greatest difficulty in keeping his face expressionless. The first thing he noticed was that her eyes were large and green, lively and searching. The whites were clear, and the lashes long and densely curled.

Mansur tore away his gaze and addressed Sir Guy again. 'Forgive my ignorance but I speak no English,' he apologized. 'I do not understand what it was Your Excellency said.'

The girl spoke in beautiful classical Arabic, making music of the words: 'My father speaks no Arabic. With your forbearance I will translate for him.'

Mansur bowed again. 'I compliment you, my lady. Your command of our tongue is perfection. I am Prince Mansur ibn al-Salil al-Malik, and I come as the messenger of my father, the Caliph.'

'I am Verity Courtney, the consul general's daughter. My father bids you welcome aboard the *Arcturus*.'

'We are honoured by the emissary of such a powerful monarch, and such an illustrious nation.' For a while longer they exchanged compliments and expressions of esteem and respect, but Verity Courtney managed not to acknowledge any royal titles or honours. She was weighing him as carefully as he was her. She was much more handsome than when he had seen her through the lens of a telescope. Her complexion was lightly sun-gilded but otherwise of English perfection, and her features were strong and determined, without being heavy or coarse. Her neck was long and graceful, her head perfectly balanced upon it. When she smiled politely her mouth was large and her lips full. Her two upper front teeth were slightly misaligned, but the imperfection was arresting and attractive.

Mansur asked if there was anything that they needed that he might be able to supply. Sir Guy told Verity, 'We are short of water, but don't let him know it.'

She relayed the request: 'A ship always needs water, *effendi*. It is not a pressing need, but my father would be grateful for your generosity.' Then she gave Mansur's answer to her father.

'The Prince says he will send out the water tender immediately.'

'Don't call him a prince. He is a dirty little rebel, and Zayn will feed him to the sharks. The water he sends out to us will probably be half camel piss.'

Verity did not even blink at her father's choice of words. Obviously she was accustomed to his phraseology. She turned back to Mansur. 'Of course, *effendi*, the water will be sweet and potable? You would not send us camel's piss?' she asked not in Arabic but in English. It was so artlessly done, her tone so level and her green eyes so candid that Mansur might have been taken in, had he not been ready for it. Yet he was so taken aback by those words on her ladylike lips that he only just managed to keep his own expression polite but neutral. He cocked his head slightly in blank enquiry. 'My father is grateful for your generosity.' She switched back to Arabic, having carried out this test of his linguistic skills.

'You are honoured guests,' Mansur replied.

'He speaks no English,' Verity said to her father.

'See what the blighter is after. They're a slippery bunch of eels, these wogs.' It was only recently that a secretary at Government House had penned this acronym for Worthy Oriental Gentleman, and as a mildly derogatory term it had been adopted throughout the Company.

'My father asks after the health of your father.' Verity avoided saying the forbidden word 'Caliph'.

'The Caliph is blessed with the strength and vigour of ten ordinary men.' Mansur emphasized his father's title. He was enjoying the battle of wits. 'It is a virtue embodied in the royal blood of Oman.'

'What does he say?' Sir Guy demanded.

'He is trying to make me acknowledge that his father is the new ruler.' Verity smiled and nodded.

'Make the correct response.'

'My father hopes that your father will enjoy a hundred more summers in such robust health and in the sunshine of God's favour, and that his conscience will always lead him in the loyal and honourable path.'

'The Caliph, my father, wishes that your father shall have one hundred strong and noble sons, and that all his daughters grow to be as beautiful and clever as the one who stands before me now.' It was unsubtle and bordering on insolence, except of course that he was a prince and might take such liberties. He saw the quick shadow of annoyance in the depths of her green eyes.

Aha! he thought, without a smile of triumph. First blood to me.

But her riposte was quick and pointed. 'May all your father's sons be blessed with good manners and show respect and courtesy towards all women,' she replied, 'even if it is not in their true nature.'

'What's all that about?' Sir Guy demanded.

'He is being solicitous of your health.'

'Find out when his rascally father will see me. Warn him that I will brook no more nonsense from them.'

'My father enquires when he may present his compliments and duty in person to your illustrious father.'

'The Caliph would welcome such an occasion. It would also be an opportunity for him to enquire how it is that the consul general's daughter speaks the language of the Prophet with such a mellifluous tongue.'

Verity almost smiled. He was such a beautiful man. Even his insults were titillating, and his manner was so engaging that, despite herself, she could not take real offence. The simple answer to his implied question was that since her childhood on Zanzibar island, where her father had at one

539

time been stationed, she had been fascinated by all things Oriental. She had learned to love the Arabic language with its poetic, expressive vocabulary. This was, however, the first time she had ever been even vaguely attracted to an Oriental man.

'If your honoured father would receive me and my father I would be pleased to respond to any question of his personally, rather than send my answers through one of his children.'

Mansur bowed to concede that she had taken the bout. He did not smile but his eyes sparkled as he took the letter from his sleeve and handed it to her.

'Read it to me,' Sir Guy ordered, and Verity translated it into English, listened to her father's reply, then turned back to Mansur. She made no further pretence at feminine modesty but looked him directly in the eye.

'The consul general wishes to have all the members of the council present at the meeting,' Verity told him.

'The Caliph would be delighted and honoured to accede to that request. He values the advice of his councillors.'

'How long will it take to arrange this meeting?' Verity demanded.

Mansur thought for a moment. 'Three days. The Caliph would be further honoured if you would join him in an expedition into the desert to fly his falcons against the bustard.'

Verity turned to Sir Guy. 'The rebel leader wants you to go out hawking in the wilderness. I am not certain that you would be safe.'

'This new fellow would be insane to offer me any violence.' Sir Guy shook his head. 'What he is after is a chance to speak in privacy to try to win my support. You can be certain that the palace is a hive of intrigue and a nest of spies. Out in the desert I might learn something from him to my great advantage. Tell him that we will go.'

Mansur listened to her polite rendition as though he had not understood a single word that Sir Guy had said. Then he touched his lips. 'I will personally arrange everything in a

540

manner befitting the importance of the occasion. I will send a barge to collect your luggage tomorrow morning. It will be taken out to the hunting encampment to await your arrival.'

'That would be acceptable.' Verity gave Sir Guy's consent.

'We are honoured. I thirst for the day when I shall set eyes upon your face once again,' he murmured, 'as the hard-run stag thirsts after cool waters.' He backed away with a graceful gesture of farewell.

'You are flushed.' Sir Guy showed a touch of concern for his daughter. 'It is the heat. Your mother is also quite prostrated.'

'I am perfectly well. I thank you for your concern, Father,' Verity Courtney replied smoothly. She, who took great pride in her cool nerves even in the most difficult circumstances, found her emotions most confused.

As the prince went down into the royal barge, she did not want to stare after him. However, she could not leave her father standing alone by the ship's rail.

Mansur looked up at her so suddenly that she could not look away without appearing guilty. She held his gaze defiantly, but as the sail of the felucca caught the breeze and swelled out, it came between them like a screen and cut them off from each other.

Verity found herself breathlessly angry but strangely elated. I am not some brainless simpering Oriental *houri*, not some plaything for him to dally with. I am an Englishwoman and I will be treated as such, she determined silently, then turned to her father, and took a breath to steady herself before she spoke. 'Perhaps I should stay with Mother while you go to parley with the rebels. She really is feeling poorly. Captain Cornish can translate for you,' she said. She did not want to be mocked again by those dancing green eyes and that enigmatic smile.

'Don't be daft, child. Cornish doesn't know how to ask the time of day. I need you. You are coming with me, and no arguments.'

Verity was both annoyed and relieved by his insistence. At

least I will have an opportunity for another passage of arms with the pretty princeling. This time we will see who is quicker with the tongue, she thought.

Before dawn on the third morning the Caliph's barge conveyed the guests to the palace wharf, where Mansur was waiting with a large bodyguard of armed horsemen and grooms to greet them. After another lengthy exchange of compliments, he led Sir Guy to an Arab stallion with a glistening sable coat. Then the grooms led forward a chestnut mare for Verity. She seemed a tractable animal, although she had the legs and deep chest that bespoke both speed and stamina. Verity mounted astride with the ease and grace of an accomplished horsewoman. When they moved out through the city gates it was still dark, and outriders went ahead with torches to light the road. Mansur rode in close attendance on Sir Guy, elegant in his English hunting dress, Verity at her father's left hand.

She wore an intriguing mixture of English and Oriental hunting dress. Her high silk hat was held in place by a long blue scarf, the loose ends thrown back over one shoulder. Her blue coat reached below her knees but the tails were pleated to allow her freedom of movement while preserving her modesty. Beneath it she had on loose cotton trousers and soft knee-boots. Mansur had chosen for her a jewelled saddle with high pommel and cantle. At the jetty she had greeted him frostily and barely glanced at him while she chatted easily with her father. Excluded from her conversation, Mansur was able to study her quite openly. She was one of those unusual Englishwomen who flourish in the tropics. Rather than wilting and sweating and succumbing to the prickly heat, she was cool and poised. Even her costume, which might have been dowdy or outrageous on another, she wore with *élan*.

At first they rode through the date-palm groves and culti-vated fields outside the city walls where, in the first light of dawn, veiled women drew water from deep wells and carried it away in pots balanced on their heads. Herds of camels and beautiful horses drank together from the irrigation canals. On the fringe of the desert they came upon encampments of tribesmen who had come in from the wilderness in response to the Caliph's summons to arms. They came out of their tents and shouted loyal greetings to the prince and fired joy shots in the air as he passed.

But soon they were out in the true desert. When the day broke over the dunes, they were all awed by its majesty. The fine dustclouds suspended in the air reflected the sun's rays and set the eastern sky on fire. Although Verity rode with her head thrown back to gaze upon this celestial splendour, she was acutely aware that the prince was watching her. His importunity no longer annoyed her so intensely. Despite herself, she was beginning to find his attention amusing, although she was determined not to give him the slightest encouragement.

Ahead of them a large group of riders came over the dunes to meet them. The huntsmen led them. Their horses were gaily caparisoned in the gold and blue colours of the caliphate, and they carried hooded falcons on their wrists. Behind them came the musicians, with lutes, horns and the big bass drums suspended on each side of their saddles, then a rabble of grooms leading spare horses, water-carriers and other retainers. They welcomed the consul general with shouting and musket shots, fanfares and the booming beat of the drums, then fell in behind the prince's party.

After several hours' riding, Mansur led them across a wide, arid plain to where a steep valley fell away to a dry riverbed far below. On the top of these cliffs stood a weird cluster of massive rock monoliths. As they drew closer Verity realized that they were the remains of an ancient city that was perched above the valley, guarding a long-forgotten trade route.

'What ruins are these?' Verity asked Mansur, the first words she had spoken directly to him all that morning.

'We call it Isakanderbad, the City of Alexander. The Macedonian passed this way three thousand years ago. His army built this fortress.'

They rode in among the tumbled walls and monuments where once mighty armies had celebrated their triumphs. Now they were inhabited only by the lizard and the scorpion.

However, a flock of servants had arrived during the preceding days, and in the courtyard where, perhaps, the conqueror had once held sway, they had set up the hunting camp, a hundred coloured pavilions furnished with all the luxuries and amenities of a royal palace. There were servants to meet the guests too. Perfumed water was poured for them from golden ewers so that they might wash away the dust of the ride and refresh themselves.

Then Mansur led them to the largest of the grand tents. When they entered Verity saw it was hung with draperies of gold and blue silk, and that the floors were covered with precious rugs and cushions.

The Caliph and his councillors rose to greet them. Verity's skills as an interpreter were tested by the exchanges of compliments and good wishes. Nevertheless she took the opportunity to study the Caliph, al-Salil.

Like his son he was red-bearded and handsome, yet there were the marks of care and sorrow etched deeply into his features, and silver threads in his beard, which he had not covered with henna dye. There was something else she found impossible to fathom. She felt a sense of *déjà vu* when she looked into his eyes. Was it simply that Prince Mansur so closely resembled him? She thought not. It was more than that. Added to this disconcerting impression, something strange was taking place between her father and al-Salil also. They stared at each other as though they were not strangers meeting for the first time. There was a brittle tension between them. It was as though the summer thunderstorms were brewing and the air was heavy with humidity and the sense that the lightning would flash out at any moment.

Al-Salil led her father to the centre of the tent and seated him on a pile of cushions. He took the place beside him. Servants brought them aniseed-flavoured sherbet in golden goblets, and they nibbled at sugared dates and pomegranates.

The silk draperies kept out the worst of the desert heat,

and the conversation was polite. The royal cooks served the midday meal. Dorian helped Sir Guy to titbits from huge salvers, which overflowed with saffron rice, tender lamb and baked fish, then waved away what remained to be taken to his retinue seated in ranks outside the pavilion.

Now the talk became more earnest. Sir Guy nodded at Verity to come to sit between him and al-Salil. Then, while the sun rose to its zenith and outside all the world drowsed in the heat, they conversed in low tones. Sir Guy warned al-Salil of how fragile was the alliance of desert tribes that he was building. 'Zayn al-Din has enlisted the support of the Sublime Porte in Constantinople. Already there are twenty thousand Turkish troops in Zanzibar, and the ships to convey them to these shores as soon as the monsoon turns.'

'What of the English Company? Will they side with Zayn?' al-Salil asked.

'They have not yet committed themselves,' Sir Guy replied. 'As you are probably aware, the governor in Bombay awaits my recommendation before he decides.' He might just as well have used the word 'order' rather than 'recommendation'. Al-Salil and every one of his council could be in no doubt as to where the power lay.

Verity was so absorbed with her work of translating that again Mansur could study her intimately. For the first time he became aware of strange depths and undercurrents between her and her father. Could it be that she was afraid of him? he wondered. He could not be certain, but he sensed something dark and chilling to the spirit.

As they talked on through the heat of the afternoon, Dorian listened, nodded and gave the appearance of being moved by Sir Guy's logic. In reality he was listening for the hidden truths and meanings behind the flowery phrases that Verity translated to them. Gradually he was starting to understand how his half-brother had achieved such power and circumstance.

He is like a serpent, he twists and turns, and always you are aware of the venom in him, Dorian thought. In the end he nodded wisely and made reply: 'All of what you say is true. I can only pray to God that your wisdom and benign interest in these dire affairs of Oman will lead us to a just and lasting solution. Before we go further I would like to assure Your Excellency of the deep gratitude I feel towards you personally and on behalf of my people. I hope that I will be able to demonstrate these warm feelings in a more substantial manner than by mere words.' He saw the avaricious gleam in his brother's eye.

'I am not here for material rewards,' Sir Guy replied, 'but we have a saying in my country that the workman is worthy of his wage.'

'It is an expression that we in this country understand well,' Dorian said. 'But now the heat passes. There will be time for us to speak again on the morrow. We can ride out to fly my falcons.'

The hawking party, a hundred horsemen strong, left Isakanderbad and rode along the edge of the cliff that looked down upon the dry river-course hundreds of feet below. The lowering sun cast mysterious blue shadows over the splendid chaos of tumbled walls and cliffs, and serpentine wadis.

'Why would Alexander choose such a wild and desolate place to build a city?' Verity wondered aloud.

'Three thousand years ago there was a mighty river and the valley floor would have been a garden of green,' Mansur replied.

'It is sad to think that so little is left of such a mighty enterprise. He built so much and it was destroyed in a single lifetime by the lesser men who inherited it from him.'

'Even Isakander's tomb is lost.' Gradually Mansur lured her into conversation, and slowly she lowered her guard and responded to him more readily. He was delighted to find in her a companion who shared his love of history, but as their discussion deepened he found that she was a scholar and her knowledge exceeded his own. He was content to listen to her rather than express his own opinions. He enjoyed the sound of her voice, and her use of the Arabic language.

The huntsmen had scouted the desert for days before and they were able to lead the Caliph to the most likely area in which they might find game. This was a wide, level plain, studded with clumps of low saltbush. It stretched away to the limit of the eye. Now, as it cooled, the air was sweet and clear as a mountain stream, and Verity felt alive and vital. Yet there was a restlessness in her, as though something extraordinary was about to happen, something that might change her life for ever.

Suddenly al-Salil called for a gallop and the horns rang out. They spurred forward together like a squadron of cavalry. Hoofs drummed on the hard-baked sand, and the wind sang past Verity's ears. The mare ran lightly under her, seeming to skim the ground like a swallow in flight, and she laughed. She looked over at Mansur, who rode beside her, and they laughed together for no other reason than that they were young and full of the joy of life.

Suddenly there was a shriller horn blast. A shout of excitement went up from the huntsmen. Ahead of the line a pair of bustards had been started from the cover of the saltbushes by the thunder of hoofs. They ran with their necks out-thrust, their heads held low to the ground. They were huge birds, larger than a wild goose. Although their plumage was cinnamon brown, blue and dark red it was so cunningly blended to match the desert terrain that they seemed ethereal and as insubstantial as wraiths.

At the sound of the horn the line of riders reined in. The horses milled, circled and chewed their bits, eager to run again, but they held their places in the line while al-Salil rode forward with a falcon on his wrist. It was a desert saker, the loveliest and fiercest of all falcons.

In the short time since they had been in Oman, Dorian had made this particular bird his favourite. It was a tercel, and therefore the more beautiful gender of the species. At three years of age, it was at the peak of its strength and swiftness. He had named it Khamseen, after the furious desert wind.

With the line of horsemen halted, the bustards had not been driven into flight. They had gone back into cover in the saltbush. They must have been lying flat against the earth with their long necks thrust out. They remained still as the desert rocks that surrounded them, concealed from the eyes of the hunters by their colouring.

Al-Salil walked his mount slowly towards the patch of scrub where they had last been seen. Excitement built in the line of watchers. Although Verity did not share the passion of the true falconer, she found her breath coming short and the hand that held the reins was trembling slightly. She glanced sideways at Mansur and his features were rapt. For the first time she felt herself completely in tune with him.

Suddenly there was a harsh, croaking cry, and from under the front hoofs of al-Salil's stallion a huge body launched itself into flight. Verity was astonished at how swiftly and strongly the bustard rose into the air. The whistling beat of the wings carried clearly in the silence. Their span was as wide as the full stretch of a man's arms, blunt at the tips and deep as they hurled the bird aloft.

The watchers began a soft chant as the Caliph slipped the hood off the tercel's marvellously savage head. It blinked its yellow eyes and looked to the sky. The bass drummer began a slow beat that boomed out across the plain, exciting both watchers and falcon.

'Khamseen! Khamseen!' they chanted. The tercel saw the bustard outlined against the hard blue and bated against the jesses that restrained him. He hung for a moment upside down, beating his wings as he struggled to be free. The Caliph lifted him high, slipped the jesses and launched him into the air.

On swift blade-sharp wings the tercel rose, higher and higher, circling. His head moved from side to side as he watched the huge flapping bird that sped across the plain below him. The drummer increased the beat and the watchers raised their voices: 'Khamseen! Khamseen!'

The tercel reached the heights, a tiny black shape on sickle wings against the steely blue, towering over his massive prey. Then, abruptly, he cocked his wings back and dropped like a javelin, plummeting towards the earth. The drummer beat a frenetic crescendo, then abruptly cut it short.

In the silence they heard the wind fluting over the wings, and the tercel's stoop was so swift as to cheat the eye. He hit the bustard with a sound like the clash of fighting stags' antlers. The bustard seemed to burst into a cloud of feathers that streamed away on the breeze.

A triumphant cry went up from a hundred throats. Verity found that she was gasping as though she had surfaced from a deep dive below the sea.

Al-Salil recovered his falcon, fed him the bustard's liver and stroked him while he gulped it down. Then he called for another bird. With it on his wrist, he rode ahead with Sir Guy and most of his councillors. In the passion of the hunt that gripped them all, there was no discussion. Verity was no longer needed to translate for them, and she lingered with Mansur. Subtly he slowed his horse and she kept pace with him, so rapt in their talk that she seemed not to realize they were falling further and further behind the Caliph's party.

The antagonism between them evaporated as they talked, and both were animated by the other's proximity. When Verity laughed it was a fetching sound that delighted Mansur, and her handsome, rather austere features were enlivened almost to the point of beauty.

Slowly they forgot the large, colourful entourage in which they rode, and became isolated in the midst of the multitude. A distant shout and the beat of the war drum jerked them back to reality. Mansur rose in his stirrups and shouted with astonishment, 'Look! Do you not see them?' The men around them were shouting and the horns blared out; the drummers beat a frenzy.

'What is it? What has happened?' His change of mood was infectious and Verity pressed up close beside him. Then she saw what had caused the pandemonium. On the far slope of the valley the small party of huntsmen led by al-Salil was at

549

full gallop. While casting for bustard they had put up much more dangerous game.

'Lions!' Mansur cried. 'Ten at least, maybe more! Come, follow me. We must not miss this sport.' Verity pushed her mare to keep pace with him as they raced down their side of the valley.

The pride that al-Salil and his hunters were driving before them, were swift, tawny shapes darting through the patches of saltbush, flitting in and out of the steep-sided wadis that rent the tortured desert ground.

The Caliph had passed his falcon to one of the hunters, and they had all snatched their long weapons from the lance-bearers. They were in full chase after the pride, their cries thin and faint with distance. Then there was a sudden terrible roar of pain and fury as al-Salil leaned from the saddle and speared one of the swift shapes. Verity saw the lion bowled over by the lance thrust, rolling and bellowing in a cloud of pale dust. Al-Salil cleared his weapon with an expert backward sweep and rode on after his next victim, leaving the downed lion grunting its last with the lung blood pumping from its jaws. The riders coming up behind him lanced the dying beast again and again.

Then another of the huntsmen scored with the lance, and another, and all became a wild confusion of racing horses and fleeing yellow cats. The hunters shouted each time they hit. The horses whinnied and shrilled under them, driven mad by the smell of lion blood mingled with the roaring of the wounded cats. The horns blew, the drums pounded and the dust shrouded it all.

Mansur snatched a lance from the bearer who rode behind him and galloped after his father. Verity kept pace with him but the hunt swept away over the crest of the hill before they could join in with the sport.

They passed two dead lions stretched out among the saltbush. Their carcasses were riddled with wounds, and the horses shied at the terrifying scent. By the time they reached the ridge and looked over, the hunt was scattered across the plain. Almost a mile away, they could make out al-Salil's distinctive figure in his flowing white robes leading the hunt, but there was no longer any sign of the lion pride. They had disappeared like brown smoke into the vastness of the desert.

'Too late,' Mansur lamented, and reined in his mount. 'They have run away from us. We will simply use up the horses to no profit if we try to chase after them.'

'Your Highness!' In her agitation Verity did not seem aware that she had used his title. 'I had a glimpse of one of the lions breaking away along the ridge.' She pointed off towards the left. 'It seemed to be heading back towards the river.'

'Come, then, my lady.' Mansur turned his stallion back. 'Show me where you saw it.'

She led him along the high ground, and then at an angle off the skyline. Within a quarter of a mile they were out of sight of the rest of the entourage, cantering alone through the wilderness. The excitement was still high in both of them, and they laughed together without reason. Verity's hat blew from her head and when Mansur would have turned back to retrieve it, she called, 'Leave it! We shall find it later.' She tossed her blue silk scarf into the air. 'This will mark the spot for us when we return.'

As she cantered on she shook out her hair. Until now she had covered it with a wide-meshed silk net. Mansur was astonished by its length as it floated over her shoulders in a dense honey-brown cloud, thick and lustrous in the soft evening sunlight. With her hair down her appearance was completely altered. She seemed to have become a wild thing, free and unfettered by the restraints of society and convention.

Mansur had fallen a little behind her, but he was content to follow and watch her. He felt a deep longing welling within him. This is my woman. This is the one I have waited and longed for. As he thought it, he caught a flicker of movement ahead of her running horse. It might have been the flit of the wings of one of the drab little thrushes, but he knew it was not.

He concentrated his attention and the complete picture leaped into his mind. It was a lion: the lash of its tail had alerted him. It was crouching in a shallow gully directly in

Verity's path. It was flattened against the ground, which was the same pale brown as its sleek hide. Its ears were laid flat against its skull, so that it looked like a monstrous serpent coiled to strike. Its eyes were an implacable gold. There was pink froth on its thin black lips, and a lance wound high in its shoulder, which had angled down to pierce the lung.

'Verity!' Mansur screamed. 'It's there, right in your path. Turn back! For God's sake, turn back!'

She looked back over her shoulder, her green eyes wide with surprise. He did not realize that he had shouted at her in English. Perhaps she was so taken aback by his change of language that she did not understand the import. She made no effort to check her mare, and galloped on towards the crouching lion.

Mansur spurred his stallion to the top of his speed, but he had dropped too far back to catch them. At the last moment the mare sensed the presence of the lion, and shied violently to one side. Verity was almost hurled from the saddle, but she snatched at the pommel and prevented herself going right over. She lost her seat, however, and one foot was out of its stirrup. As she was thrown forward over the mare's neck she hung on with both arms. The mare threw her head at the stench of the lion and the reins were jerked from Verity's hand. She was no longer in control.

The lion charged at the mare from the side. It was uttering deep chesty grunts and with each one bloody froth burst from its lips. The mare pivoted away and Verity was flung to one side, hanging down her flank with one foot trapped in the stirrup. The lion sprang upwards with both front paws reaching out, the claws fully extended, great yellow hooks that could slice through hide and muscle to the bone.

It struck the mare with a force that sent her staggering back on her haunches, but the lion's claws were sunk into her hindquarters. The mare shrilled with terror and agony and kicked out with both back legs. Verity was trapped between the two plunging bodies and her screams cut across Mansur's nerves. It sounded as though she was mortally wounded.

His stallion was already at full charge. Mansur couched his

lance and steered the horse under him with his heels, altering the angle of his attack, reaching forward with the bright lance-head dancing before him like a silver insect. The lion humped up over the mare's back, hanging on to her with the strength of those massive forelegs as she reared and bucked. It was roaring in a continuous bellow of sound. Its flanks were roped with muscle and the rack of its ribs was clearly outlined beneath the skin. He aimed the lance just behind the straining shoulder. It struck cleanly exactly at the spot he had intended. He ran the steel in with the impetus of the stallion's weight. It was almost effortless, just the jar as the steel touched bone, then glided on to transfix the lion from shoulder to shoulder. The beast arched its spine backwards in mortal agony, and the shaft of the lance snapped like a reed. The mare tore herself free of the hooked claws and raced away, the blood from her wounds slicked down her quarters. Still writhing and contorting the lion rolled in the low scrub.

Verity was half under the mare, clinging to the side of her neck, one foot still trapped in a stirrup. If she lost her grip she would be thrown to the ground and dragged along, with the back of her head bouncing along on the stones until her skull cracked open like an eggshell. She had no more breath to spare for screams. She hung on with all her strength, as the mare bolted.

Despite the bloody gashes in her hindquarters the horse ran hard. She was mad with terror, her eyeballs rolled back until the red lining of the sockets glared and silver ropes of saliva trailed from her open mouth. Verity tried to pull herself back into the saddle but her efforts merely goaded the mare to greater speed. In extreme terror she seemed endowed with fresh strength.

Mansur dropped the broken stub of the lance and shouted at the stallion, hammering his heels into the animal's heaving flanks, whipping him across the shoulders with the loose ends of his reins, but he could not catch the mare. They raced back down the slope, and at the bottom the mare turned towards the ancient riverbed. Mansur sent the stallion after her.

For half a mile they ran on, and the gap between the horses

never changed, until the mare's dreadful injuries began to tell. Her stride shortened almost imperceptibly and her back hoofs began to throw outside the line of her run.

'Hold hard, Verity!' Mansur shouted encouragement. 'I am gaining on you now. Don't let go!'

Then he saw the brink of the precipice open directly ahead of the mare, and he looked down the sheer wall of rock into the river valley two hundred feet below. Black despair clamped down on his heart as he imagined mare and girl hurled out over the cliff and dropping to the rocks far beneath.

He drove the stallion on with the strength of his arms and legs, and fierce resolve in his heart. The mare weakened visibly and the gap between them closed, but only slowly. At the last moment the mare saw the earth open ahead of her and tried to turn away, but as her front hoofs bit into the loose earth of the rim it broke away under her. She reared and teetered in wild panic, then toppled backwards.

As the mare went over Mansur threw himself from the back of the stallion and on the edge of the precipice he reached out and grabbed Verity's ankle. He was almost jerked out over the drop, but then her stirrup leather snapped and her leg was free. Still her weight dragged him face down on the sill, but he held on with all his strength. The mare fell away under them, dropping fifty feet before striking the cliff face and screaming in terror as she bounded out into the void.

Verity swung like a pendulum, dangling upside down from his right hand by one leg. The skirts of her coat fell over her head, but she dared not move, knowing that it might break his precarious grip on her ankle. She could hear his harsh panting above her, but she dared not look up. Then his voice reached her. 'Stay like that. I am going to pull you up.' His voice was strangled with the effort.

Even in her dreadful predicament she took note that he was still speaking English, unaccented and sweet in her ears, the voice of home. If I must die, let that be the last sound I hear, she thought, but could not trust her own voice to reply to him. She looked down through dizzying space to the valley floor so far below her. Her head swam with vertigo, but she hung quiescent and felt his hard fingers biting into her ankle through the soft leather of her boot. Above her Mansur grunted with the effort, and the rough rock of the cliff scraped against her hip as she was drawn upwards a few inches by his strength.

Blindly Mansur groped backwards with one leg and found a narrow cleft in the rock. He shoved his knee and thigh deeply into it. It anchored him, and now he could release his left hand with which he had been clinging to a precarious hold. He reached down over the sill of the cliff and locked both hands on to Verity's ankle.

'I have you now with both hands.' His voice was harsh with the effort. 'Courage, girl!' More decisively she was pulled upwards. He paused to gather himself.

'And a tiger!' Mansur gasped out the old nautical exhortation to encourage himself and her.

She wanted to scream at him to shut his mouth, to eschew the childish nonsense and use all his strength to lift her. She knew that the difficult part still lay ahead when he had to heave her backwards over the rock rim. He pulled again and she was dragged up another short space. There was a pause and she felt him adjusting and strengthening his position, using his hips to wriggle backwards, trying to wedge his other leg into the cleft in the rock. He pulled again more strongly from his enhanced position, and she was lifted higher.

'God love you for this,' she whispered, just loud enough for him to hear, and he heaved again so hard that she felt her leg might be pulled out of its socket in her hip.

'Nearly there, Verity,' he said, and pulled, but this time she did not move. A small shrub had taken root in a crack in the cliff face. Now its branches had hooked into her breeches. He pulled again but he could not budge her. She was firmly held by the wiry bush.

'Can't move you,' Mansur grunted. 'Something holding you.'

'It's a bush, catching my legs,' she whispered.

'Try to reach it,' he ordered.

'Hold me!' she replied, and bent her body at the waist,

555

reaching up with one hand. She felt the branches under her fingers, and made a quick grab at them.

'Got them?' he demanded.

'Yes!' But her grip was one-handed and tenuous. Then her heart turned to ice in her chest as she felt the boot he was holding begin to slide slowly off her foot.

'Boot's coming off!' she sobbed out.

'Give me your other hand,' he panted. Before she could refuse she felt him release one hand from her ankle and reach down along her leg. Her foot slid further out of the soft leather boot.

'Your hand!' he pleaded. His fingers were scrabbling urgently down her thigh towards where the bush had come up against her and blocked her way. She felt the back of her boot ride down under her heel.

'Boot's going! I shall fall!'

'Your hand! For the love of God, give me your hand.'

She lunged upwards and their fingers locked. She still had a grip on the bush with her other hand. Mansur was hanging on to the ankle of the boot, but now his right hand was linked to hers. Verity was doubled up, suspended by both arms and one leg. The skirts of her coat fell away from her face so she could see again. His face above her was flushed and swollen. His beard was dark, sodden with sweat. It dripped into her upturned face. Neither dared move.

'What must I do?' she said, but before he could answer it was decided for them. The boot slid off her foot. Her lower body dropped forcefully, then flicked round. Now she was stretched out arms upwards and feet down. Although the jerk had loosened her grip, she was still clinging to his right hand and to the bush.

Both were drenched with sweat, which greased their skin. His fingers began to slide through hers.

'I can't hold on to you,' she gasped.

'The bush,' he said. 'Don't let go of the bush.'

Though she felt as though he were crushing the bones of her fingers, their grip parted like a faulty chain link, and she dropped again until the bush broke her fall. It cracked and bent with her weight.

'It will not hold,' she screamed.

'I can't reach you.' He was groping for her with both hands and she was stretching up with her free hand, but she was just beyond his reach.

'Pull! You must pull yourself up so I can get you,' he grated. She felt the ice in her heart numbing her muscles. She knew it was over. He saw the despair in her eyes, saw her grip on the bush start to fail. She was going to let go.

He snarled at her savagely, trying to shock her into a last effort, 'Pull, you feeble creature! Pull, damn your lily liver!'

The insults stung her and anger gave her the strength for one more attempt. But she knew it was useless. Even if she could reach him their sweat-slimy hands could not hold together. She lunged for the branch and found a double hold, but the bush could no longer bear her weight. It crackled and snapped as it tore.

'I am going!' she sobbed.

'No, damn you, no!' he shouted, but the bush gave way. She started to fall, but suddenly both her wrists were seized and held. Her fall was arrested with a strength that made the joints of her upper arms pop in their sockets.

Mansur had made his last effort. He had freed his legs from the cleft in which he had wedged them, and threw himself forward over the lip of the cliff. At the full stretch of body and arms he had just reached her. He was hanging head down, only his toes hooked into the rock cleft held him. But he had to raise her before she slipped through his fingers again. He braced his elbows against the face of the cliff and slowly bent his arms, raising her until they were face to face. His features were swollen and contorted with the agony of his straining muscles, and with the rush of blood into his inverted head. 'I cannot lift you higher,' he breathed, with their lips almost touching. 'Climb up my body. Use me as a ladder.'

She locked one arm through his, the bend of her elbow through the bend in his. This left his other hand free. He reached down and took hold of her leather belt and pulled her a little higher. She grabbed his belt buckle and they pulled together. He reached lower and took a handful of the seat of her breeches. She hooked her other arm between his legs and again they heaved. Now her face was level with his waist and she could see over the top of the cliff. He reached down, linked his fingers together and made a stirrup for her bare foot. With the purchase this gave her she could drag herself up and over the lip.

She sprawled on the rock for only an instant, then whipped round. 'Can you get back?' she gasped. He was fully extended, powerless to pull himself backwards and regain the crest.

He was almost too far gone to articulate coherently. 'Get the horse,' he gasped. 'Rope on saddle. Pull me back with the horse.'

She glanced around and saw the stallion a quarter of a mile away, trotting back up the valley. 'Your horse is gone.'

Mansur reached backwards and tried to find a fingerhold on the rock, but it was smooth. There was a tiny rasping sound as the toe of one boot moved in the rock crack. He slid forward an inch towards the edge of the cliff. Then his foot caught again. She was frozen with horror. His toehold was all that held him from the drop. She seized his ankle with both hands, but she knew it was hopeless. She could never hope to hold the weight of such a big man. She tried to brace herself as she watched his foot slip again and then his hold in the cleft broke. He slid forward irresistibly, and his ankle was plucked from her hands.

He shouted as he went over the edge, and she flung herself forward across the rock sill to peer down, expecting to see him falling away with his robes ballooning around him. Then she stared in disbelief. The hem of his white robe had snagged on a shard of granite on the lip of the cliff. It had broken his fall, and now he was swinging like a pendulum just below her, dangling over that dizzying void. She stretched down with one hand to try to reach him.

'Give me your hand!' she called. She was weak with her own efforts to escape, and her hand shook wildly.

'You will never hold me.' He looked up at her, and there was no fear in his eyes.

That touched her deeply. 'Let me try,' she pleaded.

'No,' he said. 'One of us will go, not both.'

'Please!' she whispered, and the hem of his robe tore with a sharp, ripping sound. 'I could not bear it if you died for me.'

'Worth it,' he said softly, and she felt her heart break. She sobbed and looked behind her. Then hope bloomed again. She slid back from the edge and wedged herself firmly into the rock cleft. She reached back over her shoulders and seized a double handful of her dense brown hair, pulled it forward and twisted it into a loose rope that hung below her waist. Then she threw herself flat on to the rock sill. She was just able to see over the edge. The rope of her hair tumbled forward.

'Take my hair,' she shouted. He swivelled his head and stared up at her as it brushed lightly against his face.

'Do you have purchase? Can you hold me?'

'Yes, I am wedged into the rock cleft.' She tried to sound confident, but she thought, Even if I can't we will go together. He twisted her hair round his wrist, and with a final crack of tearing cloth the hem of his robe gave way. She had just time to brace herself before the shock of his full weight dropping on to her hair half stunned her. Her head was jerked forward and her cheek slammed into the rock with a force that jarred her teeth. She was pinned down. She felt the vertebrae in her neck popping, as though she were hanged on the gallows.

Mansur hung on the rope of her hair only for the seconds it took him to orient. Then he climbed up, hand over hand, swiftly as a topyard sailor going up the main shrouds. She screamed involuntarily for it seemed that her scalp was being torn from her skull. But then he reached past her, found a handhold in the rock cleft and heaved himself over the rim of the cliff.

He turned instantly, seized her in his arms and dragged her back to safety. He held her to his chest and pressed his face against the top of her head, knowing how intense must be the agony of her scalp. She lay in his arms, weeping as though in bitter mourning. He rocked her gently as though she were an infant, mumbling incoherent words of comfort and gratitude. After a while she stirred against him and he thought she was trying to escape his embrace. He opened his arms to free her, but she reached up and slipped her arms around the back of his neck. She pressed herself to his chest, and their bodies seemed to melt together like hot wax through their sweat-soaked clothing. Her sobbing stilled and then, without pulling away from him, she lifted her face and looked into his eyes. 'You saved my life,' she whispered.

'And you saved mine,' he replied. The tears still cascaded down her face and her lips were trembling. He kissed her, and her lips opened without resistance. Her tears tasted of salt, and her mouth of fragrant herbs. Her hair fell in a tent over them. It was a lingering kiss, and ended only when they were forced to breathe.

'You are not an Arab,' she whispered. 'You are an English-man.'

'You have found me out,' he said, and kissed her again.

When they drew apart, she said, 'I am so confused. Who are you?'

'I will tell you,' he promised, 'but later.' He sought her lips again, and she gave them willingly.

After a while she placed both her hands on his shoulders and pushed him back gently. 'Please, Mansur, we must stop this. If we don't something will happen that will spoil everything before it has begun.'

'It has begun already, Verity.'

'Yes, I know it has,' she said.

'It began when first I laid eyes on you on the deck of the *Arcturus*.'

'I know,' she said again, and stood up quickly. With both hands she flung the glorious profusion of her hair back from her face and over her shoulders.

'They are coming.' She pointed back up the valley at the band of horsemen who were galloping towards them.

As they rode back to Isakanderbad, al-Salil and Sir Guy listened to Verity's account of the near tragedy. When al-Salil asked Mansur for his version of events, Mansur replied quite naturally in Arabic, and Verity was obliged to go along with the deception that he spoke no English. She translated for her father his praises of her courage and resourcefulness, and could omit none of his hyperbole now that she knew Mansur understood every word.

At the end Sir Guy smiled tightly and nodded to Mansur. 'Please tell him that we are in his debt.' Then his expression turned bleak. 'You were at fault. You should not have been alone in his company, child. Your behaviour was scandalous. It will not happen again.' Once again Mansur saw fear in her eyes.

The sun had set and it was almost dark when they reached the encampment. Verity found her tent lit with lamps whose wicks floated in perfumed oil and her clothing from the ship had been unpacked. Three handmaidens were waiting to attend her. When she was ready for her bath they poured warm, perfumed pitchers of water over her, and giggled as they marvelled at the whiteness and beauty of her naked body.

The evening meal was laid out under a dazzle of stars, and the desert air had cooled. They sat cross-legged on cushions while the musicians played softly. After they had eaten, servants offered hookahs to the Caliph and Sir Guy. Only al-Salil indulged. Sir Guy lit a long black cheroot from the gold case that Verity carried for him. Politely she offered one to Mansur. 'Thank you, my lady, but I have never found tobacco to my taste.'

'I agree with you. I also find the odour of the smoke unpleasant in the extreme.' Instinctively she had lowered her voice, even though her father spoke no Arabic.

Now Mansur was certain she was terrified of him. There was more to her feelings than simply that Sir Guy was a daunting figure, hard and unyielding, and Mansur knew he would have to be circumspect in what he now had in mind. He kept his voice on the same even level when he spoke again. 'At the end of this street there lies an ancient temple to Aphrodite. The moon rises a little before midnight. Although dedicated to a pagan deity, in the moonlight the temple is very lovely.'

Verity had not heard him, or so it seemed from her lack of reaction. She turned back to translate a remark that Sir Guy had made to al-Salil, and the two men continued their earnest conversation. They were discussing the extent of the Caliph's gratitude to Sir Guy for his intervention with the Company and the British government. In what manner could the Caliph best demonstrate it? al-Salil asked. Sir Guy suggested delicately that five lakhs of gold rupees might be appropriate, which should be followed by an annual payment of another lakh.

The Caliph began to understand how his brother had amassed such vast wealth. It would take two oxcarts to carry that amount of gold. The treasury in Muscat no longer held a tenth of that amount, but he did not inform Sir Guy of this. Instead he brought the subject to a close. 'These are matters we can discuss again, for I hope to enjoy many more days of your company. But now, if we are to rise again before the sun tomorrow, we should repair to our sleeping mats. May pleasant dreams attend your slumbers.'

Verity took her father's arm as he escorted her to her tent with torch-bearers leading them through the encampment. In turmoil, Mansur watched her go: he had no indication that she would honour their assignation.

Later, dressed in a dark cloak, he waited in the temple of Aphrodite. Through a hole in the dilapidated roof the moonlight played full on the statue of the goddess. The pearly marble glowed as though with internal life. Both her arms were missing, for the ages had taken their toll, but the figure was graceful and the battered head smiled in eternal ecstasy.

Mansur had stationed Istaph, his trusted coxswain from the *Sprite*, on the roof to keep guard. Now Istaph whistled softly. Mansur caught his breath and his pulse beat faster. He stood up from his seat on one of the tumbled stone blocks and moved to the centre of the temple so that she would see him at once and not be startled by his sudden appearance from out of the shadows. He saw the dim light of the lamp she carried as she came down the narrow alley, stepping over the rubble and debris of three thousand years.

At the entrance she paused and looked across at him, then set her lamp in a niche in the doorway and threw back her hood. She had braided her hair in a single rope that hung down over one shoulder, and in the moonlight her face was as pale as that of the goddess. He let his own cloak fall open to hang from his shoulders, and went to meet her. He saw that her expression was serious and remote.

When he was within arm's length she put out a hand to stop him coming closer. 'If you touch me I shall have to leave at once,' she said. 'You heard my father's rebuke. I was never again to be alone with you.'

'Yes, I heard. I understand your predicament,' he assured her. 'I am grateful you have come.'

'What happened today was wrong.'

'I am to blame,' he said.

'There is no blame on either of us. We had been close to death. Our expressions of relief and gratitude towards each other were only natural in the circumstances. However, I said foolish things. You must forget my words. This is the last time we shall meet like this.'

'I shall fall in with your wishes.'

'Thank you, Your Highness.'

Mansur switched to English. 'Will you not at least treat me as a friend and call me Mansur, and not by the title that sits so uncomfortably on your lips?'

She smiled, and answered in the same language. 'If that is indeed your true name. It seems to me that you are a great deal more than you seem, Mansur.'

'I have promised to explain it to you, Verity.'

'Yes, indeed you have. That is why I have come.' Then she added, as though she was trying to convince herself, 'And for no other reason.'

She turned away and took a seat on a fallen stone block

just large enough to accommodate her alone, and she gestured to another at a discreet distance. 'Will you not be seated and make yourself at ease? It seems to me that your tale will take some telling.' He sat, facing her. She leaned forward with one elbow on her knee and her chin in the palm of her hand. 'You have all of my attention.'

He laughed and shook his head. 'Where to begin? How will I ever make you believe me?' He paused to gather his thoughts. 'Let me start with the most preposterous. If I can convince you of those parts of it, then the rest of the medicine will not be so difficult for you to swallow.'

She inclined her head in invitation, and he drew breath. 'Like yours my English surname is Courtney. I am your cousin.'

She burst out laughing. 'In all fairness, you did warn me. None the less 'tis bitter medicine that you are trying to dole out to me.' She made as if to rise. 'I see that this is but a prank, and you take me for the fool.'

'Wait!' he entreated. 'Give me a fair hearing.' She sank back on the stone. 'Have you heard the names Thomas and Dorian Courtney?' The smile vanished from her lips and she nodded wordlessly. 'What have you heard?'

She thought for a moment, her expression troubled. 'Tom Courtney was a terrible rogue. He was my father's twin brother. He murdered his other brother, William, and had to fly from England. He died somewhere in the African wilderness. His grave is unmarked and his passing unmourned.'

'Is that all you know of him?

'No, there is more,' Verity admitted. 'He is guilty of something even more heinous.'

'What is worse than the murder of your own brother?'

Verity shook her head. 'I know none of the details, only that it was so foul a deed that his name and his memory are blackened for ever. I do not know the full extent of his wickedness, but since we were children we have been forbidden to mention his name.'

'When you say we, Verity, who is the other person?'

'My older brother, Christopher.'

'It pains me to be the one to tell you, but what you have

been told about Tom Courtney is but a sad travesty of the truth,' Mansur said, 'but before we discuss it further, please tell me what you know of Dorian Courtney.'

Verity shrugged. 'Very little, for there is little to know. He was my father's youngest brother. No, that is not correct, he was my father's half-brother. In a tragic turn of events he fell into the hands of Arab pirates when he was but a child of ten or twelve years. Tom Courtney, that craven rogue, was to blame for his abduction and did nothing to prevent it, or to save him. Dorian died of fever, neglect and a broken heart while he was a captive in the lair of the pirates.'

'How do you know all this?'

'My father told us about it, and with my own eyes I have seen Dorian's grave in the old cemetery on Lamu island. I placed flowers upon it and said a prayer for his poor little soul. I take comfort in the words of Christ, "Suffer little children to come to me". I know he rests in the bosom of Jesus.'

In the moonlight Mansur saw a tear tremble on her bottom eyelid. 'Please don't weep for little Dorian,' he said quietly. 'Today you rode out hawking in his company and you dined this very evening at his board.'

She recoiled so violently that the tear fell from her eyelid and slid down her cheek. She stared at him. 'I do not understand.'

'Dorian is the Caliph.'

'If this be true, which it cannot be, we are cousins.'

'Bravo, coz! You have arrived at where we started our conversation.'

She shook her head. 'It cannot be ... yet there is something about you—' She broke off, then began again: 'At our very first meeting I felt something, an affinity, a bond that I could not explain to myself.' She looked distraught. 'If all this is a jest, then it is a cruel one.'

'No jest, I swear it to you.'

'I need more than that to convince me.'

'There is more, a great deal more. You shall have as much of it as you can possibly desire. Shall I tell you first how Dorian was sold by the pirates to the Caliph al-Malik, and how the Caliph came to love him so that he adopted him as his own son? Shall I tell you how Dorian fell in love with his adoptive half-sister Princess Yasmini and they eloped together? How she bore him a son, whom they named Mansur? How Yasmini's half-brother Zayn al-Din became caliph after the death of al-Malik? How, not a year past, Zayn al-Din sent an assassin to murder my mother Yasmini?'

'Mansur!' Verity's face was as white as the marble Aphrodite's. 'Your mother? Zayn al-Din murdered her?'

'This is the main reason we have returned to Oman, my father and I. To avenge my mother's death, and to deliver our people from tyranny. But now I must tell you the truth about my uncle Tom. He is not the monster you paint him.'

'My father told us—'

'I last saw Uncle Tom scarcely a year ago, hale and flourishing in Africa. He is a kind person, brave and true. He is married to your aunt Sarah, your mother Caroline's younger sister.'

'Sarah is dead!' Verity exclaimed.

'She is very much alive. If you knew her you would love her as I do. She is so much like you, strong and proud. She even looks a great deal like you. She is tall and very beautiful.' He smiled and added softly, 'She has your nose.' Verity touched her own and smiled faintly.

'With such a nose as mine she cannot be so beautiful.' The little smile faded. 'They told me – my mother and father told me they were all dead, Dorian, Tom and Sarah . . .' Verity covered her eyes with one hand as she tried to assimilate what he had told her.

'Tom Courtney made two mistakes in his life. He killed his brother William in a fair fight, defending himself when Black Billy tried to murder him.'

'I heard that Tom stabbed William while he slept.' She dropped her hand and stared at him.

'Tom's other mistake was to father your brother Christopher. That is the reason your mother and father hated him so.'

'No.' She leaped to her feet. 'My brother is no bastard! My mother is no whore!'

'Your mother conceived in love. That is not harlotry,' Mansur said, and she sank down again. She reached across the gap between them and laid her hand on his arm. 'Oh, Mansur! This is too much for me to endure. Your words tear my world apart.'

'I do not tell you this to torment you, Verity, but for both our sakes.'

'I do not understand.'

'I have fallen in love with you,' Mansur said. 'You asked who I am, and because I love you I must tell you.'

'You delude yourself and me,' she whispered. 'Love is not something that falls like manna from the sky, full formed and complete. It grows between two persons—'

'Tell me you feel nothing, Verity.'

She would not reply. Instead she sprang to her feet and looked to the night sky as if seeking escape. 'The dawn is breaking. My father must not learn I have been with you. I must go back to my tent at once.'

'Answer my question before you go,' he insisted. 'Tell me you feel nothing and I will trouble you no further.'

'How can I tell you that when I know not what I feel? I owe you my life, but beyond that I cannot yet tell.'

'Verity! Give me one small grain of hope.'

'No, Mansur. I must go! Not another word.'

'Will you come to meet me here again, tomorrow evening?'

'You do not know my father—' She stopped herself. 'I can promise you nothing.'

'There is so much more that I must tell you.'

She laughed shortly, then stopped herself. 'Have you not told me sufficient to last me a lifetime?'

'Will you come?'

'I will try. But only to hear the rest of your story.' She snatched up the lamp and pulled the hood of her cloak over her head, covering her face, and ran from the temple.

In the dawn the Caliph rode out with his guests and all his entourage to fly the falcons. They killed three times before the heat came down and they were forced back into the shelter of the tents.

During the noonday heat Sir Guy spoke to the council, explaining to them how he could save Oman from the tyrant, and from the clutches of the Turk and the Mogul. 'You must place yourselves under the suzerainty of the English monarch and his Company.'

The desert sheikhs listened and argued among themselves. They were free men, and proud. At last Mustapha Zindara asked for all of them, 'We have driven out the jackal from our sheepfold. Shall we now allow the leopard to take his place? If this English monarch wants us as his subjects, will he come to us so that we can see him ride and wield the lance? Will he lead us into battle as al-Salil has done?'

'The English king will hold his shield over you, and protect you from your enemies.' Sir Guy avoided a direct answer.

'And what is the price in gold of his protection?' Mustapha Zindara asked.

Al-Salil had seen that Mustapha's temper was rising like the heat outside the tent. He looked across at Verity and said gently, 'I ask your father for his indulgence. We must discuss all he has told us, and I must explain to my people what it means, and set their fears at rest.' He turned to his councillors. 'The heat has passed and the huntsmen have found much game on the high ground across the river. We shall talk more on the morrow.'

Mansur found that Verity was avoiding him assiduously. She would not even glance in his direction. Whenever he came close to her she turned all her attention on her father or the Caliph. He saw how she looked on Dorian in a changed

568

light now that she knew he was her uncle. She stared into his face and watched his eyes when he spoke to her. She followed his every gesture with attention, yet she would not even glance in Mansur's direction. During the afternoon's hunt she would not allow him to separate her from her father, but rode close at Sir Guy's side. In the end Mansur was forced to contain himself until the evening meal. He was not hungry and it seemed interminable. Only once did he catch Verity's eyes and, with a tilt of his head, asked a silent question of her. She arched an eyebrow enigmatically, and gave him no reply.

When at last the Caliph dismissed the company, Mansur escaped to his own tent with relief. He waited until all was quiet, for he knew that even if she intended to keep the assignation she would not move before then. That night there was a restless feeling in the camp with men passing back and forth, loud voices and singing. It was well after midnight before Mansur could leave his own tent, and start for the temple. Istaph was waiting for him beside the stone doorway. 'Is all well?' Mansur asked.

Istaph came closer and whispered, 'There are others abroad this night.'

'Who are they?'

'Two men came out of the desert while the Caliph and his guests were at dinner. They hid themselves in the horselines. When the English *effendi* and his daughter left the company, the girl did not go to her own tent as she did last night. Instead she went with her father to his. Then the two strangers came secretly to them.'

'They are set on mischief?' Mansur demanded, with horror. Was Verity to die as his own mother had, under the assassin's blade?

'No!' Kumrah assured him quickly. 'I heard the *effendi* greet them when they entered and they are together still.'

'You are certain you have never seen these men before tonight?'

'They are strangers. I do not know them.'

'How were they dressed?'

'They wore Arab robes, but only one was an Omani.'

'How did the other look?'

Kumrah shrugged. 'I saw him only for a moment. It is not possible to tell much from a man's face alone, but he was a *ferengi*.'

'A European?' Mansur exclaimed, with surprise. 'Are you sure?'

Istaph shrugged again. 'I am not sure, but so it seemed to me.'

'They are still in the tent of the consul? Is the woman with them?' Mansur demanded.

'They were all still there when I came to meet you here.'

'Come with me, but we must not be seen,' Mansur said decisively.

'There are watchmen only on the outer perimeter of the camp,' Istaph answered.

'We know where they are. We can avoid them.' Mansur turned back and went quietly down the narrow alley, the way he had come. He made as if he was returning to his own tent, then ducked behind a pile of ancient masonry and waited there until he was certain they had not been seen or followed. Then he and Istaph crept up silently behind Sir Guy's pavilion. There was light within, and Mansur could hear voices.

He recognized Verity's. She was speaking to her father, clearly translating, 'He says that the rest will arrive within the week.'

'A week!' Sir Guy's voice was louder. 'They should have been ready at the beginning of the month.'

'Father, lower your voice. You will be heard throughout the entire camp.'

For a while their voices sank to a soft mumble and they spoke with suppressed urgency. Then another voice spoke in Arabic. Even though it was so low and muted that he could not make out the words, Mansur knew he had heard it before, but where and when he could not be sure.

In a barely audible whisper Verity translated for Sir Guy, and his voice rose again sharply. 'He must not even think of it now. Tell him it could dash all our plans. His private concerns must wait until afterwards. He must restrain his pugnacious instincts until the main business has been taken care of.'

Mansur strained his ears but could catch only snatches of what followed. At one stage Sir Guy said, 'We must sweep up the whole shoal in our net. We must not allow a single fish to slip through.'

Then, abruptly, Mansur heard the strangers take leave of him. Once again the familiar Arab voice tugged at his memory. This time it whispered the formal words of farewell.

I know him, Mansur thought. He was certain of this, but still could not place him. The second stranger spoke for the first time. Istaph had been correct. This was a European speaking Arabic with a German or guttural Dutch accent. He could not remember having heard it before. He ignored it, and tried to concentrate instead on exchanges between Sir Guy and the Arab. There was silence, and he realized that the strangers had left Sir Guy's pavilion as quietly as they had come. He jumped up from where he was crouched and ran to the corner of the tent wall. Then he had to shrink back, for not ten paces away Sir Guy and Verity were standing at the entrance talking quietly and looking in the direction in which their visitors had gone. If Mansur and Istaph tried to follow, Sir Guy would spot them. Father and daughter remained in the doorway for some minutes longer before they went back inside. By this time the strange visitors had vanished among the closely huddled pavilions of the encampment.

Mansur turned to Istaph, who was close behind him. 'We must not let them get away. Search the far side of the camp, down towards the river, and see if they went that way. I shall take the northern perimeter.'

He broke into a run. Something about the stranger's voice had filled him with a sense of foreboding. I have to find out who that Arab is, he thought.

When he reached the last ruined buildings he saw two of the night watchmen standing together in the shadows cast by the wall. They were leaning on their jezails and talking quietly. He called to them, 'Did two men pass this way?'

They recognized his voice and ran to him. 'No, Highness,

'no man passed us.' It seemed that they had been awake and alert, so Mansur had to believe them.

'Shall we raise the alarm?' one demanded.

'No,' Mansur said. 'It was nothing. Return to your post.'

The strangers must have gone down towards the river. He ran back through the dark camp and, in the moonlight, saw Istaph running back towards him along the causeway. He sprinted to meet him and called to him while still far off, 'Have you found them?'

'This way, Highness.' Istaph's voice was harsh with exertion. Together they raced down the hillside, then Istaph turned off the path and led Mansur towards a clump of thorn trees.

'They have camels,' he gasped.

As he said it two riders burst from the clump of trees. Mansur came up short and stood panting, gazing after them as they rode diagonally across the hillside below him. They passed not more than a pistol shot from where he stood. Their mounts were both beautiful racing camels and carried bulky saddlebags and waterbags for a desert crossing. They were ghostly in the silvery moonlight, moving away in uncanny silence towards the open desert.

In desperation Mansur bellowed after them, 'Stop! In the Caliph's name, I order you to halt!'

Both riders turned swiftly in their high saddles at the sound of his voice. They stared back at him. Mansur recognized them both. He had not seen the man with the European features, whom Istaph had called the *ferengi*, for some years. However, it was the Arab who commanded his attention. He had thrown the hood of his cloak upon his shoulders and, for a fleeting moment, the slanting rays of the moon struck full into his face. He and Mansur stared at each other for a heartbeat, then the Arab leaned forward over the neck of his camel and, with the long riding stick he carried, urged it into the long, elegant gait that covered the ground at an astonishing speed. His dark cloak billowed behind him as he whirled away down the valley with his *ferengi* companion riding hard behind him.

A shock of recognition and disbelief paralysed Mansur's

legs. He stood and stared after them Then, black thoughts swirled through his head and seemed to batter his senses like the flapping wings of vultures, until at last he rallied himself. I must get back to my father and warn him of what is afoot, he thought. But he waited while the camels dwindled into the distance, flitting like moths across the moonlit landscape, and then were gone.

Mansur ran all the way. He had to stop in the shadow of the walls to regain his breath. Then he went on swiftly but quietly among the tents so as not to raise the alarm. There were two sentries at the door to the Caliph's, but at a quiet word from Mansur they sheathed their swords and stood aside to let him pass. He went through into the inner chamber of the pavilion. A single oil lamp was burning on a metal tripod that shed a soft light.

'Father!' he called.

Dorian sat up from his sleeping mat. He wore only a light loincloth and his naked body was slim and muscled, like an athlete's, in the lamplight. 'Who is it?' he called.

'It is Mansur.'

'What ails you at this hour?' Dorian had recognized the urgency in his tone.

'There were two strangers in our camp this night. They were with Sir Guy.'

'Who were they?'

'I recognized them both. One was Captain Koots from the garrison at Good Hope, the man who pursued Jim across the wilderness.'

'Here in Oman?' Dorian came fully awake. 'It does not seem possible. Are you certain?'

'I am even more certain of the other man. His face is graven upon my mind until the day I die.'

'Tell me!' Dorian commanded.

'It was the assassin, Kadem ibn Abubaker, the swine who murdered my mother.'

'Where are they now?' Dorian's voice was harsh.

'They fled into the desert before I could confront them.'

'We must follow at once. We cannot let Kadem escape

again.' The glazed pink knife-scar on Dorian's chest caught the lamplight as he reached for his robes.

'They are mounted on racing camels,' Mansur answered. 'We have none, and they were headed into the dunes. We can never hope to catch them in the sands.'

'Nevertheless we must try.' Dorian raised his voice and shouted for the guards.

The dawn was a lemon and orange glow in the eastern sky before bin-Shibam had gathered together a punitive party of his desert warriors and they were all mounted and ready to ride. They swept down the causeway from the camp to where Mansur had seen the fugitives disappear. The ground was sun-baked and stony and held no tracks of the camels passing, but they could not afford further time for the skilled huntsmen to search every inch.

With Mansur leading, they followed the direction in which Kadem had headed into the wilderness. Within two hours' ride they saw the dunes rising ahead of them, in flowing and fantastic shapes. The slip faces down which the sand cascaded were blue and purple and amethyst in the early light. The crests were sharp and sinuous as the back of a gigantic iguana.

Here they found the tracks of two camels trodden into deep saucers in the liquid sand where they had climbed the first dune and disappeared over the crest. They tried to follow, but the horses sank over their hocks with each pace and, in the end, even Dorian had to admit that they were defeated.

'Enough, bin-Shibam!' he told the grizzled old warrior. 'We cannot go on. Wait for me here.'

Dorian would not allow even Mansur to accompany him as he rode up the face of the next dune. His tired horse had to lunge upwards with each pace and only reached the crest with great effort. There he dismounted. From the sand valley below Mansur watched his father. He was a tall, lonely figure staring out into the desert with the early-morning breeze blowing his robes out behind him. He stood like that for a long time, then sank to his knees in prayer. Mansur knew he was praying for Yasmini, and his own sorrow for the loss of his mother welled up almost to suffocate him.

At last Dorian remounted and came down the dune with his stallion sliding in the soft-running sands on braced haunches and stiff front legs. He said not a word as he passed them, and rode on with his chin sunk on his chest. They fell in behind him and he led them back to Isakanderbad.

Dorian dismounted in the horselines and the grooms took his stallion. He strode to Sir Guy's tent with Mansur close behind him. His intention was to confront his half-brother and disclose his true identity, to throw in his face the ancient memories of his vicious treatment of Tom, Sarah and himself as a child, and to demand from him a full explanation of the nocturnal and clandestine presence of Kadem ibn Abubaker in the camp.

Before he reached the tent he realized that things had changed during their absence. A party of strangers was gathered before the entrance. They all wore seafaring dress and were heavily armed. At their head was Captain William Cornish of the *Arcturus*. Dorian was so angry that he almost hailed him in English. With an effort he prevented his anger boiling over, but it simmered dangerously close to the surface.

Mansur followed close behind him as he stormed into the tent. Sir Guy and Verity stood in the centre of the room. They were in riding garb, and were deep in conversation. Both of them looked up, startled, at the precipitate entrance of the two grim-faced figures.

'Ask them what they want,' Guy said to his daughter. 'Make them understand that this behaviour is insulting.'

'My father welcomes you. He hopes nothing is seriously amiss.' Verity was pale and seemed distraught.

Dorian made a perfunctory gesture of greeting, then glanced around the tent. The handmaidens were packing the last of Sir Guy's possessions.

'You are leaving?'

'My father has received tidings of the gravest import. He must return to the *Arcturus* and sail at once. He asks me to present his most sincere apologies. He tried to inform you of this change in his plans, but he was informed that you and your son had left Isakanderbad.'

'We were in pursuit of bandits,' Dorian explained, 'but we are desolate that your honoured father must leave before we have reached an accord.'

'My father is also put out. He asks you to accept his thanks for the generosity and hospitality you have extended to him.'

'Before he leaves I would be most grateful for his assistance. We have learned that there were dangerous bandits in the camp last night. Two men, one an Arab, the other a European, perhaps a Dutchman. Did your father speak to these men? I have had a report that they were seen leaving this tent during the night.'

Sir Guy smiled at the question, but the smile was on his lips only and his eyes were cold. Verity said, 'My father wishes to assure you that the two men who came to the camp last night were not bandits. They were the messengers who brought him the news that has necessitated his change of plans. They were with him for a short time only.'

'Does your father know these men well?' Dorian insisted. Sir Guy's reply was without obvious guile.

'My father has never seen them before.'

'What were their names?'

'They did not give their names, nor did my father ask. Their names were of no interest or importance. They were merely messengers.'

Mansur was watching Verity's face intently as she answered these questions. Her expression was calm, but there was a latent tension in her voice, and shadows in her eyes as though dark thoughts lurked in her mind. She avoided looking at Mansur. He sensed that she was lying, perhaps for her father's sake and perhaps for her own.

'May I ask His Excellency the nature of the message they brought him?'

Sir Guy shook his head regretfully. Then he drew from his inner pocket a parchment packet that bore the heavily embossed royal coat-of-arms with the legend 'Honi soit qui mal y pense' and two red wax seals. 'His Excellency regrets that this is an official, privileged document. Any foreign power who attempted to seize it would be committing an act of war.'

'Please assure His Excellency that no one is contemplating an act of war.'

Dorian dared press the matter no further. 'I much regret His Excellency's sudden departure. I wish him a safe journey and a swift return to Oman. I hope I shall be allowed to ride in company with him upon the first mile of his journey?'

'My father would be greatly honoured.'

'I will leave you now to make your final preparations. I shall wait with a guard of honour on the perimeter of the camp.'

Both men bowed to each other as the Caliph withdrew. As he left the tent Verity shot a single, anguished glance at Mansur. He knew that, at last, she was desperate to talk to him.

Sir Guy and Verity, escorted by Captain Cornish and his armed seamen, rode up to where Dorian and Mansur waited beside the eastern road to escort them. Dorian had brought his anger firmly under control. They set out again in company. Although Mansur fell in beside her, Verity stayed close to her father, translating the polite but inconsequential conversation between him and Dorian. But as they topped the first rise, the wind off the sea blew into their faces, cool and refreshing. As though to adjust it, Verity loosened the scarf that held her high hat in place. She seemed to lose her grip on it, and the breeze snatched it from her head. It tumbled away down the hillside, rolling like a wheel on its stiff brim.

Mansur turned his horse and raced after it. He leaned far out of the saddle and grabbed the hat from the ground without checking the stallion's speed. He turned back and handed it to Verity as she rode to meet him. She nodded her thanks, and as she replaced it on her head she used the silk scarf to veil her face for a moment. She had contrived to separate them from the rest of the party by at least a hundred paces.

'We have but a moment before my father becomes suspicious. You did not come last night,' she said. 'I waited for you.'

'I could not,' he replied, and he would have explained further, but she cut him off brusquely.

'I have left a letter under the pedestal of the goddess.'

'Verity!' Sir Guy called sharply. 'Come here, child! I need you to interpret.'

With her hat again firmly on her head, the brim tilted to a saucy angle, Verity kicked her mare forward and trotted up beside her father's horse. She did not look directly at Mansur again, not even when, with an exchange of compliments, the two bands of horsemen parted. Sir Guy went on towards Muscat while the Caliph and his escort turned back to Isakanderbad.

By the merciless light of midday the goddess's expression was melancholy and her beauty marred by the ravages of millennia. With one last glance around the temple to make certain that he was unobserved, Mansur went down on one knee before her. Wind-blown sand was piled along one side of the pedestal base. Someone had arranged five small chips of white marble in the shape of an arrowhead. It pointed at a spot where the sand had been recently disturbed, then carefully smoothed over again.

He swept away the sand. There was a narrow crack between the marble base of the statue and the stone flags of the floor. When he lowered his face to floor level he saw that a folded sheet of parchment had been pushed deep into the crack. He had to use his dagger to prise it out. He unfolded the sheet and saw that both sides were written upon in an elegant, feminine script. He refolded the sheet, hid it in his sleeve, hurried back to his own tent and went into the inner room. He spread out the letter on his sleeping mat and pored over it. There was no salutation.

I hope you will be there tonight. If you are not I will leave this for you. I heard the alarm a short while ago and the horsemen riding out, and I must believe that you went with them. I suspect that you are chasing the two men who came to my father this night. They are generals in the army of Zayn al-Din. One is named Kadem ibn Abubaker. The other is a renegade Dutchman whose name I do not know. They command the Turkish infantry who will lead the assault on Muscat. The news they brought my father is that, at this very moment, the fleet and the transports carrying Zayn's army are no longer lying in Zanzibar roads. They sailed two weeks ago, and they are already at anchor off Boomi island. My father and I will return on board the *Arcturus* with all despatch so that we are not trapped in the city when the Turks attack. It is my father's purpose to join Zayn's fleet, so that he might be present when Zayn enters the city.

Mansur felt his heart turn cold with dread. Boomi island lay a mere ten sea miles from the entrance to Muscat harbour. The enemy had come secretly upon them, and the city lay under a terrible threat. He read on quickly:

Zayn himself is aboard the flagship. He has fifty great dhows and seven thousand Turkish soldiers on board. They plan to land on the peninsula and march on the city from the landward side, to surprise the defences and avoid the batteries of cannon on the seaward walls. By the time you read this, they may have already launched their attack. Zayn has another fifty dhows crammed with troops and the munitions of war following. They will be in Muscat within the next week.

Mansur was so stricken that he could barely bring himself to read the rest of the letter before rushing out to warn his father.

It is with deep sadness and guilt that I must tell you that my father's offer of assistance to the junta was a ruse to lull them and to keep the desert sheikhs in Muscat until Zayn could fall upon them and capture all of them together. They will receive no mercy from him. Nor shall you and

579

your father. I knew nothing of this until an hour ago. I truly believed that the offer of British protection my father made was genuine. I am ashamed by what he has done to his brothers, Tom and Dorian, down the years. I knew nothing of this either, not until you told me of it. I have always known he was an ambitious man, but I had no idea of the true extent of his ruthlessness. I wish there was some way in which I could make amends.

'There is, Verity, Oh, yes, there is,' Mansur whispered, as he read on.

There is more that it pains me to relate. I learned tonight that Kadem ibn Abubaker is the villain who assassinated your mother, Princess Yasmini. He boasted of the heinous murder. Tonight he wanted to kill your father and you also. My father prevented him doing so, not on grounds of compassion but lest the plot he has hatched with Zayn al-Din to recapture the city be jeopardized. If my father had not stopped him, I swear to you on my hope of salvation that I would have managed to warn you somehow. You cannot know how deep is my repugnance for the deeds my father has committed. In one short hour I have come to hate him. I fear him even more. Please forgive me, Mansur, for the hurt we have done you.

'You are not to blame,' he whispered, and turned over the sheet of parchment. He read the last few lines.

Last night you asked me if I did not feel anything between you and me. I would not answer you then, but I answer you now. Yes, I do.

If we never meet again, I hope you will always believe that I never intended to cause you hurt. Your affectionate cousin, Verity Courtney.

They drove the horses without mercy, riding in full force back to Muscat. They were still too late. As they came within sight of the city towers and minarets they heard the cannon fire and saw the dun smoke of battle sully the sky above the harbour.

With Dorian, al-Salil, at the head of the troop they drove the exhausted horses through the palm groves, and now they could hear musket fire, shouting and screaming below the city walls. Onwards they raced, and the roadway ahead was crammed with women, children and old men fleeing the city. They turned off and galloped on through the groves, while the din of battle grew louder. At last they saw the glint of spearheads, scimitars and bronze Turkish helmets surging forward towards the city gates.

They flogged the last ounce of speed from their horses, and in a tight column they raced for the gates. The Turks ran through the palm grove to head them off. The gates were swinging closed.

'The gates will shut before we can reach them!' Mansur called to his father.

Dorian ripped off his turban. 'Show them who we are!' he cried. Mansur pulled off his own turban and they rode on with their bright red hair streaming behind them like banners.

A cry went up from the parapets: 'Al-Salil! It is the Caliph!'

The gates began slowly to open again as the men on the winches bent to the handles.

The Turks saw that they could not cut them off on foot. Their cavalry had not yet arrived: it was following in the second fleet. They halted and unslung their short recurved bows. The first flight of arrows rose dark against the blue and hissed like a pitful of serpents as it fell among the racing horses. One was struck, and went down as though it had run full-tilt into a tripwire. Mansur turned back, hauled Istaph from the saddle of the floundering horse, swung him up on to his stallion's withers and raced on. The gates started to close again the moment the Caliph had galloped through. Mansur shouted to the winchmen as he came through the storm of Turkish arrows. They seemed not to hear him and inexorably the gates continued to shut in his face.

Then, suddenly, Dorian turned back into the opening and stopped his horse full in the path of the great mahogany gates, which creaked to a standstill. Mansur galloped through with inches to spare. The gates slammed as the wave of Turkish attackers reached them, and the defenders on the parapets above fired muskets and arrows down into them. They fled back into the palm grove.

Dorian galloped at once through the narrow alleys to the mosque and climbed the spiral staircase to the top balcony of the tallest minaret. On one side he had a sweeping view over the harbour and peninsula, and on the other over cultivated fields and groves. Earlier he had devised a system of flag signals to communicate with the gunners on the parapets and his two ships in the bay so that he could co-ordinate their actions.

From this height he could make out through his telescope the forest of masts of Zayn al-Din's fleet showing above the high ground of the peninsula. He lowered the glass and turned to Mansur. 'Our ships are still safe,' he pointed to the *Sprite* and the *Revenge* at anchor, 'but as soon as Zayn brings his war dhows round the peninsula and enters the bay they will be exposed and vulnerable. We must bring them close in under the protection of the battery on the sea wall.'

'How long can we hold out, Father?' Mansur lowered his voice and spoke in English so that bin-Shibam and Mustapha Zindara, who had followed them, could not understand him.

'We have not had enough time to finish the work on the south wall,' Dorian replied. 'They will discover our weak places soon enough.'

'Zayn almost certainly knows of them already. The city is swarming with his spies. Look!' Mansur pointed at the corpses hanging on the outer wall like washing. 'Although Mustapha Zindara is taking care of as many as he can lay his hands on, no doubt he has overlooked one or two.'

Dorian surveyed the gaps in the defences, which had been hurriedly stopped up with timber balks and gabions filled with sand. The repairs were temporary, and would not withstand a determined attack by seasoned troops. Then he lifted his spyglass and ran the lens over the palm groves to the south of the city. Suddenly he stiffened and handed the glass to Mansur. 'The first attack is gathering already.' They could make out the sparkle of sunlight on the helmets and spearheads of the Turkish troops, who were massing under cover of the groves. 'Mansur, I want you to go aboard the *Sprite* and take overall command of both our ships. Bring them in as close to the shore as is safe. I want your guns to cover the approaches to the south wall.'

Later, Dorian watched him being rowed out to the *Sprite* in the longboat. Almost as soon as he stepped aboard, both ships swung round as their anchor cables were hauled in. Under topsails they sailed deeper into the bay, Mansur in the *Sprite* leading Batula in the *Revenge*.

In the light breeze they were barely under steerage way, and they loafed in over the sparkling water, their hulls dappled turquoise green by the reflection of sunlight off the white sand of the lagoon bottom. Then Dorian looked to the south, and saw the first wave of the Turkish assault swarming across the open fields towards the walls. He ordered a red flag hoisted to the pinnacle of the minaret: the prearranged signal to the squadron that an attack was imminent. He saw Mansur look up at the flag, waved down at him and pointed to the south. Mansur waved back in acknowledgement, and sailed on sedately.

Then the ships turned in succession just below the harbour wall. Dorian watched the gunports fall open and the guns run out, like the fangs of a snarling monster. Mansur's tall figure was pacing along the gundeck. He paused occasionally to speak to his crew as they gathered tensely around the gun carriages.

The south wall and its approaches were still hidden by the angle of the tall stone ramparts, but as the *Sprite* cleared the range and angled in towards the beach the view opened before Mansur's eyes.

The Turks were bunched up as they carried in the long scaling ladders. Some of them looked across the narrow strip of water as the two pretty little ships emerged from behind the citadel walls. The Turkish infantry had never seen the effect of shot from a naval nine-pounder. Some even waved, and Mansur ordered his crews to wave back to lull their fears.

It happened with dreamlike deliberation. Mansur had time to walk down his deck and lay each gun with his own hand, turning down the elevation screws. He found it difficult to convince some of his crew that the power of the guns was not enhanced when the screws were turned up to maximum. Closer and closer they crept in towards the beach and Mansur listened with one ear to the leadsman in the chains calling the soundings: 'By the mark, five.'

'Close enough,' Mansur murmured, and then to Kumrah, 'Bring her up a point.'

The *Sprite* settled on the new course parallel to the shore. 'We will now serve out a taste of Mr Pandit Singh's very best,' he murmured, without lowering the glass. The *Sprite*'s guns began to bear by the bows. Still he waited. Mansur knew that the first broadside would do the most damage. After that the enemy would scatter into cover.

They were so close that through the lens he could see the links in the chain-mail of the nearest Turks and the individual feathers in the plumed helmets of the officers.

He lowered the glass and walked back down the battery. Every gun was bearing and the gun-crews were watching him, waiting on his command. He lifted the scarf of scarlet silk in his right hand, and held it high.

'Fire!' he shouted, and snapped it down.

Kadem ibn Abubaker and Herminius Koots, that unlikely couple, stood on a rocky eminence and looked across the open ground towards the southern ramparts of the city. Their staff were gathered around them, among them the Turkish officers whose authority they had usurped when Zayn al-Din had promoted them.

They watched the assault troops moving forward in three columns of two hundred men each. They carried the scaling ladders, and on their shoulders were strapped the round bronze targes to defend them against the missiles that would rain down on them from the walls as soon as they were within range. Close behind them, in massed quarter columns, followed the battalions that would surge forward to exploit any foothold they won on the parapets. 'It is worth the risk of losing a few hundred men against the chance of a quick break-in,' Koots said.

'We can afford the loss,' Kadem agreed. 'The rest of the fleet will arrive within days, another ten thousand men. If we fail today, we can begin the formal siege works on the morrow.'

'You must prevail on your revered uncle, the Caliph, to bring his warships round to begin the blockade of the bay and the harbour.'

'He will give the order as soon as he has seen the outcome of this first assault,' Kadem assured the Dutchman. 'Have faith, General. My uncle is a seasoned commander. He has been waging war on his enemies since the day he ascended the Elephant Throne. The treacherous revolution of these pork-eating swine we see before us,' he pointed to the lines of defenders on the city wall, 'was the only defeat he has ever suffered – through treason and betrayal within his own court. It will not happen again.'

'The Caliph is a great man. I never said different,' Koots assured him hastily. 'We shall hang those traitors by their own entrails on the walls of the city.'

'With God's favour, thanks be to God,' Kadem intoned.

The first tenuous bond between them had been tempered to steel links over the two years they had been together. That terrible journey, forced upon them after they were routed by Jim Courtney in the disastrous night attack, was one that lesser men could not have survived. They had braved disease and starvation across thousands of leagues of wild country. Their horses died of sickness and exhaustion, or had been killed by hostile tribesmen. They had covered the last stages on foot through swamps and mangrove forest before they reached the coast again. There they had come across a fishing village. They attacked it in the night and slaughtered all the men and children at once, but they killed the five women and the three little girls only after Koots and Oudeman had expended their pent-up lust on them. Kadem ibn Abubaker had kept aloof from this orgy. He had prayed upon the beach while the women screamed and sobbed, then gave one last shriek as Koots and Oudeman slit their throats.

They had embarked in the captured fishing-boats that were nothing more than ancient, dilapidated outrigger canoes. After another arduous journey, they at last reached Lamu harbour. There they prostrated themselves before Zayn al-Din in the throne room of his palace.

Zayn al-Din had welcomed his nephew warmly. He had thought him dead, and was delighted by the tidings he brought of Yasmini's execution. As Kadem had promised, the Caliph looked with favour on Kadem's new companion and listened to accounts of his ruthless warlike talents with attention.

As a trial he had sent Koots with a small force to subdue the remaining strongholds of the rebels who still held out upon the African mainland. He expected him to fail, as all the others before him had done. However, true to his reputation, within two months Koots had brought all the ringleaders back to Lamu in chains. There, with his own hands and in Zayn's royal presence, he had disembowelled them alive. As his reward Zayn gave him half a lakh of gold rupees from the plunder, and his pick of the female slaves he had captured. Then he had promoted him to general and given him command of four battalions of the army that he was assembling to attack Muscat.

'The Caliph comes to us now. As soon as he arrives you can order the assault to begin.' Kadem turned and went to meet the palanquin that eight slaves were carrying up the hill. It was covered with a sun canopy of gold and blue, and when they set it down Zayn al-Din stepped out.

He was no longer the chubby child whom Dorian had thrashed in the harem on Lamu island and whose foot he had maimed in the struggle to protect Yasmini from the torments Zayn had heaped upon her. He still limped, but the puppy-fat had fallen away long ago from his frame. A lifetime of intrigue and constant strife had hardened his features as it had sharpened his wits. His eyes were quick and acquisitive, his manner imperious. If it were not for the cruel lines of his mouth and the fierce cunning in his dark eyes, he might have been handsome. Kadem and Koots prostrated themselves before him. In the beginning Koots had found this form of respect abhorrent. However, like the Oriental attire he had adopted, it had become part of his new existence.

Zayn gestured to his two generals to rise. They followed him to the brow of the hill, and looked down over the open ground on which the assault force was drawn up. Zayn studied the dispositions of the troops with a practised eye. Then he nodded. 'Proceed!' His voice was high-pitched, almost girlish. When he had first heard it, Koots had despised Zayn for it, but the voice was the only feminine thing about him. He had fathered a hundred and twenty-three children, and only sixteen were girls. He had slain his enemies in thousands, many with his own sword.

'One red rocket.' Koots nodded to his aide-de-camp. Swiftly the order was relayed down the back slope of the hill to the signallers. The rocket sparkled like a ruby as it rose into the cloudless sky on a long silver tail of smoke. From the foot of the hill they heard faint cheering, and the massed troops swarmed forward towards the walls. A slave stood in front of Zayn, who rested his long brass telescope on the man's shoulder, using him as a living bipod.

587

The leading ranks of Turks had reached the ditch below the walls when suddenly the *Sprite* came into view from behind the stone ramparts. She was followed almost immediately by the *Revenge*. Zayn and the officers switched their telescopes to the two ships.

'Those are the ships in which the traitor, al-Salil, arrived in Muscat,' snapped Kadem. 'Our spies warned us of their presence.'

Zayn said nothing, but his features altered at the mention of the name. He felt a stab of pain in his crippled foot, and the acid taste of hatred rose in the back of his throat.

'Their guns are run out.' Koots stared at them through the glass. 'They have our battalions in enfilade. Send a galloper to warn them,' he snarled at his aide-de-camp.

'We have no horses,' the man reminded him.

'Go yourself!' Koots seized his shoulder and shoved him away down the slope. 'Run, you useless dog, or I shall have you shot from a cannon's mouth.' His Arabic was becoming more fluent every day. The man raced away down the slope, shouting, waving his arms and pointing towards the small squadron of warships. However, the Turks were fully launched upon the attack, and none looked back.

'Signal the recall?' Kadem suggested, but they all knew it was too late for that. They watched in silence. Suddenly the leading ship erupted in a cloud of white powder smoke. She heeled slightly to the broadside of her long black cannons, then came back on even keel, but her hull was blotted out by the billowing smoke cloud. Only her masts showed high above it. The thunderous sound of the blast reached their ears only seconds after the discharge, then rolled away in diminishing echoes among the distant hills.

The watchers on the hilltop turned their telescopes back to the dense pack of humanity on the plain below. The havoc shocked even these old soldiers, who were hardened to the carnage of the battlefield. The grape-shot spread so that each blast cut a swathe twenty paces wide through the massed battalions. Like the scythe blade through a field of ripe wheat, it left not a single one standing in its path. Chain-mail and bronze armour offered the same protection as a sheet of brittle parchment. Severed heads, bearded and still wearing their soup-bowl helmets, were tossed into the air. Torsos, with arms and legs torn off, were piled upon each other. The cries of the dying and wounded carried clearly to the men on the hilltop.

The *Sprite* put up her helm and tacked round into the open waters of the bay. The *Revenge* sailed serenely into her place. On shore the survivors stood in stunned dismay, unable to fathom the extent of the disaster that had swept through their ranks. As the *Revenge* levelled her cannon on them, the moans of the wounded were drowned out by the survivors' wails of despair. Few had the presence of mind to throw themselves flat against the earth. They dropped the scaling ladders, turned their backs on the menace of the guns and ran.

The *Revenge* loosed her broadside upon them. Her shot swept the field. She put up her helm and followed her sister ship round.

The *Sprite* completed her tack across the wind, then came back on the other leg, offering her port battery to the fleeing Turks. Meanwhile her starboard battery had reloaded with canvas bags of grape, and the gunners were standing ready to take their next turn.

Like dancers performing a stately minuet, the two ships went through a series of elaborate figures-of-eight. Each time their guns bore they loosed another thunderclap of smoke, flame and cast-iron grape-shot across the narrow strip of open water.

After the *Sprite* had completed her second pass, Mansur snapped his telescope shut and told Kumrah, 'There is nothing more to fire at. Run in the guns, take her out into the bay.' The two ships sailed back blithely to their anchorage under the protection of the guns on the parapets of the city walls.

Zayn and his two generals surveyed the field. Corpses littered the ground, thick as autumn leaves.

'How many?' asked Zayn, in his high girlish voice.

'Not more than three hundred,' Kadem hazarded.

'No, no! Fewer.' Koots shook his head. 'A hundred and fifty, two hundred at the most.'

'They are only Turks, and another hundred dhows full of them will arrive before the week is out.' Zayn nodded dispassionately. 'We must begin digging the approach trenches and throw up a wall of gabions filled with sand along the bayside to protect our men from the ships.'

'Will Your Majesty order the fleet to take up a blockading station across the entrance to the bay?' Kadem asked respectfully. 'We must bottle up those two ships of al-Salil and, at the same time, prevent supplies of food reaching the city by sea.'

'The orders have already been given,' Zayn told him loftily. 'The English consul will place his own ship at the head of the fleet. His is the only vessel to match those of the enemy for speed. Sir Guy will prevent them breaking out through our blockade and escaping to the open ocean.'

'Al-Salil and his bastard must not be allowed to escape.' Kadem's eyes lit with the dark mesmeric glare as he said the name.

'My own hatred for him exceeds yours. Abubaker was my brother and al-Salil murdered him. There are other old scores, too, almost as compelling, which I still have to settle with him,' Zayn reminded him. 'Despite this setback, we have the noose round his neck. Now we will draw it tight.'

Over the next weeks Dorian watched the development of the siege from his command post on the minaret. The enemy fleet sailed round the peninsula and deployed across the entrance to the bay, just out of range of the batteries on the walls or even of the long nine-pounders on the two schooners. Some of the larger, less manoeuvrable dhows were anchored on the twenty-fathom line where the sea bottom shelved in. The more nimble vessels patrolled back and forth in the deeper waters, ready to seize any supply ships trying to enter the bay, or to intercept the two schooners if they tried to break through.

The graceful hull and the elegant raked masts of the

Arcturus hovered in the distance, sometimes hidden by the cliffs, sometimes dropping below the horizon. At intervals Dorian heard the distant rumble of her cannons as she fell on some unfortunate small vessel attempting to bring supplies in to Muscat. Then she reappeared from a different quarter. Mansur and Dorian discussed her as they watched her through their telescopes.

'She points well up into the wind when she is close-hauled, unlike any of the dhows. She can carry a spread of canvas nearly half as large again as either of our ships. She has eighteen guns to our twelve,' Dorian murmured. 'She is a lovely ship.'

Mansur found himself wondering if Verity was aboard her. Then he thought, If Sir Guy is there, of course she must be with him. She is his voice. He could not do without her. He thought of having to turn his guns on the *Arcturus* if Verity were standing on the open deck. I will worry about that when the time comes, he decided, then answered his father. 'The *Sprite* and the *Revenge* are able to point higher. Between them they have twenty-four guns to Sir Guy's eighteen. Both Kumrah and Batula know these waters like lovers. Ruby Cornish is a babe in arms compared to them.' Mansur smiled with the reckless abandon of youth. 'Besides, we will make our stand here. We will send Zayn and his Turks running like curs with live coals tucked under their tails.'

'I wish I had the same confidence.' Dorian turned his spyglass inland, and they watched the besieging army inch inexorably towards the walls. 'Zayn has done this many times before. He will make few mistakes. See how he has begun to sap forward? Those trenches and the lines of gabions will protect his assault forces until they are right under the walls.' Each day he instructed Mansur on the ancient science of siege-making. 'See there, they are bringing up their great guns to position them in the emplacements they have prepared. Once they begin firing in earnest they will smash through the weak spots in our defences and shoot away any repairs faster than we can make them. When they have opened the breaches they will rush them from the head of the assault trenches.'

They watched the guns being dragged forward by the teams of oxen. Weeks earlier the remainder of Zayn's fleet had arrived from Lamu and had landed his horses, draught animals and the rest of his men on the other side of the peninsula. Now his cavalry patrolled the palm groves and the foothills of the interior. Their dust was always visible.

'What can we do?' Mansur sounded less certain of the outcome.

'Very little,' Dorian replied. 'We can sortie and raid the earthworks. But they are expecting us to do that. We will take heavy losses. We can shoot away a few of the gabions, but they will repair any damage we can inflict within hours.'

'You sound despondent,' Mansur said, accusingly. 'I am unaccustomed to that, Father.'

'Despondent?' Dorian said. 'No, not of the eventual outcome. However, I should never have allowed Zayn to trap us in the city. Our men do not fight well from behind walls. They love to be the attackers. They are the ones losing heart. Mustapha Zindara and bin-Shibam are having difficulty keeping them here. Even they want to be out in the open desert, fighting the way they know best.'

That night a hundred of bin-Shibam's men threw open the city gates and, in a tight group, galloped through the Turkish lines and escaped into the desert. The guards were only just able to close the gates before the attackers rushed to exploit this opportunity.

'Could you not have stopped them going?' Mansur demanded, next morning.

Bin-Shibam shrugged at his lack of understanding, and Dorian answered him. 'The Saar do not accept orders, Mansur. They follow a sheikh just as long as they agree with what he asks of them. If they don't, they go home.'

'Now that it has begun, more will leave. The Dahm and the Awamir are restless also,' Mustapha Zindara warned.

At dawn the following day the enemy batteries in their deep, heavily fortified emplacements began to bombard the southern wall. Counting the flashes and the spurts of gunsmoke with each discharge, Dorian and Mansur determined that there were eleven guns of cavernous calibre. The stone balls they fired must have weighed well over a hundred pounds each. It was possible to watch the flight of the massive projectiles with the naked eye. Mansur timed the rate of fire: it took almost twenty minutes for each gun to be swabbed, loaded, primed, then run out, relaid and fired. Once the enemy guns had ranged in, the massive balls smashed into their target with disturbing accuracy, each one striking within a few feet of its predecessor. A single ball might crack a block in the wall, and the second, striking on the same spot, dislodged it entirely. If it struck the timber balks, which the defenders had used to repair the weak sections, it splintered them to toothpicks. By nightfall of the first day two breaches had been knocked through the walls. As soon as it was dark, teams of workmen under Mansur's command rushed forward to begin the repairs.

With the dawn the bombardment began again. By noon the repairs had been swept away, and the stone balls were chipping away to enlarge the breaches. Dorian's gunners dragged half of their guns round from the harbour side to reinforce the battery on the south wall, and steadily returned the fire. However, Zayn's guns were well set in their emplacements, with deep banks of sand-filled gabions protecting them. Only the gaping bronze muzzles were visible, and these were tiny targets to hit at such ranges. When the defenders' balls struck the gabions, the sand-filled baskets of woven cane absorbed the shot so completely that it made almost no impression at all.

However, half-way through the afternoon they scored their first direct hit. One of their twenty-pound iron balls struck the extreme left-hand gun full on the muzzle. The bronze rang like a church bell, and even that weight of metal was hurled backwards off its carriage, crushing the gun-crew behind it to mincemeat. The barrel stuck straight up in the air. On the city walls the gunners cheered themselves hoarse, and redoubled their efforts. But by dusk they had not achieved another hit, and the breaches in the walls gaped wide.

As soon as the moon set, bin-Shibam and Mansur led a

sortie into the enemy lines. They took twenty men each and crept up on the battery emplacement. Even though the Turks were expecting the raid, Mansur's party had almost reached the wall of the emplacement before they were spotted and one of the sentries fired his musket. The ball hummed past Mansur's head and he shouted at his men, 'Follow me!'

As he scrambled in through the embrasure, jumped up on the barrel of the gun and ran along the top of it, he stabbed at the throat of the man who had fired the shot at him. He dropped the musket he was trying to reload and grabbed the naked blade with both hands. When Mansur pulled it back the steel ran through the man's fingers, severing flesh and tendons to the bone. Mansur jumped over his twitching body and down among the Turkish gunners, who were dulled with sleep, and struggling out of their blankets. He killed another, and wounded a third before they ran howling with terror into the night. His men followed him in to join the attack. While they were busy, Mansur plunged the point of one of the iron spikes he carried in his pouch into the touch-hole of the gun, and another of his men drove it home with a dozen lusty blows of the hammer.

Then they ran down the connecting trench to the adjoining emplacement. Here the gunners were fully awake, waiting to meet them with pikes and battleaxes. Within seconds they were a shouting, struggling mass, and Mansur knew they would never be able to reach the second gun. More of the enemy were rushing up the communication trench from the rear to repel them.

'Back!' Mansur yelled, and they clambered over the front wall, just as Istaph and the other grooms rode up with horses. They galloped back through the city gates with bin-Shibam coming in close behind them.

There they found they had lost five men killed and another dozen wounded. In the dawn light they saw that the Turks had stripped the corpses of the missing men and displayed them on the front wall of the emplacement. Between them, Mansur and bin-Shibam had managed to spike only two of the guns, and the remaining eight opened fire again. Within hours the stone balls had ripped away all the repairs that had been thrown up during the night. In the middle of the afternoon a single lucky shot brought twenty feet of wall tumbling down in a heap of masonry and rubble. Surveying the damage from the top of the minaret, Dorian estimated, 'Another week at the latest, and Zayn will be ready to launch his attack.'

That night two hundred of the Awamir and the Dahm saddled their horses and rode out of the city. The next day, as was customary, the muezzin gave his wailing call to the faithful from the minaret of the main mosque in the city. Both sides responded: the big guns stopped firing, the Turks took off their round helmets and knelt among the palm groves, while on the parapets the defenders did the same. Before he joined in the worship, Dorian smiled ironically at the notion that both sides prayed to the same God for the victory.

This time there was a new development to the ritual. After the prayers Zayn's heralds rode around the perimeter of the walls shouting a warning to the defenders on the parapets: 'Hear the words of the true Caliph. "Those of you who wish to leave this doomed city may do so without let. I grant you pardon for their treachery. You may take with you your horse and your weapons and return to your tents and your wives. Any man who brings me the head of the incestuous usurper al-Salil, I will reward with a lakh of gold rupees."'

The defenders jeered at them. However, that night another thousand warriors rode out through the gates. Before they went, two of the lesser sheikhs came to take their leave of Dorian. 'We are not traitors or cowards,' they told him, 'but this is not a fight for a man. Out in the desert we will ride with you unto death. We love you as we loved your father, but we will not die here like caged dogs.'

'Go with my blessing,' Dorian told them, 'and may you always find favour in the sight of God. Know you that I will come to you again.'

'We shall wait for you, al-Salil.'

The next day, at the time of prayers when the guns fell silent the heralds circled the walls again.

'The true Caliph Zayn al-Din has declared a sack of the

city. Any man or woman who is found within the walls when the Caliph enters will be put to death by torture.'

This time only a few voices jeered back. That night almost half of the remaining defenders left. The Turks lined the road as they passed and made no effort to prevent them.

'You are distracted, my darling.' Caroline Courtney watched her daughter's face quizzically. 'What is it that troubles you so?'

Apart from a vague greeting, Verity had not spoken to her mother since she had come up on the deck of the *Arcturus* from her father's great cabin. The meeting with the Caliph's military commander, Kadem ibn Abubaker, had lasted most of the morning. Now Verity stood at the ship's side and watched the fast felucca conveying the general back to the shore. She had translated Abubaker's report to her father, and relayed to him the Caliph's orders to tighten the blockade of the bay to prevent any enemy ships escaping when at last the city was captured from the usurper.

She sighed and turned to her mother. 'The siege is entering its final stages, Mother,' she answered dutifully. The two had never been close. Caroline was a nervous, hysterical woman. She was dominated by her husband and had little time or energy remaining for her role as mother. Like a child, she seemed unable to concentrate on a single matter for any extended period, and her mind flitted from one subject to the next like a butterfly in a spring garden.

'I will be so relieved when this awful business is over and your father has dealt properly with this al-Salil rascal. Then we can have done with the whole dreadful business and go back home.' For Caroline, home was the consulate in Delhi. Behind the stone walls, in the manicured gardens and cool courtyards with bubbling fountains, she was safe and shielded from the cruel, alien world of the Orient. She scratched at her throat, and moaned softly. There was a scarlet rash on the white skin. The humid tropical airs and confinement in the hot little cabin had aggravated her prickly heat again.

'Shall I help you with some of the cooling lotion?' Verity asked. She wondered how her mother could so easily make her feel guilty. She went to where Caroline lay on the wide hammock that Captain Cornish had had rigged for her in a corner of the quarter-deck. A canvas sun-screen shaded her, but allowed the cooling airs of the trade wind to flow over her plump, moist body.

Verity knelt beside her and dabbed the white liquid on to the inflamed and itching rash. Caroline waved a hand languidly. Her diamond rings were deeply embedded in pasty white skin. The slim brown Indian maid in her beautiful silk sari knelt on the opposite side of the hammock from Verity and offered her a dish of sweetmeats. Caroline picked out a pink cube of Turkish Delight. When the maid began to rise to her feet Caroline stopped her with a peremptory snap of her fingers and selected two more of the flower-flavoured jellies and popped them into her mouth. She chewed with unbridled pleasure, and the fine white icing sugar dusted her lips.

'What do you suppose will happen to al-Salil and his son Mansur if they are captured by Kadem ibn Abubaker?' Verity asked mildly.

'I have no doubt that it will be something utterly detestable,' Caroline said, without interest. 'The Caliph does beastly things to his enemies, trampling by elephants, shooting from cannon.' She shuddered and reached for the glass of honey sherbet that the maid offered her. 'I really do not want to discuss it.' She sipped, and brightened. 'If this business is over by the end of the month, then we might be back in Delhi for your birthday. I am planning a ball for you. Every eligible bachelor in the Company will attend. It is high time we found a husband for you, my dear. By the time I was your age, I had been married four years and had two children.'

Suddenly Verity was angry with this vapid, fatuous woman as she had never been before. She had always treated her mother with weary deference, making allowance for her gluttony and other weaknesses. Not until her meeting with Mansur had she understood the depths of her mother's subservience to her father, the guilt that had placed her in his power. But now she was outraged by her smug, mindless complacency. Her anger boiled over before she could check it.

'Yes, Mother,' she said bitterly. 'And the first of those two children was Tom Courtney's bastard.' No sooner were the words past her lips than she wished them back.

Caroline stared at her with huge, swimming eyes. 'Oh, you wicked, wicked child! You have never loved me!' she whimpered and a mixture of sherbet and half-chewed Turkish Delight dribbled down the front of her lace blouse.

All Verity's sense of deference vanished. 'You do remember Tom Courtney, Mother?' Verity asked. 'And what tricks the two of you played while you were on passage to India in Grandfather's ship the *Seraph*?'

'You never— Who told you? What have you heard? It isn't true!' Caroline blubbered hysterically.

'What about Dorian Courtney? Do you remember how you and my father left him to rot in slavery when he was a child? How you and Father lied to Uncle Tom? How you told him that Dorian had died of the fever? You told me the same lie. You even showed me the grave on Lamu island where you said he was buried.'

'Stop this!' Caroline clapped her hands over her ears. 'I will not listen to such filth.'

''Tis filth, is it, Mother?' Verity asked coldly. 'Then who do you think is this al-Salil, whom you wish trampled by elephants or shot from a cannon? Do you not know that he is Dorian Courtney?'

Caroline stared at her, her face white as buttermilk, the inflamed rash more evident in contrast. 'Lies!' she whispered. 'All terrible wicked lies.'

'And, Mother, al-Salil's son is my cousin, Mansur Courtney. You want a husband for me? Look no further. If ever Mansur does me the honour of asking me to marry him, I shall not hesitate. I shall fly to his side.'

Caroline let out a strangled shriek, and fell out of the

hammock on to the deck. The maid and two of the ship's officers ran forward to help her to her feet. As soon as she was up, she struggled out of their grip, the fat quivering beneath her lace and pearl-studded dress, and heaved herself to the companionway that led down to the great cabin.

Sir Guy heard her shrieks of anguish and rushed out of the doorway in his shirtsleeves. He seized his wife's arm and drew her into the cabin.

Verity waited alone by the ship's rail for the retribution that she knew must surely follow. She stared beyond the rest of the blockading fleet of war dhows, into the entrance of Muscat bay to the distant spires and minarets of the city.

In her mind she went over once again the dreadful news that Kadem ibn Abubaker had brought to her father, and which she had translated to him. Muscat would be in the hands of Zayn al-Din before the month was out. Mansur was in the most dire danger, and there was nothing she could do to help him. Her dread and frustration had led her to the gross indiscretion with her mother she had just perpetrated. 'Please, God!' she whispered. 'Do not let anything befall Mansur.'

Within the hour her father's steward came to summon her.

In the cabin her mother sat in the seat below the stern window. She held a moist, crumpled handkerchief, wiped her eyes and blew her nose loudly.

Her father stood in the centre of the cabin. He was still in his shirtsleeves. His expression was severe and hard. 'What poisonous lies have you been telling your mother?' he demanded.

'No lies, Father,' she answered him defiantly. She knew what the consequences of provoking him must be, but she felt a reckless abandon.

'Repeat them to me,' Sir Guy ordered. In quiet, measured tones she described to him all that Mansur had told her. At the end he was silent. He went to the stern window and stared out at the low swells of the azure sea. He did not look at his wife. The silence drew out. Verity knew that this silence was one of his ploys to intimidate her and force her to lower her defences and her resistance to him.

'You kept this from me,' he said at last. 'Why did you not tell me at once what you had learned? That was the duty you owe to me, child.'

'You do not deny any of it, Father?' she asked.

'I do not have to deny or affirm anything to you. I am not on trial. You are.'

Silence fell again. It was hot and airless in the cabin, and the ship rolled sickeningly on the slow, greasy undulations of the current. She felt breathless and nauseated, but was determined not to show it.

Sir Guy spoke again: 'You have given your mother a severe shock with these wild stories.' Caroline sobbed dramatically and blew her nose again. 'A fast packet boat arrived from Bombay this morning. I am sending her back to the consulate.'

'I will not go with her,' Verity said evenly.

'No,' Sir Guy agreed. 'I will keep you here. It might be a summary example for you to witness the execution of the rebels in whom you have expressed such an unhealthy interest.' He was silent again for a while as he considered how much Verity knew of his affairs. Her knowledge was so extensive that it might prove lethal if she chose to use it against him. He dared not let her escape his immediate control.

'Father, these rebels are your own brother,' Verity broke the silence, 'and his son.'

Sir Guy showed no reaction. Instead he went on quietly, 'It seems, from what your mother tells me, you have been playing the harlot with the younger Arab. Have you forgotten that you are an Englishwoman?'

'You demean yourself by making that accusation.'

'You demean me and your family by your unconscionable behaviour. For that alone you must be punished.'

He went to his desk and picked up the whalebone riding crop that lay upon it. He turned back to her. 'Disrobe!' he ordered. She stood motionless, her face expressionless.

'Do as your father orders,' said Caroline, 'you blatant hussy.' She had stopped weeping and her tone was vindictive and gloating.

'Disrobe at once,' Guy said again, 'or I shall summon two of the seamen to do it for you.'

Verity lifted her hands to her throat and untied the ribbon that held her blouse closed. When at last she stood naked before them she raised her chin defiantly, shook out her hair and let it hang forward over her shoulders to screen her proud young breasts, and cover her pudenda.

'Lie face down over the daybed,' her father ordered.

She went to it with a firm tread. She stretched out on the buttoned green leather. The lines of her body were sweet and smooth as those of a Michelangelo marble. I will not cry out, she told herself, but her muscles convulsed instinctively as the whip hissed and clapped across her buttocks. I will not grant him that pleasure, she promised herself, and closed her eyes as the next stroke fell across the back of her thighs. It stung like the bite of a scorpion. She bit her lip until blood seeped salty and metallic into her mouth.

At last Sir Guy stood back, his breath fast and ragged with the effort. 'You may dress yourself, you shameless harlot,' he gasped.

She sat up slowly, and tried to ignore the fire that raged down her back and her legs. The front of her father's breeches was on a level with her eyes and she smiled with cold contempt as she noticed the tumescent evidence of his arousal.

He turned away hurriedly and threw the whip on to the desk top. 'You have been deceitful and disloyal to me. I can no longer trust you. I shall keep you confined to your cabin until such time as I have decided what additional punishment is appropriate,' he warned her.

Dorian and Mansur stood with the sheikhs on the balcony of the minaret, and watched the plumes and tops of the bronze soup-bowl helmets of the Turkish assault troops showing above the parapets as they moved up the approach trenches. As they massed below the walls Zayn al-Din's heavy batteries redoubled their rate of fire. They had changed their ammunition. Instead of stone balls, they swept the parapets and breaches with cartloads of fist-sized pebbles and cast-iron potlegs. The guns fell silent and the Turkish trumpeters sounded the charge; the drums pounded out an urgent beat.

A mass of shrieking Turks erupted from the head of the trenches. As they raced forward across the last few yards before the breaches, the guns of the defenders on the parapets blazed down upon them, and the archers loosed flights of arrows.

The leading attackers were across the open ground before the gunners could reload. They left dead and wounded littered upon the shot-torn earth, but wave after wave ran forward to take the place of the fallen.

They clambered over the rubble and the shattered stone blocks, and swarmed through the breaches. As soon as they were through they found themselves in a maze of narrow alleys and dead-end lanes. Dorian had ordered barricades built across every one. The Turks had to take each by storm, running into a hail of close-range musket fire as they charged. As soon as they scaled an obstruction, the defenders ran back to the next line of defence and the Turks were forced to attack again. It was gruelling and bloody work, but gradually Mansur and bin-Shibam's depleted forces were driven back into the main souk, and the Turks were able to outflank them, and reach the main city gate. They slaughtered the men who tried to defend the winches and forced the gates wide. Kadem and Koots, at the head of two thousand Turks, were waiting outside and the moment the gates swung open they rushed in.

From the top of the minaret Dorian saw them pouring like floodwaters down the narrow streets. He was relieved that over the past months he had been able to spirit most of the women and children out of the city and into the desert, for they would have been lambs to these wolves. As soon as the gates were open, he ordered the hoisting of the previously prepared flag signal to the *Sprite* and the *Revenge*. Then he turned to his councillors and captains. 'It is over,' he told them. 'I thank you for your courage and loyalty. Take your men and escape if you can. We will fight again another day.' One at a time they came forward to embrace him.

Bin-Shibam was covered with dust and black with smoke; his robe was stained with the dried blood of half a dozen flesh wounds. It mingled with the blood of the Turks he had slain. 'We shall wait for your return,' he said.

'You know where you can find me. Send a messenger to me when all is in readiness. I shall return to you at once,' Dorian told him, 'if God is willing. Praise God.'

'God is great,' they replied.

The horses were waiting in the lanes before the small north gate. When it was thrown open Mustapha Zindara, bin-Shibam and the rest of the council rode out at the head of their men. They fought their way through the attackers who raced forward to cut them off, then galloped away through the palm groves and irrigated fields. Dorian watched them go from the minaret. He heard footsteps on the marble stairs and turned with his sword in his hand. For a moment he hardly recognized his own son under the coating of grime and soot.

'Come, Father,' Mansur said, 'we must hurry.'

Together they ran down the stairs to where Istaph and ten men were waiting for them in the mosque.

'This way.' An imam stepped from the shadows and gesticulated. They hurried after him, and he led them through a labyrinth of passages until they reached a small iron gate. He unlocked it and Mansur kicked it open.

'Stay with God's blessing,' Dorian told the imam.

'Go with God's blessing,' he replied, 'and may He bring you swiftly back to Oman.'

They ran through the door and found themselves in a gloomy alleyway so narrow that the latticed balconies of the top floors of the deserted buildings almost met overhead.

'This way, Majesty!' Istaph had been born in the city, and these alleys had been his childhood playground. They raced after him and burst out into the sunlight again. The open waters of the harbour lay before them, and the *Sprite*'s longboat was waiting out in the bay to take them off. Mansur shouted and waved to Kumrah who stood at the helm. The oarsmen pulled together and the longboat shot in towards them.

At that moment there was an angry din behind them. A

mob of Turkish and Omani attackers poured out from the mouth of one of the alleys on to the wharf. They charged towards them, their front rank bristling with long pikes and bright-edged weapons. Dorian glanced over his shoulder and saw that the longboat was still a pistol shot away across the green waters. 'Stand together!' he cried, and they formed a tight circle at the head of the landing steps, shoulder to shoulder, facing outwards.

'Al-Salil!' shouted the Arab who led the attack. He was tall and lean, and he moved like a leopard. His long, lank hair whipped out behind him and his beard curled on to his chest.

'Al-Salil!' he shouted again. 'I have come for you.' Dorian recognized that fierce, fanatical glare.

'Kadem.' Mansur recognized him at the same moment, and his voice rang with the force of his hatred.

'I have come for you also, you bastard puppy of a dog and an incestuous bitch in heat!' Kadem shouted again.

'You must take me first.' Dorian stepped forward a pace, and Kadem hurled himself upon him. Their blades clashed as Dorian blocked the cut for his head, and then sent a riposte at Kadem's throat. Steel rang and scraped on steel. It was the first time they had matched blades, but Dorian knew at once that Kadem was a dangerous opponent. His right arm was quick and powerful, and in his left hand he held a curved dagger, poised to strike through any opening.

'You murdered my wife!' Dorian snarled, as he thrust again.

'I give thanks that I was able to do that duty. I should have killed you also,' Kadem answered, 'for my father's sake.'

Mansur fought at Dorian's right hand and Istaph on the left, guarding his flanks but careful not to block or impede his sword arm. Step by step they gave ground, retreating to the head of the landing, and the attackers pressed them hard.

Dorian heard the bows of the longboat bump against the stone wall below them, and Kumrah shouted, 'Come, al-Salil!'

The steps were greasy with green algae and Kadem, seeing Dorian about to escape his vengeance a second time, leaped in furiously. Dorian was driven back another pace on to the top step, and his right foot slipped on the greasy surface. He went down on one knee and was forced to save his balance by dropping his point for an instant. Kadem saw his chance. He launched himself, all his weight on his right foot, lunging for Dorian's heart.

The moment his father had gone down, Mansur anticipated Kadem's response. He turned, poised and ready. Kadem swung his body forward and for an instant his left flank was open as he launched himself into the attack. Mansur hit him, going in under his raised arm. He put all his anger, hatred and grief for his mother behind the thrust. He expected to feel his point slide in deeply, that clinging reluctance of living flesh opening to the steel. Instead his sword arm jarred to the strike of steel on the bone of Kadem's ribs, and his wrist twisted slightly as the point was deflected. Nevertheless, the thrust ran along the outside of Kadem's ribcage, and up under his scapula. It touched no vital organ but the force of it spun Kadem sideways, throwing off-line the thrust he aimed at Dorian. Kadem reeled away, and Mansur pulled his blade free and struck again. But with a violent effort Kadem blocked the second blow, and Dorian leaped back to his feet.

Father and son went at Kadem together, eager for the kill. Blood was pouring from the wound under Kadem's arm and cascading down his flank. The shock of the blow and the realization that he was in mortal danger from two skilled swordsmen blanched his face a dirty treacle colour.

'*Effendi!*' Kumrah shouted, from the longboat. 'Come! We will be trapped. There are more Turks coming.' The enemy was thronging out of the mouth of the alleyway, and rushing towards them.

Realizing their predicament, Dorian hesitated and that was all Kadem needed to break off and leap out of play. Instantly two swarthy, armoured Turks jumped forward in his place and rushed at Dorian. When he struck at them his blade skidded off their chain-mail.

'Enough!' Dorian grunted. 'Get back to the boat!' Mansur feinted at the bearded face of one of the Turks, and when he ducked back Mansur stepped across to cover his father.

'Run!' he snapped, and Dorian bounded down the steps.

Istaph and the others were already on board, and Mansur was left alone at the head of the landing. A line of pikes and scimitars pressed him back. He had a glimpse of Kadem ibn Abubaker glaring at him from the back row of the attackers; the wound had not dimmed his hatred.

'Kill him!' he screamed. 'Let not the pig-swine escape.'

'Mansur!' He heard his father call from the bows of the longboat. Yet he knew that if he tried to run down the steps one of the pike men would send a thrust into his exposed back. He turned and jumped, launching himself out over the stone edge of the wharf. He dropped ten feet and landed feet first on one of the thwarts. The heavy planking cracked under his weight, and he toppled forward. The longboat rocked violently and Mansur almost went over the side, but Dorian grabbed and steadied him.

The oarsmen heaved together and the longboat shot away. Dorian looked back over the stern just as Kadem staggered to the edge of the wharf. He had dropped his sword and was clutching the wound under his arm. The blood flowed through his fingers. 'You shall not escape my vengeance!' he shrieked after them. 'You have my father's blood on your hands and your conscience. I have sworn your death in the sight of Allah. I will follow you to the gates of hell.'

'He does not understand the true meaning of hatred,' Dorian whispered. 'One day I hope to teach it to him.'

'I share your oath,' said Mansur, 'but now we have to get our ships out of the bay and into the open sea, with Zayn's entire fleet to oppose us.'

Dorian shook himself, throwing off the debilitating throes of grief and hatred. He turned to look at the mouth of the bay. Four of the big war-dhows were anchored in sight, and two more under sail.

'No sighting of the *Arcturus*?' he asked Mansur.

'Not these past three days,' Mansur replied, 'but we can be sure she is not far off, lurking just below the horizon.'

Dorian went up on to the deck of the *Revenge*, then called down to Mansur in the longboat. 'We must try at all times to keep one another in sight, but there is sure to be fighting. Should we become separated, you know the rendezvous.'

Mansur waved at him. 'Sawda island, north tip. I will wait for you there.' He broke off at the sullen boom of a cannon, and looked back at the city walls above the harbour. Powder smoke bloomed on the parapet but was swiftly blown aside by the wind. Moments later a fountain of spray leaped from the surface of the sea close alongside the *Sprite*.

'The enemy have seized the batteries,' Dorian shouted. 'We must get under way at once.'

Another cannon shot bellowed out before Mansur reached the *Sprite*. Although this ball fell well short, Mansur knew that the gunners would soon have the range.

'Pull!' he shouted to the rowers. 'Pull or you will be forced to swim!'

The crew of the *Sprite*, urged on by the fall of shot around them, had the anchor cable singled up and the falls dangling overside from the davits, ready to retrieve the longboat. As Mansur bounded up on to the deck, he ordered the jib set to bring her round to face the entrance to the bay. As the *Sprite* turned on to the wind Kumrah broke out all sails to the royals.

The evening offshore wind had set in and was blowing steadily from the west. It was on their best point of sailing and they flew down towards the mouth of the bay. As they came up with the *Revenge*, she backed her mainsail to allow the *Sprite* to take the lead. The entrance was treacherous with hidden shoals, but Kumrah knew these waters better even than Batula in the *Revenge*. He would lead them out.

Mansur had not realized until then how swiftly the day had sped away. The sun was already low on the peaks of the mountains behind them, and the light was rich and golden. The batteries on the parapets of Muscat were still blazing away at them, and one lucky shot punched a neat hole in the mizzen topmast staysail, but they drew steadily out of range and could look ahead to the blockading ships across the entrance. Two of the war-dhows had hoisted their anchors, set their huge lateen sails and were moving out into the channel to meet them. Their passage through the water was sluggish compared to the two much smaller schooners, and they fell away noticeably even though they were not pointing high up into the stiff evening breeze. In contrast, the two schooners had set all sail and were tearing down the length of the bay.

Mansur looked along his deck and saw that his gunners were all at their action stations, although they had not yet run out the guns, which were loaded with round-shot. The slow-match was smouldering in the sand tubs and the men were laughing and talking excitedly. The days of gunnery practice and their successful attack on the Turkish infantry had imbued them with confidence. They were chafed by the inactivity of the last few weeks while they had been forced to lie at anchor, but now that Mansur and al-Salil were back in command of the flotilla they were eager for a fight.

Kumrah made a small adjustment to their course. Although Mansur trusted his judgement, he felt a twinge of unease. On this heading Kumrah would take them into the boiling white surf below the cliffs that guarded the entrance to the bay.

The nearest war-dhow altered her course towards them as soon as Kumrah's turn became apparent. They began to converge swiftly. Mansur raised his glass and studied the dhow. It was crammed with men. They lined the windward rail and brandished their weapons. She had already run out her big guns.

'She is armed with short-barrelled Ostras,' Kumrah told Mansur.

'I do not know them.'

'That does not surprise me. They must be older than your grandfather.' Kumrah laughed. 'And with a great deal less power.'

'Then it seems we are in greater danger of striking the reef than receiving a ball from those ancient weapons,' Mansur said pointedly. They were still charging straight in towards the cliffs.

'Highness, you must have faith in Allah.'

'In Allah I have faith. I worry only about the captain of my ship.'

Kumrah smiled and held his course. The dhow fired her first ragged broadside from all fifteen of her starboard guns. The range was still too far by half. Mansur spotted the fall of only one shot, and that was short by half a musket. However, the faint cheering of the dhow's crew carried to them faintly.

Still the huge dhow and the two small ships converged. Gradually as they bore down on the breaking white water the cheering from the dhow subsided and the pugnacious display with it.

'You have terrified the enemy, as you have me,' said Mansur. 'Do you intend scuttling us on the reef, Kumrah?'

'I fished these waters as a boy, as did my father and his father before me,' Kumrah assured him. The reef was still dead ahead, and they were closing rapidly. The dhow fired another broadside, but it was clear that the gunners were distracted by the menace of the coral. Only a single large stone ball howled over the *Sprite* and severed a mizzen shroud. Quickly Kumrah sent two men to replace it.

Then, without reducing sail, Kumrah steered into a narrow channel in the reef that Mansur had not noticed. It was barely wide enough to accept the beam of the schooner. As they tore through, Mansur stared with dread fascination overside and saw huge mushroom heads of coral skimming by less than a fathom below the churning surface. Any one of them would have ripped the *Sprite*'s belly out of her.

This was too much for the nerves of the dhow captain. Mansur could see him in the stern of his ship, screaming and gesticulating wildly. His crew deserted their posts at the guns and scrambled to take in the billowing lateen sail and bring their ship on to the other tack. With the sail down they had to run the boom back to bring its butt round the mast, then home again on the port side. This was a laborious business and while they were about it the dhow wallowed helplessly.

'Stand by to go about!' Kumrah gave the order and his men ran to the stays. He was staring ahead, shading his eyes with one hand, judging his moment finely. 'Up helm!' he called to his helmsman, who spun the wheel until the spokes blurred. The *Sprite* pirouetted and shot through the dogleg turn in the channel. They raced out of the far end into the deeper water, and the helpless dhow wallowed directly ahead of them with her sail in disarray and her guns unmanned.

'Run out the starboard guns!' Mansur gave the order, and the lids of the gunports crashed open. They crossed the dhow's stern so closely that Mansur could have thrown his hat on to her deck.

'Fire as you bear!'

In quick succession the cannons roared out, and each ball smashed into the dhow's stern. Mansur could see the timbers shatter and burst open in clouds of flying wood splinters. One of them as long as his arm pegged like an arrow into the mast beside his ear. At that range not a single shot missed the mark, and the iron balls raked through the dhow from stem to stern. There were screams of terror and agony from the crew as the *Sprite* sailed on past her into the open sea.

Following her closely through the channel in the coral, the *Revenge* bore down on the stricken vessel in her turn. As she passed she raked her again, and the dhow's single mast toppled and fell overside.

Mansur looked ahead. The way was clear. Not one of the other dhows was in position to head them off. Kumrah's seemingly suicidal manoeuvre had taken them by surprise. 'Run in the guns!' he ordered. 'Close the ports and secure the gun tackles.'

He looked back and saw the *Revenge* only half a cable's length behind them. A long way back the dismasted dhow was drifting on to the reef, driven before the wind. She struck and heeled over violently. Through the glass Mansur saw her crew abandon her. They were leaping over the side, hitting the water with tiny white splashes, then striking out for the shore. Mansur wondered how many would survive the rip current at the foot of the cliffs, and the sharp fangs of the coral.

He backed his mainsail and let the *Revenge* come up alongside, close enough to enable his father to hail them through the speaking trumpet: 'Tell Kumrah never to play that trick on us again! He took us through the gates of hell.'

Kumrah made a deep and penitent obeisance, but Dorian

lowered the trumpet and saluted his cool head and nerves. Then he lifted the trumpet again. 'It will be dark in an hour. I shall burn a single lantern in my stern port for you to keep your station on me. If we should become separated during the night, the rendezvous will be the same as always, Sawda island.'

The *Revenge* forged ahead and the *Sprite* fell in behind her. Weeks before Dorian had decided on their final destination. There was only one port in all the Ocean of the Indies open to them now. Zayn had all the Fever Coast and the harbours of Oman under his thrall. The Dutch had Ceylon and Batavia. The English East India Company controlled all the coast of India. Sir Guy would close that to them. There remained only the safe haven of Fort Auspice in Nativity Bay. There they would be able to gather their reserves and make plans for the future. He had marked the chart and given Mustapha Zindara and bin-Shibam the sailing directions for Fort Auspice: they would send a ship to find him there as soon as they had united the desert tribes and made all the preparations for his return. They would need gold rupees and strong allies. Dorian was as yet uncertain as to where he would find men and money, but there would be time to ponder this later.

He turned to his immediate concerns, and the course that he set now was east by south-east to clear the Gulf of Oman. Once they were into the open ocean they could steer directly for Madagascar and pick up the Mozambique current to carry them southwards. Mansur took up close station on the *Revenge* and they sailed on beneath a sunset of awe-inspiring grandeur. Mountainous anvil-headed thunderclouds marched along the darkling western horizon to the sound of distant thunder, and the sinking sun costumed them with suits of rosy gold and glittering cobalt blue.

Yet all this beauty could not lift from Mansur's shoulder the sudden oppressive weight of the melancholia that bore down upon him. He was leaving the land and the people he had swiftly learned to love. The promise of a kingdom and of the Elephant Throne had been snatched from them. Yet all that was of little account when he thought of the woman he had lost before he had won her. He took from the inner pocket of his robe the letter he carried close to his heart, and read yet again her words: 'Last night you asked me if I did not feel anything between you and me. I would not answer you then, but I answer you now. Yes, I do.'

It seemed to him that those were the most beautiful words ever written in the English language.

Darkness fell with the dramatic suddenness that is seen only in the tropics, and the stars showed through the gaps left in the high canopy of the stormclouds. Within a short time they were closed by the rolling thunderheads and the darkness was complete, except for the tiny firefly of light that was the lantern on the stern of the *Revenge*.

Mansur leaned on the compass pinnacle and let himself lapse into romantic fantasy, dreaming half the night away without seeking his bunk. Suddenly, he was roused by a stroke of forked lightning that flew from the cloud ceiling to the surface of the sea, and was followed immediately by a sky-shattering thunderclap. For an instant the *Revenge* appeared out of the darkness ahead, shimmering in vivid blue light, each detail of her rigging and sails stark and clear. Then the darkness fell over her again even more heavily than before.

Mansur jumped erect from his slouch over the binnacle and ran to the starboard rail. In that blinding lightning flash he thought he had seen something else. It had been an evanescent flash of reflected light, almost on the far horizon.

'Did you see it?' he shouted at Kumrah, who stood beside him at the rail.

'The *Revenge*?' Kumrah answered, from the darkness, and his tone was puzzled. 'Yes, Highness. She is not more than a single cable's length ahead. There – you can see the glimmer of her stern light still.'

'No, no!' Mansur cried. 'Not on our bow. Abaft our beam. Something else.'

'Nay, master. I saw nothing.'

Both men peered out into the night, and again the lightning cracked overhead like a gigantic whip, then thunder deafened them and seemed to shiver the surface of the dark sea with its monstrous discharge. In that fleeting moment of diamond-sharp clarity Mansur saw it again.

'There!' Mansur seized Kumrah's shoulder and shook him violently. 'There! Did you see it this time?'

'A ship! Another ship!' Kumrah cried. 'I saw it clear.'

'How far off?'

'Two sea miles, no more than that. A tall ship. Square-rigged. That is no dhow.'

''Tis the *Arcturus*! Lying here in ambuscade.' Desperately Mansur looked to his father's ship, and saw that the tell-tale lantern still burned on her stern. 'The *Revenge* has not seen the danger.'

'We must catch up with her and warn her,' Kumrah exclaimed.

'Even if we clap on all our canvas we will not overhaul the *Revenge* and be within hail of her in less than a hour. By then it may be too late.' Mansur hesitated a moment longer, then made his decision: 'Beat to action quarters. Fire a gun to alert the *Revenge*. Then bring her on to the starboard tack and run in to intercept the enemy. Do not light the battle lanterns until I give the order. God grant we can take the enemy by surprise.'

The war drums boomed out into the dark, and as the crew scrambled to their stations a single peremptory gunshot thudded. As the *Sprite* came about, Mansur peered across at the other ship, waiting for her to extinguish her lantern or show some sign that she had taken heed of the warning, but at that instant the thunderclouds burst open and the rain teemed down. All was lost in the warm, smothering cascade of water. It seemed to fill the air they breathed, cutting out any faint glimmer of light and muting all sound other than the roar of the heavy drops on the canvas overhead and the deck timbers underfoot.

Mansur ran back to the binnacle and took a hasty bearing, but he knew that it was not accurate, and that the enemy ship might also have spotted them and changed her course and heading. His chances of coming upon her in this deluge were remote. They might pass each other by half a pistol shot without either being aware of the other's presence.

'Turn the hourglass and mark the traverse-board,' he ordered the helmsman. Perhaps he could intercept her on dead reckoning. Then he snapped at Kumrah, 'Put two good men on the wheel.'

He hurried to the bows, and through the sheets of blinding rain tried for a glimpse of the stern lantern of the *Revenge*. He took little comfort from the fact that he could see and hear nothing.

'God grant that Father is aware of the danger, and that he has doused the lantern. Otherwise it might guide Sir Guy to him, and he could be taken unawares.' He considered firing another gun to emphasize the urgency of the danger, but discarded the idea almost at once. A second gun would confuse the warning. His father might be led to believe that the *Sprite* had already engaged an enemy. It might alert the *Arcturus* and bring her down upon them. Instead he sailed on into the darkness and the torrents of blood-warm rain.

'Send your sharpest lookouts aloft,' he ordered Kumrah grimly, 'and have the gunners ready to run out on the instant. We will not have much warning if we come upon the enemy.'

The hourglass was turned twice, and still they sailed on in darkness, every man aboard straining all his senses for some warning of the enemy ship. And the rain never let up.

The enemy might have sailed on without spotting us, Mansur thought. He pondered the chances and the choices that were open to him. Or she might have turned to intercept us, and have passed us close at hand. She might even now be creeping up on the unsuspecting *Revenge*.

He reached a decision, and called to Kumrah, 'Heave the ship to, and warn every man to keep his eyes peeled and his ears open.'

They lay dark and silent, and another hour passed, measured by the soft slide of the sand in the hourglass. The rain abated, and the freshening breeze veered into the north, bringing with it the spicy odour of the desert, which was still not far off. The rain ceased. Mansur was about to give the order to set sail again, when a flickering glow lit the darkness far over their stern. It played like candlelight on the underbelly of the lowering cloud masses. Mansur held his breath and counted slowly to five. Then came the sound, the unmistakable rumbling roar of the guns.

'The *Arcturus* has slipped by us and she has found the *Revenge*. They are engaged,' he shouted. 'Wear ship and bring her round on to the port tack.'

With the night breeze on their quarter the *Sprite* tore through the darkness, both Mansur and Kumrah straining to coax every knot of speed from her. Ahead of them the flickering light and rumble of gun salvos grew brighter and louder as they sailed towards them.

'God grant we are in time,' Mansur prayed, and as he stared ahead the wind of their passage in his face brought tears to his eyes, or it may have been some other emotion. The two persons he loved most were caught up in that maelstrom of shot and flame, and he was still powerless to intervene. Even though the *Sprite* lay well over and ran before the breeze like a stag hard pressed by the hounds, she was still too slow for Mansur's heart.

Yet the distance between them narrowed steadily and, standing in the bows, balancing to the ship's urgent motion, Mansur was at last able to make out the shapes of the two ships. They were locked in conflict, lit by the muzzle flashes of their cannon.

Mansur saw that they were on the opposite tack to the *Sprite*, crossing their bows at an acute angle, so he yelled to Kumrah to bring the *Sprite* round two points on to an interception course. Now the range began to close more rapidly, and he could make out the more intimate details of the battle.

In the *Revenge*, Dorian had somehow wrested the weather gauge from Captain Cornish, and was holding him off, frustrating his efforts to bring the *Arcturus* alongside and to board him. But Cornish was blocking any effort that Dorian might make to bring the *Revenge* before the wind on to her best point of sailing and to run away from his superior adversary. In this formation the two ships were almost perfectly matched for speed, and the *Revenge* could not evade the bigger ship for much longer. In a duel of attrition like this the heavier weight of cannon must tell in the end.

However, the *Sprite* was closing rapidly, and soon she would throw her own weight into the unequal contest. The balance then would swing in their favour – if Mansur could reach them before the *Arcturus* grappled and boarded the smaller ship.

Closer and closer Mansur edged the *Sprite* towards the two ships. Even though his impulse was to rush in recklessly and hurl himself at the *Arcturus*, he restrained his warlike instincts, and manoeuvred across the wind.

He knew that he was still shrouded in the night, invisible to the captains and crews of either ship. He must take the utmost advantage of the surprise element. There were many minutes still before he was in position to put up his helm and charge out of the darkness, to cross the *Arcturus*'s stern, then to grapple and board her from across her port quarter. Mansur watched the development of the conflict through the lens of his spyglass.

Although the guns were firing steadily, the range was still too long for them to inflict telling damage on each other. He saw that a number of the *Revenge*'s shots had smashed holes in her opponent's hull above the waterline. The shattered timbers were bright with fresh splinters. There were rips and holes in some of her sails, and a few spars had been knocked away in her rigging, but all her guns were firing steadily.

Opposite her the *Revenge* was in no worse a case. In the light of the cannons, Mansur could pick out his father's figure in the distinctive green robes as he directed his gunners. Batula stood beside the helm, endeavouring to milk the last turn of speed from his ship.

Then Mansur turned his glass back on the quarter-deck of the *Arcturus*. With dread he searched for a glimpse of Verity's tall slim figure. He felt a small lift of relief when he could not find her, although he guessed that Sir Guy had confined her below decks where she would have some protection from the screaming round-shot.

Then he picked out Captain Cornish's face, red and angry in the glare of gunfire. He was pacing his deck with ponderous dignity, occasionally shooting a glance at his adversary, then turning back to harangue his gunners through the speaking trumpet he held to his lips. Even as Mansur watched, a lucky shot from the *Revenge* took away a spar in the *Arcturus*'s rigging and her main course came billowing down across the quarter-deck, smothering officers and helmsman under its heavy canvas folds.

There were a few moments of pandemonium as the crew rushed to hack away the flapping canvas. The fire from her batteries dwindled, and the blinded helmsman allowed her head to pay off a point before the wind as he tried to struggle out from under the sail. Then, from the far side of the quarter-deck, Mansur saw Sir Guy Courtney run forward into Cornish's place, and take command. Mansur heard faintly his shouts and saw that order was being swiftly restored. He must act at once to take advantage of the moment. He called an order to Kumrah, who was already poised for it. The *Sprite* turned like a polo pony and charged out of the darkness. She passed close under the stern of the *Revenge* and Mansur jumped up in the shrouds and called across the narrow gap of water to Dorian, 'Father!' Dorian spun round with a startled expression as the *Sprite* appeared miraculously out of the darkness so close at hand. 'I will cross his bows and rake him. Then I will board him from his port side. You close from the other hand and split his force.' Dorian's features lit with the old battle madness and he grinned at Mansur as he waved acknowledgement.

Mansur ordered the guns run out as he steered boldly across the *Arcturus*'s bows. For almost five minutes, which seemed a lifetime, he came directly under her fire, but her gun-crews were still in disarray and only three balls crashed into the *Sprite*'s upper deck. Although they ripped open the heavy planking and the splinters buzzed like a swarm of hornets, not a single man of the *Sprite*'s crew was struck down. Then he was under the *Arcturus*'s bows and screened from her fire by her own hull.

Mansur ran forward as his guns began to bear, then walked back along his battery, making certain that each one was aimed true before he gave the order to fire. One after the other the huge bronze weapons bellowed flame and shot, then crashed back against their tackles. Every ball struck home.

Mansur had cut his attack a shade too fine, and he passed so closely under Arcturus's bows that the larger ship's bowsprit snagged in the *Sprite*'s mizzen mast shrouds and snapped off, but the hulls missed each other by only an arm's length before the *Sprite* was past.

Immediately he was clear Mansur spun the *Sprite* round and laid her neatly alongside the *Arcturus*. The lids of the gunports on her port side were still closed, for the *Arcturus* was unprepared for an attack from this quarter. As the grappling irons were hurled over the *Arcturus*'s bulwarks and the two hulls were lashed together, Mansur fired another point-blank salvo from his starboard battery, then led his men across in a howling berserker rush. The gun-crews of the *Arcturus* turned to face them, but no sooner were they locked in the desperate hand-to-hand fighting than the *Revenge* took advantage of her weather gauge and came gliding in to grapple on to her starboard side. The *Arcturus*'s batteries on that side had not been reloaded after the last discharge, and the crews had abandoned them to meet Mansur's attack. The *Arcturus* was caught in the jaws of the barracuda.

The fighting raged back and forth across the main deck, but the combined crews of the two schooners outnumbered that of the larger *Arcturus* and slowly they began to wrest the upper hand. Mansur sought out Cornish and the two locked blades. Mansur tried to drive him back across the deck, and pin him against the shrouds. But Ruby Cornish was a wily old dog sailor. He came back at Mansur hard and fast, and they circled each other.

Dorian killed a man with a quick thrust, then looked around for Guy. He was not certain what he would do if he found him. Perhaps, deep in his heart, he longed for a battlefield reconciliation. He could not see him in the ruck of fighting men, but he realized that the battle was swinging in their favour. The crew of the *Arcturus* were giving up the fight. He saw two throw aside their weapons and, quick as rabbits, scuttle down the nearest hatchway. When a crew ran below decks they were beaten.

'In God's Name the battle is ours,' he exhorted the men around him. 'Have at them!' His voice filled them with fresh strength and they threw themselves at the enemy. Dorian looked for Mansur, and saw him on the far side of the deck. He was heavily engaged with Cornish. There was blood on his robe but Dorian hoped that it was not his own. Then he saw Ruby Cornish break off, and run back to attempt to rally his fleeing men. Mansur was too exhausted to follow him and rested on his sword. In the light of the battle lanterns, sweat shone on his face and his chest heaved with the effort of breathing. Dorian shouted across the deck to him, 'What happened to Guy? Where is my brother? Have you seen him?'

'No, Father,' Mansur shouted back hoarsely. 'He must have run below with the rest of them.'

'We have them beaten,' Dorian cried. 'It will take one last charge, and the *Arcturus* is ours. Come on!'

The men around him gave a ragged cheer and started forward, but then they came up short again as Guy Courtney's high-pitched yell cut through the hubbub of the battle. He stood at the rail of the poop deck. In one hand he carried a burning length of slow-match and on the other shoulder he balanced a keg of black powder. The bung had been knocked from the keg and a thick trail of powder poured from it to the deck at his feet.

'This powder trail runs to the ship's main powder magazine,' he shouted. Though he spoke in English his meaning was clear to every Arab seaman aboard. The fighting ceased and all stared at him, aghast. A deathly silence fell over the *Arcturus*'s deck.

'I will strike this ship, and blow up every one of you with it,' Guy screamed, and lifted the smoking, spluttering slow-match high. 'As God is my witness, I shall do it.'

'Guy!' Dorian shouted up at him, 'I am your brother, Dorian Courtney!'

'I know it well!' Guy yelled back, and there was a bitter, hard edge to his voice. 'Verity has confessed her deceit and complicity to me. That will not save you.'

'No, Guy!' Dorian cried. 'You must not do it.'

'There is naught you can say to dissuade me,' Guy shouted back, and hurled the powder keg down on to the deck at his feet. It burst open. Gunpowder spilled across the deck. Slowly he brought down the flaring slow-match and a wail of fear went up from the crowded main deck. One of the men from the *Revenge* turned and raced back to the ship's side. He sprang across the narrow gap, to the illusory safety of the deck of his own ship.

His example was infectious. They fled back to the smaller ships. As soon as they were aboard they hacked with their swords at the grappling lines that held them bound to the doomed *Arcturus*.

Only Kumrah, Batula and a few other staunch sailors stood their ground beside Dorian and Mansur.

'It's a ruse! He will not do it,' Dorian told them. 'Follow me!' But as he ran to the foot of the ladder that led up to the poop deck, Guy Courtney hurled the slow-match into the powder trail. In a dense, hissing tail of smoke the gunpowder ignited and ran back swiftly along the deck until it reached the open hatchway and shot down into the interior of the ship.

The pluck of even the stalwart captains and their officers deserted them, and they turned and ran. The last of the grappling lines were parting, popping like cotton threads. In a moment the two smaller ships would be free of the *Arcturus* and drift away into the night.

'Even if it is a ruse, we shall still be stranded here,' Mansur called to his father. There were hostile sailors all around them. Their predicament would prove fatal.

'Not a moment to lose,' Dorian shouted back. 'Run for it, Mansur.'

Both of them turned and leaped across to the decks of their own ships, just as the last grappling lines parted and the hulls drifted apart. On the poop deck Guy Courtney stood alone. The powder smoke swirled in clouds around him, giving him a satanical appearance. The sparks of burning powder and debris took hold in the rigging and ran up the shrouds.

The first cannon salvo had jarred the timbers of the hull and startled Verity awake. The *Arcturus* had come to battle stations so silently that in her barred cabin she had not realized what was happening on deck until this moment. She scrambled from her bunk and turned up the wick on the lantern that hung on gimbals from the deck above. She reached for her clothing and pulled on a cotton shirt and the breeches she preferred to skirts and petticoats when she needed freedom of movement.

She was busy with her boots when the hull heeled sharply to the next broadside of cannon. She ran to the door of her cabin and beat upon it with her fists. 'Let me out!' she screamed. 'Open this door!' But there was no one to hear her.

She picked up the heavy silver candelabrum from the table and tried to break open the door panels so that she could reach the locking bar on the outside, but the sturdy teak timbers resisted her efforts. She was forced to give up and retreat to the far side of her cabin. She opened the porthole and peered out. She knew that escape by this route was hopeless. She had considered it many times during the weeks of her captivity. The surface of the sea creamed by close below her face, and it was six feet to the rail of the deck above her. She gazed out into the night and tried to follow the battle by the flare and flicker of gunfire. She caught glimpses of the

621

other ship that was engaging them, and recognized it at once as the *Revenge*. She could see no sign of Mansur's ship.

She winced every time the cannon salvos roared out from the deck above her cabin, or when an enemy ball crashed into their hull. The battle seemed to rage interminably, and her senses were dulled by the uproar. The stench of burnt powder permeated her cabin like some dreadful incense burned to the god Mars, and she coughed in its acrid fumes.

Then, suddenly, she saw another dark apparition appear silently out of the darkness, another ship.

'The *Sprite*!' she whispered, and her heart bounded. Mansur's ship! She had thought never to see it again. Then it began to fire upon them, and she was so excited that she felt no fear at all. One after another the iron round-shot smashed into the *Arcturus*, and each time she shuddered to the strike.

Then, abruptly, Verity was flung to the deck as a ball ripped through the bulkhead beside her doorway, and the cabin was filled with smoke and wood-dust. When it cleared she saw that the door had been shot away. She jumped to her feet, clambered through the wreckage and forced her way out into the open passageway. She heard the hand-to-hand fighting on the deck above her as the crew of the *Sprite* boarded the ship over her port rail. The shouts and cries mingled with the clash of steel blades and the report of pistols and muskets. She looked about her for a weapon but there was nothing. Then she saw that her father's door stood open. She knew he kept his pistols in the drawer of his desk, and hurried to it.

Now she stood directly below the skylight, and her father's voice carried clearly through the opening: 'This powder trail runs to the ship's main powder magazine,' he shouted. A deathly silence fell over the *Arcturus*'s deck, and Verity froze. 'I will strike this ship, and blow up every one of you with it,' her father screamed again. 'As God is my witness, I shall do it.'

'Guy!' Verity recognized the voice that answered him. 'I am your brother, Dorian Courtney!'

'I know it well!' Guy yelled back. 'Verity has confessed her deceit and complicity to me. That will not save you.'

'No, Guy!' Dorian cried. 'You must not do it.'

'There is naught you can say to dissuade me,' Guy shouted back.

Verity listened to no more. She dashed out into the passage and immediately saw the thick trail of black powder running down the treads of the companionway and along the passage to the lower deck and the magazine.

'He is telling the truth,' she cried aloud. 'He truly means to strike the ship.' She acted without hesitation. She seized one of the fire buckets that stood at the foot of the companionway. The ship's wooden hull was a mortal fire hazard, and the buckets filled with seawater were placed at every convenient point whenever the ship went into battle. Verity sloshed the water across the powder trail, washing a wide gap in it.

She was only just in time. With a sizzling rush the flames came shooting down the companionway, then checked in a cloud of blue smoke as they reached the gap she had made. She jumped upon them, stamping on the smouldering grains. Then she seized another bucket of seawater and emptied it over them. She made sure she had doused every spark before she ran up the ladder to the quarter-deck.

'Father! This is madness!' Verity cried, as she stepped out of the smoke behind him.

'I ordered you to remain in your cabin.' He rounded on her. 'You disobeyed me.'

'If I had not, you would have blown me and yourself to glory,' she shrieked at him, almost beside herself with terror at how close they had been to death.

He saw how her clothing was scorched and blackened and sodden with seawater. 'You treacherous, evil woman,' he screamed. 'You have gone over completely to my enemies.'

He struck her full in the face with a clenched fist, and sent her reeling across the deck until she crashed into the bulwark. She stared at him in horror and outrage. Since childhood she had been accustomed to the beatings with his riding crop across her legs and buttocks when she displeased him, but only twice before had he struck her with his fist. She knew in that moment that she could never let it happen again. That had been the third and last time. She wiped her mouth with the back of her hand and glanced at the thick smear of blood from her torn lips. Then she turned her head and looked down on to the deck of the *Sprite* below her.

The last grappling lines that held the two ships together parted and the *Sprite*'s sails filled with the night breeze. She began to bear away. Her deck was a shambles of shot damage, some of her crew were wounded, others scurrying to their gun stations, and still more were jumping back into her from the taller side of the *Arcturus* as the gap between them widened.

Then she saw Mansur below her on the deck of the *Sprite* and, despite her injuries and her father's rage, her heart hammered wildly against her ribs. During all the time since they had parted, she had tried to subdue her feelings for him. She had had no expectation of ever laying eyes upon him again, and thought she had succeeded in putting him out of her mind. But now, when she saw him again, handsome and tall in the light thrown by the burning rigging, she remembered the secrets he had imparted to her and the protestation of his feelings for her, and she could deny him no longer.

In the same moment he looked up and recognized her. She saw his astonishment give way immediately to grim determination. He leaped across the deck of the *Sprite* to the wheel and shoved aside the helmsman. He seized the spokes and spun it in a blur back the opposite way. The *Sprite*'s turn away to port checked and then she answered her rudder, turning back slowly. Once more her bows collided heavily against the *Arcturus*'s mid-section, but she did not rebound for Mansur held the wheel over. She began to drag down the side of the larger vessel.

Mansur shouted up at her, 'Jump, Verity! Come to me!' For a long moment she remained frozen, and then it was almost too late. 'Verity, in God's Name, you cannot deny me. I love you. Jump!'

She hesitated no longer. She came up on her feet as quick as a cat, and sprang to the top of the bulwark, balancing there for an instant with her arms outspread. Guy realized what she was about, and ran across the poop to her.

'I forbid it!' he screamed, and snatched at her leg, but she kicked away his hand. He grabbed a fistful of her shirt, and she tried to pull free, but he clung on stubbornly. As they struggled, Mansur left the wheel and ran to the *Sprite*'s side. He was directly below her, holding his arms wide in invitation.

'Jump!' he called. 'I will catch you.'

She flung herself out over the ship's side. Her father did not release his grip, and her shirt ripped, leaving him holding a handful of cloth. Verity dropped into Mansur's arms and her weight bore him to his knees, but he straightened and, for a moment, held her tightly to his chest. Then he set her on her feet and dragged her to safety. The crew's bundled hammocks had been piled along the bulwark as some protection from splinters and musket balls, and Mansur pushed her down behind this barricade. Then he ran back to the wheel and spun it the opposite way.

The two ships drew apart swiftly. The *Revenge* had also disentangled herself, and was under sail. The *Arcturus* was still ablaze, but Mansur saw Ruby Cornish striding down her deck, taking charge of the salvage. His men were swarming out of the hatchways again. Within minutes they had brought down the flaming canvas and doused it with seawater from the pumps.

With her guns reloaded and run out, the *Arcturus* turned in pursuit of the *Sprite* once more, but her rigging was heavily damaged and Cornish had not had time to bring up new canvas from the sail lockers and bend it on to the bare, scorched yards. The *Arcturus* made slow progress through the water and both the *Sprite* and the *Revenge* drew away from her.

Then, as swiftly as it had risen, the night wind died away. Almost as if they had anticipated the dawn, the clouds opened and allowed the paling stars to shine through. A hush descended on the ocean, the roiling surface seemed to freeze into a sheet of polished ice. All three of the battered ships slowed, then came to a gradual standstill. Even in the faint light of the stars they were within sight of each other, becalmed, swinging slowly and aimlessly on the silent currents beneath that glassy surface. However, the *Sprite* and the

Revenge were out of hail of each other, so Dorian and Mansur were unable to confer and decide their next course of action.

'Let the men eat their breakfast as they work, but we must repair our damage swiftly. This calm will not last long.' Mansur saw the work put in hand, then went to find Verity. She stood alone by the ship's side, staring across at the dim shape of the *Arcturus*, but she turned to him at once.

'You came,' he said.

'Because you called,' she replied softly, and held out her hand to him. He took it, and was surprised by how cool and smooth her skin was, how narrow and supple her hand.

'There is so much I want to tell you.'

'We will have a lifetime for that,' she said, 'but let me savour this first moment to the full.' They looked into each other's eyes.

'You are beautiful,' he said.

'I am not. But my heart sings to hear you say it.'

'I would kiss you.'

'But you cannot,' she answered. 'Not under the eyes of your crew. They would not approve.'

'Fortunately, we will have a lifetime for that also.'

'And I will rejoice in every minute of it.'

The dawn broke and the first shafts of sunlight beamed through the gaps in the thunderheads and turned the waters of the ocean to glowing amethyst. It played full upon the three ships. They lay motionless, like toys on a village pond. The sea was glassy smooth, its surface marred only by the skittering flight of the flying fish and the swirls of the great silver and gold tuna that pursued them.

The shot-torn sails hung slack and empty. From each ship the sounds of the carpenters' hammers and saws rang out as they hurriedly repaired the battle damage. The sailmakers laid out the damaged canvas on the decks and squatted over it, long needles flying as they cobbled up the tears and rents. They all knew that this respite would not last long, that the morning breeze would rise and the next phase of the conflict must begin.

Through the telescope Mansur watched the crew of the *Arcturus* extinguish the last flames, then send new spars aloft to replace the broken bowsprit and the yards that had been burned or shot away.

'Is your mother aboard the *Arcturus*?' Mansur asked Verity.

'Six weeks ago my father sent her back to the safety of the consulate in Bombay,' Verity answered. She did not want to think about Caroline now, or of the circumstances in which she had last seen her. To change the subject she asked, 'Will you fight again?'

'Are you afraid?' he asked.

She turned to him. Her eyes were green and her gaze was direct. 'That question is unkind.'

'Forgive me,' he said at once. 'I do not doubt your courage, for you proved it to me last night. I wanted only to know your feelings.'

'I am not afraid for myself. But my father is aboard the other ship, and you are on this one.'

'I saw him strike you.'

'He has struck me many times before, but he is still my father.' Then she lowered her eyes. 'More important than that, though, you are now my man. I am afraid for both of you. But I will not flinch.'

He reached out and touched her arm. 'I will do my utmost to avoid further battle,' he assured her. 'I would have done so last night but my own father was in danger. I had no choice but to come to his aid. However, I doubt that Sir Guy will let you and me escape without he does everything in his power to prevent it.' He nodded grimly towards the distant *Arcturus*.

'Here comes the morning wind,' she said. 'Now my father's intentions will be made plain.'

The wind scoured the polished azure surface with cats' paws. The *Arcturus*'s sails bulged and she began to glide forward. All her yards were standing, and bright new canvas had replaced much of that which had been scorched and blackened. The wind left her behind and she slowed gradually, then came once more to a standstill. Her mainsail flapped and drooped. The squall of wind came on and picked up the two smaller ships, carried them a short distance, then dropped them.

Again stillness and silence fell on the three vessels. All their sails were set, and the upper yardmen were poised to make the final adjustments when the wind came again.

This time it came out of the east, hard and steady. It caught up the *Arcturus* first and bore her on. The instant she had steerage way she put up her helm and charged straight towards the two smaller ships. Her guns were still run out and her intentions manifest.

'I am afraid your father is spoiling for a fight.'

'And so are you!' Verity accused him.

'You misjudge me.' He shook his head. 'I have already taken the prize. Sir Guy has nothing more that I want from him.'

'Then let us hope that the wind reaches us before he does.' As Verity spoke it puffed against her cheek and blew a long strand of hair across her eyes. She tucked it back into the silk hairnet. 'Here it comes.'

The wind struck the *Sprite* and she heeled to it. Her canvas slatted and her blocks rattled as her sails filled and bulged. They could feel the force of it in the eager trembling of the deck beneath their feet and, despite the exigencies of the moment, Verity laughed aloud with excitement. 'We are off!' she cried, and for a moment clung to his arm. Then she saw Kumrah's disapproving expression and stepped back. 'I need no chaperon aboard this ship for I have a hundred already.'

The *Sprite* raced down towards the *Revenge*, which still lay becalmed, but then the wind reached her also. The two ships bore away together, the *Revenge* leading by two cables' length. Mansur looked back over the stern at the pursuit.

'With the wind coming from this quarter your father can never catch us,' he told Verity exultantly. 'We will run him below the horizon before nightfall.' He took her arm and led her gently towards the companionway. 'I can safely leave the deck to Kumrah now, and we can go below to find suitable accommodation for you.'

'There are too many eyes here,' she agreed, and followed him willingly.

At the bottom of the ladder he turned her to face him. She was only a few inches shorter than he was, and the thick, lustrous coils of her hair made the difference even less obvious. 'There are no other eyes here,' he said.

'I fear I have been gullible,' her cheeks blushed pink as rose petals, 'but you would never take advantage of my innocence, would you, Your Highness?'

'I am afraid you may have overestimated my chivalry, Miss Courtney. It is my intention to do exactly that.'

'I suppose that it would be of no avail if I should scream, would it?'

'I am very much afraid that it would not,' he said.

She swayed towards him. 'Then I shall save my breath,' she whispered, 'for perhaps I will find better employment for it later.'

'Your lip is swollen.' He touched it gently. 'I will not hurt you?'

'We Courtneys are a hardy lot,' she said.

He kissed her, but softly.

It was Verity who pulled him closer, and parted her swollen lips to him. 'It hurts not at all,' she said, and he lifted her in his arms and carried her through into his cabin.

Kumrah stamped three times on the deck above Mansur's bunk. He sat up quickly. 'I am wanted on deck,' he said.

'Not as much as you are wanted here,' she murmured, with drowsy contentment, 'but I know that when duty calls I must let you go for the moment.'

He stood up and she watched him, her eyes growing bigger and her interest quickening. 'I have never seen a man in his natural state before,' she said. 'Only now do I realize I have been deprived, for 'tis a sight much to my liking.'

'I could think of far better,' he demurred, and stooped to kiss her belly. It was smooth as cream and her navel was a neat pit in the taut sleek muscle. He thrust the tip of his tongue into it.

She sighed and writhed voluptuously. 'You must stop that at once, or I shall never let you go.'

He straightened and then his eyes flew wide with alarm. 'There is blood on the sheet. Have I injured you?'

She raised herself on one elbow, looked down at the bright stain and smiled complacently. 'It is the flower of my maidenhood, which I bring to you as proof that I have always belonged to you and to none other.'

'Oh, my darling.' He sat on the edge of the bunk and smothered her face with kisses.

She pushed him away. 'Go to your duty. But come back to me the instant it is done.'

Mansur ran up the ladder and it seemed that his feet were winged, but he stopped at the head of the companionway in alarm. He had expected to see the *Revenge* still far ahead of him, for in speed she had the edge on the *Sprite*, but she was almost alongside. He snatched up his telescope from its bucket beside the binnacle and strode to the side. He saw at once that the *Revenge* sat low in the water, and that all her pumps were manned. Seawater was spurting white over the side from the outlet pipes. As he watched in consternation, Dorian appeared on deck, stepping out from the hatch over the main hold. Mansur snatched up the speaking trumpet and hailed him. His father looked across, then came to the near rail.

'What's amiss?' Mansur called again.

'We have taken a ball below the waterline, and we are taking in water faster than the pumps can discharge it.' His father's reply was faint on the wind.

So great was the disparity in speed between the two ships that in the short time that Mansur had been on deck the *Sprite* had gained a few yards on the *Revenge*. Already his father's voice carried more clearly across the gap. He looked back over the stern and judged that the *Arcturus* had lost little

630

distance in the hours that he and Verity had been below. She was making much better speed through the water than the crippled *Revenge*.

'What can I do to assist you?' he asked his father. There was a long pause.

'I have shot an angle on the *Arcturus*'s mainmast every hour,' Dorian called back. 'At this rate she will be within cannon shot before nightfall. Even in the darkness we cannot hope to elude her.'

'Can we repair the damage?'

'The shot-hole is awkwardly placed.' Dorian shook his head. 'If we heave to, *Arcturus* will be upon us before we can plug it.'

'What, then, must we do?'

'Unless something unforeseen happens, we shall be forced to fight again.'

Mansur thought about Verity in the cabin below this deck, and had a picture of that perfect pale body torn to bloody tatters by round-shot. He forced the image from his mind. 'Wait!' he called to Dorian, then beckoned to Kumrah.

'What can we do, old friend?' They talked quickly and earnestly, but while they did so the *Revenge* dropped back a little further and Mansur was obliged to order a reef in his main sail to slow the *Sprite* enough to keep his station with the *Revenge*. Then he hailed his father. 'Kumrah has a plan. Conform to me as best you are able, but I will moderate my speed if you fall too far behind.'

Kumrah brought the *Sprite*'s bows around another three points into the west until they were on a direct heading for Ras al-Had, the point of land where the gulf opened out into the ocean proper.

For the rest of that morning Mansur kept his crew busy repairing the battle damage they had suffered, cleaning and servicing the guns, bringing up more round-shot from the orlop deck, filling the powder bags to replace that which had been fired away. Then, with block and tackle, they hoisted one of the guns up from the main deck to the poop where the carpenters had made a temporary gunport for it. Trained back over the stern the cannon could now be used as a stern chaser to bring the *Arcturus* under fire as soon as she drew within range.

Almost imperceptibly the *Revenge* was settling lower in the water and losing speed as the men at the pumps battled to hold at bay the inflow of water through her pierced hull. Mansur closed in on her and they passed a line across. Then he was able to send over twenty fresh seamen to relieve the *Revenge*'s crew, who were exhausted from the unremitting work at the pump handles. At the same time he sent over Baris, one of Kumrah's junior officers, a young Omani who was also a native of this coast and knew every rock and reef almost as intimately as Kumrah did. While the two ships sailed in such close company, Mansur explained to his father the plan he and Kumrah had devised.

Dorian understood at once that this was perhaps their best chance, and he endorsed it without hesitation. 'Go to it, lad,' he called back, through the speaking trumpet.

Within the next hour Mansur was obliged to take in another reef so as not to head-reach on the *Revenge* during the night. As darkness fell he gazed back at the *Arcturus* and calculated that she had closed the gap between them to only a little over two sea miles.

It was almost midnight before he went below to his cabin, but even then Mansur and Verity could not sleep. They made love as though it would never happen again, then lay naked in each other's arms, sweating in the tropical night, and they talked softly. Sometimes they laughed and more than once Verity wept. There was so much they had to tell, their whole lifetimes to relate to each other. At last, though, even their new love could no longer keep them awake, and they slept with their limbs entwined.

An hour before first light Mansur slipped from their bunk and left her to go back on deck. But within minutes Verity, too, came up the companionway and took a place in the angle of the quarter-deck and the poop, where she could be near him but unobtrusive.

Mansur ordered the cooks to give the men their breakfast

and while they ate he went down the deck and spoke to them, giving them encouragement, making them laugh and others smile, even though they knew that the *Arcturus* was close behind them in the darkness and they would soon be called upon to fight her again.

As soon as the dawn sky began to pale Mansur and Kumrah were at the stern rail on the poop deck beside the stern chaser. The lantern on the main truck of the *Revenge* showed close astern, but as the circle of their vision opened they all stared beyond her for the first glimpse of the *Arcturus*. They were not disappointed. As the light strengthened they caught the loom of her against the still dark horizon, and Mansur had to check himself from giving voice to his disappointment. She had gained almost a mile on them during the hours of darkness, and now she was within long cannon shot. Even as Mansur stared at her through the lens of his telescope there was a flash from her bows, and a puff of white smoke.

'Your father is firing at us with bow chasers. Though I fancy the range is a trifle too long for him to do us any real damage for a while yet,' Mansur told Verity.

At that moment there was a hail from the masthead: 'Land ho!' and they left the stern and went up into the bows to scan ahead with the spyglass.

'You excel yourself, Captain,' Mansur told Kumrah. 'Unless I am very much mistaken, that is Ras al-Had dead ahead.' They went back to the chart table beside the traverse-board and pored over the chart. This masterpiece of the cartographer's art had been drawn up by Kumrah himself, the work of a lifetime spent on the sea.

'Where is this Kos al-Heem?' Mansur asked. The name meant the Deceiver in the dialect of the Omani coast.

'I have not marked it on the chart.' Kumrah pricked the waxed leather with the point of his dividers. 'Some things are best kept from the eyes of the world. But it is here.'

'How much longer to run?' Mansur asked.

'If this wind holds, we will be there an hour after noon.'

'By then the *Arcturus* will have overhauled the *Revenge*.' Mansur glanced across at his father's ship.

633

'If it is God's will,' said Kumrah, with resignation, 'for God is great.'

'We must try to shield the *Revenge* from the fire of the *Arcturus* until we reach the Deceiver.' Mansur gave Kumrah his orders, then went back to the stern where the gun-crew were gathered around the nine-pounder.

Kumrah shortened sail again and dropped back until he could interpose the *Sprite* between the other two ships. During that time the *Arcturus* fired twice with her bow chaser. Both shots fell short. However, the *Arcturus*'s next splashed heavily alongside the *Revenge*.

'Very well.' Mansur nodded. 'We can try a ranging shot at her now.'

He chose a round-shot from the locker, rolling it under his foot to check its symmetry. Then he measured the charge of powder with care, and had his crew swab the bore carefully to remove as much powder residue as possible.

Once the gun was loaded and run out he stood behind it and noted how the stern of the *Sprite* lifted and yawed as she rode over the swells. He calculated the adjustments necessary to counteract these movements. Then, slow-match in hand, he stood well clear of the breech and watched for the next swell. As the *Sprite* kicked up her heels and lifted her stern, like a flirtatious girl swishing her skirts, he pressed the burning end of the match to the quill of powder in the touch-hole. The elevation would give the iron ball the extra carry.

The long cannon bellowed and slammed back into its tackle. Verity and Kumrah were watching for the fall of shot.

Seconds later they picked out the tiny feather of white that jumped from the surface of the dark sea. 'Short by a hundred yards and about three degrees left,' Verity called sharply.

Mansur grunted and wound the elevation screw to its maximum height. They fired again. 'Under again, but on line.' They kept firing steadily.

The *Revenge* had joined in the bombardment. The *Arcturus* closed in slowly, firing her bow chasers as she came on. However, by the middle of the morning none of the ships had managed a hit, although some of the shot had fallen close.

Mansur and his gun-crew were stripped to the waist in the rising heat: their bodies were shining with sweat, and their faces were blackened with gunsmoke. The barrel of the cannon was too hot to touch. The wet swab sizzled and steamed as it was thrust down the bore. For the twenty-third time that morning they ran out the long nine-pounder and Mansur laid it with care. The *Arcturus* appeared much taller as he squinted at it over the sights. He stood back and waited for the pitch and roll of the hull under him before he fired.

The gun carriage bounded back violently and slammed against its tackle. This time, though they strained their eyes through the lens, there was no splash of falling shot. Instead Verity saw shattered timbers explode from the *Arcturus*'s bows and one of her chaser cannon knocked from its carriage and upended.

'"A hit! A very palpable hit!"'

'Say Miss Verity and the Bard!' Mansur laughed and gulped down a mouthful from the water dipper before laying the next shot.

Seemingly in retaliation, the *Arcturus* dropped a ball from the remaining bow chaser so close under the *Sprite*'s stern that a fountain of spray rose high into the air, then cascaded over them, drenching them to the skin.

All this time the rocky cape of Ras al-Had was rising higher out of the sea, and *Arcturus* was slowly overhauling them from astern.

'Where is Kos al-Heem?' Mansur asked impatiently.

'You will not see it until you are about to strike. That is how it was given the name, but these are the landmarks. The white streak in the cliff face, there. The tip of the egg-shaped rock that stands to the left of it, there!'

'I want you to take the helm now, Kumrah. Luff her a little and spill your wind. I want to let the *Arcturus* close up to us, without making it obvious that it is deliberate.'

The raging duel between the ships carried on. Mansur hoped to distract Cornish's attention from the hazard ahead, and to let the *Revenge* draw further ahead. The *Arcturus* came on eagerly, and within the hour she was so close that through the glass Mansur and Verity could recognize the burly figure and distinctive features of Captain Ruby Cornish.

'And there is Sir Guy!' Mansur had been about to say 'your father', but he changed the words at the last moment. He did not want to emphasize the relationship of his enemy to his love.

In comparison to Ruby Cornish, Guy Courtney cut a slim, elegant figure. He had changed his attire, and even in this heat he wore a cocked hat and a blue coat with scarlet lapels, tight-fitting white breeches and black boots. He stood staring across at them. His expression was set and hard, and there was a deadly purpose about him that chilled Verity to the marrow: she well knew this mood of his and dreaded it like the cholera.

'Kumrah!' Mansur called to him. 'Where is this Deceiver? Where is Kos al-Heem? Is it something you dreamed after a pipe of hashish?'

Kumrah glanced at the *Revenge*, which had forged slowly ahead. She was now leading them by a quarter of a sea mile.

'The Caliph, your revered father, is almost upon the Deceiver.'

'I can see no sign of it.' Minutely Mansur studied the waters ahead of the other ship, but the swells marched on inexorably, and there was no break or check in their ranks; no swirl nor flurry of white water that he was able to descry.

'That is why it is called the Deceiver,' Kumrah reminded him. 'It keeps its secrets well. It has murdered a hundred ships and more, including the galley of Ptolemy, the general and favourite of the mighty Isakander. It was only by God's favour that he survived the wreck.'

'God is great,' Mansur murmured automatically.

'Praise God,' Kumrah agreed and, as he spoke, the *Revenge* abruptly put up her helm and turned her bows into the wind. With all her sails backed and shuddering, she hove to.

'Ah!' cried Kumrah. 'Baris has found and marked the Deceiver for us.'

'Run out the port battery and prepare to come about on the starboard tack,' Mansur ordered. While the crew ran to their battle stations, he eyed the approaching *Arcturus*.

636

She was rushing in towards them jubilantly, with every stitch of canvas set. Even as he watched, Mansur saw the lids of her gunports crash open and the muzzles of her cannon poke out menacingly along her sides. He turned and strode forward until he had a full view of the *Revenge*, hove-to dead ahead; she also had run out her guns, offering battle.

Mansur went back to the helm. He was conscious that from the angle below the poop Verity was watching him intently. Her expression was calm and she showed no fear.

'I would like you to go below, my love,' he told her quietly. 'We will very soon be under fire.'

She shook her head. 'The ship's timbers offer no protection from nine-pound iron balls. This I know from experience,' she replied, with a naughty sparkle in her eyes, 'when you fired upon me.'

'I have never apologized for my bad manners in so doing.' He smiled back at her. 'It was unforgivable. But I swear I will make it up to you in spades and trumps.'

'All other things apart, from now on my place is at your side, not cowering under the bunk.'

'I shall always treasure your presence,' he said, and turned to look back at the *Arcturus*. She was within easy cannon shot at last. Now he must engage all her attention, and lure her on at the top of her speed. Kumrah was watching for his order.

'Up helm,' Mansur snapped, and the *Sprite* turned like a dancer. Suddenly she had turned her full broadside on the *Arcturus*.

'Steady, gunners!' Mansur shouted, through the trumpet. 'Make good your aim!' One after the other the captains raised their right arms to show that they had laid their pieces true.

'Fire!' Mansur cried, and the broadside bellowed out like a single clap of thunder. Gunsmoke poured back across the deck in a thick grey cloud, but was almost at once blown away by the wind and they could see a single spout of seawater rise from under the *Arcturus*'s bows, but the rest of the broadside smashed into her stem, tearing holes in her timbers. The ship seemed to tremble to these terrible blows but came on without a check in her speed.

'Bring her about on the old course,' Mansur ordered, and the *Sprite* obeyed her helm at once. They sped away towards where the *Revenge* lay waiting for them. Bows on to them, the *Arcturus* had not been able to fire her own broadside in return, but the manoeuvre had cost the *Sprite* almost all of her lead, and the enemy was scarcely more than a cable's length behind her. She fired her bow chaser, and the *Sprite* shuddered as the ball struck her stern and tore through her hull.

Kumrah was staring ahead with slitted eyes, but Mansur could see no sign of the Deceiver. Kumrah called a correction to the helm and the man on the wheel eased her over to port a trifle. This cleared the range for the *Revenge*, and now she could fire without fear of hitting the *Sprite*. She was still present-ing her broadside to the enemy, and disappeared momentarily behind the curtain of her own gunsmoke as she let fly with all her cannon.

The range was long but she hit with at least some of her shot. The *Arcturus* was so close by now that Mansur could hear the iron round-shot strike against her timbers like heavy hammer strokes.

'That will invite all Cornish's attention,' Verity said, and her voice was clear in the sudden silence that followed the broadside. Mansur did not answer. He was gazing ahead with a worried frown.

'Where is this triple-damned Deceiver—' He broke off as he saw the sparkle of bright specks like drifting snowflakes deep in the blue waters directly under their bows. They were so unexpected that for a moment he was at a loss. Then it dawned upon him.

'Fusiliers!' he exclaimed. These shoals of tiny, jewelled fish always hung over submerged reefs, even out here in the mid-water at the edge of the continental shelf. The shoals scattered as the *Sprite*'s hull cut through them, and Mansur saw the dark, terrible shadows rising from the depths, like blackened fangs, directly in the ship's path. Kumrah stepped across and pushed away the helmsman. Then he took the wheel of his ship in lover's hands to steer her through.

Mansur saw the dark shapes harden as they rushed down

upon them. They were three horns of granite that reached up from dark waters to within a fathom of the sunlit surface. So sharp were the points that they offered little resistance to the flow and push of currents and waves. This accounted for the lack of surface turbulence.

Instinctively Mansur held his breath as Kumrah steered into the centre of this cruel crown of stone. He felt Verity's hand on his arm as she clung to him for comfort, her fingernails digging painfully into his flesh.

The *Sprite* touched the rock. To Mansur it felt as though he had ridden a horse at full gallop through the forest and a thornbush had tugged at his sleeve. The deck shuddered softly under his feet, and he heard the granite horn rasp against their bottom timbers. Then the *Sprite* pulled herself free and they were through. Mansur let the air out of his lungs with a sigh, and beside him Verity cried, 'That was as close as I ever want to be.'

Mansur seized her hand and they ran back to the stern rail. They watched the *Arcturus* run into the trap at full tilt. Despite her battle damage and her soot-blackened rigging she presented a beautiful picture, with every sail drawing and a tall white bow wave sparkling and curling back from her forefoot.

She hit the stone pinnacles and stopped dead in the water, transformed in a single instant from a thing of airy grace to a shambles. Her foremast snapped off level with the deck and half her yards came tumbling down. Her underwater timbers crackled and roared as they shattered and she hung in the water like part of the reef. The granite horns of the Deceiver were driven deep into her belly. The top yardsmen in her rigging were hurled from their perches, like pellets from a slingshot, to splash into the water half a pistol shot from the ship's side. The rest of her crew were skittled down the deck to slam into the masts and bulwarks. Their own cannons were turned against them as they were catapulted into the unyielding metal with the full impetus of the ship's way. Arms, legs and ribs broke like green twigs, and skulls cracked like eggs dropped on to a stone-flagged floor. The crews of the two smaller vessels lined the sides, and stared in awe at the devastation they had wrought, too overwhelmed to cheer the destruction of the enemy.

Mansur hove to alongside his father's ship. 'What now, Father?'

'We cannot leave Guy in such a state,' Dorian shouted back. 'We must render what help we can. I shall go across in the longboat.'

'No, Father!' Mansur called back. 'You can spend no more time here. Your ship is also in extremes. You must go on to find the safe harbour at Sawda island, where we can repair the underwater damage before she founders and sinks.'

'But what of Guy and his men?' Dorian hesitated. 'What is to become of them?'

'I shall take care of that business,' Mansur promised. 'You can be certain that I will not let your brother, Verity's father, perish here.'

Dorian and Batula conferred quickly, and then Dorian returned to the *Revenge*'s side. 'Very well! Batula agrees that we must get into safe anchorage before another storm brews up. We cannot ride out rough seas in the shape we are now in.'

'I shall take off the survivors from the *Arcturus*, and follow you with all speed.'

Dorian put the *Revenge* once more before the wind, and headed in towards the mainland. Mansur handed over command to Kumrah, and went down into the longboat. He stood in the stern sheets as they rowed in towards the stranded and heavily listing *Arcturus*. As soon as they were within easy hail he ordered the boat crew to rest on their oars. '*Arcturus*! I have a surgeon with me. What help do you need?'

Cornish's red face appeared over the top of the canted bulwark. 'We have many broken limbs. I need to get the wounded back to the infirmary on Bombay island, or they will die.'

'I am coming on board!' Mansur shouted back.

But another voice rang out angrily: 'Stand off, you filthy rebel scum!' Sir Guy Courtney was clinging to the main shrouds with one hand. His other arm was thrust into the front of his jacket, using it as a makeshift sling. He had lost his hat, and fresh blood caked his hair and the side of his face from the deep lacerations in his scalp. 'If you try to board this ship I shall fire into you.'

'Uncle Guy!' Mansur called. 'I am your brother Dorian's son. You must allow me to help you and your men.'

'In God's Holy Name, you are no kith or kin of mine. You are a heathen bastard, an abductor and violator of innocent English womanhood.'

'Your men need help. You yourself are wounded. Let me take you and your men to the port of Bombay island.'

Guy did not reply but staggered along the listing deck to the nearest cannon. He snatched a smoking slow-match from the sand tub. The heavy weapon still poked its gleaming bronze barrel through the open gunport, but Mansur was not alarmed. The weapon was harmless. The angle of the deck pointed the muzzle down into the water close alongside.

'Listen to reason, Uncle. My father and I wish you no harm. You are of our blood. See! I am unarmed.' He held up his open hands to prove it. But with a chill of horror he realized that Guy was not intending to fire the great cannon. Instead he seized the long handle of the murderer that sat squat and ugly in its gimbal fixed to the bulwark: it was a hand-cannon, designed to repel enemy boarders, loaded with a hatful of lead goose-shot. At short range its name described its gruesome capabilities accurately.

The longboat was close under the side of the *Arcturus*. Guy swivelled the murderer towards them and squinted over the crude notch-and-pin sights at Mansur. The flared muzzle of the gun seemed to leer at them obscenely.

'I gave you fair warning, you lecherous swine.' He thrust the burning match into the touch-hole.

'Down!' shouted Mansur, and flung himself on to the deck. His crew was slow to follow his example and the blast of goose-shot swept through them. In the screams of the wounded Mansur pulled himself upright again. His shirt was splashed by the brains of his coxswain, and three dead men lay piled

641

against the boat's side. Two others were clutching their wounds and struggling in puddles of their own blood. Seawater spurted in through the holes the goose-shot had torn in the planking.

Mansur rallied those of the crew who were unharmed. 'Pull back for the *Sprite*!' and they flung themselves on the oars with a will. From the stern sheets Mansur shouted back at the figure that still clung to the handle of the smoking hand-cannon: 'Rot your black soul, Guy Courtney. You bloody butcher! These were unarmed men on an errand of mercy.'

Mansur stormed back on to the deck of the *Sprite*. His face was white and set with rage. 'Kumrah,' he snarled, 'get our dead and wounded on board, then load all our guns with grape. I am going to give that murderous swine a taste of his own dung.'

Kumrah brought the *Sprite* round on to the port tack and at Mansur's direction steered in to pass the stranded wreck of the *Arcturus* at a distance of a hundred paces, the optimum range in which the grape would wreak the most slaughter.

'Stand by to fire as you bear!' Mansur called to his gunners. 'Sweep her deck clean. Kill them all. When you have done we will put fire into her and burn her down to the water-line.' He was still trembling with rage.

The crew of the *Arcturus* saw death coming down upon them, and scattered across the deck. Some ran below and others threw themselves over the side and thrashed around clumsily in the water. Only Captain Cornish and his master Sir Guy Courtney stood four-square and faced the *Sprite*'s gaping broadside.

Mansur felt a light touch on his arm and glanced down. Verity stood beside him. Her face was pale but expressionless. 'This is murder,' she said.

'Your father is the murderer.'

'Yes. And he is my father. If you do this thing, you will never wash his blood from your conscience or from mine, not if we live a hundred years. This might be the one act that will destroy our love.'

Her words struck deep as a dagger. He looked up and saw

the number-one gunner about to touch off his weapon, the smoking slow-match only inches from the flash-hole. 'Hold your fire!' Mansur roared at him, and the man lifted his hand. All the gun captains turned to look back at Mansur. He took Verity by the hand and led her to the rail. He raised the speaking trumpet to his lips.

'Guy Courtney! You are saved only by the intervention of your daughter,' he called across.

'That treacherous bitch is no daughter of mine. She is naught but a common street whore.' Guy's face was livid, the clotted blood upon it dark crimson in contrast. 'Filth and filth have found their own level in the cesspool. Take her, and a black pox on both of you.'

With an effort that strained all his natural instincts, Mansur kept his temper from boiling over again. 'I thank you, sir, for your daughter's hand in marriage. A boon so graciously granted is one I will guard with my life.' Then he looked to Kumrah. 'We will leave them here to rot. Lay the ship on a course for Sawda island.'

As they drew away Ruby Cornish touched his forehead in a salute, silently acknowledging his defeat and Mansur's compassion in holding his fire.

They found the *Revenge* lying at anchor in the tiny bay, enclosed by the cliffs of Sawda island. This grim buttress of black rock reared three hundred feet sheer from the deep waters at the edge of the continental shelf, six miles off the coast of the Arabian peninsula. Kumrah had chosen it for good reasons. The island was uninhabited and isolated from the mainland, secure from casual discovery by an enemy. The bay was sheltered from the easterly gales. The enclosed waters were calm, and the narrow beach of black volcanic sand made a good platform on which to careen a ship's hull. There was even a secret seep of sweet water from a cleft at the foot of the cliff.

As soon as they dropped anchor, Mansur had himself and

Verity rowed across to the *Revenge*. Dorian was at the entry-port to welcome him aboard.

'Father, there is no call for me to present your niece Verity to you. You are well enough acquainted already.'

'My greetings and respect, Your Majesty.' Verity dropped him a curtsy.

'Now at last we are able to converse in English, and I can greet you as your uncle.' He embraced her. 'Welcome to your family, Verity. I know there will be much opportunity for us to come to know each other better.'

'I hope so, Uncle. But I realize that now you and Mansur have much else to do.'

Standing on the open deck they swiftly devised a plan of action, and at once set it in motion. Mansur brought the *Sprite* alongside his father's ship and they lashed the hulls together. Now all the pumps of both ships could be applied to pumping out the flooded hull. At the same time they dragged a sheet of the heaviest canvas under the *Revenge*'s hull. The pressure of the water held it firmly in place, plugging the underwater shot hole. With the inflow choked off they were able to dry out the hull within a few hours.

Then they hoisted all her heavy cargo out of her – cannon, powder and shot, spare canvas, masts and spars – and deck-loaded the *Sprite*. Relieved of her burden the *Revenge* floated high and light as a cork. With the boats they towed her on to the beach and, with the help of the tide, careened her over so that the shot damage was exposed. The carpenters and their mates fell to work.

It took two days and nights working by the light of the battle lanterns for them to complete the repairs. When they had finished, the replaced section of timber was stronger than the original. They took the opportunity to scrape the weed from her hull, recaulk her joints and renew the copper sheeting that kept the shipworm from attacking her underwater timber. When they floated her off she was tight and dry. They warped her out into the bay, reloaded her cargo and remounted her weapons. By evening they had topped up all the water-kegs of both ships from the spring, and were ready to sail. However,

Dorian decreed that the crews had earned a respite of two days to celebrate the Islamic festival of Id, a joyous occasion when an animal is sacrificed and the flesh shared among the celebrants.

That evening they assembled on the beach, and Dorian killed one of the milk goats that were kept in a cage on board the *Revenge*. Its meagre flesh provided only a mouthful for each of them, but they supplemented it with fresh fish roasted on the coals while the musicians among the crews sang, danced and praised God for their escape from Muscat, and their victory over the *Arcturus*. Verity sat between Dorian and Mansur on silk prayer mats spread on the black sand.

Like most people who came to know Dorian, Verity couldn't resist the warmth of his spirit, his quiet humour. She empathized with the tragic loss of his wife, and the sadness with which it had marked him.

He was equally taken by her lively intelligence, the courage she had demonstrated so amply, and her forthright, pleasing manner. Now, as he studied her in the firelight he thought, She has inherited all the virtues of both her parents – her mother's beauty before it was marred by gluttony, Guy's bright mind. She has been spared their failings – Caroline's shallow, fatuous personality, and Guy's avaricious and vicious instincts, his dearth of humanity. Then he put aside deep thoughts and picked up the light mood. They laughed and sang together, clapping and swaying in time to the music.

When at last the musicians faltered, Dorian dismissed them with thanks and a gold coin for their trouble. But the three were too elated for sleep. They were to sail on the morrow for Fort Auspice. Mansur began to describe to Verity the life they would live in Africa, and the relatives she would meet there for the first time. 'You will love Aunt Sarah and Uncle Tom.'

'Tom is the best of us three brothers,' Dorian agreed. 'He was always the leader, while Guy and myself—' He broke off as he realized that Guy's name would throw a pall over their mood. The awkward silence drew out and none of them knew how to break it.

Then Verity spoke: 'Yes, Uncle Dorian. My father is not a

good man, and I know that he is ruthless. I cannot hope to excuse his murderous behaviour when he fired on the long-boat. Perhaps I can explain why it happened.'

The two men were silent and embarrassed. They stared into the coals of the fire and did not look at her. After a while she resumed, 'He was desperate that no one should discover the cargo he carries in the main hold of the *Arcturus*.'

'What cargo is that, my dear?' Dorian looked up.

'Before I answer, I must explain to you how my father has amassed such a fortune as to exceed that of any potentate in the Orient, save perhaps the Great Mogul and the Sublime Porte in Constantinople. He is a power-broker. He uses his position as consul general to enthrone and dethrone kings. He wields the power of the English monarchy and the English East India Company to deal in armies and nations as some men deal in cattle and sheep.'

'Those powers you speak of, the monarchy and the Company, are not in his gift,' Dorian demurred.

'My father is a conjuror, a master of illusion. He can make others believe what he wants them to believe, although he cannot even speak the languages of his client kings and emperors.'

'For that he uses you,' Mansur interjected.

She inclined her head. 'Yes, I was his tongue, but his is the gift of political perception.' She turned to Dorian. 'You, Uncle, have listened to him and you must have understood how persuasive he can be and how uncanny his instincts are.'

Dorian nodded silently, and she went on, 'Had you not been forewarned you would have been eager to sample his wares, even though his fee was exorbitant. Well, Zayn al-Din has paid many times more than that to him. The sheer genius of my father is that not only was he able to milk Zayn but the Sublime Porte and the East India Company have paid him almost as much again to act as their emissary. For the work he has done in Arabia during these last three years my father has received fifteen lakhs in gold specie.'

Mansur whistled, and Dorian looked grave. ''Tis almost a

646

quarter of a million guineas,' he said softly, 'an emperor's ransom.'

'Yes.' Verity dropped her voice to a whisper. 'And all of it is stored in the main hold of the *Arcturus*. That is why my father would have died rather than allow you to board his ship, why he was prepared to strike his powder magazine when that cargo was threatened.'

'Sweet heavenly angels, my love,' Mansur whispered, 'why did you not tell us this before?'

She looked steadily into his eyes. 'One reason only. I have lived all my adult life with a man whose soul is consumed by greed. I know full well the effects of that corrosive affliction. I did not want to infect the man I love with the same disease.'

'That would never happen,' Mansur said hotly. 'You do me an injustice.'

'My darling,' she replied, 'if you could but see your own face at this very moment.' Shamefaced Mansur dropped his eyes. He knew that her arrow had struck close to the mark, for he could feel the emotions she had warned of churning in his guts.

'Verity, my dear,' Dorian intervened, 'would it not be a rich justice if we could use Zayn al-Din's blood-soaked gold to topple him from the Elephant Throne and set his people free?'

'This is what I have been brooding on endlessly since I threw in my lot so irrevocably with you and Mansur. The reason I have told you about the gold on board the *Arcturus* is because I reached the same conclusion as you. Please, God, that if we seize that blood money, we use it in a noble cause.'

From afar they saw that much of the *Arcturus*'s damaged rigging had been replaced or repaired, but as they sailed closer it became clear that she still lay impaled upon the granite horns of the Deceiver like a sacrifice on the altar of Mammon. Closer still they saw a small, forlorn group standing at the foot of the mainmast on the heavily canted deck.

Through the lens of the telescope Dorian picked out the burly figure and bright features of Ruby Cornish.

It was obvious that the *Arcturus* offered no threat. She was immobilized and the heavy list in her deck rendered her batteries useless. The cannons along her port side pointed into the water and the starboard side at the sky. However, Dorian took no chances: he ordered both the *Revenge* and the *Sprite* cleared for action and the guns run out. They closed in and hove to on each side of the *Arcturus*, covering her with their broadsides.

As soon as he was within hail Dorian called across to Cornish. 'Will you yield your ship, sir?'

Ruby Cornish was astonished to be addressed by the rebel Caliph in perfect English, toned with the sweet accents of Devon. He recovered swiftly, removed his hat and stepped to the rail, balancing there against the listing deck. 'You leave me no choice, Your Majesty. Do you wish to take my sword as well?'

'No, Captain. You fought bravely and acquitted yourself with honour. Please keep it.' Dorian was hoping for Cornish's co-operation.

'You are gracious, Your Majesty.' Cornish was mollified by these compliments. He clapped his hat back on his head and tightened his sword-belt. 'I await your instructions.'

'Where is Sir Guy Courteney? Is he below decks?'

'Nine days ago Sir Guy took the ship's boats and a party of my best men. He set off for Muscat where he purposes to find assistance. He will return as speedily as is possible to salvage the *Arcturus*. In the meantime, he left me to guard the vessel and protect her cargo.' This was a long message to shout, and Cornish's face was as bright as a jewel by the time he had finished.

'I am sending a boarding party to you. I intend to salvage your vessel and float her off the reef. Will you co-operate with my officers?' Cornish fidgeted for a moment, then seemed to make up his mind.

'Majesty, I have yielded to you. I will follow your orders.'

They laid the *Sprite* and the *Revenge* along each side of the

Arcturus and unloaded her, divesting her of her cannon, shot and water. Then they ran the heaviest anchor cables under her hull as slings. They tightened these with the windlasses on the *Revenge* and the *Sprite* until they were rigid as bars of iron. The *Arcturus* lifted slowly, and they heard the timbers popping and crackling as the granite horns eased their grip in her vitals. The tides were only two days from high springs, and in these waters the tidal variation was almost three fathoms. Before making the final effort, Dorian waited until slack water was at the bottom of the ebb. Then he sent every able-bodied man to his place at the pumps. At his signal they threw themselves on the long handles. The bilge water flew in sheets over the sides, faster than the inflow through rents in the *Arcturus*'s hull. As she lightened, she strained to tear herself free of the rock. The rising tide added its irresistible impulse to the buoyancy of the hull and, with a last, terrible rending sound from below, the *Arcturus* slowly righted and floated free.

Immediately all three vessels set their mainsails and, still lashed together, glided out of the Deceiver's clutches. With fifty fathoms of water under their hulls Dorian brought the linked vessels slowly around on a course for Sawda island. Then he placed an armed guard over the hatches of the *Arcturus*'s main hold with strict orders that no man be allowed to pass.

The steering was clumsy and erratic, and the three ships staggered along like drinking companions returning homeward from a night of revelry. As the dawn broke they had raised the black massif of Sawda over the horizon, and before noon they had dropped anchor in the bay.

The first task was to draw a heavy canvas sail under the *Arcturus*'s hull and cover the terrible tears through her bottom timbers; only then could the pumps of all three ships dry her out. Before they warped her into the beach to careen her and complete the repairs, Dorian, Mansur and Verity went aboard her.

Verity went directly to her own cabin. She was appalled by the damage that the battle had wrought. Her clothing was in disarray, torn by wood splinters, stained by seawater. Perfume bottles had shattered, powder pots cracked, and the contents had spilled over her petticoats and stockings. However, all of this could be replaced. It was her books and manuscripts that were her prime concern. Chief of these was a set of rare, beautifully illustrated and centuries-old volumes of the *Ramayana*. This had been a personal gift from Muhammad Shah, the Great Mogul, in recognition of her services as interpreter during his negotiations with Sir Guy. She had already translated the first five volumes of this mighty Hindu epic into English.

Among her other treasures was a copy of the Qur'an. This had been given to her by Sultan Obied, when she and her father had last visited him in the Topkapi Saray Palace in Constantinople. The gift had been made on condition that she translate it into English. This was reputed to be one of the original copies of the authoritative text revisions commissioned by the Caliph Uthman in AD 644 to 656, twelve years after the death of Muhammad, and it was known as the Uthmanic Recension. True to her promise to the Sultan, Verity had almost completed the translation of this seminal work. Her manuscripts were an investment of two years' painstaking labour. With her heart in her mouth she dragged out the chest in which she kept them from under a pile of fallen timbers and other debris. She exclaimed with relief when she opened the lid and found them undamaged.

In the meantime Dorian and Mansur were searching Sir Guy's great cabin next door. Ruby Cornish had handed over the key to them. 'I have removed nothing,' he told them. They found him as good as his word. Dorian took custody of the *Arcturus*'s logbooks and all her other papers. In the locked drawers of Guy's desk they found his private papers and his journals.

'These will afford us much valuable evidence about my brother's activities,' Dorian said, with grim satisfaction, 'and of his dealings with Zayn al-Din and the East India Company.'

Then they went back on deck, and broke open the seals on the hatches of the main hold. They lifted off the covers and went down into it. They found it filled with great quantities of muskets, swords and lance heads, new and unused, still packed in the manufacturers' grease. There was also powder and shot by the ton, twenty light field-artillery pieces, and much other military stores.

'Enough to start a war or a revolution,' Dorian remarked drily.

'Which is Uncle Guy's purpose,' Mansur agreed.

Much of this had been damaged by seawater. It was a lengthy business to clear the hold of this cargo, but at last they were down to the deck timbers, and there was no trace of the gold Verity had promised them.

Mansur climbed out of the hot, fetid hold, and went to find her. She was in her cabin. He paused in the entrance. In this short time she had restored the shambles of her cabin to a remarkable state of order and cleanliness. She sat at the mahogany desk under the skylight. She was no longer clad like an orphan in his oversized cast-off clothing. Instead she was wearing a fresh blue organza dress with leg-o'-mutton sleeves and trimmed with fine lace. Around her throat was a lustrous string of pearls. She was reading a book in a jewelled, engraved silver cover, and making notes in another with a plain vellum cover. Mansur saw that the pages were closely written with her small, elegant script. She looked up at him and smiled sweetly. 'Ah, Your Highness, do I have your attention for the moment? I am greatly honoured.'

Despite his disappointment in finding the hold bare, Mansur gaped at her in admiration. 'There is not a shadow of doubt in my mind that you are the most beautiful woman I have ever laid eyes upon,' he said, with awe in his tone. In this setting she seemed to him a perfect jewel.

'While you, sir, are rather sweaty and grubby.' She laughed at him. 'But I am sure that is not what you came to hear.'

'There isn't a single coin down there,' he said lamely.

'Have you taken the trouble to look beneath the floor-boards, or should that be the deck? I am a little at sea with these nautical terms, if you will forgive the play on words.'

'I love you more each hour, my clever darling,' he cried, and ran back to the hold, shouting for the carpenters to come to him.

V erity waited until the banging and hammering in the hold ceased abruptly and she heard the squeal of timbers being prised loose. Then she laid aside the *Ramayana* and went up on deck. She strolled across to the open hatch. She was just in time to watch the first chest being brought reverentially out of its snug hiding-place beneath the deck. It was so weighty that it took the combined strength of Mansur and five hefty seamen to lift it. As one of the carpenters unscrewed the lid, seawater poured out through the joints, for the chest had been submerged since the ship had run on to the horns of the Deceiver.

There were exclamations of astonishment and wonder as Mansur lifted off the lid. From directly above, Verity caught the wanton shine of pure gold before the men crowded forward and cut off her view. She gazed instead at Mansur's bare back. His muscles were oiled with sweat, and when he reached down to pick out one of the bright yellow bars, she glimpsed the tuft of coppery hair in his armpit.

The sight of the gold had not moved her in the least, but his body did. She felt that strange but particular feeling melting her loins, and had to go back to her book in an attempt to alleviate it. This helped not at all. The warm and pleasant sensation grew stronger.

'You have become a shameless and lascivious woman, Verity Courtney,' she whispered primly, but her smug little smile gave the lie to her self-deprecatory tone.

Mansur and Dorian removed fifteen chests of gold from the bilges of the *Arcturus*. When they weighed them they found that, as Verity had said, each one contained a lakh of the precious metal.

'My father is a neat, fastidious man,' Verity explained. 'Originally the gold was delivered to him from the treasuries of Oman and Constantinople in a profusion of coins of various dates and empires and denominations, in bars, beads and coils of wire. My father had it melted down and recast into standard bars of ten pounds weight, with his crest and the assayed purity stamped into each.'

'This is a vast fortune,' Dorian murmured, as the fifteen chests were lowered into the hold of the *Revenge*, where they would be under his direct charge. 'My brother was a rich man.'

'Do not feel sorry on his behalf,' Verity said. 'He is a rich man still. This is but a small part of his wealth. There is much more than this in the strongroom of the consulate in Bombay. It is zealously guarded by my brother, Christopher, who sets greater store by it even than my father does.'

'You have my word on it, Verity, that what we do not use in the struggle to free Muscat from Zayn's baleful thrall will be returned to the treasury in Muscat whence most of it was stolen. It will be used for the benefit of my people.'

'I trust your word on that, Uncle, but the truth is that I am sickened by it, for I have been party to its acquisition by a man who prizes it above humanity.'

Once the gold was out of her they could warp the *Arcturus* on to the beach and careen her. Then the work went swiftly, for they had gathered much experience from the repairs they had carried out on the *Revenge*. This time they were also able to call upon the expertise of Captain Cornish. He cherished his ship like a beautiful mistress, and his advice and assistance were given unstintingly. Dorian came more and more to rely on him, although by rights he was an enemy prisoner-of-war.

In his own bluff, bucolic manner Ruby Cornish was Verity's

ardent admirer. He sought the first opportunity to be alone with her. This was while she was sitting on the black sands of the beach, sketching the scene as the workmen swarmed over the careened hull of the *Arcturus*. The patterns of lines and ropes stretched over the graceful hull reminded her of a spider's web, and the contrast of clean white planed timbers against the jagged black rock intrigued her.

'May I take a few minutes of your time, Mistress Courtney?' Cornish stood before her and doffed his hat, holding it across his chest. Verity looked up from her easel and smiled as she laid aside her pencils.

'Captain Cornish! What a pleasant surprise. I thought you had quite forgotten me.'

Cornish turned an impossible shade of scarlet. 'I have come to beg a favour of you.'

'You have only to ask, Captain, and I will do my best on your behalf.'

'Mistress, at the moment I am without employment, as my ship has been seized by Caliph al-Salil, who, I understand, is an Englishman and related to you.'

'It is all very confusing, I agree, but, yes, al-Salil is my uncle.'

'He has expressed the intention of sending me back to Bombay or to Muscat. I have lost your father's ship, which was in my charge,' Cornish went on doggedly, 'and, begging your pardon, your father is not a man who forgives readily. He will hold me directly responsible.'

'Yes, I rather suspect he may do so.'

'I would not like to explain the loss of the ship to him.'

'That might indeed be prejudicial to your continued good health.'

'Mistress Verity, you have known me since you were a young girl. Could you find it in your conscience to recommend me to your uncle, the Caliph, for continued employment as the captain of the *Arcturus*? I think you know that in the circumstances I will be loyal to my new employer. In addition, it would give me the greatest pleasure to think that our long acquaintance will not end here.'

They had, indeed, known each other for several years. Cornish was a fine seaman, and a loyal servant. She also had a special affection for him, in that he had on many occasions proved himself her staunch but discreet ally. Whenever possible he had shielded her from her father's perverted malice.

'I shall see what can be done, Captain Cornish.'

'You are very kind,' he muttered gruffly, clapped his hat back on his head and saluted her. Then he stamped away through the loose black sand.

Dorian did not have to ponder long on the request. As soon as the *Arcturus* was refitted and floated off the beach, Cornish resumed command of her. Only ten of his seamen refused to come with him. When the little flotilla sailed from Sawda island, it headed south-west to pick up the warm, benign waters of the Mozambique current which, with the monsoon winds, bore them rapidly southwards along the Fever Coast.

Some weeks later, they hailed a large trading dhow on an easterly heading. When Dorian exchanged news with him, her captain explained that he was on a trading expedition to the distant ports of Cathay. He was delighted to add the ten reluctant seamen from the *Arcturus* to his own crew. Dorian was content with the knowledge that it might take years for their report to filter back to Muscat, or to the English consulate in Bombay.

Then they set all sail that the monsoon winds would allow, and went on southwards, through the channel between the long island of Madagascar and the African mainland. Slowly the wild, unexplored coastline unfolded on their right hand, until at last they raised the high whale-backed bluff that guarded Nativity Bay, and sailed in through the narrow entrance.

It was the middle of the day, but there was no evidence of human presence at the fort: no smoke from chimneys, no washing flapping on the lines, no children playing on the beach. Dorian was concerned for the welfare of his family. It was almost three years since they had sailed away and much might have happened in that time. There were many enemies, and in their absence the fort might have been overwhelmed by man, famine or pestilence. Dorian fired a gun as they glided in towards the beach, and was relieved to see the sudden stir of activity around the fort. A row of heads popped up along the parapet, the gates were flung open and a motley crowd of servants and children ran out. Dorian lifted his telescope and trained it on the gates. His heart leaped with joy as he saw the big, bear-like figure of his brother Tom striding through, and heading down the path towards the beach, waving his hat over his head. He had not reached the edge of the water before Sarah followed him, running out of the gates. When she caught up with him, she linked her arm through his. Her happy cries of welcome carried across the water to the ships as they anchored.

'You were right again,' Verity told Mansur. 'If that is my aunt Sarah, I already like her passing fair.'

'Can we trust this man?' Zayn al-Din asked, in his high, feminine voice.

'Your Majesty, he is one of my best captains. I vouch for him with my own life,' Muri Kadem ibn Abubaker replied. Zayn had bestowed upon him the title of Muri, High Admiral, after the capture of Muscat.

'You might have to do just that.' Zayn stroked his beard as he studied the man they were discussing. He was prostrated before the throne, his forehead pressed to the stone floor. Zayn made a gesture with his bony forefinger.

Kadem translated it at once. 'Lift your head. Let the Caliph see your face,' he told his captain, and the man sat back on his heels. However, his eyes were downcast for he dared not look directly into the eyes of Zayn al-Din.

Zayn studied his face carefully. The man was young enough still to have the vigour and dash of a warrior, but old enough to have tempered it with experience and judgement. 'What is your name?'

'I am Laleh, Your Majesty.'

'Very well, Laleh,' Zayn nodded, 'let us hear your report.'

'Speak,' Kadem ordered.

'Majesty, on the orders of Muri Kadem, six months ago I sailed south along the Africa mainland, until I reached the bay known by the Portuguese as the Nativity. I had been sent by the Muri to ascertain if, as our spies had told us, this was indeed the hiding place of al-Salil, the traitor and enemy of the Caliph and the people of Oman. At all times I was at great pains to make certain that my dhow should not be seen from the shore. During the day I cruised well below the horizon. Only after nightfall did I approach the entrance to the bay. If it so please Your Majesty.' Laleh prostrated himself again, his forehead pressed to the stone floor.

The men seated on cushions facing the throne were all listening intently. Sir Guy Courtney sat closest to the Caliph. Despite the loss of his ship, and the huge fortune in gold it contained, his power and influence were undiminished. He remained the chosen emissary of both the English East India Company and King George of England.

Sir Guy had found a new interpreter to replace Verity, a writer of long employment in the Bombay headquarters of the Company. He was a lanky, balding fellow, his skin pitted with smallpox scars, and his name was Peter Peters. Although his grasp of half a dozen languages was excellent, Sir Guy could not trust him as he had his daughter.

Below Sir Guy sat Pasha Herminius Koots. He also had been promoted after the capture of the city from al-Salil. Koots had accepted Islam, for he knew full well that without Allah and His Prophet he could never be fully inducted into the Caliph's favour. He was now the supreme commander of the Caliph's army. All three men, Kadem, Koots and Sir Guy, had pressing political and personal reasons to be present at this war council.

Zayn al-Din made an impatient gesture, and Muri Kadem stirred Captain Laleh with his toe. 'Continue, in the name of the Caliph.'

'May Allah always smile upon him, and shower him with good fortune,' Laleh intoned, and sat up again. 'During the night I went ashore and hid myself in a secret place on the bluff above the bay. I sent my ship away so that it should not be seen by the followers of al-Salil. From this place I watched over the stronghold of the enemy, if it so please you, Your Majesty.'

'Continue!' This time Kadem did not wait for the Caliph to give the word, and kicked Laleh in the ribs.

He gasped, and went on hurriedly, 'I beheld three ships at anchor in the bay. One of these was the tall ship that was captured from the English *effendi*.' Laleh turned his head to indicate the consul, and Sir Guy frowned darkly to be reminded of his loss. 'The other vessels were those in which al-Salil fled after his defeat by the illustrious Caliph Zayn al-Din, beloved of the Prophet.' Laleh prostrated himself again, and this time Kadem caught him a full swing of his nailed sandals.

Laleh bounced upright and his voice was wheezy with the pain of his bruised ribcage. 'Towards evening I saw a small fishing-boat leave the bay and anchor on the reef outside the mouth. When darkness fell the three men of the boat-crew began fishing by lantern-light. When I went back on board my dhow I sent my men to capture them. They killed one man when he fought against capture, but they took the two others prisoner. I towed the fishing-boat many leagues offshore before filling it with ballast stones and scuttling it. I did this so that al-Salil would believe it had been overwhelmed by the sea during the night and the men drowned.'

'Where are these prisoners?' Zayn demanded. 'Bring them before me.'

Muri Kadem clapped his hands and the two men were led in by the guards. They were dressed only in filthy loincloths and their emaciated bodies bore the marks of heavy beatings. One had lost an eye. The raw, black-scabbed pit was uncovered, except for the metallic blue flies that swarmed into it. Both shuffled along under the weight of the leg irons that were riveted to their ankles.

The guards threw them full length on the flags at the foot of the throne. 'Abase yourselves before the favourite of the

Prophet, the ruler of Oman and all the islands of the Ocean of the Indies, Caliph Zayn al-Din.' The prisoners writhed before him and whined their protestations of fealty and duty.

'Majesty, these are the men I captured,' Laleh said. 'Unfortunately the one-eyed rogue lost his wits but the other, who is named Omar, is made of stouter stuff and he will be able to answer any questions you may deign to ask him.' Laleh unhooked from his belt a long hippopotamus-hide whip and uncoiled it. As soon as he shook out the lash, the idiot prisoner began gibbering and drooling with terror.

'I have learned that both these men were sailors aboard the ship commanded by al-Salil. They have been in his service for many years and know much of that traitor's affairs.'

'Where is al-Salil?' Zayn al-Din demanded. Laleh cracked the whiplash, and the one-eyed idiot defecated down his own legs with terror. Zayn turned away his face with disgust and ordered the guards, 'Take him out and kill him.' They dragged him, shrieking, from the throne room and Zayn turned all his attention on Omar, and repeated the question: 'Where is al-Salil?'

'Majesty, when last I saw him, al-Salil was at Nativity Bay, in the fort that they call Auspice. He had with him his son, his elder brother and their women.'

'What are his intentions? How long will he remain in this place?'

'Majesty, I am a humble seaman. Al-Salil did not discuss these matters with me.'

'Were you with al-Salil when the ship called *Arcturus* was captured? Did you see the gold chests that were part of her cargo?'

'Majesty, I was with al-Salil when he lured the *Arcturus* on to the rocks called the Deceiver. I was one of those who lifted the gold chests out of the hold and carried them on board the *Revenge*.'

'The *Revenge*?' Zayn demanded.

Omar explained hurriedly, 'That is the name of the flagship of al-Salil.'

'Where are those gold chests now?'

'Majesty, they were taken ashore as soon as the ships anchored in Nativity Bay. Once again I helped to carry them. We placed them in a strongroom under the foundations of the fort.'

'How many men are with al-Salil? How many of these are fighting men who are trained in the use of the sword and musket? How many cannon does al-Salil have? Are there only the three ships you have spoken of or does the traitor have others?' In his squeaky little voice, Zayn questioned Omar patiently, often repeating his questions. Whenever Omar faltered or hesitated Laleh sent the lash curling and snapping across his ribs. By the time Zayn sat back and nodded with satisfaction, blood was dripping from the freshly opened wounds that criss-crossed the seaman's back.

Zayn turned his attention from the prisoner to the three men who sat on silk cushions below his throne. He studied their faces, and a knowing smile twitched at his lips. They were like a circle of hungry hyena watching a great black-maned lion feed, waiting to rush in and gobble the scraps after he had eaten his fill.

'It may be that I have neglected to ask this wretch questions, the answers to which are important to our deliberations?' He turned the statement into a question, and looked at Sir Guy.

Peters translated, and Sir Guy made a small bow before he replied, 'Your Majesty's questions have shown his deep perception and understanding. There are a few small items of intelligence, personal matters, of which this loathsome creature might have knowledge. With your gracious permission?' He bowed again.

Zayn waved at him to continue. Peters turned to Omar and put the first question to him. It was a laborious business, but slowly Sir Guy drew from him every detail of the treasure and the strongroom where it was stored. At last he was satisfied that all his lost gold was in Fort Auspice and that none had been hidden in some other secret location. His only remaining concern was how to regain possession of it without having to relinquish inordinate amounts to his allies, who sat with him before the throne of Zayn al-Din. He would find the solution to this problem later. For the moment he put it aside, and instead questioned Omar minutely on the identity of every *ferengi* who was within the walls of Fort Auspice. Omar's pronunciation of the names was barely recognizable, but he understood enough to be certain that Tom and Sarah Courtney were with Dorian and Mansur.

The years had done little to dim the bitter hatred he harboured for his twin brother. He remembered vividly the adolescent adoration he had felt towards Caroline, and his devastation when he spied upon Tom and Caroline's midnight coupling in the powder magazine of the old *Seraph*. Of course he had married Caroline in the end, but she came to him as Tom's reject, carrying Tom's bastard in her belly. He had tried to expunge his hatred of Tom with the subtle torments he had inflicted upon Caroline over the years of their marriage. Although time had taken the heat out of it, the hatred persisted, hard and cold as obsidian from an extinct volcano.

Then his questions moved on to Mansur Courtney and Verity. Verity was the other great love of his life, but it was a dark, twisted love. He longed to possess her in every way, even those beyond law and nature. Her voice and beauty assuaged some deep hunger in his soul. However, he had never known such transports as when he sent the whip cracking over her sweet, pale flesh and watched the crimson welts rise on her perfect skin. Then his love for her had been fierce and all-consuming. Mansur Courtney had stolen the paragon of his desire away from him.

'What of the *ferengi* woman who was captured by al-Salil during the battle with my ship?' Sir Guy's voice trembled with the pain the question caused him.

'Does the *effendi* refer to his own daughter?' Omar asked, with childlike naïvety. Sir Guy could not bring himself to answer, but he nodded abruptly.

'She has become the woman of al-Salil's son, Mansur,' Omar replied. 'They share the same sleeping quarters and spend much time laughing and speaking privately together.' He hesitated before he could bring himself to recount a matter so indelicate, but then he went on, 'He treats her as an equal, even though she is a woman. He allows her to walk ahead of him and to interrupt him when he is speaking, and he embraces and caresses her in the sight of others. Although he is of Islam, he behaves towards her like an infidel.'

Sir Guy's stomach churned with the acid of outrage and anger. He thought of Verity's body, so pale and perfect. His imagination ran out of his control. He was unable to close his mind to the vivid images that assailed him, of the filthy and obscene acts Verity and Mansur performed together. He shuddered with disgust and with the perverse arousal that seized his loins in an agonizing vice. When I capture her I will flog her until the white skin hangs from her body in tatters, he promised himself. And as for the swine who has perverted her, I shall make him scream for the mercy of death.

His imaginings were so vivid that he was afraid the men around him must sense them as powerfully as he did. He could stomach no more.

'I have finished with this piece of excrement, Your Majesty.' He scrubbed his hands in the bowl of warm water scented with flower petals that stood beside him, as if cleansing himself from the repulsive contact.

Zayn al-Din looked at Pasha Koots. 'Is there aught you wish to know from the prisoner?'

'If Your Majesty graciously permits.' He bowed. At first the questions he had for Omar were those that would concern a soldier. He wanted to know how many sailors had been on board the three ships, and how many men were in the fort, how loyal they were, and how prepared to fight. He asked about the armaments, the placement of the cannon and the field guns that had been captured from the holds of the *Arcturus*. How much powder did al-Salil have in his magazine, how many muskets?

Then his questions changed. 'The one you call Klebe, the Hawk, and whose *ferengi* name is Tom, you say you know him?'

'Yes, I know him well,' Omar agreed.

'He has a son.'

'Him I know also. We call him Somoya, for he is like the storm wind,' Omar told him.

'Where is he?' Koots asked, with a stony face, although behind the mask his anger burned brightly.

'I have heard it said within the fort that he has gone on a journey into the interior of the country.'

'Has he gone to hunt ivory?' Koots asked.

'They say that Somoya is a mighty hunter. He has a great store of ivory in the fort.'

'Have you seen this store with your own eyes?'

'I have seen the five capacious storerooms of the fort packed to the rafters with its abundance.'

Koots nodded with satisfaction. 'That is all I wish to know at present, but there will be many more questions later.'

Kadem bowed to his uncle. 'Your Majesty, I request that this prisoner be given into my personal charge and custody.'

'Take him away. Make sure he does not die, not yet at least. Not until he has served his purpose.' The guards hauled Omar to his feet and dragged him out through the great bronze doors. Zayn al-Din looked at Laleh, who had crept away, trying to efface himself among the shadows at the rear of the throne room. 'You have done good work. Now go and prepare your ship for sea. I will need your services as a scout when you lead the fleet to this Nativity Bay.'

Laleh retreated backwards, bowing and making obeisance with each few steps towards the doors.

When the guards and all lesser men had gone, a silence fell on the council. All three waited for Zayn's next pronouncement. He seemed sunk in a deep reverie, like that of the bhang smoker. But at last he roused himself, and looked to Kadem ibn Abubaker.

'You are bound by a blood oath to avenge the death of your father at the hands of al-Salil.'

Kadem bowed deeply. 'That oath is more dear to me than my life.'

'Your soul has been desecrated by al-Salil's brother, Tom Courtney. He wrapped you in the skin of a pig, and threatened to bury you alive in the same grave as the obscene animal.'

Kadem ground his teeth at the memory. He could not bring himself to admit how he had been defiled and humiliated, but he sank to his knees. 'I beg you, my Caliph and brother of my father, to allow me to seek satisfaction for these terrible wrongs that have been perpetrated against me by these two diabolical brothers.'

Zayn nodded thoughtfully, and turned to Sir Guy. 'Consul General, your daughter has been abducted by the son of al-Salil. Your magnificent ship has been pirated and your great store of wealth stolen from you.'

'All this is true, Majesty.'

Zayn turned at last to Pasha Herminius Koots. 'You have suffered humiliation and your honour has been besmirched at the hands of this same family.'

'I have suffered all these afflictions.'

'As for me, the list of my own grievances against al-Salil goes back to my childhood,' Zayn al-Din said. 'It is too long and painful for me to recite here. We have a common purpose, and that is the eradication of this nest of venomous reptiles and pork-eaters. We know that they have accumulated a considerable store of gold and ivory. Let that be only the pepper sauce that piques our appetite for retribution.' He paused again, and looked from one to the other of his generals.

'How long will you need to draw up a battle plan?' he asked them.

'Mighty Caliph, before whom all your enemies are turned into dust and ashes, Pasha Koots and I will not sleep or eat until we are able to lay the battle order before you for your approval,' Kadem promised.

Zayn smiled. 'I would have accepted nothing less from you. We will meet here again after tomorrow's evening prayers to hear your plan.'

'We will be ready for you at that hour,' Kadem assured him.

The war council continued by the light of five hundred lamps, whose wicks floated in perfumed oils to drive away the clouds of mosquitoes that, as soon as the sun touched the horizon, swarmed from the swamps and cesspools outside the city walls.

Peter Peters fell into his accustomed place behind Sir Guy Courtney as they made their way through the labyrinth of passages towards the royal harem at the rear of the vast sprawling palace. The walls smelt of rot, fungus and two hundred years of neglect. Rats scurried away ahead of the torch-bearers as they escorted the Caliph to his bedchamber, and the tramp of the bodyguard echoed hollowly from the domes and cavernous recesses of the walls.

The Caliph kept up a high-pitched monologue, and Peters translated the words almost as they fell from his lips. When the Caliph paused, Peters translated Sir Guy's response just as swiftly. At last they reached the doors to the harem where a party of armed eunuchs waited to take over the escort duty, for no natural man other than the Caliph was permitted beyond this point.

The aroma of incense floated from behind the ivory screens and mingled with the scent of lusty young womanhood. Listening intently, Peters fancied he heard the whisper of small bare feet on the flags and the sound of girlish laughter tinkling like tiny golden bells. His fatigue fell away as the cat's claws of lust pricked at his manhood. The Caliph could go to his delights and Peters did not envy him: tonight the palace vizier had promised him something special. 'She is a daughter of the Saar, the fiercest of all the tribes of Oman. Although she has seen only fifteen summers she is peculiarly gifted. She is a creature of the desert, a gazelle with pubescent breasts and long slim legs. She has the face of a child and the instincts of a harlot. She delights in the wiles and wonders of love. She will open to you all three of her passageways to bliss.' The vizier sniggered. It was part of his duty to learn every personal detail of every inhabitant of the palace. He knew full well in which direction lay Peter Peters's tastes. 'Even through the forbidden nether passage she will welcome you. She will treat you like the great lord you truly are, *effendi*.' He knew how much this worthless little clerk enjoyed being given that title.

When at last Sir Guy dismissed him, Peters hurried to his own quarters. In Bombay he lived in three tiny cockroach-infested rooms at the back of the Company compound. The only female companions he could afford on his miserly salary were the women of the night in their cheap, gaudy saris and brass bangles, their lips and gums stained bloody crimson as sword wounds from betel nut, smelling of cardamom, garlic, curry and the musk of their unwashed genitals.

Here in the palace of Muscat he was treated with honour. Men called him *effendi*. He had two house slaves to wait upon his every whim. His quarters were sumptuous, and the girls the vizier sent to keep him company were young, sweet and compliant. There was always a new one available as soon as he tired of the old.

When he reached his bedchamber Peters felt the chill of disappointment slide down his spine, for the room was empty. Then he caught the smell of her, like the perfume of a citrus orchard in blossom. He stood in the centre of the room and searched it with his eyes, waiting for her to show herself. For a while nothing moved, and there was no sound except the rustle of the leaves of the tamarind tree that stood on the terrace below the balcony.

Softly Peters quoted a stanza of the Persian poet: '"Her bosom shines like the snowfields of Mount Tabora, her buttocks are bright and round as rising moons. The dark eye that nestles between them gazes implacably into the depth of my soul."'

The curtains that screened the balcony stirred and the girl giggled. It was a childlike sound, and he knew even before he set eyes on her that the vizier had not overstated her age. When she stepped out from behind the curtains, the moonlight struck through the flimsy stuff of her robe and the outline of her body was waiflike. She came to him and rubbed herself against him like a cat. When he stroked her small rounded backside through the thin cloth she purred.

'What is your name, my pretty child?'

'I am called Nazeen, *effendi*.' The vizier had instructed her carefully as to Peters's special tastes, and her skills far surpassed her tender years. Many times during the remainder of that long night she made him bawl and bleat like a weaning calf.

In the dawn Nazeen curled into his lap as he sat in the centre of the mattress of goose down. She selected one of the ripe loquats from the silver dish that stood beside the bed, and bit it in half with her small white teeth. She spat out the glossy brown pip and placed the rest of the sweet fruit between Peters's lips. 'You made me wait so long last night before you came to me. I thought my heart would break.' She pouted.

'I was with the Caliph and his generals until after midnight.' Peters could not resist the urge to impress her.

'The Caliph himself?' She stared at him with awe. Her eyes were huge and dark. 'Did he speak to you?'

'Of course.'

'You must be a great lord in your own country. What did the Caliph want of you?'

'He wanted my opinion and advice on matters of the utmost secrecy and importance.' She wriggled excitedly in his naked lap, and giggled as she felt him swell and stiffen under her. She rose on to her knees and reached down behind herself with both hands. She spread her tight brown buttocks, then sank back into his lap.

'I do so love secrets,' she whispered, and thrust her pink tongue deep into his ear.

Nazeen spent five more nights with Peters, and when they were not otherwise engaged they talked a great deal – or, more accurately, Peters talked and the girl listened.

On the fifth morning when he came to fetch her, while it was still dark, the vizier promised Peters, 'She will return to you again tonight,' and led her away by the hand to a side gate of the palace, where an old man of the Saar waited, kneeling patiently beside an equally ancient camel. The vizier swathed Nazeen in a dark camel-hair shawl and lifted her on to the dilapidated saddle.

The city gates opened with the sunrise, and there followed

the usual exodus and influx of desert folk who had come in to sell their wares, or who were returning into the vast wilderness: pilgrims and petty officials, traders and travellers. Among those leaving were the two riders on the old camel. There was nothing about them to excite interest or envy. Nazeen looked like the old man's grandchild. It was not easy to tell her gender under the shabby robe that covered her head and body. They rode away through the palm groves and none of the guards at the gate bothered to watch them go.

A little before noon the travellers spied a goatherd squatting on a crag of the barren hills. His herd of a dozen motley beasts was spread out among the rocks below him, nibbling at the desiccated twigs of the saltbush. The goatherd was playing a mournful little tune on his reed pipes. The old rider halted his camel and prodded its neck with his goad until it hissed, bellowed a protest and knelt in the sand. Nazeen slipped off its back and ran lightly up the rocky crag, throwing back the hood of her robe as she went towards the goatherd.

She prostrated herself before him and kissed the hem of his robe. 'Mighty Sheikh bin-Shibam, father of all my tribe, may Allah sweeten every day of your life with the perfume of jasmine blossom.'

'Nazeen! Sit up, child. Even here in the wilderness there may be eyes watching us.'

'My lord, I have much to relate,' Nazeen babbled. Her dark eyes sparkled with excitement. 'Zayn is sending no less than fifteen war-dhows!'

'Nazeen, draw a deep breath, then speak slowly but miss nothing, not a word of what the *ferengi* Peters has told you.'

As she prattled away bin-Shibam's face darkened with concern. Little Nazeen had an extraordinary memory, and she had been able to milk the most minute details from Peters. Now she effortlessly recited the numbers of men and the names of the dhow captains whose ships would carry them southwards. She gave him the exact date and state of the tide on which the fleet would sail, and the date on which they expected to arrive at Nativity Bay. When she finished, the sun was half-way down the sky. However bin-Shibam had one last question for her: 'Tell me, Nazeen, has Zayn al-Din announced who is to command the expedition? Is it to be Kadem ibn Abubaker or the *ferengi* Koots?'

'Great Sheikh, Kadem ibn Abubaker is to command the ships, and the *ferengi* Koots the warriors who go ashore. But Zayn al-Din in person will sail with the fleet and take the supreme command.'

'Are you sure, child?' he demanded. It seemed too great a stroke of good fortune.

'I am certain. He told his war council, and these are the exact words that Peters repeated to me, "My throne will never be secure as long as al-Salil still lives. I want to be there at the day of his death, and to wash my hands in his heart blood. Only then will I believe that he is dead."'

'As your mother has said to me, Nazeen, you are worth a dozen warriors in the battle against the tyrant.'

Nazeen hung her head shyly. 'How is my mother, great Sheikh?'

'She is well cared-for, as I promised. She asked me to tell you how much she loves you and how proud she is of what you are doing.'

Nazeen's dark eyes glowed with pleasure. 'Tell my mother that I pray for her every day.' Nazeen's mother was blind: the flies had laid their eggs under her eyelids, and the maggots had burrowed into her eyeballs. Without Nazeen she would long ago have been abandoned, for the desert life is pitiless. Now, however, she lived under the personal protection of Sheikh bin-Shibam.

Bin-Shibam watched the girl go back down the hill and mount behind the camel rider. They set off again in the direction of the city. He felt no guilt or remorse for what he had required Nazeen to do. When it was over, when al-Salil sat once more upon the Elephant Throne, he would find her a good husband. If that was what she wanted.

Bin-Shibam smiled and shook his head. He sensed that she was one of those born with a natural talent and appetite for her vocation. Deep down, he knew that she would never give up the excitement of the city for the austere, aesthetic life of the tribe. She was not a woman who would place herself willingly under the domination of a husband.

'That little one could take care of a hundred men. Perhaps I could do better for her simply by taking care of her blind mother, and leaving her to work out her own destiny. Go in peace, little Nazeen, and be happy,' he whispered after the distant shape of the camel, as it disappeared in the purple haze of fading day. Then he whistled and after a while the true goatherd came out of his hiding-place among the rocks. He knelt before bin-Shibam and kissed his sandalled feet. Bin-Shibam shrugged off the faded robe, and handed it back to him.

'You heard nothing. You saw nothing,' he said.

'I am deaf, blind and dumb,' the goatherd agreed. Bin-Shibam gave him a coin, and the man wept with gratitude.

Bin-Shibam crossed the ridge and went down to where he had left his own camel knee-haltered. He mounted, turned her head southwards, and rode through the night and the following day without pause. He ate a handful of dates and drank thick curds of camel's milk from the skin bladder that hung behind his saddle. He even prayed on the march.

In the evening he smelt the sea salt. Still without check he rode on through the night. In the dawn the ocean lay spread before him like an infinite shield of silver. From the hills he saw the fast felucca anchored just off the beach. The captain, Tasuz, was a man who had proven himself many times over. He sent a small boat to the beach to fetch bin-Shibam aboard.

Bin-Shibam had brought with him writing materials. He sat cross-legged on the deck with the scroll before him and wrote down all that Nazeen had been able to tell him. He ended with the words, 'Majesty, may God grant you victory and glory. I shall wait with all the tribes to welcome you when you return to us.' By the time he had finished, the day was far spent. He gave the scroll to Tasuz. 'Surrender this only into the hands of Caliph al-Salil. Give your own life rather than this scroll to another,' he ordered. Tasuz could neither read nor write, so the report was safe with him. He already had detailed sailing directions for Nativity Bay. Like many illiterate people, he had an infallible memory. He would not forget a single detail.

'Go with God, and may He fill your sail with His sacred breath.' Bin-Shibam dismissed him.

'Stay with God, and may angels spread their wings over you, great sheikh,' Tasuz replied.

It was one hundred and three days later that Tasuz picked out the towering whale-backed bluff that his sailing orders had described, and as he steered into the lagoon he recognized the three tall ships that he had last seen anchored in Muscat harbour.

The entire Courtney family were gathered in the refectory, the central room in the main block of Fort Auspice where they spent much of their leisure time. It had taken Sarah four years to furnish it to its present state of homely comfort. The floor and all the furniture had been lovingly made by the carpenters from indigenous timber, stinkwood, tambootie and blackwood, magnificently grained and polished with beeswax to a warm lustre. The women had embroidered the cushions and stuffed them with wild kapok. The floors were covered with tanned animal skins. The walls were decorated with framed paintings, most of which had been executed by Sarah and Louisa, although Verity, during her short stay at the fort, had made a substantial contribution to the gallery. Sarah's harpsichord had pride of place against the main wall, and now that Dorian and Mansur were back the family choir was at full strength once again.

This evening there was no singing. They were concerned with far more dire affairs. They sat in intent silence and listened to Verity translate into English the long, detailed report that Tasuz had brought them from bin-Shibam in the north. Only one member of the family was less than enthralled by this recital.

George Courtney was now almost three, highly mobile and articulate, harbouring no doubts about his needs and desires and unafraid to make them known. He circled the table with his chubby buttocks showing under the vest that was his only garment. In front his uncircumcised penis waggled like a small white worm. George was accustomed to having the full attention of all, from the lowliest black servant to that godlike being, Grandpa Tom.

'Wepity!' He tugged imperiously at Verity's skirts. He was still having difficulty with the pronunciation of her name. 'Talk to me too!'

Verity faltered. George was not easily appeased. She broke off the recital of lists of men, ships and cannon, and looked down at him. He had his mother's golden hair, and his father's green eyes. He looked so angelic that he squeezed her heart and awakened in her instincts so deep-seated that she had only recently become aware of them. 'I will tell you a story after,' she offered.

'No! Now!' said George.

'Don't be a pest,' said Jim.

'Georgie baby, come to Mama,' said Louisa.

George ignored both his parents. 'Now, Wepity, now!' he said again, his voice rising. Sarah reached into the pocket of her apron and brought out a piece of shortbread. She showed it to him under the table. For the moment George lost all interest in Verity, dropped on to all fours, and shot among their feet to snatch the bribe out of his grandmother's hand.

'You have a wonderful way with children, Sarah Courtney.' Tom grinned at her. 'Just spoil 'em rotten, an't that so?'

'I learned the art from dealing with you,' she answered tartly. 'For you are the greatest baby of all.'

'Will you two stop squabbling for a moment? You're worse than Georgie by far,' Dorian told them. 'There's an empire at stake and all our lives at risk, while you are playing at being doting grandparents.'

Verity raised her voice and took up from where she had been interrupted, and they all became serious again. At last she read out bin-Shibam's final salutation to his Caliph. '"Majesty, may God grant you victory and glory. I shall wait with all the tribes to welcome you when you return to us."'

Tom broke the silence at last. 'Can we trust this fellow? How did he find out so much?'

'Yes, brother, we can trust him,' Dorian replied. 'I do not know how he has come by this news, I only know that if bin-Shibam says it is so, then it must be true.'

'In that case we cannot remain here to be attacked by an overwhelming fleet of war-dhows crammed with battle-hardened Omani troops. We will have to move on.'

'Do not even think it, Tom Courtney,' said Sarah. 'I have spent my whole married life on the move. This is my home, and this creature Zayn al-Din will not drive me out of it. I am staying here.'

'Woman, will you not listen to reason for once in your life?'

'I hate to take sides in such a domestic furore,' Dorian took his pipe out of his mouth and smiled at them fondly, 'but Sarah is right. We will never be able to run far enough to escape the wrath of Zayn and the men with him. Their enmity will encompass oceans and continents.'

Tom frowned darkly and tugged at one large ear. Then he sighed. 'Maybe you're right, Dorry. The hatred they bear this family goes back too far. Sooner or later we must stand and face them.'

'We will never have such an opportunity presented to us again,' Dorian went on. 'Bin-Shibam has given us Zayn al-Din's complete battle plan. Zayn will come to fight us on our own ground. When he disembarks his army it will be at the end of a voyage of two thousand leagues. He will have only those of his horses that have survived the rigours of the journey. We, on the other hand, will be prepared, our men rested, armed and well mounted.' Dorian laid his hand on his brother's shoulder. 'Believe me, Tom, this is our best chance and probably the only one we will get.'

'You think like a warrior,' Tom conceded, 'while I think like a merchant. I relinquish command to you. The rest of us, Jim and Louisa, Mansur and Verity, will follow your orders. I would like to say the same for my dear wife, but following orders has never been one of her strengths.'

'Very well, Tom, I accept the task. We have but a little

time to lay our plans,' Dorian said, 'and will need to take advantage of every minute of it. My first concern will be to survey the field, to pick out those areas where we are strongest and avoid those where we are weakest.'

Tom nodded approval. He liked the way Dorian had so swiftly taken the reins. 'Go on, brother. We are all listening.'

Dorian spoke through puffs of tobacco smoke. 'We know from bin-Shibam that when Zayn brings his ships into the lagoon and bombards the fort, it will be a diversion. The main force under Koots's command will land on the coast and march overland to surround us and prevent us breaking out to retreat inland. What we have to do first is find the most likely spot for Koots to land, then survey the route he will be forced to take to reach the fort.'

The next day Dorian and Tom went on board the *Revenge* and sailed in a northerly direction along the coast. They stood together at the chart table, studying the coastline as it passed, refreshing their memories as to all the salient features.

'Koots must try to land as close to the fort as possible. Every mile he is forced to march will compound his difficulties ten times over,' Dorian muttered.

This was a dangerous, treacherous coast: the steeply shelving beaches and rocky headlands were exposed to a high surf and open to sudden gales. Nativity Bay was almost the only secure harbour within a hundred miles. The one other possible landing was at the mouth of a large river, which ran into the sea only a few miles north of the entrance to Nativity Bay. The local tribes called this river Umgeni. Large war-dhows would not be able to negotiate the shallow bar at the entrance, but smaller boats could do so with ease.

'That is where Koots will land,' Dorian told Tom with finality. 'In his longboats, he could send five hundred men up the river in a few hours.'

Tom nodded. 'However, once he got them ashore, they would still face a march of many miles through rugged country to reach the fort.'

'We had best find out just how rugged it really is,' Dorian said, and he put the *Revenge* about and they sailed back

674

southwards, keeping as close inshore as the wind and tide would allow. They stood at the starboard rail and studied the shore through their telescopes.

There was a continuous sweep of beach all the way, sugary brown sands pounded by an unremitting surf. 'If they stuck to the beach, carrying their own armour, weapons and supplies, they would make heavy weather of marching through that deep sand,' Tom opined. 'What is more they would be vulnerable for the whole march to the cannonade of our ships.'

'Added to which is that, if he is trying to surprise us, Koots would never send them along the open beach. He knows we would spot such a large force at once. He must detour inland,' Dorian decided. 'Tell me, brother, the bush above the beach seems impenetrable. Is it really so?'

'It is very thick, but not impenetrable,' Tom told him. 'Also there are marshy and swampy areas. The bush is infested with buffalo and rhino, and the swamps are filled with crocodile. However, there are game paths along a ridge of slightly higher ground that runs parallel to the shore, about two cables' length inland from the beach. It remains dry and firm at all seasons and states of the tide.'

'Then we must go over the ground carefully and mark that path,' Dorian said, and they sailed back into the bay. The following morning, accompanied by Jim and Mansur, they rode along the beach until they reached the mouth of the Umgeni river.

'That was easy going.' Mansur checked his pocket watch. 'We covered the ground in less than three hours.'

'That may be so. But the enemy will be marching on foot, not mounted,' Jim pointed out, 'and we will have them in easy grape-shot range from the ships.'

'Yes,' Dorian acknowledged. 'Tom and I have already agreed that they must move inland. We want to scout that route now.'

They followed the south bank of the Umgeni river upstream for a mile or so until it entered the hills and the banks became steep and high, making the going difficult even for their small party.

'No, they will not come this far inland. They will be trying to invest the fort with all the speed they can. They must cut through the littoral swamps,' Dorian decided.

They returned downstream, and Jim pointed out the beginning of the low causeway through the swamps. The trees along it were taller than the surrounding forest. They left the river, and headed towards it. Almost immediately the horses plunged into the black mud of the mangrove swamps. They were forced to dismount and lead them through until they reached the ridge of firmer ground. Even here there were potholes of treacherous mud hidden under an innocuous-seeming scum of green slime. The bush grew so densely that the horses were unable to force their way through. The twisted stems of ancient milkwood trees formed serried ranks like armoured warriors and their branches hung down and entwined with the amatimgoola shrub, whose long, sturdy thorns could pierce the leather of their boots and inflict deep, painful wounds.

They were forced to move along the game paths that crisscrossed this jungle, which were nothing more than narrow tunnels of vegetation forged by buffalo and rhinoceros. The thorny roofs were so low that again they were forced to dismount and lead the horses. Even then they had to stoop and the thorns rasped on their empty saddles, scoring the leather. The mosquitoes and biting midges rose in black clouds from the mudholes and swarmed around their sweating faces, crawling into their ears and nostrils.

'When Kadem and Koots drew up their battle plan, neither of them had tried to march through this.' Tom lifted his hat and mopped his face and shiny pate.

'We can make him pay for every yard in heavy coin,' Jim said. Until now, he had been silent since they left the beach. 'In here it will all be close work, hand to hand. Bows and spears will have the advantage over muskets and cannon.'

'Bows and spears?' Dorian demanded, with sudden interest. 'Who will wield them?'

'My good friend and brother in blood and war, King Beshwayo and his bloodthirsty savages,' said Jim proudly.

'Tell me about him,' Dorian ordered.

'It's a long story, Uncle. It will have to wait until we get back to the fort. That is, if we can ever find our way home through this hellish tangle.'

That evening, after dinner, all the family remained in the refectory. Sarah stood behind Tom's chair with one arm draped over his shoulder. At intervals she rubbed the mosquito bites on his bald pate. When she did that, he closed his eyes in quiet enjoyment. At the other end of the table Dorian sat with Mansur on one side of him and his hookah on the other.

Verity had never looked upon herself as a domesticated creature, but since her arrival at Fort Auspice she had found a deep satisfaction in homemaking and caring for Mansur. She and Louisa, who were so different in nearly every way, had taken to each other from their first meeting. Now they moved quietly around the big room, clearing away the dinner dishes, serving endless cups of coffee to their menfolk, or coming to sit close to them and listen to their talk, from time to time adding their own opinions to the conversation. Louisa was well occupied with Master George. This was the time of the day that they all enjoyed most.

'Tell me about Beshwayo,' Dorian ordered Jim, and he laughed,

'Ah! You have not forgotten.' He picked up his son from the floor and placed him comfortably in his lap. 'You have raised enough hell for one day, my boy. Now I am going to tell a story,' he said.

'Story!' said George, and subsided at once. He laid his golden curls against Jim's shoulder, and thrust his thumb into his mouth.

'After you and Mansur sailed away in the *Revenge* and the *Sprite*, Louisa and I loaded up our wagons and set off into the wilderness to look for elephant and try to make contact with the tribes so that we could open trade with them.'

'Jim makes it sound as though I went willingly,' Louisa protested.

'Come now, Hedgehog, be honest. You have been bitten by the wander bug as deeply as I have.' Jim smiled. 'But let me go on. I knew that there were many large war parties of Nguni coming down with their herds from the north.'

'How did you discover that?' Dorian demanded.

'Inkunzi told me, and I sent Bakkat out far northwards to read the sign.'

'Bakkat I know well, of course. But Inkunzi? I only vaguely remember the name.'

'Then let me remind you, Uncle. Inkunzi was Queen Manatasee's chief herdsman. When I captured her cattle, he came with me rather than be parted from his beloved animals.'

'Of course! How could I ever forget it, Jim boy. Wonderful story.'

'Inkunzi and Bakkat guided us into the hinterland to find the other rampaging tribes of Nguni. Some were hostile and dangerous as nests of poisonous cobras or man-eating lions. We had a few scrapes with them, I can tell you. Then we came across Beshwayo.'

'Where did you find him?'

'About two hundred leagues north-west of here,' Jim explained. 'He was bringing his tribe and all their cattle down the escarpment. Our meeting was most propitious. I had just come upon three big elephant bulls. I did not know that Beshwayo was spying upon us from a nearby hilltop. He had never seen mounted men or a musket before. For me it was a most fortunate hunt. I was able to drive the elephant out of the thick forest into the open grassland. There, I rode them down one after the other, with Bakkat loading and passing me the guns. I managed to kill all three within a two-mile gallop on Drumfire. From his lookout Beshwayo watched it all. Afterwards he told me that it had been his intention to attack the wagons and massacre us all, but having seen the way I shot and rode he decided against it. He's a forthright rascal, is King Beshwayo.'

'He's a terrifying monster of a man,' Louisa corrected him. 'That is why he and Jim get along so well together.'

'Not true.' Jim chuckled. 'It was not I who won him over.

It was Louisa. He had never seen hair like hers, or anything to match this cub to whom she had just given birth. Beshwayo loves cattle and sons.' They both looked down fondly at the child in his arms. George had not been able to stay the course. The comforting warmth of his father's body and the sound of his voice was always a powerful soporific and he had fallen into a deep sleep.

'By this time I had learned enough of the Nguni language from Inkunzi, to be able to converse with Beshwayo. Once he had changed his warlike intentions, and prevented his warriors attacking the wagons, he set up his kraal close to us and we camped together for several weeks. I showed him the delights of cloth, glass beads, mirrors and the usual trifles of trade. These he enjoyed, but he was wary of our horses. Try as I might, I could not prevail on him to mount one. Beshwayo is fearless, except when invited to take part in equestrian activity. However, he was fascinated by the power of gunpowder, and I was required to demonstrate it to him at every opportunity, as if he needed further convincing after watching the elephant hunt.'

Louisa tried to lift George out of his father's arms and take him to his bed, but as she touched him he came fully awake and let out a bellow of protest. It took some minutes and the reassurances of the entire family to quieten him again to the point where Jim could resume his tale.

'As we came to know each other better, Beshwayo confided in me that he was having his differences with another Nguni tribe called the Amahin. These were a cunning, unscrupulous bunch of rogues who had committed the unforgivable sin of stealing several hundred of Beshwayo's cattle. This sin was compounded by the fact that in the process they had murdered a dozen or so of his herd-boys, of whom two were his sons. Beshwayo had not yet been able to avenge his sons and recover his cattle because the Amahin were ensconced in an impregnable natural fortress, which the erosion of the ages had carved from the sheer wall of the escarpment face. Beshwayo offered me two hundred head of prime cattle if I would assist him to assault the fortress of the Amahin. I told him that as I

679

now looked upon him as my friend, I would be pleased to fight alongside him without payment.'

'No payment, except the exclusive right of trade with his tribe,' Louisa smiled softly, 'and the right to hunt ivory through all the king's domain, and a treaty of alliance in perpetuity.'

'Perhaps I should have said little payment, rather than none at all,' Jim admitted, 'but let us not be pedantic. I took Smallboy and Muntu and the rest of my fellows and we rode with Beshwayo to the lair of the Amahin. I discovered that it was a massif of rock detached from the main escarpment and secured on all sides by sheer cliffs. The only avenue of approach was across a bridge of rock so narrow that it would allow the passage of only four men at a time. It was overlooked by the Amahin from the higher ground on the far side, and they were able to shower rocks, stones and poisoned arrows on any attackers who attempted to force the passage. Some hundred or so of Beshwayo's men had perished already, shot with poisoned arrows or their skulls crushed by rocks. I found a place on the face of the main escarpment from which my fellows were able to fire upon the defenders. The Amahin proved a doughty lot. Our musket balls served to dampen their ardour a little, but did not prevent them sweeping the attackers off the exposed bridgeway as soon as they ventured on to it.'

'I am certain that at this stage you conceived the solution to the insoluble, great military genius that you are.' Mansur laughed, and Jim grinned back at him.

'Not so, coz. I was at my wits' end, so naturally I did what we all do in these cases. I sent for my wife!' All three women applauded this gem of wisdom with such merry laughter that George was startled awake again and added his voice to the uproar. Louisa picked him up, helped him find his thumb and he collapsed back into oblivion.

'I had never heard of a Roman testudo until Louisa explained it. She had read of it in Livy. Although many of Beshwayo's men carried shields of rawhide, their use was frowned upon by the king as unmanly. Each warrior fights as an individual and not as part of a formation, and in the moment of greatest danger he is wont to throw aside his shield and hurl himself unprotected upon his enemy, relying on the fury of his charge and his fearsome aspect to drive his enemy from the field and carry him through unscathed. Beshwayo was at first appalled by such cowardly tactics as we suggested. In his view only women hid behind shields. However, he was desperate to avenge his sons and retrieve his stolen cattle. His men learned swiftly how to overlap their shields and hold them above their heads to form the tortoiseshell of protection. My men kept up a lively fire on the Amahin, and under their testudo Beshwayo's *impis* charged across the bridge. As soon as they had a foothold on the far side, we galloped across on the horses, firing from the saddle. The Amahin had never seen a horse before, nor had they faced cavalry, but by now they had learned of the power of our firearms. They broke at our first charge. Those Amahin warriors who did not leap from the cliffs voluntarily were helped to do so by Beshwayo's.'

'You will be pleased to know that the Amahin women did no jumping. They stayed with their children and most found husbands among Beshwayo's men soon after the end of the battle,' Louisa assured Sarah and Verity.

'Sensible creatures,' said Sarah, and stroked Tom's head. 'I would have done the same.'

Tom winked at Jim. 'Take no notice of your mother. She has a good heart. The only pity is that it does not match her tongue. Go on with the story, lad. I have heard it before, but it's a good one.'

'It was a rewarding day for all those who took part,' Jim resumed, 'except the Amahin warriors. Apart from a score of cattle that the Amahin had killed and feasted upon, we recovered the rest of the stolen herd and the king was delighted. He and I shared millet beer from the same pot, but only after we had diluted it with our commingled blood. We are now brothers of the warrior blood. My enemies are his enemies.'

'Having heard that account, there is no doubt in my mind that I should leave the defence of the swamps between here and the Umgeni river to you and your blood-brother Besh-wayo,' Dorian told him. 'And God help Herminius Koots when he tries to find his way through.'

'Just as soon as the wagons are made ready I shall leave to find Beshwayo and enlist his support and that of his spearmen,' Jim agreed.

'I hope, husband, that you do not intend to leave me here, while you wander off into the blue yet again?' Louisa asked sweetly.

'How can you think so poorly of me? Besides, I would meet with a cold welcome at the kraal of Beshwayo if I did not have you and Georgie with me.'

Bakkat went out into the hills to summon Inkunzi. The chief herder and his helpers wandered at large with the cattle herds, and no one else would have been able to find him as readily as the little Bushman. In the meantime Smallboy greased the wheel hubs of the wagons and brought in the draught oxen. Within five days Inkunzi had come into the fort with two dozen Nguni warriors and they were ready to leave.

The rest of the family stood on the palisade and watched the wagon train head for the hills. Louisa and Jim rode ahead on Trueheart and Drumfire. George was tucked into the leather carrying sling on his father's back. He waved one chubby little arm at them. 'Bye-bye, Grandpapa! Bye-bye, Grandmama! 'Bye, Uncle Dowy. 'Bye, Manie and Wepity!' he sang out, and his curls danced and sparkled to Drumfire's easy canter. 'Don't cry, Grandmama. Georgie will come back soon.'

'You heard your grandson,' said Tom gruffly. 'Stop blubbering, woman!'

'I am doing no such thing,' Sarah snapped. 'A midge flew into my eye, that is all.'

Bin-Shibam had warned Dorian in his report that it was Zayn's intention to set sail from Muscat as soon as the south-easterly *kusi* winds swung round the compass and became the *kaskazi*, blowing steadily out of the north-east to wing his fleet down the coast. That time of change was only weeks away. However, there were worrying signs. Already the black-headed gulls had arrived in their dense flocks to set up their nesting colonies on the heights of the bluff. They were the harbingers of an early change in season. For all Dorian knew Zayn's fleet might already be at sea.

Dorian and Mansur sent for their ships' captains. They studied the chart together. Although Tasuz was illiterate he could understand the shapes of islands and mainland and the arrow symbols of winds and currents, for these were the elements that guided his existence.

'At first, when the enemy leave Oman they will keep well offshore, to pick up the *kaskazi* wind and the main flow of the Mozambique current,' Dorian said, with certainty. 'It would take a large fleet to find them in that great expanse of water.' He spread his hand on the chart. 'The only place that you will be able to waylay them is here.' He moved his hand southwards on to the fish-shaped island of Madagascar. 'Zayn's fleet will be forced through the narrows of the channel between the mainland and the island, like sand through the hourglass. You will guard the narrows. Your three ships can cover the inshore passage, for such an assembly of war-dhows will be spread out over many miles. You will also be able to enlist the help of the local fishermen to help you keep watch.'

'When we discover the fleet should we attack them?' Batula asked, and Dorian laughed.

'I know you would enjoy that, you old *shaitan*, but you must keep your ships well below the horizon and out of sight of the enemy at all times. You must not let Zayn know that his advance has been discovered. As soon as you sight his fleet you will break off all contact and hurry back here as fast as wind and current can bring you.'

'What of the *Arcturus*?' asked Ruby Cornish, with a peeved expression. 'Am I also to act as a guard dog?'

'I have not forgotten you, Captain Cornish. Your ship is the most powerful, but not as fast as the *Sprite* and the *Revenge*, or even Tasuz's little felucca. I want you here in Nativity Bay and you can be sure that when the time comes I will have much employment for you.' Cornish looked suitably mollified, and Dorian went on, 'Now, I want to go over the plans to engage the enemy as soon as they show themselves in the offing.' They spent the rest of that day and most of the night in conclave, going over every conceivable eventuality.

'Our fleet is so small, and the enemy so numerous, that our success will depend on each ship working in concert with the others. At night I will use signal lanterns and, during the day, smoke and Chinese rockets. I have drawn up a list of the signal codes we will employ, with copies for Batula and Kumrah written out fair in Arabic by Mistress Verity.'

In the dawn the three little ships, *Sprite*, *Revenge* and Tasuz's felucca, took advantage of the ebb of the tide and the offshore wind and sailed out of the bay, leaving only the *Arcturus* at anchor under the guns of the fort.

Beshwayo had moved his kraal fifty miles further downriver, but Bakkat had no difficulty in leading them directly to it, for every footpath and all the cattle tracks fanned out from it like the strands of a web, with King Beshwayo, the royal spider, at the centre. The lush and rolling grasslands through which they rode were heavily populated by his herds.

Regiments of the king's warriors were guarding the cattle. Many had fought with Jim against the Amahin. They all knew that Beshwayo had made him his blood-brother, and their greetings were enthusiastic. Each regimental *induna* detached fifty men to join the escort that led the wagons towards the royal kraal. The swiftest runners raced ahead to alert the king of their imminent arrival.

Thus Jim's entourage was several hundred strong by the time they crossed the last ridge and looked down into the basin of hills where Beshwayo's new kraal stood. It was laid out in an enormous circle, divided internally into rings within rings like an archery target. Jim guessed that it might take even Drumfire almost half an hour to gallop around the outer circumference.

The kraal was surrounded by a high stockade, and at its heart was a vast cattle pen in which all the royal herds could be contained. Beshwayo liked to live close to his beasts, and he had explained to Jim how the inner enclosure also served as a fly trap. The insects laid their eggs in the fresh cattle dung where they were trodden under the hoofs of the milling herd and could not hatch.

The outer circles of the kraal were filled with the closely spaced beehive huts that housed Beshwayo's court. The king's bodyguard lived in the smaller huts. The larger huts of the king's numerous wives stood within an enclosure of woven thorn branches. In a separate smaller enclosure were fifty elaborate structures that housed the *indunas*, Beshwayo's councillors and senior captains, and their families.

All these were dwarfed by the king's palace. It could not, by any stretch of semantics, be called a hut: it stood as tall as an English country church – it did not seem possible that sticks and reeds could have been built up so high without collapsing. Every single reed used in its construction had been selected by the master thatchers. It was a perfect hemisphere.

'It looks like the egg of the roc!' Louisa exclaimed. 'See how it catches the sunlight.'

'What's a roc, Mama?' demanded George, from the sling on his father's back. 'An't that the same as a stone?' He had picked up that form of negative from his grandfather, and clung to it stubbornly despite her protests.

'A roc is a huge and fabulous bird,' Louisa answered.

'Can I have one, please?'

'Ask your father.' She smiled sweetly at Jim.

He pulled a wry face. 'Thank you, Hedgehog. No peace for me for the next month.' To distract George he touched Drumfire with his heels and they trotted down the last hill. The escorting warriors burst into a full-throated anthem of praise to their king. Their voices were deep and melodious, stirring the blood with their magnificence. The long column of men, horses and wagons snaked down across the golden grassland, the warriors keeping perfect step. Their headdresses waved and nodded in unison; each regiment had its own totem: heron, vulture, eagle and owl, and they wore the feathers of their clan. Around their upper arms they wore the cow tails of honour, awarded by Beshwayo for killing an enemy in combat. Their shields were matched, some dappled, some black, others red, while a few of the élite regiments carried pure white ones. They beat upon them with their *assegais* as they approached the kraal across a parade-ground. At the far end of this wide expanse the imposing figure of Beshwayo waited for them, seated on a carved ebony stool. He was stark naked, displaying to all the world the proof that the dimensions of his manhood exceeded those of any of his subjects. His skin was anointed with beef fat and he shone in the sunlight like a beacon. The captains of his regiments were drawn up behind him, his *indunas* crowned with the rings of authority on their shaven heads, his witch doctors and his wives.

Jim reined in and fired a musket shot into the air. Beshwayo loved to be saluted thus, and he let forth a bull bellow of laughter. 'I see you, Somoya my brother!' he shouted, and his voice carried three hundred yards across the parade-ground.

'I see you, great black bull!' Jim shouted back, and urged Drumfire into a gallop. Louisa pushed Trueheart up alongside him. Beshwayo clapped his hands with delight to see the horses run. In the sling on his father's back George was kicking and struggling with excitement to be free.

'Beshie!' he yelled. 'My Beshie!'

'You had best let him down,' Louisa called across to Jim, 'before he does you or himself an injury.'

Jim hauled the stallion to a skidding halt on his haunches, lifted the child out of the sling with one hand and leaned out of the saddle to lower him to the ground. George took off at a run straight at the Great Bull of Earth and the Black Thunder of the Sky.

King Beshwayo came to meet him half-way, picked him up and hurled him high into the air. Louisa gasped and closed her eyes in trepidation, but George shrieked with delight as the king caught him before he hit the ground, and sat him firmly upon his gleaming muscular shoulder.

That night Beshwayo slaughtered fifty fat oxen and they feasted and drank huge clay pots of frothing beer. Jim and Beshwayo boasted and laughed and told each other amazing tales of their feats and adventures.

'Manatasee!' Beshwayo encouraged Jim. 'Tell me again how you killed her. Tell me how her head sailed up into the air like a bird.' He demonstrated with an extravagant sweep of his arms.

Louisa had heard the story repeated so often, for it was Beshwayo's favourite, that she pleaded the duties of mother-hood as an excuse to leave the royal presence. She carried George, protesting sleepily, to his cot in the wagon.

Beshwayo listened to Jim's account of the battle with even more pleasure than the first time he had heard it. 'I wish I had met that mighty black cow,' he said, when the tale was told. 'I would have put a fine son in her belly. Can you imagine what a mighty warrior he would have been, with such a father and mother?'

'Then you would have been forced to live with Manatasee, the raging lioness.'

'No, Somoya. After she had given me my son, I would have made her head fly even higher into the sky than you did.' He roared with laughter and thrust the beer pot into Jim's hands.

When at last Jim came to join her in the cardell bed, Louisa had to help him climb over the afterclap. He collapsed on the mattress, and she removed his boots for him. The next morning it required two mugs of strong coffee before Jim announced dubiously that, if she nursed him well, he might just survive the day.

'I hope so, my darling husband, for I am sure you recall that this very day the king has invited you to attend the Festival of the First Flowers,' she told him, and Jim groaned.

'Beshwayo drank twice as much of that infernal brew as I did. Do you not think he may have the good sense to cancel the festival?'

'No,' said Louisa, with an angelic smile. 'I do not think he will for here come his *indunas* to escort us.'

They led Louisa and Jim back to the parade-ground. The

open expanse was lined with dense ranks of young warriors dressed in all the finery of feathers and animal-skin kilts. They sat upon their shields, silent and still as statues carved from anthracite. At the entrance to the great kraal, carved stools were set out for Jim and Louisa beside the empty stool of the king. Behind that the king's wives were squatting in double ranks. Many were beautiful young women, and nearly all were in some stage of gravidity, from a gentle swelling to full bloom, breasts bursting with abundance, belly buttons popping out. They exchanged knowing smiles with Louisa, and watched the antics of golden-headed George, their dark eyes swimming with the strength of their maternal feelings.

Louisa sighed and leaned across to Jim on his stool. 'Does not a woman have a peculiar type of beauty when she is to have a baby?' she asked ingenuously.

Jim groaned. 'You pick the oddest times to become subtly suggestive,' he whispered. 'Think you not that one George is about all this world can stomach?'

'She might be a girl,' Louisa pointed out.

'Would she look like you?' Despite the glare he opened his eyes a little wider.

'As like as not.'

'That bears some thought,' he conceded, but at that moment there sounded from within the walls of the kraal a shattering fanfare of kudu-horn trumpets and a crash of drums. Instantly the warriors sprang to their feet and their voices echoed against the hills with the royal salute, 'Bayete! Bayete!'

The king's musicians came out through the gates, rank upon rank, dipping and swaying, flirting their headdresses like the courtship dancing of crowned cranes, stamping until the dust powdered their legs to the knees. Then they froze in mid-step and the only movement was the ruffle of the feathers in their headdresses.

King Beshwayo paced out through the gates. He wore a simple kilt of white cow tails, and war rattles on his ankles and wrists. His head was shaven and his skin had been polished with a mixture of fat and red-ochre clay. His tread was stately. He shimmered like a god as he walked.

He reached his place and looked upon his subjects with such a terrible mien that they shrank before his gaze. Then, suddenly, he hurled the spear he carried into the air. Driven by his massive shoulders it rose to an impossible height. It reached its zenith and then, in a graceful parabola, fell back to peg its glittering head into the sun-baked clay of the parade-ground.

Still there was no sound, no man or woman moved. Then a single voice broke the silence: sweetly and softly it rose from the riverbed at the far end of the parade-ground. A sigh went up from the throats of all the assembled warriors and their feathers danced as they turned their heads towards that sound.

A line of young maidens came shuffling up and over the river bank. Each one had her hands on the hips of the girl in front of her and followed her movements with mirror-like precision. They wore very short skirts of combed grass and crowns of wild flowers. Their breasts were bare and shining with oil. They kept snaking out of the riverbed, until it seemed they were not individuals but a single sinuous creature.

'These are the first flowers of the tribe,' Louisa said softly. 'Each one has seen her moon for the first time, and now they are ready for marriage.'

The girl who led the line of dancers reached the end of the first verse of the song, and all the others came in together with the chorus. Their voices soared high, then fell and languished, and rose again, achingly pure, cleaving the hearts of their listeners. The line of dancing virgins came to a halt before the ranks of young warriors. They turned to face them, and the song changed. The rhythm became as urgent as the act of love, the words suggestive and lewd.

'How sharp are your spears?' they asked the warriors. 'How long the shaft? How deep your thrust? Can you stab to the heart? Will blood flow when you pull out your blade from the wound?'

Then they began to dance again, at first swaying like long grass in the wind, then throwing back their heads and laughing with white teeth and flashing eyes. They held out their breasts, one cupped in each hand, and offered them to the young men.

Then they retreated and whirled away until their skirts flew waist high. They wore nothing beneath them, and they had plucked their pudenda so that their unmasked clefts were clearly defined. Then they faced away from the men, and bowed over until their foreheads touched their knees, writhing and rolling their hips.

The warriors danced in time to the girls, working themselves into a storm of lust. They stamped until the earth jumped under their feet. They shook their shoulders. Their eyes rolled back in their skulls and froth creamed on their contorted lips. They thrust their hips into the air like mating dogs, and their engorged sexes probed rigidly through the fur strips of their kilts.

Suddenly Beshwayo sprang high from his stool and landed on legs as straight and powerful as the trunks of two leadwood trees. 'Enough!' he bellowed.

Warriors and maidens, everyone on the parade, threw themselves to the ground and lay still as death, no sound or movement but the quivering of headdress feathers and grass skirts, the panting of their breath.

Beshwayo strode along the ranks of girls. 'These are my prime heifers,' he roared. 'These are the treasures of Beshwayo.' He gazed down on them with a fierce, possessive pride.

'They are beautiful and strong. They are full women. They are my daughters. From their hot wombs will come forth regiments of my warriors to conquer all the earth, and their sons shall shout my name to the skies. Through them my name will live for ever.' He threw back his head and let forth such a volume of sound from the barrel of his chest that it rang and echoed off the hills. 'Beshwayo!'

Not another person moved and the echoes faded away into silence. Then Beshwayo turned and strode back along the regiments of prostrated warriors. 'Who are these?' The question was filled with contempt. 'Are these men who grovel before me in the dust?' he bellowed, with mocking laughter. 'No!' he answered himself. 'Men stand tall and are full of pride. These are little children. Are these warriors?' he demanded of the sky, and laughed at the absurdity of the question. 'These are not warriors. Warriors have quenched their spears in the blood of the king's enemies. These are but snot-nosed children.' He walked down the line and spurned them with his foot.

'Stand up, you small boys!' he cried. They leaped to their feet with the agility of acrobats, their young bodies forged to perfection by a lifetime of rigorous training. Beshwayo shook his head with contempt. He walked away. Then, suddenly, he leaped high in the air and landed with the elegance of a panther. 'Stand up, my daughters,' he shouted, and the girls rose and swayed before him like a field of dark lilies.

'See how their beauty outshines the sun. Can the king allow those unweaned calves to mount his beautiful heifers?' he harangued them. 'No, for there is nothing between their legs of any account. These magnificent cows need bulls of power. Their wombs crave the seed of great warriors.'

He strode back down the alley between them. 'The sight of these young calves so displeases me that I am sending them away. They shall not look upon my heifers again until they have become bulls.'

'Go!' he bellowed at them. 'Go! And do not return until you have washed your spears in the blood of the king's enemies. Go! And return only when you have killed your man and wear the cow tail on your right arm.' He paused and looked down on them with disdainful hauteur. 'The sight of you displeases me. Be gone!'

'*Bayete*!' they shouted, with a single voice, and again, '*Bayete*! We have heard the voice of the Black Thunder of the Sky, and we will obey.'

In a close column they swung away, keeping perfect step, singing the praises of Beshwayo. Like a dark serpent, they wound up the slope of the hill and disappeared over the crest. Beshwayo strode back and took his seat on the carved stool. He was scowling hideously, but without changing his expression he said softly to Jim, 'Did you see them, Somoya? They are young lions and hot for blood. These are the finest fruits of any circumcision year in all my reign. No enemy can

691

stand against them.' He turned on his stool towards Louisa. 'Did you see them, Welanga? Is there any maiden in all my realm who can resist them?'

'They are fine young men,' she agreed.

'Now I lack only an enemy to send them against.' Beshwayo's scowl became even more terrifying. 'I have scoured the land for twenty days' march in every direction, and found no more fodder for my spears.'

'I am your brother,' said Jim. 'I cannot allow you to suffer such lack. I have an enemy. Because you are my brother, I shall share this enemy with you.' Beshwayo stared at him for a long moment. Then he let fly such a bellow of laughter that all his *indunas* and his pregnant wives cachinnated in slavish imitation of him.

'Show me our enemy, Somoya. Like a pair of black-maned lions on a gazelle, you and I shall devour him.'

Three days later, when the wagons started back for the coast, Beshwayo went with them, singing his war anthems at the head of his new regiments and their battle-hardened *indunas*.

Faithful to Dorian's orders, once the *Sprite* and the *Revenge* entered the Mozambique channel, the two ships separated. Kumrah sailed up the west coast of the island of Madagascar, and Batula along the east coast of the African mainland. They called at each of the fishing villages along the way. From the headmen of these villages they hired, for payment of beads, rolls of copper wire and other stores such as fishing line, rope and bronze nails, a motley flotilla of feluccas and outrigger fishing-dhows. By the time they met again at the rendezvous off the north tip of the long island they were like ducks followed by a straggling line of ducklings. Most of these craft were ancient and decrepit and many could only be kept afloat by constant bailing.

Batula and Kumrah placed them in a thin screen from island to mainland, then took their own ships well to the south so that they were only just able to maintain visual contact with them. In this way they hoped to prevent the desertion of any of the frail vessels, and to receive their signals when Zayn's convoy of war-dhows appeared on the northern horizon, without being forced to reveal their own presence. They hoped that if Zayn's lookouts spotted one or two of these tiny vessels they would think them nothing more than innocent fishing-craft, the likes of which were common in these offshore waters.

The weeks passed slowly in such unrewarding activity. There was constant attrition among the scouting vessels. They were unsuited for such long periods at sea. The crews mutinied against the perils, discomfort and boredom, or their boats fell apart, or the rough weather of the *kaskazi* drove them into port. The screen became so perilously thin that in the heavy seas or in darkness even such a large fleet as Zayn's might slip through the holes in it unremarked.

Batula had placed Tasuz in the most likely position, within sight of the low blue outline of the African mainland. He guessed that Zayn would keep well within reach of the Omani trading settlements that for centuries had been sited at every convenient river mouth and sheltered bay and lagoon along this coast. From these bases Zayn would be able to revictual his ships with fresh water and supplies.

Batula fretted away these long, uneventful days. In the first light of each dawn he climbed to the main truck of the *Revenge* and stared into the dispersing darkness for the first sight of Tasuz's felucca. He was never disappointed. Even in the worst weather when all the other small craft had been driven to seek shelter, Tasuz was doggedly holding his position. Although his ship seemed at times to be buried under the grey, breaking swells of the Mozambique current, his dirty lateen sail always reappeared out of the gloom.

This morning the wind had dropped to a gentle zephyr. A bank of sea fret covered the horizon, and the current had settled into long swells that marched down from the north. Batula searched anxiously for his first sight of the felucca, but he was unprepared when the ghostly outline of the lateen sail

693

appeared out of the mist less than a sea mile dead ahead. 'She is flying the blue!' he exclaimed, with excitement. The long blue banner at her masthead writhed like a flying serpent in the gentle airs. It was the sky blue of al-Salil's colours. 'It is the signal. Tasuz has discovered the approach of the enemy fleet.'

He was aware at once of the danger. The sea mist would disperse as soon as the sun rose, and it would be a day of bright sunshine with visibility stretching to the horizon. He could not be certain how far behind the felucca was the enemy fleet.

He slid down the shrouds so rapidly that the rope scorched his palms, and as his feet hit the deck he shouted his orders to bring the ship about and head her southwards. Tasuz followed in his wake, but rapidly the speed of the felucca narrowed the gap. Within the hour the two ships were close together, and Tasuz shouted his report across to Batula: 'There are at least five large ships coming straight down the channel. There may be others following them. I cannot tell for certain, but I thought I glimpsed beyond them the peaks of other sails just showing over the horizon.'

'When did you last have sight of them?' Batula shouted back.

'At last light yesterday evening.'

'Did they hail you or try to intercept?'

'They paid me no heed. I think they took me for a coastal trader or a fisherman. I did not alter course until darkness hid me from them.'

Tasuz was a good man. Without arousing the suspicions of the enemy, he had been able to slip away from them and warn the two larger ships.

'The mist is beginning to lift, *effendi*,' the lookout called down to the deck, and Batula saw that it was thinning and breaking up. He seized his telescope and clambered back to the main truck. He had hardly settled himself there before the mist rolled aside like a translucent curtain and the morning sun burst through.

Swiftly he swept his lens across the northern horizon.

Beyond the felucca the channel seemed deserted, a wide blue expanse of water. Madagascar was out of sight to the east. Africa was an ethereal blue shadow in the west, and outlined against it he picked out the top sails of the *Sprite* holding her station. They were the only two ships in sight.

'We have run clear away from the enemy during the night.' His heart sang with relief. Then he turned his eye northwards again with more attention and studied the sharp line of the horizon.

'Ah!' he grunted, and then, 'Ah, yes!' He saw the tiny specks of white flash momentarily in the lens like the wings of a gull, then disappear. The leading ships of Zayn's fleet were there, hull down, showing only the very tops of their sails.

He hailed the felucca again. 'Tasuz, go across to the *Sprite* with all speed and recall her. Fire a gun to catch her attention—' He broke off and stared across at the distant schooner. 'No! You need not do it. Kumrah has already seen what we are about. He hastens to join us.'

Perhaps Kumrah had already seen the enemy sails to the north or he might have been alerted by the *Revenge*'s unusual behaviour. Whatever the reason, he had come about and was heading southwards with all sail set.

During the rest of that day the *kaskazi* wind increased in strength until, once more, it was blowing with its customary vigour and the ships were flying on course for Nativity Bay. By noon there was no longer any sight of Zayn's ships on the empty sea they left behind them. By late afternoon Kumrah had steered across on a converging course and the two schooners were in close company, but Tasuz in the felucca was almost out of sight ahead.

Batula watched his lateen sail grow tiny and disappear at last in the dusk. He stooped once more over his chart and made his calculations. 'With this wind Tasuz should reach Nativity Bay in seven more days. It will take us ten, and Zayn will be three or four behind us. We will be able to bring al-Salil fair warning.'

Zayn al-Din sat cross-legged on a bed of cushions and silk prayer mats, which were piled on the lee deck of his flagship under a canvas screen, spread to shelter him from the sun and from the wind and spray that blew back every time the *Sufi* thrust her shoulder into the green swells. The name of the flagship signified the mysticism central to fundamental Islamic thought. She was a ship of force, the most formidable in the entire Omani fleet. Rahmad, the captain who commanded her, had been selected by the Caliph himself for this venture.

Rahmad prostrated himself. 'Majesty, the whaleback that guards the bay in which lies the stronghold of the traitor is in sight.'

Zayn nodded with satisfaction and dismissed him, then turned to Sir Guy Courtney, who sat opposite. 'If Rahmad has brought us directly to our destination without sight of land for twenty days, he has done well. Let us see if it is truly so.' The two stood up and crossed to the weather rail. Rahmad and Laleh bowed respectfully as they approached.

'What do you make of the landfall?' Zayn demanded of Laleh. 'Is this the same bay in which you discovered the ships of al-Salil?'

'Great one, it is the same. This is indeed the lair of al-Salil. From the height of that very headland I looked down upon the bay where he has built his fort and where he anchors his ships.'

With a deep bow, Rahmad handed Zayn his brass telescope. Zayn al-Din balanced easily against the ship's motion. Over the past months his sea-legs had grown strong. He levelled the telescope and studied the distant shore. Then he closed the glass with a snap and smiled. 'We can be certain that our arrival has struck fear into the heart of your traitorous brother and mine. We have not been forced to grope around within sight of the shore to take our bearings. We have given him no warning of our presence and will appear suddenly before him, in all our multitudes and power. By now he must know in his heart that at last retribution has found him out.'

'He has had no time to hide his stolen booty,' Sir Guy agreed happily. 'His ships will still be at anchor in the bay, and this wind will hold them landlocked until we attack.'

'What the English *effendi* says is right. The wind is steady out of the east, mighty Caliph.' Rahmad looked up to the huge sail. 'It will bear us in on this single tack. We will be able to enter the mouth of the lagoon before noon.'

'Where is this river Umgeni in which the main force of Pasha Koots will disembark and go ashore?'

'Majesty, it is not plain to see from this distance. There, slightly to the north of the entrance to the bay.' Abruptly Rahmad broke off, and his expression changed. 'There is a ship!' He pointed. It took Zayn a few moments to pick out the fleck of canvas against the background of the land.

'What ship is it?'

'I cannot be certain. A felucca, perhaps. It is small, but that type is fast on the wind. See! It is coming up and escaping out to sea.'

'Can you send one of our ships to capture it?' Zayn asked.

Rahmad looked dubious. 'Majesty, we have no vessel in the fleet fast enough to catch her in a stern chase. She has a lead of many miles. She will be over the horizon in an hour.'

Zayn thought for a moment, and then shook his head. 'It can do us no harm. The lookouts on the bluff must already have given the alarm to the enemy, and the felucca can pose no additional threat even to the smallest of our vessels. Let her go.'

Zayn turned away and looked back at his own ships. 'Make the signal to Muri Kadem ibn Abubaker,' he ordered.

Zayn had divided the fleet into two divisions. He had taken personal command of the first. This comprised the five largest war-dhows, all armed with heavy batteries of cannon.

At every opportunity since leaving Oman, Kadem ibn Abubaker and Koots had come on board the *Sufi* to attend his war councils. Zayn had been able to adjust his plans to take into account every new detail of intelligence they had gathered at all their ports of call along the way. Now, on the eve of battle, there was no need for Zayn to summon his commanders for another meeting. Every man knew in perfect detail what Zayn required of him. Like most good plans it was simple.

Zayn's first division would sail directly into Nativity Bay, and fall upon the enemy ships they found anchored there. With their superior numbers and firepower, and the advantage of surprise, they would engage them at close range and overpower them swiftly. Then all their guns would be turned upon the fort. In the meantime Kadem would land the infantry in the river mouth and Koots would march them swiftly round to attack the fort from the rear. As soon as Koots launched his attack, Sir Guy would lead a second landing party from the ships in the bay to support him. He had volunteered for this duty: he wanted to be there when the attackers broke into the treasury under the fort where his fifteen chests of gold bars were stored. He wanted to protect his property from looting.

There was one possible flaw in this plan. Would the rebel ships be in the bay? Zayn had not jumped to a hasty conclusion. He had gathered all the intelligence from his spies in every port and harbour in the Ocean of the Indies, including Ceylon and the Red Sea. Not one had been able to report a sighting of al-Salil's ships during the many months since his capture of the *Arcturus*. It seemed that they had vanished without trace.

'They could not have disappeared from the sight of so many eyes,' Zayn reasoned. 'They are hiding, and there is only one place for them to hide.' He wanted to believe this, but doubt itched like a flea in his undershirt. He wanted a final assurance. 'Send for the holy mullah. We shall ask him to pray for guidance. Then I will ask Kadem ibn Abubaker for a sign.' Mullah Khaliq was a saint of vast sanctity and power. His prayers had been a shield to Zayn over the years, and his faith had lit the way to victory in some of his darkest hours.

Kadem ibn Abubaker had the gift of prophecy, one of the reasons that Zayn al-Din valued him so highly. He relied on the revelations that sprang from him.

In the great cabin of the *Sufi*, the three, caliph, mullah and admiral, prayed together through that long night. Khaliq's expression was rapt, his single eye glittering, as he recited the most holy texts in his nasal, singsong voice.

While he listened and made the responses, Kadem ibn Abubaker felt himself falling into that familiar dreamlike state. He knew that the angel of God was near. Just before break of dawn he fell into a sudden, heavy sleep, and the angel came to him. Gabriel lifted him out of his body and bore him up on white, rustling wings to a high place, a mountain shaped like the back of a whale.

The angel pointed down and his voice echoed weirdly in Kadem's head: 'Behold, the ships are in the bay!'

They floated on a circle of bright waters, and on the deck of the largest stood a tall, familiar figure. When Kadem recognized al-Salil, the hatred flowed through his veins like poison. Al-Salil raised his bare head and looked up at him; his hair and his beard were red gold.

'I shall destroy you!' Kadem shouted down at him, and as he said the words al-Salil's head burst into flame, and burned like a torch. The flame leaped up into the rigging, and spread swiftly, consuming everything, man and ships. The waters of the bay boiled, the steam rose in a great cloud and blotted out the dream.

Kadem woke with a deep sense of religious joy, and found himself once more in the great cabin with Zayn al-Din and Khaliq watching him for the sign.

'My uncle, I have seen the ships,' he told his caliph. 'The angel has shown them to me. They are in the bay and they shall be destroyed by fire.'

After that Zayn had no more doubts. The angel would deliver his enemy to him. Now he looked across the white flecked sea at the distant mountain.

'Al-Salil is here. I can smell him in the wind, and taste him in my mouth,' he muttered. 'I have waited a lifetime for this moment.'

Peter Peters translated his words and Sir Guy agreed at once. 'I have the same conviction. I shall stand once more on the deck of my lovely *Arcturus* before this day is done.' While Peters relayed this, Sir Guy had another thought that was almost as poignant. Not only would he recover his ship but his daughter too. Verity would come back to him. Even if she was no longer virgin, sullied and dirtied, no matter. His breath rasped in his throat as he imagined how she must be punished, and how sweet would be the reconciliation that followed. Their previous close and happy state would be restored. She would love him again, as he still loved her.

'Majesty, Muri Kadem's division is heaving to,' Rahmad reported.

Zayn roused himself, and walked back to the stern. This was how he had planned it. Kadem had the five smaller war-dhows under his command and the fifteen troop transports and supply ships. None of the transports was armed: they were merchant vessels Zayn had commandeered for this expedition, crammed with soldiers.

Kadem would lie offshore until the first division entered the bay and attacked the rebel fort. When he heard the guns open up, that would be the signal for him to take in the second division, and to land Koots and his troops in the Umgeni river mouth. When Koots had secured the landing, they could bring in the supply ships that were transporting the horses and land them through the surf. The cavalry would follow the infantry, and mop up any survivors who tried to fly from the doomed fort.

However, the long voyage in the heavy seas of the *kaskazi* had been terribly hard on the horses. They had already lost almost two in every five, and those that had survived were in poor condition. Weak and emaciated, they could still be used to pursue the fugitives. However, it would take many weeks for them to recover fully.

Many of the infantry were in scarcely better condition. The ships were overcrowded and the troops were ravaged by sea-sickness, the half-rotted rations they had to eat, and the water that was thick with green slime. However, Koots would stiffen them up once he had them ashore. Koots could get a corpse to stand up and fight until it was killed again. Zayn smiled wolfishly.

They left the second division hove-to and Zayn's division forged ahead, straight for the entrance to the bay. As they closed in under the brooding height of the bluff, Zayn could pick out the calmer water of the channel. On either side of it the white surf broke, lashed into a fury by the onshore wind.

'They cannot escape us,' he gloated. 'Even if they spot us now, it will be too late for them.'

'I long for sight of my *Arcturus*.' Sir Guy stared ahead eagerly. Verity might still be aboard. He imagined her lying on her bunk in the beautifully decorated cabin, her long hair trailing over her shoulders and her soft white bosom.

'May I beat to quarters, my caliph?' Rahmad asked respectfully.

'Do so!' Zayn nodded. 'Run out the guns. By now the enemy must have seen us. They will be waiting for us in their ships and on the parapets of the fort.'

With all her great cannon loaded, and the gun crews crouching behind them, the *Sufi* led the line of warships up the centre of the channel. Laleh was the pilot, for he was the only one aboard who knew the channel well. He stood beside the helmsman at the wheel and listened to the chant of the man in the bows who was calling the soundings. The bulk of the bluff towered at their left hand, and on their right spread the jungle and mangroves of the littoral. Laleh judged the turn in the channel and gave the order to the helm.

The *Sufi* slatted her canvas, then filled it again with a subdued thunder, and they were round the rump of the bluff. But their speed through the water was scarcely diminished. Zayn stared ahead eagerly: he seemed to snuffle the air like a hunting dog hard on the heels of his quarry. Before them opened the wide sweep of the inner waters of the bay. Slowly Zayn's warlike glare faded and was replaced by an expression of disbelief. The vision that the angel had shown Kadem could not have been false.

'They are gone!' Sir Guy whispered.

The waters of the bay were empty. There was not even a fishing-boat at anchor in its whole wide expanse. The silence was ominous.

Still the line of five ships tore on, straight towards the walls of the fort on which the muzzles of the enemy guns stared at them blankly from a mile away. Zayn fought off the sense of foreboding that threatened to debilitate him. The angel had shown Kadem a vision, yet the ships were gone. He closed his eyes and prayed aloud: 'Hear me, Holiest of All. I pray you, great Gabriel, answer me.' Both Sir Guy and Rahmad looked at him strangely. 'Where are the ships?'

'In the bay!' He heard the voice reverberate in his head, but there was a sly, sardonic tone to it. 'The ships that shall burn are already in the bay.'

Zayn looked back, and saw that the fifth and last of his war-dhows was coming through the deep-water channel into the bay.

'You are not Gabriel,' Zayn blurted. 'You are the *shaitan* Iblis, the Fallen One. You have lied to us.' Rahmad stared at him in astonishment. 'You showed us our own fleet,' Zayn cried out. 'You have led us into a trap. You are not Gabriel. You are the Black Angel.'

'Nay, great caliph,' Rahmad protested. 'I am the most loyal of all your subjects. I would never think to lead you into a trap.'

Zayn stared at him. Rahmad's consternation was so comical that he was forced to laugh, but it was a bitter sound. 'Not you, you poor fool. Another more cunning than you.'

A single cannon shot boomed out across the waters of the bay, and forced Zayn's attention back to the present. Powder smoke rolled from the parapet of the fort and the ball struck the water and ricocheted across the surface of the bay. It crashed into the hull of the *Sufi* and there was a scream of agony from the lower decks.

'Anchor the fleet in line and open fire on the fort,' Zayn ordered. He felt a sense of relief that at last the battle had begun.

As each of the war-dhows dropped anchor and took in its

canvas, it rounded up to the wind, and turned its starboard battery on the fort. One after another they opened the bombardment and the heavy stone balls kicked showers of dust and loose earth from the glacis, or smashed into the log walls. It was immediately obvious that the fortifications could not withstand such furious fire for long. The timbers shattered and burst open to each massive impact.

'I had been made to believe that it was an impregnable fortress,' Sir Guy watched the effects of the bombardment with grim satisfaction, 'but those walls will be down before nightfall. Peters, tell the caliph that I must assemble the assault party at once to be ready to go ashore as soon as the fort is breached.'

'The traitor's defence is pathetically inadequate.' Zayn had to shout above the crash and thunder of the guns. 'I can see only two cannon returning our fire.'

'There!' Sir Guy shouted back. 'One of their guns has been hit.' Both men focused their glasses on the gaping hole that had been blown in the parapet of log poles. They could see that the gun carriage had been overturned, and the broken body of one of the enemy gunners was hanging like beef on a butcher's hook from the splintered stumps.

'Sweet Name of Allah!' Rahmad shouted. 'They are deserting the fort. They have given up. They are running for their very lives.'

The gates of the fort were dragged open and out rushed a panic-stricken mob. They scattered into the jungle, leaving the gates wide, the parapet deserted. The enemy guns fell silent as the last gunner fled his post.

'At once!' Zayn turned to Sir Guy. 'Take your battalion ashore and storm the fort.'

The enemy's capitulation had taken them all by surprise. Zayn had expected them to put up a more determined resistance. Valuable time was wasted while the boats were launched, and the assault party scrambled down into them.

Guy stood impatiently at the head of the gangway, shouting orders at the detachment of men he had chosen as his own. They were all hard men: he had seen them at work and they were like a pack of hunting dogs. Added to that, many of them understood and even spoke a little English. 'Come, waste no more time! Your enemy is getting clean away from you. Every minute and your booty is being taken.'

They understood that, and for those who did not Peters repeated it in Arabic. From somewhere Peters had found a sword and pistol and they were belted around his skinny waist, sagging so that the point of the scabbard dragged on the deck, and his jacket was pulled out of shape. He cut an absurd figure.

The bombardment raged on without pause, and the great stone balls crashed mercilessly into the ruined walls of the fort. The last few defenders fled back into the forest, and the building was deserted. But at last all the boats were loaded and Guy and Peters scrambled down into the largest.

'Pull!' Guy shouted. 'Straight for the beach.' He was desperate to reach the treasury, and his gold chests. As soon as they were half-way across, the ships ceased firing for fear of hitting them. A heavy silence fell over the bay, while the small boats streamed towards the beach. Guy's longboat was first to reach it. As the bows touched the sand he leaped out and waded ashore.

'Come on!' he yelled. 'Follow me!' With the information they had wrung out of Omar, the prisoner captured by Laleh, he had been able to draw up a detailed map of the interior of the fort. He knew exactly where he was going.

As soon as they were through the open gates, he sent men up to the parapets to secure the walls, and others to search the buildings to make sure none of the enemy remained. Then he hurried to the powder magazine. The defenders might have placed a time fuse to blow it up. Four of the men with him carried heavy crow-bars and prised the door off its hinges. The magazine was empty. This should have been a warning to Guy, but he could think of nothing but the gold. He ran to the main building. The staircase that led down to the strongrooms was concealed behind the fireplace in the kitchens. It was cunningly built and even though he knew it was there it took him some time to find it. Then he kicked open the door and went down the circular staircase. An iron grating set in the arched ceiling let in a little light, and he stopped in astonishment at the foot of the stairs. The long low room ahead of him was filled to the roof with neatly stacked ivory.

'The devil take me, but Koots was right! There's tons of the stuff here. If they abandoned such a wealth of ivory, then did they also leave my gold?'

Omar had explained how Tom Courtney had used the ivory to conceal the door to the inner strongroom. But Guy would not rush ahead blindly: before going further he waited for one of his captains to come down the stairwell and report to him. The man was panting with exertion and excitement, but there was no blood on his clothing or the blade of his weapon. 'Ask him if they have secured the fort,' Guy ordered, but the man knew enough English to understand the question.

'All gone, *effendi*. Nothing! No man or dog left inside the walls.'

'Good!' Guy nodded. 'Now get twenty of the men down here to clear the ivory from the right-hand wall of this chamber.'

The most massive tusks had been used to cover the entrance to the inner strongroom and it took almost two hours of hard work to reveal the small iron door, and another hour to batter it open.

As the door toppled out of its frame and crashed to the stone floor in a dense cloud of dust, Guy stepped forward and peered into the room. As the dust settled the interior was revealed. With a stab of angry disappointment he saw that the room was bare.

No, not quite bare. A sheet of parchment was nailed to the far wall. The writing on it was in a distinctive bold hand, which he recognized immediately, even after nearly two decades. Guy tore down the sheet and scanned it swiftly. His face darkened and twisted with fury.

RECEIPT FOR GOODS

I, the undersigned, gratefully acknowledge fair
receipt of the following goods from Sir Guy Courtney:
15 Chests of Fine Gold bars.
Signed on behalf of Courtney Brothers Trading
Company at Nativity Bay this 15th day of November in
the year 1738,
Thomas Courtney esq

Guy crumpled the sheet in his fist and hurled it at the wall. 'God rot your thieving soul, Tom Courtney,' he said, quivering with fury. 'You dare to mock me? You shall find the interest that I will collect from you to be far from any joke.'

He stormed back up the stairs and climbed to the parapet overlooking the bay.

The flotilla of dhows still rode at anchor. He saw that they were unloading the horses, lifting them out of the holds, swinging them overside then lowering them to the water and turning them loose to swim to the beach. A considerable herd was already ashore, and the grooms were tending them.

He saw Zayn al-Din standing by the rail of the *Sufi*. Guy knew he should go back aboard to report to him, but first he had to control his anger and frustration. 'No *Arcturus*, no Verity and, more important still, no gold. Where have you hidden with my gold, Tom Courtney, you bitch-born lecher? Was it not enough that you rutted on the belly of my wife, and saddled me with your bastard? Now you rob me of what is rightfully mine.'

He looked down from the parapet and his eyes followed the wagon track that ran out through the open gates of the fort and immediately forked. One track ran down to the beach, the other turned inland. It wound its way through patches of denser forest and swamp and, convoluted as a scotched serpent, climbed the far hills to vanish over the crest.

'Wagons!' Guy whispered. 'You would need wagons to carry away fifteen lakhs of gold.' He rounded on Peters. 'Tell these men to follow me.' He led them at a run through the gates of the fort, and down to the head of the landing where the horses stood. The grooms were unloading the saddlery from the boats.

'Tell them I will need twenty horses,' he told Peters, 'and I will pick the men I want to go with me.' He hurried among them and slapped each of those he chose on the shoulder. They were all heavily armed and carried extra powder flasks. 'Tell them to fetch saddles from the boats.'

When the head groom realized that Sir Guy intended to take the best of his horses, he shouted a protest into his face. Guy tried to push him away, shouting back at him in English, but the man grabbed his arm and shook it violently, still protesting. 'I've no time to argue,' Guy said, drew the pistol from his belt and cocked the hammer. He thrust the muzzle into the groom's startled face and fired into his open mouth. The man collapsed. Guy stepped over his twitching corpse and ran to the horse that one of his men was holding ready for him.

'Mount!' he shouted, and Peters and twenty Arabs followed his example. He led them off the beach, along the wagon trail, heading into the hills and the hinterland. 'Hear me, Tom Courtney,' he said, 'and hear me well! I am coming to retrieve my stolen gold. Nothing that you or anyone else can do will stop me.'

From the quarter-deck of the *Sufi*, Zayn al-Din watched with anticipation as Sir Guy led his men into the deserted fort. There was no sound of fighting, and no further sight of the fugitives who had escaped from the fort. He waited impatiently for a report from Sir Guy as to what was taking place within the walls. After an hour he had to send a man ashore to enquire. He returned with a message. 'Mighty Caliph, the

English *effendi* has discovered that the fort has been stripped of all furniture and stores except much ivory. There is a hidden door in the cellars below the building. His men are forcing it open, but it is of iron and very strong.'

An hour passed during which Zayn ordered the horses to be sent ashore. Then, suddenly, Sir Guy appeared on the parapet of the fort. Zayn could tell at once from his demeanour that he had been unsuccessful. Then, abruptly, Sir Guy seemed to become galvanized. He rushed out of the fort followed by most of his detachment. Zayn expected him to come back to report to him and was puzzled when he did not, but then Sir Guy's men began to saddle most of the horses. There was a scuffle on the beach and a pistol shot rang out. Zayn saw a body lying on the sand. To his astonishment, Sir Guy and most of his men mounted and rode up from the water's edge then out along the wagon road.

'Stop them!' he snapped at Rahmad. 'Send a messenger ashore immediately to order those men to return.' Rahmad shouted to his boatswain, but before he could give the man his instructions Sir Guy's desertion became irrelevant.

A cannon shot startled them all. The echoes duplicated themselves along the cliffs of the bluff. Zayn jerked round and stared across the waters of the bay to where smoke still hung in the air. A hidden cannon had fired upon them from the tangle of dense vegetation that covered the slope of the bluff. He could not see the weapon, even though he searched through the lens of his spyglass. It was too cunningly concealed, probably in some deep emplacement dug into the hillside.

Then, suddenly, his view through the glass was momentarily obscured by a tall spout of water that leaped up directly in front of him. He dropped the glass to see that a cannonball had struck close alongside the anchored *Sufi*. As he stared, a strange phenomenon took place before his eyes. In the centre of the spreading ripples where the enemy cannon-ball had sunk, the shallow water began to seethe and boil, like a kettle, and steam rose in a dense cloud from the surface. For a long moment Zayn was at a loss to explain it. Then it came to him in a dread flash. 'Red-hot shot! The pork-eaters are firing heated shot!' He trained his glass on the hillside where the smoke still drifted. Now that he was searching for it, he saw a shimmering column of heated air rising into the sky, like a desert mirage. There was no visible smoke. He knew what that meant.

'Charcoal furnaces!' he exclaimed. 'Rahmad, we must get our ships out to sea at once. This is a terrible trap we are in. The entire flotilla will be in flames within the hour unless we can clear the bay at once.'

In a wooden ship, fire was the most terrifying hazard. Rahmad shouted his orders, but before they could get the anchor aboard, another red-hot iron ball hurtled down towards them from the heights of the bluff. It left a trail of sizzling sparks behind it and struck the last dhow in the line of anchored ships. It plunged through her maindeck deep into her hull, shedding splinters of red-hot iron in its path which buried themselves deep in the dry planking. Almost immediately they began to smoulder. Then the air reached them. With miraculous rapidity dozens of fires blossomed in the hull, and spread swiftly.

On board the *Sufi* all was pandemonium as men rushed to the pumps and the anchor capstan, and still others clambered aloft to set the sails. The anchor broke out of the sandy bottom, Rahmad set his lateen sail and the ship came round slowly towards the exit from the bay. Then a hail rang out from the lookout at the *Sufi*'s masthead. It was wild and incoherent. 'Deck below! In the Name of Allah! Beware, it is the curse of *shaitan*.'

Zayn looked up, and his voice was shrill with anger as he shouted, 'What have you seen? Make your report clear, you imbecile.' But the man was still jabbering, and pointing over the bows towards the exit channel from the bay.

Every man on deck followed the direction of his out-thrust arm. A groan of superstitious terror went up from them. 'A sea monster! The great snake from the depths that devours ships and men!' screamed a voice, and men dropped to their knees to pray, or simply stared in mute terror at the ophidian

709

creature that uncoiled from one side of the channel. Its massive body seemed to undulate in endless humps as it swam through the water towards the far bank.

'It will attack us!' Rahmad shouted in terror. 'Kill it! Shoot it! Open fire!'

The gun-crews scrambled to their cannons, and the guns roared out from every ship in the squadron. Smoke and flame flew in sheets. Tall columns of seawater sprang up in a forest around the swimming monster. In such a storm of shot some of the balls struck home. Clearly they heard the crack of impact. However, the creature swam on without any sign that it was injured. The head reached the far shore but the long serpentine body stretched from one bank of the channel to the other and bobbed and rolled in the flow and push of the current. The cannon-balls fell about it like hail. Some glanced off the surface and ricocheted out to sea.

Zayn was the first man aboard to recover his wits. He ran to the near rail and stared at the thing through the lens of his telescope. Then he shrieked, in his high, penetrating voice, 'Cease fire! Stop this madness!' The bombardment petered out.

Rahmad ran to his caliph's side. 'What is it, Majesty?'

'The enemy have drawn a boom across the mouth of the bay. We are bottled in here like pickled fish in a tub.'

As he spoke another heated shot came flying from high on the slope of the bluff, glowing sparks snapping and popping in the air behind it. It plunged into the water only feet from their stern. Zayn looked about him. The first ship that had been hit was burning furiously. Even as he watched its great lateen sail caught fire and the flames engulfed it swiftly. The canvas collapsed over the deck trapping shrieking men under its weight, and incinerating them like insects in the flue of an oil lamp. Without the push of its sail, the vessel started a slow and aimless turn across the bay until it struck the beach and heeled over steeply. The surviving men of the crew sprang over the side and splashed and crawled ashore.

Yet another heated shot came swooping towards the *Sufi* in a smoking parabola. It passed only feet from their mainmast, then flew on to smash into the other war-dhow that sailed beside them. Almost at once her deck split open and tall flames burst out through her timbers. Her crew were already at the pumps, but the streams of water they aimed at the fire had no effect. The flames jumped higher.

'Steer closer to that ship. I will speak to her captain,' Zayn ordered Rahmad. The *Sufi* veered across to her, and as they drew alongside the burning ship Zayn called to the captain, 'Your ship is stricken and doomed. You must use it to clear an avenue of escape for the other ships of the squadron. Ram the enemy boom. Break it open.'

'As you command, Majesty!' The captain ran to the wheel and pushed aside the helmsman. While the other three ships backed their sails and let him forge ahead of them, he steered straight at the line of massive logs attached to a heavy ship's cable that sealed off the channel. Smoke and flame streamed back from the burning hull.

The officers on the deck of the *Sufi* cheered aloud as it struck, and the heavy log boom was plucked below the surface. The dhow heeled over. The top of her mast snapped off and her flaming sail ballooned down over the deck. She had stopped dead in the water, but even though her sail and rigging were in a shambles, she came slowly back on an even keel. Then the line of heavy logs that made up the boom surfaced again. They were intact. They had resisted the dhow's charge. The ship itself swung round aimlessly. She no longer had steerage way. She was not answering her rudder.

'She is mortally damaged below the waterline,' Rahmad said softly. 'See? She is already sinking by the bows. The boom has torn the guts clean out of her. The flames will devour the hull to the waterline.'

The crew of the doomed vessel had managed to launch two of their boats. They clambered down into them, and rowed for the shore. Zayn looked back at the rest of his squadron. Another of his ships was in flames. It headed towards the shore and piled on to the sand with its sails and rigging burning like a funeral pyre. Then another dhow was hit, and black smoke billowed into the sky above her. The blaze drove most of her crew into the bows. A few were overpowered by the smoke, collapsed on the deck and fire swept over them. The rest leaped over the side. Those who were able to swim struck out for the beach, but the others drowned almost at once.

There was a shout of fear from the officers clustered around Zayn and they all looked up towards the heights of the bluff. Another red hot ball came sparkling in a meteoric arc towards them. This one could not miss them.

The thunder of the cannon echoed from the cliffs of the tall bluff, and rolled out across the waters to where Kadem ibn Abubaker lay hove to a mile off the mouth of the Umgeni river.

'The Caliph has begun his attack on the fort. Good! Now you must land your battalions,' Kadem told Koots, then turned to shout an order to the helm: 'Bring her back on the wind.' Obediently the dhow came round to the thrust of the big lateen, and they headed in towards the beach. The rest of the convoy followed his lead.

The transports were towing their boats, which were already packed with armed men. Others were waiting on the decks of the ships for their turn to embark in the boats as they returned empty from the beach. They sailed into the stain of yellow-brown effluent that poured from the mouth of the river and sullied the blue sea for miles along the coast. Both Kadem and Koots studied the beach through their glasses as they approached.

'Deserted!' Koots grunted.

'There is no reason for it to be otherwise,' Kadem told him. 'You will meet no opposition until you reach the fort. According to Laleh, the enemy guns are all aimed to fire out across the bay to cover the entrance channel. They are not sited to meet any attack from the landward side.'

'One quick rush while the enemy is busy with the attacking dhows and we will be over the walls and into the fort.'

'*Inshallah!*' Kadem agreed. 'But you must move swiftly. My uncle, the Caliph, is already engaged. You must drive your men hard to encircle the fort before any of the defenders can escape with the booty.'

The crew took in the sail, and the anchor went overside. A cable's length beyond the first line of breakers the dhow settled quietly to ride the long swells running into the beach.

'And now, my old comrade in arms, it is time for us to part,' Kadem said, 'but always remember your promise to me, if you should be so fortunate as to capture al-Salil or his puppy.'

'Yes, I shall remember it well.' Koots smiled like a cobra. 'You want them for yourself. I swear, if it is within my power, I shall deliver them to you. For myself I want only Jim Courtney and his pretty wench.'

'Go with God!' Kadem said, and watched Koots go down into the crowded boat and head for the shore. A swarm of small craft followed him. As they approached the river mouth, the swells sent them swooping in over the sandbar that guarded it. As soon as they were into the protected water, the boats turned into the bank. From each one twenty men jumped overside into the waist-deep water and waded ashore, their weapons and packs held high.

They assembled in their platoons above the high-water mark and squatted in patient ranks. The empty boats returned to the anchored ships, the oarsmen driving them through the lines of waves at the river mouth. As soon as they were alongside the transports the next wave of men swarmed down into them from the high deck. As the boats ferried back and forth, and more and more men went ashore, the stretch of beach grew more crowded, but still none ventured into the thick jungle beyond.

Kadem watched through his telescope and began to fret. What is Koots doing? he wondered. Every minute now, the enemy will be rallying. He is throwing away his chances. Then he turned his head and listened. The distant sound of the bombardment had ceased and there was silence from the direction of the bay. What has happened to the Caliph's attack? Surely he could not have overpowered the fort so swiftly. He looked back at the men on the beach. As for Koots, Kadem thought, he must move now. He cannot afford to waste more time.

Since he had landed, Koots had been able to form a better estimate of the kind of terrain that lay ahead of him, and had been most unpleasantly surprised. He had sent scouting parties into the bush to find the easiest way through, but they had still not returned. Now he was waiting anxiously at the edge of the jungle, thumping a clenched fist into the palm of the other hand with frustration. He understood as well as Kadem how dangerous it was to allow the momentum of his attack to dissipate, but on the other hand he dared not rush into the unknown.

Would it be better to take them along the beach? he wondered, and looked along the sweep of honey-brown sand. Then he glanced at his own feet. He was ankle-deep in it and the effort of walking even a few paces was demanding. Such a march under heavy packs would exhaust even the hardest of his men.

An hour past low tide, he estimated. Soon the tide will be in full flow. It will flood the sand and force us off it and into the bush.

While he still hesitated, one of the scouting parties pushed their way through the thick wall of vegetation and into the open. 'Where have you been?' Koots bellowed at the leader. 'Is there a way through?'

'It is very bad for three hundred yards. There is a deep swamp directly ahead. One of my men was taken by a crocodile. We tried to save him.'

'You idiot.' With his scabbard Koots struck the man across the side of the head, and he dropped to his knees in the sand. 'Is that what you have been doing all this time, trying to save another useless bastard like yourself? You should have let the crocodile have him. Did you find a path?'

The man came to his feet, swaying slightly and holding his injured face. 'Have no fear, Pasha *effendi*,' he mumbled. 'After the swamp there is a spur of dry ground that leads towards the south. There is an open path running along it, but it is narrow. It will take only three men abreast.'

'Any sign of the enemy?'

'None, great Pasha, but there are many wild beasts.'

'Lead us to the path at once, or I will find a crocodile for you also.'

'If we attack them now, we will sweep them with a single charge back into the sea whence they came,' said Beshwayo, fiercely.

'No, great king, that is not our purpose. There are still many more of them coming ashore. We want all of them,' said Jim, in a reasonable tone. 'Why kill a few of them when, if we wait awhile, we will kill them all?'

Beshwayo chuckled and shook his head so that the earrings Louisa had given him jangled. 'You are right, Somoya. I have many young warriors seeking the right to wed and I do not want to deprive them of that honour.'

Jim and Beshwayo had waited on the hills above the coast from where they had an uninterrupted view out to sea. They watched Zayn's fleet sail in and separate into two divisions. The five largest ships sailed into the bay, and the gunsmoke billowed up as they began to bombard the fort. It seemed that this was the signal for which the second, larger division had been waiting out at sea, for they immediately came directly in towards the mouth of the Umgeni river. Jim waited until they anchored close inshore. He watched them launch their boats, filled with men, and send them in towards the beach.

'Here is the meat I promised you, mighty black lion,' Jim told Beshwayo.

'Then let us go down to the feast, Somoya, for my belly growls with hunger.'

The *impis* of young warriors poured down on to the flat

lands of the littoral strip. Silently as a pride of panthers they moved into their forward positions. Jim and Beshwayo ran ahead of the leading *impi* to the lookout position. They climbed high into the branches of the tall wild fig tree they had chosen days before. Its twisted serpentine air-roots and branches formed a natural ladder, and the bunches of yellow fruit and dense foliage sprouted directly from the trunk to screen them effectively. From their perch in one of the main forks they had a view through the foliage along the entire sweep of the beach south of the river mouth.

Jim had his eye to his spyglass. Suddenly he exclaimed in astonishment, 'Sweet Mother Mary, if it's not Koots himself, all dressed up like a Mussulman grandee. No matter what his disguise, I would know that evil jib anywhere.'

He spoke in English, and Beshwayo scowled. 'Somoya, I do not understand what you say,' he rebuked Jim. 'Now that I have taught you to speak the language of heaven, there is no reason for you still to jabber like a monkey in that strange tongue of yours.'

'Do you see that man on the beach down there in the headdress with the bright and shining band, the one closest to us? He is speaking to the other two. There! He has just struck one in the face.'

'I see him,' Beshwayo said. 'Not a good blow, for his victim is standing up again. Who is he, Somoya?'

'His name is Koots,' Jim answered grimly, 'my enemy to the death.'

'Then I will leave him for you,' Beshwayo promised.

'Ah, it seems as though at last they have all their troops ashore, and that Koots has made up his mind to move.'

Even above the sound of the surf breaking on the sandbar, they could hear the Arab captains shouting their orders. The squatting ranks rose to their feet, hefting their weapons and packs. Quickly they formed up into columns and began to move into the bush and swamp. Jim tried to count them, but could not do so accurately. 'Over two hundred,' he decided.

Beshwayo whistled and two of his *indunas* climbed up to him swiftly. They wore the head-rings of their rank, their short beards were grizzled and their bare chests and arms carried the scars of many battles. Beshwayo gave them a rapid string of orders. To each they replied in unison, '*Yehbo, Nkosi Nkulu!* Yes, great king!'

'You have heard me,' Beshwayo told them. 'Now obey!'

Beshwayo dismissed them, and they slid down the trunk of the wild fig and disappeared into the undergrowth. Minutes later, Jim saw the surreptitious movements in the bush below as the regiments of Beshwayo warriors began to creep forward. They were well spread out, and even from above there was only the brief flash of oiled dark skin, or the glint of bare steel as they closed in quietly on each flank of the marching Omani columns.

A detachment of Turks in their bronze bowl-shaped helmets passed almost directly under the fig tree in which they sat, but they were so intent on finding their way through the matted bush that none looked up. Suddenly there was a commotion of grunts, breaking branches and splashing mud. A small herd of buffalo, disturbed in their mud wallows, burst out of the swamp and thundered away in a solid mass of black, mud-caked bodies and curved, gleaming horns, smashing a road through the forest. There was a scream and Jim saw the body of one of the Arabs tossed high as he was gored by the old cow buffalo that led the herd. Then they were gone.

A few of his companions gathered about the man's crushed body, but the captains yelled at them angrily. They left him lying where he had fallen and went on. By this time the leading platoons had disappeared into the jungle, while the rear echelons were only just leaving the open beach and starting into the swamp.

Once they were into the bush, none of them was able to see further ahead than the man in front of him, and they followed each other blindly. Already they were falling into mudholes in the swamp, and losing any but the most general sense of direction as they were forced to skirt the densest patches of thorny scrub. The insects swarmed off the algae-green puddles that steamed in the heat. The Turks sweated under their steel mail. The bronze helmets reflected arrows of light. The officers had to raise their voices to keep contact with their platoons, and any attempt at stealth was abandoned.

On the other hand, this was the kind of terrain in which the Beshwayo hunted and fought best. They were invisible to the columns of Koots's men. They shadowed them on each flank. The indunas never uttered a word of command. To guide their impis in for the kill, they used only birdcalls or the piping of tree frogs, which sounded so natural that it was difficult to believe they issued from a human throat.

Beshwayo listened to these sounds intently. Cocking his huge shaven head first on one side then the other, he understood what they were telling him as if they spoke in plain language. 'It is time, Somoya,' he said at last. He threw back his head and filled his lungs; his barrel chest swelled, then contracted at the force with which he uttered the high, chanting cry of a fish-eagle. Almost immediately, from far out and much closer at hand, his cry was repeated from a dozen places in the thick jungle below where they sat. His indunas were acknowledging the king's order to attack.

'Come, Somoya!' said Beshwayo softly. 'Unless we are quick we will miss the sport.' When Jim reached the ground he found Bakkat squatting beside the trunk of the fig tree.

He greeted Jim with a sparkling grin. 'I heard the fish eagle cry. So, now there is work to do, Somoya.' He handed Jim his sword belt. Jim buckled it about his waist, then thrust the pair of double-barrelled pistols through the leather loops. Like a dark shadow Beshwayo had already disappeared into a dense stand of reeds. Jim turned back to Bakkat. 'Koots is here. He leads the enemy brigade,' he told him. 'Find him for me, Bakkat.'

'He will be at the head of his troops,' Bakkat said. 'We must circle out around the main fighting so that we are not trapped in it, like a bull elephant in quicksand.'

Suddenly the jungle around them echoed and resonated with the clamour of fighting men: the thudding reports of musket and pistol, the thunder of assegai and kerrie drumming on rawhide shield, wild splashing in the swamps, and the

718

crackle of breaking brush as men charged through it. Then the war chant of Beshwayo's men was answered by shouted challenges in Arabic and Turkish.

Bakkat darted away, avoiding the sounds of battle, circling out towards the river to get ahead of the Omani brigades. Jim ran hard to keep up with him. Once or twice he lost sight of him in the denser patches of jungle, but Bakkat whistled softly to lead him on.

They reached the spur of dry ground at the far side of the swamp. Bakkat found a narrow game path and ran back along it. After a few hundred paces he stopped again, and they both stood listening. Jim was panting like a dog, and his shirt was dark with sweat, plastered to his body like a second skin. The battle was so close that, underlying the uproar, they could clearly make out the more intimate sounds of death, the crunch of a skull splitting at the blow from a *kerrie*, the grunt as a spearman thrust home, the hiss of a scimitar blade through the air, the gush of blood spilling upon the earth, the thud of a falling body, the groans and laboured breath of the maimed and dying.

Bakkat looked at Jim, and made a gesture of closing in upon the battle, but Jim raised a hand to restrain him and cocked his head. His breath was returning swiftly. He loosed his pistols in their loops, and drew his sword.

Suddenly there was a bull-like bellow from the thickets close at hand. 'Come, my sons! Come, the children of heaven! Let us devour them!'

Jim grinned, it could be none other than Beshwayo. He was answered by another voice, crying out in heavily accented Arabic: 'Steady! Steady! Hold your fire! Let them come in close!'

'That's him!' Jim nodded at Bakkat. 'Koots!'

They left the game path and plunged into the undergrowth. Jim forced his way through a wall of thorns, and before him stretched an opening of bright green swamp grass. In its centre there was a tiny island not more than twenty paces across. On this last refuge Koots was making his stand with a dozen of his men, Arabs in mud-soaked robes and Turks in splattered half-armour. They had formed a ragged line, some kneeling, others standing with their muskets at high port. Koots was striding up and down behind the second rank, carrying his musket at the trail. A bloody cloth was wrapped round his forehead, but he was grinning like a skull, a fearsome rictus that exposed his clenched teeth.

Across the narrow neck of swamp they were confronted by a mass of Beshwayo's warriors, with the Great Bull at their head. Beshwayo threw back his head and gave one last bellow: 'Come, my children. This way lies the road to glory!' He bounded forward into the pools, scummed with thick clumps of stinking green algae. His warriors raced after him and the swamp exploded into spray under their charge.

'Steady!' Koots shouted. 'One shot and they will be on us.'

Beshwayo never faltered: he galloped forward, straight into the levelled muskets like a charging buffalo.

'The mad fool,' Jim lamented. 'He knows the power of the gun.'

'Wait!' Koots called, quite softly. 'Wait for it!' Jim saw that he had chosen the king, and was aiming at his chest. He snatched one of his pistols from the loop on his belt and fired instinctively, without seeing the iron sights. It was a forlorn effort. Koots did not even flinch as the ball flew past his head. Instead, his voice rang out harshly, 'Fire!' The volley crashed out, and in the smoke Jim saw at least four of the charging warriors go down, two killed outright, the others thrashing around in the mud. Their companions ran over the top of them. Jim searched desperately for a glimpse of Beshwayo. Then as the smoke cleared he saw him untouched and undaunted still in the front of the charge, bawling lustily as he came: 'I am the Black Death. Look upon me, and know fear!' He hurled himself into the front rank of Arabs, and knocked two flat on to the earth with a sweep of his shield. He stood over them and stabbed down so swiftly that his blade blurred. Each time he drew it out again a bright crimson tide followed the steel.

Koots threw aside his empty musket, and whirled round. He crossed the island with long, loping strides and plunged into the swamp, heading straight back towards where Jim stood. Jim stepped out from the thicket of thorns. He drew his sword, and waited for him at the edge of marshy ground. Koots recognized him and stopped ankle deep in the mud.

'The Courtney puppy!' He was still smiling. 'I have waited long for this moment. Keyser will still pay good gold guilders for your head.'

'You'll have to reap it first.'

'Where is your blonde whore? I have something for her also.' Koots took a handful of his crotch and shook it lewdly.

'I will hack it off and take it to her,' Jim promised him grimly.

Koots glanced over his shoulder. His men were all dead. With slashes of the *assegai*, the Beshwayo were disembowelling their corpses, allowing their spirits to escape: a last tribute to men who had fought well. But some had already started in pursuit of Koots, splashing towards him through the swamp.

Koots hesitated no longer. He came straight at Jim, stepping high through the mud, still smiling, those pale eyes staring into Jim's face to read his intentions. His first thrust came with no warning, straight at Jim's throat. Jim touched his blade, just enough to turn it off line so that the point flew over his shoulder. In the moment that Koots was at full extension, he shot his own blade forward, steel rasped on steel, and guided Jim's point home. He felt the hit, cloth and flesh splitting, then the shock of bone. Koots leaped back.

'*Liefde tot* God!' His smile had given way to a startled expression. Fresh blood spread on his muddy shirt-front. 'The puppy has become a dog.'

Surprise gave way to anger and he rushed at Jim again. Their blades clashed and scraped as he tried to drive Jim back, so that he could find firm footing. But Jim stood solid, and kept him pinned in the soft mud. It clung to Koots's boots and hampered each step he took.

'I am coming, Somoya,' shouted Beshwayo, as he bounded across the narrow neck of swamp.

'I do not take the food from your mouth,' Jim shouted back. 'Leave me this morsel.'

Beshwayo stopped and held up his hand, to restrain his men who swarmed eagerly after him.

'Somoya is hungry,' he said. 'Let him eat in peace.' And he laughed.

Koots dropped back a pace, trying to draw Jim forward into the mud. Jim smiled into his pale eyes and, with a scornful flick of his head, declined the invitation. Koots circled left and as soon as Jim turned to meet him he broke the other way, but he was slow in the mud. Jim hit him again, raking his flank. Beshwayo's men roared approval.

'You bleed as freely as the great pig you are,' Jim taunted him. The blood was sliding down Koots's leg and dripping into the mud. He glanced down at it and his expression was grim. Both wounds were shallow and light, but together they would drain him swiftly. Jim lunged at him.

When Koots jumped back he felt the weakness in his legs. He knew he must try for a quick decision. He looked at the man who confronted him, and for one of the few times in his life he felt a twinge of fear. This was no longer the stripling he had chased across half of Africa. This was a man, tall and broad-shouldered, forged like steel in the furnace of life.

Koots gathered his courage and the last of his strength and rushed at Jim, trying by sheer weight and strength to drive him back. Jim stood to meet him. It seemed that only an evanescent barrier of darting metal separated them. The clash and scrape of the blades rose to a dreadful crescendo. Beshwayo's warriors were enthralled by this novel form of combat. They recognized the skill and strength it demanded, and they chanted encouragement, drumming their *assegais* upon their shields, dancing and swaying with excitement.

It could not last much longer. Koots's pale eyes were covered by the sheen of despair. Sweat diluted the blood that streamed down his side. He felt the slackness in his wrist, and the give of his muscles when he tried to press Jim harder. Jim blocked his next desperate thrust high in the natural line of attack, and locked their blades in front of their eyes. They stared at each other through the cross of silver formed by the quivering steel. They formed a statue group that seemed carved from marble. The Beshwayo sensed the high drama of the moment and fell silent.

Koots and Jim both knew that whichever one tried to break away would expose himself to the killing stroke. Then Jim felt Koots break. Koots shifted his feet and, with a heave of both shoulders, tried to throw Jim back and disengage. Jim was ready for it, and as Koots released, Jim shot forward like the strike of an adder. Koots's eyes flew wide, but they were colourless and blind. His fingers opened, and he let his sword drop into the mud.

Jim stood with his wrist locked and the point of his own steel buried deep in Koots's chest. He felt the hilt thump softly in his hand, and thought for an instant that it was his own pulse. Then he realized that his blade had transfixed Koots's heart, and it was the pumping of his opponent's lifeblood that he could feel transmitted up the blade.

Koots's expression was puzzled. He opened his mouth to speak, then closed it again. Slowly his knees buckled and, as he sagged, Jim allowed him to slip off the blade. He fell face down in the mud, and Beshwayo's men roared like a pride of lions at the kill.

Weeks before, the three ships, *Revenge*, *Sprite* and *Arcturus*, had sailed out of Nativity Bay on the dawn tide. They left Tasuz in his little felucca within sight of the bluff to watch for the arrival of Zayn's fleet while they went on to lie in ambush out of sight of land below the eastern horizon. The endless days that followed were of unrelieved monotony and uncertainty, patrolling back and forth along the edge of the oceanic shelf, watching for Tasuz to summon them to battle.

Ruby Cornish in the *Arcturus* made his sun shot at noon each day, but the instincts of Kumrah in the *Sprite* and Batula in the *Revenge* were almost as accurate as his navigational instruments at keeping them on their station.

Mansur spent almost all the hours of daylight high in *Arcturus*'s main top, watching the horizon through the lens of his telescope until his right eye was bloodshot with the strain and the glare of the sun off the water. Each evening, after an early dinner with Cornish, he went to Verity's cabin. He sat late at her writing bureau. She had given him the key to the drawers when they parted on the beach of Nativity Bay. 'No one else has ever read my journals. I wrote them in Arabic, so that neither my father nor my mother could decipher them. You see, my darling, I never trusted either of them very far.' She laughed as she said it. 'I want you to be the first to read them. Through them you will be able to share my life and my innermost thoughts and secrets.'

'I feel humble that you should do me such great honour.' His voice choked as he said it.

'It is not about honour, it is about love,' she replied. 'From now onwards, I shall never keep a secret from you.'

Mansur found that the journals spanned the last ten years of her life, since she had turned nine. They were a monumental record of a young girl's emotions as she groped her way towards womanhood. He sat late each night, and by the light of the oil lamp he shared her yearnings and her bewilderment at life, her girlish disasters and petty triumphs. There were outpourings of joy, and others of such poignancy that his heart ached for her. There were dark, enigmatic passages when she pondered her relationship with her parents. He felt his flesh creep when she hinted fearfully at the unspeakable as she wrote of her father. She spared no detail when she described the punishments he had inflicted on her, and his hands shook with anger as he turned the perfumed pages. There were other passages that brought him up short with their brilliant revelations. Always her fresh, inspired use of words amazed him. At times she made him laugh aloud, and at others his vision blurred with tears.

The last pages of the penultimate volume covered the period from their first meeting on the deck of the *Arcturus* in Muscat harbour until their parting on the road back from Isakanderbad. At one point she had written of him, 'Though he does not yet know it, already he owns a part of me. From this time onwards our footsteps will be printed side by side in the sands of time.'

When at last she had burnt out his emotions with her words, he blew out the lamp and went dazed with emotional exhaustion to her bunk. The rich fragrance of her hair still lingered on her pillow and the sheets were perfumed by her skin. In the night he woke and reached for her, and when he realized that she was not there the agony made him groan. Then he hated his own father for not allowing her to stay with him, and sending her away in the wagons with Sarah, Louisa and little George into the wild hills of the hinterland.

No matter how little he had slept he was always on *Arcturus*'s deck when eight bells sounded in the middle watch, and before the first blush of dawn he was at the masthead, watching and waiting.

As the most powerful but slowest ship in the squadron, the *Arcturus* kept the windward station, and Mansur had the sharpest pair of eyes on board. It was he who spotted the tiny fleck of the felucca's sail as she came up over the horizon. The moment that they were certain of her identity Ruby Cornish brought the *Arcturus* about and they ran down to intercept her.

Tasuz answered his hail: 'Zayn al-Din is here, with twenty-five great dhows.' Then he turned and led the squadron back towards the African mainland, which now lay low on the horizon, dark blue and as menacing as some monster of the deep. Again it was Mansur who first picked out the shapes of the enemy flotilla anchored off the mouth of the Umgeni river. Their sails were furled and their dark hulls blended with the background of hills and forest.

'They are lying exactly where your father expected them.' Cornish studied them carefully as they raced down upon them. 'They are already sending their boats in to the beach. The attack has begun.'

Swiftly they closed the gap, and it seemed that the enemy were so intent on their landing that they were neglecting the watch they should have kept on the open sea behind them.

'Those are the five war-dhows of the escort.' Mansur pointed them out. 'The others are transports.'

'We have the weather gauge.' Cornish smiled comfortably and his face glowed with satisfaction. 'The same wind that blows to our advantage has them pinned against the lee shore. If they hoist their anchors they will go aground almost immediately. We have Kadem ibn Abubaker at our mercy. How should we proceed, Your Highness?' Cornish looked at Mansur. Dorian had given his son the overall command of the squadron: Mansur's royal rank dictated that. The Arab captains would not have understood or accepted any other in place of him.

'My instinct is to go straight at the war-dhows while we have them at our mercy. If we can destroy them, the transports will fall into our laps like overripe fruit. Would you agree, Captain Cornish?'

'With all my heart, Your Highness.' Cornish showed his appreciation of Mansur's tact by touching the brim of his hat.

'Then, if you please, let us close with the other ships so that I may pass the order to them. I shall allot an enemy ship to each. We in the *Arcturus* will engage the largest of them,' Mansur pointed to the dhow in the centre of the line of anchored ships, 'for that is almost certainly commanded by Kadem ibn Abubaker. I shall board immediately and capture it, while you sail on and do the same to the next in line.'

The *Sprite* and the *Revenge* were sailing a little ahead, backing their sails slightly so as not to head-reach too far on the *Arcturus*. Mansur hailed them, and pointed out which of the dhows were their separate targets. As soon as they understood what he wanted of them they barged ahead, charging at the line of anchored ships.

At last the enemy saw them coming, and confusion spread swiftly through their fleet. Three of the transports were occupied with landing the horses they were carrying. They were winching them out of the holds with slings passed under their bellies, then lowering them over the side into the water. When they reached it, they turned them loose to swim unaided. The sailors waiting for them in the small boats drove them into the breaking surf to fight their way to the beach as best they were able. Already more than a hundred of the sick, exhausted animals were in the water, struggling to keep afloat.

When they saw the tall ships bearing down on them with all their guns run out, the captains of the horse transports panicked. With a few axe strokes they severed their anchor cables, and tried to bear away. Two collided, and in the confusion they drifted into the line of heaving white surf. Still locked together, the waves broke over their decks. One capsized and took the other with it. The surface of the water was covered with wreckage, struggling men and horses. One or two of the other troop ships managed to cut their cables and hoist their sails. It was close work but they cleared the lee shore and made good their offing.

'They are unarmed and no danger to us,' Mansur told Cornish. 'Let them go. We can run them down later. First we must deal with the war-dhows.' He left Cornish, and went forward to take command of the boarding party. The five war-dhows had kept their positions at anchor. They were too large and ungainly to risk the dangerous manoeuvre of trying to clear the lee shore in the face of such a powerful enemy. They had no option but to stay and fight.

The *Arcturus* ran straight at the largest. Mansur stood in the bows and surveyed the deck of the other ship as the gap between them closed. 'There he is!' he shouted suddenly, and pointed with his sword. 'I knew he must be here!'

The ships were so close that Kadem heard his voice and glared back at him. The shaft of pure hatred that passed between them was almost tangible.

'One broadside, Captain Cornish,' Mansur looked back at the quarter-deck, 'and we will board her over her bows through the smoke.' Cornish waved acknowledgement and steered his ship in.

The direction of the wind held Kadem's dhow with her bows pointing out to sea, her stern towards the beach. Although the Omani crew ran out their guns defiantly, they could not bring them to bear. Cornish crossed the bows of Kadem's dhow to rake her at point-blank range. The *Arcturus* stood higher out of the water than the dhow, and her guns were able to fire down on her. Cornish had loaded with grape-shot, and the broadside crashed out. A thick bank of grey gunsmoke shot through with lumps of burning wadding billowed out and obscured her open deck. The wind blew it aside and revealed a scene of utter devastation. The timbers of the dhow's deck had been ripped as though by the claws of a monstrous cat. The gunners were piled in bloody heaps upon their unfired weapons. The splintered scuppers ran crimson with their blood.

Mansur looked for Kadem in the carnage. With a small jolt of disbelief he saw that he was unharmed and still on his feet, trying to muster the stunned survivors of that terrible blast of iron balls. Skilfully Cornish let the hulls of the two ships kiss, then held them together with a delicate play on the helm. Mansur led his boarders across in a rush, and Cornish toyed with the wheel and disengaged. Leaving Mansur and his men to seize the dhow, he sailed on down the line of anchored ships to attack the next war-dhow before it could escape out to sea. He had a respite of a few minutes to look round and see how the other two ships were faring.

After battering them with unrelenting broadsides at close range, the crews of the *Revenge* and the *Sprite* had boarded their chosen adversaries. Three more of the troop transports had drifted into the surf and capsized; some of the others were still at anchor. Cornish counted six more who had avoided the attackers and were clawing desperately out to sea. Then he looked back over his stern and saw the bitter fighting that surged over the deck of Kadem's anchored dhow. He thought he saw Mansur in the front of the battle, but it was so fluid and confused that he could not be sure. The prince might have done better to let me give them a few more doses of grape, before he boarded, he thought, and then with admiration, but he is a hotblood. Kadem ibn Abubaker murdered his mother. Honour allows him no other course than to go after him, man to man.

The *Arcturus* was coming down fast on the next war-dhow in the line, and Cornish gave her all his attention. 'The same medicine, lads,' he called to his gunners. 'A goodly draught of the grape, and then we will board her.'

Although the grape-shot had killed or wounded half of the men on the deck of Kadem ibn Abubaker's ship, the moment Mansur's boarding party swung across from the *Arcturus*, Kadem shouted the order and the rest of his crew came pouring out of the hatchways from the lower decks and launched themselves into the fight.

In numbers boarders and defenders were almost evenly matched. They were so closely packed that there was scarce enough space in which to swing the sword or thrust with the pike. They surged back and forth, slipping on the bloody decks, shouting and hacking at each other.

Mansur looked for Kadem in the ruck, but almost immediately he was confronted by three men. They came at him in a rush. Mansur hit one low in the chest, driving his point up under the ribs. He heard the air hiss from the man's punctured lungs before he toppled to the deck. Mansur only just had time to recover his blood-smeared blade and come back on guard before the other two were upon him.

One of these was a wiry fellow whose long arms were roped with stringy muscle. His naked chest was tattooed with a *sura* from the Qur'an. Mansur recognized him: he had fought beside him on the ramparts of Muscat. He feinted, then cut overhand at Mansur's head. Mansur blocked him and locked his blade. He swung him round like a shield to hold off his comrade, who was trying to intervene.

'So, Zaufar! You could not wait for the return of al-Salil, your true caliph,' Mansur snarled into his face. 'Last time we met I saved your life. This time I shall take it from you.'

Zaufar leaped back in consternation. 'Prince Mansur, is it you?' In reply Mansur pulled off his turban and shook out his copper golden hair.

'It is the prince,' Zaufar screamed. His comrades paused and drew back. They stared at Mansur.

'It is the son of al-Salil,' one cried. 'Yield to him!'

'He is the spawn of the traitor! Kill him!' a pot-bellied rogue bellowed, and forced his way through their ranks. Zaufar turned and sent a thrust deeply into his bulging gut. In a moment the enemy was divided against each other. Mansur's men rushed forward to take advantage of the confusion.

'Al-Salil!' they shouted, and some of the dhow's crew took up the cry, while the others yelled back defiantly, 'Zayn al-Din!'

With so many of Kadem's men changing sides, those still loyal to him were outnumbered and they were swept back down the deck. Mansur led the charge, his face and robe splattered by the blood of his victims, his eyes ferocious. He searched for Kadem in the rabble. As he fought his way forward more of the enemy recognized him. They threw down their weapons and grovelled on the deck.

'Mercy in the name of al-Salil!' they screamed.

At last Kadem ibn Abubaker stood alone at the stern rail of the dhow. He stared across at Mansur.

'I have come for retribution,' Mansur called to him. 'I have come to purge your evil soul with steel.' He started forward again and the men between them shrank out of his way. 'Come, Kadem ibn Abubaker, meet me now.'

Kadem reared back, then swung forward and hurled his scimitar at Mansur's head. The curved blade, clotted with the blood of his victims, cartwheeled through the air with a vicious whirring sound. Mansur ducked under it and it went on to thud into the base of the mast.

'Not now, puppy. First I will kill your dog-sire, then only will I have time to deal with you.'

Before Mansur realized what he was about, Kadem pulled his robe over his head and threw it to the deck. He wore only a loincloth round his waist. His torso was lean and hard. Under his arm was the raised purple scar of the sword-thrust that Mansur had inflicted on him on the quay at Muscat harbour. Kadem turned to the rail and leaped far out. He hit the water, went under, then surfaced and struck out strongly for the beach.

Mansur ran down the deck to the stern, stripping off his own clothing as he went. He dropped his sword, but thrust the curved dagger still in its gold and silver sheath into the back of his loincloth where it would not hamper his swimming stroke. He knotted it there securely. Then, with hardly a check, he dived head first over the rail. Both Mansur and Jim had learned to swim in the turbulent waters of the Benguela current that sweeps the shores of Good Hope. As mere lads the two had kept the household of High Weald supplied with abalone and giant crayfish. They took these not by pot or net, but dived for them in the deep waters of the reef. At the end of many hours spent in the icy waters they would race each other back to the shore dragging the bulging sacks of their catch through the water with them.

Mansur came to the surface and, with a shake of his head, flicked his sodden mane out of his eyes. He saw Kadem fifty yards ahead of him. From experience, he knew that, even though they were accomplished seamen, few Arabs learned to swim, so he was surprised by how strongly Kadem forged through the water. Mansur struck out after him, swinging into a powerful overhead rhythm.

He heard the cries of encouragement from his men on the dhow, but he ignored them and put all his heart, sinew and muscle into the effort. Every dozen strokes he snatched a glance ahead and saw that he was slowly closing in on Kadem.

As they drew nearer to the beach the swells started to hump under them. Kadem reached the break-line first. The tumbling white surf caught and smothered him, then threw him up again, coughing and disoriented. Now, instead of going with the current, he fought against it.

Mansur looked behind him, and saw the next set of waves rearing their backs against the blue of the sky. He stopped swimming and hung in the water, treading gently and paddling with his hands. He watched the first wave come down to him, then let it pass under him. It lifted him so that he had a clear view of Kadem only thirty yards ahead. The wave went on and dropped Mansur into its trough. The next wave came at him, taller and more powerful.

'The first a piddle, the second a fountain, the third will wash you up the mountain.' He almost heard Jim call the doggerel to him as he had so often before while they played together in the surf. 'Wait for the third wave!'

Mansur let the second lift him even higher than the first. From the top he saw Kadem tumble end over end in the boil of the leading wave, his legs and then his flailing arms flashing out of the creaming surf. The wave sped on and left him struggling in its wake. Mansur looked back and saw the third wave bearing down on him. It arched up like the portals of the sky, its crest trembled, translucent green.

He turned with it and began to swim again, kicking hard and tearing at the water with both hands, building up his momentum. The wave picked him up and he found himself caught in its high frontal wall, racing onwards with his head and the top half of his body free.

Kadem was still floundering in the break and Mansur steered towards him with arms and legs, cutting across the face of the wave. At the last moment Kadem saw him and his eyes flew wide with astonishment. Mansur filled his own lungs with air and crashed into him. He locked his arms and legs around Kadem's body, as both of them were swallowed by the wave and carried deep beneath the surface.

Mansur felt his eardrums creak with the pressure and the pain was like a skewer being driven through his skull. He did not release his grip on Kadem, but he swallowed extravagantly and his eardrums made a popping sound as the pressure released. They were driven still deeper and he touched the bottom with one foot. All the time he was tightening his grip around Kadem's chest like the coils of a python.

They sank to the bottom and rolled together along the sandy floor. Mansur opened his eyes and looked upwards. His vision was blurred, and the surface seemed as remote as the stars. He gathered all his strength and squeezed again. He felt Kadem's ribs creaking and bending in the circle of his arms. Then suddenly Kadem opened his mouth wide with the agony of it, and there was an explosive rush of air out of his throat.

Drown, you swine! Mansur thought, as he watched the

silver bubbles of expelled wind racing up towards the surface. But he should have been ready for the last extremes of a dying animal. Somehow Kadem planted both feet on the sandy bottom, and thrust with all the strength of his legs. Still locked together they shot upwards, and the speed of their ascent increased as they approached the surface.

They broke out, and Kadem sucked in air. It gave him new strength, and he twisted in Mansur's arms and reached for his face with hooked fingers. His nails were sharp as augers and they raked Mansur's forehead and cheeks, groping for his eyes.

Mansur felt one hard fingertip force aside his tightly closed eyelid, and slip deeply into the socket. The pain was beyond belief as the nail scored his eyeball and Kadem began to prise it out of Mansur's skull. Mansur released his grip and jerked his head away just before the eyeball popped clean out. He was half blinded by the blood that welled up out of the wound. He emptied his lungs in a scream of agony. With renewed strength Kadem heaved himself on top of Mansur. He locked one arm around his throat in a strangler's grip and forced him under. He was kicking and driving his knees into Mansur's lower body, smothering him with blows and holding his head below the surface. Mansur's lungs were empty, and the urge to breathe was as powerful as the will for life. Kadem's arm was an iron band around his neck. He knew that he would waste the last of his strength if he continued to grapple with him.

He reached behind his back with one hand and drew his dagger from its scabbard. With his left hand he groped under the edge of Kadem's ribcage seeking the lethal point. With all his remaining strength he drove the dagger into the indentation below the sternum. The knife-maker had curved the steel to facilitate just this kind of disembowelling stroke, and the edge was so sharp that Kadem's tensed stomach muscles could offer little resistance to it. The steel ran into its full length, until Mansur felt the hilt strike against Kadem's lowest rib. Then he drew the razor edge down and like a purse opened Kadem's belly from his ribs to his pelvic bone.

With a massive convulsion of his whole body Kadem released his strangling grip, and broke away, rolling on to his

733

back. He floundered on the surface and with both hands tried to stuff his bulging entrails back into the gaping wound. In blue and slippery ropes they kept pouring out and unwinding, until they tangled in his legs as he kicked to stay afloat. His face pointed to the sky and his mouth gaped in a silent cry of anger and despair.

Mansur looked around for him, but his injured eye was blurred and the image of Kadem's face was faceted, like the multiple reflections in a cracked mirror. Pain filled Mansur's skull so that it felt as though it was about to burst. With dread of what he might find, he touched his face. His relief was immense when he found that his eye was still in its socket, not hanging out on his cheek.

Another wave broke over Mansur's head and when he surfaced again he had lost sight of Kadem. He saw something more horrifying. The mouths of these African rivers that poured effluent and offal into the sea were the natural feeding grounds of the Zambezi shark. Mansur knew them well, and instantly recognized the distinctive blunt dorsal fin that sliced towards him, drawn by the taint of blood and split intestines. The next wave lifted the beast high, and for a moment Mansur saw its shape clearly outlined in the window of green water. It seemed to stare at him with an implacable dark eye. There was a kind of obscene beauty in the hard, sculpted lines of its body, and the sleek coppery hide. Its tail and fins were shaped like giant blades, and its mouth seemed set in a cruel, calculating sneer.

With a flick of its tail it shot past Mansur, brushing lightly against his legs. Then it was gone. Its disappearance was even more terrifying than its presence. He knew it was circling under him. This was the prelude to an attack. He had spoken to a few survivors of encounters with these ferocious animals, all missing limbs or bearing other hideous mutilations, and they had all told the same tale. 'They touch you first, and then they hit you.'

Mansur rolled on to his belly, ignoring the pain in his eye socket. Fortuitously another wave rolled down upon him and he swam with it until he felt it lift him, carry him in its arms like an infant, and bear him swiftly in towards the beach. He felt the sand under his feet and staggered up the slope with successive waves crashing into him.

He was cupping one hand over his eye, grunting with the pain, and as soon as he was above the high-water line he dropped to his knees. He ripped a strip from his loincloth and wrapped it round his head, knotting it tightly over the eye to try to ease the agony.

Then he peered back into the churning surf. Fifty yards out, he saw something pale break through the surface and realized it was an arm. There was a disturbance under it, a ponderous, weighty movement in the discoloured waters. The arm vanished again, seeming to be plucked under.

Mansur stood up unsteadily and saw that there were now two sharks feeding on Kadem's corpse. They fought over it like a pair of dogs with a bone. As they worried it, they drove themselves with thrashing tails into the shallow water. At last a larger wave threw the lump of tattered flesh that was all that remained of Kadem Abubaker high up the beach, and left it stranded. The sharks prowled along the edge of the surf for a while then dived and vanished again.

Mansur went down to gaze upon the remains of his enemy. Great half-moons of flesh had been bitten out of his body. The seawater had washed away the blood, so that his stomach cavity was a clean pink pit, his dangling entrails pale and shining. Even in death his eyes were fixed in a malevolent stare, and his mouth in a snarl of hatred.

'I have fulfilled my duty,' Mansur whispered. 'Perhaps now my mother's shade can find peace.' He prodded the mutilated corpse with his foot. 'As for you, Kadem ibn Abubaker, half your flesh is in the belly of the beast. You can never find peace. May your suffering last through all eternity.'

He turned away and looked out to sea. The battle was almost over. Three of the war-dhows had been captured, and the blue banners of al-Salil flew at their mastheads. The wreckage of one more was mingled with that of the transports, being battered to kindling in the surf. *Arcturus* was pursuing the remaining war-dhow out to sea, and her cannons boomed out as she overtook it. The *Revenge* was following the fleeing transports, but they were already scattered over a wide swathe of ocean.

Then he saw the *Sprite* hovering off the mouth of the river, and waved to it. He knew good, faithful Kumrah was searching for him, and that even from this distance he would recognize the colour of his hair. Almost at once he was proved right as he saw the *Sprite* lower a boat and send it in through the surf to pick him up. His vision was still blurred, but he thought he recognized Kumrah himself in the bows.

Mansur looked from the approaching boat back along the beach. Thrown upon the sands, scattered over a mile at the water's edge, were the carcasses of drowned men and horses from the destroyed dhows. Some of the enemy had survived. Men squatted singly or stood in small disconsolate groups along the shore, but it was clear that there was no fight left in them. Stray horses wandered about at the edge of the jungle.

He had lost his dagger in the surf. He felt utterly vulnerable, half blind, naked and unarmed. Trying to ignore the pain in his eye, Mansur ran to one of the nearest corpses. It still wore a short robe and a weapon was strapped around its waist. Mansur stripped off these pathetic relics and pulled the robe over his head. Then he drew the scimitar from its sheath and tested the blade. It was of fine Damascus steel. To test the edge he shaved a few hairs from his wrist before he ran the blade back into its scabbard. For the first time he became aware of a distant hubbub of voices. These came from the depths of the vegetation above the beach.

It's not over yet! he realized. Just then a rabble of running men burst out of the jungle. They were almost a furlong further up the beach, between him and the river mouth, but he saw that they were a mixed bunch of Arabs and Turks. They were being driven down towards the water's edge by a pack of Beshwayo's warriors. The stabbing spears flashed, then were buried in living flesh, and the triumphant shouts of the warriors mingled with the screams and desperate cries of the enemy.

'*Ngi dhla!* I have eaten!'

Mansur realized the fresh danger he was in. Beshwayo's forces were in a killing frenzy. None would recognize him as friendly: he was just another pale, bearded face and they would stab him with as much glee as they would any one of the Omani.

The wet sand along the edge of the water was hard and compacted. He ran along it towards the river mouth. The Arab survivors of the battle realized they were being driven into the sea and they turned at bay. In a last bitter stand they faced Beshwayo's men. There was only a narrow gap behind them but Mansur raced through it, although the pain in his eye made him grunt at each pace. He was almost clear, and the boat from the *Sprite* was through the surf and into the calm water. It would be on the beach before he reached it.

Then there was a shout behind him and he glanced back. Three of the black warriors had spotted him. They had left the surrounded Arabs to their comrades, and they were racing after him, yelping with excitement, hounds on the scent of the hare.

From ahead there were shouts of encouragement: 'We are here, Highness. Run, in the Name of God!' He recognized the voice and saw Kumrah in the bows of the boat.

Mansur ran, but his ordeal in the surf and the agony in his eye weakened him, and he could hear bare feet slapping on the wet sand close behind him. He could almost feel the glide of the steel through his flesh as an *assegai* stabbed between his shoulder-blades. Kumrah, in the boat, was thirty paces ahead, but that might just as well have been thirty leagues. He could hear the hoarse breathing of one man close behind his shoulder. He had to turn to face them and defend himself. He drew the scimitar from its scabbard and spun round.

The leading warrior was so close that he had already drawn back his *assegai*, low underhand, for the killing stroke. But with Mansur at bay he checked his rush, and called softly to his two companions, 'The horns of the bull!' This was their favourite tactic. They fanned out on each side of him, and in that instant Mansur was surrounded. Whichever way he turned his back would be exposed to a long blade. He knew he was a dead man, but he rushed at the man before him. Before he could cross blades with him he heard Kumrah shout behind him: 'Down, Highness!' Mansur did not hesitate but threw himself flat on the sand.

His adversary stood over him and lifted the *assegai* high. '*Ngi dhla!*' he screamed.

Beshwayo's men had not yet realized the effects of close-range musketry. Before the warrior could make the stroke, a volley of musket fire swept over where Mansur lay. A ball hit the warrior in his elbow and his arm broke like a green twig. The *assegai* flew from his grip and he reeled back as another ball slapped into his chest. Mansur rolled over swiftly to face the other two warriors but one was on his knees clutching his belly and the other was on his back, kicking convulsively, half his head shot away.

'Come, Prince Mansur!' Kumrah called, through the veil of gunsmoke that had enveloped the boat. It blew aside, and Mansur saw that every man of the crew had fired the volley that had saved him. He dragged himself to his feet and staggered to the boat. Now that mortal danger was past he lacked the strength to pull himself over the gunwale, but many strong hands reached out for him.

Tom and Dorian had knelt side by side in the gun emplacement and rested their telescopes on the parapet. They studied Zayn's squadron of ships, which were anchored in a group below the walls of the fort on the far side of the bay and bombarding the walls.

Dorian had sited the long nine-pounder cannons with great care. From this height they could bring every part of the bay under fire. Once it came through the entrance no ship was safe from them. It had been a Herculean task to get the guns up to this eyrie. The sides of the bluff were too high and steep, and the guns too heavy, to lift them straight up from the shore.

Tom had cut a track through the thick forest along the

rising spine of the ridge and, using this as a ramp, he had dragged the guns up with teams of oxen until they were directly above the chosen site. Then, on heavy anchor cable, he lowered them down into the concealed emplacements. Once the guns were sited they ranged them on targets set up around the shore of the bay. Their first shots had flown far over and crashed into the forest beyond.

Once they were satisfied with the position of the guns, they built the charcoal furnace fifty paces from the powder magazine to reduce the danger of sparks flying from one to the other. They plastered the furnace with river clay. They made the bellows with fifty tanned ox hides, sealing the seams with tar. A gang of cooks, labourers and riff-raff worked the handles to force air into the furnace. Once it reached full blast, it was not possible to look with the naked eye into the white-hot glare of the interior so Dorian had smoked a sheet of glass with the flame of an oil lamp: peering through this, they could judge when the shot was hot enough. Then they manhandled each cannon ball out of the furnace with long-handled tongs. The men doing the job wore thick leather mittens and aprons to protect them from the heat. They dropped each glowing ball into a specially prepared cradle, with long handles. These were carried by two men across to the gun, which was waiting with its barrel raised to the maximum possible elevation.

Once the ball was dropped down the muzzle, it was not long before it burned away the wet wads and spontaneously ignited the powder charge behind them. A premature discharge while the barrel was pointed skywards would tear it off its carriage, wreck the gun emplacement and kill or maim the gun-crews. This allowed only the briefest respite to lay the gun on its target and fire it. Then the whole dangerous, lengthy process had to be repeated. After a few shots the barrel overheated until it was on the point of bursting and the recoil was monstrous; it had to be sponged out and buckets of sea-water poured down the sizzling muzzle before they dared ram a fresh charge of powder into it.

Over the previous weeks, while they awaited the arrival of Zayn al-Din's fleet, Dorian had instructed and exercised the

739

gunners in handling hot shot. They had encountered all these complications for themselves and learned by hard experience, which culminated with the explosion of one of the guns. Two men had been killed by flying fragments of the bronze barrel. All of the crews now had a deep respect for the glowing cannon-balls, and none was looking forward to firing the remaining three weapons in earnest.

The foreman had come from the furnace to report to Dorian with an expression of awe and dread: 'We have twelve balls ready, mighty Caliph.'

'You have done well, Farmat, but I am not yet ready to open fire. Keep the furnaces hot.' He and Tom turned back to continue their surveillance of the action taking place below them. The bombardment from Zayn's ships covered the whole bay and the edges of the forest with smoke, but through it they saw the defenders abandon the fort and run out through the gates.

'Good!' said Dorian, with satisfaction. 'They have remembered their orders.' He had ordered a token defence of the fort merely to lure Zayn's fleet deep into the bay.

'I hope they remembered to spike the guns on the parapets before they left,' Tom growled. 'I do not fancy them being turned on us.'

The bombardment died away, and they watched the boats filled with the assault party leave the war-dhows and head in for the beach, to occupy the deserted fort. Both Tom and Dorian recognized Guy Courtney in the bows of the leading boat.

'His Britannic Majesty's honourable consul general in the flesh!' Dorian exclaimed. 'The scent of the gold was too strong for him to ignore. He has come in person to retrieve it.'

'My beloved twin brother!' Tom agreed. 'It does my heart good to see him again after all these years. When we last parted he was trying to kill me. It seems that things have changed not at all since then.'

'It will not take him long to find that the cupboard is bare,' Dorian said, 'so now it is time to slam the door shut behind them.' He called to the runner who waited eagerly at the back of the redoubt for just this summons. He was one of Sarah's orphans, and he rushed forward grinning widely and trembling with eagerness to please. 'Go down to Smallboy, and tell him it is time to close the gate.' Dorian had barely finished speaking before the boy had jumped over the wall and was racing down the steep pathway. Dorian had to shout after him, 'Don't let them see you!'

Smallboy and Muntu waited with the teams of oxen already hitched to the heavy anchor cable. This was strung out across the entrance of the bay to the heavy piles of logs on the far bank. The slack cable was weighted to lie on the bottom of the channel until pulled taut. The war-dhows had sailed in over it without being aware of its presence under their keels.

The boom was made up of seventy huge logs. Many had been felled the previous year and stacked in the sawmill yard at the back of the fort, ready to be sawn into planks. Even with this stockpile, they were still short of twenty logs to span the channel.

Jim and Mansur had taken every available man into the forest to cut down more of the giant trees, and Smallboy's ox teams had dragged them to the beach. There, they had bolted them lengthwise to the spare anchor cable that they had lifted out of *Arcturus*'s orlop. The cable was almost twenty inches in diameter and had a test strain of over thirty tons. The logs, some of them three feet in diameter and forty feet in length, were strung along this massive hemp rope like pearls on a necklace. They would form a barricade that Tom and Dorian calculated would resist the onslaught of even the largest of Zayn's dhows. The heavy line of logs would tear out a ship's bottom before it could break through.

As soon as Zayn's fleet was sighted from the top of the bluff Smallboy and Muntu inspanned the ox teams and led them round to the south bank of the entrance channel. They kept the teams hidden in the dense bush, and watched the five big dhows sail past within easy pistol shot of where they lay. When the messenger lad had come racing down from the gun emplacements with the order from Dorian, he was so out of breath and wild with excitement that he was incoherent. Smallboy had to grab him by the shoulders and shake him. 'Master Klebe says to close the gate!' the child had squeaked.

Smallboy fired his long whiplash and the ox teams took the strain, then plodded away with the end of the boom cable. As it came up taut, the cable rose to the surface of the channel and the oxen had to lean into the traces. The line of logs answered the pull. They slithered down the far bank from where they had been stacked, and snaked across the channel. The head of the boom reached the north side of the channel, and Smallboy chained it fast to the trunk of a huge tambootie hardwood. The mouth of the bay was corked up tightly.

Tom and Dorian had watched as Guy led his shore party at a rush through the gates of the captured fort and disappeared from their view. Then they turned their telescopes on the entrance to the bay and saw the massive cable rise to the surface of the channel as the oxen drew it tight.

'We can load the first gun,' Dorian told his gunners, who responded without marked enthusiasm. The gun captain relayed the order to the foreman in charge of the furnace. It was a lengthy business to fish the first shot from the furnace, and while they waited Tom kept a watch on the enemy.

Suddenly he called to Dorian. 'Guy is back on the parapet of the fort. He must have discovered the epistle I left for him in the treasury.' He chuckled aloud. 'Even from this distance I can see he's fit to burst with rage.' Then his expression changed. 'Now what's the crafty swine up to? He is heading back to the beach. He is saddling up the horses that have come ashore. There is some kind of fracas. By God! You will not believe this, Dorry. Guy has shot one of his own men.' The distant pop of the pistol shot carried to them on the heights, and Dorian left the cannon to join Tom.

'He has mounted.'

'He is taking at least twenty men with him.'

'Where in the name of the devil is he going?'

They watched the troop of horsemen, with Guy at the head, set out along the wagon road. It dawned on both Tom and Dorian at the same moment.

'He has seen the wagon tracks.'

'He is going after the wagons and the gold.'

'The women and little George! They are with the wagons. If Guy catches them—' Tom broke off. The thought was too painful to express. Then he went on bitterly, 'I blame myself. I should have considered this possibility. Guy does not give up readily.'

'The wagons have had a start of many days. They will be leagues away by now.'

'Only twenty miles,' Tom said bitterly. 'I told them to go as far as the river gorge, and make laager there.'

'It's my fault more than yours,' said Dorian. 'The safety of the women should have been my first concern. What a fool I am.'

'I must go after them.' Tom jumped to his feet. 'I must stop them falling into Guy's clutches.'

'I will ride with you.' Dorian stood up beside him.

'No, no!' Tom shoved him back. 'The battle is in your hands. Without you all is lost. You cannot desert your command. That goes for Jim and Mansur too. They must not come rushing after me. I can take care of brother Guy without their help. You must keep the lads here with you until the job is done. Give me your word on it, Dorry.'

'Very well. But you must take Smallboy and his musketeers with you. By the time you reach them, their job with the boom will be done.' He slapped Tom on the shoulder. 'Ride for all you are worth, and God go with you every step of the way.' Tom sprang over the bank of the gun emplacement and ran to where the horses were tethered.

As Tom galloped away down the track, two men came staggering from the furnace. They carried between them by its long handles the cradle on which lay the cannon-ball red as a ripe apple. Dorian could spare only one more quick glance after his elder brother, then hurried to supervise the gunners as they began the dangerous task of coaxing the ball into the muzzle of the gun. As it rolled down the smooth bore, two gunners rodded it up hard against the wet wadding and it sizzled and hissed. Clouds of steam poured out of the muzzle as they lowered the barrel.

Dorian wound down the elevation screw himself, trusting no other with this precise adjustment. Two other men with crowbars levered the barrel, traversing it as Dorian called to them, 'Left, and a hair more left!' Then, satisfied that the largest enemy dhow lay exactly in his sights, Dorian yelled, 'Stand clear!' and seized the lanyard. The gun-crew responded to his command with alacrity. Dorian yanked the lanyard, and the huge gun leaped like a wild animal charging the bars of its cage.

They could all follow the flight of the sparkling ball as it arced out across the waters of the bay, then fell towards the anchored dhow. A ragged cheer went up as they thought it must strike, then turned into a groan of disappointment as a tall white fountain jumped up close alongside the dhow's hull.

'Wet her down well!' Dorian had ordered. 'You have seen what will happen if you do not.'

He scrambled out of the emplacement and ran to the second gun. Already the next ball was being carried from the furnace and the crew was waiting for him. Before they could load and lay the gun, the five vessels had fled their moorings and were headed back across the bay towards the channel. Dorian peered over the sights. He had marked the angles of elevation in white paint on the gauge, and the men on the crow-bars nudged the long barrel round. He fired.

This time there was a roar of triumph from every man on

the hill as, even from this range, they saw the shower of bright sparks as the ball struck the hull of one of the dhows and the shot ripped through her timbers. Dorian ran to the third gun, leaving the crews of the other two sponging out. By the time they had loaded again, the stricken dhow was blazing like a bonfire on Guy Fawkes night.

'They are trying to break through the boom!' one of the men shouted, as they saw the burning ship steer into the entrance channel and, without checking its speed, bear down on the line of floating logs. They cheered again as it struck the boom, the mast tumbled down and the fire spread through her. Her crew leaped over the sides.

Dorian was bathed in sweat as he worked over the guns, loading and laying. Even though the crews doused them with buckets of water, the metal still crackled like a frying pan, and at each successive shot the guns leaped more violently on their carriages. However, within the next hour they fired another twenty hot balls, and four of the dhows were ablaze. The vessel that had struck the boom had burned down to the waterline, another drifted aimlessly across the bay, abandoned by her crew, who had rowed ashore in the boats. Two more had been beached and the crews had abandoned them to burn while they escaped into the forest, all too aware that the ships' magazines were crammed with kegs of black powder. Only the largest dhow had so far escaped the fire Dorian aimed at it. But it was locked into the bay, and could only tack back and forth across the open water.

'You can't dodge me for ever,' Dorian muttered. As the next ball was carried from the furnace, he spat on it for luck. The globule of saliva hit the heated metal and disappeared in a puff of steam, and at the same moment a huge shockwave of hot air blew across the hillside. It thumped painfully into their eardrums, and every man stared down into the bay in awe.

The drifting dhow had blown up as the powder in her magazine ignited. A tall mushroom-shaped cloud of smoke boiled up into the sky until it reached higher than the hilltop. Then, as if in sympathy, one of the beached dhows blew up with even greater force. The blast tore across the bay and lifted creaming waves from the surface. It raced through the forest above the beach, flattening the smaller trees, tearing off branches from the larger trees, raising a storm of dust, leaves and twigs. The men who watched it were struck dumb by the extent of the damage they had created. They did not cheer again but stood and gaped.

'One more left.' Dorian broke the spell. 'There she is, pretty as a bride on her wedding day.' He pointed down at the big dhow as she came about and started back towards the beach below the fort.

The cradle men lifted the ball, smoking and crackling, to roll it into the muzzle of the gun. Before they could do so another shout went up from every man: 'She is scuttling herself. Praise God and his angels, the enemy has had enough.'

The captain of the remaining dhow had seen the fate of the rest of the squadron. He made no effort to tack again but bore straight down on the sloping beach. At the last moment the dhow dropped her sail and went aground with such force that they heard her belly timbers snapping. She canted over heavily and lay quiescent, transformed in the instant from a thing of grace to a broken hulk. Her crew swarmed out of her, and left her lying abandoned at the water's edge.

'Enough!' Dorian called to his men. 'We have no more need of that.' With obvious relief they tipped the hot ball out on to the earth. Dorian scooped a ladleful from one of the buckets of drinking water and poured it over his head, then wiped his streaming face in the crook of his arm.

'Behold!' screamed the foreman of the furnace and pointed down. Immediately there was an excited clamour from the gun-crews, as they recognized the tall figure in cloud-white robes who clambered down from the stranded dhow and, with his distinctive limp, led his men along the beach towards the fort.

'Zayn al-Din!' they shouted.

'Death and damnation to the tyrant!'

'Power and glory to al-Salil.'

'God has given us the victory. God is great.'

'No.' Dorian jumped to the top of the emplacement wall

where they could all see him. 'The victory is not ours yet. Like a wounded jackal into his hole, Zayn al-Din has taken refuge in the fort.'

They saw the enemy seamen who had escaped from the other ships creep out of the forest, then hurry more boldly after Zayn al-Din. They streamed into the deserted fort after him.

'We must smoke him out,' Dorian told them, and jumped down from the wall. He called his gun captains to him and gave them swift orders. 'No more need for heated shot. Use only cold balls, but keep up a lively fire on the walls of the fort. Give them no rest. I am going down to round up all our men and lay siege to the fort. They have no food or water. We left no powder in the magazine, and the guns on the parapets have been spiked. Zayn cannot hold out for more than a day or two.'

A groom had already saddled his horse and Dorian rode down with every man who could be spared from the guns trooping after him. The men who had put up the token defence of the fort were waiting at the bottom of the hill to swell his ranks. He sent them to surround the building and make certain that none of the enemy could escape.

He saw Muntu coming through the forest from the direction of the entrance channel, and rode to meet him. 'Where is Smallboy?'

'He has taken ten men and gone with Klebe to follow the wagons.'

'Have you opened the boom, so that our ships can re-enter the bay?'

'Yes, master. The channel is clear.' Dorian lifted his telescope and checked the entrance. He saw that Muntu had severed the cable and the current had pushed the boom aside.

'Well done, Muntu. Now take your oxen.' He pointed down the shore to where Zayn's dhow lay stranded. 'Get the cannon out of that ship, and drag them round to cover the fort. We will pound the enemy from all sides. Knock a breach through the walls, so that when Jim arrives with Beshwayo's *impis* they can storm in and finish the business.'

By late afternoon the captured cannons from the stranded dhow had been towed by the oxen into position and the first shots knocked clods of earth and shattered timbers from the walls of the fort. They kept up the bombardment all night, giving the besieged enemy no rest.

In the dawn the *Sprite* sailed into the bay through the channel. She was followed by the *Arcturus* and the *Revenge*, shepherding all the captured Omani dhows and transports ahead of them. The warships anchored, and immediately turned all their guns on the fort. The three long nine-pounders on the heights of the bluff and the captured carronades from Zayn's own ships were already hammering away. Between them they directed a withering fire on the fort.

No sooner had the *Revenge* dropped her anchor than Mansur came ashore. Dorian was waiting to greet him on the beach, and ran forward when he saw his son's head swathed in the bandage. He embraced him and asked anxiously, 'You are hurt. How badly?'

'A scratch on my eyeball.' Mansur shrugged it off. 'It is almost healed. But Kadem, who inflicted the injury, is dead.'

'How did he die?' Dorian demanded, holding him at arm's length and staring into his face.

'By the knife. The same way that he murdered my mother.'

'You killed him?'

'Yes, Father. I killed him, and he did not die an easy death. My mother is avenged.'

'No, my son. There is still another. Zayn al-Din is holding out within the fort.'

'Can we be certain he is in there? Have you seen him with your own eyes?' They both stared along the shore at the battered palisades of the building. They could make out the heads of a few doughty defenders behind the parapets. However, Zayn had no artillery and most of his men were crouching behind the walls. The thudding of their muskets was a feeble response to the thunder of the cannon.

'Yes, Mansur. I have seen him. I will not leave this place until he also has paid the price in full, and gone to join his minion Kadem ibn Abubaker in hell.'

They both became aware of a new sound, faint at first but growing louder with every minute. Half a mile down the shores of the bay a dense column of men trotted out of the forest. They ran in a precise military formation. Like the foam on the crest of a dark wave, their feather headdresses danced in rhythm to their step. The early sunlight sparkled on their *assegais*, and on their oiled torsos. They were singing, a deep warlike chant that thrilled the blood and rumbled across the top of the forest. A lone horseman rode at the head of the leading column. He was mounted on a dark stallion whose long mane and tail streamed back in the wind of his canter.

'Jim on Drumfire.' Mansur laughed. 'Thank God he's safe.' A diminutive figure ran beside one of Jim's stirrups, and beside the other a giant of a man.

'Bakkat and Beshwayo,' said Dorian. Mansur ran to meet Jim, who swung down from the saddle and took him in a bear-hug.

'What is this rag you wear, coz? Is it some new fashion you have struck upon? It suits you not at all, you should take my word on it.' Then he turned to Dorian with his arm still around Mansur's shoulder.

'Uncle Dorry, where is my father?' His expression changed to dread. 'He is not hurt or killed? Tell me, I beg of you.'

'Nay, Jim lad. Breathe easy. Our Tom is impervious to shot and steel. As soon as his work here was done, he went to take care of the women and little Georgie.'

Dorian knew that if he told them the full truth about Guy's intervention, he would not be able to fulfil his promise to Tom and keep the boys with him. They would rush off immediately to defend their womenfolk. Quickly he glossed over his deception. 'But what of your side of the battle?'

'It is over, Uncle Dorry. Herminius Koots, who commanded the enemy, is dead. I saw to that myself. Beshwayo's men have cleared the forests of the rest of them. The pursuit took all of yesterday and most of the night. They chased some of the Turks a league up the beach and over the hills before they caught up with them.'

'Where are the prisoners?' Dorian demanded.

'Beshwayo does not understand the meaning of that word, and I was unable to educate him.' Jim laughed. But Dorian did not laugh with him: he could imagine the slaughter that had taken place in the forest, and his conscience troubled him. Those Omani who had perished under the *assegais* were his own subjects. He could not rejoice in their deaths. His anger towards Zayn al-Din flared even higher. Here was more blood for which he must pay.

Jim did not notice his uncle's expression. He was still buoyed up by the wild excitement of battle and intoxicated with the taste of victory. 'Look at him now.' He pointed to where Beshwayo was already parading his *impis* before the walls of the fort.

The guns had knocked a wide breach through them and Beshwayo strode down the ranks, stabbing his *assegai* towards the breach and haranguing his warriors: 'My children, some of you have not yet earned the right of marriage. Did I not give you opportunity enough? Were you slow? Were you unlucky?' He paused and glared at them. 'Or were you afraid? Did you piss down your own legs when you saw the feast I laid for you?'

His *impis* shouted an angry denial. 'We are thirsty still. We hunger still.'

'Give us to eat and drink again, Great Black Bull.'

'We are your faithful hunting dogs. Let us slip, great king. Let us run!' they pleaded.

'Before Beshwayo can send in an *impi* through the breach,' Jim said to Dorian, 'you must order the batteries to cease firing so as not to endanger his men.'

Dorian sent his runners out to the gun captains with the order. One after the other the batteries ceased firing. It took the message longer to reach the three guns on the heights of the bluff, but at last a tense, heavy silence fell over the bay.

The only movement was the waving of the feather head-dresses of the Beshwayo. The Arab defenders on the parapets looked down on this array, poised so menacingly before their walls, and their desultory musket-fire dried up. They stared bleakly upon implacable death.

Then, abruptly, a ram's-horn trumpet blared out from the walls of the fort. The ranks of black warriors stirred restlessly. Dorian turned his telescope to see a flag waved from the parapets.

'Surrender?' Jim smiled. 'Beshwayo does not understand that word either. A white flag will not save one of the men inside those walls.'

'Not a surrender.' Dorian shut his telescope. 'I know the man waving that flag. His name is Rahmad. He is one of the Omani admirals, a good sailor and a brave man. He was not able to choose the master he serves. He will not cravenly surrender. He wants to parley.'

Jim shook his head impatiently. 'I cannot keep Beshwayo in check much longer. What is there to speak about?'

'I intend to find out,' Dorian said.

'By God, Uncle! You cannot trust Zayn al-Din. This might be a trap.'

'Jim is right, Father,' cried Mansur. 'Don't give yourself into Zayn's power.'

'I must speak to Rahmad, if there is some small chance that I can end the bloodshed now and save the lives of those wretches trapped within the walls.'

'Then I must go with you,' said Jim.

'I also.' Mansur stepped up beside him.

Dorian's expression softened and he placed a hand on each of their shoulders. 'Stay here, both of you. I will need someone to avenge me, if things go awry.' He dropped his hands and loosened his sword-belt. He handed the weapon to Mansur. 'Keep this for me.' Then he looked at Jim: 'Can you hold your friend Beshwayo and his hunting hounds on a leash for just a little longer?'

'Be quick, Uncle. Beshwayo is not famous for his forbearance. I know not how long I can hold him.' Jim went with Dorian to where Beshwayo stood at the front of his *impis*, and spoke to him earnestly. At last Beshwayo grunted reluctantly, and Jim told Dorian, 'Beshwayo agrees to wait until you return.'

Dorian strode through the ranks of the Beshwayo *impis*. They opened before him, for those warriors recognized the quality of nobility in him. Dorian's step was measured and stately as he strode towards the walls and stopped within easy pistol shot. He looked up at the figure on the parapet.

'Speak, Rahmad!' he ordered.

'You remember me?' Rahmad sounded amazed.

'I know you well. I would not have trusted you otherwise. You are a man of honour.'

'Majesty!' Rahmad bowed deeply. 'Mighty Caliph.'

'If you address me thus, why do you fight against me?'

Rahmad seemed for a moment overcome with shame. Then he raised his head. 'I speak not only for myself but for every man within these walls.'

Dorian raised his hand to stop him. 'This is strange, Rahmad. You speak for the men? You do not speak for Zayn al-Din? Explain this to me.'

'Mighty al-Salil, Zayn al-Din is . . .' Rahmad seemed to search for the right words. 'We have requested Zayn al-Din to demonstrate to us and all the world that he, not you, is indeed the Caliph of Oman.'

'In what way can he prove this?'

'In the traditional manner, when two men have an equal claim to the throne. In the sight of God, and before all this array, man to man in single combat, we have requested Zayn al-Din to fight to the death to prove that claim.'

'You propose a duel between us?'

'We have taken an oath of allegiance to Zayn al-Din. We cannot surrender his person to you. We are bound to defend him with our own lives. However, if he were defeated in a traditional duel, we would be released from our vow. Gladly then we would become your liege men.'

Dorian understood their dilemma. They were holding Zayn al-Din prisoner, but they were unable to execute him or hand him over. He must kill Zayn himself in single combat. The alternative would be for him to allow the Beshwayo to slaughter Rahmad and all the Omani.

'Why should I place myself in such peril? You and Zayn al-Din are in my power.' Dorian pointed at the black ranks of Beshwayo. 'Why should I not send them in to massacre you all here and now?'

'A lesser man might do that. I know you will not, for you are the son of Sultan Abd Muhammad al-Malik. You will not desecrate our honour, or your own.'

'What you say is true, Rahmad. It is my destiny to unite the kingdom of Oman, not split it asunder. I must take up that destiny with honour. I will fight Zayn al-Din for the caliphate.'

With white ash the Omani elders and headmen marked out the duelling ring on the hard-baked ground below the walls of the fort. This was a circle twenty paces in diameter.

All the Arabs who had fought with Zayn al-Din and been trapped within the fort now lined the parapets. Dorian's forces, including the crews from the captured dhows who had declared their loyalty to him, were drawn up on the bayside of the ring, facing the opposing forces on the walls of the fort.

Jim had explained the rules and the object of the duel to Beshwayo, and he was enthralled. He no longer resented being deprived of the right to storm the fort and wipe out the defenders. For him this gladiatorial contest was even greater sport.

'This is a fine way to solve a dispute, Somoya. It is truly a warrior's thing. I shall make it my own custom in the future.'

The entire Beshwayo army squatted in ranks behind Dorian's legions. The high parapet and the slope of the ground afforded every man present an unobstructed view of the ring.

Dorian, flanked by Jim and Mansur, stood at the forefront

of this array, facing the closed gates of the fort. He wore only a simple white robe and his feet were bare. In accordance with the rules of the contest he was unarmed.

There was another blast on the ram's horn and the gates of the fort swung open. Four men marched out and came down the hill. They were in half-armour, bronze helmets and chain-mail overshirts, with greaves protecting their lower legs. They were big men with cold eyes and brutal faces, the executioners of the Omani court. Torture and death were their vocation. They took up their positions at the four points of the circle, and leaned on the hilts of their drawn swords.

There was a pause and then another trumpet blast. A second procession came down the slope. It was led by Mullah Khaliq. Behind him came Rahmad and four other tribal headmen. Then, with an escort of five armed men, the tall figure of Zayn al-Din limped after them. They stopped on the far side of the ring, facing Dorian.

Rahmad advanced into the centre of the ring. 'In the Name of the One God and his True Prophet we are met here this day to decide the fate of our nation. Al-Salil!' He bowed towards Dorian. 'And Zayn al-Din.' He turned and bowed again. 'This day one of you will die and the other will ascend the Elephant Throne of Oman.'

He held out his hands and the two headmen who flanked him passed Rahmad a pair of scimitars. Rahmad stabbed the point of one of these weapons into the earth just inside the ash line of the ring, and left it standing upright. Then he crossed the circle and placed the other weapon exactly opposite it.

'Only one of you will be permitted to leave this ring alive. The four referees,' he pointed to the waiting executioners, 'have been strictly charged with the duty of killing immediately whichever of you is driven or thrown outside this line of ashes.' He touched the line with the toe of his sandal. 'Now Mullah Khaliq will lead the prayers begging for the guidance of God in these affairs.'

The holy man's voice droned in the silence as he commended the combatants to God and their fate. Dorian and

Zayn stared across the ring at each other. Their faces were expressionless but their eyes burned with hatred and anger. The mullah ended his prayer: 'In God's Name let it begin!'

'In God's Name, make ready!' Rahmad called.

Jim and Mansur lifted the loose robe over Dorian's head. He wore only a white loincloth under it. Where the sun had not touched him his skin was smooth and white as cream in a jug. At the same time his escort helped Zayn remove his robe. Now he wore only a loincloth, and his skin was the colour of old ivory. Dorian knew that Zayn was his senior by only two years. They were both in their middle forties, and the effects of age were becoming apparent on their bodies. There were streaks of grey in their hair and beards, and a fleshiness round their waistlines. However, their limbs were clean and hard and their movements were lithe as they stepped into the ring. Even the impediment in Zayn's step seemed more sinister than inhibiting. They were matched in height but Zayn was the heavier man, bigger boned and wider in the shoulder. Since childhood both had been trained in the warrior's way, but they had matched against each other once only before this day. However, they had been children then, and they and the world about them were altered.

They stood just out of arm's reach of each other. Neither spoke, but they assessed each other carefully. Rahmad stepped between them. He carried a length of silken cord, light as gossamer and strong as steel. He had measured its length and cut it precisely five paces shorter than the diameter of the ring.

Rahmad went to Zayn first. Though he knew full well that he was left-handed, Rahmad asked formally, 'Which hand?'

Disdaining a reply Zayn proffered his right hand. Rahmad tied the end of the cord round his wrist. He was a sailor and the knot would neither tighten nor slip, yet it would hold like a steel cuff. Rahmad came to Dorian with the other end of the cord. Dorian gave him his left hand and he tied it with the same type of knot. The two combatants were linked together: only the death of one could part them now.

'Mark your swords!' Rahmad ordered them, and they

glanced back at the scimitar that stood behind each man on the perimeter of the ring. The silk cord was too short to allow them simultaneously to reach a weapon.

'A blast on the ram's horn will begin this contest, but only death will end it,' intoned Rahmad. He and the four headmen left the ring. A terrible silence descended on the field. Even the breeze seemed to still, and the gulls ceased their mewing cries. Rahmad looked to the trumpeter on the parapet and raised his hand. The trumpeter lifted the curled horn to his lips. Rahmad dropped his hand and the blast sobbed and echoed off the cliffs of the bluff. A huge wave of sound swept over the ring as every man in the convocation shouted together.

Neither contestant moved. They faced each other still, leaning back on the cord, keeping it taut, taking the strain, assessing each other's weight and strength, the way a fisherman feels a heavy fish after the strike. Neither could reach his scimitar unless he could force the other to give ground. They strained silently. Suddenly Dorian darted forward, and Zayn reeled back as the cord went slack. Then he whirled and ran for his sword. Grimly Dorian noted the slight clumsiness as he turned into his crippled side. Dorian ran after him and gathered in a double arm's length of the slack in the cord. He gained the centre of the ring, and shortened the length of cord between them by almost half. From this position he dominated the ring, but he had sacrificed precious ground for that. Zayn was reaching out for the hilt of his scimitar. Dorian took a turn of the cord round his wrist and planted his feet. He anchored the cord and Zayn came up hard against the end of it with such force that it snapped him round on to his bad side. For a moment he was off-balance and Dorian heaved him backwards and gained another arm's length of the cord.

Abruptly Dorian changed the angle of his pull. He made himself the fulcrum around which Zayn pivoted. Like the stone on the end of a slingshot, Dorian used the impetus to launch Zayn towards the white ash line, straight at one of the executioners who waited with drawn sword to meet him. As it seemed he must be hurled backwards out of the ring, Zayn found purchase with his stronger leg and checked the slingshot effect. He teetered on the line and raised a puff of white ash, but he managed to stop himself going out. The executioner stood behind him with the blade raised to make the stroke. Now there was slack in the cord and Dorian had lost the leverage. He raced forward to crash into Zayn with his shoulder and drive him that last yard across the line. Zayn saw him coming, braced his legs and dropped his shoulder to meet him.

They came together with a force that jarred every bone in their bodies, and stood like a carving in marble, straining and grunting. Dorian had the heel of his right hand under Zayn's chin and forced his head back. Slowly Zayn's spine arched over the line, and the executioner moved forward a pace to meet him as he stepped over it. Zayn drew a hissing breath and summoned the last vestige of his strength. His face seemed to darken and swell with the effort, but slowly his back straightened. He pushed Dorian back a step.

The noise was deafening. A thousand voices joined in, and the Beshwayo warriors were dancing and drumming on their shields. A hurricane of sound swept over the ring. Zayn exerted his greater weight and gradually worked his shoulder down under Dorian's armpit, then suddenly heaved upwards. He took the weight off Dorian's legs and forced him to lose traction and grip. The bare soles of his feet skidded in the dust, and he was driven back a yard, then another. Dorian was pitting all his strength against Zayn's thrust. Abruptly Zayn jumped back. Dorian staggered forward off-balance. Swift as a lizard on his crippled foot Zayn darted away, straight back to where his sword was pegged into the earth.

Dorian tried to snatch up the slack in the cord to restrain him again, but before he could bring it tight Zayn had reached the weapon and had a firm grip on the hilt. Dorian jerked him backwards, but Zayn came willingly, rushing at him with the point of the blade levelled at Dorian's throat. Dorian ducked under it and they circled each other. They were still linked by the umbilical cord of silk.

Zayn was laughing silently, but it was a sound without joy.

He mock-charged at Dorian, forcing him to dodge back, and as soon as he had made slack in the cord for the move Zayn darted to where Dorian's scimitar was still standing at the far end of the circle. Before Dorian could bring the rope tight, Zayn had grabbed the second weapon out of the ground. Now he turned to face Dorian with a blade in each hand.

A silence fell over the multitude and they watched in awful fascination as Zayn stalked Dorian round the ring, while the executioners shadowed him from behind, waiting for him to step out of the ash circle. Watching him carefully, Dorian realized that though he favoured his left hand Zayn was almost as dexterous with his right. As if to demonstrate this he rushed forward and cut right-handed at Dorian's head. When Dorian ducked out of the stroke he thrust with his left and Dorian could not avoid it. Although he twisted aside, the point scored his ribs and the crowd howled to see blood spurt.

Mansur clutched at Jim's arm with such strength that his fingernails cut through the skin. 'He is hurt. We must stop it.'

'No, coz,' Jim said softly. 'We cannot intervene.'

The pair in the ring kept turning, as though the cord that linked them was a spoke of a wheel. Dorian still held the slack of the line between his hands.

Zayn was quivering with eagerness for the kill, his mouth working, his eyes burning darkly. 'Bleed, pig, and when you have shed your last drop, I will hack your carcass into fifty pieces and send each bit to the furthest corners of my empire so that all men will know the penalty for treachery.'

Dorian did not reply. He held his end of the cord lightly in the fingers of his right hand. With total concentration he watched Zayn's eyes for the signal that he would charge again. Zayn feigned a move with his bad leg, then sprang forward off his strong side. It was exactly what Dorian had anticipated. He flicked out the bight in the cord, and then, with a snap of his wrist, shot the loop forward like a whiplash. The silk cord slashed across Zayn's right eye with such force that the blood vessels burst, the pupil and the cornea shattered, and in an instant the eyeball was transformed into a fragile pink sack of jelly.

Zayn screamed, high-pitched and shrill as a girl. He dropped both swords and cupped his hands over his injured eye. He stood blind and shrieking in the centre of the ring. Dorian stooped and picked up one of the scimitars. As he came upright again, as gracefully as a dancer, he drove the point into Zayn's belly.

The shriek was cut off from Zayn's lips. One hand was still clasped over his eye but with the other hand he groped down and found the gaping wound in his guts from which blood, intestinal gas and detritus bubbled. He sank forward on to his knees and bowed his head. His neck was stretched forward. Dorian raised the scimitar on high, then swung it down. The air fluted, softly as the call of a mourning dove, over the steel, which found the joint of the vertebrae and sheared through. Zayn's head jumped from his shoulders and thumped on to the hard-baked earth. His trunk remained kneeling for a moment, with the severed arteries pumping, then toppled forward.

Dorian stooped, took a handful of the silver-streaked hair, then lifted high the severed head. The eyes were wide open and darted from side to side with a louche expression.

'Thus I avenge the Princess Yasmini. Thus I claim the Elephant Throne of Oman,' Dorian shouted in triumph.

A thousand voices joined in the cry: 'Hail to al-Salil! Hail to the Caliph!'

Beshwayo's *impis* leaped to their feet and, led by the king himself, thundered out the royal salute: '*Bayete, Inkhosi! Bayete!*'

Dorian dropped the head, and reeled from the effects of his wound. The blood was still streaming down his flank and he might have fallen, had not Mansur and Jim rushed into the ring and supported him at each side. They half carried him into the fort. The rooms had been stripped of every stick of furniture, but they took Dorian to his own bedroom and laid him on the bare floor. Mansur ordered Rahmad to call Zayn al-Din's personal surgeon, who had been waiting at the door for this summons. He hurried in at once.

While he bathed the wound and stitched it closed with cat-gut, Dorian spoke softly to Mansur and Jim. 'Tom made me give my word that I would not tell you this until the fighting here was over. Now I am released from that promise. As soon as our defenders abandoned the fort, our brother Guy came ashore with a squad of armed men. They stormed into the fort. When Guy found that we had emptied the treasury, he came out on to the parapet and saw the wagon tracks. He must have realized we had sent the gold away. Zayn had already landed his horses on the beach by this time. Guy commandeered mounts for himself and twenty of his men, and rode out along the wagon road. There can be no doubt that he intends to capture the wagons.' The two young men stared at him aghast.

Jim found his voice first. 'The women! Little Georgie!'

'As soon as we realized what was happening, Tom took Smallboy and his musketeers. They chased after Guy.'

'Oh, God!' Mansur groaned. 'That was yesterday. There is no way of telling what has happened since then. Why did you not tell us before?'

'You know why I could not, but now I am freed of my promise to Tom.'

As he turned to Mansur, Jim's voice cracked with anxiety for his family – Sarah, Louisa and Georgie: 'Are you with me, coz?'

'Will you let me go, Father?'

'Of course, my son, and all my blessings with you,' Dorian replied.

Mansur sprang to his feet. 'I am with you, coz!' They ran to the door.

Jim was already shouting for Bakkat: 'Saddle up Drumfire. We ride at once.'

In addition to being at a safe distance from the coast, the gorge was a lovely place. Sarah had chosen it as the campsite for that reason. The river came down out of the mountains in a series of cascades and waterfalls. The pools below each of these were clear and placid, filled with yellow fish. Tall trees shaded the site of their laager. Flowering fruits in the leafy canopy attracted birds and vervet monkeys.

Although Tom had prevailed on Sarah to cache most of the furniture and her other possessions within a few miles of the fort, in the same hiding-place as some of the ivory, Sarah had insisted on loading all her real treasures on to the wagons. She did not look upon the chests of gold bars that Tom had foisted on her as being of especial importance. When they reached the campsite she had not even bothered to have them unloaded. When Louisa and Verity politely queried the wisdom of this, Sarah laughed. 'Wasted effort. We will just have to load them all up again when it's time to go home.'

On the other hand, she spared no effort in providing the camp with all the comforts of home. Chief of these was a fine mud-walled kitchen and refectory. The roof was a masterpiece of the thatcher's art. The floor was plastered with clay and cow dung. Sarah's harpsichord had pride of place in the centre of the room and every evening they gathered around it to sing while Sarah played.

During the days they picnicked beside the pool, and watched George swim like a naked little fish, and applauded as he jumped in from the high bank with the loudest splash he could make. They painted and sewed. Louisa gave George riding lessons, perched up on Trueheart's back like a flea. Verity worked on her translations of the Qur'an and the *Ramayana*. Sarah took George with her to collect wild flowers. Back in the laager she sketched the plants and wrote descriptive notes of them to add to her collection. Verity had brought a box of her favourite books from her cabin in the *Arcturus*, and she read aloud to the other women. They marvelled over James Thomson's *Seasons* and giggled together like schoolgirls over *Rage on Rage*.

Some mornings Louisa left George in the care of Sarah and Intepe, the lily, while she and Verity went out riding. This was an arrangement that suited George very well. Grandmama Sarah was an unending source of biscuits, toffee and other delights. She was also a captivating raconteur. Gentle Intepe was in George's thrall and obeyed his lordly instructions without quibble. She was now Zama's wife and had already borne him one lusty son. The baby was still at her breast, but her older boy was George's liege man. Zama had made for each of them a miniature bow, and a sharpened stick to use as a spear. They spent a great amount of time hunting around the perimeter of the camp. To date they had only achieved one kill: a fieldmouse had made the mistake of running under George's feet and, in an effort to avoid it, he had stood on its head. They cooked the tiny carcass in the flames of a large fire they built expressly for the purpose, and devoured the scorched, blackened flesh with relish.

These seemed idyllic days, but they were not. A dark shadow hung over the camp. Even in the midst of laughter the women would fall suddenly silent and look back along the wagon track that led down to the coast. When they mentioned the names of the men they loved, which they did often, their eyes were sad. In the night they started up at the whicker of one of the horses, or the sound of hoofs in the darkness. They called from one wagon to the other: 'Did you hear aught, Mother?'

'It was only one of our own horses, Louisa. Sleep now. Jim will come soon.'

'Are you well, Verity?'

'As well as you, but I miss Mansur as much as you miss Jim.'

'Do not fret, girls,' Sarah calmed them. 'They are Courtneys and they are tough. They'll be back soon.'

Every four or five days a rider came up from Fort Auspice with a leather satchel over his shoulder that contained letters for them. His arrival was the highlight of their lives. Each of the women seized the letter addressed to her and rushed to her own wagon to read it alone. They emerged much later, flushed and smiling, filled with ephemeral high spirits to discuss the news they had received. Then they began the long, lonely wait until the rider came again.

Intepe's grandfather, Tegwane, was the night-watchman. At his age he slept little and took his duties seriously. He prowled endlessly around the wagons on his stork thin legs with his spear over his shoulder. Zama was the camp overseer. He had eight men under him, including the wagon drivers and the armed *askari*. Izeze, the flea, was growing into a robust youth, and a fine musket shot. He was the sergeant of the guard.

On Jim's orders Inkunzi had moved all the cattle herds up from the coast into the hills where they would be safe from any incursion by Zayn al-Din's expeditionary force. He and all his Nguni herders were close at hand if any emergency arose.

After twenty-eight days in the river camp the women should have felt secure, but they did not. They should have been able to sleep soundly, but they were not. The premonition of evil hung over them all.

That particular night Louisa had not been able to sleep. She had hung a blanket over George's cot to shield him from the light, while she lay on the cardell bed propped up on her pillows and read Henry Fielding by the light of the oil lamp. Suddenly she cast aside the book and rushed to the afterclap of the wagon. She pulled open the curtains and listened until she was certain, then she called, 'Rider coming. It must be the mail.'

The lamps in the other wagons flared as the wicks were turned up, and all three women jumped down and stood in a huddle in front of the kitchen. They were talking excitedly as Zama and Tegwane piled logs on the fire and a shower of sparks flew upwards.

Sarah was the first to grow uneasy. 'There is more than one horse.' She cocked her head to listen.

'Do you think it may be the men?' Louisa asked eagerly.

'I don't know.'

'Perhaps we should take precautions,' Verity suggested. 'We should not presume that because they are mounted and come without stealth they are friendly.'

'Verity is right. Louisa, fetch Georgie! Everyone else into the kitchen! We will lock ourselves in there until we know who they are.'

Louisa gathered up the skirts of her nightgown and raced back to her wagon, her long pale hair flying out behind her.

Intepe came running from her hut with her children, and Sarah and Verity shepherded them into the kitchen. Sarah snatched a musket from the rack and stood at the doorway.

'Hurry, Louisa!' she shouted urgently. The sound of hoofs swelled louder, and out of the night galloped a large band of horsemen. They charged into the camp and reined in, their horses milling about, knocking over buckets and chairs, kicking up a haze of dust in the firelight.

'Who are you?' Sarah called sharply, still standing foursquare in the doorway. 'What do you want with us?'

The leader of the band rode towards her and pushed his hat on to the back of his head so that she could see he was a white man. 'Put down that gun, woman. Get all your people out here in the open. I am taking charge here.'

Verity stepped up beside Sarah. 'It's my father,' she told Sarah softly. 'Guy Courtney.'

'Verity, you treacherous child. Come out of there. You have much to answer for.'

'You leave her be, Guy Courtney. Verity is under my protection.'

Guy laughed bitterly as he recognized her. 'Sarah Beatty, my beloved sister-in-law. It's been many a long year since we parted.'

'Not long enough for my taste,' Sarah told him grimly. 'I'll have you know that I am no longer Beatty, but Mrs Tom Courtney. Now be gone and leave us alone.'

'You should not boast of marriage to such a black rogue and lecher, Sarah. However, I cannot leave so soon. You have in your possession things that have been stolen from me. My gold and my daughter. I have come to reclaim them.'

'You will have to kill me before you get your hands on either of them.'

'That would cause me no hardship, I assure you.' He laughed again and looked back at Peters. 'Tell the men to search the wagons.'

'Stop!' Sarah raised the musket.

'Shoot!' Guy invited her. 'But I swear it will be the last thing you ever do.'

While Sarah hesitated, Guy's men jumped off their horses and rushed to the wagons. There was a shout and Peters told Guy, 'They have found the gold chests.'

Then there was a scream and two of the Arabs dragged Louisa from her wagon. She had George in her arms and she was struggling wildly with her captors. 'Leave me! Leave my baby.'

'Who is this brat?' Guy reached down, grabbed the child by one arm and tore him from Louisa's grip. He looked at Sarah across the fire. 'Do you know anything about this little bastard?'

Verity tugged surreptitiously at the back of Sarah's night-dress, and whispered urgently, 'Don't let him know what George means to you. He will use him ruthlessly.'

'So, my darling daughter is conniving with her father's enemies. Shame on you, child.' His eyes swivelled back to Sarah's face. He saw that it had turned frosty pale, and he smiled coldly. 'No relation of yours, Sarah? You make no claim to him? Then let's get rid of him.'

He leaned from the saddle and dangled George over the flames of the campfire. The child felt the heat on his bare legs and shrieked at the pain. Louisa screamed as loudly, and Verity shouted, 'No, Daddy, please let him go.'

'No, Guy, no.' Sarah's reaction was the strongest of all. She rushed forward. 'He is my grandson. Please, do not hurt him. We will do as you say, only let Georgie go.'

'That is so much more reasonable.' Guy lifted the child away from the flames.

'Give him to me, Guy.' Sarah held up both arms to him. 'Please, Guy.'

'Please, Guy!' He mimicked her. 'That is much more civil. But I fear I must keep young George with me to make certain that you do not have a change of heart. Now, I want all your servants to throw down their weapons and come out from wherever they are hiding with their hands over their heads. Give them the order!'

'Zama! Tegwane! Izeze! All of you. Do as he says,' Sarah ordered. They came shuffling out reluctantly from among the wagons and the surrounding trees. Guy's men grabbed their muskets, tied their hands behind their backs and led them away.

'Now, Sarah, you, Verity and this other wench,' he pointed at Louisa, 'get back inside the hut. Remember, I have this fine fellow with me.' He pinched George's cheek between his nails until the tender skin tore and the child shrieked in pain. The women struggled in the arms of the men who held them, but they were dragged back into the kitchen. The door slammed shut, and two of Guy's men stood guard over it.

Guy swung down from the saddle and threw his reins to one of the men. He dragged George along with him and when the child balked he stooped over him and shook him until his teeth rattled together and he lost his breath so that he could no longer yell. 'Shut your mouth, you little swine, or I will shut it for you.' He straightened up and called to Peters, 'Tell them to unload the gold chests. I want to check the contents for myself.'

It took longer than Guy expected for his men to manhandle the heavy crates out of the wagons and unscrew the lids, but when he stood over them at last and gazed down on the shining yellow bars his face took on a deeply religious expression. 'It's all here,' he whispered dreamily, 'every last ounce.' Then he roused himself. 'Now, it remains only to get it safely back to the ships. We will need at least two of these wagons.' He tucked George under one arm, and strode across to where the servants huddled under armed guard. 'Which of you are the wagon drivers?' He picked them out. 'Go with my men and bring in your oxen. Inspan them to these two wagons. Work quickly. If you try to escape you will be shot.'

As soon as the kitchen door slammed shut behind them Sarah turned to the girls. Verity was pale but calm. Louisa was shaking and weeping softly.

'Verity, you stay by the door and warn us if anyone tries to open it.' She put one arm round Louisa. 'Come, darling, be brave. This won't help George.'

Louisa straightened her shoulders and sniffed back her tears. 'What do you want me to do?'

'Help me.' Sarah went across to the military chest that stood against the side wall. She rummaged in the bottom drawer and brought out a blue leather case. When she opened it a pair of silver duelling pistols lay in their velvet-lined nests. 'Tom taught me to shoot with these.' She handed one to Louisa. 'Help me load.'

Now that she had a task, Louisa pulled herself together quickly and loaded the weapon with swift, sure hands. Sarah had watched her at practice and knew that Jim had made her an expert shot.

'Hide it in your bodice,' Sarah ordered, and tucked the other pistol down the front of her night clothes. She went back to the door and listened. 'Have you heard anything?'

'The two Arab guards are talking,' Verity whispered back.

'What are they saying?'

'There has been fighting at the bay. They are very worried. While they were on the road here they heard the sound of a battle raging behind them, heavy cannon fire and a number of explosions that they think were Zayn's ships blowing up. They are discussing deserting my father and trying to make a run for it to the coast. They don't want to be abandoned here if Zayn is defeated.'

'So all is not lost, then. Tom and Dorian are still fighting.'

'It sounds as if that is what is happening,' Verity agreed.

'Keep listening, Verity. I want to try the window.'

Sarah left her at the door and placed a chair under the single high window. While Louisa held it steady she climbed on to it. She lifted aside the edge of the kudu-skin curtain that covered it and peered out.

'Can you see George?' Louisa's voice shook.

'Yes, Guy has him. He looks frightened but not badly hurt.'

'My poor baby,' Louisa sobbed.

'Now, don't start that again,' Sarah snapped. To keep the

767

minds of the two girls occupied, she began a commentary of all that she could see taking place outside. 'They are unloading the gold chests from the wagons and opening the lids. Guy is checking them.'

She described how, once the chests had been sealed and reloaded into the two wagons, the drivers brought in the ox teams and, under the scrutiny of Guy's henchmen, inspanned them.

'They are ready to leave,' Sarah said with relief. 'Guy has all that he came for. Surely he must give George back to us now and leave us in peace.'

'I don't think he will do that, Aunt,' Verity disagreed reluctantly. 'I think we are his passport back to the coast. From what I overheard the guards saying, our men are still fighting. My father will know that as long as he has us women and Georgie as his hostages they will be powerless to attack him.'

Within minutes she was proved right. There was a tramp of feet outside and the door was thrown open. Five Arabs crowded through it and one spoke harshly to Verity. She translated for the others: 'He says we must dress quickly in warmer clothes and be ready to leave at once.'

They were led to their wagons and the guards stood over them as they pulled on heavy coats over their nightdresses and hastily threw a few necessities into a valise. Then the three were led out to where horses had been saddled for them. The two wagons carrying the gold were drawn up one behind another, pointed back along the track. Guy was at the head of his men.

'Let me take George from you,' Sarah pleaded.

'Once, long ago, you played me for the fool, Sarah Beatty. It will not happen again. I shall keep your grandson firmly under my hand.' He drew the dagger from the sheath on his belt and held the blade to George's throat. The child was too terrified to cry out. 'You must not doubt for a minute that I shall slit his throat without compunction if you give me cause. If we meet Tom or Dorian or any of their vile brood on the road you will tell them that. Now hold your tongue.'

They mounted the horses that Zama, Izeze and Tegwane were holding for them. As Louisa settled on Trueheart's back she leaned forward and whispered to Zama, 'Where are Intepe and her children?'

'I have sent them into the forest,' he answered quietly. 'No one tried to stop them.'

'Thank God for that at least.'

Guy called out the order to advance, and Peters repeated it in a loud voice. The trek whips popped and the wagons rolled forward. Guy led the convoy, with George carried awkwardly on his hip. The escort of Arabs forced the women to follow close behind him. They crowded them together so that their knees touched. The rumble of the wheels and the creak and rattle of equipment covered Sarah's voice as she whispered to the girls, 'Have you the pistol ready, Louisa?'

'Yes, Mother. I have my hand upon it.'

'Good. Then this is what we must do.' She went on speaking softly, and the two girls murmured acknowledgement. 'Wait for my word,' Sarah warned them. 'Our only chance is to take them by surprise. We must act in concert to have any chance of success.'

The cavalcade wound down the hills towards the littoral. The horses were constrained to the speed of the plodding oxen. After a while nobody spoke. Captors and prisoners rode in a lethargic silence, which slowly became torpor. George had long ago sunk into an exhausted sleep. His head lolled on Guy's shoulder. Every time Sarah looked at him her heart squeezed with dread.

Every once in a while she would reach across and touch one of the girls to keep them awake and alert. She had been studying the horses that the Arab captors rode. They were thin and in poor condition, and she guessed they had endured a long, debilitating voyage in small ships. They would be no match for the mounts that she and the girls rode. Of their three horses Trueheart was the swiftest. Louisa was a light weight to carry and she and Trueheart would run away from any of them, even if she was carrying George with her.

The Arab riding next to Sarah let his head drop forward

on his chest. He started to slide sideways out of the saddle. Sarah knew that he had fallen asleep. Before he toppled from his horse's back, the man's head flew up as he woke with a start.

They are all exhausted, Sarah told herself. They have had no rest since they left the coast. Their horses are in no better case. It is nearly time for us to break away, and make a run for it.

In the moonlight she recognized this section of the road. They were approaching a ford over one of the tributaries of the main river. On the outward journey up from Fort Auspice, Zama and his men had spent days digging out the banks. It was a narrow and steep crossing that the wagons could only negotiate with difficulty. She knew that they would not find a better place at which to make the break. She estimated that there was still an hour of darkness to cover their escape, and by that time she hoped they would be clear of the weakened, exhausted horses of their pursuers.

She reached stealthily across to each of the girls in turn. She squeezed their hands and shook them lightly to alert them. The three pressed their mounts gently and moved up together until they were riding within touching distance of the rump of Guy's horse.

Sarah reached under her coat and slipped the duelling pistol out of her bodice. She used the folds of her sheepskin coat to muffle the click as she drew back the hammer to half-cock. The trigger of the weapon was set very lightly and she dared not cock it fully until the moment of firing. Fifty yards ahead she saw the gap in the river bank appear out of the darkness, with the road running down into it. She waited until Guy reined in his horse as he studied the cutting that led down to the ford.

Before Guy could call out, Sarah deliberately rode into his horse. The girls on each side of her pressed forward, and for a moment there was confusion as the horses bumped each other and milled about.

'Keep your damned horses under control,' Guy exclaimed with annoyance.

Then another voice roared from the darkness of the cutting just ahead. 'Stand where you are! I have fifty muskets loaded with goose-shot trained on you.'

'Tom!' Sarah exulted. 'It's Tom!' Of course he had heard the wagons from a mile off, and he would choose the river crossing to ambush them.

'Tom Courtney!' Guy shouted back. 'I have your grandson, and my dagger to his throat. My men have your wife Sarah, and the other women of your family. Stand aside and let us pass if you want any of them alive.'

To reinforce the threat he lifted George off his shoulder and held him up with both hands. 'It's your grandfather, child. Speak to him. Tell him you are safe.' He pricked George's arm with the dagger. From behind Guy's shoulder Sarah saw the blood start on the white skin, black and shiny in the moonlight.

'Grandpapa!' George shrieked at the top of his lungs. 'There is a horrid man hurting me.'

'By God, Guy! You touch a hair of that child's head and I'll kill you with my bare hands,' Tom's voice rang out with angry frustration.

'Hear the piglet squeal,' Guy shouted back, and pricked George again. 'Throw down your weapons and show yourselves, or I will send you your grandson's guts on a silver tray.'

Sarah drew the pistol from under her coat and cocked the hammer. She reached forward and pressed the muzzle into the small of Guy's back at the level of the kidneys. She fired and the shot was muffled by Guy's clothing and flesh. Guy's back arched in his agony as the ball shattered his vertebrae. He loosened his grip and George fell out of his raised hands.

'Now, Louisa!' Sarah screamed.

But Louisa did not need the order. She leaned out of the saddle and caught George as he fell. She clasped him to her bosom and kicked her heels into Trueheart's ribs. 'Ha! Ha!' she shouted to the mare. 'Run, Trueheart! Run!'

Trueheart jumped forward. One of the Arabs reached out to seize her, but Louisa fired the second pistol into his bearded face, and he fell backwards out of the saddle. Verity turned her horse in behind Trueheart to screen George and his mother from any musket bullets fired by the escort. She was only just quick enough. One of the Arabs, more alert than his companions, threw up his jezail and the long flame of the discharge ripped through the darkness. Sarah heard the ball strike flesh. Verity's horse collapsed under her, and she was thrown forward over its head.

Sarah spurred forward just as Guy toppled backwards and fell limply from the saddle into her path. Her horse tried to jump over him, but one of the metal-shod hoofs struck Guy's temple and she heard the brittle bone break like ice. Her horse recovered its balance and Sarah steered it towards where Verity was struggling to her feet.

'I am coming, Verity!' Sarah called to her, and made an arm for her. Verity hooked hers through Sarah's as the horse swept past her. Neither of them had the strength to swing Verity up astride, but she managed to throw her free arm over the horse's withers and cling on desperately as they followed Trueheart down into the river ford.

'Tom!' Sarah yelled. 'It's us. Don't shoot!'

The rest of the Arab escort had recovered their wits and were galloping after Sarah in a tight band. Suddenly a volley of musket fire erupted from the edge of the bank where Smallboy and the rest of Tom's men were lying. Three horses went down in a tangle, and the rest of the Arabs reined in and turned back. They raced for the shelter of the wagons and huddled behind them.

Tom jumped down from the bank and, as Sarah reined in, he seized her and Verity and dragged them down. He pulled them into safety behind the bank.

'Louisa!' Sarah gasped. 'Catch Louisa and George.'

'No one can catch Trueheart when she has the bit between her teeth. But they are safe out there as long as we keep the Arabs pinned down here.' Tom embraced Sarah. 'By God, I'm pleased to see you, woman.'

Sarah pushed him away. 'There'll be plenty of time for that nonsense later, Tom Courtney. You still have work to do here.'

'Right you are!'

Tom ran back to the top of the bank, and called to the dark wagons behind which the Arabs were sheltering: 'Guy! Do you hear me?'

'He's dead, Tom,' Sarah interrupted him. 'I shot him.'

'Then you beat me to it,' Tom said grimly. 'I was looking forward to it myself.' He realized that Verity was standing beside him, 'I'm sorry, my dear. He was your father.'

'If I had had a pistol in my hand, I would have done it myself,' Verity said calmly. 'What he has done to me over the years is of no account, but when he started torturing Georgie . . . No, Uncle Tom, he deserved that and more.'

'You are a brave girl, Verity.' He hugged her spontaneously.

'We Courtneys are made of rawhide,' she said, and hugged him back. Tom chuckled and released her.

'Now, if you call those blackguards out from behind the wagons, I would be much obliged. You can tell them that we will not harm them and they will have free passage back to the coast as long as they abandon the wagons. Tell them I have a hundred men with me, which is a lie. If they don't surrender we will attack and wipe them out to the man.'

Verity called the message across to them in Arabic. There was a delay while they discussed what she had said. She could hear their heated voices and she caught some of the words. Some were arguing that the *effendi* was dead, and there was no reason to remain here. Others were talking about the amount of gold, and what Zayn al-Din would do when he learned that they had lost it. One loud voice reminded them of the sounds of battle they had heard coming from the bay. 'Perhaps Zayn al-Din is dead also,' the speaker said.

Guy Courtney's body was still lying where it had fallen and the dawn light was strengthening so that Verity could see her father's dead face. Despite her brave words she had to turn away her eyes.

At last one of the Arabs called back their reply: 'Let us go in peace and we will hand over our weapons and surrender the wagons.'

J im and Mansur pushed their horses hard, riding through the
night. They were leading spare horses and when their
mounts tired they changed saddles quickly and went on.
They rode mostly in silence, locked in their own thoughts,
which were darker than the night. When they spoke it was
mostly in monosyllables or in curt sentences, and their eyes
were fixed ahead.

'Less than six miles to the laager at the gorge,' Jim said, as
they climbed a steep rise. In the first light of morning he
recognized the tree that stood on the skyline. 'We will be
there in an hour.'

'Please God!' said Mansur, and they rode up on to the crest
and looked ahead. They saw the river winding below them,
but then the first rays of the sun touched the belly of the cloud
and lit the valley with dramatic suddenness. They both saw
the dust at the same moment.

'Rider coming at the gallop!' Jim exclaimed.

'Only a messenger rides like that,' Mansur said softly. 'Let
us hope he has favourable tidings.'

They both reached for their telescopes, and for a moment
were struck speechless as they picked up the rider in the lens.

'Trueheart!' Jim shouted.

'In the Name of God! It's Louisa on her back. Look at her
hair shine in the sunlight,' Mansur agreed. 'She carries something in her arms. It's Georgie.'

Jim waited for no more. He turned loose the spare horse he
was leading and shouted to Drumfire, 'Run, my lovely! Run
with all your heart.'

Mansur could not keep pace with them as they raced down
the track.

George saw them coming and wriggled and twisted in
Louisa's arms like a fish. 'Papa!' he screamed. 'Papa!'

Jim jumped down from Drumfire's back the moment the
horse slid to a halt, lifted them down from Trueheart's saddle

and hugged them both, crushing Louisa and George to his chest.

Mansur rode up. 'Where is Verity? Is she safe?'

'At the ford of the river with the wagons. Tom and Sarah have her.'

'God love you, Louisa.' Mansur spurred on, and left Louisa and Jim weeping with happiness in each other's arms, and George tugging with both hands at Jim's beard.

They dug a grave for Guy Courtney beside the wagon road, and wrapped his body in a blanket before they lowered him into it.

'He was a vile bastard,' Tom murmured, in Sarah's ear. 'He deserved to be left for the hyena, but he was my brother.'

'And my brother-in-law on both sides – and I was the one who killed him. That will be on my conscience for the rest of my life.'

'Let it sit lightly, for you are without guilt,' Tom said, and they looked across to where Verity and Mansur stood hand in hand on the far side of the open grave.

'We are doing the right thing, Thomas,' Sarah said.

'It does not feel like it,' he grunted. 'Let's get it over with and head out for Fort Auspice. Dorian is wounded, and even if he is now a king, he needs us with him.'

They left Zama and Muntu to fill in the grave and cover it with rocks to stop the hyena digging it open, and Mansur and Verity followed them down the hill to where Smallboy had the two gold wagons inspanned. Mansur and Verity walked hand in hand, but though her face was pale Verity's eyes were dry.

Jim and Louisa were waiting at the wagons. Both had refused to attend the burial. 'Not after what he did to Louisa and Georgie.' Jim scowled when Tom had suggested it. Now Jim looked enquiringly at his father, and Tom nodded. 'It is done.'

They mounted and turned the horses' heads down towards the coast and Fort Auspice.

It took several weeks to repair the stranded war-dhow, the *Sufi*, and float her off the beach. Rahmad and his crew took her out and anchored her in the middle of the bay. Already the captured transport dhows were ready for the long voyage back to Muscat, their holds crammed with ivory.

Dorian leaned heavily on Tom's shoulder as he hobbled down to the beach. The wound he had received from Zayn al-Din was not yet entirely healed and Sarah was in close attendance on her royal patient. When they were settled in the longboat, Jim and Mansur rowed them out to the *Arcturus*. Verity and Louisa, with George chirping on her hip, were waiting to welcome them aboard. Verity had the farewell banquet laid out on trestle tables on the quarter-deck. They laughed and ate and drank together for the last time, but Ruby Cornish was watching for the turning of the tide. At last he stood up regretfully and said, 'Forgive me, Your Majesty, but the tide and the wind stand fair.'

'Give us one last toast, brother Tom,' Dorian said.

Tom stood up just a trifle unsteadily. 'A swift and safe voyage. May we all meet again, and that right soon.'

They drank the toast and embraced, then those who were remaining at Fort Auspice went down into the longboat. From the beach they watched the *Arcturus* weigh anchor. Dorian was at the rail supported by Mansur and Verity. Suddenly he began to sing, his voice as strong and beautiful as ever:

'Farewell and adieu to you, fair Spanish ladies,
Farewell and adieu to you, ladies of Spain,
For we've received orders to sail for old England,
But we hope in a short time to see you again.

The *Arcturus* led the fleet of dhows out through the channel. When the mainland was a low blue outline on the horizon Ruby Cornish came to where Dorian sat against the windward rail. 'Your Majesty, we have made good our offing.'

'Thank you, Captain Cornish. Will you be good enough to lay the ship on course for Muscat? We have some unsettled business there.'

The wagons were loaded and Smallboy and Muntu led the oxen in from the pasture and inspanned them. 'Where are you going?' Sarah asked.

Louisa shook her head. 'Mother, you must ask that of Jim, for I know not the answer.'

They both looked at him and he laughed. 'Beyond the next blue horizon,' he replied, picking up George and placing him on his shoulder. 'But fear not, we will be back soon enough with the wagons groaning under the weight of the ivory and diamonds they carry.'

Tom and Sarah stood on the parapet of Fort Auspice and watched the wagon convoy wind away up the hills, heading into the hinterland. Jim and Louisa were in the van, with Bakkat and Zama riding a short distance behind them. Intepe and Letee were walking beside the lead wagon, the children clustered about their legs.

At the crest of the hill Jim turned in the saddle and waved back at them. Sarah whipped off her bonnet and waved it furiously until they dropped out of sight over the far side.

'Well, Thomas Courtney, it's just you and I again,' she said softly.

'I like it well enough that way,' he said, and placed his arm round her waist.

Jim looked ahead and his eyes shone with wanderlust. Perched on his shoulders George yelled, 'Horsy! Giddy-up, horsy.'

'Hedgehog, you have given birth to a monster,' Jim said.

Louisa leaned across and squeezed his arm, smiling secretively. 'I shall hope to do better on my next attempt.'

Jim stopped dead in his tracks, and stared back at her. 'No, you aren't! Are you?'

'Oh yes, I am!' she replied.

'Why did you not tell me before this?'

'Because you might have left me behind.'

'Never!' he said, with great force.

THE DARK
OF THE SUN

This book is for my wife and the jewel of my life

MOKHINISO

with all my love and gratitude for the enchanted years
that I have been married to her

'I don't like the idea,' announced Wally Hendry, and belched. He moved his tongue round his mouth getting the taste of it before he went on. 'I think the whole idea stinks like a ten-day corpse.' He lay sprawled on one of the beds with a glass balanced on his naked chest and he was sweating heavily in the Congo heat.

'Unfortunately your opinion doesn't alter the fact that we are going.' Bruce Curry went on laying out his shaving tackle without looking up.

'You shoulda told them to keep it, told them we were staying here in Elisabethville – why didn't you tell them that, hey?' Hendry picked up his glass and swallowed the contents.

'Because they pay me not to argue.' Bruce spoke without interest and looked at himself in the fly-spotted mirror above the washbasin. The face that looked back was sun-darkened with a cap of close-cropped black hair; soft hair that would be unruly and inclined to curl if it were longer. Black eyebrows slanting upwards at the corners, green eyes with a heavy fringe of lashes and a mouth which could smile as readily as it could sulk. Bruce regarded his good looks without pleasure. It was a long time since he had felt that emotion, a long time since his mouth had either smiled or sulked. He did not feel the old tolerant affection for his nose, the large slightly hooked nose that rescued his face from prettiness and gave him the air of a genteel pirate.

'Jesus!' growled Wally Hendry from the bed. 'I've had just about a gutsful of this nigger army. I don't mind fighting

– but I don't fancy going hundreds of miles out into the bush to play nursemaid to a bunch of bloody refugees.'

'It's a hell of a life,' agreed Bruce absently and spread shaving-soap on his face. The lather was very white against his tan. Under a skin that glowed so healthily that it appeared to have been freshly oiled, the muscles of his shoulders and chest changed shape as he moved. He was in good condition, fitter than he had been for many years, but this fact gave him no more pleasure than had his face.

'Get me another drink, André.' Wally Hendry thrust his empty glass into the hand of the man who sat on the edge of the bed.

The Belgian stood up and went across to the table obediently.

'More whisky and less beer in this one,' Wally instructed, turned once more to Bruce and belched again. 'That's what I think of the idea.'

As André poured Scotch whisky into the glass and filled it with beer Wally hitched around the pistol in its webbing holster until it hung between his legs.

'When are we leaving?' he asked.

'There'll be an engine and five coaches at the goods yard first thing tomorrow morning. We'll load up and get going as soon as possible.' Bruce started to shave, drawing the razor down from temple to chin and leaving the skin smooth and brown behind it.

'After three months of fighting a bunch of greasy little Gurkhas I was looking forward to a bit of fun – I haven't even had a pretty in all that time – now the second day after the ceasefire and they ship us out again.'

'C'est la guerre,' muttered Bruce, his face twisted in the act of shaving.

'What's that mean?' demanded Wally suspiciously.

'That's war,' Bruce translated.

'Talk English, Bucko.'

It was the measure of Wally Hendry that after six months

in the Belgian Congo he could neither speak nor understand a single word of French.

There was silence again, broken only by the scraping of Bruce's razor and the small metallic sound as the fourth man in the hotel room stripped and cleaned his FN rifle.

'Have a drink, Haig,' Wally invited him.

'No, thanks.' Michael Haig glanced up, not trying to conceal his distaste as he looked at Wally.

'You're another snotty bastard – don't want to drink with me, hey? Even the high-class Captain Curry is drinking with me. What makes you so goddam special?'

'You know that I don't drink.' Haig turned his attention back to his weapon, handling it with easy familiarity. For all of them the ugly automatic rifles had become an extension of their own bodies. Even while shaving Bruce had only to drop his hand to reach the rifle propped against the wall, and the two men on the bed had theirs on the floor beside them.

'You don't drink!' chuckled Wally. 'Then how did you get that complexion, Bucko? How come your nose looks like a ripe plum?'

Haig's mouth tightened and the hands on his rifle stilled.

'Cut it out, Wally,' said Bruce without heat.

'Haig don't drink,' crowed Wally, and dug the little Belgian in the ribs with his thumb, 'get that, André! He's a tee-bloody-total! My old man was a teetotal also; sometimes for two, three months at a time he was teetotal, and then he'd come home one night and sock the old lady in the clock so you could hear her teeth rattle from across the street.'

His laughter choked him and he had to wait for it to clear before he went on.

'My bet is that you're that kind of teetotal, Haig. One drink and you wake up ten days later; that's it, isn't it? One drink and – pow! – the old girl gets it in the chops and the kids don't eat for a couple of weeks.'

Haig laid the rifle down carefully on the bed and looked at Wally with his jaws clenched, but Wally had not noticed. He went on happily.

'André, take the whisky bottle and hold it under Old Teetotal Haig's nose. Let's watch him slobber at the mouth and his eyes stand out like a pair of dog's balls.'

Haig stood up. Twice the age of Wally – a man in his middle fifties, with grey in his hair and the refinement of his features not completely obliterated by the marks that life had left upon them. He had arms like a boxer and a powerful set to his shoulders. 'It's about time you learned a few manners, Hendry. Get on your feet.'

'You wanta dance or something? I don't waltz – ask André. He'll dance with you – won't you, André?'

Haig was balanced on the balls of his feet, his hands closed and raised slightly. Bruce Curry placed his razor on the shelf above the basin, and moved quietly round the table with soap still on his face to take up a position from which he could intervene. There he waited, watching the two men.

'Get up, you filthy guttersnipe.'

'Hey, André, get that. He talks pretty, hey? He talks real pretty.'

'I'm going to smash that ugly face of yours right into the middle of the place where your brain should have been.'

'Jokes! This boy is a natural comic.' Wally laughed, but there was something wrong with the sound of it. Bruce knew then that Wally was not going to fight. Big arms and swollen chest covered with ginger hair, belly flat and hard-looking, thick-necked below the wide flat-featured face with its little Mongolian eyes; but Wally wasn't going to fight. Bruce was puzzled: he remembered the night at the road bridge and he knew that Hendry was no coward, and yet now he was not going to take up Haig's challenge.

Mike Haig moved towards the bed.

'Leave him, Mike.' André spoke for the first time, his

4

voice soft as a girl's. 'He was only joking. He didn't mean it.'

'Hendry, don't think I'm too much of a gentleman to hit you because you're on your back. Don't make that mistake.'

'Big deal,' muttered Wally. 'This boy's not only a comic, he's a bloody hero also.'

Haig stood over him and lifted his right hand with the fist, bunched like a hammer, aimed at Wally's face.

'Haig!' Bruce hadn't raised his voice but its tone checked the older man.

'That's enough,' said Bruce.

'But this filthy little—'

'Yes, I know,' said Bruce. 'Leave him!' With his fist still up Mike Haig hesitated, and there was no movement in the room. Above them the corrugated iron roof popped loudly as it expanded in the heat of the Congo midday, and the only other sound was Haig's breathing. He was panting and his face was congested with blood.

'Please, Mike,' whispered André. 'He didn't mean it.'

Slowly Haig's anger changed to disgust and he dropped his hand, turned away and picked up his rifle from the other bed.

'I can't stand the smell in this room another minute. I'll wait for you in the truck downstairs, Bruce.'

'I won't be long,' agreed Bruce as Mike went to the door.

'Don't push your luck, Haig,' Wally called after him. 'Next time you won't get off so easily.'

In the doorway Mike Haig swung quickly, but, with a hand on his shoulder, Bruce turned him again.

'Forget it, Mike,' he said, and closed the door after him.

'He's just bloody lucky that he's an old man,' growled Wally. 'Otherwise I'd have fixed him good.'

'Sure,' said Bruce. 'It was decent of you to let him go.' The soap had dried on his face and he wet his brush to lather again.

'Yeah, I couldn't hit an old bloke like that, could I?'

'No.' Bruce smiled a little. 'But don't worry, you frightened the hell out of him. He won't try it again.'

'He'd better not!' warned Hendry. 'Next time I'll kill the old bugger.'

No, you won't, thought Bruce, you'll back down again as you have just done, as you've done a dozen times before. Mike and I are the only ones who can make you do it; in the same way as an animal will growl at its trainer but cringe away when he cracks the whip. He began shaving again.

The heat in the room was unpleasant to breathe; it drew the perspiration out of them and the smell of their bodies blended sourly with stale cigarette smoke and liquor fumes.

'Where are you and Mike going?' André ended the long silence.

'We're going to see if we can draw the supplies for this trip. If we have any luck we'll take them down to the goods yard and have Ruffy put an armed guard on them overnight,' Bruce answered him, leaning over the basin and splashing water up into his face.

'How long will we be away?'

Bruce shrugged. 'A week – ten days'. He sat on his bed and pulled on one of his jungle boots. 'That is, if we don't have any trouble.'

'Trouble, Bruce?' asked André.

'From Msapa Junction we'll have to go two hundred miles through country crawling with Baluba.'

'But we'll be in a train,' protested André. 'They've only got bows and arrows, they can't touch us.'

'André, there are seven rivers to cross – one big one – and bridges are easily destroyed. Rails can be torn up.' Bruce began to lace the boot. 'I don't think it's going to be a Sunday school picnic.'

'Christ. I think the whole thing stinks,' repeated Wally moodily. 'Why are we going anyway?'

'Because,' Bruce began patiently, 'for the last three

6

months the entire population of Port Reprieve has been cut off from the rest of the world. There are women and children with them. They are fast running out of food and the other necessities of life.' Bruce paused to light a cigarette, and then went on talking as he exhaled. 'All around them the Baluba tribe is in open revolt, burning, raping and killing indiscriminately. As yet they haven't attacked the town but it won't be very long until they do. Added to which there are rumours that rebel groups of Central Congolese troops and of our own forces have formed themselves into bands of heavily-armed *shufta*. They also are running amok through the northern part of the territory. Nobody knows for certain what is happening out there, but whatever it is you can be sure it's not very pretty. We are going to fetch those people in to safety.'

'Why don't the U.N. people send out a plane?' asked André.

'No landing field.'

'Helicopters?'

'Out of range.'

'For my money the bastards can stay there,' grunted Wally. 'If the Balubas fancy a little man steak, who are we to do them out of a meal? Every man's entitled to eat and as long as it's not me they're eating, more power to their teeth, say I.' He placed his foot against André back and straightened his leg suddenly, throwing the Belgian off the bed on to his knees.

'Go and get me a pretty.'

'There aren't any, Wally. I'll get you another drink.' André scrambled to his feet and reached for Wally's empty glass, but Wally's hand dropped on to his wrist.

'I said *pretty*, André, not *drink*.'

'I don't know where to find them, Wally.' André's voice was desperate. 'I don't know what to say to them even.'

'You're being stupid, Bucko. I might have to break your arm.' Wally twisted the wrist slowly. 'You know as well as I do that the bar downstairs is full of them. You know that, don't you?'

'But what do I say to them?' André's face was contorted with the pain of his twisted wrist.

'Oh, for Christ's sake, you stupid bloody frog-eater – just go down and flash a banknote. You don't have to say a dicky bird.'

'You're hurting me, Wally.'

'No? You're kidding!' Wally smiled at him, twisting harder, his slitty eyes smoky from the liquor, and Bruce could see he was enjoying it. 'Are you going, Bucko? Make up your mind – get me a pretty or get yourself a broken arm.'

'All right, if that's what you want. I'll go. Please leave me, I'll go,' mumbled André.

'That's what I want.' Wally released him, and he straightened up massaging his wrist.

'See that she's clean and not too old. You hear me?'

'Yes, Wally. I'll get one.' André went to the door and Bruce noticed his expression. It was stricken beyond the pain of a bruised wrist. What lovely creatures they are, thought Bruce, and I am one of them and yet apart from them. I am the watcher, stirred by them as much as I would be by a bad play. André went out.

'Another drink, Bucko?' said Wally expansively. 'I'll even pour you one.'

'Thanks,' said Bruce, and started on the other boot. Wally brought the glass to him and he tasted it. It was strong, and the mustiness of the whisky was ill-matched with the sweetness of the beer, but he drank it.

'You and I,' said Wally, 'we're the shrewd ones. We drink 'cause we want to, not 'cause we have to. We live like we want to live, not like other people think we should. You and I got a lot in common, Bruce. We should be friends, you and I. I mean us being so much alike.' The drink was working in him now, blurring his speech a little.

8

'Of course we are friends – I count you as one of my very dearest, Wally.' Bruce spoke solemnly, no trace of sarcasm showing.

'No kidding?' Wally asked earnestly. 'How's that, hey? Christ, I always thought you didn't like me. Christ, you never can tell, isn't that right? You just never can tell,' shaking his head in wonder, suddenly sentimental with the whisky. 'That's really true? You like me. Yeah, we could be buddies. How's that, Bruce? Every guy needs a buddy. Every guy needs a back stop.'

'Sure,' said Bruce. 'We're buddies. How's that, hey?'

'That's on, Bucko!' agreed Wally with deep feeling, *and I feel nothing*, thought Bruce, *no disgust, no pity – nothing. That way you are secure; they cannot disappoint you, they cannot disgust you, they cannot sicken you, they cannot smash you up again.*

They both looked up as André ushered the girl into the room. She had a sexy little pug face, painted lips – ruby on amber.

'Well done, André,' applauded Wally, looking at the girl's body. She wore high heels and a short pink dress that flared into a skirt from her waist but did not cover her knees.

'Come here, cookie.' Wally held out his hand to her and she crossed the room without hesitation, smiling a bright professional smile. Wally drew her down beside him on to the bed.

André went on standing in the doorway. Bruce got up and shrugged into his camouflage battle-jacket, buckled on his webbing belt and adjusted the holstered pistol until it hung comfortably on his outer thigh.

'Are you going?' Wally was feeding the girl from his glass.

'Yes.' Bruce put his slouch hat on his head; the red, green and white Katangese sideflash gave him an air of artificial gaiety.

'Stay a little – come on, Bruce.'

9

'Mike is waiting for me.' Bruce picked up his rifle.

'Muck him. Stay a little, we'll have some fun.'

'No, thanks.' Bruce went to the door.

'Hey, Bruce. Take a look at this.' Wally tipped the girl backwards over the bed, he pinned her with one arm across her chest while she struggled playfully and with the other hand he swept her skirt up above her waist.

'Take a good look at this and tell me you still want to go!'

The girl was naked under the skirt, her lower body shaven so that her plump little sex pouted sulkily.

'Come on, Bruce,' laughed Wally. 'You first. Don't say I'm not your buddy.'

Bruce glanced at the girl, her legs scissored and her body wriggled as she fought with Wally. She was giggling.

'Mike and I will be back before curfew. I want this woman out of here by then,' said Bruce.

There is no desire, he thought as he looked at her, *that is all finished*. He opened the door.

'Curry!' shouted Wally. 'You're a bloody nut also. Christ, I thought you were a man. Jesus Christ! You're as bad as the others. André, the doll boy. Haig, the rummy. What's with you, Bucko? It's women with you, isn't it? You're a bloody nut-case also!'

Bruce closed the door and stood alone in the passage. The taunt had gone through a chink in his armour and he clamped his mind down on the sting of it, smothering it.

It's all over. She can't hurt me any more. He thought with determination, remembering her, the woman, not the one in the room he had just left but the other one who had been his wife.

'The bitch,' he whispered, and then quickly, almost guiltily, 'I do not hate her. There is no hatred and there is no desire.'

The lobby of the Hotel Grand Leopold II was crowded. There were gendarmes carrying their weapons ostentatiously, talking loudly, lolling against walls and over the bar; women with them, varying in colour from black through to pastel brown, some already drunk; a few Belgians still with the stunned disbelieving eyes of the refugee, one of the women crying as she rocked her child on her lap; other white men in civilian clothes but with the alertness about them and the quick restless eyes of the adventurer, talking quietly with Africans in business suits; a group of journalists at one table in damp shirtsleeves, waiting and watching with the patience of vultures. And everybody sweated in the heat.

Two South African charter pilots hailed Bruce from across the room.

'Hi, Bruce. How about a snort?'

'Dave. Carl.' Bruce waved. 'Big hurry now – tonight perhaps.'

'We're flying out this afternoon.' Carl Engelbrecht shook his head. 'Back next week.'

'We'll make it then,' Bruce agreed, and went out of the front door into the Avenue du Kasai. As he stopped on the sidewalk the white-washed buildings bounced the glare into his face. The naked heat made him wince and he felt fresh sweat start out of his body beneath his battle-suit. He took the dark glasses from his top pocket and put them on as he crossed the street to the Chev three-tonner in which Mike Haig waited.

'I'll drive, Mike.'

'Okay.' Mike slid across the seat and Bruce stepped up into the cab. He started the truck north down the Avenue du Kasai.

'Sorry about that scene, Bruce.'

'No harm done.'

'I shouldn't have lost my temper like that.'

Bruce did not answer, he was looking at the deserted buildings on either side. Most of them had been looted and all of them were pock-marked with shrapnel from the mortar bursts. At intervals along the sidewalk were parked the burnt out bodies of automobiles looking like the carapaces of long-dead beetles.

'I shouldn't have let him get through to me, and yet the truth hurts like hell.'

Bruce was silent but he trod down harder on the accelerator and the truck picked up speed. *I don't want to hear*, he thought, *I am not your confessor – I just don't want to hear.* He turned into the Avenue l'Etoile, headed towards the zoo.

'He was right, he had me measured to the inch,' persisted Mike.

'We've all got our troubles, otherwise we wouldn't be here.' And then, to change Mike's mood, 'We few, we happy few. We band of brothers.'

Mike grinned and his face was suddenly boyish. 'At least we have the distinction of following the second oldest profession – we, the mercenaries.'

'The oldest profession is better paid and much more fun,' said Bruce and swung the truck into the driveway of a double-storeyed residence, parked outside the front door and switched off the engine.

Not long ago the house had been the home of the chief accountant of Union Minière du Haut, now it was the billet of 'D' section, Special Striker Force, commanded by Captain Bruce Curry.

Half a dozen of his black gendarmes were sitting on the low wall of the verandah, and as Bruce came up the front steps they shouted the greeting that had become traditional since the United Nations intervention.

'U.N. – Merde!'

'Ah!' Bruce grinned at them in the sense of companionship that had grown up between them in the past months. 'The cream of the Army of Katanga!'

He offered his cigarettes around and stood chatting idly for a few minutes before asking, 'Where's Sergeant Major?' One of the gendarmes jerked a thumb at the glass doors that led into the lounge and Bruce went through with Mike behind him.

Equipment was piled haphazardly on the expensive furniture, the stone fireplace was half filled with empty bottles, a gendarme lay snoring on the Persian carpet, one of the oil paintings on the wall had been ripped by a bayonet and the frame hung askew, the imbuia-wood coffee table tilted drunkenly towards its broken leg, and the whole lounge smelled of men and cheap tobacco.

'Hello, Ruffy,' said Bruce.

'Just in time, boss.' Sergeant Major Ruffararo grinned delightedly from the armchair which he was overflowing. 'These goddam Arabs have run fresh out of folding stuff.' He gestured at the gendarmes that crowded about the table in front of him. 'Arab' was Ruffy's word of censure or contempt, and bore no relation to a man's nationality.

Ruffy's accent was always a shock to Bruce. You never expected to hear pure Americanese come rumbling out of that huge black frame. But three years previously Ruffy had returned from a scholarship tour of the United States with a command of the idiom, a diploma in land husbandry, a prodigious thirst for bottled beer (preferably Schlitz, but any other was acceptable) and a raving dose of the Old Joe.

The memory of this last, which had been a farewell gift from a high yellow sophomore of U.C.L.A., returned most painfully to Ruffararo when he was in his cups; so painfully that it could be assuaged only by throwing the nearest citizen of the United States.

Fortunately, it was only on rare occasions that an American and the necessary five or six gallons of beer were assembled in the same vicinity so that Ruffy's latent race antipathy could find expression. A throwing by Ruffy was an unforgettable experience, both for the victim and the spectators. Bruce vividly recalled that night at the Hotel Lido when he had been a witness at one of Ruffy's most spectacular throwings.

The victims, three of them, were journalists representing publications of repute. As the evening wore on they talked louder; an American accent has a carry like a well-hit golf ball and Ruffy recognized it from across the terrace. He became silent, and in his silence drank the last gallon which was necessary to tip the balance. He wiped the froth from his upper lip and stood up with his eyes fastened on the party of Americans.

'Ruffy, hold it. Hey!' – Bruce might not have spoken. Ruffy started across the terrace. They saw him coming and fell into an uneasy silence.

The first was in the nature of a practice throw; besides, the man was not aerodynamically constructed and his stomach had too much wind resistance. A middling distance of twenty feet.

'Ruffy, leave them!' shouted Bruce.

On the next throw Ruffy was getting warmed up, but he put excessive loft into it. Thirty feet; the journalist cleared the terrace and landed on the lawn below with his empty glass still clutched in his hand.

'Run, you fool!' Bruce warned the third victim, but he was paralysed.

And this was Ruffy's best ever, he took a good grip – neck and seat of the pants – and put his whole weight into it. Ruffy must have known that he had executed the perfect throw, for his shout of 'Gonorrhoea!' as he launched his man had a ring of triumph to it.

Afterwards, when Bruce had soothed the three Americans, and they had recovered sufficiently to appreciate the fact that they were privileged by being party to a record throwing session, they all paced out the distances. The three journalists developed an almost proprietary affection for Ruffy and spent the rest of the evening buying him beers and boasting to every newcomer in the bar. One of them, he who had been thrown last and farthest, wanted to do an article on Ruffy – with pictures. Towards the end of the evening he was talking wildly of whipping up sufficient enthusiasm to have a man-throwing event included in the Olympic Games.

Ruffy accepted both their praise and their beer with modest gratitude; and when the third American offered to let Ruffy throw him again, he declined the offer on the grounds that he never threw the same man twice. All in all, it had been a memorable evening.

Apart from these occasional lapses, Ruffy had a more powerful body and happier mind than any man Bruce had ever known, and Bruce could not help liking him. He could not prevent himself smiling as he tried to reject Ruffy's invitation to play cards.

'We've got work to do now, Ruffy. Some other time.'

'Sit down, boss,' Ruffy repeated, and Bruce grimaced resignedly and took the chair opposite him.

'How much you going to bet?' Ruffy leaned forward.

'Un mille.' Bruce laid a thousand-franc note on the table; 'when that's gone, then we go.'

'No hurry,' Ruffy soothed him. 'We got all day.' He dealt the three cards face down. 'The old Christian monarch is in there somewhere; all you got to do is find him and it's the easiest mille you ever made.'

'In the middle,' whispered the gendarme standing beside Bruce's chair. 'That's him in the middle.'

'Take no notice of that mad Arab – he's lost five mille already this morning,' Ruffy advised.

Bruce turned over the right-hand card.

'Mis-luck,' crowed Ruffy. 'You got yourself the queen of hearts.' He picked up the banknote and stuffed it into his breast pocket. 'She'll see you wrong every time, that sweet-faced little bitch.' Grinning, he turned over the middle card to expose the jack of spades with his sly eyes and curly little moustache. 'She's been shacked up there with the jack right under the old king's nose.' He turned the king face up. 'Look you at that dozy old guy – he's not even facing in the right direction.'

Bruce stared at the three cards and he felt that sickness in his stomach again. The whole story was there; even the man's name was right, but the jack should have worn a beard and driven a red Jaguar and his queen of hearts never had such innocent eyes. Bruce spoke abruptly. 'That's it, Ruffy. I want you and ten men to come with me.'

'Where we going?'

'Down to Ordinance – we're drawing special supplies.'

Ruffy nodded and buttoned the playing cards into his top pocket while he selected the gendarmes to accompany them; then he asked Bruce, 'We might need some oil; what you think, boss?'

Bruce hesitated; they had only two cases of whisky left of the dozen they had looted in August. The purchasing power of a bottle of genuine Scotch was enormous and Bruce was loath to use them except in extraordinary circumstances. But now he realized that his chances of getting the supplies he needed were remote, unless he took along a substantial bribe for the quartermaster.

'Okay, Ruffy. Bring a case.'

Ruffy came up out of the chair and clapped his steel helmet on his head. The chin straps hung down on each side of his round black face.

'A full case?' He grinned at Bruce. 'You want to buy a battleship?'

'Almost,' agreed Bruce; 'go and get it.'

Ruffy disappeared into the back area of the house and returned almost immediately with a case of Grant's Stand-

16

fast under one arm and half a dozen bottles of Simba beer held by their necks between the fingers of his other hand.

'We might get thirsty,' he explained.

The gendarmes climbed back into the back of the truck with a clatter of weapons and shouted cheerful abuse at their fellows on the verandah. Bruce, Mike and Ruffy crowded into the cab and Ruffy set the whisky on the floor and placed two large booted feet upon it.

'What's this all about, boss?' he asked as Bruce trundled the truck down the drive and turned into the Avenue l'Etoile. Bruce told him and when he had finished Ruffy grunted noncommittally and opened a bottle of beer with his big white chisel-blade teeth; the gas hissed softly and a little froth ran down the bottle and dripped onto his lap.

'My boys aren't going to like it,' he commented as he offered the open bottle to Mike Haig. Mike shook his head and Ruffy passed the bottle to Bruce.

Ruffy opened a bottle for himself and spoke again. 'They going to hate it like hell.' He shook his head. 'And there'll be even bigger trouble when we get to Port Reprieve and pick up the diamonds.'

Bruce glanced sideways at him, startled. 'What diamonds?'

'From the dredgers,' said Ruffy. 'You don't think they're sending us all that way just to bring in these other guys. They're worried about the diamonds, that's for sure!'

Suddenly, for Bruce, much which had puzzled him was explained. A half-forgotten conversation that he had held earlier in the year with an engineer from Union Minière jumped back into his memory. They had discussed the three diamond dredgers that worked the gravel from the bed of the Lufira swamps. The boats were based on Port Reprieve and clearly they would have returned there at the beginning of the emergency; they must still be there with three or four months' recovery of diamonds on board. Something like

17

half a million sterling in uncut stones. That was the reason why the Katangese Government placed such priority on this expedition, the reason why such a powerful force was being used, the reason why no approaches had been made to the U.N. authorities to conduct the rescue.

Bruce smiled sardonically as he remembered the humanitarian arguments that had been given to him by the Minister of the Interior.

'It is our duty, Captain Curry. We cannot leave these people to the not-so-tender mercy of the tribesmen. It is our duty as civilized human beings.'

There were others cut off in remote mission stations and government outposts throughout southern Kasai and Katanga; nothing had been heard of them for months, but their welfare was secondary to that of the settlement at Port Reprieve.

Bruce lifted the bottle to his lips again, steering with one hand and squinting ahead through the windscreen as he drank. All right, we'll fetch them in and afterwards an ammunition box will be loaded on to a chartered aircraft, and later still there will be another deposit to a numbered account in Zurich. Why should I worry? They're paying me for it.

'I don't think we should mention the diamonds to my boys.' Ruffy spoke sadly. 'I don't think it would be a good idea at all.'

Bruce slowed the truck as they ran into the industrial area beyond the railway line. He watched the buildings as they passed, until he recognized the one he wanted and swung off the road to stop in front of the gate. He blew a blast on the hooter and a gendarme came out and inspected his pass minutely. Satisfied, he shouted out to someone beyond the gate and it swung open. Bruce drove the truck through into the yard and switched off the engine.

There were half a dozen other trucks parked in the yard, all emblazoned with the Katangese shield and surrounded by gendarmes in uniforms patchy with sweat. A white lieutenant leaned from the cab of one of the trucks and shouted.

'Ciao, Bruce!'

'How things, Sergio?' Bruce answered him.

'Crazy! Crazy!' Bruce smiled. For the Italian everything was crazy. Bruce remembered that in July, during the fighting at the road bridge, he had bent him over the bonnet of a Land Rover and with a bayonet dug a piece of schrapnel out of his hairy buttocks – that had also been crazy.

'See you around,' Bruce dismissed him and led Mike and Ruffy across the yard to the warehouse. There was a sign on the large double doors *Dépôt Ordinance – Armée du Katanga* and beyond them at a desk in a glass cubicle sat a major with a pair of Gandhi-type steel-rimmed spectacles perched on a face like that of a jovial black toad. He looked up at Bruce.

'Non,' he said with finality. 'Non, non.' Bruce produced his requisition form and laid it before him. The major brushed it aside contemptuously.

'We have not got these items, we are destitute. I cannot do it. No! I cannot do it. There are priorities. There are circumstances to consider. No, I am sorry.' He snatched a sheaf of papers from the side of his desk and turned his whole attention to them, ignoring Bruce.

'This requisition is signed by Monsieur le Président,' Bruce pointed out mildly, and the major laid down his papers and came round from behind the desk. He stood close to Bruce with the top of his head on a level with Bruce's chin.

'Had it been signed by the Almighty himself, it would be of no use. I am sorry, I am truly sorry.'

Bruce lifted his eyes and for a second allowed them to wander over the mountains of stores which packed the interior of the warehouse. From where he stood he could identify at least twenty items that he needed. The major noticed the gesture and his French became so excited that Bruce could only make out the repeated use of the word 'Non'. He glanced significantly at Ruffy and the sergeant major stepped forward and placed an arm soothingly about the major's shoulders; then very gently he led him, still protesting, out into the yard and across to the truck. He opened the door of the cab and the major saw the case of whisky.

A few minutes later, after Ruffy had prised open the lid with his bayonet and allowed the major to inspect the seals on the caps, they returned to the office with Ruffy carrying the case.

'Captain,' said the major as he picked up the requisition from the desk. 'I see now that I was mistaken. This is indeed signed by Monsieur le Président. It is my duty to afford you the most urgent priority.'

Bruce murmured his thanks and the major beamed at him. 'I will give you men to help you.'

'You are too kind. It would disrupt your routine. I have my own men.'

'Excellent,' agreed the major and waved a podgy hand around the warehouse. 'Take what you need.'

– 3 –

Again Bruce glanced at his wristwatch. It was still twenty minutes before the curfew ended at 06.00 hours. Until then he must fret away the time watching Wally Hendry finishing his breakfast. This was a spectacle without much appeal, for Hendry was a methodical but untidy eater.

'Why don't you keep your mouth closed?' snapped Bruce irritably, unable to stand it any longer.

'Do I ask you your business?' Hendry looked up from his plate. His jowls were covered with a ginger stubble of beard, and his eyes were inflamed and puffy from the previous evening's debauchery. Bruce looked away from him and checked his watch again.

The suicidal temptation to ignore the curfew and set off immediately for the railway station was very strong. It required an effort to resist it. The least he could expect if he followed that course was an arrest by one of the patrols and a delay of twelve hours while he cleared himself; the worst thing would be a shooting incident.

He poured himself another cup of coffee and sipped it slowly. Impatience has always been one of my weaknesses, he reflected; nearly every mistake I have ever made stems from that cause. But I have improved a little over the years – at twenty I wanted to live my whole life in a week. Now I'll settle for a year.

He finished his coffee and checked the time again. Five minutes before six, he could risk it now. It would take almost that long to get out to the truck.

'If you are ready, gentlemen.' He pushed back his chair and picked up his pack, slung it over his shoulder and led the way out.

Ruffy was waiting for them, sitting on a pile of stones in one of the corrugated iron goods sheds. His men squatted round a dozen small fires on the concrete floor cooking breakfast.

'Where's the train?'

'That's a good question, boss,' Ruffy congratulated him, and Bruce groaned.

'It should have been here long ago,' Bruce protested, and Ruffy shrugged.

'*Should have been* is a lot different from *is*.'

'Goddammit! We've still got to load up. We'll be lucky if we get away before noon,' snapped Bruce. 'I'll go up to the station master.'

'You'd better take him a present, boss. We've still got a case left.'

21

'No, hell!' Bruce growled. 'Come with me, Mike.'

With Mike beside him they crossed the tracks to the main platform and clambered up on to it. At the far end a group of railway officials stood chatting and Bruce fell upon them furiously.

Two hours later Bruce stood beside the coloured engine driver on the footplate and they puffed slowly down towards the goods yard.

The driver was a roly-poly little man with a skin too dark for mere sunburn and a set of teeth with bright red plastic gums.

'Monsieur, you do not wish to proceed to Port Reprieve?' he asked anxiously.

'Yes.'

'There is no way of telling the condition of the permanent way. No traffic has used it these last four months.'

'I know. You'll have to proceed with caution.'

'There is a United Nations barrier across the lines near the old aerodrome,' protested the man.

'We have a pass.' Bruce smiled to soothe him; his bad temper was abating now that he had his transport. 'Stop next to the first shed.'

With a hiss of steam brakes the train pulled up beside the concrete platform and Bruce jumped down.

'All right, Ruffy,' he shouted. 'Let's get cracking.'

Bruce had placed the three steel-sided open trucks in the van, for they were the easiest to defend. From behind the breast-high sides the Bren guns could sweep ahead and on both flanks. Then followed the two passenger coaches, to be used as store rooms and officer's quarters; also for accommodation of the refugees on the return journey. Finally, the locomotive in the rear, where it would be least vulnerable and would not spew smoke and soot back over the train.

The stores were loaded into four of the compartments, the windows shuttered and the doors locked. Then Bruce set about laying out his defences. In a low circle of sandbags on the roof of the leading coach he sited one of the Brens and made his own post. From here he could look down over the open trucks, back at the locomotive, and also command an excellent view of the surrounding country.

The other Brens he placed in the leading truck and put Hendry in command there. He had obtained from the major at Ordinance three of the new walkie-talkie sets; one he gave to the engine driver, another to Hendry up front, and the third he retained in his emplacement; and his system of communication was satisfactory.

It was almost twelve o'clock before these preparations were complete and Bruce turned to Ruffy who sat on the sandbags beside him.

'All set?'

'All set, boss.'

'How many missing?' Bruce had learned from experience never to expect his entire command to be in any one place at any one time.

'Eight, boss.'

'That's three more than yesterday; leaves us only fifty-two men. Do you think they've taken off into the bush also?' Five of his men had deserted with their weapons on the day of the ceasefire. Obviously they had gone out into the bush to join one of the bands of *shufta* that were already playing havoc along the main roads: ambushing all unprotected traffic, beating up lucky travellers and murdering those less fortunate, raping when they had the opportunity, and generally enjoying themselves.

'No, boss. I don't think so, those three are good boys. They'll be down in the cité indigène having themselves some fun; guess they just forgot the time.' Ruffy shook his head. 'Take us about half an hour to find them; all we do is go down and visit all the knock-shops. You want to try?'

'No, we haven't time to mess around if we are going to

make Msapa Junction before dark. We'll pick them up again when we get back.' Was there ever an army since the Boer War that treated desertion so lightly, Bruce wondered.

He turned to the radio set beside him and depressed the transmit button.

'Driver.'

'Oui, monsieur.'

'Proceed – very slowly until we approach the United Nations barrier. Stop well this side of it.'

'Oui, monsieur.'

They rolled out of the goods yard, clicking over the points; leaving the industrial quarter on their right with the Katangese guard posts on the Avenue du Cimetière intersection; out through the suburbs until ahead of them Bruce saw the U.N. positions and he felt the first stirring of anxiety. The pass he carried in the breast pocket of his jacket was signed by General Rhee Singh, but before in this war the orders of an Indian general had not been passed by a Sudanese captain to an Irish sergeant. The reception that awaited them could be exciting.

'I hope they know about us.' Mike Haig lit his cigarette with a show of nonchalance, but he peered over it anxiously at the piles of fresh earth on each side of the tracks that marked the position of emplacements.

'These boys have got bazookas, and they're Irish Arabs,' muttered Ruffy. 'I reckon it's the maddest kind of Arabs there is – Irish. How would you like a bazooka bomb up your throat, boss?'

'No, thanks, Ruffy,' Bruce declined, and pressed the button of the radio.

'Hendry!'

In the leading truck Wally Hendry picked up his set and, holding it against his chest, looked back at Bruce.

'Curry?'

'Tell your gunners to stand away from the Brens, and the rest of them to lay down their rifles.'

24

'Right.'

Bruce watched him relaying the order, pushing them back, moving among the gendarmes who crowded the forward trucks. Bruce could sense the air of tension that had fallen over the whole train, watched as his gendarmes reluctantly laid down their weapons and stood empty-handed staring sullenly ahead at the U.N. barrier.

'Driver!' Bruce spoke again into the radio. 'Slow down. Stop fifty metres this side of the barrier. But if there is any shooting open the throttle and take us straight through.'

'Oui, monsieur.'

Ahead of them there was no sign of a reception committee, only the hostile barrier of poles and petrol drums across the line.

Bruce stood upon the roof and lifted his arms above his head in a gesture of neutrality. It was a mistake; the movement changed the passive mood of the gendarmes in the trucks below him. One of them lifted his arms also, but his fists were clenched.

'U.N. – merde!' he shouted, and immediately the cry was taken up.

'U.N. – merde! U.N. – merde!' They chanted the war cry – laughing at first, but then no longer laughing, their voices rising sharply.

'Shut up, damn you,' Bruce roared and swung his open hand against the head of the gendarme beside him, but the man hardly noticed it. His eyes were glazing with the infectious hysteria to which the African is so susceptible; he had snatched up his rifle and was holding it across his chest; already his body was beginning to jerk convulsively as he chanted.

Bruce hooked his fingers under the rim of the man's steel helmet and yanked it forward over his eyes so the back of his neck was exposed; he chopped him with a judo blow and the gendarme slumped forward over the sandbags, his rifle slipping from his hands.

Bruce looked up desperately; in the trucks below him the hysteria was spreading.

'Stop them – Hendry, de Surrier! Stop them for God's sake.' But his voice was lost in the chanting.

A gendarme snatched up his rifle from where it lay at his feet; Bruce saw him elbow his way towards the side of the truck to begin firing; he was working the slide to lever a round into the breech.

'Mwembe!' Bruce shouted the gendarme's name, but his voice could not penetrate the uproar.

In two seconds the whole situation would dissolve into a pandemonium of tracer and bazooka fire.

Poised on the forward edge of the roof, Bruce checked for an instant to judge the distance, and then he jumped. He landed squarely on the gendarme's shoulders, his weight throwing the man forward so his face hit the steel edge of the truck, and they went down together on to the floor.

The gendarme's finger was resting on the trigger and the rifle fired as it spun from his hands. A complete hush followed the roar of the rifle and in it Bruce scrambled to his feet, drawing his pistol from the canvas holster on his hip.

'All right,' he panted, menacing the men around him. 'Come on, give me a chance to use this!' He picked out one of his sergeants and held his eyes. 'You! I'm waiting for you – start shooting!'

At the sight of the revolver the man relaxed slowly and the madness faded from his face. He dropped his eyes and shuffled awkwardly.

Bruce glanced up at Ruffy and Haig on the roof, and raised his voice.

'Watch them. Shoot the first one who starts it again.'

'Okay, boss.' Ruffy thrust forward the automatic rifle in his hands. 'Who's it going to be?' he asked cheerfully, looking down at them. But the mood had changed. Their attitudes of defiance gave way to sheepish embarrassment and a small buzz of conversation filled the silence.

'Mike,' Bruce yelled, urgent again. 'Call the driver, he's trying to take us through!'

The noise of their passage had risen, the driver accelerating at the sound of the shot, and now they were racing down towards the U.N. barrier.

Mike Haig grabbed the set, shouted an order into it, and immediately the brakes swooshed and the train jolted to a halt not a hundred yards short of the barrier.

Slowly Bruce clambered back on to the roof of the coach.

'Close?' asked Mike.

'My God!' Bruce shook his head, and lit a cigarette with slightly unsteady hands. 'Another fifty yards—!' Then he turned and stared coldly down at his gendarmes.

'Canaille! Next time you try to commit suicide don't take me with you.' The gendarme he had knocked down was now sitting up, fingering the ugly black swelling above his eye. 'My friend,' Bruce turned on him, 'later I will have something for your further discomfort!' Then to the other man in the emplacement beside him who was massaging his neck, 'And for you also! Take their names, Sergeant Major.'

'Sir!' growled Ruffy.

'Mike.' Bruce's voice changed, soft again. 'I'm going ahead to toss the blarney with our friends behind the bazookas. When I give you the signal bring the train through.'

'You don't want me to come with you?' asked Mike.

'No, stay here.' Bruce picked up his rifle, slung it over his shoulder, dropped down the ladder on to the path beside the tracks, and walked forward with the gravel crunching beneath his boots.

An auspicious beginning to the expedition, he decided grimly, tragedy averted by the wink of an eye before they had even passed the outskirts of the city.

At least the Mickies hadn't added a few bazooka bombs to the altercation. Bruce peered ahead, and could make out the shape of helmets behind the earthworks.

Without the breeze of the train's passage it was hot again, and Bruce felt himself starting to sweat.

'Stay where you are, Mister.' A deep brogue from the emplacement nearest the tracks; Bruce stopped, standing on the wooden crossties in the sun. Now he could see the faces of the men beneath the helmets: unfriendly, not smiling.

'What was the shooting for?' the voice questioned.

'We had an accident.'

'Don't have any more or we might have one also.'

'I'd not be wanting that, Paddy.' Bruce smiled thinly, and the Irishman's voice had an edge to it as he went on. 'What's your mission?'

'I have a pass, do you want to see it?' Bruce took the folded sheet of paper from his breast pocket.

'What's your mission?' repeated the Irishman.

'Proceed to Port Reprieve and relieve the town.'

'We know about you.' The Irishman nodded. 'Let me see the pass.'

Bruce left the tracks, climbed the earth wall and handed the pink slip to the Irishman. He wore the three pips of a captain, and he glanced briefly at the pass before speaking to the man beside him.

'Very well, Sergeant, you can be clearing the barrier now.'

'I'll call the train through?' Bruce asked, and the captain nodded again.

'But make sure there are no more accidents – we don't like hired killers.'

'Sure and begorrah now, Paddy, it's not your war you're a-fighting either,' snapped Bruce and abruptly turned his back on the man, jumped down on to the tracks and waved to Mike Haig on the roof of the coach.

The Irish sergeant and his party had cleared the tracks

and while the train rumbled slowly down to him Bruce struggled to control his irritation – the Irish captain's taunt had reached him. Hired killer, and of course that was what he was. Could a man sink any lower?

As the coach drew level with where he stood, Bruce caught the hand rail and swung himself aboard, waved an ironical farewell to the Irish captain and climbed up on to the roof.

'No trouble?' asked Mike.

'A bit of lip, delivered in music-hall brogue,' Bruce answered, 'but nothing serious.' He picked up the radio set.

'Driver.'

'Monsieur?'

'Do not forget my instructions.'

'I will not exceed forty kilometres the hour, and I shall at all times be prepared for an emergency stop.'

'Good!' Bruce switched off the set and sat down on the sandbags between Ruffy and Mike.

Well, he thought, here we go at last. Six hours run to Msapa Junction. That should be easy. And then – God knows, God alone knows.

The tracks curved, and Bruce looked back to see the last white-washed buildings of Elisabethville disappear among the trees. They were out into the open savannah forest.

Behind them the black smoke from the loco rolled sideways into the trees; beneath them the crossties clattered in strict rhythm, and ahead the line ran arrow straight for miles, dwindling with perspective until it merged into the olive-green mass of the forest.

Bruce lifted his eyes. Half the sky was clear and tropical blue, but in the north it was bruised with cloud, and beneath the cloud grey rain drifted down to meet the earth. The sunlight through the rain spun a rainbow, and the cloud shadow moved across the land as slowly and as darkly as a herd of grazing buffalo.

29

He loosened the chin strap of his helmet and laid his rifle on the roof beside him.

'You'd like a beer, boss?'

'Have you any?'

'Sure.' Ruffy called to one of the gendarmes and the man climbed down into the coach and came back with half a dozen bottles. Ruffy opened two with his teeth. Each time half the contents frothed out and splattered back along the wooden side of the coach.

'This beer's as wild as an angry woman,' he grunted as he passed a bottle to Bruce.

'It's wet anyway.' Bruce tasted it, warm and gassy and too sweet.

'Here's how!' said Ruffy.

Bruce looked down into the open trucks at the gendarmes who were settling in for the journey. Apart from the gunners at the Brens, they were lying or squatting in attitudes of complete relaxation and most of them had stripped down to their underwear. One skinny little fellow was already asleep on his back with his helmet as a pillow and the tropical sun beating full into his face.

Bruce finished his beer and threw the bottle overboard. Ruffy opened another and placed it in his hand without comment.

'Why we going so slowly, boss?'

'I told the driver to keep the speed down – give us a chance to stop if the tracks have been torn up.'

'Yeah. Them Balubas might have done that – they're mad Arabs all of them.'

The warm beer drunk in the sun was having a soothing effect on Bruce. He felt at peace, now, withdrawn from the need to make decisions, to participate in the life around him.

'Listen to that train-talk,' said Ruffy, and Bruce focused his hearing on the clickety-clack of the crossties.

'Yes, I know. You can make it say anything you want it to,' agreed Bruce.

'And it can sing,' Ruffy went on. 'It's got real music in it, like this.' He inflated the great barrel of his chest, lifted his head and let it come.

His voice was deep but with a resonance that caught the attention of the men in the open trucks below them. Those who had been sprawled in the amorphous shapes of sleep stirred and sat up. Another voice joined in humming the tune, hesitantly at first, then more confidently; then others took it up, the words were unimportant, it was the rhythm that they could not resist. They had sung together many times before and like a well-trained choir each voice found its place, the star performers leading, changing the pace, improvising, quickening until the original tune lost its identity and became one of the tribal chants. Bruce recognized it as a planting song. It was one of his favourites and he sat drinking his lukewarm beer and letting the singing wash round him, build up into the chorus like storm waves, then fall back into a tenor solo before rising once more. And the train ran on through the sunlight towards the rain clouds in the north.

Presently André came out of the coach below him and picked his way forward through the men in the trucks until he reached Hendry. The two of them stood together, André's face turned up towards the taller man and deadly earnest as he talked.

'Doll boy,' Hendry had called him, and it was an accurate description of the effeminately pretty face with the big toffee eyes; the steel helmet he wore seemed too large for his shoulders to carry.

I wonder how old he is; Bruce watched him laugh suddenly, his face still turned upwards to Hendry; not much over twenty and I have never seen anything less like a hired killer.

'How the hell did anyone like de Surrier get mixed up in this?' His voice echoed the thought, and beside him Mike answered.

'He was working in Elisabethville when it started, and he couldn't return to Belgium. I don't know the reason but I guess it was something personal. When it started his firm closed down. I suppose this was the only employment he could find.'

'That Irishman, the one at the barrier, he called me a hired killer.' Thinking of André's position in the scheme of things had turned Bruce's thoughts back to his own status. 'I hadn't thought about it that way before, but I suppose he's right. That is what we are.'

Mike Haig was silent for a moment, but when he spoke there was a stark quality in his voice.

'Look at these hands!' Involuntarily Bruce glanced down at them, and for the first time noticed that they were narrow with long moulded fingers, possessed of a functional beauty, the hands of an artist.

'Look at them,' Mike repeated, flexing them slightly; 'they were fashioned for a purpose, they were made to hold a scalpel, they were made to save life.' Then he relaxed them and let them drop on to the rifle across his lap, the long delicate fingers incongruous upon the blue metal. 'But look what they hold now!'

Bruce stirred irritably. He had not wanted to provoke another bout of Mike Haig's soul-searching. Damn the old fool – why must he always start this, he knew as well as anyone that in the mercenary army of Katanga there was a taboo upon the past. It did not exist.

'Ruffy,' Bruce snapped, 'aren't you going to feed your boys?'

'Right now, boss.' Ruffy opened another beer and handed it to Bruce. 'Hold that – it will keep your mind off food while I rustle it up.' He lumbered off along the roof of the coach still singing.

'Three years ago, it seems like all eternity,' Mike went on as though Bruce had not interrupted. 'Three years ago I was a surgeon and now this—' The desolation had spread to his eyes, and Bruce felt his pity for the man deep down where he kept it imprisoned with all his other emotions. 'I was good. I was one of the best. Royal College. Harley Street. Guy's.' Mike laughed without humour, with bitterness. 'Can you imagine my being driven in my Rolls to address the College on my advanced technique of cholecystectomy?'

'What happened?' The question was out before he could stop it, and Bruce realized how near to the surface he had let his pity rise. 'No, don't tell me. It's your business. I don't want to know.'

'But I'll tell you, Bruce, I want to. It helps somehow, talking about it.'

At first, thought Bruce, I wanted to talk also, to try and wash the pain away with words.

Mike was silent for a few seconds. Below them the singing rose and fell, and the train ran on through the forest.

'It had taken me ten hard years to get there, but at last I had done it. A fine practice; doing the work I loved with skill, earning the rewards I deserved. A wife that any man would have been proud of, a lovely home, many friends, too many friends perhaps; for success breeds friends the way a dirty kitchen breeds cockroaches.'

Mike pulled out a handkerchief and dried the back of his neck where the wind could not reach.

'Those sort of friends mean parties,' he went on. 'Parties when you've worked all day and you're tired; when you need the lift that you can get so easily from a bottle. You don't know if you have the weakness for the stuff until it's too late; until you have a bottle in the drawer of your desk; until suddenly your practice isn't so good any more.'

Mike twisted the handkerchief around his fingers as he

33

ploughed doggedly on. 'Then you know it suddenly. You know it when your hands dance in the morning and all you want for breakfast is *that*, when you can't wait until lunchtime because you have to operate and that's the only way you can keep your hands steady. But you know it finally and utterly when the knife turns in your hand and the artery starts to spurt and you watch it paralysed – you watch it hosing red over your gown and forming pools on the theatre floor.' Mike's voice dried up then and he tapped a cigarette from his pack and lit it. His shoulders were hunched forward and his eyes were full of shadows of his guilt. Then he straightened up and his voice was stronger.

'You must have read about it. I was headlines for a few days, all the papers. But my name wasn't Haig in those days. I got that name off a label on a bottle in a bar-room.

'Gladys stayed with me, of course, she was that type. We came out to Africa. I had enough saved from the wreck for a down payment on a tobacco farm in the Centenary block outside Salisbury. Two good seasons and I was off the bottle. Gladys was having our first baby, we had both wanted one so badly. It was all coming right again.'

Mike stuffed the handkerchief back in his pocket, and his voice lost its strength again, turned dry and husky.

'Then one day I took the truck into the village and on the way home I stopped at the club. I had been there often before, but this time they threw me out at closing time and when I got back to the farm I had a case of Scotch on the seat beside me.'

Bruce wanted to stop him; he knew what was coming and he didn't want to hear it.

'The first rains started that night and the rivers came down in flood. The telephone lines were knocked out and we were cut off. In the morning—' Mike stopped again and turned to Bruce.

'I suppose it was the shock of seeing me like that again, but in the morning Gladys went into labour. It was her first and she wasn't so young any more. She was still in labour the next day, but by then she was too weak to scream. I remember how peaceful it was without her screaming and pleading with me to help. You see she knew I had all the instruments I needed. She begged me to help. I can remember that; her voice through the fog of whisky. I think I hated her then. I think I remember hating her, it was all so confused, so mixed up with the screaming and the liquor. But at last she was quiet. I don't think I realized she was dead. I was simply glad she was quiet and I could have peace.'

He dropped his eyes from Bruce's face.

'I was too drunk to go to the funeral. Then I met a man in a bar-room, I can't remember how long after it was, I can't even remember where. It must have been on the Copperbelt. He was recruiting for Tshombe's army and I signed up; there didn't seem anything else to do.'

Neither of them spoke again until a gendarme brought food to them, hunks of brown bread spread with tinned butter and filled with bully beef and pickled onions. They ate in silence listening to the singing, and Bruce said at last:

'You needn't have told me.'

'I know.'

'Mike—' Bruce paused.

'Yes?'

'I'm sorry, if that's any comfort.'

'It is,' Mike said. 'It helps to have – not to be completely alone. I like you, Bruce.' He blurted out the last sentence and Bruce recoiled as though Mike had spat in his face.

You fool, he rebuked himself savagely, *you were wide open then. You nearly let one of them in again.*

Remorselessly he crushed down his sympathy, shocked at the effort it required, and when he picked up the radio the gentleness had gone from his eyes.

'Hendry,' he spoke into the set, 'don't talk so much. I put you up front to watch the tracks.'

From the leading truck Wally Hendry looked round and forked two fingers at Bruce in a casual obscenity, but he turned back and faced ahead.

'You'd better go and take over from Hendry,' Bruce told Mike. 'Send him back here.'

Mike Haig stood up and looked down at Bruce.

'What are you afraid of?' his voice softly puzzled.

'I gave you an order, Haig.'

'Yes, I'm on my way.'

– 4 –

The aircraft found them in the late afternoon. It was a Vampire jet of the Indian Air Force and it came from the north.

They heard the soft rumble of it across the sky and then saw it glint like a speck of mica in the sunlight above the storm clouds ahead of them.

'I bet you a thousand francs to a handful of dung that this Bucko don't know about us,' said Hendry with anticipation, watching the jet turn off its course towards them.

'Well, he does now,' said Bruce.

Swiftly he surveyed the rain clouds in front of them. They were close; another ten minutes' run and they would be under them, and once there they were safe from air attack for the belly of the clouds pressed close against the earth and the rain was a thick blue-grey mist that would reduce visibility to a few hundred feet. He switched on the radio.

'Driver, give us all the speed you have – get us into that rain.'

'Oui, monsieur,' came the acknowledgement and almost immediately the puffing of the loco quickened and the clatter of the crossties changed its rhythm.

'Look at him come,' growled Hendry. The jet fell fast

against the backdrop of cloud, still in sunlight, still a silver point of light, but growing.

Bruce clicked over the band selector of the radio, searching the ether for the pilot's voice. He tried four wavelengths and each time found only the crackle and drone of static, but with the fifth came the gentle sing-song of Hindustani. Bruce could not understand it, but he could hear that the tone was puzzled. There was a short silence on the radio while the pilot listened to an instruction from the Kamina base which was beyond the power of their small set to receive, then a curt affirmative.

'He's coming in for a closer look,' said Bruce, then raising his voice, 'Everybody under cover – and stay there.' He was not prepared to risk another demonstration of friendship.

The jet came cruising in towards them under half power, yet incredibly fast, leaving the sound of its engine far behind it, sharklike above the forest. Then Bruce could see the pilot's head through the canopy; now he could make out his features. His face was very brown beneath the silver crash helmet and he had a little moustache, the same as the jack of spades. He was so close that Bruce saw the exact moment that he recognized them as Katangese; his eyes showed white and his mouth puckered as he swore. Beside Bruce the radio relayed the oath with metallic harshness, and then the jet was banking away steeply, its engine howling in full throttle, rising, showing its swollen silver belly and the racks of rockets beneath its wings.

'That frightened seven years' growth out of him,' laughed Hendry. 'You should have let me blast him. He was close enough for me to hit him in the left eyeball.'

'You'll get another chance in a moment,' Bruce assured him grimly. The radio was gabbling with consternation as the jet dwindled back into the sky. Bruce switched quickly to their own channel.

'Driver, can't you get this thing moving?'

'Monsieur, never before has she moved as she does now.'

Once more he switched back to the jet's frequency and listened to the pilot's excited voice. The jet was turning in a wide circle, perhaps fifteen miles away. Bruce glanced at the piled mass of cloud and rain ahead of them; it was moving down to meet them, but with ponderous dignity.

'If he comes back,' Bruce shouted down at his gendarmes, 'we can be sure that it's not just to look at us again. Open fire as soon as he's in range. Give him everything you've got, we must try and spoil his aim.'

Their faces were turned up towards him, subdued by the awful inferiority of the earthbound to the hunter in the sky. Only André did not look at Bruce; he was staring at the aircraft with his jaws clenching nervously and his eyes too large for his face.

Again there was silence on the radio, and every head turned back to watch the jet.

'Come on, Bucko, come on!' grunted Hendry impatiently. He spat into the palm of his right hand and then wiped it down the front of his jacket. 'Come on, we want you.' With his thumb he flicked the safety catch of his rifle on and off, on and off.

Suddenly the radio spoke again. Two words, obviously acknowledging an order, and one of the words Bruce recognized. He had heard it before in circumstances that has burned it into his memory. The Hindustani word 'Attack!'

'All right,' he said and stood up. 'He's coming!'

The wind fluttered his shirt against his chest. He settled his helmet firmly and pumped a round into the chamber of his FN.

'Get down into the truck, Hendry,' he ordered.

'I can see better from here.' Hendry was standing beside him, legs planted wide to brace himself against the violent motion of the train.

'As you like,' said Bruce. 'Ruffy, you get under cover.'

'Too damn hot down there in that box,' grinned the huge Negro.

'You're a mad Arab too,' said Bruce.

'Sure, we're all mad Arabs.'

The jet wheeled sharply and stooped towards the forest, levelling, still miles out on their flank.

'This Bucko is a real apprentice. He's going to take us from the side, so we can all shoot at him. If he was half awake he'd give it to us up the bum, hit the loco and make sure that we were all shooting over the top of each other,' gloated Hendry.

Silently, swiftly it closed with them, almost touching the tops of the trees. Then suddenly the cannon fire sparkled lemon-pale on its nose and all around them the air was filled with the sound of a thousand whips. Immediately every gun on the train opened up in reply. The tracers from the Brens chased each other out to meet the plane and the rifles joined their voices in a clamour that drowned the cannon fire.

Bruce aimed carefully, the jet unsteady in his sights from the lurching of the coach; then he pressed the trigger and the rifle juddered against his shoulder. From the corner of his eye he saw the empty cartridge cases spray from the breech in a bright bronze stream, and the stench of cordite stung his nostrils.

The aircraft slewed slightly, flinching from the torrent of fire.

'He's yellow!' howled Hendry. 'The bastard's yellow!'

'Hit him!' roared Ruffy. 'Keep hitting him.'

The jet twisted, lifted its nose so that the fire from its cannons passed harmlessly over their heads. Then its nose dropped again and it fired its rockets, two from under each wing. The gunfire from the train stopped abruptly as everybody ducked for safety; only the three of them on the roof kept shooting.

Shrieking like four demons in harness, leaving parallel lines of white smoke behind them, the rockets came from about four hundred yards out and they covered the distance in the time it takes to draw a deep breath, but the pilot had dropped his nose too sharply and fired too late. The rockets exploded in the embankment of the tracks below them.

The blast threw Bruce over backwards. He fell and rolled, clutching desperately at the smooth roof, but as he went over the edge his fingers caught in the guttering and he hung there. He was dazed with the concussion, the guttering cutting into his fingers, the shoulder strap of his rifle round his neck strangling him, and the gravel of the embankment rushing past beneath him.

Ruffy reached over, caught him by the front of his jacket and lifted him back like a child.

'You going somewhere, boss?' The great round face was coated with dust from the explosions, but he was grinning happily. Bruce had a confused conviction that it would take at least a case of dynamite to make any impression on that mountain of black flesh.

Kneeling on the roof Bruce tried to rally himself. He saw that the wooden side of the coach nearest the explosions was splintered and torn and the roof was covered with earth and pebbles. Hendry was sitting beside him, shaking his head slowly from side to side; a small trickle of blood ran down from a scratch on his cheek and dripped from his chin. In the open trucks the men stood or sat with stunned expressions on their faces, but the train still raced on towards the rain storm and the dust of the explosions hung in a dense brown cloud above the forest far behind them.

Bruce scrambled to his feet, searched frantically for the aircraft and found its tiny shape far off above the mass of cloud.

The radio was undamaged, protected by the sandbags from the blast. Bruce reached for it and pressed the transmit button.

'Driver, are you all right?'

'Monsieur, I am greatly perturbed. Is there—'

'You're not alone,' Bruce assured him. 'Keep this train going.'

'Oui, monsieur.'

Then he switched to the aircraft's frequency. Although his ears were singing shrilly from the explosions, he could hear that the voice of the pilot had changed its tone. There was a slowness in it, a breathless catch on some of the words. He's frightened or he's hurt, thought Bruce, but he still has time to make another pass at us before we reach the storm front.

His mind was clearing fast now, and he became aware of the complete lack of readiness in his men.

'Ruffy!' he shouted. 'Get them on their feet. Get them ready. That plane will be back any second now.'

Ruffy jumped down into the truck and Bruce heard his palm slap against flesh as he began to bully them into activity. Bruce followed him down, then climbed over into the second truck and began the same process there.

'Haig, give me a hand, help me get the lead out of them.'

Further removed from the shock of the explosion, the men in this truck reacted readily and crowded to the side, starting to reload, checking their weapons, swearing, faces losing the dull dazed expressions.

Bruce turned and shouted back, 'Ruffy, are any of your lot hurt?'

'Couple of scratches, nothing bad.'

On the roof of the coach Hendry was standing again, watching the aircraft, blood on his face and his rifle in his hands.

'Where's André?' Bruce asked Haig as they met in the middle of the truck.

'Up front. I think he's been hit.'

Bruce went forward and found André doubled up, crouching in a corner of the truck, his rifle lying beside him

41

and both hands covering his face. His shoulders heaved as though he were in pain.

Eyes, thought Bruce, he's been hit in the eyes. He reached him and stooped over him, pulling his hands from his face, expecting to see blood.

André was crying, his cheeks wet with tears and his eyelashes gummed together. For a second Bruce stared at him and then he caught the front of his jacket and pulled him to his feet. He picked up André's rifle and the barrel was cold, not a single shot had been fired out of it. He dragged the Belgian to the side and thrust the rifle into his hands.

'De Surrier,' he snarled, 'I'm going to be standing beside you. If you do that again I'll shoot you. Do you understand?'

'I'm sorry, Bruce.' André's lips were swollen where he had bitten them; his face was smeared with tears and slack with fear. 'I'm sorry. I couldn't help it.'

Bruce ignored him and turned his attention back to the aircraft. It was turning in for its next run.

He's going to come from the side again, Bruce thought; this time he'll get us. He can't miss twice in a row.

In silence once more they watched the jet slide down the valley between two vast white mountains of cloud and level off above the forest. Small and dainty and deadly it raced in towards them.

One of the Bren guns opened up, rattling raucously, sending out tracers like bright beads on a string.

'Too soon,' muttered Bruce. 'Much too soon; he must be all of a mile out of range.'

But the effect was instantaneous. The jet swerved, almost hit the tree tops and then over-corrected, losing its line of approach.

A howl of derision went up from the train and was immediately lost in the roar as every gun opened fire. The jet loosed its remaining rockets, blindly, hopelessly, without a chance of a hit. Then it climbed steeply, turning away into the cloud ahead of them. The sound of its engines receded, was muted by the cloud and then was gone.

Ruffy was performing a dance of triumph, waving his rifle over his head. Hendry on the roof was shouting abuse at the clouds into which the jet had vanished, one of the Brens was still firing short ecstatic bursts, someone else was chanting the Katangese war cry and others were taking it up. And then the driver in the locomotive came in with his whistle, spurting steam with each shriek.

Bruce slung his rifle over his shoulder, pushed his helmet on to the back of his head, took out a cigarette and lit it, then stood watching them sing and laugh and chatter with the relief from danger.

Next to him André leaned out and vomited over the side; a little of it came out of his nose and dribbled down the front of his battle-jacket. He wiped his mouth with the back of his hand.

'I'm sorry, Bruce. I'm sorry, truly I'm sorry,' he whispered.

And they were under the cloud, its coolness slumped over them like air from an open refrigerator. The first heavy drops stung Bruce's cheek and then rolled down heavily washing away the smell of cordite, melting the dust from Ruffy's face until it shone again like washed coal.

Bruce felt his jacket cling wetly to his back.

'Ruffy, two men at each Bren. The rest of them can get back into the covered coaches. We'll relieve every hour.' He reversed his rifle so the muzzle pointed downwards. 'De Surrier, you can go, and you as well, Hendry.'

'I'll stay with you, Bruce.'

'All right then.'

The gendarmes clambered back into the covered coaches still laughing and chattering, and Ruffy came forward with a groundsheet and handed it to Bruce.

'The radios are all covered. If you don't need me, boss, I

got some business with one of those Arabs in the coach. He's got near twenty thousand francs on him; so I'd better go and give him a couple of tricks with the cards.'

'One of these days I'm going to explain your Christian monarchs to the boys. Show them that the odds are three to one against them,' Bruce threatened.

'I wouldn't do that, boss,' Ruffy advised seriously. 'All that money isn't good for them, just gets them into trouble.'

'Off you go then. I'll call you later,' said Bruce. 'Tell them I said "well done", I'm proud of them.'

'Yeah. I'll tell them,' promised Ruffy.

Bruce lifted the tarpaulin that covered the set.

'Driver, desist before you burst the boiler!'

The abandoned flight of the train steadied to a more sedate pace, and Bruce tilted his helmet over his eyes and pulled the groundsheet up around his mouth before he leaned out over the side of the truck to inspect the rocket damage.

'All the windows blown out on this side and the woodwork torn a little,' he muttered. 'But a lucky escape all the same.'

'What a miserable comic-opera war this is,' grunted Mike Haig. 'That pilot had the right idea: why risk your life when it's none of your business.'

'He was wounded,' Bruce guessed. 'I think we hit him on his first run.'

Then they were silent, with the rain driving into their faces, slitting their eyes to peer ahead along the tracks. The men at the Brens huddled into their brown and green camouflage groundsheets, all their jubilation of ten minutes earlier completely gone. They are like cats, thought Bruce as he noticed their dejection, they can't stand being wet.

'It's half past five already.' Mike spoke at last. 'Do you think we'll make Msapa Junction before nightfall?'

'With this weather it will be dark by six.' Bruce looked up at the low cloud that was prematurely bringing on the night. 'I'm not going to risk travelling in the dark. This is the edge of Baluba country and we can't use the headlights of the loco.'

'You going to stop then?'

Bruce nodded. What a stupid bloody question, he thought irritably. Then he recognized his irritation as reaction from the danger they had just experienced, and he spoke to make amends.

'We can't be far now – if we start again at first light we'll reach Msapa before sun-up.'

'My God, it's cold,' complained Mike and he shivered briefly.

'Either too hot or too cold,' Bruce agreed; he knew that it was also reaction that was making him garrulous. But he did not attempt to stop himself. 'That's one of the things about this happy little planet of ours: nothing is in moderation. Too hot or too cold, either you are hungry or you've overeaten, you are in love or you hate the world—'

'Like you?' asked Mike.

'Dammit, Mike, you're as bad as a woman. Can't you conduct an objective discussion without introducing personalities?' Bruce demanded. He could feel his temper rising to the surface, he was cold and edgy, and he wanted a smoke.

'Objective theories must have subjective application to prove their worth,' Mike pointed out. There was just a trace of an amused smile on his broad ravaged old face.

'Let's forget it then. I don't want to talk personalities,' snapped Bruce; then immediately went on to do so. 'Humanity sickens me if I think about it too much. De Surrier puking his heart out with fear, that animal Hendry, you trying to keep off the liquor, Joan—' He stopped himself abruptly.

'Who is Joan?'

'Do I ask you your business?' Bruce flashed the standard reply to all personal questions in the mercenary army of Katanga.

'No. But I'm asking you yours – who is Joan?'

All right. I'll tell him. If he wants to know, I'll tell him.
Anger had made Bruce reckless.

'Joan was the bitch I married.'

'So, that's it then!'

'Yes – that's it! Now you know. So you can leave me alone.'

'Kids?'

'Two – a boy and a girl.' The anger was gone from Bruce's voice, and the raw naked pain was back for an instant. Then he rallied and his voice was neutral once more.

'And none of it matters a damn. As far as I'm concerned the whole human race – all of it – can go and lose itself. I don't want any part of it.'

'How old are you, Bruce?'

'Leave me alone, damn you!'

'How old are you?'

'I'm thirty.'

'You talk like a teenager.'

'And I feel like an old, old man.'

The amusement was no longer on Mike's face as he asked.

'What did you do before this?'

'I slept and breathed and ate – and got trodden on.'

'What did you do for a living?'

'Law.'

'Were you successful?'

'How do you measure success? If you mean, did I make money, the answer is yes.'

I made enough to pay off the house and the car, he thought bitterly, *and to contest custody of my children, and finally to meet the divorce settlement. I had enough for that, but, of course, I had to sell my partnership.*

'Then you'll be all right,' Mike told him. 'If you've

succeeded once you'll be able to do it again when you've recovered from the shock; when you've rearranged your life and taken other people into it to make you strong again.'

'I'm strong now, Haig. I'm strong *because* there is no one in my life. That's the only way you can be secure, on your own. Completely free and on your own.'

'Strong!' Anger flared in Mike's voice for the first time. 'On your own you're *nothing*, Curry. On your own you're so weak I could piss on you and wash you away!' Then the anger evaporated and Mike went on softly, 'But you'll find out – you're one of the lucky ones. You attract people to you. You don't have to be alone.'

'Well, that's the way I'm going to be from now on.'

'We'll see,' murmured Mike.

'Yes, we'll see,' Bruce agreed, and lifted the tarpaulin over the radio.

'Driver, we are going to halt for the night. It's too dark to proceed with safety.'

– 5 –

Brazzaville Radio came through weakly on the set and the static was bad, for outside the rain still fell and thunder rolled around the sky like an unsecured cargo at sea.

' – Our Elisabethville correspondent reports that elements of the Kantangese Army in the South Kasai province today violated the ceasefire agreement by firing upon a low-flying aircraft of the United Nations command. The aircraft, a Vampire jet fighter of the Indian Air Force, returned safely to its base at Kamina airfield. The pilot, however, was wounded by small arms fire. His condition is satisfactory.

'The United Nations Commander in Katanga, General

Rhee, has lodged a strong protest with the Kantangese government—' The announcer's voice was overlaid by the electric crackle of static.

'We winged him!' rejoiced Wally Hendry. The scab on his cheek had dried black, with angry red edges.

'Shut up,' snapped Bruce, 'we're trying to hear what's happening.'

'You can't hear a bloody thing now. André, there's a bottle in my pack. Get it! I'm going to drink to that coolie with a bullet up his—'

Then the radio cleared and the announcer's voice came through loudly.

' – at Senwati Mission fifty miles from the river harbour of Port Reprieve. A spokesman for the Central Congolese Government denied that the Congolese troops were operating in this area, and it is feared that a large body of armed bandits is taking advantage of the unsettled conditions to—' Again the static drowned it out.

'Damn this set,' muttered Bruce as he tried to tune it.

' – stated today that the removal of missile equipment from the Russian bases in Cuba had been confirmed by aerial reconnaissance—'

'That's all that we are interested in.' Bruce switched off the radio. 'What a shambles! Ruffy, where is Senwati Mission?'

'Top end of the swamp, near the Rhodesian border.'

'Fifty miles from Port Reprieve,' muttered Bruce, not attempting to conceal his anxiety.

'It's more than that by road, boss, more like a hundred.'

'That should take them three or four days in this weather, with time off for looting along the way,' Bruce calculated. 'It will be cutting it fairly fine. We must get through to Port Reprieve by tomorrow evening and pull out again at dawn the next day.'

'Why not keep going tonight?' Hendry removed the

48

bottle from his lips to ask. 'Better than sitting here being eaten by mosquitoes.'

'We'll stay,' Bruce answered. 'It won't do anybody much good to derail this lot in the dark.' He turned back to Ruffy. 'Three-hour watches tonight, Sergeant Major. Lieutenant Haig will take the first, then Lieutenant Hendry, then Lieutenant de Surrier, and I'll do the dawn spell.'

'Okay, boss. I'd better make sure my boys aren't sleeping.'

He left the compartment and the broken glass from the corridor windows crunched under his boots.

'I'll be on my way also.' Mike stood up and pulled the groundsheet over his shoulders.

'Don't waste the batteries of the searchlights, Mike. Sweep every ten minutes or so.'

'Okay, Bruce.' Mike looked across at Hendry. 'I'll call you at nine o'clock.'

'Jolly good show, old fruit.' Wally exaggerated Mike's accent. 'Good hunting, what!' and then as Mike left the compartment, 'Silly old bugger, why does he have to talk like that?'

No one answered him, and he pulled up his shirt behind.

'André, what's this on my back?'

'It's a pimple.'

'Well, squeeze it then.'

Bruce woke in the night, sweating, with the mosquitoes whining about his face. Outside it was still raining and occasionally the reflected light from the searchlight on the roof of the coach lit the interior dimly.

On one of the bottom bunks Mike Haig lay on his back. His face was shining with sweat and he rolled his head from side to side on the pillow. He was grinding his teeth – a sound to which Bruce had become accustomed, and he preferred it to Hendry's snores.

'You poor old bugger,' whispered Bruce.

From the bunk opposite, André de Surrier whimpered.

In sleep he looked like a child with dark soft hair falling over his forehead.

– 6 –

The rain petered out in the dawn and the sun was hot before it cleared the horizon. It lifted a warm mist from the dripping forest. As they ran north the forest thickened, the trees grew closer together and the undergrowth beneath them was coarser than it had been around Elisabethville.

Through the warm misty dawn Bruce saw the water tower at Msapa Junction rising like a lighthouse above the forest, its silver paint streaked with brown rust. Then they came round the last curve in the tracks and the little settlement huddled before them.

It was small, half a dozen buildings in all, and there was about it the desolate aspect of human habitation reverting to jungle.

Beside the tracks stood the water tower and the raised concrete coal bins. Then the station buildings of wood and iron, with the large sign above the verandah:

MSAPA JUNCTION. Elevation 963m.

There was an avenue of casia flora trees with very dark green foliage and orange flowers; and beyond that, on the edge of the forest, a row of cottages.

One of the cottages had been burned, its ruins were fire blackened and tumbled; and the gardens had lost all sense of discipline with three months' neglect.

'Driver, stop beside the water tower. You have fifteen minutes to fill your boiler.'

'Thank you, monsieur.'

With a heavy sigh of steam the loco pulled up beside the tower.

'Haig, take four men and go back to give the driver a hand.'

'Okay, Bruce.'

Bruce turned once more to the radio.

'Hendry.'

'Hello there.'

'Get a patrol together, six men, and search those cottages. Then take a look at the edge of the bush, we don't want any unexpected visitors.'

Wally Hendry waved an acknowledgement from the leading truck, and Bruce went on:

'Put de Surrier on.' He watched Hendry pass the set to André. 'De Surrier, you are in charge of the leading trucks in Hendry's absence. Keep Hendry covered, but watch the bush behind you also. They could come from there.'

Bruce switched off the set and turned to Ruffy. 'Stay up here on the roof, Ruffy. I'm going to chase them up with the watering. If you see anything, don't write me a postcard, start pooping off.'

Ruffy nodded. 'Have some breakfast to take with you.' He proffered an open bottle of beer.

'Better than bacon and eggs.' Bruce accepted the bottle and climbed down on to the platform. Sipping the beer he walked back along the train and looked up at Mike and the engine driver in the tower.

'Is it empty?' he called up at them.

'Half full, enough for a bath if you want one,' answered Mike.

'Don't tempt me.' The idea was suddenly very attractive, for he could smell his own stale body odour and his eyelids were itchy and swollen from mosquito bites. 'My kingdom for a bath.' He ran his fingers over his jowls and they rasped over stiff beard.

He watched them swing the canvas hose out over the loco. The chubby little engine driver clambered up and sat astride the boiler as he fitted the hose.

A shout behind him made Bruce turn quickly, and he saw Hendry's patrol coming back from the cottages. They were dragging two small prisoners with them.

'Hiding in the first cottage,' shouted Hendry. 'They tried to leg it into the bush.' He prodded one of them with his bayonet. The child cried out and twisted in the hands of the gendarme who held her.

'Enough of that.' Bruce stopped him from using the bayonet again and went to meet them. He looked at the two children.

The girl was close to puberty with breasts like insect bites just starting to show, thin-legged with enlarged knee-caps out of proportion to her thighs and calves. She wore only a dirty piece of trade cloth drawn up between her legs and secured around her waist by a length of bark string, and the tribal tattoo marks across her chest and cheeks and forehead stood proud in ridges of scar tissue.

'Ruffy.' Bruce called him down from the coach. 'Can you speak to them?'

Ruffy picked up the boy and held him on his hip. He was younger than the girl – seven, perhaps eight years old. Very dark-skinned and completely naked, as naked as the terror on his face.

Ruffy grunted sharply and the gendarme released the girl. She stood trembling, making no attempt to escape.

Then in a soothing rumble Ruffy began talking to the boy on his hip; he smiled as he spoke and stroked the child's head. Slowly a little of the fear melted and the boy answered in a piping treble that Bruce could not understand.

'What does he say?' urged Bruce.

'He thinks we're going to eat them,' laughed Ruffy. 'Not enough here for a decent breakfast.' He patted the skinny little arm, grey with crushed filth, then he gave an order to one of the gendarmes. The man disappeared into the coach and came back with a handful of chocolate bars. Still talking, Ruffy peeled one of them and placed it in the boy's mouth. The child's eyes widened appreciatively at the taste and he chewed quickly, his eyes on Ruffy's face, his answers now muffled with chocolate.

At last Ruffy turned to Bruce.

'No trouble here, boss. They come from a small village about an hour's walk away. Just five or six families, and no war party. These kids sneaked across to have a look at the houses, pinch what they could perhaps, but that's all.'

'How many men at this village?' asked Bruce, and Ruffy turned back to the boy. In reply to the question he held up the fingers of both hands, without interrupting the chewing.

'Does he know if the line is clear through to Port Reprieve? Have they burnt the bridges or torn up the tracks?' Both children were dumb to this question. The boy swallowed the last of his chocolate and looked hungrily at Ruffy, who filled his mouth again.

'Jesus,' muttered Hendry with deep disgust. 'Is this a crèche or something. Let's all play ring around the roses.'

'Shut up,' snapped Bruce, and then to Ruffy, 'Have they seen any soldiers?'

Two heads shaken in solemn unison.

'Have they seen any war parties of their own people?'

Again solemn negative.

'All right, give them the rest of the chocolate,' instructed Bruce. That was all he could get out of them, and time was wasting. He glanced back at the tower and saw that Haig and the engine driver had finished watering. For a further second he studied the boy. His own son would be about the same age now; it was twelve months since – Bruce stopped himself hurriedly. That way lay madness.

'Hendry, take them back to the edge of the bush and turn them loose. Hurry up. We've wasted long enough.'

'You're telling me!' grunted Hendry and beckoned to the

two children. With Hendry leading and a gendarme on each side they trotted away obediently and disappeared behind the station building.

'Driver, are your preparations complete?'

'Yes, monsieur, we are ready to depart.'

'Shovel all the coal in, we've gotta keep her rolling.' Bruce smiled at him, he liked the little man and their stilted exchanges gave him pleasure.

'Pardon, monsieur.'

'It was an imbecility, a joke – forgive me.'

'Ah, a joke!' The roly-poly stomach wobbled merrily.

'Okay, Mike,' Bruce shouted, 'get your men aboard. We are—'

A burst of automatic gunfire cut his voice short. It came from behind the station buildings, and it battered into the heat-muted morning with such startling violence that for an instant Bruce stood paralysed.

'Haig,' he yelled, 'get up front and take over from de Surrier.' That was the weak point, and Mike's party ran down the train.

'You men.' Bruce stopped the six gendarmes. 'Come with me.' They fell in behind him, and with a quick glance Bruce assured himself that the train was safe. All along its length rifle barrels were poking out protectively, while on the roof Ruffy was dragging the Bren round to cover the flank. A charge by even a thousand Baluba must fail before the fire power that was ready now to receive it.

'Come on,' said Bruce and ran, with the gendarmes behind him, to the sheltering wall of the station building. There had been no shot fired since that initial burst, which could mean either that it was a false alarm or that Hendry's party had been overwhelmed by the first rush.

The door of the station master's office was locked. Bruce kicked and it crashed open with the weight of his booted foot behind it.

54

I've always wanted to do that, he thought happily in his excitement, ever since I saw Gable do it in *San Francisco*.

'You four – inside! Cover us from the windows.' They crowded into the room with their rifles held ready. Through the open door Bruce saw the telegraph equipment on the table by the far wall; it was clattering metallically from traffic on the Elisabethville-Jadotville line. Why is it that under the stimulus of excitement my mind always registers irrelevances? Which thought is another irrelevancy, he decided.

'Come on, you two, stay with me.' He led them down the outside wall, keeping in close to its sheltering bulk, pausing at the corner to check the load of his rifle and slip the selector on to rapid fire.

A further moment he hesitated. What will I find around this corner? A hundred naked savages crowded round the mutilated bodies of Hendry and his gendarmes, or . . . ?

Crouching, ready to jump back behind the wall, rifle held at high port across his chest, every muscle and nerve of his body cocked like a hair-trigger, Bruce stepped sideways into the open.

Hendry and the two gendarmes stood in the dusty road beyond the first cottage. They were relaxed, talking together, Hendry reloading his rifle, cramming the magazine with big red hands on which the gingery hair caught the sunlight. A cigarette dangled from his lower lip and he laughed suddenly, throwing his head back as he did so and the cigarette ash dropped down his jacket front. Bruce noticed the long dark sweat stain across his shoulders.

The two children lay in the road fifty yards farther on.

Bruce was suddenly cold, it came from inside, a cramping coldness of the guts and chest. Slowly he straightened up and began to walk towards the children. His feet fell silently in the powder dust and the only sound was his own breathing, hoarse, as though a wounded beast followed close behind him. He walked past Hendry and the two gendarmes without looking at them; but they stopped talking, watching him uneasily.

He reached the girl first and went down on one knee beside her, laying his rifle aside and turning her gently on to her back.

'This isn't true,' he whispered. 'This can't be true.'

The bullet had taken half her chest out with it, a hole the size of a coffee cup, with the blood still moving in it, but slowly, oozing, welling up into it with the viscosity of new honey.

Bruce moved across to the boy; he felt an almost dreamlike sense of unreality.

'No, this isn't true.' He spoke louder, trying to undo it with words.

Three bullets had hit the boy; one had torn his arm loose at the shoulder and the sharp white end of the bone pointed accusingly out of the wound. The other bullets had severed his trunk almost in two.

It came from far away, like the rising roar of a train along a tunnel. Bruce could feel his whole being shaken by the strength of it, he shut his eyes and listened to the roaring in his head, and with his eyes tight closed his vision was filled with the colour of blood.

'Hold on!' a tiny voice screamed in his roaring head. 'Don't let go, fight it. Fight it as you've fought before.'

And he clung like a flood victim to the straw of his sanity while the great roaring was all around him. Then the roar was muted, rumbling away, gone past, a whisper, now nothing.

The coldness came back to him, a coldness more vast than the flood had been.

He opened his eyes and breathed again, stood up and walked back to where Hendry stood with the two gendarmes.

'Corporal,' Bruce addressed one of the men beside Hendry; and with a shock he heard that his own voice was calm, without any trace of the fury that had so nearly carried him away on its flood.

'Corporal, go back to the train. Tell Lieutenant Haig and Sergeant Major Ruffararo that I want them here.'

Thankfully the man went, and Bruce spoke to Wally Hendry in the same dispassionate tone.

'I told you to turn them loose,' he said.

'So they could run home and call the whole pack down on us – is that what you wanted, Bucko?' Hendry had recovered now, he was defiant, grinning.

'So instead you murdered them?'

'Murdered! You crazy or something, Bruce? They're Balubes, aren't they? Bloody man-eating Balubes!' shouted Hendry angrily, no longer grinning. 'What's wrong with you, man? This is war, Bucko, war. C'est la guerre, like the man said, c'est la guerre!' Then suddenly his voice moderated again. 'Let's forget it. I did what was right, now let's forget it; what's two more bloody Balubes after all the killing that's been going on? Let's forget it.'

Bruce did not answer, he lit a cigarette and looked beyond Hendry for the others to come.

'How's that, Bruce? You willing we just forget it?' persisted Hendry.

'On the contrary, Hendry, I make you a sacred oath, and I call upon God to witness it.' Bruce was not looking at him, he couldn't trust himself to look at Hendry without killing him. 'This is my promise to you: I will have you hanged for this, not shot, hanged on good hemp rope. I have sent for Haig and Ruffararo so we'll have plenty of witnesses. The first thing I do once we get back to Elisabethville will be to turn you over to the proper authorities.'

'You don't mean that!'

'I have never meant anything so seriously in my life.'

'Jesus, Bruce—!'

Then Haig and Ruffy came; they came running until they saw, and they stopped suddenly and stood uncertainly in the bright sun, looking from Bruce to the two frail little corpses lying in the road.

'What happened?' asked Mike.

'Hendry shot them,' answered Bruce.

'What for?'

'Only he knows.'

'You mean he – he just killed them, just shot them down?'

'Yes.'

'My God,' said Mike, and then again, his voice dull with shock, 'my God.'

'Go and look at them, Haig. I want you to look closely so you remember.'

Haig walked across to the children.

'You too, Ruffy. You'll be a witness at the trial.'

Mike Haig and Ruffy walked side by side to where the children lay, and stood staring down at them. Hendry shuffled his feet in the dust awkwardly and then went on loading the magazine of his rifle.

'Oh, for Chrissake!' he blustered. 'What's all the fuss? They're just a couple of Balubes.'

Wheeling slowly to face him Mike Haig's face was a yellowish colour with only his cheeks and his nose still flushed with the tiny burst of veins beneath the surface of the skin, but there was no colour in his lips. Each breath he drew sobbed in his throat. He started back towards Hendry, still breathing that way, and his mouth was working as he tried to force it to speak. As he came on he unslung the rifle from his shoulder.

'Haig!' said Bruce sharply.

'This time – you – you bloody – this is the last—' mouthed Haig.

'Watch it, Bucko!' Hendry warned him. He stepped

back, clumsily trying to fit the loaded magazine on to his rifle.

Mike Haig dropped the point of his bayonet to the level of Hendry's stomach.

'Haig!' shouted Bruce, and Haig charged surprisingly fast for a man of his age, leaning forward, leading with the bayonet at Hendry's stomach, the incoherent mouthings reaching their climax in a formless bellow.

'Come on, then!' Hendry answered him and stepped forward. As they came together Hendry swept the bayonet to one side with the butt of his own rifle. The point went under his armpit and they collided chest to chest, staggering as Haig's weight carried them backwards. Hendry dropped his rifle and locked both arms round Haig's neck, forcing his head back so that his face was tilted up at the right angle.

'Look out, Mike, he's going to butt!' Bruce had recognized the move, but his warning came too late. Hendry's head jerked forward and Mike gasped as the front of Hendry's steel helmet caught him across the bridge of his nose. The rifle slipped from Mike's grip and fell into the road, he lifted his hands and covered his face with spread fingers and the redness oozed out between them.

Again Hendry's head jerked forward like a hammer and again Mike gasped as the steel smashed into his face and fingers.

'Knee him, Mike!' Bruce yelled as he tried to take up a position from which to intervene, but they were staggering in a circle, turning like a wheel and Bruce could not get in.

Hendry's legs were braced apart as he drew his head back to strike again, and Mike's knee went up between them, all the way up with power into the fork of Hendry's crotch.

Breaking from the clinch, his mouth open in a silent scream of agony, Hendry doubled up with both hands holding his lower stomach, and sagged slowly on to his knees in the dust.

Dazed, with blood running into his mouth, Mike fumbled with the canvas flap of his holster.

'I'll kill you, you murdering swine.'

The pistol came out into his right hand; short-barrelled, blue and ugly.

Bruce stepped up behind him, his thumb found the nerve centre below the elbow and as he dug in the pistol dropped from Mike's paralysed hand and dangled on its lanyard against his knee.

'Ruffy, stop him,' Bruce shouted, for Hendry was clawing painfully at the rifle that lay in the dust beside him.

'Got it, boss!' Ruffy stooped quickly over the crawling body at his feet, in one swift movement opened the flap of the holster, drew the revolver and the lanyard snapped like cotton as he jerked on it.

They stood like that: Bruce holding Haig from behind, and Hendry crouched at Ruffy's feet. The only sound for several seconds was the hoarse rasping of breath.

Bruce felt Mike relaxing in his grip as the madness left him; he unclipped his pistol from his lanyard and let it drop.

'Leave me, Bruce. I'm all right now.'

'Are you sure? I don't want to shoot you.'

'No, I'm all right.'

'If you start it again, I'll have to shoot you. Do you understand?'

'Yes, I'll be all right now. I lost my senses for a moment.'

'You certainly did,' Bruce agreed, and released him.

They formed a circle round the kneeling Hendry, and Bruce spoke.

'If either you or Haig start it again you'll answer to me, do you hear me?'

Hendry looked up, his small eyes slitted with pain. He did not answer.

'Do you hear me?' Bruce repeated the question and Hendry nodded.

'Good! From now on, Hendry, you are under open arrest.

I can't spare men to guard you, and you're welcome to escape if you'd like to try. The local gentry would certainly entertain you most handsomely, they'd probably arrange a special banquet in your honour.'

Hendry's lips drew back in a snarl that exposed teeth with green slimy stains on them.

'But remember my promise, Hendry, as soon as we get back to—'

'Wally, Wally, are you hurt?' André came running from the direction of the station. He knelt beside Hendry.

'Get away, leave me alone.' Hendry struck out at him impatiently and André recoiled.

'De Surrier, who gave you permission to leave your post? Get back to the train.'

André looked up uncertainly, and then back to Hendry.

'De Surrier, you heard me. Get going. And you also, Haig.'

He watched them disappear behind the station building before he glanced once more at the two children. There was a smear of blood and melted chocolate across the boy's cheek and his eyes were wide open in an expression of surprise. Already the flies were settling, crawling delightedly over the two small corpses.

'Ruffy, get spades. Bury them under those trees.' He pointed at the avenue of casia flora. 'But do it quickly.' He spoke brusquely so that how he felt would not show in his voice.

'Okay, boss. I'll fix it.'

'Come on, Hendry,' Bruce snapped, and Wally Hendry heaved to his feet and followed him meekly back to the train.

Slowly from Msapa Junction they travelled northwards through the forest. Each tree seemed to have been cast from the same mould, tall and graceful in itself, but when multiplied countless million times the effect was that of numbing monotony. Above them was a lane of open sky with the clouds scattered, but slowly regrouping for the next assault, and the forest shut in the moist heat so they sweated even in the wind of the train's movement.

'How is your face?' asked Bruce and Mike Haig touched the parallel swellings across his forehead where the skin was broken and discoloured.

'It will do,' he decided; then he lifted his eyes and looked across the open trucks at Wally Hendry. 'You shouldn't have stopped me, Bruce.'

Bruce did not answer, but he also watched Hendry as he leaned uncomfortably against the side of the leading truck, obviously favouring his injuries, his face turned half away from them, talking to André.

'You should have let me kill him,' Mike went on. 'A man who can shoot down two small children in cold blood and then laugh about it afterwards—!' Mike left the rest unsaid, but his hands were opening and closing in his lap.

'It's none of your business,' said Bruce, sensitive to the implied rebuke. 'What are you? One of God's avenging angels?'

'None of my business, you say?' Mike turned quickly to face Bruce. 'My God, what kind of man are you? I hope for your sake you don't mean that!'

'I'll tell you in words of one syllable what kind of man I am, Haig,' Bruce answered flatly. 'I'm the kind that minds my own bloody business, that lets other people lead their own lives. I am ready to take reasonable measures to prevent others flouting the code which society has drawn up for us, but that's all. Hendry has committed murder; this I agree is a bad thing, and when we get back to Elisabethville I will bring it to the attention of the people whose business it is. But I am not going to wave banners and quote from the Bible and froth at the mouth.'

'That's all?'

'That's all.'

'You don't feel sorry for those two kids?'

'Yes I do. But pity doesn't heal bullet wounds; all it does is distress me. So I switch off the pity – they can't use it.'

'You don't feel anger or disgust or horror at Hendry?'

'The same thing applies,' explained Bruce, starting to lose patience again. 'I could work up a sweat about it if I let myself loose on an emotional orgy, as you are doing.'

'So instead you treat something as evil as Hendry with an indifferent tolerance?' asked Mike.

'Jesus Christ!' grated Bruce. 'What the hell do you want me to do?'

'I want you to stop playing dead. I want you to be able to recognize evil and to destroy it.' Mike was starting to lose his temper also; his nerves were taut.

'That's great! Do you know where I can buy a second-hand crusader outfit and a white horse, then singlehanded I will ride out to wage war on cruelty and ignorance, lust and greed and hatred and poverty—'

'That's not what I—' Mike tried to interrupt, but Bruce overrode him, his handsome face flushed darkly with anger and the sun. 'You want me to destroy evil wherever I find it. You old fool, don't you know that it has a hundred heads and that for each one you cut off another hundred grow in its place? Don't you know that it's in you also, so to destroy it you have to destroy yourself?'

'You're a coward, Curry! The first time you burn a finger you run away and build yourself an asbestos shelter—'

'I don't like being called names, Haig. Put a leash on your tongue.'

Mike paused and his expression changed, softening into a grin.

'I'm sorry, Bruce. I was just trying to teach you—'

'Thank you,' scoffed Bruce, his voice still harsh; he had not been placated by the apology. 'You are going to teach me, thanks very much! But what are you going to teach me, Haig? What are you qualified to teach? "How to find success and happiness" by Laughing Lad Haig who worked his way down to a lieutenancy in the black army of Katanga – how's that as a title for your lecture, or do you prefer something more technical like: "The applications of alcohol to spiritual research—"'

'All right, Bruce. Drop it, I'll shut up,' and Bruce saw how deeply he had wounded Mike. He regretted it then, he would have liked to unsay it. But that's one thing you can never do.

Beside him Mike Haig was suddenly much older and more tired looking, the pouched wrinkles below his eyes seemed to have deepened in the last few seconds, and a little more of the twinkle had gone from his eyes. His short laughter had a bitter humourless ring to it.

'When you put it that way it's really quite funny.'

'I punched a little low,' admitted Bruce, and then, 'perhaps I should let you shoot Hendry. A waste of ammunition really, but seeing that you want to so badly,' Bruce drew his pistol and offered it to Mike butt first, 'use mine.' He grinned disarmingly at Mike and his grin was almost impossible to resist; Mike started to laugh. It wasn't a very good joke, but somehow it caught fire between them and suddenly they were laughing together.

Mike Haig's battered features spread like warm butter and twenty years dropped from his face. Bruce leaned back against the sandbags with his mouth wide open, the pistol still in his hand and his long lean body throbbing uncontrollably with laughter.

There was something feverish in it, as though they were trying with laughter to gargle away the taste of blood and hatred. It was the laughter of despair.

Below them the men in the trucks turned to watch them, puzzled at first, and then beginning to chuckle in sympathy, not recognizing the sickness of that sound.

'Hey, boss,' called Ruffy. 'First time I ever seen you laugh like you meant it.'

And the epidemic spread, everyone was laughing, even André de Surrier was smiling.

Only Wally Hendry was untouched by it, silent and sullen, watching them with small expressionless eyes.

They came to the bridge over the Cheke in the middle of the afternoon. Both the road and the railway crossed it side by side, but after this brief meeting they diverged and the road twisted away to the left. The river was padded on each bank by dense dark green bush; three hundred yards thick, a matted tangle of thorn and tree fern with the big trees growing up through it and bursting into flower as they reached the sunlight.

'Good place for an ambush,' muttered Mike Haig, eyeing the solid green walls of vegetation on each side of the lines.

'Charming, isn't it,' agreed Bruce, and by the uneasy air of alertness that had settled on his gendarmes it was clear that they agreed with him.

The train nosed its way carefully into the river bush like a steel snake along a rabbit run, and they came to the river. Bruce switched on the set.

'Driver, stop this side of the bridge. I wish to inspect it before entrusting our precious cargo to it.'

'Oui, monsieur.'

The Cheke river at this point was fifty yards wide, deep, quick-flowing and angry with flood water which had almost covered the white sand beaches along each bank. Its bottle-green colour was smoked with mud and there were whirlpools round the stone columns of the bridge.

'Looks all right,' Haig gave his opinion. 'How far are we from Port Reprieve now?'

Bruce spread his field map on the roof of the coach between his legs and found the brackets that straddled the convoluted ribbon of the river.

'Here we are.' He touched it and then ran his finger along the stitched line of the railway until it reached the red circle that marked Port Reprieve. 'About thirty miles to go, another hour's run. We'll be there before dark.'

'Those are the Lufira hills.' Mike Haig pointed to the blue smudge that only just showed above the forest ahead of them.

'We'll be able to see the town from the top,' agreed Bruce. 'The river runs parallel to them on the other side, and the swamp is off to the right, the swamp is the source of the river.'

He rolled the map and passed it back to Ruffy who slid it into the plastic map case.

'Ruffy, Lieutenant Haig and I are going ahead to have a look at the bridge. Keep an eye on the bush.'

'Okay, boss. You want a beer to take with you?'

'Thanks.' Bruce was thirsty and he emptied half the bottle before climbing down to join Mike on the gravel embankment. Rifles unslung, watching the bush on each side uneasily, they hurried forward and with relief reached the bridge and went out into the centre of it.

'Seems solid enough,' commented Mike. 'No one has tampered with it.'

'It's wood.' Bruce stamped on the heavy wild mahogany timbers. They were three feet thick and stained with a dark chemical to inhibit rotting.

'So, it's wood?' enquired Mike.

'Wood burns,' explained Bruce. 'It would be easy to burn

66

it down.' He leaned his elbows on the guard rail, drained the beer bottle and dropped it to the surface of the river twenty feet below. There was a thoughtful expression on his face.

'Very probably there are Baluba in the bush' – he pointed at the banks – 'watching us at this moment. They might get the same idea. I wonder if I should leave a guard here?'

Mike leaned on the rail beside him and they both stared out to where the river took a bend two hundred yards downstream; in the crook of the bend grew a tree twice as tall as any of its neighbours. The trunk was straight and covered with smooth silvery bark and its foliage piled to a high green steeple against the clouds. It was the natural point of focus for their eyes as they weighed the problem.

'I wonder what kind of tree that is. I've never seen one like it before.' Bruce was momentarily diverted by the grandeur of it. 'It looks like a giant blue gum.'

'It's quite a sight,' Mike concurred. 'I'd like to go down and have a closer—'

Then suddenly he stiffened and there was an edge of alarm in his voice as he pointed.

'Bruce, there! What's that in the lower branches?'

'Where?'

'Just above the first fork, on the left—' Mike was pointing and suddenly Bruce saw it. For a second he thought it was a leopard, then he realized it was too dark and long.

'It's a man,' exclaimed Mike.

'Baluba,' snapped Bruce; he could see the shape now and the sheen of naked black flesh, the kilt of animal tails and the headdress of feathers. A long bow stood up behind the man's shoulder as he balanced on the branch and steadied himself with one hand against the trunk. He was watching them.

Bruce glanced round at the train. Hendry had noticed their agitation and, following the direction of Mike's raised arm, he had spotted the Baluba. Bruce realized what Hendry was going to do and he opened his mouth to shout, but before he could do so Hendry had snatched his rifle off his shoulder, swung it up and fired a long, rushing, hammering burst.

'The trigger-happy idiot,' snarled Bruce and looked back at the tree. Slabs of white bark were flying from the trunk and the bullets reaped leaves that fluttered down like crippled insects, but the Baluba had disappeared.

The gunfire ceased abruptly and in its place Hendry was shouting with hoarse excitement.

'I got him, I got the bastard.'

'Hendry!' Bruce's voice was also hoarse, but with anger, 'Who ordered you to fire?'

'He was a bloody Baluba, a mucking big bloody Baluba. Didn't you see him, hey? Didn't you see him, man?'

'Come here, Hendry.'

'I got the bastard,' rejoiced Hendry.

'Are you deaf? Come here!'

While Hendry climbed down from the truck and came towards them Bruce asked Haig:

'Did he hit him?'

'I'm not sure. I don't think so, I think he jumped. If he had been hit he'd have been thrown backwards, you know how it knocks them over.'

'Yes,' said Bruce, 'I know.' A .300 bullet from an FN struck with a force of well over a ton. When you hit a man there was no doubt about it. All right, so the Baluba was still in there.

Hendry came up, swaggering, laughing with excitement.

'So you killed, hey?' Bruce asked.

'Stone dead, stone bloody dead!'

'Can you see him?'

'No, he's down in the bush.'

'Do you want to go and have a look at him, Hendry? Do you want to go and get his ears?'

Ears are the best trophy you can take from a man, not as

68

good as the skin of a black-maned lion or the great bossed horns of a buffalo, but better than the scalp. The woolly cap of an African scalp is a drab thing, messy to take and difficult to cure. You have to salt it and stretch it inside out over a helmet; even then it smells badly. Ears are much less trouble and Hendry was an avid collector. He was not the only one in the army of Katanga; the taking of ears was common practice.

'Yeah, I want them.' Hendry detached the bayonet from the muzzle of his rifle. 'I'll nip down and get them.'

'You can't let anyone go in there, Bruce. Not even him,' protested Haig quietly.

'Why not? He deserves it, he worked hard for it.'

'Only take a minute.' Hendry ran his thumb along the bayonet to test the edge. My God! He really means it, thought Bruce; he'd go into that tangled stuff for a pair of ears – he's not brave, he's just stupendously lacking in imagination.

'Wait for me, Bruce, it won't take long.' Hendry started back.

'You're not serious, Bruce?' Mike asked.

'No,' agreed Bruce, 'I'm not serious,' and his voice was cold and hard as he caught hold of Hendry's shoulder and stopped him.

'Listen to me! You have no more chances – that was it. I'm waiting for you now, Hendry. Just once more, that's all. Just once more.'

Hendry's face turned sullen again.

'Don't push me, Bucko.'

'Get back to the train and bring it across,' said Bruce contemptuously and turned to Haig.

'Now we'll have to leave a guard here. They know we've gone across and they'll burn it for a certainty, especially after that little fiasco.'

'Who are you going to leave?'

'Ten men, say, under a sergeant. We'll be back by

nightfall or tomorrow morning at the latest. They should be safe enough. I doubt there is a big war party here, a few strays perhaps, but the main force will be closer to the town.'

'I hope you're right.'

'So do I,' said Bruce absently, his mind busy with the problem of defending the bridge. 'We'll strip all the sandbags off the coaches and build an emplacement here in the middle of the roadway, leave two of the battery-operated searchlights and a case of flares with them, one of the Brens and a couple of cases of grenades. Food and water for a week. No, they'll be all right.'

The train was rolling down slowly towards them – and a single arrow rose from the edge of the jungle. Slowly it rose, curving in flight and falling towards the train, dropping faster now, silently into the mass of men in the leading truck.

So Hendry had missed and the Baluba had come up stream through the thick bush to launch his arrow in retaliation. Bruce sprang to the guard rail and, using it as a rest for his rifle, opened up in short bursts, searching the green mass and seeing it tremble with his bullets. Haig was shooting also, hunting the area from which the arrow had come.

The train was up to them now and Bruce slung his rifle over his shoulder and scrambled up the side of the truck. He pushed his way to the radio set.

'Driver, stop the covered coaches in the middle of the bridge,' he snapped, and then he switched it off and looked for Ruffy.

'Sergeant Major, get all those sandbags off the roof into the roadway.' While they worked, the gendarmes would be protected from further arrows by the body of the train.

'Okay, boss.'

'Kanaki.' Bruce picked his most reliable sergeant. 'I am leaving you here with ten men to hold the bridge for us.

Take one of the Brens, and two of the lights—' Quickly Bruce issued his orders and then he had time to ask André:

'What happened to that arrow? Was anyone hit?'

'No, missed by a few inches. Here it is.'

'That was a bit of luck.' Bruce took the arrow from André and inspected it quickly. A light reed, crudely fletched with green leaves and with the iron head bound into it with a strip of rawhide. It looked fragile and ineffectual, but the barbs of the head were smeared thickly with a dark paste that had dried like toffee.

'Pleasant,' murmured Bruce, and then he shuddered slightly. He could imagine it embedded in his body with the poison purple-staining the flesh beneath the skin. He had heard that it was not a comfortable death, and the iron-tipped reed was suddenly malignant and repulsive. He snapped it in half and threw it out over the side of the bridge before he jumped down from the truck to supervise the building of the guard post.

'Not enough sandbags, boss.'

'Take the mattresses off all the bunks, Ruffy.' Bruce solved that quickly. The leather-covered coir pallets would stop an arrow with ease.

Fifteen minutes later the post was completed, a shoulder-high ring of sandbags and mattresses large enough to accommodate ten men and their equipment, with embrasures sited to command both ends of the bridge.

'We'll be back early tomorrow, Kanaki. Let none of your men leave this post for any purpose; the gaps between the timbers are sufficient for purposes of sanitation.'

'We shall enjoy enviable comfort, Captain. But we will lack that which soothes.' Kanaki grinned meaningly at Bruce.

'Ruffy, leave them a case of beer.'

'A whole case?' Ruffy made no attempt to hide his shocked disapproval of such a prodigal order.

'Is my credit not good?'

'You credit is okay, boss,' and then he changed to French to make his protest formal. 'My concern is the replacement of such a valuable commodity.'

'You're wasting time, Ruffy!'

– 8 –

From the bridge it was thirty miles to Port Reprieve. They met the road again six miles outside the town; it crossed under them and disappeared into the forest again to circle out round the high ground taking the easier route into Port Reprieve. But the railroad climbed up the hills in a series of traverses and came out at the top six hundred feet above the town. On the stony slopes the forest found meagre purchase and the vegetation was sparser; it did not obscure the view.

Standing on the roof Bruce looked out across the Lufira swamps to the north, a vastness of poisonous green swamp grass and open water, disappearing into the blue heat haze without any sign of ending. From its southern extremity it was drained by the Lufira river. The river was half a mile wide, deep olive-green, ruffled darker by eddies of wind across its surface, fenced into the very edge of the water by a solid barrier of dense river bush. In the angle formed by the swamp and the river was a headland which protected the natural harbour of Port Reprieve. The town was on a spit of land, the harbour on one side and a smaller swamp on the other. The road came round the right-hand side of the hills, crossed a causeway over the swamp and entered the single street of the town from the far side.

There were three large buildings in the centre of the town opposite the railway yard, their iron roofs bright beacons in the sunlight; and clustered round them were perhaps fifty smaller thatched dwellings.

Down on the edge of the harbour was a long shed,

obviously a workshop, and two jetties ran into the water. The diamond dredgers were moored alongside; three of them, ungainly black hulks with high superstructures and blunt ends.

It was a place of heat and fever and swamp smells, an ugly little village by a green reptile river.

'Nice place to retire,' Mike Haig grunted.

'Or open a health resort,' said Bruce.

Beyond the causeway, on the main headland, there was another cluster of buildings, just the tops were showing above the forest. Among them rose the copper-clad spire of a church.

'Mission station,' guessed Bruce.

'St Augustine's,' agreed Ruffy. 'My first wife's little brudder got himself educated there. He's an attaché to the ministry of something or other in Elisabethville now, doing damn good for himself.' Boasting a little.

'Bully for him,' said Bruce.

The train had started angling down the hills towards the town.

'Well, I reckon we've made it, boss.'

'I reckon also; all we have to do is get back again.'

'Yessir, I reckon that's all.'

And they ran into the town.

There were more than forty people in the crowd that lined the platform to welcome them.

We'll have a heavy load on the way home, thought Bruce as he ran his eye over them. He saw the bright spots of women's dresses in the throng. Bruce counted four of them. That's another complication; one day I hope I find something in this life that turns out exactly as expected, something that will run smoothly and evenly through to its right and logical conclusion. Some hope, he decided, some bloody hope.

The joy and relief of the men and women on the platform was pathetically apparent in their greetings. Most of the women were crying and the men ran beside the train like small boys as it slid in along the raised concrete platform. All of them were of mixed blood, Bruce noted. They varied in colour from creamy yellow to charcoal. The Belgians had certainly left much to be remembered by.

Standing back from the throng, a little aloof from the general jollification, was a half-blooded Belgian. There was an air of authority about him that was unmistakable. On one side of him stood a large bosomy woman of his own advanced age, darker skinned than he was; but Bruce saw immediately that she was his wife. At his other hand stood a figure dressed in a white open-necked shirt and blue jeans that Bruce at first thought was a boy, until the head turned and he saw the long plume of dark hair that hung down her back, and the unmanly double pressure beneath the white shirt.

The train stopped and Bruce jumped down on to the platform and laughingly pushed his way through the crowds towards the Belgian. Despite a year in the Congo, Bruce had not grown accustomed to being kissed by someone who had not shaved for two or three days and who smelled strongly of garlic and cheap tobacco. This atrocity was committed upon him a dozen times or more before he arrived before the Belgian.

'The Good Lord bless you for coming to our aid, Monsieur Captain.' The Belgian recognized the twin bars on the front of Bruce's helmet and held out his hand. Bruce had expected another kiss, so he accepted the handshake with relief.

'I am only glad that we are in time,' he answered.

'May I introduce myself – Martin Boussier, district manager of Union Miniére Corporation, and this is my wife, Madame Boussier.' He was a tall man, but unlike his wife, sparsely fleshed. His hair was completely silver and his skin folded, toughened and browned by a life under the equatorial sun. Bruce took an instant liking to him. Madame

Boussier pressed her bulk against Bruce and kissed him heartily. Her moustache was too soft to cause him discomfort and she smelled of toilet soap, which was a distinct improvement, decided Bruce.

'May I also present Madame Cartier,' and for the first time Bruce looked squarely at the girl. A number of things registered in his mind simultaneously: the paleness of her skin which was not unhealthy but had an opaque coolness which he wanted to touch, the size of her eyes which seemed to fill half her face, the unconscious provocation of her lips, and the use of the word *Madame* before her name.

'Captain Curry – of the Katanga Army,' said Bruce. She's too young to be married, can't be more than seventeen. She's still got that little girl freshness about her and I bet she smells like an unweaned puppy.

'Thank you for coming, monsieur.' She had a throatiness in her voice as though she were just about to laugh or to make love, and Bruce added three years to his estimate of her age. That was not a little girl's voice, nor were those little girl's legs in the jeans, and little girls had less under their shirt fronts.

His eyes came back to her face and he saw that there was colour in her cheeks now and sparks of annoyance in her eyes.

My God, he thought, I'm ogling her like a matelot on shore leave. He hurriedly transferred his attention back to Boussier, but his throat felt constricted as he asked:

'How many are you?'

'There are forty-two of us, of which five are women and two are children.'

Bruce nodded, it was what he had expected. The women could ride in one of the covered coaches. He turned and surveyed the railway yard.

'Is there a turntable on which we can revolve the locomotive?' he asked Boussier.

'No, Captain.'

They would have to reverse all the way back to Msapa Junction, another complication. It would be more difficult to keep a watch on the tracks ahead, and it would mean a sooty and uncomfortable journey.

'What precautions have you taken against attack, monsieur?'

'They are inadequate, Captain,' Boussier admitted. 'I have not sufficient men to defend the town – most of the population left before the emergency. Instead I have posted sentries on all the approaches and I have fortified the hotel to the best of my ability. It was there we intended to stand in the event of attack.'

Bruce nodded again and glanced up at the sun. It was already reddening as it dropped towards the horizon, perhaps another hour or two of daylight.

'Monsieur, it is too late to entrain all your people and leave before nightfall. I intend to load their possessions this evening. We will stay overnight and leave in the early morning.'

'We are all anxious to be away from this place; we have twice seen large parties of Baluba on the edge of the jungle.'

'I understand,' said Bruce. 'But the dangers of travelling by night exceed those of waiting another twelve hours.'

'The decision is yours,' Boussier agreed. 'What do you wish us to do now?'

'Please see to the embarkation of your people. I regret that only the most essential possessions may be entertained. We will be almost a hundred persons.'

'I shall see to that myself,' Boussier assured him, 'and then?'

'Is that the hotel?' Bruce pointed across the street at one of the large double-storeyed buildings. It was only two hundred yards from where they stood.

'Yes, Captain.'

'Good,' said Bruce. 'It is close enough. Your people can

spend the night there in more comfort than aboard the train.'

He looked at the girl again; she was watching him with a small smile on her face. It was a smile of almost maternal amusement, as though she were watching a little boy playing at soldiers. Now it was Bruce's turn to feel annoyed. He was suddenly embarrassed by his uniform and epaulettes, by the pistol at his hip, the automatic rifle across his shoulder and the heavy helmet on his head.

'I will require someone who is familiar with the area to accompany me, I want to inspect your defences,' he said to Boussier.

'Madame Cartier could show you,' suggested Boussier's wife artlessly. I wonder if she noticed our little exchange, thought Bruce. Of course she did. All women have a most sensitive nose for that sort of thing.

'Will you go with the captain, Shermaine?' asked Madame Boussier.

'As the captain wishes.' She was still smiling.

'That is settled then,' said Bruce gruffly. 'I will meet you at the hotel in ten minutes, after I have made arrangements here.' He turned back to Boussier. 'You may proceed with the embarkation, monsieur.' Bruce left them and went back to the train.

'Hendry,' he shouted, 'you and de Surrier will stay on board. We are not leaving until the morning but these people are going to load their stuff now. In the meantime rig the searchlights to sweep both sides of the track and make sure the Brens are properly sited.'

Hendry grunted an acknowledgement without looking at Bruce.

'Mike, take ten men with you and go to the hotel. I want you there in case of trouble during the night.'

'Okay, Bruce.'

'Ruffy.'

'Sa!'

'Take a gang and help the driver refuel.'

'Okay, boss. Hey, boss!'

'Yes.' Bruce turned to him.

'When you go to the hotel, have a look-see maybe they got some beer up there. We're just about fresh out.'

'I'll keep it in mind.'

'Thanks, boss.' Ruffy looked relieved. 'I'd hate like hell to die of thirst in this hole.'

The townsfolk were streaming back towards the hotel. The girl Shermaine walked with the Boussiers, and Bruce heard Hendry's voice above him.

'Jesus, look what that pretty has got in her pants. What ever it is, one thing is sure: it's round and it's in two pieces, and those pieces move like they don't belong to each other.'

'You haven't any work to do Hendry?' Bruce asked harshly.

'What's wrong, Curry?' Hendry jeered down at him. 'You got plans yourself? Is that it, Bucko?'

'She's married,' said Bruce, and immediately was surprised that he had said it.

'Sure,' laughed Hendry. 'All the best ones are married; that don't mean a thing, not a bloody thing.'

'Get on with your work,' snapped Bruce, and then to Haig, 'Are you ready? Come with me then.'

– 9 –

When they reached the hotel Boussier was waiting for them on the open verandah. He led Bruce aside and spoke quietly.

'Monsieur, I don't wish to be an alarmist but I have received some most disturbing news. There are brigands armed with modern weapons raiding down from the north.

78

The last reports state that they had sacked Senwati Mission about three hundred kilometres north of here.'

'Yes,' Bruce nodded, 'I know about them. We heard on the radio.'

'Then you will have realized that they can be expected to arrive here very soon.'

'I don't see them arriving before tomorrow afternoon; by then we should be well on our way to Msapa Junction.'

'I hope you are right, Monsieur. The atrocities committed by this General Moses at Senwati are beyond the conception of any normal mind. He appears to bear an almost pathological hatred for all people of European descent.' Boussier hesitated before going on. 'There were a dozen white nuns at Senwati. I have heard that they—'

'Yes,' Bruce interrupted him quickly; he did not want to listen to it. 'I can imagine. Try and prevent these stories circulating amongst your people. I don't want to have them panic.'

'Of course,' Boussier nodded.

'Do you know what force this General Moses commands?'

'It is not more than a hundred men but, as I have said, they are all armed with modern weapons. I have even heard that they have with them a cannon of some description, though I think this unlikely. They are travelling in a convoy of stolen vehicles and at Senwati they captured a gasoline tanker belonging to the commercial oil companies.'

'I see,' mused Bruce. 'But it doesn't alter my decision to remain here overnight. However, we must leave at first light tomorrow.'

'As you wish, Captain.'

'Now, monsieur,' Bruce changed the subject, 'I require some form of transport. Is that car in running order?' He pointed at a pale green Ford Ranchero station wagon parked beside the verandah wall.

'It is. It belongs to my company.' Boussier took a key ring

from his pocket and handed it to Bruce. 'Here are the keys. The tank is full of gasoline.'

'Good,' said Bruce. 'Now if we can find Madame Cartier—'

She was waiting in the hotel lounge and she stood up as Bruce and Boussier came in.

'Are you ready, madame?'

'I await your pleasure,' she answered, and Bruce looked at her sharply. Just a trace of a twinkle in her dark blue eyes suggested that she was aware of the double meaning.

They walked out to the Ford and Bruce opened the door for her.

'You are gracious, monsieur.' She thanked him and slid into the seat. Bruce went round to the driver's side and climbed in beside her.

'It's nearly dark,' he said.

'Turn right on to the Msapa Junction road, there is one post there.'

Bruce drove out along the dirt road through the town until they came to the last house before the causeway. 'Here,' said the girl and Bruce stopped the car. There were two men there, both armed with sporting rifles. Bruce spoke to them. They had seen no sign of Baluba, but they were both very nervous. Bruce made a decision.

'I want you to go back to the hotel. The Baluba will have seen the train arrive; they won't attack in force, we'll be safe tonight. But they may try and cut a few throats if we leave you out here.'

The two half-breeds gathered together their belongings and set off towards the centre of town, obviously with lighter hearts.

'Where are the others?' Bruce asked the girl.

'The next post is at the pumping station down by the river, there are three men there.'

Bruce followed her directions. Once or twice as he drove

he glanced surreptitiously at her. She sat in her corner of the seat with her legs drawn up sideways under her. She sat very still, Bruce noticed. I like a woman who doesn't fidget; it's soothing. Then she smiled; this one isn't soothing. She is as disturbing as hell! She turned suddenly and caught him looking again, but this time she smiled.

'You are English, aren't you, Captain?'

'No, I am a Rhodesian,' Bruce answered.

'It's the same,' said the girl. 'You speak French so very badly that you had to be English.'

Bruce laughed. 'Perhaps your English is better than my French,' he challenged her.

'It couldn't be much worse,' she answered him in his own language. 'You are different when you laugh, not so grim, not so heroic. Take the next road to your right.'

Bruce turned the Ford down towards the harbour.

'You are very frank,' he said. 'Also your English is excellent.'

'Do you smoke?' she asked, and when he nodded she lit two cigarettes and passed one to him.

'You are also very young to smoke, and very young to be married.'

She stopped smiling and swung her legs off the seat.

'Here is the pumping station,' she said.

'I beg your pardon. I shouldn't have said that.'

'It's of no importance.'

'It was an impertinence,' Bruce demurred.

'It doesn't matter.'

Bruce stopped the car and opened his door. He walked out on to the wooden jetty towards the pump house, and the boards rang dully under his boots. There was a mist coming up out of the reeds round the harbour and the frogs were piping in fifty different keys. He spoke to the men in the single room of the pump station.

'You can get back to the hotel by dark if you hurry.'

'Oui, monsieur,' they agreed. Bruce watched them set off up the road before they went to the car. He spun the starter motor and above the noise of it the girl asked:

'What is your given name, Captain Curry?'

'Bruce.'

She repeated it, pronouncing it 'Bruise', and then asked:

'Why are you a soldier?'

'For many reasons.' His tone was flippant.

'You do not look like a soldier, for all your badges and your guns, for all the grimness and the frequent giving of orders.'

'Perhaps I am not a very good soldier.' He smiled at her.

'You are very efficient and very grim except when you laugh. But I am glad you do not look like one,' she said.

'Where is the next post?'

'On the railway line. There are two men there. Turn to your right again at the top, Bruce.'

'You are also very efficient, Shermaine.' They were silent again, having used each other's names. Bruce could feel it between them, a good feeling, warm like new bread. But what of her husband, he thought, I wonder where he is, and what he is like. Why isn't he here with her?

'He is dead,' she said quietly. 'He died four months ago of malaria.'

With the shock of it, Shermaine answering his unspoken question and also the answer itself, Bruce could say nothing for the moment, then:

'I'm sorry.'

'There is the post,' she said, 'in the cottage with the thatched roof.'

Bruce stopped the car and switched off the engine. In the silence she spoke again.

'He was a good man, so very gentle. I only knew him for a few months but he was a good man.'

She looked very small sitting beside him in the gathering dark with the sadness on her, and Bruce felt a great wave of tenderness wash over him. He wanted to put his arm round her and hold her, to shield her from the sadness. He searched for the words, but before he found them, she roused herself and spoke in a matter-of-fact tone.

'We must hurry, it's dark already.'

At the hotel the lounge was filled with Boussier's employees; Haig had mounted a Bren in one of the upstairs windows to cover the main street and posted two men in the kitchens to cover the back. The civilians were in little groups, talking quietly, and their expressions of complete doglike trust as they looked at Bruce disconcerted him.

'Everything under control, Mike?' he asked brusquely.

'Yes, Bruce. We should be able to hold this building against a sneak attack. De Surrier and Hendry, down at the station yard, shouldn't have any trouble either.'

'Have these people,' Bruce pointed at the civilians, 'loaded their luggage?'

'Yes, it's all aboard. I have told Ruffy to issue them with food from our stores.'

'Good.' Bruce felt relief; no further complications so far.

'Where is old man Boussier?'

'He is across at his office.'

'I'm going to have a chat with him.'

Unbidden, Shermaine fell in beside Bruce as he walked out into the street, but he liked having her there.

Boussier looked up as Bruce and Shermaine walked into his office. The merciless glare of the petromax lamp accentuated the lines at the corners of his eyes and mouth, and showed up the streaks of pink scalp beneath his neatly combed hair.

'Martin, you are not still working!' exclaimed Shermaine, and he smiled at her, the calm smile of his years.

'Not really, my dear, just tidying up a few things. Please be seated, Captain.'

He came round and cleared a pile of heavy leatherbound

ledgers off the chair and packed them into a wooden case on the floor, went back to his own chair, opened a drawer in the desk, brought out a box of cheroots and offered one to Bruce.

'I cannot tell you how relieved I am that you are here, Captain. These last few months have been very trying. The doubt. The anxiety.' He struck a match and held it out to Bruce who leaned forward across the desk and lit his cheroot. 'But now it is all at an end; I feel as though a great weight has been lifted from my shoulders.' Then his voice sharpened. 'But you were not too soon. I have heard within the last hour that this General Moses and his column have left Senwati and are on the road south, only two hundred kilometres north of here. They will arrive tomorrow at their present rate of advance.'

'Where did you hear this?' Bruce demanded.

'From one of my men, and do not ask me how he knows. There is a system of communication in this country which even after all these years I do not understand. Perhaps it is the drums, I heard them this evening, I do not know. However, their information is usually reliable.'

'I had not placed them so close,' muttered Bruce. 'Had I known this I might have risked travelling tonight, at least as far as the bridge.'

'I think your decision to stay over the night was correct. General Moses will not travel during darkness – none of his men would risk that – and the condition of the road from Senwati after three months neglect is such that he will need ten or twelve hours to cover the distance.'

'I hope you're right.' Bruce was worried. 'I'm not sure that we shouldn't pull out now.'

'That involves a risk also, Captain,' Boussier pointed out. 'We know there are tribesmen in close proximity to the town. They have been seen. They must be aware of your arrival, and might easily have wrecked the lines to prevent our departure. I think your original decision is still good.'

'I know.' Bruce was hunched forward in his chair, frowning, sucking on the cheroot. At last he sat back and the frown evaporated. 'I can't risk it. I'll place a guard on the causeway, and if this Moses gentleman arrives we can hold him there long enough to embark your people.'

'That is probably the best course,' agreed Boussier. He paused, glanced towards the open windows and lowered his voice. 'There is another point, Captain, which I wish to bring to your attention.'

'Yes?'

'As you know, the activity of my company in Port Reprieve is centred on the recovery of diamonds from the Lufira swamps.'

Bruce nodded.

'I have in my safe' – Boussier jerked his thumb at the heavy steel door built into the wall behind his desk – 'nine and a half thousand carats of gem-quality diamonds and some twenty-six thousand carats of industrial diamonds.'

'I had expected that.' Bruce kept his tone non-committal.

'It may be as well if we could agree on the disposition and handling of these stones.'

'How are they packaged?' asked Bruce.

'A single wooden case.'

'Of what size and weight?'

'I will show you.'

Boussier went to the safe, turned his back to them and they heard the tumblers whirr and click. While he waited Bruce realized suddenly that Shermaine had not spoken since her initial greeting to Boussier. He glanced at her now and she smiled at him. I like a woman who knows when to keep her mouth shut.

Boussier swung the door of the safe open and carried a small wooden case across to the desk.

'There,' he said.

Bruce examined it. Eighteen inches long, nine deep and twelve wide. He lifted it experimentally.

'About twenty pounds weight,' he decided. 'The lid is sealed.'

'Yes,' agreed Boussier, touching the four wax imprints.

'Good,' Bruce nodded. 'I don't want to draw unnecessary attention to it by placing a guard upon it.'

'No, I agree.'

Bruce studied the case a few seconds longer and then he asked:

'What is the value of these stones?'

Boussier shrugged. 'Possibly five hundred million francs.' And Bruce was impressed; half a million sterling. Worth stealing, worth killing for.

'I suggest, monsieur, that you secrete this case in your luggage. In your blankets, say. I doubt there will be any danger of theft until we reach Msapa Junction. A thief will have no avenue of escape. Once we reach Msapa Junction I will make other arrangements for its safety.'

'Very well, Captain.'

Bruce stood up and glanced at his watch. 'Seven o'clock, as near as dammit. I will leave you and see to the guard on the causeway. Please make sure that your people are ready to entrain before dawn tomorrow morning.'

'Of course.'

Bruce looked at Shermaine and she stood up quickly. Bruce held the door open for her and was just about to follow her when a thought struck him.

'That mission station – St Augustine's, is it? I suppose it's deserted now?'

'No, it's not.' Boussier looked a little shamefaced. 'Father Ignatius is still there, and of course the patients at the hospital.'

'Thanks for telling me.' Bruce was bitter.

'I'm sorry, Captain. It slipped my mind, there are so many things to think of.'

'Do you know the road out to the mission?' he snapped at Shermaine. *She* should have told him.

'Yes, Bruce.'

'Well, perhaps you'd be good enough to direct me.'

'Of course.' She also looked guilty.

Bruce slammed the door of Boussier's office and strode off towards the hotel with Shermaine trotting to keep pace with him. You can't rely on anyone, he thought, not anybody!

And then he saw Ruffy coming up from the station, looking like a big bear in the dusk. With a few exceptions, Bruce corrected himself.

'Sergeant Major.'

'Hello, boss.'

'This General Moses is closer to us than we reckoned. He's reported two hundred kilometres north of here on the Senwati road.'

Ruffy whistled through his teeth. 'Are you going to take off now, Boss?'

'No, I want a machine-gun post on this end of the causeway. If they come we can hold them there long enough to get away. I want you to take command.'

'I'll see to it now.'

'I'm going out to the mission – there's a white priest there. Lieutenant Haig is in command while I'm away.'

'Okay, boss.'

– 10 –

'I'm sorry, Bruce. I should have told you.' Shermaine sat small and repentant at her end of the Ranchero.

'Don't worry about it,' said Bruce, not meaning it.

'We have tried to make Father Ignatius come in to town. Martin has spoken to him many times, but he refuses to move.'

Bruce did not answer. He took the car down on to the causeway, driving carefully. There were shreds of mist lifting out of the swamp and drifting across the concrete ramp. Small insects, bright as tracer in the headlights, zoomed in to squash against the windscreen. The froggy chorus from the swamp honked and clinked and boomed deafeningly.

'I have apologized,' she murmured.

'Yes, I heard you,' said Bruce. 'You don't have to do it again.'

She was silent, and then:

'Are you always so bad-tempered?' she asked in English.

'*Always*,' snapped Bruce, 'is one of the words which should be eliminated from the language.'

'Since it has not been, I will continue to use it. You haven't answered my question: are you always so bad-tempered?'

'I just don't like balls-ups.'

'What is *balls-up*, please?'

'What has just happened: a mistake, a situation precipitated by inefficiency, or by somebody not using his head.'

'You never make balls-up, Bruce?'

'It is not a polite expression, Shermaine. Young ladies of refinement do not use it.' Bruce changed into French.

'You never make mistakes?' she corrected herself. Bruce did not answer. That's quite funny, he thought – never make mistakes! Bruce Curry, the original balls-up.

Shermaine held one hand across her middle and sat up straight.

'Bonaparte,' she said. 'Cold, silent, efficient.'

'I didn't say that—' Bruce started to defend himself. Then in the glow from the dash light he saw her impish expression and he could not stop himself; he had to grin.

'All right, I'm acting like a child.'

'You would like a cigarette?' she asked.

'Yes, please.'

She lit it and passed it to him.

'You do not like—' she hesitated, 'mistakes. Is there anything you do like?'

'Many things,' said Bruce.

'Tell me some.'

They bumped off the end of the causeway and Bruce accelerated up the far bank.

'I like being on a mountain when the wind blows, and the taste of the sea. I like Sinatra, crayfish thermidor, the weight and balance of a Purdey Royal, and the sound of a little girl's laughter. I like the first draw of a cigarette lit from a wood fire, the scent of jasmine, the feel of silk; I also enjoy sleeping late in the morning, and the thrill of forking a queen with my knight. Shadows on the floor of a forest please me. And, of course, money. But especially I like women who do not ask too many questions.'

'Is that all?'

'No, but it's a start.'

'And apart from – mistakes, what are the things you do not like.'

'Women who ask too many questions,' and he saw her smile. 'Selfishness except my own, turnip soup, politics, blond pubic hairs, Scotch whisky, classical music and hangovers.'

'I'm sure that is not all.'

'No, not nearly.'

'You are very sensual. All these things are of the senses.'

'Agreed.'

'You do not mention other people. Why?'

'Is this the turn-off to the mission?'

'Yes, go slowly, the road is bad. Why do you not mention your relationship to other people?'

'Why do you ask so many questions? Perhaps I'll tell you some day.'

She was silent a while and then softly:

'And what do you want from life – just those things you have spoken of? Is that all you want?'

'No. Not even them. I want nothing, expect nothing; that way I cannot be disappointed.'

89

Suddenly she was angry. 'You not only act like a child, you talk like one.'

'Another thing I don't like: criticism.'

'You are young. You have brains, good looks—'

'Thank you, that's better.'

' – and you are a fool.'

'That's not so good. But don't fret about it.'

'I won't, don't worry,' she flamed at him. 'You can—' she searched for something devastating. 'You can go jump out of the lake.'

'Don't you mean into?'

'Into, out of, backwards, sideways. I don't care!'

'Good, I'm glad we've got that settled. There's the mission, I can see a light.'

She did not answer but sat in her corner, breathing heavily, drawing so hard on her cigarette that the glowing tip lit the interior of the Ford.

The church was in darkness, but beyond it and to one side was a long low building. Bruce saw a shadow move across one of the windows.

'Is that the hospital?'

'Yes.' Abruptly.

Bruce stopped the Ford beside the small front verandah and switched off the headlights and the ignition.

'Are you coming in?'

'No.'

'I'd like you to present me to Father Ignatius.'

For a moment she did not move, then she threw open her door and marched up the steps of the verandah without looking back at Bruce.

He followed her through the front office, down the passage, past the clinic and small operating theatre, into the ward.

'Ah, Madame Cartier.' Father Ignatius left the bed over which he was stooping and came towards her.

'I heard that the relief train had arrived at Port Reprieve. I thought you would have left by now.'

'Not yet, Father. Tomorrow morning.'

Ignatius was tall, six foot three or four, Bruce estimated, and thin. The sleeve of his brown cassock had been cut short as a concession to the climate and his exposed arms appeared to be all bone, hairless, with the veins blue and prominent. Big bony hands, and big bony feet in brown open sandals.

Like most tall, thin men he was round-shouldered. His face was not one that you would remember, an ordinary face with steel-rimmed spectacles perched on a rather shapeless nose, neither young nor old, nondescript hair without grey in it, but there was about him that unhurried serenity you often find in a man of God. He turned his attention to Bruce, scrutinizing him gently through his spectacles.

'Good evening, my son.'

'Good evening, Father.' Bruce felt uncomfortable; they always made him feel that way. If only, he wished with envy, I could be as certain of one thing in my life as this man is certain of everything in his.

'Father, this is Captain Curry.' Shermaine's tone was cold, and then suddenly she smiled again. 'He does not care for people, that is why he has come to take you to safety.'

Father Ignatius held out his hand and Bruce found the skin was cool and dry, making him conscious of the moistness of his own.

'That is most thoughtful of you,' he said smiling, sensing the tension between them. 'I don't want to seem ungrateful, but I regret I cannot accept your offer.'

'We have received reports that a column of armed bandits are only two hundred kilometres or so north of here. They will arrive within a day or two. You are in great danger, these people are completely merciless,' Bruce urged him.

'Yes,' Father Ignatius nodded. 'I have also heard, and I am taking the steps I consider necessary. I shall take all my staff and patients into the bush.'

'They'll follow you,' said Bruce.

'I think not.' Ignatius shook his head. 'They will not waste their time. They are after loot, not sick people.'

'They'll burn your mission.'

'If they do, then we shall have to rebuild it when they leave.'

'The bush is crawling with Baluba, you'll end up in the cooking pot.' Bruce tried another approach.

'No.' Ignatius shook his head. 'Nearly every member of the tribe has at one time or another been a patient in this hospital. I have nothing to fear there, they are my friends.'

'Look here, Father. Don't let us argue. My orders are to bring you back to Elisabethville. I must insist.'

'And my orders are to stay here. You do agree that mine come from a higher authority than yours?' Ignatius smiled mildly. Bruce opened his mouth to argue further; then, instead, he laughed.

'No, I won't dispute that. Is there anything you need that I might be able to supply?'

'Medicines?' asked Ignatius.

'Acriflavine, morphia, field dressings, not much I'm afraid.'

'They would help, and food?'

'Yes, I will let you have as much as I can spare,' promised Bruce.

One of the patients, a woman at the end of the ward, screamed so suddenly that Bruce started.

'She will be dead before morning,' Ignatius explained softly. 'There is nothing I can do.'

'What's wrong with her?'

'She has been in labour these past two days; there is some complication.'

'Can't you operate?'

'I am not a doctor, my son. We had one here before the trouble began, but he is here no longer – he has gone back to Elisabethville. No,' his voice seemed to carry helpless regret for all the suffering of mankind, 'No, she will die.'

'Haig!' said Bruce.

'Pardon?'

'Father, you have a theatre here. Is it fully equipped?'

'Yes, I believe so.'

'Anaesthetic?'

'We have chloroform and pentothal.'

'Good,' said Bruce. 'I'll get you a doctor. Come on, Shermaine.'

– 11 –

'This heat, this stinking heat!' Wally Hendry mopped at his face with a grubby handkerchief and threw himself down on the green leather bunk. 'You notice how Curry leaves me and you here on the train while he puts Haig up at the hotel and he goes off with that little French bit. It doesn't matter that me and you must cook in this box, long as he and his buddy Haig are all right. You notice that, hey?'

'Somebody's got to stay aboard, Wally,' André said.

'Yeah, but you notice who it is? Always you and me – those high society boys stick together, you've got to give them that, they look after each other.' He transferred his attention back to the open window of the compartment. 'Sun's down already, and still hot enough to boil eggs. I could use a drink.' He unlaced his jungle boots, peeled off his socks and regarded his large white feet with distaste. 'This stinking heat got my athlete's foot going again.'

He separated two of his toes and picked at the loose scaly skin between. 'You got any of that ointment left, André?'

'Yes, I'll get it for you.' André opened the flap of his pack, took out the tube and crossed to Wally's bunk.

'Put it on,' instructed Wally and lay back offering his feet. André took them in his lap as he sat down on the bunk and went to work. Wally lit a cigarette and blew smoke towards the roof, watching it disperse.

'Hell, I could use a drink. A beer with dew on the glass and a head that thick.' He held up four fingers, then he lifted himself on one elbow and studied André as he spread ointment between the long prehensile toes.

'How's it going?'

'Nearly finished, Wally.'

'Is it bad?'

'Not as bad as last time, it hasn't started weeping yet.'

'It itches like you wouldn't believe it,' said Wally.

André did not answer and Wally kicked him in the ribs with the flat of his free foot.

'Did you hear what I said?'

'Yes, you said it itches.'

'Well, answer me when I talk to you. I ain't talking to myself.'

'I'm sorry, Wally.'

Wally grunted and was silent a while, then:

'Do you like me, André?'

'You know I do, Wally.'

'We're friends, aren't we, André?'

'Of course, you know that, Wally.'

An expression of cunning had replaced Wally's boredom.

'You don't mind when I ask you to do things for me, like putting stuff on my feet?'

'I don't mind – it's a pleasure, Wally.'

'It's a pleasure, is it?' There was an edge in Wally's voice now. 'You like doing it?'

André looked up at him apprehensively. 'I don't mind it.' His molten toffee eyes clung to the narrow Mongolian ones in Wally's face.

'You like touching me, André?'

André stopped working with the ointment and nervously wiped his fingers on his towel.

'I said, do you like touching me, André? Do you sometimes wish I'd touch you?'

André tried to stand up, but Wally's right arm shot out and his hand fastened on André's neck, forcing him down on to the bunk.

'Answer me, damn you, do you like it?'

'You're hurting me, Wally,' whispered André.

'Shame, now ain't that a shame!'

Wally was grinning. He shifted his grip to the ridge of muscle above André's collar bone and dug his fingers in until they almost met through the flesh.

'Please, Wally, please,' whimpered André, wriggling face down on the bunk.

'You love it, don't you? Come on, answer me.'

'Yes, all right, yes. Please don't hurt me, Wally.'

'Now, tell me truly, doll boy, have you ever had it before? I mean for real.' Wally put his knee in the small of André's back, bearing down with all his weight.

'No!' shrieked André. 'I haven't. Please, Wally, don't hurt me.'

'You're lying to me, André. Don't do it.'

'All right. I was lying.' André tried to twist his head round, but Wally pushed his face into the bunk.

'Tell me all about it – come on, doll boy.'

'It was only once, in Brussels.'

'Who was this beef bandit?'

'My employer. I worked for him. He had an export agency.'

'Did he throw you out, doll boy? Did he throw you out when he was tired of you?'

'No, you don't understand!' André denied with sudden vehemence. 'You don't understand. He looked after me. I had my own apartment, my own car, everything. He wouldn't have abandoned me if it hadn't been for – for what happened. He couldn't help it, he was true to me. I swear to you – he loved me!'

Wally snorted with laughter, he was enjoying himself now.

'Loved you! Jesus wept!' He threw his head back, for the laughter was almost strangling him, and it was ten seconds before he could ask: 'Then what happened between you and your true blue lover? Why didn't you get married and settle down to raise a family, hey?' At the improbability of his own sense of humour Wally convulsed with laughter once more.

'There was an investigation. The police – ooh! you're hurting me, Wally.'

'Keep talking, mamselle!'

'The police – he had no alternative. He was a man of position, he couldn't afford the scandal. There was no other way out – there never is for us. It's hopeless, there is no happiness.'

'Cut the crap, doll boy. Just give me the story.'

'He arranged employment for me in Elisabethville, gave me money, paid for my air fare, everything. He did everything, he looked after me, he still writes to me.'

'That's beautiful, real true love. You make me want to cry.'

Then Wally's laughter changed its tone, harsher now. 'Well, get this, doll boy, and get it good. I don't like queers!' He dug his fingers in again and André squealed.

'I'll tell you a story. When I was in reform school there was a queer there that tried to touch me up. One day I got him in the shower rooms with a razor, just an ordinary Gillette razor. There were twenty guys singing and shouting in the other cubicles. He screamed just like they were all screaming when the cold water hit them. No one took any notice of him. He wanted to be a woman, so I helped him.' Hendry's voice went hoarse and gloating with the memory.

'Jesus!' he whispered. 'Jesus, the blood!' André was sobbing now, his whole body shaking.

'I won't – please, Wally, I can't help it. It was just that one time. Please leave me.'

'How would you like me to help you, André?'

'No,' shrieked André. And Hendry lost interest; he released him, left him lying on the bunk and reached for his socks.

'I'm going to find me a beer.' He laced on his boots and stood up.

'Just you remember,' he said darkly, standing over the boy on the bunk. 'Don't get any ideas with me, Bucko.' He picked up his rifle and went out into the corridor.

Wally found Boussier on the verandah of the hotel talking with a group of his men.

'Where's Captain Curry?' he demanded.

'He has gone out to the mission station.'

'When did he leave?'

'About ten minutes ago.'

'Good,' said Wally. 'Who's got the key to the bar?'

Boussier hesitated.

'The captain has ordered that the bar is to remain locked.'

Wally unslung his rifle.

'Don't give me a hard time, friend.'

'I regret, monsieur, that I must obey the captain's instructions.'

For a minute they stared at each other, and there was no sign of weakening in the older man.

'Have it your way, then,' said Wally and swaggered through the lounge to the bar-room door. He put his foot against the lock and the flimsy mechanism yielded to the pressure. The door flew open and Wally marched across to the counter, laid his rifle on it and reached underneath to the shelves loaded with Simba beer.

The first bottle he emptied without taking it from his

lips. He belched luxuriously and reached for the second, hooked the cap off with the opener and inspected the bubble of froth that appeared at its mouth.

'Hendry!' Wally looked up at Mike Haig in the doorway.

'Hello, Mike.' He grinned.

'What do you think you're doing?' Mike demanded.

'What does it look like?' Wally raised the bottle in salutation and then sipped delicately at the froth.

'Bruce has given strict orders that no one is allowed in here.'

'Oh, for Chrissake, Haig. Stop acting like an old woman.'

'Out you get, Hendry. I'm in charge here.'

'Mike,' Wally grinned at him, 'you want me to die of thirst or something?' He leaned his elbows on the counter. 'Give me a couple more minutes. Let me finish my drink.'

Mike Haig glanced behind him into the lounge and saw the interested group of civilians who were craning to see into the bar-room. He closed the door and walked across to stand opposite Hendry.

'Two minutes, Hendry,' he agreed in an unfriendly tone, 'then out with you.'

'You're not a bad guy, Mike. You and I rubbed each other up wrong. I tell you something, I'm sorry about us.'

'Drink up!' said Mike. Without turning Wally reached backwards and took a bottle of Remy Martin cognac off the shelf. He pulled the cork with his teeth, selected a brandy balloon with his free hand and poured a little of the oily amber fluid into it.

'Keep me company, Mike,' he said and slid the glass across the counter towards Haig. First without expression, and then with his face seeming to crumble, Mike Haig stared at the glass. He moistened his lips, again older and tired-looking. With a physical wrench he pulled his eyes away from the glass.

'Damn you, Hendry.' His voice unnaturally low. 'God

98

damn you to hell.' He hit out at the glass, spinning it off the counter to shatter against the far wall.

'Did I do something wrong, Mike?' asked Hendry softly. 'Just offered you a drink, that's all.'

The smell of spilt brandy arose, sharp, fruity with the warmth of the grape, and Mike moistened his lips again. The saliva jetting from under his tongue, and the deep yearning aching want in his stomach spreading outwards slowly, numbing him.

'Damn you,' he whispered. 'Oh, damn you, damn you,' pleading now as Hendry filled another glass.

'How long has it been, Mike? A year, two years? Try a little, just a mouthful. Remember the lift it gives you. Come on, boy. You're tired, you've worked hard. Just one – there you are. Just have this one with me.'

Mike wiped his mouth with the back of his hand, sweating now across the forehead and on his upper lip, tiny jewels of sweat squeezed out of the skin by the craving of his body.

'Come on, boy.' Wally's voice hoarse with excitement; teasing, wheedling, tempting.

Mike's hand closed round the tumbler, moving of its own volition, lifting it towards lips that were suddenly slack and trembling, his eyes filled with mingled loathing and desire.

'Just this one,' whispered Hendry. 'Just this one.'

Mike gulped it with a sudden savage flick of his arm, one swallow and the glass was empty. He held it with both hands, his head bowed over it.

'I hate you. My God, I hate you.' He spoke to Hendry, and to himself, and to the empty glass.

'That's my boy!' crowed Wally. 'That's the lad! Come on, let me fill you up.'

Bruce went in through the front door of the hotel with Shermaine trying to keep pace with him. There were a dozen or so people in the lobby, and an air of tension amongst them. Boussier was one of them and he came quickly to Bruce.

'I'm sorry, Captain, I could not stop them. That one, that one with the red hair, he was violent. He had his gun and I think he was ready to use it.'

'What are you talking about?' Bruce asked him, but before Boussier could answer there was the bellow of Hendry's laughter from behind the door at the far end of the lobby; the door to the bar-room.

'They are in there,' Boussier told him. 'They have been there for the past hour.'

'Goddam it to hell,' swore Bruce. 'Now of all times. Oh, goddam that bloody animal.'

He almost ran across the room and threw open the double doors. Hendry was standing against the far wall with a tumbler in one hand and his rifle in the other. He was holding the rifle by the pistol grip and waving vague circles in the air with it.

Mike Haig was building a pyramid of glasses on the bar counter. He was just placing the final glass on the pile.

'Hello, Bruce, old cock, old man, old fruit,' he greeted Bruce, and waved in an exaggerated manner. 'Just in time, you can have a couple of shots as well. But Wally's first, he gets first shot. Must abide by the rules, no cheating, strictly democratic affair, everyone has equal rights. Rank doesn't count. That's right, isn't it Wally?' Haig's features had blurred; it was as though he were melting, losing his shape. His lips were loose and flabby, his jowls hung pendulously as an old woman's breasts, and his eyes were moist.

He picked up a glass from beside the pyramid, but this

glass was nearly full and a bottle of Remy Martin cognac stood beside it.

'A very fine old brandy, absolutely exquisite.' The last two words didn't come out right, so he repeated them carefully. Then he grinned loosely at Bruce and his eyes weren't quite in focus.

'Get out of the way, Mike,' said Hendry, and raised the rifle one-handed, aiming at the pile of glasses.

'Every time she bucks, she bounces,' hooted Haig, 'and every time she bounces you win a coconut. Let her rip, old fruit.'

'Hendry, stop that,' snapped Bruce.

'Go and get mucked,' answered Hendry and fired. The rifle kicked back over his shoulder and he fell against the wall. The pyramid of glasses exploded in a shower of fragments and the room was filled with the roar of the rifle.

'Give the gentleman a coconut!' crowed Mike.

Bruce crossed the room with three quick strides and pulled the rifle out of Hendry's hand.

'All right, you drunken ape. That's enough.'

'Go and muck yourself,' growled Hendry. He was massaging his wrist; the rifle had twisted it.

'Captain Curry,' said Haig from behind the bar, 'you heard what my friend said. You go and muck yourself sideways to sleep.'

'Shut up, Haig.'

'This time I'll fix you, Curry,' Hendry growled. 'You've been on my back too long – now I'm going to shake you off!'

'Kindly descend from my friend's back, Captain Curry,' chimed in Mike Haig. 'He's not a howdah elephant, he's my blood brother. I will not allow you to persecute him.'

'Come on, Curry. Come on then!' said Wally.

'That's it, Wally. Muck him up.' Haig filled his glass again as he spoke. 'Don't let him ride you.'

'Come on then, Curry.'

'You're drunk,' said Bruce.

'Come on then; don't talk, man. Or do I have to start it?'

'No, you don't have to start it,' Bruce assured him, and lifted the rifle butt-first under his chin, swinging it up hard. Hendry's head jerked and he staggered back against the wall. Bruce looked at his eyes; they were glazed over. That will hold him, he decided; that's taken the fight out of him. He caught Hendry by the shoulder and threw him into one of the chairs. I must get to Haig before he absorbs any more of that liquor, he thought, I can't waste time sending for Ruffy and I can't leave this thing behind me while I work on Haig.

'Shermaine,' he called. She was standing in the doorway and she came to his side. 'Can you use a pistol?'

She nodded. Bruce unclipped his Smith & Wesson from its lanyard and handed it to her.

'Shoot this man if he tries to leave that chair. Stand here where he cannot reach you.'

'Bruce—' she started.

'He is a dangerous animal. Yesterday he murdered two small children and, if you let him, he'll do the same to you. You must keep him here while I get the other one.'

She lifted the pistol, holding it with both hands and her face was even paler than was usual.

'Can you do it?' Bruce asked.

'Now I can,' she said and cocked the action.

'Hear me, Hendry.' Bruce took a handful of his hair and twisted his face up. 'She'll kill you if you leave this chair. Do you understand? She'll shoot you.'

'Muck you and your little French whore, muck you both. I bet that's what you two have been doing all evening in that car – playing "hide the sausage" down by the riverside.'

Anger flashed through Bruce so violently that it startled him. He twisted Hendry's hair until he could feel it coming away in his hand. Hendry squirmed with pain.

'Shut that foul mouth – or I'll kill you.'

He meant it, and suddenly Hendry knew he meant it.

'Okay, for Chrissake, okay. Just leave me.'

Bruce loosened his grip and straightened up.

'I'm sorry, Shermaine,' he said.

'That's all right – go to the other one.'

Bruce went to the bar counter, and Haig watched him come.

'What do you want, Bruce? Have a drink.' He was nervous. 'Have a drink, we are all having a little drink. All good clean fun, Bruce. Don't get excited.'

'You're not having any more; in fact, just the opposite,' Bruce told him as he came round the counter. Haig backed away in front of him.

'What are you going to do?'

'I'll show you,' said Bruce and caught him by the wrist, turning him quickly and lifting his arm up between his shoulder-blades.

'Hey, Bruce. Cut it out, you've made me spill my drink.'

'Good,' said Bruce and slapped the empty glass out of his hand. Haig started to struggle. He was still a powerful man but the liquor had weakened him and Bruce lifted his wrist higher, forcing him on to his toes.

'Come along, buddy boy,' instructed Bruce and marched him towards the back door of the bar-room. He reached round Haig with his free hand, turned the key in the lock and opened the door.

'Through here,' he said and pushed Mike into the kitchens. He kicked the door shut behind him and went to the sink, dragging Haig with him.

'All right, Haig, let's have it up,' he said and changed his grip quickly, thrusting Haig's head down over the sink. There was a dishtowel hanging beside it which Bruce screwed into a ball; then he used his thumbs to open Haig's jaws and wedged the towel between his back teeth.

'Let's have all of it.' He probed his finger down into Haig's throat. It came up hot and gushing over his hand,

and he fought down his own nausea as he worked. When he had finished he turned on the cold tap and held Haig's head under it, washing his face and his own hand.

'Now, I've got a little job for you, Haig.'

'Leave me alone, damn you,' groaned Haig, his voice indistinct beneath the rushing tap. Bruce pulled him up and held him against the wall.

'There's a woman in childbirth at the mission. She's going to die, Haig. She's going to die if you don't do something about it.'

'No,' whispered Haig. 'No, not that. Not that again.'

'I'm taking you there.'

'No, please not that. I can't – don't you see that I can't.' The little red and purple veins in his nose and cheeks stood out in vivid contrast to his pallor. Bruce hit him open-handed across the face and the water flew in drops from his hair at the shock.

'No,' he mumbled, 'please Bruce, please.'

Bruce hit him twice more, hard. Watching him carefully, and at last he saw the first flickering of anger.

'Damn you, Bruce Curry, damn you to hell.'

'You'll do,' rejoiced Bruce. 'Thank God for that.'

He hustled Haig back through the bar-room. Shermaine still stood over Hendry, holding the pistol.

'Come on, Shermaine. You can leave that thing now. I'll attend to him when we get back.'

As they crossed the lobby Bruce asked Shermaine. 'Can you drive the Ford?'

'Yes.'

'Good,' said Bruce. 'Here are the keys. I'll sit with Haig in the back. Take us out to the mission.'

Haig lost his balance on the front steps of the hotel and nearly fell, but Bruce caught him and half carried him to the car. He pushed him into the back seat and climbed in beside him. Shermaine slid in behind the wheel, started the engine and U-turned neatly across the street.

'You can't force me to do this, Bruce. I can't, I just can't,' Haig pleaded.

'We'll see,' said Bruce.

'You don't know what it's like. You can't know. She'll die on the table.' He held out his hands palms down. 'Look at that, look at them. How can I do it with these?' His hands were trembling violently.

'She's going to die anyway,' said Bruce, his voice hard. 'So you might as well do it for her quickly and get it over with.'

Haig brought his hands up to his mouth and wiped his lips.

'Can I have a drink, Bruce? That'll help. I'll try then, if you give me a drink.'

'No,' said Bruce, and Haig began to swear. The filth poured from his lips and his face twisted with the effort. He cursed Bruce, he cursed himself, and God in a torrent of the most obscene language that Bruce had ever heard. Then suddenly he snatched at the door handle and tried to twist it open. Bruce had been waiting for this and he caught the back of Haig's collar, pulled him backwards across the seat and held him there. Haig's struggles ceased abruptly and he began to sob softly.

Shermaine drove fast; across the causeway, up the slope and into the side road. The headlights cut into the darkness and the wind drummed softly round the car. Haig was still sobbing on the back seat.

Then the lights of the mission were ahead of them through the trees and Shermaine slowed the car, turned in past the church and pulled up next to the hospital block.

Bruce helped Haig out of the car, and while he was doing so the side door of the building opened and Father Ignatius came out with a petromax lantern in his hand. The harsh white glare of the lantern lit them all and threw grotesque shadows behind them. It fell with special cruelty on Haig's face.

'Here's your doctor, Father,' Bruce announced.

Ignatius lifted the lantern and peered through his spectacles at Haig.

'Is he sick?'

'No, Father,' said Bruce. 'He's drunk.'

'Drunk? Then he can't operate?'

'Yes, he damn well can!'

Bruce took Haig through the door and along the passage to the little theatre. Ignatius and Shermaine followed them.

'Shermaine, go with Father and help him bring the woman,' Bruce ordered, and they went; then he turned his attention back to Haig.

'Are you so far down there in the slime that you can't understand me?'

'I can't do it, Bruce. It's no good.'

'Then she'll die. But this much is certain: you are going to make the attempt.'

'I've got to have a drink, Bruce.' Haig licked his lips. 'It's burning me up inside, you've got to give me one.'

'Finish the job and I'll give you a whole case.'

'I've got to have one now.'

'No.' Bruce spoke with finality. 'Have a look at what they've got here in the way of instruments. Can you do it with these?' Bruce crossed to the sterilizer and lifted the lid, the steam came up out of it in a cloud. Haig looked in also.

'That's all I need, but there's not enough light in here, and I need a drink.'

'I'll get you more light. Start cleaning up.'

'Bruce, please let me—'

'Shut up,' snarled Bruce. 'There's the basin. Start getting ready.'

Haig crossed to the handbasin; he was more steady on his feet and his features had firmed a little. You poor old bastard, thought Bruce, I hope you can do it. My God, how much I hope you can.

'Get a move on, Haig, we haven't got all night.'

Bruce left the room and went quickly down the passage to the ward. The windows of the theatre were fixed and Haig could escape only into the passage. Bruce knew that he could catch him if he tried to run for it.

He looked into the ward. Shermaine and Ignatius, with the help of an African orderly, had lifted the woman on to the theatre trolley.

'Father, we need more light.'

'I can get you another lantern, that's all.'

'Good, do that then. I'll take the woman through.'

Father Ignatius disappeared with the orderly and Bruce helped Shermaine manoeuvre the trolley down the length of the ward and into the passage. The woman was whimpering with pain, and her face was grey, waxy grey. They only go like that when they are very frightened, or when they are dying.

'She hasn't much longer,' he said.

'I know,' agreed Shermaine. 'We must hurry.'

The woman moved restlessly on the trolley and gabbled a few words; then she sighed so that the great blanket-covered mound of her belly rose and fell, and she started to whimper again.

Haig was still in the theatre. He had stripped off his battle-jacket and, in his vest, he stooped over the basin washing. He did not look round as they wheeled the woman in.

'Get her on the table,' he said, working the soap into suds up to his elbows.

The trolley was of a height with the table and, using the blanket to lift her, it was easy to slide the woman across.

'She's ready, Haig,' said Bruce. Haig dried his arms on a clean towel and turned. He came to the woman and stood over her. She did not know he was there; her eyes were open but unseeing. Haig drew a breath; he was sweating a little across his forehead and the stubble of beard on the lower part of his face was stippled with grey.

He pulled back the blanket. The woman wore a short white jacket, open-fronted, that did not cover her stomach. Her stomach was swollen out, hard-looking, with the navel inverted. Knees raised slightly and the thick peasant's thighs spread wide in the act of labour. As Bruce watched, her whole body arched in another contraction. He saw the stress of the muscles beneath the dark greyish skin as they struggled to expel the trapped foetus.

'Hurry, Mike!' Bruce was appalled by the anguish of birth. I didn't know it was like this; in sorrow thou shalt bring forth children – but this! Through the woman's dry grey swollen lips burst another of those moaning little cries, and Bruce swung towards Mike Haig.

'Hurry, goddam you!'

And Mike Haig began his examination, his hands very pale as they groped over the dark skin. At last he was satisfied and he stood back from the table.

Ignatius and the orderly came in with two more lanterns. Ignatius started to say something, but instantly he sensed the tension in the room and he fell silent. They all watched Mike Haig's face.

His eyes were tight closed, and his face was hard angles and harsh planes in the lantern light. His breathing was shallow and laboured.

I must not push him now, Bruce knew instinctively, I have dragged him to the lip of the precipice and now I must let him go over the edge on his own.

Mike opened his eyes again, and he spoke.

'Caesarian section,' he said, as though he had pronounced his own death sentence. Then his breathing stopped. They waited, and at last the breath came out of him in a sigh.

'I'll do it,' he said.

'Gowns and gloves?' Bruce fired the question at Ignatius.

'In the cupboard.'

'Get them!'

'You'll have to help me, Bruce. And you also Shermaine.'

'Yes, show me.'

Quickly they scrubbed and dressed. Ignatius held the pale green theatre gowns while they dived into them and flapped and struggled through.

'That tray, bring it here,' Mike ordered as he opened the sterilizer. With a pair of long-nosed forceps he lifted the instruments out of the steaming box and laid them on the tray naming each one as he did so.

'Scalpel, retractors, clamps.'

In the meantime the orderly was swabbing the woman's belly with alcohol and arranging the sheets.

Mike filled the syringe with pentothal and held it up to the light. He was an unfamiliar figure now; his face masked, the green skull cap covering his hair, and the flowing gown falling to his ankles. He pressed the plunger and a few drops of the pale fluid dribbled down the needle.

He looked at Bruce, only his haunted eyes showing above the mask.

'Ready?'

'Yes,' Bruce nodded. Mike stooped over the woman, took her arm and sent the needle searching under the soft black skin on the inside of her elbow. The fluid in the syringe was suddenly discoloured with drawn blood as Mike tested for the vein, and then the plunger slid slowly down the glass barrel.

The woman stopped whimpering, the tension went out of her body and her breathing slowed and became deep and unhurried.

'Come here.' Mike ordered Shermaine to the head of the table, and she took up the chloroform mask and soaked the gauze that filled the cone.

'Wait until I tell you.'

She nodded. Christ, what lovely eyes she has, thought Bruce, before he turned back to the job in hand.

'Scalpel,' said Mike from across the table, pointing to it on the tray, and Bruce handed it to him.

Afterwards the details were confused and lacking reality in Bruce's mind.

The wound opening behind the knife, the tight stretched skin parting and the tiny blood vessels starting to squirt.

Pink muscle laced with white; butter-yellow layers of subcutaneous fat, and then through to the massed bluish coils of the gut. Human tissue, soft and pulsing, glistening in the flat glare of the petromax.

Clamps and retractors, like silver insects crowding into the wound as though it were a flower.

Mike's hands, inhuman in yellow rubber, moving in the open pit of the belly. Swabbing, cutting, clamping, tying off.

Then the swollen purple bag of the womb, suddenly unzipped by the knife.

And at last, unbelievably, the child curled in a dark grey ball of legs and tiny arms, head too big for its size, and the fat pink snake of the placenta enfolding it.

Lifted out, the infant hung by its heels from Mike's hand like a small grey bat, still joined to its mother.

Scissors snipped and it was free. Mike worked a little longer, and the infant cried.

It cried with minute fury, indignant and alive. From the head of the table Shermaine laughed with spontaneous delight, and clapped her hands like a child at a Punch and Judy show. Suddenly Bruce was laughing also. It was a laugh from long ago, coming out from deep inside him.

'Take it,' said Haig and Shermaine cradled it, wet and feebly wriggling in her arms. She stood with it while Haig sewed up. Watching her face and the way she stood, Bruce suddenly and unaccountably felt the laughter snag his throat, and he wanted to cry.

Haig closed the womb, stitching the complicated pattern of knots like a skilled seamstress, then the external sutures laid neatly across the fat lips of the wound, and at last the white tape hiding it all. He covered the woman, jerked the mask from his face and looked up at Shermaine.

'You can help me clean it up,' he said, and his voice was strong again and proud. The two of them crossed to the basin.

Bruce threw off his gown and left the room, went down the passage and out into the night. He leaned against the bonnet of the Ford and lit a cigarette.

Tonight I laughed again, he told himself with wonder, and then I nearly cried. And all because of a woman and a child. It is finished now, the pretence. The withdrawal. The big act. There was more than one birth in there tonight. I laughed again, I had the need to laugh again, and the desire to cry. A woman and a child, the whole meaning of life. The abscess had burst, the poison drained, and he was ready to heal.

'Bruce, Bruce, where are you?' She came out through the door; he did not answer her for she had seen the glow of his cigarette and she came to him. Standing close in the darkness.

'Shermaine—' Bruce said, then he stopped himself. He wanted to hold her, just hold her tightly.

'Yes, Bruce.' Her face was a pale round in the darkness, very close to him.

'Shermaine, I want—' said Bruce and stopped again.

'Yes, me too,' she whispered and then, drawing away, 'come, let's go and see what your doctor is doing now.' She took his hand and led him back into the building. Her hand was cool and dry with long tapered fingers in his.

Mike Haig and Father Ignatius were leaning over the cradle that now stood next to the table on which lay the blanket-covered body of the Baluba woman. The woman was breathing softly, and the expression on her face was of deep peace.

'Bruce, come and have a look. It's a beauty,' called Haig.

Still holding hands Bruce and Shermaine crossed to the cradle.

'He'll go all of eight pounds,' announced Haig proudly. Bruce looked at the infant; newborn black babies are more handsome than ours – they have not got that half-boiled look.

'Pity he's not a trout,' murmured Bruce. 'That would be a national record.' Haig stared blankly at him for a second, then he threw back his head and laughed; it was a good sound. There was a different quality in Haig now, a new confidence in the way he held his head, a feeling of completeness about him.

'How about that drink I promised you, Mike?' Bruce tested him.

'You have it for me, Bruce, I'll duck this one.' He isn't just saying it either, thought Bruce, as he looked at his face; he really doesn't need it now.

'I'll make it a double as soon as we get back to town.' Bruce glanced at his watch. 'It's past ten, we'd better get going.'

'I'll have to stay until she comes out from the anaesthetic,' demurred Haig. 'You can come back for me in the morning.'

Bruce hesitated. 'All right then. Come on, Shermaine.'

They drove back to Port Reprieve, sitting close together in the intimate darkness of the car. They did not speak until after they had reached the causeway, then Shermaine said:

'He is a good man, your doctor. He is like Paul.'

'Who is Paul?'

'Paul was my husband.'

'Oh.' Bruce was embarrassed. The mention of that name snapped the silken thread of his mood. Shermaine went on, speaking softly and staring down the path of the headlights.

'Paul was of the same age. Old enough to have learned understanding – young men are so cruel.'

'You loved him.' Bruce spoke flatly, trying to keep any trace of jealousy from his voice.

'Love has many shapes,' she answered. Then, 'Yes, I had begun to love him. Very soon I would have loved him enough to—' She stopped.

'To what?' Bruce's voice had gone rough as a wood rasp. *Now it starts*, he thought, *once again I am vulnerable*.

'We were only married four months before he – before the fever.'

'So?' Still harsh, his eyes on the road ahead.

'I want you to know something. I must explain it all to you. It is very important. Will you be patient with me while I tell you?' There was a pleading in her voice that he could not resist and his expression softened.

'Shermaine, you don't have to tell me.'

'I must. I want you to know.' She hesitated a moment, and when she spoke again her voice had steadied. 'I am an orphan, Bruce. Both my Mama and Papa were killed by the Germans, in the bombing. I was only a few months old when it happened, and I do not remember them. I do not remember anything, not one little thing about them; there is not even a photograph.' For a second her voice had gone shaky but again it firmed. 'The nuns took me, and they were my family. But somehow that is different, not really your own. I have never had anything that has truly belonged to me, something of my very own.'

Bruce reached out and took her hand; it lay very still in his grasp. You have now, he thought, you have me for your very own.

'Then when the time came the nuns made the arrangements with Paul Cartier. He was an engineer with Union Minière du Haut here in the Congo, a man of position, a suitable man for one of their girls.

113

'He flew to Brussels and we were married. I was not unhappy, for although he was old – as old as Doctor Mike – yet he was very gentle and kind, of great understanding. He did not—' She stopped and turned suddenly to Bruce, gripping his hand with both of hers, leaning towards him with her face serious and pale in the half-darkness, the plume of dark hair falling forward over her shoulder and her voice full of appeal. 'Bruce, do you understand what I am trying to tell you?'

Bruce stopped the car in front of the hotel, deliberately he switched off the ignition and deliberately he spoke.

'Yes, I think so.'

'Thank you,' and she flung the door open and went out of it and up the steps of the hotel with her long jeaned legs flying and her hair bouncing on her back.

Bruce watched her go through the double doors. Then he pressed the lighter on the dashboard and fished a cigarette from his pack. He lit it, exhaled a jet of smoke against the windscreen, and suddenly he was happy. He wanted to laugh again.

He threw the cigarette away only a quarter finished and climbed out of the Ford. He looked at his wristwatch; it was after midnight. My God, I'm tired. Too much has happened today; rebirth is a severe emotional strain. And he laughed out loud, savouring the sensation, letting it come slowly shaking up his throat from his chest.

Boussier was waiting for him in the lounge. He wore a towelling dressing-gown, and the creases of sleep were on his face.

'Are all your preparations complete, monsieur?'

'Yes,' the old man answered. 'The women and the two children are asleep upstairs. Madame Cartier has just gone up.'

'I know,' said Bruce, and Boussier went on, 'As you see, I have all the men here.' He gestured at the sleeping bodies that covered the floor of the lounge and bar-room.

'Good,' said Bruce. 'We'll leave as soon as it's light tomorrow.' He yawned, then rubbed his eyes, massaging them with his finger tips.

'Where is my officer, the one with the red hair?'

'He has gone back to the train, very drunk. We had more trouble with him after you had left.' Boussier hesitated delicately. 'He wanted to go upstairs, to the women.'

'Damn him.' Bruce felt his anger coming again. 'What happened?'

'Your sergeant major, the big one, dissuaded him and took him away.'

'Thank God for Ruffy.'

'I have reserved a place for you to sleep.' Boussier pointed to a comfortable leather armchair. 'You must be exhausted.'

'That is kind of you,' Bruce thanked him. 'But first I must inspect our defences.'

– 13 –

Bruce woke with Shermaine leaning over the chair and tickling his nose. He was fully dressed with his helmet and rifle on the floor beside him and only his boots unlaced.

'You do not snore, Bruce,' she congratulated him, laughing her small husky laugh. 'That is a good thing.'

He struggled up, dopey with sleep.

'What time is it?'

'Nearly five o'clock. I have breakfast for you in the kitchen.'

'Where is Boussier?'

'He is dressing; then he will start moving them down to the train.'

'My mouth tastes as though a goat slept in it.' Bruce moved his tongue across his teeth, feeling the fur on them.

'Then I shall not kiss you good morning, mon capitaine.'

She straightened up with the laughter still in her eyes. 'But your toilet requisites are in the kitchen. I sent one of your gendarmes to fetch them from the train. You can wash in the sink.'

Bruce laced up his boots and followed her through into the kitchen, stepping over sleeping bodies on the way.

'There is no hot water,' Shermaine apologized.

'That is the least of my worries.' Bruce crossed to the table and opened his small personal pack, taking out his razor and soap and comb.

'I raided the chicken coop for you,' Shermaine confessed. 'There were only two eggs. How shall I cook them?'

'Soft boiled, one minute.' Bruce stripped off his jacket and shirt, went to the sink and filled it. He sluiced his face and lifted handfuls of water over his head, snorting with pleasure.

Then he propped his shaving mirror above the taps and spread soap on his face. Shermaine came to sit on the draining board beside him and watched with frank interest.

'I will be sorry to see the beard go,' she said. 'It looked like the pelt of an otter, I liked it.'

'Perhaps I will grow it for you one day.' Bruce smiled at her. 'Your eyes are blue, Shermaine.'

'It has taken you a long time to find that out,' she said and pouted dramatically. Her skin was silky and cool-looking, lips pale pink without make-up. Her dark hair, drawn back, emphasized the high cheek bones and the size of her eyes.

'In India "sher" means "tiger",' Bruce told her, watching her from the corner of his eye. Immediately she abandoned the pout and drew her lips up into a snarl. Her teeth were small and very white and only slightly uneven. Her eyes rolled wide and then crossed at an alarming angle. She growled. Taken by surprise, Bruce laughed and nearly cut himself.

116

'I cannot abide a woman who clowns before breakfast. It ruins my digestion,' he laughed at her.

'Breakfast!' said Shermaine and uncrossed her eyes, jumped off the draining board and ran to the stove.

'Only just in time.' She checked her watch. 'One minute and twenty seconds, will you forgive me?'

'This once only, never again.' Bruce washed the soap off his face, dried and combed his hair and came to the table. She had a chair ready for him.

'How much sugar in your coffee?'

'Three, please.' Bruce chopped the top off his egg, and she brought the mug and placed it in front of him.

'I like making breakfast for you.' Bruce didn't answer her. This was dangerous talk. She sat down opposite him, leaned forward on her elbows with her chin in her hands.

'You eat too fast,' she announced and Bruce raised an eyebrow. 'But at least you keep your mouth closed.'

Bruce started on his second egg.

'How old are you?'

'Thirty,' said Bruce.

'I'm twenty – nearly twenty-one.'

'A ripe old age.'

'What do you do?'

'I'm a soldier,' he answered.

'No, you're not.'

'All right, I'm a lawyer.'

'You must be clever,' she said solemnly.

'A genius, that's why I'm here.'

'Are you married?'

'No – I was. What is this, a formal interrogation?'

'Is she dead?'

'No.' He prevented the hurt from showing in his face, it was easier to do now.

'Oh!' said Shermaine. She picked up the teaspoon and concentrated on stirring his coffee.

'Is she pretty?'

'No – yes, I suppose so.'

'Where is she?' Then quickly, 'I'm sorry it's none of my business.'

Bruce took the coffee from her and drank it. Then he looked at his watch.

'It's nearly five fifteen. I must go out and get Mike Haig.'

Shermaine stood up quickly.

'I'm ready.'

'I know the way – you had better get down to the station.'

'I want to come with you.'

'Why?'

'Just because, that's why.' Searching for a reason. 'I want to see the baby again.'

'You win.' Bruce picked up his pack and they went through into the lounge. Boussier was there, dressed and efficient. His men were nearly ready to move.

'Madame Cartier and I are going out to the mission to fetch the doctor. We will be back in half an hour or so. I want all your people aboard by then.'

'Very well, Captain.'

Bruce called to Ruffy who was standing on the verandah. 'Did you load those supplies for the mission?'

'They're in the back of the Ford, boss.'

'Good. Bring all your sentries in and take them down to the station. Tell the engine driver to get steam up and keep his hand on the throttle. We'll shove off as soon as I get back with Lieutenant Haig.'

'Okay, boss.'

Bruce handed him his pack. 'Take this down for me, Ruffy.' Then his eyes fell on the large heap of cardboard cartons at Ruffy's feet. 'What's that?'

Ruffy looked a little embarrassed. 'Coupla bottles of beer, boss. Thought we might get thirsty going home.'

'Good for you!' grinned Bruce. 'Put them in a safe place and don't drink them all before I get back.'

'I'll save you one or two,' promised Ruffy.

'Come along, tiger girl,' and Bruce led Shermaine out to the Ford. She sat closer to him than the previous day, but with her legs curled up under her, as before. As they crossed the causeway she lit two cigarettes and passed one to him.

'I'll be glad to leave this place,' she said, looking out across the swamp with the mist lifting sluggishly off it in the dawn, hanging in grey shreds from the fluffy tops of the papyrus grass.

'I've hated it here since Paul died. I hate the swamp and the mosquitoes and the jungle all around. I'm glad we're going.'

'Where will you go?' Bruce asked.

'I haven't thought about it. Back to Belgium, I suppose. Anywhere away from the Congo. Away from this heat to a country where you can breathe. Away from the disease and the fear. Somewhere so that I know tomorrow I will not have to run. Where human life has meaning, away from the killing and the burning and the rape.' She drew on her cigarette almost fiercely, staring ahead at the green wall of the forest.

'I was born in Africa,' said Bruce. 'In the time when the judge's gavel was not the butt of an FN rifle, before you registered your vote with a burst of gunfire.' He spoke softly with regret. 'In the time before the hatred. But now I don't know. I haven't thought much about the future either.'

He was silent for a while. They reached the turn-off to the mission and he swung the Ford into it.

'It has all changed so quickly; I hadn't realized how quickly until I came here to the Congo.'

'Are you going to stay here, Bruce? I mean, stay here in the Congo?'

'No,' he said, 'I've had enough. I don't even know what I'm fighting for.'

He threw the butt of his cigarette out of the window.

Ahead of them were the mission buildings.

Bruce parked the car outside the hospital buildings and they sat together quietly.

'There must be some other land,' he whispered, 'and if there is I'll find it.'

He opened the door and stepped out. Shermaine slid across the seat under the wheel and joined him. They walked side by side to the hospital; her hand brushed his and he caught it, held it and felt the pressure of his fingers returned by hers. She was taller than his shoulder, but not much.

Mike Haig and Father Ignatius were together in the women's ward, too engrossed to hear the Ford arrive.

'Good morning, Michael,' called Bruce. 'What's the fancy dress for?'

Mike Haig looked up and grinned. 'Morning, Bruce. Hello, Shermaine.' Then he looked down at the faded brown cassock he wore.

'Borrowed it from Ignatius. A bit long in the leg and tight round the waist, but less out of place in a sick ward than the accoutrements of war.'

'It suits you, Doctor Mike,' said Shermaine.

'Nice to hear someone call me that again.' The smile spread all over Haig's face. 'I suppose you want to see your baby, Shermaine?'

'Is he well?'

'Mother and child both doing fine,' he assured her and led Shermaine down between the row of beds, each with a black woolly head on the pillow and big curious eyes following their progress.

'May I pick him up?'

'He's asleep, Shermaine.'

'Oh, please!'

'I doubt it will kill him. Very well, then.'

'Bruce, come and look. Isn't he a darling?' She held the tiny black body to her chest and the child snuffled, its mouth automatically starting to search. Bruce leaned forward to peer at it.

'Very nice,' he said and turned to Ignatius. 'I have those supplies I promised you. Will you send an orderly to get them out of the car?' Then to Mike Haig, 'You'd better get changed, Mike. We're all ready to leave.'

Not looking at Bruce, fiddling with the stethoscope round his neck, Mike shook his head. 'I don't think I'll be going with you, Bruce.'

Surprised, Bruce faced him.

'What?'

'I think I'll stay on here with Ignatius. He has offered me a job.'

'You must be mad, Mike.'

'Perhaps,' agreed Haig and took the infant from Shermaine, placed it back in the cradle beside its mother and tucked the sheet in round its tiny body, 'and then again, perhaps not.' He straightened up and waved a hand down the rows of occupied beds. 'There's plenty to do here, that you must admit.'

Bruce stared helplessly at him and then appealed to Shermaine.

'Talk him out of it. Perhaps you can make him see the futility of it.'

Shermaine shook her head. 'No, Bruce, I will not.'

'Mike, listen to reason, for God's sake. You can't stay here in this disease-ridden backwater, you can't—'

'I'll walk out to the car with you, Bruce. I know you're in a hurry—'

He led them out through the side door and stood by the driver's window of the Ford while they climbed in. Bruce extended his hand and Mike took it, gripping hard.

'Cheerio, Bruce. Thanks for everything.'

'Cheerio, Mike. I suppose you'll be taking orders and having yourself made into a fully licensed dispenser of salvation?'

'I don't know about that, Bruce. I doubt it. I just want another chance to do the only work I know. I just want a last-minute rally to reduce the formidable score that's been chalked up against me so far.'

'I'll report you "missing, believed killed" – throw your uniform in the river,' said Bruce.

'I'll do that.' Mike stepped back. 'Look after each other, you two.'

'I don't know what you mean,' Shermaine informed him primly, trying not to smile.

'I'm an old dog, not easy to fool,' said Mike. 'Go to it with a will.'

Bruce let out the clutch and the Ford slid forward.

'God speed, my children.' That smile spread all over Mike's face as he waved.

'Au revoir, Doctor Michael.'

'So long, Mike.'

Bruce watched him in the rear-view mirror, tall in his ill-fitting cassock, something proud and worthwhile in his stance. He waved once more and then turned and hurried back into the hospital.

Neither of them spoke until they had almost reached the main road. Shermaine nestled softly against Bruce, smiling to herself, looking ahead down the tree-lined passage of the road.

'He's a good man, Bruce.'

'Light me a cigarette, please, Shermaine.' He didn't want to talk about it. It was one of those things that can only be made grubby by words.

Slowing for the intersection, Bruce dropped her into second gear, automatically glancing to his left to make sure the main road was clear before turning into it.

'Oh my God!' he gasped.

'What is it, Bruce?' Shermaine looked up with alarm from the cigarette she was lighting.

'Look!'

A hundred yards up the road, parked close to the edge of the forest, was a convoy of six large vehicles. The first five were heavy canvas-canopied lorries painted dull military olive, the sixth was a gasoline tanker in bright yellow and red with the Shell Company insignia on the barrel-shaped body. Hitched behind the leading lorry was a squat, rubber-tyred 25-pounder anti-tank gun with its long barrel pointed jauntily skywards. Round the vehicles, dressed in an assortment of uniforms and different styled helmets, were at least sixty men. They were all armed, some with automatic weapons and others with obsolete bolt-action rifles. Most of them were urinating carelessly into the grass that lined the road, while the others were standing in small groups smoking and talking.

'General Moses!' said Shermaine, her voice small with the shock.

'Get down,' ordered Bruce and with his free hand thrust her on to the floor. He rammed the accelerator flat and the Ford roared out into the main road, swerving violently, the back end floating free in the loose dust as he held the wheel over. Correcting the skid, meeting it and straightening out, Bruce glanced at the rear-view mirror. Behind them the men had dissolved into a confused pattern of movement; he heard their shouts high and thin above the racing engine of the Ford. Bruce looked ahead; it was another hundred yards to the bend in the road that would hide them and take them down to the causeway across the swamp.

Shermaine was on her knees pulling herself up to look over the back of the seat.

'Keep on the floor, damn you!' shouted Bruce and pushed her head down roughly.

As he spoke the roadside next to them erupted in a rapid series of leaping dust fountains and he heard the high hysterical beat of machine-gun fire.

The bend in the road rushed towards them, just a few more seconds. Then with a succession of jarring crashes that shook the whole body of the car a burst of fire hit them from behind. The windscreen starred into a sheet of opaque diamond lacework, the dashboard clock exploded powdering Shermaine's hair with particles of glass, two bullets tore through the seat ripping out the stuffing like the entrails of a wounded animal.

'Close your eyes,' shouted Bruce and punched his fist through the windscreen. Slitting his own eyes against the chips of flying glass, he could just see through the hole his fist had made. The corner was right on top of them and he dragged the steering-wheel over, skidding into it, his off-side wheels bumping into the verge, grass and leaves brushing the side of the car.

Then they were through the corner and racing down towards the causeway.

'Are you all right, Shermaine?'

'Yes, are you?' She emerged from under the dashboard, a smear of blood across one cheek where the glass had scratched her, and her eyes bigger than ever with fright.

'I only pray that Boussier and Hendry are ready to pull out. Those bastards won't be five minutes behind us.'

They went across the causeway with the needle of the speedometer touching eighty, up the far side and into the main street of Port Reprieve. Bruce thrust his hand down on the hooter ring, blowing urgent warning blasts.

'Please God, let them be ready,' he muttered. With relief he saw that the street was empty and the hotel seemed deserted. He kept blowing the horn as they roared down towards the station, a great billowing cloud of dust rising behind them. Braking the Ford hard, he turned it in past the station buildings and on to the platform.

Most of Boussier's people were standing next to the train. Boussier himself was beside the last truck with his wife and the small group of women around him. Bruce shouted at them through the open window.

'Get those women into the train, the *shufta* are right behind us, we're leaving immediately.'

Without question or argument old Boussier gathered them together and hurried them up the steel ladder into the truck. Bruce drove down the station platform shouting as he went.

'Get in! For Chrissake, hurry up! They're coming!'

He braked to a standstill next to the cab of the locomotive and shouted up at the bald head of the driver.

'Get going. Don't waste a second. Give her everything she's got. There's a bunch of *shufta* not five minutes behind us.'

The driver's head disappeared into the cab without even the usual polite, 'Oui monsieur.'

'Come on, Shermaine.' Bruce grabbed her hand and dragged her from the car. Together they ran to one of the covered coaches and Bruce pushed her half way up the steel steps.

At that moment the train jerked forward so violently that she lost her grip on the handrails and tumbled backwards on top of Bruce. He was caught off balance and they fell together in a heap on the dusty platform. Above them the train gathered speed, pulling away. He remembered this nightmare from his childhood, running after a train and never catching it. He had to fight down his panic as he and Shermaine scrambled up, both of them panting, clinging to each other, the coaches clackety-clacking past them, the rhythm of their wheels mounting.

'Run!' he gasped, 'Run!' and with the panic weakening their legs he just managed to catch the handrail of the second coach. He clung to it, stumbling along beside the train, one arm round Shermaine's waist. Sergeant Major

Ruffararo leaned out, took Shermaine by the scruff of her neck and lifted her in like a lost kitten. Then he reached down for Bruce.

'Boss, some day we going to lose you if you go on playing around like that.'

'I'm sorry, Bruce,' she panted, leaning against him.

'No damage done.' He could grin at her. 'Now I want you to get into that compartment and stay there until I tell you to come out. Do you understand?'

'Yes, Bruce.'

'Off you go.' He turned from her to Ruffy. 'Up on to the roof, Sergeant Major! We're going to have fireworks. Those *shufta* have got a field gun with them and we'll be in full view of the town right up to the top of the hills.'

By the time they reached the roof of the train it had pulled out of Port Reprieve and was making its first angling turn up the slope of the hills. The sun was up now, well clear of the horizon, and the mist from the swamp had lifted so that they could see the whole village spread out beneath them.

General Moses's column had crossed the causeway and was into the main street. As Bruce watched, the leading truck swung sharply across the road and stopped. Men boiled out from under the canopy and swarmed over the field gun, unhitching it, manhandling it into position.

'I hope those Arabs haven't had any drill on that piece,' grunted Ruffy.

'We'll soon find out,' Bruce assured him grimly and looked back along the train. In the last truck Boussier stood protectively over the small group of four women and their children, like an old white-haired collie with its sheep. Crouched against the steel side of the truck, André de Surrier and half a dozen gendarmes were swinging and sighting the two Bren guns. In the second truck also the gendarmes were preparing to open fire.

126

'What are you waiting for?' roared Ruffy. 'Get me that field gun – start shooting.'

They fired a ragged volley, then the Bren guns joined in. With every burst André's helmet slipped forward over his eyes and he had to stop and push it back. Lying on the roof of the leading coach, Wally Hendry was firing short businesslike bursts.

The *shufta* round the field gun scattered, leaving one of their number lying in the road, but there were men behind the armour shield – Bruce could see the tops of their helmets.

Suddenly there was a long gush of white smoke from the barrel, and the shell rushed over the top of the train, with a noise like the wings of a giant pheasant.

'Over!' said Ruffy.

'Under!' to the next shot as it ploughed into the trees below them.

'And the third one right up the throat,' said Bruce. But it hit the rear of the train. They were using armour-piercing projectiles, not high explosive, for there was not the burst of yellow cordite fumes but only the crash and jolt as it struck.

Anxiously Bruce tried to assess the damage. The men and women in the rear trucks looked shaken but unharmed and he started a sigh of relief, which changed quickly to a gasp of horror as he realized what had happened.

'They've hit the coupling,' he said. 'They've sheared the coupling on the last truck.'

Already the gap was widening, as the rear truck started to roll back down the hill, cut off like the tail of a lizard.

'Jump,' screamed Bruce, cupping his hands round his mouth. 'Jump before you gather speed.'

Perhaps they did not hear him, perhaps they were too stunned to obey, but no one moved. The truck rolled back, faster and faster as gravity took it, down the hill towards the village and the waiting army of General Moses.

'What can we do, boss?'

'Nothing,' said Bruce.

The firing round Bruce had petered out into silence as every man, even Wally Hendry, stared down the slope at the receding truck. With a constriction of his throat Bruce saw old Boussier stoop and lift his wife to her feet, hold her close to his side and the two of them looking back at Bruce on the roof of the departing train. Boussier raised his right hand in a gesture of farewell and then he dropped it again and stood very still. Behind him, André de Surrier had left the Bren gun and removed his helmet. He also was looking back at Bruce, but he did not wave.

At intervals the field gun in the village punctuated the stillness with its deep boom and gush of smoke, but Bruce hardly heard it. He was watching the *shufta* running down towards the station yard to welcome the truck. Losing speed it ran into the platform and halted abruptly as it hit the buffers at the end of the line. The *shufta* swarmed over it like little black ants over the body of a beetle and faintly Bruce heard the pop, pop, pop of their rifles, saw the low sun glint on their bayonets. He turned away.

They had almost reached the crest of the hills; he could feel the train increasing speed under him. But he felt no relief, only the prickling at the corners of his eyes and the ache of it trapped in his throat.

'The poor bastards,' growled Ruffy beside him. 'The poor bastards.' And then there was another crashing jolt against the train, another hit from the field gun. This time up forward, on the locomotive. Shriek of escaping steam, the train checking its pace, losing power. But they were over the crest of the hills, the village was out of sight and gradually the train speeded up again as they started down the back slope. But steam spouted out of it, hissing white jets of it, and Bruce knew they had received a mortal wound. He switched on the radio.

'Driver, can you hear me? How bad is it?'

128

'I cannot see, Captain. There is too much steam. But the pressure on the gauge is dropping swiftly.'

'Use all you can to take us down the hill. It is imperative that we pass the level crossing before we halt. It is absolutely imperative – if we stop this side of the level crossing they will be able to reach us with their lorries.'

'I will try, Captain.'

They rocketed down the hills but as soon as they reached the level ground their speed began to fall off. Peering through the dwindling clouds of steam Bruce saw the pale brown ribbon of road ahead of them, and they were still travelling at a healthy thirty miles an hour as they passed it. When finally the train trickled to a standstill Bruce estimated that they were three or four miles beyond the level crossing, safely walled in by the forest and hidden from the road by three bends.

'I doubt they'll find us here, but if they do they'll have to come down the line from the level crossing to get at us. We'll go back a mile and lay an ambush in the forest on each side of the line,' said Bruce.

'Those Arabs won't be following us, boss. They've got themselves women and a whole barful of liquor. Be two or three days before old General Moses can sober them up enough to move them on.'

'You're probably right, Ruffy. But we'll take no chances. Get that ambush laid and then we'll try and think up some idea for getting home.'

Suddenly a thought occurred to him: Martin Boussier had the diamonds with him. They would not be too pleased about that in Elisabethville.

Almost immediately Bruce was disgusted with himself. The diamonds were by far the least important thing that they had left behind in Port Reprieve.

14

André de Surrier held his steel helmet against his chest the way a man holds his hat at a funeral, the wind blew cool and caressing through his dark sweat-damp hair. His hearing was dulled by the strike of the shell that had cut the truck loose from the rear of the train, he could hear one of the children crying and the crooning, gentling voice of its mother. He stared back up the railway line at the train, saw the great bulk of Ruffy beside Bruce Curry on the roof of the second coach.

'They can't help us now.' Boussier spoke softly. 'There's nothing they can do.' He lifted his hand stiffly in almost a military salute and then dropped it to his side. 'Be brave, ma chère,' he said to his wife. 'Please be brave,' and she clung to him.

André let the helmet drop from his hands. It clanged on to the metal floor of the truck. He wiped the sweat from his face with nervous fluttering hands and then turned slowly to look down at the village.

'I don't want to die,' he whispered. 'Not like this, not now, please not now.' One of his gendarmes laughed, a sound without mirth, and stepped across to the Bren. He pushed André away from it and started firing at the tiny running figures of the men in the station yard.

'No,' shrilled André. 'Don't do that, no, don't antagonize them. They'll kill us if you do that—'

'They'll kill us anyway,' laughed the gendarme and emptied the magazine in one long despairing burst. André started towards him, perhaps to pull him away from the gun, but his resolve did not carry him that far. His hands dropped to his sides, clenching and unclenching. His lips quivered and then opened to spill out his terror.

'No!' he screamed. 'Please, no! No! No! Oh, God have mercy.

Oh, save me, don't let this happen to me, please, God. Oh, my God.'

He stumbled to the side of the truck and clambered on to it. The truck was slowing as it ran into the platform. He could see men coming with rifles in their hands, shouting as they ran, black men in dirty tattered uniforms, their faces working with excitement, pink shouting mouths, baying like hounds in a pack.

André jumped and the dusty concrete of the platform grazed his cheek and knocked the wind out of him. He crawled to his knees, clutching his stomach and trying to scream. A rifle butt hit him between the shoulder-blades and he collapsed. Above him a voice shouted in French.

'He is white, keep him for the general. Don't kill him.' And again the rifle butt hit him, this time across the side of the head. He lay in the dust, dazed, with the taste of blood in his mouth and watched them drag the others from the truck.

They shot the black gendarmes on the platform, without ceremony, laughing as they competed with each other to use their bayonets on the corpses. The two children died quickly torn from their mothers, held by the feet and swung head first against the steel side of the truck.

Old Boussier tried to prevent them stripping his wife and was bayoneted from behind in anger, and then shot twice with a pistol held to his head as he lay on the platform.

All this happened in the first few minutes before the officers arrived to control them; by that time André and the four women were the only occupants of the truck left alive.

André lay where he had fallen, watching in fascinated skin-crawling horror as they tore the clothing off the women and with a man to each arm and each leg held them down on the platform as though they were calves to be branded, hooting with laughter at their struggling naked bodies, bickering for position, already unbuckling belts, pushing each other, arguing, some of them with fresh blood on their clothing.

But then two men, who by their air of authority and the red sashes across their chests were clearly officers, joined the crowd. One of them fired his pistol in the air to gain their attention and both of them started a harangue that slowly had effect. The women were dragged up and herded off towards the hotel.

One of the officers came across to where André lay, stooped over him and lifted his head by taking a handful of hair.

'Welcome, mon ami. The general will be very pleased to see you. It is a pity that your other white friends have left us, but then, one is better than nothing.'

He pulled André into a sitting position, peered into his face and then spat into his eyes with sudden violence. 'Bring him! The general will talk to him later.'

They tied André to one of the columns on the front verandah of the hotel and left him there. He could have twisted his head and looked through the large windows into the lounge at what they were doing to the women, but he did not. He could hear what was happening; by noon the screams had become groans and sobbing; by mid-afternoon the women were making no sound at all. But the queue of *shufta* was still out of the front door of the lounge. Some of them had been to the head of the line and back to the tail three or four times.

All of them were drunk now. One jovial fellow carried a bottle of Parfait Amour liqueur in one hand and a bottle of Harpers whisky in the other. Every time he came back to join the queue again he stopped in front of André.

'Will you drink with me, little white boy?' he asked. 'Certainly you will,' he answered himself, filled his mouth from one of the bottles and spat it into André's face. Each time it got a big laugh from the others waiting in the line. Occasionally one of the other *shufta* would stop in front of

132

André, unsling his rifle, back away a few paces, sight along the bayonet at André's face and then charge forward, at the last moment twisting the point aside so that it grazed his cheek. Each time André could not suppress his shriek of terror, and the waiting men nearly collapsed with merriment.

Towards evening they started to burn the houses on the outskirts of town. One group, sad with liquor and rape, sat together at the end of the verandah and started to sing. Their deep beautiful voices carrying all the melancholy savagery of Africa, they kept on singing while an argument between two *shufta* developed into a knife fight in the road outside the hotel.

The sweet bass lilt of singing covered the coarse breathing of the two circling, bare-chested knife fighters and the shuffle, shuffle, quick shuffle of their feet in the dust. When finally they locked together for the kill, the singing rose still deep and strong but with a triumphant note to it. One man stepped back with his rigid right arm holding the knife buried deep in the other's belly and as the loser sank down, sliding slowly off the knife, the singing sank with him, plaintive, regretful and lamenting into silence.

They came for André after dark. Four of them less drunk than the others. They led him down the street to the Union Minière offices. General Moses was there, sitting alone at the desk in the front office.

There was nothing sinister about him; he looked like an elderly clerk, a small man with the short woollen cap of hair grizzled to grey above the ears and a pair of horn-rimmed spectacles. On his chest he wore three rows of full-dress medals; each of his fingers was encased in rings to the second joint, diamonds, emeralds and the occasional red glow of a ruby; most of them had been designed for women, but the metal had been cut to enlarge them for his stubby black fingers. The face was almost kindly, except the eyes. There was a blankness of expression in them, the lifeless eyes of a madman. On the desk in front of him was a small wooden case made of unvarnished deal which bore the seal of the Union Minière Company stencilled in black upon its side. The lid was open, and as André came in through the door with his escort General Moses lifted a white canvas bag from the case, loosened the drawstring and poured a pile of dark grey industrial diamonds on to the blotter in front of him.

He prodded them thoughtfully with his finger, stirring them so they glittered dully in the harsh light of the petromax.

'Was this the only case in the truck?' he asked without looking up.

'Oui, mon général. There was only one,' answered one of André's escorts.

'You are certain?'

'Oui, mon général. I myself have searched thoroughly.'

General Moses took another of the canvas bags from the case and emptied it on to the blotter. He grunted with disappointment as he saw the drab little stones. He reached for another bag, and another, his anger mounting steadily as each yielded only dirty grey and black industrial diamonds. Soon the pile on the blotter would have filled a pint jug.

'Did you open the case?' he snarled.

'Non, mon général. It was sealed. The seal was not broken, you saw that.'

General Moses grunted again, his dark chocolate face set hard with frustration. Once more he dipped his hand into the wooden case and suddenly he smiled.

'Ah!' he said pleasantly. 'Yes! yes! what is this?' He brought out a cigar box, with the gaudy wrappers still on the cedarwood. A thumbnail prised the lid back and he beamed happily. In a nest of cotton wool, sparkling, break-

134

ing the white light of the petromax into all the rainbow colours of the spectrum, were the gem stones. General Moses picked one up and held it between thumb and forefinger.

'Pretty,' he murmured. 'Pretty, so pretty.' He swept the industrial stones to one side and laid the gem in the centre of the blotter. Then one by one he took the others from the cigar box, fondling each and laying it on the blotter, counting them, smiling, once chuckling softly, touching them, arranging them in patterns.

'Pretty,' he kept whispering. 'Bon – forty-one, forty-two. Pretty! My darlings! Forty-three.'

Then suddenly he scooped them up and poured them into one of the canvas bags, tightened the drawstring, dropped it into his breast pocket above the medals and buttoned the flap.

He laid his black, bejewelled hands on the desk in front of him and looked up at André.

His eyes were smoky yellow with black centres behind his spectacles. They had an opaque, dreamlike quality.

'Take off his clothes,' he said in a voice that was as expressionless as the eyes.

They stripped André with rough dispatch and General Moses looked at his body.

'So white,' he murmured. 'Why so white?' Suddenly his jaws began chewing nervously and there was a faint shine of sweat on his forehead. He came round from behind the desk, a small man, yet with an intensity about him that doubled his size.

'White like the maggots that feed in the living body of the elephant.' He brought his face close to André's. 'You should be fatter, my maggot, having fed so long and so well. You should be much fatter.'

He touched André's body, running his hands down his flanks in a caress.

'But now it is too late, little white maggot,' he said, and

135

André cringed from his touch and from his voice. 'For the elephant has shaken you from the wound, shaken you out on to the ground, shaken you out beneath his feet – and will you pop when he crushes you?'

His voice was still soft though the sweat oozed in oily lines down his cheeks and the dreaminess of his eyes had been replaced by a burning black brightness.

'We shall see,' he said and drew back. 'We shall see, my maggot,' he repeated, and brought his knee up into André's crotch with a force that jerked his whole frame and flung his shoulders back.

The agony flared through André's lower body, fierce as the touch of heated steel. It clamped in on his stomach, contracting it in a spasm like childbirth, it rippled up across the muscles of his chest into his head and burst beneath the roof of his skull in a whiteness that blinded him.

'Hold him,' commanded General Moses, his voice suddenly shrill. The two guards took André by the elbows and forced him to his knees, so that his genitals and lower belly were easily accessible to the general's boots. They had done this often.

'For the times you gaoled me!' And General Moses swung his booted foot into André's body. The pain blended with the other pain, and it was too strong for André to scream.

'This, for the insults,' and André could feel his testicles crush beneath it. Still it was too strong – he could not use his voice.

'This, for the times I have grovelled.' The pain had passed its zenith, this time he could scream with it. He opened his mouth and filled his empty lungs.

'This, for the times I have hungered.' Now he must scream. Now he must – the pain, oh, sweet Christ, I must, please let me scream.

'This, for your white man's justice.' Why can't I, please let me. Oh, no! No – please. Oh, God, oh, please.

'This, for your prisons and your Kiboko!'

The kicks so fast now, like the beat of an insane drummer, like rain on a tin roof. In his stomach he felt something tear.

'And this, and this, and this.'

The face before him filled the whole field of his vision. The voice and the sound of the boot into him filled his ears.

'This, and this, and this.' The voice high-pitched and within him the sudden warm flood of internal bleeding.

The pain was fading now as his body closed it out in defence, and he had not screamed. The leap of elation as he knew it. *This last thing I can do well, I can die now WITHOUT SCREAMING.* He tried to stand up, but they held him down and his legs were not his own, they were on the other side of the great numb warmth of his belly. He lifted his head and looked at the man who was killing him.

'This for the white filth that bore you, and this, and this—'

The blows were not a part of reality, he could feel the shock of them as though he stood close to a man who was cutting down a tree with an axe. And André smiled.

He was still smiling when they let him fall forward to the floor.

'I think he is dead,' said one of the guards. General Moses turned away and walked back to his seat at the desk. He was shaking as though he had run a long way, and his breathing was deep and fast. The jacket of his uniform was soaked with sweat. He sank into the chair and his body seemed to crumple; slowly the brightness faded from his eyes until once more they were filmed over, opaque and dreamy. The two guards squatted down quickly on each side of André's body; they knew it would be a long wait.

Through the open window there came an occasional shout of drunken laughter, and the red flicker and leap of flames.

15

B ruce stood in the centre of the tracks and searched the floor of the forest critically. At last he could make out the muzzle of the Bren protruding a few inches from the patch of elephant grass. Despite the fact that he knew exactly where to look for it, it had taken him a full two minutes to find it.

'That'll do, Ruffy,' he decided. 'We can't get it much better than that.'

'I reckon not, boss.'

Bruce raised his voice. 'Can you hear me?' There were muffled affirmatives from the bush on each side, and Bruce continued.

'If they come you must let them reach this spot before you open fire. I will mark it for you.' He went to a small shrub beside the line, broke off a branch and dropped it on the tracks.

'Can you see that?'

Again the affirmatives from the men in ambush. 'You will be relieved before darkness – until then stay where you are.'

The train was hidden beyond a bend in the line, half a mile ahead, and Bruce walked back with Ruffy.

The engine driver was waiting for them, talking with Wally Hendry beside the rear truck.

'Any luck?' Bruce asked him.

'I regret, mon capitaine, that she is irreparably damaged. The boiler is punctured in two places and there is considerable disruption of the copper tubing.'

'Thank you,' Bruce nodded. He was neither surprised nor disappointed. It was precisely what his own judgement had told him after a brief examination of the locomotive.

'Where is Madame Cartier?' he asked Wally.

'*Madame* is preparing the luncheon, *monsir*,' Wally told

him with heavy sarcasm. 'Why do you ask, Bucko? Are you feeling randy again so soon, hey? You feel like a slice of veal for lunch, is that it?'

Bruce snuffed out the quick flare of his temper and walked past him. He found Shermaine with four gendarmes in the cab of the locomotive. They had scraped the coals from the furnace into a glowing heap on the steel floor and were chopping potatoes and onions into the five gallon pots.

The gendarmes were all laughing at something Shermaine had said. Her usually pale cheeks were flushed with the heat; there was a sooty smudge on her forehead. She wielded the big knife with professional dexterity. She looked up and saw Bruce, her face lighting instantly and her lips parting.

'We're having a Hungarian goulash for lunch – bully beef, potatoes and onions.'

'As of now I am rating you acting second cook without pay.'

'You are too kind,' and she put her tongue out at him. It was a pink pointed little tongue like a cat's. Bruce felt the old familiar tightening of his legs and the dryness in his throat as he looked at it.

'Shermaine, the locomotive is damaged beyond repair. It is of no further use.' He spoke in English.

'It makes a passable kitchen,' she demurred.

'Be serious.' Bruce's anxiety made him irritable. 'We're stranded here until we think of something.'

'But, Bruce, you are the genius. I have complete faith in you. I'm sure you'll think of some truly beautiful idea.' Her face was solemn but she couldn't keep the banter out of her eyes. 'Why don't you go and ask General Moses to lend you his transportation?'

Bruce's eyes narrowed in thought and the black inverted curves of his eyebrows nearly touched above the bridge of his nose.

'The food better be good or I'll break you to third cook,' he warned, clambered down from the cab to the ground and hurried back along the train.

'Hendry, Sergeant Major, come here, please. I want to discuss something with you.'

They came to join him and he led the way up the ladder into one of the covered coaches. Hendry dropped on to the bunk and placed his feet on the washbasin.

'That was a quick one,' he grinned through the coppery stubble of his beard.

'You're the most uncouth, filthy-mouthed son of a bitch I have ever met, Hendry,' said Bruce coldly. 'When I get you back to Elisabethville I'm going to beat you to pulp before I hand you over to the military authority for murder.'

'My, my,' laughed Hendry. 'Big talker, hey? Curry, big, big talker.'

'Don't make me kill you now – don't do that, please. I still need you.'

'What's with you and that Frenchy, hey? You love it or something? You love it, or you just fancy a bit of that fat little arse? It can't be her titties – she ain't got much there, not even a handful each side.'

Bruce started for him, then changed his mind and swung round to stare out of the window. His voice was strangled when he spoke.

'I'll make a bargain with you, Hendry. Until we get out of this you keep off my back and I'll keep off yours. When we reach Msapa Junction the truce is off. You can do and say whatever you like and, if I don't kill you for it, I'll try my level best to see you hanged for murder.'

'I'm making no bargain with you or nobody, Curry. I play along until it suits me, and I won't give you no warning when it doesn't suit me to play along any more. And let me tell you now, Bucko, I don't need you and I don't need nobody. Not Haig or you, with your fancy too-good-to-kiss-my-arse talk; when the time comes I'm going to trim you down to size – just remember that, Curry. And don't say I didn't warn you.' Hendry was leaning forward, hands on his knees, body braced and his whole face twisting and contorted with the vehemence of his speech.

'Let's make it now, Hendry.' Bruce wheeled away from the window, crouching slightly, his hands stiffening into the flat hard blades of the judo fighter.

Sergeant Major Ruffararo stood up from the opposite bunk with surprising grace and speed for such a big man. He interposed his great body.

'You wanted to tell us something, boss?'

Slowly Bruce straightened out of his crouch, his hands relaxing. Irritably he brushed at the damp lock of dark hair that had fallen on to his forehead, as if to brush Wally Hendry out of his mind with the same movement.

'Yes,' controlling his voice with an effort, 'I wanted to discuss our next move.' He fished the cigarette pack from his top pocket and lit one, sucking the smoke down deep. Then he perched on the lid of the washbasin and studied the ash on the tip of the cigarette. When he spoke again his voice was normal.

'There is no hope of repairing this locomotive, so we have to find alternative transport out of here. Either we can walk two hundred miles back to Msapa Junction with our friends the Baluba ready to dispute our passage, or we can ride back in General Moses's trucks!' He paused to let it sink in.

'You going to pinch those trucks off him?' asked Ruffy. 'That's going to take some doing, boss.'

'No, Ruffy, I don't think we have any chance of getting them out from under his nose. What we will have to do is attack the town and wipe him out.'

'You're bloody crazy,' exclaimed Wally. 'You're raving bloody mad.'

Bruce ignored him. 'I estimate that Moses has about sixty men. With Kanaki and nine men on the bridge, Haig and

141

de Surrier and six others gone, we have thirty-four men left. Correct, Sergeant Major?'

'That's right, boss.'

'Very well,' Bruce nodded. 'We'll have to leave at least ten men here to man that ambush in case Moses sends a patrol after us, or in case of an attack by the Baluba. It's not enough, I know, but we will just have to risk it.'

'Most of these civilians got arms with them, shotguns and sports rifles,' said Ruffy.

'Yes,' agreed Bruce. 'They should be able to look after themselves. So that leaves twenty-four men to carry out the attack, something like three to one.'

'Those *shufta* will be so full of liquor, half of them won't be able to stand up.'

'That's what I am banking on: drunkenness and surprise. We'll hit them and try and finish it before they know what's happened. I don't think they will have realized how badly we were hit; they probably expect us to be a hundred miles away by now.'

'When do you want to leave, boss?'

'We are about twelve miles from Port Reprieve – say, six hours' march in the dark. I want to attack in the early hours of tomorrow morning, but I'd like to be in position around midnight. We'll leave here at six o'clock, just before dark.'

'I'd better go and start sorting the boys out.'

'Okay, Ruffy. Issue an extra hundred rounds to each man and ten grenades. I'll want four extra haversacks of grenades also.' Bruce turned to Hendry and looked at him for the first time. 'Go with the sergeant major, Hendry, and give him a hand.'

'Jesus, this is going to be a ball,' grinned Wally in anticipation. 'With any luck I'll get me a sackful of ears.' He disappeared down the corridor behind Ruffy, and Bruce lay back on the seat and took off his helmet. He closed his eyes and once again he saw Boussier and his wife standing together in the truck as it rolled back down the hill, he saw the huddle of frightened women, and André standing bareheaded staring back at him with big brown gentle eyes. He groaned softly. 'Why is it always the good ones, the harmless, the weak?'

A tap on the door roused him and he sat up quickly.

'Yes?'

'Hello, Bruce.' Shermaine came in with a multiple-decked metal canteen in one hand and two mugs in the other. 'It's lunchtime.'

'Already!' Bruce checked his watch. 'Good Lord, it's after one.'

'Are you hungry?'

'Breakfast was a century ago.'

'Good,' she said, lowered the collapsible table and began serving the food.

'Smells good.'

'I am a chef Cordon Bleu. My bully beef goulash is demanded by the crowned heads of Europe.'

They ate in silence for both of them were hungry. Once they looked at each other and smiled but returned to the food.

'That was good,' sighed Bruce at last.

'Coffee, Bruce?'

'Please.'

As she poured it she asked, 'So, what happens now?'

'Do you mean what happens now we are alone?'

'You are forward, monsieur. I meant how do we get out of here?'

'I am adopting your suggestion: borrowing General Moses's transportation.'

'You make jokes, Bruce!'

'No,' he said, and explained briefly.

'It will be very dangerous, will it not? You may be hurt?'

'Only the good die young.'

'That is why I worry. Please do not get hurt – I am starting to think I would not like that.' Her face was very

143

serious and pale. Bruce crossed quickly and stooped over her, lifting her to her feet.

'Shermaine, I—'

'No, Bruce. Don't talk. Don't say anything.' Her eyes were closed with thick black lashes interlaced, her chin lifted exposing the long smooth swell of her neck. He touched it with his lips and she made a soft noise in her throat so he could feel the skin vibrate. Her body flattened against his and her fingers closed in the hair at the back of his head.

'Oh, Bruce. My Bruce, please do not get hurt. Do not let them hurt you.'

Wanting now, urgently, his mouth hunted upwards and hers came to meet it, willing prey. Her lips were pink and not greased with make-up, they parted to the pressure of his tongue, he felt the tip of her nose cool upon his cheek and his hand moved up her back and closed round the nape of her neck, slender neck with silky down behind her ears.

'Oh, Bruce—' she said into his mouth. His other hand went down on to the proud, round, deeply divided thrust of her buttocks, he pulled her lower body against his and she gasped as she felt him – the arrogant maleness through cloth.

'No,' she gasped and tried to pull away, but he held her until she relaxed against him once more. She shook her head, 'Non, non,' but her mouth was open still and her tongue fluttered against his. Down came his hand from her neck and twitched her shirt tails loose from under her belt, then up again along her back, touching the deep lateral depression of her spine so that she shuddered, clinging to him. Stroking velvet skin stretched tight over rubber-hard flesh, finding the outline of her shoulder blades, tracing them upwards then back to the armpits, silky-haired armpits that maddened him with excitement, quickly past them to her breasts, small breasts with soft tips hardening to his touch.

144

Now she struggled in earnest, her fists beating on his shoulders and her mouth breaking from his, and he stopped himself, dropped the hand away to encircle her waist. Holding her loosely within his arms.

'That was not good, Bruce. You get naughty very quick.' Her cheeks flamed with colour and her blue eyes had darkened to royal, her lips still wet from his, and her voice was unsteady, as unsteady as his when he answered.

'I'm sorry, Shermaine. I don't know what happened then, I did not mean to frighten you.'

'You are very strong, Bruce. But you do not frighten me, only a little bit. Your eyes frighten me when they look at me but do not see.'

You really made a hash of that one, he rebuked himself. Bruce Curry, the gentle sophisticated lover. Bruce Curry, the heavyweight, catch-as-catch-can, two-fisted rape artist.

He felt shaky, his legs wobbly, and there was something seriously wrong with his breathing.

'You do not wear a brassière,' he said without thinking, and immediately regretted it, but she chuckled, soft and husky.

'Do you think I need to, Bruce?'

'No, I didn't mean that,' he protested quickly, remembering the saucy tilt of that small breast. He was silent then, marshalling his words, trying to control his breathing, fighting down the madness of desire.

She studied his eyes. 'You can see again now – perhaps I will let you kiss me.'

'Please,' he said and she came back to him.

Gently now, Bruce me boy.

The door of the compartment flew back with a crash and they jumped apart. Wally Hendry stood on the threshold.

'Well, well, well.' His shrewd little eyes took it all in. 'That's nice!'

Shermaine was hurriedly tucking in her shirt tail and trying to smooth her hair at the same time.

Wally grinned. 'Nothing like it after a meal, I always say. Gets the digestion going.'

'What do you want?' snapped Bruce.

'There's no doubt what you want,' said Wally. 'Looks like you're getting it too.' He let his eyes travel up from Shermaine's waist, slowly over her body to her face.

Bruce stepped out into the corridor, pushing Hendry back and slammed the door.

'What do you want?' he repeated.

'Ruffy wants you to check his arrangements, but I'll tell him you're busy. We can put the attack off until tomorrow night if you like.'

Bruce scowled at him. 'Tell him I'll be with him in two minutes.'

Wally leaned against the door. 'Okay, I'll tell him.'

'What are you waiting for?'

'Nothing, just nothing,' grinned Wally.

'Well, bugger off then,' snarled Bruce.

'Okay, okay, don't get your knickers in a knot, Bucko.'

He sauntered off down the corridor.

Shermaine was standing where Bruce had left her, but with her eyes bright with tears of anger.

'He is a pig, that one. A filthy, filthy pig.'

'He's not worth worrying about.' Bruce tried to take her in his arms again, but she shrugged him off.

'I hate him. He makes everything seem so cheap, so dirty.'

'Nothing between you and I could be cheap and dirty,' said Bruce, and instantly her fury abated.

'I know, my Bruce. But he can make it seem that way.' They kissed gently.

'I must go. They want me.' For a second she clung to him.

'Be careful. Promise me you'll be careful.'

'I promise,' said Bruce and she let him go.

16

They left before dark, but the clouds had come up during the afternoon and now they hung low over the forest, trapping the heat beneath them.

Bruce led, with Ruffy in the middle of the line and Hendry in the rear.

By the time they reached the level crossing the night was on them and it had started to rain, soft fat drops weeping like a woman exhausted with grief, warm rain in the darkness. And the darkness was complete. Once Bruce touched the top of his nose with his open palm, but he could not see his hand.

He used a staff to keep contact with the steel rail that ran beside him, tapping along it like a blind man, and at each step the gravel of the embankment crunched beneath his feet. The hand of the man behind him was on his shoulder, and he could sense the presence of the others that followed him like the body of a serpent, could hear the crunch of their steps and the muted squeak and rattle of their equipment. A man's voice was raised in protest and immediately quenched by Ruffy's deep rumble.

They crossed the road and the gradient changed beneath Bruce's feet so that he had to lean forward against it. They were starting up the Lufira hills.

I will rest them at the top, he thought, and from there we will be able to see the lights of the town.

The rain stopped abruptly, and the quietness after it was surprising. Now he could distinctly hear the breathing of the man behind him above the small sounds of their advance, and in the forest nearby a tree frog clinked as though steel pellets were being dropped into a crystal glass. It was a sound of great purity and beauty.

All Bruce's senses were enhanced to compensate for his lack of sight; his hearing; his sense of smell, so that he could catch the over-sweet perfume of a jungle-flower and the heaviness of decaying wet vegetation; his sense of touch, so that he could feel the raindrops on his face and the texture of his clothing against his body; then the other animal sense of danger told him with sickening, stomach-tripping certainty that there was something ahead of him in the darkness.

He stopped, and the man following him bumped into him throwing him off balance. All along the line there was a ripple of confusion and then silence. They all waited.

Bruce strained his hearing, half crouched with his rifle held ready. There was something there, he could almost feel it.

Please God, let them not have a machine-gun set up here, he thought; they could cut us into a shambles.

He turned cautiously and felt for the head of the man behind him, found it and drew it towards him until his mouth was an inch from the ear.

'Lie down very quietly. Tell the one behind you that he may pass it back.'

Bruce waited poised, listening and trying to see ahead into the utter blackness. He felt a gentle tap on his ankle from the gendarme at his feet. They were all down.

'All right, let's go take a look.' Bruce detached one of the grenades from his webbing belt. He drew the pin and dropped it into the breast pocket of his jacket. Then feeling for the crossties of the rails with each foot he started forward. Ten paces and he stopped again. Then he heard it, the tiny click of two pebbles just ahead of him. His throat closed so he could not breathe and his stomach was very heavy.

I'm right on top of them. My God, if they open up now—

Inch by inch he drew back the hand that held the grenade.

I'll have to lob short and get down fast. Five-second fuse – too long, they'll hear it and start shooting.

His hand was right back, he bent his legs and sank slowly on to his knees.

Here we go, he thought, and at that instant sheet lightning fluttered across the sky and Bruce could see. The hills were outlined black below the pale grey belly of the clouds, and the steel rails glinted in the sudden light. The forest was dark and high at each hand, and – a leopard, a big golden and black leopard, stood facing Bruce. In that brief second they stared at each other and then the night closed down again.

The leopard coughed explosively in the darkness, and Bruce tried desperately to bring his rifle up, but it was in his left hand and his other arm was held back ready to throw.

This time for sure, he thought, this time they lower the boom on you.

It was with a feeling of disbelief that he heard the leopard crash sideways into the undergrowth, and the scrambling rush of its run dwindle into the bush.

He subsided on to his backside, with the primed grenade in his hand, the hysterical laughter of relief coming up into his throat.

'You okay, boss?' Ruffy's voice lifted anxiously.

'It was a leopard,' answered Bruce, and was surprised at the squeakiness of his own voice.

There was a buzz of voices from the gendarmes and a rattle and clatter as they started to stand up. Someone laughed.

'That's enough noise,' snapped Bruce and climbed to his feet; he found the pin in his pocket and fitted it back into the grenade. He groped his way back, picked up the staff from where he had dropped it, and took his position at the head of the column again.

'Let's go,' he said.

His mouth was dry, his breathing too quick and he could feel the heat beneath the skin of his cheeks from the shock of the leopard.

I truly squirted myself full of adrenalin that time, Bruce grinned precariously in the dark, I'm as windy as hell. And before tonight is over I shall find fear again.

They moved on up the incline of the hills, a serpent of twenty-six men, and the tension was in all of them. Bruce could hear it in the footsteps behind him, feel it in the grip of the hand upon his shoulder and catch it in the occasional whiffs of body smell that came forward to him, the smell of nervous sweat like acid on metal.

Ahead of them the clouds that had crouched low upon the hills lifted slowly, and Bruce could see the silhouette of the crests. It was no longer utterly dark for there was a glow on the belly of the clouds now. A faint orange glow of reflected light that grew in strength, then faded and grew again. It puzzled Bruce for a while, and thinking about it gave his nerves a chance to settle. He plodded steadily on watching the fluctuations of the light. The ground tilted more sharply upwards beneath his feet and he leaned forward against it, slogging up the last half mile to the pass between the peaks, and at last came out on the top.

'Good God,' Bruce spoke aloud, for from here he could see the reason for that glow on the clouds. They were burning Port Reprieve. The flames were well established in the buildings along the wharf, and as Bruce watched one of the roofs collapsed slowly in upon itself in a storm of sparks leaving the walls naked and erect, the wooden sills of the windows burning fiercely. The railway buildings were also on fire, and there was fire in the residential area beyond the Union Minière offices and the hotel. Quickly Bruce looked towards St Augustine's. It was dark, no flames there, no light even, and he felt a small lift of relief.

'Perhaps they have overlooked it, perhaps they're too busy looting,' and as he looked back at Port Reprieve, his mouth hardened. 'The senseless wanton bastards!' His anger started as he watched the meaningless destruction of the town.

'What can they possibly hope to gain by this?' There were new fires nearer the hotel. Bruce turned to the man behind him.

'We will rest here, but there will be no smoking and no talking.'

He heard the order passed back along the line and the careful sounds of equipment being lowered and men settling gratefully down upon the gravel embankment. Bruce unslung the case that contained his binoculars. He focused them on the burning town.

It was bright with the light of fires and through the glasses he could almost discern the features of the men in the streets. They moved in packs, heavily armed and restless. Many carried bottles and already the gait of some of them was unsteady. Bruce tried to estimate their numbers but it was impossible, men kept disappearing into buildings and reappearing, groups met and mingled and dispersed.

He dropped his glasses on to his chest to rest his eyes, and heard movement beside him in the dark. He glanced sideways. It was Ruffy, his bulk exaggerated by the load he carried; his rifle across one shoulder, on the other a full case of ammunition, and round his neck half a dozen haversacks full of grenades.

'Looks like they're having fun, hey, boss?'

'Fifth of November,' agreed Bruce. 'Aren't you going to take a breather?'

'Why not?' Ruffy set down the ammunition case and lowered his great backside on to it. 'Can you see any of those folks we left behind?' he asked.

Bruce lifted the glasses again and searched the area beyond the station buildings. It was darker there but he made out the square shape of the truck standing among the moving shadows.

'The truck's still there,' he murmured, 'but I can't see—'

At that moment the thatched roof of one of the houses exploded upwards in a column of flame, lighting the railway yard, and the truck stood out sharply.

'Yes,' said Bruce, 'I can see them now.' They were littered untidily across the yard, still lying where they had died. Small and fragile, unwanted as broken toys.

'Dead?' asked Ruffy.

'Dead,' confirmed Bruce.

'The women?'

'It's hard to tell.' Bruce strained his eyes. 'I don't think so.'

'No.' Ruffy's voice was soft and very deep. 'They wouldn't waste the women. I'd guess they've got them up at the hotel, taking it in turn to give them the business. Four women only – they won't last till morning. Those bastards down there could shag an elephant to death.' He spat thoughtfully into the gravel at his feet. 'What you going to do, boss?'

Bruce did not answer for a minute; he swung the glasses slowly back across the town. The field gun was still standing where he had last seen it, its barrel pointing accusingly up towards him. The transports were parked before the Union Minière offices; he could see the brilliant yellow and red paint and the Shell sign on the tanker. I hope it's full, Bruce thought, we'll need plenty of gasoline to get us back to Elisabethville.

'Ruffy, you'd better tell your boys to keep their bullets away from that tanker, otherwise it'll be a long walk home.'

'I'll tell them,' grunted Ruffy. 'But you know these mad Arabs – once they start shooting they don't stop till they're out of bullets, and they not too fussy where those bullets go.'

'We'll split into two groups when we get to the bottom of the hill. You and I will take our lot through the edge of the swamp and cross to the far side of the town. Tell

Lieutenant Hendry to come here.' Bruce waited until Wally came forward to join them, and when the three of them crouched together he went on.

'Hendry, I want you to spread your men out at the top of the main street – there in the darkness on this side of the station. Ruffy and I are going to cross the edge of the swamp to the causeway and lay out on the far side. For God's sake keep your boys quiet until Ruffy and I hit them – all we need is for your lot to start pooping off before we are ready and we won't need those lorries, we'll need coffins for the rest of our journey. Do you understand me?'

'Okay, okay, I know what I'm doing,' muttered Wally.

'I hope so,' said Bruce, and then went on. 'We'll hit them at four o'clock tomorrow morning, just before first light. Ruffy and I will go into the town and bomb the hotel – that's where most of them will be sleeping. The grenades should force the survivors into the street and as soon as that happens you can open up – but not before. Wait until you get them in the open. Is that clear?'

'Jesus,' growled Hendry. 'Do you think I'm a bloody fool, do you think I can't understand English?'

'The crossfire from the two groups should wipe most of them out.' Bruce ignored Wally's outburst. 'But we mustn't give the remainder a chance to organize. Hit them hard and as soon as they take cover again you must follow them in – close with them and finish them off. If we can't get it over in five to ten minutes then we are going to be in trouble. They outnumber us three to one, so we have to exploit the element of surprise to the full.'

'Exploit the element of surprise to the full!' mimicked Wally. 'What for all the fancy talk – why not just murder the bastards?'

Bruce grinned lightly in the dark. 'All right, murder the bastards,' he agreed. 'But do it as quickly as bloody possible.' He stood up and inclined the luminous dial of his wristwatch to catch the light. 'It's half past ten now – we'll move

153

down on them. Come with me, Hendry, and we'll sort them into two groups.'

Bruce and Wally moved back along the line and talked to each man in turn.

'You will go with Lieutenant Hendry.'

'You come with me.'

Making sure that the two English-speaking corporals were with Wally, they took ten minutes to divide them into two units and to redistribute the haversacks of grenades. Then they moved on down the slope, still in Indian file.

'This is where we leave you, Hendry,' whispered Bruce. 'Don't go jumping the gun – wait until you hear my grenades.'

'Yeah, okay – I know all about it.'

'Good luck,' said Bruce.

'Your bum in a barrel, Captain Curry,' rejoined Wally and moved away.

'Come on, Ruffy.' Bruce led his men off the embankment down into the swamp. Almost immediately the mud and slime was knee-deep and as they worked their way out to the right it rose to their waists and then to their armpits, sucking and gurgling sullenly as they stirred it with their passage, belching little evil-smelling gusts of swamp gas.

The mosquitoes closed round Bruce's face in a cloud so dense that he breathed them into his mouth and had to blink them out of his eyes. Sweat dribbled down from under his helmet and clung heavily in his eyebrows and the matted stems of the papyrus grass dragged at his feet. Their progress was tortuously slow and for fifteen minutes at a time Bruce lost sight of the lights of the village through the wall of papyrus; he steered by the glow of the fires and the occasional column of sparks.

It was an hour before they had half completed their circuit of Port Reprieve. Bruce stopped to rest, still waist-deep in swamp ooze and with his arms aching numb from holding his rifle above his head.

'I could use a smoke now, boss,' grunted Ruffy.

'Me too,' answered Bruce, and he wiped his face on the sleeve of his jacket. The mosquito bites on his forehead and round his eyes burnt like fire.

'What a way to make a living,' he whispered.

'You go on living and you'll be one of the lucky ones,' answered Ruffy. 'My guess is there'll be some dying before tomorrow.'

But the fear of death was submerged by physical discomfort. Bruce had almost forgotten that they were going into battle; right now he was more worried that the leeches which had worked their way through the openings in his anklets and were busily boring into his lower legs might find their way up to his crotch. There was a lot to be said in favour of a zip fly, he decided.

'Let's get out of this,' he whispered. 'Come on, Ruffy. Tell your boys to keep it quiet.'

He worked in closer to the shore and the level fell to their knees once more. Progress was more noisy now as their legs broke the surface with each step and the papyrus rustled and brushed against them.

It was almost two o'clock when they reached the causeway. Bruce left his men crouched in the papyrus while he made a stealthy reconnaissance along the side of the concrete bridge, keeping in its shadow, moving doubled up until he came to dry land on the edge of the village. There were no sentries posted and except for the crackle of the flames the town was quiet, sunk into a drunken stupor, satiated. Bruce went back to call his men up.

He spread them in pairs along the outskirts of the village. He had learned very early in this campaign not to let his men act singly; nothing drains an African of courage more than to be on his own, especially in the night when the ghosts are on the walk-about.

To each couple he gave minute instructions.

'When you hear the grenades you shoot at anybody in

the streets or at the windows. When the street is empty move in close beside that building there. Use your own grenades on every house and watch out for Lieutenant Hendry's men coming through from the other side. Do you understand?'

'It is understood.'

'Shoot carefully. Aim each shot – not like you did at the road bridge, and in the name of God do not hit the gasoline tanker. We need that to get us home.'

Now it was three o'clock, Bruce saw by the luminous figures on his wristwatch. Eight hours since they had left the train, and twenty-two hours since Bruce had last slept. But he was not tired, although his body ached and there was that gritty feeling under his eyelids, yet his mind was clear and bright as a flame.

He lay beside Ruffy under a low bush on the outskirts of Port Reprieve and the night wind drifted the smoke from the burning town down upon them, and Bruce was not tired. For I am going to another rendezvous with fear.

Fear is a woman, he thought, with all the myriad faces and voices of a woman. Because she is a woman and because I am a man I must keep going back to her. Only this time the appointment is one that I cannot avoid, this time I am not deliberately seeking her out.

I know she is evil, I know that after I have possessed her I will feel sick and shaken. I will say, 'That was the last time, never again.'

But just as certainly I know I will go back to her again, hating her, dreading her, but also needing her.

I have gone to find her on a mountain – on Dutoits Kloof Frontal, on Turret Towers, on the Wailing Wall, and the Devil's Tooth.

And she was there, dressed in a flowing robe of rock, a robe that fell sheer two thousand feet to the scree slope below. And she shrieked with the voice of the wind along the exposed face. Then her voice was soft, tinkling like cooling glass in the Berg ice underfoot, whispering like nylon rope running free, grating as the rotten rock moved in my hand.

I have followed her into the Jessie bush on the banks of the Sabi and the Luangwa, and she was there, waiting, wounded, in a robe of buffalo hide with the blood dripping from her mouth. And her smell was the sour-acid smell of my own sweat, and her taste was like rotten tomatoes in the back of my throat.

I have looked for her beyond the reef in the deep water with the demand valve of a scuba repeating my breathing with metallic hoarseness. And she was there with rows of white teeth in the semicircle of her mouth, a tall fin on her back, dressed this time in shagreen, and her touch was cold as the ocean, and her taste was salt and the taint of dying things.

I have looked for her on the highway with my foot pressed to the floorboards and she was there with her cold arm draped round my shoulders, her voice the whine of rubber on tarmac and the throaty hum of the motor.

With Colin Butler at the helm (a man who treated fear not as a lover, but with tolerant contempt as though she were his little sister) I went to find her in a small boat. She was dressed in green with plumes of spray and she wore a necklace of sharp black rock. And her voice was the roar of water breaking on water.

We met in darkness at the road bridge and her eyes glinted like bayonets. But that was an enforced meeting not of my choosing, as tonight will be.

I hate her, he thought, but she is a woman and I am a man.

Bruce lifted his arm and turned his wrist to catch the light of the fires.

'Fifteen minutes to four, Ruffy. Let's go and take a look.'

'That's a good idea, boss.' Ruffy grinned with a show of white teeth in the darkness.

'Are you afraid, Ruffy?' he asked suddenly, wanting to know, for his own heart beat like a war drum and there was no saliva in his mouth.

'Boss, some questions you don't ask a man.' Ruffy rose slowly into a crouch. 'Let's go take a look around.'

So they moved quickly together into the town, along the street, hugging the hedges and the buildings, trying to keep in shadow, their eyes moving everywhere, breathing quick and shallow, nerves screwed up tight until they reached the hotel.

There were no lights in the windows and it seemed deserted until Bruce made out the untidy mass of humanity strewn in sleep upon the front verandah.

'How many there, Ruffy?'

'Dunno – perhaps ten, fifteen.' Ruffy breathed an answer. 'Rest of them will be inside.'

'Where are the women – be careful of them.'

'They're dead long ago, you can believe me.'

'All right then, let's get round the back.' Bruce took a deep breath and then moved quickly across the twenty yards of open firelit street to the corner of the hotel. He stopped in the shadow and felt Ruffy close beside him. 'I want to take a look into the main lounge, my guess is that most of them will be in there,' he whispered.

'There's only four bedrooms,' agreed Ruffy. 'Say the officers upstairs and the rest in the lounge.'

Now Bruce moved quickly round the corner and stumbled over something soft. He felt it move against his foot.

'Ruffy!' he whispered urgently as he teetered off balance. He had trodden on a man, a man sleeping in the dust beside the wall. He could see the firelight on his bare torso and the glint of the bottle clutched in one outflung hand. The man sat up, muttering, and then began to cough, hacking painfully, swearing as he wiped his mouth with his free hand. Bruce regained his balance and swung his rifle up to use the bayonet, but Ruffy was quicker. He put one foot on the man's chest and trod him flat on to his back once more, then standing over him he used his bayoneted rifle the way a gardener uses a spade to lift potatoes, leaning his weight on it suddenly and the blade vanished into the man's throat.

The body stiffened convulsively, legs thrust out straight and arms rigid, there was a puffing of breath from the severed windpipe and then the slow melting relaxation of death. Still with his foot on the chest, Ruffy withdrew the bayonet and stepped over the corpse.

That was very close, thought Bruce, stifling the qualm of horror he felt at the execution. The man's eyes were fixed open in almost comic surprise, the bottle still in his hand, his chest bare, the front of his trousers unbuttoned and stiff with dried blood – not his blood, guessed Bruce angrily.

They moved on past the kitchens. Bruce looked in and saw that they were empty with the white enamel tiles reflecting the vague light and piles of used plates and pots cluttering the tables and the sink. Then they reached the bar-room and there was a hurricane lamp on the counter diffusing a yellow glow; the stench of liquor poured out through the half-open window, the shelves were bare of bottles and men were asleep upon the counter, men lay curled together upon the floor like a pack of dogs, broken glass and rifles and shattered furniture littered about them. Someone had vomited out of the window leaving a yellow streak down the whitewashed wall.

'Stand here,' breathed Bruce into Ruffy's ear. 'I will go round to the front where I can throw on to the verandah and also into the lounge. Wait until you hear my first grenade blow.'

Ruffy nodded and leaned his rifle against the wall; he took a grenade in each fist and pulled the pins.

Bruce slipped quickly round the corner and along the side wall. He reached the windows of the lounge. They were tightly closed and he peered in over the sill. A little of the light from the lamp in the bar-room came through the open doors and showed up the interior. Here again there were men covering the floor and piled upon the sofas along the far wall. Twenty of them at least, he estimated by the volume of their snoring, and he grinned without humour. My God, what a shambles it is going to be.

Then something at the foot of the stairs caught his eye and the grin on his face became fixed, baring his teeth and narrowing his eyes to slits. It was the mound of nude flesh formed by the bodies of the four women; they had been discarded once they had served their purpose, dragged to one side to clear the floor for sleeping space, lying upon each other in a jumble of naked arms and legs and cascading hair.

No mercy now, thought Bruce with hatred replacing his fear as he looked at the women and saw by the attitudes in which they lay that there was no life left in them. *No mercy now!*

He slung his rifle over his left shoulder and filled his hand with grenades, pulled the pins and moved quickly to the corner so that he could look down the length of the covered verandah. He rolled both grenades down among the sleeping figures, hearing clearly the click of the priming and the metallic rattle against the concrete floor. Quickly he ducked back to the lounge window, snatching two more grenades from his haversack and pulling the pins, he hurled them through the closed windows. The crash of breaking glass blended with the double thunder of the explosions on the verandah.

Someone shouted in the room, a cry of surprise and alarm, then the windows above Bruce blew outwards, showering him with broken glass and the noise half deafening him as he tossed two more grenades through the gaping hole of the window. They were screaming and groaning in the lounge. Ruffy's grenades roared in the bar-room bursting through the double doors, then Bruce's grenades snuffed out the sounds of life in the lounge with violent white flame and thunder. Bruce tossed in two more grenades and ran back to the corner of the verandah unslinging his rifle.

A man with his hands over his eyes and blood streaming through his fingers fell over the low verandah wall and crawled to his knees. Bruce shot him from so close that the shaft of gun flame joined the muzzle of his rifle and the man's chest, punching him over backwards, throwing him spreadeagled on to the earth.

He looked beyond and saw two more in the road, but before he could raise his rifle the fire from his own gendarmes found them, knocking them down amid spurts of dust.

Bruce hurdled the verandah wall. He shouted, a sound without form or meaning. Exulting, unafraid, eager to get into the building, to get amongst them. He stumbled over the dead men on the verandah. A burst of gunfire from down the street rushed past him, so close he could feel the wind on his face. Fire from his own men.

'You stupid bastards!' Shouting without anger, without fear, with only the need to shout, he burst into the lounge through the main doors. It was half dark but he could see through the darkness and the haze of plaster dust.

A man on the stairs, the bloom of gunfire and the sting of the bullet across Bruce's thigh, fire in return, without aiming from the hip, miss and the man gone up and round the head of the stairs, yelling as he ran.

A grenade in Bruce's right hand, throw it high, watch it hit the wall and bounce sideways round the angle of the stairs. The explosion shocking in the confined space and the flash of it lighting the building and outlining the body of the man as it blew him back into the lounge, lifting him clear of the banisters, shredded and broken by the blast, falling heavily into the room below.

Up the stairs three at a time and into the bedroom

passage, another man naked and bewildered staggering through a doorway still drunk or half asleep, chop him down with a single shot in the stomach, jump over him and throw a grenade through the glass skylight of the second bedroom, another through the third and kick open the door of the last room in the bellow and flash of the explosions.

A man was waiting for Bruce across the room with a pistol in his hand, and both of them fired simultaneously, the clang of the bullet glancing off the steel of Bruce's helmet, jerking his head back savagely, throwing him sideways against the wall, but he fired again, rapid fire, hitting with every bullet, so that the man seemed to dance, a jerky grotesque twitching jig, pinned against the far wall by the bullets.

On his knees now Bruce was stunned, ears singing like a million mad mosquitoes, hands clumsy and slow on the reload, back on his feet, legs rubbery but the loaded rifle in his hands making a man of him.

Out into the passage, another one right on top of him, a vast dark shape in the darkness – kill him! kill him!

'Don't shoot, boss!'

Ruffy, thank God, Ruffy.

'Are there any more?'

'All finished, boss – you cleaned them out good.'

'How many?' Bruce shouted above the singing in his ears.

'Forty or so. Jesus, what a mess! There's blood all over the place. Those grenades—'

'There must be more.'

'Yes, but not in here, boss. Let's go and give the boys outside a hand.'

They ran back down the passage, down the stairs, and the floor of the lounge was sodden and sticky, dead men everywhere; it smelt like an abattoir – blood and ripped bowels. One still on his hands and knees, creepy-crawling towards the door. Ruffy shot him twice, flattening him.

'Not the front door, boss. Our boys will get you for sure. Go out the window.'

Bruce dived through the window head first, rolled over behind the cover of the verandah wall and came to his knees in one movement. He felt strong and invulnerable. Ruffy was beside him.

'Here come our boys,' said Ruffy, and Bruce could see them coming down the street, running forward in short bursts, stopping to fire, to throw a grenade, then coming again.

'And there are Lieutenant Hendry's lot.' From the opposite direction but with the same dodging, checking run, Bruce could see Wally with them. He was holding his rifle across his hip when he fired, his whole body shaking with the juddering of the gun.

Like a bird rising in front of the beaters one of the *shufta* broke from the cover of the grocery store and ran into the street unarmed, his head down and his arms pumping in time with his legs. Bruce was close enough to see the panic in his face. He seemed to be moving in slow motion, and the flames lit him harshly, throwing a distorted shadow in front of him. When the bullets hit him he stayed on his feet, staggering in a circle, thrashing at the air with his hands as though he were beating off a swarm of bees, the bullets slapping loudly against his body and lifting little puffs of dust from his clothing. Beside Bruce, Ruffy aimed carefully and shot him in the head, ending it.

'There must be more,' protested Bruce. 'Where are they hiding?'

'In the offices, I'd say.'

And Bruce turned his attention quickly to the block of Union Minière offices. The windows were in darkness and as he stared he thought he saw movement. He glanced quickly back at Wally's men and saw that four of them had bunched up close behind Wally as they ran.

'Hendry, watch out!' he shouted with all his strength. 'On your right, from the offices!'

But it was too late, gunfire sparkled in the dark windows and the little group of running men disintegrated.

Bruce and Ruffy fired together, raking the windows, emptying their automatic rifles into them. As he reloaded Bruce glanced back at where Wally's men had been hit. With disbelief he saw that Wally was the only one still on his feet; crossing the road, sprinting through an area of bullet-churned earth towards them, he reached the verandah and fell over the low wall.

'Are you wounded?' Bruce asked.

'Not a touch – those bastards couldn't shoot their way out of a French letter,' Wally shouted defiantly, and his voice carried clearly in the sudden hush. He snatched the empty magazine off the bottom of his rifle, threw it aside and clipped on a fresh one. 'Move over,' he growled, 'let me get a crack at those bastards.' He lifted his rifle and rested the stock on top of the wall, knelt behind it, cuddled the butt into his shoulder and began firing short bursts into the windows of the office block.

'This is what I was afraid of.' Bruce lifted his voice above the clamour of the guns. 'Now we've got a pocket of resistance right in the centre of the town. There must be fifteen or twenty of them in there – it might take us days to winkle them out.' He cast a longing look at the canvas-covered trucks lined up outside the station yard. 'They can cover the lorries from here, and as soon as they guess what we're after, as soon as we try and move them, they'll knock out that tanker and destroy the trucks.'

The firelight flickered on the shiny yellow and red paint of the tanker. It looked so big and vulnerable standing there in the open. It needed just one bullet out of the many hundred that had already been fired to end its charmed existence.

We've got to rush them now, he decided. Beyond the office block the remains of Wally's group had taken cover and were keeping up a heated fire. Bruce's group straggled up to the hotel and found positions at the windows.

'Ruffy.' Bruce caught him by the shoulder. 'We'll take four men with us and go round the back of the offices. From that building there we've got only twenty yards or so of open ground to cover. Once we get up against the wall they won't be able to touch us and we can toss grenades in amongst them.'

'That twenty yards looks like twenty miles from here,' rumbled Ruffy, but picked up his sack of grenades and crawled back from the verandah wall.

'Go and pick four men to come with us,' ordered Bruce.

'Okay, boss. We'll wait for you in the kitchen.'

'Hendry. Listen to me.'

'Yeah. What is it?'

'When I reach that corner over there I'll give you a wave. We'll be ready to go then. I want you to give us all the cover you can – keep their heads down.'

'Okay,' agreed Wally and fired another short burst.

'Try not to hit us when we close in.'

Wally turned to look at Bruce and he grinned wickedly.

'Mistakes happen, you know. I can't promise anything. You'd look real grand in my sights.'

'Don't joke,' said Bruce.

'Who's joking?' grinned Wally and Bruce left him. He found Ruffy and four gendarmes waiting in the kitchen.

'Come on,' he said and led them out across the kitchen yard, down the sanitary lane with the steel doors for the buckets behind the outhouses and the smell of them thick and fetid, round the corner and across the road to the buildings beyond the office block. They stopped there and crowded together, as though to draw courage and comfort from each other. Bruce measured the distance with his eye.

'It's not far,' he announced.

'Depends on how you look at it,' grunted Ruffy.

'There are only two windows opening out on to this side.'

'Two's enough – how many do you want?'

'Remember, Ruffy, you can only die once.'

'Once is enough,' said Ruffy. 'Let's cut out the talking, boss. Too much talk gets you in the guts.'

Bruce moved across to the corner of the building out of the shadows. He waved towards the hotel and imagined that he saw an acknowledgement from the end of the verandah.

'All together,' he said, sucked in a deep breath, held it a second and then launched himself into the open. He felt small now, no longer brave and invulnerable, and his legs moved so slowly that he seemed to be standing still. The black windows gaped at him.

Now, he thought, now you die.

Where, he thought, not in the stomach, please God, not in the stomach.

And his legs moved stiffly under him, carrying him half way across.

Only ten more paces, he thought, one more river, just one more river to Jordan. But not in the stomach, please God, not in my stomach. And his flesh cringed in anticipation, his stomach drawn in hard as he ran.

Suddenly the black windows were brightly lit, bright white oblongs in the dark buildings, and the glass sprayed out of them like untidy spittle from an old man's mouth. Then they were dark again, dark with smoke billowing from them and the memory of the explosion echoing in his ears.

'A grenade!' Bruce was bewildered. 'Someone let off a grenade in there!'

He reached the back door without stopping and it burst open before his rush. He was into the room, shooting, coughing in the fumes, firing wildly at the small movements of dying men.

In the half darkness something long and white lay against

the far wall. A body, a white man's naked body. He crossed to it and looked down.

'André,' he said, 'it's André – he threw the grenade.' And he knelt beside him.

– 17 –

Curled naked upon the concrete floor, André was alive but dying as the haemorrhage within him leaked his life away. His mind was alive and he heard the crump, crump of Bruce's grenades, then the gunfire in the street, and the sound of running men. The shouts in the night and then the guns very close, they were in the room in which he lay.

He opened his eyes. There were men at each of the windows, crouched below the sills, and the room was thick with cordite fumes and the clamour of the guns as they fired out into the night.

André was cold, the coldness was all through him. Even his hands drawn up against his chest were cold and heavy. His stomach only was warm, warm and immensely bloated.

It was an effort to think, for his mind also was cold and the noise of the guns confused him.

He watched the men at the windows with a detached disinterest, and slowly his body lost its weight. He seemed to float clear of the floor and look down upon the room from the roof. His eyelids sagged and he dragged them up again, and struggled down towards his own body.

There was suddenly a rushing sound in the room and plaster sprayed from the wall above André's head, filling the air with pale floating dust. One of the men at the windows fell backwards, his weapon ringing loudly on the floor as it dropped from his hands; he flopped over twice and lay still, face down within arm's length of André.

Ponderously André's mind analysed the sights his eyes

were recording. Someone was firing on the building from outside. The man beside him was dead and from his head wound the blood spread slowly across the floor towards him. André closed his eyes again, he was very tired and very cold.

There was a lull in the sound of gunfire, one of those freak silences in the midst of battle. And in the lull André heard a voice far off, shouting. He could not hear the words but he recognized the voice and his eyelids flew open. There was an excitement in him, a new force, for it was Wally's voice he had heard.

He moved slightly, clenching his hands and his brain started to sing.

Wally has come back for me – he has come to save me. He rolled his head slowly, painfully, and the blood gurgled in his stomach.

I must help him, I must not let him endanger himself – these men are trying to kill him. I must stop them. I mustn't let them kill Wally.

And then he saw the grenades hanging on the belt of the man that lay beside him. He fastened his eyes on the round polished metal bulbs and he began to pray silently.

'Hail, Mary, full of grace, the Lord is with thee.'

He moved again, straightening his body.

'Blessed art thou among women, and blessed is the fruit of thy womb, Jesus.'

His hand crept out into the pool of blood, and the sound of the guns filled his head so he could not hear himself pray. Walking on its fingers, his hand crawled through the blood as slowly as a fly through a saucer of treacle.

'Blessed is the fruit of thy womb, Jesus. Oh, Jesus. Pray for me now, and at the hour. Full of grace.'

He touched the smooth, deeply segmented steel of the grenade.

'Us sinners – at the day, at the hour. This day – this day our daily bread.'

He fumbled at the clip, fingers stiff and cold.

'Hallowed be thy – Hallowed be thy—'

The clip clicked open and he held the grenade, curling his fingers round it.

'Hail, Mary, full of grace.'

He drew the grenade to him and held it with both hands against his chest. He lifted it to his mouth and took the pin between his teeth.

'Pray for us sinners,' he whispered, and pulled the pin.

'Now and at the hour of our death.'

And he tried to throw it. It rolled from his hand and bumped across the floor. The firing handle flew off and rattled against the wall. General Moses turned from the window and saw it – his lips opened and his spectacles glinted above the rose-pink cave of his mouth. The grenade lay at his feet. Then everything was gone in the flash and roar of the explosion.

Afterwards in the acrid swirl of fumes, in the patter of falling plaster, in the tinkle and crunch of broken glass, in the small scrabbling noises and the murmur and moan of dying men, André was still alive. The body of the man beside him had shielded his head and chest from the full force of the blast.

There was still enough life in him to recognize Bruce Curry's face close to his, though he could not feel the hands that touched him.

'André!' said Bruce. 'It's André – he threw the grenade!'

'Tell him—' whispered André and stopped.

'Yes, André—?' said Bruce.

'I didn't, this day and at the hour. I had to – not this time.' He could feel it going out in him like a candle in a high wind and he tried to cup his hands around it.

'What is it, André? What must I tell him?' Bruce's voice, but so far away.

'Because of him – this time – not of it, I didn't.' He

stopped again and gathered all of what was left. His lips quivered as he tried so hard to say it.

'Like a man!' he whispered and the candle went out.

'Yes,' said Bruce softly, holding him. 'This time like a man.'

He lowered André gently until his head touched the floor again; then he stood upright and looked down at the terribly mutilated body. He felt empty inside, a hollowness, the same feeling as after love.

He moved across to the desk near the far wall. Outside the gunfire dwindled like half-hearted applause, flared up again and then ceased. Around him Ruffy and the four gendarmes moved excitedly, inspecting the dead, exclaiming, laughing the awkward embarrassed laughter of men freshly released from mortal danger.

Loosening the chin straps of his helmet with slow steady fingers, Bruce stared across the room at André's body.

'Yes,' he whispered again. 'This time like a man. All the other times are wiped out, the score is levelled.'

His cigarettes were damp from the swamp, but he took one from the centre of the pack and straightened it with calm nerveless fingers. He found his lighter and flicked it open – then, without warning, his hands started to shake. The flame of the lighter fluttered and he had to hold it steady with both hands. There was blood on his hands, new sticky blood. He snapped the lighter closed and breathed in the smoke. It tasted bitter and the saliva flooded into his mouth. He swallowed it down, nausea in his stomach, and his breathing quickened.

It was not like this before, he remembered, even that night at the road bridge when they broke through on the flank and we met them with bayonets in the dark. Before it had no meaning, but now I can feel again. Once more I'm alive.

Suddenly he had to be alone; he stood up.

'Ruffy.'

'Yes, boss?'

'Clean up here. Get blankets from the hotel for de Surrier and the women, also those men down in the station yard.' It was someone else speaking; he could hear the voice as though it were a long way off.

'You okay, boss?'

'Yes.'

'Your head?'

Bruce lifted his hand and touched the long dent in his helmet.

'It's nothing,' he said.

'Your leg?'

'Just a touch, get on with it.'

'Okay, boss. What shall we do with these others?'

'Throw them in the river,' said Bruce and walked out into the street. Hendry and his gendarmes were still on the verandah of the hotel, but they had started on the corpses there, using their bayonets like butchers' knives, taking the ears, laughing also the strained nervous laughter.

Bruce crossed the street to the station yard. The dawn was coming, drawing out across the sky like a sheet of steel rolled from the mill, purple and lilac at first, then red as it spread above the forest.

The Ford Ranchero stood on the station platform where he had left it. He opened the door, slid in behind the wheel, and watched the dawn become day.

– 18 –

'Captain, the sergeant major asks you to come. There is something he wants to show you.'

Bruce lifted his head from where it was resting on the steering wheel. He had not heard the gendarme approach.

'I'll come,' he said, picked up his helmet and his rifle

from the seat beside him and followed the man back to the office block.

His gendarmes were loading a dead man into one of the trucks, swinging him by his arms and legs.

'Un, deux, trois,' and a shout of laughter as the limp body flew over the tailboard on to the gruesome pile already there.

Sergeant Jacque came out of the office dragging a man by his heels. The head bumped loosely down the steps and there was a wet brown drag mark left on the cement verandah.

'Like pork,' Jacque called cheerily. The corpse was that of a small grey-headed man, skinny, with the marks of spectacles on the bridge of his nose and a double row of decorations on his tunic. Bruce noted that one of them was the purple and white ribbon of the military cross – strange loot for the Congo. Jacque dropped the man's heels, drew his bayonet and stooped over the man. He took one of the ears that lay flat against the grizzled skull, pulled it forward and freed it with a single stroke of the knife. The opened flesh was pink with the dark hole of the eardrum in the centre.

Bruce walked on into the office and his nostrils flared at the abattoir stench.

'Have a look at this lot, boss.' Ruffy stood by the desk.

'Enough to buy you a ranch in Hyde Park,' grinned Hendry beside him. In his hand he held a pencil. Threaded on to it like a kebab were a dozen human ears.

'Yes,' said Bruce as he looked at the pile of industrial and gem diamonds on the blotter. 'I know about those. Better count them, Ruffy, then put them back in the bags.'

'You're not going to turn them in?' protested Hendry. 'Jesus, if we share this lot three ways – you, Ruffy and I – there's enough to make us all rich.'

'Or put us against a wall,' said Bruce grimly. 'What makes

172

you think the gentlemen in Elisabethville don't know about them?' He turned his attention back to Ruffy. 'Count them and pack them. You're in charge of them. Don't lose any.'

Bruce looked across the room at the blanket-wrapped bundle that was André de Surrier.

'Have you detailed a burial squad?'

'Yes, boss. Six of the boys are out back digging.'

'Good,' Bruce nodded. 'Hendry, come with me. We'll go and have a look at the trucks.'

Half an hour later Bruce closed the bonnet of the last vehicle. 'This is the only one that won't run. The carburettor's smashed. We'll take the tyres off it for spares.' He wiped his greasy hands on the sides of his trousers. 'Thank God, the tanker is untouched. We've got six hundred gallons there, more than enough for the return trip.'

'You going to take the Ford?' asked Hendry.

'Yes, it may come in useful.'

'And it will be more comfortable for you and your little French thing.' Heavy sarcasm in Hendry's voice.

'That's right,' Bruce answered evenly. 'Can you drive?'

'What you think? You think I'm a bloody fool?'

'Everyone is always trying to get at you, aren't they? You can't trust anyone, can you?' Bruce asked softly.

'You're so bloody right!' agreed Hendry.

Bruce changed the subject. 'André had a message for you before he died.'

'Old doll boy!'

'He threw that grenade. Did you know that?'

'Yeah. I knew it.'

'Don't you want to hear what he said?'

'Once a queer, always a queer, and the only good queer is a dead queer.'

'All right.' Bruce frowned. 'Get a couple of men to help you. Fill the trucks with gas. We've wasted enough time already.'

They buried their dead in a communal grave, packing them in quickly and covering them just as quickly. Then they stood embarrassed and silent round the mound.

'You going to say anything, boss?' Ruffy asked, and they all looked at Bruce.

'No.' Bruce turned away and started for the trucks.

What the hell can you say, he thought angrily. Death is not someone to make conversation with. All you can say is, 'These were men; weak and strong, evil and good, and a lot in between. But now they're dead – like pork.'

He looked back over his shoulder.

'All right, let's move out.'

The convoy ground slowly over the causeway. Bruce led in the Ford and the air blowing in through the shattered windscreen was too humid and steamy to give relief from the rising heat.

The sun stood high above the forest as they passed the turn-off to the mission.

Bruce looked along it, and he wanted to signal the convoy to continue while he went up to St Augustine's. He wanted to see Mike Haig and Father Ignatius, make sure that they were safe.

Then he put aside the temptation. If there is more horror up there at St Augustine's, if the *shufta* have found them and there are raped women and dead men there, then there is nothing I can do and I don't want to know about it.

It is better to believe that they are safely hidden in the jungle. It is better to believe that out of all this will remain something good.

He led the convoy resolutely past the turn-off and over the hills towards the level crossing.

Suddenly another idea came to him and he thought about it, turning it over with pleasure.

Four men came to Port Reprieve, men without hope, men abandoned by God.

And they learned that it was not too late, perhaps it is never too late.

For one of them found the strength to die like a man, although he had lived his whole life with weakness.

Another rediscovered the self-respect he had lost along the way, and with it the chance to start again.

The third found – he hesitated – yes, the third found love.

And the fourth? Bruce's smile faded as he thought of Wally Hendry. It was a neat little parable, except for Wally Hendry. What had he found? A dozen human ears threaded on a pencil?

– 19 –

'Can't you get up enough steam to move us back to the crossing – only a few miles.'

'I am desolate, m'sieur. She will not hold even a belch, to say nothing of a head of steam.' The engine driver spread his pudgy little hands in a gesture of helplessness. Bruce studied the rent in the boiler. The metal was torn open like the petals of a flower. He knew it had been a forlorn request.

'Very well. Thank you.' He turned to Ruffy. 'We'll have to carry everything back to the convoy. Another day wasted.'

'It's a long walk,' Ruffy agreed. 'Better get started.'

'How much food have we?'

'Not too much. We've been feeding a lot of extra mouths, and we sent a lot out to the mission.'

'How much?'

'About two more days.'

'That should get us to Elisabethville.'

'Boss, you want to carry everything to the lorries? Searchlights, ammunition, blankets – all of it?'

Bruce paused for a moment. 'I think so. We may need it.'

'It's going to take the rest of the day.'

'Yes,' agreed Bruce. Ruffy walked back along the train but Bruce called after him.

'Ruffy!'

'Boss?'

'Don't forget the beer.'

Ruffy's black moon of a face split laterally into a grin.

'You think we should take it?'

'Why not?' Bruce laughed.

'Man, you talked me right into it!'

And the night was almost on them before the last of the equipment had been carried back from the abandoned train to the convoy and loaded into the trucks.

Time is a slippery thing, even more so than wealth. No bank vault can hold it for you, this precious stuff which we spend in such prodigal fashion on the trivialities. By the time we have slept and eaten and moved from one place to the next there is such a small percentage left for the real business of living.

Bruce felt futile resentment as he always did when he thought about it. And if you discount the time spent at an office desk, then how much is there left? Half of one day a week, that's how much the average man lives! That's how far short of our potential is the actuality of existence.

Take it further than that: we are capable of using only a fraction of our physical and mental strength. Only under hypnosis are we able to exert more than a tenth of what is in us. So divide that half of one day a week by ten, and the rest is waste! Sickening waste!

'Ruffy, have you detailed sentries for tonight?' Bruce barked at him.

'Not yet. I was just—'

'Well, do it, and do it quickly.'

176

Ruffy looked at Bruce in speculation and through his anger Bruce felt a qualm of regret that he had selected that mountain of energy on which to vent his frustration.

'Where the hell is Hendry?' he snapped.

Without speaking Ruffy pointed to a group of men round one of the trucks at the rear of the convoy and Bruce left him.

Suddenly consumed with impatience Bruce fell upon his men. Shouting at them, scattering them to a dozen different tasks. He walked along the convoy making sure that his instructions were being carried out to the letter; checking the siting of the Brens and the searchlights, making sure that the single small cooking fire was screened from Baluba eyes, stopping to watch the refuelling of the trucks and the running maintenance he had ordered. Men avoided catching his eye and bent to their tasks with studied application. There were no raised voices or sounds of laughter in the camp.

Again Bruce had decided against a night journey. The temptation itched within him, but the exhaustion of those gendarmes who had not slept since the previous morning and the danger of travelling in the dark he could not ignore.

'We'll leave as soon as it's light tomorrow,' Bruce told Ruffy.

'Okay, boss,' Ruffy nodded, and then soothingly, 'you're tired. Food's nearly ready, then you get some sleep.'

Bruce glared at him, opening his mouth to snarl a retort, and then closed it again. He turned and strode out of the camp into the forest.

He found a fallen log, sat down and lit a cigarette. It was dark now and there were only a few stars among the rain clouds that blackened the sky. He could hear the faint sounds from the camp but there were no lights – the way he had ordered it.

The fact that his anger had no focal point inflamed it rather than quenched it. It ranged restlessly until at last it found a target – himself.

He recognized the brooding undirected depression that was descending upon him. It was a thing he had not experienced for a long time, nearly two years. Not since the wreck of his marriage and the loss of his children. Not since he had stifled all emotion and trained himself not to participate in the life around him.

But now his barrier was gone, there was no sheltered harbour from the storm surf and he would have to ride it out. Furl all canvas and rig a sea anchor.

The anger was gone now. At least anger had heat but this other thing was cold; icy waves of it broke over him, and he was small and insignificant in the grip of it.

His mind turned to his children and the loneliness howled round him like a winter wind from the south. He closed his eyes and pressed his fingers against the lids. Their faces formed in the eye of his mind.

Christine with pink fat legs under her frilly skirt, and the face of a thoughtful cherub below soft hair cropped like a page boy.

'I love you best of all,' said with much seriousness, holding his face with small hands only a little sticky with ice cream.

Simon, a miniature reproduction of Bruce even to the nose. Scabs on the knees and dirt on the face. No demonstrations of affection from him, but in its place something much better, a companionship far beyond his six years. Long discussions on everything from religion, 'Why didn't Jesus used to shave?' to politics, 'When are you going to be prime minister, Dad?'

And the loneliness was a tangible thing now, like the coils of a reptile squeezing his chest. Bruce ground out the cigarette beneath his heel and tried to find refuge in his hatred for the woman who had been his wife. The woman who had taken them from him.

But his hatred was a cold thing also, dead ash with a stale taste. For he knew that the blame was not all hers. It was another of his failures; perhaps if I had tried harder, perhaps if I had left some of the cruel things unsaid, perhaps – yes, it might have been, and perhaps and maybe. But it was not. It was over and finished and now I am alone. There is no worse condition; no state beyond loneliness. It is the waste land and the desolation.

Something moved near him in the night, a soft rustle of grass, a presence felt rather than seen. And Bruce stiffened. His right hand closed over his rifle. He brought it up slowly, his eyes straining into the darkness.

The movement again, closer now. A twig popped under-foot. Bruce slowly trained his rifle round to cover it, pressure on the trigger and his thumb on the safety. Stupid to have wandered away from the camp; asking for it, and now he had got it. Baluba tribesmen! He could see the figure now in the dimness of starlight, stealthily moving across his front. How many of them, he wondered. If I hit this one, there could be a dozen others with him. Have to take a chance. One quick burst and then run for it. A hundred yards to the camp, about an even chance. The figure was stationary now, standing listening. Bruce could see the outline of the head – no helmet, can't be one of us. He raised the rifle and pointed it. Too dark to see the sights, but at that range he couldn't miss. Bruce drew his breath softly, filling his lungs, ready to shoot and run.

'Bruce?' Shermaine's voice, frightened, almost a whisper. He threw up the rifle barrel. God, that was close. He had nearly killed her.

'Yes, I'm here.' His own voice was scratchy with the shock of realization.

'Oh, there you are.'

'What the hell are you doing out of the camp?' he demanded furiously as anger replaced his shock.

'I'm sorry, Bruce, I came to see if you were all right. You were gone such a long time.'

'Well, get back to the camp, and don't try any more tricks like that.'

There was a long silence, and then she spoke softly, unable to keep the hurt out of her tone.

'I brought you something to eat. I thought you'd be hungry. I'm sorry if I did wrong.'

She came to him, stooped and placed something on the ground in front of him. Then she turned and was gone.

'Shermaine.' He wanted her back, but the only reply was the fading rustle of the grass and then silence. He was alone again.

He picked up the plate of food.

You fool, he thought. You stupid, ignorant, thoughtless fool. You'll lose her, and you'll have deserved it. You deserve everything you've had, and more.

You never learn, do you, Curry? You never learn that there is a penalty for selfishness and for thoughtlessness.

He looked down at the plate in his hands. Bully beef and sliced onion, bread and cheese.

Yes, I have learned, he answered himself with sudden determination. I will not spoil this, this thing that is between this girl and me. That was the last time; now I am a man I will put away childish things, like temper and self-pity.

He ate the food, suddenly aware of his hunger. He ate quickly, wolfing it. Then he stood up and walked back to the camp.

A sentry challenged him on the perimeter and Bruce answered with alacrity. At night his gendarmes were very quick on the trigger; the challenge was an unusual courtesy.

'It is unwise to go alone into the forest in the darkness,' the sentry reprimanded him.

'Why?' Bruce felt his mood changing. The depression evaporated.

'It is unwise,' repeated the man vaguely.

'The spirits?' Bruce teased him delicately.

'An aunt of my sister's husband disappeared not a short throw of a spear from my hut. There was no trace, no shout, nothing. I was there. It is not a matter for doubt,' said the man with dignity.

'A lion perhaps?' Bruce prodded him.

'If you say so, then it is so. I know what I know. But I say only that there is no wisdom in defying the custom of the land.'

Suddenly touched by the man's concern for him, Bruce dropped a hand on to his shoulder and gripped it in the old expression of affection.

'I will remember. I did it without thinking.'

He walked into the camp. The incident had confirmed something he had vaguely suspected, but in which previously he had felt no interest. The men liked him. A hundred similar indications of this fact he had only half noted, not caring one way or the other. But now it gave him intense pleasure, fully compensating for the loneliness he had just experienced.

He walked past the little group of men round the cooking fire to where the Ford stood at the head of the convoy. Peering through the side window he could make out Shermaine's blanket-wrapped form on the back seat. He tapped on the glass and she sat up and rolled down the window.

'Yes?' she asked coolly.

'Thank you for the food.'

'It is nothing.' The slightest hint of warmth in her voice.

'Shermaine, sometimes I say things I do not mean. You startled me. I nearly shot you.'

'It was my fault. I should not have followed you.'

'I was rude,' he persisted.

'Yes.' She laughed now. That husky little chuckle. 'You were rude but with good reason. We shall forget it.' She placed her hand on his arm. 'You must rest, you haven't slept for two days.'

'Will you ride in the Ford with me tomorrow to show that I am forgiven?'

'Of course,' she nodded.

'Good night, Shermaine.'

'Good night, Bruce,'

No, Bruce decided as he spread his blankets beside the fire, I am not alone. Not any more.

– 20 –

'What about breakfast, boss?'

'They can eat on the road. Give them a tin of bully each – we've wasted enough time on this trip.'

The sky was paling and pinking above the forest. It was light enough to read the dial of his wristwatch. Twenty minutes to five.

'Get them moving, Ruffy. If we make Msapa Junction before dark we can drive through the night. Home for breakfast tomorrow.'

'Now you're talking, boss.' Ruffy clapped his helmet on to his head and went off to rouse the men who lay in the road beside the trucks.

Shermaine was asleep. Bruce leaned into the window of the Ford and studied her face. A wisp of hair lay over her mouth, rising and falling with her breathing. It tickled her nose and in her sleep it twitched like a rabbit.

Bruce felt an almost unbearable pang of tenderness towards her. With one finger he lifted the hair off her face. Then he smiled at himself.

If you can feel like this before breakfast, then you've got it in a bad way, he told himself.

Do you know something, he retorted. I like the feeling.

'Hey, you lazy wench!' He pulled the lobe of her ear. 'Time to wake up.'

It was almost half past five before the convoy got under way. It had taken that long to bully and cajole the sleep out of sixty men and get them into the lorries. This morning Bruce did not find the delay unbearable. He had managed to find time for four hours' sleep during the night. Four hours was not nearly enough to make up for the previous two days.

Now he felt light-headed, a certain unreal quality of gaiety overlaying his exhaustion, a carnival spirit. There was no longer the same urgency, for the road to Elisabethville was clear and not too long. Home for breakfast tomorrow!

'We'll be at the bridge in a little under an hour.' He glanced sideways at Shermaine.

'You've left a guard on it?'

'Ten men,' answered Bruce. 'We'll pick them up almost without stopping, and then the next stop, room 201, Grand Hotel Leopold II, Avenue du Kasai.' He grinned in anticipation. 'A bath so deep it will slop over on to the floor, so hot it will take five minutes to get into it. Clean clothes. A steak that thick, with French salad and a bottle of Liebfraumilch.'

'For breakfast!' protested Shermaine.

'For breakfast,' Bruce agreed happily. He was silent for a while, savouring the idea. The road ahead of him was tiger-striped with the shadows of the trees thrown by the low sun. The air that blew in through the missing windscreen was cool and clean-smelling. He felt good. The responsibility of command lay lightly on his shoulders this morning; a pretty girl beside him, a golden morning, the horror of the

183

last few days half-forgotten – they might have been going on a picnic.

'What are you thinking?' he asked suddenly. She was very quiet beside him.

'I was wondering about the future,' she answered softly. 'There is no one I know in Elisabethville, and I do not wish to stay there.'

'Will you return to Brussels?' he asked. The question was without significance, for Bruce Curry had very definite plans for the immediate future, and these included Shermaine.

'Yes, I think so. There is nowhere else.'

'You have relatives there?'

'An aunt.'

'Are you close?'

Shermaine laughed, but there was bitterness in the husky chuckle. 'Oh, very close. She came to see me once at the orphanage. Once in all those years. She brought me a comic book of a religious nature and told me to clean my teeth and brush my hair a hundred strokes a day.'

'There is no one else?' asked Bruce.

'No.'

'Then why go back?'

'What else is there to do?' she asked. 'Where else is there to go?'

'There's a life to live, and the rest of the world to visit.'

'Is that what you are going to do?'

'That is exactly what I'm going to do, starting with a hot bath.'

Bruce could feel it between them. They both knew it was there, but it was too soon to talk about it. I have only kissed her once, but that was enough. So what will happen? Marriage? His mind shied away from that word with startling violence, then came hesitantly back to examine it. Stalking it as though it were a dangerous beast, ready to take flight again as soon as it showed its teeth.

For some people it is a good thing. It can stiffen the spineless; ease the lonely; give direction to the wanderers; spur those without ambition – and, of course, there was the final unassailable argument in its favour. Children.

But there are some who can only sicken and shrivel in the colourless cell of matrimony. With no space to fly, your wings must weaken with disuse; turned inwards, your eyes become short-sighted; when all your communication with the rest of the world is through the glass windows of the cell, then your contact is limited.

And I already have children. I have a daughter and I have a son.

Bruce turned his eyes from the road and studied the girl beside him. There is no fault I can find. She is beautiful in the delicate, almost fragile way that is so much better and longer-lived than blond hair and big bosoms. She is unspoilt; hardship has long been her travelling companion and from it she has learned kindness and humility.

She is mature, knowing the ways of this world; knowing death and fear, the evilness of men and their goodness. I do not believe she has ever lived in the fairy-tale cocoon that most young girls spin about themselves.

And yet she has not forgotten how to laugh.

Perhaps, he thought, perhaps. But it is too soon to talk about it.

'You are very grim.' Shermaine broke the silence, but the laughter shivered just below the surface of her voice. 'Again you are Bonaparte. And when you are grim your nose is too big and cruel. It is a nose of great brutality and it does not fit the rest of your face. I think that when they had finished you they had only one nose left in stock. "It is too big," they said, "but it is the only nose left, and when he smiles it will not look too bad." So they took a chance and stuck it on anyway.'

'Were you never taught that it is bad manners to poke fun at a man's weakness?' Bruce fingered his nose ruefully.

'Your nose is many things, but not weak. Never weak.' She laughed now and moved a little closer to him.

'You know you can attack me from behind your own perfect nose, and I cannot retaliate.'

'Never trust a man who makes pretty speeches so easily, because he surely makes them to every girl he meets.' She slid an inch further across the seat until they were almost touching. 'You waste your talents, mon capitaine. I am immune to your charm.'

'In just one minute I will stop this car and—'

'You cannot.' Shermaine jerked her head to indicate the two gendarmes in the seat behind them. 'What would they think, Bonaparte? It would be very bad for discipline.'

'Discipline or no discipline, in just one minute I will stop this car and spank you soundly before I kiss you.'

'One threat does not frighten me, but because of the other I will leave your poor nose.' She moved away a little and once more Bruce studied her face. Beneath the frank scrutiny she fidgeted and started to blush.

'Do you mind! Were you never taught that it is bad manners to stare?'

So now I am in love again, thought Bruce. This is only the third time, an average of once every ten years or so. It frightens me a little because there is always pain with it. The exquisite pain of loving and the agony of losing.

It starts in the loins and it is very deceptive because you think it is only the old thing, the tightness and tension that any well-rounded stern or cheeky pair of breasts will give you. Scratch it, you think, it's just a small itch. Spread a little of the warm salve on it and it will be gone in no time.

But suddenly it spreads, upwards and downwards, all through you. The pit of your stomach feels hot, then the flutters round the heart. It's dangerous now; once it gets this far it's incurable and you can scratch and scratch but all you do is inflame it.

Then the last stages, when it attacks the brain. No pain

there, that's the worst sign. A heightening of the senses; your eyes are sharper, your blood runs too fast, food tastes good, your mouth wants to shout and legs want to run. Then the delusions of grandeur: you are the cleverest, strongest, most masculine male in the universe, and you stand ten feet tall in your socks.

How tall are you now, Curry, he asked himself. About nine feet six and I weigh twenty stone, he answered, and almost laughed aloud.

And how does it end? It ends with words. Words can kill anything. It ends with cold words; words like fire that stick in the structure and take hold and lick it up, blackening and charring it, bringing it down in smoking ruins.

It ends in suspicion of things not done, and in the certainty of things done and remembered. It ends with selfishness and carelessness, and words, always words.

It ends with pain and greyness, and it leaves scar tissue and damage that will never heal.

Or it ends without fuss and fury. It just crumbles and blows away like dust on the wind. But there is still the agony of loss.

Both these endings I know well, for I have loved twice, and now I love again.

Perhaps this time it does not have to be that way. Perhaps this time it will last. Nothing is for ever, he thought. Nothing is for ever, not even life, and perhaps this time if I cherish it and tend it carefully it will last that long, as long as life.

'We are nearly at the bridge,' said Shermaine beside him, and Bruce started. The miles had dropped unseen behind them and now the forest was thickening. It crouched closer to the earth, greener and darker along the river.

Bruce slowed the Ford and the forest became dense bush around them, the road a tunnel through it. They came round one last bend in the track and out of the tunnel of green vegetation into the clearing where the road met the railway line and ran beside it on to the heavy timber platform of the bridge.

Bruce stopped the Ranchero, switched off the engine and they all sat silently, staring out at the solid jungle on the far bank with its screen of creepers and monkey-ropes hanging down, trailing the surface of the deep green swift-flowing river. They stared at the stumps of the bridge thrusting out from each bank towards each other like the arms of parted lovers; at the wide gap between with the timbers still smouldering and the smoke drifting away downstream over the green water.

'It's gone,' said Shermaine. 'It's been burnt.'

'Oh, no,' groaned Bruce. 'Oh, God, no!'

With an effort he pulled his eyes from the charred remains of the bridge and turned them on to the jungle about them, a hundred feet away, ringing them in. Hostile, silent. 'Don't get out of the car,' he snapped as Shermaine reached for the door handle. 'Roll your window up, quickly.'

She obeyed.

'They're waiting in there.' He pointed at the edge of the jungle.

Behind them the first of the convoy came round the bend into the clearing. Bruce jumped from the Ford and ran back towards the leading truck.

'Don't get out, stay inside,' he shouted and ran on down the line, repeating the instruction to each of them as he passed. When he reached Ruffy's cab he jumped on to the running board, jerked the door open, slipped in on to the seat and slammed the door.

'They've burnt the bridge.'

'What's happened to the boys we left to guard it?'

'I don't know but we'll find out. Pull up alongside the others so that I can talk to them.'

Through the half-open window he issued his orders to each of the drivers and within ten minutes all the vehicles had been manoeuvred into the tight defensive circle of the laager, a formation Bruce's ancestors had used a hundred years before.

'Ruffy, get out those tarpaulins and spread them over the top to form a roof. We don't want them dropping arrows in amongst us.'

Ruffy selected half a dozen gendarmes and they went to work, dragging out the heavy folded canvas.

'Hendry, put a couple of men under each truck. Set up the Brens in case they try to rush us.'

In the infectious urgency of defence, Wally did not make his usual retort, but gathered his men. They wriggled on their stomachs under the vehicles, rifles pointed out towards the silent jungle.

'I want the extinguishers here in the middle so we can get them in a hurry. They might use fire again.'

Two gendarmes ran to each of the cabs and unclipped the fire-extinguishers from the dashboards.

'What can I do?' Shermaine was standing beside Bruce.

'Keep quiet and stay out of the way,' said Bruce as he turned and hurried across to help Ruffy's gang with the tarpaulins.

It took them half an hour of desperate endeavour before they completed the fortifications to Bruce's satisfaction.

'That should hold them.' Bruce stood with Ruffy and Hendry in the centre of the laager and surveyed the green canvas roof above them and the closely packed vehicles around them. The Ford was parked beside the tanker, not included in the outer ring for its comparative size would have made it a weak point in the defence.

'It's going to be bloody hot and crowded in here,' grumbled Hendry.

'Yes, I know.' Bruce looked at him. 'Would you like to relieve the congestion by waiting outside?'

'Funny boy, big laugh,' answered Wally.

'What now, boss?' Ruffy put into words the question Bruce had been asking himself.

'You and I will go and take a look at the bridge,' he said.

'You'll look a rare old sight with an arrow sticking out of your jack,' grinned Wally. 'Boy, that's going to kill me!'

'Ruffy, get us half a dozen gas capes each. I doubt their arrows will go through them at a range of a hundred feet, and of course we'll wear helmets.'

'Okay, boss.'

It was like being in a sauna bath beneath the six layers of rubberized canvas. Bruce could feel the sweat squirting from his pores with each pace, and rivulets of it coursing down his back and flanks as he and Ruffy left the laager and walked up the road to the bridge.

Beside him Ruffy's bulk was so enhanced by the gas capes that he reminded Bruce of a prehistoric monster reaching the end of its gestation period.

'Warm enough, Ruffy?' he asked, feeling the need for humour. The ring of jungle made him nervous. Perhaps he had underestimated the carry of a Baluba arrow – despite the light reed shaft, they used iron heads, barbed viciously and ground to a needle point, and poison smeared thickly between the barbs.

'Man, look at me shiver,' grunted Ruffy and the sweat greased down his jowls and dripped from his chin.

Long before they reached the access to the bridge the stench of putrefaction crept out to meet them. In Bruce's mind every smell had its own colour, and this one was green, the same green as the sheen of putrefaction on rotting meat. The stench was so heavy he could almost feel it bearing down on them, choking in his throat and coating his tongue and the roof of his mouth with the oily over-sweetness.

'No doubt what that is!' Ruffy spat, trying to get the taste out of his mouth.

'Where are they?' gagged Bruce, starting to pant from the heat and the effort of breathing the fouled air.

They reached the bank and Bruce's question was answered as they looked down on to the narrow beach.

There were the black remains of a dozen cooking fires along the water's edge, and closer to the high bank were two crude structures of poles. For a moment their purpose puzzled Bruce and then he realized what they were. He had seen those crosspieces suspended between two uprights often before in hunting camps throughout Africa. They were paunching racks! At intervals along the crosspieces were the bark ropes that had been used to string up the game, heels first, with head and forelegs dangling and belly bulging forward so that at the long abdominal stroke of the knife the viscera would drop out easily.

But the game they had butchered on *these* racks were men, his men. He counted the hanging ropes. There were ten of them, so no one had escaped.

'Cover me, Ruffy. I'm going down to have a look.' It was a penance Bruce was imposing upon himself. They were his men, and he had left them there.

'Okay, boss.'

Bruce clambered down the well-defined path to the beach. Now the smell was almost unbearable and he found the source of it. Between the racks lay a dark shapeless mass. It moved with flies; its surface moved, trembled, crawled with flies. Suddenly, humming, they lifted in a cloud from the pile of human debris, and then settled once more upon it.

A single fly buzzed round Bruce's head and then settled on his hand. Metallic blue body, wings cocked back, it crouched on his skin and gleefully rubbed its front legs together. Bruce's throat and stomach convulsed as he began to retch. He struck at the fly and it darted away.

There were bones scattered round the cooking fires and a skull lay near his feet, split open to yield its contents.

Another spasm took Bruce and this time the vomit came

up into his mouth, acid and warm. He swallowed it, turned away and scrambled up the bank to where Ruffy waited. He stood there gasping, suppressing his nausea until at last he could speak.

'All right, that's all I wanted to know,' and he led the way back to the circle of vehicles.

Bruce sat on the bonnet of the Ranchero and sucked hard on his cigarette, trying to get the taste of death from his mouth.

'They probably swam downstream during the night and climbed the supports of the bridge. Kanaki and his boys wouldn't have known anything about it until they came over the sides.' He drew on the cigarette again and trickled the smoke out of his nostrils, fumigating the back of his throat and his nasal passages. 'I should have thought of that. I should have warned Kanaki of that.'

'You mean they ate all ten of them – Jesus!' even Wally Hendry was impressed. 'I'd like to have a look at that beach. It must be quite something.'

'Good!' Bruce's voice was suddenly harsh. 'I'll put you in charge of the burial squad. You can go down there and clean it up before we start work on the bridge.' And Wally did not argue.

'You want me to do it now?' he asked.

'No,' snapped Bruce. 'You and Ruffy are going to take two of the trucks back to Port Reprieve and fetch the materials we need to repair the bridge.'

They both looked at Bruce with rising delight.

'I never thought of that,' said Wally.

'There's plenty of roofing timber in the hotel and the office block,' grinned Ruffy.

'Nails,' said Wally as though he were making a major contribution. 'We'll need nails.'

Bruce cut through their comments. 'It's two o'clock

now. You can get back to Port Reprieve by nightfall, collect the material tomorrow morning and return here by the evening. Take those two trucks there – check to see they're full of gas and you'll need about fifteen men. Say, five gendarmes, in case of trouble, and ten of those civilians.'

'That should be enough,' agreed Ruffy.

'Bring a couple of dozen sheets of corrugated iron back with you. We'll use them to make a shield to protect us from arrows while we're working.'

'Yeah, that's a good idea.'

They settled the details, picked men to go back, loaded the trucks, worked them out of the laager, and Bruce watched them disappear down the road towards Port Reprieve. An ache started deep behind his eyes and suddenly he was very tired, drained of energy by too little sleep, by the heat and by the emotional pace of the last four days. He made one last circuit of the laager, checking the defences, chatting for a few minutes with his gendarmes and then he stumbled to the Ford, slid on to the front seat, laid his helmet and rifle aside, lowered his head on to his arms and was instantly asleep.

– 21 –

Shermaine woke him after dark with food unheated from the cans and a bottle of Ruffy's beer.

'I'm sorry, Bruce, we have no fire to cook upon. It is very unappetizing and the beer is warm.'

Bruce sat up and rubbed his eyes. Six hours' sleep had helped; they were less swollen and inflamed. The headache was still there.

'I'm not really hungry, thank you. It's this heat.'

'You must eat, Bruce. Try just a little,' and then she smiled. 'At least you are more gallant after having rested. It

193

is "Thank you" now, instead of "Keep quiet and stay out of the way".'

Ruefully Bruce grimaced. 'You are one of those women with a built-in recording unit; every word remembered and used in evidence against a man later.' Then he touched her hand. 'I'm sorry.'

'I'm sorry,' she repeated. 'I like your apologies, mon capitaine. They are like the rest of you, completely masculine. There is nothing about you which is not male, sometimes almost overpoweringly so.' Impishly she watched his eyes; he knew she was talking about the little scene on the train that Wally Hendry had interrupted.

'Let's try this food,' he said, and then a little later, 'not bad – you are an excellent cook.'

'This time the credit must go to M. Heinz and his fifty-seven children. But one day I shall make for you one of my tournedos au Prince. It is my special.'

'Speciality,' Bruce corrected her automatically.

The murmur of voices within the laager was punctuated occasionally by a burst of laughter. There was a feeling of relaxation. The canvas roof and the wall of vehicles gave security to them all. Men lay in dark huddles of sleep or talked quietly in small groups.

Bruce scraped the metal plate and filled his mouth with the last of the food.

'Now I must check the defences again.'

'Oh, Bonaparte. It is always duty.' Shermaine sighed with resignation.

'I will not be long.'

'And I'll wait here for you.'

Bruce picked up his rifle and helmet, and was half-way out of the Ford when out in the jungle the drum started.

'Bruce!' whispered Shermaine and clutched his arm. The voices round them froze into a fearful silence, and the drum beat in the night. It had a depth and resonance that you could feel; the warm sluggish air quivered with it. Not fixed in space but filling it, beating monotonously, insistently, like the pulse of all creation.

'Bruce!' whispered Shermaine again; she was trembling and the fingers on his arm dug into his flesh with the strength of terror. It steadied his own leap of fear.

'Baby, baby,' he soothed her, taking her to his chest and holding her there. 'It's only the sound of two pieces of wood being knocked together by a naked savage. They can't touch us here, you know that.'

'Oh, Bruce, it's horrible – it's like bells, funeral bells.'

'That's silly talk.' Bruce held her at arm's length. 'Come with me. Help me calm down these others, they'll be terrified. You'll have to help me.'

And he pulled her gently across the seat out of the Ford, and with one arm round her waist walked her into the centre of the laager.

What will counteract the stupefying influence of the drum, the hypnotic beat of it, he asked himself. Noise, our own noise.

'Joseph, M'pophu—' he shouted cheerfully picking out the two best singers amongst his men. 'I regret the drumming is of a low standard, but the Baluba are monkeys with no understanding of music. Let us show them how a Bambala can sing.'

They stirred; he could feel the tension diminish.

'Come, Joseph—' He filled his lungs and shouted the opening chorus of one of the planting songs, purposely off-key, singing so badly that it must sting them.

Someone laughed, then Joseph's voice hesitantly starting the chorus, gathering strength. M'pophu coming in with the bass to give a solid foundation to the vibrant, sweet-ringing tenor. Half-beat to the drum, hands clapped in the dark; around him Bruce could feel the rhythmic swinging of bodies begin.

Shermaine was no longer trembling; he squeezed her waist and felt her body cling to him.

Now we need light, thought Bruce. A night lamp for my children who fear the darkness and the drum.

With Shermaine beside him he crossed the laager.

'Sergeant Jacque.'

'Captain?'

'You can start sweeping with the searchlights.'

'Oui, Captain.' The answer was less subdued. There were two spare batteries for each light, Bruce knew. Eight hours' life in each, so they would last tonight and tomorrow night.

From each side of the laager the beams leapt out, solid white shafts through the darkness; they played along the edge of the jungle and reflected back, lighting the interior of the laager sufficiently to make out the features of each man. Bruce looked at their faces. They're all right now, he decided, the ghosts have gone away.

'Bravo, Bonaparte,' said Shermaine, and Bruce became aware of the grins on the faces of his men as they saw him embracing her. He was about to drop his arm, then stopped himself. The hell with it, he decided, give them something else to think about. He led her back to the Ford.

'Tired?' he asked.

'A little,' she nodded.

'I'll fold down the seat for you. A blanket over the windows will give you privacy.'

'You'll stay close?' she asked quickly.

'I'll be right outside.' He unbuckled the webbing belt that carried his pistol. 'You'd better wear this from now on.'

Even at its minimum adjustment the belt was too large for her and the pistol hung down almost to her knee.

'The Maid of Orleans.' Bruce revenged himself. She pulled a face at him and crawled into the back of the station wagon.

A long while later she called softly above the singing and the throb of the drum.

'Bruce.'

'Yes?'

196

'I wanted to make sure you were there. Good night.'
'Good night, Shermaine.'

Bruce lay on a single blanket and sweated. The singing had long ago ceased but the drum went on and on, never faltering, throb-throb-throbbing out of the jungle. The searchlights swept regularly back and forth, at times lighting the laager clearly and at others leaving it in shadow. Bruce could hear around him the soft sounds of sleep, the sawing of breath, a muted cough, a gabbled sentence, the stirring of dreamers.

But Bruce could not sleep. He lay on his back with one hand under his head, smoking, staring up at the canvas. The events of the preceding four days ran through his mind: snatches of conversation, André dying. Boussier standing with his wife, the bursting of grenades, blood sticky on his hands, the smell of death, the violence and the horror.

He moved restlessly, flicked away his cigarette and covered his eyes with his hands as though to shut out the memories. But they went on flickering through his mind like the images of a gigantic movie projector, confused now, losing all meaning but retaining the horror.

He remembered the fly upon his arm, grinning at him, rubbing its legs together, gloating, repulsive. He rolled his head from side to side on the blanket.

I'm going mad, he thought, I must stop this.

He sat up quickly hugging his knees to his chest and the memories faded. But now he was sad, and alone. So terribly alone, so lost, so without purpose.

He sat alone on the blanket and he felt himself shrinking, becoming small and frightened.

I'm going to cry, he thought, I can feel it there heavy in my throat. And like a hurt child crawling into its mother's lap, Bruce Curry groped his way over the tailboard of the station wagon to Shermaine.

'Shermaine!' he whispered, blindly, searching for her.

'Bruce, what is it?' She sat up quickly. She had not been sleeping either.

'Where are you?' There was panic in Bruce's voice.

'Here I am – what's the matter?'

And he found her; clumsily he caught her to him.

'Hold me, Shermaine, please hold me.'

'Darling.' She was anxious. 'What is it? Tell me, my darling.'

'Just hold me, Shermaine. Don't talk.' He clung to her, pressing his face into her neck. 'I need you so much – oh, God! How I need you!'

'Bruce.' She understood, and her fingers were at the nape of his neck, stroking, soothing.

'My Bruce,' she said and held him. Instinctively her body began to rock, gentling him as though he were her child.

Slowly his body relaxed, and he sighed against her – a gusty broken sound.

'My Bruce, my Bruce.' She lifted the thin cotton vest that was all she wore and, instinctively in the ageless ritual of comfort, she gave him her breasts. Holding his mouth to them with both her arms clasped around his neck, her head bowed protectively over his, her hair falling forward and covering them both.

With the hard length of his body against hers, with the soft tugging at her bosom, and in the knowledge that she was giving strength to the man she loved, she realized she had never known happiness before this moment. Then his body was no longer quiescent; she felt her own mood change, a new urgency.

'Oh yes, Bruce, yes!' Speaking up into his mouth, his hungry hunting mouth and he above her, no longer child, but full man again.

'So beautiful, so warm.' His voice was strangely husky, she shuddered with the intensity of her own need.

'Quickly, Bruce, oh, Bruce.' His cruel loving hands, seeking, finding.

'Oh, Bruce – quickly,' and she reached up for him with her hips.

'I'll hurt you.'

'No – yes, I want the pain.' She felt the resistance to him within her and cried out impatiently against it.

'Go through!' and then, 'Ah! It burns.'

'I'll stop.'

'No, No!'

'Darling. It's too much.'

'Yes – I can't – oh, Bruce. My heart – you've touched my heart.'

Her clenched fists drumming on his back. And in to press against the taut, reluctantly yielding springiness, away, then back, away, and back to touch the core of all existence, leave it, and come long gliding back to it, nuzzle it, feel it tilt, then come away, then back once more. Welling slowly upwards scalding, no longer to be contained, with pain almost – and gone, and gone, and gone.

'I'm falling. Oh, Bruce! Bruce! Bruce!'

Into the gulf together – gone, all gone. Nothing left, no time, no space, no bottom to the gulf.

Nothing and everything. Complete.

Out in the jungle the drum kept beating.

Afterwards, long afterwards, she slept with her head on his arm and her face against his chest. And he unsleeping listened to her sleep. The sound of it was soft, so gentle breathing soft that you could not hear it unless you listened very carefully – or unless you loved her, he thought.

Yes. I think I love this woman – but I must be certain. In fairness to her and to myself I must be entirely certain, for I cannot live through another time like the last, and because I love her I don't want her to take the terrible wounding of a bad marriage. Better, much better to leave it now, unless it has the strength to endure.

Bruce rolled his head slowly until his face was in her hair, and the girl nuzzled his chest in her sleep.

But it is so hard to tell, he thought. It is so hard to tell at the beginning. It is so easy to confuse pity or loneliness with love, but I cannot afford to do that now. So I must try to think clearly about my marriage to Joan. It will be difficult, but I must try.

Was it like this with Joan in the beginning? It was so long ago, seven years, that I do not know, he answered truthfully. All I have left from those days are the pictures of places and the small heaps of words that have struck where the wind and the pain could not blow them away.

A beach with the sea mist coming in across it, a whole tree of driftwood half buried in the sand and bleached white with the salt, a basket of strawberries bought along the road, so that when I kissed her I could taste the sweet tartness of the fruit on her lips.

I remember a tune that we sang together, 'The mission bells told me that I mustn't stay, South of the border, down Mexico way.' I have forgotten most of the words.

And I remember vaguely how her body was, and the shape of her breasts before the children were born.

But that is all I have left from the good times.

The other memories are clear, stinging, whiplash clear. Each ugly word, and the tone in which it was said. The sound of sobbing in the night, the way it dragged itself on for three long grey years after it was mortally wounded, and both of us using all our strength to keep it moving because of the children.

The children! Oh, God, I mustn't think about them now. It hurts too much. Without the children to complicate it, I must think about her for the last time; I must end this woman Joan. So now finally and for all to end this woman who made me cry. I do not hate her for the man with whom she went away. She deserved another try for happiness. But I hate her for my children and for making shabby the love that I could have given Shermaine as a new thing. Also, I pity her for her inability to find the happiness for which she hunts so fiercely. I pity her for her coldness of body and of mind, I pity her for her prettiness that is now almost gone (it goes round her eyes first, cracking like oil paint) and I pity her for her consuming selfishness which will lose her the love of her children.

My children – not hers! My children!

That is all, that is an end to Joan, and now I have Shermaine who is none of the things that Joan was. I also deserve another try.

'Shermaine,' he whispered and turned her head slightly to kiss her. 'Shermaine, wake up.'

She stirred and murmured against him.

'Wake up.' He took the lobe of her ear between his teeth and bit it gently. Her eyes opened.

'Bon matin, madame.' He smiled at her.

'Bonjour, monsieur,' she answered and closed her eyes to press her face once more against his chest.

'Wake up. I have something to tell you.'

'I am awake, but tell me first if I am still dreaming. I have a certainty that this cannot be reality.'

'You are not dreaming.'

She sighed softly, and held him closer.

'Now tell me the other thing.'

'I love you,' he said.

'No. Now I am dreaming.'

'In truth,' he said.

'No, do not wake me. I could not bear to wake now.'

'And you?' he asked.

'You know it—' she answered. 'I do not have to tell you.'

'It is almost morning,' he said. 'There is only a little time.'

'Then I will fill that little time with saying it—' He held her and listened to her whispering it to him.

No, he thought, now I am certain. I could not be that wrong. This is my woman.

– 22 –

The drum stopped with the dawn. And after it the silence was very heavy, and it was no relief.

They had grown accustomed to that broken rhythm and now in some strange way they missed it.

As Bruce moved around the laager he could sense the uneasiness in his men. There was a feeling of dread anticipation on them all. They moved with restraint, as though they did not want to draw attention to themselves. The laughter with which they acknowledged his jokes was nervous, quickly cut off, as though they had laughed in a cathedral. And their eyes kept darting back towards the ring of jungle.

Bruce found himself wishing for an attack. His own nerves were rubbed sensitive by contact with the fear all around him.

If only they would come, he told himself. If only they would show themselves and we could see men not phantoms.

But the jungle was silent. It seemed to wait, it watched them. They could feel the gaze of hidden eyes. Its malignant presence pressed closer as the heat built up.

Bruce walked across the laager to the south side, trying to move casually. He smiled at Sergeant Jacque, squatted beside him and peered from under the truck across open ground at the remains of the bridge.

'Trucks will be back soon,' he said. 'Won't take long to repair that.'

Jacque did not answer. There was a worried frown on his high intelligent forehead and his face was shiny with perspiration.

'It's the waiting, Captain. It softens the stomach.'

'They will be back soon,' repeated Bruce. If this one is worried, and he is the best of them, then the others must be almost in a jelly of dread.

Bruce looked at the face of the man on the other side of Jacque. Its expression shrieked with fear.

If they attack now, God knows how it will turn out. An African can think himself to death, they just lie down and die. They are getting to that stage now; if an attack comes they will either go berserk or curl up and wail with fear. You can never tell.

Be honest with yourself – you're not entirely happy either, are you? No, Bruce agreed, it's the waiting does it.

It came from the edge of the clearing on the far side of the laager. A high-pitched inhuman sound, angry, savage.

Bruce felt his heart trip and he spun round to face it. For a second the whole laager seemed to cringe from it.

It came again. Like a whip across aching nerves. Immediately it was lost in the roar of twenty rifles.

Bruce laughed. Threw his head back and let it come from the belly.

The gunfire stammered into silence and others were laughing also. The men who had fired grinned sheepishly and made a show of reloading.

It was not the first time that Bruce had been startled by the cry of a yellow hornbill. But now he recognized his laughter and the laughter of the men around him, a mild form of hysteria.

'Did you want the feathers for your hat?' someone shouted and the laughter swept round the laager.

The tension relaxed as the banter was tossed back and forth. Bruce stood up and brought his own laughter under control.

No harm done, he decided. For the price of fifty rounds of ammunition, a purchase of an hour's escape from tension. A good bargain.

He walked across to Shermaine. She was smiling also.

'How is the catering section?' He grinned at her. 'What miracle of the culinary art is there for lunch?'

'Bully beef.'

'And onions?'

'No, just bully beef. The onions are finished.'

Bruce stopped smiling.

'How much is left?' he asked.

'One case – enough to last till lunchtime tomorrow.'

It would take at least two days to complete the repairs to the bridge; another day's travel after that.

'Well,' he said, 'we should all have healthy appetites by the time we get home. You'll have to try and spread it out. Half rations from now on.'

He was so engrossed in the study of this new complication that he did not notice the faint hum from outside the laager.

'Captain,' called Jacques. 'Can you hear it?'

Bruce inclined his head and listened.

'The trucks!' His voice was loud with relief, and instantly there was an excited murmur round the laager.

The waiting was over.

They came growling out of the bush into the clearing. Heavily loaded, timber and sheet-iron protruding backwards from under the canopies, sitting low on their suspensions.

Ruffy leaned from the cab of the leading truck and shouted.

'Hello boss. Where shall we dump?'

'Take it up to the bridge. Hang on a second and I'll come with you.'

Bruce slipped out of the laager and crossed quickly to Ruffy's truck. He could feel his back tingling while he was in the open and he slammed the door behind him with relief.

'I don't relish stopping an arrow,' he said.

204

'You have any trouble while we were gone?'

'No,' Bruce told him. 'But they're here. They were drumming in the jungle all night.'

'Calling up their buddies,' grunted Ruffy and let out the clutch. 'We'll have some fun before we finish this bridge. Most probably take them a day or two to get brave, but in the end they'll have a go at us.'

'Pull over to the side of the bridge, Ruffy,' Bruce instructed and rolled down his window. 'I'll signal Hendry to pull in beside us. We'll off-load into the space between the two trucks and start building the corrugated iron shield there.'

While Hendry manoeuvred his truck alongside, Bruce forced himself to look down on the carnage of the beach.

'Crocodiles,' he exclaimed with relief. The paunching racks still stood as he had last seen them, but the reeking pile of human remains was gone. The smell and the flies, however, still lingered.

'During the night,' agreed Ruffy as he surveyed the long slither marks in the sand of the beach.

'Thank God for that.'

'Yeah, it wouldn't have made my boys too joyful having to clean up that lot.'

'We'll send someone down to tear out those racks. I don't want to look at them while we work.'

'No, they're not very pretty.' Ruffy ran his eyes over the two sets of gallows.

Bruce climbed down into the space between the trucks.

'Hendry.'

'That's my name.' Wally leaned out of the window.

'Sorry to disappoint you, but the crocs have done the chore for you.'

'I can see. I'm not blind.'

'Very well then. On the assumption that you are neither blind nor paralysed, how about getting your trucks un-loaded?'

'Big deal,' muttered Hendry, but he climbed down and began shouting at the men under the canvas canopy.

'Get the lead out there, you lot. Start jumping about!'

'What were the thickest timbers you could find?' Bruce turned to Ruffy.

'Nine by threes, but we got plenty of them.'

'They'll do,' decided Bruce. 'We can lash a dozen of them together for each of the main supports.' Frowning with concentration, Bruce began the task of organizing the repairs.

'Hendry, I want the timber stacked by sizes. Put the sheet-iron over there.' He brushed the flies from his face. 'Ruffy, how many hammers have we got?'

'Ten, boss, and I found a couple of handsaws.'

'Good. What about nails and rope?'

'We got plenty. I got a barrel of six-inch and—'

Preoccupied, Bruce did not notice one of the coloured civilians leave the shelter of the trucks. He walked a dozen paces towards the bridge and stopped. Then unhurriedly he began to unbutton his trousers and Bruce looked up.

'What the hell are you doing?' he shouted and the man started guiltily. He did not understand the English words, but Bruce's tone was sufficiently clear.

'Monsieur,' he explained, 'I wish to—'

'Get back here!' roared Bruce. The man hesitated in confusion and then he began closing his fly.

'Hurry up – you bloody fool.'

Obediently the man hastened the closing of his trousers. Everyone had stopped work and they were all watching him. His face was dark with embarrassment and he fumbled clumsily.

'Leave that.' Bruce was frantic. 'Get back here.'

The first arrow rose lazily out of the undergrowth along the river in a silent parabola. Gathering speed in its descent, hissing softly, it dropped into the ground at the man's feet and stuck up jauntily. A thin reed, fletched with green leaves, it looked harmless as a child's plaything.

'Run,' screamed Bruce. The man stood and stared with detached disbelief at the arrow.

Bruce started forward to fetch him, but Ruffy's huge black hand closed on his arm and he was helpless in its grip. He struck out at Ruffy, struggling to free himself but he could not break that hold.

A swarm of them like locusts on the move, high arching, fluting softly, dropping all around the man as he started to run.

Bruce stopped struggling and watched. He heard the metal heads clanking on the bonnet of the truck, saw them falling wide of the man, some of the frail shafts snapping as they hit the ground.

Then between the shoulders, like a perfectly placed banderilla, one hit him. It flapped against his back as he ran and he twisted his arms behind him, vainly trying to reach it, his face twisted in horror and in pain.

'Hold him down,' shouted Bruce as the coloured man ran into the shelter. Two gendarmes jumped forward, took his arms and forced him face downwards on to the ground.

He was gabbling incoherently with horror as Bruce straddled his back and gripped the shaft. Only half the barbed head had buried itself – a penetration of less than an inch – but when Bruce pulled the shaft it snapped off in his hand leaving the steel twitching in the flesh.

'Knife,' shouted Bruce and someone thrust a bayonet into his hand.

'Watch those barbs, boss. Don't cut yourself on them.'

'Ruffy, get your boys ready to repel them if they rush us,' snapped Bruce and ripped away the shirt. For a moment he stared at the crudely hand-beaten iron arrowhead. The poison coated it thickly, packed in behind the barbs, looking like sticky black toffee.

'He's dead,' said Ruffy from where he leaned over the bonnet of the truck. 'He just ain't stopped breathing yet.'

The man screamed and twisted under Bruce as he made the first incision, cutting in deep beside the arrowhead with the point of the bayonet.

'Hendry, get those pliers out of the tool kit.'

'Here they are.'

Bruce gripped the arrow-head with the steel jaws and pulled. The flesh clung to it stubbornly, lifting in a pyramid. Bruce hacked at it with the bayonet, feeling it tear. It was like trying to get the hook out of the rubbery mouth of a cat-fish.

'You're wasting your time, boss!' grunted Ruffy with all the calm African acceptance of violent death. 'This boy's a goner. That's no horse! That's snake juice in him, fresh mixed. He's finished.'

'Are you sure, Ruffy?' Bruce looked up, 'Are you sure it's snake venom?'

'That's what they use. They mix it with kassava meal.'

'Hendry, where's the snake bite outfit?'

'It's in the medicine box back at the camp.'

Bruce tugged once more at the arrowhead and it came away, leaving a deep black hole between the man's shoulder blades.

'Everybody into the trucks, we've got to get him back. Every second is vital.'

'Look at his eyes,' grunted Ruffy. 'That injection stuff ain't going to help him much.'

The pupils had contracted to the size of match heads and he was shaking uncontrollably as the poison spread through his body.

'Get him into the truck.'

They lifted him into the cab and everybody scrambled aboard. Ruffy started the engine, slammed into reverse and the motor roared as he shot backwards over the intervening thirty yards to the laager.

'Get him out,' instructed Bruce. 'Bring him into the shelter.'

The man was blubbering through slack lips and he had started to sweat. Little rivulets of it coursed down his face and naked upper body. There was hardly any blood from the wound, just a trickle of brownish fluid. The poison must be a coagulant, Bruce decided.

'Bruce, are you all right?' Shermaine ran to meet him.

'Nothing wrong with me.' Bruce remembered to check his tongue this time. 'But one of them has been hit.'

'Can I help you?'

'No, I don't want you to watch.' And he turned from her. 'Hendry, where's that bloody snake bite outfit?' he shouted.

They had dragged the man into the laager and laid him on a blanket in the shade. Bruce went to him and knelt beside him. He took the scarlet tin that Hendry handed him and opened it.

'Ruffy, get those two trucks worked into the circle and make sure your boys are on their toes. With this success they may get brave sooner than you expected.'

Bruce fitted the hypodermic needle on to the syringe as he spoke.

'Hendry, get them to rig some sort of screen round us. You can use blankets.'

With his thumb he snapped the top off the ampoule and filled the syringe with the pale yellow serum.

'Hold him,' he said to the two gendarmes, lifted a pinch of skin close beside the wound and ran the needle under it. The man's skin felt like that of a frog, damp and clammy.

As he expelled the serum Bruce was trying to calculate the time that had elapsed since the arrow had hit. Possibly seven or eight minutes; mamba venom kills in fourteen minutes.

'Roll him over,' he said.

The man's head lolled sideways, his breathing was quick

and shallow and the saliva poured from the corners of his mouth, running down his cheeks.

'Get a load of that!' breathed Wally Hendry, and Bruce glanced up at his face. His expression was a glow of deep sensual pleasure and his breathing was as quick and shallow as that of the dying man.

'Go and help Ruffy,' snapped Bruce as his stomach heaved with disgust.

'Not on your Nelly. This I'm not going to miss.'

Bruce had no time to argue. He lifted the skin of the man's stomach and ran the needle in again. There was an explosive spitting sound as the bowels started to vent involuntarily.

'Jesus,' whispered Hendry.

'Get away,' snarled Bruce. 'Can't you let him die without gloating over it?'

Hopelessly he injected again, under the skin of the chest above the heart. As he emptied the syringe the man's body twisted violently in the first seizure and the needle snapped off under the skin.

'There he goes,' whispered Hendry, 'there he goes. Just look at him, man. That's really something.'

Bruce's hands were trembling and slowly a curtain descended across his mind.

'You filthy swine,' he screamed and hit Hendry across the face with his open hand, knocking him back against the side of the gasoline tanker. Then he went for his throat and found it with both hands. The windpipe was ropey and elastic under his thumbs.

'Is nothing sacred to you, you unclean animal?' he yelled into Hendry's face. 'Can't you let a man die without—'

Then Ruffy was there, effortlessly plucking Bruce's hands from the throat, interposing the bulk of his body, holding them away from each other.

'Let it stand, boss.'

'For that—' gasped Hendry as he massaged his throat. 'For that I'm going to make you pay.'

Bruce turned away, sick and ashamed, to the man on the blanket.

'Cover him up.' His voice was shaky. 'Put him in the back of one of the trucks. We'll bury him tomorrow.'

– 23 –

Before nightfall they had completed the corrugated iron screen. It was a simple four-walled structure with no roof to it. One end of it was detachable and all four walls were pierced at regular intervals with small loopholes for defence.

Long enough to accommodate a dozen men in comfort, high enough to reach above the heads of the tallest, and exactly the width of the bridge, it was not a thing of beauty.

'How you going to move it, boss?' Ruffy eyed the screen dubiously.

'I'll show you. We'll move it back to the camp now, so that in the morning we can commute to work in it.'

Bruce selected twelve men and they crowded through the open end into the shelter, and closed it behind them.

'Okay, Ruffy. Take the trucks away.'

Hendry and Ruffy reversed the two trucks back to the laager, leaving the shelter standing at the head of the bridge like a small Nissen hut. Inside it Bruce stationed his men at intervals along the walls.

'Use the bottom timber of the frame to lift on,' he shouted. 'Are you all ready? All right, lift!'

The shelter swayed and rose six inches above the ground. From the laager they could see only the boots of the men inside.

'All together,' ordered Bruce. 'Walk!'

Rocking and creaking over the uneven ground the structure moved ponderously back towards the laager. Below it the feet moved like those of a caterpillar.

The men in the laager started to cheer, and from inside the shelter they answered with whoops of laughter. It was fun. They were enjoying themselves enormously, completely distracted from the horror of poison arrows and the lurking phantoms in the jungle around them.

They reached the camp and lowered the shelter. Then one at a time the gendarmes slipped across the few feet of open ground into the safety of the laager to be met with laughter, and back-slapping and mutual congratulation.

'Well, it works, boss,' Ruffy greeted Bruce in the uproar.

'Yes.' Then he lifted his voice. 'That's enough. Quiet down all of you. Get back to your posts.'

The laughter subsided and the confusion became order again. Bruce walked to the centre of the laager and looked about him. There was complete quiet now. They were all watching him. I have read about this so often, he grinned inwardly, the heroic speech to the men on the eve of battle. Let's pray I don't make a hash of it.

'Are you hungry?' he asked loudly in French and received a chorus of hearty affirmatives.

'There is bully beef for dinner.' This time humorous groans.

'And bully beef for breakfast tomorrow,' he paused, 'and then it's finished.'

They were silent now.

'So you are going to be truly hungry by the time we cross this river. The sooner we repair the bridge the sooner you'll get your bellies filled again.'

I might as well rub it in, decided Bruce.

'You all saw what happened to the person who went into the open today, so I don't have to tell you to keep under cover. The sergeant major is making arrangements for

212

sanitation – five-gallon drums. They won't be very comfortable, so you won't be tempted to sit too long.'

They laughed a little at that.

'Remember this. As long as you stay in the laager or the shelter they can't touch you. There is absolutely nothing to fear. They can beat their drums and wait as long as they like, but they can't harm us.'

A murmur of agreement.

'And the sooner we finish the bridge the sooner we will be on our way.'

Bruce looked round the circle of faces and was satisfied with what he saw. The completion of the shelter had given their morale a boost.

'All right, Sergeant Jacque. You can start sweeping with the searchlights as soon as it's dark.'

Bruce finished and went across to join Shermaine beside the Ford. He loosed the straps of his helmet and lifted it off his head. His hair was damp with perspiration and he ran his fingers through it.

'You are tired,' Shermaine said softly, examining the dark hollows under his eyes and the puckered marks of strain at the corners of his mouth.

'No. I'm all right,' he denied, but every muscle in his body ached with fatigue and nervous tension.

'Tonight you must sleep all night,' she ordered him. 'I will make the bed in the back of the car.'

Bruce looked at her quickly. 'With you?' he asked.

'Yes.'

'You do not mind that everyone should know?'

'I am not ashamed of us.' There was a fierceness in her tone.

'I know, but—'

'You said once that nothing between you and I could ever be dirty.'

'No, of course it couldn't be dirty. I just thought—'

'Well then, I love you and from now on we have only one bed between us.' She spoke with finality.

Yesterday she was a virgin, he thought with amazement, and now – well, now it's no holds barred. Once she is roused a woman is more reckless of consequences than any man. They are such wholesale creatures. But she's right, of course. She's my woman and she belongs in my bed. The hell with the rest of the world and what it thinks!

'Make the bed, wench.' He smiled at her tenderly.

Two hours after dark the drum started again. They lay together, holding close, and listened to it. It held no terror now, for they were warm and secure in the afterglow of passion. It was like lying and listening to the impotent fury of a rainstorm on the roof at night.

– 24 –

They went out to the bridge at sunrise, the shelter moving across the open ground like the carapace of a multi-legged metallic turtle. The men chattered and joked loudly inside, still elated by the novelty of it.

'All right, everybody. That's enough talking,' Bruce shouted them down. 'There's work to do now.'

And they began.

Within an hour the sun had turned the metal box into an oven. They stripped to the waist and the sweat dripped from them as they worked. They worked in a frenzy, gripped by a new urgency, oblivious of everything but the rough-sawed timber that drove white splinters into their skin at the touch. They worked in the confined heat, amidst the racket of hammers and in the piney smell of sawdust. The labour fell into its own pattern with only an occasional grunted order from Bruce or Ruffy to direct it.

By midday the four main trusses that would span the gap in the bridge had been made up. Bruce tested their rigidity by propping one at both ends and standing all his men on the middle of it. It gave an inch under their combined weight.

'What do you think, boss?' Ruffy asked without conviction.

'Four of them might just do it. We'll put in king-posts underneath,' Bruce answered.

'Man, I don't know. That tanker weights plenty.'

'It's no flyweight,' Bruce agreed. 'But we'll have to take the chance. We'll bring the Ford across first, then the trucks and the tanker last.'

Ruffy nodded and wiped his face on his forearm; the muscles below his armpits knotted as he moved and there was no flabbiness in the powerful bulge of his belly above his belt.

'Phew!' He blew his lips out. 'I got the feeling for a beer now. This thirst is really stalking me.'

'You've got some with you?' Bruce asked as he passed his thumbs across his eyebrows and squeezed the moisture from them so it ran down his cheeks.

'Two things I never travel without, my trousers and a stock of the brown and bubbly.' Ruffy picked up the small pack from the corner of the shelter and it clinked coyly. 'You hear that sound, boss?'

'I hear it, and it sounds like music,' grinned Bruce. 'All right, everybody.' He raised his voice. 'Take ten minutes.'

Ruffy opened the bottles and passed them out, issuing one to be shared between three gendarmes. 'These Arabs don't properly appreciate this stuff,' he explained to Bruce. 'It'd just be a waste.'

The liquor was lukewarm and gassy; it merely aggravated Bruce's thirst. He drained the bottle and tossed it out of the shelter.

'All right.' He stood up. 'Let's get these trusses into position.'

'That's the shortest ten minutes I ever lived,' commented Ruffy.

'Your watch is slow,' said Bruce.

Carrying the trusses within it, the shelter lumbered out on to the bridge. There was no laughter now, only laboured breathing and curses.

'Fix the ropes!' commanded Bruce. He tested the knots personally, then looked up at Ruffy and nodded.

'That'll do.'

'Come on, you mad bastards,' Ruffy growled. 'Lift it.'

The first truss rose to the perpendicular and swayed there like a grotesque maypole with the ropes hanging from its top.

'Two men on each rope,' ordered Bruce. 'Let it down gently.' He glanced round to ensure that they were all ready.

'Drop it over the edge, and I'll throw you bastards in after it,' warned Ruffy.

'Lower away!' shouted Bruce.

The truss leaned out over the gap towards the fire-blackened stump of bridge on the far side slowly at first, then faster as gravity took it.

'Hold it, damn you. Hold it!' roared Ruffy with the muscles in his shoulders humped out under the strain. They lay back against the ropes, but the weight of the truss dragged them forward as it fell.

It crashed down across the gap, lifted a cloud of dead wood ash as it struck, and lay there quivering.

'Man, I thought we'd lost that one for sure,' growled Ruffy, then turned savagely on his men.

'You bastards better be sharper with the next one – if you don't want to swim this river.'

They repeated the process with the second truss, and again they could not hold its falling length, but this time they were not so lucky. The end of the truss hit the far side, bounced and slid sideways.

'It's going! Pull, you bastards, pull!' shouted Ruffy.

The truss toppled slowly sideways and over the edge. It hit the river below them with a splash, disappeared under the surface, then bobbed up and floated away downstream until checked by the ropes.

Both Bruce and Ruffy fumed and swore during the lengthy exasperating business of dragging it back against the current and manhandling its awkward bulk back on to the bridge. Half a dozen times it slipped at the crucial moment and splashed back into the river.

Despite his other virtues, Ruffy's vocabulary of cursing words was limited and it added to his frustration that he had to keep repeating himself. Bruce did much better – he remembered things that he had heard and he made up a few.

When finally they had the dripping baulk of timber back on the bridge and were resting, Ruffy turned to Bruce with honest admiration.

'You swear pretty good,' he said. 'Never heard you before, but no doubt about it, you're good! What's that one about the cow again?'

Bruce repeated it for him a little self-consciously.

'You make that up yourself?' asked Ruffy.

'Spur of the moment,' laughed Bruce.

'That's 'bout the dirtiest I ever heard.' Ruffy could not conceal his envy. 'Man, you should write a book.'

'Let's get this bridge finished first,' said Bruce. 'Then I'll think about it.'

Now the truss was almost servile in its efforts to please. It dropped neatly across the gap and lay beside its twin.

'You curse something good enough, and it works every time,' Ruffy announced sagely. 'I think your one about the cow made all the difference, boss.'

With two trusses in position they had broken the back of the project. They carried the shelter out and set it on the trusses, straddling the gap. The third and fourth trusses were dragged into position and secured with ropes and nails before nightfall.

When the shelter waddled wearily back to the laager at dusk, the men within it were exhausted. Their hands were bleeding and bristled with wood splinters, but they were also mightily pleased with themselves.

'Sergeant Jacque, keep one of your searchlights trained on the bridge all night. We don't want our friends to come out and set fire to it again.'

'There are only a few hours' life left in each of the batteries.' Jacque kept his voice low.

'Use them one at a time then.' Bruce spoke without hesitation. 'We must have that bridge lit up all night.

'You think you could spare a beer for each of the boys that worked on the bridge today?'

'A whole one each!' Ruffy was shocked. 'I only got a couple cases left.'

Bruce fixed him with a stern eye and Ruffy grinned.

'Okay, boss. Guess they've earned it.'

Bruce transferred his attention to Wally Hendry who sat on the running-board of one of the trucks cleaning his nails with the point of his bayonet.

'Everything under control here, Hendry?' he asked coolly.

'Sure, what'd you think would happen? We'd have a visit from the archbishop? The sky'd fall in? Your French thing'd have twins or something?' He looked up from his nails at Bruce. 'When are you jokers going to get that bridge finished, instead of wandering around asking damn-fool questions?'

Bruce was too tired to feel annoyed. 'You've got the night watch, Hendry,' he said, 'from now until dawn.'

'Is that right, hey? And you? What're you going to do all night, or does that question make you blush?'

'I'm going to sleep, that's what I'm going to do. I haven't been lolling round camp all day.'

Hendry pegged the bayonet into the earth between his feet and snorted.

'Well, give her a little bit of sleep for me too, Bucko.'

Bruce left him and crossed to the Ford.

'Hello, Bruce. How did it go today? I missed you,' Shermaine greeted him, and her face lit up as she looked at him. It is a good feeling to be loved, and some of Bruce's fatigue lifted.

'About half finished, another day's work.' Then he smiled back at her. 'I won't lie and say I missed you – I've been too damn busy.'

'Your hands!' she said with quick concern and lifted them to examine them. 'They're in a terrible state.'

'Not very pretty, are they?'

'Let me get a needle from my case. I'll get the splinters out.'

From across the laager Wally Hendry caught Bruce's eye and with one hand made a suggestive sign below his waist. Then, at Bruce's frown of anger, he threw back his head and laughed with huge delight.

– 25 –

Bruce's stomach grumbled with hunger as he stood with Ruffy and Hendry beside the cooking fire. In the early morning light he could just make out the dark shape of the bridge at the end of the clearing. That drum was still beating in the jungle, but they hardly noticed it now. It was taken for granted like the mosquitoes. 'The batteries are finished,' grunted Ruffy. The feeble yellow beam of the searchlight reached out tiredly towards the bridge.

'Only just lasted the night,' agreed Bruce.

'Christ, I'm hungry,' complained Hendry. 'What could I do to a couple of fried eggs and a porterhouse steak.'

At the mention of food Bruce's mouth flooded with saliva. He shut his mind against the picture that Wally's words had evoked in his imagination.

'We won't be able to finish the bridge and get the trucks across today,' he said, and Ruffy agreed.

'There's a full day's work left on her, boss.'

'This is what we'll do then,' Bruce went on. 'I'll take the work party out to the bridge. Hendry, you will stay here in the laager and cover us the same as yesterday. And Ruffy, you take one of the trucks and a dozen of your boys. Go back ten miles or so to where the forest is open and they won't be able to creep up on you. Then cut us a mountain of firewood; thick logs that will burn all night. We will set a ring of watch fires round the camp tonight.'

'That makes sense,' Ruffy nodded. 'But what about the bridge?'

'We'll have to put a guard on it,' said Bruce, and the expressions on their faces changed as they thought about this.

'More pork chops for the boys in the bushes,' growled Hendry. 'You won't catch me sitting out on the bridge all night.'

'No one's asking you to,' snapped Bruce. 'All right, Ruffy. Go and fetch the wood, and plenty of it.'

Bruce completed the repairs to the bridge in the late afternoon. The most anxious period was in the middle of the day when he and four men had to leave the shelter and clamber down on to the supports a few feet above the surface of the river to set the king-posts in place. Here they were exposed at random range to arrows from the undergrowth along the banks. But no arrows came and they finished the job and climbed back to safety again with something of a sense of anticlimax.

They nailed the crossties over the trusses and then roped everything into a compact mass.

Bruce stood back and surveyed the fruit of two full days' labour.

'Functional,' he decided, speaking aloud. 'But we certainly aren't going to win any prizes for aesthetic beauty or engineering design.'

He picked up his jacket and thrust his arms into the sleeves; his sweaty upper body was cold now that the sun was almost down.

'Home, gentlemen,' he said, and his gendarmes scattered to their positions inside the shelter.

The metal shelter circled the laager, squatting every twenty or thirty paces like an old woman preparing to relieve herself. When it lifted and moved on it left a log fire behind it. The ring of fires was completed by dark and the shelter returned to the laager.

'Are you ready, Ruffy?' From inside the shelter Bruce called across to where Ruffy waited.

'All set, boss.'

Followed by six heavily armed gendarmes, Ruffy crossed quickly to join Bruce and they set off to begin their all-night vigil on the bridge.

Before midnight it was cold in the corrugated iron shelter, for the wind blew down the river and they were completely exposed to it, and there was no cloud cover to hold the day's warmth against the earth.

The men in the shelter huddled under their gas capes and waited. Bruce and Ruffy leaned together against the corrugated iron wall, their shoulders almost touching, and there was sufficient light from the stars to light the interior of the shelter and allow them to make out the guard rails of the bridge through the open ends.

'Moon will be up in an hour,' murmured Ruffy.

'Only a quarter of it, but it will give us a little more

light,' Bruce concurred, and peered down into the black hole between his feet where he had prised up one of the newly laid planks.

'How about taking a shine with the torch?' suggested Ruffy.

'No.' Bruce shook his head, and passed the flashlight into his other hand. 'Not until I hear them.'

'You might not hear them.'

'If they swim downstream and climb up the piles, which is what I expect, then we'll hear them all right. They'll be dripping water all over the place,' said Bruce.

'Kanaki and his boys didn't hear them,' Ruffy pointed out.

'Kanaki and his boys weren't listening for it,' said Bruce.

They were silent then for a while. One of the gendarmes started to snore softly and Ruffy shot out a huge booted foot that landed in the small of his back. The man cried out and scrambled to his knees, looking wildly about him.

'You have nice dreams?' Ruffy asked pleasantly.

'I wasn't sleeping,' the man protested. 'I was thinking.'

'Well, don't think so loudly,' Ruffy advised him. 'Sounds though you sawing through the bridge with a cross cut.'

Another half hour dragged itself by like a cripple.

'Fires are burning well,' commented Ruffy, and Bruce turned his head and glanced through the loophole in the corrugated iron behind him at the little garden of orange flame-flowers in the darkness.

'Yes, they should last till morning.'

Silence again, with only the singing of the mosquitoes and the rustle of the river as it flowed by the piles of the bridge. Shermaine has my pistol, Bruce remembered with a small trip in his pulse, I should have taken it back from her. He unclipped the bayonet from the muzzle of his rifle, tested the edge of the blade with his thumb, and slid it into the scabbard on his web-belt. Could easily lose the rifle if we start mixing it in the dark, he decided.

'Christ, I'm hungry,' grunted Ruffy beside him.

'You're too fat,' said Bruce. 'The diet will do you good.' And they waited.

Bruce stared down into the hole in the floorboards. His eyes began weaving fantasies out of the darkness, he could see vague shapes that moved, like things seen below the surface of the sea. His stomach tightened and he fought the impulse to shine his flashlight into the hole. He closed his eyes to rest them. I will count slowly to ten, he decided, and then look again.

Ruffy's hand closed on his upper arm; the pressure of his fingers transmitted alarm like a current of electricity. Bruce's eyelids flew open.

'Listen,' breathed Ruffy.

Bruce heard it. The stealthy drip of water on water below them. Then something bumped the bridge, but so softly that he felt rather than heard the jar.

'Yes,' Bruce whispered back. He reached out and tapped the shoulder of the gendarme beside him and the man's body stiffened at his touch.

With his breath scratching his dry throat, Bruce waited until he was sure the warning had been passed to all his men. Then he shifted the weight of his rifle from across his knees and aimed down into the hole.

He drew in a deep breath and switched on the flashlight. The beam shot down and he looked along it over his rifle barrel.

The square aperture in the floorboards formed a frame for the picture that flashed into his eyes. Black bodies, naked, glossy with wetness, weird patterns of tattoo marks, a face staring up at him, broad sloped forehead above startlingly white eyes and flat nose. The long gleaming blade of a panga. Clusters of humanity clinging to the wooden piles like ticks on the legs of a beast. Legs and arms and shiny trunks merged into a single organism, horrible as some slimy sea-creature.

Bruce fired into it. His rifle shuddered against his shoulder and the long orange spurts from its muzzle gave the picture a new flickering horror. The mass of bodies heaved, and struggled like a pack of rats trapped in a dry well. They dropped splashing into the river, swarmed up the timber piles, twisting and writhing as the bullets hit them, screaming, babbling over the sound of the rifle.

Bruce's weapon clicked empty and he groped for a new magazine. Ruffy and his gendarmes were hanging over the guard rails of the bridge, firing downwards, sweeping the piles below them with long bursts, the flashes lighting their faces and outlining their bodies against the sky.

'They're still coming!' roared Ruffy. 'Don't let them get over the side.'

Out of the hole at Bruce's feet thrust the head and naked upper body of a man. There was a panga in his hand; he slashed at Bruce's legs, his eyes glazed in the beam of the flashlight.

Bruce jumped back and the knife missed his knees by inches. The man wormed his way out of the hole towards Bruce. He was screaming shrilly, a high meaningless sound of fury.

Bruce lunged with the barrel of his empty rifle at the contorted black face. All his weight was behind that thrust and the muzzle went into the Baluba's eye. The foresight and four inches of the barrel disappeared into his head, stopping only when it hit bone. Colourless fluid from the burst eyeball gushed from round the protruding steel.

Tugging and twisting, Bruce tried to free the rifle, but the foresight had buried itself like the barb of a fish hook. The Baluba had dropped his panga and was clinging to the rifle barrel with both hands. He was wailing and rolling on his back upon the floorboards, his head jerking every time Bruce tried to pull the muzzle out of his head.

Beyond him the head and shoulders of another Baluba appeared through the aperture.

Bruce dropped his rifle and gathered up the fallen panga; he jumped over the writhing body of the first Baluba and lifted the heavy knife above his head with both hands.

The man was jammed in the hole, powerless to protect himself. He looked up at Bruce and his mouth fell open.

Two-handed, as though he were chopping wood, Bruce swung his whole body into the stroke. The shock jarred his shoulders and he felt blood splatter his legs. The un-tempered blade snapped off at the hilt and stayed imbedded in the Baluba's skull.

Panting heavily, Bruce straightened up and looked wildly about him. Baluba were swarming over the guard rail on one side of the bridge. The starlight glinted on their wet skins. One of his gendarmes was lying in a dark huddle, his head twisted back and his rifle still in his hands. Ruffy and the other gendarmes were still firing down over the far side.

'Ruffy!' shouted Bruce. 'Behind you! They're coming over!' and he dropped the handle of the panga and ran towards the body of the gendarme. He needed that rifle.

Before he could reach it the naked body of a Baluba rushed at him. Bruce ducked under the sweep of the panga and grappled with him. They fell locked together, the man's body slippery and sinuous against him, and the smell of him fetid as rancid butter.

Bruce found the pressure point below the elbow of his knife arm and dug in with his thumb. The Baluba yelled and his panga clattered on the floorboards. Bruce wrapped his arm round the man's neck while with his free hand he reached for his bayonet.

The Baluba was clawing for Bruce's eyes with his fingers, his nails scored the side of Bruce's nose, but Bruce had his bayonet out now. He placed the point against the man's chest and pressed it in. He felt the steel scrape against the bone of a rib and the man redoubled his struggles at the sting of it. Bruce twisted the blade, working it in with his wrist, forcing the man's head backwards with his other arm.

225

The point of the bayonet scraped over the bone and found the gap between. Like taking a virgin, suddenly the resistance to its entrance was gone and it slid home full length. The Baluba's body jerked mechanically and the bayonet twitched in Bruce's fist.

Bruce did not even wait for the man to die. He pulled the blade out against the sucking reluctance of tissue that clung to it and scrambled to his feet in time to see Ruffy pick another Baluba from his feet and hurl him bodily over the guard rail.

Bruce snatched the rifle from the gendarme's dead hands and stepped to the guard rail. They were coming over the side, those below shouting and pushing at the ones above.

Like shooting a row of sparrows from a fence with a shotgun, thought Bruce grimly, and with one long burst he cleared the rail. Then he leaned out and sprayed the piles below the bridge. The rifle was empty. He reloaded with a magazine from his pocket. But it was all over. They were dropping back into the river, the piles below the bridge were clear of men, their heads bobbed away downstream.

Bruce lowered his rifle and looked about him. Three of his gendarmes were killing the man that Bruce had wounded, standing over him and grunting as they thrust down with their bayonets. The man was still wailing.

Bruce looked away.

One horn of the crescent moon showed above the trees; it had a gauzy halo about it.

Bruce lit a cigarette and behind him those gruesome noises ceased.

'Are you okay, boss?'

'Yes, I'm fine. How about you, Ruffy?'

'I got me a terrible thirst now. Hope nobody trod on my pack.'

About four minutes from the first shot to the last, Bruce guessed. That's the way of war, seven hours of waiting and boredom, then four minutes of frantic endeavour. Not only of war either, he thought. The whole of life is like that.

Then he felt the trembling in his thighs and the first spasm of nausea as the reaction started.

'What's happening?' A shout floated across from the laager. Bruce recognized Hendry's voice. 'Is everything all right?'

'We've beaten them off,' Bruce shouted back. 'Everything under control. You can go to sleep again.'

And now I have got to sit down quickly, he told himself.

Except for the tattoos upon his cheeks and forehead the dead Baluba's features were little different from those of the Bambala and Bakuba men who made up the bulk of Bruce's command.

Bruce played the flashlight over the corpse. The arms and legs were thin but stringy with muscle, and the belly bulged out from years of malnutrition. It was an ugly body, gnarled and crabbed. With distaste Bruce moved the light back to the features. The bone of the skull formed harsh angular planes beneath the skin, the nose was flattened and the thick lips had about them a repellent brutality. They were drawn back slightly to reveal the teeth which had been filed to sharp points like those of a shark.

'This is the last one, boss. I'll toss him overboard.' Ruffy spoke in the darkness beside Bruce.

'Good.'

Ruffy heaved and grunted, the corpse splashed below them and Ruffy wiped his hands on the guard rail, then came to sit beside Bruce.

'Goddam apes.' Ruffy's voice was full of the bitter tribal antagonism of Africa. 'When we get shot of these U.N. people there'll be a bit of sorting out to do. They've got a few things to learn, these bloody Baluba.'

And so it goes, thought Bruce, Jew and Gentile, Catholic and Protestant, black and white, Bambala and Baluba.

He checked the time, another two hours to dawn. His nervous reaction from physical violence had abated now; the hand that held the cigarette no longer trembled.

'They won't come again,' said Ruffy. 'You can get some sleep now if you want. I'll keep an eye open, boss.'

'No, thanks. I'll wait with you.' His nerves had not settled down enough for sleep.

'How's it for a beer?'

'Thanks.'

Bruce sipped the beer and stared out at the watch fires round the laager. They had burned down to puddles of red ash but Bruce knew that Ruffy was right. The Baluba would not attack again that night.

'So how do you like freedom?'

'How's that, boss?' The question puzzled Ruffy and he turned to Bruce questioningly.

'How do you like it now the Belgians have gone?'

'It's pretty good, I reckon.'

'And if Tshombe has to give in to the Central Government?'

'Those mad Arabs!' snarled Ruffy. 'All they want is our copper. They're going to have to get up early in the morning to take it. We're in the saddle here.'

The great jousting tournament of the African continent. I'm in the saddle, try to unhorse me! As in all matters of survival it was not a question of ethics and political doctrine (except to the spectators in Whitehall, Moscow, Washington and Peking). There were big days coming, thought Bruce. My own country, when she blows, is going to make Algiers look like an old ladies' sewing circle.

26

Thε sun was up, throwing long shadows out into the clearing, and Bruce stood beside the Ford and looked across the bridge at the corrugated iron shelter on the far bank.

He relaxed for a second and let his mind run unhurriedly over his preparations for the crossing. Was there something left undone, some disposition which could make it more secure?

Hendry and a dozen men were in the shelter across the bridge, ready to meet any attack on that side.

Shermaine would take the Ford across first. Then the lorries would follow her. They would cross empty to minimize the danger of the bridge collapsing, or being weakened for the passage of the tanker. After each lorry had crossed, Hendry would shuttle its load and passengers over in the shelter and deposit them under the safety of the canvas canopy.

The last lorry would go over fully loaded. That was regrettable but unavoidable.

Finally Bruce himself would drive the tanker across. Not as an act of heroism, although it was the most dangerous business of the morning, but because he would trust no one else to do it, not even Ruffy. The five hundred gallons of fuel it contained was their safe-conduct home. Bruce had taken the precaution of filling all the gasoline tanks in the convoy in case of accidents, but they would need replenishing before they reached Msapa Junction.

He looked down at Shermaine in the driver's seat of the Ford.

'Keep it in low gear, take her over slowly but steadily. Whatever else you do, don't stop.'

She nodded. She was composed and she smiled at him. Bruce felt a stirring of pride as he looked at her, so small and lovely, but today she was doing man's work. He went on. 'As soon as you are over, I will send one of the trucks after you. Hendry will put six of his men into it and then come back for the others.'

'Oui, Monsieur Bonaparte.'

'You'll pay for that tonight,' he threatened her. 'Off you go.'

Shermaine let out the clutch and the Ford bounced over rough ground to the road, accelerated smoothly out on to the bridge.

Bruce held his breath, but there was only a slight check and sway as it crossed the repaired section.

'Thank God for that,' Bruce let out his breath and watched while Shermaine drew up alongside the shelter.

'Allez,' Bruce shouted at the coloured engine driver who was ready at the wheel of the first truck. The man smiled his cheerful chubby-faced smile, waved, and the truck rolled forward.

Watching anxiously as it went on to the bridge, Bruce saw the new timbers give perceptibly beneath the weight of the truck, and he heard them creak loudly in protest.

'Not so good,' he muttered.

'No—' agreed Ruffy. 'Boss, why don't you let someone else take the tanker over?'

'We've been over that already,' Bruce answered him without turning his head. Across the river Hendry was transferring his men from the shelter to the back of the truck. Then the shelter started its tedious way back towards them.

Bruce fretted impatiently during the four hours that it took to get four trucks across. The long business was the shuttling back and forth of the corrugated iron shelter, at least ten minutes for each trip.

Finally there was only the fifth truck and the tanker left on the north bank. Bruce started the engine of the tanker and put her into auxiliary low, then he blew a single blast

230

on the horn. The driver of the truck ahead of him waved an acknowledgement and pulled forward.

The truck reached the bridge and went out into the middle. It was fully loaded, twenty men aboard. It came to the repaired section and slowed down, almost stopping.

'Go on! Keep it going, damn you,' Bruce shouted in impotent anger. The fool of a driver was forgetting his orders. He crawled forward and the bridge gave alarmingly under the full weight, the high canopied roof rocked crazily, and even above the rumble of his own engine Bruce could hear the protesting groan of the bridge timbers.

'The fool, oh, the bloody fool,' whispered Bruce to himself. Suddenly he felt very much alone and unprotected here on the north bank with the bridge being mutilated by the incompetence of the truck driver. He started the tanker moving.

Ahead of him the other driver had panicked. He was racing his engine, the rear wheels spun viciously, blue smoke of scorched tyres, and one of the floorboards tore loose. Then the truck lurched forward and roared up the south bank.

Bruce hesitated, applying the brakes and bringing the tanker to a standstill on the threshold of the bridge.

He thought quickly. The sensible thing would be to repair the damage to the bridge before chancing it with the weight of the tanker. But that would mean another day's delay. None of them had eaten since the previous morning. Was he justified in gambling against even odds, for that's what they were? A fifty-fifty chance, heads you get across, tails you dump the tanker in the middle of the river.

Then unexpectedly the decision was made for him.

From across the river a Bren gun started firing. Bruce jumped in his seat and looked up. Then a dozen other guns joined in and the tracer flew past the tanker. They were firing across towards him, close on each side of him. Bruce struggled to drag from his uncomprehending brain an explanation of this new development. Suddenly everything was moving too swiftly. Everything was confusion and chaos.

Movement in the rear-view mirror of the tanker caught his eye. He stared at it blankly. Then he twisted quickly in his seat and looked back.

'Christ!' he swore with fright.

From the edge of the jungle on both sides of the clearing Baluba were swarming into the open. Hundreds of them running towards him, the animal-skin kilts swirling about their legs, feather headdresses fluttering, sun bright on the long blades of their pangas. An arrow rang dully against the metal body of the tanker.

Bruce revved the engine, gripped the wheel hard with both hands and took the tanker out on to the bridge. Above the sound of the guns he could hear the shrill ululation, the excited squealing of two hundred Baluba. It sounded very close, and he snatched a quick look in the mirror. What he saw nearly made him lose his head and give the tanker full throttle. The nearest Baluba, screened from the guns on the south bank by the tanker's bulk, was only ten paces away. So close that Bruce could see the tattoo marks on his face and chest.

With an effort Bruce restrained his right foot from pressing down too hard, and instead he bore down on the repaired section of the bridge at a sedate twenty miles an hour. He tried to close his mind to the squealing behind him and the thunder of gunfire ahead of him.

The front wheels hit the new timbers, and above the other sounds he heard them groan loudly, and felt them sag under him.

The tanker rolled on and the rear wheels brought their weight to bear. The groan of wood became a cracking, rending sound. The tanker slowed as the bridge subsided, its wheels spun without purchase, it tilted sideways, no longer moving forward.

A sharp report, as one of the main trusses broke, and Bruce felt the tanker drop sharply at the rear; its nose pointed upwards and it started to slide back.

'Get out!' his brain shrieked at him. 'Get out, it's falling!' He reached for the door handle beside him, but at that moment the bridge collapsed completely. The tanker rolled off the edge.

Bruce was hurled across the cab with a force that stunned him, his legs wedged under the passenger seat and his arms tangled in the strap of his rifle. The tanker fell free and Bruce felt his stomach swoop up and press against his chest as though he rode a giant roller coaster.

The sickening drop lasted only an instant, and then the tanker hit the river. Immediately the sounds of gunfire and the screaming of Baluba were drowned out as the tanker disappeared below the surface. Through the windscreen Bruce saw now the cool cloudy green of water, as though he looked into the windows of an aquarium. With a gentle rocking motion the tanker sank down through the green water.

'Oh, my God, not this!' He spoke aloud as he struggled up from the floor of the cab. His ears were filled with the hiss and belch of escaping air bubbles; they rose in silver clouds past the windows.

The truck was still sinking, and Bruce felt the pain in his eardrums as the pressure built up inside the cab. He opened his mouth and swallowed convulsively, and his eardrums squeaked as the pressure equalized and the pain abated. Water was squirting in through the floor of the cab and jets of it spurted out of the instrument panel of the dashboard. The cab was flooding.

Bruce twisted the handle of the door beside him and hit it with his shoulder. It would not budge an inch. He flung all his weight against it, anchoring his feet on the dashboard and straining until he felt his eyeballs starting out of their sockets. It was jammed solid by the immense pressure of water on the outside.

'The windscreen,' he shouted aloud. 'Break the windscreen.' He groped for his rifle. The cab had flooded to his waist as he sat in the passenger's seat. He found the rifle and brought it dripping to his shoulder. He touched the muzzle to the windscreen and almost fired. But his good sense warned him.

Clearly he saw the danger of firing. The concussion in the confined cab would burst his eardrums, and the avalanche of broken glass that would be thrown into his face by the water pressure outside would certainly blind and maim him.

He lowered the rifle despondently. He felt his panic being slowly replaced by the cold certainty of defeat. He was trapped fifty feet below the surface of the river. There was no way out.

He thought of turning the rifle on himself, ending the inevitable, but he rejected the idea almost as soon as it had formed. Not that way, never that way!

He flogged his mind, driving it out of the cold lethargic clutch of certain death. There must be something. Think! Damn you, think!

The tanker was still rocking; it had not yet settled into the ooze of the river bottom. How long had he been under? About twenty seconds. Surely it should have hit the bottom long ago.

Unless! Bruce felt hope surge into new life within him. The tank! By God, that was it.

The great, almost empty tank behind him! The five-thousand-gallon tank which now contained only four hundred gallons of gasoline – it would have a displacement of nearly eighteen tons! It would float.

As if in confirmation of his hope, he felt his eardrums creak and pop. The pressure was falling! He was rising.

Bruce stared out at green water through the glass. The silver clouds of bubbles no longer streamed upwards; they seemed to hang outside the cab. The tanker had overcome the initial impetus that had driven it far below the surface, and now it was floating upwards at the same rate of ascent as its bubbles.

The dark green of deep water paled slowly to the colour of Chartreuse. And Bruce laughed. It was a gasping hysterical giggle and the sound of it shocked him. He cut it off abruptly.

The tanker bobbed out on to the surface, water streamed from the windscreen and through it Bruce caught a misty distorted glimpse of the south bank.

He twisted the door handle and this time the door burst open readily, water poured into the cab and Bruce floundered out against its rush.

With one quick glance he took in his position. The tanker had floated down twenty yards below the bridge, the guns on the south bank had fallen silent, and he could see no Baluba on the north bank. They must have disappeared back into the jungle.

Bruce plunged into the river and struck out for the south bank. Vaguely he heard the thin high shouts of encouragement from his gendarmes.

Within a dozen strokes he knew he was in difficulties. The drag of his boots and his sodden uniform was enormous. Treading water he tore off his steel helmet and let it sink. Then he tried to struggle out of his battle-jacket. It clung to his arms and chest and he disappeared under the surface four times before he finally got rid of it. He had breathed water into his lungs and his legs were tired and heavy.

The south bank was too far away. He would never make it. Coughing painfully he changed his objective and struck upstream against the current towards the bridge.

He felt himself settling lower in the water; he had to force his arms to lift and fall forward into each stroke.

Something plopped into the water close beside him. He paid no attention to it; suddenly a sense of disinterest had come over him, the first stage of drowning. He mistimed a breath and sucked in more water. The pain of it goaded him into a fresh burst of coughing. He hung in the water, gasping and hacking painfully.

Again something plopped close by, and this time he lifted his head. An arrow floated past him – then they began dropping steadily about him.

Baluba hidden in the thick bush above the beach were shooting at him; a gentle pattering rain of arrows splashed around his head. Bruce started swimming again, clawing his way frantically upstream. He swam until he could no longer lift his arms clear of the surface and the weight of his boots dragged his feet down.

Again he lifted his head. The bridge was close, not thirty feet away, but he knew that those thirty feet were as good as thirty miles. He could not make it.

The arrows that fell about him were no longer a source of terror. He thought of them only with mild irritation.

Why the hell can't they leave me alone? I don't want to play any more. I just want to relax. I'm so tired, so terribly tired.

He stopped moving and felt the water rise up coolly over his mouth and nose.

'Hold on, boss. I'm coming.' The shout penetrated through the grey fog of Bruce's drowning brain. He kicked and his head rose once more above the surface. He looked up at the bridge.

Stark naked, big belly swinging with each pace, thick legs flying, the great dangling bunch of his genitals bouncing merrily, black as a charging hippopotamus, Sergeant Major Ruffararo galloped out along the bridge.

He reached the fallen section and hauled himself up on to the guard rail. The arrows were falling around him, hissing down like angry insects. One glanced off his shoulder

236

without penetrating and Ruffy shrugged at it, then launched himself up and out, falling in an ungainly heap of arms and legs to hit the water with a splash.

'Where the hell are you, boss?'

Bruce croaked a water-strangled reply and Ruffy came ploughing down towards him with clumsy overarm strokes.

He reached Bruce.

'Always playing around,' he grunted. 'Guess some guys never learn!' His fist closed on a handful of Bruce's hair.

Struggling unavailingly Bruce felt his head tucked firmly under Ruffy's arm and he was dragged through the water. Occasionally his face came out long enough to suck a breath but mostly he was under water. Consciousness receded and he felt himself going, going.

His head bumped against something hard but he was too weak to reach out his hand.

'Wake up, boss. You can have a sleep later.' Ruffy's voice bellowed in his ear. He opened his eyes and saw beside him the pile of the bridge.

'Come on. I can't carry you up here.'

Ruffy had worked round the side of the pile, shielding them from arrows, but the current was strong here, tugging at their bodies. Without the strength to prevent it Bruce's head rolled sideways and his face flopped forward into the water.

'Come on, wake up.' With a stinging slap Ruffy's open hand hit Bruce across the cheek. The shock roused him, he coughed and a mixture of water and vomit shot up his throat and out of his mouth and nose. Then he blenched painfully and retched again.

'How's it feel now?' Ruffy demanded.

Bruce lifted a hand from the water and wiped his mouth. He felt much better.

'Okay? Can you make it?'

Bruce nodded.

'Let's go then.'

With Ruffy dragging and pushing him, he worked his way up the pile. Water poured from his clothing as his body emerged, his hair was plastered across his forehead and he could feel each breath gurgle in his lungs.

'Listen boss. When we get to the top we'll be in the open again. There'll be more arrows – not time to sit around and chat. We're going over the rail fast and then run like hell, okay?'

Bruce nodded again. Above him were the floorboards of the bridge. With one hand he reached up and caught an upright of the guard rail, and he hung there without strength to pull himself the rest of the way.

'Hold it there,' grunted Ruffy and wriggled his shiny wet bulk up and over.

The arrows started falling again; one pegged into the wood six inches from Bruce's face and stood there quivering. Slowly Bruce's grip relaxed. I can't hold on, he thought, I'm going.

Then Ruffy's hand closed on his wrist, he felt himself dragged up, his legs dangled. He hung suspended by one arm and the water swirled smoothly past twenty feet below.

Slowly he was drawn upwards, his chest scraped over the guard rail, tearing his shirt, then he tumbled over it into an untidy heap on the bridge.

Vaguely he heard the guns firing on the south bank, the flit and thump of the arrows, and Ruffy's voice.

'Come on, boss. Get up.'

He felt himself being lifted and dragged along. With his legs boneless soft under him, he staggered beside Ruffy. Then there were no more arrows; the timbers of the bridge became solid earth under his feet. Voices and hands on him. He was being lifted, then lowered face down on to the wooden floor of a truck. The rhythmic pressure on his chest as someone started artificial respiration above him, the warm gush of water up his throat, and Shermaine's voice. He could not understand what she was saying, but just the sound of it was enough to make him realize he was safe. Darkly through the fog he became aware that her voice was the most important sound in his life.

He vomited again.

Hesitantly at first, and then swiftly, Bruce came back from the edge of oblivion.

'That's enough,' he mumbled and rolled out from under Sergeant Jacque who was administering the artificial respiration. The movement started a fresh paroxysm of coughing and he felt Shermaine's hands on his shoulders restraining him.

'Bruce, you must rest.'

'No.' He struggled into a sitting position. 'We've got to get out into the open,' he gasped.

'No hurry, boss. We've left all the Balubes on the other bank. There's a river between us.'

'How do you know?' Bruce challenged him.

'Well—'

'You don't!' Bruce told him flatly. 'There could easily be another few hundred on this side.' He coughed again painfully and then went on. 'We're leaving in five minutes, get them ready.'

'Okay.' Ruffy turned to leave.

'Ruffy!'

'Boss?' He turned back expectantly.

'Thank you.'

Ruffy grinned self-consciously. ''At's all right. I needed a wash anyway.'

'I'll buy you a drink when we get home.'

'I won't forget,' Ruffy warned him, and climbed down out of the truck. Bruce heard him shouting to his boys.

'I thought I'd lost you.' Shermaine's arm was still round his shoulders and Bruce looked at her for the first time.

'My sweet girl, you won't get rid of me that easily,' he assured her. He was feeling much better now.

'Bruce, I want to – I can't explain—' Unable to find the

words she leaned forward instead and kissed him, full on the mouth.

When they drew apart, Sergeant Jacque and the two gendarmes with him were grinning delightedly.

'There is nothing wrong with you now, Captain.'

'No, there isn't,' Bruce agreed. 'Make your preparations for departure.'

From the passenger seat of the Ford Bruce took one last look at the bridge.

The repaired section hung like a broken drawbridge into the water. Beyond it on the far bank were scattered a few dead Baluba, like celluloid dolls in the sunlight. Far downstream the gasoline tanker had been washed by the current against the beach. It lay on its side, half-submerged in the shallows and the white Shell insignia showed clearly.

And the river flowed on, green and inscrutable, with the jungle pressing close along its banks.

'Let's get away from here,' said Bruce.

Shermaine started the engine and the convoy of trucks followed them along the track through the belt of thick river bush and into the open forest again.

Bruce looked at his watch. The inside of the glass was dewed with moisture and he lifted it to his ear.

'Damn thing has stopped. What's your time?'

'Twenty minutes to one.'

'Half the day wasted,' Bruce grumbled.

'Will we reach Msapa Junction before dark?'

'No, we won't. For two good reasons. Firstly, it's too far, and secondly, we haven't enough gas.'

'What are you going to do?' Her voice was unruffled, already she had complete faith in him. I wonder how long it will last, he mused cynically. At first you're a god. You have not a single human weakness. They set a standard for you, and the standard is perfection. Then the first time you fall short of it, their whole world blows up.

'We'll think of something,' he assured her.

'I'm sure you will,' she agreed complacently and Bruce grinned. The big joke, of course, was that when she said it he also believed it. Damned if being in love doesn't make you feel one hell of a man.

He changed to English so as to exclude the two gendarmes in the back seat from the conversation.

'You are the best thing that has happened to me in thirty years.'

'Oh, Bruce.' She turned her face towards him and the expression of trusting love in it and the intensity of his own emotion struck Bruce like a physical blow.

I will keep this thing alive, he vowed. I must nourish it with care and protect it from the dangers of selfishness and familiarity.

'Oh, Bruce, I do love you so terribly much. This morning when – when I thought I had lost you, when I saw the tanker go over into the river—' She swallowed and now her eyes were full of tears. 'It was as though the light had gone – it was so dark, so dark and cold without you.'

Absorbed with him so that she had forgotten about the road, Shermaine let the Ford veer and the offside wheels pumped into the rough verge.

'Hey, watch it!' Bruce cautioned her. 'Dearly as I love you also, I have to admit that you're a lousy driver. Let me take her.'

'Do you feel up to it?'

'Yes, pull into the side.'

Slowly, held to the speed of the lumbering vehicles behind them, they drove on through the afternoon. Twice they passed deserted Baluba villages beside the road, the grass huts disintegrating and the small cultivated lands about them thickly overgrown.

241

'My God, I'm hungry. I've got a headache from it and my belly feels as though it's full of warm water,' complained Bruce.

'Don't think you're the only one. This is the strictest diet I've ever been on, must have lost two kilos! But I always lose in the wrong place, never on my bottom.'

'Good,' Bruce said. 'I like it just the way it is, never shed an ounce there.' He looked over his shoulder at the two gendarmes. 'Are you hungry?' he asked in French.

'Mon Dieu!' exclaimed the fat one. 'I will not be able to sleep tonight, if I must lie on an empty stomach.'

'Perhaps it will not be necessary.' Bruce let his eyes wander off the road into the surrounding bush. The character of the country had changed in the last hundred miles. 'This looks like game country. I've noticed plenty of spoor on the road. Keep your eyes open.'

The trees were tall and widely spaced with grass growing beneath them. Their branches did not interlock so that the sky showed through. At intervals there were open glades filled with green swamp grass and thickets of bamboo and ivory palms.

'We've got another half hour of daylight. We might run into something before then.'

In the rear-view mirror he watched the lumbering column of transports for a moment. They must be almost out of gasoline by now, hardly enough for another half hour's driving. There were compensations however; at least they were in open country now and only eighty miles from Msapa Junction.

He glanced at the petrol gauge – half the tank. The Ranchero still had sufficient to get through even if the trucks were almost dry.

Of course! That was the answer. Find a good camp, leave the convoy, and go on in the Ford to find help. Without the trucks to slow him down he could get through to Msapa Junction in two hours. There was a telegraph in the station office, even if the junction was still deserted.

'We'll stop on the other side of this stream,' said Bruce and slowed the Ford, changed into second gear and let it idle down the steep bank.

The stream was shallow. The water hardly reached the hubcaps as they bumped across the rocky bottom. Bruce gunned the Ford up the far bank into the forest again.

'There!' shouted one of the gendarmes from the back seat and Bruce followed the direction of his arm.

Standing with humped shoulders, close beside the road, bunched together with mournfully drooping horns, heads held low beneath the massive bosses, bodies very big and black, were two old buffalo bulls.

Bruce hit the brakes, skidding the Ranchero to a stop, reaching for his rifle at the same instant. He twisted the door handle, hit the door with his shoulder and tumbled out on to his feet.

With a snort and a toss of their ungainly heads the buffalo started to run.

Bruce picked the leader and aimed for the neck in front of the plunging black shoulder. Leaning forward against the recoil of the rifle he fired and heard the bullet strike with a meaty thump. The bull slowed, breaking his run. The stubby forelegs settled and he slid forward on his nose, rolling as he fell, dust and legs kicking.

Turning smoothly without taking the butt from his shoulder, swinging with the run of the second bull, Bruce fired again, and again the thump of bullet striking.

The buffalo stumbled, giving in the legs, then he steadied and galloped on like a grotesque rocking horse, patches of baldness grey on his flanks, big-bellied, running heavily.

Bruce shifted the bead of the foresight on to his shoulder and fired twice in quick succession, aiming low for the heart, hitting each time, the bull so close he could see the bullet wounds appear on the dark skin.

The gallop broke into a trot, with head swinging low, mouth open, legs beginning to fold. Aiming carefully for the head Bruce fired again. The bull bellowed – a sad lonely sound – and collapsed into the grass.

The lorries had stopped in a line behind the Ford, and now from each of them swarmed black men. Jabbering happily, racing each other, they streamed past Bruce to where the buffalo had fallen in the grass beside the road.

'Nice shooting, boss,' applauded Ruffy. 'I'm going to have me a piece of tripe the size of a blanket.'

'Let's make camp first.' Bruce's ears were still singing with gunfire. 'Get the lorries into a ring.'

'I'll see to it.'

Bruce walked up to the nearest buffalo and watched for a while as a dozen men strained to roll it on to its back and begin butchering it. There were clusters of grape-blue ticks in the folds of skin between the legs and body.

A good head, he noted mechanically, forty inches at least.

'Plenty of meat, Captain. Tonight we eat thick!' grinned one of his gendarmes as he bent over the huge body to begin flensing.

'Plenty,' agreed Bruce and turned back to the Ranchero. In the heat of the kill it was a good feeling: the rifle's kick and your stomach screwed up with excitement. But afterwards you felt a little bit dirtied; sad and guilty as you do after lying with a woman you do not love.

He climbed into the car and Shermaine sat away from him, withdrawn.

'They were so big and ugly – beautiful,' she said softly.

'We needed the meat. I didn't kill them for fun.' But he thought with a little shame, I have killed many others for fun.

'Yes,' she agreed. 'We needed the meat.'

He turned the car off the road and signalled to the truck drivers to pull in behind him.

27

Later it was all right again. The meat-rich smoke from a dozen cooking fires drifted across the camp. The dark tree tops silhouetted against a sky full of stars, the friendly glow of the fires, and laughter, men's voices raised, someone singing, the night noises of the bush – insects and frogs in the nearby stream – a plate piled high with grilled fillets and slabs of liver, a bottle of beer from Ruffy's hoard, the air at last cooler, a small breeze to keep the mosquitoes away, and Shermaine sitting beside him on the blankets.

Ruffy drifted across to them, in one hand a stick loaded with meat from which the juice dripped and in the other hand a bottle held by the throat.

'How's it for another beer, boss?'

'Enough.' Bruce held up his hand. 'I'm full to the back teeth.'

'You're getting old, that's for sure. Me and the boys going to finish them buffalo or burst trying.' He squatted on his great haunches and his tone changed. 'The trucks are flat, boss. Reckon there's not a bucketful of gas in the lot of them.'

'I want you to drain all the tanks, Ruffy, and pour it into the Ford.'

Ruffy nodded and bit a hunk of meat off the end of the stick.

'Then first thing tomorrow morning you and I will go on to Msapa in the Ranchero and leave everyone else here. Lieutenant Hendry will be in charge.'

'You talking about me?' Wally came from one of the fires.

'Yes, I'm going to leave you in charge here while Ruffy and I go on to Msapa Junction to fetch help.' Bruce did not look at Hendry and he had difficulty keeping the loathing out of his voice. 'Ruffy, fetch the map will you?'

They spread it on the earth and huddled round it. Ruffy held the flashlight.

'I'd say we are about here.' Bruce touched the tiny black vein of the road. 'About seventy, eighty miles to Msapa.' He ran his finger along it. 'It will take us about five hours there and back. However, if the telegraph isn't working we might have to go on until we meet a patrol or find some other way of getting a message back to Elisabethville.'

Almost parallel to the road and only two inches from it on the large-scale map ran the thick red line that marked the Northern Rhodesian border. Wally Hendry's slitty eyes narrowed even further as he looked at it.

'Why not leave Ruffy here, and I'll go with you.' Hendry looked up at Bruce.

'I want Ruffy with me to translate if we meet any Africans along the way.' Also, thought Bruce, I don't want to be left on the side of the road with a bullet in my head while you drive on to Elisabethville.

'Suits me,' grunted Hendry. He dropped his eyes to the map. About forty miles to the border. A hard day's walk.

Bruce changed to French and spoke swiftly. 'Ruffy, hide the diamonds behind the dashboard of your truck. That way we are certain they will send a rescue party, even if we have to go Elisabethville.'

'Talk English, Bucko,' growled Hendry, but Ruffy nodded and answered, also in French.

'I will leave Sergeant Jacque to guard them.'

'NO!' said Bruce. 'Tell no one.'

'Cut it out!' rasped Hendry. 'Anything you say I want to hear.'

'We'll leave at dawn tomorrow,' Bruce reverted to English.

'May I go with you?' Shermaine spoke for the first time.

'I don't see why not.' Bruce smiled quickly at her, but Ruffy coughed awkwardly.

'Reckon that's not such a good idea, boss.'

'Why?' Bruce turned on him with his temper starting to rise.

'Well, boss,' Ruffy hesitated, and then went on, 'you, me and the lady all shoving off towards Elisabethville might not look so good to the boys. They might get ideas, think we're not coming back or something.'

Bruce was silent, considering it.

'That's right,' Hendry cut in. 'You might just take it into your head to keep going. Let her stay, sort of guarantee for the rest of us.'

'I don't mind, Bruce. I didn't think about it that way. I'll stay.'

'She'll have forty good boys looking after her, she'll be all right,' Ruffy assured Bruce.

'All right then, that's settled. It won't be for long, Shermaine.'

'I'll go and see about draining the trucks.' Ruffy stood up. 'See you in the morning, boss.'

'I'm going to get some more of that meat.' Wally picked up the map carelessly. 'Try and get some sleep tonight, Curry. Not too much grumble and grunt.'

In his exasperation, Bruce did not notice that Hendry had taken the map.

– 28 –

It rained in the early hours before the dawn and Bruce lay in the back of the Ranchero and listened to it drum on the metal roof. It was a lulling sound and a good feeling to lie warmly listening to the rain with the woman you love in your arms.

He felt her waking against him, the change in her breathing and the first slow movements of her body.

There were buffalo steaks for breakfast, but no coffee. They ate swiftly and then Bruce called across to Ruffy.

'Okay, Ruffy?'

'Let's go, boss.' They climbed into the Ford and Ruffy filled most of the seat beside Bruce. His helmet perched on the back of his head, rifle sticking out through the space where the windscreen should have been, and two large feet planted securely on top of the case of beer on the floor.

Bruce twisted the key and the engine fired. He warmed it at a fast idle and turned to Hendry who leaned against the roof of the Ford and peered through the window.

'We'll be back this afternoon. Don't let anybody wander away from camp.'

'Okay.' Hendry breathed his morning breath full into Bruce's face.

'Keep them busy, otherwise they'll get bored and start fighting.'

Before he answered Hendry let his eyes search the interior of the Ford carefully and then he stood back.

'Okay,' he said again. 'On your way!'

Bruce looked beyond him to where Shermaine sat on the tailboard of a truck and smiled at her.

'Bon voyage!' she called and Bruce let out the clutch. They bumped out on to the road amid a chorus of cheerful farewells from the gendarmes round the cooking fires and Bruce settled down to drive. In the rear-view mirror he watched the camp disappear round the curve in the road. There were puddles of rainwater in the road, but above them the clouds had broken up and scattered across the sky.

'How's it for a beer, boss?'

'Instead of coffee?' asked Bruce.

'Nothing like it for the bowels,' grunted Ruffy and reached down to open the case.

Wally Hendry lifted his helmet and scratched his scalp. His short red hair felt stiff and wiry with dried sweat and there was a spot above his right ear that itched. He fingered it tenderly.

The Ranchero disappeared round a bend in the road, the trees screening it abruptly, and the hum of its motor faded.

Okay, so they haven't taken the diamonds with them. I had a bloody good look around. I guessed they'd leave them. The girl knows where they are like as not. Perhaps – no, she'd squeal like a stuck pig if I asked.

Hendry looked sideways at Shermaine; she was staring after the Ranchero.

Silly bitch! Getting all broody now that Curry's giving her the rod. Funny how these educated Johnnies like their women to have small tits – nice piece of arse though. Wouldn't mind a bit of that myself. Jesus, that would really get to Mr High Class Bloody Curry, me giving his pretty the business. Not a chance though. These niggers think he's a god or something. They'd tear me to pieces if I touched her. Forget about it! Let's get the diamonds and take off for the border.

Hendry settled his helmet back on to his head and strolled casually across to the truck that Ruffy had been driving the day before.

Got a map, compass, coupla spare clips of ammo – now all we need is the glass.

He climbed into the cab and opened the cubby hole.

Bet a pound to a pinch of dung that they've hidden them somewhere in this truck. They're not worried – think they've got me tied up here. Never occurred to them that old Uncle Wally might up and walk away. Thought I'd just sit here and wait for them to come back and fetch me –

take me in and hand me over to a bunch of nigger police aching to get their hands on a white man.

Well, I got news for you, Mr Fancy-talking Curry!

He rummaged in the cubbyhole and then slammed it shut.

Okay, they're not there. Let's try under the seats. The border is not guarded, might take me three or four days to get through to Fort Rosebery, but when I do I'll have me a pocket full of diamonds and there's a direct air service out to Ndola and the rest of the world. Then we start living!

There was nothing under the seats except a greasy dust-coated jack and wheel spanner. Hendry turned his attention to the floorboards.

Pity I'll have to leave that bastard Curry. I had plans for him. There's a guy who really gets to me. So goddam cocksure of himself. One of them. Makes you feel you're shit – fancy talk, pretty face, soft hands. Christ, I hate him.

Viciously he tore the rubber mats off the floor and the dust made him cough.

Been to university, makes him think he's something special. The bastard. I should have fixed him long ago – that night at the road bridge I nearly gave it to him in the dark. Nobody would have known, just a mistake. I shoulda done it then. I shoulda done it at Port Reprieve when he ran out across the road to the office block. Big bloody hero. Big lover. Bet he had everything he ever wanted, bet his Daddy gave him all the money he could use. And he looks at you like that, like you crawled out of rotting meat.

Hendry straightened up and gripped the steering wheel, his jaws chewing with the strength of his hatred. He stared out of the windscreen.

Shermaine Cartier walked past the front of the truck. She had a towel and a pink plastic toilet bag in her hand; the pistol swung against her leg as she moved.

Sergeant Jacque stood up from the cooking fire and

moved to intercept her. They talked, arguing, then Shermaine touched the pistol at her side and laughed. A worried frown creased Jacque's black face and he shook his head dubiously. Shermaine laughed again, turned from him and set off down the road towards the stream. Her hair, caught carelessly at her neck with a ribbon, hung down her back on to the rose-coloured shirt she wore and the heavy canvas holster emphasized the unconsciously provocative swing of her hips. She went out of sight down the steep bank of the stream.

Wally Hendry chuckled and then licked his lips with the quick-darting tip of his tongue.

'This is going to make it perfect,' he whispered. 'They couldn't have done things to suit me better if they'd spent a week working it out.'

Eagerly he turned back to his search for the diamonds. Leaning forward he thrust his hand up behind the dashboard of the truck and it brushed against the bunch of canvas bags that hung from the mass of concealed wires.

'Come to Uncle Wally.' He jerked them loose and, holding them in his lap, began checking their contents. The third bag he opened contained the gem stones.

'Lovely, lovely grub,' he whispered at the dull glint and sparkle in the depths of the bag. Then he closed the drawstring, stuffed the bag into the pocket of his battle-jacket and buttoned the flap. He dropped the bags of industrial diamonds on to the floor and kicked them under the seat, picked up his rifle and stepped down out of the truck.

Three or four gendarmes looked up curiously at him as he passed the cooking fires. Hendry rubbed his stomach and pulled a face.

'Too much meat last night!'

The gendarme who understood English laughed and translated into French. They all laughed and one of them called something in a dialect that Hendry did not understand. They watched him walk away among the trees.

As soon as he was out of sight of the camp Hendry started to run, circling back towards the stream.

'This is going to be a pleasure!' He laughed aloud.

– 29 –

Fifty yards below the drift where the road crossed the stream Shermaine found a shallow pool. There were reeds with fluffy heads around it and a small beach of white river sand, black boulders, polished round and glossy smooth, the water almost blood warm and so clear that she could see a shoal of fingerlings nibbling at the green algae that coated the boulders beneath the surface.

She stood barefooted in the sand and looked around carefully, but the reeds screened her, and she had asked Jacque not to let any of his men come down to the river while she was there.

She undressed, dropped her clothes across one of the black boulders and with a cake of soap in her hand waded out into the pool and lowered herself until she sat with the water up to her neck and the sand pleasantly rough under her naked behind.

She washed her hair first and then lay stretched out with the water moving gently over her, soft as the caress of silk. Growing bold the tiny fish darted in and nibbled at her skin, tickling, so that she gasped and splashed at them.

At last she ducked her head under the surface and, with the water streaming out of her hair into her eyes, she groped her way back to the bank.

As she stooped, still half blinded, for her towel Wally Hendry's hand closed over her mouth and his other arm circled her waist from behind.

'One squeak out of you and I'll wring your bloody neck.' He spoke hoarsely into her ear. She could smell his breath, warm and sour in her face. 'Just pretend I'm old Bruce – then both of us will enjoy it.' And he chuckled.

Sliding quickly over her hip his hand moved downwards and the shock of it galvanized her into frantic struggles. Holding her easily Hendry kept on chuckling.

She opened her mouth suddenly and one of his fingers went in between her teeth. She bit with all her strength and felt the skin break and tasted blood in her mouth.

'You bitch!' Hendry jerked his hand away and she opened her mouth to scream, but the hand swung back, clenched, into the side of her face, knocking her head across. The scream never reached her lips for he hit her again and she felt herself falling.

Stunned by the blows, lying in the sand, she could not believe it was happening, until she felt his weight upon her and his knee forced cruelly between hers.

Then she started to struggle again, trying to twist away from his mouth and the smell of his breath.

'No, no, no.' She repeated it over and over, her eyes shut tightly so she did not have to see that face above her, and her head rolling from side to side in the sand. He was so strong, so immensely powerful.

'No,' she said, and then, 'Ooah!' at the pain, the tearing stinging pain within, and the thrusting heaviness above.

And through the pounding, grunting, thrusting nightmare she could smell him and feel the sweat drip from him and splash into her upturned unprotected face.

It lasted forever, and then suddenly the weight was gone and she opened her eyes.

He stood over her, fumbling with his clothing, and there was a dullness in his expression. He wiped his mouth with the back of his hand and she saw the fingers were trembling. His voice when he spoke was tired and disinterested.

'I've had better.'

Swiftly Shermaine rolled over and reached for the pistol

that lay on top of her clothes. Hendry stepped forward with all his weight on her wrist and she felt the bones bend under his boot and she moaned. But through pain she whispered. 'You pig, you filthy pig,' and he hit her again, flat-handed across the face, knocking her on to her back once more.

He picked up the pistol and opened it, spilling the cartridges into the sand, then he unclipped the lanyard and threw the pistol far out into the reed bed.

'Tell Curry I say he can have my share of you,' he said and walked quickly away among the reeds.

The white sand coated her damp body like icing sugar. She sat up slowly holding her wrist, the side of her face inflamed and starting to swell where he had hit her.

She started to cry, shaking silently, and the tears squeezed out between her eyelids and matted her long dark lashes.

– 30 –

Ruffy held up the brown bottle and inspected it ruefully.

'Seems like one mouthful and it's empty.' He threw the bottle out of the side window. It hit a tree and burst with a small pop.

'We can always find our way back by following the empties,' smiled Bruce, once more marvelling at the man's capacity. But there was plenty of storage space. He watched Ruffy's stomach spread on to his lap as he reached down to the beer crate.

'How we doing, boss?'

Bruce glanced at the milometer.

'We've come eighty-seven miles,' and Ruffy nodded.

'Not bad going. Be there pretty soon now.'

They were silent. The wind blew in on to them through

the open front. The grass that grew between the tracks brushed the bottom of the chassis with a continuous rushing sound.

'Boss—' Ruffy spoke at last.

'Yes?'

'Lieutenant Hendry – those diamonds. You reckon we did a good thing leaving him there?'

'He's stranded in the middle of the bush. Even if he did find them they wouldn't do him much good.'

'Suppose that's right.' Ruffy lifted the beer bottle to his lips and when he lowered it he went on. 'Mind you, that's one guy you can never be sure of.' He tapped his head with a finger as thick and as black as a blood-sausage. 'Something wrong with him – he's one of the maddest Arabs I've found in a long time of looking.'

Bruce grunted grimly.

'You want to be careful there, boss,' observed Ruffy. 'Any time now he's going to try for you. I've seen it coming. He's working himself up to it. He's a mad Arab.'

'I'll watch him,' said Bruce.

'Yeah, you do that.'

Again they were silent in the steady swish of the wind and the drone of the motor.

'There's a railway.' Ruffy pointed to the blue-gravelled embankment through the trees.

'Nearly there,' said Bruce.

They came out into another open glade and beyond it the water tank of Msapa Junction stuck up above the forest.

'Here we are,' said Ruffy and drained the bottle in his hand.

'Just say a prayer that the telegraph lines are still up and that there's an operator on the Elisabethville end.'

Bruce slowed the Ford past the row of cottages. They were exactly as he remembered them, deserted and forlorn. The corners of his mouth were compressed into a hard angle as he looked at the two small mounds of earth beneath the

255

casia flora trees. Ruffy looked at them also but neither of them spoke.

Bruce stopped the Ford outside the station building and they climbed out stiffly and walked together on to the verandah. The wooden flooring echoed dully under their boots as they made for the door of the office.

Bruce pushed the door open and looked in. The walls were painted a depressing utility green, loose paper was scattered on the floor, the drawers of the single desk hung open, and a thin grey skin of dust coated everything.

'There she is,' said Ruffy and pointed to the brass and varnished wood complexity of the telegraph on a table against the far wall.

'Looks all right,' said Bruce. 'As long as the lines haven't been cut.'

As if to reassure him, the telegraph began to clatter like a typewriter.

'Thank God for that,' sighed Bruce.

They walked across to the table.

'You know how to work this thing?' asked Ruffy.

'Sort of,' Bruce answered and set his rifle against the wall. He was relieved to see a Morse table stuck with adhesive tape to the wall above the apparatus. It was a long time since he had memorized it as a boy scout.

He laid his hand on the transmission key and studied the table. The call sign for Elisabethville was 'EE'.

He tapped it out clumsily and then waited. Almost immediately the set clattered back at him, much too fast to be intelligible and the roll of paper in the repeater was exhausted. Bruce took off his helmet and laboriously spelled out, 'Transmit slower.'

It was a long business with requests for repetition. 'Not understood' was made nearly every second signal, but finally Bruce got the operator to understand that he had an urgent message for Colonel Franklyn of President Tshombe's staff.

'Wait,' came back the laconic signal.

And they waited. They waited an hour, then two.

'That mad bastard's forgotten about us,' grumbled Ruffy and went to the Ford to fetch the beer crate. Bruce fidgeted restlessly on the unpadded chair beside the telegraph table. He reconsidered anxiously all his previous arguments for leaving Wally Hendry in charge of the camp, but once again decided that it was safe. He couldn't do much harm. Unless, unless, Shermaine! No, it was impossible. Not with forty loyal gendarmes to protect her.

He started to think about Shermaine and the future. There was a year's mercenary captain's pay accumulated in the Crédit Banque Suisse at Zurich. He made the conversion from francs to pounds – about two and a half thousand. Two years' operating capital, so they could have a holiday before he started working again. They could take a chalet up in the mountains, there should be good snow this time of the year.

Bruce grinned. Snow that crunched like sugar, and a twelve-inch-thick eiderdown on the bed at night.

Life had purpose and direction again.

'What you're laughing at, boss?' asked Ruffy.

'I was thinking about a bed.'

'Yeah? That's a good thing to think about. You start there, you're born there, you spend most of your life in it, you have plenty of fun in it, and if you're lucky you die there. How's it for a beer?'

The telegraph came to life at Bruce's elbow. He turned to it quickly.

'Curry – Franklyn,' it clattered. Bruce could imagine the wiry, red-faced little man at the other end. Ex-major in the third brigade of the Legion. A prime mover in the O.A.S., with a sizeable price still on his head from the De Gaulle assassination attempt.

'Franklyn – Curry,' Bruce tapped back. 'Train unserviceable. Motorized transport stranded without fuel. Port

Reprieve road. Map reference approx—' He read the numbers off the sheet on which he had noted them.

There was a long pause, then:

'Is U.M.C. property in your hands?' The question was delicately phrased.

'Affirmative,' Bruce assured him.

'Await air-drop at your position soonest. Out.'

'Message understood. Out.' Bruce straightened from the telegraph and sighed with relief.

'That's that, Ruffy. They'll drop gas to us from one of the Dakotas. Probably tomorrow morning.' He looked at his wristwatch. 'Twenty to one, let's get back.'

Bruce hummed softly, watching the double tracks ahead of him, guiding the Ford with a light touch on the wheel.

He was contented. It was all over. Tomorrow the fuel would drop from the Dakota under those yellow parachutes. (He must lay out the smudge signals this evening.) And ten hours later they would be back in Elisabethville.

A few words with Carl Engelbrecht would fix seats for Shermaine and himself on one of the outward-bound Daks. Then Switzerland, and the chalet with icicles hanging from the eaves. A long rest while he decided where to start again. Louisiana was under Roman-Dutch Law, or was it Code Napoléon? He might even have to rewrite his bar examinations, but the prospect pleased rather than dismayed him. It was fun again.

'Never seen you so happy,' grunted Ruffy.

'Never had so much cause,' Bruce agreed.

'She's a swell lady. Young still – you can teach her.'

Bruce felt his hackles rise, and then he thought better of it and laughed.

'You going to sign her up, boss?'

'I might.'

Ruffy nodded wisely. 'Man should have plenty wives – I got three. Need a couple more.'

'One I could only just handle.'

'One's difficult. Two's easier. Three, you can relax. Four, they're so busy with each other they don't give you no trouble at all.'

'I might try it.'

'Yeah, you do that.'

And ahead of them through the trees they saw the ring of trucks.

'We're home,' grunted Ruffy, then he stirred uncomfortably in his seat. 'Something going on.'

Men stood in small groups. There was something in their attitude: strain, apprehension. Two men ran up the road to meet them. Bruce could see their mouths working, but could not hear the words.

Dread, heavy and cold, pushed down on the pit of Bruce's gut.

Gabbled, incoherent, Sergeant Jacque was trying to tell him something as he ran beside the Ford.

'Tenente Hendry – the river – the madame – gone.' French words like driftwood in the torrent of dialect.

'Your girl,' translated Ruffy. 'Hendry's done her.'

'Dead?' The question dropped from Bruce's mouth.

'No. He's hurt her. He's – you know!'

'Where's she?'

'They've got her in the back of the truck.'

Bruce climbed heavily out of the car. Now they were silent, grouped together, not looking at him, faces impassive, waiting.

Bruce walked slowly to the truck. He felt cold and numb. His legs moved automatically beneath him. He drew back the canvas and pulled himself up into the interior. It was an effort to move forward, to focus his eyes in the gloom.

Wrapped in a blanket she lay small and still.

'Shermaine.' It stuck in his throat.

'Shermaine,' he said again and knelt beside her. A great

livid swelling distorted the side of her face. She did not turn her head to him, but lay staring up at the canvas roof.

He touched her face and the skin was cold, cold as the dread that gripped his stomach. The coldness of it shocked him so he jerked his hand away.

'Shermaine.' This time it was a sob. The eyes, her big haunted eyes, turned unseeing towards him and he felt the lift of escape from the certainty of her death.

'Oh, God,' he cried and took her to him, holding the unresisting frailty of her to his chest. He could feel the slow even thump of her heart beneath his hand. He drew back the blanket and there was no blood.

'Darling, are you hurt? Tell me, are you hurt?' She did not answer. She lay quietly in his arms, not seeing him.

'Shock,' he whispered. 'It's only shock,' and he opened her clothing. With tenderness he examined the smoothly pale body; the skin was clammy and damp, but there was no damage.

He wrapped her again and laid her gently back on to the floor.

He stood and the thing within him changed shape. Cold still, but now burning cold as dry ice.

Ruffy and Jacque were waiting for him beside the tailboard.

'Where is he?' asked Bruce softly.

'He is gone.'

'Where?'

'That way.' Jacque pointed towards the south-east. 'I followed the spoor a short distance.'

Bruce walked to the Ford and picked up his rifle from the floor. He opened the cubby hole and took two spare clips of ammunition from it.

Ruffy followed him. 'He's got the diamonds, boss.'

'Yes,' said Bruce and checked the load of his rifle. The diamonds were of no importance.

'Are you going after him, boss?'

Bruce did not answer. Instead he looked up at the sky. The sun was half way towards the horizon and there were clouds thickly massed around it.

'Ruffy, stay with her,' he said softly. 'Keep her warm.'

Ruffy nodded.

'Who is the best tracker we've got?'

'Jacque. Worked for a safari outfit before the war as a tracker boy.'

Bruce turned to Jacque. The thing was still icy cold inside him, with tentacles that spread out to every extremity of his body and his mind.

'When did this happen?'

'About an hour after you left,' answered Jacque.

Eight hours start. It was a long lead.

'Take the spoor,' said Bruce softly.

– 31 –

The earth was soft from the night's rain and the spoor deep trodden, the heels had bitten in under Hendry's weight, so they followed fast.

Watching Sergeant Jacque work, Bruce felt his anxiety abating, for although the footprints were so easy to follow in these early stages that it was no test of his ability, yet from the way he moved swiftly along – half-crouched and wholly absorbed, occasionally glancing ahead to pick up the run of the spoor, stooping now and then to touch the earth and determine its texture – Bruce could tell that this man knew his business.

Through the open forest with tufted grass below, holding steadily south by east, Hendry led them straight towards the Rhodesian border. And after the first two hours Bruce knew they had not gained upon him. Hendry was still eight hours ahead, and at the pace he was setting eight hours' start was something like thirty miles in distance.

Bruce looked over his shoulder at the sun where it lay wedged between two vast piles of cumulonimbus. There in the sky were the two elements which could defeat him.

Time. There were perhaps two more hours of daylight. With the onset of night they would be forced to halt.

Rain. The clouds were swollen and dark blue round the edges. As Bruce watched, the lightning lit them internally, and at a count of ten the thunder grumbled suddenly. If it rained again before morning there would be no spoor to follow.

'We must move faster,' said Bruce.

Sergeant Jacque straightened up and looked at Bruce as though he were a stranger. He had forgotten his existence.

'The earth hardens.' Jacque pointed at the spoor and Bruce saw that in the last half hour the soil had become gritty and compacted. Hendry's heels no longer broke the crust. 'It is unwise to run on such a lean trail.'

Again Bruce looked back at the menace of gathering clouds.

'We must take the chance,' he decided.

'As you wish,' grunted Jacque, and transferred his rifle to his other shoulder, hitched up his belt and settled the steel helmet more firmly on his head.

'Allez!'

They trotted on through the forest towards the south-east. Within a mile Bruce's body had settled into the automatic rhythm of his run, leaving his mind free.

He thought about Wally Hendry, saw again the little eyes and round them the puffy folded skin, and the mouth below, thin and merciless, the obscene ginger stubble of beard. He could almost smell him. His nostrils flared at the memory of the rank red-head's body odour. Unclean, he thought, unclean mind and unclean body.

His hatred of Wally Hendry was a tangible thing. He could feel it sitting heavily at the base of his throat, tingling in his fingertips and giving strength to his legs.

And yet there was something else. Suddenly Bruce grinned: a wolfish baring of his teeth. That tingling in his fingertips was not all hatred, a little of it was excitement.

What a complex thing is a man, he thought. He can never hold one emotion – always there are others to confuse it. Here I am hunting the thing that I most loathe and hate, and I am enjoying it. Completely unrelated to the hatred is the thrill of hunting the most dangerous and cunning game of all, man.

I have always enjoyed the chase, he thought. It has been bred into me, for my blood is that of the men who hunted and fought with Africa as the prize.

The hunting of this man will give me pleasure. If ever a man deserved to die, it is Wally Hendry. I am the plaintiff, the judge and the executioner.

Sergeant Jacque stopped so suddenly that Bruce ran into him and they nearly fell.

'What is it?' panted Bruce, coming back to reality.

'Look!'

The earth ahead of them was churned and broken.

'Zebra,' groaned Bruce, recognizing the round uncloven hoof prints. 'God damn it to hell – of all the filthy luck!'

'A big herd,' Jacque agreed. 'Spread out. Feeding.'

As far ahead as they could see through the forest the herd had wiped out Hendry's tracks.

'We'll have to cast forward.' Bruce's voice was agonized by his impatience. He turned to the nearest tree and hacked at it with his bayonet, blazing it to mark the end of the trail, swearing softly, venting his disappointment on the trunk.

'Only another hour to sunset,' he whispered. 'Please let us pick him up again before dark.'

Sergeant Jacque was already moving forward, following the approximate line of Hendry's travel, trying vainly to recognize a single footprint through the havoc created there by the passage of thousands of hooves. Bruce hurried to join him and then moved out on his flank. They zigzagged slowly ahead, almost meeting on the inward leg of each tack and then separating again to a distance of a hundred yards.

There it was! Bruce dropped to his knees to make sure. Just the outline of the toecap showing from under the spoor of an old zebra stallion. Bruce whistled, a windy sound through his dry lips, and Jacque came quickly. One quick look, then:

'Yes, he is holding more to the right now.' He raised his eyes and squinted ahead, marking a tree which was directly in line with the run of the spoor. They went forward.

'There's the herd.' Bruce pointed at the flicker of a grey body through the trees.

'They've got our wind.'

A zebra snorted and then there was a rumbling, a low blurred drumming of hooves as the herd ran. Through the trees Bruce caught glimpses of the animals on the near side of the herd. Too far off to show the stripes, looking like fat grey ponies as they galloped, ears up, black-maned heads nodding. Then they were gone and the sound of their flight dwindled.

'At least they haven't run along the spoor,' muttered Bruce, and then bitterly: 'Damn them, the stupid little donkeys! They've cost us an hour. A whole priceless hour.'

Desperately searching, wild with haste, they worked back and forth. The sun was below the trees; already the air was cooling in the short African dusk. Another fifteen minutes and it would be dark.

Then abruptly the forest ended and they came out on the edge of a vlei. Open as wheatland, pastured with green waist-high grass, hemmed in by the forest, it stretched ahead of them for nearly two miles. Dotted along it were clumps of ivory palms with each graceful stem ending in an untidy cluster of leaves. Troops of guinea-fowls were scratching and chirruping along the edge of the clearing, and near the far end a herd of buffalo formed a dark mass as they grazed beneath a canopy of white egrets.

In the forest beyond the clearing, rising perhaps three hundred feet out of it, stood a kopje of tumbled granite. The great slabs of rock with their sheer sides and square tops looked like a ruined castle. The low sun struck it and gave the rock an orange warmth.

But Bruce had no time to admire the scene; his eyes were on the earth, searching for the prints of Hendry's jungle boots.

Out on his left Sergeant Jacque whistled sharply and Bruce felt the leap of excitement in his chest. He ran across to the crouching gendarme.

'It has come away.' Jacque pointed at the spoor that was strung ahead of them like beads on a string, skirting the edge of the vlei, each depression filled with shadow and standing out clearly on the sandy grey earth.

'Too late,' groaned Bruce. 'Damn those bloody zebra.' The light was fading so swiftly it seemed as though it were a stage effect.

'Follow it.' Bruce's voice was sharp with helpless frustration. 'Follow it as long as you can.'

It was not a quarter of a mile farther on that Jacque rose out of his crouch and only the white of his teeth showed in the darkness as he spoke.

'We will lose it again if we go on.'

'All right.' Bruce unslung his rifle with weary resignation. He knew that Wally Hendry was at least forty miles ahead of them; more if he kept travelling after dark. The spoor was cold. If this had been an ordinary hunt he would long ago have broken off the chase.

He looked up at the sky. In the north the stars were fat and yellow, but above them and to the south it was black with cloud.

'Don't let it rain,' he whispered. 'Please God, don't let it rain.'

The night was long. Bruce slept once for perhaps two hours and then the strength of his hatred woke him. He lay flat upon his back and stared up at the sky. It was all dark with clouds; only occasionally they opened and let the stars shine briefly through.

'It must not rain. It must not rain.' He repeated it like a prayer, staring up at the dark sky, concentrating upon it as though by the force of his mind he could control the elements.

There were lions hunting in the forest. He heard the male roaring, moving up from the south, and once his two lionesses answered him. They killed a little before dawn and Bruce lay on the hard earth and listened to their jubilation over the kill. Then there was silence as they began to feed.

That I might have success as well, he thought. I do not often ask for favours, Lord, but grant me this one. I ask it not only for myself but for Shermaine and the others.

In his mind he saw again the two children lying where Hendry had shot them. The smear of mingled blood and chocolate across the boy's cheek.

He deserves to die, prayed Bruce, so please don't let it rain.

As long as the night had been, that quickly came the dawn. A grey dawn, gloomy with low cloud.

'Will it go?' Bruce asked for the twentieth time, and this time Jacque looked up from where he knelt beside the spoor.

'We can try now.'

They moved off slowly with Jacque leading, doubled over to peer short-sightedly at the earth and Bruce close behind him, bedevilled by his impatience and anxiety, lifting his head every dozen paces to the dirty grey roof of cloud.

The light strengthened and the circle of their vision opened from six feet to as many yards, to a hundred, so they could make out the tops of the ivory palms, shaggy against the grey cloud.

Jacque broke into a trot and ahead of them was the end of the clearing and the beginning of the forest. Two hundred yards beyond rose the massive pile of the kopje, in the early light looking more than ever like a castle, turreted and sheer. There was something formidable in its outline. It seemed to brood above them and Bruce looked away from it uneasily.

Cold and with enough weight behind it to sting, the first raindrop splashed against Bruce's cheek.

'Oh, no!' he protested, and stopped. Jacque straightened up from the spoor and he too looked at the sky.

'It is finished. In five minutes there will be nothing to follow.'

Another drop hit Bruce's upturned face and he blinked back the tears of anger and frustration that pricked the rims of his eyelids.

Faster now, tapping on his helmet, plopping on to his shoulders and face, the rain fell.

'Quickly,' cried Bruce. 'Follow as long as you can.'

Jacque opened his mouth to speak, but before a word came out he was flung backwards, punched over as though by an invisible fist, his helmet flying from his head as he fell and his rifle clattering on the earth.

Simultaneously Bruce felt the bullet pass him, disrupting the air, so the wind of it flattened his shirt against his chest, cracking viciously in his ears, leaving him dazedly looking down at Sergeant Jacque's body.

It lay with arms thrown wide, the jaw and the side of the head below the ear torn away; white bone and blood bubbling over it. The trunk twitched convulsively and the hands fluttered like trapped birds. Then flat-sounding through the rain he heard the report of the rifle.

The kopje, screamed Bruce's brain, *he's lying in the kopje!*

And Bruce moved, twisting sideways, starting to run.

Wally Hendry lay on his stomach on the flat top of the turret. His body was stiff and chilled from the cold of the night and the rock was harsh under him, but the discomfort hardly penetrated the fringe of his mind. He had built a low parapet with loose flakes of granite, and he had screened the front of it with the thick bushy stems of broom bush.

His rifle was propped on the parapet in front of him and at his elbow were the spare ammunition clips.

He had lain in this ambush for a long time now – since early the preceding afternoon. Now it was dawn and the darkness was drawing back; in a few minutes he would be able to see the whole of the clearing below him.

I coulda been across the river already, he thought, *coulda been fifty miles away*. He did not attempt to analyse the impulse that had made him lie here unmoving for almost twenty hours.

Man, I knew old Curry would have to come. I knew he would only bring one nigger tracker with him. These educated Johnnies got their own rules – man to man stuff, and he chuckled as he remembered the two minute figures that he had seen come out of the forest in the fading light of the previous evening.

The bastard spent the night down there in the clearing. Saw him light a match and have hisself a smoke in the night – well, I hope he enjoyed it, his last.

Wally peered anxiously out into the gradually gathering dawn.

They'll be moving now, coming up the clearing. Must get them before they reach the trees again. Below him the clearing showed as a paleness, a leprous blotch, on the dark forest.

The bastard! Without preliminaries Hendry's hatred

returned to him. *This time he don't get to make no fancy speeches. This time he don't get no chance to be hoity-toity.*

The light was stronger now. He could see the clumps of ivory palms against the pale brown grass of the clearing.

'Ha!' Hendry exclaimed.

There they were, like two little ants, dark specks moving up the middle of the clearing. The tip of Hendry's tongue slipped out between his lips and he flattened down behind his rifle.

Man, I've waited for this. Six months now I've thought about this, and when it's finished I'll go down and take his ears. He slipped the safety catch; it made a satisfying mechanical click.

Nigger's leading, that's Curry behind him. Have to wait till they turn, don't want the nigger to get it first. Curry first, then the nigger.

He picked them up in his sights, breathing quicker now, the thrill of it so intense that he had to swallow and it caught in his throat like dry bread.

A raindrop hit the back of his neck. It startled him. He looked up quickly at the sky and saw it coming.

'Goddam it,' he groaned, and looked back at the clearing. Curry and nigger were standing together, a single dark blob in the half-light. There was no chance of separating them. The rain fell faster, and suddenly Hendry was overwhelmed by the old familiar feeling of inferiority; of knowing that everything, even the elements, conspired against him; the knowledge that he could never win, not even this once.

They, God and the rest of the world.

The ones who had given him a drunk for a father.

A squalid cottage for a home and a mother with cancer of the throat.

The ones who had sent him to reform school, had fired him from two dozen jobs, had pushed him, laughed at him, gaoled him twice – They, all of them (and Bruce Curry who was their figurehead), they were going to win again. Not even this once, not even ever.

'Goddam it,' he cursed in hopeless, wordless anger against them all.

'Goddam it, goddam it to hell,' and he fired at the dark blob in his sights.

– 33 –

As he ran Bruce looked across a hundred yards of open ground to the edge of the forest.

He felt the wind of the next bullet as it cracked past him.

If he uses rapid fire he'll get me even at three hundred yards.

And Bruce jinked his run like a jack-rabbit. The blood roaring in his ears, fear driving his feet.

Then all around him the air burst asunder, buffeting him so he staggered; the vicious whip-whip-whip of bullets filled his head.

I can't make it.

Seventy yards to the shelter of the trees. Seventy yards of open meadowland, and above him the commanding mass of the kopje.

The next burst is for me – it must come, now!

And he flung himself to one side so violently that he nearly fell. Again the air was ripping to tatters close beside him.

I can't last! He must get me!

In his path was an ant-heap, a low pile of clay, a pimple on the open expanse of earth. Bruce dived for it, hitting the ground so hard that the wind was forced from his lungs out through his open mouth.

The next burst of gunfire kicked lumps of clay from the top of the ant-heap, showering Bruce's back.

He lay with his face pressed into the earth, wheezing

with the agony of empty lungs, flattening his body behind the tiny heap of clay.

Will it cover me? Is there enough of it?

And the next hail of bullets thumped into the ant-heap, throwing fountains of earth, but leaving Bruce untouched.

I'm safe. The realization came with a surge that washed away his fear.

But I'm helpless, answered his hatred. *Pinned to the earth for as long as Hendry wants to keep me here.*

The rain fell on his back. Soaking through his jacket, coldly caressing the nape of his neck and dribbling down over his jaws.

He rolled his head sideways, not daring to lift it an inch, and the rain beat on to the side of his face.

The rain! Falling faster. Thickening. Hanging from the clouds like the skirts of a woman's dress.

Curtains of rain. Greying out the edge of the forest, leaving no solid shapes in the mist of falling liquid mother-of-pearl.

Still gasping but with the pain slowly receding, Bruce lifted his head.

The kopje was a vague blue-green shape ahead of him, then it was gone, swallowed by the eddying columns of rain.

Bruce pushed himself up on to his knees and the pain in his chest made him dizzy.

Now! he thought. *Now, before it thins,* and he lumbered clumsily to his feet.

For a moment he stood clutching his chest, sucking for breath in the haze of water-filled air, and then he staggered towards the edge of the forest.

His feet steadied under him, his breathing eased, and he was into the trees.

They closed round him protectively. He leaned against the rough bark of one of them and wiped the rain from his face with the palm of his hand. The strength came back to him and with it his hatred and his excitement.

271

He unslung the rifle from his shoulder and stood away from the tree with his feet planted wide apart.

'Now, my friend,' he whispered, 'we fight on equal terms.' He pumped a round into the chamber of the FN and moved towards the kopje, stepping daintily, the weight of the rifle in his hands, his mind suddenly sharp and clear, vision enhanced, feeling his strength and the absence of fear like a song within him, a battle hymn.

He made out the loom of the kopje through the dripping rain-heavy trees and he circled out to the right. There is plenty of time, he thought. I can afford to case the joint thoroughly. He completed his circuit of the rock pile.

The kopje, he found, was the shape of a galleon sinking by the head. At one end the high double castles of the poop, from which the main deck canted steeply forward as though the prow were already under water. This slope was scattered with boulders and densely covered with dwarf scrub, an interwoven mass of shoulder-high branches and leaves.

Bruce squatted on his haunches with the rifle in his lap and looked up the ramp at the twin turrets of the kopje. The rain had slackened to a drizzle.

Hendry was on top. Bruce knew he would go to the highest point. Strange how height makes a man feel invulnerable, makes him think he is a god.

And since he had fired upon them he must be in the turret nearest the vlei, which was slightly the higher of the two, its summit crowned by a patch of stunted broom bush.

So now I know exactly where he is and I will wait half an hour. He may become impatient and move; if he does I will get a shot at him from here.

Bruce narrowed his eyes, judging the distance.

'About two hundred yards.'

He adjusted the rear-sight of the FN and then checked the load, felt in the side pocket of his jacket to make sure the two extra clips of ammunition were handy, and settled back comfortably to wait.

'Curry, you sonofabitch, where are you?' Hendry's shout floated down through the drizzling rain and Bruce stiffened. *I was right – he's on top of the left-hand turret.*

'Come on, Bucko. I've been waiting for you since yesterday afternoon.'

Bruce lifted the rifle and sighted experimentally at a dark patch on the wall of the rock. It would be difficult shooting in the rain, the rifle slippery with wet, the fine drizzle clinging to his eyebrows and dewing the sights of the rifle with little beads of moisture.

'Hey, Curry, how's your little French piece of pussy? Man, she's hot, that thing, isn't she?'

Bruce's hands tightened on the rifle.

'Did she tell you how I gave her the old business? Did she tell you how she loved it? You should have heard her panting like a steam engine. I'm telling you, Curry, she just couldn't get enough!'

Bruce felt himself start to tremble. He clenched his jaws, biting down until his teeth ached.

Steady, Bruce my boy, that's what he wants you to do.

The trees dripped steadily in the silence and a gust of wind stirred the scrub on the slope of the kopje. Bruce waited, straining his eyes for the first hint of movement on the left-hand turret.

'You yellow or something, Curry? You scared to come on up here? Is that what it is?'

Bruce shifted his position slightly, ready for a snap shot.

'Okay, Bucko. I can wait, I've got all day. I'll just sit here thinking about how I mucked your little bit of French. I'm telling you it was something to remember. Up and down, in and out, man it was something!'

Bruce came carefully up on to his feet behind the trunk of the tree and once more studied the layout of the kopje.

If I can move up the slope, keeping well over to the side, until I reach the right-hand turret, there's a ledge there that will take me to the top. I'll be twenty or thirty feet from him, and at that range it will all be over in a few seconds.

He drew a deep breath and left the shelter of the tree.

Wally Hendry spotted the movement in the forest below him; it was a flash of brown quickly gone, too fast to get a bead on it.

He wiped the rain off his face and wriggled a foot closer to the edge.

'Come on, Curry. Let's stop buggering about,' he shouted, and cuddled the butt of his rifle into his shoulder. The tip of his tongue kept darting out and touching his lips.

At the foot of the slope he saw a branch move slightly, stirring when there was no wind. He grinned and snuggled his hips down on to the rock. *Here he comes*, he gloated, *he's crawling up, under the scrub.*

'I know you're sitting down there. Okay, Curry, I can wait also.'

Half-way up the slope the top leaves of another bush swayed gently, parting and closing.

'Yes!' whispered Wally, 'Yes!' and he clicked off the safety catch of the rifle. His tongue came out and moved slowly from one corner of his mouth to the other.

I've got him, for sure! There – he'll have to cross that piece of open ground. A couple a yards, that's all. But it'll be enough.

He moved again, wriggling a few inches to one side, settling his aim into the gap between two large grey boulders; he pushed the rate-of-fire selector on to rapid and his forefinger rested lightly on the trigger.

'Hey, Curry, I'm getting bored. If you are not going to come up, how about singing to me or cracking a few jokes?'

Bruce Curry crouched behind a large grey boulder. In front of him were three yards of open ground and then the shelter of another rock. He was almost at the top of the slope and Hendry had not spotted him. Across the patch of open ground was good cover to the foot of the right-hand turret.

It would take him two seconds to cross and the chances were that Hendry would be watching the forest at the foot of the slope.

He gathered himself like a sprinter on the starting blocks.

'Go!' he whispered and dived into the opening, and into a hell storm of bullets. One struck his rifle, tearing it out of his hand with such force that his arm was paralysed to the shoulder, another stung his chest, and then he was across. He lay behind the far boulder, gasping with the shock, and listened to Hendry's voice roaring triumphantly.

'Fooled you, you stupid bastard! Been watching you all the way up from the bottom.'

Bruce held his left arm against his stomach; the use of it was returning as the numbness subsided, but with it came the ache. The top joint of his thumb had caught in the trigger guard and been torn off; now the blood welled out of the stump thickly and slowly, dark blood the colour of apple jelly. With his right hand he groped for his handkerchief.

'Hey, Curry, your rifle's lying there in the open. You might need it in a few minutes. Why don't you go out and fetch it?'

Bruce bound the handkerchief tightly round the stump of his thumb and the bleeding slowed. Then he looked at the rifle where it lay ten feet away. The foresight had been knocked off, and the same bullet that had amputated his thumb had smashed into the breech, buckled the loading handle and the slide. He knew that it was damaged beyond repair.

'Think I'll have me a little target practice,' shouted Hendry from above, and again there was a burst of automatic fire. Bruce's rifle disappeared in a cloud of dust and flying rock fragments and when it cleared the woodwork of the rifle was splintered and torn and there was further damage to the action.

Well, that's that, thought Bruce, *rifle's wrecked, Shermaine has the pistol, and I have only one good hand. This is going to be interesting.*

He unbuttoned the front of his jacket and examined the welt that the bullet had raised across his chest. It looked like a rope burn, painful and red, but not serious. He rebuttoned his jacket.

'Okay, Bruce Baby, the time for games is over. I'm coming down to get you.' Hendry's voice was harsh and loud, filled with confidence.

Bruce rallied under the goading of it. He looked round quickly. *Which way to go? Climb high so he must come up to get at you. Take the right-hand turret, work round the side of it and wait for him on the top.*

In haste now, spurred by the dread of being the hunted, he scrambled to his feet and dodged away up the slope, keeping his head down using the thick screen of rock and vegetation.

He reached the wall of the right-hand turret and followed it round, found the spiral ledge that he had seen from below and went on to it, up along it like a fly on a wall, completely exposed, keeping his back to the cliff of granite, shuffling sideways up the eighteen-inch ledge with the drop below him growing deeper with each step.

Now he was three hundred feet above the forest and could look out across the dark green land to another row of kopjes on the horizon. The rain had ceased but the cloud was unbroken, covering the sky.

The ledge widened, became a platform and Bruce hurried across it round the far shoulder and came to a dead end. The ledge had petered out and there was only the drop below. He had trapped himself on the side of the turret – the summit was unattainable. If Hendry descended to the forest floor and circled the kopje he would find Bruce completely at his mercy, for there was no cover on the narrow ledge. Hendry could have a little more target practice.

Bruce leaned against the rock and struggled to control his breathing. His throat was clogged with the thick saliva of exhaustion and fear. He felt tired and helpless, his thumb throbbed painfully and he lifted it to examine it once more. Despite the tourniquet it was bleeding slowly, a wine-red drop at a time.

Bleeding! Bruce swallowed the thick gluey stuff in his throat and looked back along the way he had come. On the grey rock the bright red splashes stood out clearly. He had laid a blood spoor for Hendry to follow.

All right then, perhaps it is best this way. At least I may be able to come to grips with him. If I wait behind this shoulder until he starts to cross the platform, there's a three hundred foot drop on one side, I may be able to rush him and throw him off.

Bruce leaned against the shoulder of granite, hidden from the platform, and tuned his ears to catch the first sound of Hendry's approach.

The clouds parted in the eastern sector of the sky and the sun shone through, slanting across the side of the kopje.

It will be better to die in the sun, thought Bruce, *a sacrifice to the Sun god thrown from the roof of the temple*, and he grinned without mirth, waiting with patience and with pain.

The minutes fell like drops into the pool of time, slowly measuring out the ration of life that had been allotted to him. The pulse in his ears counted also, and his breath that he drew and held and gently exhaled – how many more would there be?

I should pray, he thought, *but after this morning when I prayed that it should not rain, and the rains came and saved me, I will not presume again to tell the Old Man how to run things. Perhaps he knows best after all.*

Thy will be done, he thought instead, and suddenly his

277

nerves jerked tight as a line hit by a marlin. The sound he had heard was that of cloth brushing against rough rock.

He held his breath and listened, but all he could discern was the pulse in his ears and the wind in the trees of the forest below. The wind was a lonely sound.

Thy will be done, he repeated without breathing, and heard Hendry breathe close behind the shoulder of rock.

He stood away from the wall and waited. Then he saw Hendry's shadow thrown by the early morning sun along the ledge. A great distorted shadow on the grey rock.

Thy will be done. And he went round the shoulder fast, his good hand held like a blade and the weight of his body behind it.

Hendry was three feet away, the rifle at high port across his chest, standing close in against the cliff, the cup-shaped steel helmet pulled low over the slitty eyes and little beads of sweat clinging in the red-gold stubble of his beard. He tried to drop the muzzle of the rifle but Bruce was too close.

Bruce lunged with stiff fingers at his throat and he felt the crackle and give of cartilage. Then his weight carried him on and Hendry sprawled backwards on to the stone platform with Bruce on top of him.

The rifle slithered across the rock and dropped over the edge, and they lay chest to chest with legs locked together in a horrible parody of the love act. But in *this* act we do not procreate, we destroy!

Hendry's face was purple and swollen above his damaged throat, his mouth open as he struggled for air, and his breath smelt old and sour in Bruce's face.

With a twist towards the thumb Bruce freed his right wrist from Hendry's grip and, lifting it like an axe, brought it down across the bridge of Hendry's nose. Twin jets of blood spouted from the nostrils and gushed into his open mouth.

With a wet strangling sound in his throat Hendry's body

arched violently upwards and Bruce was thrown back against the side of the cliff with such force that for a second he lay there.

Wally was on his knees, facing Bruce, his eyes glazed and sightless, and the strangling rattling sound spraying from his throat in a pink cloud of blood. With both hands he was fumbling his pistol out of its canvas holster.

Bruce drew his knees up on to his chest, then straightened his legs in a mule kick. His feet landed together in the centre of Hendry's stomach, throwing him backwards off the platform. Hendry made that strangled bellow all the way to the bottom, but at the end it was cut off abruptly, and afterwards there was only the sound of the wind in the forest below.

For a long time, drained of strength and the power to think, Bruce sat on the ledge with his back against the rock.

Above him the clouds had rolled aside and half the sky was blue. He looked out across the land and the forest was lush and clean from the rain. *And I am still alive.* The realization warmed Bruce's mind as comfortably as the early sun was warming his body. He wanted to shout it out across the forest. *I am still alive!*

At last he stood up, crossed to the edge of the cliff and looked down at the tiny crumpled figure on the rocks below. Then he turned away and dragged his beaten body down the side of the turret.

It took him twenty minutes to find Wally Hendry in the chaos of broken rock and scrub below the turret. He lay on his side with his legs drawn up as though he slept. Bruce knelt beside him and drew his pistol from the olive-green canvas holster; then he unbuttoned the flap of Hendry's bulging breast pocket and took out the white canvas bag.

He stood up, opened the mouth of the bag and stirred the diamonds with his forefinger. Satisfied, he jerked the drawstring closed and dropped them into his own pocket.

In death he is even more repulsive than he was alive, thought Bruce without regret as he looked down at the corpse.

The flies were crawling into the bloody nostrils and clustering round the eyes.

Then he spoke aloud.

'So Mike Haig was right and I was wrong – you can destroy it.'

Without looking back he walked away. The tiredness left him.

– 34 –

Carl Engelbrecht came through the doorway from the cockpit into the main cabin of the Dakota.

'Are you two happy?' he asked above the deep drone of the engines, and then grinning with his big brown face, 'I can see you are!'

Bruce grinned back at him and tightened his arm around Shermaine's shoulders.

'Go away! Can't you see we're busy?'

'You've got lots of cheek for a hitch-hiker – bloody good mind to make you get out and walk,' he grumbled as he sat down beside them on the bench that ran the full length of the fuselage. 'I've brought you some coffee and sandwiches.'

'Good. Good. I'm starving.' Shermaine sat up and reached for the thermos flask and the greaseproof paper packet. The bruise on her cheek had faded to a shadow with yellow edges – it was almost ten days old. With his mouth full of chicken sandwich Bruce kicked one of the wooden cases that were roped securely to the floor of the aircraft.

'What have you got in these, Carl?'

'Dunno,' said Carl and poured coffee into the three plastic mugs. 'In this game you don't ask questions. You fly out, take your money, and let it go.' He drained his mug and stood up. 'Well, I'll leave you two alone now. We'll be in Nairobi in a couple of hours, so you can sleep or something!' He winked. 'You'll have to stay aboard while we refuel. But we'll be airborne again in an hour or so, and the day after tomorrow, God and the weather permitting, we'll set you down in Zurich.'

'Thanks, old cock.'

'Think nothing of it – all in the day's work.'

He went forward and disappeared into the cockpit, closing the door behind him.

Shermaine turned back to Bruce, studied him for a moment and then laughed.

'You look so different – now you look like a lawyer!'

Self-consciously Bruce tightened the knot of his Old Michaelhouse tie.

'I must admit it feels strange to wear a suit and tie again.' He looked down at the well-cut blue suit – the only one he had left – and then up again at Shermaine.

'And in a dress I hardly recognize you either.' She was wearing a lime-green cotton frock, cool and crisp looking, white high-heel shoes and just a little make-up to cover the bruise. A damn fine woman, Bruce decided with pleasure.

'How does your thumb feel?' she asked, and Bruce held up the stump with its neat little turban of adhesive tape.

'I had almost forgotten about it.'

Suddenly Shermaine's expression changed, and she pointed excitedly out of the perspex window behind Bruce's shoulder.

'Look, there's the sea!' It lay far below them, shaded from blue to pale green in the shallows, with a round of white beach and the wave formation moving across it like ripples on a pond.

'That's Lake Tanganyika.' Bruce laughed. 'We've left the Congo behind.'

'Forever?' she asked.

'Forever!' he assured her.

281

The aircraft banked slightly, throwing them closer together, as Carl picked out his landmarks and altered course towards the north-east.

Four thousand feet below them the dark insect that was their shadow flitted and hopped across the surface of the water.